# ENCYCLOPAEDIA OF LINGUISTICS, INFORMATION AND CONTROL

EDITOR-IN-CHIEF

A. R. MEETHAM
NATIONAL PHYSICAL LABORATORY, TEDDINGTON

ASSOCIATE EDITOR

R. A. HUDSON
UNIVERSITY COLLEGE, LONDON

PERGAMON PRESS
OXFORD · LONDON · EDINBURGH · NEW YORK
TORONTO · SYDNEY · PARIS · BRAUNSCHWEIG

Pergamon Press Ltd., Headington Hill Hall, Oxford
4 & 5 Fitzroy Square, London W.1
Pergamon Press (Scotland) Ltd., 2 & 3 Teviot Place, Edinburgh 1
Pergamon Press Inc., Maxwell House, Fairview Park, Elmsford, New York 10523
Pergamon of Canada Ltd., 207 Queen's Quay West, Toronto 1
Pergamon Press (Aust.) Pty. Ltd., 19a Boundary Street, Rushcutters Bay, N.S.W. 2011, Australia
Pergamon Press S.A.R.L., 24 rue des Écoles, Paris 5e
Vieweg & Sohn GmbH, Burgplatz 1, Braunschweig

Copyright © 1969
Pergamon Press Ltd.

First edition 1969

Library of Congress Catalog Card No. 68–18528

PRINTED IN HUNGARY
08 012337 6

# CONTENTS

| | |
|---|---|
| Adaptive control theory  B. R. GAINES | 1 |
| Adaptive threshold elements  C. H. MAYS | 9 |
| Algebraic manipulation using lists  J. E. SAMMETT | 12 |
| Algorithms for processing algorithms  R. A. BROOKER | 15 |
| Animal exploratory behaviour  A. WATSON | 18 |
| Animal learning  J. A. DEUTSCH | 21 |
| Animal motivation  D. DEUTSCH and J. A. DEUTSCH | 24 |
| Assembly languages  J. R. PETERS | 26 |
| Attention  T. B. MULHOLLAND | 28 |
| Automata, finite-state  M. A. ARBIB | 32 |
| Automata, infinite-state  M. A. ARBIB | 35 |
| Character recognition  M. C. CLOWES | 41 |
| Cochlear mechanics  I. C. WHITFIELD | 44 |
| Communication theory  P. M. WOODWARD | 46 |
| Computational linguistics: introduction  D. G. HAYS | 49 |
| Computational linguistics: machine translation  D. M. YATES | 51 |
| Computer language design requirements  J. C. HARWELL | 54 |
| Computer operating systems  R. N. NEEDHAM | 57 |
| Computer peripherals and their control  E. C. P. PORTMAN | 58 |
| Computer simulation of human thought processes  J. FELDMAN | 60 |
| Computers, multiaccess to  M. E. WANTMAN | 63 |
| Computers, stochastic  B. R. GAINES | 66 |
| Concept formation by artificial intelligence  E. HUNT | 76 |
| Concept identification—information processing approaches  M. I. POSNER | 80 |
| Conceptual behaviour  R. C. HAYGOOD and L. E. BOURNE JR. | 84 |
| Control: basic elements  J. A. FORMBY | 89 |
| Control by hybrid computers  L. NORONHA | 92 |
| Control by the maximum principle  S. SHAPIRO | 101 |
| Control by model reference  J. F. MEREDITH | 106 |
| Control by stationary filtering and prediction (Wiener)  A. P. ROBERTS | 109 |
| Control, hierarchical  J. D. PEARSON | 113 |
| Control, hill-climbing in  K. C. NG | 115 |
| Control, identification techniques for  P. EYKHOFF | 119 |
| Control, invariance and  J. D. ROBERTS | 126 |
| Control of aircraft as two non-interacting systems  R. D. MILNE | 128 |
| Control of an economic system  R. STONE | 129 |
| Control of respiration, self-adaptive  I. P. PRIBAN | 132 |
| Control, on–off  P. H. HAMMOND | 136 |
| Control, predictive, using fast-time models  I. LEFKOWITZ and J. D. SCHOEFFLER | 140 |
| Control, sensitivity and  J. D. ROBERTS | 147 |
| Control, stability and  C. T. LEONDES | 149 |
| Control systems, multivariable  R. J. KAVANAGH | 151 |
| Control systems, sampled data  E. I. JURY | 155 |
| Data transmission  G. D. ALLERY | 159 |
| Discrete models for forecasting and control  G. E. P. BOX and G. M. JENKINS | 162 |
| Dynamic programming  O. L. R. JACOBS | 168 |
| Error correcting codes  J. L. MASSEY | 173 |
| Eye movements  R. W. DITCHBURN | 176 |
| Fact retrieval  J. M. FOSTER | 180 |

| | |
|---|---|
| Fixed stores and control by microprogram  G. G. SCARROTT | 181 |
| Gestalt psychology  C. R. EVANS | 185 |
| Grammar (structural)  J. E. BUSE | 186 |
| Graphical communication  K. V. ROBERTS | 207 |
| Hearing  N. GUTTMAN | 211 |
| Homeostasis  I. P. PRIBAN | 213 |
| Homeostasis in the single cell  R. J. GOLDACRE | 217 |
| Information space  N. REAM | 221 |
| Information storage and retrieval  P. K. T. VASWANI | 223 |
| Information theory in psychological measurement  E. R. F. W. CROSSMAN | 232 |
| Inland trunk systems  R. H. FRANKLIN | 238 |
| Language varieties: language and dialect  J. T. WRIGHT | 243 |
| Language varieties: register  J. ELLIS and J. N. URE | 251 |
| Language varieties: stylistics  J. SPENCER | 259 |
| Learning machines: a unified view  J. H. ANDREAE | 261 |
| Linguistic form: algebraic linguistics  E. SHAMIR | 270 |
| Linguistic form: generative grammar  E. BACH | 272 |
| Linguistic form: paradigmatic  R. A. HUDSON | 273 |
| Linguistic form: syntagmatic  R. A. HUDSON | 276 |
| Linguistic form: system and structure  R. A. HUDSON | 278 |
| Linguistic form: transformational theory  E. BACH | 280 |
| Local networks  E. C. SWAIN | 284 |
| Magnetic recording  C. D. MEE | 291 |
| Man-machine communication and ergonomics  E. R. F. W. CROSSMAN | 301 |
| Man-machine in control systems  G. W. LANGE | 307 |
| Models for human memory  D. A. NORMAN | 311 |
| Nerve and muscle, initiation and conduction of impulses in  B. L. GINSBORG | 314 |
| Nervous system, role of pulse distribution in information flow  H. ROSS | 316 |
| Neuronal nets  J. D. COWAN | 320 |
| Non-neural elements in receptor systems  B. LYNN | 337 |
| Optimization, automatic  S. J. WAJC and D. J. WILDE | 342 |
| Optimization of industrial processes  A. HAZLERIGG | 345 |
| Pattern recognition  G. H. BALL | 349 |
| Perception of colour  L. WHEELER | 358 |
| Perception of sound  B. MCA. SAYERS | 365 |
| Perception, stereopsis as an aspect of  B. JULESZ | 368 |
| Perception, visual  B. H. CRAWFORD | 373 |
| Perceptual breakdown with stabilized images  C. R. EVANS | 388 |
| Phonetics, acoustic  D. B. FRY | 391 |
| Phonetics, articulatory  J. C. WELLS | 393 |
| Phonetics, auditory  J. C. WELLS | 396 |
| Phonetics, experimental  D. B. FRY | 399 |
| Phonology: contrast and opposition  K. KOHLER | 401 |
| Phonology: distinctive features  E. M. HIGGINBOTTOM | 404 |
| Phonology: phonemes and broad transcription  K. KOHLER | 409 |
| Phonology: prosodic features  E. M. HIGGINBOTTOM | 411 |
| Problem solving  A. NEWELL | 413 |
| Prosthetic limbs  N. D. RING | 416 |
| Pseudonoise sequences  D. EVERETT | 419 |
| Pseudo-random binary signals, use of, in correlation analysis of dynamic systems  P. A. N. BRIGGS | 433 |
| Psychological limiting factors in human performance  W. T. SINGLETON | 437 |
| Psychological linguistics: psycholinguistic studies of syntax  J. C. MARSHALL | 439 |
| Psychological linguistics: psychological aspects of semantic structure  C. J. MARSHALL | 442 |
| Psychological linguistics: theories of learning in relation to language  R. J. WALES | 444 |
| Psychology, use of models (learning)  G. PASK | 447 |
| Random signals and noise  P. R. WETHERALL and P. M. WOODWARD | 453 |
| Receptors as transducers  D. R. INMAN | 455 |
| Receptors in joints and muscles  P. B. C. MATTHEWS | 460 |
| Receptors: relation between the stimuli and the activity in single primary units  A. IGGO | 463 |

# ENCYCLOPAEDIA OF LINGUISTICS, INFORMATION AND CONTROL

| | | | |
|---|---|---|---|
| 77 | Nervous system, role of pulse distribution in information flow 109 | 110 | Relations between languages: introduction |
| 78 | Neuronal nets 9, 75 | 111 | Relations between languages: bilingualism |
| 79 | Non-neuronal elements in receptor systems 106, 107, 109 | 112 | Relations between languages: comparative philology |
| 80 | Optimization, automatic 11, 32, 38 | 113 | Relations between languages: lingua franca |
| 81 | Optimization of industrial processes 28, 31, 38, 46 | 114 | Relations between languages: loan and loan words |
| 82 | Pattern recognition 12, 20, 23, 78, 126 | 115 | Relations between languages: semantic change |
| 83 | Perception of colour 86 | 116 | Relations between languages: typological and areal classifications 61 |
| 84 | Perception of sound 13, 130 | 117 | Reliable computation with unreliable elements 47 |
| 85 | Perception, stereopsis as an aspect of | 118 | Scientific documentation 58 |
| 86 | Perception, visual 83 | 119 | Semantics: introduction 115 |
| 87 | Perceptual breakdown with stabilized images 51, 78 | 120 | Semantics: context and collocation |
| 88 | Phonetics, acoustic | 121 | Semantics: field theories 67, 115 |
| 89 | Phonetics, articulatory | 122 | Semantics: meaning and reference |
| 90 | Phonetics, auditory | 123 | Semantics: sign and symbol 145 |
| 91 | Phonetics, experimental | 124 | Sensory discrimination, measurement of 54, 127 |
| 92 | Phonology: contrast and opposition 70, 89, 90, 94 | 125 | Sensory processes 13, 54, 86, 124 |
| 93 | Phonology: distinctive features 70 | 126 | Similarity 23, 64, 82, 129 |
| 94 | Phonology: phonemes and broad transcription 89, 90, 145 | 127 | Simulation of traffic problems using chain-code random generators 98, 99 |
| 95 | Phonology: prosodic features | 128 | Sorting techniques 138 |
| 96 | Problem solving 138, 142 | 129 | Speech 90 |
| 97 | Prosthetic limbs | 130 | Speech perception 84, 90, 134 |
| 98 | Pseudonoise sequences 140 | 131 | Speech recognition, automatic 14 |
| 99 | Pseudorandom binary signals, use of, in correlation analysis of dynamic systems 33 | 132 | Speech synthesis 66, 88, 134 |
| | | 133 | Stacks 50 |
| 100 | Psychological limiting factors in human performance 73, 74 | 134 | Statistics of languages: introduction 15, 58, 65, 66, 135 |
| 101 | Psychological linguistics: psycholinguistic studies of syntax 66, 70 | 135 | Statistics of language: structure of written English words 145 |
| 102 | Psychological linguistics: psychological aspects of semantic structure 67, 68, 70, 119, 120, 121 | 136 | Subscriber's telephone set, design considerations of 130 |
| | | 137 | Switching and control in telephony 60, 71, 139, 140, 141 |
| 103 | Psychological linguistics: theories of learning in relation to language 65, 66, 69, 70 | 138 | Symbol manipulation by digital computer 3, 15, 16, 58, 143 |
| 104 | Psychology, use of models (learning) 6, 10, 64 | 139 | Telecommunication, economy in 14, 44, 130 |
| 105 | Random signals and noise 14, 47, 98, 117 | 140 | Telecommunication, global 44, 98 |
| 106 | Receptors as transducers 13, 76, 79 | 141 | Telecommunication system planning, international 60 |
| 107 | Receptors in joints and muscles 41, 76 | 142 | Theorem proving by machine 96, 144 |
| 108 | Receptors: relation between the stimuli and the activity in single primary units 76 | 143 | Timetabling 138 |
| | | 144 | Unsolvable problems 4, 10, 11, 66, 142 |
| 109 | Receptors: representation of information about stimuli in populations 83 | 145 | Writing 123 |

| | |
|---|---|
| Receptors: representation of information about stimuli in populations  M. F. Land | 467 |
| Relations between languages: introduction  T. Bynon | 470 |
| Relations between languages: bilingualism  N. V. Smith | 473 |
| Relations between languages: comparative philology  T. Bynon | 475 |
| Relations between languages: lingua franca  N. V. Smith | 480 |
| Relations between languages: loans and loanwords  T. Bynon | 482 |
| Relations between languages: semantic change  N. C. W. Spence | 484 |
| Relations between languages: typological and areal classifications  N. V. Smith | 486 |
| Reliable computation with unreliable elements  J. D. Cowan | 489 |
| Scientific documentation  H. East and J. Martyn | 496 |
| Semantics: introduction  G. N. Leech | 499 |
| Semantics: context and collocation  N. C. W. Spence | 503 |
| Semantics: field theories  N. C. W. Spence | 504 |
| Semantics: meaning and reference  N. C. W. Spence | 507 |
| Semantics: sign and symbol  N. C. W. Spence | 510 |
| Sensory discrimination, measurement of  M. Treisman | 512 |
| Sensory processes  I. C. Whitfield | 525 |
| Similarity  E. A. Newman | 535 |
| Simulation of traffic problems using chain-code random generators  M. G. Hartley | 539 |
| Sorting techniques  L. K. Grodman | 543 |
| Speech  N. Guttman | 545 |
| Speech perception  M. P. Haggard | 548 |
| Speech recognition, automatic  D. R. Hill | 552 |
| Speech synthesis  M. P. Haggard | 559 |
| Stacks  M. R. Wetherfield | 563 |
| Statistics of language: introduction  I. J. Good | 567 |
| Statistics of language: structure of written English words  J. L. Dolby and H. L. Resnikoff | 581 |
| Subscriber's telephone set, design considerations of  F. E. Williams | 584 |
| Switching and control in telephony  S. Welch | 590 |
| Symbol manipulation by digital computer  B. Raphael | 594 |
| Telecommunication, economy in  B. J. Vieri | 599 |
| Telecommunication, global  R. J. Halsey | 604 |
| Telecommunication system planning, international  H. Williams | 607 |
| Theorem proving by machine  J. A. Robinson | 616 |
| Timetabling  E. D. Barraclough | 619 |
| Unsolvable problems  D. M. R. Park | 623 |
| Writing  J. Mountford | 627 |
| Index/Glossary | 635 |

# LIST OF CONTRIBUTORS

ALLERY, G. D. *(London)*
ANDREAE, J. H. *(Christchurch, N.Z.)*
ARBIB, M. A. *(Stanford, California)*
BACH, E. *(Austin, Texas)*
BALL, G. H. *(Menlo Park, California)*
BARRACLOUGH, E. D. *(Newcastle upon Tyne)*
BOX, G. E. P. *(Wisconsin, U.S.A)*
BRIGGS, P. A. N. *(Teddington, Middx.)*
BROOKER, R. K. *(Manchester)*
BUSE, J. E. *(Cranleigh, Surrey)*
BYNON, T. *(London)*
CLOWES, M. C. *(Oxford)*
COWAN, J. *(Chicago, Ill.)*
CRAWFORD, B. H. *(Teddington, Middx.)*
CROSSMAN, E. R. F. W. *(Berkeley, California)*
DEUTSCH, D. *(New York)*
DEUTSCH, J. A. *(New York)*
DITCHBURN, R. W. *(Reading)*
DOLBY, J. L. *(Los Altos, California)*
ELLIS, J. *(Accra, Ghana)*
EVANS, C. R. *(Teddington, Middx.)*
EVERETT, D. *(Bangor, Caernarvonshire)*
EYKHOFF, P. *(Eindhoven)*
FELDMAN, J. *(Irvine, California)*
FORMBY, J. A. *(Birmingham)*
FOSTER, J. M. *(Aberdeen)*
FRANKLIN, R. H. *(London)*
FRY, D. B. *(London)*
GAINES, B. R. *(Essex)*
GINSBORG, B. L. *(Edinburgh)*
GOLDACRE, R. J. *(London)*
GOOD, I. J. *(Blacksburg, Va.)*
GRODMAN, L. K. *(Philadelphia)*

GUTTMAN, N. *(New Jersey)*
HAGGARD, M. P. *(Cambridge)*
HALSEY, R. J. *(Radlett, Herts.)*
HAMMOND, P. H. *(Teddington, Middx.)*
HARWELL, J. C. *(London)*
HARTLEY, M. *(Manchester)*
HAYGOOD, R. C. *(Kansas)*
HAYS, D. G. *(Santa Monica, California)*
HAZLERIGG, A. *(Teddington, Middx.)*
HIGGINBOTTOM, E. M. *(Bloomington, Indiana)*
HILL, D. R. *(Harlow, Essex)*
HUDSON, R. A. *(London)*
HUNT, E. *(Los Angeles, California)*
IGGO, A. *(Edinburgh)*
INMAN, D. R. *(London)*
JACOBS, O. L. R. *(Oxford)*
JULESZ, B. *(New Jersey)*
JURY, E. I. *(Los Angeles, Calif.)*
KAVANAGH, R. J. *(New Brunswick, Canada)*
KOHLER, K. *(Edinburgh)*
LAND, M. F. *(London)*
LANGE, G. W. *(Teddington, Middx.)*
LEECH, G. N. *(London)*
LEFKOWITZ, I. *(Cleveland, Ohio)*
LEONDES, C. T. *(Los Angeles, California)*
LYNN, B. *(London)*
MARSHALL, J. *(Edinburgh)*
MARTYN, J. *(London)*
MASSEY, J L. *(Notre Dame, Indiana)*
MATTHEWS, P. B. C. *(Oxford)*
MAYS, H. *(Palo Alto, California)*
MEE, C. D. *(New York)*
MEREDITH, J. F. *(Cheltenham, Glos.)*

MILNE, R. D. *(London)*
MOUNTFORD, J. *(London)*
MULHOLLAND, T. B. *(Bedford, Mass.)*
NEEDHAM, R. M. *(Cambridge)*
NEWELL A. *(Pittsburgh)*
NEWMAN, E. A. *(Teddington, Middx.)*
NG, K. C. *(Warwick)*
NORMAN, D. A. *(Cambridge, Mass.)*
NORONHA, L. *(Burgess Hill, Sussex)*
PARK, D. M. R. *(Oxford)*
PASK, G. *(Richmond, Surrey)*
PEARSON, J. D. *(McClean, Virginia)*
PETERS, J. *(London)*
PORTMAN, E. C. P. *(Manchester)*
POSNER, M. I. *(Eugene, Oregon)*
PRIBAN, I. P. *(Teddington, Middx.)*
RAPHAEL, B. *(Menlo Park, California)*
REAM, N. *(London)*
RESNIKOFF, H. L. *(Houston, Texas)*
RING, N. *(Chailey, Sussex.)*
ROBERTS, A. P. *(Belfast)*
ROBERTS, J. D. *(Cambridge)*
ROBERTS, K. V. *(Abingdon, Berks)*
ROBINSON, J. A. *(Houston, Texas)*
ROSS, H. *(Birmingham)*
SAMMETT, J. E. *(Cambridge, Mass.)*
SAYERS, B. McA. *(London)*
SCARROTT, G. G. *(Bracknell, Berks)*
SHAMIR, E. *(Jerusalem, Israel)*
SHAPIRO, S. *(New York)*
SINGLETON, W. I. *(Birmingham)*
SMITH, N. V. *(London)*

SPENCE, N. C. W. *(London)*
SPENCER, J. *(Leeds)*
STONE, R. *(Cambridge)*
SWAIN, E. C. *(London)*
TREISMAN, M. *(New Jersey)*
URE, J. *(Accra, Ghana)*
VASWANI, P. K. T. *(Teddington, Middx.)*
VIERI, B. J. *(Hayes, Middx.)*
WAJC, S. J. *(Brussels)*

WALES, R. J. *(Edinburgh)*
WANTMAN, M. *(London)*
WATSON A. *(Cambridge)*
WELCH, S. *(London)*
WELLS, J. C. *(London)*
WETHERFIELD, M. R. *(Kidsgrove, Staffs.)*
WHEELER, L. *(Hayward, California)*
WHITFIELD, I. C. *(Birmingham)*

WILDE, D. J. *(Stanford, California)*
WILLIAMS, F. E. *(London)*
WILLIAMS, H. *(London)*
WOODWARD, P. M. *(Gt. Malvern. Worcs.)*
WRIGHT, J. T. *(Basildon, Essex)*
YATES, D. M. *(Teddington, Middx.)*

# FOREWORD

HISTORIANS are already at work, no doubt, assessing the effects on society of computers and control systems. Although their task will be difficult, it is slight compared with any examination of the effects of computers and control systems on thinking. To take one interesting index of mental activity as an example, the Transactions of the Institute of Electrical and Electronics Engineers are now published in 32 parts, enough for 32 bound volumes a year, and their titles range alphabetically from Aerospace and Electronic Systems to Vehicular Communications. Five years ago there were 23 parts and 15 years ago only 7 parts. The rate of growth must have been about 15 per cent per annum.

The number of electrical engineers in the world must have grown at a comparable rate, and no doubt they find it hard to keep informed about each other's progress; but at least they share a common technical language, and they underwent a common training up to their second or third year in the university. A more difficult problem in current awareness occurs when they find themselves studying the work of people with different training, such as physicists, mathematicians, computer scientists, systems consultants, economists, psychologists, physiologists, documentalists and students of linguistics. In their turn, these specialists have interests in aspects of electrical engineering, as well as in each other's ideas and developments.

This encyclopaedia aims to help human communications in the wide area which is being opened up by computers and by the new thinking they have generated. The boundaries between disciplines are invisible and even non-existent, but the differences in basic training remain, and many good intentions to get to grips with an article or a report are frustrated by narrowness of training and ignorance of the best sources of information at a general enough level of language. The encyclopaedia has been compiled with exactly this difficulty in view, and its contributors come from all the specialist groups mentioned in the preceding paragraph.

The contributors have cooperated by selecting an important aspect of their own speciality, and describing it in terms which will be understood by anyone interested with a similar length of training but a different occupation. Many have written articles because they want to have a copy of the encyclopaedia for their own use. Their attitude has been most heartening, for the best reason for adding another book to the corpus is the assurance that it will be read.

To expose the common feature of all the articles, it is only necessary to point out that the signal is as fundamental in its own way as the atom. Indeed without signals there would be nothing to discuss, not even atoms, and no way of performing the discussion. The attached diagram shows how the encyclopaedia might be classified, with signals at the point of origin.

The question of a title for the encyclopaedia has been difficult, and in the end a moderately euphonious one was retained which covered a fair part of the above classification. Its word order is of no consequence. What both the title and the classification fail to convey are the many surprising cross-linkages between articles with apparently no association. Anyone who chooses to look up the references to learning, language, machine intelligence, data processing or control, for example, will finds this out for himself.

The articles in linguistics hang more strongly together, and seem to be more weakly linked with the rest, than any others. They certainly have a right to be included, because applied linguistics both uses advanced data processing techniques and is useful to them. Linguistic terminology frequently occurs in most descriptions of computer functions; documents and other utterances are potentially the most prolific source of data for data-hungry computers. I am therefore particularly indebted to Professor R. H. Robins for the following introductory account of general linguistics.

## General Linguistics

*General linguistics* as an academic subject sprang from a number of sources, notably from the nineteenth century study of comparative philology in British and continental universities, from anthropological work, especially that of American scholars in the field of American-Indian cultures, from certain developments in philosophy that involved a closer attention to questions of philosophical language, and from the experiences and the needs of teachers of modern languages.

Linguistics first achieved substantial recognition as an independent subject in America between the two world wars; this was followed by its recognition after the second world war in Britain and the rest of Europe. The growth of linguistic studies in recent years over much of the world has been phenomenal.

The objectives of linguistics are, quite simply, the study, the analysis, and the understanding of man's faculty of communicating by language, as witnessed by the languages of the world, living and dead, colloquial and literary, written and unwritten. Linguistics thus takes its place within the study of man, and in this context it is complementary both to literary studies and to the study of one's own language or of foreign languages (modern or classical).

Linguistics (the adjective 'general', though in frequent use, adds little to the title) envisages the study of language in two dimensions: the working of languages at any given time as self-contained systems of communication (descriptive or synchronic linguistics) and the historical changes that languages undergo in the course of time (historical or diachronic linguistics). Both of these dimensions involve and are involved in the major subdivisions of the subject:

    phonetics and phonology (the study of speech sounds and their functioning in languages),

    grammar (in the strict sense: syntax and morphology, the study of sentence structure and word structure),

    semantics (the study of vocabulary and meaning).

The relations between these subdivisions (or levels, as they are sometimes called) are differently interpreted by different groups of linguists, for example the transformational-generative grammarians as compared with their immediate predecessors in the United States and elsewhere.

'Applied linguistics' covers all aspects of the application of the theory and techniques of linguistics to specific practical purposes, e.g. modern language teaching, speech therapy, information retrieval, communications technology, and machine translation. In language teaching, linguistics has most to offer in the provision of material; languages can most effectively be taught to the extent that they have been accurately and systematically described; the role of phonetics in the teaching of pronunciation and its ability formally to describe intonation (previously left to be 'picked up'), and the role of grammatical analysis in contrastive studies of two or more languages are obvious examples of the place of applied linguistics in language teaching. In the different aspects of communications technology, the findings of general linguistics have proved to be of great value in making clear the communicative essentials at different levels that must be carried by the channel and which determine the requirements of the equipment, e.g. distinctive features in speech production and reception; syntactic structures, word forms, and word frequencies in the sentences of different languages.

A frequent mistake is the identification of applied linguistics with general linguistics. A proper understanding of what Bloomfield, one of the greatest linguists of all time, called 'the strangeness, beauty, and import of human speech', as well as fruitful applications of the science will best be achieved through the existence of a body of linguists disinterestedly concentrating on the study of language for its own sake, who are also always ready to make available their findings to those whose interests bring them into contact with the working of language. (End of comments by Prof. R. H. Robins.)

The organization of the encyclopaedia is inevitably a compromise. Browsers will find that related articles often occur in sequence, because the titles have been arranged to have some important keyword at the beginning, but no such device can put every article into all the groups to which it belongs. To supplement these partly fortuitous results of alphabetical arrangement, nearly every article ends with the advice *See also*, and a short list of related articles.

*Index-glossary*. Further help in searching for information is available in the index-glossary, which contains all the keywords of titles and subheadings as well as specialist words of the text. To facilitate reference back, the latter have been printed in italics on their first significant occurrence in an article.

A large number of words and expressions have been given a brief explanation, as well as a reference to articles where more extended treatment may be found. They form the glossary component of the index-glossary and will be helpful in most cases where understanding is impeded by the appearance of an unfamiliar word or, perhaps more commonly, by a word or phrase used in a specialized way. Examples of the latter practice are Process, Pulse, Read, Register and Tree, and there are many others. One difficulty often encountered when reading an unaccustomed subject, particularly if it is concerned with engineering or data-processing, is that of deciding whether some common-looking word is in fact being used with an uncommon or particular meaning, and in such cases of doubt the glossary will usually help.

I am indebted to several colleagues for assistance in preparing glossary entries, and where it has seemed appropriate their name has been appended to the entry in question. In other cases, entries have been taken verbatim from an article, and here the author's name has been included together with the title of his article. All the glossary entries concerned with linguistics are the work of Dr. R. A. Hudson, who has also selected the numerous index terms in this field.

*Acknowledgements*. I am deeply grateful to many people for their assistance in this project: at the National Physical Laboratory to the Director, Dr. J. V. Dunworth, the Superintendent of Autonomics Division, Mr. D. W. Davies and his predecessor Prof. A. M. Uttley and other members of staff including in particular Mr. P. H. Hammond and Mr. E. A. Newman; to Mr. B. R. Gaines, Cambridge University Psychology Dept., Dr. J. A. B. Gray now Second Secretary of the Medical Research Council, Prof. M. A. K. Halliday, Communications Research Centre University College, London, Mr. R. J. Halsey, recently Director of the Post Office Research Station, Dr. I, P. Priban, Medical Research Council, Prof. R. H. Robins, School of Oriental and African Studies, London University, Mr. C. J. Spratt, Post Office Engineering Dept., and Prof. I. C. Whitfield, Neurocommunications Research Unit, Birmingham University.

My best thanks to all referees, and warmest greetings to the contributors of articles, whose names and affiliations are listed in the preceding pages, followed by their articles in the list of contents. My sincere admiration to Dr. R. A. Hudson who came enthusiastically to the rescue when I was submerged by a torrent of linguistics articles. Finally we both join in thanking Mr. S. Crimmin of Pergamon Press, with whom it is always a pleasure to collaborate, for all his work in producing the book.

A. R. MEETHAM

# A

**ADAPTIVE CONTROL THEORY (The Structural and Behavioural Properties of Adaptive Controllers).**

## 1. Introduction

The term '*adaptive*' has long been applied in the biological sciences to denote the plasticity of behaviour shown by an organism in its struggle to survive in a novel or changeable environment (Stanier 1953 Sommerhof 1950). More recently control engineers have designed controllers with a similar ability to modify their behavioural strategies in the face of unpredictable changes in the controlled plant or its input, and they have used the term 'adaptive' to qualify both this type of controller and its behaviour. The aptness of a common description for biological and synthetic systems remains to be demonstrated by future studies coupling the disciplines of biology and control-engineering, but research on 'adaptive control' exists in its own right as a body of experimental, practical and theoretical work central to modern automatic control, and it is the foundations of this work which form the subject of this review.

As in all novel fields of research the terminology of adaptive control has varied widely, and at one time the variety of applications of the term 'adaptive' made it potentially meaningless. It is now accepted that 'adaption' is a very rich concept with both structural and behavioural connotations which must themselves be further qualified, and also that it is not an ontogenic property of a controller but rather a triadic relationship between controller, controlled system, and the purpose of the controller. Since the last is 'arbitrarily' assigned by the designer or observer, the application of the term 'adaptive' depends on their point of views, (Mishkin and Braun 1961) and every controller is in some sense 'adaptive'. However, once a point of view has been defined and agreed, the extent and nature of a controller's adaptivity can be determined by well-defined procedures, and it is these which are the concern of adaptive control theory.

The synthesis of adaptive controllers is very well documented, both by specialist papers on the design and performance of specific controllers, and in review papers which attempt an overall survey and classification of adaptive control schemes (Truxal 1963; Aseltine *et al*. 1958; Donaldson and Kishi 1965). The evaluation of adaptive controllers in various environments, and the general problem of comparing the behaviour of different adaptive and learning controllers, have not been studied so intensively, since the variety of adaptive control schemes has been small and their behaviour simple. Now that complex learning controllers are being simulated, and adaptive controllers are being applied to non-linear and noisy environments where their approach to optimality is not uniform or may not necessarily occur, there is a growing interest in the *evaluation* and manipulation *of adaptive behaviour*. The literature on this is brief and dispersed, and this article is intended to summarize and expand it.

The next section introduces the concept of an adaptive controller as a device for the selection and implementation of a control policy from a set of allowable policies. The means for performing this selection give rise to different adaptive control structures, but the structure of a particular controller is arbitrary to the extent that the classification of allowable policies may be varied. In the third section the behaviour of such controllers is analysed by segmenting their interaction with the environment into elements called 'tasks'. The manner in which the controller's satisfactoriness varies whilst performing a sequence of tasks gives rise to various modes of adaptive behaviour, but the mode of adaption shown by a particular segment of behaviour is arbitrary to the extent that the classification of tasks may be varied. In the fourth section a state-description of adaptive behaviour is used to define the 'adaption-automaton' of a controller for a set of tasks, and the previous definitions are stated formally in terms of the structure of this automaton. Finally, in the fifth section, 'training' is introduced as a means of fabricating a controller by varying the initial task sequence given to an adaptive controller. This is equivalent to control of the adaption-automaton, and the strategies used in this control give rise to different types of training.

## 2. The Structure of Adaptive Controllers

In synthesizing a controller for a novel environment the designer has available a body of knowledge about the behaviour of a class of controllers in various environments. If one of these controllers will perform sufficiently well in the given environment then the design problem is solved, and the designer selects that controller. If none of the controllers is uniformly satisfactory for all possible conditions of the environment, then it may be possible to find a *set* of controllers at least one of which is satisfactory for each condition. If the designer is able to synthesize a device which implements the appropriate 'controller' (or rather 'control policy') according to the environmental conditions then his overall control system is an *adaptive controller*. The adaptive controller thus automates the selection of a control policy, previously performed by the designer, and is in that sense a 'self-organizing system'. The two-level structure of an adaptive controller is illustrated in Fig. 1: the lower level is coupled to the environment by its

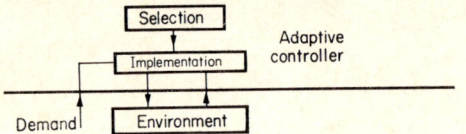

FIG. 1. *Adaptive controller*.

effector/receptor system, and receives information about the condition demanded in the environment; it implements a control policy (mapping between its inputs and outputs) which is specified by the upper level.

The strategy used by the upper level in selecting one control policy from the allowed set of policies may be used to distinguish different adaptive control structures. A major distinction is that between open-loop and closed-loop adaptive controllers (Carruthers and Levenstein 1963): an *open-loop adaptive controller* utilizes information obtained by 'identifying' the environment or demand-signal to select its control policy; a *closed-loop adaptive controller* utilizes information obtained by measuring the performance of its present and past control policies to select its next control policy. Thus the first type of controller implements a mapping from estimates of environment and demand conditions to its control policies, and relies upon the correctness both of these estimates and of the mapping. Whereas the second type of controller actually tests the appropriateness of its control policy and hence obtains feedback about the effects of its adaptive strategy. The two types of adaption are most powerful in combination, as illustrated in Fig. 2, since open-loop adaption can rapidly cope with expected environmental changes but

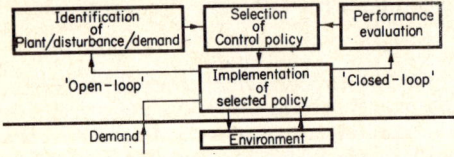

FIG. 2. *Structure of an adaptive controller*.

closed-loop adaption is necessary to check that this is operating correctly and to change it, perhaps by 'trial-and-error', if it is not.

The open-loop adaptive structure can be further classified by considering the canonical forms of the environment and of the system which is generating demand signals. Any physical system may be represented as a state-determined automaton with an output and a partially controllable input (that is a controllable input plus disturbance). A controller which identifies some property of the state of this automaton has been called, 'system-variable adaptive', and if it identifies

the transitions of the automaton it has been called, 'system-characteristic adaptive' (Aseltine *et al*. 1958). A controller identifying some property of the demand signal has been called 'input-signal adaptive', although a better name would be 'demand-signal adaptive'. Six such distinctions may be made, although in practice they merge into one another since, for example, the effect of a disturbance may be ascribed to an unobservable distinction between states.

Closed-loop adaptive structures may be further classified into those which change their control policy randomly until one is found which gives a satisfactory performance, and those which change their control policy according to definite rules dependent on past policies and their performances. The former may be said to adapt by an 'evolutionary' process (Ashby 1960; Bremmerman *et al*. 1965), and the latter may be said to be 'hill-climbing systems'.

The structural definition of an adaptive controller as one having the form of Fig. 1 does not define the class of control policies from which the upper level may select, and since one control policy may often be regarded as a class of simpler policies the definition contains an arbitrary element. This arbitrariness is not apparent in the literature because the class of linear controllers (and in particular PID controllers) has been the only one of practical interest. Thus the relay controller has been classified as 'passively adaptive' (Aseltine *et al*. 1958) since its describing function (equivalent linear controller) has a gain varying inversely with the magnitude of the error, and hence the simple relay controller may be said to 'select' a control policy from the class of linear controllers consisting of a pure gain. If, instead of this class, one considered the class of control policies as 'linear-plus-relay and linear controllers', then the relay controller would no longer have an adaptive control structure, but the dual-mode controller would still be 'passively adaptive'.

Even the simple servo becomes an adaptive controller if the class of control policies is taken to be, 'those with a fixed output voltage'. This is not a trivial example, because the transient behaviour of the simple servo forms a good approximation to the behaviour of many adaptive loops, and also it offers an interesting case of the distinction between open- and closed-loop adaption: consider the very different effects of reversing the sign of the input to a simple servo and to a human operator in a tracking situation; the former now has positive feedback and oscillates, showing that it is only open-loop, system-variable adaptive; the latter changes the sign of his output (in less than half a second) showing that the human operator is closed-loop adaptive (Young *et al*. 1964).

The arbitrariness in the structural definition of an adaptive controller is not a defect, but rather central to the importance of adaptive concepts in the design of controllers. If the class of control policies were fixed then the 'adaptive controller' could be fully investigated until all its applications and its limitations were completely known, as has happened to the 'linear controller' at present. However, this is not so, for the 'adaptive controllers' of today will become the 'control policies' of tomorrow, and adaption may be seen as a design tool for extending the range of application of the available class of controllers.

### 3. The Behaviour of Adaptive Controllers

Even if a closed-loop adaptive controller is operating correctly and is always eventually able to select a satisfactory control policy, it may take so long to do this that it is worthless as a controller. Thus the designer is faced with the problem of not only evaluating the control policy of the adaptive controller but also evaluating its adaptivity in varying this policy appropriately. If the upper level of the adaptive controller were linear or permitted a linear approximation then its behaviour could be analysed conventionally on the basis of stability, time constants, and so on. However, the possibility of such an analysis is rare since, even if the lower level implements linear policies, the upper level tends to be designed as a discrete, decision-taking controller which does not permit a linear approximation. This section outlines a theory of controller behaviour which is applicable to these more general forms of adaptive controller as well as to the simpler linear, time-varying, controllers.

*3.1. Segmentation of the controller environment interaction into 'Tasks'.* The expected behaviour of an adaptive controller when coupled to an environment is that, if its control policy is not satisfactory for the condition of the environment, then it will eventually become satisfactory. Thus it must be possible to segment its interaction with the environment into two phases, in the first of which it is not satisfactory and in the second of which it has become so. This segmentation of the interaction between controller and environment into units, for which the controller is or is not satisfactory, is extended in the definition of a 'task' to form the basis for a taxonomy of adaptive behaviour.

A 'task' is a segment of the interaction between controller and environment for which it is possible to say whether or not the controller has performed satisfactorily. Equivalence relationships between tasks (so that it is possible to say, for instance, that an interaction consists of the same task repeated several times) are arbitrary, but will in practice follow from the natural relationships between different types of controlled system. A 'task' will typically consist of some specification of the plant parameters, initial conditions and period of interaction, together with a tolerable performance level below which a control policy is not satisfactory.

The importance of this segmentation into 'tasks' may be seen by considering the effect of performing a 'task' on the upper level of the adaptive controller. At the beginning of the interaction this level will be in some state which causes it to implement a particular control policy. At the end of the interaction it will be in another state, and it will be possible to say whether the overall control policy which has been implemented is satisfactory or not. If the controller is deterministic and the task is reasonably defined then the final state of the upper level will depend only on its initial state and the 'task' given to it. Thus the 'task' may be considered to be an 'input', in some sense, to the upper level of the adaptive controller. The description of the adaptive behaviour of the controller in terms of its performance of task sequences is then based on a state-description of the upper level of the controller, and this is applicable both to linear and non-linear controllers.

The segmentation of an interaction into tasks may be performed in many ways: the time of interaction between controller and environment may be fixed; a criterion for the termination of an interaction in terms of the behaviour itself may be given; the interaction may be terminated as soon as a decision can be made about the satisfactoriness of the controller. The 'termination' itself may be purely conceptual, a convenient division of a continuous sequence of behaviour into separate sub-sequences, or it may have a physical reality in that the plant is modified at the termination of an interaction. The next sub-section describes one example of the segmentation of an interaction into tasks.

*3.2. An example of a set of tasks for a single-input, single-output controller.* Consider the stable, noiseless second-order plant shown in Fig. 3, consisting of two

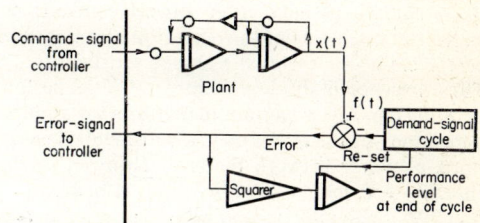

FIG. 3. *Example of a 'task' for testing the adaptivity of a controller.*

integrators in cascade with feedback from the output; its parameters are the gain, undamped natural frequency, and damping ratio. Let a task be defined by ascribing values to these three paramaters and the two initial values of the integrators, together with a time-varying demand signal, $f(t)$ for $0 \leq t < T$, and a decision procedure such that the interaction is satisfactory if and only if:

$$\frac{1}{T}\int_{t_0}^{t_0+T}[f(t_0+t)-x(t_0+t)]^2\,dt < E^2,$$

where $t_0$ is the time at which the interaction starts, $x(t)$ is the output of the plant, and $E > 0$ is some tolerance on the r.m.s. error.

To test the adaptivity of a controller to the plant and demand conditions specified by such a task, it is connected to the plant and the demand-signal cycled with period $T$. After every cycle the task is complete, and the r.m.s. error during that cycle determines whether or not the controller has performed satisfactorily. If the controller is adaptive, the r.m.s. error in each cycle might be expected to decrease, and hence (by suitable choice of $E$) the controller will be unsatisfactory initially, but after a number of repetitions of the task it will become satisfactory and remain so. Many other forms of adaptive behaviour might arise, however: the controller could be always satisfactory or always unsatisfactory; it could start by being satisfactory and become unsatisfactory; it could vary between being satisfactory and being unsatisfactory, never settling at one or the other. If other tasks with different values of the plant parameters of demanded signal were interpolated, then the adaptive behaviour would become richer still. It is the description of this variety of possible behaviours which concerns the behavioural theory of adaption.

*3.3. Varieties of adaptive behaviour*. If a task is regarded as an 'input' to the upper level of an adaptive controller, and the satisfactoriness of its performance as an 'output', then, whilst the general theory of controllers considers all possible input sequences, the theory of adaptive controllers places especial emphasis on the effects of the repetition of a single input (for example the cycling of a task described in the example above); an adaptive system is characterized by its changing response to the same situation. This prompts the following definitions:

*Acceptability*—an interaction between controller and environment consisting of the repetition of a single task is *acceptable* if it is eventually always satisfactory.

Thus, in an acceptable interaction, the initial performance of the controller does not matter and for a number of repetitions of the task it may be satisfactory, unsatisfactory, or waver between the two. However, it must eventually become satisfactory and remain so; an acceptable interaction is one which reaches a *stable* condition of satisfactoriness.

*Adapted*—an interaction between controller and environment consisting of the repetition of a single task is *immediately acceptable* if it is always satisfactory; an immediately acceptable interaction is obviously acceptable. A controller in such a condition that it would have an immediately acceptable interaction with a task is *adapted* to that task.

The concepts of acceptability and adaptedness concern the controller's interaction with a single task, but the adaptivity of the controller is generally required because the particular task it must perform is incompletely specified or may change. The possible varieties of adaptive behaviour in a control situation involving a number of tasks are many, but there are three of particular interest which will be discussed in the following sub-sections.

*3.4. Potential adaption*. Very often an adaptive controller is used to perform a single task which will not change, but whose characteristics are unknown in advance. It must be capable of having an acceptable interaction with any of a range of tasks, but need not necessarily be capable of adapting to a sequence of different tasks. This prompts the following definition:

*Potential adaption*—a controller in such a condition that it will have an acceptable interaction with any one of a set of tasks is *potentially adaptive* to that set of tasks.

A potentially adaptive controller fulfils one aim of adaptive design in compensating for the designer's ignorance about the task to be performed. It will not necessarily fulfil another major aim by performing satisfactorily in a changing situation, since there is no implication that having adapted to one task it remains potentially adaptive to the others. Potential adaption is implied in statements like, 'a shoe adapts itself to the shape of a foot', and is the weakest form of goal-attainment to merit the designation 'adaptive'.

*3.5. Compatible adaption*. A controller which is designed to perform satisfactorily in a changing situation must not only adapt to its immediate task but must also remain potentially adaptive to other tasks which it may meet. This prompts the following definition:

*Compatibly adapted*—a controller is *compatibly adapted* to a task with respect to a set of tasks if, in an interaction consisting of a repetition of the task, it is not only always satisfactory but also potentially adaptive to the set of tasks.

A controller which is to be of use in a changing situation must be potentially adaptive to all those tasks which it is required to perform satisfactorily, no matter what tasks it has previously performed. This prompts the following definition:

*Compatibly adaptive*—a controller is *compatibly adaptive* to a set of tasks if, given any sequence of tasks from that set, it remains potentially adaptive to the set of tasks.

Thus a controller which is compatibly adaptive to a set of tasks will have an acceptable interaction with any one of those tasks, and no matter how it becomes adapted to one of them it will be compatibly adapted with respect to the remainder.

*3.6. Joint adaption*. A controller which is compatibly adaptive to a set of tasks is not necessarily able to become adapted simultaneously to all of them. It is, however, quite possible for two tasks to be so similar that a controller which is adapted to one may also be adapted to the other. This prompts the following definition:

*Jointly adapted*—a controller is *jointly adapted* to a set of tasks if, given any sequence of tasks from that set, it remains adapted to every member of the set.

Thus a controller which is jointly adapted to a set of tasks will be always satisfactory given any sequence of those tasks. This is a very strong condition, and an even stronger one is that when a controller adapts to one of a set of tasks it should eventually become jointly adapted to all of them:

*Jointly adaptive*—a controller is jointly adaptive to a set of tasks if it is both compatibly adaptive to the set and, during an acceptable interaction with any task in the set, it eventually becomes jointly adapted to the whole set.

*3.7. Inter-relationships between different types of adaptive behaviour.* The preceding definitions of adaptive behaviour have been given in order of increasing strength, for if a controller is jointly adaptive to a set of tasks it is also compatibly adaptive to them, and if a controller is compatibly adaptive to a set of tasks it is also potentially adaptive to them.

Jointly Adaptive $\Rightarrow$ Compatibly Adaptive $\Rightarrow$ Potentially Adaptive. These three modes of adaption are by no means exhaustive, and it will have been obvious that many variations are possible, defining other forms of adaptive behaviour. However, most of these would be regarded as pathological, in that no advantage is gained by designing them into the controller, and the three chosen for discussion are especially important in forming explicata of the common stereotypes of adaptive behaviour.

The definitions of *adapted, compatibly adapted, jointly adapted*, and *potentially, compatibly* and *jointly adaptive*, may be used to define binary relationships on the set of tasks, relative to a controller in a given condition; for example, $task_1$ is related to $task_2$ if the controller is compatibly adapted to $task_1$ with respect to $task_2$. All six relationships are reflexive, and only that induced by 'compatibly adapted' is not symmetric. However, only 'adapted' and 'potentially adaptive' induce relationships which are also transitive (and hence are equivalence relationships). For instance, a controller may be jointly adapted to $task_1$ and $task_2$, and also jointly adapted to $task_2$ and $task_3$, but given a sequence containing $task_1$ and $task_3$ there is no reason why even its potential adaptation to both tasks should not disappear. It is this lack of equivalence relationships which gives adaptive behaviour its extraordinary richness. A controller which shows no 'pathological' behaviour is rare, although the more drastic forms will be designed out if possible; for example, the relationship induced by 'compatibly adaptive' ought to be one of equivalence, for no sequence of normal tasks should be able to destroy a controller's ability to adapt to one of them.

*3.8. Arbitrariness and triviality in the definitions of 'adaptive'.* Just as the structural definition of an 'adaptive controller' contains an arbitrary element, because the classification of allowable control policies is left undefined, so do the behavioural definitions of 'adapted' and 'adaptive' contain an arbitrary element because the classification of tasks is left undefined. This arbitrariness need cause no confusion provided it is realized that at some stage in the discussion of an adaptive controller and its behaviour both these classifications must be agreed. Much early controversy over the application of the term 'adaptive' arose because the 'obvious', tacit classifications of one engineer were not those of another, or because disagreement over such classifications was wrongly ascribed to the definition of adaption itself.

Even when the arbitrariness in the definitions is accepted there remains the possibility that some types of adaptive structure and adaptive behaviour may be 'trivial'. Open-loop adaptive controllers have no feedback from their performance by which to guide their adaption, and it has been suggested that they be treated as 'unusual' non-linear but 'non-adaptive' controllers (Raible 1963). In the behavioural definitions of 'adaptive', 'jointly adaptive' is a very strong condition which is often trivial in practice—the tasks to which a controller becomes jointly adapted are equivalent and need not be distinguished. 'Potentially adaptive' is a very weak condition which again may often be regarded as trivial, because it is satisfied by systems showing an irreversible descent to equilibrium. 'Compatibly adaptive' adds the requirement of reversibility, and is closest to what is commonly regarded as being 'really adaptive'. However, although a compatibly adaptive controller shows the behaviour which one would expect, it may still do so 'trivially' by being adapted to all its tasks all the time, and hence showing no adaptive dynamics—it is just a very good, but static, controller!

In testing the behaviour of an artifact (or animal) for 'adaption' or 'learning' it may be desirable to eliminate this 'trivial' adaption; it is meaningful, for example, to ask whether an animal performs well in two different situations because it has a policy suited to both, or because it changes its policy according to the situation. To force the controller to show adaptive dynamics, one might say that it is 'really adaptive' to a task if it has an acceptable, but not immediately acceptable, interaction consisting of the repetition of that task. This is bound to occur if a controller is compatibly, but not jointly, adaptive to a pair of tasks, for there will then be a sequence of the tasks which causes it to become adapted to one but not the other. It has been suggested that a crucial test for 'learning' may be constructed by requiring an artifact to be compatibly adapted to two tasks, which are so defined that it is *logically* impossible for it to be jointly adaptive to them (Martens 1959).

## 4. State-Descriptions of Adaptive Behaviour and 'Adaption-Automata'

Although the definitions of various modes of adaptive behaviour have used the term 'condition' of a controller in such a way to imply that this is the 'state' of the upper level of an adaptive controller, there is no need to introduce structural considerations into state-descriptions of adaptive behaviour and the term 'condition' may be taken as what is actually defined. Such a view is taken in this section in order to introduce the concept of an 'adaption-automaton', and the preceding definitions are embedded in the automaton structure. A clearer picture of the inter-relationships between the various modes of adaption is then possible.

The mechanics for the introduction of a state-description into a system defined extensively by its behaviour are well-known (Zadeh 1964) and will be outlined only briefly. The object so far defined is a set of tasks, with relationships between them defined by the effect of sequences of tasks on the satisfactoriness of the controller environment interaction. The state of the controller should then be a description enabling its satisfactoriness to be predicted for each member of any sequence of tasks. Thus a description of the condition of a controller will be called its 'state' at the start of a sequence of tasks if it completely determines the satisfactoriness of the controller for each task in the sequence. If such a description is available of the controller at the termination of any task, it is said to have a complete state-description. If two descriptions of the conditions of a controller always predict identical sequences of satisfactoriness they are said to be equivalent. A complete state-description under the quotient mapping induced by this equivalence is said to be a minimal state-description.

This is merely a definition of 'state' for a fully controllable (not necessarily observable) state-determined automaton with inputs. The existence of a complete state-description implies that there is a minimal state description such that the state of the controller at the beginning of a task and the task itself together determine its state at the end of the task and the satisfactoriness of its performance. Thus there is defined an automaton whose state is a description from the minimal state-description of the controller, whose input is a task and whose output is the binary variable 'satisfactory' or 'not satisfactory'. This is the *adaption-automaton* of the controller for the set of tasks. It is not a finite-state machine, but considerations of acceptability give it many of the properties of one; for example, the output must retain the same value after a finite number of repetitions of a task for which the controller is potentially adaptive, and hence the states from then on are in some way equivalent. In the next-section the previously defined modes of adaption will be re-phrased in terms of the structure of the adaption-automaton.

*4.1. Adaption-automata.* An adaption automaton has a possibly infinite set of states, probably a finite set of inputs (tasks) and two outputs (satisfactory $0^+$, unsatisfactory $0^-$). A typical state will be represented by the letter, $s$ ($s_1$, $s_2$ etc. if there are several); a typical input by the letter, $t$ ($t_1$, $t_2$ etc. if there are several); and the outputs by symbols, $0^+$, $0^-$. Let an automaton in state $s$, be given a task $t$, such that its next state is $s'$ and its output is $o$. We have the transition mapping:

$$s' = \sigma(s, t)$$

and the output mapping:

$$o = \theta(s, t).$$

Since we are interested in the effects of sequences of inputs, especially those generated by the repetition of a single task or by any means from a set of tasks, it is important to have a clear notation distinguishing between tasks, sets of tasks, sequences of tasks and sets of sequences of tasks. A sequence consisting of task $t_1$ followed by task $t_2$ will be written $t_1 t_2$ (with the obvious extension to longer sequences); a sequence consisting of the task $t$ repeated $n$ times will be written $t^n$. A typical set of tasks will be represented by the letter, $T(T_1, T_2$ etc.); a typical sequence of tasks will be represented by the letter, $u(u_1, u_2$ etc.). The set of sequences generated by the set of tasks, $T$, as free generators, will be written $U(T)$; that is, $U(T)$ is the set of all sequences of tasks which may be formed using the members of $T$. The mapping, $\sigma$, has an obvious extension from tasks to task sequences:

$$\text{if} \quad T = tT', \quad \text{then} \quad \sigma(s, T) = \sigma(\sigma(s, t), T').$$

*4.2. Adaption sets.* Let

$$W(T) \equiv \{s \mid \forall t \in T, \; \theta(s, t) = 0^+\};$$

that is, $W(T)$ is the set of states such that the controller will have a satisfactory interaction given any task from the set, $T$.
Let

$$A(t) \equiv \{s \mid \forall n, \; \sigma(s, t^n) \in W(t)\};$$

that is, $A(t)$ is the set of states in which the controller is adapted to the task, $t$.
Let

$$P(T) \equiv \{s \mid \forall t \in T, \; \exists N: \sigma(s, t^N) \in A(t)\};$$

that is, $P(T)$ is the set of states in wich the controller is potentially adaptive to the set of tasks, $T$.
Let

$$C_A(t, T) \equiv \{s \mid \forall t \in T, n, \; \sigma(s, t^n) \in W(t) \cap P(T)\};$$

that is, $C_A(t, T)$ is the set of states in which the controller is compatibly adapted to the task, $t$, with respect to the set of tasks, $T$.

Let $C(T) \equiv \{s \mid \forall t \in T, \; u \in U(T), \; \sigma(s, u) \in P(T)\};$

that is, $C(T)$ is the set of states in which the controller is compatibly adaptive to the set of tasks, $T$.
Let

$$J_A(T) \equiv \{s \mid \forall t \in T, \; u \in U(T), \; \sigma(s, u) \in A(t)\};$$

that is, $J_A(T)$ is the set of states in which the controller is jointly adapted to the set of tasks, $T$.
Let

$$J(T) \equiv \{s \mid \exists N: \forall t \in T, \; u \in U(T), \; \sigma(s, ut^N) \in J_A(T)\}$$

that is, $J(T)$ is the set of states in which the controller is jointly adaptive to the set of tasks, $T$.

This defines all the various modes of adaption previously described—they now appear as constraints on the structure of the adaption-automaton. There are many inclusion relationships between the adaption sets, of which the following are the most important:

$$W(T_1 \cup T_2) = W(T_1) \cap W(T_2);$$
$$P(T_1 \cup T_2) = P(T_1) \cap P(T_2);$$
$$C(T_1 \cup T_2) \subset C(T_1) \cap C(T_2);$$
$$J(T_1 \cup T_2) \subset J(T_1) \cap J(T_2);$$
$$A(t) \subset W(t) \cap P(t);$$

This last relationship is illustrated in Fig. 4: the space of all states is split into overlapping regions, $W(t)$, $P(t)$, $A(t)$; performance of the task, $t$, causes a transition from one state in the space to another; it is shown that the trajectory generated by a repetition of the task, $t^n$, starting at $X$ in $P(t)$, must eventually enter $A(t)$ and, once in,

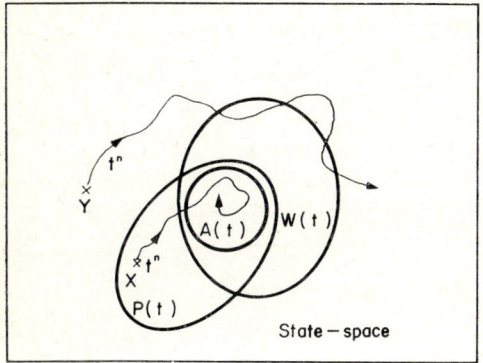

FIG. 4. *Behaviour of adaption–automaton for single task.*

it cannot escape; whereas a similar trajectory starting at $Y$ outside $P(t)$ cannot enter $A(t)$, and if it should enter $W(t)$ must always leave it again. Thus $A(t)$ is the maximum set contained in $W(t)$ which is closed under the operator, $t$; it is the maximum 'trapping set' of $W(t)$ under $t$. Similarly $P(t)$ is the maximum trapping set for the whole space under $t$, which contains no non-transient states outside $W(t)$.

Further important relationships are:

$$C_A(t, T) = A(t) \cap P(T);$$
$$P(t_1 \cup t_2) \supset A(t_1) \cap A(t_2) \supset J_A(t_1 \cup t_2);$$
$$P(T) \supset C(T) \supset J(T).$$

Some of the relationships between potential, compatible and joint adaption for two tasks are illustrated in Fig. 5: the space of all states is split into regions $A(t_1)$, $A(t_2)$, $P(t_1 \cup t_2)$, $C(t_1 \cup t_2)$, $J(t \cup t_2)$; since the state $X_0$ is within $P(t_1 \cup t_2)$ but outside $C(t_1 \cup t_2)$, trajectories of the form $t_1^n$ or $t_2^n$ will eventually reach $A(t_1)$ or $A(t_2)$ respectively, but leave $P(t_1 \cup t_2)$ in so doing; this loss of potential adaptivity may not take place immediately (as in the trajectory from $X_0$ to $X_1$), as is shown by the trajectory from $X_0$ to $X_2$ under $t_2^n$ which enters $A(t_2)$ within $P(t_1 \cup t_2)$ and hence is within $C_A(t_1 \cup t_2)$—on taking advantage of its adaptivity to $t_1$, however, it reaches $X_3$ where it has lost the possibility of returning to $A(t_2)$; $C(t_1 \cup t_2)$ is the maximum trapping set of $P(t_1 \cup t_2)$ under $t_1$ and $t_2$, and hence a trajectory starting from $Y_1$ within $C(t_1 \cup t_2)$ cannot escape from $P(t_1 \cup t_2)$ no matter what sequence of tasks it is given. $J_A(t_1 \cup t_2)$ is the maximum trapping set within $C(t_1 \cup t_2)$ which is contained in the intersection of $A(t_1)$ and $A(t_2)$, and $J(t_1 \cup t_2)$ is the maximum trapping set within $C(t_1 \cup t_2)$ which contains no non-transient states outside $J_A(t_1 \cup t_2)$.

The possible modes of adaptive behaviour are many, and only a few have been illustrated. It will have been apparent, however, that certain modes of behaviour are to be preferred—it would be pleasant to build a controller that always settled in $J_A(T)$, or, more realistically, that always remained in $C(T)$. This might

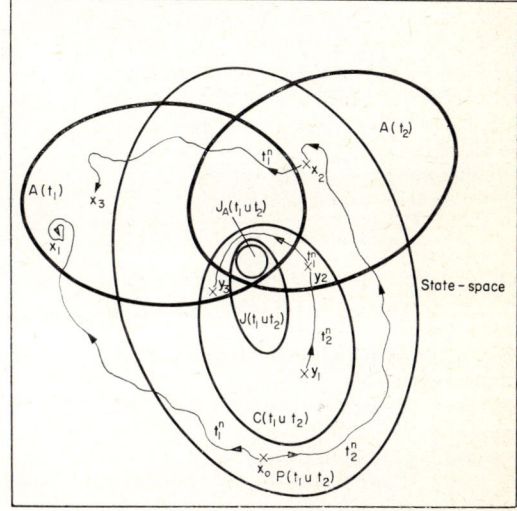

FIG. 5. *Behaviour adaption–automaton for two tasks.*

not be possible at the design stage, however, and the initial state of a controller could be outside $P(T)$! Such a controller might well be very attractive if it were cheap to fabricate, and there existed a sequence of tasks which would cause it to enter $C(T)$ (where $T$ is the set of tasks it is required to perform). This sequence of tasks would be a 'training' sequence given to the controller for the sole purpose of shaping its response to later tasks, and the possibility of 'training' adaptive controllers will be considered in the next section.

## 5. Strategies for Training

It has been assumed that the tasks given to the controller are those which it is required to perform satisfactorily, and hence the emphasis has been on task sequences consisting of a repetition of the same task; such a sequence is called a *fixed training sequence* for the task. The success of fixed training depends upon the controller being at least potentially adaptive to the task it has to perform, or, more strongly, compatibly adaptive to the set of tasks it has to perform. The selection of tasks by the trainer in fixed training involves no observation of the condition of the adaption-automaton, and the controller is given only those tasks which it is required to perform satisfactorily.

In *open-loop training* the trainer still does not observe the controller, but prepares it for adaption to the main tasks by giving it an initial sequence of auxiliary, or training, tasks for which it is not required to be satisfactory. Let:

$$P(T \mid u) \equiv \{s \mid \sigma(s, u) \in P(T)\};$$

that is, $P(T \mid u)$ is the set of states from which the training sequence, $u$, takes the controller to a state where it is potentially adaptive to the set of tasks, $T$. A controller whose adaption-automaton is in one of these states may not adapt to a task, $t \in T$, when given the fixed training sequence, $t^n$, but will do so if given the open-loop training-sequence $ut^n$; such a controller is said to be *potentially open-loop trainable* by the task sequence, $u$, for the set of tasks, $T$.

Similar conditional-adaption sets may be defined for *compatibly open-loop trainable*:

$$C(T \mid u) \equiv \{s \mid \sigma(s, u) \in C(T)\};$$

and for *jointly open-loop trainable*.

$$J(T \mid u) \equiv \{s \mid \sigma(s, u) \in J(T)\}.$$

There is obviously an even greater variety of modes of adaption with which to contend in conditionally adaptive situations—one may question whether a particular open-loop training sequence is always applicable, whether it can be harmful to the adaptivity toward some tasks, and so on. This variety is so great that it is not worthwhile treating it in a general terminology, and recourse must be made to the specific properties of the adaption-automaton under consideration.

*5.1. Training as a control problem.* An open-loop training sequence would be chosen to make the conditional-adaption sets as large as possible, so that they include all the possible initial states of the adaption-automaton. Some general restrictions, such as $P(T \mid u) \supset \supset P(T)$, may also be applied to ensure that the training does not destroy adaptivity which is already present. However, it may not be possible to find a single training sequence which has all the properties desired, and hence it may be necessary to apply different training sequences dependent on the initial condition of the controller. The only output from the adaption-automaton is a performance measure, the satisfactoriness of an interaction, and a trainer which utilizes this output in selecting the initial training sequence is said to be a *performance-feedback trainer*. A typical training strategy for this type of trainer would be to give one task until it is performed satisfactorily, and then another, and so on until the required task is being performed satisfactorily.

If other outputs from the adaption-automaton are made available and the trainer uses these in selecting the initial training sequence, then it is said to be a *feedback-trainer*. At this level of complexity training is itself a control problem: there is an 'environment', physically the controller, conceptually its adaption-automaton, whose inputs are tasks and one of whose outputs is the satisfactoriness of the previous interaction; the control problem is to take the automaton from an initial state, where the controller is not adapted to the task, to a final state where the controller is adapted to the task (or potentially, compatibly, or jointly, adapted to a set of tasks); the performance measure for this control problem may be based on the number of tasks given before the controller is adapted, or it may be a more complex cost function based on the cost of giving irrelevant tasks and so on.

The feedback-trainer solves this control problem by utilizing information about the state of the controller's adaption-automaton in selecting the task to be given to it. A stationary feedback-trainer implements a mapping between the state of the adaption-automaton at the end of a task and the next task to be given. This mapping will be a function of the tasks which the controller is required to perform satisfactorily, but, considering only one such task, let the mapping be:

$$t = \tau(s),$$

so that the transition and output equations may be written:

$$s' = \sigma(s, \tau(s)) = \sigma s, \quad \text{say};$$
$$0 = \theta(s, \tau(s)) = \theta s, \quad \text{say}.$$

If the trainer is successful then ultimately the task should always be the required one, $t_0$ say, and the output should be always satisfactory—that is, for some $N$:

$$\forall n > N \quad \tau(\sigma^n s) = t_0$$
$$\theta \sigma^n s = 0^+.$$

If these conditions are not fulfilled then it may still be possible for the task sequence to contain $t_0$ frequently with a satisfactory interaction, and this mode of behaviour (which is shown in the symbiosis of animals and plants) may be advantageous if continual performance of a single task is not required (Schrodt 1965).

## 6. Summary and Conclusions

Adaptive controllers have a two-level structure in which the upper level selects a control-policy and the lower level implements it. The class of control-policies from which the upper level selects has generally been that of linear differential operators, but it is central to the importance of adaptive concepts in design that this class expands as our knowledge increases. The upper level of an *open-loop adaptive controller* utilizes information obtained by identifying the environment or demand-signal to select a control-policy. The upper level of a *closed-loop adaptive controller* utilizes information obtained by measuring the performance of its present and past control policies to select its next control policy.

The evaluation of the controller's adaptive strategy depends on the segmentation of its interaction with the environment into 'tasks', so that the behaviour of the controller may be regarded as the performance of a sequence of tasks for each of which it is, or is not, satisfactory. This evaluation reduces to an analysis of the stability, settling time, and so on, of the upper level regarded as a (highly non-linear) controller, which would be quite general were it not for the importance in adaptive control of input sequences consisting of the repetition of a single task. This leads to the definition of modes of behaviour which are peculiarly important to adaptive control theory.

A controller is *adapted* to a task if, given that task an indefinite number of times in sequence, it is always satisfactory. A controller is *potentially adaptive* to a set of tasks if, given any one of the tasks a number of times in sequence, it eventually becomes adapted to it. A controller is *compatibly adaptive* to a set of tasks if, given any sequence of the tasks, it remains potentially adaptive to them all; this is the explicatum of 'adaptive' nearest to its general usage. A special case of this, jointly adaptive, is so strong as to imply some triviality in the definition of the tasks—a controller is *jointly adaptive* to a set of tasks if in adapting to any one of them it eventually becomes adapted to all.

The *adaption-automaton* of a controller's adaptive behaviour is based on a state-description of the controller which enables its satisfactoriness for each of a sequence of tasks to be predicted. The definitions of different modes of adaption may be regarded as descriptions of the adaption-automaton's gross structure, and represent common behaviour in non-pathological controllers.

*Training* a controller consists of the manipulation of the inputs (tasks) to its adaption-automaton in order to force it into a condition where it is adapted to a particular task (or compatibly or jointly adaptive to a set of tasks). If the controller is already potentially adaptive to the task then *fixed training* may be used, in which it is given only the task for which it is required to be satisfactory. In *open-loop training* an initial sequence of auxiliary tasks, independent of the adaption-automaton's initial state, is given to the controller in order to make it potentially adaptive to the required task. In *performance-feedback training* the satisfactoriness of past interactions is used to select the training sequence given to the controller, and in *feedback training* general information about the state of the controller's adaption automaton is used in this selection.

The early adaptive controllers were too simple for training techniques to be of practical importance, but future '*learning machines*' may become commercially viable only as a general-purpose control-element which is fabricated uniformly and *trained* for a specific application. '*Teaching machines*' for the human adaptive controller (Gaines 1966) illustrate the use of training to synthesize a controller by manipulation of its initial environment rather than its internal structure, and the converse situation has been realized in which the human operator is used to train a learning-machine (Widrow and Smith 1964). Adaptive controllers were originally conceived for their insensitivity to variations in the controlled system, but the opportunities they offer for synthesis through 'training' may well become their main attraction.

*See also:* Control: basic elements. Learning machines. Automata, finite-state.

*Bibliography*

ASELTINE, MANCINI and SARTURE (1958) *A survey of adaptive control systems, Trans. I.R.E.*, AC-**6**, Dec., 102.
ASHBY (1960) *Design for a Brain*, London: Chapman and Hall.
ASHBY (1964) *The set theory of mechanism and homeostasis*, Yearbook of Soc. for Gen. Systems Res., Vol. 9.
BREMMERMANN, ROGSON and SALAFF (1965) *Search by Evolution*, in *Biophysics and Cybernetic Systems*, New York: Spartan Press.
CARRUTHERS and LEVENSTEIN (Eds.) (1963) *Adaptive Control Systems*, Oxford: Pergamon Press.
DONALDSON and KISHI (1965) *Review of adaptive control system theories and techniques* in *Modern Contro Systems Theory*, New York: McGraw-Hill.
GAINES (1967) *Teaching machines for perceptual-motor skills*, Nat. Prog. Learn. Conf. Loughborough (1966) in *Aspects of the Technology of Teaching)*, London: Methuen.
MARTENS (1959) *Two notes on Machine learning, Inf. and Control*, **2** (4) Dec., 364.
MISHKIN and BRAUN (1961) *Adaptive Control Systems*, New York: McGraw-Hill.
RAIBLE (1963) *Comments on 'An approach to self-adaptive control', Trans. I.E.E.E.*, Ac-**8** (3), July, 270.
SCHRODT (1965) *Controlled cycle operations, Ind. Engng. Chem.*, **4** (1), Feb., 108.
SOMMERHOF (1950) *Analytical Biology*, Oxford: The University Press.
STANIER (1953) *Adaptation in Micro-organisms* (1953) 3rd. Symp. Soc. Gen. Microbiol., Cambridge: The University Press.
TOLMAN (1925) *Purpose and Cognition: the determiners of animal learning, Psychol. Rev.*, July.
TRUXAL (1963) *Adaptive control*, Survey paper, 2nd Congr. Intern. Fed. Automatic Control.
WIDROW and SMITH (1964) *Pattern recognizing control systems*, in *Computer and Information Sciences*, New York: Spartan Press.
YOUNG, GREEN, ELKIND and KELLY (1964) *Adaptive dynamic response characteristics of the human operator in simple manual control, Trans. I.E.E.E.* HFE, **5** (1), Sept., 6.
ZADEH (1963) *On the definition of adaptivity, Proc. I.E.E.E.*, **51** (3), March, 469.
ZADEH (1964) *The concept of state in system theory*, in *Views on General Systems Theory*, New York: Wiley.

B. R. GAINES

**ADAPTIVE THRESHOLD ELEMENTS.** *I. Introduction.* The term adaptive, as used herein, is meant to describe the behaviour of a system that automatically changes its internal structure so that the response of the system to a set of sample inputs is modified in a desired manner. The goal of an adaptation process is to produce a system structure that responds correctly to new inputs. For example, if the adaptive system has been adapted (or trained) to classify written samples of the letters $A$ and $B$, the system should respond correctly to new samples.

Figure 1 shows a block diagram of an adaptive system. In this figure, a set of input variables, represented by the vector **X**, is presented to the system along with a desired response for the set. The internal structure is then modified so that the response to this pattern vector

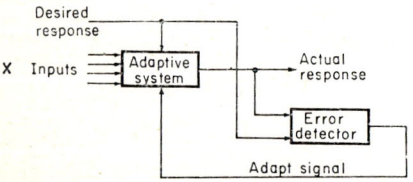

FIG. 1. *Adaptive system.*

is more nearly correct. If the desired response is supplied by some external agency, the adaptation process is called 'learning with a teacher'. If the desired response is based on the present input and its response, or on some function of past inputs and responses, the adaptation process is called 'learning without a teacher'.

The mechanization of the adaptive system discussed here is that of an adaptive threshold element (ATE) as shown in Fig. 2. The weights $w_1$ to $w_n$, represented by the vector **W**, are adjustable. An additional input $x_0$ is always equal to 1 and it is connected to $w_0$, the threshold weight. The vector representation of the weights

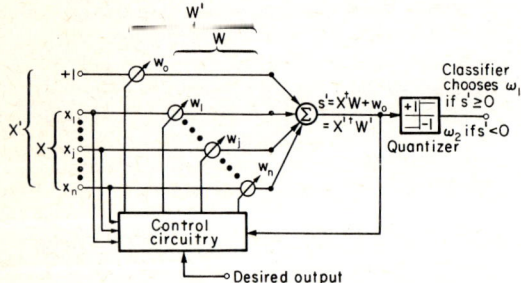

FIG. 2. *Adaptive threshold element.*

$w_0$ to $w_n$ is **W'** and the vector **X** with an extra element equal to 1 is represented by **X'**.

The input variables are weighted by their corresponding weights and the resulting products are summed. The output of the summer, $s'$ is quantized so that the quantized output is equal to 1 if the sum is greater than or equal to zero and is equal to $-1$ otherwise.

It should be noted that the summer output is equal to the inner product of the vector's **X'** and **W'**. Thus a particular value of **W'** establishes a hyperplane in the space of input variables. If the **X'** vector lies on one side of the hyperplane (or actually on it) the output of the quantizer is 1; and if it is on the other side, the output is $-1$.

Threshold elements have been physically realized in several ways (Nagy 1963). These have included electrochemical techniques, magnetic techniques, summing amplifiers and digital computer simulations. Although it is possible to make digital hardware to implement adaptation algorithms, there has been little work in this direction.

There are several possible uses for threshold elements. For instance, a threshold element can be adapted to realize a solution to a set of linear inequalities. If the inputs are binary values, normally 1 and $-1$ are used, it is possible to use the threshold element as a logic element; thus, threshold elements can be used to realize switching functions. Statistical problems requiring separation of multi-dimensional gaussian distributions with equal covariance matrices have optimum solutions consisting of hyperplanes. It is possible to adapt threshold elements to the optimum hyperplane by use of samples from the distributions.

*II. Error functions.* Most adaptation algorithms are methods for searching error functions for a minimum (Koford and Groner 1966). If the error surface is suitably defined, there will be no local minima, only a global minimum. The three most popular error functions have been the sum of the squared errors, the sum of the squared one-sided errors, and the sum of the magnitudes of the one-sided errors (Mays 1964).

The sum of the squared errors is best described in matrix notation. A set of input pattern vectors to be classified can be collected into a matrix $A$, where every row of the matrix represents a different pattern vector. The analogue outputs of the threshold element can be written as $S' = AW'$. The desired analogue responses of the threshold element is represented by a vector **D**. Generally, if the number of pattern vectors is greater than the number of weights, the equation $AW' = D$ will not have a solution. An error vector is defined as $\mathbf{E}_1 = AW' - \mathbf{D}$. The sum of the squared errors is equal to

$$f_1(\mathbf{W'}) = \mathbf{E}_1^t \mathbf{E}_1 = (AW' - \mathbf{D})^t (AW' - \mathbf{D}).$$

The error function $f_1$ has a calculable weight vector giving minimum error, namely $\mathbf{W'} = (A^t A)^{-1} A^t \mathbf{D}$. This weight vector is equal to the solution of $AW' = \mathbf{D}$ if a solution exists; in that case $f_1 = 0$. Thus minimizing the sum of the squared error will yield a solution of a set of simultaneous linear equations.

The one sided error is equal to $\mathbf{E}_2 = 1/2(|AW' - \mathbf{D}| - (AW' - \mathbf{D}))$, where $|AW' - \mathbf{D}|$ is a vector with elements equal to the absolute values of the corresponding elements of $AW' - \mathbf{D}$. The sum of the one-sided squared errors is $f_2(\mathbf{W'}) = \mathbf{E}_2^t \mathbf{E}_2$. If the inequality $AW' \geq \mathbf{D}$ has a solution, the minimum value of $f_2$ is 0.

The sum of the magnitude of the one-sided errors is

$$f_3(w') = \mathbf{J}^t \mathbf{E}_2 = \tfrac{1}{2} \sum_{i=1}^{m} \{|A_i \mathbf{W'} - d_i| - (A_i \mathbf{W'} - d_i)\}$$

where **J** is a vector with all elements equal to 1, $A_i$ is a row of $A$, $d_i$ is an element of $D$ and $m$ is the number of rows of $A$.

All the above error functions represent multidimensional surfaces in the space of weights. Their minima are found by algorithms that move the weight vector approximately in the direction of negative gradient. The gradient of each of the function is:

$$\nabla f_1(\mathbf{W}') = \frac{df_1(\mathbf{W}')}{d\mathbf{W}'} = 2A^t \mathbf{E}_1$$

$$\nabla f_2(\mathbf{W}') = 2A^t \mathbf{E}_2$$

$$\nabla f_3(\mathbf{W}') = \sum_{i=1}^{m} A_i^t \text{ sgn } (A_i \mathbf{W}' - \mathbf{D}) = A^t \text{ sgn } (A\mathbf{W}' - \mathbf{D})$$

where sgn $(x) = 0$ for $x < 0$ and $= 1$ for $x \geq 0$.

If the time derivative of $\mathbf{W}'$ is equal to the negative gradient $\left(\text{i.e. } \frac{d\mathbf{W}'}{dt} = -\nabla f(\mathbf{W}')\right)$ the weight vector will move in a direction that causes the error to be decreased at a maximum rate. Weight vectors governed by these differential equations will cause the error to be minimized as $t$ approaches infinity (Mays 1965).

To normalize the above inequalities, $A_i$ and $d_i$ were multiplied by $-1$ when the desired output was negative. Thus $d_i$ is always positive.

*III. Iterative procedures.* Rather than writing a differential equation, one can write a difference equation so that $\mathbf{W}'(k+1) = \mathbf{W}'(k) - \mu \nabla f(\mathbf{W}'(k))$. For sufficiently small $\mu$ this equation will converge to a minimum error solution. A further simplification leads to the algorithms normally used with adaptive threshold elements. The difference equation is modified so that the weight vector is corrected for one pattern at a time. For example, the procedure associated with $f_1$ gives

$$\mathbf{W}'(k+1) = \mathbf{W}'(k) - 2\mu A_i^t (A_i \mathbf{W}'(k) - d_i) \text{ and}$$

$$\mathbf{W}'(k+2) = \mathbf{W}'(k+1) - 2\mu A_{i+1}^t (A_{i+1} \mathbf{W}'(k+1) - d_{i+1}).$$

This procedure is repeated for all the sample pattern vectors many times. The minimum error can be approached as closely as desired by making $\mu$ sufficiently small (Koford and Groner 1966). It has been proven many times for error functions $f_2$ and $f_3$ that one pattern at a time adaptation will solve the inequality $A\mathbf{W}' \geq \mathbf{D}$ if a solution exists (Novikoff 1962; Rosenblatt 1962; Singleton 1962).

The quantity $\mu$ in the above equation is called a proportionality constant for error functions $f_1$ and $f_2$ and an increment size for error functions $f_3$. Because of the susceptibility of the quantizer to noise, it is desirable to satisfy the inequality $A\mathbf{W}' \geq \mathbf{D}$ rather than $A\mathbf{W}' \geq \mathbf{O}$. If all the elements of $\mathbf{D}$ are equal to a scalar, this scalar is called the *dead zone*. When using error functions $f_2$ it is desirable to use an '*adapt level*' to determine how much of a correction to make in the weight vectors. A decision to adapt is made on the basis of the dead zone, but a correction is made on the basis of the adapt level (larger than the dead zone).

All the above parameters of adaptation algorithms have an effect on convergence rate and the sensitivity of the weights to noise (Mays 1964). In general, parameters giving rapid convergence will result in weights very sensitive to noise and vice versa.

*IV. Uses for adaptive threshold elements.* One of the most interesting uses of the ATE is for separation of multidimensional distributions. With regard to ATE's, the statistical problem receiving the most analysis has been the case of two gaussian distributions with different means but equal covariance matrices. If the two distributions have equal probability of occurrence, the optimum decision theory solution (Koford and Groner 1966) is:

$$w_0 = -\tfrac{1}{2}(M_1 + M_2)^t \mathbf{W}$$
$$\mathbf{W} = \Phi^{-1}(M_1 - M_2)$$

Where $M_1$ and $M_2$ are the means of the two distributions and $\Phi^{-1}$ is the inverse of the covariance matrix.

If the means and covariance matrix are unknown, but equal numbers of samples from each distribution are available, the best decision theory solution is to replace the true means and covariance matrix by their sample values. Normally these sample values must be computed, the covariance matrix inverted and the weights calculated as above. Using the ATE, the adaptation algorithm corresponding to error function $f_1$ will cause the weight vector to converge to the optimum solution (Koford and Groner 1966).

Adaptation using a fixed sample set is called '*adaptation with data repeating*'. If the samples are used and then discarded, the adaptation is called '*adaptation without data repeating*'. An analysis of adaptation without data repeating, when the data are samples from gaussian distributions shows that the expected weight vector equals the optimum decision theory solution when the sum of squared errors algorithms is used (Mays and Koford 1965). The case that has been analysed requires that the desired responses be exactly correlated with the distribution from which the sample input patterns were taken.

The requirement that the desired output be exactly correlated with the sample is a rather severe restriction. One of the original advantages purported for adaptive systems was that they could automatically adapt to give optimum performance with changing input statistics, without supplying a desired output exactly correlated with the input. For the case of adaptation without a teacher as applied to ATE's, the concept of bootstrapping has been conceived. *Bootstrap adaptation* consists of setting the desired digital response equal to the actual digital response. There has been no satisfactory theoretical analysis of this procedure, but experimental results (unreported) indicate that sufficiently slow changes in statistics can be followed so that nearly optimum separation is maintained.

As noted above, ATE's divide input space by a hyperplane. Many problems require non-linear rather than linear separating surfaces. For example, two gaussian distributions with unequal covariance matrices require a quadratic separating surface for optimum separation. Networks of ATE's have been proposed as piecewise linear approximations of non-linear surfaces. No theoretically satisfactory adaptation algorithms have been found for non-trivial networks. (A non-trivial network is defined as one for which the desired response does not uniquely determine the output of individual ATE's in a network.) However, experimental work has been encouraging in that convergence to a satisfactory solution usually occurs.

ATE's have been used experimentally for many pattern classification and prediction problems (Widrow et al. 1963). Experiments have included attempts to predict weather with inputs representing barometric pressure at several geographic locations. Coded forms of electrocardiograms have been used as inputs with the desired output being an indication of a normal or abnormal heart condition. Speech (King and Tunis 1966) and sonar recognition experiments have been performed. Inputs represented spectral energy in different frequency bands and desired responses were either word identification or identification of the source of sonar energy. These experiments were interesting but no practical applications have yet come from them.

*See also:* Information space. Pattern recognition.

*Bibliography*

KING J. H. Jr. and TUNIS C. J. (1966) *Some Experiments in Spoken Word Recognition, IBM J. Res. Dev.* **10,** No. 1, January.

KOFORD J. S. and GRONER G. F. (1966) *The Use of Adaptive Threshold Elements to Design a Linear Optimal Pattern Classifier, I.E.E.E. Trans. on Information Theory,* Vol. IT-12, No. 1, 42, January.

MAYS C. H. (1964) *Effects of Adaptation Parameters on Convergence Time and Tolerance for Adaptive Threshold Elements, I.E.E.E. Trans. on Electronic Computers,* Vol. EC-13, No. 4, August.

MAYS C. H. (1965) *The Relationship of Algorithms Used with Adjustable Threshold Elements to Differential Equations, I.E.E.E. Trans. on Electronic Computers,* Vol. EC-14, No. 1, 62, February.

MAYS C. H. and KOFORD J. S. (1965) *Adaption of a Linear Classifier Without Data Repeating, I.E.E.E. Record of the* 1965 *International Space Electronics Symposium,* pp, 11-C1 to 11-C7, Nov. 2, 3, 4.

NAGY G. (1963) *A Survey of Analog Memory Devices, I.E.E.E. Trans. on Electronic Computers,* Vol. EC-12, No. 2, August.

NOVIKOFF A. (1962) *On Convergence Proofs for Perceptions, Proceedings of the Symposium on Mathematical Theory of Automata,* Polytechnic Institute of Brooklyn, April.

ROSENBLATT F. (1962) *Principles of Neurodynamics: Perception and Theory of Brain Mechanisms,* Washington, D. C.: Spartan Books.

SINGLETON R. C. (1962) *A Test for Separability as Applied to Self Organizing Machines,* Self Organizing Systems, Washington, D. C.: Spartan Books.

WIDROW B. et al. (1963) *Practical Applications for Adaptive Data Processing Systems, I.E.E.E. Wescon Convention,* Paper 11.4.

C. H. MAYS

**ALGEBRAIC MANIPULATION USING LISTS.** In order to discuss algebraic manipulation using lists, it is important to understand what is meant by algebraic manipulation, what its main subdivisions are, the relation of their overall implementation to lists, and why this subject is important. The last item will be discussed first.

Ever since the availability of digital computers, they have been used for doing tedious numerical calculations. The technologies of science, engineering, and even some areas of mathematics have been significantly influenced by the ability of the computer to do vast amounts of arithmetic rapidly and accurately. A few simple and independent attempts were made as early as 1953 by Kahrimanian and Nolan to use the computer to do formal differentiation. However, there was then a hiatus with very little work done in the area of algebraic manipulation until the subject began to receive increasingly more attention from 1959 on. Evidence of the importance of this subject is the well attended and successful Symposium on Symbolic and Algebraic Manipulation sponsored by the ACM Special Interest Committee on this subject, held in Washington, D.C. in March 1966. (Communications of the ACM 1966).

Algebraic manipulation (often referred to as formula manipulation) involves the handling of mathematical expressions in a formal fashion or for the purpose of producing a formal result, rather than dealing with numeric values. Algebraic manipulation has increased enormously in importance over the past years, for two primary reasons. The first has been the increasing realization that a vast amount of analytic work previously (and even currently) being done by hand, can be done equally well or better by computer. There are problems which require days, weeks, months, and sometimes years of straightforward hand manipulations; many of these problems require no more knowledge than high school algebra or how to take a derivative. Since this type of work is just as tedious and error prone as numerical calculations, it is not only logical, but desirable, and often necessary, to use a computer. Examples of problems requiring computer assistance include such things as generating series involving thousands of terms, analytic solution of linear and differential equations, expansion and rearrangement of large expressions, etc.

The second reason for the increasing importance of algebraic manipulation is the development of techniques which permit reasonably efficient programs —either system or specific application—to be written. First and foremost of these techniques is the manipulation of lists in various ways. Although the two most significant list processing systems are IPL–V (Newell *et al.* 1964) and LISP (McCarthy *et al.* 1962), only LISP has been used to any extent in doing algebraic manipulation, and that work has usually *not* been motivated by a desire to solve specific problems. However, the *basic concepts* of list processing (which are assumed known to the readers of this article) have been used widely.

Before discussing the specific use of lists, it is necessary to have a better understanding of what is meant by algebraic manipulation, and which of its major subareas are affected by the use of lists.

The main subdivisions for *algebraic manipulation* are batch and on-line systems, where the distinction is whether or not the system is designed to permit the user to interact with it. This has no direct effect on the use of lists. A major subset of algebraic manipulation is the handling of polynomials (including rational functions). In most cases, they are stored internally as numerical arrays, representing the coefficients and exponents. Lists do not provide any significant advantage and hence are seldom used; Collins' PM system (Collins 1966) is a notable exception to this statement. Hence, we need only consider systems providing some type of general algebraic manipulation capability.

The types of facilities needed and many of the technical issues are discussed in the author's paper (Sammet 1967a). A vital facet of algebraic manipulation from the user's viewpoint is the need to have the algebraic manipulation commands intermingled with the normal numerical, loop control, and input/output facilities of a numerical language. This principle is best illustrated by FORMAC (Sammet 1964), which is an extension of FORTRAN IV on the 7090. The new capabilities provided for the user include such things as differentiation, performing addition, subtraction, multiplication, and division of expressions, substituting expressions for variables, removing parentheses by applying the distributive and multinomial laws, finding coefficients of variables, evaluating expressions, matching expressions, simplifying expressions, as well as others. (See Bond *et al.* 1964 for a description of the language.) FORMAC has been successfully used to solve a wide variety of practical problems (see Tobey 1966), and in fact is the only system in this area known to the author which has received extensive usage in a wide variety of situations and problems.

Another approach to providing algebraic manipulation facilities is that taken by Formula ALGOL (Perlis *et al.* 1966). Here, the user is presented with a new data type added to ALGOL to represent the formulae, but is not provided with many facilities directly. However, the system does include list and string processing commands, so that the user can write his own procedures to perform the types of manipulation that he needs.

In order to clarify the type of manipulation under discussion, it must be re-emphasized that we are dealing with the handling of expressions in a formal fashion, as distinguished from considering their numeric values. If we talk about the expression $(A+B)^2$ we are concerned with the fact that we have the sum of two elements which is to be squared, and we have no interest in the numeric value. Even more specifically, $A$ and $B$ are *not assigned* numeric values. One of the common types of things that one does is to remove parentheses in expressions by applying the distributive law. Thus, $(A-B)(A+B)$ would normally result in $A^2 - B^2$.

Historically, *lists* have been used in situations where the size of a particular item, or the number of items, is generally unpredictable within any reasonable limits at the start of the program. The manipulation of algebraic expressions is an excellent illustration of a field with these characteristics.

There are a number of reasons for needing lists in doing algebraic manipulation. The first is the general impossibility of knowing how many final expressions will result from a particular computation. In the numeric case, the desired result may be a list of items which satisfy some particular criteria; in the non-numeric, or algebraic, case this situation can also arise. For example, one might want all expressions which are cubic in a particular variable, or all expressions which involve the second derivative of a variable. One significant difference between the numeric and algebraic case is that in the former you know how much space an item requires, and there are techniques for outputting such results which don't apply to the algebraic case. While this particular motivation for needing lists certainly exists, it is actually less important than the next three.

The second reason for needing lists is the impossibility of predicting the size of a particular expression. The size of the result cannot be determined in advance, particularly since some extremely complicated looking expressions can actually reduce to a single term. Any reader who doubts this should write down some arbitrary expressions and differentiate them, or predict the size of the derivative of $\frac{x^2 + \sin x \log x}{x^3 - \cos x}$. Equally striking results—either in terms of very large or very small results—can come from removing the parentheses on complicated expressions.

The third—and probably the most important—reason for needing lists is the constant change of size of an expression as it is being created. This is best illustrated by again considering the expansion of the expression $(A-B)(A+B)$. In multiplying out, the terms generated are $A^2$, $-AB$, $+AB$, and $B^2$. If we assume that some type of simplification process takes place whereby the two intermediate terms are cancelled, then we have the final result $A^2 - B^2$. The essential point here is that the amount of space required for the intermediate expression (i.e. before any simplification) may exceed the amount required for either the initial or final version by a considerable factor. There have been cases in which problems could not be made to run to completion for just this reason; in other words, the input expression fitted in memory, and the result was known to be small enough to fit, but the intermediate results required so much room that the problem could not be finished.

A fourth—and very vital—reason for needing lists is the fact that most algorithms for manipulating expressions require constant insertion and deletion of elements.

This is particularly true in such things as simplification, where terms are frequently deleted.

While of course it is theoretically possible to perform all these operations by storing the component parts of an expression sequentially, the constant movement would be prohibitive in time. On the other hand, the normal disadvantages of lists apply here also. For one thing, each element normally takes up twice as much space as it would otherwise, because you need either all or part of a word for a pointer to the next element; depending upon the particular type of lists used, two pointers may be needed. The second major disadvantage is that you cannot easily obtain any particular character in an expression without scanning at least part of the string sequentially. Fortunately, this is not a major disadvantage, since in many (although certainly not all) cases, one wants to proceed sequentially anyhow.

The lists that have been referred to above are those needed for storage of expressions. There are a few other instances in which relatively small lists are needed for other purposes. For example, if one needs to keep a history of certain characteristics of an expression while scanning it, a *push-down list* is normally a technique for this. Depending upon the internal representation, a push-down list may be needed to translate to *Polish* from *infix*, since the former is a very convenient way of representing expressions internally. It is very important to realize that Polish representation of an algebraic expression is not the same thing as using lists for an algebraic expression. Either one can be used without the other. In particular, the expressions could be stored in BCD form using lists (although this would be terribly slow).

Having determined the fact that lists are either necessary or extremely desirable, there are a number of issues which need to be considered in determining just what type of lists should be used. The first is whether a simple chain, or a list structure is to be used. In the former case, there are no sublists. As an illustration of the difference between these representation, consider Figs. 1a and 1b, where 1a shows a Polish representation of an expression in a simple chain, and 1b shows the equivalent formula expressed with a list structure. The primary advantage to a list structure over a chain is that it does not require scanning through the entire

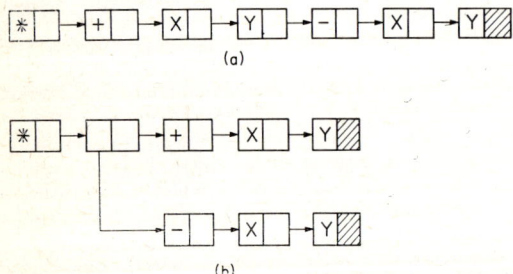

FIG. 1. *Polish representation of* $(X+Y)(X-Y)$. a) *Chain;*
b) *List structure.*

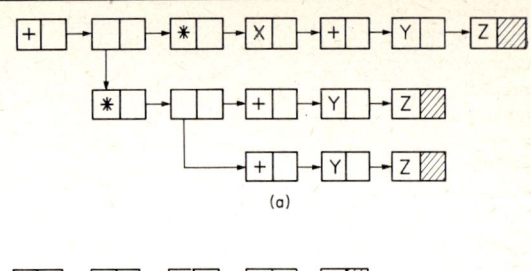

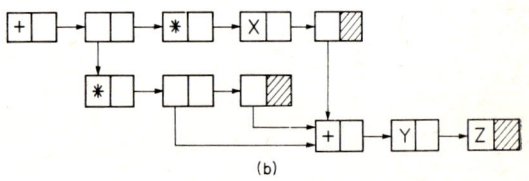

FIG. 2. *Polish representation of* $x(Y+Z)+(Y+Z)(Y+Z)$.
a) *Without common sublist;* b) *With common sublist.*

expression in order to examine any portion of it. In other words, certain decisions can be made based on the operators, and only the necessary part of the list need be scanned. List structures also permit the use of common sublists, and this is a very key issue in determining an effective representation. The primary advantage to the common sublist (as shown in Figs. 2a and 2b) is that expressions need not be repeated. The disadvantage is that a vast amount of bookkeeping is needed in order to keep things straight. This is true even when all expressions are considered to be in the primary storage medium, and becomes even more complicated when some type of secondary storage is used. In both figures, it is assumed that a word normally contains one pointer and an item of data, although it may contain two pointers. The method used for determining the use of 'across' versus 'down' pointers is that 'across' pointers are used unless both of the two items governed by an operator are themselves operators, i.e. unless both nodes in the tree representation are operators. This is an arbitrary decision, and many other possibilities are available. For example, the basic word might contain two pointers and an item of data, or 'down' pointers might be used for each horizontal level in a tree representation. The choices depend heavily upon the structure of a computer word and the instructions available for manipulation of parts of a word.

Other possibilities for the type of lists include symmetric lists (Weizenbaum 1963) and threaded lists (Perlis and Thornton 1960). There appears to be no particular value in having a symmetric list for doing algebraic manipulation. Similarly, threaded lists are not of particular advantage, although some algorithms could make effective use of them.

In any list processing system, one of the key issues is the 'free list' (i.e. the unused storage space) and how locations are returned to the free list. It is characteristic of algebraic manipulation (and many other list processing) problems, that the ability to successfully handle a particular problem may depend entirely on the size of the free list. There are generally two ways in which expressions which are no longer needed for active processing can be returned to the free list. One is to have the user specify when he is through with a particular expression and then have the system return the storage positions to the free list. The alternative is to have the system do it automatically, whenever the free list is empty; in this case, the system will scan each expression to determine which are no longer in use and then those will be returned to the free list. It is important to note that the use of common sublists presents certain problems in handling the free list, because it is always necessary to do elaborate bookkeeping to make sure when a 'common' sublist is not being used by anything and thus can be erased.

It has only been possible to provide an extremely brief view of a complicated subject in this article. Algebraic manipulation is becoming a subject of major importance, and the techniques for efficient systems are therefore of prime concern. Further information can be found in the many additional articles given in the author's annotated descriptor based bibliography (Sammet 1966).

*See also:* Computer language design requirements. Symbol manipulation by digital computer.

*Bibliography*

BOND E., AUSLANDER M., GRISOFF S., KENNEY R. MYSZEWSKI M., SAMMET J. E., TOBEY R. G. and ZILLES S. (1964) *FORMAC — An Experimental FORmula Manipulation Compiler, Proceedings of the ACM National Conference*, K2.1-1 — K2.1-11, August.
*Communications of the ACM* (1966) **9**, No. 8, August.
*Communications of the ACM* (1966) **9**, No. 10, October.
COLLINS G. E. (1966) *PM, A System for Polynomial Manipulation, Communications of the ACM* **9**, No. 8, August.
MCCARTHY J., ABRAHAMS P., EDWARDS D., HART T. and LEVIN M. (1962) *LISP* 1.5 *Programmers' Manual*, Computation Center and Research Laboratory of Electronics, M.I.T., Cambridge, Massachusetts, August.
NEWELL A., TONGE F., FEIGENBAUM E., GREEN B. F. and MEALY G. H. (Eds.) (1964) (2nd Edn) *Information Processing Language V Manual*, Englewood Cliffs, New Jersey: Prentice-Hall.
PERLIS A. J. and THORNTON C. (1960) *Symbol Manipulation by Threaded Lists, Communications of the ACM* **3**, No. 4, April.
PERLIS A. J., ITURRIAGA R. and STANDISH T. A. (1966) *A Definition of Formula Algol*, Carnegie Institute of Technology, March (Presented at the SICSAM Symposium).
SAMMET J. E. and BOND E.R. (1964) *Introduction to FORMAC, I. E. E. E. Trans. on Electronic Computer*, **EC-13**, No. 4, August.
SAMMET J. E. (1967) *Formula Manipulation by Computer*, (To appear in *Advances in Computers*, Vol. 8, New York Academic Press.
SAMMET J. E. (1966) *An Annotated Descriptor Based Bibliography on the Use of Computers for Non-Numerical Mathematics, Computing Reviews* **7**, No. 4, July.
TOBEY F. G. (1965) *Eliminating Monotonous Mathematics with FORMAC*, Poughkeepsie, N. Y.: IBM, Systems Development Division, Technical Report No. TR00. 1365, November.
WEIZENBAUM J. (1963) *Symmetric List Processor, Communications of the ACM* **6**, No. 9, September.

J. E. SAMMETT

**ALGORITHMS FOR PROCESSING ALGORITHMS.** *Introduction.* A frequent task of the professional programmer is to *modify* a computer program—a *process* described in some well defined language—with a view to making it shorter, or faster, or use less storage space, or to adapt it to some special requirements. The question arises as to what extent the computer itself can be made to perform such activities. The practical answer of course is that it is only possible to a limited extent. If it could match the ingenuity which is sometimes put into this activity by the human programmer we should have gone a long way to making a machine 'think', and while this may eventually be possible, it is not something which is going to mteraialise in the near future. In this article we are concerned with methods which are or can be used in present day compilers to improve the quality of the object program.

The fact that the human programmer 'understands' the *algorithm* to be processed, and that he can if necessary recast it so as to employ an entirely different method, should not deter us from seeking ways to make purely local improvements to a program without knowing the overall picture. Indeed many such modifications are often made by people who have no wish to know what the program is about!

A program which processes an algorithm must clearly 'understand' in some way the language in which it is written in, even if, as we have just said, it does not attempt a reconstruction in terms of some internal mental imagery. It must at least be able to check the grammatical construction of the subject program, and to make certain equivalence preserving transformations on individual statements, or groups of statements. If it can do this, then it may by a series of such transformations gradually bring the program to a more acceptable form. Such a description could also apply to a *compiler* regarding it as a program which gradually transforms the original 'high level' statements into the desired machine language form. Some compilers do in fact work in precisely this way: they subject the original text to a series of 'passes', in each of which some characteristic transformation is made on relevant statements, the final pass yielding the object program.

Most tranformations are preferably performed while

the program is still in a high level state. Thus for instance changing $A := B \times C + B \times D$ to $A := B \times (C+D)$, thereby saving a multiplication, will be more effective if the quantities in question are matrices and not scalars. In general high level *language* is more '*transparent*': it would be much more difficult to apply such transformations if statements are first crudely translated into machine code symbolism. To take another example, one may infer from the statements $A := B^T B$ that $B^T B$ is a symmetric matrix and thereby avoid computing unnecessary elements, but it would be an almost impossible task at machine code level. In short the advantages conferred by a high level language are precisely the notational advantages of mathematics.

On the other hand, however, certain transformations or refinements can only be done at machine code level because they depend intimately on the structure of the machine.

Consider the statements $a := b+c;\ d := a+e$ which translate into

fetch   $b$
add   $c$
store   $a$
fetch   $a$    ←   redundant
add   $e$
store   $d$

Eliminating the redundant 'fetch' we have

fetch   $b$
add   $c$
store   $a$
add   $e$
store   $d$

This can only be done in the latter stages of compiling because the original language does not allow the writer to take advantage of the fine structure of the machine—even if he were so inclined. The above simplification would not of course be possible if the second statement were *labelled*, for example

$$a := b+c;\ L1 : d := a+e$$

because if there is a jump to the label $L1$ then the 'fetch $a$' is not redundant.

*Replacement of common subexpressions*. A group of statements such as the following (again none of them must be labelled)

$$u := 1 + \cos\,(\mathrm{sqrt}\,(1+p \times q))$$
$$v := q$$
$$w := \mathrm{sqrt}\,(1+p \times q) + \sin\,(\mathrm{sqrt}\,(1+p \times q))$$

could be replaced by

$$t := \mathrm{sqrt}\,(1+p \times q)$$
$$u := 1 + \cos\,(t)$$
$$v := q$$
$$w := t + \sin\,(t)$$

which form of expression is certainly more economical in symbols, and is the kind of substitution which a compiler must perform if it is to yield an optimized object code.

The original author of the algorithm will have done something on these lines himself, partly to avoid writer's cramp, and generally to tidy up the expression of the algorithm. Economy of expression does not always imply economy of execution, however. It may be convenient to use a single short symbol over and over again in spite of the fact that it may refer to a complicated function which is time consuming to evaluate.

Certain precautions must be observed when performing the foregoing operations. For example if the original statements were

$$u := 1 + \cos\,(\mathrm{sqrt}\,(1+p \times q))$$
$$v := q$$
$$w := \mathrm{sqrt}\,(1+p \times q) + \sin\,(\mathrm{sqrt}\,(1+p \times q))$$

then the subexpression 'sqrt$(1+p \times q)$' would no longer be 'common' to the 1st and 3rd statements because its value may have changed as a result of the assignment $p := q$. It would still be common to both terms of the third statement. Thus we could write

$$u := 1 + \cos\,(\mathrm{sqrt}\,(1+p \times q))$$
$$p := q$$
$$t := \mathrm{sqrt}\,(1+p \times q)$$
$$w := t + \sin\,(t).$$

In this case the danger was fairly obvious. It is not always so.

If a *subroutine call* had appeared in place of $p = q$ we would either have had to check that it did not interfere with $p$ or $q$ or else forego the optimization. A much less obvious source of danger is the possible side effects of function subroutines which may alter critical variables. This is of course very unlikely but it means investigating every *function call* in an expression. An extreme example of this is the fact that in Algol $a \uparrow 2$ may not give the same result as $a \times a$! Algol has often been criticized on precisely these grounds, i.e. for the lack of transparency. Common subexpressions may not of course be recognizable as such, e.g. $1 + p \times q$ may appear elsewhere as $q \times p + 1$ or $1 + q \times p$ or $p \times q + 1$. Clearly there is considerable scope for the application of the *commutative, associative, and distributive rules* governing the elementary operators, to rearrange the form of an expression (or group of expressions) in order to optimize it in some way, e.g. to minimize its length as such, or the implied processing or storage space involved. (This last is not particularly important.) Part of this activity may be machine oriented (e.g. computing $a + b \times c$ as $b \times c + a$ in order to avoid *dumping* the *accumulator*) but a good deal of such processing could be expected to be of general utility. In fact of course there is no limit to the mathematical identities and theorems which could be used to simplify the calculation and once again we must restrain our ambition and confine ourselves to the use of fairly elementary devices which can be simply applied. (As a matter of interest even the rules of association and distribution do not always hold with finite arithmetic units. Thus, e.g. $a+b-a = a$ is not necessarily true on a *floating point* machine, and $a\times(b\times c) = (a\times b)\times c$ does not always hold on either *fixed* or floating point machines. A disastrous loss of accuracy could in fact result from playing about with such relations in a superficial way.) There is one type of expression, however, where rearrangement will not lead to trouble, and that is one in which the *operands* are all integers and the *operators* do not include division. Array subscript expressions fall in this class, and as we shall see in the next section, have a special significance for the efficiency of the program.

*Inner loops and subscripting.* If it is the purpose of the processor to reduce the execution time of the algorithm, then clearly the greatest effect is going to be achieved by concentrating on those *statements* which are obeyed most frequently, i.e. those areas of the program usually referred to as the *inner loops*. Fortunately in most *algorithmic languages* the *loops* are usually designated as such, and moreover permit of a nested structure so that there is no difficulty in recognizing which are the most important. There are of course exceptions, when for one reason or another the author has chosen to ignore the formal cycle facilities and 'programs' his own.

In addition to improving the statements in the inner loops we can also remove unnecessary calculation from within an inner loop to a position outside it. For example

$$a := 0$$
$$\text{cycle } i := 1, 1, 100$$
$$\quad \text{cycle } j := 1, 1, 100$$
$$\quad\quad a := a + b[j] \times \cos(i \times r/100)$$
$$\quad \text{repeat}$$
$$\text{repeat}$$

$$a := 0$$
$$\text{cycle } i := 1, 1, 100$$
$$\quad t := \cos(i \times r/10)$$
$$\quad \text{cycle } j := 1, 1, 100$$
$$\quad\quad a := a + b[j] \times t$$
$$\quad \text{repeat}$$
$$\text{repeat}$$

This rearrangement is not equivalent to

$$\sum_{i=1}^{100} \sum_{j=1}^{100} b[j] \times \cos(i \times r/10) \rightarrow \sum_{i=1}^{100} \cos(i \times r/10) \sum_{j=1}^{100} b[j]$$

but it is a considerable improvement on the original form.

If we can recognize the summation operator (either by making it a special feature of a language or by grammatical analysis of the program) we can apply the rules relating to its use, e.g.

$$\sum_i \lambda \times a[i] \rightarrow \lambda \times \sum_i a[i] \quad \sum_{i=1}^n (a[i]+b) \rightarrow n\times b + \sum_{i=1}^n a[i]$$

$$A = \sum_{i=1}^n a[i]; \quad B = \sum_{i=1}^n b[i]; \quad C = \sum_{i=1}^n c[i] \rightarrow$$

$$(A, B, C) = \sum_{i=1}^n (a[i], b[i], c[i]).$$

There is another particularly useful type of optimization that is associated with cycles, namely the efficient computation of *subscript expressions*. It can be illustrated as follows

$$u := 0; \quad v := 0$$
$$\text{cycle } i := 1, 1, 10$$
$$\quad \text{cycle } j := 1, 1, 10$$
$$\quad\quad u := u + U[10 \times i + j - 11]$$
$$\quad\quad v := v + V[10 \times i + j - 11]$$
$$\quad \text{repeat}$$
$$\text{repeat}$$

The expression $10 \times i + j - 11$ being linear in the cycle indices $i, j$, can be computed by 'incrementing' as follows

$$u := 0; \quad v := 0; \quad si := 0$$
$$\text{cycle } i := 1, 1, 10$$
$$\quad si := si + 10$$
$$\quad sj := si$$
$$\quad \text{cycle } j := 1, 1, 10$$
$$\quad\quad sj := sj + 1$$
$$\quad\quad u := u + U[sj - 11]$$
$$\quad\quad v := v + V[sj - 11]$$
$$\quad \text{repeat}$$
$$\text{repeat}$$

Such modifications to the program are only possible of course under certain restrictive conditions, similar to these relating to the utilization of common subexpressions. In the above example the expressions to be treated in this way are explicitly displayed, but in practice they would be implicit in the notation for 2-dimensional array elements, e.g. $U[i, j]$ and $V[i, j]$.

A rather elegant processing scheme which accomplishes much of what we have been describing has been developed by A. Glennie who has employed it very successfully in two FORTRAN compilers S2 and S3. We can only describe here the basic essentials of the scheme. It consists of representing a simple chain of statements as sentences in an operator precedence grammar. For example

$$a := b*c+d$$
$$e := a+d$$
$$f := g*(d+c*b)$$

is represented by the following binary tree structure(s).

|      | left operand | right operand | operator |
|------|------|-------|----|
| 1    | 0 | a | 0 |
| 2    | 0 | b | 0 |
| 3    | 0 | c | 0 |
| 4    | 0 | d | 0 |
| 5    | 2 | 3 | * |
| 6    | 4 | 5 | + |
| 7    | 1 | 6 | := |
| 8    | 4 | 7 | + |
| 9    | 0 | e | 0 |
| 10   | 9 | 8 | := |
| 11   | 0 | f | 0 |
| 12   | 0 | g | 0 |
| (5) 13′ | 2 | 3 | * |
| (6) 13″ | 4 | 5 | + |
| 13   | 12 | 6 | * |
| 14   | 11 | 13 | := |

*Notes*

1. The trees are binary structures and represent both the explicit and the implicit bracketed structure of the original expressions.
2. There is one entry in the list for each node (sub-expression) and is defined by the two operands and the node operator. If the node is commutative (e.g. *, +) the entry is converted to standard form with the lower tree entry as the left operand [entries 6, 8, 13′ have been so converted].
3. Before each node is actually entered in the list we check to see whether it is already present, and if this is the case its entry number is used in place of the new entry which can then be omitted (as in the case of 13′ 13″).
4. Wherever a variable appears on the r.h.s. of an assignment we must refer always to its latest value, i.e. to the most recent assignment made to that variable. Thus in the entry no. 8 the right operand refers not to the original $a$ (entry no. 1) but to the latest assignment to it (entry no. 7). This automatically takes care of the situation described earlier on, where possible common subexpressions are invalidated because of interfering assignments—as would be the case, e.g. if the statement $e := a+d$ was replaced by $c := a+d$.
5. The list permits of other kinds of operations and may undergo considerable rearrangement before it is eventually used for compiling instructions. (Certain additional flags are associated with each node for this purpose.)

There is of course a good deal more to the scheme than can even be hinted at here, but there is one point which is rather interesting and that is the way in which the node list is searched for a previous occurrence of a given node. It is done in the same way that identifiers one often looked up in a dictionary. We first form a hash address from the node information (which is probably unique) and then search from that position until either the entry is found or we encounter a zero.

*Conclusion.* We have described some of the processes which compilers can apply to programs in the course of translating them into machine language. No mention has been made of the more far reaching transformations suggested by Ianov and others.

It should be pointed out that the more an algorithm departs from its original form as a result of modifications such as we have been discussing, the more difficult it becomes to monitor in the event of a run time fault. This is, in the author's opinion, a very serious objection to such processing and if used at all it should certainly be an optional facility that can be switched on or off as necessary. It would be preferable to use a more powerful, concise, and transparent language, in which monitoring is closely related to the facilities provided.

*See also;* Computer language design requirements. Control, identification techniques for. Symbol manipulation by digital computer.

*Bibliography*

NIEVERGELT J. (1965) *On the Automatic Simplification of Computer Programs, Comm. A.C.M.,* **8,** June, 366.
IANOV I. I. (1960) *The logical schemes of Algorithms* in *Problems of Cybernetics* **1,** 82, Oxford: Pergamon Press.
RUTLEDGE J. D. (January, 1964) *J. A.C.M.* **12,** *On Ianov Program Schemata* 1.
COOPER D. C. *The Equivalence of Certain Computations,* Research Report, Computation Centre: Carnegie Institute of Technology.

R. A. BROOKER

**ANIMAL EXPLORATORY BEHAVIOUR.** Cats are not the only creatures to suffer the lethal effects of curiosity; and the saying is no empty adage. The question "why do animals explore" therefore seems of particular interest. But this is a very wide question, and for present purposes discussion will be limited to the particular case of exploratory behaviour exhibited by laboratory rats in maze-type environments. It is unlikely that any conclusions drawn from these studies will be found to have complete generality for other species and situations. Of course it will be satisfactory if any light is thrown on other examples by these investigations; but such an outcome must by no means be presupposed.

The question above is complex. In this discussion,

two aspects only will be considered. First, is it or is it not the case that such behaviour is under the control of motivational processes? Second, if it is under such control, what motivation is involved? 'Motivational process' is here used in the same or a closely similar sense to that set out in the article on Animal Motivation in this volume. For present purposes behaviour is regarded as controlled by a motivational mechanism 'X' if it can be shown that it is initiated by some factor 'A' and terminated by some factor 'B' (or goal); the motivation 'X' is identified by the identification of 'B' and an adequate specification of the process involves also the identification of 'A'. It seems convenient to examine exploratory behaviour by a process of elimination.

1. Is exploratory behaviour independent of motivational control and also of the nature of the environment, except in so far as the latter provides the necessary physical circumstances for the activity to be exhibited? If the behaviour did prove to be of this nature it would seem that as a classification term, "exploratory" would be a misnomer. Thus, it may be supposed that rats are so constructed that they automatically move at random in any adequate space unless other forms of behaviour, for instance eating, are dominant. Any hypothesis of this kind appears incapable of explaining basic characteristics of the behaviour observed. First the amount and duration of locomotion is found to vary with the size of the maze used for the test (e.g. Montgomery 1951). Second, the behaviour is orderly in the sense that the animal moves in such a way that it tends to visit in turn those parts of the environment which have least recently been visited. Third, if the animal has had previous experience of the maze and a change is made in some part, the rat on a subsequent trial will tend to prefer that part which has been changed (e.g. Dember 1956). The second of these objections might be met by appeal to the concept of reactive inhibition. This implies that, a particular response having been made, a state of inhibition persists for a limited time which tends to prevent the recurrence of that response. An alternative response is therefore formed and the degree of order-lines of response and the apparently systematic sequence in which different parts of the maze one visited during exploration would merely be a consequence of systematic response selection. Whatever may be the value of the concept of the reactive inhibition in other contexts, this account seems incorrect. For, first, it has been shown (e.g. Montgomery 1951) that during a single exposure in a maze there is not in fact this kind of order-lines of direction of bodily turns made by the animal, although the usual systematic selection of places in the maze is found. And, second, it has been shown (e.g. Montgomery 1952; Walker et al. 1955) that, where a maze is so designed that over a series of discrete trials the rat may at the choice point either alternate the places he visits or the bodily responses he makes, alternation of place rather than of response is found.

It may be concluded that the behaviour we have termed "exploratory" is not independent both of motivational control and of the particular stimulus characteristics of the environment explored.

2. Is the behaviour only under the control of the immediate stimuli in the environment, without the added contribution of any motivational control? In this case the behaviour might reasonably be regarded as exploratory, although it would be limited in the sense that the rat would merely react to stimuli as it encountered them and would not, in any way, actively seek out remote parts of his environment. It seems clear that any view of this kind could not provide a complete account of the behaviour of satiated rats in a new environment. Perhaps the most serious difficulty for this kind of theory stems from the consequence that it implies that animals could not seek out a novel stimulus in an otherwise familiar environment. Various experiments have shown that in mazes in which a familiar initial area leads by one path towards a more novel, complex or variable area and an alternative path leads only to a stable and familiar alley, rats have a marked preference for the former path (e.g. Montgomery 1954; Still 1966). It has been suggested that such experiments may indicate only a preference for complexity (Berlyne and Slater 1957). But this explanation is hardly adequate in the case of Still's experiment and a repetition of Berlyne's experiment (Watson and Ryder, in preparation) suggests that the conclusion is erroneous. It is concluded that not all cases of exploratory behaviour are explicable without reference to any motivational process. For the fact that rats will seek out, as an apparent goal, a novel stimulus from a familiar environment seems to demand some motivational process which selects such stimuli as goals before they are encountered.

3. If motivational control is required what is the motivation? Could it be a need only for physical exercise irrespective of the nature of the environmental stimuli. In this case the initiating factor or factors might be thought to arise from some aspect of the normal living circumstances of the animal and the terminating factors would presumably be produced in some way by the physical process of exercise. This view, however, would encounter the same difficulties of order-lines etc., mentioned above in relation to the hypothesis that the behaviour merely constituted an 'automatic', tendency to locomotion. Further, experiment does not suggest that deprivation of opportunity for exercise in the home environment influences the amount of exploratory behaviour subsequently shown in mazes (Montgomery 1953).

4. Is the motivation special to this class of behaviour in the sense that it controls only such activities? This hypothesis, to be meaningful, requires the specification of the initiating and terminating factors. It might be supposed that initiating factors are produced when the rat encounters stimuli which are, to the particular animal, novel and the 'goal' of such behaviour is familiarity, or simply elimination of the initiating novelty. Against this view, it may be argued that it presents no explanation of the kind of exploratory behaviour referred to above in which the rat finds his way through

a familiar environment in order to reach a novel or complex stimulus. For, in this case, the motivation would not be 'switched on' until the novel stimulus was attained and hence the rat could not selectively prefer those paths through the familiar parts of the maze which lead to the novel circumstance. Further, it is not entirely clear why, when faced with a choice between novelty and familiarity, rats should choose the former, since the appearance of novelty would initiate the motivation which should then, on this view, lead the animal to select familiar stimuli as a goal. It may be concluded that this formulation, although making allowance for the clearly motivated character of the activity and the importance of the novelty of stimuli encountered, does not do so in a way which predicts the observed character of the behaviour.

5. Could the hypothesis of a special 'exploratory' motivation be formulated in some other way? The obvious alternative is to suppose that the initiating factor arises from some characteristic of the animal's normal living circumstances, perhaps from the absence of novel stimuli, and that novelty serves as the terminating factor or goal. This hypothesis would account for all the evidence mentioned above. Now, it would seem implausible to assume that the initiating and terminating processes would be all or none in character; that is, that the animal would not seek novelty at all until a certain degree of deprivation was reached, when it would begin such activity with maximum vigour and that no reception of novelty of less than a certain amount would have any effect in terminating the behaviour until a certain critical level was reached, when it would cease abruptly. No known aspects of exploratory behaviour would seem to support such a supposition. If, therefore, it is assumed instead that the onset and diminution of the motivation are gradual as, for instance, in the case of hunger with increasing deprivation and consumption of food, we should expect to be able to detect these deprivation and satiation effects. There seems to be no satisfactory evidence in the case of rats for any such deprivation effect, while experimental results suggest the absence of any satiation effect. Thus it has been shown that rats who are exposed to one novel maze 'A' and immediately afterwards to another, also novel, maze 'B' explore 'B' no less than do rats who have not had preliminary experience in 'A' (Halliday 1966). It may be concluded again that experimental findings do not support this formulation of a motivation specific to exploratory behaviour. Similar considerations apply to the hypothesis that rats are so constituted that they seek a prescribed level of novel stimulation, a motivational or 'arousal' state being initiated when the actual level of stimulation differs from the prescribed optimum. The 'goal' of this motivation is supposed to be attainment of the optimum. Although this hypothesis seems unsatisfactory for the above reasons, it has the interesting implications that animals would sometimes avoid novelty—namely when it is excessive. This possibility will be mentioned again below.

6. If no satisfactory account can be given of exploratory behaviour in terms of a motivation specific to that behaviour may it be that such activity is controlled by slight residual degrees of other motivations? This possibility, in the case of such motivations as hunger, thirst and sex has not been examined experimentally as thoroughly as could be wished. According to such a hypothesis, exploratory behaviour represents a systematic search in a novel environment for food, water, etc., under the control of one or more of such motivations. An explanation of this kind somewhat elaborated, would be consistent with much, perhaps all, of the evidence so far considered. It seems clear, however, that at least in the case of hunger the explanation lacks complete generality. It appears that sex differences complicate the issue here, but in the case of female rats it has been shown that and increase of food deprivation diminishes, rather than enhances exploratory behaviour (Montgomery 1953a; Chapman and Lery 1957). If such behaviour represented a search for food, the contrary findings would be expected. This is not, of course, to say that hungry animals may not search their environment with food as the goal of behaviour, in a similar or identical manner to that in which satiated animals explore such environments; and it is clear that the issue is complicated by sex and other variables. It is claimed only that not all examples of exploratory behaviour can be attributed to the operation of residual degrees of hunger.

If the same conclusion holds in the case of other motivations similar to hunger, and on this point experimental evidence is insufficient, the situation might be summarized as follows: Exploratory behaviour is controlled by a motivational process, in the sense described above, and is also governed by the nature, and particularly novelty, of the stimuli, immediate or remote, in the environment. This motivational process, however, has not been satisfactorily formulated as a motivation specific to this kind of behaviour, neither has it been possible to identify it with other motivations such as hunger etc. The question remains, what is the specification of the motivation involved?

7. There is no established answer to this question. The process of elimination above, however, has omitted one major possibility. It is clear that animals avoid and escape from noxious stimuli, and in so doing their behaviour is selective in a way which is often called fear, thought the use of the name is seriously misleading. For present purposes, it is necessary to assume only that there exists a motivational process which is initiated by painful stimuli, and others associated with pain, and terminated by a goal constituted by stimuli which are dissociated from pain. It is further assumed, first, that novel stimuli will elicit this motivation because they have not, in the animal's experience, been dissociated from pain; and, second, that the animal has a choice of strategies of behaviour in that it may, if possible, withdraw from the novel stimuli or, by exploration, eliminate their novelty and hence convert them into stimuli dissociated from pain. On this view, although exploration involves acquisition of information

about the environment, this is a 'goal' of the behaviour only in so far as it is a necessary means for achieving 'safety'. And the motivation is identical with that involved when the rat escapes from a noxious stimulus. Clearly, such an account requires much amplification. But it may be of interest that, for instance, the prediction may be deduced that under certain circumstances more 'fear provoking' environments will induce enhanced exploration. This prediction appears to be confirmed (Halliday 1967).

*Bibliography*

BERLYNE D. E. and SLATER J. (1957) *Perceptual curiosity, exploratory behaviour and maze learning*, J. Comp. Physiol. Psychol. **50**, 228.
CHAPMAN R. M. and LEVY N. (1957) *Hunger drive and reinforcing effect of novel stimuli*, J. Comp. Physiol. Psychol. **50**, 233.
DEMBER W. N. (1956) *Response by the rat to environmental change*, J. Comp. Physiol. Psychol. **49**, 93.
HALLIDAY M. S. (1966) *Effect of previous exploratory activity on the exploration of a simple maze*, Nature, **209**, 432.
HALLIDAY M. S. (1967) *The effects of variation of intertrial interval on exploration of elevated and enclosed mazes*, Quart. J. Exp. Psychol. (in press).
MONTGOMERY K. C. (1951) *The relation between exploratory behaviour and spontaneous alternation in the white rat*, J. Comp. Physiol. Psychol. **45**, 50.
MONTGOMERY K. C. (1952) *A test of two explorations of spontaneous alternation*, J. Comp. Physiol. Psychol. **45**, 287.
MONTGOMERY K. C. (1953) *The effect of activity deprivation on exploratory behaviour*, J. Comp. Physiol. Psychol. **46**, 438.
MONTGOMERY K. C. (1953a) *The effect of hunger and thirst drives on exploratory behaviour*, J. Comp. Physiol. Psychol. **46**, 315.
MONTGOMERY K. C. (1954) *The role of exploratory drive in learning*, J. Comp. Physiol. Psychol. **47**, 60.
STILL A. W. (1966) *Spontaneous alternation and exploration in rats*, Nature, **210**, 657.
WALKER E. L., DEMBER W. N., EARL R. A. and KAROLY A. J. (1955) *Choice alternation: I. Stimulus versus place versus response*, J. Comp. Physiol. Psychol. **48**, 19.

A. WATSON

**ANIMAL LEARNING.** First we shall discuss what mechanism of learning seems to be operating in animals. Second we shall review the evidence about the physiological nature of the change which underlies learning.

One of the most influential views about the mechanism of learning stems from *Pavlov*. This is the view that learning consists of a linkage of a stimulus to a response under certain conditions. These views were given prominence by the work of Pavlov on the conditioned reflex. Pavlov's procedure was to pair a neutral stimulus (conditioned stimulus) such as a bell, with a stimulus of some biological significance (unconditioned stimulus) such as food or shock, which evoked a response. After a number of pairings of the two stimuli, Pavlov observed that the neutral stimulus would come to evoke the same (or similar) response as the unconditioned stimulus. Pavlov assumed that what had happened during training was a linkage between the *afferent* message produced by the conditioned stimulus and brain loci producing the efferent message, eventuating the original response. Though Pavlov conducted a large number of experiments which he interpreted in this framework, he never sufficiently varied the conditions of the basic experiment actually to test his theoretical interpretation. Instead he set an example which has been followed by most learning theorists. He experimentally measured and so made quantitative the processes he had assumed. Pavlov's basic ideas have been adopted by a large number of theorists, among them Thorndike, Guthrie and Hull. This is in spite of the fact that there is a large amount of compelling evidence against his paradigm. The notion that has become widespread as a result of Pavlov's work is that the occurrence together of a stimulus and a response under certain conditions alters the nervous system in such a way that on the next occasion that the stimulus occurs, the response will occur also. On this view, at least two predictions follow about learning. The first is that learning should not occur without the execution of responses. The second prediction is that a learned habit should be critically dependent on the responses made during learning. It is difficult to see how other responses could be substituted. Against the first prediction is the finding that animals can learn just by being shown. Gleitman (1955) pulled rats along in a plexiglass car and gave them a shock when the car was in a particular place. On being released, the rats avoided the place where they had been shocked. Other experimenters have also taken rats through mazes in various other vehicles, and have been able to show considerable learning of the route although the movements necessary for performance were not made during learning. In another set of experiments, rats were allowed to explore a maze randomly. They were then made hungry and fed at an arbitrarily chosen point. On being placed hungry at another point, they were able to make their way to the point where they had been previously fed, making many fewer errors than other rats that had not explored the maze. In a case like this then the rat is able to synthesize a whole new sequence of actions. It is also possible to show in experiments on sensory preconditioning that an animal learns about the sequence of two stimuli simply when they are together in time. With regard to the second prediction that responses made during learning are critical, it has shown that animals when they are prevented from making the original response execute another response which leads to the same end result.

In spite of the evidence against the view that learning consist of a linkage of an afferent channel (stimulus) with an efferent channel (response), many suggestions have been made about the conditions under which such a linkage of stimulus and response takes place. It has been thought that simple repetition would produce such a linkage. However such a view is almost certainly wrong. Nevertheless such an assumption is frequently made in speculations about the neural basis of learning when it is postulated that repeated *firing* of a neural circuit leads to an enhanced probability of such firing in the future. However, on the behavioural level the repetition of a habit tends to make its future occurrence unlikely unless each repetition is accompanied by a *reward*. This observation has led to the theory that for a stimulus-response linkage to occur, a reward is necessary.

However, in view of what has already been said learning does not consist of a stimulus-response linkage and it does seem that it can occur without reward from the experiments on random exploration and sensory preconditioning. Instead, it seems most probable, as Tolman stressed, that animals, rather like ourselves, simply learn what leads to what, and that they will utilize such a cognitive map when they are appropriately *motivated* to obtain a reward. It turns out that what was thought to be necessary for learning, such as a response or a reward, was only necessary as a sign to the observer that learning had taken place. In other words we only know that an animal has learned if it performs and it will only perform if rewarded. Far from making a theory of learning more difficult the realization that performance and reward are unimportant in learning removes constraints on the mechanism that has to be hypothesized and leads to a simple system, such as that which has been proposed by Deutsch (1960). This can also account for the flexibility with which learned information is used.

What can animals learn? First, there is a question which engineers tend to ask, namely what is the information storage capacity of a given animal, such as the rat. Unfortunately this is a question which it is not possible to answer. One of the reasons is that the rate of acquisition is limited and storage capacity cannot even be approached because the rate of input is slow. But we cannot even make a statement about the rate of input because the rate varies not according to the information content of the task but according to somewhat obscure conditions under which learning takes place. For instance, simple visual discriminations may take a rat two thousand trials to learn in a maze. However, the same discrimination will only take thirty trials on a Lashley jumping stand. Similarly, when we ask what animals at various phylogenetic levels can learn, the conditions of training are of great importance. Comparisons between different animals are almost meaningless, except in a gross or shadowy way, because it is impossible to equate environment between species. The same physical environment may yet be different worlds to a rat and a pigeon. Bitterman has attempted to obviate this last difficulty in the following way. He uses tasks that consist of learning about second order information in a discrimination. For instance, a rat may be taught that one side of a T-maze contains a reward whereas the other is empty. When the rat has learned this task, reversal takes place. The position of the reward is switched to the previously empty arm and the animal is required to relearn. Bitterman finds that rats learn more quickly after each successive reversal, whereas fish do not. Similar other interesting phylogenetic trends have been found by him.

It is of course a natural assumption to expect better learning from animals with larger and more elaborate nervous systems. However, the possession of a larger nervous system may simply be due to a larger perceptual capacity rather than any improved learning system. It is of interest to note here that on tasks which we may be reasonably sure are well within the perceptual capacity of different species, rates of learning appear to be much the same. However, even here comparisons may be very deceptive, because rates of learning may be determined by extraneous factors. For instance, the limit on rate of learning may lie in the fact that in most tasks there is a large number of irrelevant cues which are accidentally rewarded and that it is bound to take a number of trials to learn which cues are most highly correlated with reward even if all the information about each trial is retained perfectly and acted upon in the optimal manner. According to this argument, animals with a more complex sensory and perceptual apparatus could be slower in learning simple discriminations than organisms which divide the environment into fewer categories. (This can be observed for instance with children.) There are also differences in learning rate which depend on the category to be discriminated. If a category, such as brightness, is preferred and relevant, learning will be much faster. The literature on various learning phenomena is very large and the reader is referred to Hilgard and Marquis' Conditioning and Learning by Kimble (1961).

Turning now to the physiological substrates of learning, it has been possible to induce animals to learn habits to obtain an intracranial electrical stimulus. This phenomenon, first described by Olds and Milner in 1954, bears a striking resemblance to learning for a normal reward. However, animals seem quickly to lose interest once the electrical current has been switched off. Deutsch (1960) from the learning system mentioned above, predicted that two pathways were involved, one with reward functions and the other with motivational functions. It has since been possible to show that two populations of nerve fibres are stimulated to produce the phenomenon. The population with a shorter refractory period (and so consisting of thicker fibres) subserves a reward function whereas the group with a longer refractory period (and so made up of thinner fibres) appears to subserve the motivation to obtain the reward. Stimulation of fibre tracts coursing through the medial forebrain bundle produces such learning. As yet the destination of such tracts is undetermined.

It seems clear that during learning some change must take place within the nervous system, because an animal reacts differently after learning has taken place. The nature of this change has been the subject of much speculation and some research. It appears that only very recent memories are vulnerable to *electroconvulsive shock*. If the shock is administered more than about 20 minutes after training, the learned habit is remembered. Such results have given rise to the notion that initially learning may be stored by *reverberating activity* (Hebb) and then later by a different process. At a later time measures which abolish temporarily all electrical activity, such as freezing or *ischemia*, fail to have an effect on a memory. Whether the notion of reverberating circuits is correct (and this writer is inclined to doubt it) the evidence shows clearly that a memory trace does change in some way with time. It has been suggested that permanent storage in the nervous system is accomplished by coding the information on large molecules, such as those of DNA or RNA, which are already known to store genetic information. Perhaps the most dramatic piece of evidence for such a view comes from experiments which extract RNA from animals that have learned a particular habit. Such RNA is then injected into the peritoneal cavity of animals which have not been trained. It is claimed that upon being injected such animals act as if they had been trained. It should be stressed, however, that these claims have not been substantiated in many other laboratories. It has also been shown that RNA injected into the peritoneum does not reach the brain or does so in negligible quantities only. Further, even direct injection of the 'educated' RNA into the brain substance has failed to produce learning transfer. Perhaps the strongest presumptive evidence that macromolecules are involved in memory storage comes from the work of Flexner, Flexner and Stellar on the injection of puromycin, a protein synthesis inhibitor, into the temporal region of the brain in mice. Such injections are capable of disrupting memory of habits learned days before. However, inhibition of protein synthesis interferes indirectly with all kinds of other systems, so that the observed effects need not be due to inhibition of protein synthesis *per se*.

Another view of memory storage, almost as old as the notion of the *synapse* itself, is that the substrate of learning consists of changes at a synapse. It has been widely suggested that certain synapses which prior to learning were non-functional, would after learning begin to conduct. Though plausible, such a view has until recently lacked evidence. However, work by Deutsch and his collaborators (1966) has done much to confirm the synaptic conductance theory. It has been shown that injections of anticholinesterase into the brain of rats at different times after learning produced variable degrees of amnesia. For instance three days after learning there was no amnesia, whereas 14 days later amnesia was complete. On the other hand, injection of an anticholinergic substance produces the reverse pattern. There was amnesia if the drug was injected one day after learning but no amnesia seven days later. If a synapse gradually increases the amount of acetylcholine (a well-known transmitter) utilized during transmission, then it should be most vulnerable to an anticholinergic at the beginning of such an increase, but most vulnerable to anticholinesterase when the level of acetylcholine during transmission is high. An anticholinesterase causes accumulation of acetylcholine and such accumulation beyond a certain point produces block of synaptic conduction. An anticholinergic on the other hand lessens the effectiveness of any given level of acetylcholine, thus producing blockage of transmission most readily where amounts of acetylcholine are low.

Further it seems that the same synapse is used for different degrees of learning of the same habit. It has been thought that as a habit continues to be practised, a larger amount of neural tissue becomes involved. However, if a habit is pratised only moderately it is much less vulnerable to the effects of the same dose of anticholinesterase than a habit of the same age which is very well practised. That is, the habit when better learned is much worse retained after injection. This can readily be explained if we assume that the amount of acetylcholine released at a synapse during transmission increases as a function of original training. Perhaps the most dramatic demonstration of this is as follows. When the effective amount of acetylcholine during transmission is low as in myasthenia gravis, anticholinesterase is used to produce more efficient transmission by allowing acetylcholine to accumulate. We would therefore expect that if habits were only weakly learned, anticholinesterase, (in the same dose as in the previous experiments) would actually improve memory for such habits. This turns out to be the case. For instance animals scoring about 67 per cent correct in the last 10 trials before injection, improve to 85 per cent in the first 10 trials after injection. An operated control group without drug scores 9 per cent less in the first 10 trials after operation than in the last 10 before.

Learning is often thought to produce a permanent modification in the nervous system, and this has been an argument for implicating large molecules such as are used for genetic information. Yet animals forget. This has been variously explained by assuming that habits acquired after the original habit interfered in some way. However, it has been possible to show that with *forgetting* there is a lessening susceptibility of memory to anticholinesterase injection. In fact, when forgetting is almost complete, memory is restored by such injections. This tends to show that there is a decrease after a certain point in the amount of transmitter at a synapse subserving a learned habit and that such a physiological decrease probably underlies forgetting.

*See also:* Animal exploratory behaviour. Attention.

*Bibliography*

DEUTSCH J. A. (1960) *The Structural Basis of Behaviour*, Chicago: The University Press.
DEUTSCH J. A., HAMBURG M. D. and DAHL H. (1966) *Anticholinesterase—induced amnesia and its temporal aspects, Science*, **151**, 221.

GLEITMAN H. (1955) *Place learning without prior performance*, J. Compl. Physiol. Psychol. **48,** 77.
KIMBLE G. A. (1961) *Hilgard and Marquis' Conditioning and Learning,* New York: Appleton—Century Inc.

J. A. DEUTSCH

**ANIMAL MOTIVATION.** The topic of animal *motivation* includes the study of such *states* as hunger, thirst, sex, fear, rage, maternal behaviour and curiosity. Many of these states may be brought on by deprivation of certain substances or by the injection of certain other substances. When animals are in such states they will seek out goals, such as the ingestion of food. Such goals are specifically selected by the state animals are in without previous learning. Once such goals have been selected, an animal may seek to attain such goals either through the utilization of prior learning or the execution of unlearned behaviour sequences. However, learning itself can occur without the presence of any obvious motivation. Learned information can also be utilized by the animal in pursuit of whatever goal is set by its motivational state, independent of the motivation during which it was originally learned.

*Peripheral structures and the initiation of emotional states.* According to one school of thought, motivational states or drives are initiated by activity in peripheral bodily structures. It has been suggested, for instance, that hunger arises as a result of stomach contractions. Thirst is considered to be produced by dryness of the mouth, sexual behaviour by changes in the genitalia, and fear and rage by activity in the viscera. However, the overwhelming body of evidence is against this hypothesis.

Studies on the role of stomach contractions in hunger have shown these to have very little effect. Animals with their stomachs removed or denervated still show normal food motivation. Further, when the salivary glands of animals are extirpated, there results no increase in average daily water intake, though one can assume that the mouths of these animals are drier than normal. It has also been found that the removal of peripheral structures affected by sex hormones leaves sexual motivation unimpaired.

Investigators studying fear and rage behaviour have injected epinephrine into animals and observed the effect of this treatment on *avoidance learning.* Epinephrine mimics the action of the sympathetic nervous system and so such an injection should have the same effect as increased activity in visceral structures (though it also has other effects, which complicates the picture). However, the body of these studies does not allow a definite conclusion on this point. Different experimenters have found either a decrease, or an increase, or no change in avoidance learning with epinephrine injection. Others have studied the effect of adrenal demedullation on avoidance learning. Since the adrenal medulla secretes epinephrine and norepinephrine, such an operation should produce the equivalent of lessened activity in the viscera. However, these experiments also have yielded conflicting results. Although some studies failed to find an effect of demedullation on avoidance learning, it was concluded from others that such operates perform fewer avoidance responses than controls.

A very compelling study on this issue has recently been performed by Wenzel. She injected a group of mice for the first eight days after birth with an antiserum causing atrophy of the sympathetic ganglia. Two and a half months later they were trained in a shock-avoidance and a food-getting task. No difference was found between the performance of this group of mice and that of saline-injected controls. This study therefore argues forcibly against the hypothesis of peripheral autonomic discharge as a cause of avoidance learning.

*Central structures and the initiation of motivational states.* Recently a considerable amount of evidence has accumulated showing that motivational states are produced by activity in circumscribed regions in the central nervous system. It has been shown for instance that electrical stimulation in the lateral *hypothalamus* can produce marked increases in eating. It has even been shown that tasks acquired to obtain food can be elicited by such stimulation (e.g. Coons, Levak and Miller 1965). Chemical stimulation with epinephrine in the lateral hypothalamus can also elicit eating. Furthermore, lesion studies involving this region have produced effects to be expected from the stimulation studies. Anand and his coworkers have shown that bilateral extirpation of the lateral hypothalamic region produces aphagia in rats, cats and monkeys.

Analogous findings have been obtained in the investigation of thirst. Microinjections of hypertonic saline into hypothalamic regions induces water drinking in goats, cats and rats. Further, drinking can be obtained by electrical stimulation of these structures; and by injection of carbachol. In addition, lesions in the region of the hypothalamus produce a partial or complete loss of thirst.

The investigation of sexual behaviour has produced similar results. Electrical stimulation of a circumscribed hypothalamic region has produced coordinated sexual behaviour. Injection of male sex hormone into this brain site in quantities too small to have an effect elsewhere, also has this effect (though other behaviour may also be elicited by this procedure, such as nest-building, retrieving and grooming of young, digging and so on). Further, the placing of small quantities of oestrogen into the hypothalamus of ovariectomized cats produces behavioural signs of oestrus. Finally, restricted hypothalamic lesions have been found to abolish integrated mating behaviour, even with adequate supplies of the appropriate hormone, and intact genital development and secondary sexual characteristics.

A very large number of studies have been performed attempting to identify the structures responsible for fear and rage behaviour. Fear and rage have been produced in animals by electrical stimulation of many brain stem and rhinencephalic placements. Notable amongst these

recognition. It seems reasonable that items which have not been attended to will not be as well remembered. These methods have been widely used in appraising attention for many years (Woodworth and Schlosberg 1954).

Eye movements and fixations and pupillary diameter during attention have been used in the study of the efficacy of various visual displays. Special cameras photograph the eye. The developed film can be projected back onto the original display permitting a determination of pupillary diameter and the places toward which the eye was directed during fixation and, the sequence and duration of these (Woodworth and Schlosberg 1954; Hess 1965).

The organized, complex response to a novel stimulus which involves postural adjustments, head positioning, receptor positioning and concomitant changes in the EEG, in cardiac, respiratory and circulatory responses, and in the GSR, is known as the *orienting reflex or response* and has been extensively studied by Russian researchers (Sokolov 1963). The EEG component of the orienting response is an especially useful indicator of shifts of the attentional process. Following a stimulus which is novel, intense, significant or some combination of these, the brain rhythm shifts from a slower (8–13 c/s), synchronous, higher amplitude rhythm to a faster, desynchronized and lower amplitude rhythm. (Sometimes only an attenuation of the 8–13 c/s rhythm may occur.) After removal of the stimulus, the synchronous 8–13 c/s '*alpha*' *rhythm* associated with relaxed wakefulness returns.

Repetition of the stimulus causes a reduction of EEG activation response, the so-called *habituation* (Sharpless and Jasper 1956; Mulholland and Runnals 1964). Changes also occur in the transitory, more localized cortical evoked potentials (Hernández-Peón 1960). The rate of habituation of cortical activation and of cortical evoked potentials is a function of stimulus information. The more redundant the stimulus the more rapid response it habituates providing that the stimulus has no great emotional significance (Fox 1964). The cortical evoked potentials also vary as a function of the selective *orienting* of the animal or selective attention of the human (Garcia-Austt *et al.* 1964; Guerrero-Figueroa, and Heath 1964; Haider *et al.* 1964; Spong *et al.* 1965).

In his interpretation of the orienting reflex Sokolov (1963) stresses the role of a brain model of the stimuli. The magnitude of the orienting response is assumed to be proportional to the difference between the brain representation of the present stimulus and the nervous model of prior stimuli. The nervous model is described as a multidimensional memory trace representing the intensity, quality and temporal characteristics of the previous stimuli. If a new stimulus differs from prior ones by a just-noticeable-difference, the orienting response is reinstated. The EEG components of the orienting reflex follow the same rule. The duration of activation decreases with repetition of the stimulus, while the delay or *latency* of the activation increases.

With a change of stimulation, duration increases, latency decreases (Sharpless and Jasper 1956). Electrophysiological studies of brain electrical activity during various states of attention have been reviewed by Lindsley (1960) and Oswald (1962).

Recordings of brain activity can be from the scalp, the cortex or deeper in the brain (Hill and Parr 1963; Bures *et al.* 1960). Mulholland and Runnals (1962, 1963) have utilized a method which connects the EEG response to the attentional stimulus by means of an external path and back to brain via the appropriate receptor (Shipton 1949; Walter and Walter 1949; Corriol and Gastaut 1950; Hewlett 1951; Turton 1952; Storm v. Leeuwen 1959). The advantages of 'feedback electroencephalography' include a controlled contingency between the EEG and onset and offset of the stimulus, a controlled schedule of stimulation, and a rapid production of a series of EEG activation responses.

The *galvanic skin response* (GSR) is utilized in studies of the orienting response and attention. This response can be recorded as a brief change in the resting potential difference between palmar skin and the skin on the back of the forearm. Increases in the magnitude of GSR follows presentation of novel, intense or emotionally significant stimuli. A summary of the application of the GSR to studies of the orienting response is given in Oswald (1962) and in Sokolov (1963). More comprehensive discussions of the method are presented by Wang (1957) and Silverman *et al.* (1959). Application of these various methods have yielded results which though not synthesized to the satisfaction of everyone interested in this problem, do permit some generally valid descriptions of the attention process.

First, attention is a process of selecting inputs which reflects *phylogenetic and ontogenetic determinants*, the inherent organization of the nervous system as well as determinants developed out of our life experience (Lashley 1954). This involves a selection among sensory modalities (visual, auditory, etc.) and selection within a particular mode. These processes may involve adjustments of the positioning and the operating characteristics of the receptor (Sokolov 1963) or a selective gating or blocking of stimuli not attended to (Bruner 1957). For instance, the cortical electrical activity evoked by a click stimulus is attenuated if the cat orients toward a significant visual olfactory stimulus such as a mouse (Hernandez-Peon *et al.* 1956; Hernandez-Peon *et al.* 1961). Within a sense modality, there is also a selective process (Woodworth and Schlosberg 1954). The specificity of attention can be indexed by a change in the EEG specific to the attentional stimulus. For instance, Mulholland and Runnals (1963) found that if the subject were required to 'pay attention' to the 15th flash in a series of flashes, the duration of the EEG response increased as time for the 'target' stimulus was approached and decreased after it had occurred.

The selectivity of inputs includes a selective response to discriminated aspects of a stimulus complex, e.g. we can attend to a particular instrument and its melodic line in a symphony while the rest is background. This kind of selectivity is likely to be missed, especially in animal studies, if only the orienting behaviour is evaluated (Mackintosh 1965).

A second characteristic of attention is its instability, though this variation is not primarily random. Verbal reports of shifts of attention as well as eye movement recordings indicate that the duration of attention to a particular stimulus ranges from as little as 0.1 sec to 5 sec (Woodworth and Schlosberg 1954). Shifts of attention, both voluntary and otherwise reflect the motivational determinants of the perceptual process. Stimuli which are desired, hated or feared, interesting or beautiful, loved or owned are selectively attended to. Only with effort can we attend to the familiar, emotionally or motivationally indifferent stimulus.

Fluctuations in the appearance of ambiguous visual stimuli, in the perceived intensity of the stimulus, in the performance of continuous work have been considered in relation to the problem of 'fluctuations of attention' (Guilford 1927; Philpott 1932; Woodworth and Schlosberg 1954). Non-random variation in the duration of successive EEG activation responses have been interpreted in relation to the quasi-periodic fluctuations in psychological processes (Morrell and Morrell 1962). The various instabilities exhibited by complex, adaptive biological control processes such as attention, reflect variation in a number of parameters not yet understood nor properly evaluated. The basic requirements for a rigorous analysis of biological control systems can be found in Stark (1959); Young and Stark (1965); and Stark et al. (1965). Hopefully, these studies will become paradigms for the study of problems like 'fluctuation of attention'.

The problem of shifts of attention includes as a special case those shifts that occur when we must attend to two or more things at once. Studies on the interaction of simultaneous performance illustrate this problem. Woodworth and Schlosberg (1954) conclude from their review that the evidence does not support the hypothesis that two attentive acts can occur simultaneously. By inference some rapid sampling or scanning process occurs whereby the attentional process involves first one stimulus then another.

In discussions of attention the question arises concerning the upper limit of things that can be apprehended in a brief time, the so-called attention-span. For instance the number of dots accurately apprehended in a 200 ms exposure is between 5 and 7. For larger numbers, errors increase. However, the process is different. With larger numbers of objects a reclassification into groups and a counting of the groups occurs, i.e. there is a reduction of information. The function errors of number $<7$, called 'subitizing' is discontinuous with the function errors of number $>7$ (Kaufman et al. 1949).

The question of optimum levels of attention has not been investigated as thoroughly as have the questions concerning limits of attention. Bruner (1957) suggests that for sensory thresholds both too little or too much attention yields higher threshold measures. Malmo (1962) and Duffy (1962), show that the kinds of extreme arousal associated with maximal alertness and attention may yield a degradation of performance. Surprisingly, there is little research on the question of optimum levels of attention in relation to learning. In Duffy's (1962) comprehensive review of activation and behaviour there is only one study on this problem (Obrist 1950). Sokolov (1963) notes the interaction of the orienting and conditioned reflexes but the few experimental studies cited point out the need for definitive research on this important topic. It is generally agreed that inattention is associated with less efficient learning. However, it is difficult to devise a control experiment whereby the material to be learned is presented when the subject is not attentive (orienting) and removed when alertness or attention (orienting) increases. Feedback electroencephalography can be adapted to provide a method for this kind of study (Rosenman 1964).

When a stimulus is briefly presented or continued, the attentional process subjectively increases, then decreases. As of now little is known about the growth and decay of the attentional process following a single impulse stimulation nor following a step change of stimulation, and this remains a problem for future research. Stark (1956) and Young and Stark (1965), provide a paradigm for experimental study of this kind of problem in their control engineering studies of pupillary function and eye movement.

The current neurophysiological interpretation of attention results from the demonstration by Moruzzi and Magoun (1949) that stimulation of the central *brain stem reticular substance* produced a behaviour and EEG response like that seen when the animal was 'alerting to attention' following a normal sensory stimulation. Later studies showed that the reticular activating system participated in the response to every sensory input. In general input information proceeds through relays to the cortex. In addition, collateral signals from these primary neural cables proceed to the brain stem and then upward through the upper brain stem and the *thalamus* projecting in a diffuse way to the cortex. If the projections from the reticular system are interrupted, the animal does not exhibit wakefulness nor can it be aroused by intense stimuli even though recordings from cortex show the arrival of information along the more direct route from the receptors (Lindsley et al, 1949). The concept of a cortical-subcortical feedback regulatory system including inhibitory and facilitory processes, which controls the level of central nervous system arousal and activation is fundamental for the neurophysiological interpretation of attention (Jasper et al. 1958).

The current interest in autonomics and intelligent machines (Turing 1956; Uttley et al. 1959) which utilize analogues of processes of thinking and perceiving prompts the question concerning an analogue of attention. Such an autonomic attentive system would include a device for selecting, receiving, weighting, gating and filtering multiple inputs from a variety of transducers. The various input sampling and filtering functions would themselves be dynamically readjusted as a function of the decisions and results of processing, storing and utilizing the input information. In this way the system would always select, receive, process, store and retrieve information as a function of its relevance and significance. The significance of input information would be developed on the basis of the efficiency of the adaptation of the system to its (fluctuating) environment and its success in reaching the goals established for or by it. To accomplish this the system would construct an updated model of the environment in terms of its significance for the actions and goals of the system (Craik 1943) as well as in terms of its uncertainty and redundancy.

*Bibliography*

BERLYNE D. E. (1960) *Conflict Arousal and Curiosity*, New York: McGraw-Hill.
BROADBENT D. E. (1958) *Perception and Communication*, Oxford: Pergamon Press.
BRUNER J. S. (1957) *Neural mechanisms in perception* Psychol. Rev. **64**, 340.
BUREŠ J., PETRÁŇ M. and ZACHAR J. (1960) *Electrophysiological Methods in Biological Research*, New York: Academic Press.
CORRIOL J. and GASTAUT H. (1950) *Le circuit déclancheur électronique de H. Shipton & W. Grey Walter, Son application en electroencephalographie clinique*, Rev. Neurol. **82**, 608.
CRAIK K. J. W. (1943) *The Nature of Explanation*, Cambridge: The University Press.
DUFFY E. (1962) *Activation and Behaviour*, New York: Wiley.
FOX S. S. (1964) *Evoked potential habituation rate and sensory pattern preference as determined by stimulus information*, J. Comp. Physiol. Psychol. **58**, 225.
GARCIA-AUSTT E., BOGACZ H. and VANZULLI A. (1964) *Effects of attention and inattention upon visual evoked response*, Electroenceph. Clin. Neurophysiol., **17**, 136.
GUERRERO-FIGUEROA R. and HEATH R. G. (1964) *Evoked responses and changes during attentive factors in man*, Archives Neurol. **10**, 74.
GUILFORD J. P. (1927) *Fluctuations of attention with weak visual stimuli*, Amer. J. Psychol. **38**, 534.
HEIDER M., SPONG P. and LINDSLEY D. B. (1964) *Attention vigilance and cortical evoked potentials in humans*, Science **145**, 180.
HERNÁNDEZ-PEÓN R., SCHERRER H. and JOUVET M. (1956) *Modification of electric activity in cochlear nucleus during 'attention' in unanaesthetized cats*, Science, **123**, 331.
HERNÁNDEZ-PEÓN R. (1960) *Neurophysiological correlates of habituation and other manifestations of plastic inhibition*, Electroenceph. Clin. Neurophysiol., Supplement 13, 101.
HERNÁNDEZ-PEÓN R., BRUST-CARMONA H., PEÑALOZA-ROJAS J. and BACH-Y-RITA G. (1961) *The efferent control of afferent signals entering the central nervous system*, Ann. N. Y. Acad. Sci. **89**, 866.
HESS E. H. (1965) *Attitude and pupil size*, Scientific American **212** (4), 46.
HEWLETT M. G. T. (1951) *An electronic trigger mechanism*, Electroenceph. Clin. Neurophysiol., **3**, 513.
HILL D. and PARR G. (Eds.) (1963) *Electroencephalography*, New York: MacMillan.
JASPER H. H., PROCTOR L. D., KNIGHTON R. S., NOSHAY W. C. and COSTELLO R. T. (Eds.) (1958) *Reticular formation of the brain*, Boston: Little, Brown.
KAUFMAN E. L., LORD N. W., REESE T. W. and VOLKMANN J. (1949) *The discrimination of visual numbers*, Amer. J. Psychol. **62**, 498.
KLINE N. S. (Ed.) (1961) *Pavlovian Conference on higher nervous activity*, Ann. N. Y. Acad. Sci., **92**, 813.
LASHLEY K. S. (1954) *Dynamic processes in perception*, in (E. D. Adrian *et al.* Eds.) *Brain Mechanisms and Consciousness*, Oxford: Blackwell.
LINDSLEY D. B. (1960) *Attention, consciousness, sleep and wakefulness*, in (Field J., Magoun H. W. and Hall V. E. Eds.) *Handbook of Physiology*, Section 1: Neurophysiology, Vol. III. 1553, Washington, D. C.: American Physiological Society.
LINDSLEY D. B., BOWDEN J. W. and MAGOUN H. W. (1949) *Effect on the EEG of acute unjury to the brain stem activating system*, Electroenceph. Clin. Neurophysiol., **1**, 475.
LURIA A. R. (1961) *The role of speech in the regulation of normal and abnormal behavior*, New York: Pergamon Press.
MACKINTOSH N. J. (1965) *Selective attention in animal discrimination learning*, Psychol. Bull., **64**, 124.
MALMO R. B. (1962) *Activation*, in (Bachrach A. J. Ed.) *Experimental Foundations of Clinical Psychology*, 386, New York: Basic Books.
MORRELL L. and MORRELL F. (1962) *Non-random oscillation in the response-duration curve of electrographic activation*, Electroenceph. Clin. Neurophysiol., **14**, 724.
MORUZZI G. and MAGOUN H. W. (1949) *Brain stem reticular formation and activation of the EEG*, Electroenceph. Clin. Neurophysiol. **1**, 451.
MULHOLLAND T. and RUNNALS S. (1962) *Evaluation of attention and alertness with a stimulus brain feedback loop*, Electroenceph. Clin. Neurophysiol. **14**, 847.
MULHOLLAND T. and RUNNALS S. (1963) *The effect of voluntarily directed attention on successive cortical activation responses*, J. Psychol., **55**, 427.
MULHOLLAND T. and RUNNALS S. (1964) *Cortical activation during steady and changing visual stimulation*, Electroenceph. Clin. Neurophysiol. **17**, 371.
OBRIST W. D. (1950) *Skin resistance and electroencephalographic changes associated with learning*, unpublished Ph. D. Thesis, Northwestern University.
OSWALD I. (1962) *Sleeping and Waking*, Amsterdam: Elsevier.
PHILPOTT S. J. F. (1932) *Fluctuations in human output*, Brit. J. Psychol. Monogr., Suppl. XVII, 1.
ROSENMAN M. (1964) *Relationship between learning and*

*attention as determined in a brain-stimulus feedback loop*, Unpublished Laboratory Report, Perception Laboratory, V. A. Hospital, Bedford, Mass.

ROSVOLD H. E., MIRSKY A. F., SARASON I., BRANSOME E. D. and BECK L. H. (1956) *A continuous performance test of brain damage*, J. Consult. Psychol. **20**, 343.

SHARPLESS S. and JASPER H. H. (1956) *Habituation of the arousal reaction*, Brain. **79**, 655.

SHIPTON H. W. (1949) *An electronic trigger circuit as an aid to physiological research*, J. Brit. Inst. Radio Engrs. **4**, 374.

SILVERMAN A. J., COHEN S. I. and SHMAVONIAN B. M. (1959) *Investigation of psychophysiologic relationships with skin resistance measures*, J. Psychosomatic Res. **4**, 65.

SOKOLOV Y. N. (1963) *Perception and the conditioned reflex*, (Trans. from Vospriyatiye Uslovnyi Refleks, Moscow Univ. Press. Moscow. 1958) Oxford: Pergamon Press.

SOKOLOV Y. N. (1963) *Higher nervous functions: The orienting reflex*, in (Hill, V., Sonnenschein R. and Grese, A. Eds.) Ann. Rev. Physiol. **25**, 545.

SPONG P., Haider M. and Lindsley D. B. (1965) *Selective attentiveness and cortical evoked responses to visual and auditory stimuli*, Science, **148**, 395.

STARK L. (1959) *Stability, oscillations and noise in the human pupil servomechanism*, Proc. Inst. Radio. Engs., **47**, 1925.

STARK L., KUPFER C. and YOUNG L. R. (1965) *Physiology of the visual control system*, CR-238, Washington, D. C.; National Aeronautics and Space Administration.

STORM VAN LEEUWEN (1959) Personal communication.

TURING A. M. (1956) *Can machines think?* in (E. Newman Ed.) The World of Mathematics, New York: Simon & Schuster.

TURTON E. C. (1952) *An electronic trigger used to assist in the EEG diagnosis of epilepsy*, Electroenceph. Clin. Neurophysiol., **4**, 83.

UTTLEY A. *et al.* (1959) *The Mechanization of Thought Processes*, National Physical Laboratory, Symposium No. 10, London: Her Majesty's Stationery Office.

WALTER V. J. and WALTER W. G. (1949) *The central effects of rhythmic sensory stimulation*, Electroenceph. Clin. Neurophysiol., **1**, 57.

WANG G. H. (1957) *The galvanic skin reflex: A review of old and recent works from a physiologic point of view*, Amer. J. Phys. Med. **36**, 295; (1958) **37**, 35.

WOODWORTH R. S. and SCHLOSBERG H. (1954) *Experimental Psychology*, New York: Henry Holt.

YOUNG L. R. and STARK L. (1965) *Biological Control-Systems — A Critical Review and Evaluation, Developments in Manual Control*, CR-190, Washington, D. C.: National Aeronautics and Space Administration.

T. B. MULHOLLAND

**AUTOMATA, FINITE-STATE.** *1. Basic definitions.* For a more general view, and historical sketch, of automata theory, see the article *Automata, infinite-state*. This article describes some of the mathematical theory centred on an automaton (or machine) abstractly described as a quintuple $M = (X, Y, Q, \lambda, \delta)$ where $X$ is a finite set of inputs, $Y$ is a finite set of outputs, $Q$ is a (not necessarily finite) set of states, $\lambda : Q \times X \to Q$ is the next-state function, and $\delta : Q \times X \to Y$ is the next-output function. The interpretation of an automaton is as a system such that if at time $t$ it is in state $q$ and receives input $x$, then at time $t+1$ it will be in state $\lambda(q, x)$ and emit output $\delta(q, x)$.

We introduce $X^*$, the set of all finite sequences of input symbols, and include in it $\Lambda$, the 'empty string' of 0 symbols. $X^*$ is a semigroup under concatenation (i.e. concatenation is associative $(x_1 x_2) x_3 = x_1 (x_2 x_3)$) and has identity $\Lambda$. We then extend the applicability of $\lambda, \delta$, so that $\lambda$ maps $Q \times X^*$ into $Q$, whilst $\delta$ maps into $Y$, by repeated application of the equalities (Fig. 1.).

$$\lambda(q, x'x'') = \lambda(\lambda(q, x'), x'')$$
$$\delta(q, x'x'') = \delta(\lambda(q, x'), x'')$$

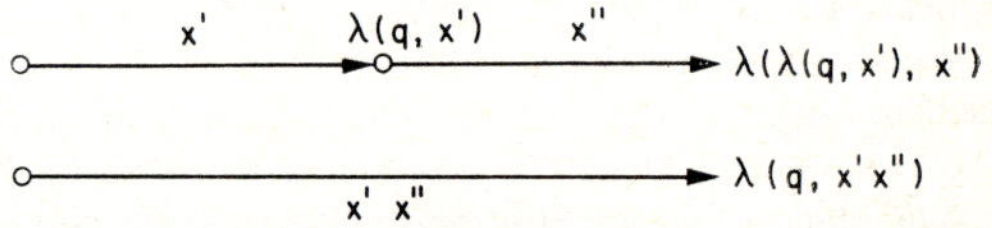

FIG. 1

We may associate with each state $q$ of a machine M the way it produces an output for each input string. This is expressed by the function $M_q : X^* \to Y$, where $M_q(x) = \delta(q, x)$. Clearly M behaves the same if started in two states $q, q'$, with the same input output function, i.e. if $M_q(x) = M_{q'}(x)$ for all input strings $x$. So if our interest in M is in its external behaviour, we may replace it by its reduced form which has one state for each *distinct* function $M_q$. Let $M$ in state $q$ have input-output function $f$, and let $q'$ be a state *reachable* from $q$, i.e. we can find $x \varepsilon X^*$ such that $\lambda(q, x) = q'$. Then $q'$ has function $g = M_{q'}$ where

$$M_{q'}(x') = M_{\lambda(q, x)}(x') = \delta(\lambda(q, x), x') = \delta(q, xx')$$
$$= f(xx') = fL_x(x')$$

where $L_x : X^* \to X^*$ is the 'left multiplication by $x$' function: $L_x(x') = xx'$.

Then in our reduced form for M, we replace each state reachable from $q$ by its input-output function $fL_x$—and the reduced form (restricted to states reachable from $q$) has finitely many states just in case there are only finitely many distinct functions $fL_x$ (so that infinitely many strings $x \varepsilon X^*$ must yield the same $fL_x$). Thus our interest centres on machines of the form

$$M(f) = (X, Y, Q_f, \lambda_f, \delta_f)$$

where $f$ is a given function mapping $X^*$ to $Y$, and where
$$Q_f = \{g : X^* \to Y \mid g = fL_x \text{ for some } x\varepsilon X^*\}$$
$$\lambda_f(g, x) = gL_x$$
$$\delta_f(g, x) = g(x),$$
especially in the case when $f$ is such that $Q_f$ is a finite set.

With such a machine $M(f)$, we associate a semigroup $S_f$, namely the collection of transformation of the state set $Q_f$ induced by the input strings to $M(f)$, i.e. $s_f = \{s : Q_f \to Q_f \mid \exists x\varepsilon X^* \text{ such that } s(q) = \lambda(q, x)$ for all $q\varepsilon Q\}$

This semigroup is finite if and only if $Q_f$ is finite. If $M$ is not in reduced form, we associate with it (and some specified starting state $q$) the semigroup of the reduced machine $M(f)$ where $f$ is just $M_q$.

We may introduce a function $i_f : S_f \to Y$ by the definition $i_f(s) = f(x)$ if $s(q) \equiv \lambda(q, x)$. This does not depend on the choice of $x$. We may then define a new 'semigroup machine' with 'state-output' $i_f$ as
$$[M(S_f, i_f) = (S_f, S_f, Y, \lambda, \delta)]$$
where $\lambda(s, s') = s \cdot s'$ (where the · denotes semigroup multiplication) and $\delta(s, s') = i_f(s \cdot s')$.

We may also introduce the semigroup machine of $S_f$ itself as simply $M(S_f) = (S_f, S_f, S_f, \cdot, \cdot)$.

**2. Regular events.** A subset $E$ of $X^*$ is called *realizable* if there is a machine $M$ with a specificied starting state $q_0$, and a specified output (call it 1, say) such that $E = \{x\varepsilon X^* \mid \delta(q, x) = 1\}$. Consider the characteristic function of $E$, $\chi_E : X^* \to \{0, 1\}$ defined by
$$\chi_E(x) = \begin{cases} 1 & \text{if } x\varepsilon E \\ 0 & \text{if } x\bar{\varepsilon}E \end{cases}.$$

Then $E$ is realizable if and only if $M(\chi_E)$ has only a finite number of states. Kleene has introduced a natural language for describing subsets of $X^*$. The idea of a regular set is defined inductively as follows:

1. The empty set, the set containing only $\Lambda$, and any set containing a single symbol of $X$, are all regular.
2. If $E$ and $F$ are regular sets then so are the *union* of $E$ and $F$ ($E \cup F = \{x \mid x\varepsilon E \text{ or } x\varepsilon F\}$), the *concatenation* of $E$ and $F$ ($E \cdot F = \{ef \mid e\varepsilon E \text{ and } f\varepsilon F\}$), and the *iterate* of $E$, ($E^* = \Lambda \cup E \cup E^2 \cup E^3 \cup \ldots$).
3. No set is regular unless it can be obtained from the sets of (1) by a finite number of applications of the operations of (2).

Kleene (1956) proved that a set is realizable if and only if it is regular.
For example, the regular set
$$10^* \cup (0 \cup 10^*1) \cdot (1 \cup 0^*1)^* \, 0^*0$$
can be obtained as the set of strings for which $\delta(q_1, x) = 1$ in the following machine (an arrow marked $a/b$, leading from circle $q$ to circle $q'$ denotes that $\lambda(q, a) = q'$ whilst $\delta(q, a) = b$) (Fig. 2).

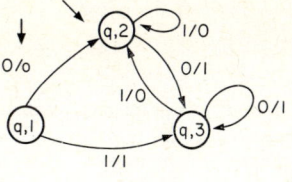

FIG. 2

From a more abstract point of view, we introduce the notion of regular expressions, where we make explicit the idea that a regular expression is in a *meta*language and serves to *denote* a regular event.

If $X = \{x_1 \ldots, x_n\}$ we introduce a new set of symbols $\bar{x}_1 \ldots, \bar{x}_n$, as well as $\bar{\Lambda}$ and $\bar{\varphi}$. We then say a string on the alphabet of symbols $\{\bar{x}_1, \ldots, \bar{x}_n, \bar{\Lambda}, \bar{\varphi}, +, 0, *\}$ is a *regular expression* if it can be obtained from the expressions $\bar{x}_1, \ldots, \bar{x}_n, \bar{\Lambda}, \bar{\varphi}$, by a finite number of the combinations $\alpha, \beta \to \alpha+\beta$; $\alpha, \beta \to \alpha \cdot \beta$; $\alpha \to \alpha^*$. Let $L$ be the set of regular expressions, and let $K$ be the set of subsets of $X^*$. Then we define the function $|\ | : L \to K$ by induction

$$|\bar{\varphi}| = \varphi; \quad |\bar{\Lambda}| = \Lambda; \quad |\bar{x}_i| = x_i, \quad i = 1, \ldots, n.$$
$$|\alpha+\beta| = |\alpha| \cup |\beta|; \quad |\alpha \cdot \beta| = |\alpha| \cdot |\beta|; \quad |\alpha^*| = |\alpha|^*,$$

We read '$|\alpha| = E$' as '$\alpha$ denotes the set $E$' and observe that a set is regular if it may be denoted by a regular expression. We often write $\alpha\beta$ for $\alpha \cdot \beta$.

For regular expressions $\alpha$, $\beta$ we write $\alpha \equiv \beta$ (read: $\alpha$ and $\beta$ are identical), if $\alpha$ and $\beta$ are exactly the same symbols; and we write $\alpha = \beta$ (read: $\alpha$ and $\beta$ are equal), if $\alpha$ and $\beta$ denote the same sets, i.e. $|\alpha| = |\beta|$. For example $\bar{0}^*\bar{0}+\bar{0}+\bar{1} = \bar{1}+\bar{0}^*$. We observe the following identities, for all regular expressions $\alpha$, $\beta$, $\gamma$:

$A_1 : \alpha+(\beta+\gamma) = (\alpha+\beta)+\gamma \quad A_2 : \alpha(\beta\gamma) = (\alpha\beta)\gamma$
$A_3 : \alpha+\beta = \beta+\alpha \quad A_4 : (\alpha+\beta)\gamma = \alpha\gamma+\beta\gamma$
$A_5 : \alpha(\beta+\gamma) = \alpha\beta+\alpha\gamma \quad A_6 : \alpha+\alpha = \alpha \quad A_7 : \bar{\Lambda}\alpha = \alpha$
$A_8 : \bar{\varphi}\alpha = \varphi \quad A_9 : \alpha+\bar{\varphi} = \alpha \quad A_{10} : \alpha^* = \bar{\Lambda}+\alpha^*\alpha$
$A_{11} : \alpha^* = (\bar{\Lambda}+\alpha)^*$.

Salomaa (1966) has shown that *all* equalities for regular expressions may be obtained from the equalities $A_1 - A_{11}$ by repeated applications of the two rules of inference:

R 1 (Substitution): Assume that $\gamma'$ is the result of replacing an occurrence of $\alpha$ by $\beta$ in $\gamma$. Then from the equations $\alpha = \beta$ and $\gamma = \delta$ one may infer the equation $\gamma' = \delta$ and the equation $\gamma' = \gamma$.

R 2 (Solution of equations): Assume that $\Lambda \notin |\beta|$. Then from the equations $\alpha = \alpha\beta+\gamma$ one may infer the equation $\alpha = \gamma\beta^*$.

However, Redko (1964) has shown that if we allow only the rule of substitution, no finite collection of axioms suffices for the deduction of all regular expression inequalities. If we augment the equalities $A_1 - A_{11}$, by the denumerable set of axioms

$$\alpha^* = \bar{\Lambda} + \alpha + \alpha^2 + \ldots + \alpha^{k-1} + \alpha^k \alpha^*, \quad k = 1, 2, 3, \ldots$$

(where $\alpha^2 = \alpha \cdot \alpha$, $\alpha^3 = \alpha \cdot \alpha \cdot \alpha$, etc.) then from this collection one may deduce all equalities of regular expressions by applications of $R_1$ alone.

We note that if $\alpha$ is a regular expression with $n$ letters (in the sense that $\bar{0}\bar{1}^* + \bar{0}^*\bar{1}\bar{0}^*$ has five letters, not two) then there is an automaton with no more than $2^n$ states which realises $|\alpha|$.

3. *Simulation and divisibility*. We say that the machine $M$ *simulates* the machine $M'$ if, provided we encode and decode the input and output appropriately, $M$ can process strings just as $M'$ does. We require the encoder and decoder to be memoryless (i.e. operate symbol by symbol) in order to make $M$ do all the computational work involving memory.

4. *Loop-free decomposition theory*. It is well known that any finite automaton may be simulated by a network of *modules* (i.e. *one-state* finite automata) provided we allow loops in the network ~ such constructions form the central theme of any text on switching theory. In fact we may use copies of just one module (the *Sheffer stroke module*) to build such a network. In other words, a very simple set of components suffices for the construction of arbitrary finite automata *if loops are allowed*. In this section we describe some theorems on the restrictions following from the outlawing of loops between machines (of course, there may be loops in the internal structure of the machines we are combining).

Given machines $M'$ and $M$, and a map $Z : X' \times Y \to X$, we define $M' \times M$, the semi-direct product of $M'$ and $M$ with connecting map $Z$, by Fig. 4.

To get *series* composition (albeit preserving the output of $M$) we make $Z$ independent of $X'$; to get *parallel* composition we take $Z(x', y)$ to be just $x'$.

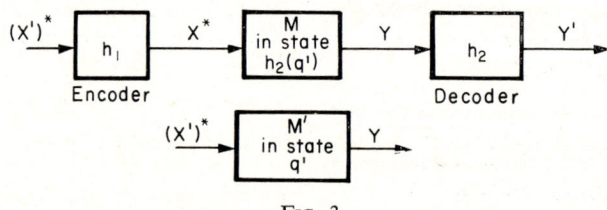

Fig. 3

If $M$ simulates $M'$, we write $M' | M$ and say that $M'$ *divides* $M$. If both $M | M'$ and $M' | M$ we say that $M$ and $M'$ are *weakly equivalent*. The utility of semigroups in finite automata theory is emphasized by the result that $M(S_f, i_f)$ is weakly equivalent to $M(f)$. It turns out that semigroups, as well as machines, have a natural concept of divisibility. We say a semigroup $S$ *divides* a semigroup $S'$ if there is a subsemigroup $S''$ of $S$ of which $S'$ is the image under a homomorphism $Z$:

$$S' \supseteq S'' \xrightarrow{Z} S.$$

If $S$ and $S'$ have associated maps $i : S \to Y$, $i' : S' \to Y'$, then we say that $(S, i)$ divides $(S', i')$ if the situation above holds, and there is a further mapping $H : Y \to Y'$ such that

$$i(Z(s)) = H(i'(s)) \quad \text{for all} \quad s \varepsilon S.$$

The important tie-up between the machine and semigroup concepts of divisibility is that the machine $M(g)$ divides the machine $M(f)$ with each started in their initial state, if and only if the pair $(S_g, i_g)$ divides the pair $(S_f, i_f)$.

Our precise notion of loop-free composition is that of repeated formation of semi-direct products, as well as memoryless codings to obtain machines simulable by such combinations. We let $SD(M)$ denote the set of machines obtainable in this fashion, from a set $M$ of machines.

We say that a machine $N$ is *irreducible* if for *any* collection $M$ of machines for which $N \varepsilon SD(M)$, there actually exists a machine in $M$, with semigroup $S$, such that $M(S)$ simulates $N$, i.e. $N$ cannot be replaced by a combination of machines with "smaller" semigroups.

We call $M$ an *identity-reset machine* if an input either acts as a reset, returning the machine to a state determined by that input ($\lambda(q,x) = q_x$, $\forall q \varepsilon Q$) or else acts as an identity, leaving the state unchanged ($\lambda(q,x) = q$, $\forall q \varepsilon Q$).

Of special importance is the two-state identity reset machine, which we call the 'flip-flop' $F$: It has states $\{q_0, q_1\}$ and inputs $\{e, x_0, x_1\}$ with $\lambda(q, e) = q$ ($e$ is the identity), and $\lambda(q, x_i) = q_i$ ($x_i$ resets to state $q_i$); and with state and output equal. We note that any identity-reset machine may be obtained by loop-free synthesis from copies of $F$. $F$ has semigroup $U_3 = \{I, r_0, r_1\}$ whose elements are the state-maps corresponding to $e$, $x_0$, $x_1$ respectively. We let UNITS denote the set of semigroups which divide $U_3$. In fact.

$$\text{UNITS} = \{U_0, U_1, U_2, U_3\}$$

where $U_0 = \{1\}$, $U_1 = \{1, r_0,\}$ and $U_2 = \{r_0, r_1\}$.

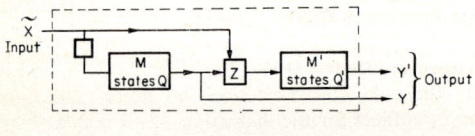

Fig. 4

Then we owe to Krohn and Rhodes (1965) the following elegant results:

1. A machine $M(f)$ is irreducible if and only if $S_f$ is an element of UNITS or is a simple group (i.e. has no non-trivial normal subgroup).

2. Given a machine $M(f)$, we can realize it by loop-free synthesis from flip-flops and from the machines of (not necessarily all) the simple groups which divide semigroup $S_f$.

The reader may find a full proof and exposition of this result in Arbib's chapters in Kalman, Falb, and Arbib (1966). Another wellknown approach to loop-free decomposition, via lattice theory, may be found in the work of Hartmanis and Stearns (1964).

5. *References.* There are many other topics in finite-state automata theory, even if we restrict ourselves to the rather abstract approach taken above. Rather than try to give frustratingly brief accounts of such topics, we have included below certain uncited works which give some indication of further areas of research. Harrison's text contains an excellent bibliography, which mentions most important papers published up to 1964.

*See also:* Automata, infinite-state. Learning machines: a unified view.

*Bibliography*

ARBIB M. A. (1965) *A Common Framework for Automata Theory and Control Theory, J. SIAM Control,* Ser. A., **3**, No. 2, 206.

ARBIB M. A. (1964) *Brains, Machines, and Mathematics,* New York: McGraw-Hill.

ARBIB M. A. (Ed.) (1967) *The Algebraic Theory of Machines, Languages and Semigroups,* New York: Academic Press.

BÜCHI J. R. (1960) *Weak Second-Order Arithmetic and Finite Automata, Z. Math. Logik Grundlagen Math.* **6**, 66.

CLIFFORD A. H. and PRESTON J. B. (1961) *The Algebraic Theory of Semigroups,* Providence, R. I.: Amer. Math. Soc.

GINSBURG S. (1962) *An Introduction to Mathematical Machine Theory,* Reading, Mass: Addison-Wesley.

HARRISON M. A. (1965) *Introduction to Switching and Automata Theory,* New York: McGraw-Hill.

HARTMANIS J. and STEARNS R. E. (1964) *Pair Algebra and Its Application to Automata Theory, Inform. Control,* **7**, 485.

KALMAN R. E., FALB P. L. and ARBIB M. A. (1967) *Topics in Mathematical System Theory,* New York: McGraw-Hill.

KLEENE S. C. (1956) *Representation of Events in Nerve Nets and Finite Automata,* in *Automata Studies,* Princeton: The University Press.

KROHN K. B. and RHODES J. L. (1965) *Algebraic Theory of Machines I. Trans. Am. Math. Soc,* **116**, 450.

RABIN M. O. and SCOTT D. (1959) *Finite Automata and Their Decision Problems, IBM J. Res. Develop.* **3**, 114.

RABIN M. O. (1963) *Probabilistic Automata, Inform. Control,* **6**, 230.

REDKO V. N. (1964) *On defining relations for the algebra of regular events, Ukrain. Mat. Ž.* **16**, 120. (Russian).

SALOMAA A. (1966) *Two Complete Axiom Systems for the Algebra of Regular Events, J. ACM* **13**, 158.

SCHUTZENBERGER M. P. (1961) *On the definition of a family of automata, Inform. Control,* **4**, 245.

M. A. ARBIB

**AUTOMATA, INFINITE-STATE.** *1. Historical* Modern abstract automata theory may be said to start with the simultaneous publications of Turing (1936) and Post (1936), who gave independent—and equivalent—formulations of machines which could carry out any effective procedure provided that they were adequately programmed. (Of course such a statement is informal—we cannot prove that the formally defined class of procedures implementable by *Post* or *Turing machines* will be the same as our intuitive hazy notions of effective procedure. Suffice to say that it has been proved equivalent with many other formal classes, and that no one has produced a procedure which is intuitively effective but cannot be translated into a program for one of their machines.) This work tied in with the work on foundations of mathematics being done by Kleene, Church and Gödel. (For a full account, see Kleene (1952), for a semi-technical exposition see Arbib 1964.)

The basic idea of the Post and Turing formalisms is as follows. The machine consists of a control box in which may be placed a finite program; a potentially infinite tape, divided lengthwise into squares (i.e. depending on our choice of mathematical fiction, we may consider the tape as comprising an infinite string of squares of which all but finitely many are blank; or as a finite tape, to the ends of which arbitrarily many new squares may be added as required); and a device for scanning, or printing on, one square of the tape at a time, and for moving the tape, all under the command of the control box.

We start the machine with a finite string (i.e. sequence) of symbols from some alphabet $X$ (we denote by $X^*$ the set of all such strings) on the tape, and with a program in the control box. The symbol scanned, and the instruction now being executed, determine what new symbol shall be printed on the square, how the tape shall be moved and what instruction is to be executed next. *If* and when the machine stops, the result of our computation, a new string from $X^*$, may be read off the tape.

In 1943, McCulloch and Pitts published their paper in which they introduced nets of formalized neurons, and showed that such nets could carry out the control operations of a Turing machine—providing, if you will, a formal "brain" for the formal machine which could carry out any effective procedure (cf. Arbib 1964). These nets comprised synchronized elements, each capable of some Boolean function, such as 'and', 'or', and 'not'. It was his knowledge of these networks that inspired von Neumann in establishing his logical design, for digital computers with stored programs, which is of basic importance to the present day. In 1948, von Neumann (1951) added to the computational and logical questions of automata theory, the new questions of construction and self-reproduction.

1956 saw the publication of 'Automata Studies', and the emergence of automata theory as a relatively autonomous discipline. Besides the 'infinite-state' Turing-Post machines, much interest centred on finite-state automata, which studied, essentially, the input-output behaviour of the Turing machine control box without regard for its interaction with data stored on a potentially infinite tape. Since then, the two branches of automata theory have progressed more or less separately. For the rest of this article, we concentrate on 'infinite-state machines—other material may be found in the article *Automata, finite-state*.

2. *Many notions of effectiveness.* Let Z be a Turing machine, specified by its program, i.e. list of instructors. We may associate with Z a numerical function $f_Z$ simply by placing a number $n$ suitably encoded as a string $\langle n \rangle$ on the tape and start Z scanning the leftmost square of $\langle n \rangle$. If and when Z stops, we decode the result to obtain the number $f_Z(n)$. If Z never stops, we leave $f_Z(n)$ undefined. (Of course, we can only associate $f_Z$ with Z after we have chosen our encoding and decoding.) *Turing's Hypothesis* (also called *Church's thesis*) is that a function is effectively compatable if and only if it is an $f_Z$, for some Z.

Many other attempts have been made to formalize the notion of effectiveness. Each formalization has yielded a class of procedures equivalent to those implementable by Post-Turing machines (or a subclass thereof). We briefly give examples of two such approaches.

The first is that of *recursion*. Starting with the simple functions

$N(x) = 0$      the constant function with value zero

$S(x) = x+1$      the successor function, and

$U_j(x_1, \ldots, x_n) = x_j$ which selects the $j^{\text{th}}$ of $n$ arguments, we build up new functions by the three operations of

Composition: given functions $h, g_1, \ldots, g_n$ form the new function

$f(x_1, \ldots, x_n) = h(g_1(x_1, \ldots, x_n), \ldots, g_m(x_1, \ldots, x_n))$

Recursion: Given functions $g, h$ form the new function

$f(0, x_2, \ldots, x_n) = g(x_2, \ldots, x_n)$

$f(x+1, x_2, \ldots, x_n) = h(x, f(x, x_2, \ldots, x_n), x_2, \ldots, x_n)$

Minimization: given the function $g$, form the new function

$f(x_1, \ldots, x_n) = \mu y[g(x_1, \ldots, x_n) = 0]$

the least $y$ such that $g(x_1, \ldots, x_n, y)$ is zero whereas $g(x_1, \ldots, x_n, z)$ is defined but non-zero for $z < y$.

The class of functions so obtained is called *partial recursive*: recursive because of the importance of the recursion scheme, partial because the use of minimization leads to functions not defined for all values of their arguments. Amazingly enough, a function is partial recursive if and only if it is an $f_Z$, i.e. it can be computed by a Turing machine Z. For a proof of this equivalence, and a host of extra details see the books by Kleene (1952), and Davis (1958).

Another approach is via the formalization of schemes much more akin to present-day programmed computers. For instance, Shepherdson and Sturgis (1963), introduce the *limited register machine*, *LRM*, which has at any moment of time, only a finite number, $N$, of registers, but also has the facility of adding and deleting registers. Each register can store any number. $\langle n \rangle$, $\langle n' \rangle$ henceforth denote the contents of register $n$ before and after carrying out the instruction. In the instructions listed below, the subscript $N$ means that the instruction is to be applied when the number of registers is $N$, and is to leave all registers unchanged, save where the instruction specifies to the contrary. The possible instructions for LRM are (for $N = 1, 2, 3, \ldots; n = 1, 2, \ldots, N$):

$P_N(n)$:      Add 1 to $\langle n \rangle$ $(1 = 1, \ldots, k)$.

$D_N(n)$:      Subtract 1 from $\langle n \rangle$.

$J_N(n)$ [E1]:      jump to exit 1 if $\langle n \rangle \neq 0$.

$N \rightarrow N+1$:      bring in a new register, numbered $N+1$.

$N \rightarrow N-1$:      remove register $N$.

We define a *program* as a finite sequence of instructions from the above list, numbered serially.

A *computation* of the LRM starts with the specification of a program, of the number of registers, and of their contents. The machine starts by executing instruction 1 ... When it has executed instruction $k$, it always proceeds to instruction $k+1$, unless instruction $k$ was of the form $J_N(n)$ [$l$] and $\langle n \rangle$ was $\neq 0$, in which case the machine next executes instruction $l$. The computation *halts* if the machine is sent to an instruction number which is outside the domain of the program. We only consider programs in which $N$-register instructions are to be executed when and only when there actually are $N$ registers.

Then, for each partial recursive function $f$ on $n$ arguments and each set of natural numbers $x_1, \ldots, x_n, y$, $N(y \neq x_i$ for $i = 1, \ldots, n; x_1, \ldots, x_n, y < N)$ there exists a program $R_N(y = f(x_1, \ldots, x_n))$ for LRM such that if $\langle x_1 \rangle, \ldots, \langle x_n \rangle$ are the initial contents of registers $x_1, \ldots, x_n$, then if $f(\langle x_1 \rangle, \ldots, \langle x_n \rangle)$ is undefined the machine will not stop; if $f(\langle x_1 \rangle, \ldots, \langle x_n \rangle) = m$, say, the machine will stop with the final contents of register $y$ equal to $m$, and with the final contents of all registers 1, 2, ..., $N$ except register $y$ the same as their initial contents. At the start and end of computation, LRM will have exactly $N$ registers. For the proof of this result, and a discussion of similar approaches to the problem, see the lucid paper of Sheperdson and Sturgis (1963).

Still other approaches are due to Church, Post and Markov.

**3. Universal machines and undecidability.** Since each Turing machine is described by a finite list of instructions, it is easy to show that we may *effectively* enumerate the Turing machines

$$Z_1, Z_2, Z_3, \ldots$$

so that, given $n$ we may effectively find $Z_n$, and given the list of instructions for $Z$, we may effectively find the $n$ for which $Z = Z_n$.

This implies that we can effectively enumerate all partial recursive functions as

$$f_1, f_2, f_3, \ldots$$

simply by setting $f_n = f_{Z_n}$.

Say that $f_n$ is *total* if $f_n(x)$ is defined for all $x$. We might ask: Is there an effective procedure for telling whether or not $f_n$ is total; i.e. does there exist a total recursive function $h$ such that $f_n$ is total if and only if $n = h(m)$ for some $m$? The answer is 'NO'. For if such an $h$ existed, define $f$ by

$$f(n) = f_{h(n)}(n) + 1.$$

Then $f$ is total recursive, and so $f = f_{h(m)}$ for some $m$.

Then $f_{h(m)}(m) = f_{h(m)}(m) + 1$, a contradiction! This is just one example of the many things we can prove to be undecidable by any effective procedure. To say that we cannot effectively tell that $f_n$ is *total*, is just the same as saying that we cannot tell effectively when $Z_n$ will stop computing no matter what tape it is started on. We may thus say that 'the halting problem for Turing machines is unsolvable'.

A most interesting result of Turing's paper is that there is a *universal* Turing machine, i.e. one which when given a coded description of $Z_n$ on its tape, as well as the data $x$, will then proceed to compute $f_n(x)$, if it is defined. This is obvious if we accept Turing's hypothesis, for given $n$ and $x$ we find $Z_n$ effectively, and then use it to compute $f_n(x)$, and so there should exist a Turing machine to implement the effective procedure of going from the *pair* $(n, x)$ to the value $f_n(x)$. A proper proof takes somewhat longer!

**4. Difficulty of computation.** A Turing machine may blithely assure us that a problem is effectively solvable and that it will eventually solve it—but the Universe may disappear before it finishes the computation. One reaction to this contretemps is to follow Sheperdson and Sturgis in searching for more natural models intermediate between finite-automata and full-fledged Turing machines, and to study the problem areas they characterize. Such is the work relating automata and context-free languages (see *Linguistic form: algebraic linguistics*, Schutzenberger (1963); and the forthcoming book by S. Ginsburg on the mathematical theory of context-free languages); and the work on linear-bounded automata,

trades-off between determinism and non-determinism, number of tapes, etc. (see Hartmanis *et al.* (1965), and the excellent review article by Fischer (1965)). Here we content ourselves with recalling a few results due to Rabin (1960), Ritchie (1963), and Blum (1964).

Let $F_0$ be the class of all *total* functions computable by Turing machines in which every instruction requires that the tape be moved right, whatever printing and state-changes are involved. When the machine moves off the portion of tape initially printed on, its subsequent behaviour is completely determined by its state at that moment. Thus if the machine has states $q_j (j = 1, \ldots, n)$, the result of computation will be of the form $yz_j$, where $y$ is printed on the initial portion of tape, and $z_j (j = 1, \ldots, n)$ is the expression printed if the machine goes off the initial portion in state $q_j$. We thus see that it is not unreasonable terminology to speak of $F_0$ as the class of 'functions computable by finite automata'.

We say a function $f$ is obtained from the function $g$ by an *explicit* transformation if

$$f(x_1, \ldots, x_n) = g(\xi_1, \ldots, \xi_k)$$

each $\xi_j$ is an $x_i$ or a constant.

Then $F_0$ contains addition (though *not* multiplication) and is closed under explicit transformations and composition (cf. Sec. 2). It thus includes all linear functions. Ritchie takes $F_0$ as a basic class since its functions are computed 'as swiftly as possible'—as soon as the input has been scanned, the output is printed.

Ritchie then defines, inductively, $F_i (i = 1, 2, 3, \ldots)$ to be the class of functions computable by Turing machines which use in their computations an amount of tape bounded by a function in $F_{i-1}$. Thus he measures the complexity of a Turing machine in terms of the amount of tape required for the computation. $F$, the denumerable union of the $F_i$'s, is then called the class of *predictably computable functions*.

Let
$$f_0(x) = x$$
$$f_1(x) = 2^x$$
$$f_{L+1}(x) = 2^{f_L(x)}$$

Ritchie proves that $f_L(x)$ is in $F_L$ but not in $F_{L+1}$, for each $L$. In contrast to the recursion introduced in Sec. 2, let us now say that $h$ is obtained from the functions $f, g$ and $j$ by *limited* recursion if

$$h(0, x_2, \ldots, x_n) = g(x_2, \ldots, x_n)$$
$$h(x+1, x_2, \ldots, x_n) = f(x, h(x, x_2, \ldots, x_n), x_2, \ldots, x_n)$$
and $\quad h(x_1, \ldots, x_n) \leq j(x_1, \ldots, x_n) \quad$ for *all* $\quad x_1, \ldots, x_n$.

Kalmar has defined as function to be *elementary* if it can be obtained in a finite number of operations of composition and *limited* recursion beginning with the functions of the following list

(1) $S(x) = x+1$
(2) $N(x) = 0$
(3) $U^n(x_1, \ldots, x_n) = x_j \quad 1 \leq j \leq n$
(4) $xy$

(It may be proved that 'most' partial recursive functions are not elementary, for example

$$e_4(x, y) = \left. \begin{matrix} x^{x^{\cdot^{\cdot^{\cdot^{x}}}}} \end{matrix} \right\} y \text{ times.}$$

Ritchie's main theorem is that $F$ is just the class of functions elementary in the sense of Kalmar! He also gives a machine-independent characterization of each $F_j$, which shows they are closed under explicit transformations.

Let now $Z_1, Z_2, Z_3, \ldots$ be an enumeration of Turing machines with a fixed alphabet, and fixed choice of encoding and decoding functions; and let $f_1, f_2, f_3, \ldots$ be the corresponding enumeration of the partial recursive functions. Let $F_n(x)$ be the number of steps $Z_n$ takes to compute $f_n(x)$. (Thus if we find $m$ and $n$ such that $f_m(x) \equiv f_n(x)$, we will not expect, in general, that $F_m(x) = F_n(x)$ for any given $x$.) The functions $F_n(x)$ are partial recursive, and satisfy (i) For all $n$ and $x$, $f_n(x)$ is defined if and only if $F_n(x)$ is defined. (ii) There exists a total recursive function $\alpha$ such that for all $n$ and $x$

$$\alpha(n, x, y) = \begin{cases} 1 & \text{if } F_n(x) = y. \\ 0 & \text{else} \end{cases}$$

To see (ii), we use Turing's hypothesis, noting that we may find $\alpha(n, x, y)$ effectively by supplying $Z_n$ with input $x$, and letting it run for $y$ steps.

Rabin has shown there are functions which are arbitrarily hard to compute. We shall state a related result. First notice, that, given $h(x)$, it is easy to find a function $f$ such that no matter *what* machine $Z_n$ computes it, we will have $F_n(x) \geq h_n(x)$, by having it take at least $h(x)$ steps, just to write $f(x)$ on the tape. To make the question interesting, we must ask if there is a function which takes a long time to *compute*. The answer in the affirmative may be stated:

Let $h(x)$ be any partial recursive function. There exists a function $f(x)$, defined just for those $x$ for which $h(x)$ is defined, *taking only the values 0 and 1*, and such that for any machine $Z_n$ which computes $f$, we have

$$F_n(x) \geq h(x) \quad \text{for all but finitely many } x.$$

Suppose $Z_L$ and $Z_j$ both compute $f$. We shall say $Z_j$ is no faster than $Z_L$ if

$$F_L(x) \leq F_j(x) \quad \text{for all but finitely many } x.$$

The latter phrase merely ensures that our comparison is not vitiated by any purely transient advantage that $Z_j$ may have, e.g. in ordinary computer terminology, due to a *table look-up* which allows the machine to obtain $f(x)$ very quickly for the finitely many $x$ in the table.

One question that immediately arises is: Does every partial recursive function $f$ have a fastest program, i.e. is there a $Z_n$ computing $f$ such that any $Z_m$ computing $f$ is no faster than $Z_n$? The answer to this question is negative—there are very many functions with no fastest program. In fact, Blum's speed-up theorem says much more.

Let $r(x, y)$ be any total recursive function. Let $Z_m$ and $Z_n$ both compute $f$. We shall say $Z_m$ is an *r-speed-up* of $Z_n$ if

$$r(x, F_m(x)) < F_n(x) \quad \text{for all but finitely many } x.$$

Thus $Z_m$ is faster than $Z_n$ if it has an $e$-speed-up $Z_n$ for $e(x, y) \equiv y$.

Since we may choose $r(x, y)$ to grow very quickly indeed, e.g.

$$r(x, y) = 2^{3^{5^{7^{x+y}}}}$$

we see that an $r$-speed-up of $Z_n$ may be very much faster indeed.

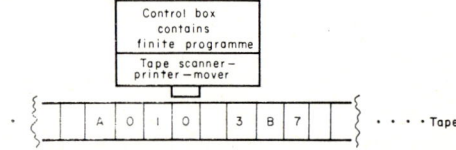

Fig. 1

The speed-up theorem tells us that no matter how large we choose $r$ to be, we may find a $0-1$ valued function $f$ such that *any* $Z_n$ for $f$ has an $r$-speed-up $Z_m$ which computes $f$, and so *ad infinitum*. This is a most surprising result, and the proof is a long one. We close with a warning, in which is implicit a whole programme of research on difficulty of computation. We must discourage the reader who wishes to treat the speed-up theorem as a truth about real computers, rather than partial recursive functions—the $r$-speed-up fails for finitely many $x$, and this finitude may well contain all those integers (e.g. $0 \leq x < 2^{32}$) that we consider in a real computer. And yet the theorem is not without interest!

5. *Self-reproducing automata.* DNA → RNA and RNA → enzyme transductions, while important biologically, are of little interest to the experienced automata theorist. The challenging questions seem to be further up the hierarchy: 'How can a complex multicellular automaton grow from a single cell, given that a finite program can be executed within each cell?' Such a question as this is non-trivial, and becomes a fit topic for automata theory, though it must be confessed that, at present, the emphasis is on ingenious programming of cellular arrays rather than on weaving a rich texture of theorems.

It should perhaps be emphasized that the theory of automata is usually concerned with devices which transform information from an input string to an output string, changes in the automaton being regarded as incidental. In studying self-reproducing automata, the emphasis shifts to the way in which initial information serves to regulate the growth and change in structure of an automaton. It will be of some interest to see what contribution the latter approach can make to our more classical problems. The study of self-reproduction is but one chapter in a thorough-going study of growing automata.

If one thinks of a machine making another machine, one has the idea that machine reproduction (in a very broad sense) implies a degradation of complexity—a complex machine builds a simpler machine. But in biological systems, the complexity of an offspring seems much the same as that of the parent; and evolution talks about machines producing more complicated machines. So, we pose the question of reproduction, 'How, starting from one fixed kind of finite automaton as basic cell, can we design an automaton of arbitrary complexity with the computational ability of a Universal Turing machine, and which can also reproduce itself?'

We have seen that it is possible to program a universal Turing machine which, given for any Turing machine Z, a suitable encoded description $e(Z)$, would simulate any computation which Z could execute.

This *suggested* to von Neumann the existence of an automaton A which when furnished with the description of any other automaton M (composed from some suitable collection of elementary parts) would construct a copy of M.

He outlined how one could use such a 'universal constructor' A to solve the problem of self-reproduction: To build an aggregate out of our elementary parts in such a manner that 'if it is put into a reservoir in which there float all these elements in large numbers, it will then begin to construct other aggregates, each of which will at the end turn out to be another automaton exactly like the original one'.

However, there is a great gap between the known universal computer and the posited universal constructor. For our universal Turing machine only simulates symbolic operations—any physical realization of such a machine would use components of a nature and complexity quite different from that of the tape symbols. This point requires some emphasis. Von Neumann's 1951 paper has left many people with the impression that there is no new logical problem here—that the existence of a self-reproducing machine is reducible to an instance of the recursion theorem of recursive function theory. This is not so. There are two fixed point theorems to prove.

One might suspect that, given a list of elementary parts, a universal constructor for machines comprising only those parts might itself have to be constituted of a more complex variety of components. The proof that this suspicion is wrong gives us the first fixed point theorem: There does exist a set of components from which may be built a universal constructor for automata built from that very set of parts.

The universal constructor A, supplied with a description of an automaton, will build a copy of that automaton. However, A is *not* self-reproducing: A, supplied *with* a copy of its own description, will build a copy of A *without* its own description. The passage from a universal constructor to a 'self-constructor' *is*, in essence, a fixed-point theorem reducible to the recursion theorem.

Von Neumann gave the first construction of a self-reproducing automaton in a manuscript on 'The Theory of Automata: Construction, Reproduction, Homogeneity' which was incomplete at the time of his death, and which A. W. Burks has since edited for publication by the University of Illinois Press. He replaced the reservoir in which the organism floated by a 'tessellation' of identical cells, which were finite automata with only 29 states (von Neumann 1966).

The trouble is that it is very complicated to program something with such simple components. For instance, you can't just have two wires crossing. One way of solving the cross-over problem is to code messages so that, when a message comes to a crossing, it goes both ways, but only a decoder in the desired direction will be able to 'understand' the message. Another way is to introduce a large array of cells such that if you put a pulse in any corner, it will come out of the opposite one. Thatcher (1965) has since produced a polished version of von Neumann's scheme, using the same set of components.

Arbib (1965) has shown how to reduce the complexity of the programming immensely, but only at the cost of more complicated *modules*. The living cell, with its synthetic machinery involving hundreds of metabolic pathways can rival any operation of our module, as well as being under the control of DNA molecules, we believe, with far more bits of information than our cell can store. So, perhaps we lose biological significance by unduly limiting the information content of the module.

Basic to the problems of replication (perhaps a better term than self-reproduction in view of our above remarks) are

(i) *Cell reproduction:* This we have not touched on—our constructions rest on the assumption that we can produce new cells at will, our only problem being to ensure that they contain the proper instructions.

(ii) *Organism replication:* Given cell reproduction, how do we replicate an organism? This is the topic we treat—and it makes sense to subsume a lot of hard work in (i) by using complicated cells. In fact, we might hypothesize that multicellular organisms can evolve (by whatever mechanism) only when there are complicated reproducing cells available.

Contrasting the automaton models of reproduction and organism reproduction, we would see that

1. The automaton program is embedded in a *string* of cells, whereas the biological program is a string stored *in each* cell.

2. The automaton requires a complete specification of its offspring, whereas 'Nature uses' an incomplete

specification. Further, automaton reproduction constructs a passive configuration, i.e. sets up all the cells with their internal program, and only then activates the machine. Contrast the living, growing embryo. The machine construction relies on passivity of components, and demands that any subassembly stay fixed and inactive until the whole structure is complete. The biological development depends on active interaction and induction between subassemblies.

Finally, let us note two distinct problems of evolution. One is, starting from a relatively unstructured universe, how do you get cells. The next evolutionary problem is how do cells start aggregating. We think at the present moment it is relatively easy, at least qualitatively, to get the idea of cells competing for various nutrients in the environment, cooperating to form aggregates, and these aggregates then evolving in a classical domineering fashion. The question of where the cells came from is a very different and very difficult one. What tesselation models study is how, assuming you can place any component you like in the construction area, to reproduce a whole multi-cellular organism. But we haven't touched on the question of how to get whatever component one wants up there; and the question of how reproducing cells evolved in the first place. Codd (1965) considers tessellations with even simpler components than von Neumann's. So a pure automata problem is to embed von Neumann's or Arbib's modules in Codd's model, where one cell is simulated as an aggregate of Codd's cells with appropriate change of time scale. Perhaps we can approach the cellular evolution problem by imagining a sub-tessellation with components comparable to the macromolecules of biology, and consider reproduction of our modules as aggregates of these pseudomacromolecules. Our constructions would then treat arrays of arrays.

*See also:* Computers, stochastic. Linguistic form: algebraic lingiustics. Unsolvable problems.

*Bibliography*

ARBIB M. A. (1964) *Brains, Machines and Mathematics*, New York: McGraw-Hill.
ARBIB M. A. (1966) *A Simple Self-Reproducing Universal Automaton; Information and Control.*
ARBIB M. A. and BLUM M. (1965) *Machine Dependence of Degrees of Difficulty*, Proc. Amer. Math. Soc., **16**, 442.
BLUM M. (1964) *A Machine-Independent Theory of Recursive Functions*, Doctoral Thesis, Cambridge, Mass.: Massachusetts Institute of Technology.
BURKS A. W. and WANG H. (1957) *The Logic of Automata*, J. ACM, Part I: 193, Part II: 279.
DAVIS M. (1958) *Computability and Unsolvability*, New York: McGraw-Hill.
FISCHER P. C. (1965) *Multi-tape and Infinite-State Automata-A Survey*, Communications of the ACM, **8**, No. 12, Dec.
HARTMANIS J., LEWIS P. M. and STEARNS R. E. (1965) *Classifications of Computations by Time and Memory Requirements*, Proc. IFIP Int. Congr. Vol. 1, 31.
HENNIE F. C. (1961) *Iterative Arrays of Logical Circuits*, Cambridge, Mass.: M.I.T. Press.
KLEENE S. C. (1952) *Introduction to Mathematics*, Princeton, N. J.: van Nostrand.
MCCULLOCH W. S. and PITTS W. (1943) *A Logical Calculus of the Ideas Immanent in Nervous Activity*, Bull. Math. Biophys. **5**, 115.
MYHILL J. (1964) *The Abstract Theory of Self-Reproduction*, in *Views on General Systems Theory* (M. D. Mesarovic, Ed.), New York: Wiley, 106.
POST E. L. (1936) *Finite Combinatory Processes—Formulation I*, J. Symbolic Logic, **1**, 103.
RABIN M. O. (1960) *Degree of Difficulty of Computing a Function*, Jerusalem: Hebrew University.
RITCHIE R. W. (1960) *Classes of Predictably Computable Functions*, Trans. Amer. Math. Soc., **106**, 139.
SCHÜLTZENBERGER M. P. (1963) *On Context-free Languages and Push-Down Automata*, Information and Control, **6**, 246.
SHANNON C. E. and MCCARTHY J. (Eds.) (1956) *Automata Studies*, Princeton: The University Press.
SHEPERDSON J. C. and STURGIS H. E. (1963) *Computability of Recursive Functions*, J. ACM, **10**, 217.
THATCHER J. W. *Universality in the von Neumann Cellular Model*, to appear in a book, (Ed. A. W. Burks) on *Cellular Automata*.
TURING A. M. (1936) *On Computable Numbers*, Proc. London Math. Soc., Ser. 2, **42**, 230, **43**, 544.
VON NEUMANN J. *The Theory of Self-Reproducing Automata*, (Ed. A. W. Burks) University of Illinois Press.
VON NEUMANN J. (1951) *The General and Logical Theory of Automata*, in *Cerebral Mechanisms in Behaviour*, Proc. of the Hixon Symp. (L. A. Jeffress, Ed.), New York: Wiley.

M. A. ARBIB

# C

**CHARACTER RECOGNITION.** The phrase 'character recognition' refers to the process by which information encoded in the form of legible printed or written symbols (alphabetic and numeric) is converted into symbols used in computer systems. A recent survey (Feidelman 1966) lists some 30 reading machines (including both optical and magnetic readout systems) now commercially available. A major U.S. manufacturer has 100 or more optical readers in regular commercial use, at prices beginning at £30,000. The basic principles involved in all these devices may best be understood by considering a particular—but typical—example. For brevity we shall not consider magnetic ink character recognition at all.

*Recognition—a paradigm.* In one commercial application the continuous printed tape (journal tape) generated by a cash register is scanned and the information in each line, e.g. 'item of sale', 'mode of payment', 'amount' etc., converted into a coded form which is punched on paper tape or cards. Alternatively, the reading device may be coupled directly to the computer being used to process the information for example for stock control, automatic customer billing, preparation of sales digests and so on. Thus the process of character recognition is one phase of a larger system, in this case a management information service.

In the application cited above, the characters to be read are restricted to the numerals plus a few special symbols, printed in a single style on a continuous strip of paper; machines have been on the market for several years priced at £40,000 and upwards which perform this task reliably and with acceptably low error rates (say 1 character in error per 10,000 read) (Feidelman 1966). The 'hardware' of such a reading device may be considered in three parts concerned with *Transport, Scanning* and Recognition respectively (Fig. 1). The transport mechanism for this device resembles that used in a magnetic tape recorder, and does not present any great technical problems. The scanning or 'sensing' component comprises a Cathode Ray Tube (CRT) and one or more photomultipliers. The spot on the face of the CRT is caused to execute a 'TV' raster scan which is imaged onto the tape by a lens system. As the image of the spot traverses the paper the intensity of the light reflected varies as it moves over blank paper or inked regions. This reflected light is collected by the photomultipliers whose time-varying output is thus a one-dimensional representation of the two-dimensional light/dark pattern on the tape. This output—the so-called video waveform—may then be processed so as, for example, to adjust its maximum and minimum excursus to have the values 0 and 100 respectively. It is then converted into a pulse train by classifying contiguous segments of the waveform as one or zero according as the average value of the waveform in a segment is greater or less than 50. (It is conventional to regard 'black' as having the binary value 1 and white as 0.) The effect of this processing is to convert the ink pattern which *varies continuously* in space and degree of reflectance, into a two-dimensional array of elements. The duration of each segment is such that typically a numeral would occupy a substantial region of a binary matrix, 30 elements high by 15 wide.

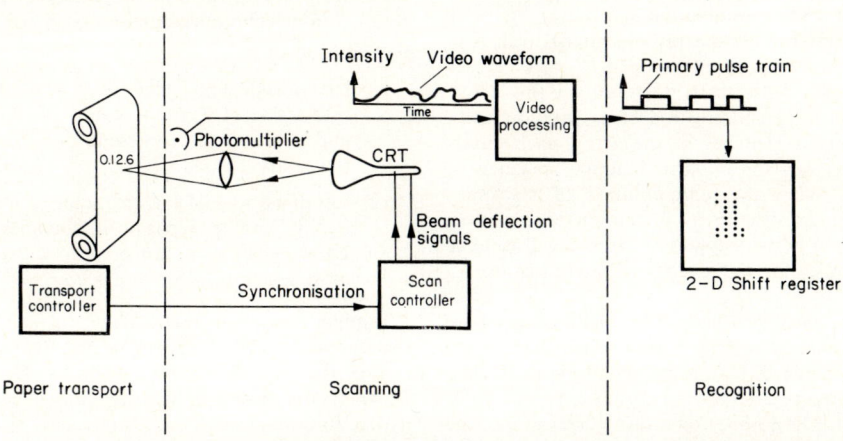

FIG. 1. *Schematic diagram of device to read characters printed on a journal tape.*

Consider the representation of two numerals 5 and 6 (Fig. 2), illustrated for simplicity on matrices smaller than the 30×15 typically employed. Denote the elements of the matrix $X(1,1)$, $X(2,2)$, $X(i,j)$, ... $X(I, J)$, according to the convention indicated, (Fig. 2a). Then we may discriminate one numeral from the other by noting that for the '5':

$$X(7,1) = X(8,1) = 0; \quad X(2,2) = X(2,3) = 1$$

whereas for the '6':

$$X(7,1) = X(8,1) = 1; \quad X(2,2) = X(2,3) = 0.$$

If the problem was merely to distinguish '5' from '6' we would use as definitions of these symbols:

$(\text{Def})_5 \equiv X(2,2) \cdot X(2,3) \cdot \overline{X}(7,1) \cdot \overline{X}(8,1)$
$(\text{Def})_6 \equiv X(7,1) \cdot X(8,1) \cdot \overline{X}(2,2) \cdot \overline{X}(2,3).$

These are *boolean discriminant functions* having the value 0 or 1. Thus in Fig. 2(b) $(\text{Def})_5 = 1$, $(\text{Def})_6 = 0$ and in Fig. 2(c) $(\text{Def})_5 = 0$, $(\text{Def})_6 = 1$.

To discriminate between ten or more symbols, definitions having a larger number of terms will be required (Greanias 1962); such an increase is generally desirable since $(\text{Def})_5$ would be satisfied if *only* $X(2,2) = 1$ and $X(2,3) = 1$, which would be the case if an accidental

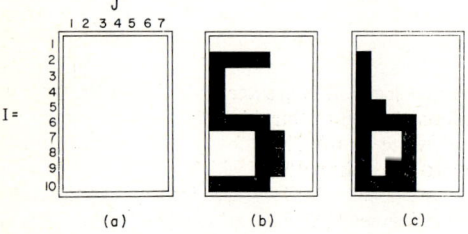

FIG. 2. *Illustrating matrix representation of two characters '5' and '6'.*

black *spot* occurred on the journal tape at that point. In mechanical terms a recognition scheme of this kind is based upon the use of an array of switches (relays or 'flip-flops') which may be either open ($= 0$) or closed ($= 1$). The video pulse train is stored on this array. Logical circuits corresponding to $(\text{Defs})_{0-9}$ are connected to the appropriate switches of the array, each circuit computing precisely the boolean function specified by the definition. When the representation of a scanned numeral is fed onto the array in the correct position, one and only one of the recognition circuits will yield an output thus indicating the identity of the numeral.

*Recognizing 'noisy' characters.* The definitions whose form we have indicated above were based upon some idealised or standard matrix representation of each character. In practice actual representations will differ from the ideal in a number of ways. For example, the character may appear misaligned with respect to the standard position, or together with part of some other character or mark, or misshapen due to under- or over-inking. Overcoming these problems is the central task in character recognition.

Variation in inking and small amounts of misalignment will have the effect of changing the values of some but not all the elements of a representation. The boolean discriminant function requires all of the elements specified in it to have their stated values: it is a sensitive detector of small differences between patterns and in consequence sensitive to small amounts of 'noise'. A less sensitive and therefore more reliable discriminant function *sums* the weighted values of selected matrix elements:

$$S_r = \sum_{i,j} (a_{ij})_r X(i,j)$$

where $r$ has the values 0, 1, 2 ... 9 corresponding to the symbol classes being discriminated. Sensitivity to inking variations may be further reduced by cutting out the binarization of the video signal and treating the values of $X$ as continuous. This is essentially the discriminant function computed by simple optical systems employing 'templates' (Rabinow 1962).

The elements $X(1,1)$, $X(1,2)$, ... $X(i,j)$, ... regarded as variables define a space. If we regard the value of each $X$ as independent of all the others then we have a signal space with orthogonal dimensions. Each linear discriminant function $S_r = f(X(i,j))$ is thus a *plane* in this hyperspace, marking off a region of space (the $r$-th region) into which the scanning procedure maps the characters from the $r$-th class. Establishing optimum methods of partitioning such a space, together with the discovery of 'good' dimensions for the space (i.e. ones which produce maximum separation of character classes) constitute the central problems in the theory of Pattern Recognition (see *Pattern recognition*).

*Registration techniques.* Misalignment of the character representation will of course introduce gross changes in the values of elements entering into a definition. *Accurate registration* of the representation is therefore essential for the success of this method of recognition. Registration techniques commonly in use centre upon detection of:

(1) left- or right-hand edges of the character—to separate a line of characters into individual symbols and position the representation horizontally on the matrix,

(2) top or bottom of the character to position it vertically, and to separate a document into lines. Thus registration can be seen to be part of the more general problem of *segmentation*.

Using a raster with vertical lines the left hand edge of the character will be indicated by the occurrence of '1's in the binarized video waveform. The picture line in which this occurs is then fed into column 1 of the matrix followed by successive lines until all columns are filled. Vertical registration may then be accomplished by shifting the pattern up (or down) until an appropriately constructed definition of 'top' (or 'bottom') is satisfied. Shifting is facilitated by coupling the flip-flops in a way which permits the values of a row of elements to be rewritten on an adjacent row one higher (or lower) in the matrix. This type of matrix is called a *two-dimensional shift register*.

For segmentation and registration to be reliable it is important that characters should be clearly separated when printed, and that the paper surrounding a character should be free of ink spots etc. which might be 'mistaken' for the boundary of the symbol. Both to maintain a reliable representation of the character and to achieve good segmentation and registration, it is essential that the *quality* of the printing should be as high as possible. Thus the control of print quality has been a major factor in the development of practical reading machines. Related to the control of print quality, there have been changes in the style and spacing of characters. Thus the characters are more angular in appearance and are

```
ABCDEFGHIJKLMNOPQRSTUVWXYZ
0123456789
    .  PERIOD
    ,  COMMA
    ;  SEMI-COLON
    "  QUOTATION MARK
    ?  QUESTION MARK

THE TYPEWRITER IS DESIGNED TO GIVE CLEAR
SPACES BETWEEN EACH CHARACTER.
```

FIG. 3. *A sample of typescript recognized by the Control Data 915 page reader.*

more widely separated along the line (Fig. 3). The earliest machine readable characters of this kind—the Selfchek numerals—are regarded for recognition purposes as a combination of horizontal and vertical strokes as shown in the Table (from Heasly and Fisher

|  | 0 | 1 | 2 | 3 | 4 | 5 | 6 | 7 | 8 | 9 |
|---|---|---|---|---|---|---|---|---|---|---|
| **Horizontal** | | | | | | | | | | |
| Top | + | − | + | + | − | + | − | + | + | + |
| Middle | − | − | + | + | + | + | − | − | + | + |
| Bottom | + | − | + | + | − | + | + | − | + | − |
| **Short Vertical** | | | | | | | | | | |
| Upper Left | | | − | − | + | − | + | − | + | + |
| Lower Left | | | + | − | − | − | + | − | + | − |
| Upper Right | | − | + | | | − | − | + | + | |
| Lower Right | | − | | | + | + | − | + | | |
| **Long Vertical** | | | | | | | | | | |
| Left | + | + | | | + | | | | | |
| Right | | + | | + | + | | | | | |

1962). By restricting the geometry of the character in this way, we ensure that any 'black' element of the matrix representation will have a context of black elements either horizontally or vertically. The value of any picture element is therefore correlated with those of its

neighbour and this can be utilized to improve the reliability of the black/white decision for the element and therefore to provide a greater reliability in the *detection* of features of the character. This use of 'context' in judging the form of symbols appears to be an important factor in our ability to ignore poor printing quality. The use of feature descriptions rather than picture elements is another way of looking at the problem of selecting the best dimensions of the classificatory space. One of the most successful devices for the recognition of handwritten numerals, used just such a feature analysis (Greanias *et al.* 1963).

*Format.* Concurrently with development of greater control over the shape, spacing and quality of characters it has proved essential to control the format of the printed information. On a journal tape, the information on any line is formatted into groups of different types—for example 'customer account number' or 'amount'. Digits appearing elsewhere may be superfluous or irrelevant. On a unit document there will usually be a great deal of pre-printed text which is of no significance, therefore only certain *areas* of the document need be read. To specify these areas to the scanner a 'picture' specifying the regions to be scanned may be prepared on a plug-in board (Heasly and Fischer 1962). Thus a batch of documents of the same type is read under the control of one format specification which is changed when a new batch is to be processed.

A technique having greater flexibility (but requiring a more sophisticated machine, the Control Data Corporation 915 page reader, with associated computer) scans a fixed location on the document in which a number is pre-printed. This number is a code for the document format; having read the number the device uses it to locate from computer memory the information needed to control its subsequent scan of the document.

Of course neither of these procedures are applicable in cases where the format changes continuously in an unpredictable fashion, as for example it would in a book containing illustrations, diagrams and equations. The resolution of this problem clearly lies outside the domain of pattern recognition conceived solely as the assignment of bounded patterns to defined classes. What is needed is a method of pre-scanning the document to recover some general description of its contents such as would identify regions containing text, diagrams etc. This description could then be used by the machine to decide on an appropriate scan pattern in a manner analogous to the method used by the Control Data 915 page reader. To recover such a description we need to know the defining characteristics of pictorial objects much more complex than single characters, namely of diagrams, text, equations, pictures, footnotes etc. This wider view of documents as 'pictures' is being investigated by Kirsch (1964) and others as a problem in syntax analysis. It is also essential to the automation of picture processing tasks where measurement is the objective (e.g. bubble-chamber photographs, Narasimhan (1964), chromosome studies, Ledley (1964)).

*Conclusion.* Reading machines capable of recognizing a full set of alphabetic and numeric symbols of a defined style, quality, spacing and format are commercially available. The restrictions encountered are not serious in many commercial data processing applications where rigid control of document preparation is practicable. However, reliable multi-font capability with uncontrolled quality and format has yet to be demonstrated. It is inevitable that such a device will be an integral part of a powerful computer-controlled data processing system.

*See also:* Pattern recognition. Speech recognition, automatic.

*Bibliography*

FEIDELMAN L. A. (1966) *A survey of the character recognition field*, Datamation, **12**, 2, 45.
GREANIAS E. C. (1962) *Some important factors in the utilization of optical character readers*, 129 in *Optical Character Recognition*, (Eds Fischer G. L., Pollock, D. K., Raddack B., Stevens M. E.), Washington D. C.: Spartan Books.
GREANIAS E. C., MEAGHER P. F., NORMAN P. J. and ESSINGER P. (1963) *The recognition of handwritten numerals by contour analysis*, IBM J. Res. and Development, **7**, 1, 14.
HEASLY C. C. and FISCHER G. L. (1962) *Some elements of optical scanning*, 15, in *Optical Character Recognition*, (Eds. Fischer G. L., Pollock D. K., Raddack B., Stevens M. E.) Washington, D. C.: Spartan Books.
KIRSCH R. A. (1964) *Computer interpretation of English text and picture patterns*, I.E.E.E. Trans. Electronic Computers EC–14, 363.
LEDLEY R. S. (1964) *High speed automatic analysis of biomedical pictures*, Science **146**, 3641, 216.
NARASIMHAN R. (1964) *Labeling schemata and syntactic descriptions of pictures*, Inform. and Control **7**, 151.
RABINOW M. (1962) *Developments in character recognition machines at Rabinow Engineering Company*, 27, in *Optical Character Recognition*, (Eds. Fischer G. L., Pollock D. K., Raddack B., Stevens M. E.) Washington, D. C.: Spartan Books.

M. B. CLOWES

**COCHLEAR MECHANICS.** The basilar membrane and its associated structures (the organ of Corti), form the analytic mechanism of the internal ear. The membrane in man is about 35 mm long and about 0·15 mm across at its widest point. It varies about six-fold in width, and some hundred fold in stiffness, from one end to the other, the narrower, stiffer end being at the base of the cochlea, adjacent to the stapes and the round window (Fig. 1).

The membrane is immersed in fluid which is set into vibration by the piston-like action of the stapes. The stapes is in turn linked via the other ossicles of the middle ear to the ear drum, which receives the aerial pressure changes of the original sound wave. The whole system, ear drum, ossicles, internal ear fluid, serves as a matching device to transfer the aerial sound energy to the basilar membrane.

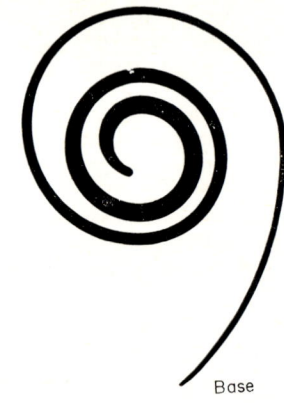

FIG. 1. *Projection of the spiral arrangement of the basilar membrane showing how it becomes broader from the basal to the apical region.*

The cochlear duct is divided into three parts, the scala vestibuli (SV), the scala media (SM) and the scala tympani (ST) (Fig. 2). Reissner's membrane divides the scala vestibuli from the scala media, while the basilar membrane divides scala media from scala tympani. The fluid in scala media, (for reasons probably connected with the transducer action of the hair cells) has a differ-

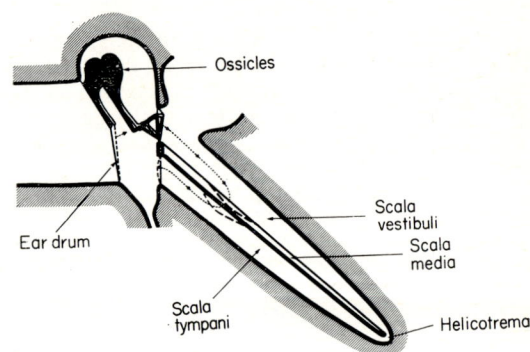

FIG. 2. *Diagram to show the relation of the cochlear ducts to the basilar membrane and to the ossicles.*

ent chemical composition from that in scala vestibuli and scala tympani. Reissner's membrane, which is a thin uniform sheet, serves merely to separate these two fluids, and plays no part in the mechanics of the cochlea. For our purpose we can regard the basilar membrane as the partition separating the fluid in contact with the stapes from the fluid in the scala tympani in contact with the round window. At the apex of the cochlear ducts, remote from the stapes, is a narrow passage, the helicotrema, connecting scala vestibuli with scala tympani, and serving to equalize the static pressure on the two sides of the partition.

If we move the stapes inwards very slowly, fluid flows through the helicotrema into the scala tympani causing the round window to bulge outwards. Moving the stapes outwards reverses the process and causes the round window to bulge inwards. If we now begin to move the stapes in and out rather more rapidly (say 30–50 c/s) the fluid cannot move sufficiently fast through the narrow helicotrema and instead an effective transfer takes place by displacement of the basilar membrane along its whole length (Fig. 3 c), the less stiff parts being displaced most. The point of transfer between movement through the helicotrema and displacement of the basilar membrane, sets the low frequency response limit of the transducer system.

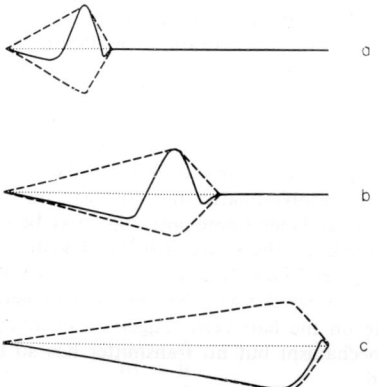

FIG. 3. *'Instantaneous' picture of the displacement of the basilar membrane (full line) from its resting position (dotted). The dashed line shows the amplitude limits of the travelling wave.* (a) *high frequency (10 kc/s);* (b) *intermediate frequency (1 kc/s);* (c) *low frequency (50 c/s).*

As the frequency of movement of the stapes is gradually increased further, the basilar membrane no longer vibrates in phase with the stapes, but travelling waves start to develop. The phase of the displacement lags progressively along the membrane, in relation to the driving force, from the base to the apex. As the wave travels along the membrane it increases gradually in amplitude and then dies out rather rapidly. As the driving frequency is increased, the position of the maximum and of the subsequent decay retreats further and further towards the basal end. The membrane thus acts as a progressive *low-pass filter*—high frequencies excite only the basal region, while lower frequencies excite progressively more and more of it, spreading towards the apical end.

The travelling wave itself can perhaps be visualized more readily if a transient is applied to the system by displacing the stapes step-wise. In response to this, a 'bulge' travels along the membrane with a gradually decreasing velocity which varies from about 100 m/sec near the stapes to 2 m/sec at the apex. This transient response is, of course, an important feature of the system. The mechanics of the basilar membrane in fact represent a good compromise between a purely frequency analytic system which would be completely phase insensitive (such as the old Helmholtz resonator model), and a broadly tuned phase-sensitive system unsuited to frequency discrimination. The versatility of the auditory system is seen in the marked distinction it makes in its response to a single pulse and to continous white noise; both have the same frequency spectrum, the components differing only in phase, yet one is heard as a 'click' and the other as a rushing sound.

It must be emphasized that the direction of travel of the wave, from the basal to the apical end, is a property determined solely by the graduation in the parameters of the basilar membrane itself, and is in no way due to the stapes being situated at the basal end. The vibration is transferred from the stapes to the fluid of the scala, and it is this latter which acts on membrane. Since the speed of sound in the fluid is some 1500 m/sec, the pressure wave can travel the whole length of the cochlea in about 20 microseconds. This compares with about 2 milliseconds for the time taken by the wave to travel from end to end of the basilar membrane. Thus for practical purposes, the pressure is applied simultaneously to all parts of the membrane, irrespective of the position of the stapes. It is, of course, for this reason that hearing by bone conduction is possible, since by this route the vibration is applied all over the bony walls of the cochlea.

We have so far considered the movements of the whole cochlear partition in response to various stimulus conditions. We must now turn to the way in which these movements are caused to stimulate the hair cells, and thus eventually to excite the auditory nerve fibres. The adequate stimulus for a hair cell, whether in the cochlea or the vestibular labyrinth, appears to be deflexion of the hairs in a particular direction; this direction is determined by the position of the kinocilium or the basal body. Figure 4 shows the cochlear partition

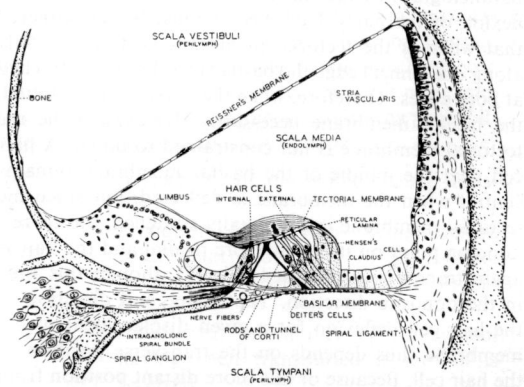

FIG. 4. *Transverse section of the cochlear duct showing structure of the organ of Corti.*

The information rate for a noisy channel may be arrived at, intuitively, by considering the effect of the arrival of one symbol at the receiving end. The ignorance removed is

$$I = \text{(initial uncertainty)} - \text{(final uncertainty)} \quad (5)$$
$$= -\log p(i) - (-\log p_j(i))$$
$$= \log \frac{p_j(i)}{p(i)}. \quad (6)$$

Averaging over all $i$ and $j$ we obtain the average information communicated per symbol

$$\bar{I} = \sum_i \sum_j p(i,j) \log \frac{p_j(i)}{p(i)}. \quad (7)$$

By the laws of probability, we have

$$p(i,j) = p(i)p_i(j) = p(j)p_j(i) \quad (8)$$

and using this, (7) may be written symmetrically in $i$ and $j$, thus

$$\bar{I} = \sum_i \sum_j p(i,j) \log \frac{p(i,j)}{p(i)p(j)}. \quad (9)$$

This is a generalization of (3), reducing to it when $i$ is always equal to $j$, but reducing to zero if $i$ and $j$ are statistically independent. The information rate, $R$, for a communication channel is simply

$$R = m\bar{I} \quad (10)$$

where $m$ is the number of symbols per unit time. All these formulae would merely be empty definitions if it were not for a coding theorem, also due to Shannon, which shows that it is possible to use noisy channels for almost error-free communication. This is in spite of the fact that the individual transmitted symbols $i$ are not always equal to the received symbols $j$. Shannon proves that a source of (say) binary digits can be communicated with an arbitrarily small proportion of errors by suitable encoding into a sequence of the transmitted symbols and decoding from the resulting (imperfectly corresponding) sequence of received symbols, provided that the information rate of the source is less than that of the channel. The coding may be difficult, as it cannot generally be done digit by digit or symbol by symbol. Long sequences must be done at a time, and a delay is thereby introduced, but the rate $R$ can always be approached.

An important result for the engineer and applied physicist is obtained when (9) is generalized to continuous signals. The sums become integrals and the sampling theorem of waveform analysis is invoked to replace the notion of symbols per second by amplitudes or 'signal values' per second. It is well known that a frequency band of width $W$ can transmit $2W$ independent signal values per second. The information rate for a channel of bandwidth $W$ is then

$$R = 2W \iint p(x,y) \log \frac{p(x,y)}{p(x)p(y)} \, dx \, dy \quad (11)$$

where $x$ and $y$ denote transmitted and received signal values. The units of $R$ are bits/sec if the logarithm is base 2. This expression can be simplified when the received signal has merely suffered the addition of a random fluctuation, i.e.

$$y = x + n, \quad (12)$$

and the integral may readily be evaluated if $n$ is 'white Gaussian', $p(x)$ is suitably chosen and $n$ is statistically independent of $x$. For best use of the channel, $p(x)$ should be chosen to maximize $R$, though unless constraints are introduced, $R$ would be infinite. With a constraint on mean signal power

$$P = \overline{x^2} \quad (13)$$

it can be shown that $x$ (and hence $y$ also) is Gaussian. Writing the mean noise power as

$$N = \overline{n^2} \quad (14)$$

the expression (11) yields the maximum information rate, or *channel capacity*

$$C = R_{\max} = W \log \left(1 + \frac{P}{N}\right). \quad (15)$$

This is probably the best known and most widely used result of the theory; it had been less rigorously anticipated by W. G. Tuller before his untimely death in an air accident.

If the noise is purely thermal, we have classically

$$N = W \cdot kT \quad (16)$$

where $kT$ has its usual meaning. The expression (15) increases with $W$, and as $W$ tends to infinity, it asymptotically approaches the limit

$$C = P/kT \quad (17)$$

natural units of information per unit time. It follows that, on average, a signal of energy $E$ cannot yield, in the presence of undular thermal noise, a quantity of information greater than $E/kT$ natural units.

The further elaborations and recent advances in the subject are more specialized and are mainly concerned with coding. The source is generally not a quasi-random stream of binary digits and its statistics will not generally happen to correspond to those of the optimized channel. The coder and decoder required for purposes of statistical matching would in general be quite complex electronic machines. A summary of fairly recent advances has been given in a book by R. M. Fano.

*See also:* Error correcting codes. Information theory in psychological measurement, Random signals and noise. Telecommunication, economy in.

*Bibliography*

FANO R. M. (1961) *Transmission of Information: a statistical Theory of Communication*, Cambridge, Mass.: M.I.T. Press.
SHANNON C. E. and WEAVER W. (1949) *The Mathematical*

*Theory of Communication*, Illinois: The University Press. This book consists mainly of a reprint of Shannon's original papers in the Bell System Technical Journal.

SCHWARTZ L. S. (1963) *Principles of Coding, Filtering and Information Theory*, London: Cleaver-Hume Press.

P. M. WOODWARD

**COMPUTATIONAL LINGUISTICS: INTRODUCTION.** This is a technical term intended to embrace all uses of computers in which the machine is under the control of a program embodying principles of linguistic theory. Since many of these uses are components of the research process in linguistics, computational linguistics is not a professional subspecialty but rather a set of techniques useful to all linguists (Mel'chuk 1963). Other uses of the computer that must be guided by linguistic theory have commercial value; indeed, the growth of the field must be attributed to the eagerness of the potential clientele. Other terms used with the same or approximately the same meaning are *automatic language processing* and *mechanolinguistics*.

*Applications*. Much of the work in computational linguistics can be traced to origins in machine translation. A squib in a popular magazine, published in the United States around the turn of the century, stated the goal, and semi-automatic dictionaries were conceived in France and the USSR during the 1930's. Dictionary lookup is not the whole of translation, however, and the essential ingredients of automatic computation (an instruction vocabulary, conditional instructions, and treatment of the program uniformly with the data) were not invented until the 1940's. Toward the end of that decade, Warren Weaver (1955) circulated a memorandum reviving the lost dream, and numerous attempts, mostly superficial but some nevertheless expensive, were made. Nowhere in the world were linguists quick to seize upon the computer in spite of a few very early statements that clearly expressed the fundamental importance of automatic symbol manipulation to a science dealing exclusively with symbol systems (thus Hockett 1952).

While machine translation was occupying what must be described retrospectively as an inordinate amount of attention, given the inherent difficulty of the task, the low cost of human translation, the small amount of translation actually purchased each year, and the widespread use of English in science and commerce, other applications had quieter beginnings but quickly outranked translation in several respects. The first to achieve commercial significance was *automatic typographic composition*. The contribution of linguistics to this field is essential, but well-nigh trivial; the late development of linguistic theory and empirical knowledge therefore did not delay the applications. Programming techniques had to reach a certain level of sophistication; high-speed and error-free devices for the physical preparation of printing masters had to be invented; and the cost of computation had to fall below a certain ceiling. All of these requirements were satisfied by the early 1960's, and the result was a sweeping alteration of the methods and even the financial structure of the publishing industry. Firms originally devoted to computing began to offer typographic services, and there were mergers of publishing houses with computer manufacturers and television broadcasters.

Simultaneously with the development of phototypesetting equipment for output and computer programs for line justification and page composition, hardware for input and programs for file management were advancing. Techniques for coupling many keyboards to a computer simultaneously were introduced, and opened the way to an inevitable vertical enlargement of the computer's role. The author or his secretary would prepare copy with computer assistance; thereafter, the computer would participate in every step up to platemaking. Editorial processes would alter the text stored in the computer, but the work of copying a typewritten page at a keyboard would disappear entirely.

The field of *scientific documentation*, with the operationally identical fields of legal research, humanistic scholarship, etc., offered other applications of computational linguistics. Bibliographies were growing rapidly as the pursuit of knowledge accelerated after World War II; the purely mechanical-clerical tasks of interfiling new entries among old ones could be automated with ease, and early small-scale experiments led to immense operating systems such as MEDLARS, the medical bibliography system at the (U.S.) National Library of Medicine. Many large periodical bibliographies for scientific and technological fields adopted automatic systems, libraries began experimenting with computer-based catalogues of their holdings, and the (U.S.) Library of Congress began in 1966 to experiment with distribution of their catalogue entries for new books by magnetic tape shipped to subscribing libraries.

Simple economic considerations showed that neither card catalogues nor printed books or periodicals could permanently survive as guides to published literature. With ever decreasing costs for computation, storage, and access hardware, there would perforce come a time when it would be cheaper to store bibliographic information in computer memory and print portions of it on demand for the individual scientist or scholar. Indeed, this prediction seemed equally valid for all kinds of knowledge.

In commerce and government, applications of computational linguistics include the management of files of information of all kinds, with ready access provided for managers who must base their decisions on the known facts. Maintenance of handbooks, processing of correspondence, and other tasks were conceived and attempted.

In the social and psychological sciences and the study of literature, applications of computational linguistics include content analysis, i.e. determination of the psychological, social, historical, or stylistic significance of a text.

These applications can be graded into three broad categories. Those requiring little linguistic knowledge could be pursued as soon as the art of computation was sufficiently advanced; typesetting and the processing of bibliographies therefore led the whole field. Those requiring much linguistic knowledge, but nothing more, were slower to advance; and those requiring something additional were slowest of all. The basis required for machine translation, or automatic determination of the topic of a scientific article, might be debated; but the basis required for truly automatic programming, problem solving, content analysis, and many other conceivable applications was indubitably broad, calling for integration of linguistic theory with mathematics and those branches of philosophy devoted to the roots and structure of knowledge.

*Linguistic research.* Considered as a scientist, the linguist has the objective of decsribing one portion of reality: natural languages, their syntactic structures, lexical composition, and use as vehicles of communication, emotional expression, social integration, and artistic creation by the human beings who use them. As soon as the art of computation had progressed far enough for the computer to be recognizable as a symbol manipulator, a few linguists began to apply it as a tool in their research. Widespread use had to wait on several things: self identification of linguists as scientists, technical facilities permitting easy use of the computer, and explication of the methodology of linguistic research.

The traditional method of the school in linguistics sometimes called 'American' is distributional analysis, and the traditional tool of distributional analysis is the *concordance*, often realized as a file of slips, each bearing the transcription of an utterance and each filed under some lexical item or syntactic feature. Concordances have been prepared over the centuries for many texts in many languages. They have served linguists, literary scholars, and theologians well, but they were prepared at great human cost until the computer was put into service. Now a concordance can be prepared almost as quickly as a text can be transcribed at a typewriter. In fact, once a text has been transcribed it is somewhat pointless to make a complete concordance of the items contained in it; rather, a linguist or other student can call, when the occasion arises, for a concordance of those items of interest to him, sub-classified according to criteria pertinent to his research subject.

Concordances are sometimes made from text in its barest, most straightforward form; they need not be, however, for the text can be stored in the computer in parallel with a translation, a paraphrase, a grammatical interpretation, syntactic annotations, or other additional information. The arrangement of the concordance can be conditioned to elements of these parallel texts as appropriate to the research in hand.

If a linguist has even partial knowledge of the language he is studying, he may be able to realize it in the form of an automatic dictionary, automatic system for sentence structure determination (parser), automatic semantic interpreter or content analyser, etc. If his knowledge is only partial, any system he may develop and apply to his corpus must certainly fail from time to time. These failures become the subject of investigation; perhaps they can be identified automatically, or perhaps they must be discovered by perusal of the results. Whichever the case, once they have been noted they can be classified according to the lexical, syntactic, or other environments in which they occur. The linguist's ingenuity is then the only limiting factor in automation of error analysis. If his ingenuity is high, he may even find a way to close the research loop, as Pendergraft has attempted to do, putting the results of automatic analysis back into the partially developed dictionary or parsing system and making a new attack on the same or a different corpus. Garvin (1962) has distinguished three grades of computer participation in linguistic research. The first is purely clerical, as when the computer makes a concordance; here scarcely any linguistic theory is involved in the design of the computer program. The intermediate stage is that of computer testing of systems (dictionaries, parsers, etc.) obtained by any research technique whatsoever; here, linguistic theory is involved in program design. The highest degree of computer participation is achieved when the linguist's theory of the nature of natural languages is combined with a metatheoretical explication of the research process itself; by adding methodological to theoretical considerations, the linguist frees his program from human intervention during the whole research procedure.

Other categorizations of computer participation are conceivable. The computer may serve to process data acquired by the linguist in the field or by collection of texts; the computer can itself be programmed to collect data, perhaps by means of a console at which an informant can be interrogated and through which he can submit his answers directly to the computer. The analytic program provided for the computer may be based entirely on logical considerations about the nature of language and of the linguistic theory being used, or statistical considerations may enter as well. Automatic classification or clumping techniques fall in the latter domain, and have already proved useful (e.g. Sparck Jones 1964). Both the files of data on which linguistic analyses are based and the results of analysis (dictionaries, grammars, and thesauri among others) are so voluminous and so difficult to control that the computer must henceforth be recognized as the indispensable tool of the linguist who would pursue his task beyond rather superficial levels.

*Components of linguistic systems.* Whether the computer is used for linguistic research or for some application, certain programs or files of material are necessary. These components recur widely; the progress of the field depends largely on universal availability of these components in good form.

The purpose of an *input processor* is to isolate and eliminate characteristics of the input that are peculiar to the nature of the device used for input preparation. A text may come from a card punch, a paper-tape punch, the input device of an automatic typesetting system, an automatic print reader, or some other source. For further processing, for archiving, or for interchange among research centres it is most desirable to make text conform to a standard independent of the physical nature, and conventions for use, of such devices. One proposal for a standard, allowing for indefinitely many varieties of characters and providing simple encoding of typographic features such as change of face or font, was proposed in 1965 by Kay and Ziehe (1965).

Archival storage of text ready for processing is necessary if students and linguists without funds or energy to prepare their own materials are to make use of the computer as an analytic instrument. If each linguist must prepare his own material, he can spend as much time and money on this one step as he might in completing a small piece of research. The development of archives covering many languages and many kinds of text is therefore of great importance to the advancement of the art.

For many processes, a *dictionary* is necessary. A dictionary may contain morphological, syntactic, semantic, psychological, or other information about the units that can occur in a text. By automatic consultation of a dictionary the research linguist learns what is known about the individual units in his text, thus reserving his efforts for the solution of real problems; the operator of an applied system, for machine translation, indexing, or some other purpose cannot proceed without dictionary lookup, which provides the inputs to his further processors.

*Parsers* are programs that apply grammatical theory and the known facts of syntax to a text, relying on information about individual items obtained from dictionary lookup. They provide descriptions of the syntactic relationships among items, up to the boundaries of the free utterance or sentence. These relationships are used, for example, in semantic analysis.

*Stratal conversion* is called for by theories that apportion the description of a language among several strata; these programs convert the representation of a text from syntactic to semantic (sememic), or from any stratum to any adjacent stratum. Dictionary lookup is only one example of a stratal converter (Lamb 1965).

As the outcome of linguistic research, a *grammar* is the basis for description of a language, as for example to students. As part of a system for linguistic computation, it is the file of specific facts about a given language that a universal parsing program must have in order to carry out its work on a given text.

Other components are being developed and will be invented in the future: as a wider variety of components comes into existence, new applications will be invented by recombination. A machine translation system, for example, might consist of input processor, dictionary consultation program, parser, one or more stratal converters, and various components for translating on a high stratum and synthesizing in the output language. A system for automatic content analysis in psychology might consist of the same several components of a machine translation system, up to analysis of text on the highest linguistic stratum, followed not by a translator but by an interpreter of psychological content. Some of these components exist only in imagination at the time of writing, but when they are realized there will surely be other inventions to occupy the linguist who would seek an ever wider range of applications, concomitant with widening knowledge of human speech.

*Bibliography*

GARVIN P. L. (1962) *Computer Participation in Linguistic Research, Language*, **38**, 385, Oct.–Dec.
HOCKETT C. F. (1952) *Review of Harris, Methods in Structural Linguistics, American Speech*, **27**, 117.
KAY M. and ZIEHE T. W. (1965) *Natural Language in Computer Form*, RM-4390, The Rand Corporation, Santa Monica, California, February.
LAMB S. M. (1965) *The Nature of the Machine Translation Problem, J. Verbal Learning and Verbal Behavior*, **4**, 196, June.
MEL'CHUK I. A. (1963) *Machine Translation and Linguistics*, in (O S. Akhmanova *et al.*) *Exact Methods in Linguistic Research*, University of California Press, Berkeley.
SPARCK JONES K. (1964) *Synonymy and Semantic Classification*, Ph. D. Thesis, University of Cambridge.
WEAVER W. (1955) *Translation*, in (William N. Locke and A. Donald Booth, Eds.) *Machine Translation of Languages*, 15, New York: Wiley.

D. G. HAYS

**COMPUTATIONAL LINGUISTICS: MACHINE TRANSLATION.** To what extent can translation from one natural language to another be performed by a machine? Are the 'translations' so produced of sufficiently high quality to be useful? How can the process best take advantage of the latest state of knowledge in linguistics and in the study of the languages concerned? It is the goal of research in machine translation (MT) to supply answers to these questions, besides, of course, actually making a machine translate.

Either spoken or written language may be involved, but the great majority of workers have so far devoted their attention to written language. This is because it is straightforward to convert a written text to machine-readable form, and to produce printed output automatically; the corresponding processes in spoken language can not yet be performed by a machine, and indeed are by no means fully understood.

The machine used must be a versatile manipulator of symbols, and the only such machine at present is the digital computer. The kernel of any practical machine translation process must therefore be a computer program, and in this article we will mainly be concerned with the nature of this program.

*The development of MT.* The routine nature of certain aspects of translation is evident to any translator. The realization that it should therefore be possible to construct a machine to perform these functions is generally attributed to the Russian P. P. Smirnov-Trojanskij, writing in 1933. His plans were premature, and it was not until the earliest computers were in use, in 1946, that the idea reappeared, independently. A. D. Booth and Warren Weaver were the principal figures in the initial discussions, and in 1949 Weaver distributed a 'memorandum' (reprinted in Locke and Booth, 1955), which caught the imagination of many research authorities and thus effectively launched machine translation.

The work mushroomed, particularly in the United States: by 1958 there were about twenty groups active in the field. Much money was spent, some of it in the hope of quick returns, which was not fulfilled. In retrospect this appears to have been due firstly to insufficient coordination of the work: the field tackled was too broad, and even so there was considerable duplication of effort; and secondly to the fact that linguistics was not sufficiently advanced to have a clear claim to be the theoretical foundation on which the technology of MT should be built.

Since 1960 the pattern of research has been rationalized somewhat; some of the less promising branches have been pruned; others are more fertile, and a certain amount of fruit has been gathered in the form of usable translations. Meanwhile the general validity of the use of computers to process natural language data has been demonstrated, so that the subject of *Computational Linguistics* is now firmly established and MT finds its proper place within it. Linguistics has developed considerably in the period since 1950, no doubt partly stimulated by MT itself; it is now generally accepted that an MT project should be organised in accordance with the principles of linguistic theory. (This is not of course to say that MT processes should mirror those of human translation, about which, in any case, very little is known.) What is not, unfortunately, generally accepted is the nature of these principles.

*MT as applied linguistics*. In linguistic science there are at present several schools of thought, each using their own model of language. Since they are all studying aspects of a single phenomenon it is reasonable to assume that their views are only apparently in conflict, and that in time all will be related, one model being established as the most suitable for MT, others being appropriate to other uses. Until this is done there will be as many approaches to MT as there are theories of language; fortunately these approaches have a certain measure of common ground.

*Translation* is a transformation from one set of symbols to another (hence the appropriateness of computers, since they are symbol-manipulators). This transformation is such that *meaning* is invariant, or rather is changed as little as possible. The nature of meaning is far from being fully understood, but certain facts are known about it. The first of these concerns words: a word in the source language has an area of meaning which *in general* will be covered by a small set of words in the target language. (This intentionally begs several questions, but is nevertheless valid: witness the usefulness of an ordinary bilingual dictionary.) The second concerns grammar: it is demonstrably a useful approximation to the truth to say that a particular syntactic pattern or structure in the source language has the same 'meaning' as, and is accordingly to be translated into, a certain structure in the target language.

*Outline of an MT system*. If MT is to use these facts the process must first identify the basic items or 'words' in the text. This is done by consulting a *dictionary*, of course in a machine-readable form. Secondly the process must find any grammatical patternings into which these items enter. These patternings will be expressed in terms of the particular model chosen; the more powerful the model the nearer to 'meaning' these statements of pattern or structure will be. This process (finding patterns and expressing them in terms of the chosen model) is a fundamental one in MT and is called analysis.

Following the analysis there will need to be a transformation of the pattern-statement into one appropriate to the target language.

The final stage, *synthesis*, takes this pattern-statement and generates from it, using facts about the target language, a string of characters which is the system's attempt at a translation of the original text.

Thus a four-stage process is proposed, each stage being carried out by a computer program:

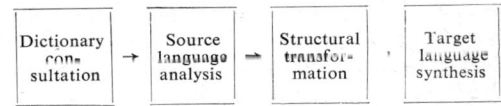

This plan is generally accepted by the various groups in the field. They differ considerably, however, both on the central question of the nature of the 'pattern-statement', and, therefore, on the techniques appropriate within each program.

For instance, to a worker in transformational grammar the analysis would have the task of discovering the list of phrase-structure and transformational rules which would generate each observed source-language sentence; the structural transformation would convert this list, according to certain rules, into one appropriate to the target language; and the synthesis would 'obey' this list to produce the required output string.

To a worker in stratificational grammar the grammars of the two languages, once written, would include analysis and synthesis processes, each proceeding in steps from one stratum to the next. All that would be needed in addition would be the structural transformation from one language to the other on the highest stratum reached (and if this was high enough perhaps no such transformation would be needed).

*Practical MT*. In a practical MT system the first step is to put the text in a machine-readable form. At present this is a typing operation, producing punched paper tape or cards; eventually a reading machine may be developed, or the printers of journals might be persuaded to produce such a tape, in a standard code, as a by-product of the typesetting process.

Many groups restrict themselves to scientific texts, since this is where the greatest demand lies; also in them there is little of that underlying cultural difference which, in the extreme case, may make a non-scientific text impossible to translate adequately.

After any initial processing of the text (for instance marking probable boundaries between stem and affix in inflected languages), the first major program is the *dictionary consultation*. Various techniques have been devised: a common method is to have the dictionary on magnetic tape, sort the text words into alphabetical order, run through text and dictionary simultaneously, appending relevant entries to each text word, and finally re-sort to text order. Sorting can be avoided if a large random-access store is available; Lamb (1961) devised an elegant method which avoids sorting even for a comparatively small random-access store, though at some cost in the complexity of, for instance, dictionary amendments. IBM constructed a special 'photostore' for use as a random-access dictionary, a disk on which a complete dictionary was inscribed photographically on an annular area of about 15 in.$^2$ (for details, see Bowers and Fisk 1965). This is one of the relatively few instances of major hardware developed, at least initially, for MT.

Whatever dictionary technique is used, the process must cater for idioms like 'alternating current', where the two words act as a single linguistic item; and also for compound words like 'microelectronic' which it may well be convenient to consider as containing two linguistic items. The output from the dictionary consultation is often called *augmented text*.

Two main techniques are available in *analysis*. One is to incorporate the grammar in the program. This is powerful but makes for complex programming and requires close cooperation between linguist and programmer. The other is to construct a grammar in a tabular form, and have a general program, independent of the particular grammar and using it as part of its data. This method may be restrictive, some grammatical ideas not being convenient to express in tabular form; but it should simplify the program and also the division of responsibilities between the workers. It is too early to judge between these methods: both have merits and both have been used successfully.

Most analysis programs make several passes through each sentence, each pass looking for a different set of features. One technique, devised by Mrs. Ida Rhodes of the U.S. National Bureau of Standards and developed by the group at Harvard University, is an exception to this 'multi-pass' rule, and deserves particular mention. It is called *predictive analysis* (Rhodes 1961), and consists of moving along the sentence from left to right, and after each word making an informed guess as to what the structure will be, modifying this guess in the light of what actually appears next. Often several possibilities have to be 'kept in mind'. The method is attractive, partly perhaps because human analysis apparently works predictively. It has proved successful in practice.

Less can be said about the stage of *structural transformation*. As implied above, it should become less important as more powerful models are used; it is also less complex if the pair of languages being studied are closely related. Much work, for instance, has been done on Russian to English, where the transformations would consist of modifications to the given Russian structure. For an unrelated pair such as Chinese and English, the transformations would presumably need to be much more drastic, far fewer linguistic categories being shared between the two languages.

The tasks of *synthesis* are principally to determine the order of words in the output; to select equivalents from the short list in each dictionary entry (where any grammatical or collocational criteria exist for doing this); to insert 'function' words, such as an auxiliary verb to express a particular tense; and finally to provide inflected endings for the words where needed. The synthesis must incorporate in its final stage format-control processes to determine lines, paragraphs, pages, etc., in the final output. This may be on a line printer direct from the computer, or off-line via magnetic tape, paper tape or cards. The output may include a copy of the original or not depending on the use to which it is to be put.

How much useful translation has been produced by machines so far? This is difficult to discover, partly for security reasons: if MT research is financed by military authorities they are naturally not prepared to say exactly what use they are making of the results. Certainly however, machine translations have been produced which are good enough to be useful, and in the United Kingdom, as this article is written, potential users are cooperating in an evaluation experiment by submitting papers and assessing the usefulness of the machine translation results.

The economics of machine translation also involve many unknown quantities, but it has been estimated that MT running costs would be rather less than the cost of human translation. The punching of text is the major item on the MT side, so that a cheap reading machine would alter this balance considerably.

Machine translation is a long-term challenge to the computer scientist, the linguist, and the philosopher, and not least to their powers of cooperation. It is therefore involved with the relations between science and the humanities in a unique way. It has provoked violent enthusiasms and denunciations during its short life, and it will be fascinating to see how it develops.

*See also:* Symbol manipulation by digital computer.

*Bibliography*

BOOTH A. D. (Ed.) (1967) *Machine Translation*, Amsterdam: North-Holland (in press).
BOWERS D. M. and FISK M. B. (1965) *The World's Fair machine translator, Computer Design*, April.

Delavenay E. (1960) *Introduction to Machine Translation*, London: Thames and Hudson.
Garvin P. L. (Ed.) (1963) *Natural Language and the Computer*, New York: McGraw-Hill.
Lamb S. M. and Jacobsen W. H. (1961) *A high-speed large capacity dictionary system*, Mechanical Translation, **6,** Nov.
Locke N. and Booth A. D. (1955) *Machine Translation of Languages*, London: Chapman and Hall.
Mounin G. (1964) *La machine à traduire*, The Hague: Mouton.
Rhodes I. (1961) *A new approach to the mechanical syntactic analysis of Russian*, Mechanical Translation, **6,** Nov.
Proceedings of the 1961 International Conference on machine translation of languages and applied language analysis, (1962) London: H. M. Stationery Office.

D. M. Yates

**COMPUTER LANGUAGE DESIGN REQUIREMENTS.** A programming language is a coherent set of instructions from which a selection may be made by the programmer in order to instruct the computer on the method which it is to adopt in the solution of a problem. Since the computer is already provided with an order code which constitutes a set of instructions, any program written in a programming language other than the machine language will require to be translated from the 'source' language into the 'object' language which the computer will perform directly. The process concerned is called translation or compilation and a program called a translator or compiler is provided in order to make the programming language a working instrument.

In considering the merit of a programming language there are three aspects to be taken into account. They are first the efficacy of the programming language as a tool for problem solution, second the standard of competence displayed by the translator or compiler which converts the source program into machine language, and third the efficiency, measured probably in money cost, of the machine language object program.

Several fields of application have already been established for programming languages. There is, however, no reason to suppose that computer languages might not be designed to cover the whole range of human thinking. The fields in which the most advanced development work has been done, and in which most languages exist, are commercial data processing, scientific computation, simulation of complex situations, and numerical control of machine tools. Languages are beginning to appear for real time processes in a computer; for example, for process control of industrial plant, and for the 'conversational mode' (in which the computer and the user at a typewriter console are regarded as being in conversation with each other). One's choice of programming language will be made with regard to the field of application with which one is concerned.

Most languages are *procedural* in nature, that is they consist of a sequence of imperatives which are executed by the computer in the order of their statement. This technique of proceeding from instruction to instruction is particularly useful since in this way the relationship, in time, of commands to each other can be used to govern the logical relationships of mathematical and other arguments, and also to prescribe the spatial layout of different elements on a page of printed paper. However, since logical and spatial relationships can be expressed without using the technique of procedural statement some languages provide for a large proportion of *declarative* or, in the grammatical sense, *indicative*, statements. Where large volumes of complex data are to be processed it is an advantage in a language that as much as possible of the solution process should be defined (or declared) rather than expressed in commands. The theoretical ideal of having an input state of affairs which is mapped into an output state of affairs is hardly likely to be felt practicable and in fact all computer languages have some procedural element.

The general requirement of a programming language is that it should be a conceptual tool suited to the needs of its user. In the widest view the user is going to process information. In the science of cybernetics the word 'information' is given a very wide meaning indeed. Most current programming languages simply process data which is generally organized into quite a small number of kinds of information. The data upon which current commercial and scientific languages operate comprises numbers (complex, real, integer), alphanumerical strings (ordinary words and sentences), and boolean variables (two-state variables having the value true or false). It is generally also possible to operate upon single digits as items of data, for example numerals and letters. (The word 'data' is used as a singular noun rather than a Latin plural.)

Statements in a procedural language are made up of various combinations of operators and operands, and the operands are the elements of data just mentioned. The technique of using operators and operands is particularly suitable for present-day computers in which each instruction comprises an executable function coupled with the address of the register upon whose content the function is to be executed. Much of the modern structure of computer languages has been erected upon this concept of an operator which may be referred to by some mnemonic and an operand to which may be given a symbolic name. The simplest (assembly) languages use this technique to provide a one-to-one correspondence with the machine code in which the program is performed. At a higher level greater complexity of operation is provided so that several machine instructions are executed for each operator in the language and much more complex data references can be made. Operators are built into computer languages in three main ways. They may be imperative, active verbs in what seems a natural language sentence. They may be mathematical operators (plus, minus, etc.) appearing in an assignment statement in which the operand on the left of an equal sign is the receiving variable. Or they may be a place in a table whose rows and columns have been given special significance for the purposes of the language.

Statements in any language are couched in a form of some sort, and the form can be used to give or to add meaning so as to alter the meaning of a statement as a whole. Since the same can be said of syntactical structure in natural language this phenomenon is referred to as the *syntax of the language* and it can be expressly used by the designer of the language to carry some of the burden of meaning and by the implementor of its translator to ascertain the intended meaning. When written in a program a statement of a language is generally contained within a paragraph, a block, or a table, depending upon the superficial nature of the language. Thus groups of statements can be put together to form quite large units of performance for a computer.

Equally the data upon which the program is to work can be organized into larger and more complex structures. The variables of algebra can be grouped into vectors forming an array which may have many dimensions and each variable may be uniquely indicated by a series of subscripts. Business data in which the variables are called 'fields' each containing an element of information such as a name, an amount or an account number, is organized into groups called records, and records are held in very large numbers as files. It is possible, and sometimes necessary, to provide for extensive facilities in business data description. Fields can be referenced by their names, if those are unique, otherwise by reference to the record in which they reside and to the file in which the record resides. The reader will observe that addressing a mathematical variable by its co-ordinates or subscripts within an array is quite a different data-access process from referencing a field within a record within a file. Both types are not found together in all mathematical and business languages. Besides those two there are a number of other techniques for accessing data. These other techniques, however, are not in general use and it will take several years of experimentation before data structures can be found which have integrity enough to stand up to the logical probing of any set of operators likely to be able to manipulate the data in a useful manner.

One programming language may make automatic a feature which in another language may require a number of express statements to be made by the user. Such a piece of 'automaticity' may extend even to the sequence in which the statements are performed. For example, in a simple case a program may consist of a sequence of statements which are performed, subject to certain conditions, every time a record is input to the computer. The programmer is not required to complete a program loop in which the last statement is connected to the first statement by means of a branch instruction. Such a program may contain no branch instruction whatever, each statement being selected for performance upon the truth or falsity of a number of conditions associated with the statement. In such a language the input of data and the output of data are handled by the system in accordance with the description of those parts of the data given on appropriate forms. The statements written by the user are caused to be performed by the system whenever it recognizes predetermined input or output situations. The experienced computer programmer, accustomed to the procedural nature of most programming languages, may find that use of such a language imposes such difficulties upon his accustomed modes of thinking that he finds the language extremely difficult to use. On the other hand a tabulator user for example, accustomed to think in terms of punched cards passing through a machine with a cycle of prescribed events to be executed as each card is processed, might find such a language particularly apt for his accustomed ways of thinking. From this it might be thought that a language which makes everything automatic, is the most powerful language and the most useful. This, however, is not the case, as, if carried to its logical conclusion, it would mean that a language consisting of a single statement 'solve the problem' would be the most powerful and the most useful.

Computer programming, at its present stage, is not sufficiently developed for it to be said that computers can solve problems. What they can do is to carry out the stated solution process, and it is for this that a programming language must contain suitable tools. The tools (or techniques) should be suited to the tasks which programs written in the language are to perform. They should make automatic the features which are common to the various tasks. They might make special provision for tasks of special importance, for example sorting in business data processing. There should be a clear syntax or structure to the language. The language should be consistent, harmonious, and its parts should be really proportionate to each other. The language should have the features which it requires to cover the area of its intended work. It is no disadvantage if it is not logically complete, since logical completeness may make it easier to remember but not necessarily easier to use and the disproportionate patterns of reality may make a logically complete language appear to contain much that is irrelevant and inappropriate to the tasks which it is called upon to perform. Similarly, a language should not have too many features since then it will appear as a clutter of facilities, a rag-bag of tricks. The user should have at his command a tool which is at once precise in its effect and sufficiently robust not to lead to the consequences which automata frequently impose upon people like the Sorcerer's Apprentice who forgot to provide for a terminating condition. People after all are only human.

One of the most important aspects of any computer language is the use it makes of names. Naming is one of mankind's oldest techniques but it is associative and it does not recognize functional differences in the things named. This indiscriminate use of the powerful tool of naming is what makes some languages rather difficult to use correctly. The many aspects of naming cannot be discussed here, but one example may be useful. Very simply, contrast the meaning of a name given to a variable or a field whose value is held in computer memory so that its name is virtually synonymous with its address in that memory, with the name of a field or variable contained within a record which occurs many hundreds of times upon a magnetic tape where the name is not synonymous with any address except that in which any given record is at some time held in the computer memory. The difference between calling as input the next record on a file and calling as input the named record on a file is one which experienced programmers are accustomed to, but which a beginner may find very deceptive. Much of the difficulty of learning and using a computer language lies in perceiving and utilizing differences of that sort.

The foregoing may be considered the intrinsic aspects of a computer language. They are concerned with its power for expressing a sequence of actions which the computer is to carry out and of describing the data upon which it is to carry them out. A program written in a given language requires to be compiled or translated into the language of the computer. This is done by a compiler or translator program which transmutes the user's 'source' program, treated simply as if it were input data, into an 'object' program as if it were output data. The operating characteristics of both the translator program and of the object program will be of considerable importance to the user.

The operating characteristics of most importance are the running time on the computer and the amount of memory space required. Besides those two the user may find that other operating characteristics seriously interfere with his use of any particular computer language.

It might be thought reasonable for a small program to be translated in one minute and a large program in twenty minutes and for the translator to operate satisfactorily on the second smallest size of memory available in the computer concerned. However, the computer user with the smallest possible computer configuration would be unable to use the computer language at all since the translator would not work on this machine. The average number of times which a source program has to be presented for translation before it is free from errors is between five and ten. The computer user with many large programs to translate will calculate the required amount of machine time for this purpose according to the quoted times for the compiler which he intends to use. And he may be dismayed at the result.

The amount of computer memory required to enable an object program to be performed varies with the program concerned as well as with the efficiency of the translator program. Clearly a computer user must be able to have his object programs performed. Apart from inefficiency in the translator which causes unduly elaborate object programs to be produced the design of the language may be such as to compel the user to adopt a programming strategy not best suited to the machine. Conversely, a good language will invite the user to adopt an effective strategy and a good translator will convert that into a first class object program which wastes neither space nor time in performance. For this reason the 'expansion ratio' which was for some years used as a measure of power of a translator is inappropriate.

In producing an object program the translator may be able to economize in the memory requirement of the object program or to increase the speed of the object program, but not to do both at the same time. In such a case it is common to optimize time rather than space because it is easier for a user simply to buy more computer memory than it is to change his computer so that it will run faster. For very small computer configurations the reverse is usually the case; the object program has to be squeezed into the small memory available even if this means that it takes longer in performance.

There are other features of a programming language which need not be, but may be, intrinsic to it. These are, documentation, error diagnosis and correction, and operating and monitoring. Those three subjects must be dealt with in any translating system. Documentation must be provided since a large program may require many amendments before it is free from errors, and throughout this time the programmer must work with a continually updated version; and when the program is complete a clear statement of what it does must be available to all who wish to use it. Diagnostic and program development aids must be provided because of the difficulty which human beings find in writing programs correctly even in the simplest source language.

The criteria of usefulness of a programming language and its associated system of translation are (a) the efficacy of the language as a tool for the definition and organization of data and for the processing and transformation generally to which the data is to be subject, (b) the operating characteristics of the translator and (c) the operating characteristics of the object program. Some languages are not translated into object programmes but are interpreted directly (or after some minor intermediate process) for immediate performance. In such a case translation and the object-time performance may be regarded as being a single process. Programming 'packages' exist which contain a large number of associated facilities useful in a particular computer application. Use of the programs in the package is governed by a number of general directives provided by the user. Such directives for any single application package together constitute a programming language and should be judged on this basis.

A prospective user may, if he knows what he wants, commission the construction of a language of his own from an experienced software firm; or he may choose an existing language which suits his requirements and commission the implementation of an efficient translator for it on the computer of his choice; or he may, at least cost to himself, study the existing computers, the languages offered by their manufacturers, and the translators offered for them, and then choose that trinity of computer, language and translator which he feels gives him the best advantage.

*See also:* Algebraic manipulation using lists. Algorithms for processing algorithms.

J. C. HARWELL

**COMPUTER OPERATING SYSTEMS.** A computer operating system is a body of software designed to organize the flow of work through a machine in such a way that the various parts of the installation are kept working smoothly and are as fully utilized as possible. The operating system may also have the task of ensuring that certain kinds of job pass through the machine at high priority, so that rapid results may be obtained.

The need for operating systems arises from a variety of factors, including

(1) the mismatch in speed between input and output peripherals and the programs which consume or produce the information passed through the peripherals;
(2) the aims, in the interests of efficiency, of avoiding idle intervals between the conclusion of one job and the initiation of the next;
(3) the need for mechanized bookkeeping to ensure that the large amount of output which can issue from a big computer is properly sorted out, to ensure that such auxiliary stores as magnetic tapes, cards, and disks, are safely organized and to keep accounting records;
(4) the need to cater as automatically as possible for malfunctions in peripheral and other hardware.

*Operating small computers.* All of the above factors arise essentially from the increase in size and speed of computer installations. Many small machines have been, or still are, operated on the following basis.

A user approaches the machine, checks visually that things are in order (there is enough paper in the printer, there are enough tape drives switched on, and they have the right tapes mounted), inserts his input material in a card or paper tape reader, manipulates keys or buttons, and awaits events. Perhaps he has to perform various handling operations on his input (new reels of tape, new decks of cards), or perhaps he has to manipulate switches to control the course of his program. All of these manipulations involve waiting time, during which the machine is idle. The program runs; it produces output on peripherals which are directly coupled to the machine and essentially to the user's program, which is held up if the output is produced faster than the device can take it. When the program terminates, the user gathers up his effects and removes them, looks at the wall clock, signs the log, and another user takes his place.

It is to be emphasized that there is nothing intrinsically wrong in this way of using a machine, provided that the aggregate of all the hold-up and waiting times is negligible by comparison with the time taken to perform the actual instructions of the job. If a machine is used typically for jobs which require input of 20 cards, reading of 50 feet of magnetic tape, 4 hours straight arithmetic computation, and printing of 6 numbers, there is no point whatever in having an operating system, no matter how fast and glossy the computer.

That situation is, however, quite atypical; in many installations it would be common for the idle and waiting times for the usual run of work to exceed the useful time by a large factor if such a simple way of using the machine were adopted.

*Buffering technique.* The technique used in most operating systems is to buffer the input and output; that is, to divorce the transfer of information through the peripherals from its consumption or production by a user program. Input material, for example, may be transferred from a card reader to a magnetic tape or disk, and from thence to a user program, the gain coming from the fact that the tape or disk can deliver the data at a rate more likely to be in accord with the rate of consumption. Output goes in a similar way. Provided that the actions of the peripheral itself impose little or no cost on the system, delays due to speed mismatches can in general be obviated. It is, however, important to realize that all that this buffering achieves is an averaging operation. No amount of buffering will avoid output hold-ups in the long run if the computer produces twice as much output per day as the printer can print. The same remark goes for almost all the positive benefits of an operating system; it does its best to smooth out the requirements for all the various parts of the machine, but no amount of smoothing will obscure a basic deficiency somewhere.

*Multiprogramming.* A different kind of smoothing is achieved by multiprogramming, which means nothing more than having several user programs in the rapid access store of the machine at once, so that control can be switched from one to the other if the first gets held up for any reason. The classical reason for hold-ups is waiting for magnetic tapes, disks, or similar auxiliary stores, to finish a search or data transfer. It should be noticed that this is essentially different from the hold-ups involved in direct use of slow peripherals as described above. In that case we could avoid the inefficiency by anticipation and buffering, and that was possible because there was available some faster device for transferring data to or from the rapid-access store than the slow peripherals themselves. In the case of the fastest device available or a particular machine (usually some magnetic device) bufferage is only possible using the core-store itself, which may not exist in large enough amounts, and the element of anticipation crucial to the other kind of buffering is often absent. In this case, the only way to avoid idle time is to change to executing another program. Notice here that the smoothing performed is much more local. It depends on the behaviour of those programs available ready to run just now, and if, as is mostly the case, the number is fairly small, the danger of 'conspiracy' is not negligible.

as barrel or hammer printers and card punches require access to the data for the whole line or card several times, so that the transfer must be repeated from the beginning. This may be affected automatically by *recharging* the control word, at the end of the transfer, to its original value, which has been retained in a suitable *recharge word*. An alternative method which again trades equipment for time is to use a *buffer store* into which the transfer is done and which the peripheral reads repeatedly with its own autonomous control circuits.

In some systems, the transfers are of fixed length and in some cases from fixed areas of the store, this reduces the required complexity of the control word and the operations to be performed on it, but with an accompanying loss of flexibility.

These additional hardware units may be special purpose, designed for one specific peripheral or set of peripherals or may be made more general purpose by allowing some measure of conditional operation and by making the peripheral do those operations peculiar to itself. By adopting a *Standard Interface* between the peripheral and the peripheral control part of the processor, both the programming and design of the machine may be simplified at the expense of a complication to the peripheral which has to deal with most of its own special requirements.

The peripheral control section of the data processor may be implemented by using a small digital computer, which is used principally for handling the peripherals, hence regaining a great part of the flexibility which would otherwise have been lost.

*Control of transfers.* The initiation, termination and checking of transfers may also be handled in a variety of ways, trading equipment for speed. The factors to be considered are the degree of checking that is required and the complexity of the desired operations. Electromechanical peripheral equipment is liable to errors due to 'foreign bodies' and to wear and tear. The effect of these errors may vary from occasionally inaccurate data to a complete cessation of activity. In order to detect the former, the data may be held in a redundant form and checks performed to ensure that only permitted combinations occur, usually a simple odd-even count or *parity check* is considered sufficient. In some cases a *check-sum*, which is the sum of all the units of data in the transfer, is written with the data and checked on reading, or the medium may be read twice and the corresponding data units compared. Information about the *status* of the peripheral, such as power-on, media present, feeding in progress, data check fail and so on, may be made available to the processor. A program may then be written, which by *interrogating* the peripheral, may attempt in the case of a data check error, to do a re-read or re-write and, if this *repeat* procedure fails, or cannot be performed, stop the machine and/or inform the operator of the fault.

In controlling the transfer, some of the operations may be performed by additional hardware, at increased cost, to reduce the amount of computer time used.

A facility which may be implemented in this way is the *chained* transfer, in which a number of peripheral transfers (on one mechanism) may follow one another automatically, once started by a single initiation, and if no errors are detected by the check circuits, a single termination sequence is sufficient. There is hence a reduction in computer time per character transferred, but there must, of course, be enough store to hold all the data or the computer must calculate the data fast enough to keep safely ahead of the peripherals. This technique is particularly useful for the type of peripheral which cannot be stopped, such as an experiment or a magnetic tape unit reading tapes recorded without inter-block gaps.

The author wishes to thank I.C.T. for permission to publish this article and to acknowledge all other workers in the Data Processing field for the various ideas which are described.

E. C. P. PORTMAN

**COMPUTER SIMULATION OF HUMAN THOUGHT PROCESSES.** The study of human thought processes is directed toward understanding the complex processes humans use in solving problems. A partial list of these processes includes heuristic search, induction, learning, pattern recognition, natural language processing, and information storage and retrieval.

*Media of model representation and techniques of model exploration.* The traditional strategy for the study of any process consists of three steps: constructing a model of the process, determining the implications of the model, and comparing the behaviour of the model with the behaviour of the process. Models can be represented in different media (e.g. natural language, mathematical notation, electromechanical components, computer programming languages), and their implications determined with techniques associated with each medium (Simon and Newell 1956). The choice of a medium depends on the nature of the model and the nature of the medium. The nature of the medium is a function of three variables: the difficulty of constructing models, the ability to determine the implications of statements, and the difficulty of determining the implications of models. Models represented in natural language are relatively easy to construct. However, because of the ambiguity of the statements and the difficulties involved in handling large sets of statements, implications are difficult to determine. The language of mathematics is more rigorous and the use of appropriate mathematical techniques enables the determination of implications. However, considerable mathematical skills are required to use these techniques and suitable techniques are not available for treating large, complex models. Physical models require specialized skills for construction and exploration and have been used to advantage by those possessing these skills.

The representation of models as computer programs and the use of modern digital computers to determine the implications of these models appear to be particularly suited to the study of complex processes. The representation media—computer programming languages—permit considerable flexibility in statement of models but do not require extensive preparation on the part of the user. For models represented as computer programs, the computer system detects ambiguous statements and determines the implications of large, complex systems. While the use of the computer in this fashion has been hailed as a development comparable to that of the microscope, computer simulation is more accurately viewed as a technique for model representation and exploration especially suited to the study of large, complex processes.

The technique of computer simulation has been applied to the study of human thought processes in a direct fashion by developing models of these processes for problem solving, concept formation, learning, and decision making. Most of these models have been characterized by the use of the subject's verbal description of his behaviour as the target behaviour for the model and the information processing level of explanation.

*Target behaviour.* Since human thought processes are not themselves directly observable, the model builder assesses the sufficiency of the model by comparing the behaviour of the model with the behaviour emitted by the subject. In a short period of time, a human can emit a considerable amount of detectable information ranging from the electrical activity of neurons to the verbal description of his problem-solving processes. Generally, research in human thought processes utilizes the overt behaviour of the subject (e.g. verbal responses, button pushing) as the target behaviour. In most cases the researcher actually tries to predict some function of the target behaviour. The functions of the data which are usually studied are summary statistics, e.g. the mean probability of a response over the last 100 trials, the number of trials to criterion, the distribution of errors over subtasks. While such functions of the data are well defined, the selection of a function is a matter of judgment. For example, if the behaviour of interest is a time series of symbols, is the desired function the number of $x$ symbols, the number of $x$ symbols given $x$ symbols on immediately preceding trials, etc.? One solution to this problem is not to select any function but to use the target behaviour itself, e.g. the entire time series of symbols.

In a number of studies of human thought processes utilizing computer models, the primary datum is the protocol of the subject's verbal explanations of his problem-solving procedure—his explanation of why he takes the particular steps that he takes. Information gleaned from these protocols has been used in constructing models, and the protocols themselves have been used as the target data of models. The selection of a medium for model representation does not force the selection of target behaviour. However, the relationship between computer models and subject protocols is not completely fortuitous. Computer simulation provides a technique which permits at least a first approximation to the representation of the complex processes underlying thought. The protocols provide considerably more information about these processes than any record of physical manipulations, e.g. chess moves. The data represented in the protocol have been adopted as the target data because they offer a more exacting and detailed test for the model.

As target data these verbal explanations create two problems. A perfect match of these target data would require that the model generate an identical string of prose statements. To attempt such a match introduces language requirements in addition to the substantive requirements of the processes involved in solving problem of concern. No model has yet reached this zenith, and most researchers work with a coded representation of the verbal statements. The second difficulty derives from the omissions in the verbal statements. The verbal statements are extremely useful for what they say (the question of the validity of these statements can, of course, only be answered indirectly); however, subjects clearly do not report all of their activity or processing. Since the researcher can obtain a complete record from the model, a comparison involves decisions about what the subject revealed and what he did not reveal.

*Level of explanation.* A phenomenon can be explained at several different levels. If a driver is asked to explain why an automobile moves, he might explain the phenomenon in terms of his actions—press the starter button, put the car in gear, and depress the accelerator pedal. The automobile mechanic and automotive engineer explain the same movement in different terms—at a different level. While the selection of a level of explanation is often made on pragmatic grounds—the driver does not usually have to concern himself with the inner workings of the internal combustion engine—the selection of a level of explanation is the option of the explainer.

Human thought processes are currently being studied at several different levels of explanation. Again the technique of computer simulation does not force the level of explanation. Nevertheless, much of the work in computer simulation of thought processes uses the level of explanation which subjects use in describing their own problem-solving efforts. These models manipulate—compare, transform, combine, and copy—the symbols which comprise the expressions or represent the objects that are being dealt with. Patterns of symbols are sought and related to other patterns of symbols. This level of explanation is referred to as the symbol manipulation or information processing level. The relationship of these information processes to more fundamental physiological processes is generally left unspecified.

The selection of this level of explanation is related to the use of protocols to develop models and as target behaviour. The information processing level is also related to the level of explanation of computer languages and central processors which are generally described in terms of symbol manipulation.

*Goodness-of-fit.* Since the behaviour of models is almost never in perfect agreement with the behaviour of subjects, the question of the adequacy of models arises. Two statistical issues—goodness-of-fit and parameter estimation—are of interest. While these issues are relevant to all models, regardless of the medium of representation, research with computer models of human thought processes has highlighted certain aspects of these issues.

Counting the number of agreements between the behaviour of the model and the data is the most straightforward way of measuring the goodness-of-fit of model to data. Such a count only has meaning when compared to the corresponding count on alternative models. Common statistical tests make comparisons to alternative naive models. Often complex models, such as those usually represented in computer programs do not compare favourably to simpler models in terms of these raw counts for particular sets of data. In fact the ultimate agreement between model and data is obtained when the data is treated as a model of itself. However, this ultimate agreement will usually hold for only a single subject in a single repetition of an experiment. This extreme case indicates the need for testing models over a broad range of data and the need to develop models which better represent the underlying processes than naive models.

Counting presupposes some agreement on the target data. Where the researcher does not wish to select an arbitrary function of the target data or otherwise code the data, it is has been suggested that judges be employed to determine whether they can distinguish the behaviour of the model from the data. In the crudest form of this test the judges might be presented with pairs of data sets and asked to discriminate between the behaviour of the subjects and the behaviour of the model. While such a test may be intuitively appealing, its scientific value is small because of the gross nature of the judgments. The test can be made more powerful by using experienced judges and suitable foils so that the question is whether the model's behaviour is a good approximation to that of a particular subject or class of subjects (Abelson 1966).

Another problem with simple counting arises because in most models the current values of most variables depend on earlier values. For example, the response at time $t$ may depend on events and responses at times preceding $t$. Hence a discrepancy (or agreement) between the model's behaviour and the data at trial $t$ may be spurious because it was determined by a discrepancy between the behaviour of the model and the data at trial $t$-$i$. In some cases it is possible to set the model back-on-the-track, i.e. adjust the model and/or its behaviour so that the model's behaviour at trial $t$ is not affected by its previous errors. This procedure is also useful in attributing errors to those components of the model that are responsible for the errors.

*Parameter estimation.* Models consist of two components—structure and parameter. For example, in a linear model $y = ax+b$, there are two parameters—$a$ and $b$. The usual procedure is to estimate these values from the data in accordance with some standard statistical criterion. There are two issues here—estimating the values of the parameters and determining how much information the estimation of parameters extracts from the data. These problems are of particular concern for computer models because virtually all of the work on parameter estimation has been on models consisting of systems of equations. Although a computer program is formally a system of difference equations, a program is not usually thought of as a system of equations. For example, a program may contain a table indicating the relationship between program statements or variables. The values in this table might be estimated from the data by compiling frequency counts (Reitman 1965). However, the determination of how much information has been extracted by the estimation procedure is a more difficult task and is complicated even more because model builders often try to fit different structures to the data.

Most of the work with computer models of human thought processes has been essentially curve-fitting. Much attention has been focused on getting the model to fit and little attention has been given to the niceties of parameter estimation. The most promising approach to this problem is one which places goodness-of-fit and parameter estimation on the same scale by measuring the information (in a formal sense) in the data, the information extracted by the parameters, and the information explained by the structure. An interesting result: it is possible to extract less information from a set of data by estimating $n$ parameters than by estimating $m$ (less than $n$) parameters. In the first case the structure explains more information (Hanna 1965).

Another interesting approach to the problems of parameter estimation, goodness-of-fit, and identification of the model components which generate errors is to modify the model until it fits the first data set. Then modify the model again until it fits the second data set, etc. Such a procedure is consistent with the methodological approach which views research as an effort in model estimation. In this view new data is used to refine the model. The amount and type of changes to the model provide information on those components of the model which remain invariant over time and subjects (structure) and those components which change (parameters). Unfortunately the model adjustments made in this procedure are usually not unique.

*Limitations.* While the technique of computer simulation may be the most important recent development in the study of human thought processes, the most severe limitation on the development of models of thought processes is the lack of understanding of these processes. The understanding of thought processes and the development of models of these processes have a circular relationship. An understanding of the processes is required to construct a model; and the construction of the model and the study of the model contribute to the understanding.

Many of the computer models that have been developed have been accompanied by significant empirical work on thought processes, and the development of additional models will stimulate an increasing amount of empirical research on thought. The related research in artificial intelligence—the development of computer programs to solve problems—will also provide stimulation to further empirical work.

The development of computer models of thought has also been impeded by rigidity in the representation of data and models. (The material in this paragraph is adapted from Newell 1962.) The major need is for more flexible representation. This limitation is perhaps most clearly seen in problems of storage allocation. It is usually desirable to avoid *a priori* decisions on storage allocation and postpone these decisions until the program is executed. Then the program can allocate storage as determined by the program's needs to record, process, and store information. The storage allocation problem has been largely solved by the use of list memories of various types. However, several other problems have only been partially solved. There is a need to be able modify large, complex programs more easily than the present state-of-the-art permits. There is a conflict between the need to provide sub-programs with access to large data bases and the need to protect the security of these data bases. Programs must have greater capabilities for accepting and using information which the programmer may desire to provide at some point in time. Programs like organizations suffer from the centralization-decentralization dilemma. Sub-programs have to be able to take actions because they have better information, while higher-order programs must retain some control.

The computer hardware and software (programming languages and systems) limitations have been the least vexing restrictions. Nevertheless, these limitations have been a serious source of inconvenience. A major source of inconvenience stems from the early uses of computers to manipulate numbers. Although computers are in principal generalized information processors, most of them have been adapted to facilitate numerical work. Even with the development of special languages more suitable for simulation of cognitive processes than machine languages and early compilers, discrepancies between the needs of these languages and the design of most computers have taken a heavy toll in speed and storage capacity. A second serious inconvenience derives from the incompatibility of computers. Even programs written in what is ostensibly the same language rarely can be run on different machines without program changes. The difficulties in communicating models expressed as programs are increased by the difficulty in transferring programs from machine to machine. A third difficulty is inherent in the time lag between submission and return of jobs in conventional batch-processing systems. The nature of computer models is that they are never completed. The programmer is constantly making minor and major changes; he would prefer instantaneous feedback on the consequences of these changes. The most promising development in the hardware-software field has been time-sharing. The resulting reduction in turn-around time has opened up new vistas. A fourth difficulty is the size and speed of computers. Many of the models of human thought processes have been large programs requiring rather large amounts of computer time and memory. Recent increases in the speed of central processors and the size of memories coupled with paging systems which provide system coordination of information stored in different types of memories are welcome additions.

*See also:* Concept formation by artificial intelligence. Concept identification—information processing approaches. Learning machines: a unified view. Pattern recognition.

*Bibliography*

ABELSON R. P. (1966) *Simulation of social behavior*, in (G. Lindzey and E. Aronson Eds.), *Handbook of Social Psychology*, Reading, Mass: Addison-Wesley.
DREYFUS H. L. (1965) *Alchemy and Artificial Intelligence*, Santa Monica: Rand.
FEIGENBAUM E. A. and FELDMAN J. (1963) *Computers and Thought*, New York: McGraw-Hill.
FELDMAN J. (1962) *Computer simulaion of cognitive processes*, in (H. Borko Ed.) *Computer Applications in the Behavioral Sciences*, Englewood Cliffs: Prentice-Hall.
MILLER G. A., GALANTER E. and PRIBRAM K. H. (1960) *Plans and the Structure of Behavior*, New York: Holt.
NEWELL A. (1962) *Some problems of basic organization in problem-solving programs*, in (M. C. Yovits, G. T. Jacobi and G. D. Goldstein Eds.), *Self-organizing Systems*, Washington: Spartan Books.
REITMAN W. R. (1965) *Cognition and Thought*, New York: Wiley.
SIMON H. A. (1961) *Modeling Human Mental Processes*, *Proceedings of the Western Joint Computer Conference*, Los Angeles.
SIMON H. A. and NEWELL A. (1956) *Models: their uses and limitations*, in (L. D. White Ed.), *The State of the Social Sciences*, Chicago: The University Press.

J. FELDMAN

## COMPUTERS, MULTIACCESS TO.

*1. What is Multiaccess?*

The important aspect of multiaccess systems is not how many users there are, but what kind of access each user has.

A user informs the computer that he wants service by pushing an attention button on his *terminal*. This signal is recognized by the computer and it then devotes some of its power to this user.

As soon as the user's program terminates, the computer removes it from active consideration and devotes its attention to the requests of other users.

To a user the significant difference between the batch processing mode of operation and multiaccess operation is that under batch processing there is no opportunity to interact with a running program. All decisions must be clearly specified in advance. If some error, like omission of an important statement, has been made, the program cannot be executed.

In a multi-access environment errors and ambiguities can be clarified as they are detected. If a control statement is missing the user can be asked to supply it at execution time. Any such oversights can be corrected almost immediately. In addition, a running program can ask a user for input and pause until it is supplied. In this way decisions which were not programmed in advance can be made on-line, or new input data can be supplied to a processing program.

## 2. Traditional Access to Computers

In the twenty years since the introduction of electronic computers there have been three basic approaches to computer usage. Initially the computer and all its associated equipment were dedicated to one individual at a time. He would sit at the operator's console and try to control his program by various means, such as watching the patterns of lights on the console display or listening to a speaker that could be driven from different sources.

Running a program was like driving a temperamental car; you had to know just which noises were important and what they meant.

As computers became more expensive, it became uneconomic to allow the computer to be idle while a programmer-operator sat at the console and tried to debug his program.

Operating systems were devised which automatically ran a job with a minimum of human intervention and which moved smoothly from one task to the next without stopping. Programmers were isolated from the computer, and all direct communication to a program was handled by a skilled operator. The time between submitting a job to the dispatcher and receiving the processed job back (turnaround time) varied from one hour to two days, depending on the loading of the machine.

## 3. Motivation for Multiaccess

The motivation behind the development of multi-access was twofold:
1. Programmers were becoming more expensive and computer hardware becoming cheaper. This made it economically desirable to make computing power more accessible to programmers.
2. The ability to interact with a running program might provide programs and applications in areas that were previously untouched by computers. These areas include education, information retrieval (automated libraries), medicine (aid to diagnosis and drug prescription) and experimental psychology to name a few.

The goals were to be reached principally by providing computing power as it was needed, on demand.

Project MAC at M.I.T. was the first large-scale effort in the multi-access direction. Its principal contribution has been to show that multiaccess is technically feasible and that the improved accessibility of the computer is a significant factor in reducing total solution time.

The actual benefits which have been realized have exceeded the expectations of its founders. The gains include:
1. Turn-around times are reduced by about two orders of magnitude, leading to much faster overall job completion.
2. The productivity and creativeness of programmers is enhanced by eliminating the long delay between the inception of an idea and its testing. A programmer can test something new in a few minutes instead of several hours.
3. Information, including programs and data, is stored centrally. This relieves the users from having to keep track of their files, as well as simplifying file maintenance procedures.
4. One user can make a program or data file accessible to other users. Information or results generated by one person can be almost immediately made available to someone else.

Thus, multiaccess techniques provide the virtues of both previous approaches without the drawbacks of either. They give the programmer the illusion of having a computer all to himself, but do not tie up any equipment if he wants to take time off to think.

## 4. Special Requirements for a Multiaccess System

*(a) File system.* A multiaccess computer installation requires considerably more than a conventional computer in the way of equipment and 'executive systems' to operate it. The most important requirement for effective operation is a good file maintenance system. It must handle very diverse storage requirements, from the high speed and low capacity required for temporary storage of an active program to the high capacity and low speed storage required for archival storage of infrequently-used programs.

These diverse needs require a hierarchy of storage devices. At present the range of devices runs from 'slow' core for the fast, small storage, and data cells for slow, bulk storage. The terms fast, slow, big and small are intentionally vague; what we consider fast or big today may seem slow or small in the not-too-distant future.

*(b) Communications control.* Communication between remote terminals and the computer is generally handled by a multiplexer, which keeps track of all messages between the terminals and the computer. Input and output must be routed correctly, as an invidual user of the system should be unaware that perhaps a hundred other terminals are being serviced at the same time as his own.

*(c) Security.* In a traditional (non-multiaccess) computer operation a program goes from start to

finish without being interrupted. There are no problems of security from another program, as no other can gain the attention of the computer. In a multiaccess environment a program may be interrupted several times by the executive system, and safeguards must be provided to assure that no other program can intentionally or unintentionally tamper with it.

*(d) Executive system.* The *'executive'* *program* of a multiaccess computer exercises much more control than does a conventional operating system. It must prevent any particular user program from 'hogging' the machine; it must keep a close watch over all input and output to guarantee other users' information; it must control the central information storage system.

When discussing the complexities of the executive system one should bear in mind that these complexities are not at all apparent to the users of the system. In fact, it is the complexity of the executive, in assuming many chores previously left to the programmers, that makes a multiaccess system simple to use.

*1. Time slicing.* The executive prevents any particular program from taking a disproportionate share of the processor's time by automatically interrupting it at frequent intervals (perhaps 10 times a second). A user program cannot prevent this interrupt from occurring.

At each interrupt the executive decides by examining its scheduling algorithm, whether this program should continue to run.

If another program is to be executed, the complete machine status of the interrupted program is saved for resumption at a later time.

All this scheduling and interrupting is hidden from the users; the only noticeable effect is that a program will take more time to run, as it is being interrupted continually. Typically a 10-second batch job might be completed in one to two minutes, even though the processor time taken was still 10 seconds.

*2. Input-output control.* The executive prevents user programs from performing input or output directly. This guarantees protection of files from unauthorized access, because the executive routines that must be used can check to see that the user is allowed access to the information he is trying to obtain. If a user attempts to do I/O himself the executive notes this fact and stops execution of that program.

*3. Storage management.* A user is concerned not with the physical location of his programs and data, but with using them. He will be happy to leave with the executive the decision as to where a particular file will be kept. The user does not even have to know what hardware is available to the executive.

This is a natural extension of the executive, as it must already supervise all input and output as mentioned above. In general the faster storage devices (core and drum) are reserved for frequently-used information, while slower devices (disk, data cells and magnetic tape) are used for less active information.

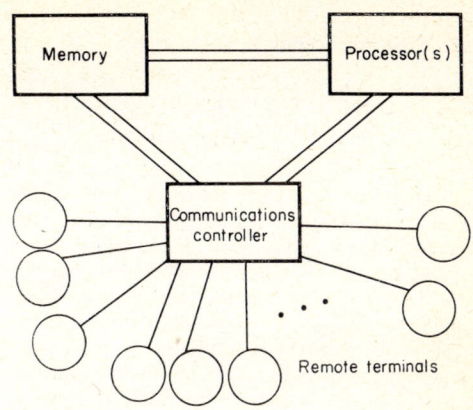

*Components of a multiaccess system. Memory includes all storage devices available to the system. Users communicate only with the Communications Controller, which relays to and output from the system.*

## 5. The Economics of Multiaccess

It is easy to determine the cost of a multiaccess system; it consists of the hardware cost, software cost, and cost of executive overhead time. It is much more difficult to put a money value on the benefits to be gained. How much programmer time can be saved? How much is higher creativity and productivity worth? What is the money value of an application like aid to medical diagnosis or drug prescription?

The situation is somewhat analogous to the growth of the modern telephone system. Telegraph offices were centrally located, and messages were transmitted from one office to another. If a person wanted to send a message he composed it beforehand and brought it to the telegraph office. It was transmitted to the receiving station, and thence was delivered to the recipient. An exchange of messages could take hours.

Contrast this with the telephone system. Each subscriber has a 'remote terminal' of his own, and shares the central office switching equipment. The investment that could not be justified for one user is quite economical when it is shared by many. Even though there is no intermediary between a user and the switching equipment, it is easy to use. An exchange of information takes less than a minute.

The economics of multiaccess will probably work out like the economics of telephone systems. The initial capital investment is very high, but the potential gains are also high. We may well get to the stage where remote terminals for computers are as common as telephones are today.

*See also:* Computer operating systems. Computer peripherals and their control. Problem solving.

M. E. WANTMAN

**COMPUTERS, STOCHASTIC (Stochastic Automata—Their Application to Computing).**

*1. Introduction*

There is a large class of problems which are intractable for present analog and digital computers. They arise in the control of chemical plant, in the control of aircraft, missiles and spacecraft, in the simulation of economic systems, and generally in the real-time simulation and control of large, complex systems. Analog computers are not suitable for these problems because of the large number of operational amplifiers required (a reasonable upper limit at present is 400 amplifiers, sufficient to simulate about 30 non-linear, fourth-order differential equations), and particularly because of the defects, size and expense of analog multipliers and integrators. Digital computers are not suitable for these problems because their bandwidth is limited by the use of a central processor to compute sequential solutions of differential equations. Williams (1965) has reviewed these difficulties in the context of process control and demonstrated the impossibility of simulating even a simple, linearized model of a multi-plate distillation column in real time with presently available computers. His diagram illustrating the applicability of digital and analog computers to processes of different orders (number of first-order differential equations) and time-constants is reproduced in Fig. 1. As Williams remarks, 'It is truly unfortunate to note the number of chemical process systems which fall into the lower right hand corner of Fig. 1', and a similar remark may be applied to many other systems of great practical importance.

There have been many attempts to design computers which combine the parallel operation of analog computers with the simplicity and accuracy of digital computers. Parallel digital differential analysers (Leondes 1959) using incremental digital stores to simulate the analog integrator (serial DDA's offer only economic advantages over the general purpose digital computer), and hybrid computers (Connelly 1962; Truitt 1964) in which a digital computer controls the operation of an analog computer have been the most successful to date, but their computing elements are as complex as those of conventional computers and it remains economically infeasible to simulate large, complex systems.

The main performance measures of a computer are size and range of possible problems, speed and accuracy of solution, and the physical size, reliability and cost of the computer. There are strong interactions between these measures and it is unlikely that any one form of computer will ever be optimal on all counts. The simulation of complex plant and multivariable control systems requires large numbers of computing elements such as multipliers, summers and integrators, working simultaneously and costing little. However, these elements do not have to compute a solution quickly or accurately, for a bandwidth of 10 c/s and an overall accuracy of 1 per cent is adequate in the simulation of economic and chemical processes, and in control systems where feedback operates a computational accuracy of 10 per cent may be ample. In these situations it should be possible to trade the accuracy of the digital computer and the speed of the analog computer for computing size and economy, and the stochastic computer is the most promising attempt to do this so far.

The stochastic computer was developed for the type of problem where the availability of large numbers of low-cost computing elements is more important than the speed and accuracy of computation. Information within the computer is carried through modulation of the statistics of digital 'noise', and the theory underlying its computational processes is that of Markov chains and stochastic automata. Research on the latter has been oriented towards their applications in the design of reliable digital computers and the literure is heavily biased to this point of view. The next section follows the evolution of stochastic automata as a natural derivative of state-determined machines, and outlines the main theoretical results. A brief indication is given of how the theory may be applied to problems of computer reliability, but the main section of this review describes the positive, rather than preventive, applications of stochastic automata to computing.

*2. Digital Computer Theory*

The basic mathematical object used to represent the behaviour of a digital computer is the finite-state automaton (McNaughton 1961; Rabin and Scott 1959). The essential features of this object are a finite set of states, inputs and outputs, together with mappings from all state-input pairs to the sub-set of states and the sub-set of outputs. In a 'noiseless' or perfectly reliable computer the input sequence is uniquely specifiable by a control (program or data) tape, and the input sequences to

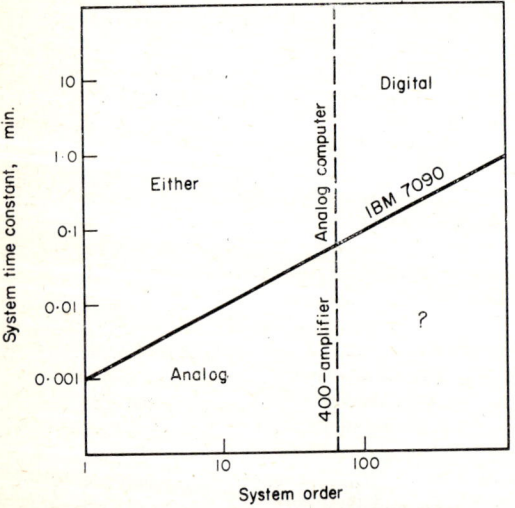

Fig. 1. *Applicability of analog and digital computers to process simulation.*

the automaton can be treated as a representation of the actual 'input' to the computer. If the digital computer is imperfect then a distinction must be made between the specified 'input' and the actual 'input'. We shall call the former a control and reserve the term input for the latter; in a perfectly reliable computer there is a trivial isomorphism between controls and inputs.

The automaton taken to represent an unreliable computer is generally larger than that representing the equivalent reliable computer, for each of its controls gives rise to a set of possible inputs, and its state set must contain states which arise through component failure. In practice the finite-state automaton subsuming all possible faults is so large and unwieldy that a statistical approximation to its behaviour is more useful. The mathematical object developed as a statistical representation of an unreliable computer is the stochastic automaton, and the theory of such objects treats transitions between hyperstates (statistics of state distributions) in much the same way that deterministic automata theory treats transitions between states. The theory of stochastic automata is best approached through the matrix representation of finite deterministic automata, and this is outlined in the next section.

*2.1. Matrix representation of finite automata.* Any finite automaton may be represented by a set of matrices, each matrix corresponding to an input and containing only ones and zeros, which define the transitions between its states and the relationships between its states and outputs. The element in the $i$th row and $j$th column of a transition matrix for a particular input will be one if that input would cause the automaton in its $i$th state to transit to its $j$th state (at the occurrence of a clock pulse). Similarly the $ij$th element of the output matrix for a particular input will be a one if that input gives rise to the $j$th output when the automaton is in its $i$th state. Since a state and input give rise to a unique output and next state, these matrices are characterized by having a single one in every row, and are therefore particular examples of probability matrices (whose rows sum to unity). This representation of a finite automaton reduces it to a semigroup of matrices with its behaviour determined by matrix multiplication.

Let the set of possible inputs to an automaton be:

$$(I_i), \quad 0 < i \leqslant N;$$

the set of possible states be:

$$(S_i), \quad 0 < i \leqslant M;$$

and the set of possible outputs be:

$$(O_i), \quad 0 < i \leqslant P.$$

Let the state of the automaton be $S$, its ouput $O$, its input $I$, and the state after the next clock pulse $S'$. We have the transition mapping:

$$S' = \sigma(S, I);$$

and the output mapping:

$$O = \theta(S, I).$$

The $M \times M$ transition matrices, $(P^k)$, may now be defined. If $P^k \equiv (p_{ij}^k)$ is the transition matrix corresponding to an input $I_k$ then:

$$p_{ij}^k = \begin{cases} 1 \Leftrightarrow S_j = \sigma(S_i, I_k) \\ 0 \quad \text{otherwise.} \end{cases}$$

Similarly the $M \times P$ output matrices, $(O^k)$, where $O^k \equiv (o_{ij}^k)$ corresponds to the input $I_k$, may be defined:

$$o_{ij}^k = \begin{cases} 1 \Leftrightarrow O_j = \theta(S_i, I_k) \\ 0 \quad \text{otherwise.} \end{cases}$$

The existence and uniqueness of the output and next state imply:

$$\sum_{j=1}^{M} p_{ij}^k = 1$$

$$\sum_{j=1}^{P} o_{ij}^k = 1.$$

Having defined the transition and output matrices, we may consider the behaviour of the automaton to be determined entirely by the rules of matrix multiplication. For example, the sequence of inputs, $I_{\lambda_1}$ followed by $I_{\lambda_2}$ and so on up to $I_{\lambda_n}$, applied when the automaton is in state $S_i$, leads to state $S_j$ if and only if:

$$(P^{\lambda_1} P^{\lambda_2} P^{\lambda_3} \ldots P^{\lambda_n})_{ij} = 1,$$

and the output of the automaton will then be $O_j$ if and only if:

$$(P^{\lambda_1} P^{\lambda_2} \ldots P^{\lambda_n} O^{\lambda_n})_{ij} = 1.$$

These equations could be reduced to matrix/vector equations by defining the state of the automaton to be an $M$-vector whose $i$th element is unity if its state is $S_i$, and zero otherwise, and defining the output of the automaton to be a $P$-vector whose $i$th element is unity if its output is $O_i$, and zero otherwise. Transitions between states are determined by post-multiplying the present state vector by the transition matrix corresponding to the input, and the output is determined by post-multiplying it with the output matrix corresponding to the input. This matrix representation of finite automata is cumbersome in practice, but ideal for the conceptual transition from 'noise' at the input to stochastic automata.

*2.2. Stochastic automata.* Consider now a set of 'controls' to the automaton which do not specify the input exactly but rather give rise to probability distributions over the inputs. If the present state and control are known then the probability of occurrence of each input may be used to calculate the probability that the next state will be a given state. Thus only the state distribution, or expectation of a given state, can be predicted. This distribution will be called a complete hyperstate, and the theory of stochastic automata concerns the matrix representation of transitions between complete hyperstates.

Let the set of controls to the automaton be:

$$(C_i) \quad 0 < i \leqslant Q,$$

and let the application of the control $C_i$ give rise to a probability $v_i^j$ that the input $I_j$ will occur. Since some input must occur we have:

$$\sum_{j=1}^{N} v_i^j = 1.$$

If the automaton is in state $S_i$ when the control is $C_k$ then the probability, $\pi_{ij}^k$, that it will next be in state $S_j$ is:

$$\pi_{ij}^k = \sum_{r=1}^{N} v_k^r p_{ij}^r.$$

Thus if the hyperstate of the automaton is the distribution $(\Pi_i)$, where $\Pi_i$ is the probability that the automaton is in the state $S_i$, then the hyperstate $(\Pi_i')$ after a control $C_k$ is given by:

$$\Pi_j' = \sum_{i=1}^{M} \Pi_i \pi_{ij}^k = \sum_{i=1}^{M} \Pi_i \sum_{r=1}^{N} v_k^r p_{ij}^r.$$

The matrices $\Pi^k \equiv (\pi_{ij}^k)$ are probability matrices since their elements are non-negative and:

$$\sum_{j=1}^{M} \pi_{ij}^k = 1;$$

they may be regarded as generalizations of the matrices $P^k$.

Probabilistic output matrices relating controls, hyperstates and outputs may similarly be defined. This structure of controls, hyperstates, outputs and probability matrices is a stochastic automaton. It is interesting to note that we may regard the stochastic automaton either as a special case of the finite automaton in which probability distributions are assigned to incompletely specified inputs, or as a generalization of the matrix representation of finite automata in which arbitrary probability matrices replace those previously containing only ones and zeros.

*2.3. Markov chains.* The discrete transitions of a system from condition to condition are said to form a Markov chain (Takács 1960; Kemény and Snell 1960) of the $n$th order if the probability of a transition to a new condition depends only on the previous $n$ conditions. A Markov chain of the zeroth order is called a Bernoulli sequence, and is distinguished by the statistically independent generation of its elements. If the controls to a stochastic automaton are constant, or form a Bernoulli sequence, then the state sequences are Markov chains of the first order, and the output sequences are Markov chains generally of higher order (the output chains are first order if there is an inverse mapping from output-input pairs to states). If the controls are functions of previous outputs, or are generated in set sequence, then both states and outputs may form Markov chains of higher order. In stochastic computers processing Markov chains, much of the simplicity of computation would be lost if the order of the chains increased at each stage of processing, and stochastic computing elements are designed to receive and emit Bernoulli sequences.

The relationship between the average behaviour of an ensemble of stochastic automata, which is the conceptual basis for their operation, and the average behaviour over a number of transitions, which is the practical means for observing their operation, depends on the ergodicity of the Markov process generating the transitions. A hyperstate is said to be stationary for a transition if it does not change under that transition, and a sequence of transitions with one and only one stationary hyperstate is said to be ergodic. Stationary hyperstates in the stochastic computer correspond to steady states in the analog computer, having similar properties in that they are far more tractable theoretically than the transient, non-ergodic behaviour, and often act as 'solutions' in a computation.

*2.4. Computer reliability.* This section is a digression from the main theme but the literature on stochastic automata is concerned mainly with computer reliability and the results obtained must be considered relative to this. Deterministic automata theory investigates the set of input sequences which will take the automaton from a given initial state to one of a set of final states (these are usually included as part of the definition of the 'automaton'); these sequences are called the input tapes 'accepted' by the automaton and are said to define an 'event'. With stochastic automata one may consider only the probability that a control sequence will take the automaton from a given initial state to one of the given final states, and define the set of control tapes, accepted by a stochastic automaton to be those for which this probability is greater than a threshold, $\delta$, $0 \leq \delta \leq 1$.

To determine by experiment whether a given control tape is accepted by a stochastic automaton with threshold, $\delta$, requires more and more instances as the actual probability of transition to one of the given final states approaches $\delta$. It is only if this probability is bounded away from $\delta$ for all possible control tapes that an experiment of pre-determined length may be used to decide whether a tape is accepted by the automaton with any required confidence; a threshold with this property is said to be isolated.

Rabin (1963) and Paz (1966) have shown that for every stochastic automaton with an isolated threshold there is a deterministic automaton which is equivalent in that it accepts the same set of control tapes. However, the deterministic automaton may be less economical in storage, requiring more internal states than the stochastic automaton. There is of course no real gain in storage since an external store is required for the results of the series of experiments which determine whether the stochastic automaton 'accepts' a particular tape. However, this result has its practical applications, for example, in the 'Enhancetron', a waveform averager described in Section 3.1. The first stage of the 'Enhancetron' may be regarded as a two-state, stochastic automaton, receiving input tapes of unit length (in fact analog voltages, but taken to be finely quantized for the sake of this example). The shift of storage burden is an advantage in this application because an external store is already needed for the averaging process.

Whilst the statistical approximation to the behaviour of an unreliable computer through stochastic automata reduces the large input set to a smaller control set, it leaves the state set unchanged. This is a serious defect, since consideration of the states arising through faults in a computer, especially one with much redundancy, leads to a very large state set and an unwieldy automaton. One would like to group the states of the automaton in some way, but so doing generally leads to a Markov chain which is not of first order and hence equally unwieldy. Keményi and Snell (1960) call a transition matrix 'lumpable' if states can be grouped without raising the order of the chain, but the conditions for lumpability are highly restrictive. Pierce (1965) has considerably generalized their results by obtaining probability bounds on the hyperstates after grouping even when the matrix is not lumpable.

The first application of the theory of stochastic automata to computer design was that of von Neumann (Shannon and McCarthy 1956) who showed that under certain conditions arbitrary reliability could be obtained from a computer made of unreliable components through the use of parallel redundancy. This result bears a striking resemblance to Shannon's coding theorem for a discrete channel and the work of Winograd and Cowan (1963) shows that this resemblance is more than superficial. In practice digital computers are still designed with little redundancy and with error-detection rather than error-correction, and work on computer reliability is more suggestive of the advantages of brain-like, homeostatic artifacts, than of new developments in conventional computers (Cowan 1965).

### 3. The Use of Noise in Data-Processing

The application of the theory of stochastic automata to the design of reliable computers has been purely negative—the stochastic properties are a defect to be overcome rather than an essential feature of the computer. The emphasis of the remainder of this review is on the converse situation where probabilistic behaviour is used constructively and randomness is essential to the performance of the computer. Before introducing the general notion of stochastic representations of quantity, two simple examples are given of the advantageous introduction of noise into computers.

#### 3.1 Round off error in analog-digital convertors.

A simple example of data-processing where the addition of a little noise can do a lot of good is in the avoidance of the cumulative effects of round-off error in analog to digital convertors. A successive-approximation digital voltmeter takes a sequence of decisions of the type: is the input voltage above half-scale range?—if so set the most significant digit and subtract half-scale voltage from the input; is the remainder above quarter-scale range?— if so etc. The least significant digit, the $N$th say, is set in the same way by comparison of the $(N-1)$th remainder

with $2^{-N}$ times the full-scale range, and the residual remainder is neglected. This residue or round-off error can have a maximum magnitude slightly less than $2^{-(N+1)}$ times the full-scale range (FSR).

Suppose now that a sequence of $M$ readings of a fixed voltage are averaged to obtain the best estimate of its value. There is no reason to suppose that the round-off errors will cancel, and indeed if the voltage is fixed and the convertor is accurate the errors will all be the same in magnitude and sign. Thus the mean error, $\varepsilon$, in the result is still bounded by:

$$-\text{FSR}/2^{N+1} < \varepsilon < +\text{FSR}/2^{N+1},$$

and the averaging has made no reduction in the round-off error.

Consider now the effect of adding to the input voltage another, $V$, whose magnitude lies in the same range as the round-off error, and which is selected at random uniformly in this range each time a conversion is made. This added voltage is too small to affect any but the least significant digit, but the latter is now dependent on both the input voltage and the random voltage. The greater the round-off error in deterministic conversion the less the probability that the least significant digit will be set in random conversion. Thus there will a tendency for errors in the least significant digit in random conversion to cancel out on averaging. That this tendency is exact may be shown by determining the expected state of the least significant digit (LSD) and hence its expected value. Let the remainder after determination of the $(N-1)$th digit be $E$, $0 \leq E < \text{FSR}/2^N$. The LSD is one if $E+V$ exceeds $\text{FSR}/2^{N+1}$, and since $V$ is evenly distributed over its range:

$$p(\text{LSD} = 1) = p(E+V > \text{FSR}/2^{N+1}) = \frac{E}{\text{FSR}/2^N}.$$

Thus the expected value represented by the LSD is:

$$p(\text{LSD} = 1)\ \text{FSR}/2^N = E,$$

and the average of a set of readings of the input voltage plus random noise has no bias or round-off error. It will of course have a variance since it is based on a finite sample of a random process, and it may be shown to have an approximately normal distribution with a variance:

$$\sigma^2 = \frac{|\varepsilon|\ (\text{FSR}/2^N - |\varepsilon|)}{4M}.$$

Thus the standard deviation of the random conversion is less than the round-off error of the deterministic conversion and goes to zero as the number of readings becomes large.

This technique has been used to good effect in the 'Enhancetron', (Schumann 1965) a device for averaging evoked potentials to decrease the effects of noise, or for averaging any phase-locked voltage waveform. Averaging devices for this purpose must use digital stores since analog integrators have too short a leakage time-constant. The normal practice is to sample the waveform at regular intervals, convert it into a twelve-bit digital form, and add this into a digital store corresponding to the particular sampling instant. The Enhancetron is remarkable in that it converts to a single bit, using random conversion to prevent the tremendous round-off error which would otherwise accrue. The block diagram of Fig. 2 illustrates its operation: the incoming waveform

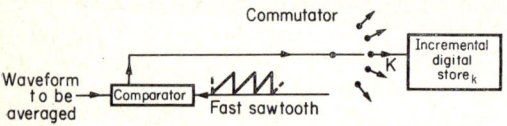

FIG. 2. *Principle of 'Enhancetron'*.

form is compared with a sawtooth (simulating a uniform random distribution) in a comparator; the output is commutated around a ring of digital stores; at a clock pulse the appropriate store is incremented by one unit if the output of the comparator is ON and decremented otherwise; the ring of stores will eventually average out the noise at the input and the noise of random conversion, and contain a sampled representation of any repetitive signal whose phase is locked to their cycling rate. Thus the use of random conversion has replaced a twelve-bit analog to digital convertor by a simple comparator, and replaced twelve-bit binary addition by simple incrementing/decrementing; both considerable economies.

3.2. *The polarity coincidence correlator* (Veltman and Van den Bos 1965). One of the most frequent computations on the analog computer is to cross-correlate two waveforms. Given two voltage waveforms with zero means it is required to compute their co-variance:

$$C_T = \frac{1}{T} \int_0^T U(t)V(t) \, dt,$$

which is an awkward function because it involves integration over extended intervals and multiplication, both of which tax analog computing elements to their utmost. If the waveforms have almost Gaussian distributions, it may be shown that the correlation between their heavily limited forms (in which only their signs are taken into account) is uniquely related to $C_T$. If:

$$P_T = \frac{1}{T} \int_0^T \text{sgn}(U(t)) \, \text{sgn}(V(t)) \, dt,$$

then as $T \to \infty$ $C_T \to a \sin\left(\frac{\pi}{2} P_T\right)$, where $a$ is a constant dependent on the variance of $U$ and $V$.

This non-linear relationship does not necessarily hold for non-Gaussian distributions, and does not yield a simple additive effect if uncorrelated noise is added to the waveforms. Despite these limitations the polarity coincidence correlator is very attractive because multiplication of two numbers whose modulus is unity can be carried out by a simple gate or relay, and if the waveforms are sampled at regular intervals the integration may be carried out digitally by a reversible counter; thus both analog multiplier and integrator may be replaced by economical and reliable digital devices.

The limitations can be completely removed if the polarity coincidence correlator is converted to a simple stochastic computer by adding to the input voltages randomly varying voltages with zero means and uniform distributions. Let $A(t)$ be a random waveform uniformly distributed in a range greater than that of $U(t)$ and having a $\delta$-function autocorrelation, and let $B(t)$ be a similar uncorrelated waveform for $V(t)$. Let $P_{T,N}$ be the sampled polarity coincidence correlation of $(U+A)$ against $(V+B)$:

$$P_{T,N} = \frac{1}{N} \sum_{i=0}^{N-1} \{\text{sgn}(U[iT/N] + A[iT/N]) \, \text{sgn}(V[iT/N] + B[iT/N])\}.$$

Then it may be shown that as $T \to \infty$:

$$C_T \to a \lim_{N \to \infty} P_{T,N}, \quad \text{where } a \text{ is a constant.}$$

Thus the polarity coincidence correlator gives an unbiased estimate proportional to the covariance of the input signals no matter what their distribution, provided the signals are sampled rapidly enough over a sufficient period. The addition of random noise again introduces additional variance into the estimate, but this can be made negligible by taking a longer sample of the waveforms or sampling more often; thus the power of this correlator may be less than that of a normal cross-correlator but its accuracy is the same.

A block diagram of one realization of a polarity coincidence correlator with added noise is shown in Fig. 3: the random waveforms are again approximated by very

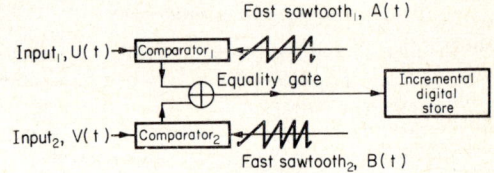

FIG. 3. *Polarity coincidence correlator*.

fast anharmonic sawtooths feeding inputs to comparators, on the other side of which are the waveforms to be correlated; the logic levels out of the comparator are fed to an equality gate whose output is ON only when its inputs are equal; the output from this gate represents the product of the signs of the signals plus noise, and this is used to determine whether a binary counter shall increment or decrement at a clock pulse (sampling instant); the state of the counter eventually represents the covariance between the inputs. This is a digital circuit, more economical in its realization than an analog multiplier and integrator, and is the classic example of the advantages to be gained through the intentional introduction of noise into data-processors. The full exploitation of these advantages in the stochastic computer depends on the use of general stochastic representations of quantity, and these are described in the next section.

### 4. Stochastic Representation of Quantity

The basic principle of the stochastic computer is to use the generating probability of Bernoulli sequences of logic levels to carry information. In the first example above, the probability that the least significant digit would be set was proportional to the voltage to be represented by the LSD, and hence the LSD's in a sequence of readings form a stochastic representation of this voltage. This is called the 'asymmetric binary representation' and its most general form is:

given any quantity $E$ in the range $0 \leqslant E \leqslant V$, represent it by a Bernoulli sequence of binary logic levels with generating probability:

$$p(\text{ON}) = E/V.$$

Thus the maximum voltage is represented by a logic level always ON, zero voltage by it being always OFF, and values in between by some probability that it will be ON.

A second representation was exemplified by the polarity coincidence correlator where both positive and negative voltages had to be represented. The representation used was an example of the 'symmetric binary representation' whose most general form is:

given any quantity in the range $-V \leqslant E \leqslant +V$, represent it by a Bernoulli sequence of binary logic levels with generating probability:

$$p(\text{ON}) = \frac{E+V}{2V} = \tfrac{1}{2}E/V + \tfrac{1}{2}.$$

Thus the maximum positive voltage is represented by a logic level always ON, maximum negative voltage by it being always OFF, and zero voltage by a random sequence with equal probability of ON or OFF.

Many other forms of stochastic representation are possible, and those which have definite representations of infinite quantities are especially interesting. A binary representation may be regarded as a mapping from a line, the range of an analog variable, to the interval [0, 1], the range of probabilities. There is a natural 'distance' between two probabilities, defined by the reciprocal of the length of experiment necessary to distinguish between them. This gives the natural topology of the interval to the range of probabilities, so that it is usual for the mapping of an analog variable into this range to be monotonic, if not continuous. The computing elements described in the remainder of this paper operate in the binary symmetric representation.

*4.1. Comparison of stochastic and other forms of representation.* Stochastic representations of quantity may be compared with those which characterize other forms of computer. The most direct representation is that of the analog computer where continuous voltage levels replace analog quantities. In the digital computer a quantity is represented by an ordered set of binary logic levels or binary word. The DDA and pulse-counting computers represent a quantity by the number of ON logic levels occurring during an interval. In the stochastic computer only the probability of occurrence of a logic-level carries information.

If one compares the efficiency of these representations, in terms of the number of levels required to carry information to a precision of one part in $N$, then:

the analog computer requires one continuous level;
the digital computer requires $\log_2 kN$ ordered binary levels;
the pulse-counting computer or DDA requires $kN$ unordered binary levels;
and the stochastic computer requires $kN^2$ unordered binary levels—where $k > 1$ is a constant representing the effects of round-off error or variance, $k = 10$ say. This progression from $1 : \log_2 N : N : N^2$ shows the stochastic computer to be by far the least efficient in its representation of quantity, but it is through this inefficiency that it gains in simplicity and economy. In the polarity coincidence correlator, for example, a simple equality gate performs multiplication, whereas multiplication in the analog computers requires several operational amplifiers—in the digital computer a complex central processor and sub-routine—and in the DDA two integrators. The next sections describe stochastic computing elements to perform the complete range of analog computing functions, inversion, multiplication, addition, integration and so on.

### 5. Stochastic Computing Elements

The elements of a stochastic computer consist of logic units, gates, and storage devices, together with random generators whose outputs are Bernoulli sequences of logic levels. For convenience in exposition the stochastic computer will be assumed to run synchronously, so that the inputs, outputs and states of elements within the computer change only at the occurrence of a 'clock pulse'. The properties of the most common binary elements are shown in Fig. 4, together with their graphic symbols. The logical computations performed by the computing elements induce arithmetical computations in the quantities represented by their input lines, and these depend on the particular representation in use.

*5.1. Stochastic invertors, multipliers and isolators.* Consider the simple logical invertor (Fig. 4a) whose output is the complement of its input. The relationship between the probability that its input will be ON and the probability that its output will be ON is:

$$p_{\text{out}}(\text{ON}) = 1 - p_{\text{in}}(\text{ON}).$$

In the binary symmetric representation the relationship between these probabilities and the quantities they represent is:

$$p_{\text{in}}(\text{ON}) = \tfrac{1}{2} + \tfrac{1}{2}E_{\text{in}}/V$$
$$p_{\text{out}}(\text{ON}) = \tfrac{1}{2} + \tfrac{1}{2}E_{\text{out}}/V,$$

hence $\quad E_{\text{out}} = -E_{\text{in}},$

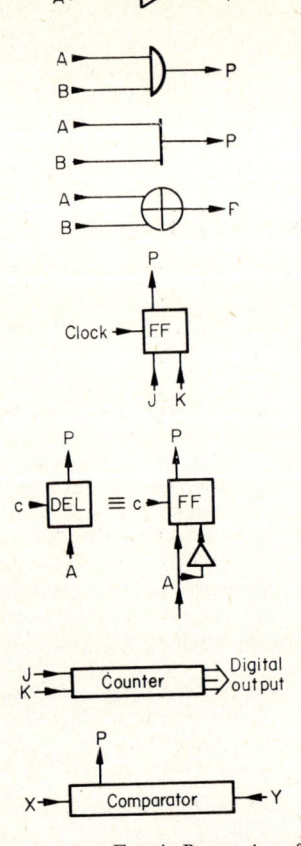

(a) *Logical Invertor* $P = \bar{A}$, the output is the complement of the input.

(b) *AND Gate* $P = A.B$, the output is ON $\Longleftrightarrow$ both inputs are ON.

(c) *OR Gate* $P = A \wedge B$, the output is ON $\Longleftrightarrow$ either or both inputs are ON.

(d) *Equality Gate* $P = A.B \wedge \bar{A}.\bar{B}$, the output is ON if the inputs are the same.

(e) *JK Flip-Flop* The output is the same as the internal state of the flip-flop. At a clock pulse the state becomes ON if the J line alone is ON, and OFF if the K line alone is ON. It complements if they are both on, and remains the same if they are both OFF.

(f) *Unit Delay* $P(t) = A(t-1)$, the JK flip-flop is connected so that its output reproduces its input delayed through one clock pulse.

(g) *Counter* A store with states $S_0 \ldots S_N$; in state $S_k$ at a clock pulse, it goes to state $S_{k+1}$ if its J line is on alone, and to state $S_{k-1}$ if its K line is on alone; otherwise it remains in the same state.

(h) *Comparator* $P \equiv (X \geq Y)$, the output is determined by the relative magnitude of the (analog or digital) quantities at the inputs.

FIG. 4. *Properties of binary elements used in the stochastic computer.*

so that the logical invertor acts to give the negative of a number (in other representations it may subtract the number from a constant or compute its reciprocal).

The equality gate (Fig. 4d) is used to carry out multiplication in the binary symmetric representation. Consider the two input streams to represent quantities $E_{in}, E'_{in}$, by probabilities $p_{in}, p'_{in}$. The output is ON when the inputs are both ON or both OFF, and hence:

$$p_{out}(ON) = p_{in}(ON)p'_{in}(ON) + [1 - p_{in}(ON)][1 - p'_{in}(ON)]$$

so that

$$E_{out} = E_{in}E'_{in}/V.$$

An important phenomenom is illustrated by the use of a stochastic multiplier as a squarer. It is not sufficient to short-circuit the inputs of the equality gate together, for its output will then always be ON. This difficulty arises because the multiplier inputs must be statistically independent if the probability of their conjunction is to be the product of their generating probabilities. Fortunately an independent replication of a Bernoulli sequence may be obtained by delaying it through one event, and Fig. 5 illustrates a squarer utilizing a flip-flop as a delay, (Fig.

4f), and an equality gate as a multiplier. The flip-flop used in this way is a stochastic 'isolator', performing no computation but statistically isolating two cross-correlated lines.

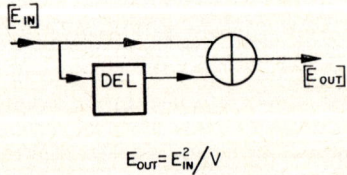

$E_{OUT} = E_{IN}^2/V$

FIG. 5. *Stochastic squarer.*

The necessity for stochastic isolation in the squarer is an example of a general principle applying to all stochastic computation. It is assumed that whenever sequences of logic levels are brought together at the inputs of a computing element they are independent Bernoulli sequences; that is they are neither cross-correlated nor autocorrelated. Both these conditions may be neglected to advantage in pseudo-random realizations of the computer, but isolation must normally be used to maintain statistical independence.

### 5.2. Stochastic addition.

Having seen how readily inversion and multiplication are effected by simple gates, one is tempted to assume that a similar gate may be used to perform addition. However, this is not so and a stochastic logic element must be introduced to effect addition in the symmetric binary representation. Consider the situation when one input is always ON, representing the maximum positive quantity, and the other is always OFF, representing the maximum negative quantity. The sum of the quantities represented by the inputs is zero, and hence the output must be random, with equal chances of being ON or OFF. A probabilistic output cannot be obtained from a deterministic gate with constant inputs, so that stochastic behaviour must be built into the gate itself.

One realization of a stochastic adder in the binary symmetric representation is illustrated in Fig. 6: flip-flop$_1$ is in a random state which is transferred to flip-

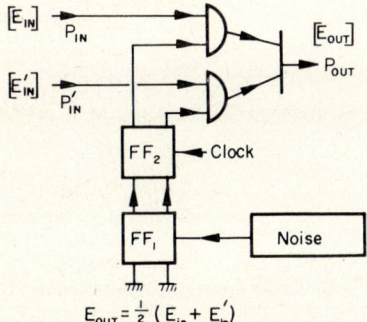

FIG. 6. *Stochastic adder.*

flop$_2$ at a clock pulse; dependent on the state of flip-flop$_2$, one or the other of the input lines is reproduced at the output. Thus the probability that the output will be ON is half the sum of the generating probabilities of the inputs:

$$p_{\text{out}}(\text{ON}) = \tfrac{1}{2} p_{\text{in}}(\text{ON}) + \tfrac{1}{2} p'_{\text{in}}(\text{ON}),$$

and hence:

$$E_{\text{out}} = \tfrac{1}{2}(E_{\text{in}} + E'_{\text{in}}).$$

A multi-input adder may be realized by reproducing any one of its inputs at random as the output, and a weighted adder may be realized by biasing the probabilities that given inputs will be reproduced at the output.

### 5.3. Stochastic integrators, the ADDIE, and Interface.

Integration in the Polarity Coincidence Correlator (Fig. 3) is realized by a counter which increments its count by unity when its input is ON, and decrements it by unity when its input is OFF. However, the counter itself has the third possibility of not changing its count,

and this is used to advantage in the two-input summing integrator illustrated in Fig. 7: the counter changes its state at a clock pulse only if the 'hold' line is ON; it

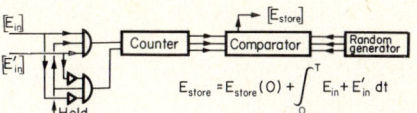

FIG. 7. *Stochastic two-input summing integrator.*

increments by unity if both its inputs are ON, and decrements by unity if they are both OFF; otherwise it remains in the same state. With both inputs joined together the two-input integrator behaves as the incremental digital store previously described.

A stochastic output from the integrator, representing the stored quantity, is obtained by comparing its count with a randomly varying digital quantity, uniformly distributed over the range of the store. If the store has $N+1$ possible states, $S_0 \ldots S_N$, then when it is in state $S_k$ the probability that its output will be ON at the next clock pulse is:

$$p_{\text{out}}(\text{ON}) = k/N.$$

The integrator with unity feedback illustrated in Fig. 8b is called an ADDIE, and performs the important

(a) Integrator symbol    (b) Integrator connected as ADDIE

FIG. 8.

function of exponentially averaging the quantity represented by its input line. The count in its store is an unbiased estimator of the generating probability of its input, and it may be read out in analog or digital form as the natural outward interface of the stochastic computer. The count in an $N+1$ state ADDIE, with an input of constant generating probability, $p$, is approximately normally distributed with a variance:

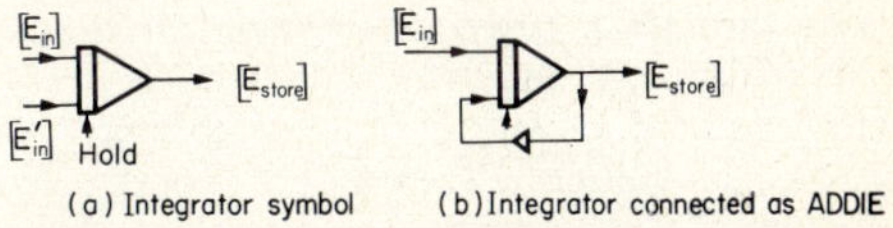

$$\sigma^2 = p(1-p)N,$$

and hence the standard deviation of the quantity represented, $\sigma(E)$, expressed as a fraction of the range is:

$$\frac{\sigma(E)}{|V|} = \frac{1}{N^{\frac{1}{2}}}\left[1-\left(\frac{E}{V}\right)^2\right]^{\frac{1}{2}} \leq \frac{1}{N^{\frac{1}{2}}}.$$

Thus quantities within the stochastic computer may be read out to any required accuracy by using ADDIE's with many states, but the more states the longer the time-constant of smoothing and the lower the bandwidth of the computer. Hence variables within the computer may be regarded as degraded by Gaussian noise, whose power increases with the bandwidth required from the computer.

The integrator or ADDIE may be used to realize arbitrary functions by imposing suitable non-linear relationships between the count in its store and stochastic output. For example if all counts above the mid-level give rise to an ON output, and all those below it give rise to an OFF output, then the input/output relationship approximates to a discontinuous relay or switching-function. Integrators with their hold lines OFF may be used to store a constant during integration, and thus act as a 'potentiometer' if coupled to a multiplier.

The inward interface of the stochastic computer consists of comparators, one side of which accepts the analog or digital input, and the other side of which is driven by a random analog or digital waveform; these have been described for both the 'Enhancetron' and the polarity coincidence correlator. In the binary symmetric representation the random waveform will have a uniform distribution over the range of the inputs, symmetrical about zero; other representations may be obtained by transforming the input or biasing the random distribution.

### 6. Applications of Stochastic Computing Elements

The stochastic computing elements described form a complete set in the binary symmetric representation: invertor, adder, multiplier, integrator, function generator, inward and outward interfaces. These may be made available through a patch-board identical to that in conventional analog computers, so that the elements may be interconnected at will to simulate specific systems. Stochastic computing elements are constructed of such simple digital circuits, however, that many elements can be fabricated on a single chip of an integrated circuit, and to take full advantage of the compactness and economy offered it is desirable for interconnexions between elements to should be fabricated on the same chip. Thus practical computing units tend to be fairly large complexes of the basic elements interconnected to perform a specific computation. Some simple examples of such complexes are given in the concluding sections.

*6.1. A second-order transfer function.* A stable second-order transfer function with variable natural frequency and damping-ratio is shown in Fig. 9: two integrators

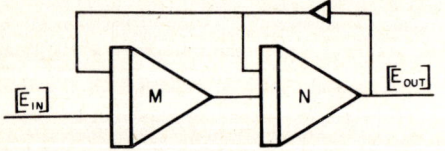

FIG. 9. *Second-order transfer function.*

are connected in series, and inverted feedback from the final output is taken to both their inputs. If the first integrator has $(M+1)$ states and the second has $(N+1)$ states, then the transformation realized is:

$$\frac{MN}{f^2} \ddot{E}_{\text{out}} + \frac{M}{f} \dot{E}_{\text{out}} + E_{\text{out}} = E_{\text{in}},$$

where $f$ is the clock frequency.

This is a stable second-order transfer function with:

$$\text{undamped natural frequency} = \frac{f}{2\pi(MN)^{\frac{1}{2}}},$$

$$\text{damping ratio} = \tfrac{1}{2}(M/N)^{\frac{1}{2}}.$$

A simulated response of this stochastic computing unit to a step in position and velocity is shown in Fig. 10, for $M = N = 2000$, corresponding to a damping

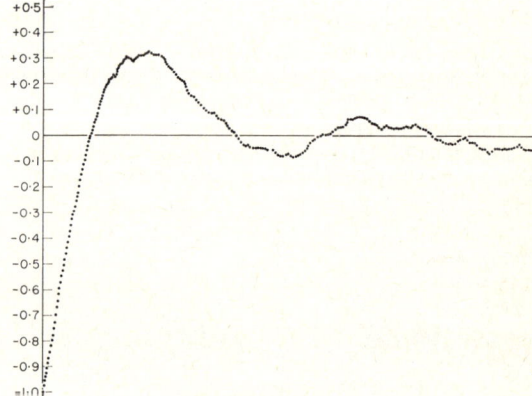

FIG. 10. *Response of stochastic second-order transfer function.*

ratio of $\tfrac{1}{2}$. Gaussian noise, superimposed on the normal overshoot and oscillatory decay, can clearly be seen.

*6.2. Steepest descent computer.* The most ubiquitous of computing configurations is that of 'steepest descent', (Donaldson and Kishi 1965; Tou and Wilcox 1964) and its uses range from implicit four-quadrant division to parameter identification and pattern recognition. Its usage is normally restricted by the number of multipliers and storage elements required for its implementation, but these requirements make it ideal for stochastic realization.

It is required to find weights, $w_1 \ldots w_N$, for inputs, $x_1 \ldots x_N$, which give the best approximation (in terms of r.m.s. error) to the required output, $y$, by a weighted sum of the inputs, $z$. That is to find $\{w_i\}$ such that:

$$\overline{(e^2)} = \frac{1}{T} \int_0^T (z-y)^2 \, dt \quad \text{is minimized,}$$

where $z = w_1 x_1 + w_2 x_2 + \ldots + w_N x_N$.

It may be shown that the best values of the weights can be established on-line through the computation (assuming no secondary minima):

$$\dot{w}_i = \alpha x_i (y - z), \quad \text{where } \alpha > 0 \text{ is the slope of descent.}$$

A stochastic computer realizing this computation is shown in Fig. 11: the weights are represented by the outputs of integrators (only one section is shown), whose inputs receive feedback from the error between actual and required output which is multiplied by the

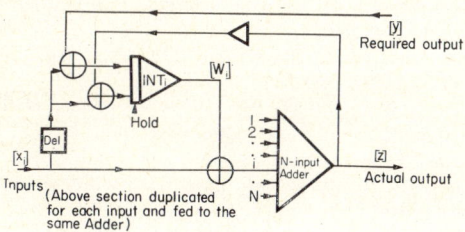

FIG. 11. *Steepest descent computer.*

appropriate input. When the 'hold' lines of the integrators are ON the computer makes a steepest descent approach to the best linear relationship between inputs and required output, and when the 'hold' lines are OFF the 'actual output' simulates the 'required output' by using this relationship. Note the need for isolation of the input feedback, and the use of three multipliers for each weight. Stochastic computing elements allow by far the most economical realization of the steepest descent computer.

*6.3. Partial differential equations and neural nets.* Analog computers have one natural independent variable and that is time. Partial differential equations involving several independent variables are usually solved iteratively on a hybrid computer, or through a discrete approximation on the digital computer. The use of stochastic computing elements makes it feasible to simulate the equations by spatial arrays of special-purpose computing elements, with one spatial dimension for each independent variable, and these arrays bear an interesting resemblance to 'neural nets'. A stochastic solution of Laplace's equation will be used to illustrate this technique.

Laplace's equation in two dimensions:

$$\frac{\partial^2 u}{\partial x^2} + \frac{\partial^2 u}{\partial y^2} = 0, \quad \text{with boundary}$$

conditions on a closed curve, may be simulated by expressing it in discrete form:

$$u(x-\varepsilon, y) - 2u(x, y) + u(x+\varepsilon, y) + u(x, y-\varepsilon) - 2u(x, y) + u(x, y+\varepsilon) = 0.$$

If $u(x, y)$ is represented as the output of a stochastic integrator, then the above relationship can be enforced by feedback to its input, assuming other integrators are representing neighbouring grid-points. A suitable computing element, the 'Laplacian', is shown in Fig. 12: an ADDIE receives the output of an adder, which sums the peripheral terms of the above equation, together with the normal inverted feedback from its output; the value represented by the ADDIE can settle only when the above equation is satisfied. Networks of these units, interconnected as shown in Fig. 13, can be used to solve Laplace's equation in two-dimensions for arbitrary shapes and boundary conditions.

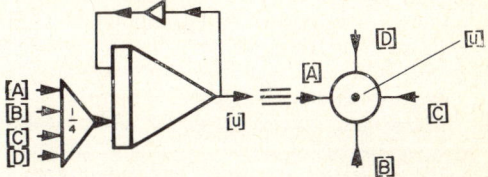

FIG. 12. *Two-dimensional Laplacian element.*

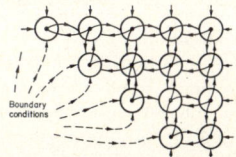

FIG. 13. *Net of Laplacians.*

The properties of these spatial arrays have interesting resemblances to those of the 'neural nets' simulated by Farley and Clark (1954) and Beurle (1956), and the computing elements themselves are reminiscent of the 'neurons' of Harmon (1961) and other workers. Neurons in the brain are known to show stochastic behaviour, and it is possible that stochastic computing may provide not only a new impetus to work on neural nets, but also a reasonable model of some cortical functions; for example, the cross-correlational processes of visual disparity and auditory formant separation.

## 7. Summary and Conclusions

The place for the stochastic computer in the diagram of Fig. 1. should now be clear, and is shown in Fig. 14.

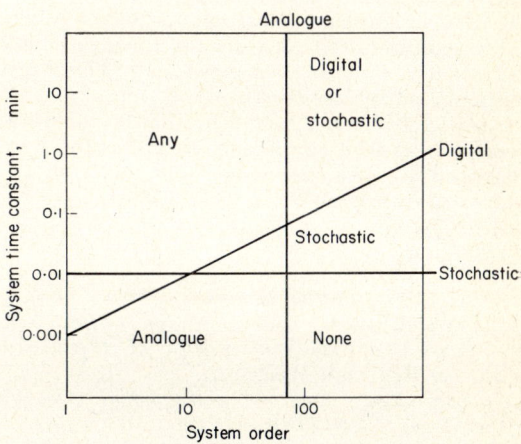

FIG. 14. *Applicability of analog, digital and stochastic computers to process simulation.*

The main limitation is its speed, and systems suitable for simulation by a stochastic computer lie above a horizontal line cutting the time axis at approximately 0·01 minutes. There remains an area in the lower right hand corner which is intractable for all forms of computer, but this is now bounded by a horizontal rather than a sloping line, implying that the stochastic computer suffers no loss in speed as the size of problem increases. It is interesting to note that advances into the missing area of large, fast systems are largely independent of increases in the speed or size of digital computers; sequential processing is a grave disadvantage in the simulation of systems with many interacting components.

The diagram is anomalous in making it appear that analog and stochastic computers are everywhere alternatives to the digital computer. Figure 14 represents the physical constraints in real-time process simulation, and neglects the many applications where the digital computer proves cheaper, more flexible and easier to use. A combination of the three types of computer in a hybrid stochastic computer would prove very powerful in control applications; the digital computer providing flexible sequencing and supervision of operations, the analog computer providing fast but simple models for iterative optimization, and the stochastic computer providing real-time, realistic simulation for identification of process states and dynamics.

The application of complex adaptive controllers has been inhibited by the lack of suitable hardware, and the ease of multiplication and storage in the stochastic computer offers opportunities for parameter optimization which have not previously been available. The development of learning machines which take full advantage of the properties peculiar to stochastic hardware, and the development of stochastic computing elements to fulfil the particular requirements of learning machines are potentially the richest fields of research in both computation and control.

*Acknowledgement.* Part of this review is based on unpublished work by Dr. J. H. Andreae and the staff of the Learning Machines Department at Standard Telecommunication Laboratories, and the author would like to thank them for their co-operation, and STL for permission to publish this material.

*See also*: Automata, finite-state. Control by hybrid computers. Control, identification techniques for. Neuronal nets. Reliable computation with unreliable elements.

*Bibliography*

BEURLE (1956) *Properties of a mass of cells capable of regenerating pulses*, Trans. Roy. Soc., **B240**, Aug.
BLAKELOCK (1965) *Automatic Control of Aircraft and Missiles*, New York: Wiley.
CONNELLY (1962) *Real-time analog-digital computation*, Trans. I.R.E, EC-**11**, (1) Feb., 31.
COWAN J. (1965) *The problem of organismic reliability*, in *Progress in Brain Research*, Vol. 17, Amsterdam: Elsevier.
DONALDSON and KISHI (1965) *Review of adaptive control systems theories and techniques*, in *Modern Control Systems Theory*, New York: McGraw-Hill.
FARLEY and CLARK (1954) *Simulation of self-organizing systems by digital computer*, Trans. I.R.E., IT-**4**, Sept., 76.
HARMON (1961) *Studies with artificial neurons*, Kybernetik, **1**, Dec., 89.
KEMENY and SNELL (1960) *Finite Markov Chains*, New York: Van Nostrand.
KORN and KORN (1964) *Electronic Analog and Hybrid Computers*, New York: Van Nostrand.
LEONDES (1959) *Digital techniques in analog computation*, in *Handbook of Automation, Computation and Control*, New York: Wiley.
MCNAUGHTON (1961) *The theory of automata—a survey*, in *Advances in Computers*, Vol. 2, New York: Academic Press.
MOORE (1964) *Sequential Machines*, New York: Addison-Wesley.
PAZ (1966) *Some aspects of probabilistic automata*, Inf. and Control, 9, (1), Jan., 26.
PIERCE (1965) *Failure-tolerant Computer Design*, New York: Academic Press.
RABIN (1953) *Probabilistic automata*, Inf. and Control, 6 (3), Sept. 230.
RABIN and SCOTT (1959) *Finite automata and their decision problems*, I.B.M.J. Res. and Dev., 3 (2), April, 114.
SHANNON and MCCARTHY (1956) *Automata studies*, Annals of Mathematics, **34**, Princeton: The University Press.
SCHUMANN (1965) *Method and apparatus for averaging a series of electrical transients*, U.S. Patent 3, 182, 181.
TAKACS (1960) *Stochastic Processes*, London: Methuen.
TOU and WILCOX (1964) *Computer and Information Sciences*, New York: Spartan Press.
TRUITT (1964) Hybrid Computation... What is it? Who needs it? *Proc. Spring Joint Computer Conf.*, 249.
VELTMAN and VAN DEN BOS (1965) *The applicability of the relay-correlator and polarity coincidence correlator in automatic control*, Proc. 2nd Congress. Intern. Fed. Automatic Control, London: Butterworths.
WILLIAMS (1965) *Process dynamics and its application to industrial process design and process control*, Proc. 2nd Congr. Intern. Fed. Automatic Control, London: Butterworths.
WINOGRAD and COWAN (1963) *Reliable Computation in the Presence of Noise*, Cambridge, Mass.: M.I.T. Press.

B. R. GAINES

**CONCEPT FORMATION BY ARTIFICIAL INTELLIGENCE.** The idea of 'concept formation by artificial intelligence' is at first a bit frightening, as it suggests an omniscient machine meditating upon the nature of the world. In fact, the problem has been redefined in such a way that the topic is not so vast, and to the sentient being neither so frightening nor so implausible. Modern references to artificial intelligence nearly all refer to a problem solving procedure which, at least in principle, can be stated as a digital computer program. There is sometimes the added implication that the program must not be derived from well known mathematical procedures. Obviously this is a subjective judgement, since ultimately any computer program is reducible to well defined mathematical operations. Whether or not one chooses to call a particular problem solution by computer an example of artificial intelligence seems to depend as much on taste as upon any formal definition.

Concept formation can be defined formally. Consider a universe of *objects*, each of which can be described by stating its *values* on every member of a set of *attributes*. For example, people might be described by age, sex, height, weight, and nationality. Now suppose that each object in the universe is assigned to exactly one set, and that the set has a name associated with it. A set of objects associated with a given name is the denotation of the name, and a rule for deciding, by examination of its attributes, whether or not a given object belongs to the denotation of a name is called the *concept* of the name. Thus a concept is simply a rule for classifying objects by examining their descriptions (Church 1958). In most *concept formation problems* the class membership of every object in a sample of the universe is made known. Call this subset the *organizing set*. By examining the organizing set, the concept learner must develop a concept which can be applied to any object in the universe. Concept formation by artificial intelligence is the specification of a mechanical procedure for doing this.

It is useful to distinguish certain classes of concept learning situations, since the manner of operation of a concept learning device depends upon the sort of situation in which it operates. One distinction is between situations in which the attributes are in some sense continuous, measurable dimensions (e.g. height and weight) and situation in which the attributes have nominal values (e.g. nationality, colour of hair). The distinction is important because if the dimensions are continuous one can represent the universe as a Euclidean space in which each point may represent an object. The idea of distance between pairs of points is meaningful, and can be used by the concept former. This special situation encompasses many practically important problems. Under the title 'pattern recognition' a specialized mathematical literature has developed. There is a third case, in which attributes are binary variables, that strictly speaking, is a special case of the nominal attribute situation. In practice, many of the methods applicable to the continuous representation may be applied to the binary, as in the binary case the universe can be conceptualized as an *n*-dimensional hypercube, where each object is associated with a corner of the cube.

A second important distinction between concept learning situations rests upon the manner in which the organizing set is presented. The feasibility of a particular concept learning procedure may depend upon whether all members of the organizing set are presented at one time, and a concept then required, or whether the organizing set is presented one item at a time and the learner required to converge upon an answer. The second type of situation is the one usually studied in psychological experiments on human concept learning and in studies of pattern recognition.

First consider the situation in which the attributes are continuous and the organizing set is presented all at one time. A graphic representation of this problem is shown in Fig. 1, with an organizing set consisting of members of three classes, represented by circles, squares, and crosses. Suppose that a point outside the organizing set (point X in Fig. 1) is designated. If one

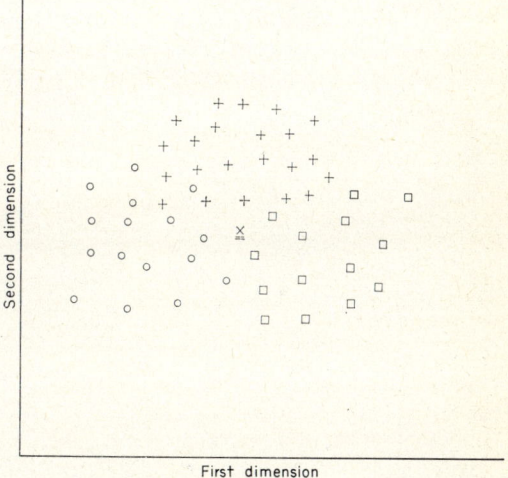

FIG. 1. *Example of a classification problem. Should one expect to find a circle, square or cross at the point marked X in this figure?*

has a concept, one should be able to assign that point to one of the three classes. Sebesteyen (1962) has formulated this as the mathematical problem of determining the density of class membership for each class and each point in the space. Given a point, one classifies the object associated with that point by determining the class which is densest (i.e. assumed to be most frequently found) at the point. The computations required to determine the density of each class over the entire space are formidable, especially if the number of attributes is large. On the other hand, the resulting decision rules can be shown to result in the lowest possible loss due to misclassification, i.e. they are optimal by a Bayesian decision criterion. In addition, if the density of each class is actually determined by a multivariate normal distribution the procedures advocated by Sebesteyen are identical to the statistical procedure of maximum likelihood classification.

An alternate procedure, which is somewhat simpler computationally, but which does not result in Bayesian optimal classification rules, is to locate a hyperplane between each pair of classes, and assign an item to a class by noting on which side of the hyperplane it falls. Formally, if we consider only two classes, and let each object be represented by a row vector, $X_k = x_{ik}$, where $x_{ik}$ is the value of the $k$th object on the $i$th attribute, then in classification one chooses a weight vector, $W = w_i$, such that one can compute the vector product

$$g(X_k) = WX', \qquad (1)$$

and assign object $k$ to class 1 or 2 depending upon whether or not $g(X_k)$ is greater than some threshold value, $L$.

In the example of Fig. 1 all classes are 'linearly separable' in the sense that there is a line (hyperplane) between each pair of classes so that (1) can be computed with some set of weights, $W$, and some threshold value, so that the number of correct classifications can be maximized. In Fig. 2 an example is given of a classi-

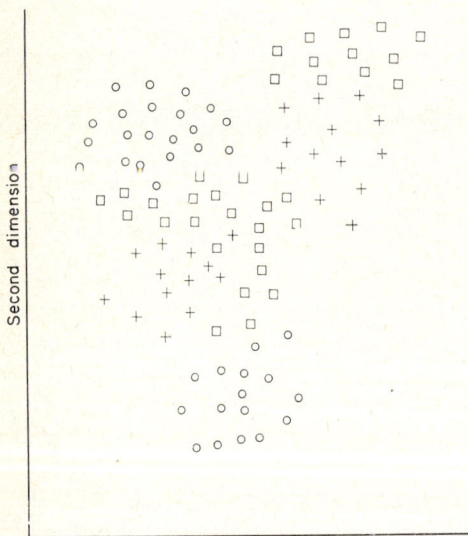

FIG. 2. *Example of a classification problem which is not linearly separable. Lines cannot be drawn such that all the circles (or squares, or crosses) are on one side of the line, and all the other figures on the other side.*

fication problem in which the classes are not linearly separable. This sort of problem can be transformed to a linearly separable problem by expanding the measurement space to include successively higher powers of the attributes. For example, in the expanded space the first $n$ dimensions would be the original dimensions, the next $n$ dimensions would be defined as the squares of the values objects had on the first $n$ dimensions, the next $n$ dimensions would be defined as the cubes, and so on. While conceptually simple, this scheme increases the computational burden drastically.

The rationale for these computations is that the organizing set will be presented once. If items are added to the organizing set, one should repeat the computations for each new addition. This is prohibitively expensive. For this reason, many pattern recognition studies have concentrated upon the definition of a procedure for converging upon the correct answer without such heavy computation. Most attention has been focussed upon problems which are linearly separable. A trial value for $W$ is chosen, and used to classify new objects. As each new object is presented the values of the components of $W$ are readjusted (i.e. the hyperplane is repositioned) until its location stabilizes. A variety of rules, sometimes called 'training procedures' have been suggested for making the necessary readjustments. The study of different training procedures has given rise to a series of difficult and interesting mathematical problems (Nilsson 1965).

If the problem is not linearly separable the adjustment procedure may be quite difficult. One approach is to adjust several hyperplanes simultaneously and to use as the classification to be made on each trial a composite of the 'recommendations' from each linear classification rule. Little is known formally about such machines, although it has been shown that they are capable of quite complex decision rules (Nilsson 1965; Rosenblatt 1962). They are also interesting because they have been proposed as models of some of the decision making processes in the central nervous system.

The case in which the attributes are nominal variables has received much less attention, both because it is harder to relate to well developed mathematical techniques and because many important practical problems can be forced into the Euclidean or binary framework without doing too much injustice to the original problem.

Uhr and Vossler (1963) report a program which makes use of a non-parametric cluster analysis to assign objects to classes. In its most primitive form, an object is described to the program as a string of binary digits (bits). Each digit thus stands for the presence or absence of a characteristic, and could be looked upon as a nominal, two valued attribute. The program does not deal directly with this bit pattern. Instead it describes the object to itself as having certain 'features', which are defined as substrings of bits which may occur within the original string. For example, if the input string were a digitized description of the letter 'A' the Uhr and Vossler program could detect the substring of bits representing the inverted 'v' at the top of the 'A'. After having obtained an abstracted description of a object by noting its features, the program compares this description to a description which it has stored of a prototypical member of each class. The object at hand is tentatively assigned to that class whose prototype description it most resembles. The prototype description is itself a composite description of all objects which have previously been designated as members of that class. Thus the prototype is continuously updated as the program is shown new objects.

The Uhr and Vossler method is quite similar to the method of classification by maximum likelihood, in the sense that in each case one measures the distance between a particular object and the idealized representative of a class of objects. Unlike the maximum likelihood method, the Uhr and Vossler definition of similarity is quite crude, and so simple computationally that it can be used in a concept learning situation in which items of an organizing set are presented one at a time. Although Uhr and Vossler make no claim that their similarity definitions are in any sense optimal, they have shown that empirically their program converges on an accurate decision rule in reasonable times over a variety of problems.

A second interesting feature of the Uhr and Vossler method is that the program has a capacity to generate the features used to describe input patterns. This is done by choosing as trial features substrings which actually occur in the input patterns, keeping statistics on their utility as measures of the distance from an object to a class representation, and replacing little used substrings (features) by new ones which are also chosen by copying the input patterns. Block, Nilsson and Duda (1964) have also investigated this method of feature generation. Such programs can, in effect, discover the attributes of objects. This is an important increase in problem solving power.

A second approach to concept formation based upon nominal attributes is one in which the concept is represented as a sequential decision rule. In establishing a concept, one first examines the organizing set to select an attribute which is in some sense a good predictor of the class membership of all objects. This attribute is then used to sort the objects in the organizing set into subsets. Within each subset, the attribute selection and sorting procedures are repeated, establishing subsubsets. The process is continued until a subset is either empty or contains only members of one class. The resulting classification process can be depicted as a sequential decision tree, in which the question asked at time $n$ depends upon the answer received to the question asked at time $n-1$. A sample problem analysed in this manner is shown in Fig. 3. Hunt, Marin and Stone

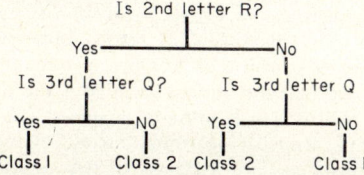

FIG. 3. *Example of a classification problem where the solution is represented as a sequential decision procedure.*

(1966) have shown that adequate sequential decision trees can be obtained for a variety of complex problems, within reasonable limits on computation, using quite simple rules for choosing the sorting attributes at each step.

A few programs have been reported which, under the title of concept formation, actually do a somewhat different task. These programs develop rules for predicting the next in a sequence of items. Two notably different approaches are those of Rosenblatt (1962) and Simon and Kotovsky (1963). Rosenblatt's proposal, part of his more general work on a type of self-organizing system which he calls a '*perceptron*', is for a machine which acts as a linear classification device which takes as its input at time $t$ both the description of the object presented at that time and some representation of the object(s) presented to it previously. One such representation is the classification response made to an object when it was presented. Such machines are, in principle, capable of learning to reproduce a sequence of responses given only a few of the original stimuli. The amount of training required before the machine can achieve reasonable performance may be considerable.

The Simon and Kotovsky program contains within it some simple transformations to map the last $n$ items in a sequence into the next item. If the sequence is actually being generated in accordance with one of the program's transformations, then this will be detected. If not, the program tries different concatenations of its transformations in an attempt to match the sequence being generated. Simon and Kotovsky proposed their program as an explanation for human problem solving behaviour on intelligence test items. An example is 'Generate the next item in the sequence a, b, c —.' They report a correspondence between the results they obtained from their program and from human problem solvers.

Many writers have remarked upon the mathematical similarity between threshold classification devices, which classify by using linear equations, and the idealized properties of neurons. While some of the models seem plausible, we do not know enough about how the brain works to make a direct test of a sophisticated concept learner at this level. At a more abstract level of 'higher mental processes' similarities have been noted between the Uhr and Vossler and the Hunt *et al.* procedures and data from the psychologist's laboratory. In addition, other programs have been proposed explicitly as models of human performance without regard for their efficiency as concept learners (Baker 1965; Johnson 1964). It seems fair to say that in a well structured situation it is possible to write a computer program which will do considerably better than a human in solving concept learning problems, but when there are possibilities for accepting alternative solutions, or of redescribing the objects in terms of some space other than the originally defined attributes, then good human problem solvers are more capable than any extant computer program.

*See also:* Concept identification–information processing approaches. Computer simulation of human thought processes. Learning machines: a unified view. Pattern recognition.

*Bibliography*

BAKER F. (1965) *Case; A program for the simulation of concept learning*, Proc. Fall Joint Computer Conf., 979.

BLOCK H., NILSSON N. and DUDA R. (1964) *Determination and direction of features in patterns*, in Tou J. and Wilcox R. (Eds.) *Computer and information sciences*, Washington: Spartan Press.

CHURCH A. (1958) *Introduction to Mathematical Logic*, Princeton: The University Press.

HUNT E., MARIN J. and STONE P. (1966) *Experiments in Induction*, New York: Academic Press.

JOHNSON E. S. (1964) *An information processing model of one kind of problem solving*, Psychol. monographs, **78**, whole 4.

NILSSON N. (1965) *Learning Machines*, New York: McGraw-Hill.

ROSENBLATT F. (1962) *Principles of Neurodynamics*, Washington: Spartan Press.

SEBESTEYEN G. (1962) *Decision Making Processes in Pattern Recognition*, New York: Macmillan.

SIMON H. and KOTOVSKY K. (1963) *Human acquisition of concepts for sequential patterns*, Psychol. Rev. **70**, 534.

UHR L. and VOSSLER C. (1963) *A pattern recognition program that generates, evaluates, and adjusts its own operators*, in Feigenbaum E. and Feldman J. *Computers and Thought*, New York: McGraw-Hill.

E. HUNT

**CONCEPT IDENTIFICATION – INFORMATION PROCESSING APPROACHES.** *Introduction.* 'The lowest form of thinking is the bare recognition of the object, the highest the comprehensive intuition of the man who sees all things as part of a *system*' (Peters 1965). This Platonic view emphasizes the hierarchical nature of the many processes by which man imposes order on his world. Psychologists have applied the word concept to any situation in which man assigns discriminably different stimuli to the same response category. The process may be closely related to rote memory, as when various simple patterns are arbitrarily assigned to the class 'letter'. Or it may involve a complex rule, as when the zoologist assigns an animal to the class 'mammal'. This enormous diversity should warn us against any simple theory or equation to summarize the many processes which must underlie such tasks.

In recent years psychologists have begun to uncover a framework which may be adequate to the exploration if not the explanation of the many levels of conceptualization. This framework is informational in the sense that it has emphasized the structural relationships among the stimuli assigned to a common category. Variables which affect the amount of information processed, such as the number of stimuli in a category, the number of relevant and irrelevant dimensions, redundancy, etc., have been of interest. The goal has been twofold. The first goal has been to develop functions relating information variables to the ability of subjects to form and utilize concepts. This has primarily involved laboratory studies of human performance. The second goal has been to identify the processes which man uses in the achievement of that performance. This goal has involved the simulation of concept attainment by computer (Hunt 1962).

This brief review will focus primarily upon empirically determined functional relations. For that reason the emphasis will be upon laboratory studies of human performance, but relevant computer simulation results will also be mentioned. The basic organization is hierarchical in consonance with the taxonomy of tasks implied by the Platonic model. Successive sections will consider rote concepts, pattern recognition, multivariate conceptualization and comprehension. Within each section generalizations are stressed which are relevant to an informational analysis and which are common across levels.

*Rote categories.* The simplest level at which man may form a concept is to assign a set of arbitrary *stimuli* to some category. In this situation, concept learning is very similar to rote learning except that more than one stimulus is mapped into the same response. For example, the stimuli 'A' and 'a' are usually given the same verbal label, although they have no obvious physical similarity. In the same way, instances of the category 'letter of the alphabet' are a set of arbitrary forms. Moreover, it is likely that many concepts which are defined formally by complex common properties of the stimuli are frequently learned and exercised in a rote manner. For example, pig and dog are instances of animal. Clearly there are similarities which exist between the denotations of these words. However, it is often more difficult to state the formal connexion between instances of a category than to make the classification. Thus, when asked to provide a *superordinate* for the word 'dog' it is likely that the rote connexion between the words 'dog' and 'animal' is the basis for the category. For this reason *rote conceptualization* may play a more important role in the human intellect than might at first be supposed.

Studies of information processing of rote categories have concerned: (1) the process of learning the categories, (2) the recall of instances belonging to already formed categories, or (3) speed of classifying familiar instances. The most general results obtained during the process of learning or memorization of the categories indicate that the critical variable is the number of stimulus words which must be assigned (stimulus information). Rate of learning varies relatively little whether instances are assigned to few or many categories (Posner 1964).

The efficiency of assigning many stimuli to one category occurs during the later recall and identification of already learned concepts. It has been shown that the recall of individual words may be increased many fold if the words fit into known categories (Cohen 1963). For recall, the number of categories (response information) into which the words may be grouped, rather than the number of individual words, seems to limit performance. This ability to group words into categories, sometimes called chunking, reduces the limitations of human memory and demonstrates the efficiency of categorization.

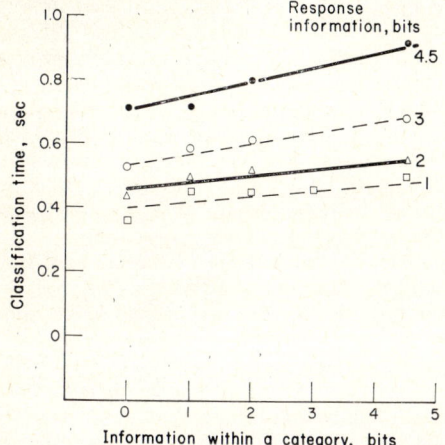

FIG. 1. *Time to classify a familiar word into its superordinate category as a function of the amount of information within the category and the response information. Adapted from Pollack (1963).*

Figure 1 illustrates the effect of varying stimulus and response information upon the time to classify familiar words (e.g. dog) into their superordinate categories (e.g. animal). Both variables are directly related to response speed and their effects are roughly linear. This experiment agrees with many studies in showing that response time increases with information transmitted. It also indicates that in classification of familiar instances the amount of information within a *response* category is an important determinant of performance.

*Pattern recognition.* Both psychologists and computer specialists have been more interested in cases where the stimuli to be assigned to a category have common characteristics. The earliest studies of this type showed that either a common element or a common relationship between elements could serve as the basis of a category. Moreover, after learning to identify instances of such categories, subjects might be completely unable to verbalize the relationship between instances.

In recent years identification of patterns with common properties has come to be called pattern recognition. The study of human pattern recognition involves man's ability to perceive similarity among stimuli, to learn to classify a set of instances and to utilize such learning in the identification of new instances.

Figure 2 illustrates a statistical process operating to distort the digit four. At each successive level of distortion the patterns appear to be more distant from a prototypical 4. It is possible to summarize the level of distortion produced by statistical processes of this type by the average amount of uncertainty which the statistical rule introduces about the location of a given element in the original. For example, a rule which allows a given element to move with equal probability to any of four adjacent positions produces 2 bits of distortion. Experiments show that the level of distortion is linearly related to perceived distance as rated by human subjects (Posner 1964). This relationship holds whether a particular rule

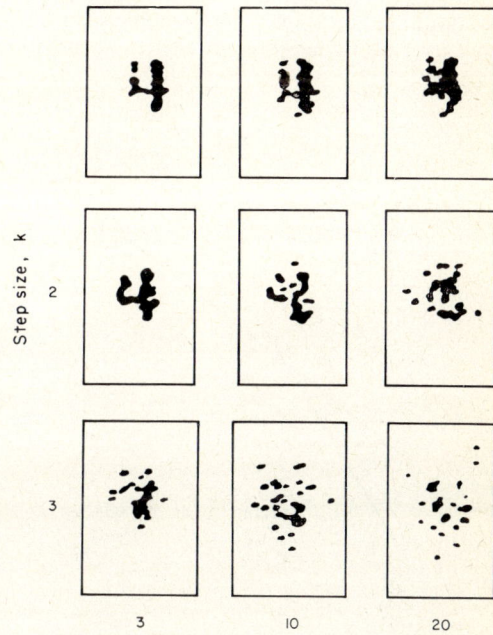

FIG. 2. *Distortion of the digit 4 by a random statistical process. From White (1962).*

leaves many or few elements in common, and appears to depend only upon the average amount of distortion introduced.

The rate at which subjects can learn to identify a set of patterns depends upon the similarity within and between categories. Differences in rate processing continue after errors of identification are eliminated. For example, Fig. 3 shows that the rate at which two patterns, for which subjects had learned a common name, were correctly identified as 'same' depends upon the level of distortion (uncertainty) between the patterns. This relationship between perceptual similarity and recognition speed maintains itself after extensive learning. It takes longer to recognize 'A' and 'a' as *same* than it does 'A' and 'A', while 'C' and 'c' lie in between. These findings, together with the relations discussed in the last paragraph, suggest that the rate of learning to identify a particular set of distortions as instances of a common pattern depends upon the amount of information within the category.

In order to recognize new instances, a subject must somehow match the new stimulus against stored information based upon his prior learning. For unfamiliar or noisy instances this process can be viewed as a serial search process through the stored exemplars. However, for highly overlearned sets, such as digits, the speed of recognition does not seem to depend upon the number of response categories (Neisser et al. 1963). The recognition of new noisy patterns may depend upon the degree of distortion as well as the number of the previously learned exemplars of the category as well as their number. High distortion categories, while difficult to learn, provide the basis for improved transfer to classification of noisy instances.

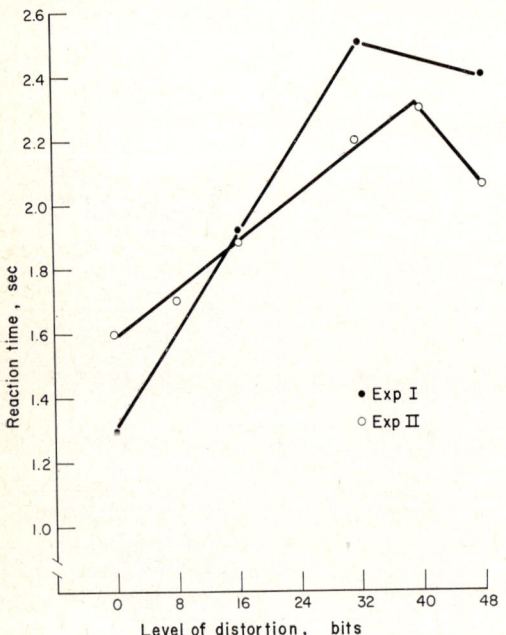

FIG. 3. *Time to recognize two patterns as having the same name as a function of the level of distortion between them (distance). From Posner* (1964).

While laboratory experiments have revealed some of the functional relations governing the difficulty of pattern recognition, they have done relatively little to uncover the details of the stored *features* which make recognition possible. Results in neurophysiology, and in the psychology of perception, have indicated that the brain may be analysing complex figures into sets of simpler configurations, such as straight lines, curves, slants, angles, etc. Efforts to model such processes in computer programs have produced results which compare favorably with human data (Uhr 1966). This approach shows some promise of providing insights into the details of the features which underlie recognition.

*Multivariate concepts.* Some psychologists have chosen to confine the term concept to those cases in which the experimenter is able to state a rule relating positive instances in terms of a combination of known dimensions. This situation is of obvious importance because many natural objects and abstract terms may be thought of as varying along a number of different dimensions. For example, the United States and Mexico are similar in being located in North America, but differ greatly in language and culture. Multivariate concept learning allows transfer of either the relevant dimensions or of the rule relating them. For example, the concept 'tall men' involves a conjunction of values of two relevant dimensions. The concept 'red flowers' involves the same rule but different dimensions, while the concept 'tall or male' involves the same dimensions but a new rule (disjunction).

Laboratory experiments have indicated how varying the dimensions and rules affects the learning of concepts. Figure 4 illustrates the effects of increasing the number of relevant dimensions (response uncertainty) and the number of irrelevant dimensions (noise) upon performance. In general, the difficulty of forming the concept increases regularly with increasing response uncertainty and with increases in the total uncertainty within a category. Providing alternative solutions *(redundant information)* tends to counteract noise and improve performance (Hunt 1962)

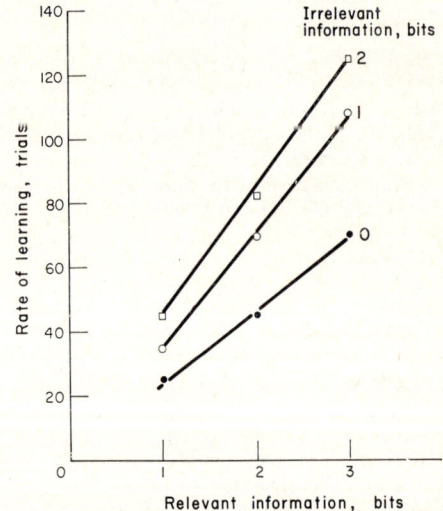

FIG. 4. *Rate of learning a multivariate concept as a function of the amount of relevant and irrelevant information. Adapted from Bulgarella and Archer* (1962).

A number of studies have compared the rate of learning different types of classification rules (Haygood and Bourne 1965). Changing rules may increase the number of dimensions that are relevant to the category, and thus increase the difficulty of forming the concept. Rules which define categories with highly dissimilar instances also tend to be difficult. For example, an exclusive disjunction is difficult because it requires grouping, within the same category, stimuli with one of the two relevant properties, while placing those with both properties in a separate category. Changes in the rule may also vary the frequency of positive instances encountered by the subject. Since subjects tend to extract much more of the potential information from positive than from negative instances (Hunt 1962), this will also affect performance.

Both laboratory and computer simulation studies have formulated and tested various models which might describe the strategies people adopt in multivariate concept learning (Hunt 1962; Reitman 1965). In the simplest such model, subjects are thought to sample randomly from a pool of hypotheses and benefit only from instances which allow them to discard their present hypothesis. Situations of high memory load and low motivation may be found for which the data are fitted by models that credit the human with such low information extraction and storage abilities. More typically, however, subjects use a positive instance as a focus which is actively modified in the light of later evidence. The early trials may be used to gain a general impression of the patterns contained within the positive category, which is then used as the basis for later hypotheses (Hunt 1962; Reitman 1965).

From an information processing viewpoint, multivariate concept formation includes as component functions short and long term memory, pattern recognition, selective attention and the ability to transform relevant information. Different problems are likely to place varying loads on these functions and to be associated with different strategies.

*Comprehension.* Both computer (Reitman 1965; Lindsay 1961) and laboratory (Posner 1965) approaches to concept identification are moving toward an analysis of comprehension. The goal is to understand how stimuli are mapped into cognitive representations which allow the subject to go beyond the information explicitly given in order to evaluate new statements.

The sentence 'all scientists and some others support the test ban' posits an inclusion relation between two elements, scientists and test ban supporters. The comprehension of this sentence is measured by the degree of transfer to new questions which are implied by the information in the relationship. Presumably the ease of comprehension depends upon the number of elements and the structure or rule which relates them, in much the same way as in the multivariate concept experiments. Many sentences, however, require complex rules relying more heavily upon prior experience. The statement 'John is Mary's brother and Jeanne is Mary's sister' implies that 'Jeanne is John's sister,' given some highly familiar rules of family relationships. Computer programs based upon knowledge of short and long term human memory limitations have been designed to make such inferences (Lindsay 1961)

The ease of comprehension depends upon the initial structure and upon the transfer situation. Comprehension requires both memory and the ability to make transformations or inferences from the stored information. Thus errors in answering a new question may be due to inexact memory, to the inability to perform the necessary transformation, or perhaps to interactions between the two (Posner 1965).

A comprehension task for which quantitative analyses are presently available involves induction of the correct state of nature from probabilistic evidence (Edwards *et al*. 1965). When actual probabilities are specified, human performance has been compared with a Bayesian statistical observer. The results of many studies indicate that human induction tends to be more conservative than that of the statistical observer, but that the extent of such conservatism depends upon the average amount of information which is conveyed by the environmental events (Posner 1965). Perception itself may be conceived as a process of induction based on the analysis of serial information (Sokolov 1963).

*See also:* Computer simulation of human thought processes. Concept formation by artificial intelligence. Pattern recognition.

*Bibliography*

BULGARELLA R. G. and ARCHER E. J. (1962) *Concept identification of auditory stimuli as a function of amount of relevant and irrelevant information*, J. Exp. Psychol., **63**, 254.

COHEN B. H. (1963) *Recall of categorized word lists*, J. Exp. Psychol., **66**, 227.

EDWARDS W., LINDMAN H. and PHILLIPS L. D. (1965) *Emerging technologies for decision making*, in *New Direction in Psychology II*, (Newcomb T. M. Ed.) New York: Holt.

HAYGOOD R. C. and BOURNE L. E. (1965) *Attribute- and rule-learning aspects of conceptual behavior*, Psychol. Rev., **72**, 175.

HUNT E. B. (1962) *Concept Learning*, New York: Wiley.

LINDSAY R. K. (1961) *Toward the development of a machine which comprehends*, University of Texas (mimeo).

NEISSER U., NOVICK R. and LAZAR R. (1963) *Searching for ten targets simultaneously*, Percept. Motor Skills, **17**, 955.

PETERS R. S. (1965) *Brett's History of Psychology*, Cambridge, Mass.: M.I.T. Press.

POLLACK I. (1963) *Speed of classification of words into super-ordinate categories*, J. Verbal Learning & Verbal Behavior, **3**, 159.

POSNER M. I. (1964) *Information reduction in the analysis of sequential tasks*, Psychol. Rev., **71**, 491.

POSNER M. I. (1965) *Memory and thought in human intellectual performance*, Brit. J. Psychol, **56**, 197.

REITMAN W. R. (1965) *Cognition and Thought,* New York: Wiley.

SOKOLOV E. N. (1963) *A probabilistic model of perception*, translated in *Soviet Psychology and Psychiatry*, **1**, 28.

UHR L. (1966) *Pattern Recognition*, New York: Wiley.
WHITE B. W. (1962) *Recognition of familiar characters under an unfamiliar transformation*, Percept. Motor Skills, **15**, 107.

M. I. POSNER

## CONCEPTUAL BEHAVIOUR.

### *1. Introduction and Definitions*

*A. Concepts and conceptual behaviour: General.* In ordinary language, the word concept has many connotations, referring among other things to inner images or ideas, to abstract relationships among environmental properties or events, to operations which an organism performs on stimulus inputs, and so forth. Among experimental psychologists, however, the term has come to have a more precise, though somewhat limiting, meaning. Henceforth, we shall understand a concept to be a principle by which all objects or events can be classified into two categories; the categories are labelled examples and non-examples, or positive and negative instances, of the concept.

Conceptual behaviour concerns the learning or the utilization of grouping (or classification) principles. Understandably, then, studies of conceptual behaviour are usually conducted within the framework of a task in which the subject (*S*) must sort or classify a given set of stimulus patterns into categories. The problem for *S* is to learn or to discover an acceptable sorting principle, using information provided by members of the stimulus set and by corrective feedback signals given after each sorting response.

*B. Conceptual structure.* Two structural features of concepts can be isolated. The first is a set of one or more specific, perceptible stimulus properties—those physical characteristics which underlie the necessary distinctions among stimuli. Conventionally, these are called the *relevant attributes* of the concept. The second is a *rule* or relation, specifying the manner in which the relevant attributes are combined in a statement of the concept. For example, consider the concept red triangle, i.e. the class of all things which are both red and triangular. Redness and triangularity are the relevant attributes and the ability to discriminate them from other attributes on the dimensions of colour and shape is obviously prerequisite to learning the concept. But the concept also entails a particular relationship between redness and triangularity, that of conjunction, or joint presence of attributes. Only those stimuli which are *both* red *and* triangular are positive instances. The same pair of attributes might be related by any number of rules, such as disjunction (red and/or triangle) or conditional (if red then triangle), but these of course are quite different concepts.

The foregoing analysis is meant only to illustrate the distinction between fundamental structural features of concepts. Any concept will admit to such an analysis, though it is clear that the description of real-life groupings may involve a wide range of attributes (some of which may be intangible qualities of events) and a variety of highly complex rules. A detailed description of many common conceptual rules has been provided by several authors (Bruner *et al.* 1956; Hunt 1962; Haygood and Bourne 1965).

*C. Types of conceptual problems.* To solve the kind of problem posed typically in experimental work, *S* somehow must learn or discover the relevant attributes and the rule of an unknown concept. While *S* does not necessarily approach the task analytically in such a way as to determine independently the attributes and the rule, his final solution must demonstrate sufficient knowledge of both components.

A conceptual problem can be simplified by converting one of the unknown components to a 'given.' The *S* might be given detailed instruction and pretraining on the rule, thus making the primary requirement a matter of learning or discovering the relevant attributes. Conversely, *S* might be given the relevant attributes during preliminary instructions, and be left with the sole task of determining the rule required to effect a solution. Most experimental studies of conceptual behaviour have employed problems in which the only unknown is the set of relevant attributes. Because the requisite discriminations among attributes (e.g. red vs. green, square vs. triangle) are typically well-known at the outset, solution depends merely on discovery of the relevant discriminations. Thus, *S*'s behaviour in such a task is best described as a selection and test, or identification, process, as opposed to a learning or formative process. Only recently has there been any indication of research interest in tasks which require the learning or discovery of conceptual rules. On the assumption that the rule is a fundamental and learnable component of any concept, it is reasonable to expect a considerable increase in research on rule learning and rule identification.

### *2. Methods Used in the Study of Conceptual Behaviour*

Experimental procedures used in the study of conceptual behaviour almost universally require *S* to discover or infer the correct concept from a series of examples and/or non-examples. While there are many variations, most procedures seem to fall into one of two classes, depending on whether *S* is a passive receiver of stimulus information or has an active role in selecting each stimulus.

*A. Reception paradigm.* The distinguishing aspect of the reception paradigm is that *S* has no control over the selection and ordering of stimuli. On each of a series of trials, *S* is presented with a stimulus, is required to classify it (positive or negative instance), and is told whether his response was correct or not (informative feedback). Trials proceed in this fashion until *S* can show an understanding of the correct classification principle, either by verbal statement or by meeting an arbitrary performance criterion such as 10 or 20 consecutive correct responses. While it is typical to display stimuli successively, allowing S to inspect only one on each trial, some experiments have used a simultaneous presentation procedure. In this method, the entire array of stimulus patterns is visible to S throughout the problem.

Conventional performance measures are the number of errors made, the number of trials taken, or the amount of time needed to reach the criterion of problem solution. In some cases, S is required to verbalize periodically his best guess about the concept at that point in the series. Under these circumstances, other potentially useful measures of performance, such as the compatibility of stated hypotheses with present or previously given information, are available.

*B. Selection paradigm.* Experiments using the selection paradigm begin with the presentation to S of the entire stimulus display (simultaneous presentation). One of these is designated by the experimenter as a positive instance, and S is asked to make a guess, i.e. state a hypothesis, about the concept. From that point on, S is free to choose the stimuli to be examined in any order he wishes. After each selection, the experimenter names its category and S revises (if necessary) his hypothesis. The selection process continues until S can name the correct concept.

This procedure provides much the same performance measures as does the reception paradigm, and in addition, allows for an analysis of possible regularities in the series of stimulus selections and stated hypotheses which might be indicative of S's strategy or plan of attack (Bruner *et al.* 1956).

*C. Procedural details.* The particular mechanics of the experimental task differ widely. The stimuli, usually visual, may be printed on cards or prepared on photographic slides to be projected on a screen. The S's response might be verbal (e.g. yes or no, plus or minus) or might consist of pushing a button to indicate the chosen category. The categories themselves might or might not be labelled by letters, numbers, nonsense syllables, and so forth. Finally, feedback can be given verbally (the experimenter saying 'right' and 'wrong') or by signal lamps placed adjacent to response pushbuttons. There is little or no evidence that any of these variations exert a significant influence on performance in conceptual problems.

It might also be noted that in some experimental problems S is required to learn not one but several problems concurrently. In this case there are several response categories, each representing a different concept. Number of concepts is, of course, a powerful variable determining task difficulty.

*Comment.* It might be noted that experimental tasks have variously been called concept formation, concept attainment, concept learning, concept utilization, concept identification, and so forth, in the literature. Unfortunately, these names do not necessarily distinguish identifiable differences either in methodology or in behaviour. Quite the opposite; all of these names have been applied to experimental tasks which are essentially the same. For practical purposes, they can be used interchangeably.

*3. Research on the Determiners of Conceptual Behaviour*

Variables which have been shown by experiment to affect conceptual behaviour will be grouped under three major headings: (a) structure of the concept to be formed or identified, (b) conditions governing the manner in which S receives information about the concept, and (c) process variables which are characteristic of S. Considerable research has been done on these variables; in the space assigned we can at best illustrate the findings.

*A. Structure of the concept. 1. Conceptual rules.* Nearly all early work (pre-1960) was done with problems utilizing conjunctive (e.g. red triangle) or simple uni-dimensional (e.g. triangular figure) concepts. Recently, however, several studies have appeared which provide a comparison of different conceptual rules. Neisser and Weene (1962) had S's learn two sets of 10 problems each of which represented a different one of 10 uni- and bidimensional (two relevant attribute) rules. They found that non-conjunctive rules are substantially harder to learn than conjunctions, which in turn are harder than uni-dimensional concepts. Most difficult were biconditional ($X$ if and only if $Y$) and exclusive disjunction ($X$ or $Y$ but not both) problems. Essentially the same order of difficulty was reported by Haygood and Bourne (1965).

Neisser and Weene pointed out that the rules can be arranged in a hierarchy representing the complexity of their symbolic expression. Order of rule difficulty is highly correlated with position in the hierarchy. However, it is also clear that problems constructed with the various rules require differing amounts of information for solution, which might account for some significant portion of the effect of this variable. Finally, in an early analysis of this problem, Bruner *et al.* (1956) noted that individuals are most familiar with, and prefer, conjunctive concepts. This analysis was confirmed experimentally by Hunt and Hovland (1960); Wells (1963) subsequently showed that this preference could be altered by training on other rules.

*2. Attributes.* The attributes used in a conceptual problem differ in saliency or obviousness. Such variation might be further compounded with S's predispositions to examine certain kinds of attributes first. These factors combine to affect problem difficulty; when an obvious attribute is relevant, the concept is more easily identified than when the same attribute is irrelevant, i.e. not involved in the concept definition (e.g. Archer 1962).

Bruner *et al.* (1956) report a study in which thematic attributes such as sex, dress, and displayed affect of human figures resulted in poorer performance than did abstract materials (geometric designs) chosen to give the same number of relevant and irrelevant attributes. The results indicated that S attitudes associated with thematic material can interfere with concept attainment.

Stimulus patterns differ in degree of compactness. A highly compacted figure is one in which all dimensions represent attributes of a single object. The opposite extreme is a distributed stimulus where each potentially relevant dimension is represented by a different figure; a commonly used example is a typewritten cluster of letters, each of which may be capital or lower case. Shepard *et al.* (1961) found that concepts defined on compacted stimuli are easier to learn than those represented by distributed stimuli. They assigned this result to two factors: (a) the verbal descriptions are longer for distributed stimuli, which might interfere with verbal learning-processes, and (b) attribute combinations are more obvious when they are part of a single object.

The conceptual problems used in almost all research have been defined on visually presented stimulus material. Lordahl (1961), however, contrasted visual and auditory stimuli for their availability as sources of relevant and irrelevant information. He found that $S$'s perform much more efficiently when the relevant attributes are visual rather than auditory, and further observed that auditory signals are much weaker sources of distraction when irrelevant to the task. On the other hand, Bulgarella and Archer (1962) reported that variation in the number of auditory stimulus dimensions has much the same effect on performance as does variation in visual dimensions. Haygood (1965) contrasted the learning of concepts that were purely visual, purely auditory, and a combination of auditory and visual attributes and observed that bimodal conjunctions were significantly more difficult than those based on either modality alone.

*B. Informational variables.* The amount of information presented to $S$, and the rate at which it is presented, exert profound effects on the ease of learning concepts. The variables to be discussed in this section frequently influence not only the manner in which information is presented, but also $S$'s ability to deal with the information efficiently.

*1. Informative feedback.* Within the paradigms used in this type of research, concept attainment is fully dependent on periodic signals to $S$ about the correctness of his responses. Information provided by these signals has been manipulated in several ways. For example, feedback may be omitted on a certain proportion of the trials or, when $S$ is required to learn several concepts concurrently, he might be told 'wrong' when an error is made, with or without indication of the correct response. Omitting signals or failing to provide corrective information both interfere with performance (Bourne and Pendleton 1958). In the case of signal omission, it is important to note that learning is delayed by more than the number of trials on which no feedback is given.

It is also possible to misinform $S$ as to the correct response. Under these circumstances, the concepts to be learned can be thought of as probabilistic rather than completely determined. Bruner *et al.* (1956) and Pishkin (1960) have shown that $S$'s can identify the relevant attributes, even with up to 40 per cent misinformative feedback. Early investigators found that $S$'s tended to distribute their responses in accord with the probability of correct feedback, a phenomenon which has been called 'probability matching.' That is, if Category A is correct for red triangles 80 per cent of the time, $S$ responds to red triangles with Category A 80 per cent of the time. Bourne (1963) subsequently presented evidence that probability matching in conceptual problems is transitory, and that most, if not all, $S$'s come to respond perfectly in accord with the relevant attributes after a sufficient amount of practice.

*2. Numbers of relevant and irrelevant attributes.* One or more stimulus attributes—the relevant attributes—are involved in the definition of any concept. Stimulus objects to which the concept applies, however, generally have other properties, and these are referred to as irrelevant attributes. The number of different attributes characterizing a stimulus population determines the information load with which $S$ must contend to solve the conceptual problem. Experiments have shown that increases in the amount of relevant information (attributes to be identified) and irrelevant information (attributes to be eliminated) both result in linear increases in problem difficulty (Bulgarella and Archer 1962). Irrelevant information appears to function as does noise in a communication channel. It makes it more difficult to detect or discriminate the relevant dimensions ('signal') from the total stimulus variability ('signal plus noise'). The interfering effects of increasing the number of relevant attributes are generally thought to result from increases in the required memory and information-processing demands on $S$.

*3. Positive vs. negative instances.* It is possible to solve any conceptual problem by inspecting only positive instances or only negative instances, provided $S$ knows the range of possible solutions. Hovland (1952) has shown that negative instances in general convey less information about the concept than positive instances. Thus under ordinary circumstances, $S$'s should learn sooner when given a high proportion of positive instances. However, Hovland and Weiss (1953) reported that more $S$'s attain concepts when presented with sequences of all positive instances than with sequences of negatives or mixed positives and negatives, even when the sequences are equated for informational content. They attributed this finding to greater difficulty in assimilating information from negative instances. Subsequently, Freibergs and Tulving (1961) demonstrated that $S$'s can learn (over a series of problems) to use negative instances as readily as positive instances to solve concept identification problems. While the general phenomenon seems fairly well established, more research is clearly needed. To date, the tasks used in this research have all been based on a conjunctive solution. For other types of rules, such as disjunction, the relative informational value of positive and negative instances is reversed. Thus $S$ might well find it easier to solve these problems with a higher proportion of negative instances.

*4. Stimulus redundancy.* Stimulus redundancy in a concept problem exists when the state of any dimension can be predicted from the state of another dimension or combination of dimensions. In the simplest case, two dimensions might be perfectly correlated, for example red patterns might always be square and green patterns triangular. In more complex cases, the state of the dimension may be contingent on the appearance of specified levels in two or more separate dimensions. Redundancy of relevant information definitely aids performance (Bourne and Haygood 1959). This appears to result primarily from the increased possibilities for solution provided by the fact that more dimensions can be used to solve the problem, though there might also be an increase in solution saliency resulting from the constant repetition of attribute combinations.

Irrelevant dimensions might also be made redundant. Introducing new redundant irrelevant dimensions retard performance, but not as much as introducing the same dimensions independently (Bourne and Haygood 1959).

*5. Memory load.* Successive presentation methods require that $S$ remember information about past stimuli. The ability of most untrained $S$'s to retain prior information is generally so poor that some theoreticians have felt justified in developing mathematical models of concept learning which assume that $S$ cannot remember anything before the last preceding stimulus (Trabasso and Bower 1964). The memory load can be lightened by making available to $S$ a record of past stimuli and their correct categorizations. The effect of increasing the number of past instances available is to improve performance, at least up to about five instances (Bourne *et al.* 1964). As would be expected, simultaneous presentation of all stimuli is superior to successive methods (Cahill and Hovland 1960).

*6. Timing variables.* In a reception problem, a trial usually represents a sequence of three clearly identifiable events: (a) the stimulus, (b) $S$'s response, and (c) informative feedback. The appearance of a new stimulus begins another trial. These events give rise to a set of time intervals which might affect performance.

The first interval, during which $S$ is allowed to observe the stimulus and formulate a response, is normally $S$-paced. Although this interval has on occasion been limited by the experimenter, there is no clear evidence of the effects of doing so. The second interval, the delay of feedback after $S$'s response, was formerly thought to be an important variable over even a brief period; it was reasoned, and some evidence seemed to support the notion, that delay of feedback was analogous to the delay of reinforcement known to be effective with lower animals. Later re-analysis and experimentation showed that delay of feedback over the intervals studied (up to 8 or 9 sec) has no effect on performance (Bourne and Bunderson 1963).

The length of time feedback is given is not known to affect performance. Presumably $S$ gains as much information as is available in the first fraction of a second, and making the signal available over a prolonged period does little to aid performance.

One intratrial time interval is known to have a considerable impact on performance. This is the postfeedback interval—the time between feedback on one trial and the appearance of the stimulus for the next. In one study, the postfeedback interval was varied from 1 to 25 sec (Bourne *et al.* 1965). Performance improved up to a point and then got worse. The point at which improvement stopped depended on task difficulty, being about 9 sec for an easy task (one irrelevant dimension) and about 17 sec for a more complex problem (five irrelevant dimensions). Somewhat similarly, distribution of practice, the interpolation of a rest between blocks of $n$ trials, also improves performance (Oseas and Underwood 1952).

At least two alternative explanations are available for the effect of increasing the postfeedback interval. First, the time might simply permit $S$ to rehearse what he has learned from the preceding trial. Secondly, the interval could permit some kind of neural consolidation or dissipation of inhibition. Evidence to distinguish between these interpretations is as yet lacking.

*C. Variables related to the subject. 1. Motivation.* Of the many variables generally grouped under the heading of motivation, few have been studied in the context of conceptual problems. What work there is has been concerned with anxiety, arousal, or generalized drive, often operationally defined by performance on a psychological test (e.g. Taylor 1953). Wesley (1953) found that anxious $S$'s showed consistently better performance than non-anxious $S$'s on simple unidimensional conceptual problems. In a later study, Romanow (1956) demonstrated little effect of anxiety with concepts of high and moderate dominance (defined as the strength of association between the category label and the particular verbal stimuli in that category). Performance of $S$'s showing high anxiety was considerably worse, however, on problems involving low-dominance (difficult) concepts. In addition, recent experiments have indicated that feedback signals associated with wrong responses have an aversive effect that reduces $S$'s willingness to offer hypotheses about problem solution (Wallace 1964). In general, the data suggest that increased drive can improve performance by causing $S$ to be more alert or 'anxious' about the solution, but can also interfere through distraction. A great deal of research is needed before these effects can be specified in more detail.

*2. Intelligence and age.* In the undergraduate college populations often used to study conceptual behaviour, the correlation between IQ and performance on conceptual problems is near zero (Byers 1963). There appear to be at least two reasons. First, these students represent a highly restricted range of intelligence, a factor which invariably attentuates correlation. Second, the tasks are relatively simple, and ordinarily can be mastered easily by individuals of average and even subnormal intelligence. Thus there is little room for superior $S$'s to demonstrate superior performance.

However, on formal grounds, it is clear that intelligence is related to conceptual behaviour. The relation can be demonstrated empirically with younger $S$'s. Osler and Fivel (1961) report a series of experiments with children of high (above 110) and medium (90 – 109) IQ, of ages 6, 10, and 14 years. Both increasing age and higher IQ were associated with more rapid concept learning.

In addition, the high IQ $S$'s seemed to learn more 'suddenly', or insightfully. In another study, Osler and Trautman (1961) found that for medium-IQ $S$'s, there was no difference between problems utilizing simple stimuli and more complex stimuli. For high-IQ $S$'s, on the other hand, a significant difference was found. These results are interpreted by the authors to mean that high intelligence in children is associated with mediational or symbolic activity which might take the form of hypothesis testing, and result in overt performance resembling insightful problem solution.

The findings of Osler and her associates are similar to those of Kendler and Kendler (1959), who also found evidence that, as children develop, simple associational processes are elaborated into (sometimes) implicit mediational events which permit a degree of 'cognitive' control over overt behaviour.

It is possible and eminently desirable that experimental work on the development of conceptual behaviour in children will prove to be consistent and integrable with the work of Piaget and his associates (see e.g. Flavell 1963). Using observation and interview methods, these workers have uncovered evidence indicating that conceptual behaviour in children emerges in a fixed sequence of stages representing increased complexity of conceptual material that can be handled. There is some indication of an increase in the influence of Piaget on research in the United States.

*3. Prior experience of subjects.* An important determiner of performance efficiency in a conceptual problem is the set of strategies, habits, and attitudes $S$ brings with him to the experimental situation. Strategies differ in efficiency, and Bruner *et al.* (1956) have shown that $S$'s who understand and are able to employ the more efficient strategies exhibit superior performance. Secondly, $S$'s typically have hierarchies of habits for dealing with stimulus materials. Salient attributes such as colour, and simple rules such as conjunction usually are more familiar to, and preferred by, $S$'s, a fact which undoubtedly interferes with performance when other attributes and rules are relevant. These habits and expectations can be modified by experience. For example, Gelfand (1958) reported a facilitating effect of prior familiarization with the relevant attributes of a concept. In addition, as already discussed in connexion with conceptual rules, Wells (1963) showed that the evident preference of naive $S$'s for conjunctive rules can be modified by practice with disjunctive rules. Finally, most studies using more than a single problem have demonstrated a significant improvement in performance from the first problem to subsequent problems, reflecting $S$'s increasing familiarity with, and skill at, the particular task at hand (see e.g. Haygood and Bourne 1965).

*4. Concluding Comment*

In this brief discussion it has not been possible to review the literature with any degree of completeness. Rather, an attempt has been made to provide a representative sampling of research methods and recent empirical findings. The interested reader can find more detailed, and more extensive, coverage of the area in several recent books, including Bruner *et al.* (1956), Hunt (1962), and Bourne (1966). In addition, a consideration of information-processing approaches to conceptual behaviour and quantitative models may be found elsewhere in this volume.

The preparation of this section was facilitated by funds made available from the United States Public Health Service, National Institute of Mental Health (Research Grants MH 08315 and MH 11283), and from the National Science Foundation (Research Grant GB 3404).

*See also:* Concept identification—information processing approaches. Information theory in psychological measurement.

*Bibliography*

Archer E. J. (1962) *Concept identification as a function of obviousness of relevant and irrelevant information,* J. Exp. Psychol., **63,** 616.

Bourne L. E. Jr. (1963) *Long term effects of misinformative feedback on concept identification,* J. Exp. Psychol. **65,** 139.

Bourne L. E. Jr. (1966) *Human Conceptual Behavior,* Boston: Allyn and Bacon.

Bourne L. E., Jr. and Bunderson C. V. (1963) *Effects of delay of informative feedback and length of postfeedback interval on concept identification,* J. Exp. Psychol., **65,** 1.

Bourne L. E., Jr., Goldstein S. and Link W. E. (1964) *Concept learning as a function of availability of previously presented information,* J. Exp. Psychol., **67,** 439.

Bourne L. E., Jr., Guy D. E., Dodd D. and Justesen D. R. (1965) *Concept identification: The effects of varying length and informational components of the intertrial interval,* J. Exp. Psychol., **69,** 624.

Bourne L E., Jr. and Haygood R. C. (1959) *The role of stimulus redundancy in the identification of concepts,* J. Exp. Psychol., **58,** 232.

Bourne L. E., Jr. and Pendleton R. B. (1958) *Concept identification as a function of completeness and probability of information feedback,* J. Exp. Psychol. **56,** 413.

Bruner J. S., Goodnow J. J. and Austin G. A. (1956) *A Study of Thinking,* New York: Wiley.

Bulgarella R. and Archer E. J. (1962) *Concept identification of auditory stimuli as a function of amount of relevant and irrelevant information,* J. Exp. Psychol., **63,** 254.

Byers J. L. (1963) *Strategies and learning set in concept attainment, Psychological Reports,* **12,** 623.

Cahill H. E. and Hovland C. I. (1960) *The role of memory in the acquisition of concepts,* J. Exp. Psychol. **59,** 137.

FLAVELL J. H. (1963) *The Developmental Psychology of Jean Piaget*, New York: Van Nostrand.
FREIBERGS V. and TULVING E. (1961) The effect of practice on utilization of information from positive and negative instances in concept identification, *Can. J. Psychol.*, **15**, 101.
GELFAND S. (1958) Effects of prior associations and task complexity upon the identification of concepts, *Psychological Reports*, **4**, 567.
HAYGOOD D. (1965) Audio-visual concept formation, *J. Educ. Psychol.*, **56**, 126.
HAYGOOD R. C. and BOURNE L. E., Jr. (1965) Attribute and rule learning aspects of conceptual behavior, *Psychol. Rev.* **72**, 175.
HOVLAND C. I. (1952) A "communication analysis" of concept learning, *Psychol. Rev.*, **59**, 461.
HOVLAND C. I. and WEISS W. (1953) Transmission of information concerning concepts through positive and negative instances, *J. Exp. Psychol.*, **45**, 165.
HUNT E. B. (1962) *Concept learning: An information Processing Problem*, New York: Wiley.
HUNT E. B. and HOVLAND C. I. (1960) Order of consideration of different types of concepts, *J. Exp. Psychol.*, **59**, 220.
KENDLER T. S. and KENDLER H. H. (1959) Reversal and nonreversal shifts in kindergarten children, *J. Exp. Psychol.*, **58**, 56.
LORDAHL D. S. (1961) Concept identification using simultaneous auditory and visual signals, *J. Exp. Psychol.* **62**, 282.
NEISSER U. and WEENE P. (1962) Hierarchies in concept attainment, *J. Exp. Psychol.*, **64**, 644.
OSEAS L. and UNDERWOOD B. J. (1952) Studies of distributed practice: V. Learning and retention of concepts, *J. Exp. Psychol.*, **43**, 143.
OSLER S. F. and FIVEL M. W. (1961) Concept attainment: I. The role of age and intelligence in concept attainment by induction, *J. Exp. Psychol.*, **62**, 1.
OSLER S. F. and TRAUTMAN G. E. (1961) Concept attainment: II. Effect of stimulus complexity upon concept attainment at two levels of intelligence, *J. Exp. Psychol.*, **62**, 9.
PISHKIN V. (1960) Effects of probability of misinformation and number of irrelevant dimensions upon concept identification *J. Exp. Psychol.*, **59**, 371.
ROMANOW C. V. (1958) Anxiety level and ego involvement as factors in concept formation, *J. Exp. Psychol.* **56**, 166.
SHEPARD R. N., HOVLAND C. I. and JENKINS H. N. (1961) Learning and memorization of classifications, *Psychological Monographs*, **75**, No. 13 (Whole No. 517).
TAYLOR J. A. (1953) A personality scale of manifest anxiety, *J. Abnorm. Soc. Psychol.*, **48**, 285.
TRABASSO T. R. and BOWER G. (1964) Memory in concept identification, *Psychonom. Sci.*, **1**, 133.
WALLACE J. (1964) Concept dominance, type of feedback and intensity of feedback as related to concept attainment, *J. Educ. Psychol.*, **55**, 159.
WELLS H. (1963) Effects of transfer and problem structure in disjunctive concept formation, *J. Exp. Psychol.* **65**, 63.
WESLEY E. L. (1953) Perseverative behavior in a concept-formation task as a function of manifest anxiety and rigidity, *J. Abnorm. Soc. Psychol.*, **48**, 129.

R. C. HAYGOOD and L. E. BOURNE, JR.

**CONTROL: BASIC ELEMENTS.** Automatic control theory has its origin in the consideration of certain simple devices such as the Watt Governor and the common ball valve. Scientists became interested in the fact that in certain circumstances a device designed to effect a steady condition might, instead, cause violent oscillations. Thus, theoretical investigation of stability and instability, based on a mathematical formulation of the problem, is the beginning of modern control theory. The development of radar and automatic devices for the control of gun fire in the Second World War provided an immense stimulus to further thought. The cessation of hostilities disclosed to the industrial and academic world an impressive array of devices and a wealth of technological knowledge, with no immediate purpose. Whereas in war-time the spirit of progress had been severely pragmatic, with the return of peace it soon became highly theoretical. Much of the new development was influenced by Norbert Wiener who brought his great mathematical talent and prestige to bear in asserting that the problem of production was virtually solved; that the means were already at our disposal to replace human toil, both physical and mental, by automative agencies. The rapid post-war development of computers and also of atomic power soon led to the concept of computer control for industrial plant.

Meanwhile, detailed theory, of a predominantly mathematical character though pursued mainly by engineers, had been making steady progress. The basic control concept is that of an error actuated device. That is to say, if a certain quantity associated with a 'plant' to be controlled has a value $c$ whereas it ought to have a value $r$, appropriate physical means may be provided to apply a signal proportional to this difference ($e = r - c$), to operate on a plant in order to reduce this difference $e$ to zero. Such a means constitutes a controller of a simple type known as a proportional controller. Alternatively, it is possible to apply a signal of the form $\int e \, dt$. Such a signal has the property of increasing with time, so long as the error exists. Yet a third type of controller applies a signal proportional to $de/dt$. These three types may be combined into a single 'three-term' controller, the action of which may be represented mathematically by the expression:

$$k_1 \int e \, dt + k_2 e + k_3 \frac{de}{dt}.$$

Commercial controllers representing this mathematical expression and operating by pneumatic, hydraulic or electrical means constitute the basic control devices available to industry.

A more complex adaptive situation would be one in which the controlling condition is a function of a set of past measurements. A system which records, calculates and acts on the results of calculations based on past records would be called a *learning control system*. A major problem in such systems is to design for economic use of recording media, and automatic access thereto.

In a more general sense a system may be said to be *self-organizing* if it can effect substantial alteration in its own structure in response to some change of circumstance. This concept appears to represent the ultimate development of control theory. It suggests problems lying beyond the scope of practical endeavour.

Although modern control theory is pre-eminently mathematical in character, it differs from mathematics itself in that mathematics is not restricted by any kind of material consideration, whereas the subject matter of control theory is essentially governed by technological and economic limitations. This circumstance has given rise to the criticism that the mathematician may be called upon to apply the most precise tools of mathematical analysis to a situation that is governed in the first instance by matters of expediency.

This paradox may be illustrated by the simple example of a domestic electric toaster. As a matter of practical convenience and economy the toaster is designed to be controlled by a timing device not directly related to the piece of toast itself. If the problem of optimum performance of a toaster were to be treated theoretically, however, it would be necessary to define an optimum condition of a piece of toast, perhaps in terms of the uniformity of tone and the colour of the bread surface. It would then be necessary to provide a multiplicity of sensing elements to monitor the toast and to determine its deviation from the prescribed condition. Whether adequate substitutes for the human eye, or indeed, the nose, exist is doubtful. Assuming such devices to be available it is still necessary to define the constitution of the bread to which they are to be applied, since a given condition of the exterior will imply a predetermined condition of the interior only in the case of a standard product. To cater for different kinds, sizes and thicknesses of bread would require an adaptive or learning toaster of most elaborate kind.

A domestic toaster no doubt differs greatly from an oil-refinery, but considerations of economy and expediency apply to the latter case also. A like question of the availability, cost and reliability of sensing devices is of paramount importance. Optimizing of cost cannot be divorced from cost of optimizing. This consideration may properly engender caution in relation to the mathematical investigation of control problems.

The primary justification of mathematical investigations is that the execution of large scale technological projects on a purely experimental basis is impracticable for both economic and safety reasons. Furthermore, the plant when constructed may be too complex and too dangerous to be controlled manually. Moreover, the difference between average and optimal performance may be so great as to make modern control techniques mandatory. Yet a further justification, which may ultimately prove paramount in the industrial field, is that automatic control destroys dependence on 'long runs' as it becomes possible to switch the plant from one mode of operation to another, eliminating the need for time consuming manual resetting, with the facility to drive the plant, without delay, into a state of maximum efficiency.

*See also:* Adaptive control theory. Contro, onoff.

J. A. FORMBY

## CONTROL BY HYBRID COMPUTERS.

### Introduction

Computers can assist in control tasks in a number of ways, but not all the applications can be called 'computer control systems'. The possible approaches range from periodic off-line calculations to continuous on-line closed-loop control under dynamic and changing conditions. The benefits of computer control both from an economic standpoint as well as from the improvement in control performance possible are now well established and are supported by evidence derived from well over 800 on-line computer control systems installed and operating around the world.

The principal logic behind the use of a computer to control a process is that irrespective of the lack of precision with which variables are measured, the ability of the computer to manipulate the data rapidly and consistently is so superior to that of a human being, that some improvement in the operation of the process is inevitable. Naturally, the improvement will be greatest when the mathematical model of the process is known to the fullest degree and when ideal instrumentation exists. Thus computational speed and the exactness and authenticity of the model of the process are the key requirements of a successful computer control system. Combined with the high reliability that present day electronic technology can endow, thus eliminating the need for redundancy, computer control systems can be a profitable investment.

Computers used in these systems can be pure analog, pure digital or hybrid computers depending upon the complexity and the nature of the control task. Pure *analog control computers* have been successfully applied to the control of processes where the control strategy is known in advance and the absence of complexity in the control requirements permits low cost, small size on-line installations. Among these are applications of analog computers to the control of the internal reflux and feed enthalpy of distillation columns, the control of product composition in stirred-tank chemical reactors, and the control of end-point tapping temperatures of Basic-Oxygen Steel Furnaces. Their significant advantages lie in their low cost, their *compatibility* with existing analog instrumentation and ready acceptance of this form of local control by plant personnel. They suffer from the disadvantage that they cannot handle the more complex control requirements of complete plants and are incapable of carrying out *data-logging* and *plant-scheduling* operations.

Pure *digital computers* have been used very widely for the control of entire steel and chemical plants and can cater for the very complex control situations involving optimization procedures, with the added ability of dealing with background tasks such as the automatic *monitoring* and logging of plant data and programmed plant scheduling, *sequencing* and *supervisory operations*. They, however, often do not meet the combined requirements of high computational speed coupled with the automatic *tailoring of the mathematical model* representing the *dynamic behaviour* of the *process*. It is to circumvent these limitations of the individual computer types and to combine their advantages that hybrid computers are now rapidly coming into the scene of computer control. The unique combination made possible by bringing together the best characteristics of both types of computer, gives the hybrid computer the ability of operating at extremely high speeds and at high accuracies—requirements demanded by the ever increasing complexity of the control tasks of today.

The purpose of this article is to introduce the basic elements of the modern hybrid computer, to point out the areas where it is needed, to examine the types of computer control systems and to illustrate the role of the hybrid computer in various industrial applications. It is envisaged that as the techniques of computer control are developed and refined and more operating experience of installed systems is acquired, its application will be extended to such plants as chemical reactors, oil refineries, steel mills, cement mills, power stations, paper mills, rubber factories, and food processing plants.

## The Elements of Hybrid Computers for Process Control

Present day hybrid computers are made up of existing general purpose analog and digital computers linked together to afford intimate data and control communication between the two basically different types of machine. The digital computer can be characterized as a *sequential machine*. That is, it operates on the digits representing its instructions and numbers in a step-by-step manner with great precision, so that each computation at one instant in time depends upon the result of the computation at the previous time step. Since the same parts of the computer are used over and over again in a computational sequence, there is no need for a multiplicity of units. The organization of a digital computer is such that it would simply comprise of three main sections (Arithmetic, Memory and Input/Output) which are time-shared by a fourth section (Control) (see Fig. 1).

In contrast to the above, the analogue computer can be characterized as a *parallel machine* with a multiplicity of computing components operating in concert. It is not solely a computer for continuous variables, but is a parallel assembly of building blocks: *integrators, multipliers, function generators* etc. for continuous variables as well as *flip-flops, logic gates, binary counters* etc. for

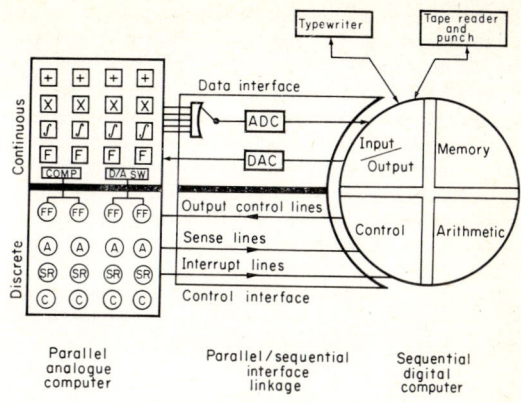

Fig. 1

discrete variables. It is organized for convenient representation of an 'analogous' physical system by means of a computer model constructed of these building blocks. Its characterization is parallel because all parts of the computational process take place simultaneously so that solutions are generated continuously rather than in a step-by-step manner (see Fig. 1). Because of this its overall computational speed can be considerably faster than that of the digital computer.

The *interface* between the digital and analog computers is intended to match and resolve the significant disparity between sequential and parallel operations. The difference between continuous voltage and discrete number is simply one of *format* and presents no fundamental problem since appropriate format converters can always be found. The real disparity of importance is that in part of the hybrid machine, many operations are taking place simultaneously while elsewhere a sequence of operations take place one at a time in a repetitive manner, so as to effect the generation of problem variables *as if* they they occurred simultaneously.

With the above points in mind, it becomes possible to formulate the basic requirements for each part of the hybrid system.

*Digital computer*. For effective use within a hybrid system the digital computer:

1. must have sufficient high internal speed for it to *appear* as though a number of calculations were taking place simultaneously.
2. must be internally organized for maximum speed in executing mathematical calculations, especially in a floating-point format.
3. must have efficient means for input and output of data *during* calculation and must include many levels of *interrupt* capability.

Some basic specifications pertaining to a digital computer intended for hybrid operation can be summarized as:

*Speed.* This is a function of memory access time and multiplication speed. Ferrite core storage gives access times of between 0·75 and 2 $\mu$secs. This means that addition times range between 1·5 and 4 $\mu$sec. Multiplication and division take longer, generally 10 to 30 $\mu$sec. Overall program speed can be increased by the use of *index registers* and a minimum of 4 is very desirable. Special instructions for subroutine entry, for executing commands out of sequence, and for testing and skipping can help increase computing speeds.

*Memory.* 8–12,000 *words* of *core memory* would suffice for most hybrid control computer applications. It should, however, have the capability of expansion to 16,000 words.

*Word structure.* A binary word of at least 24 bits gives a dynamic range of $10^6$ when the effects of round-off errors are included. *Floating-point* capability should preferably be a *hardware* rather than a *software* feature as the latter can be costly in program speed. Decimal format and character oriented machines do not offer any advantage in hybrid computation.

*Input/output.* A minimum data transfer rate of 500,000 words per minute is called for. For control applications no elaborate high-speed printer or card reader is necessary. The minimum requirement in peripheral equipment is a high speed paper-tape reader and punch and a fast automatic typewriter.

*Analog computer.* The common measure of a large analog computer is that it has 100 to 200 operational amplifiers. Analog computer features that are important for hybrid systems can be listed as:
— Integrators with electronic mode control and multiple time-scales.
— Amplifiers for *tracking* and *storing* voltages.
— Automatic, remote control and setting of *potentiometers*.
— Fast, accurate multipliers (typical accuracy 0·015 per cent, typical bandwidth 25 kc/s).
— High speed comparators with logic signal outputs.
— Analog switches under control of logic signals.

*Digital-analog interface linkage.* There are two basic requirements of the digital-analog interface:
 1. To provide data communication via format converters between the parallel and sequential machines.
 2. To provide intimate two-way control between the two machines.

1. Data communication is effected through three kinds of devices; the digital-to-analog converters (DAC) the analog-to-digital converter (ADC) and the multiplexer for time-sharing the ADC among many analog channels.

DAC—13-bit + sign binary input providing an analog output in the range ±100 volts, with an accuracy of 0·01 per cent. Total conversion time per word should be of the order of 10–50 $\mu$sec.

ADC—Analog input in the range ±100 volts produces a 13-bit + sign binary number equivalent with an accuracy of 0·025 per cent. Typical conversion time should be of the order of 4–10 $\mu$sec.

Multiplexer—Up to 128 analog channels and having a settling time of 8–12 $\mu$secs per channel.

2. The *control interface* should provide a fast and flexible means for communicating control signals to and from the analog computer. Three kinds of control lines are usually provided.

 (i) Output control lines—a condition in the digital computer program is communicated to the parallel logic on the analog.
 (ii) *Interrupt* lines—a condition in the parallel logic program interrupts the digital computer and causes it to transfer to another subroutine. This feature allows time-sharing of the digital computer among many job tasks.
 (iii) *Sense* lines—the digital computer sends out a sense signal to test the existence or absence of some condition on the analog.

*The Areas of Computer Control where Hybrid Computers are Needed*

The forté of the digital computer is the solution of algebraic equations. If the equations are *explicit*, the calculation time is easily determined. *Implicit* equations ofter require a variable length of time. Numerical integration comes as an incidental by-product of the computer's power in solving algebraic problems. Time is the only penalty. If the high precision is not needed, the integration is better done by the analog computer, for the solution of ordinary *non-linear differential equations* is its strong feature. Implementation of non-analytic, non-linear functions, such as limits, backlash, deadzone, hysteresis and arbitrary functions are amenable by both techniques, but analog is certainly more economical. For functions of two or more variables, multivariate function generator programs on the digital computer are generally used. Logic equations, decision and control functions and sequencing operations can usually be shared between parallel logic and digital computer programs depending upon the speed and complexity requirements. The solution of partial differential equations in the representation of *distributed systems* is cumbersome by either computer alone. Hybrid computers, however, can make substantial improvements in the efficiency and speed with which these systems are executed, by retaining the continuous integration facilities of the analog computer in one space dimension and solving for the other dimensions by numerical integration on the digital machine. Complex boundary conditions and complete sets of intermediate solutions can also be readily handled with hybrid computers.

With these general problem solving characteristics in mind it is not difficult to isolate the areas of computer control suited to hybrid computers. In fact, with many of the applications falling into the classes tabulated below, hybrid computers prove to be the only way of meeting the combined high-speed, *real-time*, high-precision and data-processing requirements of present-day and future *on-line* control tasks.

*Main areas for control by hybrid computer and the division of tasks between the analog and digital parts of the hybrid computer*

| Category | Control requirement | Division of control tasks | |
|---|---|---|---|
| | | Analog | Digital |
| I | Wide range of signal frequencies and precision | High frequency, low accuracy parts of the control requirement. | Low frequency, high accuracy parts of the control requirement. |
| II | Model-Reference Adaptive Control Systems | Fast reference model of system dynamics economically and conveniently performed by Analog. | Optimisation, curve-fitting and hill-climbing routines. |
| III | Fixed Strategy Control Systems | Rapid computation of predetermined Control Strategy. | Data monitoring, logging and production scheduling operations. |
| IV | Statistical Data Analysis for On-Line Model Building in Control | Preprocessing of statistical data and implementation of resultant model Transfer Functions. | Final processing of statistical data and PARAMETER SEARCH routines for determination of mathematical model |

## Types of Computer Control Systems with Applications

In the systems for which Computer Control is applicable, the computers receive data from process instruments, perform calculations to determine the best operating conditions, and transmit the results to *set-points* of conventional controllers. Alternatively, the control computer outputs can be applied directly to the actuators of the plant, thereby eliminating the need for conventional controllers. It is instructive to examine the *four* main types of computer control situations that are feasible. Industrial process plants are chosen for the purposes of comparison of the different types possible.

### Type 1. *Off-line computer control*

In an OFF–LINE Computer Control situation, readings from process instruments and results of laboratory analyses are collected by an operator and entered into the computer as data for control calculations. The results of these calculations from the computer are typed out and used as the basis for adjustments of process conditions. A typical example of the use of a system of this type is in the calculation of the charging of raw materials into the top of a *blast furnace*. Because raw material characteristics on the hot metal do not change frequently, no justification can be made for connecting the control computer on-line to the furnace. However, since these 'burdening' calculations must be carried out very accurately, a computer is needed. The use of the computer now allows more comprehensive calculations to be made to incorporate the part played by each raw material in meeting requirements for hot metal production, end-point tapping temperature, total slag volume, base-acid ratio, and sulphur and phosphorous content.

Another application of an off-line system appears in the use of a special purpose analog computer for the calculation of optimum *lengths of billet* in a rolling mill to minimise back-end wastage. The total length of the bloom, the mill-reduction factor and the flying shear tolerances are entered into the computer as potentiometer settings. A scanning system built into the computer enables the computation to proceed automatically and display the optimum cut billet length in order to eliminate back-end wastage. The operator sets the flying shear to the value displayed by the computer.

Type 1 systems have limited use and very few applications can justify a general purpose computer. To date, special purpose computers have largely dominated the scene in this type of control situation.

### Type 2. *On-line open loop—Computer linked to Controllers*

In this type of application, the computer receives its information from an operator reading the process instruments, but is connected on-line to the process so that it exercises direct control of the process. The in-built capacity for directly controlling the process from instructions fed in by the operator implies that the computer will act as a program or sequence controller where the control strategy is determined in advance. The programmed sequence of operations are entered as punched cards by the operator and the computer initiates a series of calculations according to a previously stored control strategy to compute the best operating conditions pertaining to these demands. One possible application falling under this heading is in the use of a digital computer applied to type composition and printing. The programs can then be easily extended to include the automatic operations of copy preparation, editing and preparing material for final publication.

Another example of such a computer control system is the automatic *control of optimum blending* operations at least cost in a mill producing animal feedstuffs, in order to satisfy certain constraints placed upon the level of the nutrients in the feed-mix. A fully analog system is both possible and economical in this application. For a particular animal feed a specified number of ingredients (such as wheat, maize, fish, meat, etc.) containing constituent parts (such as oil, protein, energy, etc.) which are of nutritional significance, are to be blended together. The problem posed is that, given the current prices of each of the ingredients and upper and lower constraints placed upon the ingredient and constituent levels in the mixture, what is the optimum blend of ingredients which will satisfy all these constraints and do so at minimum cost of the mix. It will be recognized that this is a problem in *Linear Programming* and can be readily and rapidly solved by an analog computer. The mathematical tool utilized in this application is through the use of the Method of Steepest Descent for achieving the optimum solution at least cost. This application thus falls under Category III for Hybrid Computer Control since the control strategy (Steepest Descent) is determined in advance.

A set of linear constraints on $n$ constituent levels can be expressed in functional form by the $n$ equations of the type

$$b_{i_{max}} > f_i(x_1\ x_2\ x_3\ \ldots\ldots\ x_m) > b_{i_{min}}$$
$$i = 1, 2, 3 \ldots\ldots n. \quad n \leq m$$

where $x_1\ x_2 \ldots x_m$ represent the quantities of the $m$ ingredients. It is now required to minimize a Cost function $C(x_1\ x_2 \ldots x_m)$, subject to the above constraints. Furthermore, the variables $x_i$ are not allowed to be negative as they represent quantities of raw material. The above equation is first transformed to $n$ pairs of conditional equations

$$f_i(x_1\ x_2\ \ldots\ x_m) - b_{i_{min}} = \begin{cases} E_{i_{min}} \text{ if the inequality is violated} \\ 0 \text{ if the inequality is satisfied} \end{cases}$$

$$f_i(x_1\ x_2\ \ldots\ x_m) - b_{i_{max}} = \begin{cases} E_{i_{max}} \text{ if the inequality is violated} \\ 0 \text{ if the inequality is satisfied} \end{cases}$$

$$i = 1, 2, 3 \ldots\ldots n.$$

In order to satisfy all these $2n$ constraints, we seek to minimize $(S)$ the sum of the squares of the errors $(E_i)$

$$S = \sum_{i=1}^{n} (E_{i_{max}} + E_{i_{min}})^2.$$

This can be realized alongside the condition for minimizing the cost function, by implementing the $m$ Steepest Descent equations, viz.

$$\frac{dx_j}{dt} = -\sum_{i=1}^{n} G_i E_i \frac{\partial E_i}{\partial x_j} - K_i \frac{\partial C}{\partial x_j}$$
$$j = 1, 2, 3 \ldots\ldots m$$

where $G_i$ determines the rate of convergence towards a *feasible* solution and $K_i$ determines the rate of convergence from a feasible solution to an *optimum* solution corresponding to minimum cost. Implementation of these Steepest Descent equations not only ensures rapid convergence, but guarantees stability of the matrix under all circumstances. Figure 2 shows the mechanization of this type of linear programming problem for solution on an analog computer. For the sake of clarity the flow-diagram is illustrated for a simple 3 ingredient, 3 constituent problem. In practice overall accuracies for a realistic $30 \times 20$ L.P. matrix is of the

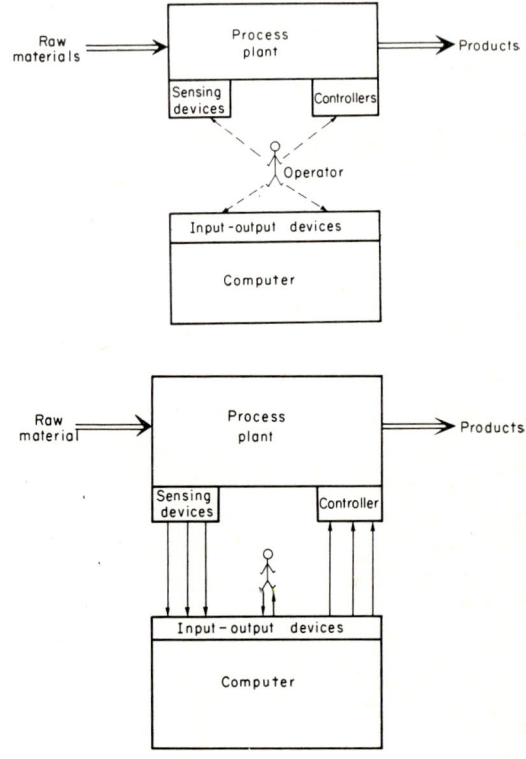

FIG. 2. *Analog program for optimum feed formulation.*

order of 0·1 per cent and is adequate for the purpose for which it is intended.

| Constituent | Ingredient | | |
|---|---|---|---|
| | Wheat | Maize | Fish |
| OIL | $b_{1\ max} > a_{11}x_1 + a_{12}x_2 + a_{13}x_3 > b_{1\ min}$ | | |
| PROTEIN | $b_{2\ max} > a_{21}x_1 + a_{22}x_2 + a_{23}x_3 > b_{2\ min}$ | | |
| ENERGY | $b_{3\ m\ x} > a_{31}x_1 + a_{32}x_2 + a_{33}x_3 > b_{3\ min}$ | | |
| | $x_1 + x_2 + x_3 = 100\%$ | | |
| COST | $C = c_1 x_1 + c_2 x_2 + c_3 x_3$ | | |

The data pertaining to 30 ingredients each analysed into its 20 constituent parts, is entered into a typewriter which automatically sets up the potentiometers on the machine and thereby fixies the composition matrix for the particular foodstuff in production at the time. Data from the mill and prior nutritional knowledge enables the operator to set in upper and lower constraints placed upon the ingredients and constituents in the mix.

For example, it may be desired to limit the contribution of wheat to a maximum of 25 per cent of the mix due to the low level of wheat in stock. Or the protein content in the feedmix should not be allowed to fall below 15 per cent in order to maintain the nutritional value of the feed. Lastly, the current prices per unit ton of the ingredients are entered into the computer. When all this data is complete, the computer will automatically seek the optimum blend to satisfy all these restrictions at minimum cost. Because of the speed of the analog computer, these results are produced almost instantaneously. The outputs of the computer giving the ingredient levels required are already in analog voltage form so that, with only simple amplification, it would be capable of directly setting the actuators in the mill that regulate the ingredient batches at each mix cycle.

*Type 3. On-line open-loop—Computer linked to sensing devices*

In this type of operation the full capabilities of a general purpose digital computer can be exploited. The computer is essentially used for data logging, and supervisory functions and operator guide calculations. Process instruments are connected via appropriate analog-to-digital converters directly to the computer inputs.

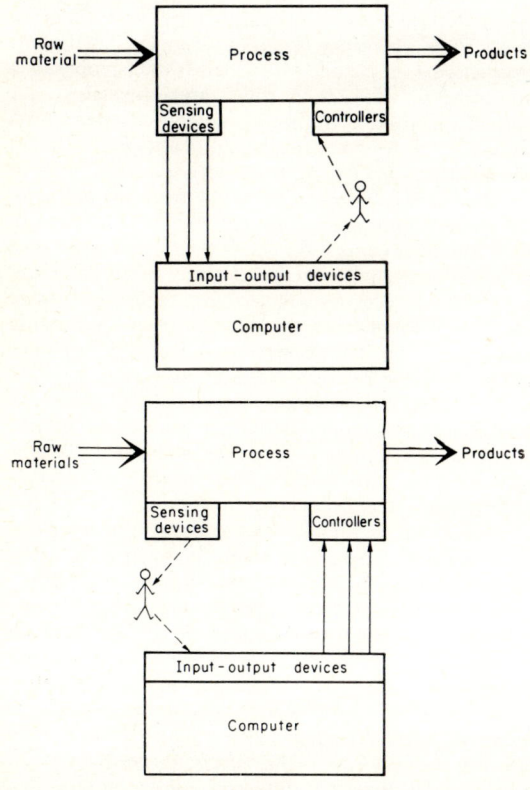

Fig. 3.

The outputs are the data as it stands or functions of the original inputs such as yields or efficiencies acting as guides or criteria of performance which may help the operator to adjust the process to achieve better operation of the plant. The loop is closed, so to speak, via the human operator. It is often possible to combine with the data-logging function much more complex computations in order to ascertain various characteristics of plant behaviour. Figure 4 shows a typical flow chart for a digital computer program combining the functions of data-logging, sequence control and the calculation of reactor parameters in a nuclear power-plant under computer control. In effect the computer continually traverses the outside loop, watching a clock and comparing the actual time with the scheduled time (stored in memory) for the performance of each function. When these times arise the program leaves the main loop, goes into a subroutine to perform the required operation, resets the time at which this operation should be repeated and returns to the main loop. Data obtained through the logging capabilities of the computer will permit verification and modification of approximate relationships before they are used to define an appropriate control scheme. Additional data collected while the system is operating can be used to bring the relationships up to date. Through this evolutionary procedure, a control policy has been developed which has effected significant improvements in the operation of the power plant when ultimate closed loop control was eventually adopted. The calculations involved with the determination of reactor parameters is carried out with the objective of producing a mathematical model of the transient behaviour of the reactor by statistical measurements. Perturbation phenomena taking place naturally in the cores of nuclear reactors manifest themselves as random fluctuations in neutron population density or as changes in core reactivity due to minute movements of control rods. If this reactor noise is continually measured and statistical analyses of these random fluctuations is carried out, considerable information regarding reactor behaviour can be obtained. For example, system time-delays, impulse responses and propagation velocities of the reactor can be derived from the cross-correlation of the time-series of the random fluctuations using known mathematical relationships. Furthermore, complete transfer functions describing steady-state behaviour and stability criteria of the neutron kinetics can be obtained from the autospectra and system phase lag measurements providing the computation can be performed. The information so gained can assist in the construction of a model of reactor behaviour enabling a control policy to be formulated which could lead to optimum computer control of the reactor under adverse transients in its operating cycle.

*Type 4. On-line closed-loop computer control*

In an On-Line Closed-Loop Computer Control system, the computer reads and records process instruments, uses these to calculate the best operating condi-

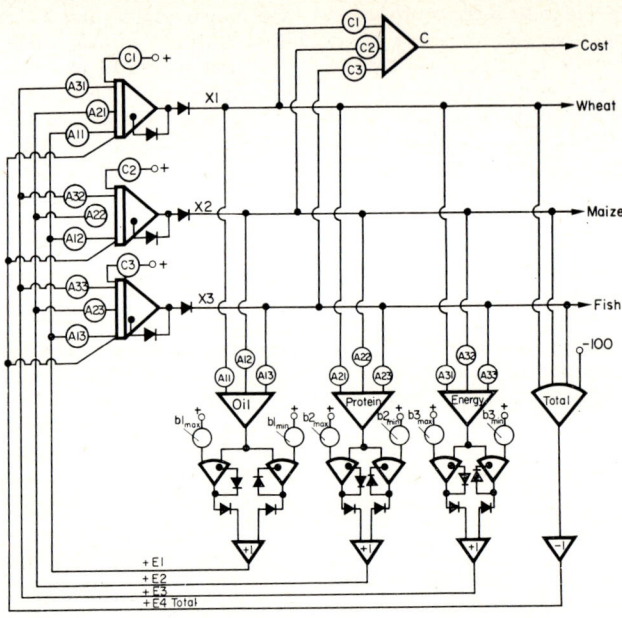

Fig. 4. *Flow-chart for Type 3 computer control of a nuclear power plant.*

tions and based on the results of these computations, makes continuous adjustments to the controllers of the plant automatically. The role of the manual operator is that of overseer rather than controller. He receives information on performance of the entire system via a typewriter output on scheduled times, on demand or when some operating condition is violated. His only interaction with the plant is to modify system objectives according to instructions which are unrelated to the correct operation of the process-computer system. Thus a complete order-book for the automatic production of the plant product can be entered via punched tapes or punched cards. In emergencies, the operator can assume control from the computer. The need for closed-loop computer control systems is established when operating and/or environmental changes occur so frequently *and* the decisions and necessary adjustments to be made depend on such complex relationships that a human operator cannot respond correctly in the time available. Random disturbances in the plant machinery are inevitable. In addition, raw material characteristics, chemical compositions, equipment efficiencies, ambient conditions and product specifications change from time to time in an unpredictable way. As with any process improvement, the justification for installing a computer control system is found in better operation, measured in turn by increased production, higher yields, better product quality or reduced raw material and utility costs. Upon these factors will depend the economic considerations for the size and extent incumbent in a computer control system.

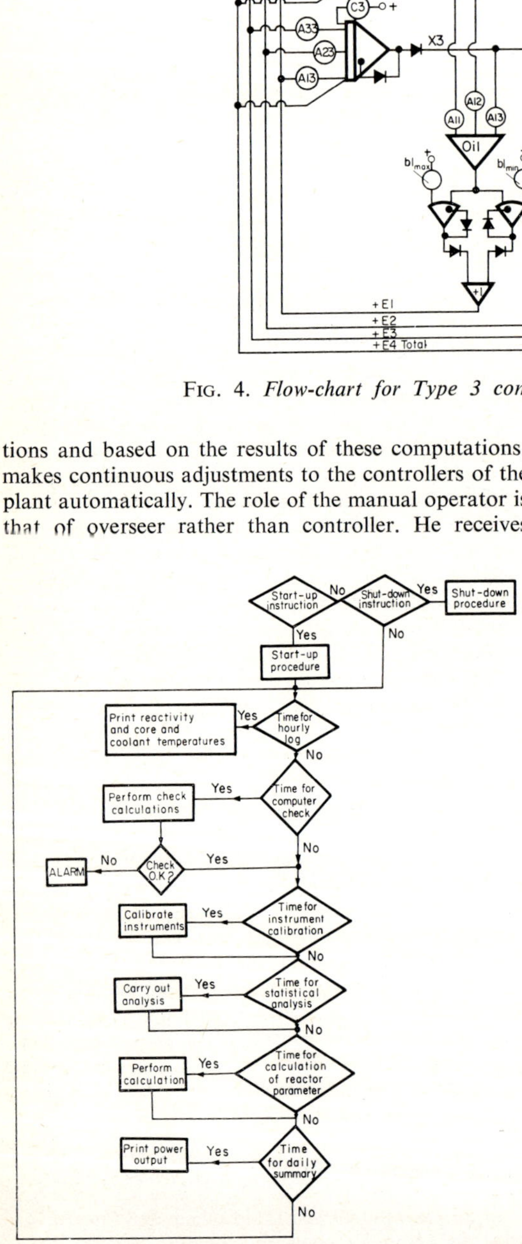

The degree of success of such a closed loop system relies upon the depth with which knowledge of the input/output relationships between many process variables are known. This is the most important, but at the same time the most difficult, aspect of closed-loop control. The relationships can be theoretical or empirical

Fig. 5

and can be best developed by a combination of theory and operating data. Theory indicates what variables are involved and gives the form of the functional relationships between these variables, while operating data permits evaluation of model parameters which are not easily fixed by theory. In many cases the computer has the added facility for alleviating certain measurement problems. For example, in a Distillation Column, it may be necessary to control the internal reflux which cannot in itself be measured. By carrying out the computations involved in heat, material and enthalpy balances using measurements made external to the column, it is possible to obtain a measure of the internal reflux for control purposes.

ing *and* kiln temperature profile is called for, and the success of one determines the success of the other.

The benefits yielded by on-line closed-loop computer control are:

1. Constant cement composition is maintained at a higher quality.
2. Higher kiln production rate.
3. Kiln lining life is appreciably lengthened, materially reducing time between overhauls.

A proposed hybrid computer control scheme is also included in Fig. 6. The analogue computer part of the hybrid system performs the feed-blending optimization computations in a few seconds, while the digital compu-

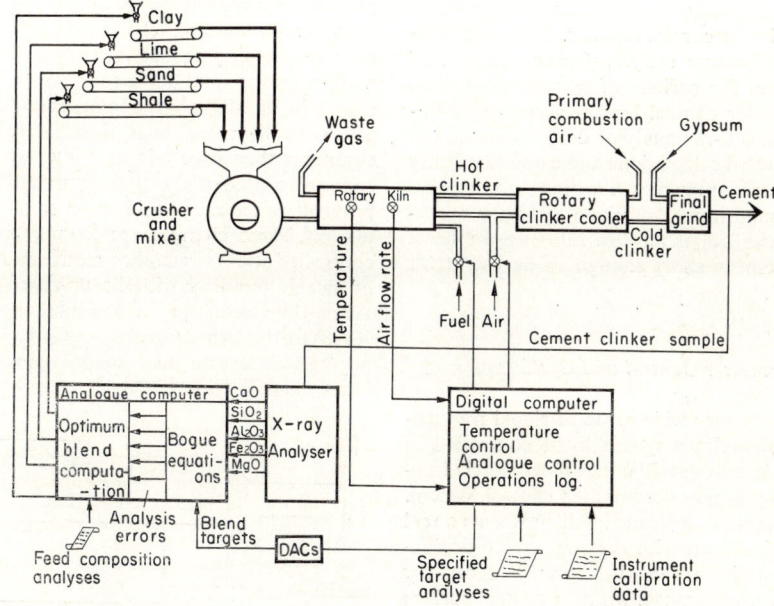

FIG. 6. *Closed-loop hybrid computer control of cement plant.*

A proposed application of a closed-loop computer control system employing both feed-forward and feed-back control is in the *production of cement*. Figure 6 shows the operations involved in the manufacture of cement employing a rotary-kiln. Raw materials flow in at one end and heat at the other. The raw materials react during their passage through the kiln and become the product. A major consequence of this is that acceptable cement can only be made if the feed of raw materials is controlled to within fine limits. Cement kiln blending systems are characterized by high material hold-ups and long delays in conveyor belt response. Both of these characteristics imply difficult control by conventional means. Furthermore, unexpectedly high temperatures cause formation of glasses in the kiln, resulting in slagging and reduction of through-put. If temperature is controlled and feed composition changes, the same thing can happen. Computer control of both feed-blend-

ter implements the feed-back control calculations needed to adjust the heat energy input to the kiln based upon measurements of air-flow rate. In addition it performs the function of overall supervision and control of the analog computer modes, as well as keeping an operations log of the plant. Furthermore it has the added capacity of being able to deal with major upsets in plant operation. For example, if a raw material feeder should fail, it is likely that the specified target blend cannot be achieved with the available raw materials. The feed-blending calculations on the analog are then instantly modified by the digital computer when this upset is detected, so as to do the best that is possible by distributing the unavoidable error evenly among the targets, on a nearly equal percent of-target basis.

Data on the oxide composition analysis of the raw materials (clay, lime, sand and shale) are initially entered into the analog computer. The analogue outputs of this computer provide the optimum feed quantities and directly set the actuators of the raw material weighfeeders at each cycle. At regular intervals of 30 seconds, a sample of the product cement clinker is also automatically analysed into its five constituent parts, on-line, using a high-speed X-ray analyser, to a precision of about 0·3 per cent. Target blend specifications, entered into the digital computer, give the required percentages of $C_3S$, $C_2S$, $C_4AF$, $C_3A$ and MgO in the manufactured cement. Empirical relationships established by Bogue enable these specifications to be algebraically related to the oxide composition of the kiln feed. This is readily performed by the analog computer and any discrepancies between these and the actual oxide composition from the X-ray analyser will generate error signals. These will in turn modify the optimum computations of the feed-rates in the correct manner. The control so achieved is stable because the *feed-forward* control of raw material caters for periods of normal operation, and carries the major control load, whereas the *feedback* control via the X-ray analyser double checks and trims the feed-forward calculations and caters for faulty feeders, inaccurate instrument calibration and poor estimates of bin composition. Additionally, kiln temperature profile is controlled via air-flow rate measurements whose time-constant is short enough to be useful for feed-back control.

## Adaptive Computer Control and Optimization

The presence of a very wide range of signal frequencies or time-constants in a system to be controlled in real time is the one characteristic that most clearly indicates the need for a hybrid computer control system. The long range flight of a ballistic missile presents a real time control environment with the position co-ordinates describing its trajectory varying by 0·001 cycles per second over most of the range, whereas control surface forces and the local dynamics of the missile may have transient frequencies as high as 100 c/s. Furthermore, a large discrepancy exists in the computational accuracy requirements between these two aspects of this problem. Navigational computation and the storage of aerodynamic data such as air-density functions, require high precision and deals with slowly changing variables. These functions are naturally best suited to the digital computer. However, *transfer-functions* of control mechanisms, such as actuators, the local aerodynamic equations of motion and the representation of non-linearities such as back-lash, dead-zone and hysteresis all exhibit rapidly changing characteristics and are more economically done on the analog computer. This is an application falling under category I in the table.

Computer control of high performance aircraft operating over wide ranges of speeds and altitudes calls for a high speed of adaption in the control system to correct for unanticipated changes in environment and aircraft operating characteristics. A scheme of adaptive control that is gaining wide acceptance, is that based upon the use of a high speed *reference model* of the system behaviour. The provision of a fast reference model enables prediction of future transient performance from measurements of past performance. The use of a hybrid computer for such a closed-loop application combined with parameter optimization based upon well established hill-climbing routines, is illustrative of the area listed as category II in the table.

Because speed of adaptation is of importance here, fast models of the aircraft dynamics and the controller are simulated on the analog computer and the response of these reference models to pilot inputs are evaluated in an iterative manner at the rate of hundreds of solutions per second. The parameters ($\lambda$) of the controller are subject to adaptation by an optimization parameter search program implemented on the digital computer (see Fig. 7.) The response of the high-speed reference analog model is compared with actual aircraft response and the errors between these two are stored in the digital computer. Based upon the errors generated by many high speed solutions, the digital computer then proceeds to carry out its optimization routine to predict the optimum changes in controller parameters required to improve some index of performance. These changes are then applied to both the controller and its reference model and the iterative sequence is repeated with its up-dated parameters. An adaptation technique as presented by Whitaker *et al.* (1958) for the yaw control system of a supersonic transport gives rise to a dual adaptive process outlined in block diagram form in Fig. 7.

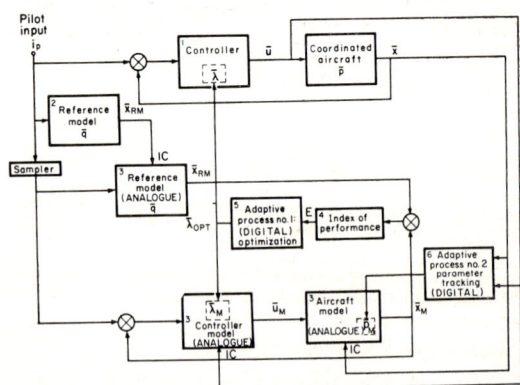

FIG. 7. *Fast reference model hybrid adaptive control system block diagram.*

Here again, a hybrid control computer is needed to deal with the combined requirements of high-speed modelling and parameter optimization. Adaptive process No. 1 is an automatic optimization program which computes $\partial E/\partial \lambda$ and the optimum value of $\lambda$. Adaptive process No. 2 is a parameter tracking program which calculates optimum parameter values ($\bar{p}M$) for the aircraft model based on measurements of actual system performance. A single index of performance $E$ was based on the integral of the error between the desired and demanded yaw angular velocity $W$.

### Conclusions

This article examined the role of hybrid computers in on-line control situations. The basic elements of the present day hybrid computer were presented and the typical specifications for a hybrid computer for On-line computer control applications laid down. The four main areas where hybrid computers are needed and the division of the main tasks between the analog and digital parts of the computer were described. This division capitalises on the high-speed and ease with which non-linear differential equations describing the behaviour of the system to be controlled, is implemented on the analog computer *and* on the efficiency and high degree of automation that the digital computer displays in executing complex control tasks such as optimization, using hill-climbing and parameter search routines. Data monitoring and logging, and production scheduling operations come as a useful by-product of the digital computer's ability to carry out stored program sequences. The four main types of computer control systems covering the entire spectrum from off-line to on-line closed-loop control were described and illustrated with examples in the nuclear power, the iron and steel, the feed-blending and the cement manufacturing industries. Model reference adaptive computer control systems show the greatest promise for hybrid control and this was elaborated through an example describing the high-speed adaptive control of a supersonic transport.

*See also:* Control, hierarchical. Control of aircraft as two non-interacting systems. Control of an economic system.

### Bibliography

FINNIGAN F. E. et al. (1963) *Modern Process Control*, Science and Technology, May.
HALBERT P. W. *Hybrid Simulation of an Aircraft Adaptive Control System*, E.A.I. Applications Study, 3.4.5h.
MARR G. R. (1965) *Cement Kiln Feed-Blend Computer Control System*, E.A.I. SAG Report, October.
NORONHA L. G. (1964) *Hybrid Computation in the Process Industry*, Process Control and Automation, July.
PURI N. N. and WEYGANDT C. N. (1963) *Multivariable Adaptive Control Systems*, I.E.E.E. Trans., May.
STOUT T. M. and ROBERTS S. M. (1960) *Some Applications of Computer Control in the Iron and Steel Industry*, Iron and Steel Engineer, March.
WHITAKER H.P. et al. (1958) *Design of Model-Reference Adaptive Control Systems for Aircraft*, Report R-164, Instrumentation Lab. M.I.T., September.
WITSENHAUSEN H. S. (1962) *Hybrid Techniques Applied to Optimisation Problems*, Spring Joint Computer Conference Proceedings, May.
*Combined Feedforward Feedback Control of a Chemical Reactor*, E.A.I. Applications Study, 6.4.3m.
*The Internal Reflux Computer*, E.A.I. Applications Study, 6.4.2m.

L. NORONHA

## CONTROL BY THE MAXIMUM PRINCIPLE.

*1. Introduction.* There is a very large class of situations in which a number of decisions are to be made—perhaps at the same time, perhaps sequentially—which affect the outcome of a particular process, and the problem arises: how to make the best possible decisions. One of a variety of mathematical techniques might be used (for example: game theory, decision theory, mathematical programming) according to the nature of the process and of the decision variables, and despite their differences, these techniques will have certain fundamental concepts in common. The 'maximum principle' is such a technique, tailored to the needs of a particular type of problem occurring in the context of control of dynamic systems.

*2. The problem.* A multiple-input, multiple-output system (Fig. 1), whose dynamic behaviour is described by a known set of ordinary differential equations, is to be guided, by suitable manipulation of the inputs during the period of operation, from some initial state to some final state. What program of inputs will achieve this in the best possible way?

The following elements are required for a proper formulation of this problem:
*(i) The input vector.* This is the collection

$$u(t) = \{u_1(t), u_2(t), \ldots u_m(t)\} \qquad (1)$$

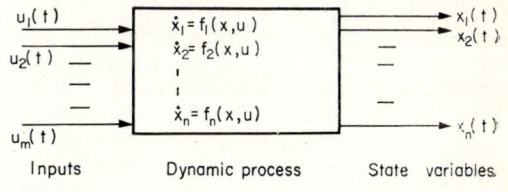

FIG. 1

of relevant input, or 'control' variables, corresponding to those variables of the physical system which are under our immediate control, and their range of variation will generally be subject to some restrictions of the type

$$A_i \leq u_i \leq B_i \quad i = 1, 2, \ldots, m. \qquad (2)$$

*(ii) The state vector.* This is the collection

$$x(t) = \{x_1(t), x_2(t), \ldots x_n(t)\} \qquad (3)$$

of the dependent variables of the system, which are controlled, directly or indirectly, by $u(t)$, according to the differential equations

$$\dot{x}_1 = f_1(x(t), u(t))$$
$$\dot{x}_2 = f_2(x)t, u(t))$$
$$\vdots$$
$$\dot{x}_n = f_n(x(t), u(t)) \quad \left(\dot{x} = \frac{dx}{dt}\right) \quad (4)$$

(Any $n$th-order differential equation can be written as a set of $n$ first-order equations.)

The 'state variables' $x_j$ might also be subject to restrictions on their range.

(*iii*) *Boundary conditions.* The initial and terminal states $x(0)$, $x(T)$ must be specified, either by completely defining each component:

$$x_1(o) = a_1 \quad x_1(T) = b_1 \quad \text{etc.}$$

or, generally, by giving $(q+r)$ algebraic equations

$$S_\alpha(x(0)) = 0 \quad \alpha = 1, 2, \ldots q \leq n. \quad (5a)$$
$$T_\beta(x(T)) = 0 \quad \beta = 1, 2, \ldots r \leq n. \quad (5b)$$

This allows the $n$ components of state $(n-q)$ degrees of freedom at $t = 0$, and $(n-r)$ degrees of freedom at $t = T$, i.e. the initial and final states are merely required to lie on hypersurfaces of dimension $(n-q)$, $(n-r)$, respectively.

(*iv*) *The performance criterion.* Some criterion must be given, according to which one input program $u(t)$, $0 \leq t \leq T$, can be regarded as 'better' than another. This will be a scalar of path-integral form

$$\int_0^T L(x(t), u(t)) \, dt \quad (6a)$$

evaluated along the path $x(t)$ corresponding to the input $u(t)$, or a terminal-point function

$$P(x(T)), \quad (6b)$$

the optimum input function being that which minimizes (or maximizes) the criterion.

(*i*) and (*ii*) are determined by the nature of the system; the engineer's role here is comparatively passive—he simply describes the system—though he must decide which variables are relevant, which can be safely neglected, and what degree of approximation is acceptable in constructing the equations. (*iii*) and (*iv*), however, allow him greater freedom to prescribe how the system is to behave, but, as ever, the price of correspondingly greater vigilance must be paid to prevent this freedom from becoming a source of grave error. For example: a machine must start up as rapidly as possible; we specify a required terminal state (velocity, say) and a criterion $T$, to be minimized. This achieved, the problem is over, yet the machine will continue to run, probably unstably, and we must not forget to specify another control regime for $t > T$, or the mathematical problem will not be a correct reflection of real requirements.

A more common pitfall lies in setting a problem which can have no solution. For example: a rocket with given amount of fuel can achieve a maximum height $H_1$. Suppose the problem is posed, to reach $H_2$ with least fuel consumption; if $H_2 > H_1$ the boundary condition cannot be met, regardless of the performance criterion: if $H_2 = H_1$ there is a solution, but the question of minimization of fuel does not arise. Only for $H_1 > H_2$ is the problem properly posed.

Further, it may occur that the problem is underspecified, admitting many solutions: if it is desired, for instance, to minimize a 'miss-distance' from a target $c$:

$$P(x(T)) = |x(T)-c|^2$$

while in fact it is possible to achieve $x(T) = c$ by a variety of paths, then the problem as posed does not really involve any minimization. Thus, for any 'completely controllable' system, which can always be made to travel between any pair of points in finite time, a terminal point criterion is meaningless, unless the available control is restricted.

Assuming that the problem is properly posed, we may restate it as follows: given a dynamic system (4), and a performance criterion (6a) or (6b), determine the input vector function (1) satisfying restrictions (2) over the interval $0 \leq t \leq T$, such that the corresponding solution (3) of (4) satisfies the boundary conditions (5a) and (5b) in such a way that the performance criterion achieves an optimum (i.e. maximum or minimum) value.

3. *The maximum principle.* The 'maximum principle' provides a straightforward technique for solving this problem. The procedure varies slightly according as the criterion is an integral or a terminal-point function, but both eventualities can be accounted for by taking for our criterion

$$\left\{\int_0^T L(x(t), u(t)) \, dt + P(x(T))\right\} \quad (7)$$

and setting either $L$ or $P$ identically equal to zero in the ensuing equations. ((7) is itself a valid criterion: it is legitimate to sum a number of different criteria—perhaps with relative weighting factors—to obtain an optimum compromise between conflicting requirements.) Define variables

$$\{p(t) = p_1(t), p_2(t), \ldots, p_n(t)\} \quad (8)$$

satisfying differential equations

$$\dot{p}_i = \frac{\partial L(x, u)}{\partial x_i} - \sum_{j=i}^{n} p_j \frac{\partial f_j(x, u)}{\partial x_i} \quad (9)$$

with boundary conditions

$$p_i(0) = \sum_{\alpha=1}^{q} \mu_\alpha \frac{\partial S_\alpha(x(0))}{\partial x_i} \quad (10a)$$

$$p_i(T) = -\frac{\partial P(x(T))}{\partial x_i} + \sum_{\beta=1}^{r} \gamma_\beta \frac{\partial T_\beta((x(T))}{\partial x_i} \quad (10b)$$

where $\mu_\alpha, \gamma_\beta$ are undetermined constants.

Construct the function

$$H(x, p, u) = -L(x, u) + \sum_{i=1}^{n} p_i f_i(x, u) \quad (11)$$

then the optimum input $u(t)$ at each instant must satisfy

$$\max_u H(x, p, u) = 0 \quad (12)$$

which, solved for $u$, gives

$$u = u(x, p). \quad (13)$$

The problem of minimizing a functional (6) with respect to a function $u(t)$ has been replaced by that of maximizing a function (11) with respect to a variable—or rather, a number of independent variables, the components of $u$. (The reversal min → max is not essential: we could just as well define $H = L + \sum p \cdot f$ and change the boundary value (10b) to $p_i = +(\partial P/\partial x) + \ldots$, then (12) would become min $H = 0$, and the sign of $p$ would be reversed throughout.)

If the criterion is simply $P(x(T))$, $L$ vanishes in (9) and (11), which do not involve $P$, so that the function $u(x, p)$ —the optimum control—is the same for all terminal point criteria. The influence of a particular criterion enters via the boundary conditions.

4. *Two important examples.* (i) *The linear regulator.* The system is

$$\dot{x}_1 = x_2$$
$$\dot{x}_2 = ax_1 + bx_2 + u, \quad (4')$$

(equivalent to $\ddot{x}_1 - b\dot{x}_1 - ax_1 = u$).

The system is to run for a fixed time $T$. Since this makes the problem time-dependent we shall introduce time as a third state variable, thus

$$\dot{x}_3 = 1.$$

Starting from

$$x_1(0) = A \quad x_2(0) = B \quad x_3(0) = 0,$$

we wish to choose $u(t)$, $0 \le t < T$ to minimize

$$\tfrac{1}{2} \int_0^T (x_2^2 + u^2) \, dt. \quad (6a')$$

The terminal constraint is simply

$$x_3 = T$$

(9) becomes

$$\dot{p}_1 = -ap_2$$
$$\dot{p}_2 = x_2 - p_1 - bp_2$$
$$\dot{p}_3 = 0. \quad (9')$$

The boundary condition functions are

$$S_1 = x_1 - A = 0$$
$$S_2 = x_2 - B = 0$$
$$S_3 = x_3 \quad = 0 \quad (5')$$
$$T_1 = x_3 - T = 0 \quad (5b')$$

$$\therefore \quad p_1(0) = \mu_1; \quad p_2(0) = \mu_2; \quad p_3(0) = \mu_3$$
$$p_1(T) = 0; \quad p_2(T) = 0 \quad p_3(T) = \gamma_1 \quad (10')$$

$$\max_u \{-\tfrac{1}{2}(x_2^2 + u^2) + p_1 x_2 + p_2(ax_1 + bx_2 + u)\} = 0 \quad (12')$$

$$\frac{\partial H}{\partial u} = -u + p_2 = 0$$

$$\therefore \quad u = p_2. \quad (13')$$

Substituting this optimum value into the system equations we could solve explicitly the simultaneous equations for $p_1(t)$, $p_2(t)$, $x_1(t)$, $x_2(t)$ finally obtaining $u$ as an explicit function of time. However, it is more useful in this case to note that the structure of the equations implies that $p(t)$ is a linear function of $x(t)$,

$$\therefore \quad p_1(t) = k_{11}(t) x_1(t) + k_{12}(t) x_2(t)$$
$$p_2(t) = k_{21}(t) x_1(t) + k_{22}(t) x_2(t) \quad (14)$$

Substituting (14) into (9'), and using (4') and (13') we obtain

$$(\dot{k}_{11} + ak_{12} + ak_{21} + k_{12} k_{21}) x_1 +$$
$$+ (\dot{k}_{12} + k_{11} + bk_{12} + ak_{22} + k_{12} k_{22}) x_2 = 0 \quad (15)$$
$$(\dot{k}_{21} + k_{11} + ak_{22} + bk_{21} + k_{21} k_{22}) x_1 +$$
$$+ (\dot{k}_{22} + k_{12} + k_{21} - 1 + 2bk_{22} + k_{22}^2) x_2 = 0.$$

Since this is true for all values of $x$, the coefficients of $x_1$, $x_2$ in (15) are identically zero, giving differential equations for the parameters $k$, which can be solved numerically, using the boundary values

$$k_{11}(T) = k_{12}(T) = k_{21}(T) = K_{22}(T) = 0$$

obtained from (10') and (14). We now have the system shown in Fig. 2. The same argument extends to the general $n$th order linear system with a quadratic performance criterion. Note that for steady-state operation, $T \to \infty$, $\dot{k} \to 0$, the equations derived from (15) are algebraic, not differential, and the feedback coefficients are constants, as in classical feedback design.

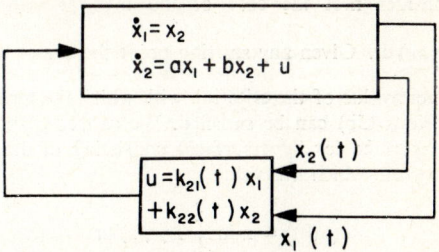

Optimum linear regulator

Fig. 2

(ii) *Linear optimum-time control.* Using the system (4') we pose the problem of reducing the system to rest at the origin, from a given initial state, in least time. We impose the constraint

$$-1 \le u \le +1$$

without which it would be possible to reach the terminal point in arbitrarily short time, using arbitrarily large values of $u$.

The criterion is
$$\min x_3(T)$$
where $T$ is implicitly defined by the two constraints
$$T_1: x_1(T) = 0$$
$$T_2: x_2(T) = 0$$

The initial constraints are
$$S_1: x_1(0) - A = 0 \quad S_2: x_2(0) - B = 0 \quad S_3: x_3(0) = 0$$
Now
$$\dot{p}_1 = -ap_2$$
$$\dot{p}_2 = -p_1 - bp_2 \qquad (9'')$$
$$\dot{p}_3 = 0$$
$$\max_u [p_1 x_2 + p_2(ax_1 + bx_2 + u) + p_3] = 0$$
$$\therefore u = \begin{cases} +1 & p_2 > 0 \\ -1 & p_2 < 0 \end{cases}$$
$$p_1(T) = v_1 \quad p_2(T) = v_2 \quad p_3(T) = -1.$$

The boundary values for $p$ remain undefined — we have four boundary conditions on $x_1$, $x_2$, sufficient to solve the four equations for $x_1$, $x_2$, $p_1$, $p_2$; (the equations for $x_3$, $p_3$ can be solved independently). The general solution for $p$ is immediately found, since the $p$-equations (9'') are decoupled from the $x$-equations, and we can derive the important result that if the eigenvalues are real, $p_2(t)$ is a function which cannot change sign more than once, so that the input switches at most once. In general, for an $n$th-order linear system with real eigenvalues, at most $(n-1)$ switches are required for optimum-time control.

5. *Geometric interpretation of the maximum principle.*
In section 3 the variables $p$ and the function $H(x, p, u)$ were introduced without explanation, but their role can be interpreted geometrically.

Consider first the case of the integral criterion, $\int_0^T L(x, u) \, dt$. Given any starting point there will be an optimum value of the criterion with which the terminal conditions (5b) can be satisfied. We can construct an entire surface (or hypersurface) consisting of starting points from which this value
$$J(x(0)) = \min \int_0^T L(x, u) \, dt$$
is the same, and the equation
$$J(x) = \text{const.}$$
actually describes such a surface. Thus, in Fig. 3, all optimum trajectories starting from $S_1$ have the same 'cost' $c_1$.

Now any optimum path has the property that the *actual* rate of increase of the criterion-value — viz. $L(x, u)$ — along it, is equal to the rate of increase of the *optimum*

criterion value, $-dJ/dt$, and it cannot, of course, be less than that.
$$\therefore \quad \min \left[ L(x, u) + \frac{dJ}{dt} \right] = 0$$
$$\text{or} \quad \min \left[ L(x, u) + \sum_{i=1}^{n} \frac{\partial J}{\partial x_i} \frac{dx_i}{dt} \right] = 0$$
$$\text{or} \quad \max \left[ -L(x, u) - \sum \frac{\partial J}{\partial x_i} f_i(x, u) \right] = 0$$
using (4).
Comparing this with (11), we can identify
$$p_i = -\frac{\partial J}{\partial x_i},$$
i.e. $p$ is the negative gradient of the constant-criterion surface. The equations (9) give the values of these gradients along the optimum trajectory as the trajectory crosses successive surfaces at the rate $-dJ/dt$.

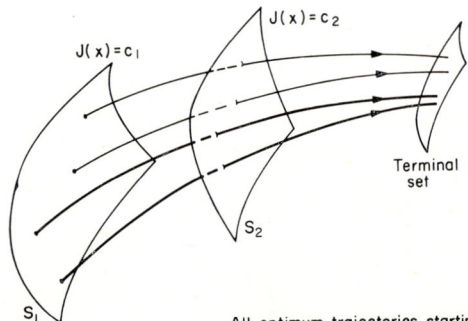

All optimum trajectories starting from $S_1$ have same criterion value, $C_1$

FIG. 3

For a terminal-point criterion, the problem is correctly posed, as explained in section 2, only if it is known that certain states cannot be reached, and the meaning of the problem is: 'go as far as possible towards minimizing the criterion'. This implies that the optimum terminal point will be at the very limit of those states which can be reached, i.e. on the boundary of the 'reachable set'. This point gives the criterion an optimum value, and this value is attainable from all points $x$ on the optimum trajectory: indeed it is attainable from all points on a surface described by
$$J(x) = \text{constant},$$
where
$$J(x) = \min P(x(T))$$
and
$$x(T) = x_0 + \int_0^T f(x, u) \, dt.$$

Our trajectory is entirely embedded in this surface, and from it it is impossible to get to points from which a smaller value (less than optimum) is attainable. Thus
$$J(x(t + \delta t)) \not< J(x(t))$$

or
$$\min \frac{dJ}{dt} = 0$$
$$\min \sum \frac{\partial J}{\partial x_i} f_i(x, u) = 0.$$

Comparing with (11) for $L(x, u) = 0$, we again identify $p$ with the negative gradient of the constant-criterion surface, which in this case also plays the role of the boundary of the reachable set.

6. *The two-point boundary-value problem.* By maximizing $H(x, p, u)$, $u$ is obtained as a function of $x$ and $p$. Substituting this into the system equations for $\dot{x}$ and the 'adjoint' equations for $\dot{p}$ we obtain a set of $2n$ differential equations in $2n$ variables with $2n$ boundary conditions (5) and (10). (Although (5) and (10) constitute $(2n+q+r)$ conditions, the $(q+r)$ constants $\mu$ and $\nu$ remain undetermined, and are eliminated.) These equations would appear to be solvable, at least numerically, enabling us to set up the control system of Fig. 4.

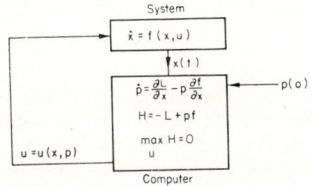

Guidance scheme based on the max. principle. But impractical owing to ignorance of p(o).

FIG. 4

Unfortunately an insurmountable difficulty arises: in order to solve differential equations numerically, initial values are needed as a starting point. In our problems only $n$ boundary values appear at $t = 0$, the others apply at $t = T$, so that $n$ of the equations have no starting points. This arises in all cases, and is inherent in the very principle of computing control for a process over an entire interval, for in computing the very first step some account must be taken of where the trajectory is going. Thus nothing can be done at $t = 0$ without using some information for $t = T$. There is clearly no way of directly overcoming this problem—at best we can circumvent it by some approximation technique.

7. *Computing techniques.* The most direct way of avoiding the issue would be to replace the 'unsolvable' problem by another, less intransigent one, sufficiently close to the original to yield satisfactory results. The simplest course is to linearize the system equations, and to replace the performance criterion by one of quadratic form, thus returning to the linear regulator problem of section 4, for which a solution is available. Obviously such crude approximation is not always tenable, in which case a technique of 'successive approximations' could be applied—that is, a sequence of approximations, each a modification of the previous, which converges to the required solution. Following on from the above, a sequence of linear equations and a sequence of quadratic criteria can often improve on the crudeness of a single approximation.

A more effective technique works on the two-point boundary-value problem directly. At $t = 0$, $n$ of our variables $(x, p)$ are unknown. If, as a first approximation, we guess a set of $n$ values, we can solve the equations, obtaining a solution which will almost certainly not satisfy the terminal conditions at $t = T$. Now construct an 'accessory' minimization problem in which the minimand is the terminal error, and the minimizing parameters are the unknown initial conditions. This can be solved by a hill-climbing technique, which involves

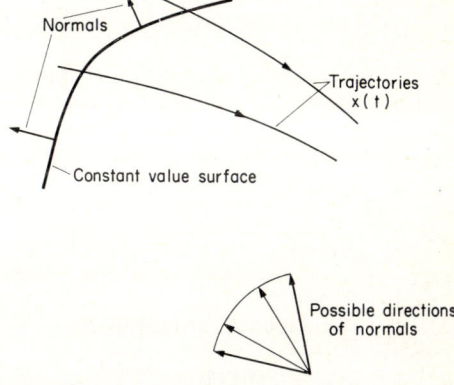

FIG. 5

determining the gradients of the terminal error with respect to variations of the initial conditions, and modifying each successive approximation by a small step in the direction of the downward gradient—the direction of steepest descent.

Determining these gradients is in itself a tedious process, involving a large number (usually $2n^2$) of accessory linear differential equations. A further handicap is the fact that, like most convergence schemes, the first approximation must be sufficiently accurate to ensure that convergence to the desired result will occur at all. In this situation the value $p(0)$ must be a normal to the constant-criterion surface, and if the surface is oriented in a certain way, there is a limited range of directions which could conceivably be normals (see Fig. 5). A choice outside this range might rule out any possibility of convergence, and often this range is so small that it is impossible to hit it merely by trial and error.

Another commonly used technique is to approximate the control function $u(t)$, modifying it at each successive iteration in the direction of steepest descent of the value of the performance criterion. This is not really a solution of the equations of the maximum principle, as it works directly on the criterion function and the system dynamics; nevertheless the equations involved turn out to be very similar. It is also subject to the usual handicap of requiring a good first approximation.

The number of different techniques that have been suggested is legion, but they all tend to become unwieldy for systems larger than 4th or 5th order. This difficulty of computation is probably the major limitation on the applicability of the maximum principle to problems of dynamic control.

*See also:* Control: basis elements. Control systems, multivariable. Optimization of industrial processes.

*Bibliography*

BALAKRISHNAN AND NEUSTADT (Eds.) (1964) *Computing Methods in Optimization Problems*, New York: Academic Press.
LEITMANN G. (Ed.) (1963) *Optimization Techniques*, New York: Academic Press.
MERRIAM C. (1963) *Optimization Theory and the Design of Feedback Control Systems*, New York: McGraw-Hill.
PAIEWONSKY B. (1965) *Optimal Control: a Review of Theory and Practice*, A.I.A.A. J., Nov.
PONTRYAGIN L. et. al. (1962) *The Mathematical Theory of Optimal Processes*, New York: Interscience.

S. SHAPIRO

## CONTROL BY MODEL REFERENCE.

### 1. Introduction

In the simplest form of closed loop control system (Fig. 1) the input vector (x) and the output vector (y) are

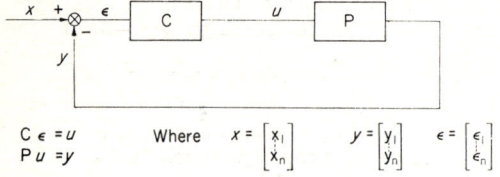

FIG. 1. *Single loop control system.*

differenced and the error vector ($\epsilon$) so formed is shaped or filtered in some manner before being applied to actuate the object or process whose response constitutes the output of the system. The response of the controlled system may be varied by altering the coefficients of the matrix ($C$) which operates upon the error vector.

The design of the control system involves the synthesis of that matrix, or in practical terms, that filter, which most nearly makes the performance of the system coincide with the design specification.

Design specifications take many forms, being most often expressed in the form of upper bounds on certain errors under particular circumstances, lower bounds on the damping of system modes and perhaps permitted ranges for the frequencies of these modes. In many instances it is possible to synthesize an ideal system whose response satisfies the given specification and this ideal system is called *the model* for the system to be designed. The output of this model when fed with the system input represents the desired or specified response for the system and is known as *model response*.

As a simple example if a specification requires the response of the system to respond to a step function with not more than say 10 per cent overshoot and that the error be first reduced to zero in approximately one second.

A suitable model would be a system having the transfer function

$$M = \frac{\omega_n^2}{S^2 + 2\varrho\omega_n S + \omega_n^2}$$

where $\omega_n = 1\cdot 2$
and $\varrho = 0\cdot 6$.

The model response may or may not be attainable by the actual system. For example a control system which is inherently of third order may have a specification which produces a model of second order in which case the system response and the model response can never be identical. In particular, the parameter values in the design which most closely matches model response will be functions of the frequency of the input. Similarly the true system may contain some non-linearity and the model be linear. In which case the design parameters for optimum response will depend upon the amplitude of the input signal. Alternatively the system and the model may be of the same order and so the design will produce a system having model response for all input spectra and amplitudes.

Techniques involving the use of a model are called *model reference* methods and they have applications in both conventional and adaptive control.

### 2. Application of Model Reference Technique to Conventional Control

Since the model response to the current system input represents the desired response the difference between this and the system output is the instantaneous system error and may be used as an additional control input.

Consider the system of Fig. 2. The process and the model have transfer functions $P$ and $M$ respectively, the input is $x$, the outputs of the system and the model

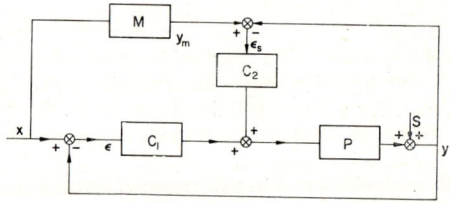

FIG. 2. *Model reference control system.*

$y$ and $y_M$ respectively. The process is actuated by the controllers $C_1$ and $C_2$. Then

$$P[C_2(Mx-y)+C_1(x-y)] = y$$

or

$$[I+C_1P+C_2P]y = [C_1+MC_2]Px \quad (1)$$

in order to obtain model response

$$(C_1+MC_2)P = (I+C_1P+C_2P)M \quad (2)$$

if $C_1 = 0$ then (2) is satisfied as $|C_2| \to \infty$ (3)
if $C_1 \neq 0$ (2) is satisfied independent of $C_2$

by $C_1 = \dfrac{M}{I-M} \cdot 1/P$ (4)

Discussion of the system defined by equation 3 is deferred to the next section.

Since in the general system model response can be obtained independently of $C_2$ this controller may be used to satisfy some other criterion.

In the system of Fig. 2, suppose that the output of the process is contaminated by additive noise, $\delta$, in such a way that only the modified output may be observed. Then equation 1 becomes

$$[1+C_1P+C_2P]y = [C_1+MC_2]Px+\delta \quad (5)$$

and if $C_1$ is chosen as in equation 4 this becomes

$$[1+C_2P(1-M)]y = M[1+C_2P(1-M)]x+(1-M)\delta. \quad (6)$$

Thus $C_2$ may be chosen to produce acceptable noise response.

However, the system defined in equation 5 is equivalent to the system of Fig. 3 if $C = C_1+C_2$ and the pre filter

$$C' = (C_1+MC_2)/C_1+C_2.$$

This equivalent system makes no use of model reference technique. The advantage which may be claimed for model reference technique is that it allows the design of demand response and noise response to be treated essentially separately, by means of $C_1$ and $C_2$ respectively.

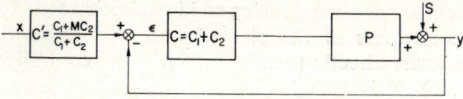

FIG. 3. *Single loop system equivalent to Fig. 2.*

Because, in the majority of important cases noise inputs are not observable, except in terms of system response, a model for noise response is not so valuable a concept. If, however, the noise input, $\delta$, is observable and $M_\delta$ is the model for this input, then $C_2$ may be chosen so that the system response to the noise is model response

by taking $C_2 = \dfrac{1-M-M_\delta}{M_\delta(1-M)} \cdot \dfrac{1}{P}$ providing $C$ is given by

equation 4. In this manner, as illustrated in Fig. 4, the controller $C_3$, operating on the error between the model response to the gust input and the true response, may be used to produce an acceptable response to some other unobservable noise input, $\delta_1$.

Ideally, if the response of the system is to match that of the model, then as the characteristics of the process $P$ vary so also must those of the controller. This is the problem of adaptive control.

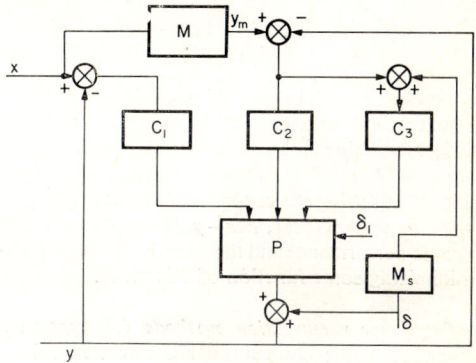

FIG. 4. *Model reference system employing two models.*

## 2. Application of Model Reference Technique to Adaptive Control

*(i) High gain systems.* Equation 3 asserts that if, in the system of Fig. 2, $C_1 = 0$ then the condition for model response is satisfied as $|C_2| \to \infty$ and this is independent of the characteristics of the process $P$. The system satisfies the equation

$$(1+C_2P)y = \delta+MC_2Px \quad (7)$$

and the frequency and damping of the system modes are given by

$$1+C_2P = 0.$$

In any practical system letting $|C_2| \to \infty$ results in instability. Consequently in order to approximate to model response the gain of the control can only be set as high as the current state of $P$ allows. To use this method an adaptive solution is essential. The most interesting application of this technique, to the control of the $X-15$, is discussed in Lindahl and McGuire (1962). In this the gain $|C_2|$ is increased so that the loop is kept in a state of oscillation, the amplitude of which is detected and used to control the gain. Careful design of $C_2$ is required to ensure that the frequency of oscillation is independent of the characteristics of $P$, because this eases the task of detecting the frequency in the presence of noise.

The advantages of such a method are:

(a) speed of the adaptive response to changes in the characteristics of P;
(b) its relative simplicity;

whereas its disadvantages are associated with:

(a) the continuous presence of a high frequency oscillation in the system;

(b) poor system behaviour in the presence of noise disturbances;
(c) ability to change only a single controller variable.

*(ii) Multiparameter systems.* If $C_1$ is non-zero then the system exhibits model response if $C_1$ takes the value

$$\frac{M}{1-M} \cdot \frac{1}{P}.$$

The process $P$ will in general contain many varying parameters and consequently the controller $C_1$ must, if perfect matching is to be attempted, contain an equal number of variable parameters. Several methods are available for setting the controller parameters correctly. In each the system error, $Mx-y$, is used as a monitor of system performance and the adaptive process consists of minimizing some function of this error.

*(a) Parameter perturbation methods* (Hammond and Duckenfield 1963; Douce and Ng 1965). In this type of system the parameters $k_i$ of the controller, Fig. 5, are perturbed by externally applied disturbances $\Delta k_i$. A function of the system error $\varepsilon_s$ is used to provide a performance index, or figure of merit, for the system. The change in performance index $(PI)$ caused by the perturbation is

$$\sum_i \frac{\partial (PI)}{\partial k_i} \Delta k_i.$$

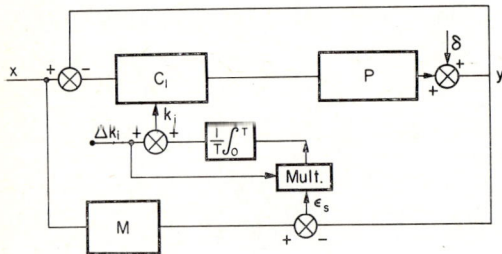

FIG. 5. *Parameter perturbation technique.*

The performance index has a minimum at points such that $\frac{\partial (PI)}{\partial k_i} = 0. \; i = 1, 2 \ldots$ and so adaptive loops are required to zero these latter quantities. If the perturbations of the individual parameters are mutually orthogonal then the individual elements of the summation $\sum_i \frac{\partial (PI)}{\partial k_i} \Delta k_i$ can be extracted and used with an adaptive control law of the form

$$\dot{k}_i = -\lambda_i \frac{\partial (PI)}{\partial k_i}$$

where $\lambda_i$ is proportional to the expectation of $(\Delta k_i)^2$. Here the model has been used to provide a continuous and instantaneous measure of the performance index.

*(b) M.I.T. Technique* (Whitaker 1963; Dymock et al. 1965). If the criterion to be minimized is the error squared, $\varepsilon_s^2$, the necessary adaptive control law for the controller parameter $k_i$ can be written

$$\dot{k}_i = -\lambda_i \frac{\partial}{\partial k_i}(\varepsilon_s^2) = -2\lambda_i \varepsilon_s \frac{\partial \varepsilon_s}{\partial k_i}.$$

Now for the system of Fig. 2 with $C_2 = 0$

$$\varepsilon_s = Mx - y = \left(M - \frac{C_1 P}{1 + C_1 P}\right)x - \frac{\delta}{1 + C_1 P}$$

and

$$\frac{\partial \varepsilon_s}{\partial k_i} = \frac{P}{(1+C_1 P)^2} \frac{\partial C_1}{\partial k_i} x + \frac{P}{(1+C_1 P)^2} \frac{\partial C_1}{\partial k_i} \cdot \delta$$

and supposing that $C_1$ is set approximately correctly

$$\frac{\partial \varepsilon_s}{\partial k_i} = M(1-M) \frac{1}{C_1} \frac{\partial C_1}{\partial k_i}(\delta - x)$$

and the component of $\partial \varepsilon_s / \partial k_i$ which results from the input $x$ is

$$-M(1-M)\frac{1}{C_1}\frac{\partial C_1}{\partial k_i}x = -(1-M)\frac{1}{C_1}\frac{\partial C_1}{\partial k_i} \cdot y_M.$$

So if the average setting of $k_i$ is to be unaffected by gusts

$$\dot{k}_i = -2\lambda \left[\left(\frac{C_1 P}{1+C_1 P} - M\right)x\right] \cdot \left[(1-M)\frac{1}{C_1}\frac{\partial C_1}{\partial k_i} y_M\right]$$

$+$ term in $x\delta$

the contribution of this latter term tends to zero as the time constant of integration is increased.

In this system therefore model output provides not only an instantaneous measure of system error, $\varepsilon_s$, but also, after filtering, a measure of the slope of the error criterion against parameter curve.

*(c) Direct identification techniques* (Dymock and Meredith 1965). In the two methods mentioned previously the optimum controller parameters are determined as the result of a hill-climbing type of process conducted upon these parameters. An alternative method of approach is to determine, using an identification technique, the parameters of the plant $P$ and then to use these parameters directly to substitute into the controller $C_1$ (Fig. 6). This technique has an advantage over the

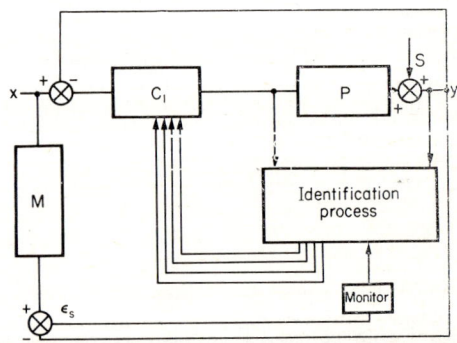

FIG. 6. *Direct identification technique with model reference providing long term monitor.*

methods previously discussed in that only optimized parameters are set into the controller. However, the method is open loop in the sense that no function of system error is used in setting the controller parameters. The most natural way to introduce this information, without returning to essentially one of the previous techniques is to employ the system error signal as a long term monitor and to initiate some self checking routine if the output of the monitor exceeds a certain threshold. In the absence of noise disturbances

$$\varepsilon_s = \frac{P}{(1+C_1 P)^2} \sum_i \frac{\partial C_1}{\partial k_i} \Delta k_i \cdot x$$

where the controller parameters are $k_i$. Clearly, those combinations of parameter errors $\Delta k_i$ which do not greatly affect the system response will be ignored in comparison with combinations which produce a serious departure from model response.

In the presence of noise it is necessary to select that portion of the system error which is correlated with $x$ and a suitable and simple measure of system error appears to be

$$\left| \frac{1}{T} \int_0^T \left( \varepsilon_s \cdot \mathrm{Sign}\, \frac{1}{1+D} x \right) \mathrm{d}t \right|$$
$$+ \left| \frac{1}{T} \int_0^T \left( \varepsilon_s \cdot \mathrm{Sign}\, \frac{D}{i+D} \cdot x \right) \mathrm{d}t \right|$$

although any which correlate $\varepsilon_s$ with a function of the input $x$ will be satisfactory.

### 4. Model Reference Technique

A specification is an attempt to summarize the requirements of a system by a small number of numerical values. It is therefore an abstraction and as such does not define a unique solution; many system designs may satisfy a given specification. In order to arrive at a specification one or both of two courses may be adopted, either the class of possible input functions is restricted to a single member, typically a step function or an impulse, and some characteristic of the response to this input is specified or the input class is defined only in a probability sense and the specification takes the form of statistical measures of the response characteristics. There is therefore less information available in the specification than is available in the response of a system which satisfies the specification.

The model, developed from a specification, is an attempt to make up for the lack of information. It is an intermediate stage in the design. The specification requests a system, to satisfy the requirements, the model provides a transfer function. Just as the system design is not specified uniquely, neither is the model. The choice of the model depends upon the characteristic of the process, $P$. It must imply a realizable and acceptable form for the controller $C$. The form will determine the order of the transfer function of $C$ and also the number of parameters of $C$ which need to be varied to maintain model response.

Having obtained the model a continuous signal is available which expresses the specification for all input signals and at all times. This is the essential feature of model reference technique. The earlier sections have indicated some applications of this technique. In the non-adaptive case the great advantage is that the design of demand response characteristics and noise response characteristics can be separated or alternatively that in the absence of noise a continuous figure of merit is available for monitoring. With adaptive systems this figure of merit is employed to modify the controller either directly as in the parameter perturbation and M.I.T. methods or in the form of a monitor with adaptive systems using direct identification techniques.

Although in this discussion the model has been thought of as a fixed parameter transfer function, it may itself be varied by either measured environmental data or, where the parameters of $P$ are being directly identified, as a function of these measurements.

*See also:* Adaptive control theory. Control of an economic system. Discrete models for forecasting and control. Control, hill climbing in Identification techniques for control.

*Bibliography*

DOUCE J. L. and NG K. C. (1965) *The Use of Pseudo-Random Binary Signals in Adaptive Control*, I.F.A.C. (Teddington) Symposium, Sept.

DYMOCK A. J., MEREDITH J. F., HALL A. and WHITE K. M. (1965) *Analysis of a Type of Model Reference Adaptive Control System*, Proc. I.E.E. **112**, No. 4, April.

DYMOCK A. J. and MEREDITH J. F. (1965) *An Adaptive Control System Employing High Speed Parameter Identification*, I.F.A.C. (Teddington) Symposium, Sept.

HAMMOND P. H. and DUCKENFIELD M. J. (1963) *Automatic Optimisation by Continuous Perturbation of Parameters*, Automatica, **1**, 147.

LINDAHL J. H. and McGUIRE W. M. (1962) *Adaptive Control Flies the X-15*, Control Engineering, Oct. 93.

WHITAKER H. P. (1963) *Use of Model Reference Adaptive Control to Achieve a Specified Performance*, M.I.T. Report, R.407, April.

J. F. MEREDITH

**CONTROL BY STATIONARY FILTERING AND PREDICTION (WIENER).** *Introduction.* Wiener (1949) studied the problems of filtering and prediction of stationary time series. The latter are randomly varying signals or quantities which have statistical averages which remain constant with time. They are also assumed to be ergodic so that ensemble and time averages are the same.

The filtering problem is to extract a randomly varying signal from another one, which is the first signal with *noise* superimposed. The noise is another randomly varying quantity so that extraction cannot be performed exactly. Wiener derived a method for finding the optimum filter when the only known data for the signal and noise are the *auto-correlation functions* or *spectral densities*. Optimum is defined in the sense that the mean square error between the filter output and the true signal is minimum. The filter can also be adapted to provide *prediction* as well; then the mean square error between the signal at a future time and the output of the filter at the present time is minimized. *Wiener filters* are absolutely optimum in the sense defined when the random variables are Gaussian. Even if they are not Gaussian, such filters are still the best in the absence of further statistical information and they are always the best *linear filters*.

Wiener's methods have been modified and extended in order to optimize the control of a process in which the *dynamics* are described by ordinary *linear differential equations*. A parallel development which makes use of *z-transforms* allows *sampled-data systems* to be optimized in a similar manner.

Finally, optimization may also be performed by what might be called state-space methods. Instead of deriving optimum transfer functions, the optimization is performed directly in terms of the *state variables* of the random signals and of the process to be controlled.

*Filter and predictor.* Suppose that the filter (Fig. 1) operates on a signal $x$ which has two components, that to be followed $r$ plus additional noise $n$. The filter must

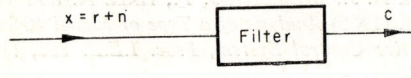

FIG. 1. *Filter.*

be designed to minimize the mean square error between the output $c$ and the value of $r$ at a future time. The error can be expressed as

$$e(t) = r(t+T) - c(t),$$

where $t$ is the present time and $T$ is the amount of prediction required. Then the quantity to be minimized is

$$\sigma^2 = E[e^2],$$

where $E$ means expected or average value of the argument, which in this case is the error squared.

In this case $\sigma^2$ can be expressed as the following integral of spectral densities.

$$\sigma^2 = \frac{1}{2\pi j} \int_{-j\infty}^{j\infty} (\Phi_{rr} - e^{-sT} H \Phi_{rx} - e^{sT} \overline{H} \Phi_{xr} + H \overline{H} \Phi_{xx}) \, ds,$$

where

$H \equiv H(s) \equiv$ the transfer function of the filter,

$\overline{H} \equiv H(-s)$, $j \equiv \sqrt{-1}$ and the letter e in the integrand denotes the exponential function.

The spectral density functions are of the form $\Phi_{yz} \equiv \Phi_{yz}(s)$, where

$$\Phi_{yz}(j\omega) = \int_{-\infty}^{\infty} \phi_{yz}(\tau) e^{-j\omega\tau} \, d\tau$$

and $\phi$ is the correlation function

$$\phi_{yz}(\tau) = E[y(t) \, z(t+\tau)];$$

here $y$ and $z$ are any two random variables.

The application of variational methods leads to the integral equation

$$\int_{-j\infty}^{j\infty} (e^{sT} \Phi_{xr} - H_0 \Phi_{xx}) \overline{H}_1 \, ds = 0,$$

which must be satisfied by the optimum filter transfer function $H_0$ for any permissible transfer function $H_1$; permissible implies stability and the operation on present and past information only. From this requirement can be derived the following expression for the optimum transfer function

$$H_0 = \frac{1}{\Phi_{xx}^+} \left[ \frac{e^{sT} \Phi_{xr}}{\Phi_{xx}^-} \right]_+.$$

To derive this expression $\Phi_{xx}$ has been divided into two factors so that $\Phi_{xx} = \Phi_{xx}^+ \cdot \Phi_{xx}^-$, where the $+$ indicates the factor with all its zeros and poles in the left half $s$-plane and the $-$ indicates the factor with all its zeros and poles in the right half $s$-plane. Finally the function

$$\left[ \frac{e^{sT} \Phi_{xr}}{\Phi_{xx}} \right] = \left[ \frac{e^{sT} \Phi_{xr}}{\Phi_{xx}} \right]_+ + \left[ \frac{e^{sT} \Phi_{xr}}{\Phi_{xx}} \right]_-,$$

where $[\,]_+$ is a function with all its poles in the left half $s$-plane and $[\,]_-$ is a function with all its poles in the right half $s$-plane.

The optimum filter transfer function can also be written in the following integral form

$$H_0 = \frac{1}{2\pi j \Phi_{xx}^+} \int_0^\infty e^{-st} \, dt \int_{-j\infty}^{j\infty} \frac{\Phi_{xr}}{\Phi_{xx}^-} e^{(t+T)u} \, du.$$

The above is not the only way in which $H_0$ can be derived. For instance, Wiener expressed $\sigma^2$ as convolution integrals involving the correlation functions and the filter weighting function (impulse response function). He then made a variation on the weighting function to obtain an integral equation for the optimum weighting function. After transformation the solution then came out by factorization as shown above. Yet another interesting method was derived by Bode and Shannon (1950).

*Optimum control.* When a physical process is to be controlled, besides having noise contaminating the input as in the filtering problem, there may also be random disturbances to the process itself. We shall assume that these disturbances can be represented by a stationary random variation of the output as indicated by $d$ in Fig. 2.

It is assumed that the dynamical operation of the process in response to an input signal $u$ can be represented by the transfer function $YPe^{-sT}$. The factor $e^{-sT}$ represents a finite time delay (distance/velocity lag) of $T$ and $P = \prod_i (s-\alpha_i)$, where the $\alpha_i$'s are any zeros of the process transfer function which lie in the right half

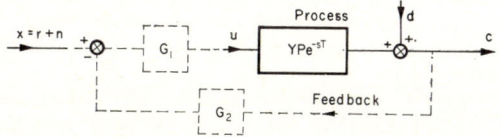

FIG. 2. *Control of a process.*

$s$-plane. $T$ and $P$ may not exist but if they do it is necessary to separate them from the rest of the transfer function since they are terms which cannot be cancelled out by the controller.

Finally, certain variables in the process must be constrained to lie within given finite bounds. We shall assume that the input $u$ must be so constrained but the method is the same whatever the variable. The only way in which the constraint can be imposed theoretically is to have $E[u^2] \leqslant L^2$ and make $L$ small enough for $u$ to rarely touch the finite bound. The optimization may then be performed by minimizing $\{\sigma^2 + \gamma E[u^2]\}$, where $\gamma$ is a positive constant, the value of which is chosen subsequently in order that the desired level of constraint $L^2$ be achieved.

Referring to Fig. 2, it can be seen that feedback from the output is essential if any counteraction to the disturbance $d$ is to be made. It will be assumed that the controller can be made with an element of transfer function $G_2$ in the feedback and another with transfer function $G_1$ in the forward path. $G_1$ and $G_2$ must be derived to optimize the output response due to the separate inputs $x$ and $d$. In order to do this and at the same time allow for the physical constraints due to $P$ and $T$, the transfer function which determines the part of the output response due to the input $x$ is written as $Pe^{-sT} H_1$ and that for the part due to $d$ as $(1+Pe^{-sT} H_2)$. Then the linear transfer functions $H_1$ and $H_2$ must be optimized.

If $x$ and $d$ are uncorrelated, we can write

$$\sigma^2 + \gamma E[u^2] = \frac{1}{2\pi j} \int_{-j\infty}^{j\infty} \left\{ \Phi_{rr} + \left(P\bar{P} + \frac{\gamma}{Y\bar{Y}}\right) H_1 \bar{H}_1 \Phi_{xx} \right.$$
$$+ \left[ (1+Pe^{-sT}H_2)(1+\bar{P}e^{sT}\bar{H}_2) + \frac{\gamma}{Y\bar{Y}} H_2 \bar{H}_2 \right] \Phi_{dd}$$
$$\left. - Pe^{-sT}H_1 \Phi_{rx} - \bar{P}e^{sT}\bar{H}_1 \Phi_{xr} \right\} ds.$$

Then by applying variational methods to both $H_1$ and $H_2$, it is possible to derive the corresponding optimum transfer functions

$$H_{1_0} = \frac{1}{\left(P\bar{P} + \frac{\gamma}{Y\bar{Y}}\right)^+ \Phi_{xx}^+} \left[ \frac{\bar{P}e^{sT}\Phi_{xr}}{\left(P\bar{P} + \frac{\gamma}{Y\bar{Y}}\right)^- \Phi_{xx}^-} \right]_+$$

and

$$H_{2_0} = \frac{1}{\left(P\bar{P} + \frac{\gamma}{Y\bar{Y}}\right)^+ \Phi_{dd}^+} \left[ \frac{\bar{P}e^{sT}\Phi_{dd}}{\left(P\bar{P} + \frac{\gamma}{Y\bar{Y}}\right)^- \Phi_{dd}^-} \right]_+.$$

Finally, the optimum control is realized by making

$$G_1 = \frac{H_{1_0}}{Y(1+Pe^{-sT}H_{2_0})} \quad \text{and} \quad G_2 = \frac{H_{2_0}}{H_{1_0}}.$$

A complete derivation of these results has been given along with some examples by Chang (1961).

Notice that if $T$ exists, the form of $G_1$ requires the simulation of a finite time delay in a feedback loop in the controller. Also the value of the constant $\gamma$ has still to be chosen to match the desired constraint on $E[u^2]$. This is not always a simple problem particularly when constraints must be imposed on more than one of the system variables (Sancho and Roberts 1965).

*Optimum sampled data system.* In a sampled data control system the control signal is fed into the process as a sequence of numbers or samples. In other words, the process has a digital controller which has a given cycling frequency resulting in a fixed sampling interval $\tau$. By using $z$-transforms, the optimum controller may be derived in a way which is analogous to the Wiener-type of optimization of a continuous control system.

To see what is involved in optimizing a sampled data system with stationary random inputs, consider the system represented diagrammatically in Fig. 3. As is

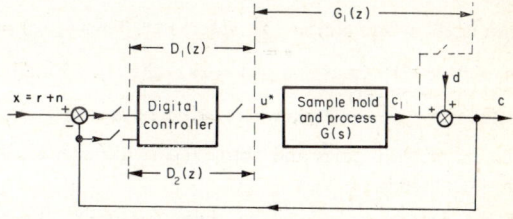

FIG. 3. *Sampled data control system.*

usual in the analysis of such systems, the control signal $u^*$ will be thought of as a sequence of impulses. Then the transfer function $G(s)$ represents not only the process but the sample-hold as well; $G_1(z)$ is the corresponding pulse transfer function. The random inputs are represented by $x$ and $d$ in the same way as in the continuous system discussed in the previous section.

The digital controller operates on $(x-c)$ and $c$ with pulse transfer functions $D_1(z)$ and $D_2(z)$, respectively. The latter allow the independent realization of the pulse transfer functions $K_1(z)$ and $K_2(z)$ such that

$$C_1(z) = K_1(z)\,X(z) + K_2(z)\,D(z),$$

where $C_1(z)$, $X(z)$ and $D(z)$ are the $z$-transforms of $c_1 = c - d$, $x$ and $d$, respectively.

Physical constraints again affect the design of the controller. To limit the value of $E[u^{*2}]$, the function $\{\sigma^2 + \gamma E[u^{*2}]\}$ is minimized and the constant $\gamma$ finally selected to give the required constraint. (A simple extension of the theory allows the constraint to be imposed on any variable which may be either sampled or continuous.) For the controller itself to be stable, the optimization must avoid cancellation of zeros of $G_1(z)$ which lie outside or on the unit circle about the origin of the $z$-plane. Let such a factor of $G_1(z)$ be

$$P(z) = \prod_{i=1}^{l}\left(1 - \frac{z}{\lambda_i}\right), \quad |\lambda_i| \geq 1.$$

Also, the controller cannot cancel out the effect of a finite time delay in the process. Assume that the delay is $T$, such that $(m-1)\tau < T \leq m\tau$.

Taking into account the above constraints, the optimum expressions for $K_1(z)$ and $K_2(z)$ may be written (Chang 1961) as

$$K_{1_0}(z) = \frac{1}{\chi(z)\,Y_1(z)}\left[\frac{\bar{G}\psi_{xr}(z)}{G_1(z^{-1})\,Y_1(z^{-1})\,\chi(z^{-1})}\right]_+$$

and

$$K_{2_0}(z) = -\frac{1}{\Delta(z)\,Y_1(z)}\left[\frac{\bar{G}\psi_{dd}(z)}{G_1(z^{-1})\,Y_1(z^{-1})\,\Delta(z^{-1})}\right]_+.$$

The + signs outside the square brackets indicate that only the partial fractions of the enclosed functions be taken which have poles inside the unit circle. $\bar{G}\psi_{xr}(z)$ and $\bar{G}\psi_{dd}(z)$ are the $z$-transforms which correspond to the Laplace-transforms $G(-s)\,\Phi_{xr}(s)$ and $G(-s)\,\Phi_{dd}(s)$, respectively. $\chi(z)$ and $\Delta(z)$ are the factors of $\theta_{xx}(z)$ and $\theta_{dd}(z)$, respectively, with zeros and poles inside the unit circle, where $\theta(z) = \sum_{n=-\infty}^{\infty}\phi(n\tau)\,z^{-n}$. Thus $\theta_{xx}(z) = \chi(z)\,\chi(z^{-1})$ and $\theta_{dd}(z) = \Delta(z)\,\Delta(z^{-1})$. Finally,

$$Y_1(z) = \frac{z^{m'}P(z^{-1})}{P(z)}\,Y(z),$$ where $m' = l + m$ and $Y(z)$ is the factor with poles and zeros inside the unit circle of the function

$$Y(z)\,Y(z^{-1}) = \frac{\bar{G}G_1(z) + \gamma}{G_1(z)\,G_1(z^{-1})};$$ here $\bar{G}G_1(z)$ is the $z$-transform corresponding to the Laplace-transform $G(-s)\,G(s)$.

*State-space approach.* The procedure for finding optimum transfer functions can be extended to systems with more inputs and outputs (Davis 1963). However, another method will now be discussed which can also be applied when there are several inputs and outputs. This differs radically in that, instead of deriving optimum transfer functions, the control signals for the process are derived directly in terms of the state variables. The problem can be studied in discrete time or continuous time but only the latter will be considered here.

Suppose that the process dynamics and the random inputs are described by a set of first order differential equations denoted by the vector equation

$$\dot{\mathbf{x}} = A\mathbf{x} + B\mathbf{u} + \boldsymbol{\xi}.$$

The elements of $\mathbf{x}$ are the state variables of the random inputs and the process. The elements of $\mathbf{u}$ are the control signal inputs to the process. $A$ and $B$ are matrices with constant elements; the elements could be functions of time but then the optimization would not be stationary. The elements of $\boldsymbol{\xi}$ are fundamental noise sources which, when operated on by linear filtering as described by the state vector equation, produce the random inputs to the system.

Florentin has shown that, if all the state variables are completely observable, the method of dynamic programming (Bellman 1957) may be used to derive the optimum control when each element of $\boldsymbol{\xi}$ is either white noise (Florentin 1961) or a Poisson series of impulses (Florentin 1963). For the sake of brevity, only the white noise case will be considered here.

The general form of quadratic cost criterion may be written as

$$\sigma^2 = \lim_{T \to \infty} E\left[\frac{1}{T}\int_0^T (\mathbf{x}'C\mathbf{x} + \mathbf{u}'D\mathbf{u})\,dt\right],$$

where $t = 0$ represents the present instant of time, $C$ and $D$ are given *positive definite symmetric matrices* and a dash is used to denote transpose. Then the optimum control $\mathbf{u}$ is

$$\mathbf{u}_0 = -\tfrac{1}{2}D^{-1}\,B'(\mathbf{z} + 2Z\mathbf{x}),$$

where $\mathbf{z}$ is a vector and $Z$ is a symmetric matrix defined by the following vector and matrix algebraic equations:

$$-ZBD^{-1}B'\mathbf{z} + A'\mathbf{z} + 2Z\mathbf{m} = 0$$

and

$$C - ZBD^{-1}B'Z + A'Z + ZA = 0,$$

where $\mathbf{m} = E[\boldsymbol{\xi}]$. Notice that $\mathbf{u}_0$ is determined as a linear function of the state vector $\mathbf{x}$.

In practice, complete observability cannot be assumed. Suppose that the variables which can be measured are

$$\mathbf{y} = M\mathbf{x} + \boldsymbol{\eta},$$

where $M$ is a constant element matrix and $\boldsymbol{\eta}$ represents white noise error incurred in measurement. Then Sancho (1966) has shown that the control $\mathbf{u}_0$ given above is still optimum in the incompletely observable case if $\mathbf{x}$ is replaced by $\hat{\mathbf{x}}$, where $\hat{\mathbf{x}}$ is the optimal estimate of $\mathbf{x}$ given $\mathbf{y}$.

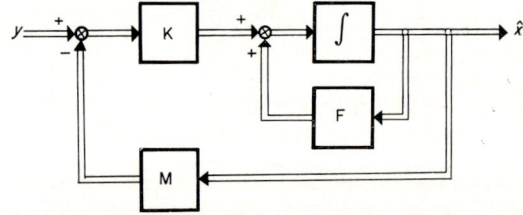

Fig. 4. *Optimal estimator.*

The optimal estimate is defined in the sense that the mean square error $E[(\mathbf{x} - \hat{\mathbf{x}})'(\mathbf{x} - \hat{\mathbf{x}})]$ is minimum. The solution to the optimal estimation problem has been given by Kalman (1963).

For simplicity, assume that $\mathbf{m} = 0$. Then $\hat{\mathbf{x}}$ must be computed continuously as indicated by the block diagram in Fig. 4. Each block in the diagram indicates the matrix multiplication of the incoming vector which is represented by the double flow line. The only exception is $\int$ which indicates the integration of the vector with respect to time. The matrices $F$ and $K$ are defined by

$$F = A - D^{-1}B'Z \quad \text{and}$$
$$K = PM'R^{-1},$$

where $P$ is defined by the algebraic matrix equation

$$FP + PF' - PM'R^{-1}MP + S = 0.$$

Assuming that $\xi$ and $\eta$ have zero mean, $R$ and $S$ are defined by

$$E[\boldsymbol{\eta}(t)\boldsymbol{\eta}'(t+\tau)] = R\delta(\tau) \quad \text{and}$$
$$E[\boldsymbol{\xi}(t)\boldsymbol{\xi}'(t+\tau)] = S\delta(\tau).$$

*See also:* Control, predictive, using fast time models. Control systems, sampled data. Information space. Random signals and noise.

*Bibliography*

BELLMAN R. (1957) *Dynamic Programming*, Princeton: The University Press.
BODE H. W. and SHANNON C. E. (1950) *A simplified derivation of linear least square smoothing and prediction theory, Proc. I.R.E.*, **38**, 417, April.
CHANG S. S. L. (1961) *Synthesis of Optimum Control Systems*, New York: McGraw-Hill.
DAVIS M. C. (1963) *Factoring the spectral matrix, I.E.E.E. Trans. on Automatic Control*, **AC-8**, 296, October.
FLORENTIN J. J. (1961) *Optimal control of continuous time, Markov, stochastic systems, J. of Electronics and Control*, **10**, 473, June.
FLORENTIN J. J. (1963) *Optimal control of systems with generalized Poisson inputs, Trans. A.S.M.E. J. of Basic Engineering*, **85**, 217, June.
KALMAN R. E. (1963) *New methods in Wiener filtering theory, Proc. of the first Symposium on Engineering Applications of Random Function Theory and Probability*, New York: Wiley.
SANCHO N. G. F. and ROBERTS A. P. (1965) *Use of a digital computer for the optimization of automatic control systems with random inputs, Int. J. Control* **1**, 501, June.
SANCHO N. G. F. (1966) *Optimization of linear stochastic control systems operating over a finite time interval, Int. J. Control.* **3**, 313.
WIENER N. (1949) *Extrapolation, Interpolation, and Smoothing of Stationary Time Series*, New York: Wiley.

A. P. ROBERTS

**CONTROL, HIERARCHICAL.** *Introduction.* A *hierarchy* is any system of persons or things in a graded order. Hierarchical (hierarchial) control refers to a collection of controllers in a graded order of command. The figure illustrates the concept most effectively.

The objective of the structure is to control the response of some system indicated by the lower rectangle in (a) and (b).

Centralized control indicated in (a) assumes that a single controller directs the whole system.

Hierarchial control in (b) assumes grades or levels of control. Level 1 consists of several individual control units which control the actual system based on informa-

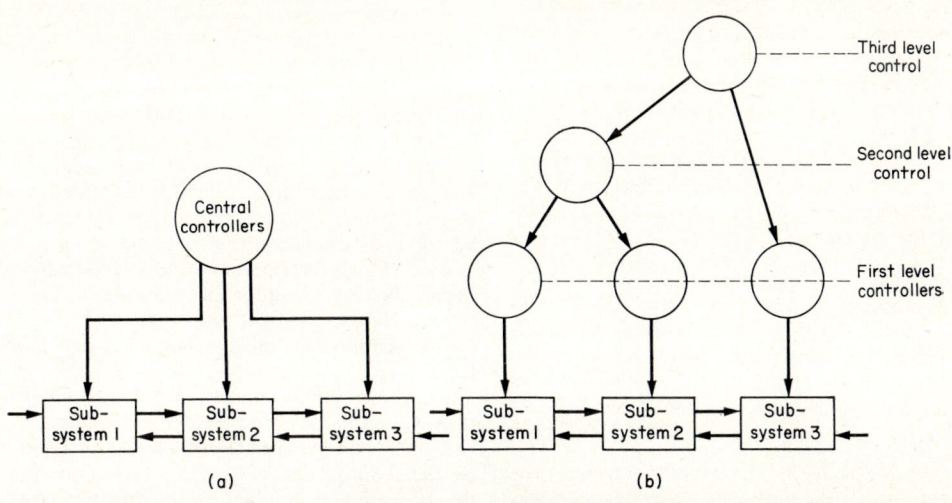

*Centralized versus hierarchical control.*

tion from the system and in general level $n$ consists of several control units which control the adjacent lower level $n-1$ based on information received from that level.

It is useful conceptually to visualize each level as constituting a system to the levels above. Thus a hierarchial control structure can be visualized as a recursive structure of levels controlling the system that each 'sees' below it, based on information provided by that system.

In practice the system may consist of many interacting units in a complex industrial situation. The precise information flow and control patterns will depend on the application, and the precise concept of level is not necessarily absolute but is relative to some sub-structure of the hierarchy, for example, level 1 of a sub-structure may directly control level 1 of some other substructure in the same hierarchy controlling a large process.

*Benefits of hierarchial control.* A hierarchial structure has certain properties which can occasionally be exploited to advantage.

*1) Economic costs of realization.* Realization costs of control tend to be proportional to some power of the degree of complexity. (Inversion of an $n \times n$ matrix requires approximately $n^3$ operations defining a specific cost.) Under these circumstances it is more economical to subdivide the control problem to take advantage of the fact that the sum of the sub-system realization costs is less than the realization cost for the sum of the sub-systems.

*2) Reliability problems.* Hierarchial structures of unreliable elements tend to be redundant. Consequently failures directly interrupt only part of the control structure. Careful design can produce better system reliability than an equivalent centralized control structure by arranging, for example, that adjacent sub-systems on the level of a given failure can take over from a faulty unit.

*3) Time scaling.* The direct costs of operating a system in real time are proportional to the rate of operation. In hierarchial situations it is possible to grade the bandwidths of the devices for control implementation such that control of rapid wide bandwidth disturbances is performed at a low hierarchial level by simple closed loop devices. More complex calculations occurring at slower rates can be done at higher levels in the hierarchy. The result is a more economic distribution of computing capacity over the hierarchy.

*4) Simplified design.* Hierarchial control can make explicit use of simplified models of lower levels often enabling reduced information flow up the levels of the hierarchy and simplifying design and implementation problems. Simplified models arise because lower level control can be used to suppress certain details from the sub-system descriptions such as disturbances, drift, noise, etc.

*General techniques for hierarchial control.* As in conventional or centralized control there are at least two approaches depending on whether a feasible, practical control policy is desired, or whether an optimum solution is desired. Since optimality inevitably requires a knowledge of the future, the optimal schemes are often impractical to realize.

In hierarchical control the approaches will be classed as direct methods or as decomposition methods, the former being the complementary set to the latter. A loose definition might be that 'Direct Methods' of synthesis are used when any kind of hierarchial situation is constructed by intuition.

*A survey of direct approaches to hierarchial control.* At present no theoretical basis exists for the synthesis of a hierarchy. Most published work is based on a simplification approach to each part of the system, aimed primarily at meeting physical constraints and achieving some kind of long term static optimum.

The aim of each local design is to suppress disturbances and make the subsystem controllable with respect to a few well chosen reference variables. This is generally done for each sub-system individually by small closed loop decision units.

At second and higher levels the problem reduces to adjusting the reference variables to meet overall objectives or performance criterion. It is generally true that the performance criterion is most sensitive to the reference variables and approximate control of the sub-system is usually quite adequate. Systematic approaches have been proposed based on examining the modes or eigenvalues of the sub-systems. The idea is that the overall response of the system is probably determined by only the dominant parts of the sub-systems. Thus by eliminating the rapidly varying or transient parts of the sub-system descriptions, a substantial reduction in system complexity can be achieved thus simplifying design.

*A survey of decomposition techniques for hierarchial control.* Decomposition techniques attempt to take a formulation of the problem of optimal control and separate it into parts pertaining to each natural division of the system. The advantage of this idea is that such subproblems have built in coordinating parameters which enable the optimum parts to solve the original problem.

Actually there are two fundamental approaches. The economic interpretation behind the first decomposition technique is that initially a price (per unit value) is defined for each interconnexion variable between the subsystems. Using these prices, a local performance economy can be established for each subsystem.

Net subsystem performance value =
(gross performance value) + (output value) − (input value).

The optimum inputs and outputs for each subsystem are then chosen to maximize the net performance value for each subsystem independently. Clearly for arbitrary prices the subproblems may make no sense and in general the best outputs are not necessarily the best inputs somewhere else.

This last observation gives rise to a second level coordination problem of adjusting the prices so that firstly, the outputs and inputs all match and secondly, the overall performance value is maximized. It is a remarkable fact that *minimizing* the sum of the maximal subsystem performance values performs both requirements simultaneously.

One inherent feature of this method of decomposition is that subproblems are essentially severed from one another and consequently a partially coordinated hierarchy designed on this basis is not physically realizable. Under these circumstances some kind of buffering is required to isolate the physical system while decomposition calculations are in progress.

An alternative decomposition method widely used in the United States electrical power industry is precisely the mathematical dual of the first method. It can only be applied to systems whose sub-processes have more degrees of freedom than outputs because it involves defining the interconnexion variables over periods of time. Each interconnexion variable between the subsystems is fixed, and this can be shown to be equivalent to setting up net cost economies for each subsystem. Each of these cost economies is minimized independently resulting in optimal subsystem operation. Each fixed input and output interconnexion variable has an associated price or per unit variable cost sensitivity. When the overall system is operating optimally the prices at input and output ends of each interconnexion must be equal. The coordinating problem for the second level is then firstly, to match these prices and secondly, to minimize overall costs. As before, this is done simultaneously by adjusting the interconnexion flows to *maximize* the sum of the minimal subsystem costs, contradictory as this may seem.

The attractive feature of this method is that a partially coordinated hierarchy based on this decomposition is always physically realizable in real time.

*General comments.* Implicit in this general discussion has been the idea that subsystems are easily recognized. This is generally not the case. Most of the techniques indicated here operate more readily if the interaction between sub-systems is weak (in fact they are ideal if there is no interaction at all). Thus one way of defining a subsystem is to isolate blocks of the system which have minimal interaction. The problem of finding blocks of minimal interaction is well known.

Finally, large scale systems on which hierarchial control is exercised usually consist of collections of small systems. In attempting to control a large system by looking in detail at its dynamics, the situation is close to that in classical physics when attempts were made to predict macro-phenomena by examining the individual atoms. Clearly some kind of 'statistical mechanics' of collections of interacting systems is lacking. Thus it is probable that the only true 'large scale technique' considered here is the approach based on simplification, which recognizes at the outset that fine microstructure of subsystems is irrelevant.

*See also:* Control by hybrid computers. Optimization of industrial processes.

*Bibliography*

ARROW K. J. (1964) *Control in Large Organizations*, Management Science, **10**, No. 3, 397 April.

BAUMOL W. J. and FABIAN T. *Decomposition, Pricing for Decentralization and External Economies*, Management Science, **11**, No. 1, 1 Sept.

BROSILOW C. B., LASDON L. S. and PEARSON J. D. (1965) *Feasible Optimization Methods for Interconnected Systems*, Proceedings, Joint Automatic Control Conference, 79, New York.

CARRÉ B. A. (1966) *The Partitioning of Network Equations for Block Iteration*, Computer, **9**, No. 1, 84, May.

COHN N. (1965) *State of the Automatic Control Art in the Electric Power Industry of the United States*, Proceedings, Joint Automatic Control Conference, 110, New York.

DANTZIG G. B. (1963) *Linear Programming and Extensions*, Princeton: The University Press.

DAVISON E. J. A. (1966) *A Method for Simplifying Linear Dynamic Systems*, IEEE Transactions on Automatic Control, Vol. AC-11, No. 1, 93, January.

KOEKIN A. I. (1965) *Optimization of Reliability and Structure of Hierarchic Control Systems*, Automatika i Telemakhanika **26**, No. 10, Part 1, 1707, Oct.

LEFKOWITZ I. (1965) *Multilevel Approach to Control System Design*, Proceedings, Joint Automatic Control Conference, 100, New York.

MILLER W. E. (1965) *Automatic Control in the Metallurgical Industry*, Proceedings, Joint Automatic Control Conference, 124, New York.

PEARSON J. D. (1965) *Multilevel Control Systems*, Proceedings, IFAC (Teddington) Symposium on Self-Adaptive Control Systems, Teddington, England.

ROSENBROCK H. H. (1966) *On the Design of linear Multivariable Control Systems*, Proceedings of IFAC, Session 1, Paper 1A, London.

ROTH J. F. (1962) *The Application of the Hierarchy System to On-Line Process Control*, Brit. I.R.E., 24, No. 2, 1, Aug.

STEWARD D. V. (1965) *Partititoning and Tearing Systems of Equations*, J. SIAM Numer. Anal., Ser. B, 2, No. 2.

J. D. PEARSON

**CONTROL, HILL CLIMBING IN.** Besides the normal input and output variables, a control system has disturbance variables occurring either as unpredictable variations of the input variables or as fluctuations in the system parameters. For example, in a chemical plant, the composition and feed rate of the input raw material may fluctuate about their normal values. The heat input may change unpredictably; the reaction rate of the process and the temperature and pressure distribution within the reactor will seldom, if ever, remain constant. Such disturbances inevitably affect the quality of the product.

If these disturbances are measurable or if the system dynamics are known, then special techniques (Aseltine et al. 1958) may be applied which will ensure optimum operation of the system under the given conditions. Practical systems, however, are usually very complex and the dynamics of these systems are generally not known in any detail. The disturbances are often not measurable. In such cases, an indirect method of control is employed. The performance itself is measured, using some suitably chosen index of performance, and trial-and-error experiments performed on the controllable parameters, for example heat input and feed rate of the raw material, to find the settings giving best performance. If the disturbances change, the parameters will be automatically adjusted to new positions to maintain optimum performance. Such trial-and-error methods are known as *hill climbing* techniques of optimization in control.

The performance index $P$ may be expressed as a function of the controllable parameters $K_i$, that is $P = f(K_i)$, and will have, in general, one or more extrema (maxima or minima) in the parameter space. Figure 1 shows typical performance contours of a two-parameter system. The object is to adjust $K_1$ and $K_2$ to the optimum values so that the extremum of $P$ is attained. (Henceforth we shall consider the extremum to be a maximum.)

Hill climbing by trial-and-error methods is a well-established technique in applied mathematics, where it is applied to problems in which the extremum of several variables is to be found. Many hill-climbing methods have been developed (Rosenbrock 1960). The basis of one of these is to measure the gradient of the multi-dimensional function by small changes applied to each variable in turn. The local direction of steepest ascent is thus determined and a small control step is initiated along this direction by suitably proportioned changes in the variables. This process is repeated at each new point until the maximum is reached.

Several difficulties are encountered in trying to apply the hill-climbing techniques of applied mathematics to control systems.

(a) The physical system takes a finite time to respond to exploratory changes in its parameters. This introduces a time delay between the application of the change and the subsequent measurement of its effect on the performance.

(b) The presence of disturbances introduces uncertainties in the measurements. It is necessary to base the performance index on time averages of functions of the system variables, thus introducing further delays in the gradient measurement.

(c) Whereas the variables of a mathematical function can be varied readily, those of a physical system have to be carefully handled, in view of the grave economic and physical results which may follow if successive erroneous adjustments are made as a result of statistical errors in measurement.

(d) The hill-climbing controller must be fast enough to track movements of the maximum resulting from external disturbances or from changes in the control system parameters.

The various hill-climbing methods used in the control field may be classified under two broad categories. The first type uses discrete exploratory steps in a logical search in the parameter space for the maximum. The results of these exploratory steps are used to initiate control steps according to a predetermined strategy. In the second type, the gradient is continuously computed, using small continuous periodic exploratory changes in the parameters. Here the adjustment in each parameter is generally made proportional to the derivative of the performance index with respect to the parameter, that is proportional to $\frac{\partial P}{\partial K}$. The system thus approaches the maximum along the line of the gradient.

*Discrete systems.* These are essentially automatic methods of carrying out the type of experiments described by Box and Wilson (1951). These are sequential search techniques, the sequence of moves following a predetermined strategy. Figure 2 shows a typical sys-

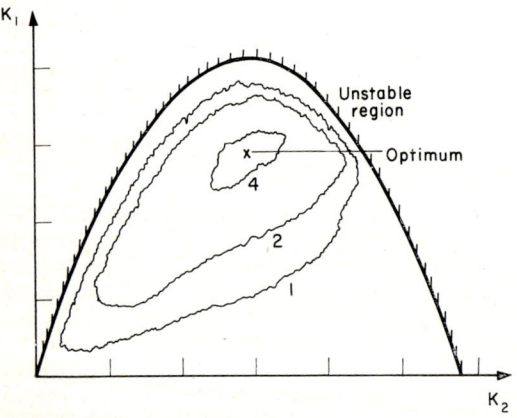

Fig. 1

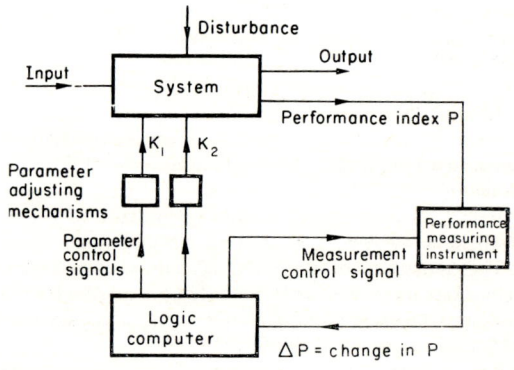

Fig. 2

tem. To illustrate some of the strategies proposed, we shall consider the problem of maximizing the system performance by controlling two parameters only.

The logic computer initiates exploratory steps in the parameters $K_1$ and/or $K_2$. The system is allowed to settle to the steady state before the change in performance is measured. The sign (and possibly the magnitude) of this steady state change is then used by the logic computer to determine the next exploratory step or adjustment step according to the strategy built into the logic.

In the simplest strategy, one parameter is subjected to an exploratory step to determine the direction of increasing $P$. The parameter is then adjusted along this direction until the maximum value of $P$ in this direction is reached. Holding this parameter constant at this value, the experiment is repeated on the other parameter and so on. The system thus approaches the optimum by a series of *alternate adjustments* in $K_1$ and $K_2$, as shown by trajectory 1 in Fig. 3.

This is illustrated in Fig. 4. At any point A along MN adjusting $K_1$ or $K_2$ does not improve $P$. An improvement will be observed only when $K_1$ and $K_2$ are adjusted together. Simultaneous exploratory steps in $K_1$ and $K_2$ are necessary, in general, to determine the direction of the gradient.

This difficulty is overcome in the following strategy (Rees 1960). Here the parameters $K_1$ and $K_2$ are adjusted such that the system makes one of eight exploratory steps in the $K_1 - K_2$ plane, as at point B in Fig. 4. These steps are taken in turn. The system is then adjusted along the direction of the step producing the greatest change in $P$ (that is along the gradient) in the steepest ascent or the gradient manner.

There are many variations of these basic techniques. Some of these have been built, with modifications, into commercial controllers. One of the earliest is the Westinghouse Company's Automex, which has been replaced by the OPCON, designed to control two parameters.

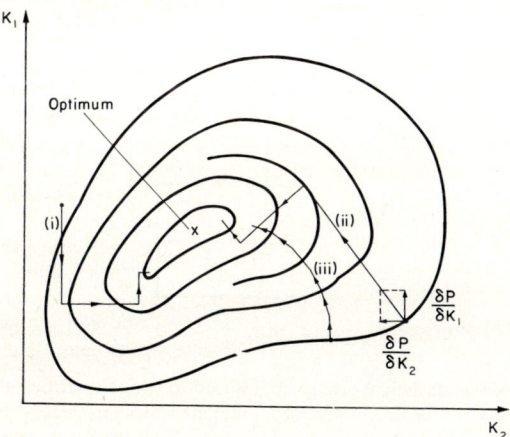

Fig. 3

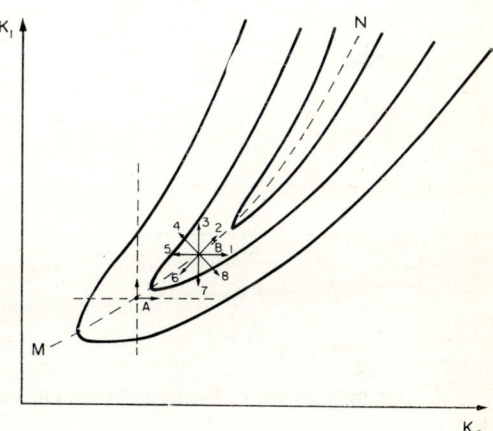

Fig. 4

A modification of this strategy is to measure the quantities $\frac{\partial P}{\partial K_1}$ and $\frac{\partial P}{\partial K_2}$ and then compute the gradient at the operating point. The system then moves along the direction of the gradient until the maximum in this direction is reached. The process is repeated at this point. This is the Method of *Steepest Ascent* (trajectory (ii) in Fig. 3).

In the *Gradient Method*, only a small adjustment is made along the gradient. At the new point, the gradient measurement is repeated. The next move is then along the new local gradient. The trajectory (iii) will therefore consist of a series of small moves along the gradient of the hill.

The Method of Steepest Ascent is most useful when the initial point is far away from the optimum. The Gradient Method is preferred when working near the optimum and for tracking a slowly moving optimum.

It is not always possible to reach the optimum by adjusting the parameters sequentially to find the gradient.

The first application of OPCON was in the control of a miniplant for the catalytic dehydrogenation of ethyl benzene in the production of styrene. The first British commercial adaptive controller is the Elliott Company's OPTIMAT which unlike the OPCON can control three parameters.

*Continuous perturbation systems.* Draper and Li (1951) proposed the use of continuous periodic perturbations in the parameter as an exploratory signal for determining the dependence of the performance index $P$ on the parameter. Referring to Fig. 5, which shows the $P-K$ characteristic for a single parameter system, the variation in $P$ resulting from a sinusoidal perturbation in $K$ changes sign as the operating point moves from one side of the optimum to the other. The magnitude of the change provides an estimate of the slope of the characteristic at the operating point.

Let the performance index be related to the parameter by the relationship $P = f(K)$. When the perturbation is introduced, the performance index $P'$ is given by

$$P' = f(K + \delta K \sin \omega t)$$
$$= f(K) + \delta K \sin \omega t \frac{\partial f}{\partial K} + \frac{(\delta K \sin \omega t)^2}{2!} \frac{\partial^2 f}{\partial K^2}$$
$$+ \ldots \ldots$$

$P'$ thus consists of the unperturbed value $P$ and terms involving $\delta K$ and higher powers of $\delta K$. The term involving $\delta K$ contains information about the magnitude and sign of the gradient of the characteristic, that is it involves the quantity $\frac{\partial f}{\partial K}$. This information may be

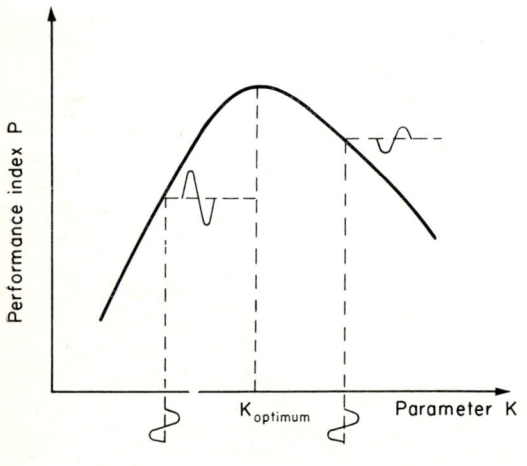

Fig. 5

obtained by multiplying $P'$ by the perturbation signal $\sin \omega t$ and averaging the product. Thus

$$\overline{P' \sin \omega t} = f(K) \overline{\sin \omega t} + \delta K \overline{\sin^2 \omega t} \; \frac{\partial f}{\partial K}$$
$$+ \ldots \ldots$$
$$= \tfrac{1}{2} \delta K \cdot \frac{\partial f}{\partial K} + \xi(t).$$

The bar denotes time averaging. $\xi(t)$ is a disturbance term due to the terms involving the odd powers of $\delta K$ and is, in general, negligible.

A complete sinusoidal perturbation system is shown in Fig. 6. The parameter is adjusted continuously at a rate proportional to the gradient, that is

$$\frac{dK}{dt} = \alpha \cdot \frac{\delta K}{T} \cdot \frac{\partial P}{\partial K}$$

where $T$ is the time constant of the integrator and $\alpha$ is a constant. Alternatively a 'sample-and-hold' operation may be interposed between the integrator and the adder so that the parameter is adjusted in steps once per cycle of the perturbation signal. Since the parameter is held constant between sampling intervals (except for the intentional perturbation), a more accurate estimate of the gradient can be obtained.

At the optimum no adjustment will be made, since $\frac{\partial P}{\partial K}$ is zero. The perturbation, however, will introduce a cyclic movement at the optimum. The consequent reduction in performance or hunting loss of the system must be kept small by using small perturbation amplitudes, usually of less than ten per cent of the maximum parameter value.

Perturbation signals other than sine waves may be employed. Square-wave perturbation is widely used, and is particularly useful, together with the sampled data control, when an on-line digital computer is employed in the gradient estimation. Random signals have been found to be of little use as perturbation signals because

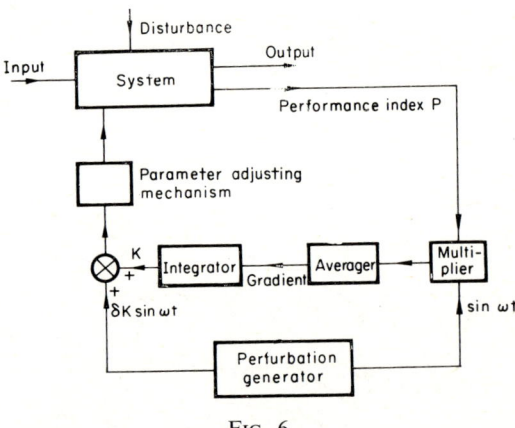

Fig. 6

of the statistical errors introduced in the estimation process. Unusually long measurement times are necessary to ensure an acceptably low noise level in the measurements.

Several parameters may be controlled simultaneously by operating a number of hill-climbing controllers in parallel (Douce and Ng 1964). In general, perturbation signals of similar frequencies are used to obtain a more or less uniform speed of operation in the controllers. The frequency separation must be made sufficiently large to keep the beat-frequency interference small.

The exact behaviour of these systems is extremely difficult to analyse. At present no comprehensive general theory has been presented. Analyses given for particular systems generally assume that the performance measure changes instantaneously with variations in the parameter, thus allowing the control system to be represented by an instantaneous non-linear relationship between the performance index and the parameter setting, as in Fig. 5. These analyses have been useful in so far as they give approximate criteria for choosing the values of the controller variables such as perturbation amplitude and frequency and gain of the controller. The stability of particular continuous perturbation systems and their behaviour in the presence of random disturbances have also been described.

The earliest application of the technique was described by Draper and Li in the optimization of the performance of an internal combustion engine. Other recent attempts have been in the control of combustion in industrial burners.

*Hill climbing with models.* A different approach to the optimization problem is used in the *model-reference* hill-climbing systems (Whitaker 1959). The technique assumes that the ideal system, or the best estimate of this, is known. The performance of the practical system is made to be as close as possible to that of the ideal system by controlling the parameters of the former. Figure 7 illustrates the technique. A dynamic model is used in

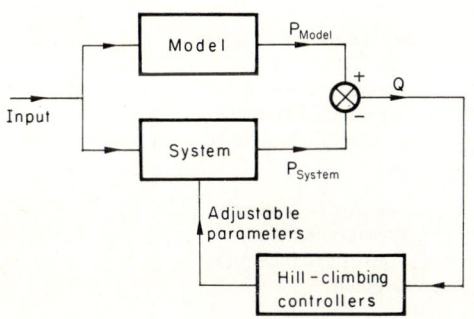

Fig. 7

parallel with the practical system and their performance measures are compared to give a new performance measure $Q$. The hill-climbing controller adjusts the system parameters to minimize $Q$. This is essentially a regulatory system. The overall performance is dependent mainly on the reliability of the model, the derivation of which is extremely difficult for all but the simplest systems.

The reverse of this technique has been used for on-line model-building or identification of the dynamics of the system (Blandhol). In this application of the hill-climbing technique, a computer model is set up which approximates in form to the expected transfer function of the system. The parameters of the model are built in as adjustable coefficients under the control of hill-climbing controllers. The model is subjected to the same input and disturbances as the system. A performance measure is formed from the difference in the responses of the model and the system, for example this may be the mean square value of the difference. The hill-climbing controllers then adjust the model coefficients to minimise this performance measure.

*See also:* Adaptive control theory. Control by model reference. Discrete models for forecasting and control. Control, identification techniques for. Optimization, automatic.

*Bibliography*

ASELTINE J. A., MANCINI A. R. and SARTURE C. W. (1958) *A Survey of Adaptive Control Systems*, I.R.E. Trans. on Automatic Control, Vol. AC-6, 102, Dec.

BLANDHOL E. *On the Use of Adjustable Models for Determination of System Dynamics*, Tech. Rep. no. 62–5-D, Division of Auto. Control, Technical University, Trondheim, Norway.

BOX G. E. P. and WILSON K. B. (1951) *On the Experimental Attainment of Optimal Conditions*, J. Roy. Statist. Soc., **13** (Series B), 1.

DOUCE J. L. and NG K. C. (1964) *A Six-channel Adaptive Computer*, Proc. I.E.E., **111**, No. 10.

DRAPER C. S. and LI Y. T. (1951) *Principles of Optimalising Control Systems and an Application to the Internal Combustion Engine*, ASME Publications, New York., Sept.

REES N. W. (1960) *Self Adaptive Systems*, Brit. Chem. Eng., **5**, Feb.

ROSENBROCK H. H. (1960) *Computer J.*, **3**, 175.

WHITAKER H. P. (1959) MIT Presentation; *Proceedings of the Self Adaptive Flight Control Systems Symposium*, 58, March.

K. C. NG

**CONTROL, IDENTIFICATION TECHNIQUES FOR.** *General aspects.* Among the tendencies in the development of control engineering there are: the growing emphasis on optimal and self-optimizing systems and: the use of control systems in applications where the environment changes rapidly and drastically.

A general aspect of these systems is the need to derive knowledge about the dynamics or non-linearities of the process under control. This need is caused by the (strong) dependence of the (optimal) operation on this knowledge. The methods used for obtaining that knowledge, mostly under normal operating conditions of the process, are called '*identification techniques*'.

Strictly speaking identification has the connotation of starting from scratch without any prior knowledge about the process. In the majority of engineering situations and in a number of cases in biology as well this is not a realistic assumption; from the structure of the 'process' and at least a partial understanding of its operation a certain amount of *a priori* information will, be available. In such cases the knowledge to be derived is reduced to numerical values of certain parameters: coefficients of differential equations governing the dynamics of the process, coefficients of a linear or a non-linear 'model' of the process, etc. Consequently the identification problem is reduced to that of (process) *parameter estimation*. Here the word estimation refers to the fact that the numerical values obtained for the parameters will be subject to uncertainty on account of disturbances (noise) and a limited observation time interval.

In some cases one is interested in a more detailed knowledge. This may be a continuous information about the state of the process which is needed for optimal control. The problem of deriving this knowledge is called *state estimation*.

In this article attention will be focused on parameter estimation, as this is the most important aspect that can be discussed in rather general terms. Most other aspects are very much dependent on the application under consideration.

The above diagram indicates the theories that are relevant for this problem together with the goals or applications for parameter estimation.

From this diagram it will be clear that the potential applications extend beyond those in control engineering. It also follows that, through stochastic-signal theory, statistics and information theory, a considerable use is made of probabilistic notions and results.

With respect to the instrumentation of the parameter estimation problem only a few requirements of a general nature can be formulated. One wants to find the characteristics of the process:

Accurately, not affected by additive noise and possible unwanted non-linearities in the system.

Rapidly, yet under the condition that the system always has to be stable.

Economically, using an instrumentation that is feasible with repects to costs.

As regards the type of instrumentation used for solving the parameter-estimating problem two different classes can be distinguished (Eykhoff 1964):

Instrumentation of mathematical relations that result explicitly in numerical quantities for the parameters. This type of instrumentation is called: '*using an explicit mathematical relation*'.

Instrumentation using a physical model, the parameters of which are controlled in such a way that the characteristics of the model approach the characteristics of the process under study in some predefined sense. This will be called: '*using a model adjustment technique*'.

The difference between these two classes is illustrated by the block diagrams Figs. 1 and 2. Depending on the

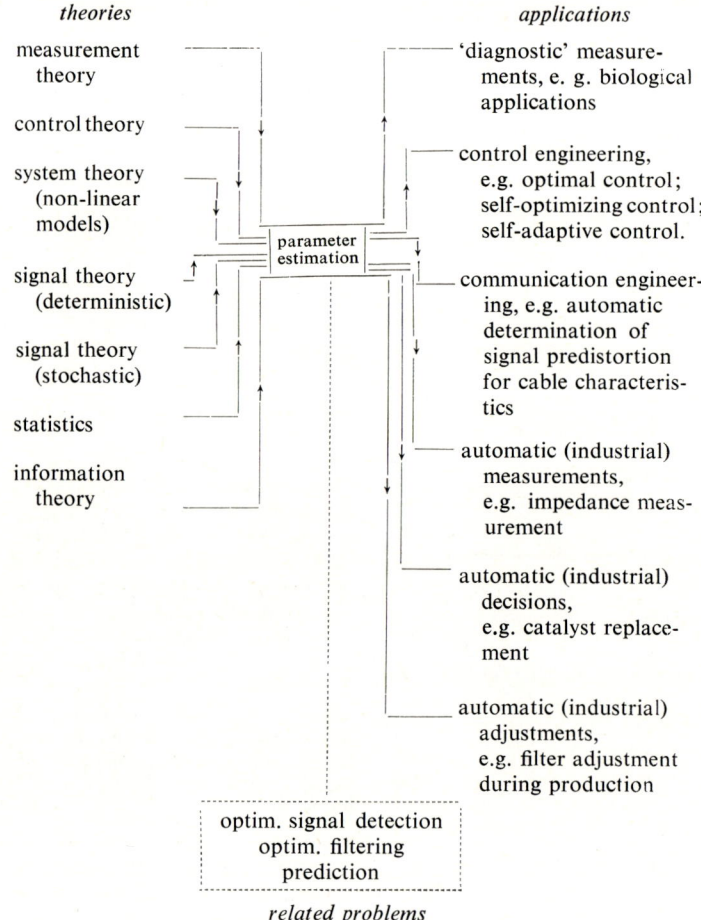

Multiply both sides of this equation with $x(t-\tau)$, representing a delayed version of the input signal:

$$y(t)\, x(t-\tau) = \int_0^\infty h(\theta)\, x(t-\theta)\, x(t-\tau)\, d\theta. \quad (30)$$

For (ergodic) stationary stochastic signals the correlation can be written as

$$\psi_{xy}(\tau) = \lim_{T\to\infty} \frac{1}{2T} \int_{-T}^{+T} x(t-\tau)\, y(t)\, dt. \quad (31)$$

Consequently by applying the operation

$$\lim_{T\to\infty} \frac{1}{2T} \int_{-T}^{+T} \ldots dt$$

to both sides of equation 30 and changing the order of integration, one arrives at

$$\psi_{xy}(\tau) = \int_0^\infty h(\theta)\, \psi_{xx}(\tau-\theta)\, d\theta = h(\tau) * \psi_{xx}(\tau). \quad (32)$$

If the input signal is white noise then its correlation function is $\psi_{xx}(\tau-\theta) = k\delta(\tau-\theta)$; the Dirac 'function'. In that case

$$\psi_{xy}(\tau) = \int_0^\infty h(\theta)\, k\delta(\tau-\theta)\, d\theta = kh(\tau), \quad (33)$$

i.e. one point of the impulse response function $h(t)$ is determined. For input signals with other correlation functions one can arrive at $h(t)$ from equation 32 by simulation of the convolution on an analog computer or by transformation to the frequency domain and curve fitting.

The averaging operation over an infinite time interval is, of course, highly impractical. In actual applications one has to restrict the correlation time to a finite interval $(0, T)$. Consequently one obtains approximations of the correlation functions that can be denoted by $\psi_{xx}(\tau, T)$ and $\psi_{xy}(\tau, T)$. These experimental 'correlation functions' show some variance (uncertainty) with respect to the theoretical correlation functions.

In the light of the discussions in the previous section it is clear that this procedure is not restricted to determining points of an impulse response function only. Depending on the type of process representation other parameters can be determined as well, e.g. coefficients of an orthogonal expansion.

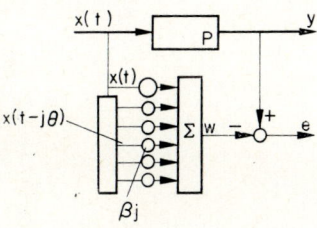

Fig. 10

It was stated before that the simple correlation technique provides us with a least squares estimation of the unknown parameters. This can be shown by the following discussion; cf. Fig. 10. The process output is $y(t)$; the output of a conceptual model, again consisting of a time delay circuit, is

$$w(t) = \sum_j \beta_j x(t-j\theta). \quad (34)$$

The mean square error between these outputs is:

$$E = \lim_{T\to\infty} \frac{1}{2T} \int_{-T}^{+T} \left\{ y(t) - \sum_j \beta_j x(t-j\theta) \right\}^2 dt. \quad (35)$$

Minimizing with respect to $\beta_i$ requires $\partial E/\partial \beta_i = 0$, which leads to

$$\lim_{T\to\infty} \frac{1}{2T} \int_{-T}^{+T} y(t) x(t-i\theta)\, dt$$

$$= \lim_{T\to\infty} \frac{1}{2T} \int_{-T}^{+T} \left\{ \sum_j \beta_j x(t-i\theta) \right\} x(t-i\theta)\, dt$$

$$= \sum_j \beta_j \lim_{T\to\infty} \frac{1}{2T} \int_{-T}^{+T} x(t-j\theta) x(t-i\theta)\, dt. \quad (36)$$

Using the definition of a correlation function given before this leads to:

$$\psi_{xy}(i\theta) = \sum_j \beta_j \psi_{xx}((i-j)\theta) \quad (37)$$

or, written in matrix form for three parameters as an example:

$$\begin{pmatrix} \psi_{xy}(0) \\ \psi_{xy}(\tau) \\ \psi_{xy}(2\tau) \end{pmatrix} = \begin{pmatrix} \psi_{xx}(0) & \psi_{xx}(-\tau) & \psi_{xx}(-2\tau) \\ \psi_{xx}(\tau) & \psi_{xx}(0) & \psi_{xx}(-\tau) \\ \psi_{xx}(2\tau) & \psi_{xx}(\tau) & \psi_{xx}(0) \end{pmatrix} \begin{pmatrix} \beta_0 \\ \beta_1 \\ \beta_2 \end{pmatrix}$$

This is the discrete version of equation 32. If the input signal is white noise then

$$\psi_{xx}((i-j)) = k\delta((i-j)\theta) = \begin{cases} 0 & \text{for } i \neq j \\ k & \text{for } i = j \end{cases}$$

and

$$\psi_{xy}(i\theta) = k\beta_i. \quad (38)$$

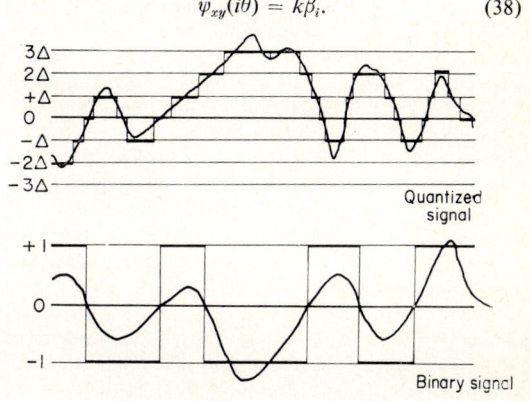

Fig. 11

The least squares properties follow from a comparison of the equations 33 and 38.

There is a host of publications on correlation techniques of which only a few are mentioned in the references (Faran and Hills 1952; Solodownikow and Uskow 1963; Lampard 1955; Balchen and Blandhol 1960).

From an engineering point of view it is preferable to operate with signals $x$ and $y$ which can assume only a limited number of levels (quantized signals; binary signals; cf. Fig. 11). For such wave forms multiplication is simpler to instrument than for pure analog signals (Faran and Hills 1952). In many cases even a coarse quantization does not influence the properties of the correlation technique very much (Watts 1962; Veltman and Van den Bos 1963).

*See also:* Control by model reference. Control by stationary fiiltering and prediction. Discrete models for for forecasting and control. Learning machines: a unified view. Pseudo–random binary signals, use of in correlation analysis of dynamic systems.

*Bibliography*

ASTRÖM K. J. and BOHLIN T. (1965) *Numerical Identification of Linear Dynamic Systems from Normal Operating Records*, Paper IFAC Symposium on 'The Theory of Self-Adaptive Control Systems' Teddington, Sept.

BALCHEN J. G. and BLANDHOL E. (1960) *On the Experimental Determination of Statistical Properties of Signals and Disturbances in Automatic Control Systems, Automatic and Remote Control*, (Proc. First Internat. Congress IFAC, Moscow, 1960) **2**, 788, London: Butterworths.

BLANDHOL E. and BALCHEN J. G. (1963) *Determination of System Dynamics by Use of Adjustable Models, Automatic and Remote Control (Proc. Second Congress IFAC*, Basle, Sept. 1963) *Theory*, 602, London: Butterworths; Munich: Oldonbourg.

DEUTSCH R. (1965) *Estimation Theory*, Englewood Cliffs, N.J.: Prentice Hall.

EYKHOFF P. (1963) *Some Fundamental Aspects of Process-Parameter Estimation, I.E.E.E. Trans.*, Vol. AC-8, no. 4, 347, Oct.

EYKHOFF P. (1964) *Process Parameter Estimation*, in (Macmillan *et al.* Eds.), *Progress in Control Engineering*, Vol. 2, London: Heywood.

FARAN J. J. and HILLS R. (1952) *Correlators for Signal Reception*, Techn. memo no. 27, Acoustics Research Laboratory, Harvard University (Mass.), Sept.

GABOR D., WILBY W. P. L. and WOODCOCK R. (1961) *A Universal Nonlinear Filter, Predictor and Simulator which Optimizes Itself by a Learning Process*, Proc. I.E.E., **108B**, no. 40, 422, July.

KOKOTOVIĆ P. V. and RUTMAN R. S. (1965) *Sensitivity of Automatic Control Systems (Survey), Automatic and Remote Control*, **26**, no. 4, 727, April.

KOKOTOVIĆ P. V. *et al.* (1966) *Sensitivity Method in the Experimental Design of Adaptive Control Systems*, paper: Third Congress IFAC, London.

LAMPARD D. G. (1955) *A New Method of Determining Correlation Functions of Stationary Time Series*, Proc. I.E.E., **102**, part C, 35.

LEVIN M. J. (1960) *Optimum Estimation of Impulse Response in the Presence of Noise*, IRE Trans., Vol. CT-7, no. 1, 50, March.

MASLOV E. P. (1964) *Application of the Theory of Statistical Decisions to the Estimation of Object Parameters, Automation and Remote Control*, **24**, no. 10, 1214, March.

MEISSINGER H. F. (1960) *The Use of Parameter Influence Coefficients in Computer Analysis of Dynamic Systems*, Proc. of the West. Joint Computer Conf., San Francisco, 181, March.

SOLODOWNIKOW W. W. and USKOW A. S. (1963) *Statistische Analyse von Regelstrecken*, Berlin: VEB Verlag Technik.

VELTMAN B. P. Th. and VAN DEN BOS A. (1963) *The Applicability of the Relay-Correlator and the Polarity-coincidence Correlator in Automatic Control, Automatic and Remote Control (Proc. Second Congress IFAC*, Basle, 1963), *Theory*, 620, London: Butterworths; Munich: Oldenbourg.

WATTS D. G. (1962) *A General Theory of Amplitude Quantization with Applications to Correlation Determination*, Proc. I. E. E, **109**, part C, no. 15. 209, March.

P. EYKHOFF

**CONTROL, INVARIANCE AND.** The '*principle of invariance*' is a mathematical principle which can be applied in a number of situations in which the basic aim is to neutralize the effects of unwanted disturbances. In general, if there is a known linear relationship between the variables $x, \ldots x_n$ of a system and certain forcing terms $u_1 \ldots u_m$ and unwanted disturbances $f_1 \ldots f_l$ and if this relation can be written in the form

$$\begin{bmatrix} a_{11} & a_{12} & \cdots & a_{1n} \\ a_{21} & a_{22} & \cdots & a_{2n} \\ \vdots & \vdots & & \vdots \\ a_{n1} & a_{n2} & & a_{nn} \end{bmatrix} \begin{bmatrix} x_1 \\ x_2 \\ \vdots \\ x_n \end{bmatrix} = \begin{bmatrix} b_1 f_1 \\ \vdots \\ b_l f_l \\ 0 \\ \vdots \\ 0 \end{bmatrix} + \begin{bmatrix} c_1 u_1 \\ \vdots \\ c_m u_m \\ 0 \\ \vdots \\ 0 \end{bmatrix}$$

then a particular variable $x_i$ is unaffected by a particular disturbance $f_j$ if the cofactor of $a_{ji}$ is zero, i.e. if the determinant

$$A_{ji} \equiv \begin{bmatrix} a_{11} & \cdots a_{1, i-1} & a_{1, i+1} & a_{1n} \\ \vdots & \vdots & \vdots & \vdots \\ a_{j-1,1} & \cdots a_{j-1, i-1} & a_{j-1, i+1} & a_{j-1, n} \\ a_{j+1,1} & \cdots a_{j+1, i-1} & a_{j+1, i+1} & a_{j+1, n} \\ \vdots & \vdots & \vdots & \vdots \\ a_{n, 1} & a_{n, i-1} & a_{n, i-1} & a_{nn} \end{bmatrix} = 0$$

In the above statement of the principle, the coefficients $a_{11} \ldots a_{nn}$ $b_1 \ldots b_l$ $c_1 \ldots c_m$ can represent either plain numbers (when applied to a problem of static equilibrium) or differential operators or 'transfer functions' (when applied to a dynamical problem).

An example of a static system is the feedback arrangement shown in Fig. 1 for a power amplifier. The box enclosed by a dotted line represents a power amplifier with high input impedance, unity gain, and output impedence $k_0$. The current drain $f$ can be regarded as a disturbing influence, and the various voltages in the circuit are related by the equations

$$\begin{bmatrix} -1 & -1 & 1 \\ 0 & -2 & 1 \\ \frac{1}{k_0} & \frac{1}{k_0}+\frac{1}{k_1} & \frac{-1}{k_0} \end{bmatrix} \begin{bmatrix} x_0 \\ x_1 \\ x_2 \end{bmatrix} = \begin{bmatrix} (k_1+k_0)f \\ 0 \\ 0 \end{bmatrix} + \begin{bmatrix} 0 \\ u \\ 0 \end{bmatrix}.$$

The principle of invariance tells us that $x_0$ is independent of $f$, i.e. the amplifier has zero output impedance when

$$\begin{bmatrix} 1-2 & 1 \\ \frac{1}{k_0}+\frac{1}{k_1} & \frac{-1}{k_0} \end{bmatrix} = 0$$

i.e. when $k_0 = k_i$.

The application of the principle to a dynamic mechanical system can be illustrated by the spring-weight assembly shown in Fig. 2 which represents a non-perfectly rigidly mounted force-measuring device. If the frame is put in an accelerating environment, the acceleration $f$ can be regarded as a 'disturbing influence' and the system is described by the set of equations:

$$\begin{bmatrix} D^2+\frac{k_1}{m_1} & -\frac{k_2}{m_1} & 0 \\ -\frac{k_1}{m_1} & D^2+\frac{k_2}{m_2}+\frac{k_3}{m_2}+\frac{k_2}{m_1} & -\frac{k_3}{m_2} \\ \frac{k_4}{m_3}-\frac{k_1}{m_1} & \frac{k_2}{m_1}-\frac{k_3}{m_3} & D^2+\frac{k_3}{m_3}+\frac{k_4}{m_3} \end{bmatrix} \times \begin{bmatrix} x_1 \\ x_2 \\ x_3 \end{bmatrix} = \begin{bmatrix} f \\ 0 \\ 0 \end{bmatrix}$$

where D denotes $d/dt$. The displacement $x_3$ is unaffected by $f$ if $A_{13} = 0$, i.e. if

$$k_1; \; k_4 = k_2 : k_3 = m_1; \; m_2.$$

The principle of invariance is applicable to the design of control loops most effectively for the control of linear multivariable systems. The 'complete' invariance (i.e. the exact vanishing of the appropriate minor $A_{ji}$) can only be attained in a control loop if the disturbing influences can be traced to a single or relatively small number of primary signals (such as mains supply variations). It is also necessary for any disturbing influence to

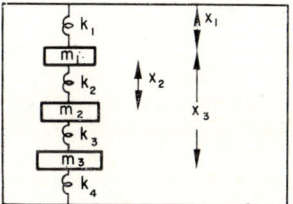

Fig. 2

act on a control loop at points which can be intercepted by measurements. The control loop shown in Fig. 3 shows this and is typical of the configurations of closed loops designed according to the principle of invariance.

The time varying signals $u \, f \, x_0 \, x_1 \, x_2$ are related by the equations:

$$\begin{bmatrix} 1 & 0 & -a_5(D) \\ a_2(D) & 1 & -a_3(D) \\ 1 & a_4(D) & -1-a_5(D) \end{bmatrix} \begin{bmatrix} x_0 \\ x_1 \\ x_2 \end{bmatrix} = \begin{bmatrix} f \\ 0 \\ 0 \end{bmatrix} + \begin{bmatrix} 0 \\ (a_1(D)+a_2(D))u \\ 0 \end{bmatrix}.$$

The output $x_0$ is unaffected by $f$ if $A_{11} = 0$, i.e. if

$$a_3(D) = \frac{1+a_5(D)}{a_4(D)}.$$

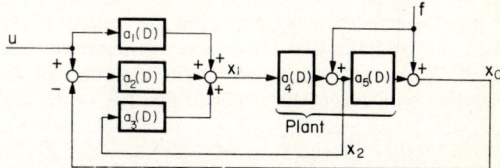

Fig. 3

Sometimes if there are several disturbing influences it is only possible to compensate a limited number of them. This condition is known as '*selective invariance*'. In other cases it is not possible to fulfil invariance conditions exactly and a condition of 'approximate invariance' or 'invariance up to $\sum$' may have to be specified, especially with non-linear plants. Invariance may be regarded in the design of control loops as a criterion which is complementary to other criteria such as 'low transient response time', 'insensitivity to parameter variations', 'high stability margins' etc. Invariance has been given a great deal of theoretical study especially in the U.S.S.R. in the early post war years. The related topics of designing multivariable control and of attaining insensitivity to plant parameter variations have however been most fruitfully studied by somewhat different approaches.

See also: Control sensitivity and

*Bibliography*

KESLEBAKIN and PETROV (1963) *Automation and Remote Control*, IFAC Congress Moscow, London: Butterworths.

J. D. ROBERTS

**CONTROL OF AIRCRAFT AS TWO NON-INTERACTING SYSTEMS.** A flexible aircraft in flight may be considered to consist of two interacting sub-systems: one sub-system represents the motion of an equivalent rigid aircraft disturbed from trimmed flight while the other represents the deformation motion of the elastic airframe situated in a uniform airstream of speed equal to the trimmed flight speed. When the deformation motion is referred to Body Mean Axes (Milne 1964) the interaction between these systems is purely aerodynamic in origin. The interaction is often weak and in that case it is possible to treat the flexible aircraft as two equivalent, non-interacting systems (Milne 1965).

The deformation of the continuous elastic airframe is usually represented by a weighted sum of suitably chosen co-ordinate functions so that the airframe system is reduced to one of finite dimension. If the co-ordinate functions are chosen to be the normal, in-vacuo, vibration modes of the airframe (Milne 1964) the deformation motion is necessarily referred to Body Mean Axes. In addition, provided the aerodynamic surfaces are of aspect ratio less than about six and the motions to be considered are not too rapid the concept of constant aerodynamic derivatives may be employed (Etkin 1959). With these assumptions the equation of first variation with respect to trimmed flight is of the form

$$\frac{d\mathbf{u}}{dt} - \mathbf{C}\mathbf{u} = \mathbf{f}(t) \qquad (1)$$

where $\mathbf{C}$ is a real, constant matrix and $\mathbf{u}(t)$ is the trajectory of the system in the state-space of $l$ dimensions. If $\mathbf{U}$ is the matrix of characteristic vectors of $\mathbf{C}$ and the characteristic roots (assumed distinct) are $\lambda^{(e)}$, $e = 1, 2, \ldots l$, the solution of (1) with initial point $\mathbf{u}(o)$ is

$$\mathbf{u}(t) = \mathbf{Y}(t)\mathbf{u}(0) + \int_0^t \mathbf{Y}(t-\tau)\mathbf{f}(\tau)\,d\tau \qquad (2)$$

where
$$\mathbf{Y}(t) = 0 \qquad t < 0,$$
$$= \mathbf{U}\,\text{diag}\,[\exp\lambda^{(e)}t]\,\mathbf{U}^{-1}, \qquad t \geq 0$$

is the principal matrix solution of (1).

Let the system equation (1) be partitioned to the form

$$\frac{d}{dt}\begin{bmatrix}\mathbf{u}_1\\\mathbf{u}_2\end{bmatrix} - \begin{bmatrix}\mathbf{C}_{11} & \mathbf{C}_{12}\\\mathbf{C}_{21} & \mathbf{C}_{22}\end{bmatrix}\begin{bmatrix}\mathbf{u}_1\\\mathbf{u}_2\end{bmatrix} = \begin{bmatrix}\mathbf{f}_1(t)\\\mathbf{f}_2(t)\end{bmatrix}, \quad \mathbf{u}(0) = \begin{bmatrix}\mathbf{u}_1(0)\\\mathbf{u}_2(0)\end{bmatrix} \qquad (3)$$

where $\mathbf{C}_{11}$ and $\mathbf{u}_1$ of dimension $m$ refer to the rigid aircraft, $\mathbf{C}_{22}$ and $\mathbf{u}_2$ of dimension $n$ refer to the elastic airframe and $l = m+n$.

The matrices $\mathbf{C}_{12}$, $\mathbf{C}_{21}$ represent the aerodynamic coupling terms. When symmetric and antisymmetric aeroplane motions are considered separately the dimension of $\mathbf{C}_{11}$ will not exceed six. The dimension of $\mathbf{C}_{22}$ will generally be not less than four (two normal vibration modes) and will usually be more. The characteristic roots of $\mathbf{C}_{22}$ may differ considerably from the normal mode roots due to the presence of the aerodynamic forces.

Let the characteristic roots of $\mathbf{C}_{11}$ and $\mathbf{C}_{22}$ form two disjoint sets which are widely separated in modulus. That is, if the roots of $\mathbf{C}_{11}$ lie on or within the circle of radius $r$ and the roots of $\mathbf{C}_{22}$ lie on or without the circle of radius $R$ then $r/R \ll 1$. In addition, let $\mathbf{C}_{12}$, $\mathbf{C}_{21}$ be small in a sense to be detailed later. With these assumptions the principal matrix solution $\mathbf{Y}(t)$ can be approximated by the sum (Milne 1965),

$$\mathbf{Y}(t) = \begin{bmatrix}\mathbf{Y}_1(t) & -\mathbf{Y}_1(t)\mathbf{C}_{12}\mathbf{C}_{22}^{-1}\\ -\mathbf{C}_{22}^{-1}\mathbf{C}_{21}\mathbf{Y}_1(t) & \mathbf{C}_{22}^{-1}\mathbf{C}_{21}\mathbf{Y}_1(t)\mathbf{C}_{12}\mathbf{C}_{22}^{-1}\end{bmatrix}$$
$$+ \begin{bmatrix}\mathbf{C}_{12}\mathbf{C}_{22}^{-1}\mathbf{Y}_2(t)\mathbf{C}_{22}^{-1}\mathbf{C}_{21} & \mathbf{C}_{12}\mathbf{C}_{22}^{-1}\mathbf{Y}_2(t)\\ \mathbf{Y}_2(t)\mathbf{C}_{22}^{-1}\mathbf{C}_{21} & \mathbf{Y}_2(t)\end{bmatrix} \qquad (4)$$

where $\mathbf{Y}_1(t)$, $\mathbf{Y}_2(t)$ are respectively the principal matrix solutions of the modified, rigid aircraft sub-system

$$\frac{d\mathbf{u}_1}{dt} - [\mathbf{C}_{11} - \mathbf{C}_{12}\mathbf{C}_{22}^{-1}\mathbf{C}_{21}]\mathbf{u}_1 = 0 \qquad (5)$$

and the elastic airframe sub-system

$$\frac{d\mathbf{u}_2}{dt} - \mathbf{C}_{22}\mathbf{u}_2 = 0. \qquad (6)$$

That is, if $\lambda_1^{(i)}$, $i = 1, 2 \ldots m$ are the characteristic roots and $\mathbf{U}_1$ is the matrix of characteristic vectors of the $m$-dimensional matrix

$$\mathbf{C}_{11} - \mathbf{C}_{12}\mathbf{C}_{22}^{-1}\mathbf{C}_{21},$$

then
$$\mathbf{Y}_1(t) = \mathbf{U}_1\,\text{diag}\,[\exp\lambda_1^{(i)}t]\mathbf{U}_1^{-1}, \quad t \geq 0. \qquad (7)$$

Similarly, if $\lambda_2^{(p)}$, $p = 1, 2 \ldots n$ are the characteristic roots and $\mathbf{U}_2$ is the matrix of characteristic vectors of the $n$-dimensional matrix $\mathbf{C}_{22}$

$$\mathbf{Y}_2(t) = \mathbf{U}_2\,\text{diag}\,[\exp\lambda_2^{(p)}t]\mathbf{U}_2^{-1}, \quad t \geq 0. \qquad (8)$$

The conditions for weak coupling are derived in Milne (1965). They require that $r/R \ll 1$ and that in $\mathbf{C}_{11} - \mathbf{C}_{12}\mathbf{C}_{22}^{-1}\mathbf{C}_{21}$ a typical element of the second matrix should be at most of the same order as the corresponding element of $\mathbf{C}_{11}$. It is also shown there that, provided these conditions are satisfied, then if the roots $\lambda_1^{(i)}$ lie on or within the circle of radius $r^*$, $r^*/R \ll 1$.

The roots $\lambda_1^{(i)}$, $\lambda_2^{(p)}$ are approximations to the roots $\lambda^{(e)}$ of the system matrix **C** while an approximation to the matrix of characteristic vectors of **C** is

$$\mathbf{U} = \begin{bmatrix} \mathbf{U}_1 & \mathbf{C}_{12}\mathbf{C}_{22}^{-1}\mathbf{U}_2 \\ -\mathbf{C}_{22}^{-1}\mathbf{C}_{21}\mathbf{U}_1 & \mathbf{U}_2 \end{bmatrix}. \quad (9)$$

The collineatory transformation $\mathbf{U}^{-1}\mathbf{C}\mathbf{U}$ gives, upon using equation

$$\mathbf{U}^{-1}\mathbf{C}\mathbf{U} = \begin{bmatrix} \mathbf{\Lambda}_1 & \mathbf{\Lambda}_1\mathbf{U}_1^{-1}\mathbf{C}_{12}\mathbf{U}_2\mathbf{\Lambda}_2^{-1} \\ \mathbf{\Lambda}_2^{-1}\mathbf{U}_2^{-1}\mathbf{C}_{21}\mathbf{U}_1\mathbf{\Lambda}_1 & \mathbf{\Lambda}_2 \end{bmatrix} \quad (10)$$

where $\mathbf{\Lambda}_1 = \mathrm{diag}\,[\lambda_1^{(i)}]$, $\mathbf{\Lambda}_2 = \mathrm{diag}\,[\lambda_2^{(p)}]$.

If **U** were the matrix of exact characteristic vectors of **C** then the right hand side of equation 10 would be exactly the characteristic roots of **C**. What the approximation achieves is a reduction of the coupling matrices by roughly the ratio $r^*/R$ and hence a reduction of the product of the coupling matrices by $(r^*/R)^2$. To this order the flexible aircraft is represented by the two non-interacting systems (5) and (6).

The response of the initially quiescent, equivalent rigid aircraft system to the input $\mathbf{f}(t)$ is, for example,

$$\mathbf{u}_1(t) = \int_0^t \mathbf{Y}_1(t-\tau)\,\{\mathbf{f}_1(\tau) - \mathbf{C}_{12}\mathbf{C}_{22}^{-1}\mathbf{f}_2(\tau)\}\,d\tau$$
$$+ \mathbf{C}_{12}\mathbf{C}_{22}^{-1} \int_0^t \mathbf{Y}_2(t-\tau)\,\{\mathbf{f}_2(\tau) + \mathbf{C}_{22}^{-1}\mathbf{C}_{21}\mathbf{f}_1(\tau)\}\,d\tau.$$

Under certain circumstances the roots of the matrix $\mathbf{C}_{22}$ need not be known in detail. Thus, provided estimates are available to show that $r/R \ll 1$ and that $\mathrm{Re}\,(\lambda_2^{p}) < \mathrm{Re}\,(\lambda_1^{(i)})$ the response of the aircraft in the state variables $\mathbf{u}_1$ for sufficiently slowly varying inputs will be given by,

$$\mathbf{u}_1(t) = \int_0^t \mathbf{Y}_1(t-\tau)\,\{\mathbf{f}_1(\tau) - \mathbf{C}_{12}\mathbf{C}_{22}^{-1}\mathbf{f}_2(\tau)\}\,d\tau$$
$$+ \mathbf{C}_{12}\mathbf{C}_{22}^{-2}\mathbf{f}_2(\tau).$$

The equivalent rigid aeroplane sub-system (5) is associated in British literature with the 'method of modified derivatives' (Taylor 1959) and in American literature with the 'quasi-static method' (Runyan et al. 1961).

The treatment of the elastic airframe system (6) forms the basis of many Aeroelastic studies. For a study of oscillatory instability (flutter) this is valid according to the conditions of weak interaction provided the flutter frequency is at least of the order of the lowest natural frequency. However, many such studies have been concerned with the static stability of the airframe system (aeroelastic divergence) and neglect of the interaction with the 'rigid' aircraft is then clearly not admissible.

*See also:* Control, stability and.

*Bibliography*

ETKIN B. (1959) *Dynamics of Flight*, New York: Wiley.
MILNE R. D. (1964) *Dynamics of the Deformable Aeroplane*, Aeronautical Research Council, R. & M. No. 3345.
MILNE R. D. (1965) *The Analysis of Weakly Coupled Dynamical Systems*, International J. Control, **2**, No. 2, 171, August.
RUNYAN H. L., PRATT K. G. and BENNET F. V. (1961) *Effects of Aeroelasticity on the Stability and Control Characteristics of Airplanes*, A.G.A.R.D. Report No. 348, April.
TAYLOR A. S. (1959) *The Present Status of Aircraft Stability Problems in the Aeroelastic Domain*, J. Roy. Aeronaut. Soc., No. 580, **63**, 227.

R. D. MILNE

**CONTROL OF AN ECONOMIC SYSTEM.** An economic system can be thought of as a vast human computer into which information is fed continuously, leading to calculations, decisions and actions. For the system to work well, the flow of information should be both full and up to date. Equally important, it should be appropriately distributed among the units responsible for the decisions: insufficient knowledge at one point will not be compensated by an excess of information at another. Given a well-regulated flow of information, it should not be impossible to build into the system a set of controlling devices which would ensure that the ultimate aim of economic activity, namely making the best possible use of all available resources, is achieved.

Viewed in this light, the study of economics is largely the study of information and control in a particular kind of self-regulating system. But borrowing the language of control-system engineering is one thing, applying its methods to economic policy is another. Before considering how far this is possible, it may be useful to indicate the various ways in which economic systems have been controlled in the past and, to a greater or lesser extent, are still controlled today.

In primitive societies, purposive economic action is limited; economic life is not clearly distinguished from life in general, economic values are not emphasized and control is largely authoritarian. People who live in such societies are likely to be more concerned with playing a role determined by their birth than with optimal economic behaviour. Powerful social forces, usually impressed by a superior class and accepted without much questioning by the inferior classes, are likely to exist which greatly reduce the scope of economic innovation, so that if ideas of potential economic value arise they may either not be recognized or not be turned to economic purposes.

Gradually, traditional attitudes give way under the impact of innovation, and free enterprise develops. Status is replaced by contract; class relationships by competitive relationships. A clearer distinction is made between economic life and life in general, economic values are greatly emphasized and control is, to a considerable extent, exercised by purposive action directed to individual gain. Although each economic unit, whether a producer or a consumer, a worker or an employer, a saver or an investor, is too small, typically, to influence the market appreciably, the universal attempt to buy cheap and sell dear generates the necessary flow of information in terms of a continually changing set of prices. Given its preferences and a knowledge of the constraints under which it operates, each unit responds to these price signals in such a way as to maximize its gain.

This is a highly simplified account of the working of a free enterprise system but it brings out an important point: such a system, in principle at least, is self-regulating. Like a biological or ecological system, it does not depend on outside control. It is to this feature that it owes its robustness. However, in the real world a number of forces conspire to diminish the effectiveness of the self-regulating process, and these give rise to a number of policies designed to make it work better. The policies pursued are of many different kinds but tend to serve a few broad purposes.

First, the dominating principle of self-interest often leads producers to act collusively in order to raise the prices of their products above the 'competitive' level. Accordingly, there are policies which, taking the competitive economy as an ideal, try to make the real world conform more closely to this ideal. The outstanding example of this type of policy is anti-trust legislation, the purpose of which is to prevent the formation of price rings and restore as far as possible the competitive self-regulation of the idealized system.

Second, while society must be on its guard against anti-social acts of collusion, there are forces other than self-interest which work against the persistence of 'perfect competition'. In most branches of production, efficiency is increased by economies of scale, so that a big unit can sell its products at a lower price than can a small unit. In these circumstances it is only a matter of time before a few big producers come to dominate the market and squeeze out their smaller competitors. The resulting state of affairs can be operated to the benefit of the community and indeed is a precondition of a wealthy society, but it does raise the possibility of monopolistic malpractices. In an attempt to prevent these without losing the advantages of economies of scale, many governments introduce schemes to regulate and control the larger units in the system, sometimes culminating in complete public control through nationalisation.

Third, small units, lacking the power to determine prices, often find it difficult to adapt themselves to sudden changes in demand. This is particularly the case in the more fragmented sectors of production, such as agriculture. Thus there is a tendency for the units in these sectors to combine in operating restriction schemes, whose purpose is to avoid temporary over-production leading to a sudden fall in prices and to the consequent ruin of many individual producers. Inevitably, this type of control causes shortages when demand rises again. The various buffer-stock schemes promoted by governments and international organizations are another form of control, intended to avoid shortages without causing hardship to the small producer.

Fourth, for many reasons the social gains or losses which follow from an individual action may not coincide with the gains or losses incurred by the person who takes the action. For example, the subscriber to a telephone confers a benefit on those who want to get in touch with him, but the user of a car inflicts a cost on other road users. To a large extent such gains and losses lie outside the activities of the market, and when public authorities become aware of the ill-effects of certain private actions, such as the congestion of streets and roads, they usually react by imposing either indiscriminate prohibitions or indiscriminate taxation. The introduction of parking meters and tolls shows that better methods of control are sometimes possible, in this case by using the price mechanism to regulate a non-market activity.

Fifth, an economic system mainly regulated by market forces has a tendency to oscillate, sometimes with very serious consequences. This gives rise to policies which use the price mechanism as a tool to be arbitrarily manipulated in an attempt to restore the balance in those parts of the system which seem to need it most. An example of this type of policy is the use of purchase tax, hire-purchase terms and interest rates to check or stimulate consumption according to the state of the balance of payments. Such policies are usually justified as short-term measures taken to avert a critical state of disequilibrium. In practice they tend to persist, causing a good deal of dislocation in other parts of the system and doing nothing to cure the basic conditions which led to the loss of balance in the first place.

Finally, we come to policies which, on social as well as economic grounds, reject the free-enterprise system altogether and try to organize the use of economic resources by means of directives emanating from a single centre. The abandonment of the principle of self-interest naturally avoids its shortcomings, but its replacement by political and administrative decisions leads to evident difficulties. Above all, the flow of information that must be absorbed by the central organism to ensure welfare and efficiency by bureaucratic means is staggeringly large.

In view of all the difficulties that experiments in economic control have brought to light, it is natural to ask whether the problem has been properly regarded by politicians and economists and whether its true nature cannot be better understood by following the thought processes used in control-system engineering and systems analysis. Of course an economic system is altogether more complex than the industrial and technical processes where these methods have had so much success, and so it is not to be expected that they can be lifted lock, stock and barrel to solve the problems of economic control. Nevertheless they provide a point of view which might eventually contribute greatly to the solution of control problems in the economic sphere.

As a very simple example, consider a proposal for maintaining full employment by varying social security contributions inversely with the level of unemployment. By this means, if unemployment rises, the retained income of those who pay the contributions rises too, they tend to spend more and thus stimulate production and reduce unemployment. Conversely, if unemployment falls, the retained income of those who pay the contributions falls, they tend to spend less and thus cause production to contract and unemployment to rise. The social security fund is so set up than it can absorb these fluctuations in its income, and in this way the changing level of spending by the contributors will tend to stabilize employment at whatever level is considered desirable.

Let us now paraphrase this problem and its solution in the language of control-system engineering. We compare our objective with the performance of the system and seek a means of bringing the performance close to the objective and keeping it there. We do this by studying the dynamics of the system, choosing a control variable and formulating a control function which gives the value to be taken by the control variable in terms of our objective and of the performance of the system. If the control function is well formulated, the changing value of the control variable will produce the desired result.

The kind of difficulties we have to face in applying such ideas as these can be seen by considering the elements in the formal description.

*(a) Objective.* In this particular example the objective, maintaining full employment, is superficially a very simple one. In practice it may not be so easy to decide just how much unemployment must be tolerated to allow for unavoidable factors such as changes of job and seasonality: if too much allowance is made for these factors, some waste of resources will be built into the system by the controlling device; if too little allowance is made, the system may become explosive, money values, but not the goods and services they represent, tending to rise without limit. Thus our objective is not simply to maintain full employment but also to avoid explosive price movements. Since in practice objectives are always composite, we have to face the essentially political problems of resolving a conflict of aims by giving appropriate weights to the different elements of which our objective is composed.

*(b) Performance.* In this example, there should be no great difficulty in measuring performance monthly and in obtaining these measures with a time-lag of about one month. If this is sufficient for the operation of a satisfactory control system, well and good. But if it proves not to be, then reliable, up-to-date measures of performance may call for a radical revision of existing methods of collecting and processing data.

*(c) Dynamics of the system.* Our knowledge of how the system works can be formalized in a model which sets out the relationships connecting the variables in terms of which the system is described. A reasonably accurate model, in which attention is paid to time-lags and to the variances of random impulses that affect the system, is needed in order to design an efficient control function. In social and economic applications our knowledge of how the system works must largely be derived from how it has worked in the past, since the scope for experimentation is limited.

*(d) Control variable.* In this example, the control variable is the rate of contribution to social security. In practice it is often necessary to consider several control variables. Further, it must be recognized that a social or economic system may not be wholly controllable, in the sense that parts of it may not be accessible to any politically acceptable control variable.

*(e) Control function.* In this example, the control function specifies the value of the control variable in terms of the objective and of a lagged value of performance, the lag arising because we cannot measure performance instantaneously. In practice, for efficient control, it would be necessary to consider not only the level of performance but also its integral and derivative with respect to time.

It may be helpful to illustrate what has just been said by means of a diagram. In order to avoid complications, income (or product), $Y$ say, will be identified with employment, so that if $Y$ is kept to a target value, $Y^*$ say, employment will be kept at its 'full' level. Also for simplicity, foreign trade, the need for intermediate production, the dependence of saving on wealth as well as on income, and a host of other factors are ignored.

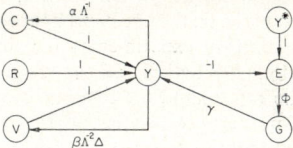

In this figure, $\alpha$, $\beta$ and $\gamma$ are parameters; $\Lambda$ is the lag operator (often written as $E$), so that $\Lambda^{-1}$ applied to a variable indicates its value in the preceding time-period; $\Delta \equiv \Lambda - 1$ is the first-difference operator; and $\Phi$ is the control function.

The left-hand side of the diagram, up to and including $Y$, illustrates the dynamics of the system. Two feedback relationships are shown: the first connecting current expenditure (consumption), $C$, with $Y$; the second connecting capital expenditure (investment), $V$, with $Y$. The first relationship states that this year a proportion, $\alpha$, of last year's income is spent on consumption, which expenditure in turn generates an equal amount of income this year. The second relationship states that this year a proportion, $\beta$, of the increase in income from two years ago to last year is spent on capital goods, which expenditure in turn generates an equal amount of income this year. Such simple relationships could not be expected to hold exactly, and so this year's income is shown as affected by a random element, $R$.

The systematic part of the model can be expressed as an autoregressive equation of the second order and will oscillate if the discriminant $\frac{1}{4}(\alpha+\beta)^2-\beta < 0$. For example, if $\alpha = 0\cdot 6$ and $\beta = 1$, the system will exhibit undamped oscillations with a period of about ten years.

The right-hand side of the diagram shows a means of controlling this system. Its performance, summarized by $Y$, is subtracted from the desired performance, $Y^*$, to give a measure of the error in performance, $E$. The control function, $\Phi$, depends on $E$ and determines the control variable, $G$, which in turn acts proportionately on $Y$.

This simple example does not presume to settle without more ado the complicated question of unemployment but to illustrate a point of view: that any control problem, if it is to be even partially solved, must be analysed in terms of the five headings, (a) through (e), given above. This is an accepted fact in the physical sciences. A better appreciation of it in the social sciences would help in the formulation of policies for economic control and discourage the endless introduction of half-thought-out measures which complicate our lives without meeting the basic conditions on which successful control depends.

*See also:* Control by model reference.

R. STONE

## CONTROL OF RESPIRATION, SELF-ADAPTIVE.

The subject of respiratory control has been studied by different types of workers concentrating on different aspects. For example, on the one hand neurophysiologists investigated mainly in experiments on animals 'respiratory reflexes' or the activity of the 'brain respiratory centre'. On the other hand the respiratory physiologist investigated such aspects as the 'work of breathing', breathing in exercise or the chemical control of ventilation. Most of these different and varied studies have been very comprehensively reviewed in the last few years (see Bibliography).

A recent study, both theoretical and experimental, attempts to bring together in the form of a model many of the different aspects studied by other workers (Priban and Fincham 1965). The object of this model is that it should explain as simply as possible the natural behaviour of the entire respiratory control system, in particular that of man.

The first mathematical model of respiratory regulation was the 'respiratory chemostat' by Gray (1946).

Actual simulation studies on computers of certain aspects of respiratory control began with the partial pressure of carbon dioxide, $p_{CO_2}$, as the only variable controlling ventilation. This model and the subsequent ones have as basic element the servomechanism. With this the controlled variable is kept at a desired level by comparison with a preset reference level through the feedback loop. The difference between the two levels or some function of this, the error signal, is used to bring about the correction. In the earliest model the blood flow was assumed to be constant, circulation times infinitely short and all tissue elements were lumped. This simple model was then progressively refined (a) by dividing the tissues into two compartments, brain and body, and considering the cerebral blood flow as a function of arterial $p_{CO_2}$; (b) by including circulation times and the control of oxygen; (c) more details of the structure and parameters of the brain medullary $CO_2$ receptor, and (d) by adjusting model parameters so that simulated responses matched the experimental ones more closely (Grodins 1963; Handbook of Physiology; Horgan and Lange 1962; Milhorn et al. 1965; Nahas 1963).

Although the performance of such models has been similar to that of the real system modelled under certain idealized conditions of operation, the inclusion of several reference levels seems unrealistic when one takes into account the necessary interaction of the respiratory control system with other physiological control systems; also, there is no experimental evidence to suggest that biological reference levels exist. The close control of the many variables of the respiratory system, even when some of the system parameters are subject to large changes, can be best explained at present in terms of the theory of self-adaptive multi-level control systems.

The most basic observations that any model has to explain are that in normal man the mean values of the relevant variables in the arterial blood, the pH, partial pressure of carbon dioxide and partial pressure of oxygen, $(p_{O_2})$, at rest and during exercise are nearly constant and that there is little variation in these values between normal individuals. These observations and others suggest that the operation of the respiratory system is controlled in such a way that the exchange of oxygen and carbon dioxide for one another between the environment and the body keeps pace exactly with the metabolic requirements of the body provided these are not too severe.

The proposed new model of the respiratory control system can account for these and many additional observations. It may be considered to consist of three interacting control loops involving:

(1) The control of the blood respiratory chemistry. The process by which for any given metabolic exchange requirement by the lungs of both oxygen and carbon dioxide the level of ventilation is kept at a minimum.

(2) The control of the activity of the respiratory muscle. The process by which for any level of ventilation demanded by the blood chemistry, a pattern of activation of the respiratory muscles is selected in which the average expenditure of energy is kept at a minimum.

(3) The control of the airway dimensions. The process by which for any alveolar gas exchange requirement the energy required to ventilate the dead space is kept at a minimum.

The three processes are co-ordinated and controlled by the over-all controller, a network of respiratory neurones in the brain. The controller predicts the activity which will keep the over-all energy expenditure of the respiratory system at the minimum. For this prediction the controller uses information fed back during previous breaths.

*Control of the blood respiratory chemistry.* An accurate description of the physico-chemical state of the blood relevant to respiration must take into account, at least, the following variables, pH or hydrogen ion concentration, the partial pressures of carbon dioxide and oxygen and the level of saturation of haemoglobin with oxygen ($S_{O_2}$) and the temperature. The chemical state is dependent upon the relative exchange flow rates of $CO_2$ and $O_2$ from the blood. They occur in one direction as the blood passes the tissue cells of the body where metabolism is occurring and in the opposite direction as the blood passes through in the lungs. The important functional respiratory characteristics of blood are largely due to the properties of haemoglobin.

When haemoglobin is oxygenated in the absence of carbon dioxide there is an acidifying effect. This effect is a function of pH and is maximal at pH 7·4. In the presence of carbon dioxide and above certain values of $p_{CO_2}$, and pH, oxygenation tends to make blood more alkaline. The presence of carbon dioxide also increases the buffer power towards addition of fixed acid or fixed base. The important functional relation between haemoglobin and the respiratory variables is shown in Fig. 1. This representation on the shape of a hill shows that the maximum number of molecules of carbon dioxide that can be exchanged per molecule of oxygen (without producing changes in the pH or $p_{CO_2}$) occurs at pH 7·4 and a $p_{CO_2} = 40$ mm Hg, the values normally found in arterial blood. The $p_{O_2}$ value and the temperature appear to be involved in determining the properties of the blood and therefore the shape of the hill. It seems that at a lower $p_{O_2}$ the base of the hill is smaller.

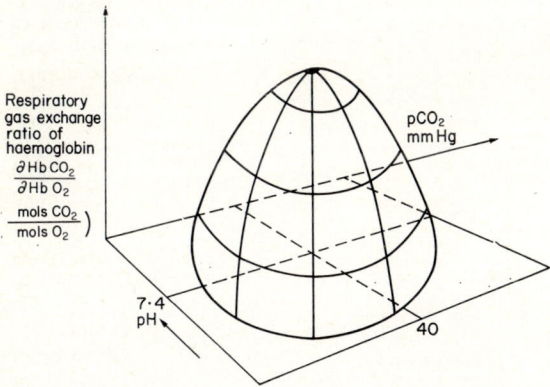

FIG. 1. *Relation between the respiratory variables of blood.*

Figure 2 shows a two-dimensional curve in which the abscissa is a composite function of pH and $p_{CO_2}$. The curve has a peak value of about 0·67, whereas a typical value for the metabolic gas exchange ratio is 0·76. This means that as blood passes through the lungs or the tissues, haemoglobin can only partly buffer against the tendency for a change in the state of the blood and, therefore, both pH and $p_{CO_2}$ will change.

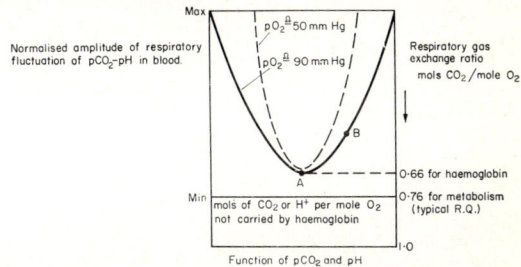

FIG. 2. *Functional respiratory and control characteristics of blood.*

The rhythmical nature of breathing produces cyclic variations in the $p_{CO_2}$ and $p_{O_2}$ values of the gases in the lungs and thus also in the gas exchange rate ratio between the blood and the gas phase. This in turn induces fluctuations in the values of $p_{CO_2}$, $p_{O_2}$ and pH of the arterial blood leaving the lungs. The mean values of these variables depend on the composition of blood entering the lungs and on the total volumes of $CO_2$ and $O_2$ exchanged. If the mean state of the blood is at point A, then the gas exchange in the lungs can be accomplished with the smallest variation about the mean state. If, however, the blood is at state B, then for the same gas exchange the variation in state will be larger.

An analysis of the fluctuations in the arterial $p_{CO_2}$ shows that these increase with increasing metabolic (exercise) carbon dioxide production. In resting man the pH fluctuations have an amplitude of 0·01 to 0·015 pH units.

Histological and physiological findings suggest that a sensor mechanism exists in the area postrema region of the brain which is capable of responding to these fluctuations in $p_{CO_2}$, pH or both. The acceptance of this hypothesis enables a complete optimizing system to be postulated (Fig. 3).

The principle of control is that ventilation is adjusted in the direction that will minimize the magnitude of the

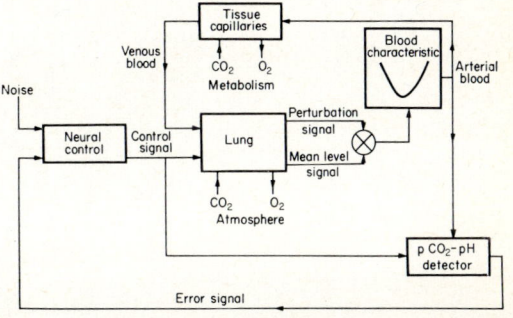

FIG. 3. *The respiratory gas exchange control system.*

fluctuations. These serve as a perturbation or test signal and when it is at a minimum, the mean values of pH and $p_{CO_2}$ are those found in normal man (Fig. 2). They are also the values at which the level of ventilation will exactly keep pace with the metabolism. The 'control signal' connexion to the sensor is necessary so that the sensor output is independent of the pattern of breathing and dependent only on the state of the blood passing through it.

*Control of the respiratory muscles.* When the duration of a breath is short and the tidal volume small, high input power is required to produce the relatively larger changes in velocity of muscle shortening. Because the 'dead space' volume of the airways has to be cleared before any useful gas exchange can occur, increased energy is required to compensate for the relative reduction in the effective gas exchange volume. Alternatively, at large tidal volumes, large movements are required for longer durations. The power required to distend the chest wall and enlarge the lungs rises steeply as the tidal volume increases. The natural frequency of breathing is found to agree with the predicted frequency at which the power necessary for a particular level of ventilation is at a minimum.

The main energy consumption in respiration is that due to the expenditure in the 'respiratory muscles'. These muscles, although referred to here as respiratory muscles, may also be involved in other functions such as limb movement or holding a load.

The physical properties and the structure of the muscular respiratory apparatus are such that considerably more energy is required for effecting unit ventilation (volume of air inspired or expired per unit time) in some parts of the system as compared with others. This property can be represented by contours of performance index values on the grid of a two-dimensional muscle map. This index is defined by the maximum number of units of ventilation obtainable per unit energy expenditure in the muscles. The contours are different for different levels of ventilation and different postures. The objective of the control process is to match the muscle activity contours with the performance index contours of highest value. The muscle activity at any instant in time is determined by a sequence of control actions involving three levels of control (Fig. 4).

A high level overall or executive controller defines the total amount of energy, $E$, to be expended in a breath and the time, $\tau$, over which it is to be dissipated. It does this by comparing the optimal predicted $E$ for a breath with the actual $E$ in that breath. The result is a prediction for the next breath in terms of energy and time. This prediction is conditioned by the response of the system during previous breaths. It is the activity that in the steady state should keep the operating point of the blood at the optimum while using a minimum of energy.

An intermediate level controller takes the orders from the higher level and produces a more detailed temporal distribution of the pattern of activity. Finally a low level controller details the spatial pattern of activity.

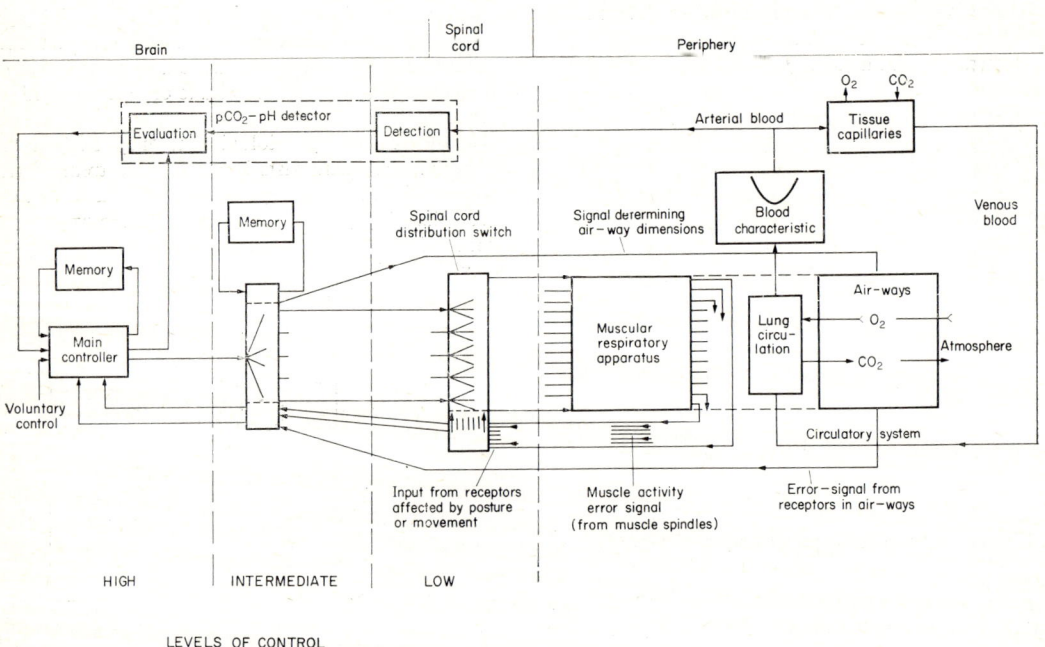

FIG. 4. *Organization of the overall respiratory control system.*

The high and intermediate levels of control are in the brain. The lower level controller is in the spinal cord and involves muscle spindles. Its action is to select those muscles, in some detail, that can effect ventilation while developing a minimum of tension. Such selection is probably accomplished by a continuous appraisal of muscle tension relative to the input signal to the muscles as determined by the muscle spindles. The output from the spindles, afferent nerve impulse activity, could in this way determine the spatial distribution of muscle activity. The output is also fed back to the highest level. If the muscles shorten and effect ventilation as predicted, no correction is required of the higher control activity. If, however, the load on the muscles has changed there is a difference between the predicted activity and the actual activity, and the feedback signal associated with this. This signal informs the brain about the new state of the muscular system and enables a new prediction to be made.

*Control of the airway dimensions.* This mechanism involves the vagus nerves which carries both the efferent fibres from the brain to the smooth muscles in the airway walls and afferent fibres coming from mechanoreceptors in the airway walls and going to the brain.

The apparent function of the airway control mechanism is to keep the airway diameter adjusted, by means of smooth muscles in its walls, to those dimensions at which the forces acting on the walls of the airway due to the main muscles of respiration are minimal. The main evidence for this comes from experiments on man. Temporary blocking of the pathway in the vagus nerve produces changes in the pattern of breathing which imply an increased energy consumption for an equal average level of ventilation.

*Overall control of respiration.* The function of the high level or main controller is the combination of functions of the three sub-systems. This is accomplished in such a way that the entire respiratory system functions with the minimum consumption of energy.

The necessity for combining the functions discussed separately become obvious when one considers that the dimensions of the airways determine both the resistance to air flow and the size of the ventilatory dead space, which determines the effectiveness of ventilation. The overall optimization ensures that the lung ventilatory gas exchange is equal to the metabolic gas exchange occurring at the level of tissues and organs. The index contours of many processes, if not all, may be represented in the shape of a hill. The overall control may be seen as a hillclimbing process involving an over-all functional hill of the respiratory system.

Consider a control sequence and begin with the operating point of blood away from the optimum (point B, Fig. 2) which may have been the result of a change in: (a) ventilation; (b) metabolism; (c) efficiency of airway control. The $p_{CO_2}$–pH detector (Fig. 4), by comparing the chemical state of the blood in the last few breaths with that in earlier breaths, obtains a measure of both the magnitude and the direction of the operating point of blood from the optimum value. This comparison enables the decision to be made whether or not a change in the energy dissipation for respiration is required to change the level of ventilation.

To resolve ventilation into tidal volume, $V_t$, and breath duration, $\tau$, the main controller uses the previous prediction, the memory of the muscle activity pattern controlling the present breath, and the error signals fed back from the muscular sub-system and airway sub-system. These error signals contain the information about the mismatch in performance with respect to the best predicted input to the sub-system. The signals from the receptors are reduced at the low and intermediate level controllers so that only the significant information about the accuracy of the prediction is fed back to the main controller. This is the converse process to that which produces an increase in resolution or detail of the control activity.

The prediction and relative adjustment of the values of $V_t$ and $\tau$ at which the mean value of energy expenditure is at a minimum for a given ventilatory demand involves information passing round in the three control loops. The existence of such a control process is suggested from an analysis of variations in $V_t$ and $\tau$ which have been observed during breathing. The values of $V_t$ and $\tau$ are positively correlated. These variations have an average cycle time of 3·6 breaths, while the cycle time expected from a random process is 3 breaths. The shortest cycle time of a controlled process of the type discussed, in which there are delays and which is subjected to random disturbances, would be expected to have a length of 3–4 breaths.

Evidently, describing the respiratory control system and other biological systems in the form of models is leading to a better understanding of complex biological mechanism. There is also a practical application in that with a model it has become possible to determine in medical diagnosis more exactly those components and parameters in a system that cause clinical impairment.

The relations between different systems and sub-systems that together comprise a living organism are discussed in more general terms in *Homeostasis*.

*See also:* Control, invariance and. Homeostasis in the single cell.

*Bibliography*

BROOKS C. McC., KAO F. F. and LLOYD B. B. (Eds.) (1965) *Cerebro-Spinal Fluid and the Regulation of Respiration*, Oxford: Blackwell.

COMROE J. E. (1965) *Physiology of Respiration*, Chicago: Year Book Medical Publishers.

CUNNINGHAM D. J. C. and LLOYD B. B. (Eds.) (1963) *The Regulation of Human Respiration*, Oxford: Blackwell.

GRAY J. S. (1946) *The multiple factor theory of the control of respiratory ventilation*, Science, **103**, 737; (1950)

*Pulmonary Ventilation and its Physiological Regulation*, Springfield, Ill.: Thomas.

GRODINS F. S. (1963) *Control theory and biological systems*, Colombia Press.

*Handbook of Physiology*, Section I, Neurophysiology Vol. 2; Section 3, Respiration, Vols. 1 and 2.

HORGAN J. D. and LANGE D. L. (1962) *Analog computer studies of periodic breathing*, I.R.E. Trans. Bio. Med. Elect. **9**, 221; (1965) *Digital Computer Simulation of Respiratory Responses to Cerebro spinal Fluid $p_{CO_2}$, in the cat, Biophysiol. J.* **5**, 935.

HUGH-JONES P. and CAMPBELL E. J. M. (Eds.) (1963) *Respiratory Physiology*, British Medical Bulletin, Vol. 19 (No. 1).

HOWELL J. B. L. and CAMPBELL E. J. M. (Eds.) (1966) *Breathlessness*, Oxford: Blackwell.

MILHORN H. T., BENTON R., ROSS R. and GUTYON A. C. (1965) *A mathematical model of the human respiratory control system, Biophysical J.*, **5**, 27.

NAHAS G. E. (Ed.) (1963) *Regulation of Respiration, Ann. N.Y. Acad. Sci.*, **109**, (2), 411.

PRIBAN I. P. and FINCHAM W. F. (1965) *Self-Adaptive Control and the respiratory system, Nature*, **208**, 339.

YAMAMOTO W. S. and BROBECK J. R. (1965) *Physiological Controls and Regulations*, Philadelphia: Saunders.

I. P. PRIBAN

**CONTROL, ON-OFF.** *Introduction.* On-off control, also and perhaps more appropriately described as *bang-bang* or *Schwartz–Weiss control*, is the principle governing the cheapest and most primitive control systems. At the same time its unique properties have been exploited in high grade control applications and it has the distinction of providing an optimal form of control under very general conditions.

The basic on-off relationship between deviation from desired state and control action is shown in Fig. 1.

This control law is the limiting case of a saturation characteristic in which the control action is proportionally related to deviation over a small range but becomes constant for larger deviations (dotted curve on Fig. 1).

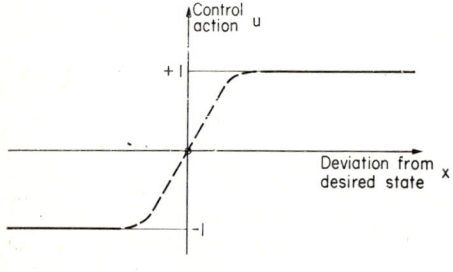

On-off control law (thick line)
u = sgn x

FIG. 1.

The on-off control law found early application in simple and inexpensive control systems. A typical example is the thermostatic temperature regulator where the desired temperature state is arranged to cause contacts mounted on a bimetallic strip to touch. These contacts switch the source of heat on and off depending on the sign of the difference between the desired and actual temperatures. Unless provision is made for actively removing heat as well as supplying it, the control action is zero when the desired temperature state is exceeded giving an asymmetrical characteristic.

Amongst the other applications of on-off control is the angular positioning of a shaft in accordance with remotely initiated demands for changes in position. Positional servomechanism to satisfy this requirement can be made using on-off elements such as electromagnetic or pneumatic relays and may have advantages of lightness and simplicity compared with the proportional amplifiers which would otherwise be necessary. (Hazen 1934; Hall 1947; La Salle 1954).

As an example consider the control of angular position of an electrically driven shaft in proportion to the magnitude and sign of a voltage (Fig. 2).

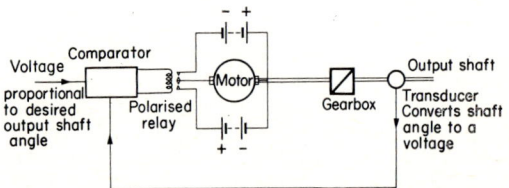

FIG. 2. *Simple relay controlled positional servomechanism.*

The control action is torque, produced by switching current to the motor; a polarized electromagnetic relay, sensitive to the direction of the drive current, is used for switching. The sign of the motor torque $T$ is determined by measuring the actual position of the controlled shaft, converting this into a proportional voltage and comparing it with the input voltage which is related to desired position. Any difference is a deviation from the desired state, or error, $e$ and the sign of this error, sgn $e$, determines the relay contact state and hence the sign of motor torque,

i.e. $T \propto \text{sgn } e$.

Clearly, when the desired angle of the output shaft has been reached and the error is zero, the relay is in a state of transition between its two possible positions. In the event of an ideal on-off characteristic being achieved (Fig. 1) it is clear that this state of transition occupies zero error range and is a physically unobtainable state. For this reason, assisted by the inevitable presence of time delays in the controller, practical on-off controllers exhibit continuous oscillations of error around the zero error point for zero input, a state known as *limit cycle oscillation*.

Limit cycle oscillations impose mechanical stresses and wear on the mechanical parts of on-off controlled mechanisms, as well as placing a limitation on the positioning accuracy which can be achieved (Uttley and Hammond 1952). The magnitude of the oscillations can be reduced, at the expense of an increase in their frequency, by adding to the error a term proportional to error rate,

i.e. $T \propto \text{sgn}\,[e + \Delta \dot{e}]$

so that switching now occurs when $\text{sgn}\,(e + \Delta \dot{e}) = 0$. Alternatively a *dead zone* may be introduced into the relay so that the control law is modified to the form shown in Fig. 3.

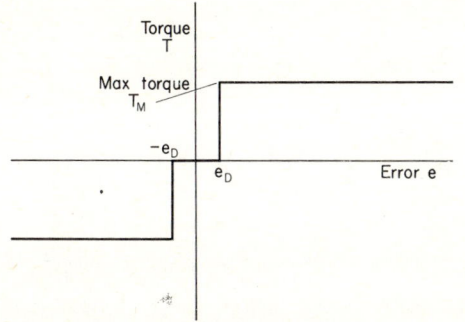

On-off control law with dead zone

FIG. 3.

By correct design the limit cycle may be eliminated in this way and the error $e$ will settle to a fixed value between $+e_D$ and $-e_D$ causing a static error in shaft positioning.

*Phase plane analysis.* The analysis of on-off controlled systems is simplified considerably by the use of the phase plane concept (Flügge-Lotz 1953; Hammond 1958; Fuller 1960). This leads to a graphical technique applicable to systems governed by certain second order non-linear differential equations and is of particular value for the analysis and synthesis of on-off controllers.

Suppose that the angle of the controlled shaft $\theta_0$ can be related to motor torque by a second order linear differential equation of the form

$$T = \frac{J\,d^2\theta_0}{dt^2} + \frac{F\,d\theta_0}{dt},$$

where $J$ is the effective moment of inertia referred to the motor shaft, $F$ is the effective speed dependent friction referred to the motor shaft.

The law of the on-off controller is

$$T = T_M \,\text{sgn}\,(\theta_i - \theta_0).$$

Hence, the non-linear equation of motion of the servomechanism is given by:

$$\frac{J\,d^2\theta_0}{dt^2} + \frac{F\,d\theta_0}{dt} = T_M \,\text{sgn}\,(\theta_i - \theta_0).$$

We have defined the error as $e = (\theta_i - \theta_0)$. So that

$$\frac{J\,d^2\theta_i}{dt^2} + \frac{F\,d\theta_i}{dt} = T_M \,\text{sgn}\,e + \frac{J\,d^2e}{dt^2} + \frac{F\,de}{dt}.$$

The servomechanism may be in a state of motion due to initial conditions in the form of previously applied demands or disturbances which have left the state variables with finite values at an arbitrary time origin. The subsequent motion is then said to be *autonomous* and the equations governing this state are obtained by setting the input angle $\theta_i$ and its derivatives to zero. A stable autonomous system, must, by definition, tend towards a state of rest or of strictly bounded motion.

The *autonomous state* is therefore defined by:

$$\frac{J\,d^2e}{dt^2} + \frac{F\,de}{dt} = -T_M \,\text{sgn}\,e.$$

The phase plane has co-ordinates which are state variables of the system; these are defined by writing down the set of first order equations governing the motion. In the present example they are:

$$\frac{J\,dv}{dt} + Fv = -T_M \,\text{sgn}\,e.$$

$$v = \frac{de}{dt}$$

so that the state variables are $v$ and $e$.

Figure 4 shows a phase plane diagram. If $e$ has an initial value $e_0$ at point A then the subsequent autonomous motion of the system can be described by the trajectory ABC where the rate of change of error $v$ tends to an asymptotic value $V_{\max} = -T_M/F$ corresponding to fric-

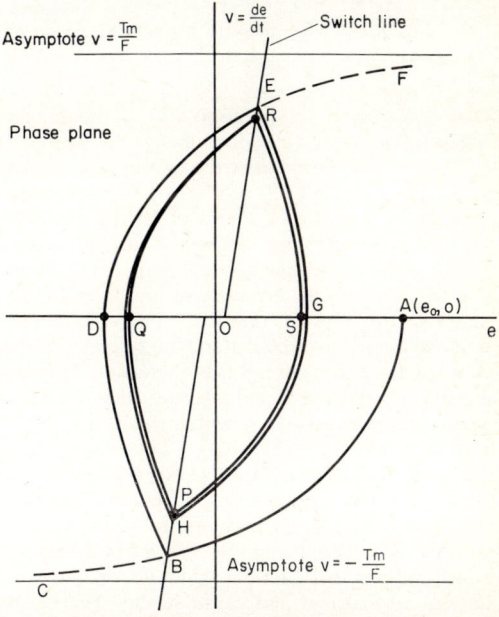

FIG. 4. *Phase plane diagram with trajectories of an on-off servomechanism.*

tion limited motor speed in one direction. At point B, however, the error has reached zero and its sign reverses. After a small time delay the relay operates and the trajectory becomes BDEF, tending to an asymtotic value of $T_M/F$. At E the relay again reverses and the subsequent course of the motion is GH, etc, finally arriving at a closed curve PQRS, representing a continuous oscillation or limit cycle. In the limit cycle a continuous fluctuation of energy from kinetic to potential form occurs in the system.

The line on which the torque reverses is called a *switch line* and is inclined at an angle to the ordinate due to the small time delay in relay operation.

If the initial conditions had been $e_0 <$ OS, i.e. within the limit cycle, then the trajectories of autonomous motion would spiral outwards from the centre, ending on the same limit cycle as before.

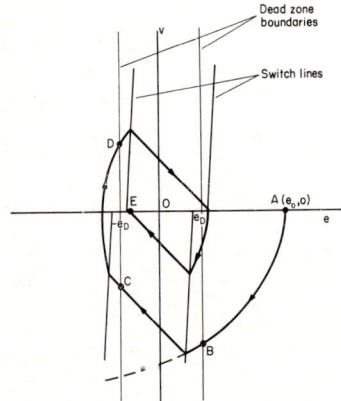

FIG. 5. *Phase plane diagram with trajectories of an on-off servomechanism having a dead zone characteristic.*

When dead zone is designed into the on-off controller the phase plane representation is as shown in Fig. 5. From an initial condition at A the output shaft accelerates towards alignment (i.e. zero error). The relay dead zone boundary is reached at B and after a short time delay the relay contacts open and motor torque becomes zero. The motor shaft then decelerates under the influence of friction until the error arrives at the value $-e_D$ at point C. After a further time delay the relay contacts close in the opposite direction and cause renewed and now reversed acceleration towards alignment. The dead zone is again entered at D and after a further overshoot the output shaft comes to rest with a small steady error at E.

The key to the design of on-off controlled systems lies in the shaping of the switch line to give a specified transient response and limit cycle amplitude.

As has already been mentioned, the introduction of a rate of change of error term into the control law can counteract time delays and cause smaller, higher frequency limit cycles. Thus let the control law be

$$T = T_M \operatorname{sgn}(e + \Delta v).$$

The reversal in motor torque will therefore occur when

$$e + \Delta v = 0.$$

This is a line through the origin of a phase plane diagram and its inclination causes switching to occur before the error becomes zero. The time delay is thus anticipated leading to greater stability and a smaller limit cycle amplitude.

*Optimal switching.* A switch line of particular significance is one which has the same shape as the trajectory BD (Fig. 4) displaced to the right, so that D coincides with the origin (Fig. 6).

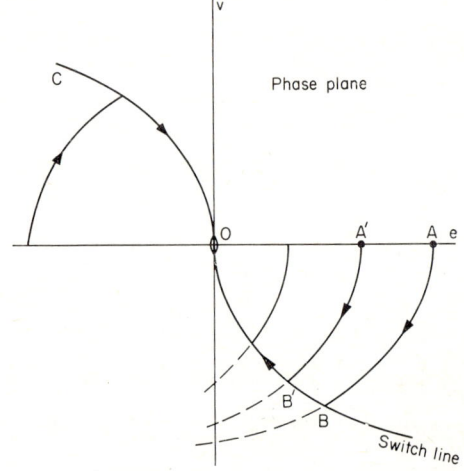

FIG. 6. *Optimal on-off control trajectories in a second-order system.*

Evidently, from Fig. 6, if switching occurs at point B, the subsequent motion follows a trajectory BO superimposed on the switch line. This special trajectory takes the system directly to the origin where zero error and zero error rate are achieved simultaneously. For any initial condition other than A, the motion will similarly arrive at the origin without overshoot.

On arriving at the origin, limit cycles will be established as before at an amplitude determined by the system time delays and other dynamical properties.

To achieve a non-linear switch boundary it is necessary to form a non-linear function of $v$ and arrange to switch when $e + f(v) = 0$.

To make analysis of the resulting motion easier the friction coefficient $F$ will be neglected. The trajectory equations are then

$$\frac{J \, d^2 e}{dt^2} = -T_M \operatorname{sgn}[e + f(v)].$$

This equation can be integrated by setting

$$\frac{d^2 e}{dt^2} = \frac{v \, dv}{de}$$

and separating the variables.

Hence the trajectories are found to be parabolas of the form:

$$\frac{v^2}{2} = -\frac{T_M}{J} \operatorname{sgn}[e+f(v)] + \text{constant of integration}.$$

For an initial condition at A (Fig. 6) a parabolic trajectory AB meets a parabolic switching boundary BOC. Similarly for any other initial state, e.g. $A^1$ the system also arrives at the co-ordinate origin with no overshoot.

In fact this method of control can be readily shown to be the fastest method of taking the given system from state A to state 0. Full acceleration is applied until the error is halfway towards zero and full deceleration over the remainder of the motion (Fig. 7).

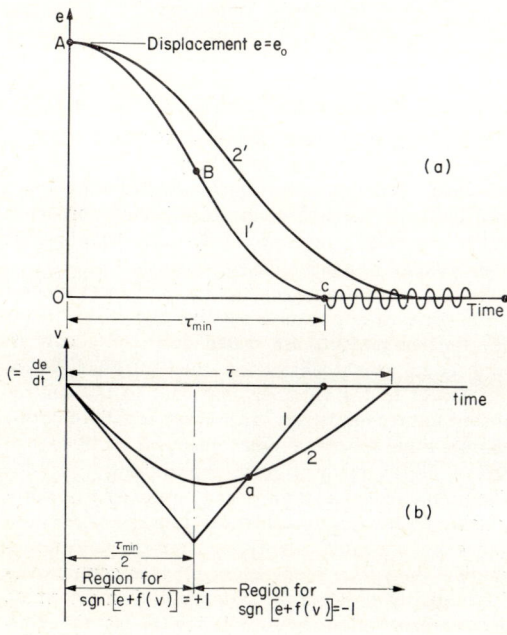

Fig. 7.

The relationship for the switch boundary BOC in this idealised case is

$$e = \frac{J}{2T_M} v|v|$$

hence the equation of motion is

$$\frac{J\,\mathrm{d}v}{\mathrm{d}t} = -T_M \operatorname{sgn}\left[e - \frac{J}{2T_M} v|v|\right]$$

To prove the optimality of the motion it is necessary to consider the velocity-time curves, also shown in Fig. 7. These are linear for the case considered since, from the equation of motion

$$v = \frac{\mathrm{d}e}{\mathrm{d}t} = -\frac{T_M t}{J} \operatorname{sgn}[e+f(v)].$$

It is now necessary to consider a system in which $|\mathrm{d}^2 e/\mathrm{d}t^2|$ does not always take its maximum value $T_M/J$

but where

$$\frac{\mathrm{d}^2 e}{\mathrm{d}t^2} = -\frac{T_M}{J} f(e, v) \text{ where } |f(e, v)| < 1.$$

For either system the area under any curve for $v$ during a transient must have a constant magnitude, equal to the displacement during the transient.

Thus
$$\int_0^\tau v \cdot \mathrm{d}t = e_0$$

were $\tau$ is the duration of the transient.

Consider curve 2 showing the velocity as a function of time for the non-on-off system which differs from the triangular shape of curve 1 (see Fig. 7b). The magnitude of the acceleration on this curve cannot exceed the maximum value given by the equation of motion as

$$\left|\frac{\mathrm{d}^2 e}{\mathrm{d}t^2}\right| = \frac{T_M}{J}.$$

Hence, during the interval $t = 0$ to $t = \tau_{\min}/2$ the slope of curve 2 in Fig. 7b must be equal to or less than that of curve 1. It follows that

$$\int_0^{\tau_{\min}/2} v\, \mathrm{d}t_{(\text{curve 2})} \leq \int_0^{\tau_{\min}/2} v\, \mathrm{d}t_{(\text{curve 1})}.$$

But the total area under the two curves in the total interval $0-\tau$ must be identical and equal to $e_0$, the common displacement. Therefore in the second interval from $\tau_{\min}/2$ onward the second curve cannot reach the abscissa without first intersecting the first curve (e.g. at point a in Fig. 7b). A second intersection is not possible since the slope of curve 2 must not exceed that of curve 1. Curve 2 therefore reaches the abscissa at a time later than $\tau_{\min}$ and curve 1 is that for minimal time transient response.

Optimal on-off control can be generalized to any order of system having a linear equation of motion of the form

$$a_0 \frac{\mathrm{d}^n x}{\mathrm{d}t^n} + a_1 \frac{\mathrm{d}^{n-1} x}{\mathrm{d}t^{n-1}} + \ldots + a_n x = u$$

where $x$ is the controlled variable, $u$ is the control action. And where $a_0 > 0$ and the roots of the characteristic equation are real, negative or zero (i.e. the system has a stable response).

The control action is restricted by the relation

$$|u| \leq u_m$$

where $u_m$ is the limiting value of $u$.

The following theorem can now be stated:

The optimal response which takes $x(t)$ from an initial to a final state in minimum time can be divided into $n$ intervals and is described by the equation

$$a_0 \frac{\mathrm{d}^n x}{\mathrm{d}t^n} + a_1 \frac{\mathrm{d}^{n-1} x}{\mathrm{d}t^{n-1}} + \ldots + a_n x = \pm u_m$$

where the sign taken by $u_m$ alternates in neighbouring intervals.

This theorem was proved by Feldbaum (1953). A proof of the second order ($n = 2$) case has already been given.

*Predictive on-off control.* From the discussion on optimal control it can be seen that the problem of taking a state variable in a dynamical system from an initial state to a final state in minimum time is that of deciding the instants at which to switch the control action from one extreme to the reverse extreme. The number of switch points in a complete optimal transient is $(n-1)$ for a system of order $n$.

The construction of a switch line for a simple second order position servomechanism was seen to depend on forming a function $v|v|$.

For higher order systems, higher order derivatives are necessary in the switching function but, in principle, the switching surface in the phase space can always be defined in terms of system variables. The shape of the switching surface is constant in a time invariant system and the best switch points can thus be predicted by an on-line computer taking as input data measurements of system variables (Adey et al. 1964). The computer output initiates the reversal of the control variable $u_m$.

Predictive control techniques have been developed which are widely applied particularly in the optimal control of space vehicles and aircraft.

The growing use of digital computers as controllers has itself encouraged the application of on-off control theory since the prediction of optimal switch points in systems of high order often requires extensive computation in the relatively short times available during the transient response.

*See also:* Control, predictive, using fast-time models. Optimization, automatic. Optimization of industrial processes.

*Bibliography*

ADEY A. J., COALES J. F. and STILES J. A. (1964) *Predictice Control of an On-off System with two control Variables, Automatic and Remote Control* (Proceedings of the Second IFAC Congress, Basle 1963) London: Butterworths.

FELDBAUM A. A. (1953) *Optimal processes in Automatic Control Systems, Avtomatika i Telemekhanika,* **14**, 5.

FLÜGGE-LOTZ I. (1953) *Discontinuous Automatic Control,* Princeton: The University Press.

FULLER A. T. (1960) *Phase Space in the Theory of Optimum Control, J. Electron. Control,* **8**, May.

HALL A. A. (1947) *The Use of Servomechanisms in Aircraft, J.I.E.E.,* **94**, Pt. IIA, No. 2, 256.

HAMMOND P. H. (1958) *Feedback Theory and its Application,* London: English Universities Press.

HAZEN H. L. (1934) *Theory of Servomechanisms, J. Franklin Inst.,* **218**, No. 3, 279.

LA SALLE J. P. (1954) *Basic principles of the bang-bang servo, Bull. Amer. Math. Soc.,* **60**.

UTTLEY A. M. and HAMMOND P. H. (1952) *The Stabilisation of On-off Controlled Servomechanisms, Automatic and Manual Control* (Ed. A. Tustin) 285, London: Butterworths.

P. H. HAMMOND

**CONTROL, PREDICTIVE, USING FAST-TIME MODELS.** *Introduction.* The essential feature of the predictive control approach is a fast-time model of the controlled system which provides a prediction of its behaviour under any specified inputs or operating conditions. This information is available in a small fraction of the time it takes the real system to respond; hence, a rapid feedback of the effects of input perturbations and control actions is provided. Thus, relatively crude control techniques based on trial and error, perturbation and iterative procedures may be implemented on the simulated system, with only the results transmitted to the real-time system.

The controlled system may be simulated on either analog, digital or hybrid computers. The dynamic relations are scaled such that $\tau = \alpha t$ where $\tau$ and $t$ denote simulated and real time, respectively, and $\alpha$ is the scaling factor (usually much smaller than one). A special case of particular interest is where $\alpha$ approaches zero and essentially only the steady-state relationships are represented by the model.

Although simulation by computer is of most general interest, there are applications involving physical models where the components are scaled down physically to yield a model which behaves like the controlled system (with respect to the variables pertinent to the control problem) but responds very much more rapidly. Pilot or bench scale models of complex chemical or biological processes are examples of such applications.

The predictive control approach appears particularly promising where (1) the analytical techniques for deriving an explicit control algorithm from the known mathematical model are inadequate; (2) it is computationally simpler to simulate the system and then determine desired control actions by stimulating the fast-time model; (3) on-line observations of the system are limited because of (a) measurement noise, (b) large sampling intervals, (c) inaccessible points of measurement; (4) dynamic lags of the system are large relative to the frequency of disturbances.

Obvious limitations to the predictive control approach include (1) enough must be known about the system in order to obtain a sufficiently accurate simulation, (2) the computation time per iteration of the system response must be small relative to the real-time response of the system. This latter point is particularly limiting in consideration of complex multivariable systems and distributed parameter systems.

The above features of the predictive control approach give rise to two general areas of application: (1) exploration in fast-time of either the manipulated input space or parameter space for results which will yield a best performance according to an appropriate criterion, (2) prediction of the future state (or behaviour) of the system from information on its present state and anticipated inputs. Specific applications to static and dynamic optimizing control, terminal control, feedforward control, hierarchical control, etc., are considered below.

While most of the applications discussed here consider only deterministic inputs to the simulated system, these are readily generalized to include the effects of random inputs. Thus, random noise generators, random number sequences, etc. provide means of simulating such inputs on the fast-time model. In like manner, random inputs may be employed in search procedures on the fast-time model to determine optimum conditions (e.g. Monte Carlo techniques).

*Regulatory control function.* The regulatory control function is associated with the problem of maintaining the outputs of the process as close as possible to their respective set-point values despite the influences of set-point changes and disturbances (see *Control: basic elements*). The predictive control approach is particularly effective in applications where the process dynamics are very complex and where there are significant interactions among the several control loops. In general, a relatively simple on-line control device is employed; the fast-time simulation provides immediate indication of the transient response of the system to any trial values of the controller inputs or parameter values.

Basically two methods of predictive control may be used here. The first method is shown in Fig. 1. A model of the system consisting of the controlled process and the complex control algorithm is simulated in fast-time.

manipulated variables are changed in a linear fashion from their values at the beginning of the prediction interval to the predicted final values at the end of the interval. In either case, the actual on-line control device is quite simple with the complex control algorithm implemented only in the fast-time simulation.

A second application of predictive control to the regulatory function recognizes that even a simple algorithm may be feasible for control of a process over a limited range of operation or disturbances. A model of the process is then simulated in fast-time together with the simple controller. The current state of the system is used as initial conditions for the simulation as before but now the controller parameters are varied in the fast-time simulation to determine the set of values yielding the best transient behaviour of the system at its current operating point.

A combination of these two methods is of course possible. Successive iterations of the fast-time simulation then update parameters in the complex simulated controller whose output is transmitted to the real-time controller as before. In this case, it is possible to compensate the complex controller for changes in process parameters or operating conditions. This might be especially suitable, for example, in keeping a multivariable controller non-interacting over a wide range of operating conditions.

Ziebolz and Paynter (1954), in a very early paper on predictive control, use the first method to control a simulator for training purposes. To simulate the motion

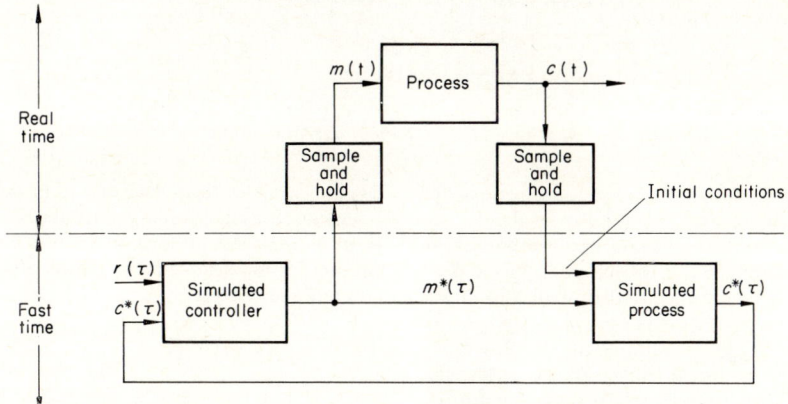

FIG. 1. *Regulatory controller based on predictive fast-time model.*

The response of the system is determined for a period into the future with the current state of the process providing the initial conditions for the model. The output of the simulated controller is sampled and translated into real-time values for the process manipulated variables. These are implemented in as simple a fashion as possible. For example, if the predicted controller outputs change only slightly during the real-time interval between predictions, the manipulated variable may be held piecewise constant. A smoother control results if the

of a ship, the dynamics of the hull, its disturbance environment, and the response of the steering system are simulated in fast-time to predict the attitude of the ship at a later time. Servos are then used to drive a physical model of the ship to this predicted attitude. This implies that the physical model need not have the same mathematical model as the actual system in order to have a realistic trainer or simulator.

Under many circumstances, a human operator is required to perform the regulatory function. The state of the system is usually displayed to the operator and he uses his experience and knowledge of the process to make changes in the manipulated variables in order to hold the process at some desired operating condition. When the process is dynamically complex or interacting, the human operator must be very skilled in order to perform adequately.

The predictive control approach appears to be an effective method of alleviating this problem. Rather than displaying just the current state of the system, the entire transient response to each considered control action is displayed to the operator by use of a fast-time model of the system. The future consequences of any change become self-evident and much less skill is necessary on the part of the operator.

controller, the operator can respond quickly enough. In this case, future dynamic response of the process is displayed for current values of the controller parameters. The operator then makes changes in the parameters and observes their effect on the dynamic response. This approach is shown in the block diagram of Fig. 3 and is similiar to the use of predictive control for adapting controller parameters described earlier but relies on a human operator to make the decision as to which parameters to change and how often (see also *Adaptive control theory*).

*State estimation by inferential means.* Predictive control is of value when it is necessary to extrapolate measurements in time or space. For example, when a process

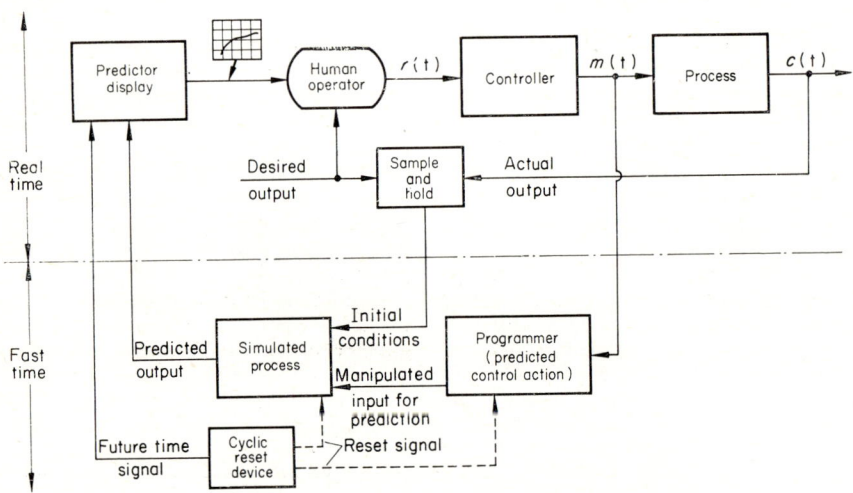

FIG. 2. *Controller input provided by human operator using predictor display.*

Kelley (1962), for example, proposes the scheme of Fig. 2 for the predictive control of submarine depth. The current state of the submarine is used as initial conditions for the simulation and the control action displayed is for diving planes assumed returned to their neutral position. The simulation is repeated many times a second so that a continuous display on the cathode-ray oscilloscope is obtained. Even when the dynamics of the submarine were oscillatory, little training was necessary before almost optimal control of depth was attained on the part of operators. A similar scheme is described for controlling the landing of a Moon vehicle where the several manipulated variables are highly interacting (Fargel and Ulbrich 1963).

If the response of the system is such that a human operator cannot regulate fast enough, predictive control suggests an alternate solution. A simple controller is supplied to do the actual regulation and the operator is assigned the task of manipulating the controller parameters so that the transient response is satisfactory. Since these parameters need be adjusted much less frequently than the variables manipulated by the on-line

has appreciable dead-time or lag in the measuring instruments, the effectiveness of feedback control is necessarily diminished whereas predictive control can compensate for the dead-time by means of a fast-time simulation of the system.

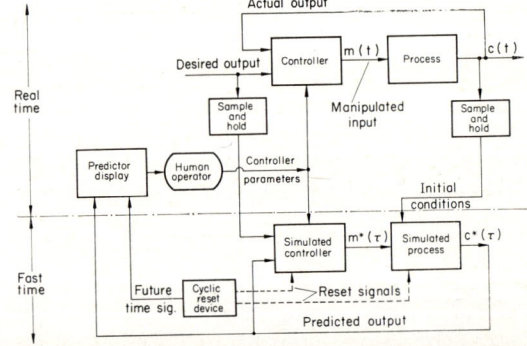

FIG. 3. *Controller parameters adjusted by human operator using predictor display.*

Consider the reactor system shown in Fig. 4. The objective is to control the production rate despite variations in catalyst activity or other disturbances. The controller can adjust the flow rate of the catalyst feed provided it can determine the actual production rate to compare with the desired rate. Calculation of production rate through a steady-state heat balance may be considerably in error, however, because of the effects of system dynamics and dead time in some measurements. These effects are taken into account by use of a fast-time dynamic model of the system with the result that an accurate measure of production rate is obtained (Tolin and Fleugel 1959).

An extension of the above methods is useful in feedforward control applications. An example described in the literature (Lupfer and Parsons 1962) is the control of a distillation column as shown in Fig. 5. Here incom-

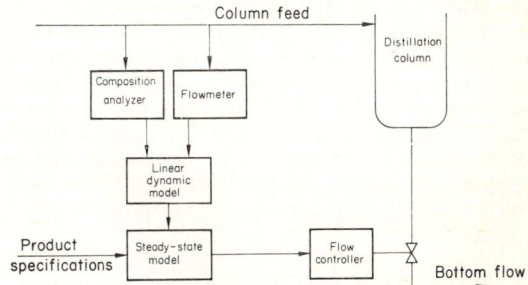

FIG. 5. *Use of predictive model to compensate for dynamic lags in feedforward control of distillation column.*

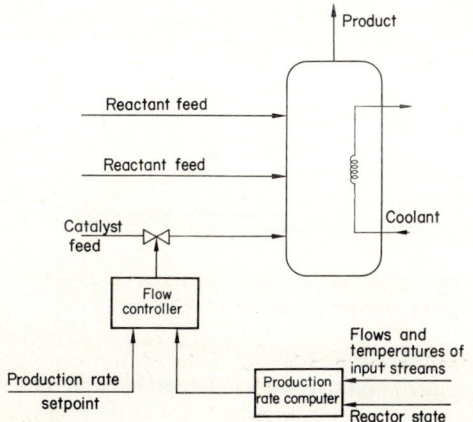

FIG. 4. *Control of reactor production rate based on predictive model.*

ing feed is measured and analysed on line. From the known product specifications, the flow rate of the bottom product is to be regulated. However, a sudden change in the incoming feed is not immediately felt in the output product because of the dynamics of the column. Consequently, the bottom product flow rate must be changed appropriately in time; this is accomplished through a fast-time model of the system which accounts for the actual hold-ups and lags of the column.

*Static optimizing control.* The principle of control based on a fast-time model may be applied to the problem of on-line optimizing control of continuous processes. The control problem consists of determining the steady-state value of **m** such that $P = F(\mathbf{m}, \mathbf{u})$ is maximized, where $P$ denotes an appropriate performance measure for the process and **u** denotes the set of disturbance inputs (assumed relatively constant between successive control instants).

In the predictive control approach, a fast-time model of the process is employed in an off-line search procedure to determine the optimal **m** for a given set of operating conditions for the process. Any of the standard hill climbing or gradient search routines (see *Control, hill climbing in*) may be employed; in general, the simulation is repeated for each iteration of the search procedure until an acceptable level of convergence is attained. The results are then transmitted as real-time inputs to the process.

A second example of extrapolation in time occurs when process measurements are available only at discrete instants of time which are too far apart to permit the control action to be held constant over the sampling interval. A fast-time model of the system, with the actual measurements used as initial conditions, permits the prediction of system variables for times between sampling instants. If the frequency of disturbances is not too high, the output of the simulation may be used to compute the continuous real-time control action to be taken.

Problems of extrapolation in space are common in process control. Often desired measurements are not directly available and must be inferred from measurements of secondary variables via a mathematical model of the system. This occurs, for example, in the control of cooling of steel ingots where the interior temperature is inferred from external temperature measurements applied to a fast-time dynamic model of the heat transfer characteristics of the system.

A second example is the strip process where sensors can often be placed only at the entrance and exit of the process. The behaviour of the strip within the process must be predicted by a fast-time model of the process together with the available terminal measurements.

The advantage of this scheme over say hill climbing in real-time is that problems of noise, dynamic lags, limitations of measurement etc., may be eliminated or significantly reduced. There is also the advantage of not having to perturb the process in searching for the optimum. The advantage over an analytical derivation of the optimal control algorithm is that often the system relationships are too complex to yield the desired result in closed form; this is particularly true for distributed systems and where there are inequality constraints.

Limitations of the predictive control approach are again the ability to simulate the process on the fast-time computer and the feasibility of an iterative search procedure from the standpoints of computing time and costs.

An interesting application of this approach lies in the case where the equations for the system cannot be written because of complexity or insufficient knowledge of the underlying mechanisms, hence, the system cannot be simulated on the computer. However, a fast-time physical model which behaves like the real system but, because of say reduced physical dimensions, is able to respond very much more rapidly may be feasible. Such an application is described by Neugroschl (1963) in connexion with the control of a sewage disposal plant.

*Dynamic optimizing control.* The predictive control approach has important application to the optimizing control of dynamic systems. The essential feature here is the prediction of the future response of the process to the manipulated inputs in order to satisfy the set of specified boundary conditions.

A fairly general formulation of the problem is as follows: determine the manipulated input $\mathbf{m}_{[t_0, t_f]}$ (restricted to an appropriately defined input space) which maximizes the performance $P$, where

$$P = \Psi[\mathbf{c}(t_f), t_f] + \int_{t_0}^{t_f} F[\mathbf{c}(\tau), \mathbf{m}(\tau)] \, d\tau \qquad (1)$$

subject to the set of constraints

$$\dot{\mathbf{c}}(t) = \mathbf{g}[\mathbf{c}(t), \mathbf{m}(t)] \qquad (2)$$

and the boundary conditions

$$\mathbf{c}(t_0) = \mathbf{c}_0$$
$$\mathbf{c}(t_f) = \mathbf{c}_f . \qquad (3)$$

Here $t_0$ and $t_f$ denote the initial and final times, respectively, and $\mathbf{c}(t)$ denotes the vector of process outputs (or states) which may be sampled and measured at the successive time instants, $t_0, t_1, \ldots t_N$.

Application of variational principles yields a set of auxiliary equations (equations 4 and 5) which must be solved simultaneously with equation 2 (see *Control by the maximum principle*).

$$\dot{\boldsymbol{\mu}}(t) = \mathbf{g}[\boldsymbol{\mu}(t), \mathbf{c}(t), \mathbf{m}(t)] \qquad (4)$$
$$0 = \mathbf{h}[\boldsymbol{\mu}(t), \mathbf{c}(t), \mathbf{m}(t)] \qquad (5)$$

where $\boldsymbol{\mu}(t)$ may be considered the set of Lagrange multipliers or co-state variables.

Equations 2, 4 and 5 may be solved simultaneously to obtain $\mathbf{m}_{[t_0, t_f]}$ and $\mathbf{c}_{[t_0, t_f]}$ if the given $\mathbf{c}_0$ is supplemented by an estimate of $\boldsymbol{\mu}_0 = \boldsymbol{\mu}(t_0)$. The computed $\mathbf{c}(t_f)$ is then compared with the specified $\mathbf{c}_f$, and the initial estimate of $\boldsymbol{\mu}_0$ is adjusted in the direction to reduce the difference. The procedure is repeated until the final error is within some arbitrary tolerance. Note that since $\mathbf{c}(t_f) - \mathbf{c}_f$ will be some function of $\boldsymbol{\mu}_0$, any of the gradient search techniques (see the preceding section on Static Optimizing Control) may be considered here. In addition, there are several methods based on first and second variations

which have been proposed for solution of the two-point boundary value problem (see *Control by the maximum principle*).

The above procedure is implemented by the predictive control scheme shown in the block diagram of Fig. 6. The open-loop procedure is modified by periodic sampling of the process output (or state); at each sample point the value $\mathbf{c}(t_n) = \mathbf{c}_n$, $n = 0, 1, 2, \ldots N$ provides the initial conditions for fast-time solution of the problem over the remaining time interval $(t_n, t_f)$. The Principle of Optimality is involved here, i.e. whatever

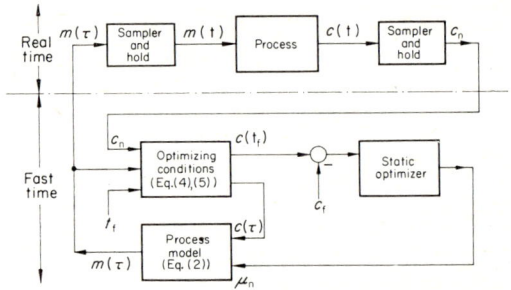

FIG. 6. *Satisfying boundary conditions in dynamic optimizing control by means of fast-time simulation.*

the action taken prior to $t_n$, the control action over the future interval $(t_n, t_f)$ is to be optimal with respect to the present state of the process. The scheme thus provides a feedback which helps compensate for (a) disturbances entering the system during the interval $(t_n, t_{n+1})$, and (b) the effects of approximations in the mathematical model. Another feature is that only the input segment $\mathbf{m}_{(t_n, t_{n+1})}$ need be stored.

The fast-time solution of the control equations (equations 4 and 5) generates $\mathbf{m}(\tau)$, $t_n \leq \tau \leq t_f$, based on the assumed $\boldsymbol{\mu}_n$ and feedback of $\mathbf{c}(\tau)$ from the fast-time model of the process (equation 2). When the gradient search on $\boldsymbol{\mu}_n$ yields (in fast-time) a $\mathbf{c}(t_f)$ sufficiently close to $\mathbf{c}_f$, the resulting segment $\mathbf{m}_{(t_n, t_{n+1})}$ is sampled and stored for (real-time) playback to the process. The procedure is repeated at each sampling instant. Note that when the intervals $(t_n, t_{n+1})$, $n = 0, 1, 2, \ldots$, are not very large, the time function $\mathbf{m}_{(t_n, t_{n+1})}$ may be replaced by the constant value $\mathbf{m}(t) = \mathbf{m}(t_n)$, $t_n \leq t < t_{n+1}$, thereby further simplifying the storage and playback problem. Another advantage is that the previously determined value for $\boldsymbol{\mu}_n$ provides a good initial estimate for $\boldsymbol{\mu}_{n+1}$. This scheme was implemented by Eckman and Lefkowitz (1957) in the application of optimizing control to a batch chemical reactor.

A special case of dynamic optimization is the 'bang-bang' controller, i.e. at any time each component of $\mathbf{m}(t)$ is either at its minimum or maximum permissible value. (This result is obtained in the case of time optimal control of linear systems, e.g. when $\Psi \equiv 0$ and $F \equiv 1$ in equation 1 and where equation 2 is linear.) Thus, the control problem reduces to the determination of the finite sequence of switching times which satisfy the given boundary conditions. This type of control is of particular interest because of the relative simplicity and low cost of the logic elements and power amplifiers.

Several methods are proposed for implementing the 'bang-bang' control algorithm based on the predictive control approach and a fast-time model. The objective in each of these methods is to reduce an error vector (deviation of the set of process outputs from the set of desired values) and its derivatives to zero in minimum time. All of the computation is done in the fast-time computer with only the switching times communicated to the real-time controller.

Chestnut *et al.* (1961) suggest a simple algorithm for determining the switching time which is based on the analysis of a second-order system with real roots. The current state of the controlled system provides the initial conditions for the fast-time model to which is applied a manipulated input of sign opposite to that acting on the system. The sign of the predicted error signal at the instant the error derivative passes through zero is observed. This sign should be the same as that of the input currently applied (in real-time). If this is not true or if the predicted error derivative does not go to zero, then the polarity of the actual manipulated input is switched. In the case of other than second-order systems with real roots, this algorithm is only approximate.

Another special case of the optimal control problem which is of particular importance is that of terminal or end-point control (e.g. $F \equiv 0$ in equation 1). The sole objective here is to control the system so that the output at some future time attains the specified value (the final time may be either fixed or conditional on some other variables attaining prescribed values. For example, the airplane landing problem (Mathews and Steeg 1956) is a terminal control problem in that the vehicle vertical velocity must become zero when the vertical height reaches zero. Using a fast-time model of the system, either the operator or the automatic controller can base current changes in the manipulated variables on future errors.

*Hierarchical control.* The general application of optimizing control to industrial processes is seriously limited by the complexity of such systems. The hierarchical control approach (Lefkowitz 1966) circumvents this limitation by the following procedure: (1) the process is characterized by an approximate mathematical model of relatively simple structure, (2) the optimizing control algorithm to be used in on-line control of the process is derived on the basis of this approximate model, (3) the parameters of the model are updated periodically or when called for by gross changes in operating conditions, (4) the adjusted parameter values are transmitted

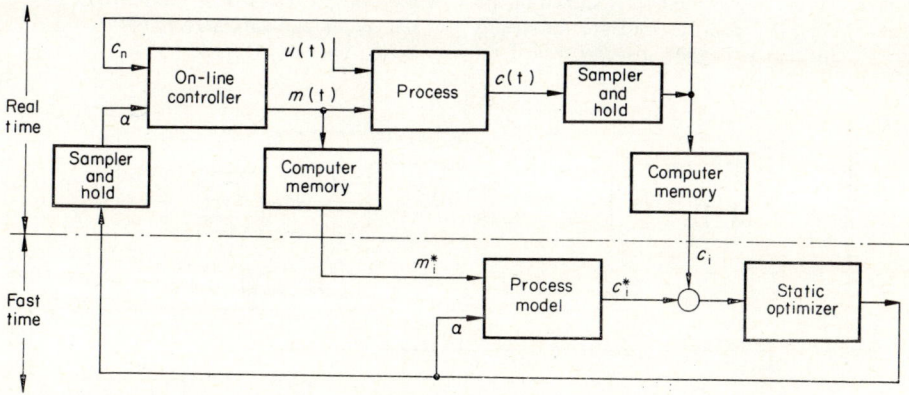

Fig. 7. *Model parameter adaptation scheme in hierarchical control approach.*

Adey *et al.* (1963) have extended the predictive control concept to higher order systems by using optimization theory to determine the form of the optimal switching curve. As in the previous method, a fast-time model of the system is searched to determine the set of switching times satisfying the desired final state. A simple, near-optimal result is derived for a sample two-input, two-output system requiring three switches.

Extensions to general higher order systems have been described (Horing 1963; Gul'ko and Kogan 1963). Coales points out, however, that near-optimal control may be achieved with quite simple models by means of the predictive control approach (Adey *et al.* 1963).

to the on-line controller. This approach is illustrated by the block diagram of Fig. 7.

The parameter adaptation is implemented by use of the fast-time model technique. Basically, the input-output data observed for the process over the past adaptation period is stored in the computer memory. The fast-time approximate model is excited by the stored set of input data and the resulting model output sequence is compared with the stored output values. The parameters are adjusted according to a least-squares or other criterion of fit. Any appropriate hill climbing or gradient procedure may be used here in the fast-time scale of the computer, e.g. the above computation procedure is repeated over and over again until convergence of the parameter values to the desired 'least-squares' set is achieved.

Let $\mathbf{x}(t)$ and $\mathbf{y}(t)$ denote the measured process input and output vectors, respectively, observed at time $t$. The mathematical model of the system is expressed in the form

$$\mathbf{y}_n^* = \mathbf{h}_n(\mathbf{y}_0^*, \mathbf{x}_1, \mathbf{x}_2, \ldots \mathbf{x}_N; \boldsymbol{\alpha}) \qquad (6)$$

where $\mathbf{y}_n^*$ denotes the set of model outputs corresponding to $t_n$ (in real time); $\mathbf{x}_1, \mathbf{x}_2, \ldots \mathbf{x}_N$ are the sampled values of the process input vectors at $t_1, t_2, \ldots t_N$, respectively; $\boldsymbol{\alpha}$ represents the set of parameters associated with the model. If now $\mathbf{y}_1, \mathbf{y}_2, \ldots \mathbf{y}_N$ denote the sequence of outputs of the real time process, the objective function for the parameter adaptation (in fast-time) may be expressed

$$\min_{\boldsymbol{\alpha}} \left[ \sum_{n=1}^{N} (\mathbf{y}_n - \mathbf{y}_n^*)^T W_n (\mathbf{y}_n - \mathbf{y}_n^*) \right] \qquad (7)$$

where $W_n$ is some appropriate weighting matrix. The resulting set of parameter values is then transmitted for incorporation into the on-line optimizing control algorithm. This procedure has been described for the optimizing control of a batch chemical process (Eckman and Lefkowitz 1960) (see also *Control, identification techniques for*).

A modification of the above method is shown in the block diagram of Fig. 8 (Burghart 1966). Here, the structure of the control algorithm is defined *a priori*, based on either an arbitrary series expansion (say a polynomial of the observed input variables), or on prior analytic considerations. The parameters associated with the assumed structure are determined such as to maximize the expected or time-averaged value of system performance. This is carried out by means of a fast-time model of the system consisting of process, controller and disturbance inputs. The simulated inputs may be based on a statistical model determined from past observations of the system (extrapolated into the next adaptive period). The result, for each iteration, is an average performance value which depends on the set of parameter values currently in the simulated controller. Thus, again a search procedure on the parameter space of the fast-time model may be implemented with the final results transmitted to the on-line controller.

A further extension of the hierarchical control approach applies to the periodic reassessment of such design decisions as relates to the choice of structure for the control algorithm (or the simplified model), the specifications of local objective functions, etc. (Lefkowitz 1966). Here, a finite number of discrete alternatives may be considered via the fast-time simulation of the overall system; that alternative is selected which yields the best result according to a meaningful criterion, e.g. maximum average performance projected over a substantial time period.

*See also:* Control by stationary filtering and prediction. Control, hierarchical. Control, on-off.

*Bibliography*

ADEY A. J., COALES J. F. and STILES J. A. (1963) *The control of two-variable on-off systems*, Proceedings IFAC, Theory, 41, Basle.

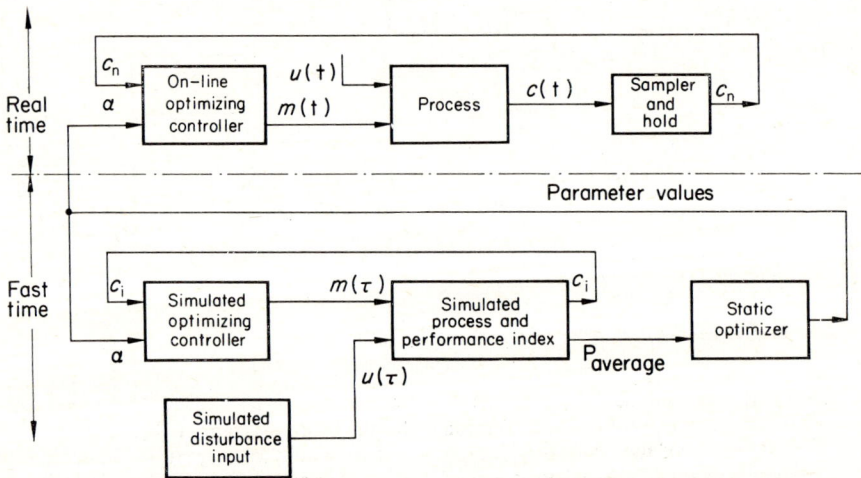

FIG. 8. *Use of fast-time simulation to determine parameter values for on-line optimizing controller.*

BURGHART J. (1966) *An adaptive technique for on-line steady-state optimizing control*, Ph.D. thesis, Case Institute of Technology, Cleveland, Ohio.

CHESTNUT H., SOLLECITO W. E. and TROUTMAN P. H. (1961) *Predictive control systems applications*, Trans. A.I.E.E. Pt. II, **80**, 128.

Eckman D. P. and Lefkowitz I. (1957) *Optimizing control of a chemical process*, Control Engng, **4**, September, 197.

Eckman D. P. and Lefkowitz I. (1960) *Principles of model techniques in optimizing control*, Proceedings IFAC, Vol. II, 970, Moscow.

Fargel L. C. and Ulbrich E. A (1963) *Aerospace simulators prove predictor displays extend manual operation*, Control Engng, **10**, August 57.

Gul'ko F. B. and Kogan B. Ya. (1963) *A method of optimal control prediction*, Proceedings IFAC, Theory, 63, Basle.

Horing S. (1963) *On the design of predictor control systems*, Proceedings IFAC, Theory, 55, Basle.

Kelley C. R. (1962) *Predictor instruments look into the future*, Control Engng., **9**, March, 86.

Lefkowitz I. (1966) *Multilevel approach applied to control system design*, ASME Trans., J. Basic Engng., **88**, June, 392.

Lupfer D. E. and Parsons J. R. (1962) *A predictive control system for distillation columns*, Chem. Eng. Progress, **58**, September, 37.

Mathews M. V. and Steeg C. W. (1956) *Final value controller synthesis*, I.R.E. Trans. on Automatic Control, **1**, May.

Neugroshl E. J. (1963) *Computer control of an activated sludge treatment plant*, Ph.D. thesis, Case Institute of Technology, Cleveland, Ohio.

Tolin E. D. and Fleugel D. A. (1959) *An analog computer for on-line reactor control*, I.S.A. J. **6**, October.

Ziebolz H. and Paynter H. M. (1954) *Possibilities of a two-time scale computing system for control and simulation of dynamic systems*, Proc. of Nat'l Electronics Conf., 215.

I. Lefkowitz and J. D. Schoeffler

**CONTROL, SENSITIVITY AND.** 'Sensitivity analysis' is concerned with the effects of alterations (especially small alterations) to the inital conditions or to the parameters in systems described by differential equations.

In a qualitative sense, the importance of sensitivity considerations in engineering design has been appreciated for a long time. An obvious illustration is the design of electronic circuits taking into account realistic tolerances of the components. Any theory of an engineering system is realistic only if the solutions of the equations are affected very little by any realistic discrepancies between the mathematical model and the actual system. Trouble can occur in particular if one fails to take into account small finite delays or other fast dynamical effects. The single stage multivibrator is a striking example in that oscillation cannot be explained without considering the 'parasitic' effects. Problems such as these led mathematicians to examine under what conditions solutions to differential equations were not 'easily disturbed' whence the concept of 'inert systems' of Andronov. It is, however, in the study of partial differential equations that the importance of 'insensitivity' has attracted most attention in mathematics; in fact the well known *conditions of Hadamard* for a boundary value problem (i.e. the problem of solving a partial differential equation given boundary conditions) to be 'properly posed' include the requirement that the solution should not be highly sensitive to small alterations in the boundary conditions. An excellent discussion of the significance of classical mathematical problems in the above and other examples of engineering design is given in Gumowski and Mira.

The quantitative study of sensitivity has been stimulated by an increasing emphasis on optimization in system design based on some mathematically defined performance index. In the field of control this is important in two main areas:

1. Sensitivity to variations in control parameters—with the aim of calculating the derivatives of the performance index with respect to the parameters (especially using analogue techniques).

2. Sensitivity to variations in the parameters of the controlled plant—with the aim of designing control systems which are not unduly affected by variations in the plant.

In general, if a system is described by a set of differential equations

$$\frac{dx_i}{dt} = f_i(a, x, t)$$

where $a$ is any parameter, then the solution of these equations (for a given set of initial conditions) will be a set of functions $x_i(a, t)$ and if we write

$$x_i^{(a)}(t) \equiv \frac{\partial}{\partial a} x_i(a, t)$$

then these variables will satisfy the set of equations:

$$\frac{dx_i^{(a)}}{dt} = \frac{\partial}{\partial a} f_i(a, x, t) + \sum_j \frac{\partial}{\partial x_j} f_i(a, x, t) x_j^{(a)}.$$

These equations can generally be set up on an analog computer with a network similar in size and structure to the network required for simulating the original equations. If a 'performance index' is defined in the form

$$v = \int_0^T L(x, t) \, dt$$

then the gradient of the performance index can be calculated with the formula

$$\frac{\partial v}{\partial a} = \sum \int_0^T \frac{\partial}{\partial x} L(x, t) \, x^{(a)}(t) \, dt.$$

The signals $\partial x_i/\partial a$ and the quantity $\partial v/\partial a$ (or sometimes the quantity $\partial (\ln v)/\partial (\ln a)$ are called 'sensitivity coefficients' or 'parameter influence coefficients'. If necessary, the 'sensitivity coefficients' can be computed simultaneously for several parameters and highly efficient optimization procedures can be used which make use of the 'gradient' of the performance index.

An example of the generation of sensitivity coefficients by analogue circuits is given in the figure. Here the diagram in bold lines represents a linear position control system with an adjustable velocity damping coefficient $a$. The performance index $v$ is generated by integrating the square of the error. The circuit in thin lines generates sensitivity coefficients for every signal (including $v$) in the network in bold lines.

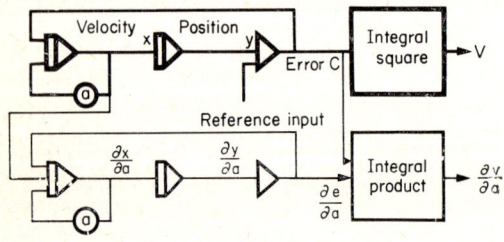

*Generation of sensitivity coefficients.*

The generation of sensitivity coefficients is not straightforward in any of the following circumstances: when the functions $f_i(a, x, t)$ contain discontinuities (as in a bang-bang servomechanism); when $a$ represents the frequency of a forcing function, when the system of equations is self-oscillating; or when infinitesimal changes in $a$ can affect the order of the system (i.e. when at least one equation is in general of the form $a\, dx_i/dt = \ldots$ and $a = 0$). Practicable methods of overcoming these difficulties have however been devised and these are described in Radanovic.

As regards the second aspect of sensitivity in control—the effect of variations in plant parameters, the first-order sensitivity coefficients do not always give adequate engineering insight. This is obvious as far as sensitivity to variations in the control parameters since the condition of optimality ensures that if $a$ is a control parameter then the first order sensitivity coefficient $\partial v/\partial a = 0$. The effect of a maladjustment $\delta a$ in $a$ is given by

$$\delta v = \tfrac{1}{2}\, \partial^2 v/\partial a^2\, \delta a^2 + 0(\delta a^3).$$

However, second order effects are not necessarily small effects as is well illustrated by the following example. In order to move a mass $m$ through a unit distance with unit available force one should apply maximum forward drive for a time $a$ and maximum reverse drive for a further time $a$ (where $a = a_0 = m^{\frac{1}{2}}$). However, if $a$ is not perfectly set, the final error will be given by

$$\frac{1}{m}(a^2 - a_0^2).$$

If the performance index is of the type

$$v = \int_0^T e(t)^2\, dt$$

then with large $T$

$$v \simeq \frac{T}{m^2}(a^2 - a_0^2)^2$$

and while $\partial v/\partial a = 0$ when $a = a_0$ the second order term

$$\frac{\partial^2 v}{\partial a^2} = \frac{8T}{m}\, \delta a^2$$

can be large if $T$ is large. The second-order effects are equally important in studying the effects of variations in the parameters of the plant being controlled. While in general here $\partial v/\partial a \neq 0$ it can be shown that its value is independent of the structure of the system chosen to achieve an optimal control strategy; for example if $(\partial v/\partial a)$ is independent of whether closed-loop or open-loop control is used. The well-known relative insensitivity of closed loop control again only shows up by considering the second-order coefficients $\partial^2 v/\partial a^2$. The reason for this is seen most clearly if we define a quantity $V_s$ which may be called the 'sub-optimality' of a control strategy by

$$V_s(a) = V_0(a) - V(a)$$

where $V_0(a)$ is the performance which would be obtained if the control strategy were optimally designed by having a true knowledge of the value of the parameter $a$. Clearly $\partial V_s/\partial a = 0$ under optimal control since $V_s$ is taking its minimum possible value of zero. Therefore $\partial v/\partial a = \partial v_0/\partial a$ and so the first-order derivative only indicates the unavoidable effect of changes in plant parameters. In the case of several parameters, the significant measure of sensitivity to small variations in plant parameters is usually given by:

$$\frac{\partial^2}{\partial a_i\, \partial a_j} V_s(a)$$

In some situations, even the second-order sensitivity coefficient will not give a true insight into the sensitivity problem. For example, a plant can tolerate a very high loop gain for a wide range of values of some parameter, but become unstable outside that range. In this case, one is explicitly interested in the sensitivity to large finite variations.

The need to take into account uncertainties in the parameters of a plant suggests that criteria of optimality might be formulated in a different way. Given any deterministic problem, one can use conventional optimal control theory to work out a control schedule as a function of time. However, optimal control theory leaves open the question of the structure of the system for realizing the optimal control schedule—for instance closed loop control and open loop control might be equally optimal. This represents a serious limitation to the practical value of optimal control theory which might be overcome by introducing the uncertainties of the plant parameters in some way. One suggestion has been to adopt performance criteria of the type

$$\min \int_0^T \left\{ L(\mathbf{x}(\mathbf{a}, t), t) + \sum_{ij} K_{ij} \frac{\partial^2}{\partial a_i\, \partial a_j} L(\mathbf{x}(\mathbf{a}, t), t) \right\} dt.$$

Another suggestion, the so-called 'game-theory' ap-ed in the transmission of digital signals. These errors result in a Binary 1 digit being changed to a Binary 0 digit or conversely. The duration of such impulsive noise or clicks may be quite small. In the case of a data circuit transmitting at 1000 bits/second, each of the binary digits will only last for 1 thousandth of a second and so a noise click lasting 1 hundredth of a second could affect 10 binary digits.

Very approximately, the long term average error rate on the switched telephone network at 1200 bits/second is 1 binary digit error in 10,000. On rented telephone circuits at a similar transmission rate the error rate is about 1 in 100,000 binary digits. On telex and telegraph rented circuits working at 50 bits/second, the error rate is about 1 in 200,000 binary digits. These error rates for some applications are quite good enough, particularly at the lower speed using telegraph circuits. However, at the higher rates on telephone type lines it will be seen that errors occur more frequently. For most types of data transmission applications therefore, it is necessary that some form of error control, i.e. error detection and possibly correction should be employed. Error control as applied to the data transmission link may be analog or digital. The term analog error control here refers to any method of determining that the received signal has departed from an acceptable form, but does not include checks involving the significance or value of the demodulated digital signals. Such a check would be digital error control.

Most analytical work on error detection has been concerned with the introduction of digital redundancy into the data and various methods of coding have been devised. The most simple arrangement is a parity check. This consists of adding a single binary digit to the information digits such that the total number of binary 1 digits are an even number. This means that all single digit errors, but only some multiple errors, would be detectable. Due to the fact that a proportion of disturbances on telephone lines used for data transmission affect adjacent signal elements, simple parity check digits do not always give sufficient protection. However, by interlacing the digits of a number of parity check groups, the effect of a burst of errors can be spread over several such groups. This reduces the chance of the burst affecting more than one digit in a group. Figure 3 illustrates a combination of row and column parity check digits applied to a group of 30 information binary digits. Examination will show that only certain combination of 4 binary digit errors or multiples of 4 binary digits in error will fail to be detected. Other different ways of combating error bursts including a rather more general approach by means of cyclic codes are used. Cyclic codes enable protection to be arranged against specific types of error bursts and are highly flexible. For a given degree of protection, quite low levels of redundancy are possible. The name derives from the method of generation which is by means of a cycling shift register. With the arrangements discussed a reduction of the undetected error rates from a tenth up to one hundred thousandth of the original error rate are possible.

Error correction after an error has been detected is achieved by requesting the transmitting end to repeat that part of the message containing the error. This may be done automatically.

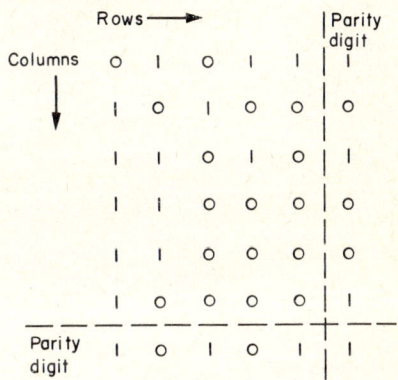

Fig. 3. *Row and column parity.*

Error correcting codes are possible but are not economic on telephone type circuits, nor do they give sufficient protection where burst types of errors occur.

Figure 4 shows the elements of a typical data transmission link including error control and modems.

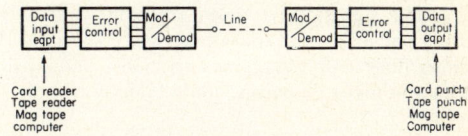

Fig. 4. *Elements of a data transmission system.*

*Use of data transmission in data processing systems.* Data processing systems set up by some national banks include data transmission as an integral part. Accounts are centralized and the branch offices send in data regarding account transactions and can request a centralized computer as to the state of a depositors account.

Air-line companies operating centralized seat reservation systems use data links from their agents' booking offices on an enquiry basis. A number of the links extend overseas.

Universities and scientific organizations by means of data links can share a computer between several colleges or users. This enables computer programs to be tested and problems solved remotely. An example of this is the project MAC (multi access computer) at the Massachusets Institute of Technology where a large number of users are equipped with keyboards for direct entry over data links to the computer. This arrangement is termed 'on-line' working as distinct from 'off-line' when direct connexion to the computer is not made.

Figure 5 shows a hypothetical data processing system using the data transmission facilities previously discussed.

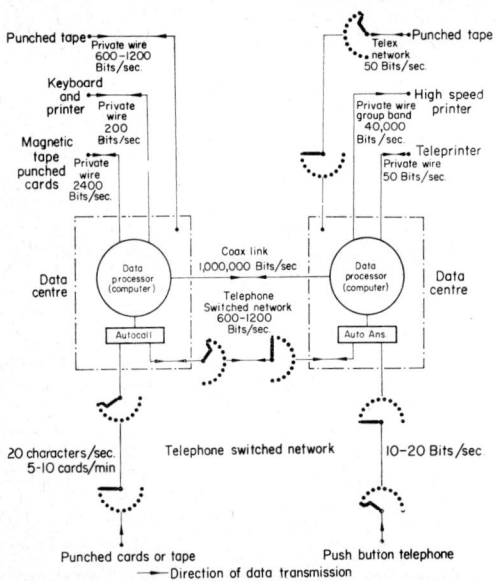

FIG. 5. *Data processing system with transmission links.*

*Further developments in data transmission.* In the U.K. and U.S.A. analog transmission of a patient's electrocardiograph signals have been transmitted over the switched network to a consultant heart specialist for diagnosis. This remote access to a specialist, and possibly later an automatic diagnosis, could be important in the future.

With new methods of pulse modulation being introduced into the telephone network the possibility of providing up to about 60,000 bits/sec in a voice channel is a prospect. By using such high speed links in combination with computer storage and switching techniques a relatively cheap, separate, flexible speed switched data network might be established on a public service basis.

*Acknowledgements.* Information in this article is based upon work carried out by the Post Office Engineering Department of the U.K. and acknowledgement is made to the Engineer-in-Chief for permission to publish.

*See also:* Magnetic recording. Telecommunication, economy in. Telecommunication, global.

*Bibliography*

ALLERY G. D. (1965) *Some aspects of data transmission,* J. Inst. P.O. Engrs., **57** (4), Jan.
BENNETT W. R. and DAVEY J. R. *Data Transmission,* New York: McGraw-Hill.
PETERSON W. W. and BROWN D. T. (1961) *Cyclic codes for error detection,* Proc. I.R.E., Jan.
SMITH N. G. (1966) *An Introduction to the Post Office Datel Services,* J. Inst. P.O. Engrs., **59** (1), April.

G. D. ALLERY

# DISCRETE MODELS FOR FORECASTING AND CONTROL.

## 1. Introduction and Summary

We first describe a class of discrete linear time series models capable of representing non-stationary as well as stationary behaviour. In control problems these models are used to describe disturbances to the system. Dynamic models which represent relationships between variables which control and are controlled are introduced later. The identification, fitting, checking and practical use of such models in forecasting and control are discussed.

The models employed are empirico-mechanistic in that while they can be interpreted as descriptions of physical phenomena having the right general character they do not claim to represent exact physical reality and are fitted to data empirically.

An important principle in the choice of such models is that, they should, while adequately representing the data, contain the fewest possible number of parameters. This is called the principle of parsimony or of parsimonious parametrization.

## 2. Time Series Models

We denote values of a time series at equispaced times $t, t-1, t-2, \ldots$, by $z_t, z_{t-1}, z_{t-2}, \ldots$. Let $B$ be the backward shift operator, $\nabla$ the backward difference operator $S = \nabla^{-1}$ the summation operator so that

$$Bz_t = z_{t-1}, \quad \nabla z_t = z_t - z_{t-1}, \quad Sz_t = \sum_{j=0}^{\infty} z_{t-j}.$$

We shall say that the series follows a linear process of order $(p, d, q)$ if

$$\varphi_p(B)(1-B)^d z_t = \theta_q(B)a_t \qquad (1)$$

where $a_t, a_{t-1}, a_{t-2}, \ldots$ are independent random deviates with zero means and all having the same variance $\sigma_a^2$, and

$$\varphi_p(B) = 1 - \varphi_1 B - \varphi_2 B^2 \ldots - \varphi_p B^p$$
$$\theta_q(B) = 1 - \theta_1 B - \theta_2 B^2 \ldots - \theta_q B^q$$

are polynomials in $B$. The *admissible parameter space* is defined by those values for which the roots of $\varphi_p(B) = 0$ and $\theta_q(B) = 0$ lie outside the unit circle. In practice the positive integers $p$, $d$, and $q$ are usually 0, 1, or 2.

If $d = 0$ the time series will be stationary and $z_t$ will be understood to refer to the *deviation* from the mean. The series most frequently needed will be non-stationary with $d = 1$ or sometimes $d = 2$. We call $\varphi_p(B)$ the stationary autoregressive operator, $\Phi_{p+d}(B) = \varphi_p(B)(1-B)^d$ the general autoregressive operator and $\theta_q(B)$ the moving average operator.

*2.1. Selection of the time series model.* Suppose we wish to determine a suitable model for a series for which $n$ consecutive observations $z_1, z_2, \ldots, z_n$ are available and where if possible $n$ should be at least 50 and preferably more than 100. In practice such model determination has to be done iteratively using a process of *identification, fitting, diagnostic checking*, refitting and rechecking till a satisfactory representation is found.

*2.2. Identification.* Equation 1 supplies too rich a class of models to permit immediate estimation. Using experience and the data therefore, we first identify a subclass of models worthy to be entertained.

The primary data-analysis tool at this stage is the sample autocorrelation functions of the original series and its differences. The sample autocorrelation coefficient at lag $k$ for $w_j = \nabla^d z_j$ is $r_k(w) = c_k(w)/c_0(w)$ with

$$c_k = n^{-1} \sum_{j=1}^{n-k} (w_j - \bar{w})(w_{j+k} - \bar{w}) \text{ and } \bar{w} = n^{-1} \sum_{j=1}^{n} w_j.$$

We shall use $\varrho_k(w)$ for the corresponding theoretical autocorrelation.

A suitable value for $d$ may now be inferred by finding the degree of differencing necessary to induce the sample autocorrelation function to damp out fairly quickly. For example, Table 1 shows the sample autocorrelation function for IBM common stock daily closing prices. While the behaviour of the original series is non-stationary, its first and higher differences behave like those of a stationary series suggesting that we set $d = 1$.

Table 2. Behaviour of theoretical autocorrelation function of $d$th difference of series for various simple models.

| Order (1, $d$, 0) | Order (0, $d$, 1) |
|---|---|
| $\varrho_k$ decays exponentially | Only $\varrho_0$ and $\varrho_1$ are non-zero |
| $\varphi_1 = \varrho_1$ | $\varrho_1 = -\theta_1/(1+\theta_1^2)$ |
| $-1 < \varphi_1 < 1$ | $-1 < \theta_1 < 1$ |
| Order (2, $d$, 0) | Order (0, $d$, 2) |
| $\varrho_1$ is mixture of exponentials or a damped sine wave | Only $\varrho_0$, $\varrho_1$ and $\varrho_2$ are non-zero |
| $\varphi_1 = \dfrac{\varrho_1(1-\varrho_2)}{1-\varrho_1^2} \quad \varphi_2 = \dfrac{\varrho_2 - \varrho_1^2}{1-\varrho_1^2}$ | $\varrho_1 = -\dfrac{\theta_1(1-\lambda_2)}{1+\theta_1^2+\theta_2^2} \quad \varrho_2 = \dfrac{-\theta_2}{1+\theta_1^2+\theta_2^2}$ |
| $\begin{cases} \varphi_2 > -1 \\ \varphi_2 + \varphi_1 > 1 \\ \varphi_2 - \varphi_1 > 1 \end{cases}$ | $\begin{cases} \theta_2 > -1 \\ \theta_2 + \theta_1 > 1 \\ \theta_2 - \theta_1 > 1 \end{cases}$ |
| Order (1, $d$, 1) | |
| $\varrho_k$ decays exponentially *after* 1st lag correlation | |
| $\varrho_1 = \dfrac{(1-\theta_1\varphi_1)(\varphi_1-\theta_1)}{1+\theta_1^2-2\varphi_1\theta_1} \quad \varrho_2 = \varrho_1\varphi_1$ | |
| $-1 < \varphi_1 < 1$ | $-1 < \theta_1 < 1$ |

identification procedure that the model $\nabla z_t = (1-\theta B)a_t$ of order (0, 1, 1) should be entertained and that a value of $\theta$ close to zero is to be expected.

*2.3. Fitting.* Using efficient statistical methods we may now fit the tentatively identified model, or to be on the safe side, a slightly overparameterized version of it.

If the additional assumption is made that the $a$'s are Normally distributed, then maximum likelihood estimates of $\varphi = (\varphi_1, \varphi_2, \ldots, \varphi_p)$ and $\theta = (\theta_1, \theta_2), \ldots$

Table 1. Sample autocorrelations for IBM common stock daily closing prices, NYSE, May 1961 – November 1962.

| 369 observations | Autocorrelations lag | | | | | | | | | | | | | | | | | | | |
|---|---|---|---|---|---|---|---|---|---|---|---|---|---|---|---|---|---|---|---|---|
| | 1 | 2 | 3 | 4 | 5 | 6 | 7 | 8 | 9 | 10 | 11 | 12 | 13 | 14 | 15 | 16 | 17 | 18 | 19 | 20 |
| $z$ | 0.99 | 0.99 | 0.99 | 0.98 | 0.98 | 0.97 | 0.97 | 0.96 | 0.95 | 0.95 | 0.94 | 0.91 | 0.93 | 0.92 | 0.92 | 0.91 | 0.90 | 0.90 | 0.89 | 0.88 |
| $\nabla z$ | 0.08 | 0.00 | −0.05 | −0.04 | −0.02 | −0.13 | 0.07 | 0.03 | −0.07 | 0.02 | 0.08 | 0.06 | −0.05 | 0.07 | −0.07 | 0.12 | 0.13 | 0.05 | 0.05 | 0.07 |
| $\nabla^2 z$ | −0.45 | −0.02 | −0.04 | −0.00 | −0.07 | 0.11 | −0.01 | 0.04 | −0.11 | 0.02 | 0.04 | 0.04 | −0.12 | 0.14 | −0.18 | −0.10 | 0.05 | −0.04 | −0.01 | 0.10 |

Values to be entertained for $p$ and $q$ may usually be deduced by inspecting the sample autocorrelations using knowledge of the behaviour of the theoretical autocorrelation function $\varrho_k$ for various types of models. The characteristics of $\varrho_k(\nabla^d z)$ for models of order (1, $d$, 0), (2, $d$, 0), (0, $d$, 1), (0, $d$, 2) and (1, $d$, 1) are shown in Table 2. The boundaries of the admissible parameter space are indicated by the inequalities. By substituting sample estimates for $\varrho_k$ in Table 2, preliminary values for the model parameters (which, however, are in general not efficient estimates) may be obtained. In the case of the IBM series for instance we might conclude from our

$\theta_q$) will be obtained by minimizing the sum of squares

$$S(\varphi, \theta) = \sum a_j^2(\varphi, \theta)$$

The value $a_j(\varphi, \theta)$ for any $\varphi$ and $\theta$ may readily be calculated recursively using

$$a_j = \theta_1 a_{j-1} + \ldots + \theta_q a_{j-q} + w_j - \varphi_1 w_{j-1} - \ldots - \varphi_p w_{j-p}$$

with $w_j = \nabla^d z_j$. To start the process off we can set $a_j = w_j = 0$ for $j \leq 0$ or more exactly a process of backward calculation (Box and Jenkins, in press) may be used.

An approximate 1-ε confidence region for $\varphi$ and $\theta$ is supplied by the contour

$$S_{1-\varepsilon}(\varphi, \theta) = S(\hat{\varphi}, \hat{\theta}) \left\{ 1 + \frac{\chi_\varepsilon^2(p+q)}{n} \right\}$$

where $\chi_\varepsilon^2(v)$ is the upper ε significance point of the Chi-square distribution having $v$ degrees of freedom.

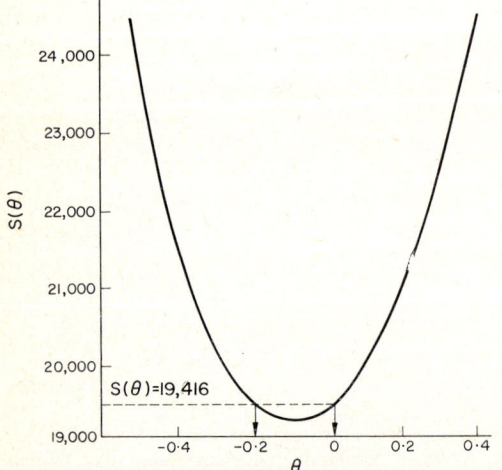

FIG. 1. *Sum of squares function for IBM data with approximate 95 per cent confidence region for $\theta$.*

Figure 1 shows a plot of $S(\theta)$ against $\theta$ for the IBM series with a minimum at $\hat{\theta} = -0.09$ and $S(\hat{\theta}) = 19,216$. The approximate 95 percent confidence limits for $\theta$ of $-0.19$ and $0.03$ are those values for which

$$S(\theta) = 19,216(1 + 3.84/369) = 19,416.$$

Least squares estimates and approximate confidence limits may be obtained without the use of graphical methods using iterative non-linear least squares procedures. However, in general graphs and contour plots of the sum of squares function $S(\varphi, \theta)$ or of sections of it are of great value in illuminating the estimation situation.

2.4. *Diagnostic checks.* If the form of the model is correct and if $\hat{\varphi}$ and $\hat{\theta}$ are close to their 'true' values then the residuals $\hat{a}_j = a_j(\hat{\varphi}, \hat{\theta})$ will be (very nearly) uncorrelated random deviates. Inadequacies of the model may therefore be shown up by examining the autocorrelation function of the estimated residuals. When the possibility of unaccounted-for periodic effects exist (as in the fitting of seasonal models) the cumulative periodogram of the residuals should also be examined.

2.5. *Seasonal models.* Time series have often to be analysed in which recurrent patterns with *known periods* occur, for example, yearly patterns in monthly sales data ($s = 12$). Here parsimony can often be achieved using multiplicative models of the type

$$\varphi_p(B)\,\Phi_P(B^s)\,(1-B)^d\,(1-B^s)^D\,z_t = \theta_q(B)\,\Theta_Q(B^s)\,a_t$$

Procedures for identifying, fitting and checking such models closely follow those described above. For instance, using these techniques it was shown that the airline passenger data of Fig. 2 was closely fitted by the model

$$(1-B)(1-B^{12})\,z_t = (1-0.4B)(1-0.6B^{12})\,a_t\,. \qquad (2)$$

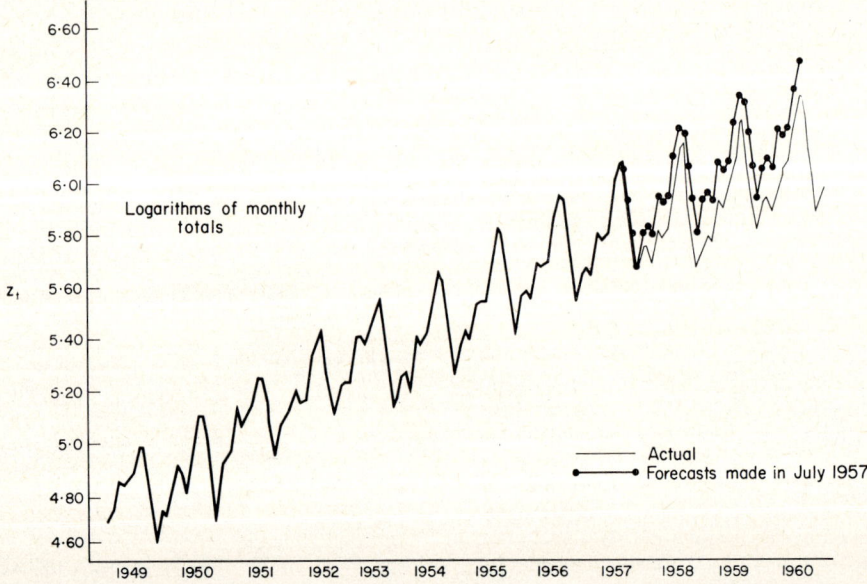

FIG. 2. *Logarithms of monthly totals of international airline passengers with forecast made at origin July 1952 for 1, 2, 3, ..., 36 months ahead.*

## 2.6. Forecasting

Suppose now that we have determined an adequate linear model for a given series and we have new data $z_t, z_{t-1}, \ldots$ from the same series extending up to the present time $t$ from which we wish to make a forecast $l$ steps ahead. We call this an *origin t forecast for lead time l*.

It may be shown that the minimum mean square error forecast for any lead time is given by

$$\hat{z}_t(l) = \underset{t}{E}(z_{t+l})$$

where $\underset{t}{E}$ is the conditional expectation at time $t$. It follows in particular that $a_t = z_t - \hat{z}_{t-1}(1)$ is the forecast error for unit lead time. Now the required expectations are easily found because

$$\underset{t}{E} z_{t+j} = \hat{z}_t(j), \quad \underset{t}{E} a_{t+j} = 0 \quad j = 1, 2, 3, \ldots$$

$$\underset{t}{E} z_{t-j} = z_{t-j}, \quad \underset{t}{E} a_{t-j} = a_{t-j} = z_{t-j} - \hat{z}_{t-j-1}(1)$$

$$j = 0, 1, 2, \ldots$$

For instance to determine the 3-month ahead forecast for the airline series we first use equation 2 to write down

$$z_{t+3} = z_{t+2} + z_{t-9} + z_{t-10} + a_{t+3} - 0.4 a_{t+2} - 0.6 a_{t-9} + \\ + 0.24 a_{t-10}.$$

Taking conditional expectations at time $t$

$$\hat{z}_t(3) = \hat{z}_t(2) + z_{t-9} + z_{t-10} - 0.6 a_{t-9} + 0.24 a_{t-10}.$$

Using these methods, forecasts made at origin July 1957 for lead times $1, 2, 3, \ldots, 36$ months ahead are shown in Fig. 2 where they may be compared with the values actually realized.

## 3. Dynamic Models

Suppose that in the study of some system such as a chemical reactor pairs of observations $(X_t, Y_t), (X_{t-1}, Y_{t-1}), \ldots$ are available of an input $X$, such as gas feed rate, and an output $Y$, such as product viscosity. Suppose further that over the interesting ranges of variation of $Y$ and $X$ there exists an approximately linear steady-state relationship

$$Y = a + gX$$

where $g$ is called the steady state *gain*.

The *dynamic* characteristics of such systems can usually be represented by difference equations of the form

$$\xi(\nabla) Y_{t+1} = a + g \eta(\nabla) X_{t-b} \qquad (3)$$

with

$$\xi(\nabla) = 1 + \xi_1 \nabla + \ldots + \xi_u \nabla^u$$
$$\eta(\nabla) = 1 + \eta_1 \nabla + \ldots + \eta_v \nabla^v$$

where $b$ represents the number of whole intervals of pure dead time (delay) in the system.

### 3.1. Fitting dynamic models (direct estimation of the transfer function)

Given data $(X_1\ Y_1), (X_2\ Y_2), \ldots, (X_n\ Y_n)$ the dynamic model may now be identified and fitted in an interative manner closely paralleling our treatment of the time series model. For instance, the simple model

$$(1 + \xi \nabla) Y_{t+1} = a + g(1 + \eta \nabla) X_t$$

or

$$Y_{t+1} = \frac{a}{1+\xi} + \frac{\xi}{1+\xi} Y_t + g \frac{1+\eta}{1+\xi} X_t - g \frac{\eta}{1+\xi} X_{t-1}$$

can represent a system whose response to a step change of $X_0$ in the input is to produce an eventual change $gX_0$ in the output which is approached exponentially at a rate depending on $\xi$ and delayed by an amount depending on $\eta$ as is illustrated in Fig. 3.

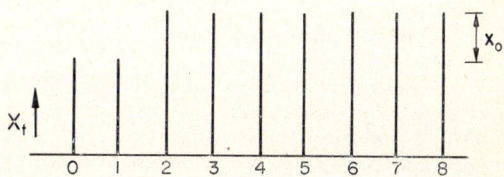

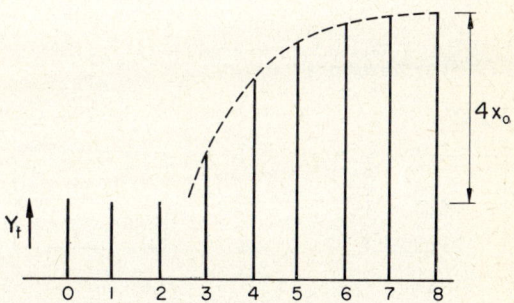

FIG. 3. Delayed exponential response to a step change produced by model $(1 + \nabla) Y_{t+1} = a + 4(1 + 0.5 \nabla) X_t$.

To fit this dynamic model we write

$$Y_{t+1} = \beta_0 + \beta_1 Y_t + \beta_2 X_t + \beta_3 X_{t-1} + e_{t+1} \qquad (4)$$

where

$$\beta_1 = \frac{\xi}{1+\xi}, \quad \beta_2 = g \frac{1+\eta}{1+\xi}, \quad \beta_3 = -\frac{g\eta}{1+\xi}. \qquad (5)$$

If the errors $e_t$ were independent normal deviates, maximum likelihood estimates $\hat{\xi}, \hat{\eta}$ and $\hat{g}$ of the parameters would be obtained by substituting standard least squares estimates for the $\beta$'s in equations (5).

In practice, the $e_t$'s would rarely be independent and we must arrive at a model by iteration.

Examination of the autocorrelation function of the residuals $\hat{e}_t$ from the least squares fit usually provides a clear indication of what would be a more suitable noise structure. For example, it might be found that the $\hat{e}_t$'s had an autocorrelation function which damped out roughly exponentially suggesting the noise model

$$(1-\varphi B)e_t = a.$$

Such a model is best fitted by writing

$$\tilde{Y}_t = Y_t - \varphi Y_t, \quad \tilde{X}_t = X_t - \varphi X_t$$

and fitting by simple linear least squares

$$\tilde{Y}_{t+1} = \beta_0(1-\varphi) + \beta_1 \tilde{Y}_t + \beta_2 \tilde{X}_t + \beta_3 \tilde{X}_{t-1} + a_{t+1}$$

for a series of values of $\varphi$ (say from $\varphi = -1$ to $\varphi = +1$ in steps of 0·1). The over-all minimum is then obtained by plotting the value of the (conditional) minimum sum of squares against $\varphi$ to obtain $\hat{\varphi}$. In more complex cases and when there are multiple inputs the parameters may be estimated by iterative non-linear least squares.

## 4. Use of Time Series Models and Dynamic Models in Control

The models we have discussed can be used as building blocks in over-all representations of dynamic systems subject to disturbance. These representation may then be used to deduce optimal control schemes which can be of the feed-forward, feed-back or mixed variety. We use for illustration the simple feed-back system outlined in Fig. 4. Here the output (viscosity) is to be maintained

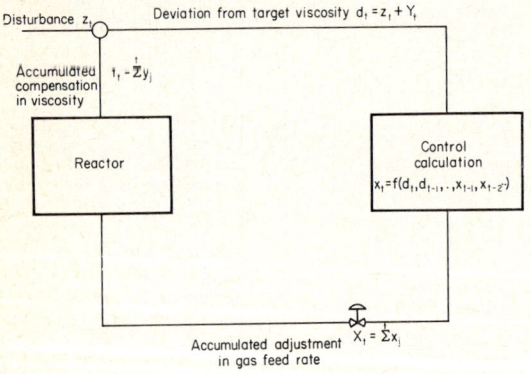

FIG. 4. *A simple feedback control system to maintain viscosity close to target by varying gas feed rate.*

close to a fixed target value by manipulating a variable $X$ (gas feed rate). In fact at time $t$ a deviation $d_t$ from target occurs because the system is infected by a disturbance $z_t$. The disturbance $z_t$ which we suppose is represented by some member of the family of models of equation 1 is defined as the deviation from target which would have accumulated by time $t$ if no control action had been applied.

We suppose also that the process dynamics are described by an equation of the form (3) so that with $y_t = Y_t - Y_{t-1}$, $x_t = X_t - X_{t-1}$ and $L_1(B)$ and $L_2(B)$ polynomials in $B$ we may write

$$L_1(B) y_{t+b+1} = g L_2(B) x_t. \quad (6)$$

Ideally, adjustments $x$ in the input gas rate $X$ would induce at any time $t+1$ an accumulated effect in output viscosity $Y_{t+1} = \sum_{j=1}^{t+1} y_j$ which was just enough to equal $-z_{t+1}$ so that there was no deviation from target. In practice a deviation

$$d_{t+1} = z_{t+1} + Y_{t+1}$$

occurs and we wish to determine a control equation $x_t = f(d_t, d_{t-1}, \ldots; x_{t-1}, x_{t-2}, \ldots)$ which enables us to compute at each stage an 'optimal' control action $x_t$ which will minimize the mean square error $E(d_t^2)$.

*4.1. Optimal control action.* In general using the dynamic model (6) which contains $b$ intervals of deadtime, action taken at time $t$ could only begin to affect the system during the interval $t+b$ to $t+b+1$. Such action can therefore be based only on that knowledge of $z_{t+b+1}$ which is available at time $t$. Consequently for optimal control $x_t$ is chosen at each stage so that

$$Y_{t+b+1} = -\underset{t}{E}(z_{t+b+1}) = -\hat{z}_t(b+1),$$

that is

$$y_{t+b+1} = -\{\hat{z}_t(b+1) - \hat{z}_{t-1}(b+1)\}. \quad (7)$$

Now using the model (1)

$$z_{t+b+1} = S^d \varphi_p^{-1}(B) \theta_q(B) a_{t+b+1} = L(B) a_{t+b+1}$$
$$= d_{t+b+1} + \hat{z}_t(b+1),$$

so that we can write

$$d_t = L_0(B) a_t \quad (8)$$

and

$$\hat{z}_t(b+1) - \hat{z}_{t-1}(b+1) = L_4(B) a_t. \quad (9)$$

Combining (6), (7), (8) and (9) we obtain the optimal control equation

$$g L_3(B) L_2(B) x_t = -L_1(B) L_4(B) d_t.$$

*4.2. An example.* In one process study it was found that the disturbance could be represented by $\nabla z_b = (1-0·5B) a_t$
and the dynamic relation by

$$(1+0·7 \nabla) y_{t+1} = 0·2(1-0·25 \nabla) x_t.$$

Thus

$$b = 0, \quad z_{t+1} = a_{t+1} + \hat{z}_t(1)$$

where $d_t = a_t$ with $\hat{z}_t(1) - \hat{z}_{t-1}(1) = 0·5 a_t$ and

$L_1(B) = 1·7 - 0·7B \quad L_2(B) = 0·75 + 0·25B$
$L_3(B) = 1 \quad\quad\quad\quad L_4(B) = 0·5 \quad\quad g = 0·2.$

The optimal control equation is therefore

$$0·2(0·75 x_t + 0·25 x_{t-1}) = -0·5(1·7 d_t - 0·7 d_{t-1}),$$

or

$$x_t = -\tfrac{1}{3}\{x_{t-1} + 17 d_t - 7 d_{t-1}\}. \quad (10)$$

The implementation of such control action can in different contexts be achieved by devices of various levels of sophistication.

uncertainty to be reduced can be completely specified by the values of a finite set of parameters called sufficient statistics.

*3.4. Number of state-variables.* A multistage decision process may have any finite number of state-variables. When the number of state-variables is greater than one it is convenient to use vector notation to replace the single state-variable $x$ and transformation $G[x, u]$ by a state vector $\mathbf{x}$ and vector function $\mathbf{G}[\mathbf{x}, u]$. The type of Dynamic Programming equation is not affected by the number of state-variables, but the dimensionality of the equation is increased by one for every additional state-variable.

*3.5. Processes operating for an indefinite time.* Some processes are required to operate over an indefinite period of future time rather than over a known finite number $N$ of stages. When the process is stationary and the number of future stages of operation is infinite the solution functions are independent of 'number of stages-to-go'; typical definitions of solution functions for such a problem are the optimal-return function

$f[c] = $ The total return from an infinite number of stages starting from state $c$ and using the optimal policy and the optimal decision function

$u[c] = $ The optimal first decision when there are an infinite number of stages-to-go and the current-state is $c$.

Because the distinction between the solution for an $N$-stage process and the solution for an $(N-1)$-stage process vanishes when $N$ goes to infinity the Dynamic Programming functional recurrence equation, for example equation 1, changes type to become a functional equation.

The corresponding continuous-time problem gives rise to partial differential expressions in which the partial derivative with respect to time, $\partial f/\partial T$, is zero. Similar types of Dynamic Programming equation arise in other problems where the operating time is indefinite although finite; for example in 'minimum time' problems where it is required to achieve some specified state as rapidly as possible.

*4. Solving Dynamic Programming Equations*

Dynamic Programming equations of appropriate type can be derived for almost any multistage decision process. The major practical limitation on the usefulness of Dynamic Programming is that these equations are not always soluble.

There are certain relatively simple processes giving rise to equations that can be solved analytically. As a general rule these processes are also soluble by other methods than Dynamic Programming and their Dynamic Programming equations can be shown to be equivalent to the equations of *Pontriagin* or to the equations of the *calculus of variations*. Although these processes are of interest in that they offer a new, Dynamic Programming, derivation of established classical results they do not fully exploit the potentialities of Dynamic Programming.

The Dynamic Programming equations for all discrete-time processes that operate over a known finite time are functional recurrence equations which happen to be very well adapted to numerical solution using a digital computer. This type of numerical solution is the standard Dynamic Programming procedure for solving all classes of multistage decision processes. The procedure gives exact solutions for processes where the Dynamic Programming equations are discrete-valued functional recurrence equations; for continuous-time processes where the equations are partial differential expressions it gives approximate solutions in the form of solutions to corresponding discrete-time processes. The functional equations of processes that operate for an indefinite time are solved numerically using a method of successive approximations. The Dynamic Programming procedure is such that in every case the numerical solution gives the optimal policy and optimal return for every possible initial state of the process; this property of the procedure is sometimes described by saying that particular processes with particular initial states are *imbedded* into a whole class of processes.

Certain advantages and disadvantages of Dynamic Programming are directly attributable to its use of a numerical solution procedure. The main advantages are that Dynamic Programming is applicable to problems described by non-analytic functions and that any restrictions on the allowable range of process variables make solution easier by restricting the amount of computation that is necessary. The main disadvantage is an inability to solve problems of high dimensionality. Although there are certain problems where the *dimensionality* of the equations can be reduced by a technique that uses a Lagrange multiplier, the limitation to problems of low dimensionality is a major limitation on the practical usefulness of Dynamic Programming.

*See also:* Control by stationary filtering and prediction. Optimization of industrial processes.

*Bibliography*

ARIS R. (1964) *Discrete Dynamic Programming*, London: Blaisdell.
BELLMAN R. E. (1957) *Dynamic Programming*, Princeton: The University Press.
BELLMAN R. E. (1961) *Adaptive Control Processes*, Oxford: The University Press.
BELLMAN R. E. and DREYFUS S. E. (1962) *Applied Dynamic Programming*, Princeton: The University Press.
BELLMAN R. E. and KALABA R. (1965) *Dynamic Pro-*

gramming and Modern Control Theory, New York: Academic Press.
DREYFUS S. E. (1965) *Dynamic Programming and the Calculus of Variations*, New York: Academic Press.
JACOBS O. L. R. (1967) *An Introduction to Dynamic Programming*, London: Chapman and Hall

ROBERTS S. M. (1964) *Dynamic Programming in Chemical Engineering and Process Control*, New York: McGraw-Hill.
TOU J. T. (1966) *Dynamic Programming and Modern Control Theory, Progress in Control Engineering*, Vol. III, London: Heywood.

O. L. R. JACOBS

# E

**ERROR CORRECTING CODES.** A simple idealization of a noisy communication channel is the memoryless *binary symmetric channel* (BSC) of Fig. 1. When a binit

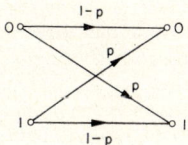

FIG. 1. *The Memoryless Binary Symmetric Channel (or BSC).*

(*bi*nary dig*it*) is transmitted, it is erroneously received with a probability $p$, $p \leq \frac{1}{2}$. The information-theoretic capacity of this channel is

$$C = 1 - H(p) \qquad \text{bits/use} \qquad (1)$$

where $H(p) = -(p)\log_2(p) - (1-p)\log_2(1-p)$ is the entropy function of a binary ensemble. The development of error correcting codes is largely a product of the study of means for transmitting information reliably over the BSC.

In *block coding*, the sender identifies each of $M$ equiprobable messages with a distinct sequence of $n$ binits which is used to transmit the message over the channel. The *code*, $X_n$, is just the set of $M$ possible transmitted $n$-tuples of binits. The message ensemble has an entropy of $\log_2(M)$ bits, hence the *code rate*, $R$, is just $\log_2(M)/n$ bits per use of the channel. Equivalently, $M = 2^{nR}$.

Let $x = (x_1, x_2, \ldots x_n)$ be a code word in $X_n$. Each $x$ can be considered as a vertex or point of the unit $n$-cube. The $R = \frac{1}{3}$ code, $X_3 = \{(0, 0, 0), (1, 1, 1)\}$ is shown in Fig. 2 by shading, the $M = 2$ points of the unit 3-cube.

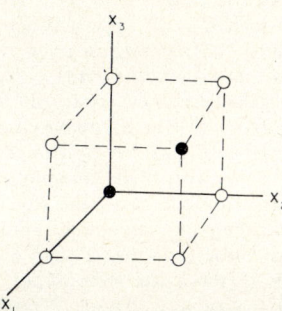

FIG. 2. *The code $X_3 = \{(0, 0, 0), (1, 1, 1,)\}$ shown as shaded vertices of the unit 3-cube.*

which are *code points*. When the point $x$ is transmitted over the BSC, the point $y = (y_1, y_2, \ldots, y_n)$ is received where $y \neq x$ if errors have occurred. When $R < 1$, not all $2^n$ vertices of the unit $n$-cube are code points. In this case more than one vertex $y$ can be *decoded* into the same vertex $x$ at the receiver, i.e. the code has the ability to correct certain errors.

The *Hamming distance*, $d(v, v')$ between vertices $v$ and $v'$ of the $n$-cube is the number of coordinates in which $v$ and $v'$ differ. The minimum distance, $d_{\min}$, of a code $X_n$ is the minimum Hamming distance between distinct code points in $X_n$. For $X_3$ in Fig. 2, $d_{\min} = 3$. A pattern of $t$ errors perturbs a code point $x$ to a point $y$ such that $d(x, y) = t$. Provided that $t \leq t_{\max} = [(d_{\min} - 1)/2]$, where the bracket denotes the integral part of the enclosed expression, $y$ will be closer to $x$ than to any other code point. Thus all patterns of $t_{\max}$ or fewer errors can be corrected by the code $X_n$. Moreover, not all patterns of $t_{\max} + 1$ or fewer errors can be corrected so that $t_{\max}$ is the guaranteed error-correcting radius of the code. The code of Fig. 2 is single-error correcting since $t_{\max} = 1$.

A major problem in coding theory is, for given $n$ and $R$, finding a code $X_n$ which (nearly) maximizes $d_{\min}$ or $t_{\max}$. Limits on the solutions of this problem can be readily established by geometric arguments. A *sphere* of radius $r$ about a vertex $v$ of the $n$-cube is the set of all vertices $v'$ such that $d(v, v') \leq r$. The volume, $V(r)$, of the sphere is the number of vertices which it contains, viz.

$$V(r) = \sum_{i=0}^{r} \binom{n}{i} = 2^{n[H(r/n) + \varepsilon]} \qquad (2)$$

where $\varepsilon$ approaches zero as $n$ approaches infinity for $(r/n) \leq \frac{1}{2}$.

Given a code $X_n$ with error-correcting radius $t_{\max}$, the spheres of radius $t_{\max}$ about each of the $M$ code points must be disjoint. Since the total volume of these spheres cannot exceed the number of vertices of the $n$-cube, $(M)V(t_{\max}) \leq 2^n$ or

$$V(t_{\max}) \leq 2^{n(1-R)} \qquad (3)$$

which is the *Hamming bound*. A code $X_n$ for which (3) holds with equality is called a *sphere-packed code*, a trivial example of which is the code $X_3$ of Fig. 2. It is known that sphere-packed codes must be exceedingly rare. The only known ($m > 2$) sphere-packed codes are the Hamming codes and the remarkable Golay code. For any $m$, there is a Hamming code with $n = 2^m - 1$, $t_{\max} = 1$, and $R = (2^m - m - 1)/(2^m - 1)$. The *Golay code* has $n = 23$, $t_{\max} = 3$, and $R = 12/23$. For large $n$, the Hamming bound becomes $H(t_{\max}/n) \leq 1 - R$, or equivalently $H(d_{\min}/2n) \leq 1 - R$. The corresponding upper bound on the attainable $d_{\min}/2n$ ratio is plotted in Fig. 3.

Given any $d \leq n$, a code $X_n$ with $d_{\min} \geq d$ can be constructed by the following procedure. Choose the first code point arbitrarily and surround it with a sphere of radius $d-1$. Choose a second code point not in this sphere and surround it with a sphere of radius $d-1$. Choose a third code point not in the *union* of the preceding spheres, etc. At least $M$ code points can be chosen provided that $(M-1)V(d-1) < 2^n$ and this code must have $d_{\min} \geq d$. Thus $V(d_{\min}) \leq 2^{n(1-R)}$ is a sufficient condition for the construction of a code $X_n$ with rate $R$ and minimum distance $d_{\min}$. This is the *Gilbert bound*. This bound states that some $d_{\min}/n$ ratio is attainable for which $H(d_{\min}/n) \geq 1 - R$. This lower bound on the attainable ratio is plotted in Fig. 3.

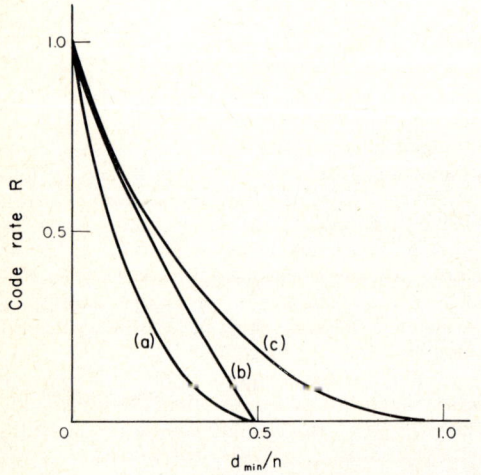

FIG. 3. *Bounds on the ratio of minimum distance $d_{\min}$ to code length n attainable with a block code with rate R:* (a) *Gilbert lowerbound;* (b) *Elias–Shannon–Gallager asymptotic upper bound;* (c) *Hamming asymptotic upper bound.*

An improved asymptotic upper bound on the $d_{\min}/n$ ratio can be found using more subtle arguments. This *Elias–Shannon–Gallager bound* states that $H(\frac{1}{2} - \frac{1}{2}\sqrt{1 - 2d_{\min}/n}) \leq 1 - R$ and is shown in Fig. 3.

The Gilbert lower bound shows that for any fixed $R$ there exists a sequence of codes $X_n$ such that $d_{\min}/n$ (or $t_{\max}/n$) approaches a non-zero constant as $n$ becomes infinite, but no closed construction procedure is known which realizes this possibility. The most powerful constructive class of codes now known, the *Bose–Chaudhuri–Hoquenghem codes*, attain the Gilbert lower bound out to code lengths $n$ of about 1000 binits.

The search for good codes is greatly simplified by the restriction to *linear codes* (also called *group codes* and *parity-check codes*.) A linear code with rate $R = k/n$ is specified by an $(n-k) \times n$ matrix $H$ with linearly independent rows. This binary matrix $H$ is called the parity-check matrix of the code. All operations with such matrices are assumed to be carried out over the binary number field, i.e. using modulo-two arithmetic. The code $X_n$ defined by $H$ is the set of $2^k$ binary row vectors $\mathbf{x} = (x_1, x_2, \ldots x_n)$ such that $Hx^T = \mathbf{0}$ where $T$ denotes 'transpose' and $\mathbf{0}$ denotes the $n-k$ dimensional vector of zeroes. Each row of the matrix $H$ specifies a *parity check* for the code since the ones in that row designate a set of coordinates whose values must sum to zero for all code words. The minimum distance of a linear code is always equal to the Hamming weight (i.e. number of non-zero positions) of the non-zero code word in $X_n$ with minimum Hamming weight. It can be shown that there exist linear codes which attain the Gilbert lower bound on the $d_{\min}/n$ ratio for all $n$ and $R$.

Decoding of linear codes is facilitated by use of the *syndrome*, $s$, which is the $n-k$ dimensional vector $\mathbf{s} = Hy^T$ where $y$ is the received point. When $x$ is transmitted, $y = x + e$ where $e$ is the error pattern and has a one in each position of $y$ where an error has occurred in transmission. Hence $s = Hy^T = H(x+e)^T = Hx^T + He^T = He^T$ so that $s$ depends only upon the error pattern. Exactly $2^{n-k}$ error patterns give the same syndrome. Optimum decoding is accomplished by decoding $y$ into $x + e$ (addition and subtraction coincide in modulo-two arithmetic) where $e$ is the most probable of the $2^{n-k}$ error patterns consistent with $s$. For the BSC, the most probable error pattern is that with the fewest ones. For an example of syndrome decoding, consider the Hamming $R = \frac{4}{7}$ code with the parity check matrix

$$H = \begin{bmatrix} 0 & 0 & 0 & 1 & 1 & 1 & 1 \\ 0 & 1 & 1 & 0 & 0 & 1 & 1 \\ 1 & 0 & 1 & 0 & 1 & 0 & 1 \end{bmatrix}. \quad (4)$$

As with any linear code, $s = He^T = 0$ when no errors occur. If a single error occurs in the $i$th position, it follows from (4) that $s = He^T = (s_1, s_2, s_3)$ where $s_1 s_2 s_3$ is the radix-two representation of the integer $i$. Since the code has $t_{\max} = 1$ and is sphere-packed, it cannot correct more than single errors. Thus the optimum decoding algorithm is simply: Change the $i$th binit of $y$ if $i = (s_1 s_2 s_3)_2 \neq 0$.

Encoding is also greatly simplified for linear codes. Any linear code is equivalent (i.e. differs by at most a permutation of the positions in the code words) to a code $X_n$ for which $H = [P : I]$ where $I$ is the $(n-k) \times (n-k)$ identity matrix. Such a code is called *systematic*. In a systematic code, the binits $x_1, x_2, \ldots x_k$ of the code word $x$ may be chosen arbitrarily and hence are called *information bits*. The parity check defined by the $i$th row of $H$ is then satisfied by choice of the *parity binit* $x_{k+i}$. Thus the parity binits are uniquely determined once the information bits have been selected.

Further encoding and decoding simplifications are possible for a *linear code* that is also *cyclic*. A linear code is cyclic if the cyclic shift, $(h_1 h_2 \ldots h_{n-1} h_n) \to (h_2 h_3 \ldots h_n h_1)$, of any row of $H$ produces another row in the row-space of $H$. For such a code, the cyclic shift of a code word $x$ produces another code word. Very simple shift-register circuits can be used to encode and to form the syndrome for cyclic codes. Moreover, the decoding algorithm need only decode the first binit, $y_1$, of the received block. The received block is then cycled and the same algorithm used to decode $y_2$, etc. The Bose–Chaudhuri–Hoquenghem (BCH) codes are cyclic codes as are many other important classes of codes, but it is not known whether there exist cyclic codes which attain the Gilbert lower bound on the $d_{\min}/n$ ratio for fixed $R$ as $n$ becomes infinite.

Cyclic codes have an interesting algebraic interpretation. The code point $x = (x_1, x_2, \ldots x_n)$ is identified with the polynomial $x(X) = x_1 X^{n-1} + x_2 X^{n-2} + \ldots + x_{n-1} X + x_n$. For any cyclic code $X_n$, there exists a polynomial $g(X)$ of degree $n-k$ which divides $X^n - 1$ such that the $2^k$ distinct multiples of $g(X)$ with degree less than $n$ are the polynomials corresponding to the $2^k$ code words in $X_n$. Conversely, any $g(X)$ which divides $X^n + 1$ generates the code words of a cyclic code. The BCH codes are formed by choosing $g(X)$ to be the minimum degree polynomial having among its roots $d-1$ consecutive powers of some specified element $\beta$, $\beta \neq 0$, of $GF(2^m)$. $GF(2^m)$ is the finite field of $2^m$ elements, all $n = 2^m - 1$ non-zero elements of which are roots of $X^n + 1$. If the $d-1$ successive powers of $\beta$ are distinct, then any multiple of $g(X)$ must have at least $d$ non-zero coefficients so that $d_{\min} \geq d$ in the corresponding cyclic code. The most important BCH codes result when $\beta$ is taken to be a primitive element of $GF(2^m)$. In this case with $d-1 = 2t$, the resulting cyclic codes have block length $n = 2^m - 1$, error-correcting radius $t_{\max} \geq t$, and at most $n-k = mt$ parity binits. The Hamming codes are the special case where $t = 1$.

Closely related to the problem of finding codes with (nearly) maximum $d_{\min}$ is the problem of finding codes for which the probability of a decoding error on the BSC is (nearly) minimum. On the BSC, the probability that $y$ is received when $x$ is transmitted decreases monotonically with $d(x, y)$. Thus the decoding error probability is minimized by a *maximum likelihood decoder* which decodes $y$ into the nearest code point $x$. The probability of a decoding error for a code $X_n$ when used on a BSC and decoded by a maximum likelihood decoder will be denoted $P(X_n)$.

One form of the noisy coding theorem of information theory states that for any rate R less than capacity $C$, there exists a sequence of codes $X_n$ with rate at least $R$ such that $P(X_n) \to 0$ as $n \to \infty$; conversely no such sequence exists if $R > C$.

The lower bound on attainable $P(X_n)$ is established from the Hamming bound on $t_{\max}$. For any code, $P(X_n)$ must be at least as great as that for a postulated sphere-packed code of the same rate $R$. A sphere-packed code, however, corrects a pattern of $t$ errors if and only if $t \leq t_{\max}$. The average number of errors in a received block is just $np$ on the BSC, and the probability that the fraction of errors differs from $p$ by any fixed amount $\varepsilon > 0$ approaches zero as $n$ becomes infinite. Thus $P(X_n)$ for the sequence of sphere-packed codes can approach zero only if $t_{\max}/n$ approaches a limit greater than $p$. Using (1), (2) and (3) this condition becomes $H(t_{\max}/n) = 1 - R \geq H(p) = 1 - C$, or simply $R \leq C$ which is the converse part of the coding theorem.

The direct part of the coding theorem was proved by Shannon using a 'random coding' argument, i.e. by showing that the average of $P(X_n)$ over all codes of rate $R$ and length $n$ approaches zero as $n$ becomes infinite provided that $R < C$. Only one constructive class of codes, the Elias iterated codes, has been found with the property that the rates approach a non-zero rate $R$ and $P(X_n)$ approaches zero as $n$ becomes infinite. But these codes require $R$ to be considerably less than $C$ and the approach of $P(X_n)$ to zero is much less rapid than is known to be attainable.

Non-block forms of coding have also been studied for the BSC. *Convolutional coding* (also called recurrent coding) is a non-block form of linear coding. In a convolutional code, the transmitted binits are generated in segments of $n_0$ binits, $k_0$ of which are information bits. The parity binits in each segment are a modulo-two sum of information binits in that segment and the preceding $m$ segments. Convolutional codes are found to have essentially the error-correcting capability of block codes of length $n = (m+1)n_0$. These codes have played an important theoretical role in *sequential decoding*, which is a form of decoding applicable to any convolutional code. Over the ensemble of all convolutional codes with rate $R = k_0/n_0$, the probability of a decoding error vanishes exponentially as $m$ is increased while the average number of decoding computations is bounded provided that $R < R_{\text{comp}} < C$ where $R_{\text{comp}}$ is the computational cut-off rate.

Codes have also been studied for many noisy communication channels besides the BSC. One such channel is the binary burst channel where errors can occur only in clusters spanning at most $b$ channel binits, such clusters being separated by at least $g$ error-free binits. For this simple channel, essentially optimum codes and simple decoding methods are known. Non-binary input channels have also been considered. Virtually all the theory of linear binary codes can be extended to linear $q$-ary codes where $q = p^m$ is the power of a prime. The code digits in this case are taken to be elements of $GF(p^m)$, the finite field of $p^m$ elements. Error correcting codes have also been developed for non-communication applications. For instance, a special type of block binary code called a *residue code* has been developed to correct the kinds of errors that commonly arise in digital circuits for the adding of integers in radix-two representation, viz. the inversion of binits in the sum and the loss or spurious generation of carry binits.

*See also:* Communication theory. Random signals and noise. Reliable computation using unreliable elements.

*Bibliography*

PETERSON W. W. (1961) *Error-Correcting Codes*, Cambridge, Mass.: M.I.T. Press; New York: Wiley.

SHANNON C. E. (1948) *The Mathematical Theory of Communication*, Bell Syst. Tech. J., **27**, 379, 623.
WOZENCRAFT J. M. and JACOBS I. M. (1966) *Principles of Communication Engineering*, New York: Wiley.

J. L. MASSEY

**EYE MOVEMENTS.** In this article eye movements means rotations of the eye ball in its orbit. These rotations are important because they produce movements of image of the visual scene across the retina. In this article we consider only the simplest situation in which the target is at a very great distance from the subject. Translational movements of the head do not then affect the retinal image and vergence movements need not be discussed.

When a subject with normal vision is erect and is looking straight forward, the two visual axes are horizontal and parallel. The eyes are then said to be in the *primary position*. Rotation about a vertical axis is called an H-rotation (Fig. 1a) because the direction of view moves in a horizontal plane: rotation about a horizontal axis which is perpendicular to the visual axis (in the primary position) is called a V-rotation; rotation about the visual axis itself is called *torsion* or T-rotation. Rotation about any other axis may be regarded as compounded of H, V, T components. The instantaneous centre of rotation for small rotations is about 14·0 mm behind the outer surface of the cornea.

The orientation of the eye ball is determined by the combined action of three opposing pairs of muscles called the *extra-ocular muscles* (Fig. 1b). (In this article we do not consider the dynamics of the action of the eye muscles. For this topic see Robinson (1964).) These are (a) the lateral rectus and medial rectus which act so as to give H-rotations when the eye is in the primary position (b) the superior rectus and inferior rectus which produce V-rotations when the eye has been rotated about 24° from the primary position (inwards) but produce rotation which has H, V and T components when the eye is in the primary position and (c) the superior oblique and the inferior oblique. These act in a vertical plane which makes an angle of about 52° with the visual axis when the eye is in the primary position. They thus affect, H, V and T rotations. A pure V-rotation can be produced by the joint action of the superior and inferior recti and the two obliques acting in the correct ratio which is about 2 : 1 in favour of the obliques. Thus the position of the eye at any moment depends on a fine balance between the action of the six muscles. This provides accurate and flexible control but carries the penalty of many possibilities of imbalance or imprecise adjustment.

It is convenient to divide eye movements into two categories:

(a) Movements made to bring an object of interest into the centre of the field of view or to avoid an excessively bright light: eye movements made to follow a moving target are included in this category.

(b) Certain small movements which remain when a well trained subject fixes his gaze as accurately as he can upon a well defined target: these are called eye movements of fixation.

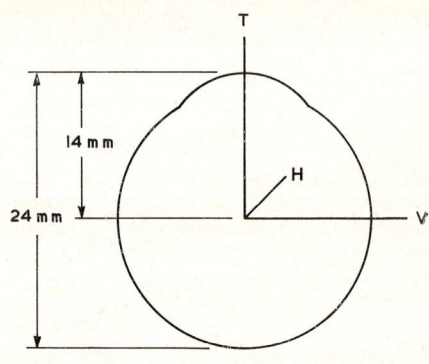

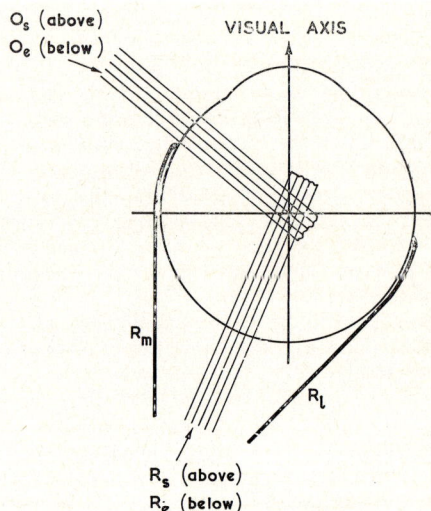

FIG. 1. (a) *Axes of rotation (H, V, T) Right eye from above, H into paper.* (b) *Extra-ocular muscles (Right eye from above)*: $R_l$ = *lateral rectus*; $R_m$ = *medial rectus*; $R_s$ = *superior rectus*; $R_e$ = *inferior rectus*; $O_s$ = *superior oblique*; $O_e$ = *inferior oblique*.

Movements of category (b) are subject to an elaborate control system but they are not consciously controlled and a naive subject is entirely unaware of their existence. Movements of category (a) are 'subject to conscious control' in that a person can decide not to make them although, in normal life, most people are conscious of these movements only to the extent that they are conscious of breathing—which also can be temporarily stopped. Whether the subject is conscious of these movements or not they are made in response to stimuli and, as with movements of category (b), the control is not a very simple one. It is convenient to discuss category (b) before category (a).

*Small eye movements of fixation.* It has been shown by many experimenters that three kinds of eye movements exist during fixation.

(i) *Saccadic movements* lasting about 25 millisec and of excursus up to 20 min arc. (Angular movements are given in minutes of arc ($2.9 \times 10^{-4}$) radian. One min arc corresponds to a movement of $5.3\ \mu$ in the retinal image of a distant object. The intercone distance in the centre of the fovea is $5.3\ \mu$.) These occur at irregular intervals ranging from 25 msec to 25 sec.

(ii) *Drifts* which occur during intersaccadic intervals. These are mainly in one direction during any one intersaccadic interval. Their speed varies up to about 5 min arc per sec.

(iii) *Tremor:* an irregular oscillatory movement of amplitude less than 1 min arc. (Some writers use the term 'tremor' for components above some chosen frequency (e.g. 30 c/s). We consider all irregular oscillatory movements together under (iii).) The movement includes components with frequencies up to 100 c/s but the main 'power' is in the frequency range below 10 c/s. Figure 2a shows a record of components of H, V, and T components of rotation. Figure 2b is a small section of a record. It has been amplified to show the oscillatory movement.

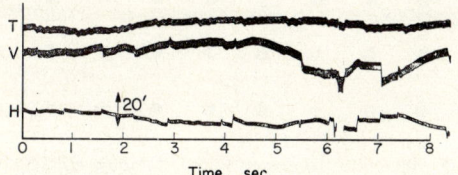

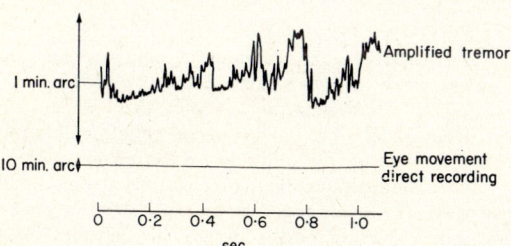

FIG. 2. (*above*) *Record of eye movements (H, V, T components). (below) Small portion of record with amplification of appropriate frequencies to show tremor.*

In regard to the magnitude $M_s$ of the saccades and the interval between them (intersaccadic interval) there is considerable variation between the performance of the same subject on different days and a much larger difference between subjects. Thus Boyce (1965) found $M_s = 3.7$ min arc and $M_s = 5.5$ min arc as median values for one subject on different days. The table shows the range of median values found by different experimenters who have tested about 30 subjects in all.

|  | Max. | Min. | Median |
|---|---|---|---|
| $M_s$ (min arc) | 4 | 1.5 | 2.7 |
| $M_d$ (min arc) | 20 | 2 | 4.7 |
| $T_{is}$ (sec) | 25 | 0.24 | 0.62 |

The table, column 1 shows the largest median value for any one subject. Column 2 shows the smallest median value for any one subject. Column 3 shows the median of the median values for different subjects.

The diameter of the Moon in the visual field is about 15 min arc. A sharp movement of this magnitude occurring in the external world would be very obvious. Yet the saccades are producing comparable retinal image movements about once a second for many observers and these are not noticed. There must therefore be some specific inhibitory action which prevents us from perceiving the retinal image movement due to involuntary saccades. Fender arranged that a signal derived from the eye movement produced a brief deflexion on a C.R.O. screen. The subject whose eye had triggered the movement could not see it even though it was clearly visible to another person. Later work by Latour (1962), Volkman (1962) and Ebbers (1965) showed that there is a reduction of the sensitivity of the visual system by a factor of between $10^2$ and $10^3$ beginning about 40 ms before a saccade and lasting till after the end of the saccade. A similar partial or total inhibition of vision occurs during large voluntary saccades.

The overall effect of the eye movements of fixation is that the retinal image of the point fixated moves so that samples of its position taken at sufficiently long intervals constitute an approximately normal bivariate distribution. The point remains about 60 per cent of the time within an elliptical area of major and minor axes about 10.0 min arc and 6.0 min arc respectively. It appears that the major axis for several subjects is nearer the vertical than the horizontal but the number of subjects tested is too small to be sure that this is typical.

This distribution suggests a control operating against random disturbances due to imperfect balance of the action of the extra-ocular muscles. Each muscle consists of bundles of fibres: any one fibre (or small group) loses tone intermittently at random intervals. There is thus a small irregular variation in the force exerted by each of two opposing muscles and this produces the tremor. In addition a gradual change in the average forces exerted by two opposed muscles will lead to a drift. *Prima facie,* it would seem likely that the saccade is a restoring movement but this will be discussed later.

Even though the movements of fixation arise from imperfection of muscle control, we still need to consider whether the resulting movements of the retinal image have any useful function. This is tested by means of devices which produce a *stabilized retinal image*. These devices arrange that a visual target moves so that its image is stationary on the retina even when the eye moves. One method is shown in Fig. 3. P, which is

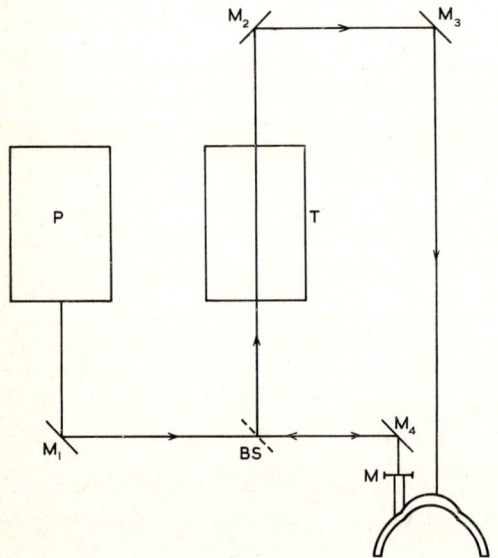

FIG. 3. *Apparatus for producing a stabilized retinal image.*

similar to a projection system forms an image of a lantern slide. Light from P falls on the mirror M, which is fixed to a tight-fitting contact lens. It then goes via the beam splitter BS and the telescopic optical system T to the eye of the observer who sees an image of the target. When the eye turns through an angle $\theta$, the beam reflected from M turns through $2\theta$. The beam emerging from T turns through $2m\theta$ where $m$ is the angular magnification of T. The movement relative to the eye is $(2m-1)\theta$ which is zero when $m = \frac{1}{2}$. It is found that when the retinal image is stabilized, the main visual discriminations fail; the target is seen intermittently and hazily like an after-image and, in some conditions, vision fails completely. The whole field goes black.

*Visual function of small eye movements.* Detailed study of vision with the stabilized images and of the effect of movements controlled by the experimenter leads to the following general picture of the visual function of small eye movements. The visual system, in common with other receptor systems responds strongly to varying stimuli and weakly to steady stimuli. The low frequency components (2 to 10 c/s) of the irregular movement cause varying stimuli for receptors lying near a boundary between light and dark regions in the retinal image (see Fig. 4). These receptors send strong signals which enable the boundary to be perceived. However, if these signals are carried by the same nerve-fibres for more than a short period ($\sim 0.1$ sec) accommodation occurs and the response falls. It is therefore advantageous to allow the mean position of a boundary to drift so that the strong signals are transferred to another set of receptors (and associated nerve tracts). This drift should be predominately in one direction. If uncompensated it would carry the point of interest outside the region of close packed cones where visual acuity is highest. Therefore intermittent corrections are needed and the saccades are suitable for this function.

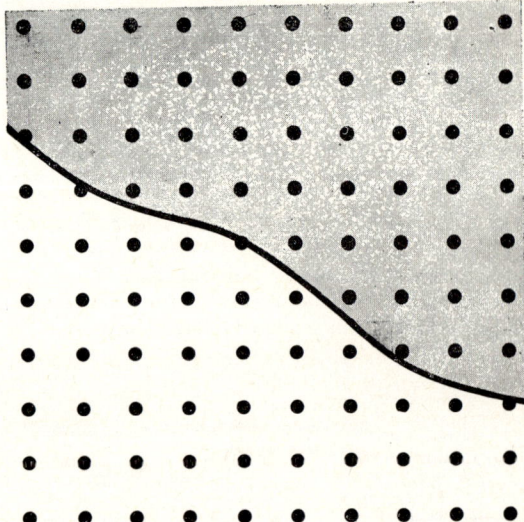

FIG. 4. *Schematic representation of boundary superimposed on an array of receptors.*

*Eye movement control systems.* A detailed study of the eye movements reveals a system of control which is somewhat more complicated than that we have so far suggested. It is now generally accepted that the control has a 'dead-space' (of radial dimension about 5 min arc). When the image of the point to be fixated lies within this region there is no 'error-signal' or only a weak one. When it strays outside this area an error signal is generated and correction occurs mainly by saccades but, in some subjects, also by successive drifts to some extent compensating each other. However, the centre of fixation is not fixed exactly but changes every few seconds by a few minutes of arc, but it always remains within about 10·0 min arc of the mean position (taken over a long time). The change from one centre of fixation to another is usually made by means of saccade. Thus the control system operates like a servomechanism which (a) uses an error signal derived from the retina, (b) has a dead space, (c) changes its 'zero' every few seconds, (d) has an information delay of about 0·15 sec (e) uses correction pulses. It appears that corrective saccades usually occur in response to error signals but, if drifts are abnormally small, saccades tend to occur at regular times.

*Eye movements when tracking a target moving continuously in a predictable path.* Fender and Nye (1961) studied the eye when following a target which moved sinusoidally. They proposed the control system shown in Fig. 5. as a result of their experiments. This postulates

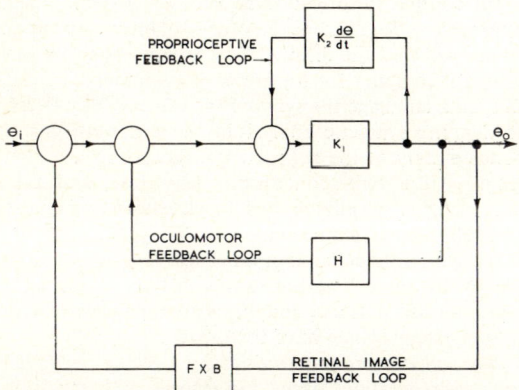

FIG. 5. *Control model (Fender and Nye).*

the existence of (a) an error signal ($F \times B$) derived from the retina (b) a signal $\left(K_2 \dfrac{d\theta}{dt}\right)$ derived from the nerves attached to the extra-ocular muscles and proportional to the angular velocity of the eye and (c) a signal ($H$) giving the difference between 'goal and achievement' in respect of any movement. The effectiveness of the signal can be reduced or increased by using the apparatus shown in Fig. 3 and varying $m$ in an appropriate way. The factor $F$ can be made equal to 0 (stabilized image) so that the system becomes open loop in respect of this signal or $F$ can be given any value between $-5$ and $+5$ (normal vision corresponds to $F = 1$). The observations of the eye movements when following targets moving with small amplitude and different frequencies could all be represented by a linear control system, of the type shown.

*Eye movements when following sharp non-predictable target movements.* Stark and Vossius and others have investigated the response of the eye to sharp movements of the target. They proposed a control system which 'sampled' the position of the eye at regular intervals of about 0·15 sec but starts a new series of samples whenever there is a sharp movement of the target. This system is not so sharply distinguished from that proposed by Fender and Nye as might be supposed on first consideration. Any continuous control system must operate like a sampling system when the movements which are being followed take place in times short compared with the time required for signals to 'round the loop' in the continuous system. Similarly a sampled data system following a smooth motion so that future position can be predicted operates like a smooth control. Boyce (1965) has tested the system proposed by Young and Stark using special series of pulses and has found that a more complicated sampling program is needed.

*Conclusion.* Control models like those described above may have two purposes (a) to summarize a complicated series of results in a relatively simple way and (b) to predict the behaviour of a biological system under conditions which have not yet been examined. The models are nearly always useful in regard to (a). They do represent the logical structure of the results from which they are constructed. They are often not successful in regard to (b) because they are inevitably very simple in relation to the biological system under examination. Logical models help as mnemonics and in the design of new experiments. They impede research if too naively accepted as representing the biological systems under conditions which have not been examined.

*See also:* Man-machine in control systems. Perceptual breakdown with stabilized images.

*Bibliography*

CLOWES M. B. and DITCHBURN R. W. (1959) *Opt. Acta* **6**, 252.
DITCHBURN R. W. (1959) Year Book Physical Society, 66.
DITCHBURN R. W. (1960) *Science*, No. 6, 47.
EBBERS (1965) Thesis (Indiana University).
FENDER D. H. and NYE P. W. (1961) *Kybernetik*, **1**, 81.
HUBEL D. H. and WIESEL T. N. (1965) *J. Neurophysiol.* **28**, 229.
LATOUR P. L. (1962) *Vision Research* **2**, 261.
RATLIFF F. and RIGGS L. A. (1950) *J. Exp. Psychol.* **40**, 687.
ROBINSON D. A. (1964) *J. Physiol.*, **194**, 245.
VOLKMAN F. C. (1962) *J. Opt. Soc. Amer.* **52**, 571.
YOUNG and STARK (1962) M.I.T. Research Laboratory of Electronics. Cambridge, Mass. Quart. Prog. Report 66, July 1962.

R. W. DITCHBURN

# F

**FACT RETRIEVAL. (Answering questions by computer about a store of data.)** Large stores of information, such as national census returns, telephone directories, encyclopaedias and the records of banks and insurance companies are of great potential value. This value is not fully realized because of the extreme difficulty of extracting facts from them on matters for which they were not designed and indexed. Questions like 'I want the telephone number of someone who lives in Grove Street, I don't know her name but I would recognize it if you mentioned it' or 'is there any correlation between age and district in Swansea?' may be difficult to answer if they have not been already provided for by a suitable index. If the facts are stored in a computer, much more elaborate searching processes are economical, but these processes have to be controlled by the questioner, who has to write what is effectively a program to answer his question.

The problems can be separated into two groups. First, the computer must read and understand the question, that is, translate it into an acceptable, legal internal representation. Second, the store must be searched to answer the question. The format of the question could vary from the most rigid, such as marks on a multiple-choice form, through something resembling a computer language, up to a restricted version of natural language. If the questioners are postulated to be untrained, then a form has some advantages, but the need to answer unforeseen questions points to a programming language for the trained operator and a subset of English with elaborate diagnostic aids for the man in the street. There has therefore been an emphasis on work on English language input of questions. This has been reviewed by Simmons (1965). It presents a problem of difficulty comparable with that of mechanical translation, though this is eased by the restricted scope of particular examples. The difficulties of searching for the information depend heavily on the form that it is in. If it is language text, as it would be in an encyclopaedia, then the difficulty is very great. If it is previously structured data, as in a census form, then the problem is more or less tractable according to the sort of question envisaged.

No large scale, highly flexible scheme seems likely to be forthcoming in the near future and all of the 20 or so programs which have been written by various authors have been experimental. A considerable variety of problems have been partly solved, or at least recognized, but because of the small size of the systems they have all avoided a principal difficulty, which is that of large scale. Nevertheless, the experiments are of considerable interest and three typical ones are described below. Quite a simple operational system could be valuable.

In any system, a set of primitive operations will be available for searching the data, and the task of the input routine is to put some of these together, with appropriate parameters, in order to form a program which will find the answer. This is very much like the job of a compiler for an ordinary computer language. In such a language the syntax has been carefully chosen so that the syntactic analysis of the programs corresponds closely to the required translation. In a natural language the correspondance is less close, and extra processing is usually needed to eliminate ambiguities and relate parts of the sentences. The distinction between syntax and semantics, which has been drawn rather strictly by some linguists, seems not to be especially useful for this purpose, and this is exemplified by several of the systems which have been made.

*Baseball* is a program written by Green *et al.* (1963) to answer questions about the records of baseball games. It consists of two parts, called the Language Analyser and the Data Processor, and it has a dictionary of words and a collection of data. The question is read and processed by the *Language Analyser*, which forms a specification list representing the content of the question. This is passed over to the Data Processor which acts, under its instructions, on the data to produce an answer. An example of a simple specification list is

```
TEAM    = ?
MONTH   = MAY
DAY     = 12
```

which represents the question 'Who played on May 12th?' The list is composed of pairs of attributes and values. The attribute may be simple, like TEAM, or it may be qualified, like [WINNING] TEAM. The value may be a list. For example, a more complex specification list is

```
SUBLIST = ([WINNING, HOME] TEAM =
        = YANKEES)
[WINNING] MARGIN = ?
DATE = [AFTER] JULY 31, 1959
```

for the question 'What were the Yankees' winning margins at home after July 1959?'

The process of producing this list is complex. First the words of the question are read and looked up in the dictionary, and their definitions are found. Then combinations of these words that form recognized idioms are located in the question and their definitions also found. For those words which have several meanings, the relevant meaning is determined. Then the phrases of the question are bracketed, with noun phrases distinguished from prepositional and adverbial phrases.

[Who] was [the winning team] (of [the May 5 Washington game])?

Other routines locate prepositions, subjects, objects, determine whether the verb is active or passive and whether the question requires a yes-no answer.

The next stage is to translate these annotated results into a specification list. The words which carry meaning are divided into content words, like 'August', which gives

MONTH = AUGUST

or 'where', which gives

CITY = ?

and operation words, like 'how many' and 'by', which alter the meaning of content words. These are all combined by an elaborate program to produce the final specification list which then passes into the Data Processor.

The entries of a specification list are arranged so that it can be applied to the record of any game. These records form the unit in which the data is stored. A process of search through game records, applying the specification list to them, and remembering and relating the individual answers, will answer the question.

The program Baseball is a simplification in several ways. First the vocabulary and the syntactic range of the questions is limited, not more than one clause is allowed and no logical connectives can be used. Second, the data base is very small and very simply organized. In particular, the fact that the answers can be obtained in terms of one sort of unit of information is a great help. Nevertheless, questions of considerable complexity can be satisfactorily answered, and there is a valuable demonstration of how difficult is the necessary language processing.

*Protosynthex* is a program which attempts to answer questions using an encyclopaedia (Simmons *et al.* 1964). It accepts an English question and tries to find sentences or articles which are relevant to answering it. The first stage is to read question and analyse it to find the content words in it and their mutual dependency relationships. A collection of words of related meanings is added and sentences or sections of the encyclopaedia are found which have the greatest number of these words. This can be done efficiently because the encyclopaedia has been appropriately indexed beforehand. The best sections are then examined to see if the dependency relationships in them correspond to those of the question. For example, the relations in 'What do worms eat?' and 'Worms eat grass' correspond exactly, but 'Worms eat their way through the ground' corresponds only partially and 'Birds eat worms' not at all. This system must be considered as a rather primitive model and success in this field seems a long way off.

A program written by Cooper (1964) attacks another of the problems of searching the data. It accepts a collection of statements, like 'magnesium burns rapidly', 'ferrous sulphide is a dark-grey compound that is brittle' and 'no metal is a non-metal' which it translates into Aristotlian forms 'all $x$ is $y$', 'not all $x$ is $y$' and so on. The questions are then read. Cooper's approach is to take the original statements as axioms and the question as a theorem to be proved. Thus the proposition 'sodium chloride is a compound' is found to be true from the statements 'sodium chloride is salt' and 'salt is a compound' and the proposition 'oxides are not white' is shown to be false by 'magnesium oxide is a white metallic oxide'. The great importance of this method is that it allows questions to be answered by combining several data statements, whereas many systems have been content to treat only questions whose answers were directly in the data. Clearly a general system must have the ability to put statements together, but this increases the difficulty of finding answers, for this is a theorem proving process, and a difficulty in these lies in knowing which are the relevant axioms to combine. In ordinary theorem proving, the axioms are usually few in number, but the axioms in fact retrieval may consist of thousands of statements, so a useful measure of relevance is vital to this approach. However, the theorem proving procedure could use quite primitive techniques and still be useful.

Considerable research must be done before a general system can be developed, though some specialized systems are being produced. In particular, work is needed on large quantities of incoherent data, on measures of relevance, on elimination of ambiguity from the questions (perhaps by on-line reference to the questioner) and on methods of inference. Text-processing systems have a long way to go before they will achieve practical utility.

*See also:* Information storage and retrieval.

*Bibliography*

COOPER W. S. (1964) *Fact retrieval and deductive question-answering information retrieval systems*, J.A.C.M. **11**, 2, 117.

GREEN B. F. Jr., WOLF A. K., CHOMSKY C. and LAUGHERY K. (1963) *Baseball: an automatic question answerer*, in *Computers and Thought*, New York: McGraw-Hill.

SIMMONS R. F., KLEIN S. and MCCONLOGUE K. L. (1964) *Indexing and dependency logic for answering English questions*, Amer. Documentation **15**, 3, 196.

SIMMONS R. F. (1965) *Answering English questions by computer: a survey*, C.A.C.M. **8**, 53.

J. M. FOSTER

**FIXED STORES AND CONTROL BY MICROPROGRAM.** *Fixed stores.* A fixed store usually means a store in which the information is written at the time of manufacture and cannot be erased or modified other than by remanufacture of that part of the store

ed for without residue. Forms like *whortle* are often described as *unique morphemes*.

The morpheme has been described as the 'minimum meaningful unit', but the validity of this definition really depends on what one understands by '*meaningful*' (Bazell 1962). If by 'meaningful' one implies something like 'possessing a constant and regular relationship to non-linguistic phenomena', then the definition is hard to justify. It is difficult to see, for instance, what constant meaning the morpheme {*ob*} has in *obtain, object, observe, obsess, obstruct*, etc. or what the meaning of the morpheme {*of*} is in such phrases as *two of them, proud of them, demand of them, boy of ten, fool of a dog, in case of fire, hard of hearing*, to take a few examples at random. If, however, by 'meaningful' one means simply 'relevant to the statement of intra-linguistic patterns', then, of course, the definition covers forms such as {*ob*} and {*of*}. A crucial test of the degree to which (semantic) meaning is regarded as relevant to the identification of morphemes arises with so-called '*homophones*', e.g. are the following one morpheme, or two, or several: /ruːt/ in *root, route*; /bɔːl/ in *ball-bearing, ballroom*; /keis/ in *suitcase, case-history, case-hardened steel, in case of fire*; /əv/ (*of*) in the seven examples quoted above? Many linguists feel that if linguistics hopes to help make possible a statement of the relationship between intra-linguistic patterns and the outside world, then to use meaning to define a key linguistic unit such as the morpheme is to introduce a confusing degree of circularity. It seems reasonable to require, therefore, that 'homophones' should be treated as single morphemes unless and until formal (distributional, intralinguistic, not semantic) evidence is produced to justify the recognition of two or more morphemes.

In most of the cases considered so far a given morpheme has been represented by the same phonological form—there has been a one-to-one relationship between the grammatical unit, the morpheme, and its phonological representation, or *MORPH*. Sometimes, however, it happens that what appears to be the same grammatical unit has different phonological representations, i.e. one morpheme appears to be represented by two or more morphs. Such morphs are termed *ALLOMORPHS*. English noun plurals provide a convenient illustration. Plural nouns share a number of distributional features which distinguish them sharply from singular nouns. For example:

| | | | |
|---|---|---|---|
| *one cat* | (*dog, horse*) | but | *two cats* (*dogs, horses*) |
| *this cat* | (*dog, horse*) | but | *these cats* (*dogs, horses*) |
| *that cat* | (*dog, horse*) | but | *those cats* (*dogs, horses*) |
| *the cat* | (*dog, horse*) *is* | but | *the cats* (*dogs, horses*) *are* |

Clearly, the -*s* suffix in *cat-s, dog-s, horse-s* performs the same grammatical function (showing that the noun is plural) in all these words, so there is a good case for increasing the generality of our grammatical statement by recognizing it as the same morpheme. It has, however, different phonological representations: /-s/ in /kæts/, /-z/ in /dɔgz/, and /-iz/ in /hɔːsiz/. We therefore group /-s ~ -z ~ -iz/ as different allomorphs of the plural morpheme. Diagrammatically:

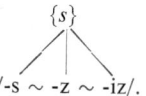

The different forms assumed by allomorphs are often determined by purely phonological factors, such as the presence or absence of voicing in neighbouring sounds, the presence or absence of stress, and so on. For example, the vast majority of English nouns form their plurals on the pattern of /kæts, dɔgz, hɔːsiz/. Here the /-iz/ suffix appears whenever the final consonant of the stem is /-s, -ʃ, -tʃ, -z, -ʒ, -dʒ/, as in /hɔːs-iz, sæʃ-iz, mætʃ-iz, rouz-iz, ruːʒ-iz, ledʒ-iz/; otherwise the voiceless suffix, /-s/, appears after voiceless stem-final sounds, as in /kæt-s/; and the voiced suffix, /-z/, appears after voiced stem-final sounds, as in /dɔg-z/. Such allomorphs are said to be *phonologically conditioned*. However, although the above rule covers most English plural forms, not all English plurals are conditioned in this way. If they were, the plurals of *ox* and *man* would be */ɔksiz/ and */mænz/ instead of /ɔksən/ and /men/. Such allomorphs may be said to be *lexically conditioned*, because the choice of the plural form does not depend in any way on the phonological characteristics of neighbouring sounds, but simply on the identity of the preceding stem. In the form /ɔks-ən/ we have no difficulty in deciding where to make our morpheme cut, and we can add the morph /-ən/ to our list of plural allomorphs, bearing in mind, of course, that it is differently conditioned from the sibilant suffixes:

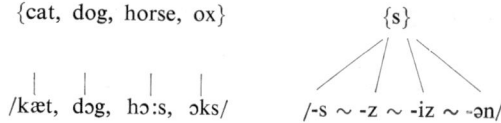

A somewhat different problem arises with plurals like *men*. If we wish the obvious distributional parallelism between *cat* : *cats* and *man* : *men* to be reflected in the morphemic analysis, then we must recognize that *men* contains two morphemes, i.e. that it comprises {*man*} plus {*s*} just as *cats* comprises {*cat*} plus {*s*}. The difficulty here (as well as with *geese, mice*, and the like) lies in dividing up the phonological representation /men/ to correspond to the two morphemes {*man*} and {*s*}. Various solutions have been proposed to cover this and similar cases. For example, the representation of the plural morpheme in *men* may be stated not in terms of the addition of a particular item, but as a process of vowel change. Diagrammatically, *man* (sg.) may be analysed as:

| {*man*} | and *men* (pl.) as: | {*man*} | + | {*s*} |
|---|---|---|---|---|
| \| | | \| | | \| |
| /mæn/ | | /mæn/ | | /æ > e/ |

—to be read as: the representation of the plural morpheme {s} is the change of the stem vowel from /æ/ to /e/. Similarly with /guːs, giːs/, /maus, mais/, and so on. Various other solutions are possible.

Sometimes, however, it is hardly possible to find individual representation for every morpheme. Take, for example, the English genitive plural form, *dogs*, (as in *he docks his dogs' tails*). Many analysts wish to regard *dogs'* as containing three morphemes: a stem morpheme, {dog}, a plural morpheme, which we symbolize as {s}, and a genitive case morpheme, which we may symbolize as {'s}. Compare *ox-en-'s*, where the three morphemes have separate representation:

{ox}    {s}    {'s}
 |       |      |
/ɔks/   /ən/   /z/.

In the genitive plural form *dogs'*, the plural and genitive morphemes are both represented by the single phoneme /z/, so it is not possible to find them separate representation:

{dog}    {s}    {'s}
  |        \    /
/dɔg/       /z/

Such morphs have been variously described as *fused*, *portmanteau*, or *cumulative*. They represent an extreme case of overlapping in the representation of two morphemes.

Occasionally one meets with a morpheme which appears to have zero (Haas 1957) as one of its allomorphs, i.e. it has an allomorph which has no phonological representation at all. The English plural *sheep* is a case in point. If, for the reasons discussed above, it is felt grammatically useful to recognize *sheep* (pl.) as composed of two morphemes (because of such parallelisms as *the cat is : the sheep is; the cats are : the sheep are*), then zero may be set up as the representation of the plural morpheme:

{sheep}    {s}
   |        |
 /ʃiːp/    /.../

Alternatively, of course, /ʃiːp/ may be regarded as a fused form:

{sheep}    {s}
     \    /
     /ʃiːp/

An extreme case of allomorphic variation arises with *suppletive allomorphs*. Because of the distributional parallelism exhibited by such forms as:

*sweet : sweeter*

*kind : kinder*

*good : better*

it is convenient to recognize /bet-/ as an allomorph of {good}, occurring before the comparative morpheme, viz.:

{good}    {er}
  |        |
/bet-/    /-ə/

It should be observed that the aim of these seemingly somewhat artificial morphophonological devices, such as fused, zero, and suppletive morphs, is to obtain a simpler grammatical statement of greater generality. This is achieved at the inevitable expense, of course, of complicating the morphophonology.

*Morphology: Root, Affix and Stem*

When we investigate the composition of words containing two (or more) morphemes, we often find that one of these can be replaced by a large number of different morphemes, whereas the other can be replaced by comparatively few forms. That morpheme which occupies the position where the greatest potentiality of substitution generally exists we refer to as the ROOT of the word. For example, in the English word *cat-s*, the first morpheme can be replaced by almost any one of hundreds of singular nouns; the second morpheme, however, can be replaced by comparatively few forms. The root of the word *cats* is therefore *cat*. Roots may be either *free* (capable of functioning as a separate word) or *bound* (incapable of functioning as a separate word). The words *de-press* and *ex-change* contain the free roots *press* and *change;* the words *de-scend* and *ex-pel* contain the bound roots *-scend* and *-pel*.

*AFFIXES* are bound forms, with a comparatively limited potentiality of replacement, which are added to roots to form different words. Affixes may be classified in two ways: by position and by function. Classified by position in relation to the root, affixes are termed *prefixes* (when they precede the root), *infixes* (when they interrupt the root), and *suffixes* (when they follow the root). English *un-dis-con-cert-ed* contains three prefixes, a root, and a suffix: *phon-eme-ic-ize* contains a root and three suffixes. Infixes can hardly be illustrated from English: the following examples are from Malagasy and show the passive infix *-in-*:

*babo* 'capture' : *b-in-abo* 'captured'

*hary* 'creation' : *h-in-ary* 'created'.

In languages like English, where several prefixes or suffixes may co-occur within a word, it is often possible to subclassify them according to their position relative to one another within the word.

Affixes may be broadly classified by function into two main types: *derivational* and *inflectional*. The combination of root plus derivational affix(es) can be replaced by a simple (monomorphemic) root form that has the same syntactic potential (eg. *em-power* and *de-press* by the simple forms *allow, press;* the nouns *paint-er* and *art-ist* by the monomorphemic noun *man*); *em-* and *de-* are derivational prefixes: *-er* and *-ist* are derivational suffixes. Similarly, *em-ploy-ment* (derivational prefix, root, derivational suffix) may be replaced in a phrase such as *he changed his employment* by a monomorphemic free form (e.g. *job*). Derivational processes introduce no new syntactic restrictions that are not already carried by other root forms: monomorphemic forms can normally be found that can have the same syntactic function as a pluri-morphemic form composed of root plus derivational affix(es). Inflectional affixes, by contrast, introduce syntactic restrictions, especially those of concord and government. English plural suffixes are inflectional: in the sentence *their son goes fishing*, if we add a plural suffix to the noun there must be a compensating alteration in the verb form: *their sons go fishing*. The word *writer* is formed from a root *(write)* plus a derivational (agentive) suffix *(-er)*. Nevertheless it has the same broad possibilities of inflection and distribution as any other English noun (e.g. *poet*): it takes plural inflection, functions as the subject and object of verbs etc. Simple form *(poet)* and derived form *(writer)* are functionally similar:

   *a poet*   : *poets*   : *the great poets are forgotten*

   *a writer*   : *writers*   : *the great writers are forgotten*

Words containing inflectional affixes, however, cannot regularly be replaced by a simple form, e.g. in

   *the great poets are forgotten*

   *the great writers are forgotten*

the inflected noun forms cannot be replaced by a simple free form such as *man*, *poet*, or *king*.

A word stripped of its inflectional affixes is described as a *STEM*. Stems may be either bound or free. The Latin singular noun forms *dominus, domine, dominum, domini, dominō, dominō* (considering only this declension) contain the bound stem *domin-*. The English words *poet, poetess, conceive* are all free stems; *poets, poetesses, conceives* are not stems, because they contain inflectional affixes. A word stripped of both inflectional and derivational affixes is a root: *-ceive* is a bound root, *poet* is a free root (as well as being both a stem and a word). Roots are either simple (monomorphemic, e.g. *bird*) or compound (consisting of two or more morphemes, e.g. *blackbird*, assuming the analyst treats this form as a single word).

Derivational affixes may either maintain or change the word-class of an underlying free root (or stem). For example, *-ling* in *princeling* derives a noun from an underlying noun form *(prince)* and is therefore (in this particular example) *class-maintaining*. On the other hand, *-ize* (in *scandalize*) derives a verb from an underlying noun and is *class-changing*. Derivational affixes may produce stems that always belong to the same class, e.g. *-ling* always produces nouns and *-ize* always produces verbs; or they may produce stems that belong to different classes, e.g. *-eer* produces a noun in *racketeer*, a verb in *electioneer*, and both a noun and a verb in *profiteer*. The same derivational affix may be added to underlying forms which belong to different classes, e.g. *-ling* is added to an underlying noun in *princeling*, to an underlying adjective in *weakling*, to an underlying verb in *fledgeling*; *-ize* is added to an underlying noun in *scandalize*, to an underlying adjective in *civilize*, and to an underlying form which is both noun and adjective in *circularize*.

*Morphology and Syntax: the Word as a Grammatical Unit*

The traditional division of grammar into morphology and syntax implies that the word-rank has particular importance in the grammatical hierarchy. A special term, MORPHOLOGY, is used to describe patterns within words, whereas patterns formed by the distribution of words, phrases and clauses are all subsumed under the heading of SYNTAX. The *validity* of the morphology: syntax division depends therefore on the ability to establish the word as a viable grammatical unit. Granted that this can be done in a given language, the *usefulness* of the division depends on establishing the primacy of the word as a grammatical unit—demonstrating that the word is central to grammatical statement in a way in which (say) the phrase and clause are not.

The *WORD* has been described as a unit possessing internal stability and positional mobility (Robins), i.e. as having a fixed composition and a relatively free distribution. This is, of course, a characterization rather than a definition. The criterion of internal stability turns mainly on the impossibility of inserting new material within the word, or of rearranging its internal parts. This obviously does not distinguish it from the morpheme, which is an even 'tighter' unit than the word, and has, in any case, no component parts to rearrange. It is true that many phrases can be interrupted by insertion (e.g. *the man* by the insertion of an adjective, *the old man*) whereas words are less interruptible, but insertions are possible within words, e.g. *kings, king-dom-s; kindness, kind-li-ness, kind-hearted-ness; southwards, south-east-wards, south-southeast-wards*, etc. It is also true that words do not generally permit rearrangement of their internal parts, e.g. one must have *seven-th*, and not *\*th-seven; kind-li-ness* and not *\*ness-li-kind*, and so on. However, this is to a considerable extent true also of phrases, e.g. we must have *the old man* and not *\*man old the; (it) might have been broken* and not *\*(it) broken been have might*, etc.

Turning to the question of positional mobility, the word undoubtedly has a measure of distributional freedom, e.g. in *the dog chased a cat* the articles are interchangeable and so are the nouns; in *great musicians, famous artists and celebrated actors* the adjectives are, like the nouns, interchangeable. The morphemes, however, cannot be exchanged so freely, e.g. one must have *music-ian-s, art-ist-s*, and *act-or-s*, and not (say) *\*music-or-s, \*art-ian-s,* or *\*act-ist-s.* Note, though, that phrases can be exchanged (*the cat chased a dog*, or *a dog chased the cat*) and it is doubtful how far positional mobility characterizes the word as distinct from the phrase. No doubt all natural languages contain certain restrictions on the distribution of words, though this may be less marked in languages with a rich system of inflections.

A well-known definition of the word is that it is a *minimum free form* (Bloomfield 1935), i.e. a form which can stand alone as an utterance (eg. *John, no, there, quick*) and which cannot be divided into two or more free forms (as can *John dear, no sir, there now, quick march*). Words, then, are free forms, as distinct from affixes, which are bound forms. This free-form criterion requires a certain amount of imaginative ingenuity in its application: one may be hard put to find situations in which forms traditionally regarded as words (such as *as, our, being, am, the, to*) appear as isolated utterances. Note that by this criterion, many forms traditionally regarded as single words (or 'compound' words) will be sequences of two words (e.g. *commonplace, borderline, blackbird, forearm, greenhouse, overtake, whitewash*), unless stress patterns are taken into account. The traditional treatment of these forms as single words appears to have been based, in part, on the semantic criterion that they possess a different meaning from the sum of their parts, e.g. that *a blackbird* is not the same thing as *a black bird*, or *a greenhouse* the same as *a green house*. Such a direct use of meaning as a divisive criterion would now be rejected, but the traditional analysis can be supported by formal criteria. These forms commute freely with what are unquestionably single words (as *blackbird* with *thrush*, or *greenhouse* with *shed*) so that *blackbird* and *thrush* exhibit the distributional limitations characteristic of single nouns, not those of adjective-plus-noun sequences, e.g. one can have *a white blackbird* but not *a white black bird;* one can have *a very black bird*, but not (now) *a very blackbird*.

Various suprasegmental criteria, notably *stress* and *juncture*, are often pressed into service to help define the word-unit. There is, of course, no reason to expect the word as a phonologically determined unit to be coterminous with the word as a grammatically determined unit, and phonological and grammatical criteria sometimes yield different results. For example, the reduction of stress in the second element of adjective-noun complexes like *blackbird, greenhouse, gentleman* could be used to classify these as single words, in contrast with the two-word sequences *black bird, green house, gentle man*, where the second element retains its stress. This would be in accord with the traditional treatment of *blackbird* etc. as one word, but perhaps at variance with the minimum free form criterion. By the stress criterion, forms such as *bird-cage, rose-bush*, would be one word, but not by the criterion of internal stability (the elements are reversible: *cage-bird, bush-rose*). It is also possible to regard *blackbird* and *gentleman* as downgraded phrases: they show the compositional characteristics of a phrase (adjective plus noun) but the distributional characteristics of a single noun, i.e. they are phrases downgraded to word-rank. If this view is taken, the stress reduction on the second element would be an overt phonological mark of downgrading, and inability to pattern with *very* would be a covert grammatical indication. Another phonological criterion sometimes employed to identify word-like units is the alleged separability of word-units by potential pause. For instance, a native speaker of the language in question may be asked to repeat a short sentence very slowly, pausing whenever he feels it is possible to do so. When the maximum break-up has been obtained, the resulting units are set up as words. The writer has not found this a very useful procedure. Different informants (especially illiterate or semi-literate speakers) make the breaks in different places in the same sentence. This is not to deny that there is, in many languages, a fair degree of correspondence between the word as defined by distributional criteria and the word as defined by phonological criteria. For example, stress may be fixed in a certain position in the grammatical word (e.g. Polish), there may be restrictions on the occurrence of certain phonemes at word-initial or word-final position (e.g. Japanese), word divisions often occur at syllable divisions (any Polynesian language) etc., but it is doubtful if phonological and grammatical criteria ever completely coincide.

It will be apparent that what is intuitively felt as a word is often, in fact, a unit which is defined by the convergence of several criteria, both grammatical and phonological. These criteria are not infrequently in conflict, with the result that given items are marginal in various ways and to different degrees. This means that the word-unit is somewhat blurred, but it does not prevent it from being an extremely useful medium for grammatical statement. In many languages, the compositional stability of words—the tendency of morphemes to cohere and move as blocks—means that the description of the composition of phrases is most easily stated via the medium of the word rather than directly in terms of morphemes. If often happens, too, that word boundaries coincide with immediate constituent boundaries. This coincidence of rank-determined and constituency-determined units, plus the partial convergence of grammatical and phonological features noticed above, give the word a certain centrality in linguistic statement. Because, however, several disparate and sometimes conflicting criteria are used to isolate the word-unit, the linguist who employs it in his grammatical statement is under an obligation (1) to state precisely what criteria he is using to isolate words, and (2) to list the order of priority in which these are applied, e.g. when two criteria are in conflict, to state which is given precedence. The criteria will no doubt be selected and ordered so as to obtain maximum simplicity in the overall account of the language. They should not be selected in order to rationalize the native speaker's intuition about words (which may be based in part on extralinguistic factors), still less to justify the spaces in an institutionalized orthography, which constitutes a different system, analysable in its own right, and only partially paralleling the spoken language.

## IA, IP, WP

*Item and Arrangement* (IA), *Item and Process* (IP), *Word and Paradigm* (WP) (Robins 1959) are labels given to three somewhat different *models* of grammatical description. The first two (IA, IP) are characterized by the assumption that no particular grammatical unit is *primary* for purposes of grammatical statement, though the morpheme is regarded as *basic*, as it is the smallest unit. It follows from this that the distinction between morphology and syntax is (theoretically) in IA and IP of no more importance than the distinction between the composition and distribution of any other unit, say the phrase or the clause. WP differs from the other two, however, in assigning the word a key role in grammar, so that the morphology-syntax division is essentially relevant to this model.

The main difference between IA and IP is essentially that of a static versus a dynamic approach to the statement of grammar. The static approach of IA deals simply with items (units of various ranks) and their arrangement relative to one another in constructions. For instance, at the morphological level, IA is likely to describe the composition of the word *inconceivable* as the *occurrence* in sequence of two prefixes, a root, and a suffix, whereas IP is more likely to describe it as the *addition* of prefixes and suffix to a root, i.e. some logical priority appears to be assigned to an underlying form, which is then regarded as subject to various processes —in this case, addition. A strict adherence to IA methods may sometimes (on the surface, at least) make morphophonological statements appear rather cumbersome. Consider, for instance, three possible IA analyses of the word *men*:

(1)   {man}   {s}
         \\   /
         /men/

i.e. /men/ is a fused morph, it being impracticable or unnecessary to state separate representations for the stem and plural morphemes. (Here no attempt is made to locate the exponency of plurality in the vowel of *men*.)

(2)   {man}   {s}
         |      |
      /mæn ~ men/  /.../

i.e. /mæn/ and /men/ are allomorphs, the latter occurring only before the plural morpheme, here represented by zero. (Here a 'representation' has been found for the plural morpheme by the artificial device of describing this representation as zero. This solution has the unfortunate effect of attributing the change in vowel from *man* to *men* as the result of the occurrence of a (phonetically) non-existent suffix.)

(3)   {man}   {s}
         |      |
      /mæn ~ m—n/  /-e-/

i.e. /mæn/ and /m-n/ are allomorphs, the latter occurring in an interrupted form when in construction with the plural morpheme, which is represented by the infix /-e-/. (This solution locates the representation of plurality correctly in the vowel form, but involves setting up a discontinuous and an infixed morph. Although English strong verbs (e.g. *shine, shone*) are susceptible to similar treatment, discontinuity and infixing are otherwise rare with English morphs.)

A typical IP analysis of the form *men* would be:

(4)   {man}   {s}
         |      |
       /mæn/  /æ > e/

where the 'becomes' sign marks the process of vowel change which is the representation of the addition of the plural morpheme. Note that all four statements make essentially the same *grammatical* analysis—the morphemic structure of *men* is given as {man} and {s} in each case. It is only in the morphophonology, in the relation of the grammatical units (the morphemes) to their phonological representations (the morphs), that the analyses differ.

The third model, WP, is much closer to traditional methods of grammatical statement. It differs from IA and IP, not so much in its insistence on stating linguistic patterns as either arrangements or processes (though process terminology is often employed in morphology and arrangement terminology in syntax), but rather by its preference for the word as the primary, focal unit of grammar. The WP model takes advantage of the fact that in many languages certain regular correspondences exist between the composition of words and their distributional behaviour, i.e. the word is treated as a focal unit precisely because morphological changes in part of a word are often linked to syntactic restrictions affecting the word as a whole. The medium for expressing this linkage is the *PARADIGM*: its purpose is to indicate the relationship between word composition and word distribution. The words in a given paradigm often consist of stem plus inflectional affix(es), though paradigms involving root and derivational affix(es) can also be useful. However, because derivational affixes tend to appear only with some members of a given word-class, whereas inflectional affixes normally affect nearly all the members of a given class, paradigms involving the latter attain greater power and generality.

An elementary type of paradigm is the English noun paradigm:

sg.   cat
pl.   cats

Like all paradigms this contains two components: (1) a statement of the morphological variation involved (here the presence or absence of the sibilant suffix), and (2) a summary of the distributional restrictions peculiar to each word in the paradigm (in this example, *sg.* and *pl.*, where *sg.* indicates the admissibility of such patterns as *this cat, the cat is* etc., and *pl.* indicates the possibility of *these cats, the cats are*, etc.). The example indicates only one category of grammatical variables, a two-term system of number, but it is quite common for paradigms to represent the intersection of several categories. Thus an adjective paradigm may reflect (say) a two-term system of number, a three-term system of gender, a four-term system of case; a verb paradigm may reflect (say) a two-term system of number, a three-term system of person, a four-term system of mood, a five-term system of tense, and so on. Identical syntactic restrictions may be marked by different morphological exponents: in this event several morphological classes may be set up, as Paradigms (or Classes) 1, 2, 3, etc. For example:

|     | (1)  | (2)  | (3) | (4)   |
|-----|------|------|-----|-------|
| sg. | cat  | ox   | man | sheep |
| pl. | cats | oxen | men | sheep |

Because syntax is normally given priority over morphology for classificatory purposes, paradigms are often conflated, so that a maximum formal differentiation exhibited by one morphological class is generalized over other classes with less formal differentiation. Thus in the English paradigms given above, the form *sheep* was listed twice, as both sg. and pl., in order to conform with the number differentiation which is morphologically marked in *cat* : *cats*, etc. Similarly, to take a fragment of two Latin paradigms:

|         | (1)     | (2)    |
|---------|---------|--------|
| gen. sg.| puellae | dominī |
| dat. sg.| puellae | dominō |
| abl. sg.| puellā  | dominō |

*puellae* is listed as both gen. and dat. because this syntactic distinction is morphologically marked in the corresponding forms *dominī, dominō*; similarly, *dominō* is listed as both dat. and abl. because this syntactic distinction is morphologically marked in the corresponding forms *puellae, puellā*. Conflated paradigms like these may be described as morphologically defective. Paradigms may also be syntactically defective, as, for example English *news*, which lacks plural distribution, or *police* which lacks singular distribution:

|     |       |        |
|-----|-------|--------|
| sg. | news  | —      |
| pl. | —     | police |

Because WP makes the word the key unit of grammar, it by-passes many of the more complicated morphophonemic statements inherent in those models which make the morpheme the immediate vehicle for the statement of distributional relations. Both the IA and IP models require that the parallelism in the syntactic behaviour of *cat* : *cats* and *man* : *men* should be reflected by a similar parallelism in the morphemic analysis, i.e. that *men* like *cats* should be treated as containing two morphemes. The precise location of the exponent of plurality in the form *men* is less relevant in WP: the exponency of sg. and pl. in the forms *man* : *men* is held to lie in the contrast between the whole word *man* and the whole word *men* in the paradigm sg. *man*, pl. *men*. It follows that the complicated apparatus of overlapping, fused, and interrupted morphs often required by IA is unnecessary in WP. Similarly, in WP there is no need to invent a zero morph in the plural *sheep* merely to maintain the parallelism in the composition of *cat* : *cats* and *sheep* : *sheep*—their distributional similarity is brought out by the paradigms:

|     |      |       |
|-----|------|-------|
| sg. | cat  | sheep |
| pl. | cats | sheep |

The irregularity in the plural form *sheep*, regarded in IA or IP as being marked by the presence or addition of a zero morph, is regarded in WP as being marked by a morphologically defective paradigm. Similarly, noun plurality, which in (say) IA is regarded as being represented by a series of allomorphs, /s/ ~ /z/ ~ /iz/ ~ /en/ ~ /../ etc., is held in WP to be carried by the contrast between five different paradigms.

*Constituent, Constitute, Construction*

If we were asked to divide the word *inconceivable* (which contains four morphemes: *in-con-ceiv-able*) into two parts in a 'natural' way, i.e. in a way which does not seem to violate the usual processes of English word-formation, we should no doubt cut it as follows: *in | conceivable*. This probably seems the natural place in which to make the division because there are a large number of forms which can be substituted for *conceivable*, e.g.

in-conceivable
-valid
-secure
-decent
-exact
-human
-firm, etc.

It also seems right because such a division is in keeping with an obvious feature of English morphology—that many adjectives can be negatived by the addition of the derivational prefix *in-*. On the other hand, a division such as *inconceiv | able* seems unnatural, because there is no form *\*inconceive* from which an adjective can be formed by the addition of *-able*. Continuing the process of bi-section, we might divide *conceivable* into *conceiv | able* on the analogy of *break-able, lov-able, find-able, count-able*, etc., and perhaps because (consciously or unconsciously) we are aware of such parallels as:

conceivable : able to be conceived
breakable   : able to be broken
countable   : able to be counted, etc.

Finally, we are left with the form *conceiv(e)*, and can only divide it into its two constituent morphemes, *con-*

and -*ceive*, on the analogy of such sets as:

*conceive* : *contain*

*receive* : *retain*

We have now reached the smallest grammatical units, the morphemes, beyond which no further grammatical division is possible. The same process may be viewed in the reverse direction, as a process of synthesis instead of analysis. If we try to reassemble the word *inconceivable*, starting with its constituent morphemes, the two morphemes which seem to be most closely linked—to cohere most tightly—are *con*- and -*ceive* (rather than (say) *in*- and *con*-, or -*ceive* and -*able*). Diagrammatically:

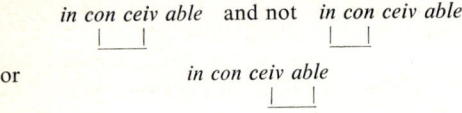

Similarly, we feel that this group *(conceive)* is more tightly linked to -*able* than to *in*-. Diagrammatically:

*in con ceiv able* and not *in con ceiv able*

Finally, we link *in*- and *conceivable*, the only remaining pair:

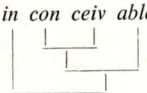

This type of diagram is known as a *tree-diagram*, but the same features of linkage or coherence between pairs of forms can be shown in other ways, e.g. by a *box-diagram*:

| inconceivable | | | |
|---|---|---|---|
| in | conceivable | | |
| in | conceiv | able | |
| in | con | ceiv | able |

or by bracketing: *(in ((con ceiv) able))*. Such diagrams can be viewed as analytic—as successively reducing a longer form—by working upwards through the tree-diagram, downwards through the box-diagram, and inwards through the brackets; and as synthetic—as successively building up the longer form—by working downwards through the tree-diagram, upwards through the box, and outwards from the innermost brackets. They all show *layers of constituency*, i.e. *inconceivable* is first analysed into *in* and *conceivable*, *conceivable* is then analysed into *conceiv* and *able*, and finally *conceiv* into *con* and *ceiv*. The first cut made in a complex form divides it into its IMMEDIATE CONSTITUENTS (Wells 1947) *(ICs)*. Thus the ICs of *inconceivable* are *in* and *conceivable*, the ICs of *conceivable* are *conceiv* and *able*, the ICs of *conceiv* are *con* and *ceiv*. A pair of ICs are said to be PARTNERS in a CONSTITUTE. Thus *in* and *conceivable* are partners in the constitute *inconceivable*, *conceiv* and *able* are partners in the constitute *conceivable*, *ceiv* and *able* are partners in the constitute *conceiv(e)*. The ULTIMATE CONSTITUENTS of any constitute are its constituent morphemes—the 'atomic' units of grammar, incapable of further subdivision. Thus the ultimate constituents of *inconceivable* are the morphemes {*in*, *con*, *ceive*, *able*}.

The example discussed above was concerned with morphological constituency, i.e. with cutting a word into successive layers of constituents. The same techniques are more often applied to the statement of syntactic constituency, i.e. the cutting of higher-ranking constitutes (e.g. phrases, clauses, sentences) into their successive constituents. For example, the sentence *the conductress refused his five-pound note* could be analysed as follows (using the tree-diagram):

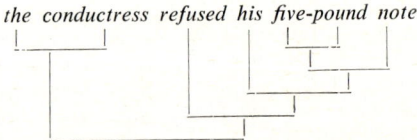

This analysis might be justified by such substitution possibilities as:

*the conductress refused his five-pound note*
*she refused his pound note*
*she refused his money*
*she refused it*
*she refused*

The ICs of this sentence are therefore *the conductress* (replaceable by *she*) and *refused his five-pound note* (replaceable by *refused*), which are the subject and predicate of the sentence. The ICs of the predicate are the verb *(refused)* and the object-phrase *(his five-pound note)*, and so on. The ultimate syntactic constituents shown in this example were the individual words, but the analysis might have been continued right down through the morphology to the individual morphemes. Thus *refused* could be further analysed as

*re fus ed*

and justified by such substitutions as:

*re fus ed*
*dropp ed*
*chang ed*
*mark ed*
*pocket ed*

while *conductress* could be analysed as:

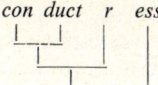

and justified by the substitutions:

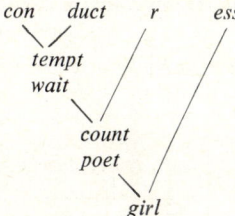

We noticed earlier that the cohesion of the word-unit is demonstrated by the fact that it nearly always forms a constituent in larger constitutes, i.e. in the constituent analysis of a phrase or sentence it is uncommon for *part* of a word to be immediately constituent with any other structure except another part of the same word, and that it is this coincidence of unit and constituency boundaries that helps to make the word such a useful unit in grammatical statement. Nevertheless, word boundaries do not always coincide with constituency divisions. For example, the sentence *old people's bones break easily* analyses as follows:

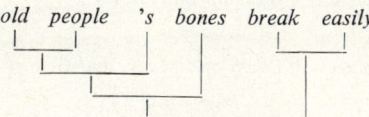

Here the possessive morpheme, {'s}, is immediately constituent not with the preceding word *(people)*, but with the phrase *old people*. Justification of this analysis may be sought both in the replaceability of the phrase *old people* by a single noun (e.g. *John—John's bones break easily*), and in the cohesion of the phrase *old people*, which moves as a block when the possessive construction is converted into a prepositional construction—*the bones of old people*. In languages where there is considerable cross-cutting (non-coincidence) of word and constituency boundaries, the value of the word as a focal unit is correspondingly reduced, and analysis in terms of the WP model less profitable.

When we investigate the constituent structure of longer stretches, we meet with a further complication of IC analysis, the appearance of DISCONTINUOUS CONSTITUENTS. In the sentence *(they) called in the police*, the IC structure is

(they) called in the police

justified by the usual substitution techniques (e.g. *(they) summoned them*). An equally common variant of this sentence is: *(they) called the police in.* Here the constituent *called... in* is interrupted by its partner, *the police.* This may be diagrammed:

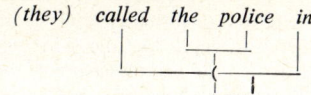

Discontinuous constituents complicate diagramming, but their recognition is essential in the analysis of many constructions.

It has been held as a general principle of IC analysis that—unless there is good reason to the contrary—ICs should be *BINARY*, i.e. that each successive IC cut should divide the constitute into two, and only two, constituents. Thus, for example, *called the police in* must be analysed into two constituents, *called ... in* and *the police*, and not (say) into three: *called | the police | in.* Similarly in *the conductress refused his fiver*, only two constituents are allowed as immediate, *the conductress | refused his fiver*, and not (say) three: *the conductress | refused | his fiver*. However, a number of cases arise where a binary division appears to be unjustified, or —at the best—highly artificial. For instance, in the command *one, two, three—go!*, an initial cut into *one, two, three | go* might be justified (cf. *ready—go!*), but there seem to be no grounds for preferring a secondary cut into *one | two three*, rather than *one two | three*, or even a discontinuous cut into *one ... three* and *two*. Similarly with a phrase like *(a) nice quiet old dog*, **a** suggested analysis is

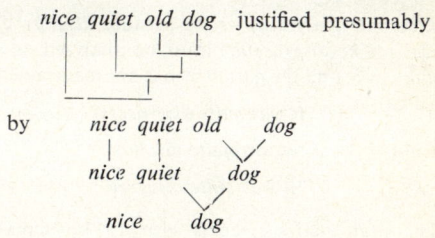

but it is hard to see why this should be preferred to (say)

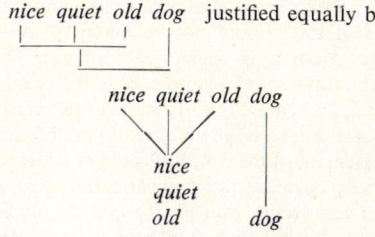

It is, of course, a condition of IC analysis that a given constituent cannot simultaneously be a partner in two different constitutes, so that it would be inadmissible in the IC approach to regard *nice, quiet,* and *old* as separately linked to the noun *dog*:

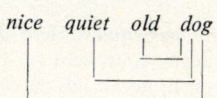

To admit such an interpretation would be to contravene a basic tenet of constituency analysis: that constituents are layered in depth like the skins on an onion.

It will be clear that the main measure of the degree of coherence between two elements is the extent to which they can be replaced by single elements, and the freedom with which they can be transferred *en bloc* to other positions in the sentence. It must be stressed, however, that mere substitutability is an inadequate criterion: grammatical comparability must be maintained in making the substitution. The substituted element must have the same broad grammatical function as the two elements it replaces, so that the resulting shorter sequence is distributionally comparable to the original longer one. For example, merely substituting a simpler form, and disregarding the necessary condition of grammatical comparability, it would be possible to justify both: (1) an analysis of *disgraceful* into *disgrace | ful* on the analogy of *hope | ful*, *help | ful*, etc., and (2) an analysis into *dis | graceful* on the analogy of *dis | allow*, *dis | agree*, etc. The first analysis is correct because *hopeful* and *helpful* must (like *disgraceful*) be analysed as *noun* (or *verb*)+ *—ful* = adj., so that the grammatical parallelism is maintained; cf.:

> it was quite disgraceful
>
> it was quite hopeful
>
> it was quite helpful

The second analysis is wrong because *disallow* and *disagree* (unlike *disgraceful*) must be analysed as *dis—* + *verb* = *verb*, and the parallelism is not maintained:

> it was quite disgraceful

but not   *it was quite disallow

or   *it was quite disagree

The first analysis seems also to be semantically 'right', i.e. *disgraceful* means something like 'full of disgrace', just as *hopeful* means 'full of hope' etc. IC groupings normally do conform to meaningful relationships, but this should not be taken to mean that constituency analysis is semantically based. The substitution techniques of IC analysis, plus the requirement that grammatical comparability be maintained, involve the consideration of a large number of possible substitutions. A statement of the conditions under which shorter sequences can be successively expanded into longer sequences (or vice versa), which is the aim of constituency analysis, necessarily reflects much of the general structure of the language.

Constitutes may be classified according to the relationship between their constituents. Such relations are basically of three types, giving rise to three main types of constitute.

*(1) Subordinative constitutes.* Here one of the constituents is syntactically equivalent (or broadly equivalent) to the whole constitute, i.e. it is the constituent which could be cited in justification of the constituency grouping. A constituent is therefore 'syntactically equivalent' when it can regularly be substituted for the constitute without otherwise disturbing the structure of the sentence. Such a constituent is described as the *HEAD* of the constitute; the other constituent is the *ATTRIBUTE*. In the following examples of subordinative constitutes, the arrow points from the attribute towards the head:

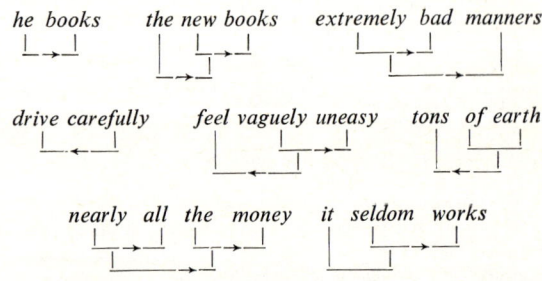

*(2) Coordinative constitutes.* Here two (or more) constituents are equivalent to the constitute: they are indicated here with an equals-sign. Where there is a coordinator (e.g. *and*), the equals-sign is placed under this; where there is no coordinator (as in *paratactic* constitutes), the equals-sign is placed between the two constituents:

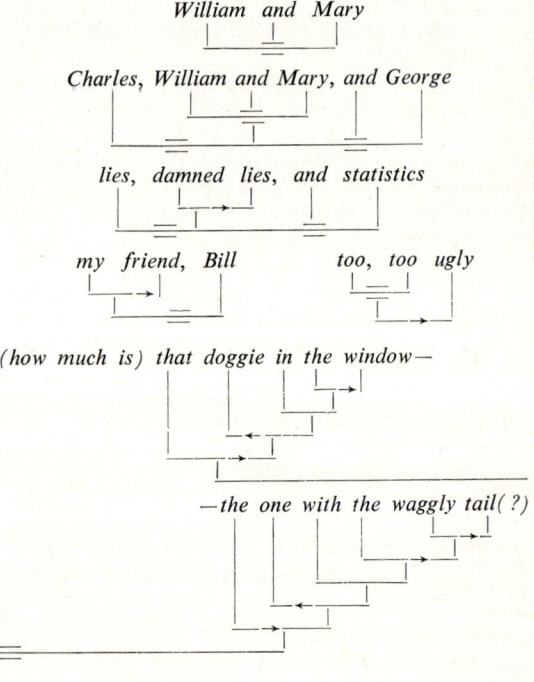

Both subordinative and coordinative constitutes share the feature that one or more of their constituents is syntactically equivalent to the constitute. For this reason both are often subsumed under the general title of *ENDOCENTRIC constitutes*. These are distinguished from *(3) EXOCENTRIC constitutes*, where no constituent is equivalent to the constitute. These are diagrammed here with a cross between the constituents:

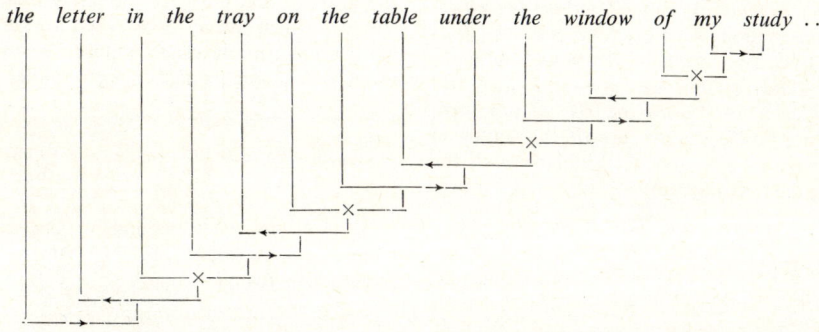

The techniques of constituency analysis bring out the underlying similarity between structures of different lengths. Thus *the angry conductress | refused his five-pound note* and *she | refused* are shown to be fundamentally similar (subject-predicate). Similarly with *in|conceivable* and *in|firm*, both of which contain the derivational prefix *in-* and a free adjective stem or root. By the same substitution procedures as are used in IC analysis it is possible to establish significant groupings of forms into classes and constructions. Forms which can be substituted for each other, i.e. those which can occupy the same box in an IC box-diagram, represent a *class* more precisely, an IC *substitution class*. For example:

| | | | | | | | | |
|---|---|---|---|---|---|---|---|---|
| | the young fool smashed the shop window<br>a big truck removed the ten-ton load<br>the angry conductress refused the five-pound note | | | | | | | |
| | the young fool<br>a big truck<br>the angry conductress | | | smashed the shop window<br>removed the ten-ton load<br>refused the five-pound note | | | | |
| the<br>a<br>the | young fool<br>big truck<br>angry conductress | | | smashed<br>removed<br>refused | | the shop window<br>the ten-ton load<br>the five-pound note | | |
| the<br>a<br>the | young<br>big<br>angry | fool<br>truck<br>conductress | | smashed<br>removed<br>refused | | the<br>the<br>the | shop window<br>ten-ton load<br>five-pound note | |
| the | young | fool | | smashed | | the | shop | window |
| a | big | truck | | removed | | the | ten-ton | load |
| the | angr | y | conductr | ess | refused | the | five-pound | note |
| the | young | fool | | smash | ed | the | shop | window |
| a | big | truck | | remov | ed | the | ten | ton | load |
| the | angr | y | conduct | r | ess | refus | ed | the | five | pound | note |
| the | young | fool | | smash | ed | the | shop | window |
| a | big | truck | | re | mov | ed | the | ten | ton | load |
| the | angr | y | con | duct | r | ess | re | fus | ed | the | five | pound | note |

Here *the young fool, a big truck* and *the angry conductress* belong to the same substitution class, as they occupy the same box; so do *smashed, removed, refused;* or *the* and *a;* or *shop, ten-ton, five-pound,* to select examples at random. Two classes (or members of classes) which are grouped together into one box at the level immediately above (i.e. the constituents in a constitute) are said to form a CONSTRUCTION, or to stand in construction. So that *the angry conductress* and *refused the five-pound note* form a construction; so do *refused* and *the five-pound note; the* and *five-pound note; five pound* and *note; five* and *pound; conductr-* and *-ess; con-* and *-duct,* and so on. On the other hand, *refused* and *the* do not form a construction, nor do *the* and *five,* nor (in this sentence) do *pound* and *note,* nor *fus-* and *-ed.* Similarly with the following (using the tree-diagram):

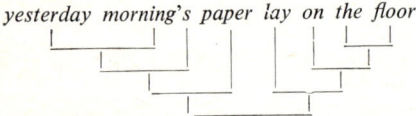

*yesterday morning's paper lay on the floor*

Here the whole sentence is a construction; so are *yesterday morning's paper, yesterday morning's, yesterday morning, lay on the floor, on the floor,* and *the floor.* On the other hand, for example, *'s paper* is not a construction, nor is *paper lay,* or *on the:* nor is *morning's,* even though it is a word.

We have already said that IC substitution classes form a constitute and it might therefore be assumed that the terms constitute and construction were synonymous. This is not quite the case. The term constitute belongs essentially to immediate constituent analysis, with its implication that constituents are usually grouped into binary constitutes. Binary grouping implies that constitutes are layered in depth, i.e. if the grouping of forms X.Y.Z. is to proceed on a binary basis, then we must first group X and Y, and then group XY with Z; or else first group Y and Z and then YZ with X, and so on:

```
          X Y Z (or)  X Y Z
layer 1: |_|           |_|
layer 2:   |___|     |___|
```

Although analysis into binary constitutes is often feasible, it is questionable whether it is always profitable to proceed on these lines. We have already discussed difficulties which arise when an attempt is made to impose a a strictly binary analysis on such sequences as *one, two, three—go!* and *nice quiet old dog,* and have partially abandoned this principle in the diagrams illustrating coordinative constitutes. An alternative approach is to dispense with the theory that grammatical structures are, in principle, bipartite, and therefore layered, and to consider them instead as potentially multipartite, and arranged more like beads on a string, i.e. as

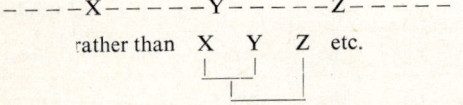

rather than X Y Z etc.

e.g. nice — — — quiet — — — old — — — dog

rather than (say) *nice quiet old dog*

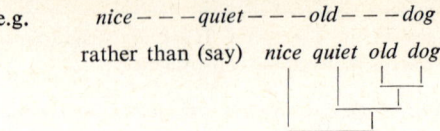

Each grammatical sequence may be considered as a single row of vacant pigeon-holes (or 'slots') into which the grammatical units (in the last example, words) are sorted in their correct order, each pigeon-hole containing a substitution class. Suitable labels may then be given to the contents of each pigeon-hole:

| DETER-MINER | NUMERAL | ADJEC-TIVE | NOUN ATTRIBUTE | NOUN HEAD |
|---|---|---|---|---|
| the | five | young | Chelsea | forwards |
| these | hundred | old | tin | cans |
| my | two | new | cotton | socks |

The labels are not intended as a guide to further sorting, but simply as a convenient means of referring to a class of forms which appear in a given pigeon-hole. The analysis of structures along these lines in known as TAGMEMIC (SLOT-FILLER) ANALYSIS. (Elson and Pickett 1962). A *tagmeme* is a *grammatical function* (or *slot*) together with the class of forms which can occupy it. In tagmemic terminology, the member of a class which appears in a given utterance is said to 'manifest' the tagmeme, e.g. in *the five young Chelsea forwards,* the form *the* manifests the determiner tagmeme, *five* manifests the numeral tagmeme, etc. It should be observed that the term 'slot' does not refer entirely to linear position, but has reference primarily to the grammatical function of the class. Thus tagmemes may be discontinuous (e.g. the predicate tagmeme in *shall (I) come?*), or may have portmanteau realization (e.g. the suffix *-s'* in *dogs'* manifests both the number and case tagmemes, which are separately realized in *ox-en-'s*). Also two different tagmemes may be manifested by identical or partially overlapping substitution classes, e.g. the noun attribute and noun head tagmemes are both manifested by noun stems *(Chelsea forwards, tin cans, cotton socks).* Note, however, that even here the difference is not simply one of order: nouns in the attribute slot are not normally inflected for number, whereas nouns in the head slot inflect freely for number: head nouns are linked to the main verb of the predicate by number concord, attribute nouns are not so linked *(the Chelsea forward is, the Chelsea forwards are).* An important distinction is between *optional* and *obligatory* *tagmemes,* e.g. in the illustration of part of the English noun phrase illustrated above, the head noun is usually obligatory and the various attributes are optional. This may be symbolized by placing a plus-sign before the obligatory tagmeme and both a plus and a minus before the optional one, e.g. ± *determiner* ± *numeral* ± *adjective* ± *noun attribute* + *noun head.* Various other symbolizations have been devised for showing more complicated relations of co-occurrence between tagmemes.

The term 'constitute' usually implies the essentially binary approach of the IC model, whereas 'construction' is commonly used more widely (as, for example, in the tagmemic model). IC analysis regards sequences of forms as successively *layered;* tagmemics recognizes a certain amount of *layering*, but considers that many sequences are best regarded as simply strung out in a line. It is useful therefore to distinguish between *immediate constituents*, which form a usually bipartite constitute (the IC approach), and *string constituents*, which form an often multipartite construction (the tagmemic approach).

### Structure, System, Class

The basic technique underlying the setting up of classes is that of substitution within a frame. For example, anyone investigating the composition of English words might encounter the following: *inconceivable, inconsolable, inconsumable, incontestable*, each of which contains four morphemes. The data could be set out as follows:

| (1) | (2) | (3) | (4) |
|---|---|---|---|
| in- | con- | -ceiv | -able |
|  |  | -sol |  |
|  |  | -sum |  |
|  |  | -test |  |

The forms (morphemes) in positions 1, 2, and 4 are constant; those in position 3 are variable. Positions 1, 2, and 4 provide a frame; position 3 contains a substitution class. The members of a substitution class are said to *COMMUTE* with one another and to form a *SYSTEM*. They stand in *paradigmatic* relationship one with the other. Note that the relationship between the members of a substitution class is a latent one: in a given frame, only one member of a substitution class may be present in an utterance containing that frame—the members of a substitution class are mutually exclusive. The example above was concerned with a substitution class of (root) morphemes within the word. Similar procedures isolate higher-ranking classes of units: thus the diagram on p. 197 identifies *smash, remov-* and *refus-* as a class of (verb) stems; *the* and *a* as a class of (determiner) words; *the young fool, a big truck, the angry conductress*, as a class of (noun) phrases, etc. (These examples are, of course, intended merely as an illustration of the technique of substitution within a frame: consideration of additional data would alter the number of classes and their membership.)

In the example with *inconceivable* etc., all the members of the frame were held constant except for the substitution class being examined. This is the most precise way in which such a class can be identified. Such a precise application of the substitution principle is impracticable for purposes of grammatical statement: the level of generality obtained is so low that any extension of the frame, or alteration in its membership, frequently results in an alteration of the membership of the substitution class. It is not therefore required that every individual lexical item in a frame should be held constant, or that every member of the substitution class should pattern with every member of the framing classes: limited combination between members of different classes would be accepted, at least in the first stage of analysis. Thus in the sequence classes:

| QUANTIFIER | DETERMINER | NUMERAL |
|---|---|---|
| all | the | eleven |
| both | my | two |
| half | those | twenty |
| ADJECTIVE | [NOUN | NOUN |
| young | Chelsea | players |
| new | cotton | socks |
| old | London | churches |

the fact that the sequences *both these twenty churches* and *all young cotton socks* may be regarded as badly-formed does not destroy the general validity of the classification. It merely limits its usefulness and serves to remind us that a complete account of a language will need to state somewhere (either in the grammar or in a dictionary) the combinational restrictions that operate between individual members of different classes.

Forms which can co-occur in a construction are said to combine with one another and to form a *STRUCTURE*. They stand in *syntagmatic* relationship one with the other. Note that the relationship between the forms in a structure may be a patent one, i.e. a given text may contain both (or all) the forms that are syntagmatically related—contrast the latent relationship which holds between the terms in a system. Classes which co-occur are said to *COLLIGATE:* the co-occurrence of the determiner, article, numeral, adjective and noun classes illustrated above represents a *colligation*. Similarly, the co-occurrence of the (very broad) morphological classes of prefix, root, and suffix in

| con- | form | -s |
|---|---|---|
| per- | -ceiv | -ed |
| de- | -tain | -ing |

illustrates a colligation. In the sentences:

*this player tackles well*
*these players tackle well*

besides the colligation of the classes of determiner, noun, verb, and adverb, we notice also the co-occurrence patterns:

this .... player ...... tackles
these .... players ..... tackle

and recognize the colligation of the subclasses of singular determiner, noun and verb, contrasting with the colligation of plural determiner, noun and verb.

Clearly, systems and structures are complementary. The existence of a system implies a structure—a structure by which the system is defined and within which it operates. In the same way, the existence of a structure presupposes the existence of systems. A stretch of speech can only be segmented into units by the possibility of substitution at given places in the utterance. Structure therefore implies systems—systems which it contains and by which it is segmented.

A substitution class is, then, a set of forms which commute within a given frame. It often happens, however, that the same set of forms can appear in a number of different frames. English noun stems, for example, appear in both the attributive and head positions in nominal phrases *(a big stone wall, a big stone)*, and adjectives appear both attributively in nominal phrases and predicatively after some verbs *(an empty house, the house looked empty)*. It is possible therefore to obtain greater generality in classification by assigning to one class forms which share a number of different syntactic positions. A class, in this enlarged sense, may be defined as a set of forms which exhibit the same (or broadly similar) distribution, i.e. which have the same colligational potential. The concept of class is probably most familiar in the term *word-classes* or (traditionally) 'parts of speech'. For instance, it is possible to recognize in English a large class of words (usually labelled *adjectives*) which can appear in the following frame:

DETERMINER NUMERAL ——— NOUNS

e.g.  the   five   young Chelsea   forwards

This is a syntactic classification: the class of adjectives is here defined by the distribution of these words within a higher-ranking unit (in this case, the noun phrase). We noticed earlier, when discussing the importance of the word as a grammatical unit, that there may be significant similarities between the composition and distribution of words. For example, many of the class of adjectives, defined distributionally as above, exhibit a similar composition: they may appear in the following paradigm:

| STEM | e.g. *young* |
| STEM-*er* | *young-er* |
| STEM-*est* | *young-est* |

These represent a morphological subclass of a major syntactic class. Many English adjectives satisfy both the syntactic and morphological requirements suggested above, e.g. *young, kind, clever, tall*. It rarely happens, however, that distributional and compositional classes are completely coterminous. For example, the words *incompetent, interesting, beautiful, exceptional*, satisfy the syntactic requirements outlined above *(the five incompetent Chelsea forwards)*, but not the morphological one *(\*incompetenter, \*incompetentest)*. However, the *incompetent*-group shares other syntactic frames with the *young*-group, e.g.

DETERMINER NOUN LINKING-VERB ———

| the | players | were | *young* |
| the | players | were | *incompetent* |

and we recognize regular correspondences between the comparative and superlative forms of the two groups:

| *young* | : | *incompetent* |
| *young-er* | : | *more incompetent* |
| *young-est* | : | *most incompetent* |

Considerations like these lead us to group *incompetent* with *young* as a member of the class of adjectives, and to recognize two subclasses: those which decline using suffixes (like *young*) and those which decline phrasally (with *more* and *most*). (This is an example of the cross-cutting of class and unit boundaries.) Furthermore, forms which satisfy certain broad syntactic requirements, as well as a set of morphological criteria, will not always meet more specific syntactic requirements. For example, while nearly all 'adjectives' will fit into the frame:

*the players are* ———,

only the positive form will fit into the slightly enlarged frame:

*the players are very* ———,

only the comparative form will fit the frame:

*the players are very much* ———,

and only the superlative form will fit the frame:

*the players are the* ——— *of all*.

In languages which possess variable words (e.g. languages with inflectional affixes), syntactic classification is given priority over morphological classification when the two are in conflict, e.g. one does not deny *incompetent* membership of the adjective class because it does not decline using -*er* and -*est*, or *sheep* membership of the class of nouns because it has no plural suffix. To give priority to purely morphological criteria might result in the absurd situation of grouping together words like *love* and *young* because of the morphological parallelism:

| love | young |
| lover | younger |
| lovest | youngest |

In any case, most languages contain at least some monomorphemic invariable words (e.g. English *by, here, since*) and these cannot be classified morphologically —except, of course, by the limiting criterion that they *are* invariable, and this may not be paralleled by any significant distributional similarities. Some linguists nevertheless find it useful to distinguish in their terminology between syntactic classes and morphological (usually inflectional) classes, by adding the suffix -*al* to the name of the syntactic class. Thus if morphological classes of (say) adjectives, verbs, nouns, are set up, the corresponding syntactic classes which are inflectionally defective in some way may be labelled adjectivals, verbals, noun-als. For example, *young* (being a member of the paradigm *young, younger, youngest*) might be called an adjective, but *incompetent*, which exhibits adjective distribution but lacks the adjective paradigm, might be labelled an adjectival. This is really only one example of a more general distinction between compositional and distributional classes, which can be drawn at all intermediate ranks in the grammatical hierarchy.

Clearly, the setting up of classes is by no means a simple operation. It is often possible to find a group of (say) words, which share a number of features of composition and distribution, and these then form the core of a given class. Usually, however, there still remain a few words which lack one or more of these features. On the strength of the limited number of features they do have in common with the core group, such words may also be assigned, with varying degrees of syntactic or morphological marginality, to membership of the same major class. Major classes may be divided into subclasses, using these irregularities in composition or distribution. For example, English nouns could be subdivided according to their various methods of forming plurals (sibilant suffixation—*cats, dogs, horses;* nasal suffixation—*oxen;* vowel change—*mice, geese,* and so on). Nouns in which the plural is not morphologically marked could be divided syntactically according to whether they pattern with singular verbs (e.g. *phonetics*), plural verbs (e.g. *police*), or both (e.g. *sheep*). Subclassification is also possible by refining the distributional criteria. For example, the frame suggested for English adjectives:

DETERMINER NUMERAL ——— NOUNS, is a very wide one, and adjectives appearing between numerals and nouns could be subclassified according to their position relative to one another. For example, a comparison of phrases like:

| (1) | (2) | (3) | (4) | (5) | |
|---|---|---|---|---|---|
| nice | big | | | | (kiss) |
| | big | new | | | (house) |
| | | new | red | | (car) |
| | | | red | English | (faces) |

suggests the techniques by which such a positional subclassification might proceed. (Here, too, there will be irregularities to be stated: some adjectives may be less rigidly fixed than others, there may be order distortion in some stereotyped sequences or under differing conditions of stress, juncture, and so on.)

A further problem of classification arises in cases of *CLASS-CLEAVAGE*. Cleavage arises when particular items are not assigned uniquely to classes by available classificatory criteria (or groups of criteria). When an item is assigned only to one class no problems arise. For instance, the English word *snail* satisfies a given set of syntactic criteria and we label it a noun. The word *deny* satisfies a quite different set of criteria and we label it a verb. A word such as *smile*, however, satisfies both sets and presents us with a problem of class-cleavage. One solution, the traditional one, is to say that *smile* is potentially both a noun and a verb (though, of course, either one or the other in a given frame), i.e. it is a member both of the word-class, noun, and of the word class, verb. This classification would be supported by the argument that since *snail* and *deny* are clearly differentiated, it seems reasonable to make *smile* conform to this distinction. This solution keeps the classificatory criteria quite distinct, at the expense of allowing the same phonological and lexical form to appear in two grammatical classes, i.e. overlapping class membership is allowed. A second solution is to keep the class membership quite distinct, i.e. to permit a given form to be a member of only one class, at the expense of allowing partial overlapping in the defining criteria. Thus if *snail* is a noun and *deny* is a verb, we must assign *smile*, which satisfies both sets of criteria, to a third word-class—we might perhaps agree to call it a 'base'. A third solution is to say that *smile*, *snail*, and *deny* are all members of the same major class. *Smile* is a core member of the class in question, i.e. it satisfies all the criteria, but *snail* and *deny* are defective members (or subclasses) of the same class, i.e. they satisfy some, but not all, of the criteria set up as definitive for the major class. Which solution is preferred is to some extent a statistical matter: if words like *smile* are a small minority compared with words like *snail* and *deny* then the first solution may commend itself; if *vice versa*, then the third solution may be preferred. The second method, with its requirement of unique class membership, sometimes makes for a neater formulation of structural processes. For instance, using the first method to state derivational processes, we can state that the nouns *princeling* and *fledgeling* are derived respectively from noun plus *-ling* and verb plus *-ling*. Faced with the form *hireling*, however, we may be in difficulty (in a taxonomic grammar) in deciding whether it is composed of noun plus *-ling* or of verb plus *-ling*. The second method gives a superficially neater solution, stating that *princeling* is noun plus *-ling*, *fledgeling* is verb plus *-ling*, and *hireling* is 'base' plus *-ling*. On the other hand, when we are presented with the overlapping not just of two sets of criteria, but with different types of overlapping between several sets of criteria (and this is often the case), then this method can become extremely complicated in its formulation and unwieldy in its application.

A distinction is sometimes drawn between *CLOSED* and *OPEN classes*. A closed class is typically a class with a strictly limited membership which cannot be increased by the addition of loan-words or new formations. The 'meaning' of a word belonging to a closed class is usually best expressed in terms of its grammatical function, e.g. by indicating how it colligates with other classes. Examples are the English articles *(a, the)* and conjunctions *(and, but)*. Open classes, by contrast, have a large membership, which is readily increased by the addition of loan-words or new formations. The 'meaning' of a word belonging to an open class can be expressed *translationally* (e.g. by listing synonyms, antonyms, etc.), or *collocationally* (by listing those members of other open classes with which it commonly associates). Examples of open classes are English nouns, verbs, and adjectives. It should be observed that the distinction between closed and open classes rests on a mixture of criteria, both statistical and diachronic. If the purely statistical criterion (i.e. the number of forms in a class) is adopted, either an arbitrary line must be drawn somewhere (e.g. classes with less than twenty members are closed, those with twenty or more are open) or we must treat the distinction as a cline between two poles (i.e. some classes are more open than others). As for the diachronic criterion (e.g. whether or not the class in question admits loanwords) it may seem questionable how far this is relevant for any descriptivist who is concerned to describe a language as if it existed in a finite state at a given time.

*Dependency, Downgrading*

The concepts of dependency and downgrading in grammar involve the notion of hierarchy or rank (see the first section). It is assumed that utterances can be segmented into units which stand in a hierarchical relation to one another, so that each higher-ranking unit is composed of one or more units from the rank immediately below it (words are composed of morphemes, phrases of words, clauses of phrases, etc). Thus the clause *the papers have disappeared* contains two phrases *(the papers* and *have disappeared)*; the first phrase contains two words *(the* and *papers)*; and the second word contains two morphemes *(paper* and *-s)*. It should be observed that the same form can belong to more than one rank-unit. For example, *paper* in *paper tears easily* is a phrase-unit, of the same rank as (say) *the paper* or *the very old paper*, as well as being a word-unit and a morpheme-unit. To take a more extreme case, in an utterance such as *shoot!*, the form *shoot* is (when supplied with the necessary suprasegmentals) a sentence, and therefore, *a fortiori*, also clause, phrase, word and morpheme.

A unit is INDEPENDENT when it is also a member of the next higher rank-unit; otherwise it is DEPENDENT. Thus the word *papers* in *the papers have disappeared* is independent, since it is also a member of the class of phrases (as in *papers have disappeared*); the word *the*, on the other hand, is dependent, since there is no phrase *the*. The distinction between free and bound morphemes discussed earlier (see section on Morphology) is also a matter of dependency: a free morpheme is one which is also a word; if not, it is a bound form. For instance, the *paper* part of the word *papers* is a free morpheme, since there is also a word *paper*, but the *-s* is a bound morpheme since there is no word *-s*. Similarly, the classic definition of the word as a minimum free form turns on the possibility of single-word sentences (or perhaps single-word utterances), i.e. it is claimed that words are the smallest units which can constitute complete sentences (or utterances). We have mentioned earlier (see section on Morphology and Syntax) the inadequacy of such a definition as a means of isolating word-like units. It will be clear that it cannot apply to all words but only to those which are independent (in the sense defined above). If a word can constitute a complete sentence, it must necessarily be able to constitute a complete phrase, but dependent words like *the* or *of* cannot (by definition) constitute complete phrases, so they cannot, *ipso facto*, constitute sentences. (It is true, of course, that it is possible to find 'quotation' or 'echo' contexts in which dependent words appear as utterances—e.g. in answer to the question *did you say 'the' or 'of'?*, but in such circumstances even dependent morphemes can appear, e.g. in answer to the question *did you say 'pre-' or 'pro-' ?*).

Likewise, the distinction between head and attribute in endocentric constructions can be described in terms of dependency, though it also involves considerations of grammatical comparability. For instance, in the adverbial phrase *very cheerfully*, the word *very* is dependent whereas the word *cheerfully* is independent—cf. *he was smiling very cheerfully* with the grammatical *he was smiling cheerfully* and the ungrammatical *\*he was smiling very*. In terms of Immediate Constituent analysis, then, *very cheerfully* is an endocentric constitute in which *very* is the attribute and *cheerfully* is the head. Similarly, in *he was smiling very cheerfully*, if we chose to treat the predicate as a rank-unit composed here of verb-phrase plus adverb-phrase, then, of course, the phrase *very cheerfully* is dependent whereas the phrase *was smiling* is independent. In IC terms, the predicate is another endocentric constitute, in which *was smiling* is the head and *very cheerfully* is the attribute. The importance of grammatical comparability becomes clear if we consider a phrase such as *brick walls*. Here both the word *brick* and the word *walls* are independent (cf. *brick walls can be ugly, brick can be ugly, walls can be ugly*). However, we can show that in this phrase *brick* is attribute and *walls* is head by comparing *brick walls are ugly* with the grammatical *walls are ugly* and the ungrammatical *\*brick are ugly*. Furthermore, we can generalize this analysis of *brick walls* (via *the brick walls*) to include also *the brick wall*, where the above text would not serve to select either *brick* or *wall* as head (cf. *the brick wall is ugly, the brick is ugly, the wall is ugly*).

The hierarchical determination of dependency discussed above is a covert distinction turning on whether or not the item in question can also be a member of a higher unit-rank. This may be reinforced more overtly by some kind of marker of the dependency. This indication may be morphological (e.g. a non-finite, as opposed to a finite verb form), lexical (e.g. the presence of a subordinating conjunction), syntactic (e.g. a change in the sequence of words or phrases as compared with the sequence in independent units), or suprasegmental (i.e. different stress, pitch and juncture patterns from those of the independent units).

Examples of morphological marking are the non-finite verb forms in the dependent clauses in: *the conductress having refused his fiver, (he left the bus); his fiver being refused, ....., grumbling at the conductress, .....*

Examples of lexical marking are the subordinators *if, when, which*, in:

> (I shall leave) if he comes
> (tell me) when it finishes
> (the books) which you ordered (have arrived)

What may be called syntactic marking of dependency occurs in such sentences as:

> (I enjoyed the talk) you gave
> (the book) you ordered (has arrived)

In these examples the dependent structures *(you gave, you ordered)* are not morphologically marked (the verbs are finite) or lexically marked (there are no subordinators though such constructions are traditionally treated as containing a zero form of *which* or *that*). Such sentences could be regarded as an amalgamation of two independent structures, e.g. *I enjoyed the talk you gave* could be regarded as being formed from two Subject—Verb—Object structures that share the same object phrase:

> *I enjoyed* )
> ) *the talk*
> *you gave* )

Similarly, with *the book you ordered has arrived*, where the shared phrase is subject of one structure and object of the other:

> (             *has arrived*
> ( *the book* )
> *you ordered*            )

If this view (essentially a transformational one) is adopted, then there is syntactic marking of dependency by a distortion in the sequence of the units in the subordinated structure, i.e. its object is 'front shifted' *(the talk you gave* instead of *you gave the talk; the book you ordered* instead of *you ordered the book)*.

As an example of the suprasegmental marking of dependency, consider the sentences:

> *the men, I knew, were late*
> *the men I knew were late*

In the first sentence, the juncture and pitch patterns, implied orthographically by the commas, mark *I knew* as the independent clause and *the men were late* as dependent; the sentence thus means roughly the same as *I knew that the men were late*. In the second sentence, the absence of such juncture and pitch patterns marks *the men were late* as the independent clause and *I knew* as dependent (attribute of the subject phrase); it means about the same as *I knew the men that were late*.

Dependency is a particular type of syntagmatic (co-occurrence) relationship. We have mentioned some others in earlier sections, notably relations of *order* (e.g. the sequence of determiner, numeral, adjectives, and nouns in English noun phrases) and relations of constituency. The partners in a constitute are, of course, linked by this very fact, but partnership is essentially a covert relationship depending on the substitution procedures by which the constitute is established. We noticed above that the relationship between the partners in an endocentric constitute (which one is head and which is attribute) may be overtly signalled by a marker. Likewise, in the sentences:

> *visiting professors is a bore*

and

> *visiting professors are a bore*

the verb form indicates that the gerund is head of the subject-phrase in the first sentence and that the noun is head in the second. When no such indication is present, the construction may be ambivalent, e.g. in:

> *visiting professors can be a bore*

the verb form does not specify the relationship between the partners, and the sentence is ambiguous.

In languages with variable word forms, syntactic relations are often marked morphologically by inflection —concord and government are typical examples. In CONCORD, the items which are linked—and this linkage can operate across constituency boundaries—are interdependent, i.e. neither or none of the items can be said to select or determine the form of the other items which are linked with it concordially. In GOVERNMENT, one of the items selects the form of the other(s). For instance, in *this dog bites* as opposed to *these dogs bite* the three items are linked by a 'thread of concord' and must all be either singular or plural. We could, if we wished, abstract this feature and state it as a feature of the whole subject predicate constitution, e.g. sg. (THIS DOG BITE) as opposed to pl. (THIS DOG BITE). We should then have to state somewhere in the grammar where the morphemes which indicate the number concord are attached, and, of course, give the morphophonological rules for their representation. An example of government is supplied by the following Old English prepositional constructions:

> ymb ðā weallas   'around the walls' *(acc.)*
> andlang ðāra wealla 'along the walls' *(gen.)*
> neah ðsēm weallum 'near the walls' *(dat.)*

Here the case form of the noun is selected by the preposition and we can say that (in these examples) *ymb* governs the accusative, *andlang* the genitive, and *nēah* the dative. Besides the exocentric governmental relationship between the preposition and the article-noun phrase, there is also an endocentric concordial relation between the inflected article and the inflected noun. In French article-noun phrases *(le crayon, la plume)* different nouns select either the masculine or the feminine form of the article. In cases like this, where the category is marked by the variable word but determined by the invariable word, it is sometimes said to be 'inherent' in the invariable form—e.g. French nouns are said to possess inherent gender. In the same way, of course, when different prepositions govern different cases, it would be reasonable to say that the prepositions possess inherent case. Sometimes the same item may select two or more different forms, usually with a difference of meaning. Compare Latin *in urbem* 'into the city' and *in urbe* 'within the city', where the preposition governs respectively the accusative and ablative cases; or French *le malade* 'the male patient' and *la malade* 'the female patient', where the noun selects masculine and feminine genders; or Maori *tāna kōrero* 'his story (-the one *he* tells)' and *tōna kōrero* 'his story (-the one about *him*)', where the noun selects the subjective and objective forms of the possessive.

Turning again to the question of rank, we recall that in the first paragraph of this section we discussed the classification of units inclusively in terms of their position on a rank-scale. We have, however, to reckon with the fact that units do not always function at their normal (classificatory) ranks. In a construction like *the papers have disappeared* there is no problem because *the papers*, considered as a member of a class of phrases, is also *functioning* as a phrase, i.e. as an immediate constituent of a clause. However, in a construction like *the book you ordered has arrived*, the clause *you ordered* is functioning as part of a lower-ranking unit, i.e. as part of the phrase *the book you ordered*. The clause *you ordered* is therefore said to be **DOWNGRADED** (or *rank-shifted*) i.e. it has the potential of functioning as a clause, within a sentence, but is here required to function within a phrase. Similarly, in *the books which you ordered have arrived*, the clause *you ordered* is overtly rankshifted by the addition of the downgrader, *which*.

It is characteristic of downgrading that it may be potentially *recursive* in its operation; that is to say, a downgraded construction may contain within itself a downgraded construction, which may contain within itself a downgraded construction, etc. In a sentence like *you know he knows they know I know*, there is successive downgrading of a subject-predicate structure to the status of object:

```
          you know (it)
                 /\
             he knows (it)
                     /\
                 they know (it)
                         /\
                      I know.
```

or, using the tree-diagram, with strict insistence on binarity:

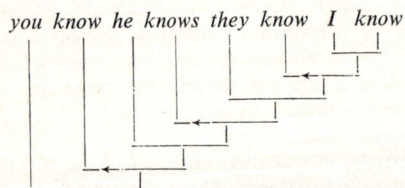

The noun phrase diagrammed on page 197 *(the letter in the tray on the table under the window of my study)* is also recursive and illustrates the use of prepositions to subordinate noun phrases to the status of attributes to the preceding noun. In derivational processes there often occurs what could be regarded as the progressive (but not usually recursive) downgrading of forms that potentially have word-status to the status of stems, e.g. in

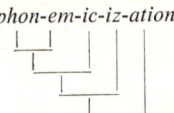

one observes the successive downgrading of the lefthand IC (a potential free form) by the right-hand derivational affix.

## Types of Linguistic Category

The term *category* has been applied in linguistics in a number of different ways, which need to be distinguished. The term is sometimes applied to general theoretical categories which are set up by (or are implicit in) a particular theoretical model of grammar. Concepts such as *unit, class, construction, transform*, are instances of such theoretical categories. The word has also been applied to the various descriptive categories which result from the application of a given model to the analysis of a particular language. *Noun, verb, subject, object*, are instances of descriptive categories which are relevant to the statement of English grammar. Even in this purely descriptive sense, the term *category* is variously used. It is frequently used to include the notion of class, e.g. some linguists speak of the categories of noun and verb, instead of the classes of noun and verb. The term is also applied to various functional relations, such as subject and object.

We observed in our discussion of concord and government that syntactic relations are often marked by morphological changes, especially inflectional affixes. The forms which display such changes are often said to carry (or expone) a category. For instance, in our examples *this dog bites* and *these dogs bite* all the words carry the category of number—a GENERIC CATEGORY. Subdivisions of a generic category are SPECIFIC CATEGORIES. The generic caregory of number in English subsumes two specific categories, usually termed *singular* (carried here by the words *this, dog* and *bites*) and *plural* (carried here by the words *these, dogs* and *bite*). To the overriding syntagmatic (concordial) rule which permits only two of the eight possible combinations of these words, we give a generic category label—*number*. To the two permitted combinations, we give the specific category labels of *singular* and *plural*.

It will be observed that terms like concord and government are universally applicable, i.e. they are general theoretical categories relevant to any language where members of two classes are syntactically interdependent (concord) or where one controls the form of the other (government). Generic and specific categories, however, are valid only for the particular language to which the term is applied and from which it takes it value. The same label (e.g. number) will doubtless be applied to situationally or referentially similar phenomena in different languages (e.g. number is usually referable to the activity of counting, but the grammatical VALUE (*valeur*) of descriptive categories varies as the distributional patterns of the units that carry them vary from language to language. This will be evident in the following brief discussion of some applications of four typical generic category terms: number, gender, case, and person.

The category of NUMBER in English usually involves a compulsory choice between two specific categories, plural and singular, e.g. between *these dogs* and *this dog*. In Rarotongan—a Polynesian language—however, the speaker has a choice between a plural (usually a small plural or 'paucal') and a general term which is indifferent as to number, e.g. *ēia puakaoa* 'these (few) dogs' and *tēia puakaoa* 'this dog, these dogs'. Although we speak of the category of number in both languages, the specific categories have different values. For example, the Rarotongan plural, which is in contrast with a general term, has a different grammatical function from the English plural, which is in contrast with a singular term. Some languages distinguish between three specific categories of number, (e.g. singular, dual, plural); or between four terms, (e.g. some Melanesian languages distinguish in the personal pronouns between singular, dual, paucal (a few), and multiple (many), as in Fijian:

| | |
|---|---|
| *kō* | you (one person) |
| *kodrau* | you (two) |
| *kodou* | you (few) |
| *konī* | you (many) |

Pronominal number in Fijian is rarely, however, a concordial category, e.g. the verb remains constant regardless of whether a singular, dual, paucal, or multiple pronoun is used as subject. Similarly in English, pronominal number is hardly a concordial category in subject—verb constructions:

*I, you, we, they* .............*go*
*he, she, it* .................*goes*

If any general rubric can be found to cover the above pronominal groupings, it is that gender-bearing pronouns (i.e. those that indicate the gender of the subject—*he, she, it*) take the verb form with a sibilant suffix, while non-gender bearing pronouns take a verb-form without this suffix. On the other hand, of course, English pronouns might be divided into two numbers concordially in the reflexive frames:

*I (you, he) kicked my- (your-, him-) self*
*we (you, they) kicked our- (your-, them-) selves*

The term GENDER is commonly applied to a classification of nouns when this is made in terms of changes in the form of words which are syntactically linked to these nouns. Typical examples are the two-term gender system of French (masculine, feminine) and the three term system of German (masculine, feminine, neuter) where the gender of the nouns is indicated by a variation in the form of articles and adjectives, e.g. German:

*der Wein* 'the wine', *süsser Wein* 'sweet wine' *(masc.)*
*die Milch* 'the milk', *frische Milch* 'fresh milk' *(fem.)*
*das Bier* 'the beer', *kaltes Bier* 'cold beer' *(neut.)*

In English it is possible to recognize three genders according to whether the singular noun is resumed by *he, she,* or *it*:

*I rang up about the BOY— HE's on HIS way*
*I rang up about the GIRL— SHE's on HER way*
*I rang up about the CAR— IT's on ITS way*

There is often some partial parallelism between grammatical gender classes and semantic classes, e.g. the limited parallelism between gender and sex in many European languages. So in English, where nouns denoting males are commonly masculine, and nouns denoting females are commonly feminine. In other languages, the gender system may reflect different semantic groupings, e.g. Fijian, where three of the four gender classes partially and imperfectly parallel a semantic grouping of nouns into edible objects, drinkable objects, and parts of the body:

*na kena uvi* 'his yam' (for eating)
*na mena tī* 'his tea' (for drinking)
*na ulu-na* 'his head' (part of the body)

The same gender distinction is also carried by some Fijian prepositions, e.g.

*na ulu kei Pita* 'Peter's yam' (the-yam-of-Peter)
*na tī mei Pita* 'Peter's tea'
*na ulu i Pita* 'Peter's head'

Semantic distinctions of animateness, size, shape, degree of abstraction or familiarity, and others are often incorporated into gender systems, but rarely is there a perfect correlation between semantic components and grammatical categories. Thus we find that *ship* is often feminine in English, *Weib* (female) is neuter in German, *sentinelle* (sentry) is feminine in French, *dio* (oyster) is —more naturally perhaps—drinkable in Fijian.

The term CASE is used when the function of a nominal form in a construction is shown by a variation in its paradigm, e.g. different case forms may be used to mark different syntactic relationships between the nominal form and the verb (as subject, object, etc.) The way in which the relationship between subject and object is signalled in different case systems has been suggested as a possible classification of these (Hockett). The term *nominative type* case system has been proposed for languages like Hindi which do not distinguish inflectionally between subject and object when both are present. The term *accusative type* has been applied to languages like Latin which distinguish inflectionally between subject (nominative case) and object (accusative case, usually). The *ergative type* is represented by languages like Eskimo, which specifically mark the subject (ergative case) when an object is present, thus freeing the nominative

clusion; for example if graphical presentation suggests a circle centred at the origin, he can establish this by displaying a table of values $\sqrt{(x_i^2+y_i^2)}$, which should be identical and equal to $a$ if his hypothesis is correct. Thus a continuous man-machine dialogue is possible.

The effective use of graphical techniques depends on the provision of a library of general-purpose subroutines. Preferably these should be built up as a hierarchy, so that each new subroutine can make use of those that have gone before. This greatly reduces the amount of programming that has to be done. In scientific calculations, subroutines or standard programs which plot and and contour arbitrary functions (Roberts 1965) are particularly useful (Fig. 4).

A typical large time-dependent calculation can lead to $10^7$ numbers, which cannot be digested by the human brain in a reasonable time; if, however, the results are displayed in animated graphical form (Zajac 1966). the eye can readily distinguish significant features of the results in a minute or so. Figure 5 shows some frames from a film which displays the motion of magnetic field lines, and combines the two techniques of animation and contour plotting. (In two dimensions, the magnetic field lines are contours of the orthogonal component of the vector potential.) Although the animated display may indeed contain more information than the brain can accept, the important features can often be made to stand out from the rest, so that the effect of a limited data transfer rate can be minimized. Here again, techniques for the effective presentation of information in other fields such as advertising might profitably be studied.

It is likely that graphical communication will be of particular importance in engineering design, and several experiments along these lines have been carried out (Sutherland 1963). The use of a light pen enables rough diagrams to be drawn on the screen, which can then be tidied up by the computer. It also enables the user to point to particular features of the display, more easily than he could do from the keyboard, and in this way to indicate his interests to the computer.

*See also:* Computer operating systems. Computers, multiaccess to.

*Bibliography*

BARGELLINI P. L. (1965) *Considerations on Man versus Machines for Space Probing, Advances in Computers*, **6,** 195 (Eds. Alt and Rubinoff), New York: Academic Press.

CORBATO F. J. and VYSSOTSKY V. A. (1965) *Introduction and Overview of the Multics System, Proceedings of the Fall Joint Computer Conference, Las Vegas*. This paper contains many references to earlier work on multi-access systems, and other papers presented at the Conference should also be consulted.

GOOD I. J. (1965) *Speculations Concerning the First Ultra-intelligent Machine, Advances in Computers* **6,** 31, (Eds. Alt and Rubinoff), New York: Academic Press.

ROBERTS K. V. (1965) *Scientific Computing and Operational Research*, Culham Laboratory Report CLM-R 45, LONDON: H.M.S.O.

SUTHERLAND I. E. (1963) *Sketchpad, a Man-Machine Graphical Communication System, Proceedings of the Spring Joint Computer Conference, Detroit*. Several other papers presented at this Conference should also be consulted.

ZAJAC E.E. (1966) *Film Animation by Computer, New Scientist*, **29,** 346.

K. V. ROBERTS

# H

**HEARING.** Hearing is the sense with which an animal detects minute molecular vibrations of his environment. Investigating the nature of hearing often requires the use of 'unnatural' sounds. This article, while necessarily omitting many, attempts to identify some hearing phenomena by correlating physical representations of these sounds with the psychological and physiological responses. The figure exhibits replicas of sound pressure-time waveforms of several useful sounds.

Wave 1 is the sinusoid, classically the work-horse laboratory and clinical auditory stimulus. There are many practical and theoretical reasons why: it is the natural wave function of a linear transmission system, which a portion of the ear appears to be. It is also relatively easy to generate over a large part of the relevant acoustic range. Nowadays, replacing the tuning fork, the electronic oscillator is the typical source.

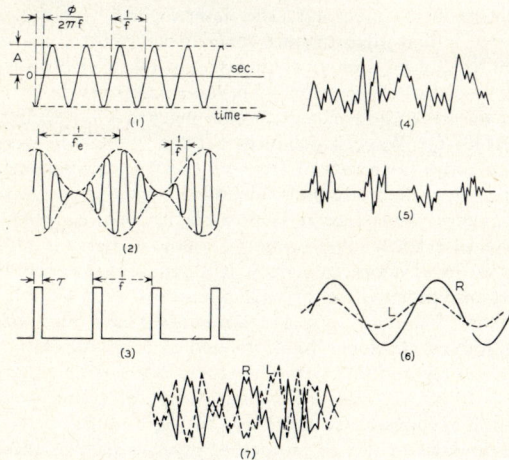

*Waves of sounds discussed in text. Each of the waveforms may be considered to be a replica of the pattern of variation in time of air pressure at an eardrum. Wave 1 is a sinusoid of amplitude A, frequency f, phase φ. The dashed line is the constant envelope. Wave 2 is a sinusoid amplitude modulated by frequency $f_e$, which appears as the envelope. Wave 3 is a pulse train whose pulse duration is τ second and fundamental frequency is f. The waveform as shown is an idealization of possible acoustic waves. Wave 4 is random noise approximated by linear segments. Wave 5 is periodically interrupted random noise. Waves 6, in which Wave L is the left ear stimulus and Wave R is the right ear stimulus, are sinusoids differing in phase and amplitude. Waves 7 are binaural random noise stimuli differing only in polarity.*

A third reason is that the parameters defining the sinusoid find basic correlates in perception. Mathematically, the sinusoid is completely described by the expression $A \sin(2\pi ft+\varphi)$. The parameter $f$ specifies the number of oscillations occurring per second, i.e. the frequency in cycles per second (c/s). The range of audible $f$ is approximately 20–16,000 c/s. Pitch is the main psychological correlate of $f$, but pitch is not necessarily proportional to $f$. Below 1000 c/s it is, so a frequency twice another has a pitch twice as high. Stability of the perception of 2:1 frequency ratios is the basis of the construction of the usual musical scale in octaves.

The amplitude $A$ is the physical correlate of loudness. Except near the lowest and highest audible sinusoids, loudness is approximately proportional to $(A-A_0)^{0.6}$, where $A_0$ is the sound pressure at the threshold of audibility. $A_0$ is near 0.0002 dyne/cm² between 600 and 7000 c/s and higher elsewhere.

The parameter $\varphi$ specifies phase, whose relation to a time reference is made clearer if the sinusoid is written $A \sin 2\pi f(t+\varphi/2\pi f)$. Phase has no relevance when the sinusoid is heard in one ear. It has relatively minor effects in most complex sounds heard monaurally, but it can have major effects in binaural hearing.

The timbre of a sinusoid is generally smooth in character. The physical correlate is the fact that the envelope of a sinusoid is constant. A signal of varying envelope is illustrated by Wave 2, in which a sinusoid of frequency $f$ is modulated in amplitude by another sinusoid of frequency $f_e$. Within certain ranges of $f$ and $f_e$, the timbre of Wave 2 is sharp, but its pitch can be matched by the low pitch of $f_e$ in the form of Wave 1. This finding is of theoretical importance because, although the spectrum of Wave 2 contains energy at three frequencies, $f-f_e$, $f$, and $f+f_e$, it does not at $f_e$. Evidently the pitch of Wave 2 is derived from the envelope, and auditory theory must account for the necessarily non-linear operation of envelope detection.

Wave 3, like Wave 2, is a complex periodic sound. Insofar as the pulse duration $\tau$ is short compared to the pulse period, the spectrum of Wave 3 consists of a series of nearly equal-amplitude harmonics (themselves sinusoids) at frequencies $f$, $2f$, $3f$, etc. Perception of Wave 3 varies widely with $f$. If $f = 1$ c/s, clicks spaced like clock ticks are heard. As $f$ increases, the clicks begin to merge into a buzz, and at about 20 c/s, Wave 3 begins to produce a sensation of pitch along with the buzz. As $f$ increases further, pitch rises and the timbre includes buzzy and tonal components. Above perhaps 400 c/s, the buzzy component vanishes and Wave 3 is as tonal and smooth as Wave 1. Upon close listening, individual low-frequency harmonics may be singled out. The pitch of Wave 3 usually corresponds to $f$ even if energy at $f$ is removed by filtering. Thus again pitch can be associated with a 'missing' spectral component.

Wave 4 is an aperiodic random wave. Its spectrum is therefore continuous rather than discrete. If its spectral bandwidth is narrow, its pitch is that of the centre frequency. If its spectrum is wide, Wave 4 is pitchless. The speech sound $s$ is an example of the Wave 4 type. In the laboratory, Wave 4 is often used to mask other sounds.

Wave 5 is somewhat more specialized. Although it is Wave 4 with gaps introduced periodically, it is not periodic. Perception of Wave 5 depends on the bandwidth, the on-off ratio, and the gap repetition rate. Notably, in yet another demonstration of envelope effects, Wave 5 can produce a pitch perception at repetition rates as high as some 800 per second.

A sound is always perceived to be somewhere. Heard monaurally, a sound is located at the stimulated ear. In free-field binaural hearing, which is our ordinary experience, a sound may be localized at any azimuth. Spatial localization depends on two factors, interaural time and amplitude differences. The Waves 6 illustrate these factors. Measured with respect to, say, the crest, Wave L leads Wave R in time. Wave L is also smaller in amplitude. If, in separate earphones, Wave L is the left-ear stimulus and Wave R is the right-ear stimulus, the location of the perceived sound will be drawn simultaneously to the left by the time difference and to the right by the amplitude difference. Provided the frequency is not too high and the time-amplitude difference too large, it is possible to balance the factors to place the sound image at $0°$ azimuth, as if the time and amplitude differences were zero. Time is not a factor in the localization of sinusoids higher than about 1500 c/s.

The localization of other waves in the figure may be manipulated in binaural hearing. At low repetition rates, the clicks in Wave 3 may be induced to appear at any azimuth. Wide-spectrum Wave 4 presented to both ears without time separation is heard as a ball of noise in the centre of the head. Introducing an interaural time difference moves the low-frequency portion of the noise to the leading side. The effect weakens if the time separation exceeds about 2 milliseconds but may persist to 50 milliseconds. Wave 5 from independent sources in separate earphones will still be localized, proving that localization can be produced by envelope effects.

Wave 7 illustrates other possibilities in binaural hearing. In this case, the stimulus in one ear is the negative of the other. This polarity inversion is equivalent to a phase shift of $\pi$ radians in all frequencies. Through earphones, wide-band Waves 7 are heard from ear to ear within the head. Interaural phase differences produce other phenomena of considerable theoretical interest. In one, termed binaural masking-level difference, the threshold of a sinusoid binaurally in phase and masked by Waves 7 may be 10–15 decibels lower than the threshold of an in-phase sinusoid marked by in-phase noise (Wave 4 in each ear). In a second phenomenon, a narrow band of noise interaurally out of phase heard together with the remaining noise interaurally in phase can induce a weak pitch perception associated with the frequencies of the narrow band. This phenomenon proves that the nervous system can extract a cue to pitch absent in the power spectrum.

A fourth physical parameter with strong psychological effects is duration. The inventory of effects of the waveforms in the figure has assumed that the stimulus duration is reasonably long. All of the waveforms of sufficient amplitude will be heard as a click if they are too short. Laboratory experiments have shown that over a wide range of $f$, Wave 1 gains full loudness in 200 milliseconds and characteristic pitch in three cycles for low $f$ and nine milliseconds for high $f$. Prolonged exposure to a complex sound results in a perceptual instability difficult to quantify.

Pitch, loudness, and timbre are the principal, though not necessarily independent, qualities of sound. It is clear that loudness is nearly independent of the others because pitch and timbre tend to retain their character over a wide range of loudnesses. It may be argued that pitch and timbre are not independent, for every sound possesses timbre but only a class of sounds have pitch.

Auditory theory has considerable information about, but has not yet proven, the physiological bases of most auditory phenomena. It has been established, for example, that pure tones are localized mechanically at characteristic places along the basilar membrane of the cochlea in the inner ear. The natural conclusion to be drawn is that pitch of pure tones is determined, at the first level of physiological analysis, by 'place'. However, the results of experiments with Wave 2 apparently compel the conclusion that pitch and 'place' are not simply related, for Wave 2 produces a pitch associated with pure tones far removed from its spectral components. Since this pitch is closely identified with the envelope frequency, and since it is possible in separate physiological experiments to observe volleys of nerve impulses at the envelope frequency, it is apparent that neural response patterns can provide pitch cues. Furthermore, inasmuch as the responses from the two ears must, for anatomical reasons, be correlated at a neural station beyond the auditory nerve, binaural localization results also force the conclusion that temporal patterns of neural responses are preserved in the auditory nerve. Discoveries in the physiology of hearing such as these indicate that, in general, the features of sound important in the psychology of hearing are extracted at low levels of the nervous system.

*See also:* Cochlear mechanics. Perception of sound.

*Bibliography*

von Békésy G. (1960) in *Experiments in Hearing* (G. Wever Ed.), New York: McGraw-Hill.
Busnel R. G. (Ed.) (1963) *Acoustic Behavior of Animals*, Amsterdam: Elsevier.
Feldtkeller R. and Zwicker E. (1956) *Das Ohr als Nachrichtenempfänger*, Stuttgart: Hirzel Verlag.
Rasmussen G. L. and Windle W. F. (Eds.) (1960) *Neural*

*Mechanisms of the Auditory and Vestibular Systems*, Springfield, Illinois: Charles C. Thomas; Toronto: The Ryerson Press; Oxford: Blackwell.

STEVENS S. S. (Ed.) (1951) *Handbook of Experimental Psychology*, New York: Wiley; London: Chapman and Hall.

STEVENS S. S. and DAVIS H. (1938) *Hearing, Its Physiology and Psychology*, New York: Wiley.

SWETS J. A. (Ed.) (1964) *Signal Detection and Recognition by Human Observers*, New York: Wiley.

TAVOLGA W. N. (Ed.) (1964) *Marine Bioacoustics*, New York: Macmillan.

WEVER E. G. (1949) *Theory of Hearing*, New York: Wiley.

WEVER E. G. and LAWRENCE M. (1954) *Physiological Acoustics*, Princeton, N. J.: The University Press; London: Oxford University Press.

N. GUTTMAN

**HOMEOSTASIS.** In 1878 Claude Bernard put forward the view that a constant *internal environment* is an essential requisite for the maintenance of life of an organism. This concept was modified by Cannon in 1929 who introduced the term *homeostasis* to describe the reactions of a living system in maintaining the internal environment relatively constant when the external environment changes. Cannon also pointed out how stable and well co-ordinated different biological mechanisms usually are. It is now accepted that we live in a continually changing external environment and that this will influence continually and to different degrees the internal environment of living organisms. The term homeostasis is now used to describe the active response to such changes which is found in all living systems (Adolph 1961; Ashby 1956, 1960; Barcroft 1934; Brookhaven 1958; Soc. for Exptl. Biol. 1964; Wiener 1961).

Generally speaking the early studies on the subject of biological control either used *systems* which were simple in themselves or the study was simplified experimentally by, for example, attempting to maintain the system in a steady state or to keep constant all but one of the variables of the system. The practical limitations to progress in the study of more complex systems have been largely due to the difficulties in recording a number of variables simultaneously. Progress was also held up by the lack of conceptual techniques for dealing with complex systems in both the design and analytical stages of investigations. Although the number of living control mechanisms that have been described in precise mathematical terms is still small, recent progress in control systems technology has provided new instrumental techniques, analytical methods and concepts (Bayliss 1966; Milsum 1966; Yamamoto and Brobeck 1966) whose use in biology should enable more rapid advances to be made in the understanding of the behaviour of complex biological systems.

Some understanding of homeostatic mechanisms may be obtained by viewing the subject either from the development aspect, using the evidence from evolution and embryology, or from the analytical aspect using results from biochemistry and physiology. By combining both these approaches a useful picture of homeostatic processes and their organization in a living organism can be obtained.

The simplest processes that could be said to be homeostatic must have been those chemical reactions the result of which were the earliest forms of primitive life. It is likely that a reaction which was performed in a laboratory in 1953 may have been one such process. A mixture of hydrogen, methane, ammonia vapour, water vapour, carbon monoxide, hydrogen sulphide and other gases believed to have existed in the Earth's primeval atmosphere were subjected for 24 hours to an electric discharge in a reaction chamber. Among other organic products found at the end of the reaction were a number of amino acids of the type identified as components of proteins. Electric storms and ultraviolet radiation may have provided the energy for the reaction in primeval times.

Similar chemical reactions are believed to have been responsible for the synthesis of large hydrocarbon molecules of the type now found in living cells. Polar lipids, fatty type substances that form films on water and which are constituents of the membranes enclosing living cells, are thought to have a similar origin. They are known to have two stable states, one in which the molecules form a thin film on water and in the other a micel, a sphere-like structure and in both the states the free energy is minimal. Disturbance of such a film on a water surface by wind may easily have been the cause that led to the formation of the spherical hollow structure and to a primitive type of cell (Goldacre 1958). Processes of the above type and many others must have contributed towards the synthesis of what we now know as biological cells and as the building blocks of living organisms.

Within the 'primitive cells' the end products of the different reactions would largely be the result of energy conversion from ultra-violet light or electrical energy to chemical energy, in the form of 'high energy' compounds. If such 'cells' provided a focus both for the absorption of inorganic molecules and for the concentration of energy they would grow. This growth could occur only up to a certain size when the force of surface tension and of the chemical bonds that maintain the cell structure become weak and the whole system becomes unstable. To attain a new stable state division into two would then be a natural occurrence. Following the division, each cell would be in a state in which the free energy was at a minimum. The above provides some basis for the generalization, that in biology, function (mechanisms, reactions) precedes and leads to the synthesis (creation) of structure (cells, organs, organisms).

Most of the above reactions can be explained in terms of the laws of physics such as thermodynamics or statistical mechanics. For example consider a simple process comprising a forward reaction and a backward reaction. In all real non-idealized systems there is always some flow of energy (and matter) from the environment into the system under consideration. The laws of irreversible (or non-equilibrium) thermodynamics permit the description of processes in which a change in the energy of the system which is time dependent moves the 'equilibrium point'. An example is the steady flow of energy from the Sun which prevents the Earth's atmosphere from reaching a state of thermodynamic equilibrium. The existence of a continuously changing physico-chemical state is implicit in the word 'ageing' which has been applied to non-living as well as living matter. The state of the variables in a reaction system changes with time in the direction in which the free energy of the system tends to be at a minimum. This state can be computed at a point in time from a knowledge of the rates of different individual reactions that make up the process together with the coefficients that are used to describe the degree of coupling, that is interaction between the different reactions. The efficient conversion of energy requires close coupling, irrespective of whether this conversion is from mechanical energy to electrical or from chemical energy to thermal energy. Living biochemical processes are complex in the sense that they involve many coupled reactions which are occurring simultaneously.

The process of evolution has gone through a long series of phases with the existing biological organisms as the result. Each phase ended when the then existing system tended to become unstable. This intermediate condition lasted until the system was constrained by a new 'higher order' system producing a new stable condition and which enabled growth to occur for a time.

The most general statement about the evolution of living systems due to Darwin is that the present state of the biological world has been arrived at by the natural selection of the fittest. Each stage of evolution must have taken considerable time because the likelihood of formation of higher order systems must in the early stages have comprised a very great random component superposed on only a small deterministic component. This is borne out by the estimates we have about the development of life and the evolution of its forms. These are after the formation of the planetary system occurring about $5 \times 10^{10}$ years ago, the first appearance of primitive organisms about $10^9$ years ago, of first mammals $5 \times 10^8$ years ago and of first man-like beings $5 \times 10^6$ years ago. Evolution in more general terms may be described as any process in which there is a gradual increase in 'hereditary' information with time. A *hereditary process* is one by which information is transmitted from one structure, the parent, to another structure, the heir, so as to result in a net increase in physical order of the over-all system comprising parent, heir and environment. As hierarchical systems have greater likelihood of evolving more quickly than non-hierarchical systems of comparable size (Simon 1962) we can conclude that the more complex forms of organization which we can find now have a hierarchical structure. We know from fossil remains that whole species have become extinct. Their homeostatic mechanisms could not have enabled them to adapt adequately to some unusually rapid change in their environment. Likely conclusions from this are that the over-all structure and function of existing organisms are the optimal ones for their particular and sometimes unique environment.

It is obvious that evolution has brought with it increasing complexity of organization of living organisms. We can now find, on the one hand definite different structures within cells which themselves perform specific functions. On the other hand we find different cells having specific functions. It is possible in principle to define the degree of complexity of a system, by, for example, the numbers of different types or classes of cell present or by the number of units within cells and by the number of levels of interaction between these. One must remember that these are relative quantities and they depend on the resolving power of the investigator or his instruments.

The wide range of tasks that man can accomplish, or in other words the wide variety of responses man may produce, makes him the most complex living organism. We will jump many stages of evolution and consider the organization of some functions in man which show hierarchical structure.

In general all cells convert one form of energy into another, i.e. chemical energy to electrical energy, mechanical energy or a different type of chemical energy, with many of these reactions occurring simultaneously. Within a cell the over-all rate of reaction is determined by the rates of the different reactions, their coupling coefficients, by enzymes and by the characteristic of the cellular structures (see *Homeostasis in the single cell*). Growth of cells and their division, with aggregations of cells, leads to the formation of organized organs and organisms. With it occurred the specialization of function of cells. This means that the cells became concerned mainly with one or a limited number of specific forms of energy conversion, for example the process of concentrating hydrochloric acid in the stomach, or the transfer of energy at receptors (see *Receptors as transducers*).

One chemical metabolic reaction called aerobic respiration, which occurs in most living cells, in fact in all mammalian cells, will serve as example. In this glucose and oxygen react to give the energy for the cell to perform its function and remain alive, and produce carbon dioxide and water as by-products.

Food (chemical energy) + oxygen = carbon dioxide + water + heat energy + stored chemical energy + work energy

$C_6H_{12}O_6 + 6 O_2 = 6 CO_2 + 6 H_2O + Q$ (calories in the form of heat) + E (calories in the form of high energy phosphate compounds) + W (calories in the form of work). For energy conversion to occur efficiently it is necessary that the concentrations of oxygen and carbon dioxide, glucose and electrolytes have certain values which are the same for most cells. These values appear to be those at which the free energy of the cell is at a minimum. In other words these reactions can usually be said to be occurring under the optimal conditions.

The energy that has become available for cell functioning by aerobic respiration is usually stored in the form of a high energy phosphate compound such as Adenosine Triphosphate. It remains available for the cell to perform its specific specialized function until required, whether for muscular activity—that is mechanical action—or the concentration of inorganic electrolytes or organic molecules in glandular cells, or for maintaining nerve cells excitable by causing them to be polarized.

If the processes within the different cells, lying within an assembly of cells, are to occur under the optimal conditions in which the free energy is minimal, then the distribution of chemical products that are to provide the energy must also be determined by the same principles. This means that the structures of the distribution systems and distribution pattern of the substances must be determined by the same principles of optimization. An examination of the respiratory system (in the widest sense) and of the circulatory system shows that there are many observations which support this explanation (Priban and Fincham 1965; Rashevsky 1960).

Respiration is the term used to describe a specific form of energy conversion (metabolism) on the molecular or cellular level and also to describe breathing, the rhythmical movement of the thoracic apparatus and ventilation of the lungs, sometimes called external respiration.

Both the circulation of blood and the ventilation of the lungs appear to be controlled in such a way that the over-all function of the system is kept at an over-all optimum, the minimum energy consumption to maintain this functioning even when the metabolism of the body is changing as for example during exercise.

The control of the different processes that together accomplish the respiratory function is based on a hierarchical organization. This has to some extent been discussed under respiratory control (see *Control of respiration, self-adaptive*).

Metabolic tissue respiration and external respiration are linked by the circulation. The distribution of oxygen to the different organs and tissues and the removal of carbon dioxide from these by the circulation of the blood appears also to involve self-optimization. It is probably accomplished by keeping the relative distribution of the cardiac output, the flow of blood from the heart, to a particular region, a function of the metabolism in this region. Such circulatory control is essential if the (ventilatory) respiratory control is to be effective. In addition it is necessary that the cardiac output and the pulmonary circulation keep pace with the overall metabolism, i.e. to balance circulation with ventilation. A feed-forward control mechanism with receptors in the mixed venous blood, regulating the heart and the pulmonary vascular bed would be the simplest mechanism to accomplish this. The circulatory requirements of the brain are exceptional; because it is without an oxygen store and its metabolism is essentially aerobic, it is critically dependent on a satisfactory oxygen supply while its functioning is absolutely essential for the survival of an organism.

The arterial chemoreceptors in the carotid body lying in the circulatory path to the brain are in a very suitable position to detect potential oxygen lack and bring about a feed-forward compensatory adjustment to the cerebral circulation as well as to the cardiac output generally and to respiration. This type of control mechanism can bring about a very rapid adjustment which over-rides the other control mechanisms (Priban and Fincham 1965).

One can generalize by saying that the physical properties and structures of most if not all living systems or their sub-systems (e.g. components and organs) are such that progressively more energy is required for their functioning towards the outer limits or boundaries of the systems. This non-linear property can be represented by contours of functional index or performance index, i.e. units of function (e.g. litres of circulation or secretion) per unit energy consumption values for a given region on a two-dimensional map of any particular system. The index contours of many of these living systems have the shape of a hill. The purpose of the control is to regulate the different functions so as to obtain coincidence of the peaks of the hills representing the different systems. In other words the functioning of the individual component systems is adjusted so that all operate at their optima. By combining the hills representing different systems the map of functional index contours of the entire system is obtained. In this context the over-all control may be seen as a hill-climbing process involving an over-all functional hill of the entire body system.

It is fair to say that the application of self-optimizing and adaptive control theory to explaining biological process, instead of *set-level control* principles, has made analogies between living systems and man made systems more realistic.

The over-all system can only remain stable when all the sub-systems are functioning in a definite order, the one imposed by evolution. These sub-systems which comprise the different control loops are now being studied and identified by their time constants, cycle times, or frequency and amplitude components.

While the evidence for hierarchical organization of the vegetative system (e.g. circulation and respiration) has been indirect, more evidence for such a structure is beginning to appear. The organization of the nervous system in the form of a hierarchical structure has been accepted for some time. Essentially this organization involves two connected decision trees. This enables the peripheral functions or processes of the body (reactions involving the conversion of energy) to be controlled and co-ordinated as a whole.

The concept of a hierarchical organization of the central nervous system which evolved by natural selection to the highest level which we now see in man was probably first introduced by Darwin in 1872. The concept was later elaborated by many other workers, in particular the neurologist Hughlings Jackson (Magoun 1960) (see also *Neuronal nets*).

The phylogenetic elaboration of living organisms with the developments of a central nervous system in a series of stages in which new super levels were added as the evolutionary scale was ascended is enabling the more complex organisms to survive in a wider range of environmental conditions. Naturally this elaboration involves together the peripheral system, the cells and organs, and the nervous system. It is a sequential elaboration of what may be considered to have begun as a simple control process which initially utilized only a very simple computer controlling quantitatively a very simple process. Once a type of control was established the stability of the system with respect to changes in the environment became better. This in turn enabled the computer to improve further. Today the best (and over-all) controller in the highest level of the central nervous system. The internal environment of the highest level is the most stable, protected against mechanical shock by bone and multiple membranes. The chemical environment is maintained optimally by a hierarchical arrangement of control loops and a 'blood brain barrier'.

In principle there is little difference between the nervous processes concerned with the vegetative functions such as respiration and those concerned with mental processes. The main difference which enables such a wide spectrum of energy as represented by light, sound, smell, and heat to be dealt with by the brain is most likely to lie in the greater number of decision levels and 'memories' that exist in the part of the brain associated with consciousness. It is this difference which enables man to have within him mental images of his past experiences with the environment. It is this which also enables him to predict the future by extrapolating forward in time from his memory of experiences.

Learning is exhibited by an animal when presented repeatedly to the same situation and the response becomes less (in that mistakes are reduced). It can be accounted for by changes in physico-chemical properties and in structure in both the peripheral system and in the nervous system. The results of such learning are transmitted from one generation to the next in the form of genes. The genes may be seen as the templates that determine how the molecules and cells are built up in definite patterns and sequences during the development of the animal.

While the initial reactions involved in the sequence leading to primitive life would have been determined mainly by random events we are now living in a period in which we can describe even complex reactions or behaviour probabilistically. That is events are tending to become more deterministic. One might expect also that if those conditions that existed on our planet just before primitive life appeared were to exist again here or elsewhere, this would lead eventually to the same chain of events. Each of the events in this chain of 'purposive' type processes may be for example, simply a chemical reaction that is moving towards the state in which the free energy is at a minimum, the growth and division of living cells, the self-optimization (also called adaptation) of biological function by minimizing the energy expenditure, learning, the natural selection of the fittest, and the maximization of a performance of functional index. The different terms that have been used to described different phenomena can probably be simplified to a single principle whatever the concepts and terminology that are used.

One may begin concluding by saying that all processes are irreversible when considered over sufficient time. This is particularly true of living processes. Throughout evolution functional capability must always have preceded morphological differentiation. This has given rise to such complex organisms as man. The process was in all probability speeded up by parallel development of complexity and these being brought together by cross fertilization.

The goal of a living organism is to bring its actual state into congruence with a 'desired or optimal' state. The more complex the system the further ahead can it predict the future.

One may finally conclude from the preceding account that so-called homeostasis can be maintained only by a multi-level hierarchical organization of self-adaptive control loops and that this organization is such that the sub-systems are optimally distributed. Considerable experimental work will have to be done to establish this for the whole organism. The emergence of a general pattern of behaviour in living systems and the use of systems research techniques, principles and concepts permits the whole subject of homeostasic control, that is of living multi-level self-adaptive control systems, to be approached more rationally.

*See also:* Animal learning. Communication theory. Homeostasis in the single cell.

*Bibliography*

ADOLPH E. F. (1961) *Early concepts of physiological regulation*, Phys. Rev. **41**, 737.
ASHBY W. R. (1956) *An Introduction to Cybernetics*, Sci. Eds.
ASHBY W. R. (1960) *Design for a Brain*, New York: Wiley.
BARCROFT J. (1934) *Features in the architecture of physiological function.*
BAYLISS L. E. (1966) *Living Control Systems*, New York: Wiley.
Brookhaven Symposia in Biology No. 10 (1958) *Homeostatic mechanisms*, New York: Brookhaven National Laboratory.
CANNON W. B. (1929) *Organization for physiological homeostatics.*
CANNON W. B. (1939) *The Wisdom of the Body*, Norton.
GOLDACRE R. J. (1958) *Surface films, their collapse on compression, the shapes and sizes of cells and the origin of life* in Surface Phenomena in Chemistry and Biology, 278, Oxford: Pergamon Press.
MAGOUN H. W. (1960) *Evolutionary concepts of brain function, Darwin and Spencer*, in Vol. 2, The Evolution of Man, (Ed. S. Tax).
MILSUM J. H. (1966) *Biological control systems analysis.*
PRIBAN I. P. and FINCHAM F. W. (1965) *Self-adaptive control and the respiratory system*, Nature **208**, 339.

RASHEVSKY N. (1960) (3rd Edn) *Mathematical Biophysics*, New York: Dover.
SIMON H. A. (1962) *The Architecture of Complexity*, Proc. Amer. Phil. Soc. **106**, 467.
Society for Experimental Biology (1964) Symposia No. 18, *Homeostasis and feedback mechanisms*.
WIENER N. (1961) *Cybernetics*, Cambridge, Mass.: M.I.T.
YAMAMOTO W. S. and BROBECK T. R. (1965) *Physiological Controls and Regulations*.

I. P. PRIBAN

**HOMEOSTASIS IN THE SINGLE CELL.** It has been stated by Claude Bernard that the indispensable condition for free existence of multicellular organisms was the constancy of the medium bathing the cells. This is achieved by the kidneys, lungs and other organs. With single cells, however, there is no means of keeping the external medium constant in composition, and those who culture for example bacteria, protozoa and tissue cells have frequently to change the medium, for the cells alter the medium by their metabolism and make it eventually unsuitable for growth. All the cells can do is to move away from the higher concentrations of harmful substances, or towards a better part of the medium, though the death of some of the cells may at first condition the medium for the rest, e.g. by absorbing poisons on their proteins. Outside the laboratory, the balance of nature adjusts the proportion of the different kinds of organisms in a mixed population, and the medium may remain fairly constant in composition because of this mutual adjustment.

On the other hand, single cells do have some mechanisms whereby they can control their own *internal* medium. For example, many fresh-water unicellular organisms, such as protozoa and some algae, have a higher salt concentration than the medium has, and tend continually to absorb water by osmosis. The extra water may be removed by a contractile vacuole, rhythmically filling and discharging to the outside. The higher salt concentration is maintained by an active transport mechanism, which uses metabolic energy (derived from ATP) to concentrate various ions against a concentration gradient. This has been much studied in the nerve cell, where potassium ions are pumped in and sodium out. As the *nerve impulse* passes along the *axon*, the membrane becomes more permeable to these ions which tend to equalise their concentrations inside and out; thereafter, the active transport mechanism builds up the inequalities again to permit the nerve once more to *fire*.

Again, an injured cell may pinch off the injured part by a local contraction. This can happen when various noxious substances are injected into the amoeba with a micropipette. While a nucleus pushed into the amoeba by the technique of nuclear transfer is retained and functions normally, a nucleus damaged by exposure to external medium is pushed out through the membrane by the cell. Some harmful substances in the external medium can enter the cell and soon afterwards become segregated into vacuoles, which may later be excreted intact into the medium. This process can be observed particularly well with certain basic dyes.

As far as can be judged by the present rather inaccurate methods of measurement, the pH of the cell remains fairly constant, in spite of small fluctuations in that of the medium, provided that these fluctuations are due to non-penetrating (i.e. strong) acids and bases rather than weak (i.e. penetrating) ones. Since many enzyme reactions are sensitive to pH and to salt concentration, it is not difficult to see how a mechanism designed to keep a constant concentration of these ions could operate by means of such sensitivity, and also why such constancy is necessary.

The existence of control mechanisms which maintain homeostasis implies the passage of information across the cell by some means or other. If, say, three quarters of the amoeba's cytoplasm is amputated, the cut seals itself instantly and the nucleus shrinks as if to preserve a definite volume ratio to the cytoplasm. How does the nucleus know the cytoplasmic volume? A possible way would be for the nucleus to respond to the concentration change of some substance put into the cytoplasm by the nucleus in a given amount, the concentration being determined by the volume of the cytoplasm.

Amoebae when unfed move at relatively high speed in a wavy exploratory path. When they find food and ingest it, their speed greatly decreases. This has the effect of concentrating the amoebae near food, like a liquid distilling from a hot to a cold surface. Thus they tend to become 'locked' on to their goal.

The old idea that organisms act only in response to external stimuli is untenable. Much of the motivation is endogenous. For example, an amoeba will move in a homogeneous medium at constant speed in one direction without reversal for a generation time (2 days in *Amoeba proteus*). All cells are goal-seeking organisations based on negative feedback creating apparent purposiveness. Such feedback mechanisms must be numerous but few have been described. The following is a brief account of fields in which some progress has been made.

*1. Amoeboid movement.* The first published account of a control mechanism in a cell based on feedback, appears to be that dealing with the speed governor in the amoeba (Goldacre 1954, 1958, 1964). In this the extent of contact of an enzyme with its substrate is influenced by the force of contraction of the motor mechanism of the cell. The enzyme produces a substance causing contraction (i.e. driving the motor) and the contraction decreases the contact of the enzyme with its substrate. Thus we have negative feedback leading to homeostasis, i.e. constant speed. By mechanically interfering with this process several new forms of amoeboid movement, unknown in nature, could be provoked. For example, by a process well-known to engineers, homeostasis can be converted into rhythm by introducing a time-lag into the feedback loop. In the amoeba this was done by mechanically flattening the cell, by screwing down the coverslip with a cell compressor. At a critical thickness of the cell, about a third of the natural thickness, the constant speed of streaming of the cytoplasm switched over into a rapid cytoplasmic oscillation. This was reversible on releasing the cell.

This contral mechanism is mechanochemical in that the enzyme is on the cell membrane, the substrate near the membrane is a non-diffusible gel from which the membrane is insulated by a fluid layer just under the cell surface except at the rear motor end, where it is absent. Contraction produces more of this insulating fluid layer (like water out of a contracting sponge) and so reduces the area of contact of membrane and substrate-gel.

*2. Feedback inhibition of enzymes.* A number of other control mechanisms are purely chemical, based on the inhibition of enzymes by substances produced further along the chain of reaction. This process, called 'feedback inhibition' was first described by Umbarger in 1956, and has since been found to be fairly widespread in cells from bacteria to mammals. The general process is as follows:

$$\begin{array}{c} \text{inhibition} \\ \overbrace{\phantom{XXXXXXXXXXXXXXXXX}} \\ E_a \quad E_b \quad E_c \quad\quad\quad E_w \\ A \longrightarrow B \longrightarrow C \longrightarrow D \longrightarrow \cdots \longrightarrow X \end{array}$$

where $E_a$, $E_b$ etc. are enzymes bringing about successive reactions on substance A through intermediates B, C, D etc. finally producing X. Substance X acts so as to inhibit not the final enzyme $E_w$ but one earlier in the chain $E_a$ and is highly specific. This arrangement has the interesting effect of preventing any unwanted accumulation of substance X, and coordinates rate of synthesis of a building-block with its rate of utilization. This may play a part in the remarkable efficiency of enzyme reactions in cells, whose yields are stated by Dixon to be 100%. Such high yields are very necessary, because many reactions involve a long chain of successive enzyme reactions. For example, the Krebs cycle has 8 successive steps in it, synthesis of proteins has hundreds and nucleic acid many tens of thousands. A chemist attempting to carry out a long synthesis with, say, 20 stages each with a yield of 50%, would finish with only about one millionth of the theoretical yield. Of course, the low activation energy of enzyme reactions, taking place at body temperature, may also contribute to the high yields in the cell.

A somewhat related phenomenon is called 'feedback repression' (Magasanik 1961) and refers to the inhibition of the *formation* of an enzyme of a biosynthetic pathway by the ultimate product. Its result is that the cell can alter its enzyme composition according to its needs. It appears to be a general mechanism for controlling the rate of synthesis of individual enzymes. Enzyme inducers appear to act by overcoming these inhibitory effects.

It has also been proposed that a cell may 'switch' from one chemical pathway to another and 'lock' itself there. For example, the final product of an enzyme chain may inhibit the synthesis of an enzyme, or its activity, in an alternate pathway.

*3. Regulator genes.* The primary function of many genes in bacteria is not to direct the formation of proteins, but to regulate the action of genes that do so (Jacob and Monod 1961). For example, $\beta$-galactosidase is formed in normal *E. coli* only when lactose is present, but when the regulator gene is defective (through mutation) the cell produces this enzyme whether lactose is present or not. In the absence of lactose, the normal cell's regulator gene prevents the other gene from functioning, and hence the cell only produces enzymes when there is something to break down. Evidence for this was derived from mating defective and normal bacteria.

*4. Cell division.* As mentioned above, a control mechanism may express itself in two ways, either by generating homeostasis or rhythm. Rhythmic cell division which occurs in many single cells in their log phase of growth such as bacteria, protozoa, vertebrate cells in tissue culture etc., appears to be a rhythm of this type (Goldacre 1958b). Numerous experiments, especially microdissection experiments, indicate that the cell nucleus influences the cytoplasm, and the cytoplasm the nucleus, feedback fashion. Since changes brought about in this way are slow, involving synthesis and growth, the feedback operates with a time lag and generates a rhythm, which expresses itself as a periodic change in the chemical and physical properties of the nucleus and cytoplasm as observed in the cell cycle. Presumably cell division is triggered off when some property exceeds a critical value, but the trigger control mechanism does not reside in either nucleus or cytoplasm but lies ultimately in the interrelationship between the two. The phase of the cell cycle can be altered by removing or adding either nuclei or cytoplasm, and correct estimates can be made of the generation time and of the effect of disturbing experimentally the ratio of cytoplasm to nucleus by the use of feedback theory, and of data obtained by microdissection (Goldacre 1960).

*5. Transmission of the genetic message and ageing.* Just as entropy tends to increase, information tends to decrease with time. The cell is faced with the problem of how to preserve its genetic message, transmitted from one generation to the next over millions of years. Some cells do not succeed in preserving it even for a few years, as shown by progressive changes in tumours maintained by passage through successive hosts in cancer research laboratories, and the progressive, even malignant, change in mammalian cells in tissue culture.

The answer to the cell's problem would appear to lie in the use of redundancy. The Shannon-Weaver (1949) theorem, developed in connexion with the problem of telephone communication in the presence of noise, has important biological applications. It shows mathematically how the degradation of a message by noise may be prevented by an increase in the redundancy of the message. Similarly the degradation of a message in the genes of a cell by biological 'noise'—thermal agitation, toxic substances, chemical mutagens, ionizing radiation, etc. may be overcome by biological redundancy. This is provided by multiplexing, by the prodigious reproductive power of many organisms, and by mating.

The cell is not built for economy, but for safety. It is not uncommon for all but one millionth or less of the progeny of an individual of some species to be destroyed in a balanced population. When there are many messages, some get through intact.

Again, in mating, which occurs from bacteria to man, a defective part of a message in one cell may be compensated for by an intact part from another cell which fuses with it. Since *somatic* cells of multicellular organisms do not normally mate, the coded instructions in their genes, their instructions to themselves, become blurred with time and the cells age.

An interesting intermediate form occurs in some protozoa. Cultures of paramecium for example divide vegetatively for months, then deteriorate. If they are mixed with a strain with which they can mate, they do so and become revitalised.

A primary event in ageing therefore, appears to be the breakdown of homeostasis. Were homeostasis effective, there would *ipso facto* be no progressive change in the cell. Old organisms have generally a reduced capacity for homeostasis. A familiar example in man is the greater adverse effect of a given amount of alcohol, tobacco, heat, cold or noise at age 50 than age 20.

*6. Cell reliability.* Owing to biological variation, cells of the same type vary considerably in their properties. Thus a particular concentration of bactericide in a pure culture of bacteria may kill most cells but leave a fraction alive which is proportional to the negative log of the dose. This is an expression of the *Weber-Fechner* Law in physiology. How does a multicellular organism function reliably when formed of such variable material? For example, the brain computes accurately although its cells are not standardized and change with time. It is even possible to remove surgically more than half of the brain without destroying specific memories or the ability to perform learned tasks. Evidently there are many more cells present than are needed for the task. But even protozoa carry out their various activities, such as mitosis, with precision. The problem of making a reliable organism out of unreliable parts is soluble again through the application of the Shannon-Weaver theorem, by multiplexing or the provision of redundancy. The same principle is used in man-made computers (with multiplexing and majority organs), and in the cell itself, with redundant organelles (over 90 per cent of the amoeba's cytoplasm, for example, can be cut away with complete recovery) and in some cases diploidy polyploidy. Redundant genetic information in the giant chromosomes of some insects such as *Chironimus* and *Drosophila* is of the order of 1000-fold.

It is to be noted that homeostasis in the cell is relative, not absolute: the condition of the cell may vary with the phase of the cell cycle, the state of differentiation and various other things such as metabolism and age. In a sense, 'homeostasis' is perhaps not so apt a term as 'goal-seeking activity' for some aspects of cell behaviour, though the underlying mechanism, negative feedback, is the same.

*7. Cell-cell interactions and cancer.* Cells in a developing embryo which are originally similar may be switched over into becoming quite different in type by interacting amongst themselves. In this way controlled growth or morphogenesis proceeds. The different kinds of differentiated cells have the same genes, as shown for example by nuclear transfer experiments and the growth, for example, of a single isolated carrot phloem cell into a whole carrot. The activity of some of the genes is inhibited by a kind of 'chemical conversation' with their neighbours, as if cell A said to cell B, 'I'm carrying out programme X, you do programme Y'. When cells are separated from close connexions with their neighbours, they may carry out quite a different programme, and even form a whole organism, as in uniovular twins, or they may become malignant. In cancer cells, the cell membrane, which is the organ of cell-cell communication, appears to be different from the normal, and the inhibition from the rest of the body, necessary for controlled normal growth, appears not to be accepted by the cell.

*8. A general cell theory.* The various cell components or organelles act and react on one another in some cases to stimulate and in others to inhibit. This arrangement has some interesting consequences. Suppose, for the sake of argument, a number of reacting components as in the figure are allowed to interact according to the arrows shown. Continuous spontaneous activity is provided by circular stimulating pathways and self-regulation and oscillation by negative feedback pathways. Behaviour was studied by building an electronic analogue (Goldacre 1960b) and recorded automatically. Activity beginning at any point created further activity according to the communication network and after a period of mounting activity which was long or short according

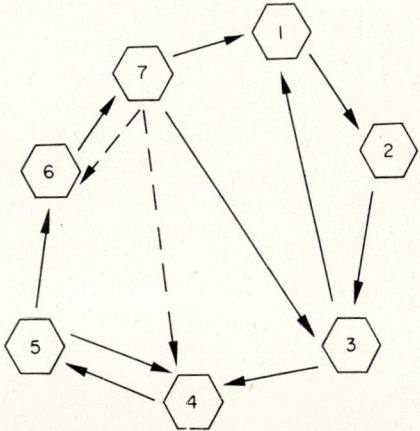

to the network, the behaviour pattern settled down to one of two states:

1. The behaviour was homeostated, i.e. either stimulating or inhibiting temporarily a component caused a temporary change in behaviour which gradually found its way back to the original behaviour.
2. The behaviour could be switched permanently to another kind by interference by the operator. This could usually be switched back by appropriate intervention.

Many other biological analogies were found in this system including the generation of head-tail polarity and left and right-handed forms. By the addition of suitable auxiliary equipment such as self-scanners and switching devices actuated by specified behaviour, the system could be made to repair and reproduce itself and grow automatically. The similarity of the behaviour of both the biological and artificial electronic systems appears to result from the common possession of a communication network with positive and negative feedback, and it is this which gives living systems many of their remarkable properties. Some examples of biological communication pathways in the cell involved in control have been indicated by Danielli (1963) in a general cell theory.

Recent progress in guided missiles and other cybernetic machines has re-emphasized that all that is essential for goal-seeking behaviour is negative feedback. The apparent purposiveness of living organisms appears to be derived from such a mechanism.

*See also:* Control of respiration, self-adaptive Homeostasis.

*Bibliography*

DANIELLI J. F. (1963) *The Theory of Cells, in Relationship to Cytoplasmic Inheritance in Amoeba by Nuclear Transfer*, Harvey Lectures, **58**, 217.

GOLDACRE R. J. (1954) *The Cell Membrane, Head-tail Polarity and the Maintenance of Cell Organisation in Amoeba proteus*, Excerpta Med., **8** (1), 408.

GOLDACRE R. J. (1958a) *The Regulation of Movement and Polar Organisation in Amoeba proteus by Intracellular Feedback*, Proc. 1st Internat. Congr. Cybernetics, Namur 1956, Paris: Gauthier Villars.

GOLDACRE R. J. (1958b) *The Regulation of Cell Division by Intracellular Feedback*, Proc. 1st Internat. Congr. Cybernetics, Namur 1956, Paris: Gauthier Villars.

GOLDACRE R. J. (1960a) *The Control of Rhythm and Homeostasis in Biology and Medicine*, Cybernetica, **1**, 117.

GOLDACRE R. J. (1960b) *Morphogenesis and Communication between Cells*, Proc. 2nd Internat. Congr. Cybernetics, Namur 1958. For details of construction of electronic analogue computer see Bean A. D., ibid., 219.

GOLDACRE R. J. (1964) *On the Mechanism and Control of Amoeboid Movement* in *Primitive Motile Systems*, (Eds. Allen and Kamiya), New York: Academic Press.

JACOB F. and MONOD J. (1961) *Genetic Regulatory Mechanisms in the Synthesis of Proteins*, J. Molec. Biol., **3**, 318; (1963) J. Molec. Biol. **6**, 306.

MAGASANIK B. (1961) in *Biological Approaches to Cancer Chemotherapy* (Ed. R. J. C. Harris), New York: Academic Press.

SHANNON C. and WEAVER W. (1949) *The Mathematical Theory of Communications*, Urbana: Illinois Press.

UMBARGER H. E. (1956) *Evidence of a Negative Feedback Mechanism in the Biosynthesis of Leucine*, Science **123**, 848; see also ibid., Cold Spring Harbor Symp. Quant. Biol., **26**, 301 (1961).

R. J. GOLDACRE

# I

**INFORMATION SPACE.** *Introduction.* The term 'space' is used in mathematics to denote the set of all possible values which a quantity or quantities may take. The space has $n$ 'dimensions' if $n$ numbers, and no more, are needed to specify exactly one element or 'point' in the space. The terminology is derived from, and the concepts are strongly influenced by, our familiar experience with three-dimensional physical space. A single point can be regarded as 0-dimensional space; points on a straight line, although infinitely numerous, form a space of one dimension (1-space) since each is specified by its distance from a given datum point. Similarly, points in a plane are the elements of 2-space, and so on.

Physical 3-space, and its subspaces planes and lines, consist of an infinite number of points, infinitely densely packed (or so we assume in elementary Geometry). The particular 'information space' considered here, however, has either a finite number of points, or an infinite number not densely packed (i. e. by moving a finite distance we only traverse a finite number of points). It is as if physical space were granular rather than continuous, so that all matter and energy were concentrated at the vertices of a crystal lattice, perhaps extending to infinity in each direction. The reason for this restriction is that information is essentially that which is communicated; now communication involves a sender, a channel, and a receiver; and no physical device acting in any of these capacities can discriminate, in a finite time, between pieces of information that differ by an arbitrarily small amount.

For example: meteorological information may include the speed and direction of wind at a station. Direction is commonly expressed as one of 8 compass points, speed as one of 13 points on the Beaufort scale. Speed and direction are independent quantities (though they may be correlated at a particular station), so the information space is a finite 2-space with $8 \times 13$ elements.

*Binary codes.* 'Coding' is here regarded as the process of assigning numbers to information, or the conversion of information from one number-scheme to another. Two-state electronic devices are so much faster and more reliable than any others, that nowadays coding virtually means expressing information as an ordered set or 'word' of binary digits or 'binits'. In the meteorological example, direction could be encoded as a 3-binit word and speed as a 4-binit word, omitting numbers 13 to 15. These numbers would together form 'binary 7-space' with a total of 512 elements, 24 of which would only be received in error.

*Distance.* Physical space, apart from its dimensionality, has a structure: given any two points we can define a 'distance' which is unchanged under certain mathematical operations, e.g. rotation of axes of coordinates. (A particular definition of distance, in 4-space, is a basic concept of relativity theory.) Distance is an example of a 'metric'; if $a, b, c$, are any three points and $D(a, b)$ is the distance between $a$ and $b$, we have:

$D(a, a) = 0$
$D(a, b) = D(b, a) > 0$ if $b \neq a$
$D(a, b) + D(b, c) \geq D(a, c)$

In the theory of codes, a metric called '*Hamming distance*' is used: if $a$ and $b$ are two $n$-digit words, $D(a, b)$ is defined as the number of digit places in which $a$ and $b$ differ. Although this metric is not restricted to binary codes, it has there a simple geometrical interpretation: we have

$$D(a, b) = (a_1 - b_1)^2 + (a_2 - b_2)^2 + \ldots + (a_n - b_n)^2$$

where $a_1 \ldots a_n$ are the digits (0 or 1) of $a$, and $b_1 \ldots b_n$ those of $b$. Hence $D(a, b)$ is the square of the Euclidean distance between points $a$ and $b$ in the space generated by $n$ perpendicular (Cartesian) axes in which each coordinate is either 0 or 1. Expressed geometrically, the set of all possible words are the vertices of a unit $n$-hypercube, and $D$ is the square of the distance between vertices $a$ and $b$.

*Detecting information errors.* The coded information received may contain errors of various kinds. We shall consider only the simple binary channel where errors consist of sending a 0 and receiving it as a 1, or vice versa. The received word may be indecipherable, i.e. be composed of no allowable set of digits; alternatively the received message may be so improbable that an error may be assumed to have occurred. We shall deal only with the first possiblity; the second is difficult to formulate mathematically and belongs more to information theory; there is the obvious pitfall that the most unlikely messages are just those which contain the most information.

Accordingly we assume that for an error to be detected it is necessary for the received word to differ from any codeword. It is clearly impossible to detect all errors, because any codeword can be changed into any other codeword by altering enough digits. However, it is reasonable to assume a reliable channel, so that the chance of a given digit being in error is small; then most received words will be in error by a few digits at worst. (It is also convenient to assume the incidence of errors is random; this is the usual assumption, but there is a theory of codes for 'bursts' of errors such as can occur when electrical transmission is affected by lightning.)

To detect up to $s$ digit errors in a word it is necessary

to have each codeword differing by at least $s+1$ digits from any other, i.e. the minimum distance between codewords must be $s+1$.

*Correcting information errors*. If the prior probability of each codeword being sent is the same, and errors occur randomly and with equal probability, then the word most likely to have been sent is the one which differs from the received word by the fewest digits. In this sense, up to $t$ digits can be 'corrected' in any received word if any two codewords differ by at least $2t+1$ digits, since there will not be more than one codeword whose distance from the received word is less than $t+1$. Such a code could alternatively be used to detect, without correcting, up to $2t$ errors.

*Codes for detecting or correcting errors*. An $n$-digit binary code for detecting or correcting errors is, in principle, constructed by selecting, from binary $n$-space, a subspace of points the specified minimum distance apart. The simplest code, which detects single errors, is constructed by adding an $n$th 'parity-check' digit to $n-1$ information digits so as to give each codeword an even (odd) number of ones; a received word containing an odd (even) number is in error. This code is extensively used in digital computers, where errors are infrequent and a faulty calculation can be repeated.

A class of codes, simple to construct but not to decode, is derived from *Hadamard matrices*. Each row of a Hadamard matrix $H_n$ of order $n > 1$ has $\frac{1}{2}n$ elements of value $+1$, and $\frac{1}{2}n$ of value $-1$; and in any pair of rows, $\frac{1}{2}n$ places are occupied by pairs of like elements and $\frac{1}{2}n$ places by unlike pairs. Hence a code in which each word has zeros (ones) in positions corresponding to the positive (negative) elements of a row of $H_n$ has distance $\frac{1}{2}n$. Except for the trivial case $n = 2$, all $n = 4m$; to many, possibly all, $m$ there corresponds a Hadamard matrix. There are $n$ codewords, and $t < m$ errors can be corrected. Another $n$ codewords can be added by changing each digit in the original words; the new words are $\frac{1}{2}n$ distant from each other and from the original words, except that each new word is $n$ distant from the word it was derived from. There is no procedure for obtaining a Hadamard matrix of any order, but given $H_n$ it is easy to construct $H_{2n}$.

Though there are interesting connexions between Hadamard matrices and geometry of regular figures in $n$-space, the difficulty of designing circuits to encode information into the required form, and to correct errors has concentrated attention on the class of codes now to be described.

*Linear group codes: Hamming codes*. A linear group code has the property that the digit-by-digit sum of any two codewords is a codeword, addition being modulo-2, i.e. $1+1 = 0$; the codewords form a mathematical group under addition. The simple parity-check code already described is a linear group code if the number of ones is even. It can be shown that any linear group code can be put into a form where the first $k$ digits are information digits and the remaining $n-k$ digits are generalized parity-check digits; there are then $2^k$ possible codewords; the value of $k$ depends on the minimum distance, but only for a few codes is the relationship known.

The best-known are the Hamming codes which correct single errors. Such a code must disclose a single error and indicate its position in the received word. For a linear code this means that a suitable set of linear operations on an 'error word' consisting of all zeros except for a one in the $i$th place must yield a pattern of digits or '*syndrome*' identifying the error. In a Hamming code the syndrome is the binary number representing the position of the error. An $r$-digit syndrome can represent $2^r - 1$ non-zero binary number representing the position of the error. An $r$-digit syndrome can represent $2^r - 1$ non-zero binary numbers, so $n = 2^r - 1$. $r$ check digits are needed to ensure that the $r$ operations give a zero syndrome when no error is present. Hence the number of information digits is $k = 2^r - r - 1$.

Associated with each codeword are $n$ words differing in one digit, the total being $(n+1)2^k = 2^n$. A Hamming code is thus 'perfect' in the sense that all single errors are corrected but no further combinations of errors are detected. Apart from a perfect triple-error-correcting code discovered by Golay, with $n = 23$, $k = 12$, the only perfect codes known are the Hamming codes and the codes derived from them by adding a single parity-check digit to detect double errors. Again, some results due to Peterson on the weights (number of ones) of Hamming codewords suggest interesting patterns in $n$-space, but these have not been explored.

*Other linear group codes*. Among other linear group codes are the Reed-Muller codes, which are a generalization of the Hamming codes and have, for given $m$ and $r$,

$$n = 2^m; \quad k = 1 + \binom{m}{1} + \binom{m}{2} + \ldots + \binom{m}{r}; \quad D = 2^{m-r}.$$

These codes, and their parity-check rules, can be interpreted geometrically in terms of interesections of hyperplanes in $n$-space.

Another generalization is the class of Bose-Chaudhuri codes, perhaps the most important linear codes so far discovered. For any $m$ and $t$, there is a Bose-Chaudhuri code with $n = 2^m - 1$ and at most $mt$ check digits, which corrects any $t$ or fewer errors. Coding is straightforward but an economical decoding scheme for these codes has yet to be found.

*Encoding and decoding circuits*. Computers, it is well known, are poor at geometry. Since practical communication systems must use electronic encoding and decoding, geometrical interest is a secondary merit in a code. Most successful mechanization has been based on the properties of 'linear switching circuits' which perform linear operations on binary words. For example, $k$ information digits may be fed into a circuit which transmits the $n$ digits of the corresponding codeword. For the Hamming codes, but for no others so far, a similar circuit will accept the $n$ received digits, and generate $k$ correct digits, if one error has occurred. (The digits are transmitted coded in 'cyclic form', involving a trivial rearrangment of the Hamming code; the theory of cyclic codes is most naturally developed using the algebra of polynomials, and it is in this form that the Bose-Chaudhuri codes appear.)

*See also:* Communication theory. Error correcting codes.

*Bibliography*

PETERSON W. W. (1961) *Error-correcting codes*, New York; Wiley. (The most comprehensive account of the subjects; the mathematics is tough but essential. Gives all the necessary references to original papers.)

N. REAM

**INFORMATION STORAGE AND RETRIEVAL.** Information storage is one of man's most fundamental activities. The only reason for storing information is to make it available when required at some later point in time. Retrieval of information is therefore an equally fundamental activity, occurring whenever a fact is withdrawn from human memory and whenever we refer to a map, dictionary, telephone directory, diary, textbook, scientific report, etc.

Although information is most commonly stored in the form of the written word it might also be in the form of diagrams, pictures or numerical data.

The efficient organization and implementation of storage and retrieval present many problems when the form of the information to be stored is at all complex, or when the amount of information involved is very great. These problems are most pressing in the area of scientific and technical information where the volume of material produced has increased alarmingly, mainly as a result of two world wars and the vast amount of scientific effort arising directly or indirectly from military defence programmes. Most of the recent advances in information storage and retrieval, especially in computerized systems, have been in the field of scientific information, but most of the methods developed would be applicable to processing other kinds of information.

*Definition of an information retrieval system.* Information is normally retrieved in response to a request, since retrieval implies purposeful recovery rather than chance discovery. An information retrieval system is therefore defined here in terms of its response to a request for information. In their raw state, requests will usually be expressed in natural language, which may not always be a suitable form for input to a mechanized system. In such cases it might be necessary to put the request into a standard form, for example, by retaining only the key words in the request. To allow for this it will be assumed that a request is first transformed into a *specification* of the characteristics of items required to be recovered from the store. The specification constitutes the standardized form of the original request, and in the special case when natural language requests are the normal form of input to a system the transformation to a specification may be thought of as leaving the request unaltered.

It is assumed that the store contains a collection of *information items*, or a collection of *descriptions* of such items. An information retrieval system is then one which compares the specification of required items with the descriptions of the stored items and retrieves, or lists, all the items which correspond in some defined way to that specification.

One of the main criteria of success of such a system is the extent to which the utilized definition of correspondence between specifications and items yields items judged by users of the system to be relevant to their requests. It is therefore usual to measure the quality of retrieval of a system in terms of the respective numbers of retrieved items judged to be relevant and non-relevant, and if available, the respective numbers of unretrieved items judged to be relevant and non-relevant.

*Methods of storing information.* Very commonly, information to be stored is in the form of texts, numerical data, diagrams or photographs. *Information* in all these forms is suited to *storage on film*. One of the main advantages of this medium is the extremely high resolution and the correspondingly high storage density offered by modern microfilm techniques. Other advantages include:

(i) convenience of handling;
(ii) the high rates at which a microfilm store can be searched by modern film scanners;
(iii) the ease with which selected items on film can be projected for display or photographically enlarged and copied.

Another development in the use of film is the *microfiche*, which consists of a small piece of microfilm (typically 35mm×60mm) on which information is stored. The use of individual microfiches instead of continuous strip film means that sorting and merging operations are possible. Equipments designed for handling microfiches also provide high speed scanning. For a review of film storage techniques see Bagg *et al.* (1962).

It is often necessary to encode information in various ways before storing it. This will be discussed in more detail in the next section. This may be necessary simply in order to use a particular form of storage, or so that the stored information can be mechanically processed. The media to be described are usually used to store coded information.

The traditional catalogue *card*, or index card, is the commonest method of *storing* coded *information*. Abstracts, subject headings, key words, etc., are entered on these cards which are then handled and searched manually.

Many organizations use punched cards for storage purposes. Coded information is stored by perforating a card with a pattern of holes which may be in any of a number of pre-determined positions in a rectangular array arranged systematically into rows and columns. The commonest format provides 960 possible hole sites arranged in 12 rows and 80 columns. A considerable range of machines is available for processing these cards. The operations provided include sorting, duplicating and verification of card punching. It is also possible to obtain a printed copy of any information, punched in an appropriate alphanumeric code. An interpreting machine will print this information along the top edge of the cards, or listing and tabulating machines may be used to produce printed sheets, the information from successive cards appearing as successive lines of print.

*Aperture cards* may be used whenever items of information are indexed or described in terms of selections of properties or attributes. To each attribute there corresponds an aperture card which, like the punched cards described above, has a large number of sites in which holes may be punched, arranged in a systematic array. The sites are numbered and are associated with accession numbers assigned to the information items stored. When a new item enters the system, all the cards corresponding to the particular attributes of that item are punched with a hole in a position determined by its accession number. The accession numbers of all items possessing any given set of attributes are found by superimposing the appropriate cards and noting the numbers of all the hole sites through which light penetrates.

Another form of *card* used for storing coded information is the *edge notched* one. Before any information is stored on them, these cards have a series of holes arranged near the perimeter, often along three edges of the cards. The coded information is stored by converting a selection of these holes into 'notches' by clipping in from the edge of the card to the holes. The usual arrangement is such that each card corresponds to one information item, the attributes of that item being coded around the edges of the card as described. A stack of these cards is searched to select those with notches in specified positions by inserting long needles through the stack in the appropriate positions and then bifurcating the stack by lifting the needles. This may be done in a single operation or the sort may be made in stages by successive bifurcations corresponding to the chosen notch positions.

The last major group of *storage media* in wide usage consists of *magnetic* devices in which information is stored as a pattern of magnetized and unmagnetized areas on a surface coated with a magnetic oxide. Magnetic tape is perhaps the most widely used in this group. This is a fairly cheap mass storage medium, ideal in cases where the whole, or a large continuous section, of a serially-arranged file has to be searched for each request. This arrangement is unsuitable unless an advantageous file organization can be found which avoids having to access the file in a random manner.

Magnetic drums provide a means of storing more limited quantities of information with a very much lower mean access time (a few milliseconds).

Capacities of perhaps one order of magnitude above those available with drums are offered by magnetic disk stores, which have mean access times comparable with drum times. Information is stored on both sides of each of a stack of disks. Because of the precision engineering involved in their construction, disk stores are extremely expensive, and this is the biggest factor limiting their use.

Although rather rare, systems have been developed for storing information on small magnetically coated cards which are handled mechanically. These are in many ways analogous to the microfiches described earlier. Pneumatic handling of magnetic cards can provide extremely high scanning rates. As with microfiches, sorting and merging of file items are possible. Once again expense has been the limiting factor. For a description of one such system see Shera *et al.* (1957, 1960).

*Symbolizing and coding information.* Most information entering storage and retrieval systems exists in a symbolic form of one sort or another, e.g. textual material and all numerical data. When it is necessary to handle information in any other form (such as pictures or diagrams) it is nearly always found to be convenient to symbolize the information before it enters the system. This is true particularly in the case of mechanized information handling, since most modern machinery is designed to process data in symbolic form.

It is often desirable to re-express symbolic information expressed in one system of signs, in terms of another system of signs. This process of transforming expressions from one system of signs to another is called coding. An example would be the transformation of a written text, expressed in the familiar system of signs of the English language, into a binary system (containing only two signs), for input to a computer.

The many coding processes employed in information storage and retrieval systems are of two basic kinds: those intended to be substantially information preserving and those designed to reduce or suppress information.

The main application of information preserving coding is the one cited in the above example, i.e. transforming information to a symbolic form suited to the proposed storage medium.

Coding procedures designed deliberately to reduce information are far more interesting and important in this context. If the idea of coding is taken to include the case of a transformation from one expression to another in the same system of signs, then the familiar concepts of summarizing, abstracting, indexing and classifying are all subsumed under this one coding process which reduces information.

There are two important, and quite distinct, reasons for wanting to reduce the amount of information contained in items entering a storage and retrieval system. The first is the obvious one of reducing the information to a more compact form so that a smaller storage capacity will suffice. This may be to reduce the cost of the store or to reduce the amount of time spent scanning the contents of the store, or both. The second reason for reducing the amount of information in stored items is to make explicit the similarity between like, but not identical, items. This leads to the concept of item descriptions which is dealt with in the following section.

*Description of information items—indexing.* The retrieval of items of information in response to a request involves comparing an item specification, derived from the request, with the stored items. However, comparison with the stored items themselves, which might be full-length papers or even books, would generally be uneconomic and intolerably slow. The usual custom, therefore, is to store, in addition to the actual items of information, *descriptions* of these items, and to use the descriptions for making any necessary comparisons during the retrieval process. The preparation of these descriptions is normally referred to as *indexing*.

Almost invariably the item descriptions are stored separate from the actual items, so that the descriptions alone need to be handled or scanned when making comparisons. In fact items and their descriptions are commonly held in different levels of storage. For example, the descriptions might be stored on a magnetic disk whilst the items are stored on magnetic tape, or even as physical objects on library shelves.

If the descriptions are to serve a useful purpose they must be brief in relation to the items to which they apply. Thus, as already noted, much of the information in the original items must be discarded. This must not be an arbitrary process, but one designed to emphasize any similarities that may exist between items. The less important information should be discarded so that items which differ mainly in unimportant aspects are given similar descriptions, the less important details not being allowed to cloud the issue. However, the problem of deciding which are the important aspects of an item of information has no simple solution. It is very dependent upon the frame of mind of the system users, upon their particular interests and the kinds of request they are likely to make. All these things are not only difficult to predict, but also very liable to change. From this point of view the ideal solution would be not to prepare descriptions of items at all, and to refer to the items themselves when processing requests. Although this was earlier rejected as being impracticable, the situation could change if mass stores and computing power become cheap enough. More immediately the best compromise seems to be to produce descriptions of items which are fairly detailed and to make the sytem sufficiently dynamic to permit the interpretation of the descriptions by the system, and the relative emphasis given to different parts of descriptions, to be modified when required.

When storing texts, the title, author and other bibliographic details naturally form a valuable part of any complete description of an item. The description of the contents of an item is the most important and also the most difficult thing to produce and very many different techniques for doing this have been tried. Traditionally this has been done by using a *classification schedule*, which is a *hierarchical* arrangement of subject headings, usually organized as a *tree structure*. Appropriate subject headings are selected from the classification tree to form item descriptions. Many libraries adopting this approach are finding it increasingly difficult to cope with the torrent of literature now being produced. Most of the inadequacies of these systems may be attributed to the fact that a tree structure is not very suitable as a basis for organizing a classification scheme. A further disadvantage of these systems is that they are not easy to mechanize. To quote Fairthorne (1958) on this subject:

'Direct mechanization of traditional library classifications is like building locomotives to run with legs.'

The general approach with most mechanical retrieval systems has been to form descriptions of items by listing their important characteristics or attributes. Any key word, group of key words, defined concept, subject heading, or other descriptive label assigned to an item in this process of listing its characteristics is called a *descriptor*. In many systems an item description consists simply of a set of descriptors of this sort. Numerous methods of forming item descriptions have been tried ranging from the free extraction of key words from the items themselves to selection from a restricted and carefully controlled set of descriptors.

One highly desirable aspect of this method of forming descriptions is that descriptors can be combined in any way at any time. New developments in interdisciplinary subject areas present no real problem. In this respect the descriptor approach scores heavily over the use of a classification schedule.

The usual way of handling a *request for information* item on some defined topic is to treat it as though it were, itself, an information item entering the system. The same procedure used for obtaining the description of an item is then used to obtain a formulation of the request in terms of descriptors. This has already been referred to as an item *specification*. The retrieval process then involves comparing this specification with the stored descriptions of items and listing those items for which a sufficiently good correspondence is observed. The retrieval strategy is dealt with in more detail in a later section.

*Fallacy of the ideal descriptor system.* When working with restricted sets of descriptors an attempt is often made to keep the set as small as possible. Speculations regarding the best one can do in this respect have led to numerous fallacious arguments about so-called 'ideal' systems, and the number of descriptors they should contain. Information theory is usually invoked to provide a basis for the argument that $N$ descriptors should be sufficient to describe, or index, a set of $2^N$ items. This is true if the descriptor set provides the maximum possible information, and in these circumstances the descriptors would have to be used orthogonally in describing the items, each being applied to exactly half the total collection.

The absurdity of this situation becomes obvious when it is realized that every possible selection of descriptors must be used to describe exactly one item in the collection. In other words the collection must contain one item on every single combination of the concepts corresponding to the descriptors. This seems to have little connexion with reality.

Such an arrangement is conceivable if the only attribute shared by all the items to which a particular descriptor is assigned is having that descriptor assigned to them. It is quite inconceivable if they are intended to share any other attributes. That is, this sort of informationally perfect set-up is, of necessity, completely devoid of semantics and divorced from reality. These are somewhat questionable properties for an 'ideal' system to possess.

*Relationships between descriptors.* Ambiguity, and consequent retrieval of irrelevant items, can arise as a result of ignoring relational information between descriptors. This is nicely illustrated by the example of the ambiguity between Venetian blinds and blind Venetians which occurs through failing to note when one descriptor is used to qualify another.

To illustrate another sort of ambiguity that could occur in a system based upon key words, consider a request for information on electrical analogues of mechanical oscillators. In the absence of relational information it would be impossible to distinguish relevant items from others which might exist dealing with mechanical analogues of electrical oscillators. *Links* (or *inter fixes*) are sometimes employed to resolve ambiguities of this sort. This simply involves indicating when a relationship exists between a pair of descriptors used in an item description or specification. Thus, an item describing electrical analogues of mechanical oscillators might have a description of the form

electrical/1      analogue/1
mechanical/2      oscillator/2

where the numbers following the descriptors are the links to indicate which descriptors are related.

The *role indicator* is another device used to help preserve relational information. As the name implies, this is used to indicate the role played by a descriptor in any particular situation. For example, a system might contain role indicators to specify the following:

(i) starting material, or input to a process
(ii) major component or constituent
(iii) process, change undergone
(iv) product, thing manufactured or fabricated.

Quite a small number of broad indicators of this sort is usually found to suffice, about a dozen being typical.

The techniques so far discussed are fairly crude and give only the briefest picture of the complicated structure of interrelationships which sometimes exist. Some people advocate a more thorough analysis of the situation and the use of highly refined indexing languages (Farradane 1963; Gardin) capable of expressing precisely all the many relationships that might be met. The description of an item is now represented as a diagram in the form of a network showing the full structure of relationships between the descriptors, and specifying the type of each relationship. An item specification produced from a request would similarly be in the form of a relational network or *graph*, to use the mathematical term for this sort of structure. The retrieval strategy must compare not only the sets of descriptors used, but also the structure of the associated graphs.

These methods are suitable when the prime aim is to achieve an exact match between the syntactic structure of a request and that of the description of any retrieved item. However, this precision is only had at the risk of missing items whose descriptions contain the desired descriptors, but do not have exactly the right syntactic structure. These will not be retrieved although they may sometimes be relevant. In fact there is some evidence that for normal retrieval purposes even links and role indicators are of doubtful value, as they are often responsible for relevant items being rejected, particularly if there is any slight inconsistency in their manner of use by indexers and library users (Montague 1964).

*Semantic association between descriptors.* Another important way in which descriptors might be connected is by semantic association. Whereas the relationships described above exist only in a particular context in which the descriptors are used, semantic associations have a more intrinsic nature.

Synonymy is perhaps the most obvious form of semantic association. It is often allowed for in key word systems by keeping lists of synonyms and, if any member of a list occurs in a request, retrieving items that feature any of the listed equivalents.

Examples of semantic associations are:

(i) part-whole          chuck-lathe
(ii) proximity          compass-ship
(iii) cause-effect      gas-explosion
(iv) similarity of function   knife-saw
(v) generic             metal-iron
(vi) synonymy           ferrous-iron

If a system is required to retrieve a maximum number of relevant items it should search for items whose descriptions contain the descriptors used in the specification, or semantically associated ones. An example should clarify this. A person requesting items on 'preventing the formation of rust on iron' might reasonably be interested in the following titles:

(A) Methods of treating the surface of metals to inhibit corrosion.
(B) A new cold galvanizing process.
(C) Applications of recently developed electroplating methods.
(D) Protective coatings for small metal parts.

Of course, semantically associated descriptors need not be given the same priority in the retrieval strategy as the primary descriptors. This point is amplified in the appropriate section.

Semantic associations are often handled by including in a system a thesaurus of words or descriptors. In this context this is an arrangement of words or descriptors designed to facilitate the selection of terms which are semantically associated with a given term. The thesaurus may be consulted in book form by users of a system, or it may be a built-in feature of a fully mechanized system. The construction of a retrieval thesaurus is a formidable task, and if accomplished manually it usually represents a great deal of painstaking work by a team of subject experts. However, efforts have been made to delegate this laborious task to machines, and the next section describes some of the techniques used.

*Statistical word associations and thesaurus construction.* Much useful information about words can be derived from studies of the way in which people use them. Statistical analysis of word usage forms the basis of a number of researches into automatic indexing and mechanical thesaurus construction. The raw data used in most of these experiments are the frequencies of occurrence of key words, and their frequencies of co-occurrence. Word counting is generally undertaken on a collection of units of written text. A unit of text might, for example, be a brief abstract of a paper or a paragraph or sentence in a longer text. The frequency of a word is usually taken to be the number of text units in which the word appears, and the frequency of co-occurrence of two words to be the number of text units featuring both words (not necessarily in juxtaposition).

A basic assumption underlying most of this work is that words found to be statistically associated in their use are also usefully associated for purposes of information storage and retrieval. The validity of this assumption will, in time, be judged by the outcome of such experiments.

Many different functions have been proposed for obtaining a measure of statistical association between two words. The classical *association factor* is obtained by evaluating the expression

$$\frac{N \cdot n_{ij}}{n_i \cdot n_j}$$

where $n_{ij}$ is the co-occurrence frequency for words $i, j$
$n_i$ is the frequency of occurrence of word $i$
$n_j$ is the frequency of occurrence of word $j$
and $N$ is the total number of text units used.

This may be interpreted as the ratio of the observed number of co-occurrences of words $i$ and $j$ to the number of co-occurrences expected assuming that the words are used with statistical independence. The logarithm of this ratio is also commonly used as a measure of association.

The function given below as another example has been used by the Cambridge Language Research Unit in applying their theory of clumps to document retrieval (Needham and Sparck Jones 1964)

$$\frac{n_{ij}}{n_i + n_j - n_{ij}}.$$

This is the ratio of the number of text units containing both words to the total number of units in which either word occurs.

Associations derived in this manner can be used to construct some sort of thesaurus, which could then be employed as a retrieval tool, or they can be utilized directly in indexing and searching algorithms. This might be done, for example, by including in an item description not only key words appearing in the item, but also these other highly associated words. To facilitate this, the word associations might be stored in the form of a square matrix having a row and column corresponding to each word, and containing the values of statistical association computed for all word pairs. Alternatively, the required storage space can be greatly reduced by fixing some threshold value of association and working with a binary association matrix which indicates the pairs of words whose association exceeds the threshold value.

To obtain statistics that are at all reliable it is generally necessary to analyse really large samples of texts, often many thousands. Even so, from the point of view of the rarer words present, a vast number of texts analysed might represent but a small and inadequate sample. As a consequence, many associations that might have been obtained from an even larger sample will be missed, and many of the associations actually obtained will be fortuitous. In other words the results will probably contain a fair amount of 'noise'. One way of attempting to combat this situation is to use the statistical associations to construct a thesaurus, or set of groups of strongly associated words. The idea here is that if there is sufficient information in the set of word associations, and not too much noise, it might be possible to arrange all, or most, of the words into groups such that there are many associative connexions within the groups, and not too many between them.

If such an arrangement of word groups can be found it can be substituted for the original matrix of associations, a pair of words now being regarded as associated if and only if they appear together in at least one group. Much of the 'noise', which existed in the form of connexions between the detected groups, is thus eliminated.

A useful interpretation is to think in terms of a graph, or network, containing a unique point to represent each word, and having a connecting line between two points if the association between the corresponding words exceeds a threshold level. The thesaurus groups then correspond to strongly interconnected sets of points in the graph, and the construction of a thesaurus entails writing a computer program to detect these sets.

One method of using a theasurus of this kind would be to use each group of associated words as a descriptor, which might be included in the description of an item if that item contains at least one, or some specified number, of words in that group. A request could be similarly processed to yield an item specification consisting of a number of these descriptors.

Descriptions of several experiments along these and similar lines are given in Nat. Bur. Stds. (1965).

*Comparison of item descriptions and specifications.* When processing a request, the item specification produced from it is compared with item descriptions in the store, and an item is retrieved whenever a satisfactory match is observed. When the specification and the descriptions are composed of simple sets of descriptors, the usual procedure is to begin by selecting only those items for which a perfect match is obtained. This may be followed by stages in which a match with all-but-one, all-but-two, and so on, of the descriptors in the specification results in the selection of items. This produces a partial rank-ordering of the selected items; those produced in the first batch (if any) matching the request perfectly, and therefore most likely to be relevant, and those produced in subsequent batches being less and less likely to be relevant. The process can be terminated either when a suitable number of items has been retrieved or when the relevance of the output has fallen to the lowest acceptable level.

Sometimes the descriptors in the specification are assigned weights (by the requester) to indicate their relative importance in expressing the request. When retrieving items which match with all-but-one of the specified descriptors the natural strategy would be to select items which lack a low weighted descriptor before items lacking a higher weighted one. This procedure gives an output with a higher degree of rank-ordering.

An even more elaborate strategy is called for if weights are assigned to the descriptors in both specification and item descriptions. Each comparison is then between two weighted sets of descriptors. If item descriptions and specifications are represented as normalized vectors in a descriptor space (containing a dimension for each descriptor in the system) an appropriate strategy is to retrieve items whose description vectors are nearest to the vector representing the specification. Once again a rank-ordered output is produced.

Increased flexibility in expressing requests may be achieved by allowing specifications to be formulated as any Boolean function of the descriptors. Descriptors in a specification may then be linked by logical connectives such as AND, OR, NOT and IF...THEN... It is a fairly trivial matter to decide whether or not the set of descriptors appearing in an item description is in accordance with a given Boolean specification. However, having selected items for which a satisfactory match is obtained, it is not at all easy to rank the remaining items according to how nearly they meet the specification. A strategy to do this, analogous to the process of successively relaxing the specification by one descriptor at a time when simple sets of descriptors are used, would involve substituting, for the original Boolean function in the specification, other functions which include it, drawn from successively higher levels of the complete Boolean lattice. However, no simple algorithm exists for generating the sequence of functions that would need to be substituted for any given Boolean function.

When expressing specifications in this way, the value of negating a descriptor is questionable. For example, if papers describing some particular type of transistor circuit are sought, but not those describing circuits which employ point-contact transistors, then if the descriptor 'point-contact' appears negated in the specification, there is a risk that papers will be rejected which mention point-contact transistors simply to compare them with other sorts of transistor with which the papers are principally concerned. This is more likely if item descriptions are prepared mechanically on the basis of key words appearing in the items.

A common requirement of a system is the ability to make generic searches. Thus, if 'insect' were one of the descriptors in a specification, an item should be selected if its description contains 'insect' or a descriptor corresponding to any particular insect species, provided of course, that the rest of the specification is suitably matched. One method of conducting a generic search is therefore to search under descriptors which are generically included by descriptors in the specification. Alternatively, when producing the description of an item, any generically inclusive ones can be added.

Arranging descriptors in a generic hierarchy also provides an extra degree of freedom useful for controlling the number of items retrieved; if too few are retrieved one or more descriptors in the specification can be replaced by other inclusive ones from a higher level in the hierarchy; if too much output is produced more specific descriptors can be substituted.

If role indicators are used they must be considered when comparing a specification and a description in addition to the usual comparison of descriptors. The situation is further complicated when links are used. In that case the retrieval strategy must ensure that the descriptors in a description stand in the same relation to one another as do those in the specification. If a very elaborate system of relational indexing is employed the process of comparison can involve quite intricate graph matching. This might involve testing to see whether two graphs are isomorphic, or whether one is contained in the other as a sub-graph.

*Search strategies involving the use of citations.* A number of common search strategies take as their starting point an item known to be relevant to the needs of the requester. Sometimes a known relevant item is simply treated as though it were a request. Any of the strategies previously described would then find other items similar to the given one.

The citations normally included in documents, to other pertinent works, can be exploited in several ways. The most obvious way is to consider those items cited by any items already known to be relevant to the request. There is a fair chance that these will be relevant. It is also useful to trace through these citation links in the reverse direction, considering items which cite another relevant one. This is particularly attractive because it provides a means of tracing documents published later than the original item known to be relevant. These methods are facilitated by the publication of citation indexes, which list, for each reference, all the other documents which cite it. These indexes are often prepared automatically and are also readily incorporated in mechanized retrieval systems.

A more subtle way of exploiting the information contained in citations is to compare the sets of citations contained in documents and to compute distances or similarities between all pairs of documents on this basis. This is analogous to computing the degree of statistical association between two words by comparing the sets of texts in which they occur. The measures discussed in that connexion are also applicable here for computing *bibliographic couplings*, as they are often called, between pairs of documents (see, for example, Salton et al. 1963; Kessler et al. 1964). A matrix containing bibliographic couplings between all pairs of items would be held in the computer store, then, starting with a known relevant item, others would be retrieved having degrees of coupling with this item in excess of some specified level.

*File Organization.* Any stored collection of information units is called a file, and the individual units are called records. In the context of information retrieval each record usually contains one information item in the collection, or one description of such an item. Each record will generally contain an additional piece of information in the form of an identification label. This will often be a number, for example a document accession number.

The most important operations on a file are:

(i) selection of a record whose identification label is given, or has given characteristics,
(ii) addition to the file of a new record

and (iii) deletion from the file of an old record.

In considering various ways of organizing the records in a file and of implementing the above operations, two factors of fundamental importance are the average time required for these operations, and the efficiency with which the store is utilized, i.e. the proportion of the total storage capacity used. These depend upon the characteristics of the storage medium and upon the chosen method of organizing the file. Two kinds of store will be considered. With the first, typified by magnetic tape, the order in which the records of a file are scanned is restricted by the nature of the store. The second kind, the random-access store, does not impose restrictions upon the scanning sequence and all records can be accessed in approximately equal times.

If the records of a file on magnetic tape are stored in arbitrary order, then the time required to access a single specified record will average out to the time taken to scan half the total length of tape occupied by the file. The scanning time can be reduced by ordering the records of a file according to their expected frequency of recall, placing those with high expected frequency near the front of the tape. Of course, this is only feasible if some basis exists, such as past history of use, for predicting future frequencies of reference to the file records. The advantage of such an arrangement depends upon the actual frequency distribution of reference to the file records as well as the accuracy with which this is predicted.

Variations upon this theme are possible. For example, if the identification label of each item consists of a set of descriptors, then the records could be arranged according to the frequency with which the various descriptors in the system are used in formulating requests. That is, there is something to be said for placing at the beginning of the tape all records whose identification labels contain the descriptor most often used in requests. The situation is not quite as simple as that, however, for if that descriptor happens to appear in the identification label of most of the records in the file, what has been gained? To analyse the situation further, suppose that $(D_1, D_2, \ldots, D_r)$ is the complete set of descriptors, for which $(P_1, P_2, \ldots P_r)$ are estimates of the probability with which they will be used in requests. Further, suppose that $(n_1, n_2, \ldots, n_r)$ are the numbers of record identification labels containing the descriptors. Now consider an arrangement in which the set of records, $n_i$ in number, whose identification labels contain the descriptor, $D_i$, is placed at the front of the file, the remaining records following in arbitrary order. Suppose that the file is to be searched for all records whose identification labels contain a given set of descriptors. Two possibilities now exist: either the request contains $D_i$, in which case only the first $n$ records of the file need be scanned, or the request does not contain $D_i$, in which case the whole file must be scanned. If the file contains $N$ records in all, the expected number of records to be scanned is given by

$$P_i n_i + (1 - P_i) \cdot N,$$
i.e. $\quad N - P_i \cdot (N - n_i).$

The expected number of records to be scanned can therefore be minimized by selecting the descriptor, $D_i$, so as to maximize the quantity $P_i \cdot (N - n_i)$. Having made this selection and placed the corresponding set of $n_i$ records at the front of the file, can the same argument now be applied to the remaining $(N - n_i)$ records on the file to select the next best descriptor, $D_j$, as $D_i$ was selected above? It can if the probabilities, $(P_1, P_2, \ldots, P_r)$, with which the descriptors are used in requests are assumed to be independent. But first, the set of descriptor assignment frequencies, $(n_1, n_2, \ldots, n_r)$, must be replaced by a new set, $(n'_1, n'_2, \ldots, n'_r)$, corresponding to the $(n - n_i)$ records on the file still to be put in order. Each new value, $n'_k$ is obtained by subtracting from the old value, $n_k$, the number of records in the set of $n$ records, already placed in the ordering, whose identification labels contain the descriptor, $D_k$. This process may be repeated to order the complete file.

*Batch processing of requests*, when tolerable, presents one of the most attractive ways of reducing the effective average scanning time per request. It is often possible to handle quite a large batch of requests and to process them with one complete scan of the file.

When using magnetic tape it is usually impracticable to adopt any file arrangement which involves the frequent insertion of new file records anywhere other than at the end of the file. It is therefore advisable to insert large batches of new items when up-dating, leaving the maximum possible time between successive up-dating runs. Any necessary deletions can conveniently be made at the same time.

When a file is stored in a random-access store (e.g. a core store or a magnetic disk), quite different file arrangements may be appropriate. One commonly used method is to arrange the file records in order according to their identification labels. Then, if the identification labels are such that all, or most, allowable labels are likely to occur (this would be so with serially-assigned numbers, but not in the case of a file of people's names, since only a minute fraction of all allowable names actually occur), each identification label can be directly related to the address of the location in which the record is stored. When a particular record is required it is obtained simply by referring to the store at the address corresponding to the given identification label. This procedure is appropriate only when searching for a file record having a completely specified identification label.

A method known as *binary searching* is applicable when most allowable identification labels are not likely to occur (e.g. when the labels are proper names). The records are kept in order of their labels, but the latter are no longer related to the store addresses at which the records are located. When searching the file for a record with a (completely) specified identification label, this specification is first compared with the label of a record at the middle of the file to ascertain which half of the file contains the required record. The specification is then compared with the label of a record at the middle of the selected half of the file to establish which quarter of the file must be searched further. The search continues in this way, halving the number of records to be searched at each stage, until the required record is found. The number of comparisons in the search is given approximately by the logarithm, to base two, of the total number of records in the file. The main disadvantage of this arrangement is the difficulty involved in inserting new records into the file and removing unwanted ones. In fact whenever the file has to be up-dated in this way it must be resorted afterwards.

Some file arrangements using a random-access store leave a number of unused storage locations distributed throughout the file, thus making it fairly simple to perform a limited amount of up-dating without any major reorganization. File systems of this type, one of which is described below, are treated in more detail in Peterson (1957).

The store is divided into a set of serially-numbered segments, each large enough to hold a fair number (say, about 100) of records. Rules are required for transforming any given identification label (of a record to be added to the file) into a series of store segment numbers in which the new record could be stored. The first segment number is obtained as an arithmetic function of the symbols of the identification label (which are ultimately reduced to numbers for computer storage). Subsequent segment numbers in the required series are usually obtained by addition of one to the previous number. Having devised a suitable set of rules for this purpose they are used to decide the segment of the store in which the new file record should be inserted. If this segment is already full, the segment given by the next number in the series is tried, and so on, until a segment is found which is not full.

A similar procedure is followed when the file is searched for a record with a (completely) specified identification label.

Although this mode of operation would eventually use up all the available storage space, the scheme becomes rather inefficient when the store is nearly full. At that stage a great deal of time is spent hunting for locations for new file records. It is therefore better to arrange that the store is never more than, say, 80 per cent full.

An important feature of this sort of file arrangement is that new records can be added to the file and existing ones deleted without affecting the rest of the file. This would make it a most attractive choice for many applications which necessitate continual up-dating of a file.

*On-line use of computers for retrieval.* Complete devotion of the powers of a modern electronic computer to library problems can be economically justified in very few cases. Only the largest libraries, which in addition to having a vast holding of books and documents, have an ample and steady supply of requests to answer, can provide this justification.

In their struggle to gain access to a computer, many libraries of more modest size and means have contented themselves with the part-time use of a machine. This has often meant that any mechanical processing of data has had to be restricted to a period of half an hour per day or less. This mode of operation, though highly unsatisfactory from the point-of-view of temporally matching the computing effort to the work load, has been encouraged by the possibility of hiring computer time and also, in the case of many libraries attached to industrial concerns and government departments, by the existence of a computer installation within the organization.

Recent advances in computers which allow time-sharing and parallel access will make mechanical processing of data a feasibility for many more libraries, even quite small ones. A computer operating in a time-sharing mode can hold several programs in its store concurrently and switch to and fro between programs so rapidly that it seems as though the programs are being run simultaneously. These machines allow transfer of information between the computer and peripheral input and output devices whilst the central processing unit is independently active. The machine is therefore capable of processing one program until it calls for input or output of data, and then, having initiated the transfer of data from or to the appropriate peripheral device, switching to another program which can occupy the central processing unit.

Operator intervention during the running of a program is entirely feasible under these circumstances. This, in itself, is a tremendous advantage in many data processing situations, including that of information retrieval. In a time-sharing system a human operator sitting at a console can interact with the machine, observing data and intermediate results visually displayed for his convenience, and taking decisions on any points better left to human judgment than to a programmed set of rules. Human skills and mechanical efficiency can thus be combined to achieve the best of the worlds of men and machines.

In any satisfactory information retrieval system it is essential to be able to integrate the library user with the computing facilities while his request is being processed. During this time the ready transference of information in both directions between the man and the computer is of the utmost importance. The human searcher is then able to modify his request in the light of the information already provided by the computer. For example, he might wish to introduce a generic term into his request, or to broaden it in some other way. If the retrieval output is too voluminous he can make his request more specific and thus confine the search to a narrower part of the document collection, or if the output is not of sufficient relevance to his interests he can attempt to express his requirements more satisfactorily. Role indicators and links might be far more worthwhile with this mode of operation, being inserted into a request only when examination of a sample of retrieved material shows it to be necessary.

With this sort of user-machine interaction it is possible to simulate many aspects of the facility to browse, which seems to rank very highly in the minds of users of conventional libraries. This is illustrated by the following description of an experimental, on-line retrieval system being developed at M.I.T. (Kessler *et al.* 1964). It operates as part of Project Mac, a mammoth experiment in Machine-Aided Cognition and Multi-Access Computing. Material in the experimental retrieval system, taken from some twenty leading physics journals, is stored on magnetic disks. The author, title, and full bibliographic details are stored for each paper appearing in these journals in addition to the list of citing references included in each paper. Programs exist for searching the collection for specific references, for papers by a given author or for papers including specified keywords in their title. In the 'browsing' mode, any page of any selected volume of a journal may be inspected.

The results of any particular type of search may be listed for subsequent inspection or output, or simply counted. Thus one could request a print-out of the details of all papers published in the *Japanese Journal of Applied Physics* between April and October, 1964, which contain the word laser in their title. Alternatively, one could instruct the machine to count the number of references to a given work which appear in any journal published since January 1966.

Programs are also provided which can be used to prepare author, title and citation indexes as required.

*Data banks and information networks.* The previous section showed how the cost of computing facilities can be shared by operating in a time-sharing mode. It also makes sense to strive to share the cost of the mass stores needed for large-scale retrieval systems. This can be done by making one physical computer storage system serve the needs of many users who require access to the same information items. One way of doing this is to construct a network of information channels linking libraries to vast central data banks. Such a network could also include centralized computer installations for processing the data on a multiaccess basis, with remote consoles situated in libraries and other locations where access to the system is required. It is possible to arrange that a library included in a network in this way could conduct its searches on the material contained in its own private store of material as well as that contained in the central stores. These satellite stores could be made available to other users, or, if desirable for security reasons, all or part of such a store could be restricted exclusively to local access.

The trend of opinion is certainly towards the development of large networks of this sort, operating on a national, and eventually, an international scale.

Users of the system at various points in the network could inspect material retrieved in response to their requests, on visual display units. They could obtain facsimile copies of selected material quickly and easily. Scientific publication in its present form of reports and journal articles might cease altogether. It is, after all, extremely inefficient from all points-of-view, save that of the publishers, to print and distribute thousands of copies of papers, many so specialized in their treatment of subjects that they are understandable by only a few dozen people in the world, a handful of whom may have sufficient interest to read them. How much more sensible only to print each copy of a paper when someone wants it. Of course, publication of articles of more general appeal should continue in more conventional form. The publication of abstracts journals is certainly increasing rapidly, but before long the publication rate will reach a level at which it is not feasible even to read all the abstracts in one's field of interest. Computer produced lists of abstracts, tailor-made to the individual's requirements, will probably be the answer.

*See also:* Fact retrieval. Scientific documentation. Statistics of language: introduction.

*Bibliography*

BAGG T., THOMAS and STEVENS M. E. (1962) *Information Selection Systems Retrieving Replica Copy: State-of-the-Art Report*, N.B.S. Technical Note 157, August.

has shown (Crossman 1961) this is not much better. As he points out, a constant channel-capacity can be obtained by taking into account information in the sequential order of message items; the value thus obtained is about 30 bits over a wide range of values of $s$. However, this formulation does not command general acceptance and the channel-capacity of immediate memory is still in doubt.

A number of studies have also shown that within wide limits redundancy in messages presented for short-term recall increases the amount of material recalled correctly but not the rate of information-transfer. For instance Aborn and Rubinstein (1952) using strings of nonsense syllables with $s = 16$ (4 bits per syllable), found that sequential constraints which reduced entropy to 1·5 bits per syllable increased the amount recalled more than 100 per cent, but produced a small net reduction in information transfer. It seems clear that human immediate memory behaves more like a store of limited information-capacity than as one holding a fixed number of items.

*(3) Choice responses.* It was known at least since the work of Merkel in 1887 that choice reactions with more alternatives take longer to make. The usual experiment for testing this employs a number of lights any one of which may go on, with corresponding keys for the subject to press as quickly as possible. In 1952 Hick pointed out that such a subject could be regarded as transmitting information about which light had been illuminated, and showed that response time depended logarithmically on the number of (equiprobable) alternatives, which would be expected if he were operating as a channel of limited capacity per unit time (rather than per stimulus as in absolute judgements).

The measured capacity was around 5·5 bits per second, and in an ingenious supplementary experiment where subjects deliberately reacted too fast for accuracy, Hick showed that increased equivocation due to errors made in premature responses just balanced the time saved, leaving a constant information-rate. Subsequent studies by Hyman (1953) and the present writer (Crossman 1953) showed that the rate was also invariant under redundancy in the 'message' input, so that here too subjects appear to be behaving as limited-capacity channels.

In this case the measured capacity varies widely with type of task; from 3 to at least 25 bits per second. The variation was at first ascribed to differences in 'compatibility' between signal and response (Fitts and Seeger 1953), but this view could not account for high capacities obtained in not obviously compatible though highly practiced everyday tasks such as typing and piano-playing (Quastler 1955). Direct studies on the effect of practice such as that by Leonard (1958) showed major increases in information-rate, and the current consensus of opinion appears to be that variations in rate over different tasks are primarily due to this factor, the 'compatible' tasks in general being more highly practised in daily life.

*(4) Motor control.* In the absence of externally supplied messages such as occur in absolute judgements, immediate memory and choice experiments, there is still a joint limitation on subjects' speed and accuracy which can be expressed as a channel-capacity. This was pointed out in 1954 by Fitts (1954). His experiments consisted of repeatedly tapping a stylus on each of two metal plates of width $w$ set a distance $a$ apart in the horizontal plane. He measured the time per tap as a function of $w$ and $a$, finding it to be proportional to the quantity $\log_2(w/2a)$, which he labelled the Index of Difficulty. This quantity measures the selectivity or information (in bits) that must be supplied in the choice of alternative motion-patterns to assure hitting a target and the maximum rate of tapping can therefore be seen as the outcome of a fixed capacity to generate information. This capacity turned out to be about 10 bits/second over a wide range of values of $w$ and $a$, and was unaffected by increasing the weight of the stylus to 2 lb.

While Fitts' exact formula has been questioned by Welford (1961) in an important review article written in 1960, the original version was certainly not far from the truth, and the existence of an informational limitation on motor performance can be taken as established. However, the question arises why information needs to be transmitted, since the targets are in full view all the time. Fitts postulated the existence of 'noise' in the motor system which would prevent exact repetition of a given motor pattern. If this view is accepted the position of the target could be regarded as a new message to be transmitted for each tap, through the noisy channel of the motor system, but the noise in question has not been directly observed. Agreement has not yet been reached on the correct answer to this question.

*(5) Perception.* Visual perception has been analysed informationally by Attneave (1954) and Archer (1954) among others and it has been shown that redundancy plays an important part. For instance figures with 'good Gestalt' are highly redundant when measured by a guessing-game like that devised by Shannon (1951) for the redundancy of English text, and hence their perception requires little information from the senses. Visual perception and memory for printed letters, words and text are also highly correlated with information-per-item as shown, for instance in the now classical paper of Miller and Selfridge (1950) on memory for short passages of different statistical approximations to English, and the more recent study by Morton (1964) on eye-voice span as a function of the same variable. (Eye-voice span is the extent to which the eye runs ahead of speech in reading aloud.)

Auditory discrimination of signals (spoken words) in noise improves with a reduction in vocabulary-size, and a definite channel-capacity can be established, its value depending on signal-to-noise ratio as theory predicts (Miller *et al.* 1951 and Garner 1962) though the capacity is very much lower than pure theory predicts.

The rate of scanning visual displays (dials) to detect out-of-tolerance readings has been predicted by

J. Senders (1955) from a knowledge of the bandwidth (frequency cutoff) and amplitude of their random variation, using the Nyquist-Shannon sampling theorem, and the predictions verified experimentally.

Thus the human receptor system has been shown to behave in various ways like an adaptive coding system capable of matching itself to the informational characteristics of its input within definite limitations of overall capacity. However, the definitive results obtained so far only scratch the surface of what seems likely to prove an extended and difficult subject.

*(6) Central processes.* Apart from the results on choice-time outlined above, information-theoretic approaches have had relatively little success in dealing with more complex central processes such as long-term memory, reorganization of stored information, decision and problem-solving, learning of new responses, and supervisory control of ongoing behaviour. As discussed below, this is probably because the message-transmission paradigm of Shannon does not fit the phenomena being analysed so well as in the case of input/output processes (perception, short-term memory, motor control, speech), and coherent results may await the application of a different kind of information-processing theory not yet fully formulated but perhaps foreshadowed by the work of McCarthy (1962) and others on the theory of automatic computation.

Meanwhile *concept formation* (the discovery by subjects of experimentally or naturally assigned regularities in categorization of multi-dimensional stimulus objects or situations) has been studied as a signal-noise problem by Hovland (1952) among others, finding that variation in irrelevant dimensions reduces speed in identifying the correct concept, as does increase in the number of alternatives possible within the relevant ones; however, a comprehensive informational analysis has not yet been attempted. Learning of sequential dependencies and statistical structure of displays generally has also attracted some attention, the observed response being a series of guesses at the next item in a sequence of values of a binary (or other) stochastic variable. It turns out that subjects can learn only the simpler kinds of structure, and hence should be able to utilize redundancy to only a limited extent (Hake and Hyman 1953), a result in line with findings of studies on redundancy in immediate memory reviewed above. Apart from these somewhat specialized areas the study of learning, which bulks so large in general psychology, has attracted very little informational analysis. This is perhaps surprising since it clearly entails the intake, storage and retrieval of information for fairly well-defined purposes.

*(7) Response processes.* While Fitts had some success with simple repetitive motion patterns, more complex skilled activity and the overall planning of effector functions have yielded little to informational analysis, though here again the problem clearly involves information transfer and processing. Data is taken in from the task being performed and/or retrieved from storage and used to direct and control muscular action. However, the attention of researchers in this field has largely been captured by the highly successful use of continuous automatic-control theory for the study of tracking performance, and this may have inhibited further attempts to develop the informational approach (see *Adaptive control theory*; *Man-machine communication and ergonomics*).

A provocative study by Pierce and Karlin in 1957 showed that target-aiming with a stylus could be performed concurrently with reading random words for a net gain in total information-rate, and isolated studies on tracking by Elkind and Sprague (1961) and the present writer (Crossman 1960) have subsequently established what appear to be channel capacities for throughput of continuous positional information in the range 2–5 bits/sec without preview and around 10 bits/sec with it. However, these estimates may need revision when better experiments can be devised an performed.

In a related area Klemmer (1957) has shown that uncertainty in the timing of discrete signals has a predictable effect on response-lag (the classical 'simple *reaction-time*'), when expressed in informational measure and combined with a similar measure of uncertainty in time-estimation: the incremental information-rate is about 50 bits/sec. Apart from these pioneer efforts there is little to report.

*(8) Language and social communication.* Although it naturally involves the various 'micro' processes discussed above, language is nowadays considered as a special topic under the heading of psycholinguistics and results will not be discussed in detail here (see *Psycholinguistic studies of syntax*). The informational concept that has proved of most use is redundancy, and Shannon (1951) himself considers redundancy of English at some length in his classical work. The human user of a native or highly-practiced foreign language has been found to make extensive use of its objectively measurable statistical structure to offset noise and cancel errors, in exactly the way that a theoretically ideal coding device would behave when designed to maximize information-transfer through a noisy channel. This is to be expected if the internal mechanisms for speech generation and perception are adapted by learning or their internal structure to maximize information-transfer in inter-personal communication, which is presumably the prime function of both spoken and written language.

This might suggest attempting to measure the information-transfer rate achieved between people using various linguistic media, a problem which does not appear to have received attention except in relatively 'peripheral' studies on the intelligibility of random words transmitted over telephone lines and in noise (e.g. Miller *et al.* 1951). Certain studies in group problem-solving of the type pioneered by Bavelas (1950) have manipulated the distribution of information among group-members, and Heise and Miller (1951) used the same format to study the effects of noise on problem-solving effectiveness, but we have no direct estimates of effective information-transfer rates reached during the solution of problems. They should not be too difficult to measure, and might throw light on important social questions of inter-personal and inter-group communication involving apparent barriers and impaired communication.

*Critique and prospects.* The foregoing survey gives no more than a birds-eye view of an extensive and in many areas still controversial body of work triggered by the introduction of information-theoretic ideas into experimental psychology. However, an evaluation of progress to date may be attempted on this basis.

It is clear that since 1948 a number of genuinely new psychological 'laws' have been discovered by applying informational concepts and measurement methods to refine and strengthen old-established experimental procedures. Many, perhaps most, of these successes have followed from three advances—(i) taking more systematic account of the context in which given signals occur, particularly the statistical structure of perceptual inputs, through measures of entropy, redundancy and so forth; (ii) integrating measures of accuracy and speed together into a combined measure of information-rate; and (iii) systematically varying the information input to experimental subjects and measuring the corresponding transmission-rates to establish channel-capacities. These procedures were exploited energetically in the decade after Shannon's work first attracted notice.

However, once the main areas outlined above had been mapped out the impetus seems to have subsided and with the possible exception of perception the initial successes have not led to the kind of self-perpetuating enquiry characteristic of scientific growing-points. The question may be asked why the application of such an apparently subtle and powerful new tool to what is clearly a complex area of interlocking problems should lack this kind of depth or 'mileage', though initial results show it to be obviously relevant. One answer might be that the relevance is no more than superficial, and another that our experimental methods are not powerful enough to tackle theoretically significant issues beyond an elementary level.

The writer feels that while both of these suggestions have some truth in them, the trouble lies more in the way the theory has been applied than in any inherent shortcoming either of theory or empirical method. With very few exceptions psychologists have taken over the new informational concepts as ready-made unitary building-bricks or coinage without paying adequate attention to their theoretical derivation or examining the precise conditions under which the theorems might be expected to apply to experimentally defined situations. This is shown by the fact that the psychological literature contains remarkably little discussion of exactly how or why Shannon's message-transmission paradigm fits specific cases. The prevailing attitude among psychologists has been one of 'suck it and see', whereas electrical engineers working in the area, such as Cherry (1957) and North (1956), have shown much more caution, discussing at length the theoretical justification for their use of such measures as entropy in connexion with human experiments.

Shannon's analysis was intended to answer a highly specific set of questions arising in the design and operation of electrical communication-systems for transmitting customers' messages and scientific data. His results are existence theorems derived by consideration of ideal operations on indefinitely long messages, using ideal devices such as coders with infinite memory, designed from a complete knowledge of signal and noise statistics. They are intended to set up criteria against which the performance of real systems may be evaluated, like the Carnot cycle of thermodynamics. But clearly one cannot expect a real system such as part of the human brain to behave in the theoretically ideal way unless the same preconditions are met. Apart from identification of message, channel and noise, and statistical stationarity, the most important assumptions are the presence of infinite (or very large) coding capacity, near-perfect knowledge of message and noise statistics embodied in the construction of the coder, and infinite permissible delay in transmission.

About the only experimental situations that come near to meeting these requirements involve 'off-line' uses of natural language (reading, communication by telegram, etc.). In all other cases one or more missing conditions prevent direct application of the theorems. Instances are signal statistics unknown to the subject in absolute judgements, lack of storage capacity for messages in choice-reaction experiments, and so forth. Best results seem to have been obtained where the conditions are most nearly met, but this need not imply that other situations are intractable.

What seems to be needed is a more analytical approach paying attention to the exact informational situation in each case, where necessary discarding Shannon's results in favour of those derived for less ideal cases by information-theorists such as Fano (1960), Wolfowitz (1964) and others.

This would undoubtedly require psychologists with more specialized preparation in this area of mathematics and more detailed working knowledge of communication systems hardware and software than has been customary. But the potential benefits are great, for in the writer's view the body of theory and technique generally subsumed under the heading of information sciences (including communication-theory, control-theory, artificial intelligence, and related areas) offers our best hope of explaining the organization and workings of the human mind at a functional rather than physiological level. Information-theory is an essential part of this structure and should be exploited to the full as a working tool in psychology.

*See also:* Communication theory. Man-machine communication and ergonomics. Psychology, use of models (learning). Statistics of language: introduction.

*Bibliography*

ABORN M. and RUBINSTEIN H. (1952) *Information theory and immediate recall*, J. exp. Psychol. **44**, 260.

ARCHER E. J. (1954) *Identification of visual patterns as a function of information load*, J. exp. Psychol. **48**, 313.

ATTNEAVE F. (1954) *Some informational aspects of visual perception*, Psychol. Rev. **61**, 183.

ATTNEAVE F. (1955) *Applications of Information Theory to Psychology*, New York: Holt, Rinehart and Winston.

BAVELAS A. (1950) *Communication patterns in task-oriented groups*, J. Acoust. Soc. Amer. **22**, 725.

BEEBE-CENTER J. G., ROGERS M. S. and O'CONNELL D. M. (1955) *Transmission of information about sucrose and saline solutions through the sense of taste*, J. Psychol. **39**, 157.

BERLYNE D. E. (1957) *Uncertainty and conflict: a point of contact between information-theory and behavior-theory concepts*, Psychol. Rev. **64**, 329.

CHERRY E. C. (1957a) *On the validity of applying communication theory to experimental psychology*, Brit. J. Psychol. **48**, 176.

CHERRY E. C. (1957b) *On Human Communication*, New York: Wiley.

CROSSMAN E. R. F. W. (1953) *Entropy and choice time: the effect of frequency unbalance on choice responses*, Quart. J. exp. Psychol. **5**, 41.

CROSSMAN E. R. F. W. (1960) *The information capacity of the human motor system in pursuit tracking*, Quart. J. exp. Psychol. **12**, 1.

CROSSMAN E. R. F. W. (1961) *Information and serial order in human immediate memory*, in (Cherry E. C. Ed.) *Information theory: 4th London Symposium*. London: Butterworths.

CROSSMAN E. R. F. W. (1964) *Information processes in human skill*, Brit. Med. Bull. **20**, 32.

ELKIND J. I. and SPRAGUE L. T. (1961) *Transmission of information in simple manual control*, HFE-2, 58, Trans Hum. Factors in Electronics.

FANO H. M. (1960) *Transmission of Information*, New York: Wiley.

FITTS P. M. and SEEGER C. M. (1953) *S-R compatibility; spatial characteristics of stimulus and response codes*, J. exp. Psychol. **46**, 199.

FITTS P. M. (1954) *The information capacity of the human motor system in controlling the amplitude of movement*, J. exp. Psychol. **47**, 391.

FITTS P. M. and POSNER M. I. (1966) *Human Performance*, New York: Wadsworth.

FRICK F. C. and MILLER G. A. (1951) *A statistical description of operant conditioning*, Amer. J. Psychol. **64**, 20.

GARNER W. R. (1962) *Uncertainty and Structure as Psychological Concepts*, New York: Wiley.

GARNER W. R. and HAKE H. W. (1951) *The amount of information in absolute judgements*, Psychol. Rev. **58**, 446.

HAKE H. W. and GARNER W. R. (1951) *The effect of presenting various numbers of steps on scale-reading accuracy*, J. exp. Psychol. **42**, 358.

HAKE H. W and HYMAN R. (1953) *Perception of the statistical structure of a random series of binary symbols*, J. exp. Psychol. **45**, 64.

HARTLEY R. V. L. (1928) *Transmission of information*, Bell Syst. Tech. J. **7**, 535.

HEISE G. A. and MILLER G. A. (1951) *Problem-solving by small groups using various communication nets*, J. abnorm. soc. Psychol. **46**, 327.

HICK W. E. (1951) *Information theory and intelligence tests*, Brit. J. Psychol. **4**, 157.

HICK W. E. (1952) *On the rate of gain of information*, Quart. J. exp. Psychol. **4**, 11.

HOVLAND C. I. A. (1952) *A communication analysis of concept learning*, Psychol. Rev. **59**, 461.

HYMAN R. (1953) *Stimulus information as a determinant of reaction time*, J. exp. Psychol. **45**, 188.

KLEMMER E. T. and FRICK F. C. (1953) *Assimilation of information from dot and matrix patterns* J. exp. Psychol. **45**, 15.

KLEMMER E. T. (1957) *Simple reaction time as a function of time uncertainty*, J. exp. Psychol. **54**, 195.

LEONARD J. A. (1958) *Partial advance information in a choice reaction task*, Brit. J. Psychol. **49**, 89.

MCCARTHY J. (1962) *Towards a Mathematical Science of Computation*, in *Information Processing 1962*, Proceedings of I.F.I.P. Congress, Amsterdam: North-Holland.

MCGILL W. J. (1954) *Multivariate information transmission*, Psychometrika **19**, 97.

MILLER G. A. and FRICK F. C. (1949) *Statistical behavioristics and sequences of responses*, Psychol. Rev. **56**, 311.

MILLER G. A. and SELFRIDGE J. A. (1950) *Verbal context and the recall of meaningful material*, Amer. J. Psychol. **63**, 176.

MILLER G. A., HEISE G. A. and LICHTEN W. (1951) *The intelligibility of speech as a function of the context of the test materials*, J. exp. Psychol. **41**, 329.

MILLER G. A. (1956) *The magical number seven, plus or minus two: some limits on our capacity for processing information*, Psychol. Rev. **63**, 81.

MORTON J. A. (1964) *The effects of context upon speed of reading, eye-movements and eye-voice span*, Quart. J. exp. Psychol. **16**, 340.

NORTH J. D. (1956) *Application of Information Theory to the human operator*, in (Cherry E. C. Ed.) *Information Theory: 3rd London Symposium*, London: Butterworths.

PIERCE J. R. and KARLIN J. E. (1957) *Reading rates and the information rate of a human channel*, Bell Syst. Tech. J. **36**, 497.

POLLACK I. (1952) *The information of elementary auditory displays*, J. Acoust. Soc. Amer. **24**, 745.

POLLACK I. (1953) *Assimilation of sequentially encoded information*, Amer. J. Psychol. **66**, 421.

POLLACK I. and FICKS I. (1954) *Information of elementary auditory displays*, J. Acoust. Soc. Amer. **26**, 155.

QUASTLER H. (Ed.) (1955) *Information Theory in Psychology: Problems and Methods*, Glencoe, Ill.: Free Press.

SENDERS J. W. (1955) *Man's capacity to use information from complex displays*, in (Quastler H. Ed.) *Information Theory in Psychology; Problems and Methods*, Glencoe, Ill.: Free Press.

SHANNON C. E. and WEAVER W. (1949) *The Mathematical Theory of Communication*, Urbana; University of Illinois Press.

SHANNON C. E. (1951) Prediction and entropy of printed English, *Bell Syst. Tech. J.* **30**, 50.

WELFORD A. T. (1961) *The measurement of sensorimotor performance; a review of twelve years progress*, Ergonomics **3**, 189.

WOLFOWITZ J. (1964) *Coding Theorems of Information Theory*, Basle: Springer-Verlag.

E. R. F. W. CROSSMAN

**INLAND TRUNK SYSTEMS.** *Introduction.* The basic techniques used for providing long distance trunk telephone circuits by line have not changed since the introduction of carrier working in the 1930's. The main developments have been in components and circuit design, leading to reduction in size and cost of equipment, greater reliability and improvement in transmission performance. This process has been accelerated in recent years by the introduction of transistors and other semiconductor devices, which has led not only to completely new concepts in equipment engineering but has opened up new fields of application on line systems; the buried repeater is a particular example.

The long distance trunk network consists of multichannel systems either line or microwave radio, circuits being assembled for transmission over these links by means of terminal translating equipment. This latter equipment is described briefly later and is common to all the systems mentioned.

*Line Systems*

*Open-wire carrier systems.* Although not used to any great extent in the United Kingdom, open-wire carrier systems still have an important place in the trunk networks of many countries. The modern open-wire line systems (Chandler 1964; Paola 1964; McPhail 1964) offer considerable advantages in sparsely populated areas where route distances may be very great and the number of circuits required is relatively small.

Because of the low attenuation of an open-wire line, systems can be operated over long distances without intermediate repeaters; a 240 mile unrepeatered 3-circuit system is typical.

The initial cost of construction of an open-wire line is in many situations considerably less than alternatives, and the cost of subsequently providing additional pairs to cater for growth in circuit requirements is also relatively small. Although on open-wire line is more susceptible to physical damage than other transmission media, the faults which occur can usually be quickly located and repaired by staff whose skill is predominantly manual rather than technical.

The attenuation/frequency characteristic of an open-wire pair varies considerably with changes in weather conditions along its route, and automatic regulation of line loss and slope is provided in the terminal equipment, and in any intermediate greater equipment, by means of variable equalizers and amplifiers controlled by line pilots.

In addition to 3 and 12-circuit systems, higher capacity systems are now available which provide up to 28 telephone circuits and 4 duplex telegraph circuits over a single pair. For certain rural subscriber applications and for short haul junctions, 60-circuit systems are available using the frequency spectrum up to 500 kHz, but special noise reducing devices are usually required to overcome the crosstalk and interference experienced at these high frequencies.

*Balanced-Pair Carrier Cable Systems*

*12 and 24-circuit systems.* The early long distance trunk network was built up on systems using separate balanced-pair carrier cables for 'go' and 'return' directions of transmission. The cables used were usually 24 pair (40 lb per mile conductors) in star quad formation. The 12 circuits were assembled as a standard C.C.I.T.T. basic group in the band 60–108 kHz before translation to the line frequency band 12–60 kHz.

It was later found possible to transmit satisfactorily up to 108 kHz and by the addition of combining and equalizing equipment, a second 12-circuit basic group could be transmitted without translation, thus providing 24 circuits in the line frequency band 12–108 kHz. The increased line loss at the higher frequencies necessitated closer spacing of repeaters, and almost all of the 12-circuit links in the United Kingdom have now been converted in this manner to 24-circuit working.

*60-circuit systems.* A few 60-circuit systems on balanced-pair cables are in use in the United Kingdom for special applications where there is a need for flexibility in supergroup units, and where, for other reasons, coaxial cable cannot conveniently be used.

An improved type of carrier quad cable is used, having low attenuation, achieved by increased separation between conductors, and good crosstalk performance, over the wider range of line frequencies (12–252 kHz). Separate 'go' and 'return' cables, 8 or 14 pairs/36 lb, are used, and the basic supergroups in the frequency range 312–552 kHz are translated to the line frequency range by means of supergroup modulating equipment (564 kHz carrier).

These cables have also been successfully used to provide short tie circuits between supergroup distribution frames in neighbouring repeater stations in large cities. No modulating equipment is required for this application, the basic supergroups being transmitted directly, but the increased crosstalk in the frequency range 312–552 kHz limits the length of such ties.

*Larger capacity systems.* Some European countries have developed carrier quad cables giving 120 circuits; refined techniques of cable design (using polystyrene or polythene insulation), manufacture and installation, give the necessary lower attenuation and reduced crosstalk couplings to permit operation at frequencies up to 552 kHz.

### Coaxial Cable

*375-type systems.* The coaxial cable most commonly used on the main trunk routes is the well known 375-type, and line systems using this cable have been standardized in many countries. The coaxial tube consists of an outer conductor, 0·375″ internal diameter, with a centre conductor located accurately within the tube by means of polythene disks at 1·3 inch intervals; the dielectric is thus mainly air (see Fig. 1). In the United Kingdom cables having up 8 tubes are available, whilst in the United States 20 tube cables are coming into use.

4 and 6 MHz coaxial systems have been standardized internationally and are in use in several countries, whilst in the United States 8 MHz systems are widely used. Systems using line frequencies up to 12 MHz (2700-circuit capacity) with repeaters spaced at 3 mile

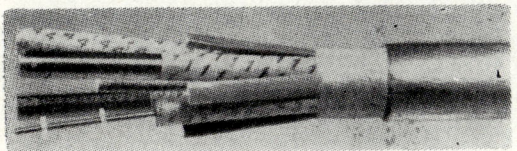

Fig. 1

intervals, are in use in the United Kingdom and elsewhere on heavy traffic trunk routes, and these systems could if necessary be used alternatively for the provision of 900 circuits together with a 625-line television channel (5·5 MHz video bandwidth).

In the United Kingdom the existing 4 MHz (Simpson and Collier 1957) and 12 MHz (Bordiss and Davis 1961) systems use valves, intermediate repeaters being housed in surface buildings. Systems now being installed are, however, transistor operated, and the intermediate repeaters are designed to be housed in buried boxes (see Fig. 2). In the United States, a transistor 18 Mc/s system has been developed with buried repeaters at intervals of 2 miles.

375 type cable possibly be further exploited by extending the transmitted frequency range to perhaps 45 MHz or even 100 MHz.

*174-type systems.* Small diameter tube coaxial cables (174-type) are being used extensively for short and medium distance trunk routes and systems have been standardized internationally providing a bandwidth up to 1·3 MHz (300-circuit capacity) and 4 MHz (960 circuit capacity). The cable is essentially air-spaced, the inner conductor being located accurately within the outer conductor,

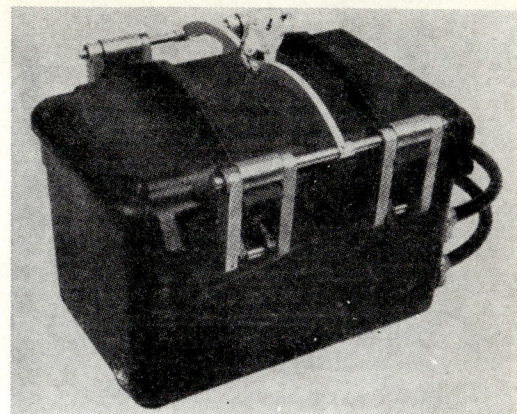

Fig. 2

different manufacturers adopting different methods. The outer conductor has an internal diameter of 0·174″.

Two steel tapes are wrapped helically around the outer conductor to reduce crosstalk at lower frequencies and add mechanical strength. Cables having up to 12 tubes are available, with interstice pairs for speakers, supervisory and alarm systems (see Fig. 3).

The 1·3 MHz (Endersby and Sixsmith 1962) and 4 MHz systems have buried transistor repeaters (see Fig. 4) spaced at 3·5 and 2·5 mile intervals respectively. A 12 MHz system (2700 circuit capacity) is under development and will have repeaters spaced at about 1·5 miles.

### Radio Relay Systems

*General.* The United Kingdom coaxial cable network which at present carries the major proportion of the telephony traffic on the trunk routes, is now being supplemented with microwave radio relay systems, and present plans are to build up a radio relay network of comparable circuit capacity to that of the cable network.

Each radio relay link provides a number of broad-band channels which can be used for telephony or 625-line television signals as explained in a later paragraph.

Early radio-relay systems operated in the v.h.f. band and had a limited traffic capacity. Subsequent developments have enabled higher frequencies to be used in the u.h.f. and s.h.f. bands thereby substantially increasing traffic capacity. Current equipment designs are making increasing use of solid state devices.

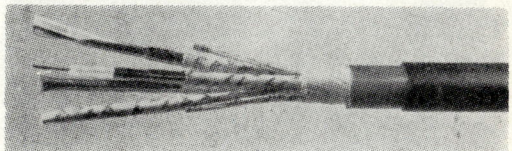

Fig. 3

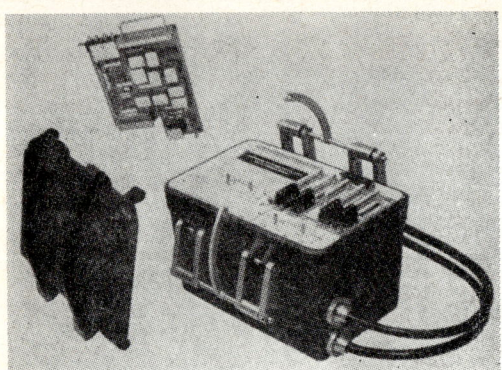

Fig. 4

*V.H.F. systems.* In the United Kingdom trunk network, v.h.f. radio-relay links have been used on a small scale to provide circuits to off-shore islands, such as the Scilly Isles and the Hebrides. They operate in the band between 150 and 185 MHz and have a traffic capacity of up to 48 telephone circuits.

Radio propagation at these frequencies is relatively tolerant of a small amount of obstruction in the radio path, and whilst line-of-sight paths are desirable, beyond-the-horizon working is feasible in certain circumstances. Path lengths of up to about 50 miles are possible. Because of these characteristics the v.h.f. band is widely used by mobile radio systems and the broadcasting services, thus restricting their use for telephony radio-relay systems.

Rhombic aerials are generally provided, separate transmit and receive aerials being required for each direction of transmission from a station. Protection against loss of traffic due to equipment failure is provided by duplication of the transmitting and receiving equipment at each station, and by providing automatic change-over facilities.

*Microwave Systems*

Microwave radio-relay links operate at radio frequencies above 1000 MHz (1 GHz) and have a large traffic-carrying capacity. Propagation of radio waves at these frequencies has much in common with that of light waves, and it is essential that radio paths between adjacent stations are unobstructed. In addition, sufficient clearance above all features of the intervening terrain must be provided, to avoid losses due to diffraction, and also to prevent obstruction which might otherwise occur during very occasional adverse meteorological conditions that unfavourably modify the normal path of the radio waves. With suitable choice of site on high ground these conditions are obtained, in general, with radio-relay stations spaced 25 to 30 miles apart.

The radio frequencies available to the British Post Office for microwave radio-relay links are:

(i) 1700–1900 MHz ⎫ 2 GHz band
(ii) 1900–2300 MHz ⎭
(iii) 3770–4200 MHz    4 GHz band
(iv) 5850–6425 MHz ⎫ 6 GHz band
(v) 6425–7110 MHz ⎭
(vi) 10700–11700 MHz  11 GHz band.

Equipment working in each of the first four frequency ranges is already in operation (see Fig. 5), and equipment working in the fifth range (6425–7110 MHz) is being installed. The 11 GHz band remains to be exploited; the main use for systems operating in this band will probably be to provide short-distance links from large main centres, such as London or Birmingham, to local centres.

The total number of broadband channels that can be accommodated in each direction of transmission in these frequency bands on any one route is as follows:

1700–1900 MHz: 2 television or 6 multichannel telephony
1900–2300 MHz: 6 television or 6 multichannel telephony
3770–4200 MHz: 6 television or 6 multichannel telephony
5850–6425 MHz: 8 television or 8 multichannel telephony
6425–7110 MHz: 16 television or 16 multichannel telephony
10700–11700 MHz: 12 television or 12 multichannel telephony

Fig. 5

The traffic-carrying capacity of each broadband channel is as follows:

1700–1900 MHz equipment: 625-line colour television, or 300 telephone circuits.
1900–2300 MHz equipment: 625-line colour television, or 600 or 960 telephone circuits.
3770–4200 MHz equipment: 625-line colour television, or 960 or 1800 telephone circuits.
5850–6425 MHz equipment: 625-line colour television, or 1800 telephone circuits.
6425–7110 MHz equipment: 625-line colour television, or 960 telephone circuits.

Future 11 GHz equipment will carry one 625-line colour television channel or up to 960 telephone circuits per broadband channel.

About a quarter of the total channel capacity of a link is allocated on a shared basis as standby or 'protection' channels to guard against loss of traffic due to failure of equipment on a channel in service; rapid-acting switches at each end of the link automatically replace the failed channel by a protection channel.

The most important future development will be the improvement of solid-state techniques to enable higher r.f. powers to be obtained from transmitters and lower noise factors from receivers.

Other likely developments include the extension of radio-relay systems to higher frequency bands and possibly, the design of systems to carry p.c.m. signals.

*Terminal Translating Equipment*

*Channel translating equipment.* Channel translating equipment (see Fig. 6) is used to assemble the voice channels for transmission over all forms of trunk, line and radio-relay systems.

Twelve audio circuits each having a nominal bandwidth of 4 kHz are assembled into the band 60–108 kc/s to form a basic group, the overall characteristics of which were standardized internationally many years ago.

The filters used in the assembly process may be of the quartz crystal, inductor/capacitor or electromechanical types. In some designs the channels are translated directly to their final positions in the 60–108 kHz band, whereas in other designs the channels are first assembled into three identical subgroups of four channels before final translation to the group band.

*Group, supergroup and broadband translating equipment.* For transmission over high-circuit-capacity coaxial line or radio-relay systems, the basic 12-circuit groups are further translated into the appropriate line or baseband frequency spectrum. The group translating equipment assembles five 12-circuit groups into the basic supergroup frequency range 312–552 kHz. These basic supergroups are then assembled by means of supergroup, hypergroup or broadband translating equipment, as necessary for application to the line or radio equipment.

*Carrier generating equipment.* In the United Kingdom, the carrier frequencies required for these translation processes are derived from a master oscillator by means of harmonic generators and conventional multiplication and division processes. Free-running crystal-controlled master oscillators, using BT- or GT-cut 124 kHz crystals having a long-term frequency stability of 2 parts in $10^7$ form the basis of most United Kingdom carrier generating equipments.

With the introduction of 12 MHz coaxial-line and the possibility of further increases in line frequencies, the

Fig. 6

frequency stability provided by this generating equipment was marginal and in consequence new carrier-generating equipment (Jones and Andrew 1964; McAllan 1964) has been developed to provide adequate stability. Three oscillator designs are now being installed in the U.K., using 2·48 MHz AT-cut, 4·96 MHz BT-cut and 64 kHz NT-cut crystals respectively. The advantages of these crystals is that their ageing period is short and that their frequency stability at the temperature-inversion point is excellent. Provided that the crystal-oven temperature is controlled within close limits, long-term frequency stability of 5 parts in $10^8$ per month, or better, should be achieved.

In the United Kingdom, frequency-generating equipments are compared with a nationally distributed 60 kHz pilot which is maintained to within 1 or 2 parts in $10^8$, thus ensuring a high standard of frequency accuracy throughout the network.

*Television equipment.* For short distances, up to about 25 miles, the direct transmission of video signals over coaxial cables (Hale and McDiarmid 1963) is generally the least expensive method. Because the screening properties of a coaxial cable become increasingly less effective at low frequencies, it is necessary, for distances longer than about 25 miles, to translate the video signal into a higher frequency band in the line-frequency spectrum if interference from external sources is to be kept to tolerable levels; this process produces its own distortion and is a surprisingly difficult and expensive operation. A number of systems (Halsey and Williams 1952) are however, in service which are suitable for the transmission of 405-line monochrome television on the standard British Post Office 4 MHz coaxial-cable systems. Microwave radio links have the advantage over coaxial cables in that the video signal modulates the intermediate-frequency carrier without prior translation.

625-line monochrome and colour television, requires a video-bandwidth defined up to about 6 MHz, and the standard 4 MHz coaxial cable system is inadequate. The general pattern of provision is therefore by microwave radio for long distances, and by direct transmission of video over coaxial cable for shorter distances. Very short temporary links, e.g. for outside broadcasts, can be provided by microwave radio or by balanced video transmission over local cables and unloaded-junction cables.

*Acknowledgements.* Acknowledgments are made to the Senior Director of Engineering of the General Post Office for permission to publish information contained in this paper, and to the Institution of Electrical Engineers for permission to quote extracts from the Proceedings, I.E.E., Vol. 111.

*See also:* Local networks. Telecommunication system planning, international.

*Bibliography*

BORDISS H. J. K. and DAVIES A.P. (1961) *A 12-Mc/s coaxial line equipment – CEL No 8A, Post Office Elect. Engrs. J.* **54**, Part 2, 73.

CHANDLER T. W. (1964) *Modern three and twelve circuit open-wire carrier telephone systems*, I.E.E. Conf. Transmission Aspects of Communications Networks, 24th Feb.

ENDERSBY J. C. and SIXSMITH J. (1962) *Coaxial line equipment for small diameter cables, Post Office Elect. Engrs. J.* **55**, Part 1, 44.

HALE H. S. and McDIARMID I. F. (1963) *Video transmission system for use with coaxial cable, Proc. I.E.E.* **110**, Part 8, 1329.

HALSEY R. J. and WILLIAMS H. (1952) *The Birmingham – Manchester – Holme Moss television cable system, Proc. I.E.E.* **99**, Part IIIA, 398.

JONES J. D. C. and ANDREW J. E. (1964) *Transistor operated carrier generating equipment with graded protection facilities*, I.E.E. Conf. Transmission Aspects of Communications Networks, 24th Feb.

McALLAN J. (1964) *New techniques in carrier supply for f.d.m. telephony*, I.E.E. Conf. Transmission Aspects of Communications Networks, 24th Feb.

McPHAIL D. C. (1964) *A fully transistorized 12-channel openwire carrier system*, I.E.E. Conf. Transmission Aspects of Communications Networks, 24th Feb.

PAOLA N. J. (1964) *Exploiting the open-wire spectrum up to 300 kilocycles per second*, I.E.E. Conf. Transmission Aspects of Communications Networks, 24th Feb.

SIMPSON W. G. and COLLIER M. E. (1957) *A new 4-Mc/s coaxial line equipment – CEL No 6A, Post Office Elect. Engrs J.* **50**, Part 1, 24.

R. H. FRANKLIN

# L

**LANGUAGE VARIETIES: LANGUAGE AND DIALECT.** *Language communities.* The branch of linguistics which deals with linguistic patterning among peoples is termed *institutional linguistics*. Although closely allied to descriptive linguistics, institutional linguistics is primarily concerned with variety in and of languages and with the correlations of linguistic variation and other classifications in society.

The category *'language'* may be defined by both linguistic and extralinguistic criteria. Among the latter is the concept introduced by institutional linguistics of *language community*. A language community may be said to comprise all those speakers who claim to speak the same language. Several distinct types of language community may thus be recognized in different parts of the world.

a) The English language community, for example, includes, according to this definition, Britain, her ex-colonial and empire territories and the USA, and is characterized by widespread mutual intelligibility between its speakers, in spite of its geographical discontinuity.

b) The Chinese on the other hand includes at least six mutually incomprehensible varieties which might otherwise be classified as separate languages. Its people are unified by an official spoken language, they have a common writing system and literature, and are governed by a powerful centralized political administration.

c) Two further instances may be cited in which although the elements of language community exist, the institutional status of any language is unrecognized.

i) The Scandinavian languages constitute independent language communities despite their mutual intelligibility and the close cultural and geographic relationship of Denmark, Norway and Sweden.

ii) The Romance group has a common parent and mutually intelligible dialects in border regions, but the institutionalized language communities remain distinctively Italian, Spanish and French.

A language may also be considered to be coextensive with a people or a political unity. Languages such as Malay, which has a majority of overseas speakers, cut across such definitions. Languages of trade and culture may be spoken across the world by speakers who have little or no contact with the country and people whose native language they ordinarily use.

*Mutual intelligibility.* The definition of 'language' by objective linguistic criteria mainly rests upon the notion of *mutual intelligibility*. A 'language' is thus said to exist when effective vocal communication can be established between two speakers. This concept is subject to considerable limitation however. Any language which is distributed over a large territory can be demonstrated to contain many varieties sufficiently divergent as to be either partly or completely incomprehensible to other speakers of the same language. An instance of the variability of inter-dialectal comprehension overtly recognized within a language community is given by Hockett. He cites tribal communities of West Africa where certain varieties are known as 'two-day dialect' or 'one-week dialect', depending on the time taken by neighbouring villages to achieve communication for everyday purposes. In the extreme case, the Dane and the Norwegian, or the Russian and the Pole, are reasonably comprehensible to each other without translation or resort to a common language.

A more rigorous definition admits to membership of a language all those varieties between which comprehension exists in an unbroken chain, provided that the constituent members share a common standard language. Thus the language continuum Flemish—Dutch—German—Swiss(-German) can be divided into recognized constituents of the order of languages, even though a series of mutually intelligible varieties may be traced from the North Sea to the Alps.

*Dialect and idiolect.* These major internal varieties in languages are termed *dialects*. Every speaker learns a particular variety of his language, which is largely determined by the region of his birth and early life. The extent and distribution of dialectal characteristics is affected by physical isolation of communities, political or religious division, social distance and mobility, all of which promote or inhibit the freedom of communication within a language community. Each language may therefore be analysed as a *dialect continuum* in which contiguous dialects exhibit closer correspondences of form than those members of the continuum which are either topographically or socially far removed. Differences between related dialects are evident at all levels of language, but local and social differentiation is more apparent in phonetic and phonological patterning than in lexical or morphological patterning. Thus adjacent dialects are never absolutely distinct from each other. Dialects which differ quite markedly in phonological inventory and exponence may show more or less complete correspondence in lexis and other levels.

The distribution of dialectal varieties patterns with socio-economic factors to define distinctive groups within a given community. In all these groups personal variations occur. The term *idiolect* has been introduced to describe individual usages. Two main aspects of the idiolect concern the linguist, namely the use of *register* and *style*. Style is variation with reference to the interpersonal tension between speaker and listener, ranging from most formal, e.g. in reading a list of minimal pairs, to most spontaneous, as in familiar discourse. Register

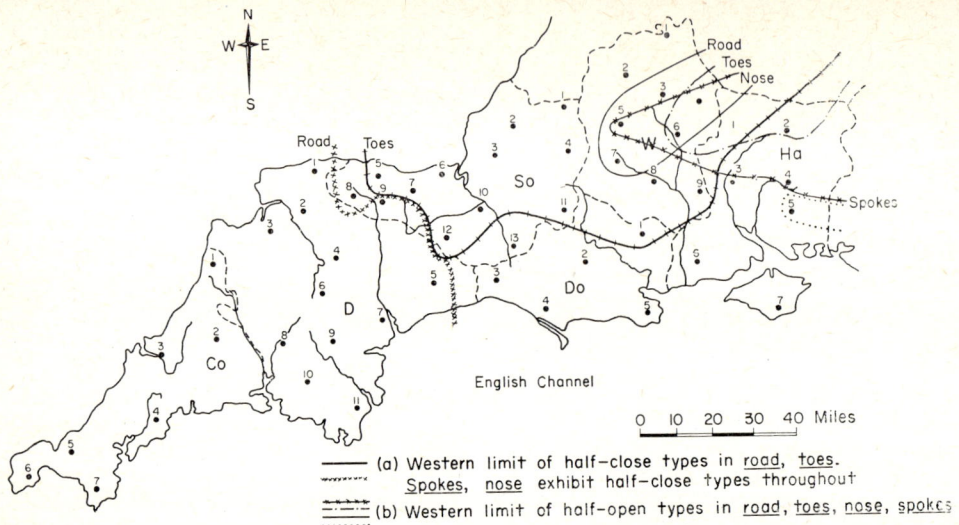

FIG. 1. *The distribution of isoglosses for nose, road, spokes and toes in the dialects of south-west-England (based on unpublished material collected for the survey of English Dialects, by permission of the director, Prof. H. Orton).*

covers variations conditioned by social context, e.g. the register of the lawyer in the courtroom, which contrasts with registers appropriate to the club or domestic environment. All idiolects thus select from a potential range of style and register in a given community, and it is his selection between these categories of variety which, in addition to idiosyncratic habits of pronunciation, marks the speech of the individual in a dialect-speaking community.

*Divergence and merging.* The distributional patterning of dialects illustrates various aspects of the characteristic changefulness of language. In isolation, dialects evolve at various rates of change and in different directions. This can readily be illustrated by comparing, for example, the development of the dialects exported to North America in the seventeenth century and after with their counterparts in England today. Even in a restricted set of words over a limited region the distribution of the respective forms may not be coterritorial. Figure 1 shows the patterning of the stressed vowels in such a set in the south west of England. Maps like this, which illuminate the lack of uniformity in dialect regions, give rise to the dictum that each form has its own history.

Changes spread more or less rapidly from a particular centre in various directions favourable to them. They are either accepted or resisted, and in time their distribution thus becomes irregular. In some directions at any time a change may advance rapidly forward; in others it may encounter strong opposition or recede in the face of other developments from different innovating centres. At its source, an innovation may have completely supplanted an original form, but at successive points removed from the centre, other forms may coexist with varying chances of success. A distributional display of the dynamics of change and borrowing may indicate that a change

has spread evenly on all fronts. But the possibility is equally likely that an innovating centre may be outside the territory covered by the borrowed feature, the centre having been included in the subsequent expansion of forms emanating from other points of origin.

It sometimes happens that history permits the dialects of a language community to remain in comparative isolation for such great lengths of time that the divergences which develop interfere with mutual intelligibility within the community. This occurred in Chinese. But dialects show an opposite tendency when regional independence gives way to improved communications. Unifying pressures may be exerted on a language so that one prestigious dialect expands at the expense of others which may either recede or disappear. Linguistic diversification is thus favoured or retarded by social forces.

Linguistic uniformity and loyalty have long been recognized as practical adjuncts of political and cultural domination. Wherever a single group in a community gains supremacy over an area greater than its regional origin, the language of that people tends to supplant that of the subjected territories. Politicians have shown a keen awareness of the advantages of linguistic uniformity to central government. In 1807, for example, the post-revolutionary régime in France conducted a linguistic survey to assess the influence of regional dialects. As a result of its findings, the government posted teachers of standard French to those departments where regional variation hindered the ready assimilation of government directives. The provincial dialects were in fact declared to be counter-revolutionary. At the same period, Scandinavian dialects were being actively fostered to counteract the cultural infiltration of northern Europe by Germany. In this century, linguistic divergence has been influenced by unifying trends in China and India.

The complete cycle of divergence and merging may be

illustrated in Chinese. The language which was originally restricted to a small part of China gradually spread over a vast territory by conquest, trade and cultural pre-eminence. This expansion inevitably loosened the ties which held together the original group. Contact between its members became more tenuous in time, so that a language community which had at one phase been more or less uniform became fragmented. The various groups eventually lost the mutual intelligibility which once united them, and developed independently. This evolutionary cycle may then take one of two courses. The dialect communities which have emerged may develop into separate language communities, as with Flemish and Dutch. Alternatively a spoken lingua franca may emerge. This was the course taken by the Chinese, where a form of northern dialect has been adopted as the common language.

The individual behaves in ways which are analogous to the divergence and merging in language communities. Every individual possesses attributes for various rôles, in some situations acting as a model, and in others as an imitator. He may move away from the influence of one group and into that of some other, successively integrating into new situations governed by different social factors. His facility for adaptation hardly ceases through life. Various groups are linked by members who act as mediators. Thus a father may be unconsciously adopting the patterns of his occupational group, whilst at the same time mediating to his family. Individual membership of a language community therefore demands flexibility not only for interpreting a considerable range of varieties, but also for modifying personal patterns according to a constantly changing environment.

Both the individual then, and the larger social constructs in which individuals collectively function, have dual rôles as imitators and imitated. But the privileged individual most often acts as a model for the unprivileged, and the social minority is most susceptible to the influence of the dominant group. Social forces reflected in language divergence and merging have been described as 'the direction of convergence of a manifold of asymmetries in social valuation, such as of the many to the few, the class to the mass, the holy to the pious, the learned to the people, the market to the farm, the town to the country, the university to the school, the metropolis to the province, the precedent to the principle, the form to the meaning'. The arrangement and tension between such polarities in society partly determine the potential success or failure of linguistic innovation. From the linguistic point of view, however, the study of dialectal variety and patterning establishes that, regardless of external influences, certain forms spread more readily than others, and some are inherently resistant to change. *A priori* reasons for this are difficult to analyse, but techniques for the actual observation of trends in linguistic change between generations and social classes have recently been refined.

For example, dialectologists in the United States have found that certain pressures currently affect the distribution of *r* in final and pre-consonantal positions. In the most conservative east coast dialects *r* is pronounced in these positions with a retracted and constricted articulation, whereas this feature is absent from the dialects of the industrial north east Midland region, where *r* is not pronounced at all in final and preconsonantal positions. Recent investigations in other regions have shown that the acceptance or rejection of this among other features of pronunciation closely corresponds with social groupings. Older people are still influenced by the *r*-dialects of the east, whilst younger generations follow the *r*-less dialects of the Midlands. The reason for this linguistic development is the recognition by the younger strata in society of a shift in the prestige centre away from the east coast to the rapidly expanding industrial cities inland. The significance of these results is that they isolate distributional criteria which have operated on the dialects quite independently of geographical factors.

*Isogloss, mapping.* The distribution of linguistic variants is most clearly revealed by a display of features recorded on large-scale maps. A separate branch of dialectology has refined the procedures of this aspect of the ordering of dialect materials, the term for which is *linguistic geography*. The dialects of a number of countries have been represented by collections of maps, generally called *dialect atlases*.

The prime object of traditional investigations was the territorial differentiation of dialects. Before maps were used for this purpose, translations of standard texts and

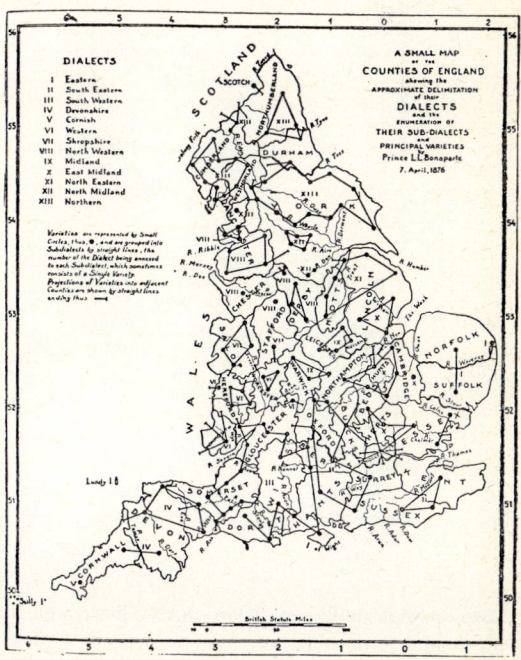

FIG. 2. *Prince L. L. Bonaparte's 'Small map'. (Reproduced from S. Pop, La Dialectologie. The original, in colour, is in the British Museum.)*

17*

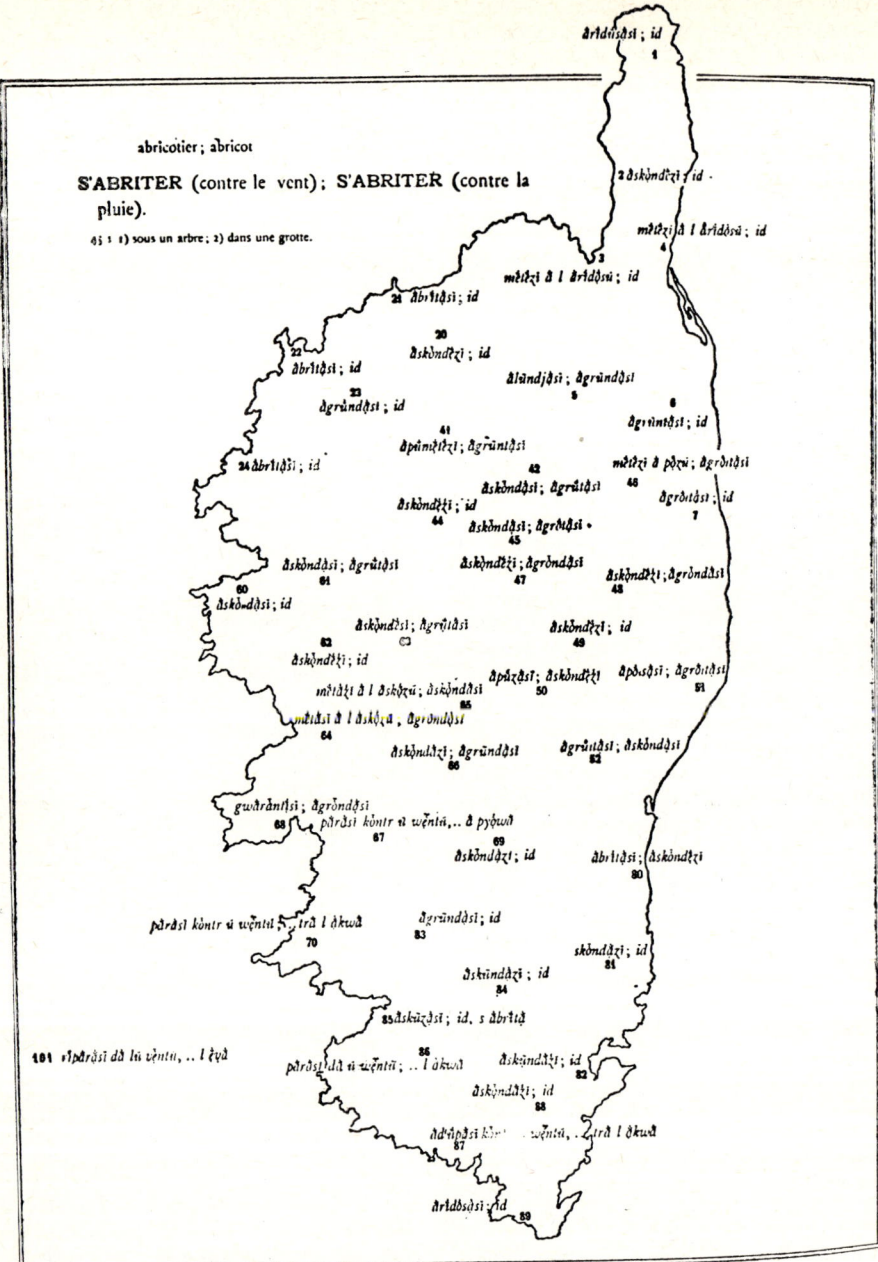

Fig. 3. J. Gilliéron and E. Edmont, L'Atlas linguistique de la France: Corse. (Reproduced from S. Pop, La Dialectologie.)

glossaries were published. These merely illustrated the individual dialects recorded, and comparative work on data from more numerous sources was impossible. Proposals for mapping dialectal variation were made to the French Royal Society of Antiquaries in 1814. Occasional maps were published, such as Prince Bonaparte's 1876 'Small Map', which represented the first attempt to subdivide the dialects of England, and inspired the more detailed work of A. J. Ellis, see Fig. 2. The first atlas, however, was the work of J. Gilliéron, entitled *Petit atlas phonétique du Valais roman* (1880). A year later G. Wenker published his *Sprachtlas von Nord- und Mittel-*

*deutschland*. These pioneers achieved dense coverage of the regions they investigated, through the agency of a single fieldworker in Gilliéron's subsequent *Atlas linguistique de la France*, and mainly by postal questionnaire in the case of Wenker. The advantages of the map as against earlier word lists and idiom inventories are obvious. A large-scale map makes possible the immediate comparison of forms distributed over a considerable territory. Gilliéron's maps included 639 numbered localities at each of which the phonetic transcription recorded by his fieldworker E. Edmont, in 1400 words and phrases, is printed directly and unretouched on separate plates, see Fig. 3. Other atlases have used printed symbols, so reducing the size of the maps without loss of clarity, and assisting interpretation of the data by the use of colour. Linguistic atlases have been published in most European countries, in America and elsewhere. More than 70 completed or projected atlases were described by Pop in 1950.

The dialect map is more than merely a graphic method of representing the geographical distribution of linguistic variation. It has been developed as a means of further analysis. The map of a single feature reveals an aspect of the relatedness of territorial units within a language community, and research has been concentrated upon finding reliable methods of evaluating the correspondences and divergences of multiple features. The common notion of the dialect as a unique and discrete entity is not immediately borne out when comparison is made between large numbers of pages in a linguistic atlas. When dialectologists first realized this fact, controversy arose as to the propriety of using the term 'dialect' to represent any kind of reality. Gaston Paris led an extremist group in the Romance field, which denied the existence of 'dialects': for them only the dialect continuum was real, and this continuum could not be divided into discrete constituents.

However, in spite of theoretical difficulties in making absolute distinctions between dialects, cartographic displays of linguistic features revealed demarcations in a way which had previously been impossible, and they continue to be utilized. The maps present evidence in such a way that it proves irresistible to draw lines signifying distribution patterns. Analogous with those drawn on weather maps, these lines on a dialect map are termed *isoglosses*. Unlike the isobar in meteorology, however, which joins points of equal atmospheric pressure, the isogloss is not usually drawn through points where similar linguistic features occur. It is more akin to a political boundary in that it includes territory uniform in respect of the linguistic form represented. The function of the isogloss is thus to show the boundaries between the territories of different features, which correspond with lines of weakness in communication.

The interpretation of isogloss patterning is a statistical procedure, since agreements between a number of features spread over a given tract of territory are at best only partial. When there is approximate correspondence for the distribution of a significant number of features, however, and the respective isoglosses follow roughly the same course, this phenomenon is referred to as *bundling*. The correlation of bundles of isoglosses and extralinguistic factors forms the basis for setting up dialect areas, which may subsequently be subdivided or expanded in accordance with the divergent patterns established by consideration of other feature-scatters. The overlapping configurations of the isoglosses within the territory of a language community show that both linguistic and physical barriers to communication are seldom complete. Such obstacles as do occur normally have the effect of retarding, rather than completely blocking, the territorial spread of a feature.

Interpretation of any isogloss must therefore be made only after careful consideration of a wide range of formal criteria. A bundle of features may predict the occurrence of other features following similar trends, but no absolute quantization is derivable, even from a sample of high statistical probability. The reason for this lies a) in the potential diversity of a bundle of features, and, possibly more importantly, b) in the absence of rigorous techniques for selecting the features to be represented by isoglosses.

a) The boundaries represented by certain isoglosses may be static over long periods of time. Others, which may coincide with the same bundle, may be transient, lending only temporary support to a possible dialect boundary. The maps so far produced in atlases give no indication of the potential internal structuring of bundles: nor can they indicate future directional trends. Some included forms may be in an expanding phase, whilst others may be recessive, so that the fact that they correspond when recorded by a fieldworker at a given time may be merely incidental. It is unfortunately the case that a line once drawn across a map gives substance to the notion of absolute divisions between adjacent localities, when it is empirically obvious that only gradual transitions occur within the language community. It must also be noted that a fieldworker can only sample the dialects of a language community. Lines drawn on a map between separate points of investigation are therefore to be interpreted as representing the probable state of affairs on the ground. Verification of their accuracy can only be made by intensive coverage. Nevertheless, the concept of the isogloss has been proved useful as a diagnostic for the relative degree of correspondence between topographical locations. Research is likely to enhance the utility of the isogloss through developing techniques of statistical validation.

b) The structure of isogloss bundles has engaged increasing attention in recent years. Whilst bundling is still regarded as a self-evident demarcation of dialect areas for many dialectologists, others have argued that a boundary based on an arbitrary selection of forms is invalid, since the configurations produced are predetermined by the restrictions imposed on the choice of inventory. Some scholars have attempted to show that isoglosses of structural significance take precedence over other criteria in cutting up a language continuum. Others have discovered important distributions based on typological comparison. Figure 4 shows the contrasting distributional display obtained when maps based on purely phonetic data are compared with those constructed from a structural analysis of each dialect. These approaches all produce reformulations of the data, but no single one has proved decisive. The view that discrete dialects are no more than a conventional assumption however, need not preclude re-interpretations of material.

Efforts have been made to establish criteria for evaluating isoglosses by reference to a) density, b) direction and c) incidence. Procedures have been based on the possibility of measurement and numerical notation for the ground covered and population affected. The theory rests partly on the premise that a linguistic atlas provides enough examples for statistical validation of the measurements taken, thus discounting the acknowledged arbitrariness of selection criteria.

a) When the number of isoglosses per unit length has been observed on a line drawn between given points, an objective statement can be formulated as to the even spread or concentration of the intersections on that line by the isoglosses. Correlations with population distribution can be validated.

b) Significance may be attached to the general trend of isoglosses. In the 19th century, A. J. Ellis apportioned the main divisions of the English dialects according to ten 'Transverse Lines' (isoglosses) from west to east, see Fig. 5. Ivič states that west-east isoglosses outnumber north-south trends in Gallo-Romance, German and Russian, whereas in South Slavonic, NNE-SSW isoglosses are most prevalent.

c) Isoglosses contrast in other ways. They may either intersect or include those produced by other forms. Social factors may also be considered. Calculations of the number of lines of communication, e.g. highways, railroads etc., crossed by each isogloss in a given region have been made. It has been shown on a limited scale that major isoglosses intersect other communication channels rather infrequently, but where isoglosses bundle it is predictable that troughs will occur in other means of communication. Isoglosses which are crossed by numerous people in their daily lives present further correlative possibilities for investigation.

*Social dialects and standards.* The spatial distribution of dialects has hitherto been central to dialectology, but some attention has been given to another important aspect of variation within language communities, namely the correlation of linguistic and socio-economic parameters. Socially determined distinctions of vocal behaviour have been recognized for a long time. The 18th century pastor of Montreux, P. Bridel, noted in

FIG. 4. Weinreich's *The Vowel in 'Man' in Language X*. Map 1: Traditional; Map 2: Structural. On map 2, a continuous single line divides areas with different phonemic inventories (shaded area distinguishing vowel length, unshaded area not distinguishing it). The double line separates areas using different phonemes in this word (difference of distribution). The dotted line separates allophonic differences.

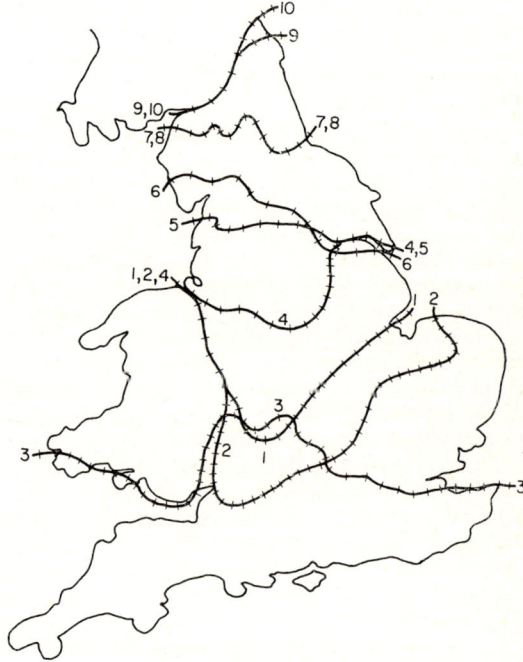

FIG. 5. English Dialect Districts according to A. J. Ellis, 1887; (reproduced from A. J. Ellis *On Early English Pronunciation: Pt. V, The Existing Phonology of English Dialects*. London, 1889).

The isoglosses determining Ellis's main dialect divisions are:

1. n. limit of [sʌm] *some*. [sʌm] reappears n. of line 8.
2. s. limit of [sʌm] *some*. Line 9 represents n. limit.
3. n. limit of retroflex *r* [ɽ].
4. s. limit of [t'] or [t'θ] for definite article. [ðə] returns n. of line 7.
5. n limit of [t'θ] in definite article.
6. s. limit of [huːs] *house*, and n. limit of [haus].
10. Limit of English and Lowland Scots.

his study of the Suisse romande patois that a barrier had arisen between the upper class who spoke French and the local people who had the patois. Louis Gauchat noted variation between different age-groups in his account of the dialect of Charmey, Switzerland, in 1899. The pressures of social conditions on the dialect of Angoumois were noted by A-L. Terracher, whose atlas included geographical, historical and social maps. Hans Kurath distinguished the informants for the *Linguistic Atlas of New England* (1939 – 42) according to their education and age. As yet, however, no full-scale assessment of socio-linguistic correlates has been attempted over anything like the same territorial range as that covered by atlases of folk speech. However, limited studies on these lines have recently been made in the United States and in Germany.

Language communities vary from relatively simple to highly complex structures. Tribal society is characterized by low diversification, minimal occupational specialization and infrequent contacts beyond immediate intra-tribal relationships. Language variation is limited, though stylistic differences are evident in ceremonial usage and story-telling for example. It has been found, however, that stylistic and dialectal diversification increase as the economic base of a society expands. Social forces, such as the division of people into agricultural or industrial specializations, stratification into a rigid class-system in which groups and individuals may be at varying stages of integration, and the development of urban regional centres, encourage the fragmentation of language varieties. The rural speaker tends to have less stylistic range than his urban counterpart and fewer register possibilities as a result of his reduced contact with a diversified society and the absence of the greater differences of environmental accompaniment in daily life to which the urbanite is required to adapt. Rural members of a speech community therefore tend to be predominantly conservative, and in remote regions what De Saussure termed *l'esprit de clocher*, or parochialism, is the most powerful cultural force. Urban life is subjected to a similar pressure, but the more mixed the segment of society in which a speaker functions, the weaker are parochial influences, and the stronger is *la force d'intercourse*, or pressures of inter-communication.

Traditional dialectology has tended to disregard intra-dialectal variation, being preoccupied with problems arising from the study of unified structures abstracted from the speech community. Comparative work on this basis has, in the main, been exclusively *diachronic*, and aberrant forms have been generally ascribed to a fundamental tendency in language for 'drift', or sporadic, and indeterminate change. Attention has only recently been given to internal variation within dialect communities. The hypothesis has been advanced that what may have been disposed of as random or 'free' variation in traditional descriptions may, if examined in a wider context, reveal a coherent structure congruent with other elements in social organization. Socio-stylistic systems of this type have been termed *sociolects*.

Social dialects have been considered to constitute part of a *communication matrix* which by definition includes not only the varieties of the given language spoken in a language community, but also the languages of minorities within the same speech community who are bilingual. Thus in Wales, Welsh has equivalent functional status with the local dialects of English in some parts, and must be considered as an integral part of the communication matrix of that region. Thus Welsh may be used in a familiar context with other Welsh speakers, but in the presence of other speakers of indeterminate linguistic affinities, a regional dialect of English, approximating to standard, may be substituted. Welsh and English are considered to be separate *codes* within the same matrix then, and the dialects of both to be *subcodes*. This approach is thus more comprehensive in scope than that of the traditional study of language communities. Fundamental to it is the view that a language is a composite comprising functionally related systems wholly describable only in terms of all the systems (both 'codes' and 'subcodes') included. It brings into prominence the dialects of those groups in society which lie between the extremes of the speakers of standards and the rural and 'traditional' dialect speakers. It is believed by some linguists that these intermediate classes act as mediators of change in the language community.

The student of dialects traditionally investigates local variation in a predetermined environment. That is, he defines the sort of dialects he is prepared to examine in advance, e.g. the fishing communities of Nova Scotia, or the indigenous working class of a given urban community. The status of the dialect within the language community is often loosely defined, and based on insufficient extralinguistic data. Descriptions of dialects which identify social groups cannot proceed adequately until the basic elements which combine to stratify and segment the social continuum have been rigorously defined. Most significant are race-cultural background, age, education, occupational class, parentage, rural–urban environment, marital status and sex. Class stratification can only be reliably established after conflation of all such taxonomic criteria. Each factor must be weighted according to priorities predetermined by the various societies investigated. Work in comparative sociology demonstrates that although unrelated societies in different parts of the world rank the individual by similar criteria and arrive at broadly the same classifications, they differ in regard to the respective values attached to the various criteria. For this reason, it is essential that all of the criteria should be included in the specification of the segment of the 'universe' to be analysed.

Besides the careful consideration of the extralinguistic environment, the study of social dialects compels an examination of stylistic varieties. Preliminary work shows that this aspect of variation is one of the most positive indicators of urban versus rural dialect. In a study of New York City dialect, Labov set up a series of empirically determined norms, designed to grade style from a maximal degree of formality, as in reading for example, to maximal informality, as in conversation with a third person. Labov showed that stylistic variation correlates with social parameters to the extent that sound changes can be reliably predicted from comparisons of the social varieties within a dialect community. He also showed that class structure may be stratified by reference to selected linguistic variables, and that the results of such procedures are borne out by correlations with socio-economic analyses. In Labov's experiments, the incidence of a given feature typically increases or diminishes directly as the degree of formality moves between informal discourse and reading style. His sociostylistic graphs show a well-defined separation between the classes. In some cases, however, intermediate social classes appear to diverge markedly from their expected norms. These deviations predict sound changes, supporting the thesis that such changes are not propagated through the direct influence of the upper class on the lowest, but through the agency of intermediate classes in the social hierarchy. In many accounts of local dialects, deviation from predictable patterns is ascribed to pressure from the standard. Labov's work emphasizes, however, that contact between polar extremes in the linguistic community is normally made indirectly through a chain of intermediaries, and then only as and when social conditions favour inter-class communications.

In many speech communities, a local or regional dialect may be sufficient for almost all purposes of communication. Some speakers of American English, for example, do not feel compelled to adapt utterances to contexts which may range from a formal lecture to discourse about the weather. Other speakers, however, may consciously or otherwise feel bound to make complicated modifications at all linguistic levels between one environment and another. American society has reached a high degree of uniformity, both socially and geographically, so far as linguistic variation is concerned through the rapid industrialization of society, the development of communications, and social mobility. America is predominantly an urban and industrial society where, in the largest cities, the indigenous population forms a numerical and cultural minority. Europe, by contrast, has not attained a similar social fluidity. It has a comparatively well defined class-structure in which differentiated speech forms indicate affinities with local, social and occupational groups. When a language community is fragmented in this way, the varieties which develop interfere with mutual intelligibility so that one particular dialect tends to emerge as being pre-eminently suitable for purposes of communication. When such a dialect has been adopted by large numbers of speakers, it acquires a prestige and may become a goal for the entire language community. Such dialects are termed the *standard language* of the speech community. They are frequently the dialect of the capital city, e.g. the Pekinese form of Chinese or the Parisian variety of French, but they may be a composite of a number of prestigious dialects as in German.

Standardization is normally achieved in grammar and lexis, and, in written language, in orthography also. When a speaker learns a spoken standard which is different from his native dialect, however, phonetic transference often occurs from the regional or social dialect to the standard, so that he may be described as speaking the standard with an *accent*. And in fact much of the provincial speech in industrial countries now consists of accents of a standard rather than traditional dialectal speech, which may vary from the standard at every level.

Britain has a considerable range of regional and social dialects, and a standard language which varies slightly, and only in minor detail, from American usage. Unique to Britain, however, is an accent of the standard which is referred to as *Received Pronunciation* (RP) in technical accounts, but more commonly as 'the Queen's English', 'Public Schools' English', 'Oxford English' or 'BBC English'. The special quality of RP is that it is a regionless accent of English. That is to say, the geographical origins of a speaker of RP remain obscure as with no other accent, even to the ear which has been trained accurately to discriminate between other varieties of spoken English. RP is an indicator of a particular social group, and in particular, it identifies a speaker's educational background, for RP is learnt in the home if the parents speak it, but otherwise it may be acquired at preparatory and public schools or at the Universities of Oxford and Cambridge. Since RP is a correlative of a desirable educational and social status, this accent has greater prestige than any other in Britain. By comparison, other accents are held in low regard, either as evidence of a provincial origin, or even as a mark of a lack of proper education. RP is subject to change, as are other varieties of pronunciation, but it remains the norm at which speakers of British English aim, and in debates as to questions of pronunciation, RP provides the model of what is commonly regarded as 'correct'.

Attempts have been made to define the common characteristics and functions of standards.

a) All share the property termed flexible stability, which is to say that modifications can and do occur in line with cultural changes within the language community. For instance, in the case of the language rivalry in Poland, the capital was moved from Cracow to Warsaw in the Middle Ages, and as a result the dialect of Cracow began to lose the prestige it had enjoyed as the seat of the monarchy, church and University. Standards also typically facilitate intellectualization. That is, they provide a range of styles and registers which allows increasing precision of communication from conversational to scientific requirements.

b) Standards perform several specific functions. They unify in a single language community various otherwise distinct dialect communities. In so doing, they differentiate a community from contingent groups which may be affiliated to other standards. Thirdly, they have a prestige function, acting as a goal for speakers of substandard varieties, and thus reinforcing the unifying function. The referential function of standards is derived from their unifying role, serving to provide a model of correctness for the community. The status as a standard reached by a given variety depends upon its intrinsic properties, upon the function of the standard in the cultural life of the speech community, and upon the attitudes of the people to it.

*See also:* Relations between languages: bilingualism. Relations between languages: lingua franca. Language varieties: stylistics.

*Bibliography*

BLOOMFIELD L. (1935) *Language*, London.
BRIGHT W. O. (1960) *Social dialects and language history*, Current Anthropology, **1**, 5, 424.
CATFORD J. C. (1957) *Vowel-Systems of Scots dialects*, Trans. Phil. Soc. 107.
GARVIN P. L. (1959) *The standard language problem*, Anthropological Linguistics, **1**, 3, 25.
GUMPERZ J. J. (1964) *Types of Linguistic communities*, in *Language in Culture and Society: A Reader in Linguistics and Anthropology* (D. H. Hymes Ed.) New York.
HILL T. (1958) *Institutional Linguistics*, Orbis **7**, 2, 441.
HOCKETT C. F. (1958) *A Course in Modern Linguistics*, New York.
IVIČ P. (1964) *Structure and typology of dialectal differentiation*, Proc. 12th Internat. Congress of Linguistics (H. G. Lunt Ed.) Cambridge, Mass. 1964, The Hague.
KURATH H. (1964) *Interrelation between regional and social dialects*, Proc. 9th Internat. Congress of Linguistics, The Hague.
LABOV W. (1963) *The social motivation of a sound change*, Word, **19**, 3, 273.
LABOV W. (1964) *The Ethnography of Communication* (J. J. Gumperz and D. H. Hymes Eds.) American Anthropologist Spec. pub., Pt. 2, 66, 6.
MARTINET A. (1964) *Elements of General Linguistics* (trans. E. Palmer), London.
MCDAVID R. I. Jr. (1948) *Post-vocalic r in South Carolina: a social analysis*, Am. Speech, **23**, 194.
PARIS G. (1888) in *Revue des patois gallo-romans*, **2**, 161.
POP S. (1950) *La Dialectologie: Aperçu historique and Methodes d'enquêtes linguistiques*, 2 Vols., Paris: Louvain.
RAY P. S. (1962) *Formal procedures of standardization*, Anthropological Linguistics, **4**, 3.
ROBINS R. H. (1964) *General Linguistics: an Introductory Survey*, London.
STANKIEWICZ E. (1957) *On discreteness and continuity in structural dialectology*, Word **13**, 44.
WEINREICH U. (1954) *Is a structural dialectology possible?* Word **10**, 388.

J. T. WRIGHT

**LANGUAGE VARIETIES: REGISTER.** Any one language has many varieties. Variations according to *user* are termed local, or social, varieties, or dialects. There are, however, also variations according to *use*; how we talk or write, what kind of language we use, depends not only on what we are talking about but on the use we are putting language to and other circumstances of the 'immediate situation of utterance'. The study of such varieties has been developed recently using the term *registers* for them.

*Development of the concept of register*. Reid (1956) put forward the concept, which he termed *register*, of differing linguistic behaviour on the part of one individual: 'For the linguistic behaviour of a given individual is by no means uniform; placed in what appear to be linguistically identical conditions, he will on different occasions speak (or write) differently according to what may be roughly described as different social situations: he will use a number of distinct 'registers'.'

Ure (1963, 1959) applied the concept in a specific connexion, and in a context of Firthian (see below) linguistic theory, to the theory of *translation:* '...the characteristic which I shall here call register, or the features in any given text which show it as belonging to the system of features, lexical, syntactical, phonological and others by which the hearer, without regard to the content of the text, can draw certain conclusions about the speaker. In the case of a dead language it may be impossible to identify register; it is often difficult for a non-native to recognize even in modern languages.' (This definition in fact could include also other variety-features than register, such as social variety and register-repertory, for which see below.) 'The problem here for the translator is always whether to attempt to find the corresponding register in his own language, if one exists, or whether to find a compromise that shall reflect with the maximum of preciseness that is intelligible the peculiarities of register of the source language.'

Hill (1958) had independently put forward an alternative terminology: *style, genre,* and *mode*. This is compared below with the more elaborated terminologies of register developed in the light of it.

Catford (1965), whose research students for purposes of applied linguistics collected statistics of various registers, mostly in English, distinguishes 'register' in a narrower sense from 'style' and 'medium'. This is also compared below. Strang (1962), partly following Catford, likewise distinguished *medium, style* and (in a narrower sense) *register*.

Dixon (1964), following J. McH. Sinclair, distinguishes kinds of register which are in fact all matters of mode.

Halliday, McIntosh and Strevens (1965) distinguish three kinds of register: *field of discourse, mode of discourse* and *style of discourse*.

We prefer, in order to accommodate all distinctions made by all the above in a unified terminology, to classify register along the four dimensions (each of which has subdivisions depending on the language) of *field, mode, role* and *formality*. These are explained and exemplified, and compared with the above terminologies, below. But first a very brief outline should be given of what may be called the 'prehistory' of the subject (before Reid) and of work proceeding on the subject in other terms, mostly in other countries.

Linguistic (and literary) scholarship has always recognized, without exhaustively systematizing, variation in the usage of linguistic items. This awareness is reflected in such terms as 'literary language', 'elevated language', 'colloquial language', etc., and in such treatments of individual linguistic items as the Shorter Oxford Dictionary's 'Words are also classifiable according to the sphere of their currency and usage', and its distinction of 'common', 'literary' and 'colloquial', and division of 'literary' into scientific, foreign and archaic, and of 'colloquial' into technical, slang, vulgar and dialectal.

In fact, the different application of say 'literary language' in English, and of 'Schriftsprache' in German, *literaturny yazyk* in Russian, for example (where it includes some non-literary registers of educated speakers), shows that differing institutional linguistic (see below) developments in different societies result in different variety-systems in different languages; and a general theory of language-variety must deploy a set of categories abstracted from such particular manifestations.

Moreover, the terminological extension of the metaphor found in 'elevated language', etc., to, for instance, the current French terminology of 'niveaux de langue' (e.g. Vinay and Darbelnet (1958)) has helped to perpetuate a normative, prescriptive, and in any case unidimensional, conception of the subject. Even after descriptive linguistics generally had been developed scientifically the subject of language-varieties and especially register lagged behind partly because of attitudes of prejudice about linguistic usage. Pioneering American work, for example, began with languages of *other* societies, especially primitive ones (where register-distinctions may be just as multiple, and in some ways more salient). For example, when Sapir wrote 'the sociologist is necessarily interested in the symbolic significance in a social sense of the linguistic differences which appear in any large community', he had *inter alia* had experience of the languages of small primitive communities and their interest to the social anthropologist. Sapir's hypothesis that language shapes social experience formed a starting point for Bernstein (1958), see below.

Bachtin (1938–9), for purposes of literary criticism and linguistic study of translation, recognized 'a continuous shifting from one level of language to another' on four different *scales* in *The Waste Land:* levels of colloquial idiom ... specifies speaker socially ... etc.; normal scale of poetic diction: 'dry, prosaic' to 'high lyrical or rhetorical pitch'; the diachronic scale: 'temporal levels perceived as such'; the diaglossal scale: shifts of language, e.g. foreign quotations. This is a most fertile application to a special topic of an implicit theory of language-variety.

Abercrombie (1963), without elaborating a full framework, brings out a fundamental distinction: the fact that a piece of language is spoken (a question merely of mode) does not guarantee it as being conversational (a question of role and also of formality), cf. below on Teaching.

Wegener (1885) had argued the differentiation of language into fields of context distinguished by general subject-matter, participants' interests, etc. (cf. *field* and also *role* below), e.g. to a huntsman other things being equal, or in a hunting context generally, the German *Löffel* (usually 'spoon') would suggest specifically 'hare's ear'. From him, through Malinowski (1935), Firth (1937, 1950, 1959) draws a concept of context of situation; he integrated this as an abstract category into a theory of levels of linguistic analysis, which included for him a developed notion of *restricted languages* (characterized partly by patterns of lexical collocation, e.g. in Wegener's example *Löffel* collocates in the restricted language with *Hase* ('hare'), but otherwise with *Gabel* ('fork')): 'Effective action and good manners require appropriateness of language in situational context. This leads to the adoption of the notion of *restricted languages*' (Firth 1959). It is the Firthian starting point which has been elaborated in the recent categorization and terminology of *register*.

Valuable work has also been done in other terms, mostly in other countries. Contributions include those by the Czechs Hausenblas (1955) and Doležel (1964), the German Koch (1963) and the Americans Ferguson and Gumperz (1960) ('There are also linguistic variations which regularly coexist in the speech of individuals, with their use reflecting some kind of situational or role differences') and Gumperz (1964) or Joos (1959, 1962) (degrees of formality): the American work in particular is associated with the development of a discipline of sociolinguistics (e.g. Hymes (1964), Fishman (1965), cf. T. Hill's institutional and sociological linguistics, also Ellis (1965)).

*The place of register in language.* Register is a linguistic category, a property relating a given text, in terms of its formal, phonological or graphological, or substantial, features to similar texts in comparable situations, and thereby to features in the situation of utterance or composition. A given language will be said to have a register-distinction at a certain point only if there are both linguistic and situational differences there. Hence Gregory (1966) categorizes language-variety as belonging to the *inter*level of *context* (on which cf. Ellis 1966a).

Thus each language has its own register-system, which may or may not cover the same range of possible situations as other languages, but which has a unique distribution of linguistic discriminations between situations. Each such system comprises relatively indelicate (general) and relatively delicate (particular) distinctions. A relatively indelicate distinction is easier to demonstrate and more accessible to less sophisticated analysis (notably without statistics); also, in general it is more likely to be alike in different languages, especially of similar culture.

(The term *register markers* is sometimes (e.g. Catford 1965) used for linguistic features distinguishing a register from other registers or (cf. Gregory 1966) from some other registers at a certain degree of delicacy; sometimes it is used only for more salient features — possible ambiguities here need resolving by definition in relation to context.)

Registers are common to different speakers, but speakers differ in the registers they possess actively and, to a certain extent, the degree of recognition and response. Cf. Firth (1959): '...an integrated personality ... would be regarded as being in command of a constellation of restricted languages, satellite languages so to speak, governed by personality in social life and the general language of the community.' The registers of a speaker constitute his register-range or repertory; this is a situational category, and is a factor influencing the developing situation of an interchange or other instance of communication: one of its effects is to determine the registers actually used by either participant.

*The classification of register.* We classify register on four principal situational dimensions. In a given language, a combination of points on these dimensions, or sub-dimensions within them, will yield a given register with linguistic characteristics. The separate dimensions are abstracted from these language-specific combinations so that we see the dimensions on the theoretical plane, as generally applicable to any language or variety, down to idiolect.

(i) The *field* dimension of register is defined as the dimension of classification of registers on which linguistic variations correlate with variations in the type of subject-matter, where the difference is not merely a direct reflection of the particular reference, e.g. 'the solution was heated' and 'I heated the solution' may (perhaps) be distinguished as belonging respectively to 'the field of science' and "general" or everyday field', whereas 'I heatted the solution' and 'I cooled the solution' may not.

Thus defined, *field* does *not* include those aspects of Halliday, McIntosh and Strevens' 'field of discourse' such as 'getting things done' or phatic communion, which are matters of role. Catford too conflates the latter and our 'field' in his narrow use of the term *register* itself ('performer's wider social role ... e.g. "scientific", "religious", "civil-service"'), as do Vinay and Darbelnet in their 'spécialisations fonctionnelles'.

(ii) The *mode* dimension of register is defined as correlating with the medium of utterance and the general communicative relation between the participants. (On subdimensions of mode, and the concept of a cline of 'isolation', see Dixon (1964).) This is a department of register which has changed rapidly in the last hundred years, with constant revolutions in the physical techniques of communication: mass-newspapers and universal literacy, telegraphy, telephony, radio, television, tape-recording. The full mode register-system of contemporary languages comprises (indelicately): printed texts, letters, tape-recordings, broadcasting, television, public speaking, telephone conversation, note-passing, spoken colloquy etc..

Halliday, McIntosh and Strevens' 'mode of discourse' includes also some distinctions, e.g. newspaper, advertising, conversation, in which role also plays a part (or, as in their example of *sports* commentary, also field); but Strang's 'medium' and partly Catford's 'medium' correspond to our 'mode', though Catford includes the 'number' as well as the (unspecified) 'nature' 'of addressees and the performer's' (unspecified) 'relation to them' under 'style'. Vinay and Darbelnet in effect include mode in 'tonalité ésthétique'.

(iii) The *role* dimension of register is defined as correlating with the social or other function of the utterance or text (on 'role' of *participant* see below). Examples are: (a) the linguistic features common to informal personal interchange, whether it occurs in the kind of spoken colloquy identifiable as informal conversation on the one hand, or in an exchange of personal letters on the other; (b) those linguistic features to be found in exposition (of varying degrees of technicality, cf. below on *stratum*): and (c) those to be found (with the provisos below) in literature as such. (Genre-distinctions within literature insofar as they are linguistic, are more delicate subdivisions of role (or of mode, but this is the case only in inner situation); but they also need to be considered in the light of the special nature of the language of literature mentioned below.)

Some contemporary languages at least temporarily (cf. Halliday, McIntosh and Strevens (1965), p. 94, on the future role of machine translation) are without the registers appropriate to certain situations already arising in the society concerned (e.g. language for education of various grades, for technical specialities (including that used in higher education), for government and administration); either the result or the cause of such a state of affairs is that the society uses another language, e.g. English and French in Africa. Unlike the differences in their ranges of mode-register, these differences between language-communities in the ranges of their role-registers are not peculiar to the modern age—as witness medieval uses of Latin in Europe, Chinese in the Far East, etc., etc. (cf. Hill, e.g. on Arabic).

With role belong largely also registers that may be called *restricted registers* (Halliday, McIntosh and Strevens' 'restricted languages' in this sense is a narrowing of Firth's use of that term); these are roles which are possible only for certain fields, so that many utterances in other registers could not be 'translated' into them, and/or their formal resources are relatively impoverished, as in the case of recipes. They may also be restricted to certain modes and formality-registers, e.g. military commands, telegrams. In fact the restrictedness of registers in this sense forms a cline, nor is there anywhere such a thing as a whole register distinguished from all other registers only by variation on one of the four dimensions.

Halliday, McIntosh and Strevens treat the factors elsewhere grouped under role as *field* or *mode* (or possibly as *style*, as in an interchange between teacher and pupil; but here they *are* also speaking of the formality consequences of the educational function). Role corresponds to Hill's *genre*, though again see also his *style*. Catford's (and Strang's *subjective*) *register* correlating with 'social role' is also a matter (social variety) of the speaker's range of registers as a person, not of the social function of the utterance; the linguistic features correlating with social variety are those permanent to the individual, and in particular societies such social varieties may be linked with specific social functions, e.g. Catford's 'professor of biochemistry'. This would cover the sexually correlating differences in Japanese, mentioned by Halliday, McIntosh and Strevens, insofar as these distinctions are not affected by the sex of the addressee (a subdivision of formality). Vinay and Darbelnet include role both in *tonalité ésthétique* and in *spécialisations fonctionnelles*.

(iv) Finally, the *formality* dimension of register (which is also affected, in particular ways that are partly more complex and subtle, by communicative and other developments in modern society), correlating with the personal relation between the participants (including their 'roles' in the sociological sense insofar as these interact). When no particular addressee is envisaged, formality is neutralized and we may speak of *neutral* or *impersonal* formality – which in a given language may share linguistic features with more formal registers, as in English, or with more informal registers as exemplified by Japanese verb endings (see O'Neill (1966) for a lucid exposition of formality in Japanese generally).

Degree of formality corresponds to *style* in the terminology of Hill, Catford, and Halliday, McIntosh and Strevens. The last, it is true, use the term 'style of discourse', and they do distinguish it from 'style' in the traditional literary sense (see below), but dangers of confusion call for a distinct term. Gregory uses 'tenor'. Vinay and Darbelnet include formality in *tonalité ésthétique*. Strang appears to conflate part of formality and role under 'style' (and to treat part as 'objective register').

*Relations of registers to linguistic features, to each other and to other varieties of language.* Linguistic features of registers can sometimes be seen to have language-external causes, e.g. tempo-conditioned (lento and allegro) forms like 'cannot' and 'can't' (see below), but otherwise they must be accepted as being in the same arbitrary type of relation to the situational features they correlate with as, in general, linguistic items are to the situational items they 'mean'. (Cf. Halliday (1966) though his formulation of the distinctions as matters of etiquette obscures this parallel of arbitrary relations.)

In the interrelations of the four dimensions with each other, already exemplified above, examples could be multiplied endlessly ('there may be syncretisms and incompatibilities between varieties' – Catford); e.g. *cannot*, given by Catford as an example of a marker of mode and also formality. The same may apply to the use of the passive in our own example: *the solution was heated/I heated the solution;* a longer section of text would narrow the range of possibilities in that a high frequency of passives would point to a scientific field, a lower one to 'formal' formality in personal relations. A principal case is the scale technical-non-technical, sometimes called *stratum*, e.g. learned article, book, popular writing, etc., this combines field, role, and formality.

Equally important are relations with other kinds of variety. Registers may draw their linguistic material from local and social varieties, as indeed from quite separate languages. Cf. Reid: 'The fundamental importance of the distinction of registers is shown by the fact that it may cut across the distinction of national or regional tongues, as when a person whose familiar conversation is carried on in Alsatian or Breton or Welsh uses French or English for administrative purposes; but it is no less significant where forms of the same national language are used in all cases.' A distinction must of course be made between cases like those mentioned above under 'role' where no one (yet) uses the native language for certain purposes, and other cases (due to national domination in the case of communities, or to more particular reasons in the case of migrated etc. bilinguals) where some individuals have registers in a second language only although others have them in the native language, e.g. Gaelic speakers who are literate only in English compared with intellectuals with a full Gaelic register-range.

This last is a case of a social variety distinguished by the range or other features of its register-system (in this case by the division of range between languages). There is another kind of register differentiation of social varieties which is more fundamental, and a matter of sociological linguistics, rather than institutional linguistics, since it characterizes a particular kind of society irrespective of the language involved. A case of such register-differentiation of social varieties investigated in detail by Bernstein (1958, 1962, 1965) is the distinction between 'restricted codes', which are possessed by all members of, e.g. British society (though unevenly distributed by role and field and even formality), and 'elaborated codes' which characterize the middle class rather than the working class (though, as Bernstein shows in his statistical results, the facts represent a cline rather than a dichotomy). (Bernstein's results need to be supplemented by comparative work on other societies, and as far as possible historical considerations, e.g. the historical 'Dissociation of Sensibility' could conceivably be formulated as a relative impoverishment of restricted codes, not suffered to the same extent in e.g. Russian culture.)

The final type of variety-dynamics is in language-contact, cf. Weinreich (1953), Stewart (1962), Fishman (1964). Registers themselves illustrate contact linguistics where a given register is transmitted to other members of the same language community; when the whole community adopt new languages or one language exerts a lesser degree of influence upon another, registers of both old and new language play a vital role in concentrating the contact at strategic points, cf. on languages lacking in registers, see above. Cf. also Ure (1963) on Rabin's 'translation stock' as 'a part of ... 'registers".

In all this, and first of all in the sheer description of registers of one language, large-scale research using enough text for significant statistics is called for. The development of computer methods in linguistic analysis should make possible the effective application of, and feedback to, variety and especially register theory.

*Register in literature.* Written language (and some kinds of recorded spoken language) and literary language present special problems which can only be treated briefly here. (Written: a term on the register dimension of mode; literary: a term on the register dimension of role, although both are treated as 'modes of discourse' in Halliday, McIntosh and Strevens.)

The difference between an utterance conveyed to the addressee as soon as performed at all, and a text composed for later communication, introduces a scale of premeditation and elaboration of the final text or act of speech (oral literature being a particular case, with improvised adaptation of remembered patterns). At or towards one end of this scale the role of addressee is mediated by forms of memory or intention; the conditions of impersonal formality mentioned above, where there is no specific addressee (in terms of personal relations), are a particular case of the abstraction of some degree of generality of (potential) addressees. Here reference may again be made to Dixon's cline of isolation mentioned above.

Literature is distinguished generally by something linguistic, 'patterning of patterns', and much literature by something semantic, namely its belonging to the category of the fictional (non-literary members of this category are exemplified by anecdotes in personal interchange). 'Indeed, the distinction between truth and falsehood is hardly material to contextual study as such, that between either and fiction being much more important. In both error or unintended falsehood and intentional lying, as much as in truth, the performer intends the addressee to fit the thesis into the universe of his ordinary experience (referentially, as distinct from any literary allusions, etc., in presentation); in fiction, on the contrary (where 'the poet lieth not, for he affirmeth nothing'), the thesis creates a secondary universe (in some complex relation, referentially and non-referentially, to the primary universe), which is one reason for the greater complexity needed in the contextual analysis of literary utterance' (Ellis 1966a).

The characteristic of being fiction, however, has in general little effect on the choice of linguistic forms, though it does in languages like Bulgarian affect the usage of the 'renarrative' system of the verb (the 'direct' mood of which is in most non-fictional registers reserved for events to which the speaker can testify). Most patterning of patterns in literary language is again in the arbitrary type of relation to the cognitive semantic content, though no doubt some correlation is demonstrable with the affective aspect.

As for the further question of what distinguishes the poetic from the literary generally, we can say briefly, that in the former the affect is rather in the language selected, while in the latter it is rather in the thesis of the (just as much selected) language.

Insofar as a general characteristic of selecting in a specially patterned kind of way from the patterns of the language at large does distinguish literature as a whole from other uses of language ('the language at large'), Reid (with his 'register... of literature (with various subdivisions)'), Vinay and Darbelnet (with their 'langue poétique', 'langue littéraire', 'langue écrite', reading downwards!), Ellis (1965) ('Role...e.g....literature...'), Halliday, McIntosh and Strevens ("'the language of literature' as a single register") and others must be allowed a 'register of literature'. (Bachtin's 'normal scale of poetic diction' precisely, as 'scale' implies shift, and, as 'normal' implies other scales.) But in giving substance to the concept of special patterning, it is immediately apparent that literature (or 'the register of literature') throughout makes use of 'other' registers (the registers of other uses of language), including *residual* features (this is so in our culture, though not necessarily in other cultures). Cf. Catford: 'a poetic genre as a super-variety characterized by potential use of features appropriate to all varieties.'

*Register in Language-Teaching and Comparison*

*The problem of learning registers.* Register variation poses a language learning problem, both to native children and to foreigners.

In both cases it is mainly a question of experience. Children have a limited experience of life and may simply not know a new situation and the variety of language associated with it. Foreign adults may know the type of situation, but not the appropriate variety of the second language.

For foreigners the problem is complicated by the fact that different languages respond to different factors in the situation and to variations in these factors. That is to say, the linguistic grouping of situations involving language differs from language community to language community.

This can lead both to difficulties in production, and to misunderstandings. Examples of such differences in the linguistic grouping of situations may be quoted from experience in a university.

German students who were attending an honours course in English Literature declared that they were astonished at the language used by their lecturers, which, they said, was merely 'coffee talk'. Similar comments were made by a Serbian who declared that 'nobody, at home, would have delivered a lecture in such language.'

The situational factors here involve social role and medium. English speakers talking about the same field of study make, it appears, relatively little difference in their language whether they are taking part in a friendly discussion or giving a lecture. On the other hand, a spoken lecture and a printed article on the same subject do exhibit more striking linguistic differences. In German and Serbo-Croat, on the other hand, the big difference would seem to be not one of medium—spoken versus written— but the difference between the social roles of conversation and exposition, whilst the difference between spoken and written texts, when both are dealing with the same subject and both are expository, would be smaller.

At the same time, we do have languages, particularly where there is close cultural and linguistic contact between them, whose registers have features that can be described as similar; indeed, we have some registers where some of the distinctive features can be described in terms of calque (cf. 'translation stock' above), and then it may be pedagogically useful to equate registers in two languages when teaching the relevant registers of the one language to speakers of the other.

*The problem of fixing transition points between registers.* It must be remembered that clear-cut divisions do not always exist to mark a change of register. In the study of register variety as in the study of local or social, or dialect, variety, there may be a continuum. In descriptive linguistics there is a convenient term for such gradations, borrowed from natural science: a *cline;* and in the study of register it may be used equally for situational and linguistic gradations.

There may, for example, be a gradual transition in subject matter. A single prolonged conversation may start with the discussion of a news item as a matter of immediate practical interest and thence gradually develop into a more academic discussion of contemporary history. If we take a set of texts in contemporary English with subject matter locatable at different places along this cline, some dealing with practical matters and the latest news that concerns us all, others more detached, academic and historical, and then submit these texts to a linguistic analysis, it is probable, provided that these texts are all produced in situations otherwise similar, that the linguistic patterning will yield a classification that puts them in an order corresponding more or less to their distribution between these two situational poles, but there is not likely to be a clear-cut division or point of transition part-way along the line.

Likewise, in relations between people, native English speakers can get more and more friendly with one another without there being any one linguistic transition point. In many languages, as in French or Russian, a change in familiarity may be marked by crossing the linguistic boundary, e.g. from *vous* to *tu* or from *vy* to *ty*, with a set of further corresponding changes in language choices.

Thus increasing the delicacy or depth of detail of a description will mean either making finer distinctions within the terms of an either/or system or making distinctions along a line of gradations that may, indelicately, appear as a cline.

For instance, we have the particular either/or system of formality in French just mentioned. This is used to mark various situational contrasts, among others the case where an acquaintanceship develops into a friendship. Here the situational transition may be accompanied by a transition from *vous* to *tu* associated with other changes of linguistic patterning; perhaps, for example, a higher frequency of *gentil* as opposed to *aimable* etc., and in grammar imperative verbs instead of *vouloir* + *bien* + infinitive. Within the register with *tu* formality there are distinctions to be made according to various criteria: family relationship irrespective of age, the relationship of senior to junior, membership of the same social group. In the second of these cases the use of *tu* will not be reciprocal. The first and second might further be differentiated by the different lexical items that occur as imperatives as well, perhaps, as by such verbs occurring with different frequencies: perhaps in the first case there is a specially high frequency of *va* and *viens* (judging by a cursory glance at the usage of Inspector Maigret). But this is only a suggestion. It illustrates the need, however, for counting, and sometimes for counting a considerable corpus of text, in order to extract data for more delicate register distinctions.

English texts covering a similar development in a situation may not be so clearly marked that one can place all of them immediately and unmistakably on one side or the other of the great divide; however, there will still be a number of linguistic features that will serve to distinguish among the texts and will yield a graded linguistic grouping to correspond to the situational grouping. (Where we have related languages or languages in contact the actual linguistic features may show a degree of comparability, e.g. *kind* as opposed to *nice*, *come (along)* together with go (+*and*+verb), which probably occur in English texts in a similar distribution to the French examples quoted above.)

The particular case of formality just discussed shows a pair of languages that respond similarly with linguistic patterning to specific situational distinctions, but the English language (i) ranges these distinctions along a cline, while French has a closed system to deal with them, and (ii) requires a more delicate analysis to identify them than French does.

Since it is typical features rather than unique ones that are the subject of register study, a minimum amount of pre-judging is inevitable as part of the preliminaries to any register study, in that texts will usually need to be grouped (using an intuitive judgment of linguistic/situational correspondences) to obtain a large enough initial corpus for study. Here, in any foreign-language or comparative register study, the help of native speakers is essential.

To distinguish between registers, or produce an inventory of registers for a given language, linguistic differences, as we have seen, must be correlated with situational ones. The question arises: is it possible to compare languages numerically, from the point of view of the number of registers that they possess?

From this there follow the two questions: is it possible to identify transition points? and how should we evaluate, quantitatively and qualitatively, the occurrence of features of linguistic patterning?

A profitable method of approach would be that of contrasting sets of texts. This method involves the choosing of paired texts or sets of texts that differ along those situational parameters that are of interest to the investigator, but that are otherwise alike in their situational provenance. A linguistic analysis will enable the investigator then to allocate those linguistic features that distinguish the texts in question to the corresponding distinguishing situational features. For example, we might contrast a set of letters with a set of phone calls (the contrast being between written and spoken, and also between more and less immediate response), all between members of a family and all dealing with, say, holiday plans.

Then to the first set of texts may be added a second, introducing one, but only one, new situational variable. For instance, letter and phone calls, with the same subject and performers, but addressed to travel agencies (thus varying the formality). One may continue with variations along all the situational parameters that have been selected for investigation, and in progressively increasing delicacy along those same parameters for as long as may be required.

*The problem of comparing register-systems.* The number and range of registers possessed by any given person in his native language will be relatable, in a certain measure, to his experience. It will not necessarily be a complete set—if indeed it ever is. Some French people may have no one to call *tu;* some people seem to have no very friendly, or informal, register. (Note that the first of these two observations is situation-based, the second language-based.) The absence in a given person of experience of the language normally deemed appropriate to the situation in which he finds himself does not, of course, by any means imply that he is unable to cope with that situation.

Something similar can be said when it comes to comparing register systems for different languages. A language may have no technical scientific register; it will still be able to accommodate the necessary register adjustments to develop such a register. It is a subject for research whether and in what way complexity of the total register-system of a language is relatable to the social complexity of the language community (certainly primitive societies may possess striking variety distinctions), or indeed at all to the sheer number of its speakers. (So also is the question of the register-range of the individual speaker.) It is not possible to evaluate the adequacy of the register-system of another language on the basis of a comparison with the register-system of one's own language.

Though they cannot be evaluated, the register systems of different languages can be compared, in terms of response to situational factors and the transition points where a change in these brings about a change in linguistic patterning.

*The problem of describing the register-system of a foreign language.* We have seen how in register study the starting point is bound to be a selection of situational factors. In a foreign-language study project the selection will be guided (1) by the needs which the first language 'consumers' of the results of the research have for information about the kinds of language appropriate to a specific set of situations, and (2) by the researcher's intuitive comparative estimation of the register systems of the two languages.

Thus a second language register description, like other kinds of linguistic description, needs to a certain extent to be made (and to a more considerable extent to be presented) afresh for each first language community.

The needs of the consumers will be unique in each case and no generalizations can usefully be made. As regards the intuition of register differences, one may usefully distinguish between those of which the unsophisticated bilingual only becomes aware in extreme cases, and those where misunderstandings may arise immediately.

As an example of the former may be quoted the differences of register along the formality parameter between English and Italian.

Two Italian prisoners of war in Britain, of reasonable intelligence and limited education, had picked up enough English to follow a simple conversation. They had been in few situations where they might have expected the equivalent of the Italian *tu*, and they had accounted for its absence by the conclusion (not uncommon among foreigners to the U.K.) that the British are more formal than most other people. But on one occasion (in 1946) when they and some British students had met, and were speaking to a cat, they were astonished at the 'formality' of the English speakers in still using *you*, although in fact the register used to the animal was characterized by all the usual markers (high frequency of imperatives and verbless clauses, lexical peculiarities, etc.), which had escaped their notice.

Here, though the example may be trivial, the point illustrated is important in demonstrating how the same situational distinctions may be reflected in a pair of languages, but at different degrees of delicacy. (Another example would be the sex-based language differences in English sought by a Japanese.)

An example of the latter kind of register difference, and a particularly difficult case, is where a pair of languages respond to the same set of factors but make cuts at different places within the set of factors, as in the private discussion/public lecturing/writing for publication' situations mentioned above, where the first two give sharply contrasting registers in Serbo-Croat and German but represent only points in a cline in the register-repertory, it seems, of many British university lecturers.

Here a detailed register description may be very useful with certain teaching problems, since it is very difficult to convince many students that it is in fact a question of the appropriate register being used: that the lectures in question are not *abnormally* frivolous—or to persuade native English speakers that the lectures they hear in the universities of Berlin and Belgrade are not abnormally ponderous.

A more general question naturally arises. Is the lecturing situation a more socially serious one in the one set of languages, is it really more relaxed in the other? This is a question for the sociologist, in the final count, but it is clear that for part of his data the sociologist must rely on the linguist: on the institutional linguist in the first place, and via him, on the descriptive linguist.

A statement of register for second language speakers and for comparative purposes needs to be linked with a situational (cultural) statement; in language teaching this can be of great importance because of the possible danger of misunderstandings and wrong evaluations.

*Conclusion: register teaching method in language and literature.* The method here adumbrated, of multi-dimensional comparison, is one suitable both for research and for native language and second language teaching.

Research in the theory and description of registers in language has still a long way to go, but this does not mean that the teacher must wait for a full description before beginning to teach. For the nature of register is to be seen as a series of combinations of situational and the corresponding linguistic features, tending to relate along a series of clines rather than to form sets of clear-cut alternatives; and, this being the case, the most profitable approach to register teaching would be, in each case, to select a set of appropriate models for study and imitation, rather than the prescriptive approach with its implication of a rigid norm. As a method, textual study, in which analysis leads to imitation, and imitation to free production, has much to recommend it; it enables research worker and teacher to proceed *pari passu*, without the considerable time delay that there would be if the latter were obliged to wait on the results obtained by the former. It is a method that has as its aim to encourage linguistic observation, such as would enable each learner eventually to abstract from the language contacts he makes in the course of his exposure to the language he is studying that unique repertory of registers deriving from individual experience and forming the idiolect of the native speaker.

A subsidiary advantage of the textual imitative approach is its value to teachers who are not native speakers of the second language, and who will, consequently, not have a fully developed intuitive knowledge of register, but who will, if they impose the requirement of a close imitation, have objective criteria for judging linguistic appropriateness.

An advantage of the contrastive textual approach is its value, in intermediate and advanced teaching, in making the transition from the known variety to the unknown.

For elementary second-language teaching, register-based linguistic analysis of texts can equally provide the teacher with a selection of material appropriate to the situational needs of the student, together with a statement of frequency of occurrence and co-occurrence of items and categories.

In certain specialized fields there is already a tradition of the application of *ad hoc* register study to language teaching, e.g. in the case of business letters (register-restricted as to formality and mode, and indelicately, field, with some delicate variations in role), and foreign languages for scientists (usually register-restricted on all four parameters). On the other hand, conversation manuals traditionally contain faked material and most often concentrate on isolated features rather than on the register properties of whole texts.

Finally in the teaching of literature, both to native and to non-native learners, a register-based approach may serve to make explicit subtle variations within the text, whether these are treated as variations within 'literary language' itself (e.g. correlating with literary genre) or borrowings from language normally occurring in a non-literary situation. Recognition of the latter is often crucial to the understanding of fiction (see section 'Register in Literature': borrowings can be demonstrated by comparing literary and non-literary texts using the methods outlined above). For in real (non-fictitious) situations, the use of register implies a response by the user to the developing language situation; it is a choice, deliberate or unconscious, which classifies this particular language situation with previous language situations having elements in common (and by means of this classification, the speaker may in fact be exercising a form of control or direction). On the other hand, in literary texts register may be found independent of the outer situation, as an element in the creation of the secondary universe of fiction; the reader with experience of language in real situations will recognize the linguistic patterning, and an analogous situation will be created in his mind.

Without such understanding of register, works of literature may remain a closed book to the learner, just as his general language study will be unreal if not related through register to situations of utterance.

*Bibliography*

ABERCROMBIE D. (1963) *Conversation and Spoken Prose*, English Language Teaching **18**, 10.
BACHTIN N. (1938–9) *English Poetry in Greek*, The Link, **1** and **2**.
BERNSTEIN B. (1958) *Some Sociological Determinants of Perception*, British Journal of Sociology **9**, 159.
BERNSTEIN B. (1962) *Language and Speech* **5**, 31, 221.
BERNSTEIN B. (1965) *A Socio-linguistic Approach to Social Learning*, in Social Science Survey (Ed. J. Gould), London: Pelican.
CATFORD J. C. (1965) *A Linguistic Theory of Translation, An Essay in Applied Linguistics*, Oxford: The University Press.
DIXON R. M. W. (1964) *On Formal and Contextual Meaning*, Acta Linguistica (Budapest) **14**, 23.
DOLEŽEL L. (1964) *Vers la stylistique structurale, L'école de Prague d'aujourd'hui*, Prague, 257.
ELLIS J. (1965) *Linguistic Sociology and Institutional Linguistics*, Linguistics **19**, 5.
ELLIS J. (1966a) *On Contextual Meaning, In Memory of J. R. Firth*, London: Longmans.
ELLIS J. (1966) *Towards a General Comparative Linguistics*, The Hague: Mouton.
ENKVIST N. E., SPENCER J. and GREGORY M. J. (1964) *Linguistics and Style*, Oxford: The University Press.
FERGUSON C. A. (1959) *Diglossia*, Word **15** (2).
FERGUSON C. A. and GUMPERZ J. J. (1960) *Introduction to 'Linguistic Diversity in South Asia'*, International Journal of American Linguistics, **26**, No. 3, Part III.
FIRTH J. R. (1937) *The Tongues of Men*, London.
FIRTH J. R. (1950) *Personality and Language in Society*, Sociological Review **42**, section 2, pp. 37–52 (= Papers in Linguistics 1935–51, London, (1957)).

Here, the system of structural descriptions is very simple, namely, each string $z$ has the structural description $z$. In order to satisfy the demands of more realistic systems, e.g. descriptions of natural languages, far more apparatus is needed. In this extended work a broader definition is necessary in which the generated objects are not constrained to be strings but may be, e.g. sets of strings, bracketed strings, strings of complex symbols, and the like. In the more usual presentations we have in place of axioms of the form '$G(xyz) \to G(xwz)$' where only $x$ and $z$ are variables, rules of the form '$y \to w$'.

The term '*generate*' has caused much confusion among linguists, as it has often been equated with 'produce' or 'synthesize' as opposed to 'accept' or 'analyse', hence other terms have sometimes been used: 'specify,' 'define,' 'enumerate' (in the sense of providing a system which could map the integers onto the sentences of the language according to some arbitrary orderly procedure).

Formal studies of such systems have been confined largely to so-calle d 'rewriting systms' (where the generated objects are strings) including especially 'phrase-structure' grammars. A number of correspondences have been proved between various kinds of generative grammars and abstract automata, e.g. Turing machines, pushdown store systems, finite automata, linear-bounded automata, etc. (see *Algebraic linguistics* and the articles on Automata). It is probably fair to say that the application of such systems to natural language description has been done most extensively within the theory of transformational grammar. Other types of generative grammars of varying degrees of explicitness include stratificational grammars, the categorial grammars of Y. Bar-Hillel and J. Lambek, the applicational-generative model of S.K. Šaumjan, the dependency grammars of D.G. Hays, and others.

The formal and empirical studies merge in attempts to show that various classes of grammars are too limited in weak or strong generative capacity to accomodate known properties of natural languages, or not limited enough to provide interesting hypothesis about the general properties of natural languages. An example of the latter argument would be the proof that a given type of system is equivalent to a Turing machine, which is actually the case with the rewriting systems considered above unless some further restrictions are placed on them. To say that a grammar for a natural language is such a system is to say nothing more than that a natural language is an arbitrary recursively enumerable set. An example of the former type of argument follows.

Given a language $L$, two strings $x$ and $y$ belong to the same *substitution class* in $L$ just in case for all strings $w$ and $z$ $wxz$ is in $L$ if and only if $wyz$ is in $L$. It was proved in Rabin and Scott (1959) that every language defined (accepted) by a finite automaton has the property that the number of such substitution classes in the language is finite. Thus, the language $L_2$ mentioned above cannot be defined by such a system, since the number of substitution classes is precisely the number of different strings in $\{a, b\}$, a denumerable infinity. If a natural language has a construction which can be described only by rules that lead to such an infinity of substitution classes, we can argue that finite automata (or their corresponding grammars) fail as candidates for the grammars of natural languages. Such structures do indeed exist: nested sentences with dependencies across the nested parts (Chomsky 1956), or sentences of the form $X$ *Verb* $Y$ where $X$ and $Y$ represent infinite classes (e.g. nounphrases) but may not be identical, and so on.

Similarly, it has been shown that natural languages have structures that cannot be described by context-free grammars or if we consider strong generative capacity, by context-sensitive grammars (Postal 1964). A basic premise of all such arguments is that natural languages are to be described as systems determining an infinite set of sentences, otherwise every language can be trivially proved to be describable by a finite automaton. That this is not a practical alternative is easy to see. On the other hand, when we move away from theory to various applications (e.g. machine translation) it is conceivable that various approximations to an adequate theory may give useable results for one purpose or another and that hence what may be an indefensible hypothesis about natural languages may have some practical use.

*Bibliography*

CHOMSKY N. (1956) *Three Models for the Description of Language. I.R.E. Transactions on Information Theory*, IT-2, 113.
CHOMSKY N. (1963) *Formal Properties of Grammars, Handbookof Mathematical Psychology*, II, 323, (Eds. R. Duncan Luce, Robert R. Buch, and Eugene Galanter) New York and London.
CHOMSKY N. and MILLER G. A. *Introduction to the Formal Analysis of Natural Languages*, ibid. 269.
POST E. (1944) *Recursively Enumerable Sets of Positive Integers and their Decision Problems, Bulletin of the American Mathematical Society*, 50, 284.
POSTAL P. M. (1964) *Limitations of Phrase Structure Grammars*, in *The Structure of Language*, (Eds. Jerry A. Fodor and Jerrold J. Katz) Englewood Cliffs, N. J.
RABIN M. and SCOTT D. *Finite Automata and their Decision Problems, IBM J. Res. Dev.* 3, No. 2, 114.
ROSENBLOOM P. C. (1950) *The Elements of Mathematical Logic*, New York.
SMULLYAN R. M. (1961) *Theory of Formal Systems*, Annals of Mathematics Studies, 47, Princeton.

E. BACH

## LINGUISTIC FORM: PARADIGMATIC.

1. The word *Paradigm*, from which the word Paradigmatic is derived, is familiar, from school-grammars of foreign languages. A paradigm is a set of items—nor-

mally words—which are similar in some respects and different in others; in particular, they all share the same stem, and normally there are two or more syntactic categories with respect to which they differ (for instance, Latin noun-paradigms are sets of words, all with the same stem, but each word being unique in its number, gender and case). The relations among the members of a paradigm represent only one particular kind of paradigmatic relation. In more general terms, *Paradigmatic relations* subsume all relations of similarity which allow us to classify items in a language as being the same or different. (*Items* are the *Constituents* of particular utterances, as described in '*Syntagmatic*', section 4.1; they are further defined in 2.4 below.)

Describing a language involves specifying in some way on the one hand all the items which are part of that language's vocabulary, and the paradigmatic relations among them; and on the other hand, the ways in which these items combine to form larger items, including sentences and complete utterances, i.e. the *Syntagmatic relations* which can hold among them.

Thus, if we are analysing a linguistic text, we can say of each item in the text (a) what paradigmatic relations it enters into, as well as (b) what its syntagmatic relations to its environment are. Take for instance the sentence:

Mary never cooks the lunch badly.

Many syntagmatic relations hold among the various constituents of this sentence; for instance *cooks* is syntagmatically related to *never*, in that *cooks* follows *never*, and to *Mary*, in that *cooks* shows concord with *Mary*. On the other hand, to give a complete analysis of this sentence we must also describe the paradigmatic relations between its constituents and items *not* in the text. For instance, *cooks* is paradigmatically related both to *cooked* and to *plans*: *cooks* and *cooked* differ in tense, but have the same stem, whereas *cooks* and *plans* are the same as far as tense is concerned, but have different stems. These are all facts about English which any complete description of the language must supply; the facts about tense will be part of the *Grammar*, while the differences between items containing *cook-* and those containing *plan-* may be better handled by the *Lexis*.

## 2. The Terms of a Paradigmatic Relation

2.1. In order to describe adequately the paradigmatic relations holding among the items of which English sentences consist, it is necessary to show some relations as each holding not between two (or more) individual items, but between two (or more) sets of items. For instance, we must show that there is a relation between *cooks* and *cooked* which also holds between *bakes* and *baked* (namely, the relation of tense); or rather, the relation of tense holds between *any* member of the set which includes *cooks* and *bakes* (the set of present-tense verbs) and *any* member of the set which includes *cooked* and *baked* (the set of past-tense verbs). Whether or not it is possible to generalize the relation between two items depends on the kind of relation involved; and if it is possible to generalize a relation by grouping items into sets, different kinds of sets will be the terms of different kinds of relations. For instance, there is a clear distinction between members and non-members of the sets 'past-tense verb' and 'present-tense verb'. Another kind of paradigmatic relation is that which distinguishes between verbs which do, and those which do not, occur with 'culinary' nouns as objects, where 'culinary' nouns include items such as *food, lunch, eggs*. The word *eat* is certainly a member of the former set, but is the word *buy?* and *hear?*

2.2 Just as words can be classified by their paradigmatic relations, as in the above examples, so can constituents bigger or smaller than words. For instance, *the lunch* can be classified as a 'noun-phrase' (like *a big fat cow* but unlike *is cooking*), and more precisely as a 'definite noun-phrase' (like *the door* but unlike *some lunch*). Likewise, smaller items, including single words, can be paradigmatically related to larger items, so that, for instance, *Mary* is also classed as a 'noun-phrase', along with *the lunch*, and *cooks* is a 'verb-phrase', along with *is cooking*. Moreover, even the whole clause (or sentence) *Mary never cooks the lunch badly* is paradigmatically related to other clauses; for instance, it is 'declarative' (like *she seems a nice girl*, but unlike *have you heard the news?*) and 'negative' (like *he wouldn't tell me*, or *no-one knew the answer*, but unlike *she seems a nice girl* and *have you heard the news?*)

2.3. In the previous examples all the paradigmatic relations have been described as though they had only two terms each; this is not in general laid down as a theoretical requirement of paradigmatic relations, though some linguists do claim that at least some kinds of paradigmatic relations are essentially binary—for instance, Chomsky (1965) describes the paradigmatic relations between formatives in terms of syntactic features which are either present or absent. On the other hand, postulating a relation with a large number of terms, say ten, implies that no two of these terms are more closely related to each other than to any of the remaining terms. In the kinds of relations that we have exemplified, it is unusual for there to be many more than two terms; the larger the number of terms appears to be, the greater the probability that a generalisation has been missed, i.e. that a feature relating some of the terms, to the exclusion of the others, has been overlooked.

2.4. No definition has so far been given to the '*Items*' which can be paradigmatically related to one another, except that they have simply been equated with the consituents of particular sentences. More precisely, items are the constituents of particular sentence-*Types* as opposed to the particular sentence-*Tokens*: *John has come* and *John has come* are two different tokens (occurences) of the same type. The question arises: when are two tokens tokens of the same type? A distinction can be drawn between *Grammatical items, Lexical items* and *Formal items*. Any two items in particular texts are tokens of the same *Grammatical* (or *Lexical*) item if there is no grammatical difference (or lexical difference, as the case may be) between them, and they are tokens of the same *Formal* item if there is *neither* a grammatical *nor* a lexical difference between them. Thus *a* and *an* in *a pear* and *an apple* are the same formal item; presumably no grammatical difference can be discovered between *tea* and *beer*, so these are the same grammatical item (though different lexical items); and no significant lexical difference would be found between *cooks* and *cooked*, so these are the same lexical item (though different grammatical items). This process of *Identifying* items, as tokens of the same or of different types, can thus be seen as the end-point of the process of *Classifying* items (Halliday 1961; Hjelmslev 1943).

### 3. Kinds of Paradigmatic Relations

Given two terms A and B of a paradigmatic relation, the relation between them is always fundamentally the same: A constrasts with B. Thus, in order to distinguish between different paradigmatic relations it is necessary to specify in which feature A differs from B; that is, given two members of A ($A_1$, $A_2$) and two of B ($B_1$, $B_2$), with respect to what feature does the proportion $A_1 : B_1 :: A_2 : B_2$ hold? This feature can be one of a very wide range of different kinds, but the basic kinds are described below.

*1. Internal features:* these are features within the contrasted items themselves, whether purely phonological *(sink : sank :: rink : rank)*, purely lexical *(He bought two teas : He bought two beers :: He drinks only tea : He drinks only beer)* or purely grammatical; if purely grammatical, the feature may be relatively trivial *(Mary's been cooking : Mary's been cooking the lunch :: The lunch has been cooking : The lunch has been cooking all the morning*, i.e. noun-phrase+verb-phrase : noun-phrase+verb-phrase+noun-phrase) or relatively important and meaningful *(The students work hard : John works the students hard :: The horse galloped : John galloped the horse*, i.e. non-causative : causative). The name *Paradigmatic Class* is used by Gleason (1955) for sets of words defined by the Paradigms of which their members form a part; this is in effect a classification of words according to the class of their stem, and therefore purely internal to the word.

*2. External features*, i.e. the total range of syntagmatic environments in which A and B respectively can occur, whether these environments are defined grammatically (e.g. in French *l'homme* : *la femme* :: *le vice* : *la vertu*, according to the gender of adjectives in whose environments they occur) or lexically (e.g. *drive* : *ride* :: *car* : *horse*).

In addition to the strictly formal, intralinguistic kinds of external feature, a paradigmatic relation could be considered to hold between sets of items used in consistently different extralinguistic contexts (ie. with consistently different *Meanings*). In many cases, the relations based on purely formal criteria seem to reflect such extralinguistic features as well; this is not coincidental,

since most linguists try to make their formal classification correspond as nearly as possible to a semantic classification. For instance the grammatical tenses are analysed in such a way that they can be correlated, with the time dimension, even if the correspondence is not a simple one. Thus, in deciding which syntagmatic environments to use as criteria for the distinction between two sets, the linguist will always choose environments which yield semantically homogeneous classes in preference to those which yield semantically heterogeneous classes. However, it is also generally accepted that the classification should be *Explicit*, in the sense that the formal or **phono**logical differences between members of A and members of B should be stated. If the distinction between A and B is basically of the internal type, then there is no problem, but when the classification becomes oriented towards the 'meaning' more than towards the 'form' it becomes harder to make it explicit. In most cases, a compromise has to be found between a semantically heterogeneous but completely explicit classification, and a semantically homogeneous but inexplicit classification.

One kind of paradigmatic relation which has not been mentioned yet is the *Transformational* (in the sense of optional, meaningful transformation—Chomsky (1957), but not (1965)). Transformational relations differ from those mentioned so far in that if A is in a transformational relation to B, then A and B can differ only grammatically, i.e. their lexical constituents must remain unchanged (cf. Bazell (1953)). For instance, there is a transformational relation between *Mary cooked the lunch* and *The lunch was cooked by Mary*, but not between the former and *The dinner was cooked by Mary*. In addition, a transformational relation implies a relatively constant difference in meaning (e.g. active : passive, statement : question) reflected by a relatively constant difference in form. If transformational relations are incorporated in a *Generative* grammar, then they also differ from other paradigmatic relations in that they are unidirectional, i.e. A is treated as a base, from which B is derived, but not vice versa.

### 4. Relations Between Paradigmatic and Syntagmatic Relations

1. The difference between syntagmatic and paradigmatic relations is that the former result from segmentation, while the latter result from sub-classification. (They have also been described as relations *in praesentia* and *in absentia* respectively, i.e. both terms of a syntagmatic relation are present in the text, while only one term in a paradigmatic relation can be in the text, the other(s) being absent.)

2. It is important to distinguish carefully between syntagmatic and paradigmatic relations, in order to avoid considerable possible confusion. For instance, when one talks of 'grouping items together', this may refer to a syntagmatic grouping of items (into a single *Constituent*), or to a paradigmatic grouping of items

(into a single Set). Likewise, if one says that *our car* is different from *John's house* in (1) and (2) below, one has to be clear that this is a syntagmatic difference—*our car* and *John's house* have different syntagmatic *Functions* (v. *Syntagmatic* 4.5), being 'object' and 'subject' respectively—and *not* a paradigmatic difference: that is, as far as the grammar of English is concerned, *our car* and *John's house* belong to the same set:

(1) We've just sold our car.
(2) John's house has a blue front-door.

3. De Saussure and Hjelmslev *et al.* imply that paradigmatic relations are at least independent of, and probably logically prior to, syntagmatic relations. They say that syntagmatic relations are relations only within the *Text*, while paradigmatic relations are relations within the *System* of the language; but since the text logically presupposes the system, but not vice versa, (Hjelmslev (1943) trans. Whitfield (1961)), paradigmatic relations must be logically prior to syntagmatic relations. J. R. Firth, on the other hand, suggested that paradigmatic and syntagmatic relations are in fact *inter*dependent, so that a given paradigmatic relation would apply only in specified syntagmatic environments. More precisely, a paradigmatic relation A : B may hold when a member of A has one function, but not when it has a different function (v. *System and structure*, 3). This means that a distinction must be drawn between those paradigmatic relations for which this restriction does hold, and those for which it does not. The former are referred to as *Systems* if they are grammatical, otherwise as *Lexical sets*, while the latter are given the name *Paradigms*. Classical paradigms of, say, a five-case nominal group '*puella pulchra : puellam pulchram : . . .*' are paradigms in this stricter sense of the word, since there is in fact no syntagmatic environment in which this paradigmatic relation could hold: that is, there is no structurally defined syntagmatic environment where all five members of the paradigm could occur.

*Bibliography*

BAZELL C. E. (1953) *Linguistic Form*, Istanbul.
CHOMSKY N. (1957) *Syntactic Structures*, The Hague.
CHOMSKY N. (1965) *Aspects of the Theory of Syntax*, Cambridge, Mass.
GLEASON H. A. (1955) *An Introduction to Descriptive Linguistics*, New York.
HALLIDAY M. A. K. (1961) *Categories of the Theory of Grammar*, Word, 17.3, 241.
HALLIDAY M. A. K. (1963) *Class in relation to the axes of chain and choice in language*, Linguistics, 2.
HJELMSLEV (1943) *Omkring sprogteoriens grundloeggelse*, Copenhagen; trans. by Whitfield (1961): Prolegomena to a Theory of Language (Madison).
DE SAUSSURE F. (1915) *Cours de Linguistique Gènèrale*, Paris; trans. by Baskin (1959), London.

R. A. HUDSON

## LINGUISTIC FORM: SYNTAGMATIC.

1. The relation between a linguistic item—say a word—and its environment (or part of its environment) in a particular utterance is a Syntagmatic relation. If we want to analyse and describe this utterance this can involve, among other things, describing some of the syntagmatic relations among its parts. For instance, in analysing the sentence:

Mary never cooks the lunch badly.

we may state the relations between *cooks* and the other parts of the sentence; for instance, it immediately follows *never* and immediately precedes *the*, but it shows concord with *Mary*, and has some kind of expectation relation with *lunch*.

We can, of course, say that *cooks* is in concord with *Mary* only on the basis of a description of English grammar in general. We cannot know that this relation holds by looking at our sentence *on its own*; rather, we must first compare it with other similar sentences, from which we can deduce such rules as those for concord between the subject and the verb. In fact, unless we know the rules of English grammar (in the broadest sense of the word 'grammar'), we cannot know even that this sentence is to be devided up into the six words *Mary*, *never*, etc.

It is clear that none of the words in our sentence is related to *cooks* in the same way that, for instance, *cooked* is; the relation between *cooks* and *cooked* is known as a *Paradigmatic* relation.

*2. The Environment of an Item*

The environment has been defined as follows: 'The *environment* or *position* of an element consists of the neighbourhood, within an utterance, of elements which have been set up on the basis of the same fundamental procedures which were used in setting up the element in question. 'Neighbourhood' refers to the position of elements before, after and simultaneous with the element in question' (Harris 1951).

Two features of this definition are worth emphasizing:

1. The elements in the environment must have been set up on the basis of the same fundamental procedures which were used in setting up the element in question. This means, for instance, that the environment of a word cannot include a set of phonemes or vice versa.

2. The elements in the environment are those before, after *and* simultaneous with the element in question. In allowing simultaneity of the element and its environment, Harris has in mind those elements which are *outside* the element in question, but which are simultaneous with it—notably intonation; some linguists, however, would interpret the definition to mean that the element in question could form a part of its own environment—thus there would be a syntagmatic relation between *cooks* and the *whole* sentence in which it occurs: *Mary never cooks the lunch badly*.

Another question, which is left unanswered in Harris' definition, is how *far* the environment extends. This is a question which cannot really be given a general answer, except possibly 'as far as it is relevant'. The extent to which the environment is relevant will depend partly on the kind of syntagmatic relation to be described (see below). In some cases, the environment may include several sentences before or after the element: in other cases, it will be only a relatively small number of words, phrases or clauses.

### 3. Elements in Syntagmatic Relations

3.1. The elements said to stand in syntagmatic relations to other elements in their environment need not always be words. For instance, *the lunch* in our example above can be treated as such an element, as can *John's charming and beutiful wife Mary* in the sentence:

John's charming and beautiful wife Mary
never cooks the lunch badly.

Both *the lunch* and *John's charming and beautiful wife Mary* are *constituents* of this sentence, whereas *cooks the* is not. The relevance of constituents for syntagmatic relations is that the elements in such relations are always constituents, and conversely all constituents are elements in syntagmatic relations.

3.2. On the other hand, in describing the totality of syntagmatic relations possible in a language—as opposed to the relations among the constituents of a particular utterance in that language—we must be able to specify the elements between which these relations can hold. Where the same relation holds between a large number of different pairs of elements—as is the case with most of the useful and interesting relations one can postulate—then one can describe this relation as holding between two *classes* of elements. For instance, one can set up two classes of elements, 'nominal phrases' and 'verbal phrases', which can stand in same the relation to each other as do *Mary* and *cooks* in our first example; then all nominal phrases are counted as instances of the same element, provided they stand in the same relation to a verbal phrase as *Mary* does in the above example. Alternatively, some kinds of syntagmatic relations can be generalized by describing their elements as abstract *functions*, rather than classes; then we go on to describe the classes of items which can 'have' these functions (see *System and structure*, section 2.4.)

### 4. Kinds of Relations

There is no space here to give more than a sketch of the main kinds of syntagmatic relations:

*1. Constituency relations*. The fundamental, atomic elements—whether words or stretches smaller than words—fall into groups (*Syntagms*—de Saussure *et al.*), each of which is a Constituent (as described in 3.1 above). We discover these constituency relations in a text by applying one of two procedures or processes: *Grouping* or *Segmentation*. The former starts with the 'ultimate constituents'—words or parts of words—and groups these together into increasingly large constituents; the latter starts with the whole sentence, which it breaks down into smaller and smaller parts. The second procedure seems to produce an analysis which is intuitively more satisfying (cf. Haas 1960).

When talking about the constituency relations among the parts of a complex item, it is useful to distinguish terminologically its Immediate, Mediate and Ultimate constituents: it can itself be referred to as the *Constitute*. Its *Ultimate constituents* are its *smallest* parts, i.e. those parts which cannot be further subdivided syntagmatically. For instance, assuming words to be atomic in this sense (which is debatable), the ultimate constituents of: *A beautiful girl appeared and all the men watched her*, are *A, beautiful*, etc. Its *Immediate constituents* (I.C.'s) are its *largest* parts, i.e. those parts which cannot be grouped into larger wholes which are smaller than the constitute itself. In our example, the sentence's immediate constituents are the clauses *A beautiful girl appeared* and *and all the men watched her*. (It is debatable whether *and* should be included with the first or second of the sentence's immediate constituents—or whether it should be included with neither of them. For the sake of the example it will be taken as a constituent with what follows it.) The sentence's *Mediate constituents* are any constituents smaller than the immediate constituents, including the ultimate constituents. In our example, one mediate constituent is *a beautiful girl*.

It is most convenient to represent the constituency relations among the parts of an item—say our sentence above—by means of a *tree*, such as the following. (The shape of the tree will depend on which description of English is presupposed.) Each *node* in the tree is said to *dominate* a constituent of the sentence (except the top node, which dominates the whole sentence).

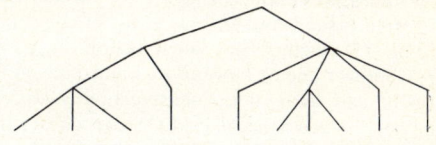

*2. Superficial relations*. The relation between two elements (A and B) can be described in terms of *linear sequence* (A follows, precedes, or is included in, B); in terms of *intonation*, *prominence* etc. (e.g. A is on a higher pitch, or has a stronger stress, than B); or in terms of *juncture features* (e.g. there is a phonetic feature in A or B showing A to be separated from B by a word-boundary). These 'superficial' relations tend to be treated as markers of other, 'deeper' relations (including constituency relations) rather than as syntagmatic grammatical relations in their own right.

*3. Part: Part relations*. Apart from the relations already described, the most important relations between one element and another element outside it are those of Selection (Bazell 1953): A selects B if the presence of A in a text implies that B must also be present. (Normally it is necessary to specify the syntagmatic relation, defined by other criteria, which must hold between A and B in order for this selection relation to apply.) A useful distinction is made by Chomsky (1965, p. 95) between *strict subcategorization rules* and *selectional rules;* these two kinds of rules reflect the two situations described by 'A selects B': either B is the name of a *class* of items which must be present if A is present (strict subcategorization rule); or B is the name of a feature which a certain class must have if it occurs with A (selectional rule). The first situation is found where, for instance, one class of verbs ('transitive') can (or must) be accompanied by a noun-object, but a second class (intransitive) cannot. The second is found, for instance, where there is *Concord* (A and B must be of the same class, e.g. adjective and noun in inflected languages) or *Government* (A determines the class of B, but is not itself of the same class, e.g. in Latin *de* 'governs' the ablative case, i.e. *de* selects nouns of the class 'ablative').

A distinction was made by Firth (1957) between *Collocation* and *Colligation;* these are the 'mutual expectation' (i.e. selection) of grammatical and lexical elements respectively. All the examples of selection given above are examples of colligation. Collocation is exemplified by the 'selection' of *beautiful* by *girl* (or vice versa) but of *handsome* by *boy* — this cannot easily be generalized to other mutually selecting pairs nor can it be stated as a hard-and-fast rule, since *a handsome girl* is possible, though less likely than *a beautiful girl*.

*4. Whole: Part relations.* Not only can we say that the nominal phrase *the lunch* consists of *the* and *lunch*, but we can also say that the noun *lunch* is an *obligatory* element in the phrase, in that every non-adjectival nominal phrase must contain a noun, whereas *the* is not obligatory in the same sense, since there are non-adjectival nominal phrases without an article. A parallel distinction is often made between three kinds of construction, according to whether the construction as a whole occurs wherever one or more of its immediate constituents (I.C's) can occur: if the construction is *exocentric*, it can occur where *none* of its I.C's can occur; if it is *coordinate endocentric*, it can occur wherever *any* of its I.C.'s can occur; if it is *subordinate endocentric*, it can occur wherever only *one* of its I.C.'s can occur (Bloomfield 1933; Bazell 1953). In the last kind of construction, only one I.C. is 'obligatory' in the sense that it determines where the constitute can occur, while the other I.C.'s are 'optional', in the sense that their presence or absence makes no difference to the places where the constitute can occur. In other words, the items in which these optional I.C.'s are present belong to exactly the same *class* as the corresponding items in which they are absent. These distinctions are clearly important; but in order to distinguish between 'optional' and 'obligatory' elements, we first have to specify exactly the class of constitute under consideration. For instance, if we consider nominal phrases in general, then *the* is optional; but if we consider a subclass of nominal phrases, 'definite nominal phrases', then *the* is obligatory, since its presence is criterial for membership of this class.

*5. Part: Whole relations* (or *Functional relations*—Haas (1966) and Juilland (1961)). Not only can we say that *the* is an immediate constituent of the phrase *the lunch*; we can also assign *the* a *function* in the whole phrase, which will be a different function from that of *lunch*. Likewise we can assign different functions to *Mary* and *the lunch* in the clause *Mary cooked the lunch* — namely subject (or actor) and object (or goal), respectively. Thus the 'functional' relation of *Mary* to *Mary cooked the lunch* is that of 'subject to clause': *Mary* is the subject of the clause rather than subject of the verb (Chomsky 1965). When the functional relation between each of the immediate constituents and the whole clause has been specified, the set of *function-labels* which can be assigned to the Immediate Constituents specifies the *structure* of the clause (using 'structure' in a technical sense—(see *System and structure* section 2.4.).

*Bibliography*

BAZELL C. E. (1953) *Linguistic Form*, Istanbul.
BLOOMFIELD L. (1933) *Language*, New York.
CHOMSKY N. (1965) *Aspects of the Theory of Syntax*, Cambridge, Mass.
FIRTH J. R. (1957) *A synopsis of Linguistic Theory 1930–1955*, in *Studies in Linguistic Analysis*, Oxford.
HAAS W. (1960) *Linguistic Structures*, Word, 16.2.
HAAS W. (1966) *Linguistic Relevance* in *In Memory of J. R. Firth*, London.
HARRIS Z. S. (1951) *Methods in Structural Linguistics*, Chicago.
JUILLAND A. (1961) *Structural Relations*, The Hague.

R. A. HUDSON

**LINGUISTIC FORM: SYSTEM AND STRUCTURE.** The use in linguistics of the words System and Structure (and their derivatives) are of three main types:

(1) System and Structure are more or less synonymous; a language as a whole has a system or structure, and this is what the linguist describes when he describes the language;

(2) a Structure is the structure of a particular item—a word or a sentence, for instance; the item is complex, and the structure shows the syntagmatic relations between it and its parts, and/or the syntagmatic relations among its parts;

(3) a System is a particular kind of paradigmatic relation, namely one which is limited to a specified environment; the system of a language (i.e. System in sense (1)) is an arrangement of a large number of such systems, intimately related to a large number of structures (in sense (2)).

*1. 'System' or 'Structure' of a Language*

All modern linguists agree that a language is structured, in the sense that it is not simply an unordered set of items; if it were such a set, then describing a language would mean listing all the possible utterances (not only words, but also sentences and even paragraphs) of the language, and knowing the language would mean having learned all these utterances, in the same way that one learns lists of words when learning a foreign language. That this is not the case is self-evident: we can all produce and understand sentences we have never seen or heard before, and there are—literally—an infinity of sentences that we can say, since it is never possible to point to the longest or most complex possible sentence of a language.

What we in fact find, when we look at the very large number of different sentences that we use, or hear others using, is *recurrent patterns* (recurrent partial similarities): even if two sentences are 'different sentences', they are not necessarily different in all respects, but may have quite a lot in common. Whatever features they have in common may well be features they share with many other possible sentences, and likewise the features distinguishing them will most likely be found to distinguish other pairs of sentences too. These features in respect of which different sentences are found to be the same or different—or more particularly those features which can be generalized—are the 'recurrent patterns' referred to above. The number of such patterns is finite, whereas the number of different sentences in which they can occur is infinite. The job of the linguist in describing a language is thus to describe these recurrent patterns, and the relations among them. It is these patterns, together with their interrelations, which constitute the System or Structure of the language.

This distinction between the underlying system or structure, and its manifestations in actual utterances, has been referred to in various ways: for de Saussure, the underlying system is *La Langue* and its various manifestations are *La Parole*—translated as *Language* and *Speaking* respectively; for Hjelmslev, the terms are *System* or *Language* and *Process* or *Text* respectively; for Chomsky, they are *Competence* and *Performance* (see de Saussure 1915; Hjelmslev 1945; Chomsky 1965). Hjelmslev (1943) also identified his System: Process distinction with the *paradigmatic: syntagmatic* distinction, whereas for de Saussure (pp 124-5) not only all *associative* (= *paradigmatic*) relations, but also many Syntagmatic relations are relations within La Langue.

A description of a language then is a description of the system or structure underlying all the utterances in that language. It will be possible to give such a description only on the basis of an adequate *model*, i.e. an adequate theory of the *kinds* of recurrent patterns to be found in a language, together with an adequate method of representing these patterns. Several different kinds of model have been offered for consideration, and so far there is no general agreement among linguists as to which of these models is the most adequate.

## 2. 'Structure' of a Particular Item

2.1. Any item (i.e. any stretch of text) which can be broken down syntagmatically into smaller items has a Structure; its structure is the totality of the relations between it and its parts, and/or among its parts. These relations are all Syntagmatic, and can be described only on the basis of a description of the underlying language system (in sense (1)). One speaks of the larger item as 'having' the structure concerned, and one can speak of its parts as 'entering into' this structure. A description of an item with reference only to its structure can be referred to as a *structural description* of the item, to be distinguished from a 'structural description' in sense (1).

2.2. In describing the structure of particular items, not all the syntagmatic relations within it need be described, or rather, not all these relations need be included in the same statement. It is useful to distinguish between those relations which are relatively *deep* and those which are relatively *surface*, in the sense of reflecting more of the meaning and more of the form of the item respectively (Chomsky 1965; Halliday 1966). Thus, one could say that in terms of their deep structures, (a) and (b) below were more similar to each other than either is to (c), while the surface structures of (b) and (c) were the same, and different from that of (a):

(a) Mary is cooking the lunch.
(b) Mary is cooking.
(c) The lunch is cooking.

2.3. The structure of an item may or may not be taken to include the structures of its *immediate constituents;* for instance, in specifying the structure of the sentence
My brother's car is red
either we can treat *my brother's car* as if it were atomic—i.e. ignore its internal structure—or we can consider its structure as contributing to the structure of the whole sentence. When describing the structure of an item, however, it is important to say which of these approaches one is adopting. Likewise, a description of an item's structure may or may not include information about the *paradigmatic relations* of its parts, as well as about their syntagmatic interrelations; only the latter are mentioned in the definition of Structure given in 2.1 above, but the former are also included as part of the structure of an item by Chomsky (1965).

2.4. Firth used the word Structure as the name for sets of sets of items in a *selection relation*, as described in *Syntagmatic* section 4.3. He called the sets which are the terms of such relations *Elements of structure*, and the elements of a particular structure were said to be *mutually expectant*. The relation between the elements of a structure was also referred to as *Colligation* (Firth 1957; Mitchell 1958).

Halliday on the other hand uses Structure as the name for sets of *functions* (rather than of sets of items); the the structure of an item is the totality of the functions of its immediate constituents. (For Function, see *Syntagmatic* 4.5.) Again, the members of these sets are called Elements of structure. Thus the structure of *My brother's car is red* is ('Subject', 'Predicator', 'Attribute-complement), rather than ('nominal phrase', 'verbal phrase', 'adjectival phrase')—'subject', etc. being the names of functions, while 'verbal phrase' etc. are the names of sets of items. A structure, in both Firth's and Halliday's use, is a set of essentially *unordered* elements, in the sense that the structure of *My brother's car is red* could equally well have been described as ('Predicator' 'Subject', 'Attribute-complement'). That is, it is not *necessary* to specify the sequence in which the elements occur, though it may in some cases be useful to do so (Halliday 1966).

### 3. 'Systems' as Restricted Paradigmatic Relations

Paradigmatic relations are essentially relations between contrasting sets of items. Given a set of items A, if any member of set A must be either a member of subset $A_1$ or a member of subset $A_2$, then there is a paradigmatic relation between $A_1$ and $A_2$. For instance, one could say that in English

(1) nominal phrases must be either singular or plural (where A = the set of nominal phrases, $A_1$ = the set of singular nominal phrases, $A_2$ = the set of plural nominal phrases);
(2) nominal phrases must be either adjectival (e.g. *beautiful*) or substantival (e.g. *a beautiful girl*);
(3) any phrase must be verbal or nominal or adverbial (where adverbial includes prepositional).

These $A_1 : A_2$ relations are, however, significantly different, in that

(1) applies only to 'countable' nominal phrases, but not to 'uncountable' or 'adjectival' phrases, such as *sugar* or *beautiful*;
(2) applies only to nominal phrases which are the complement to a verb such as *be, become*, etc.;
(3) applies only to phrases when the functions they can have are disregarded, since, for instance, a phrase which has the function 'subject' must be nominal—it can not be verbal or adverbial, because with a few statable exceptions such phrases never have the function subject.

Clearly it is necessary, in describing a paradigmatic relation between two sets, to specify under what conditions this relation applies (the Environment of the system); Firth restricted the terms System and Systemic to refer to paradigmatic relations which apply at specified elements of structure as defined in 2.4 above. Thus for Firth set A could be broken down paradigmatically into $A_1$ and $A_2$ only when set A was identified as a particular element of structure; the system $A_1:A_2$ Operates at this element of structure. This principle (known as the *polysystemic* approach, since it implies that there can be a different set of systems for each different element of structure) is one important characteristic of 'Firthian' linguistics. (See *Paradigmatic* section 4.3 and Halliday 1966.)

The relation implied by (1) above, between 'singular' and 'plural' nominal phrases, is a system in Firth's sense, but it applies not to all nominal phrases, but only to those which are 'countable'. One can say that the environment of this system is paradigmatically defined—the relation between 'countable' and 'uncountable' nominal phrases being a paradigmatic one—but needs no syntagmatic definition.

The relation implied by (2) is also a system, but is restricted to one particular syntagmatic environment—it applies only to nominal phrases with the function 'attributive complement'.

The relation implied by (3), however, is not a system at all in Firth's sense, since there is no element of structure at which it could be said to operate; thus the relation in (3) defines a *paradigm* rather than a system (see *Paradigmatic* section 4.3).

One consequence of considering systems as '*context-sensitive*', in this way, is that the presence, in a given sentence, of an item which is (a member of) one term in a system represents the result of a *free choice*. For instance, the presence of a singular countable nominal phrase represents a choice between this and a plural countable phrase, where the latter *could* have been chosen; therefore the reason why a singular rather than a plural phrase was chosen must be that 'singular' was more appropriate to the meaning than 'plural' would have been. Thus, if one can describe every grammatical feature of a sentence either as the result of a systemic choice, or as predetermined by such a choice, then there will be only a limited number of grammatical features relevant to the sentence's meaning (Bazell 1953; Firth 1957; Lyons 1963).

*Bibliography*

BAZELL C. E. (1953) *Linguistic Form*, Istanbul.
CHOMSKY N. (1965) *Aspects of the Theory of Syntax*, Cambridge, Mass.
FIRTH J. R. (1957) *A Synopsis of Linguistic Theory 1930–1955*, in *Studies in Linguistic Analysis*, Oxford.
HALLIDAY M. A. K. (1966) *Some Notes on 'Deep' Grammar*, J. Ling. 2.1.
HJELMSLEV L. (1943) *Omkring sprogteoriens grundloeggelse*, Copenhagen: trans. by Whitfield (1961), Madison.
LYONS J. (1963) *Structural Semantics*, Oxford.
MITCHELL T. F. (1958) *Syntagmatic relations in linguistic analysis*, Trans. Philol. Soc.
DE SAUSSURE F. (1915) *Cours de Linguistique Générale*, Paris; translated by Baskin (1959), London.

R. A. HUDSON

**LINGUISTIC FORM: TRANSFORMATIONAL THEORY.** Transformational theory is taken here in the sense of a linguistic theory aimed at characterizing the notion Natural Language by providing a particular type of generative grammar which has the necessary and sufficient apparatus for describing particular languages. A number of points about the form of a transformational grammar are still unsettled. The following statement chooses one of the presently available alternatives, leaving variations to be mentioned later.

A *transformational grammar* consists of four parts: a base component, a set of transformational rules, a semantic component, and a phonology. The base component generates an infinite set of structures called generalized phrase markers, which receive a semantic interpretation in the semantic component, are mapped onto a set of final derived phrase markers by the transformations, and these phrase markers receive a phonetic interpretation in the phonology. Before describing each of these parts in detail, a few technical terms will be mentioned:

1. A *category symbol* is a member of a special vocabulary of symbols for construction types and classes of forms, e.g. $S$ for 'sentence', $NP$ 'noun-phrase', $N$ 'noun'.

2. A *complex symbol* is a set of pairs $\alpha F$ where $\alpha$ is some positive integer and $F$ is some feature, that is, an element from a set specified in part by general linguistic theory, e.g. $V$ ('verb'), *Vocalic* (a phonological feature), *Animate* (a syntactic or possibly semantic feature). When, as is usual, the integer is restricted to the values $1$ and $2$, plus and minus are used: $+V$, $-V$ ('not-verb').

3. A *complex string* is a string of elements each of which is either a complex symbol or a category symbol.

4. A complex symbol $X$ is said to be *distinct from* a complex symbol $Y$ just in case there is some feature $F$ for which $X$ and $Y$ are differently specified (e.g. as $+$ and $-$). Similarly, two complex strings are distinct if at some point they contain either different category symbols or distinct complex symbols.

The *base component* consists of two parts: the base rules and the lexicon. The base rules are of several sorts:

(i) $A \to X$ where $A$ is a single category symbol, and $X$ is a string of category symbols.

(ii) $A \to [X]/Z\_\_W$ where $A$ is a single category symbol, $[X]$ is a complex symbol and $Z$ and $W$ are complex strings (possibly null) specifying the environment in which the rule is to operate ('/' stands for 'in the environment').

(iii) $[X] \to [Y]/Z\_\_W$ where $[X]$ and $[Y]$ are complex symbols and $Z$ and $W$ complex strings.

The base rules define a set of derivations in the following fashion. A string $y$ is said to *follow from* a string $x$ (with respect to a set of base rules $B$) if any of the following conditions holds:

(i') $x = z\char`\^ A\char`\^ w$; $y = z\char`\^ X\char`\^ w$; and $B$ contains rule $i$ above ($z$ and $w$ any string).

(ii') $x = z\char`\^ Z'\char`\^ A\char`\^ W'\char`\^ w$; $y = z\char`\^ Z'\char`\^ [X]\char`\^ W'\char`\^ w$; $Z'$ and $W'$ are not distinct from $Z$ and $W$ respectively; $B$ contains rule $ii$.

(iii') $x = z\char`\^ Z'\char`\^ [X']\char`\^ W'\char`\^ w$; $y = z\char`\^ Z'\char`\^ [Y']\char`\^ W'\char`\^ w$; $B$ contains rule $iii$; the stipulations of $ii'$ hold for $Z'$ and $W'$; and in addition $[X']$ is not distinct from $[X]$ while $[Y']$ is the result of adding to or changing the feature specifications of $[X']$ in just the way indicated by $[Y]$, that is, $[Y']$ is the set-theoretic union of $[X']$ and $[Y]$ minus those feature specifications of $[X']$ which are differently specified for $[Y]$.

A *derivation* is then a sequence of complex strings each of which follows from the preceding one in one of the senses above. The base rules define a set of prelexical strings consisting of just those complex strings resulting from derivations beginning with $\# S \#$ (where $\#$ is a sentence boundary element) and continuing until no further rules of the base can apply. The set is denumerably infinite because the initial symbol $S$ is introduced at appropriate places within the base rules and the rules can then reapply to each internal occurrence of $S$.

An important aim of transformational theory is to establish a simplicity metric for the evaluation of two otherwise equivalent descriptions. In connexion with this metric a number of abbreviative devices are used which are intended to convert considerations of generality to considerations of length (measured by counting symbol tokens or feature specifications). Each such abbreviation is a hypothesis about 'linguistically significant' generalizations. They include the following:

1. Braces to enclose the distinct parts of otherwise identical rules:

$$w \begin{Bmatrix} x \\ y \end{Bmatrix} z \quad \text{for} \quad \begin{matrix} w & x & z \\ w & y & z \end{matrix}$$

2. Parentheses for optional elements:

$$w \ (x) \ z \quad \text{for} \quad \begin{matrix} w & x & z \\ w & & z \end{matrix}$$

3. Greek letter variables over the specifications of features, e.g. $[\alpha F, \alpha G]$ for $[+F, +G]$ and $[-F, -G]$, or $[\alpha F, -\alpha G]$ for $[+F, -G]$ and $[-F, +G]$.

4. The symbol $CS$ ('complex symbol') in connexion with two types of abbreviative rules:

(a) $A \to CS$ to stand for all the rules
$A \to [+A, -M_1, -M_2, \ldots, -M_n, +X_i\char`\^\_\_\char`\^Y_i]/X_i\char`\^\_\_\char`\^Y_i$
where $M_j$ $(1 \leq j \leq n)$ denotes each lexical category other than $A$, and $X_i\char`\^\_\_\char`\^Y_i$ stands for each of the different environments in which $A$ can appear with respect to the substrings derived from each rule of the form $B \to \ldots A \ldots$. Such a rule is called a *strict subcategorization rule* and the environmental features *subcategorization features*.

(b) $\quad [X] \to CS/\alpha\char`\^X\char`\^\_\_\char`\^Y\char`\^\beta$

where $\alpha$ and $\beta$ are the feature specifications of complex symbols that are further defined in the rule. Such a rule is called a *selectional rule* and its new features *selectional features*. Each application of such a rule in an environment $\alpha$; $\char`\^X\char`\^\_\_\char`\^Y\char`\^\beta$; where $\alpha$; and $\beta$; are the feature specifications included in the complex symbols associated with the rule yields a feature $+[\alpha; \char`\^X\char`\^\_\_\char`\^Y\char`\^\beta;]$.

A miniature example of a set of base rules may help to make these stipulations and definitions clear:

1. $S \to NP\char`\^VP$

2. $VP \rightarrow V \begin{Bmatrix} (NP) \\ \#S\# \end{Bmatrix}$

3. $V \rightarrow CS$

4. $NP \rightarrow (Det) N$

5. $N \rightarrow CS$

6. $Det \rightarrow [+Det]$

7. $[+N] \rightarrow [\pm Animate]$

8. $[-Animate] \rightarrow [\pm Abstract]$

9. $[+V] \rightarrow CS/\alpha\hat{\ }\_\_(\beta)$ where $\alpha$ and $\beta$ are $+N$.

Thus, Rule 2 stands for these rules:

2a $VP \rightarrow V\hat{\ }NP$

2b $VP \rightarrow V\hat{\ }\#S\#$

2c $VP \rightarrow V$.

If $N$, $V$ and $Det$ are the only lexical categories, then according as 2a, 2b, or 2c is applied, Rule 3 will give the complex symbols:

$[+V, -N, -Det, +\_\_NP]$

$[+V, -N, -Det, +\_\_\#S\#]$

$[+V, -N, -Det, +\_\_]$.

Given the complex string

$\#[+Det]\hat{\ }[+N, +Animate+Det\_\_,]\hat{\ }[+V, +\_\_]\#$

Rule 9 will add to the last complex symbol the selectional feature $+[+N, +Animate, +Det\_\_]\hat{\ }\_\_$.

The *lexicon* comprises a set of entries each of which contains a phonological matrix and feature specifications of various sorts: category features, subcategorization and selectional features as illustrated above, semantic features, *rule features* (i.e. directions that a particular transformation must, may, or may not apply to structures containing the given item). Lexical items are inserted in strings according to the following convention:

(iv) If $X$ is a complex symbol occurring in the string $z\hat{\ }X\hat{\ }w$, then for every lexical entry $Y$ that is not distinct from $X$ the string $z\hat{\ }Y'\hat{\ }w$ follows from $z\hat{\ }X\hat{\ }w$, where $Y'$ is the set-theoretic union of $X$ and $Y$.

Thus, given appropriate entries we can insert in the example given above the entries corresponding to *the*, *rabbits*, and *run*. The subcategorization and selectional features for *run* will say, respectively, that it is an intransitive verb to be used with an animate subject.

With each terminated derivation from the base we associate a uniquely determined object called a *generalized phrase marker*. This may be thought of as a labelled tree diagram or bracketing constructed in the obvious way from a derivation: start with $S$ as the root and at each application of a rule $A \rightarrow B_1\hat{\ }B_2\hat{\ }\ldots\hat{\ }B_n$ add to the tree a branch of the form

$A$
$/|\backslash$
$B_1\ B_2 \ldots B_n$

If such a generalized phrase marker is not blocked by the transformational rules, then it is called the *deep structure* of the sentence to which it leads.

The deep structure forms the basis for the operation of the semantic component which provides zero, one, or several *readings* for each generated sentence, according as the sentence is semantically anomalous, unambiguous, or ambiguous. (Note that syntactic ambiguity arises when several distinct deep structures reduce to one final shape by the operation of the transformations and phonological rules.) The elements making up the reading for each sentence are the semantic features given in each lexical entry. The main device in the semantic component is a set of *projection rules* which amalgamate semantic features successively for each constituent of the generalized phrase marker.

The *transformational component* consists of a linearly ordered set of rules of a different sort. Instead of operating on strings of elements, they operate on *phrase markers*. The phrase markers are a new set of elements which result by taking the generalized phrase markers as a basis and extending the set to include the structures which result from the operation of the transformational rules. The rules operate in a cycle, first on the most embedded sentences, then on the next most embedded and so on. The ultimate result for those phrase markers that meet all the conditions set by the transformations is a *final derived phrase marker* or *surface structure* which provides the input to the phonological part of the grammar.

A *transformation* operates as follows:

1. The *structure index* of a transformation $T_j$ is a sequence of elements $A_1, A_2, \ldots, A_n$ each of which is either a *variable* (a member of a new vocabulary of elements, or a symbol (complex or otherwise).

2. A string $x$ with phrase marker $P$ is in the domain of $T_j$ with the structure index as given above if it can be subdivided into the parts $y_1, y_2, \ldots y_n$ and (for $1 \leq i \leq n$)

(i) if $A_i$ is a category symbol, then $y_i$ can be traced back to a node labelled $A_i$ in $P$;

(ii) if $A_i$ is a set of feature specifications then $y_i$ is a complex symbol containing $A_i$;

(iii) if $A_i$ is a variable, then $y_i$ is any string.

3. With each transformation there is associated a *structural change* which tells what happens to each of the parts of the phrase marker and the terminal string as analysed by the structure index. It may be that these elementary operations can be limited to one very simple operation of substitution (with deletion a special case of substitution) although the question is still open. In any case, the actual change in the phrase marker is specified by general conventions according to the type of structural change rather than *ad hoc* for each rule. The convention for substitution can be visualized as the replacement of whole branches in the phrase marker $P$ by branches occurring elsewhere in $P$ or by new terminal elements, while deletion entails the deletion of any 'higher' branches which dominate the deleted elements (where *dominates* is defined as the converse of the relation of condition *i* above).

When the above stipulations are made sufficiently precise we then define the relation *follows from* for phrase markers:

(v). A phrase marker $P'$ *follows from* a phrase marker $P$ if there is a transformation $T_i$ such that $P$ is in the domain of $T_i$ and $P'$ is the result of carrying out the structural change of $T_i$ according to the general conventions.

The sketch above allows a much too large class of possible transformations and the energies of linguists have been directed at limiting the number of possible rules as stringently as possible. One restriction, which is fairly well established, is a condition on *recoverability*: given a phrase marker $P'$ and a transformation which it has undergone it must always be possible to determine the underlying phrase marker $P$ from which $P'$ was formed. This restriction leads to the condition that deletion and substitution be limited to constant strings or to cases where the deletion or substitution is governed by the occurrence of the same item somewhere else in the phrase marker.

Suppose the miniature grammar above is extended to allow a sentence to be generated after every noun in each noun phrase (*NP*). Then we might state (roughly) a transformation for relative clauses as follows:

Structure Index: X, N, $\neq$, Y, NP, Z, $\neq$, W
$\phantom{\text{Structure Index: }}$1  2  3  4  5  6  7  8

Structural Change: $3 \succ that$, $5, 7 \succ null$ (all other parts unchanged, i.e. $1 \succ 1$ etc.).

If properly formulated (additional specification is necessary, 3...7 must be a single sentence, 5 must contain 2 etc). this rule will form (assuming further rules) *The rabbit that I shot is lying on the table* from the phrase marker associated with *the rabbit ǂ I shot the rabbit ǂ is lying on the table*. Note that the two nouns involved must be identical and that the general restriction on recoverability would rule out any transformation which did not incorporate such a condition, thus blocking *The rabbit that I am deriving is lying on the table* from the structure underlying *the rabbit ǂ I am deriving the sentence ǂ is lying on the table*. This example also illustrates one way in which the transformations can be used to block ill-formed sentences; we can state a general convention to the effect that nothing is a final derived phrase marker unless all internal occurrences of the sentence boundary ǂ have been deleted.

The final component of a transformational grammar is the *phonology*, which accepts final derived phrase markers and provides for each an 'interpretation' in terms of a phonetic description of the possible pronunciations of each well-formed sentence. As mentioned above, each lexical entry contains a phonological matrix, the columns of which stand for segments and the rows for binary specifications of universal *distinctive phonological features*. The features currently used include the following:

*vocalic:* positive for vowels and liquids
*consonantal:* positive for stops, spirants, liquids, and nasals (glides are non-vocalic, non-consonantal)
*voiced:* positive for all voiced sounds
*nasal:* positive for nasal consonants (and vowels)
*continuant:* negative for stops, affricates, trills, and taps
*grave:* positive for non-front vowels and peripheral consonants (/p k u/ are + grave, /t/ is -grave)
*diffuse:* positive for labial, dental, and alveolar ('front') consonants and high vowels
*compact:* positive for low vowels (for consonants α compact means -α diffuse)
*strident:* positive for sibilants, 'shibilants' (š) and their corresponding affricates (possibly also labiodental spirants and affricates)
*flat:* positive for rounded vowels and secondarily labialized or pharyngealized consonants.

Various further features used on occasion are *obstruent* (stops and spirants), *tense*, *stressed*, *long* and *tone* features (e.g. *high*, *low*).

In general, predictable information is omitted from lexical entries and reintroduced by *redundancy rules* of various sorts (this holds for all kinds of features mentioned above). In phonology these rules include rules filling in features predictable for separate segments (voicing for vowels), for sequences of sounds (reflecting constraints on possible clusters of consonants etc.).

To illustrate, suppose we want to give a representation of the English word *spanks*. I give a complete specification (using parentheses to indicate the bracketing of the item in the phrase marker). Specifications that can be omitted and reintroduced by redundancy rules of the first type (inherently redundant) are circled, while those that can be predicted from sequential constraints are enclosed in squares. Finally, the voicing specification of the final segment would be actually changed by a rule.

|  | ((s | p | ae | N | k) | z) |
|---|---|---|---|---|---|---|
| voc | − | − | ⊡ | − | − | − |
| cns | + | ⊡ | − | + | + | + |
| grv | ⊟ | + | − | ⊡ | + | − |
| dif | ⊞ | + | ⊖ | ⊟ | − | + |
| cmp | ⊖ | ⊖ | + | ⊕ | ⊕ | ⊖ |
| str | ⊞ | ⊖ | ⊖ | ⊖ | ⊖ | + |
| nas | ⊖ | − | ⊖ | + | ⊖ | ⊖ |
| cnt | ⊞ | − | ⊕ | − | ⊖ | + |
| vce | ⊟ | ⊡ | ⊕ | ⊕ | − | + |
| flt | ⊖ | ⊖ | ⊖ | ⊖ | ⊖ | ⊖ |

Among the rules filling in the circled specifications is the following:

$$[+\text{voc}] \rightarrow [-\text{str}].$$

Among the rules of the second sort (sequential rules) the following makes nasals homorganic to following stops:

$$\begin{bmatrix} +\text{cns} \\ -\text{voc} \\ +\text{nas} \end{bmatrix} \rightarrow \begin{bmatrix} \alpha \text{ grv} \\ \beta \text{ dif} \end{bmatrix} \bigg/ - \begin{bmatrix} -\text{cnt} \\ \alpha \text{ grv} \\ \beta \text{ dif} \end{bmatrix}$$

The phonological rules of various sorts result finally in a detailed phonetic characterization of the given sentences, hence in some instances include rules that change the binary specifications to *n*-ary ones (e.g. several degrees of stress, amount of aspiration etc.). Among the phonological rules are some which operate in a cycle, first on the smallest constituent, erasing innermost brackets at the end of the cycle, then on the next smallest constituents etc. These rules—the *transformational cycle*—account typically for phenomena of stress and other kinds of accent, sandhi, and the like.

The characterization of transformational theory given above is in most respects that of the second chapter of Chomsky (1965), while the phonological description follows the work of Morris Halle (1959, see also several papers in Fodor and Katz 1964, and Halle and Chomsky, forthcoming). It is impossible to give here more than a brief hint about the backgrounds of the theory and the differing conceptions of the theory which have existed and are constantly arising. In the last analysis, the theory must be considered the result of a remarkable convergence of independent lines of thought. It is a return to conceptions of linguistic theory which are as old as the universal grammarians of the 18th century and even ancient Indian linguistics but enriched by logico-mathematical methods and ideas of very recent times and the results of modern structural linguistics. The notion of a transformation itself is derived from work of Zellig Harris (1957, 1965), who has continued to use the idea in a different sense from that sketched above (for Harris a transformation is essentially a relation between sets of sentences rather than a kind of rule operating on phrase markers in a generative grammar).

Earlier presentations of transformational theory differ from the above sketch in a number of basic ways (Chomsky 1957; Bach 1964): In place of the base there was a set of context-sensitive phrase structure rules. The transformations included optional meaning-changing rules, whereas above everything necessary to the interpretation of the sentence must be present in the deep structure. Various systems were assumed for the ordering of the transformational rules. No semantic component had been proposed. Instead of embedding sentences in the base, so-called *generalized transformations* performed this task by operating on pairs of phrase markers. The blocking of ill-formed sentences was only implicitly a function of the transformational component, whereas now this function is explicit. At present various new suggestions are under study: a more explicit and extended use of transformations in the base (even in the system sketched above, a fully developed set of selectional rules entails the use of essentially transformational operations); the extraction of particular rules (perhaps the whole set of base rules) from individual grammars and their incorporation into general linguistic theory. In addition it is likely that the system of feature specification will be changed to include a preliminary specification in terms of a marked-unmarked distinction which will then be translated into $+/-$ feature specifications in such a way as to exploit certain universal characteristics of linguistic systems.

*See also:* Phonology: distinctive features.

*Bibliography*

BACH E. (1964) *An Introduction to Transformational Grammars*, New York, Chicago, San Francisco.
CHOMSKY N. (1957) *Syntactic Structures*, The Hague.
CHOMSKY N. (1965) *Aspects of the Theory of Syntax*, Cambridge, Mass.
FODOR J. A. and KATZ J. J. (1964) *The Structure of Language*, Englewood Cliffs, N. J.
HALLE M. (1959) *The Sound Pattern of Russian*, The Hague.
HALLE M. and CHOMSKY N. *The Sound Pattern of English*, (in press).
HARRIS Z. S. (1957) *Co-occurrence and transformation in linguistic structure*, Language **33**, 293.
HARRIS Z. S. (1965) *Transformational Theory*, Language **41**, 363.
KATZ J. J. and POSTAL P. (1964) *An Integrated Theory of Linguistic Descriptions*, Cambridge, Mass.

E. BACH

# LOCAL NETWORKS.

## *1. Introduction*

The term 'local network' is explained in the International Telegraph and Telephone Consultative Committee (C.C.I.T.T.) Manual on 'National Telephone Networks for the Automatic Service' (1964): A *local network* is used to serve a town with its surrounding rural district, an administrative area or another suitable region having the same locality as its cultural or economic centre. It often constitutes a numbering area and applies a uniform local charge rate. A local network may include one or several local exchanges.

The term *junction circuits* is explained in the same manual: The circuits interconnecting local exchanges, either directly or via tandem exchanges.

A *local exchange* is defined as: An exchange to which subscribers are connected.

A *tandem exchange* is defined as: An exchange used for connecting local exchanges within a metropolitan network.

A *local area* is defined as: The circuits connecting the subscribers' telephone instruments to the local exchange are Subscribers' Lines which together with the local exchange form the LOCAL AREA.

This article considers the planning and design of the equipment used in the local network and refers in general to United Kingdom practice.

## *2. Local Areas*

A subscriber's line consists of one pair of wires between the telephone and the local exchange although some sharing of wires is achieved by the use of shared service or line concentrators.

*2.1. Construction methods. 2.1.1. Cables.* The insulation of wires in cables may be lapped paper or extruded polythene. Copper is used for the conductor and the sizes used are $2\frac{1}{2}$, 4, $6\frac{1}{2}$, 10 and 20 lb per mile (these are equivalent to AWG 28, 26, 24, 22 and 19).

In the larger cables the pairs are made up into units of 100 pairs and the units then laid up in layers to form a circular section. Cable pairs within the units and in the smaller cables are laid up in concentric layers.

The sheathing material has previously been lead but now the sheath consists of white or black polythene (Winterborn 1958; Hayes 1961) extruded over a longitudinally applied aluminium foil either 0·3 mils or 0·6 mils thick. There is a small overlap at the edges of the aluminium foil. The object of the aluminium foil is to prevent the ingress of moisture (Glover and Hooker 1961) into the core of the cable over a long period.

Cables of sizes up to 100 pairs are insulated and sheathed with polythene; aluminium foil is not used. Black polythene, i.e. polythene in which carbon black has been incorporated, is used to sheath cables up to 100 pairs because these cables are more likely to be exposed to sunlight than the larger cables.

Wire joints are made by twisting the wires together by hand or by mechanical means and insulating with a paper or polythene sleeve. Joints in wires in local cables are generally not soldered.

*2.1.2. Underground ducts.* Cables are usually drawn into underground pipes or ducts which may be single pipes (single-way) or in multiple formation (multiple-way). Ducts are often made of glazed earthenware but fibre glass, asbestos cement, polythene, polyvinylchloride, steel and cast iron are also used.

Smaller cables are sometimes buried directly in the ground, often by mole-plough, when there is little likelihood that an additional cable will be required later.

*2.1.3. Overhead construction.* Smaller cables are erected overhead between poles. In this case polyvinylchloride is used for the sheath and a steel suspension wire is moulded in with the conductor core so that the cross-section of the cable is a figure-of-eight. Where only one overhead pair of wires is required, for example, between a pole and a house, polyvinylchloride insulation is extruded over copper coated steel wires.

*2.1.4. Cross connexion cabinets and pillars.* The need for and use of cross connexion cabinets and pillars is explained in section 2.3.2 below. Cabinets and pillars are normally erected in streets and therefore their external dimensions have to be kept as small as possible.

Three sizes of cabinet casings are available all 3′6″ high and 9″ deep. The widths are 2′, 2′9″ and 3′6″. The individual parts are separately cast in grey iron and the machined sections, after dressing with sealing compound, bolted together. The subsequent replacement of parts which may be damaged is thereby facilitated and the use of large castings with the attendant risk of distortion and breakage avoided.

The pillar casing is made of asbestos cement with consequent advantages in lightness, strength, economy and permanence without the need for a preservative finish. The cover, of hexagonal shape, is secured to the base by a single fixing bolt.

Cable pairs are terminated inside the cabinet and the pillar on terminal tags moulded in plastic cross connexion assemblies. The use of an enclosed type of construction has enabled the maximum number of cable pairs to be terminated in the minimum space. Cross connexions between cable pairs are made by means of straight 'bridging pins' or flexible 'jumper' wires and an essential feature is the simultaneous securing of both pins or wires of a pair through the medium of an insulated block and a single pressure screw. The construction of the cross connexion assembly is illustrated in Figs. 1 and 2.

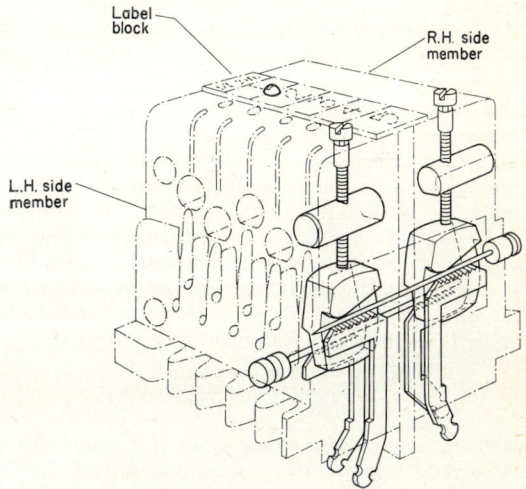

FIG. 1. *Cross connexion assembly—pin connexion.*

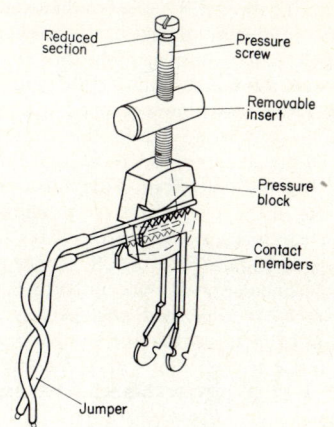

FIG. 2. *Cross connexion assembly—jumper connexion.*

Further details of cross connexion cabinets, pillars and assemblies are given in Edwards *et al.* (1946–7) and Hayward and Angell (1961).

## 2.2. Transmission and signalling requirements.

The subscribers' line must provide transmission and signalling paths so that the speech transmitted is satisfactory and the signals passed will operate the automatic apparatus at the telephone exchange. Limits are laid down for both transmission and signalling performances (see *Subscribers' apparatus*). The conductor gauge chosen for a cable route should be the most economical and lightest gauge consistent with the transmission and signalling standards adopted. This is generally achieved by the use of large light gauge cable adjacent to the exchange and small heavier gauge cables near the exchange area boundary.

### 2.2.1. Transmission.

One convenient method of assessing the transmission performance of a subscribers' line made up of sections of various conductor gauges, is the 'transmission equivalent resistance' (T.E.R.) concept (Fudge 1949), whereby all conductor gauges are converted to a common base relative to one arbitrarily chosen conductor gauge, viz. $6\frac{1}{2}$ lb. The T.E.R. of any line is then defined as the d.c. resistance of a $6\frac{1}{2}$ lb gauge line having the same grade of transmission as the line concerned. The T.E.R. of a line is expressed in ohms and its magnitude is equal to its loop resistance multiplied by a factor. If the transmission standard, in terms of a $6\frac{1}{2}$ lb gauge line, is 1000 $\Omega$, the equivalent 4 lb gauge line affording the same grade of transmission is 1250 $\Omega$. Thus, for a 4 lb gauge line the multiplying factor is

$$\frac{\text{Limit for } 6\frac{1}{2} \text{ lb}}{\text{Limit for 4 lb}} = \frac{1000}{1250} = 0.8.$$

Multiplying the d.c. resistance of any length of 4 lb cable by 0.8 gives the T.E.R. value in ohms, e.g. 2 miles of 4 lb gauge line, loop resistance 880 $\Omega$, has a T.E.R. of 704 $\Omega$. The corresponding multiplying factor for a 10 lb gauge line is 1.2.

By summating the T.E.R. values of the separate lengths of different conductor gauges comprising a line, the overall T.E.R. can be obtained and this can be directly compared with the T.E.R. limit for the type of exchange concerned. For a short line equipped with a regulated telephone, the summated T.E.R. does not give a true indication of the actual transmission performance of the circuit, i.e. line plus telephone. This, however, does not affect the use of the T.E.R. concept in determining the appropriate conductor sizes to ensure that a line is within transmission limits. The T.E.R. concept therefore simplifies the calculation of the conductor size(s) required for a particular cable and enables a single limiting transmission value to be used for any particular type of exchange. It is extremely useful in calculating the allowance and losses of private branch exchange (P.B.X.) installations.

### 2.2.2. Signalling.

In addition to the transmission considerations it is necessary to ensure that the d.c. resistance of a line does not exceed the signalling limit appropriate to the particular type of exchange. For many types of exchanges the signalling limit is 1000 $\Omega$, but for some of the older automatic exchanges it is 650 $\Omega$. Thus, particularly where lighter gauge cables are used, signalling limits may be the predominant factor.

## 2.3. Provision of plant.

### 2.3.1. Forecast of telephone growth.

The main problem in planning the local area is to decide what advance provision of cable pairs and other plant would be the most economic consistent with the objective of being able to provide a telephone where and when it is required. To assist the local line plant planning engineer a forecast is provided giving the assessed future requirements in each street, and in each large building. This forecast is usually given for 20 years or more ahead at 5 yearly intervals (e.g. 1971, 1976, 1981, 1986).

Although forecasts of bulk telephone growth can be quite accurate, deviations from forecast inevitably occur when dealing with small territorial divisions over comparatively long periods. The probability of such deviations is greater the smaller the territorial unit or group of buildings concerned. A further source of difficulty is the impossibility of forecasting which particular buildings in a group will require a telephone and in what order and, as buildings frequently change hands cessations and transfers have also to be taken into account. Changes in customer requirements may also alter considerably as a result of changes in the occupation of buildings.

### 2.3.2. Flexibility.

To cater for these possible deviations from forecast, a system has been evolved which provides maximum flexibility in the utilization of cable pairs. The exchange area is divided into cabinet areas and further sub-divided into a number of pillar areas, each served by a cross-connexion cabinet or pillar (see section 2.1.4). Cables from the exchange are terminated on the exchange (or E-side) of the cross-connexion assembly in the cabinet, and cables to pillars or distribution points (D.P.) are terminated on the distribution (or D-side) of the cross-connexion assembly. Similarly, at the pillar, cables from the cabinet are terminated on the E-side and cables to D.P.s on the D-side. Each subscriber's telephone is connected to a D.P. which consists of a terminal block located on a pole, or outside or inside a building. The layout of the cable network showing the variations in practice is illustrated in Fig. 3. The largest size of cabinet will accommodate 800 cable pairs on each of the E and D sides. The pillar will accommodate a maximum of 200 cable pairs on each side.

Full flexibility is provided at cross-connexion cabinets and pillars since any cable pair on the E-side can be cross connected by means of bridging pins or jumpers to any cable pair on the D-side (see section 2.1.4 above). D-side pairs can also be cross connected if required.

Several major advantages accrue from the use of cross connexion points with full flexibility. The ease with which 'pins' and 'jumpers' can be altered enables cables on the E-side of cabinets or pillars to be used to maximum fill before it is necessary to provide a relief cable. Hence the system can be operated with minimum spare cable pairs. Since the cable network is divided into distinct sections, the work of relief of any section can be planned and carried out independently of the other sections and furthermore provisioning periods based on the rate of growth can be applied to each section so that maximum economic advantage is obtained. Another advantage is that rearrangements of cable pairs can be confined to the cabinets and pillars.

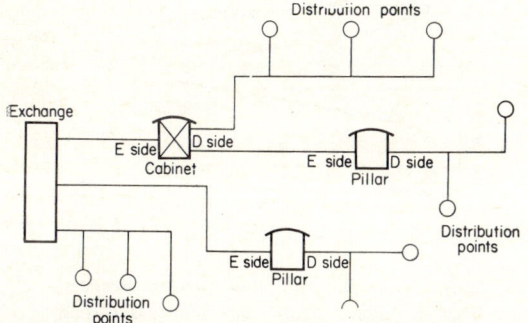

FIG. 3. *Layout of cabinets, pillars and distribution points.*

2.3.3. *Economic studies.* Local line plant planning engineers are often faced with several alternative methods of providing for a requirement and an economic cost comparison between the various methods has to be made. Initial costs are not necessarily a true indication of the relative economic merits of alternative methods and a cost comparison must take into account differing lives of plant and maintenance charges. Engineering cost comparisons generally therefore require a long-term view of costs to be taken over a period of years known as the 'costing period' using, for example, the present value of the annual charges of the various alternative methods. The use of present value of annual charges and other information on telecommunications economics has been given by Morgan (1958).

2.3.4. *Augmentation of plant.* Cable networks must be kept constantly under review in order to pin-point those parts which will require an increase in the number of cable pairs. To assist this process a graphical record is maintained for each cross connexion cabinet area showing the number of cable pairs existing and in use, together with the forecast of requirements. In some instances similar records are kept for pillar areas. A typical record is given in Fig. 4.

The need for augmentation of the plant in an area having been established the amount of relief required can be decided. The relief may consist simply of providing an additional cable to a single cross connexion cabinet but it may be more complicated and involve several cabinets as well as additional distribution points in some parts of the area. The amount of relief is decided on an economic basis and graphs are available which show for various growth rates the economic size of the initial relief cable.

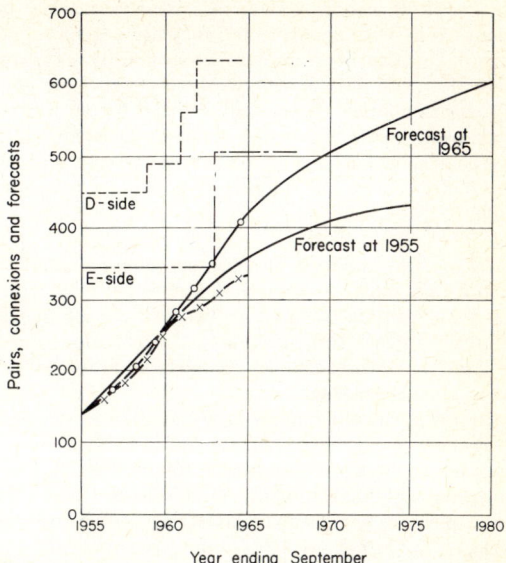

FIG. 4. *Typical growth and capacity graph for a cabinet.—forecast of growth;* –o–o– *exchange connexions;* –×–×– *cable pairs in use;* – – – – *cable pairs connected to distribution D-side;* – – – *cable pairs connected to exchange E-side.*

2.4. *Utilization of subscribers' lines.* Various methods are employed to make the maximum use of the cable pairs between subscribers' premises and the exchange. These methods may be divided broadly into two categories, for telephony and for other services.

2.4.1. *Telephony.* All the methods so far designed for sharing the use of cable pairs for telephony involve at least the provision of individual leads-in to subscribers' premises and cables connecting the leads-in to the exchange, e.g. via a cross connexion pillar or cabinet. The cost of the provision of this relatively expensive part of the subscribers' lines must be taken into account in any cost comparison between the use of the method and the provision of individual cable pairs to the exchange.

Shared service, i.e. two subscribers on one line has limited appeal to subscribers mainly because of the lack of secrecy between the parties but it is an excellent way of dealing with temporary shortages of cable pairs in a particular locality. It is not economic, generally, to include shared service in any long term plans.

The line concentrator uses common cable pairs from the exchange to a point in the cable network where automatic switching equipment (the line concentrator) is provided. Individual pairs of wires are required from the line concentrator to each telephone and additional switching equipment is necessary at the normal exchange. Savings are marginal when compared with the provision of cable pairs on a planned basis and the chief use of line concentrators is to overcome temporary shortages of cable pairs.

Subscribers' carrier systems are used extensively on long lines in some countries but they are expensive and cannot be justified at present economically on short lines. However, development work on cheaper methods of provision could make a subscribers' carrier system available in a few years time. A major problem to be overcome is the feeding of power to the carrier apparatus which ideally should be an integral part of the telephone itself.

*2.4.2. Other services.* The normal cable pair may be used for the telex service and all kinds of private wires, e.g. v.f. telegraphs, connexions between private switchboards, burglar alarms, programme distribution (music or speech). All these services are operated at frequencies up to about 10,000 Hz.

However, since loading is rarely used on subscribers' lines there is only a gradual frequency cut-off and the lines are capable of being used at frequencies considerably above 10,000 Hz, many of the services mentioned in the previous paragraph could be operated on a carrier basis.

*Carrier wired broadcast services* are relatively simple to provide and this is especially so when the demand for a particular service is large and the channel is required for continuous use. In these circumstances, in a given exchange area, it is economic to use an exclusive carrier channel for the service. Even if the average number of subscribers is relatively small, attractive savings are still possible if the service is required throughout a number of exchange areas and if the exchanges can be linked using the local carrier frequency on existing audio junctions. This avoids repeated demodulation, carrier generation and remodulation. The information broadcast may be, for example speech, music, data or telecontrol signals. Such services will all be subject to limitations due to attenuation and crosstalk but in differing degrees. Slow-speed telecontrol systems can readily be made to be very tolerant of noise and crosstalk.

*Data collection systems* and *alarm concentration systems* are generally more complex than broadcast systems. They involve frequency generators and modulators at the subscribers' terminals, inward transmission to the exchange, and monitoring, storage, interrogation and re-transmission equipment at the exchange. The equipment needed, however, is not necessarily more costly than that which would provide equivalent service on audio private wires or on subscribers' telephone lines. Alarm services can be given on telephone lines by setting up calls over the switched network, but the method is less satisfactory than the use of permanent channels between the alarm points and the monitoring point.

The possibilities of using subscribers' lines at carrier frequencies depend on the attenuation and on the crosstalk between pairs and, in the case of open wire, the amount of radio pickup. The table gives attenuation limits for 1, 70 and 140 Hz. Taking account of the way in which the various sizes of cable are distributed throughout the network, it is possible, as an approximation, to draw a single attenuation/frequency curve for a subscribers' line of 1000 $\Omega$ T.E.R. as shown in Fig. 5. This figure also shows cable pair-to-pair crosstalk/frequency curves for 50 per cent, 95 per cent and 99 per cent pairs in any one cable. Figure 6 shows similar curves for a subscribers' line of 500 $\Omega$ T.E.R.

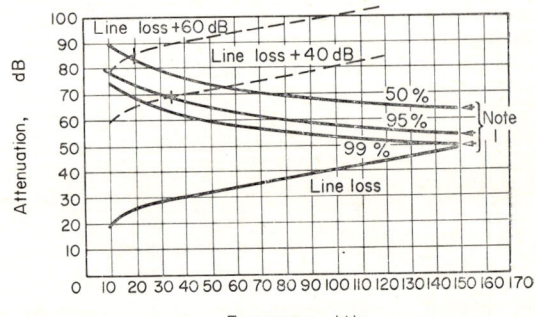

FIG. 5. *Near-end crosstalk and line-loss properties of local lines. Estimated figures for 1000 $\Omega$ T.E.R. line in cable. Note: Crosstalk — the percentages indicate the proportion of pairs in one cable.*

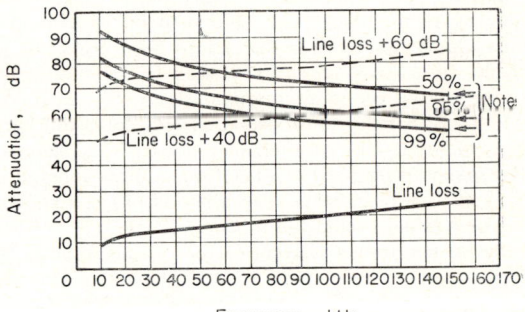

FIG. 6. *Near-end crosstalk and line-loss properties of local lines. Estimated figures for 500 $\Omega$ T.E.R. line in cable. Note: Crosstalk — the percentages indicate the proportion of pairs in one cable.*

Subscribers' lines on which cable pairs are extended by parallel open wires give poor crosstalk attenuation at carrier frequencies. Probably not better than 30 dB pair-to-pair crosstalk can be relied on at 100 Hz for one mile of open wire. Radio pickup by open wire is also a serious problem. It is possible for one mile of open wire to have an induced voltage of 1 mV from a high power radio transmitter at a distance of 30 miles, but pickup may be very much less than this, depending on the location and direction of the open wire. Improvements can be obtained by transpositions or by terminal networks, but these measures are only effective over a limited frequency band and for one source of interference.

*Subscribers' lines: Characteristics for various conductor gauges at carrier frequencies*

| Conductor | Mileage limits | | | Attenuation at 1 Hz | | Attenuation at 70 Hz | | Attenuation at 140 Hz | |
|---|---|---|---|---|---|---|---|---|---|
| lb/mile | Sig. 1000 Ω d.c. | Trans. 100 Ω T.E.R.* | Over-riding line length | dB per mile | dB at limiting length | dB per mile | dB at limiting length | dB per mile | dB at limiting length |
| Cable Copper conductors | | | | | | | | | |
| 4 | 2·3 | 2·8 | 2·3 | 2·7 | 6·2 | 13·8 | 31·5 | 17·0 | 38·9 |
| 6½ | 3·7 | 3·7 | 3·7 | 2·2 | 8·1 | 9·5 | 35·2 | 12·6 | 46·6 |
| 10 | 5·7 | 4·7 | 4·7 | 1·8 | 8·7 | 7·9 | 37·4 | 10·7 | 50·7 |
| 20 | 11·4 | 7·6 | 7·6 | 1·2 | 9·1 | 4·9 | 37·1 | 8·0 | 60·5 |
| Overhead Cadmium – Copper conductors | | | | | | | | | |
| 40 | 19·2 | 27·4 | 19·2 | 0·23 | 4·4 | 0·5 | 9·5 | – | – |
| 70 | 33·3 | 44·4 | 33·3 | 0·16 | 5·3 | 0·46 | 15·2 | – | – |

\* See Section 2.2.1.

From the above information on the properties of subscribers' lines it is possible to give approximate upper frequency limits according to the type of carrier working and the way of using the frequency spectrum. For wired broadcast systems, there is no precise upper limit, but 150 Hz, giving an attenuation of about 50 dB on the longest lines, can be considered a practical limit. For different services using the same carrier frequency bands for transmission in one direction only, the frequency is limited by both crosstalk and attenuation. The limit could be 70 Hz on the longer lines and 100 Hz on shorter lines. For services using the same carrier frequency bands in both directions, the possibilities are very limited. On the longest lines the limit is 16 Hz and on shorter lines the limit is about 60 Hz (Anderson 1964).

### 3. Junction Circuits

These are the circuits interconnecting the local exchanges, either directly or via tandem exchanges, which are used to carry telephone conversations between subscribers' lines connected to local exchanges within the same local area. They are essentially short distance circuits mainly in the range 3 to 10 miles but up to a maximum of about 25 miles. The maximum transmission loss of a junction circuit at audio frequencies should not exceed about 6·5 dB.

Junction circuits may be routed on open wire overhead lines, in aerial cable or more usually in underground cable.

*3.1. Open wire lines.* Open wire lines consisting of copper or cadmium copper wire attached to porcelain insulators at 9 'spacing' on arms attached to poles are used in sparsely populated areas where the route distances are relatively long and the number of circuits required is relatively small. The transmission loss at audio frequencies is very small, of the order of 0·1 dB per mile.

*3.2. Cable circuits.* The most usual type of cable for junction circuits has 10 or 20 lb per mile copper conductors insulated with lapped paper in a lead or polythene sheath. Four conductors are laid up together in a quad and the quads are arranged in layers around a centre core of one or more quads. In some cables the conductors are wrapped with a helix of cotopa string before the application of the paper and a core of cotopa string is inserted in the centre of the four conductors of the quad. The use of string in this fashion results in a cable having more uniform electrical characteristics. The lengths of the 'lay' of the wires within quads and of the quads themselves are varied so as to reduce parallelism and hence crosstalk between individual pairs of wires.

The transmission loss per mile of this type of cable is of the order of 1·5 dB for 10 lb and 1·0 dB for 20 lb conductor.

The transmission loss can be reduced by the introduction of loading coils. The most usual type of loading used is 88 mH coils at 2000 yd spacing. The transmission loss per mile of this type of cable is of the order of 0·7 dB for 10 lb and 0·4 dB for 20 lb conductor.

Thus, loaded type cable will be satisfactory for junction circuits up to about 9 miles for 10 lb and 17 miles for 20 lb conductor cable. Beyond these distances amplifiers (or repeaters) may be necessary. Information on this subject is given in Franklin (1964).

### 4. Acknowledgements

Acknowledgements are made to the Engineer-in-Chief of the General Post Office for permission to publish information contained in this paper and to the Institution of Electrical Engineers for permission to quote extracts from the *Proceedings I.E.E.* Vol. 111.

*See also:* Inland trunk systems. Switching and control in telephony.

*Bibliography*

ANDERSON E. W. (1964) *Local networks, Proc. I.E.E.*, **111,** 713.
EDWARDS J. J., HARDING J. P. and HUMPHRIES A. J. (1946–7) *Flexibility units for local line networks, Post. Off. Elect. Engrs. J,.* **39** (3) & (4) 100, 159.
FRANKLIN R. H. (1964) *Transmission systems for trunk and junction circuits, Proc. I.E.E.*, **111,** 700.
FUDGE G. A. E. (1949) *Introduction and application of transmission performance ratings to subscribers' networks', Post Off. Elect. Engrs.* Paper 198.
GLOVER D. W. and HOOKER E. J. (1961) *A moisture barrier for polythene sheathed cables, Post Off. Elect. Engrs. J.*, **51 (1)** 253.
HAYES H. C. S. (1961) *Polythene sheathed underground telephone cables, Post Off. Elect. Engrs. J.*, **53** (4), 250.
HAYWARD R. W. and ANGELL F. W. (1961) *A new cross connection assembly for cabinets and pillars, Post Off. Elect. Engrs. J.*, **53** (4), 254.
MORGAN T. J. (1958) *Telecommunications Economics*, London: MacDonald.
*National Telephone Networks for the Automatic Service* (1964) published by I.T.U.
WINTERBORN E. E. L. (1958) *Plastics in cables, Post Off. Elect. Engrs. J.*, **51** (1), 33.

E. C. SWAIN

# M

## MAGNETIC RECORDING.

### Applications and Techniques

*Introduction.* It is customary to consider the scope of magnetic recording as being concerned with systems in which information is stored on moving magnetic media such as tape or drums. The common method for imprinting the information is to transport the recording medium through a sharply defined recording magnetic field produced near the gap of a small electromagnet as depicted in Fig. 1 [inset (a)]. This same electro-

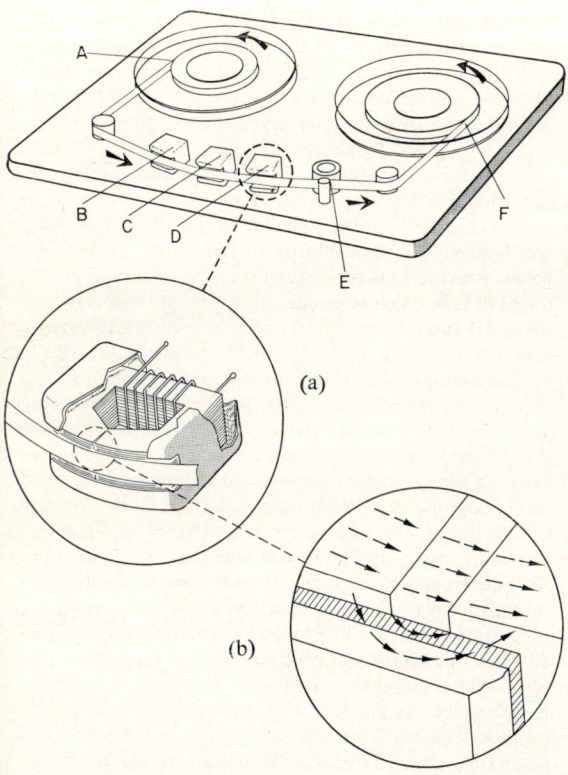

FIG. 1. *Basic tape recording and reproducing system. a) Details of magnetic reproducing head. b) Gap fringe field.*

magnet, called a recording or reproducing head, can be used in a reciprocal fashion to detect the magnetic field of a recording, and a voltage is produced across the winding which is dependent on the recorded information. However, although this system, and a number of mechanical variations, account for most of the present day magnetic recording applications, it can be expected that for future systems the mechanical motion of the storage medium will give way to electronic addressing of the recorded information. Recording and reproducing techniques already exist which demonstrate the feasibility of such future systems. Of course, completely electronically addressable storage systems, using magnetic cores or films, are used in the magnetic memories of computers, although they do not come within the scope of what is presently termed 'magnetic recording'. The definition of magnetic recording can therefore be restricted to those magnetic storage systems involving mechanical motion of either the storage medium, or the recording transducer, or of both. It cannot be expected, however, that this definition will last for very long in the future and the present division between 'magnetic recording' and 'magnetic memory' will disappear. Even within the present limited scope of magnetic recording systems which have been developed from the basic system shown in Fig. 1, the combined features of high density of recorded information, erasability of the recording, large frequency bandwidth, and moderate cost of the storage medium have permitted wide application of magnetic recording systems.

The advances in the areas of application for magnetic recording continue to be unchallenged by competing non-magnetic recording systems. Starting with sound recording, the uses for magnetic recording have expanded after World War II into video recording and digital and analogue data recording. Particularly in the case of data recording, the recording medium has developed into many different forms to achieve fast mechanical access to the recorded data. The rapid growth of the electronic computer industry has produced an ever-increasing need for data storage systems with larger and larger capacities and shorter and shorter information access times. Although much mechanical ingenuity has gone into satisfying these requirements, using the conventional system of electromagnetic recording and reproducing transducers and a thin permanent magnet recording medium, the limitations of the mechanically accessed system are quite apparent and future demands will exceed these limitations. In the area of video recording, a workable but expensive system is in commercial operation. Here, video frequencies are recorded by rapid mechanical scanning of a moving tape with a revolving recording head. Frequencies up to 10 mc/s can be recorded by this method. The cost factor is certainly retarding the natural extension of magnetic tape video recording into the home entertainment market. Cost has also regulated the impact of audio tape recording on the home market. Of all the applications discussed, however, it is only in home audio reproduction that magnetic recording has been successfully challenged by a non-magnetic system. Up to the present time, the lower cost phonograph disk system has almost equalled the quality of magnetic tape for home music reproduction. Recording of music and speech, however, is still performed on magnetic tape and transferred to disks for mass reproduction.

In addition to the above large markets for magnetic recording, there are a host of specialized applications for which it has unique advantages. A few of the many and varied uses may be mentioned here to indicate the wide scope of present day tape recording systems. For instance, magnetic tape is now used as a control medium for machine tools, and is especially useful where complicated machining operations are required on a non-mass production basis. Magnetic tape is used in commercial aircraft in the conventional way to provide background music, but has also found specialized application in aircraft crash recorders where fire and shock resistance are important. The rugged nature of tape recording systems has also found application in space satellite recording, although here the ultimate non-mechanical recording system is required. Another interesting use is in the classroom where, in addition to the conventional video recording systems, pre-recorded oscilloscope display material is used to generate complicated displays with a minimum of apparatus. An entirely new form of magnetic recording has the name 'magnetography' in which a narrow recorded track in a wide moving tape can be scanned across the tape in a controlled fashion to produce a visible trace when 'developed' with a magnetic ink. This narrow recorded track is the boundary zone between oppositely magnetized regions and is produced by a recording head with no moving parts. Thus, recording in two dimensions is achieved with mechanical motion in one direction only. Further two-dimensional recording techniques have been proposed using electron or optical beams. As yet, however, beam techniques for magnetic recording are in the early development stage. Such techniques can be expected to form the basis of future bulk memories, since they offer the combined advantages of high density of stored information, fast access to the information, and a fast reading speed.

*Magnetic recording techniques*. The conventional method of recording and reproducing on a moving magnetic medium using electromagnetic heads has been the undisputed favourite throughout the historical development of magnetic recording. Oberlin Smith first reported, in 1888, on a method for recording the undulating currents from a microphone on cotton threads in which steel clippings were embedded. Within a few years of Smith's report, Valdemar Poulsen showed that magnetic wire could also be recorded by producing tiny magnetized zones along its length. Magnetic wire was the favourite recording medium for many years, but the inability to produce a thin but strong wire restricted the ultimate information storage density. Magnetic tape provided a better solution, and, in particular, the plastic tapes coated with magnetic powder have become the most widely used magnetic storage medium. In fact, magnetic tape would probably completely dominate the scene were it not for the relatively long time required to achieve access to any part of the tape quickly.

Fast access has been achieved in a number of ways: first by increasing the speed of the medium, secondly by mechanical motion of the heads, and thirdly by using a large number of heads to record information in parallel. In this respect, magnetic drums were first developed employing many parallel information tracks. More storage capicity and mechanical motion of the recording heads has been achieved with a system using a stack of coaxially mounted magnetic disks; a key factor in the success of disks has been the development of an out-of-contact recording system employing air-floated heads. Even greater capacity has been obtained with magnetic cards or chips where relatively fast mechanical access can be obtained from a large stack. Recording and reproducing in this latter case is performed by rotary motion of the card as in the drum system. Practically every mechanical modifications of the basic recording system has now been tried and future developments rest on the emergence of some new basic systems.

*Basic recording system*. The conventional magnetic recording system will be described for the tape system shown in Fig. 1, but the basic recording and reproducing techniques are applicable to all the forms of magnetic media previously described. In the tape system of Fig. 1, a reel of tape (A) is unwound by a constant velocity tape drive (E) and is transported in contact with the magnetic erasing, recording and reproducing heads (B, C, and D respectively). All of the heads have similar design, shown in inset (a). The erasing head produces an alternating magnetic field having relatively poor resolution along the direction of tape motion. This field is sufficient to saturate the magnetic tape which becomes demagnetized on leaving the maximum field occurring in the vicinity of the gap in the head core (inset (b)). The recording head (C) has a narrower gap which produces a rapid field decrement as the tape passes beyond the field maximum. In this case, magnetization of the tape takes place if the field corresponding to the information to be recorded does not change appreciably as the tape leaves the recording gap region. Thus, the recording resolution is determined by the field decrement along the direction of tape motion. This also applies to the reproducing head (D), which is of similar design to the recording head. Narrow gap recording heads and tapes with smooth surfaces have also been developed to the stage where it is common to operate down to recorded wavelengths of 2 microns, for instance a 1·5 mc/s signal recorded at a tape speed of 120 inches per second. Such high resolution in the direction of tape motion is not approached in the transverse direction where recorded track widths of 10 mils are common.

During recording, while the tape is transported across

the gap between the high permeability poles of the recording head, the magnetization acquired by an element of tape will depend on the strength, direction and duration of the field, and on the magnetization mechanism in the tape material. Since it is desirable for the tape material to have high remanent magnetization, and yet be non-susceptible to self-demagnetization, its remanent magnetization characteristic is necessarily highly non-linear. For recording of digital information, overall system linearity is not required. However, for analogue recording the tape magnetization should be proportional to the recording signal amplitude and the most common technique for achieving linearity is to add a high frequency bias field to the signal field. The bias field must not magnetize the tape in a way which is detectable on reproduction. In effect, the resultant recording field is similar to one producing ideal or anhysteretic magnetization and linearity is thereby achieved. Immediately after being recorded, the tape is separated from the high permeability pole-pieces and is subjected to the full self-demagnetizing fields of the recorded magnetization. It then travels in contact with the reproducing head (D) where the recorded magnetic flux is shunted by the high permeability head core. Thus, magnetic flux flows through the reproducing head winding which produces a voltage proportional to its time rate of change. The recorded tape is subsequently wound up on the take-up roll (F) for storage. Further magnetic changes can occur during storage due to natural relaxation phenomena in the magnetized tape. Small magnetization changes can occur due to self-demagnetization effects, magnetization by external fields and by fields from adjacent layers in the wound-up reel. Tape materials are designed to minimize these effects which are normally very small.

*Novel recording techniques.* As has been indicated, the limitations of the conventional recording methods centre around mechanical problems of transporting relatively bulky recording heads near the storage medium. Narrow-track miniaturized heads in multi-track packages help to reduce the access time, but have not been successful in producing very high area-density recording. A promising new approach has been to use heat energy produced by an electron beam raise the temperature of the magnetic medium above its Curie point. On cooling again, a small applied magnetic field is sufficient to magnetize the medium at the local zone heated by the beam. Similar heat writing is possible on any material showing a large temperature dependence of coercive force. Since the electron beam is readily deflected to any location on a storage plate, a two-dimensional array of storage cells is achieved which can be accessed randomly. Writing speeds of $10^6$ bits/sec are forecast with bit densities of at least $10^5$ per cm$^2$.

The rapid scanning advantage of an electron beam controlled recording method may be retained in a multi-track recording head scheme which records by applying a field to the tape. In this system, the single turns of the recording heads receive their recording currents directly from an electron beam, the turns being completed outside the vacuum and each linking with a single-lamination U-shaped recording head core.

*Novel reproducing techniques.* Electron or optical beams may also be used to detect the recorded information and there is some variety in the available techniques. There is an essential distinction between these beam recording methods and the conventional electromagnetic heads. In the latter case, the output signal is proportional to the rate of change of the recorded flux linking the head. On the other hand, the deflexion of an electron beam by the surface field of a tape, or the rotation of the plane of polarization of a light beam reflected from the tape, is determined by the amplitude of the recorded flux. The beam readout schemes are known as flux-sensitive detectors and, therefore, do not require relative motion between the recorded tape and the beam in order to produce a readout signal. Electromagnetic heads have also been made flux-sensitive by modulating the head core reluctance. In another approach to flux-sensitive heads, a thin slab of semiconducting material, such as indium antimonide, is included in the head core structure: the Hall voltage being proportional to the head core flux. The electron beam and magnetic modulator heads can give large output voltages ($\sim 1 \cdot 0$ V) for large and medium output impedances respectively. On the other hand, the Hall-effect head delivers a small voltage (0·3 mV) at a low impedance output. The appliceation for flux-sensitive heads are rather specialized, the most well-known application being to check binary rocorded data immediately after recording.

Of the various electron beam techniques propssed for reading magnetic recordings, probably the most uccessful to date is one using the method of the electron mirror microscope. In this method, the electron beam is slowed down and reversed in direction, in the vicinity of the magnetic tape, by an electrode held at the cathode potential. Thus, as the beam passes through the surface field of the recording, its velocity approaches zero and the deflexion sensitivity is very high. The best optical readout method to date uses the Kerr rotation of the plane of polarization of a laser beam. Megacycle readout rates from recorded zones about 10 micron diameter are possible with both beam techniques.

*Modulation techniques.* Finally, in this section, some of the methods used to tailor the recording signal to the characteristics of the recording medium and to the application will be described. Direct recording implies that the recording field amplitude is proportional to the signal amplitude. The highest information packing density on tape can be achieved by direct recording. However, both amplitude and phase distortion occur in this method. The amplitude distortion caused by the non-linearity of the magnetization characteristic of the recording medium is avoided by the use of a bias field added to the signal field, high frequency a.c. bias being the most successful technique. Further amplitude distortion can occur due to non-uniformities in the magnetic storage medium, and these are not tolerable in video recording, for instance, where their effect is large enough to be seen on the reproduced picture. This amplitude distortion is also intolerable for some instrumentation recording applications and, in these cases, the problem is avoided by using frequency modulation or pulse width modulation. Then, the amplitude distortions of the recording system are unimportant and the signal can be recorded at the maximum level; the onus for amplitude fidelity is transferred to the constancy of the tape speed. The price paid for the advantages of frequency modulation or pulse width modulation is that the signal bandwidth is more severely limited. For instance, at speeds of 7·5 inches/sec the recorded bandwidth is 50 c/s–10 kc/s, 0–1 kc/s, and 0–150 c/s for direct, FM, and PWM recording respectively.

### The Recording Process

The recording process to be examined is the mechanism whereby an electromagnetic recording head magnetizes the tape. The magnetic field acting on an element of tape, as it passes the recording gap region, varies in direction and magnitude with the position of the element as shown in Fig. 2. On the left-hand side of the ordinate plane, the field is entirely longitudinal and rotates towards the perpendicular direction as a tape element moves away from the centre plane.

In order to understand how the tape magnetization depends on the recording field direction, reference is made to typical hysteresis loops for a conventional oxide powder tape. Figure 3a shows a family of loops for a

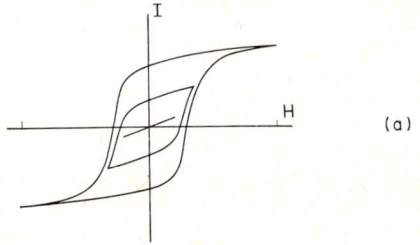

(a)

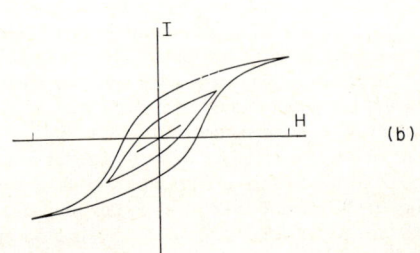

(b)

Fig. 3. *60 c/s hysteresis loops for oriented particles of $\gamma Fe_2O_3$, $H_{max} = 1,000$ Oe. a) Field applied along direction of orientation; b) Field perpendicular to (a).*

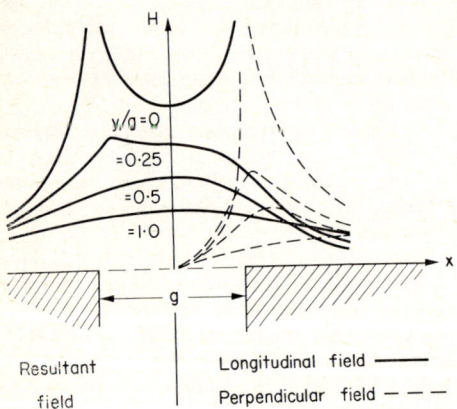

Fig. 2. *Field Distribution near a recording head gap. x = Direction of tape motion; y = Perpendicular distance from gap; g = Gap length.*

(H) the total field amplitude is plotted for different relative distances ($y/g$) from the recording head surface, where $g$ is the gap length. It is an objective of high resolution recording to produce a very rapid decrement of the recording field as the tape moves away from the gap region in the $x$ direction. Since this condition occurs near the head surface, as shown in Fig. 2, only a thin magnetic layer can be effective for short wave-length recording. The change in direction of the recording field is illustrated by plotting the longitudinal and perpendicular components of the field on the right-hand side of the ordinate in Fig. 2. It can be seen that, at the gap centre

field applied along the direction of orientation of the long axes of the elongated particles; this corresponds to the longitudinal head field direction in conventional tapes. It can be seen that, for small applied fields, a low remanent magnetization is acquired. This rapidly increases on increasing the applied field. Similarly, for a perpendicular field, the same type of highly non-linear remanent magnetization characteristic is obtained (Fig. 3b), but here lower maximum magnetization is achievable. Thus, taking account of the tape magnetization characteristics and the recording head field contour, it is expected that the recording will be primarily longitudinal for most of the tape. However, for the surface layer in contact with the recording head, large perpendicular fields are encountered which produce some perpendicular magnetization. That this is the case has been verified by examining the tape magnetization direction at various depths into the magnetic layer using a large scale model. It is an unfortunate feature of conventional recording that perpendicular recording, with relatively poor resolution, occurs in the surface layers where the maximum resolution would be obtained for longitudinal recording.

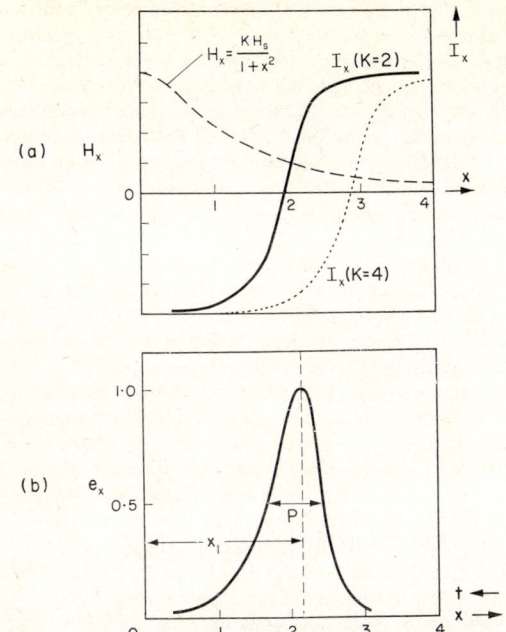

FIG. 4. *a) Recorded transition; b) Ideal reproduction for NRZ step function.*

*Digital data recording.* The simplest method of coding the recording head field is to reverse its direction. In digital data recording, a recording field of amplitude sufficient to produce magnetic saturation through the complete tape layer thickness, is reversed to record a '1' signal and remains constant to record a '0' signal. Binary information recorded in this manner is known as non-return-to-zero recording, the most common technique for digital data recording. Reproduction of this recording is achieved by using a timing signal, obtained from a separate clock track, corresponding to the time when a '1' or '0' is recorded. Self-clocking systems are also in use where the recording field is reversed at regular intervals and the '1' and '0' signals are recorded in between these clock signals.

The recording of an instantaneous reversal of the applied field will be considered initially for an infinitely thin layer of tape at a typical distance, $y = 0.5 g$, from the surface of the recording head. Considering the corresponding longitudinal field contour from Fig. 2, which is replotted in Fig. 4, and the longitudinal magnetization loops of Fig. 3a, the resulting tape magnetization on reversing the recording field can be computed for different maximum applied amplitudes. The resulting form of the magnetization transition is shown in Fig. 4a for $H_{max} = 2H_s$ (solid line) and $H_{max} = 4H_s$ (dotted line). The derivative of the magnetization change for $K = 2$ is shown in Fig 4b to be asymmetrical, and this corresponds to the reproduced waveform using an idealized reproducing head (time axis increasing to the left). As can be seen, both the width and the location of the reproduced pulse will change as the applied field maximum amplitude is increased.

Taking account of practical recording conditions, a number of factors will contribute to a widening of the reproduced pulse and a consequent decrease in the overall resolution. From the above construction of the reproduced pulse for an infinitesimally thin layer of tape, it can be expected that, due to the change in field magnitudes and contours with distance from the head, the contribution from the other tape layers will occur with different amplitudes and at different times. Also, the spatial sensitivity of the reproducing head is not an impulse function, as assumed above, but is given by the field function of Fig. 2. The reproducing head flux is approximately expressed as a convolution integral of the longitudinal field function of the head ($H_x$) and the longitudinal tape magnetization ($I_x$). For a tape of thickness, $c$, spaced a distance, $a$, from the head, the core flux $\varphi_c$ is given by

$$\varphi_c = K \int_a^{a+c} dy \int_{-\infty}^{+\infty} H_x I_x \, dx \qquad (1)$$

where $K$ is a constant. The time derivative of $\varphi_c$ then gives the reproduced waveform. Further distortion of the pulse would be caused on taking account of the perpendicular component of magnetization but this effect is relatively small. It is found, in practice, that even wider pulses than those estimated above are obtained and self- and adjacent bit-demagnetization effects must be considered to account for this. Such losses are reduced in very thin magnetic coatings with a relatively large ratio of $H_c/I_r$.

From the foregoing discussion of practical NRZ recording, it is evident that the highest resolution is obtained by adjusting the field amplitude so that the maximum longitudinal decrement occurs in the surface layer of the tape at a distance where the field has reduced to the switching fields of the particles in the tape material. In practice, larger fields are usually employed to ensure more reliable recording through the coating thickness. When faults occur in the tape coating, in the form of coating nodules or foreign particles, the tape is momentarily separated from the recording head and a 'dropout' of information occurs. To minimize the effect of dropouts, large recording fields are used and resolution is sacrificed for increased reliability. Present high density data recording on oxide powder tapes is in the range 1500–2000 flux reversals per inch. Using thin metallic coatings with high coercive force, extension up to 10,000 reversals per inch is envisaged for the future. Corresponding improvements in the resolution of the reproducing heads is required and this may be achieved by the use of narrow head gaps and electronic pulse slimming filters.

*Analogue recording.* It is possible to extend the NRZ recording system to analogue recording where amplitude linearity between the original and reproduced signals is required. This has been achieved by pulse coding the recording signal so that the width of the recorded pulses is controlled by the recording signal. Another system for analogue recording, using a tape saturating signal, is to frequency modulate a high frequency carrier which is then recorded. However, by far the most economical system for analogue recording uses direct recording of the signal in which the amplitude and frequency of the signal are linearly recorded as changes of magnetization amplitude and wave-length on the tape. A high frequency a.c. bias signal is added to the recording signal to achieve amplitude linearity. The resulting tape magnetization process is rather complicated and has been described by numerous models. Fundamentally, the recording process using a.c. bias is a modification of ideal or anhysteretic magnetization in which an alternating field, sufficient to saturate the material, is applied together with a constant field. On slowly reducing the alternating field to zero the magnetization achieved is approximately proportional to the d.c. field for magnetization levels up to about half of the saturation level.

*Anhysteretic magnetization process.* The linearization of the non-linear remanent magnetization curve, ($I_r$ vs. $H$), achieved in the anhysteretic magnetization process, is shown in Fig. 5 for oriented iron-oxide powder tape.

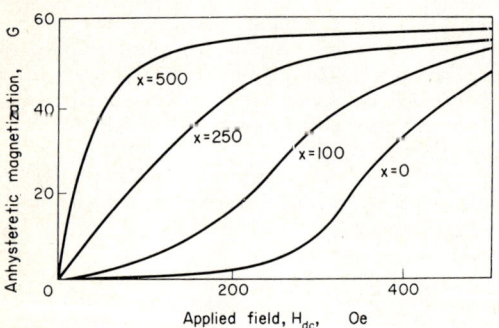

FIG. 5. *Anhysteretic remanent magnetization curves for oriented $\gamma\ Fe_2O_3$ tape, $x = $ peak a.c. field.*

For a.c. fields greater than 500 Oe a limiting condition is reached and the characteristic curve is obtained. In a.c. bias recording the anhysteretic magnetization process is modified, since the d.c. field (the recording signal) acting on a tape element, reduces in amplitude at the same rate as the a.c. bias field as the element traverses the recording head gap zone. This has little effect with respect to the anhysteretic magnetization curves of Fig. 5 until the maximum a.c. field exceeds the coercive force. Then, instead of repeating the characteristic curve for large a.c. fields, the slope of the curve is reduced but keeps the same general shape. This is easily understood since the final magnetization of the particles is determined by the amplitude and direction of the d.c. field when the total field has reduced to the particle switching field ($H'_c$).

In the case of anhysteretic magnetization this condition is always the same providing the maximum a.c. field exceeds the particle switching field. However, in the modified case, the d.c. field occurring when $H_{ac} + H_{dc} = H'_c$ will be reduced as the maximum a.c. field increases. Thus, for recording conditions the initial anhysteretic susceptibility (or the recording sensitivity) has a maximum value for a maximum a.c. field approximately equal to the particle switching field. This corresponds to an optimum a.c. bias amplitude.

It is observed that the general shape of the anhysteretic magnetization curve is similar for most hard magnetic materials. This shape reflects the distribution of internal fields acting on the particles. Whether or not a particle gets magnetized in the direction of an applied d.c. field during anhysteretic magnetization depends on whether $H_{dc}$ exceeds the local internal field due to the magnetizations of the neighbouring particles. Essentially these local internal fields will be randomly directed throughout the material and will have an amplitude distribution which determines the shape of the anhysteretic magnetization curve. Locally, the magnitude and direction of the internal field will depend on the packing density of the particles and their magnetization directions. Consequently, if the magnetization direction of one particle is changed by an external field, the local field in its vicinity will also change and the effective switching fields of neighbouring particles will be modified. One can see that the anhysteretic magnetization process does not then depend on the intrinsic particle switching fields; it depends on the internal fields and their effects on the particle switching fields. Due to the angular dependence of these effects, somewhat higher susceptibility and linearity of the anhysteretic curve is obtained when the magnetizing fields are applied in the direction of orientation of the elongated particles and this is the condition obtained in analogue recording.

*Practical conditions.* The recording process takes place in applied fields from a recording head having a distribution as shown in Fig. 2. This is more complicated than the modified anhysteretic magnetization process described above, since the magnetic coating, at different distances from the head, is subjected to fields of different amplitudes and directions. In addition, the recording field is somewhat modified by the fields from adjacent tape elements which have just been recorded. The net effect is that the actual recording process leads to a more linear characteristic than the modified anhysteretic magnetization curve. As the magnetic coating becomes relatively thicker, the long wave-length recording sensitivity increases up to a point if the a.c. bias amplitude is increased to give maximum sensitivity. Eventually, however, a limit is reached since a decrease of the magnetization of the surface layers in contact with the head occurs due to excessive a.c. bias amplitude. In fact, examination of the recorded magnetization in large scale models indicates that very low magnetization levels are achieved in the surface layers. This is due in part to the low sensitivity to perpendicular fields of the longitudinally oriented tape and also to reduction of the recording field by fields from adjacent recorded zones.

In attempting to determine the optimum dimensions of the head gap and tape thickness, for broadband linear recording with a.c. bias, it is instructive to redraw the head field distribution of Fig. 2 as contours of constant field amplitude as shown in Fig 6. As has been explained, a.c. bias recording takes place when the total applied field, $(H_{ac}+H_{dc})$, falls to a value equal to the particle switching fields. Due to variations in these particle switching fields, amounting to about $0.25\ H_c$ for typical oxide powders, recording will take place over the finite region in which the applied fields fall into this range. Recording regions corresponding to three different amplitudes of applied field are shown as shaded zones in Fig 6a and b. In Fig 6a the zones correspond to

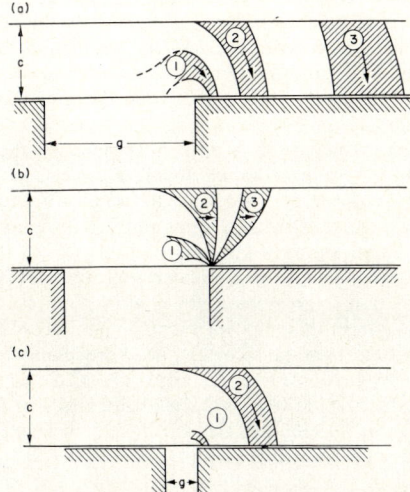

FIG. 6. *Constant recording head field contours. a) Wide gap. Resultant field; b) Wide gap. Longitudinal field; c) Narrow gap. Resultant field.*

the resultant applied field and it is seen that the narrowest longitudinal recording region, giving highest short wave-length resolution, occurs for zone (1) where the field is not sufficient to magnetize the whole coating. This leads to non-optimum recording of the long wavelengths since the whole coating thickness can contribute to the long wave-length output. Due to separation losses in reproduction, only the surface layers contribute to the short wave-length output, and remote layers are useless even if they could be recorded at short wavelengths. As can be seen, however, from Fig. 6a, if the bias amplitude is increased so that the whole of the coating is magnetized (zone 2), then the recording zone widens and the resolution of the recording deteriorates. If it were possible to produce a head in which the perpendicular field is attenuated, or a tape which is insensitive to this component, then the recording zone at the

tape surface would not extend. This is illustrated in Fig. 6b where only the longitudinal component of the constant field contours is plotted. In practice, the short wavelength recording resolution reduces so sharply with separation from the head gap that for a recorded wavelength of 2 microns the loss caused by a 0·1 micron surface roughness on the tape is about 50 per cent.

For the example shown in Fig. 6a and b, the recording head gap length is twice the coating thickness. Using a narrow gap, as shown in Fig. 6c, correspondingly narrower recording zones are possible. However, due to the increased field decrement in the perpendicular direction, indicated by the small penetration of zone (1), the overall resolution is not improved if the field is increased to magnetize the whole tape as shown by zone (2). In practice, moderately narrow gaps are used to favour the recording resolution of short wave-lengths. Thin coatings are also sought for the same reason. As the resolution requirements increase, the mechanical perfection of the gaps and of the head and tape surfaces become the limiting factor. Other losses can occur in the recording head itself and thin metallic laminations or dense ferrites are used for the head core material to minimize the eddy current losses at the bias frequency. This frequency must be high enough to avoid the intermodulation with the signal and also to obtain anhysteretic magnetization conditions.

### The Reproducing Process

A number of techniques are presently available for reproducing a magnetic recording. However, best transducing performance at moderate cost is obtained in an electromagnetic head using a high permeability core.

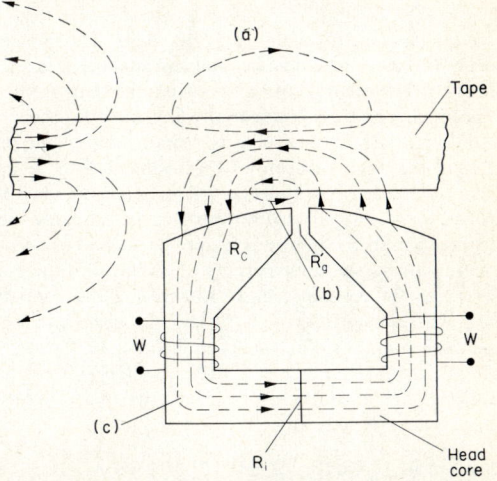

FIG. 7. *Schematic of reproduction process from a recorded tape.*

The essentials of the tape reproducing function are shown schematically in Fig. 7. The low reluctance core, having highly polished magnetic pole pieces in contact with the tape, shunts the flux external to the recorded tape through the desirable path (C) linking the head windings (W). A small fraction of the flux closes through the useless paths (a) on the remote side of the tape and (b) between the head and the tape. If the recorded wave-length exceeds the length of the pole-pieces in contact with the tape, a further loss occurs due to flux not linking the core, and, in the case of infinite recorded wave-length, the reproduced output falls to zero. The head will, of course, also deliver zero output if the frequency of a recording is reduced to zero by reducing the tape speed to zero. Under the normal reproducing conditions shown in Fig. 7, most of the magnetic flux entering the head core from the tape takes the desirable low reluctance path (C) consisting of the core reluctance ($2R_c$) and the back gap reluctance ($R_i$). However, the head gap provides a shunting reluctance ($R'_g$) which may be low when the gap length is made very short to reproduce short recorded wave-lengths. The fraction of the head core flux taking the desirable path (c) is given by

$$\frac{\varphi_c}{\varphi} = \frac{R'_g}{2R_c + R'_g + R_i}. \quad (2)$$

For high efficiency in the reproducing head the gap reluctance is usually kept high by use of a very small gap-depth; the disadvantage being the reduction in head life due to wearing of the pole-pieces. The core reluctance should be as small as possible and high permeability nickel-iron laminations are used for heads operating at relatively low frequencies. For video and pulse recording, however, the frequency losses in metal laminations are excessive and ferrite heads are superior. Other practical reproduction losses, associated with the head geometry, arise when the pole-piece length is of the same order as the recorded wave-length and when the head gap is either not straight or is misaligned with the recording.

*Reproduction of analogue recording.* The general technique used to calculate the reproducing head flux due to a sinusoidal recording is to assume that, since the reproducing process is essentially a linear one, the contribution of any tape element is proportional to the product of the magnetization of that element and the field which the head would produce at the element. In other words, a reciprocal relationship occurs and the field distribution in the gap region may be looked upon as a measure of the spatial sensitivity of the head to the magnetization in the gap region. Integrating the contribution of all elements through the tape thickness and along the tape length yields the total head core flux $\varphi_c$ as shown in equation 1. For a finite gap length ($g^1$), tape thickness ($c$) and a sinusoidal recorded magnetization ($I_x$) of wave-length $\lambda$.

$$\varphi_c = 4\pi c I_{x\,(\max)}\,[A]\,[B]\,[C] \cos \frac{2\pi vt}{\lambda} \quad (3)$$

where $v$ is the tape velocity and $A$, $B$ and $C$ are reproduction loss factors. Were it not for these losses, the reproducing head voltage would be inversely proportional to the recorded wave-length; however, all three factors reduce the short wave-length response.

$$\text{Factor A}\,(\,=(1-\exp[-2\pi c/\lambda])/(2\pi c/\lambda))$$

is called the thickness loss and refers to the attenuation of the reproducing head flux compared with that obtained when the recorded wave-length is long with respect to the coating thickness. Factor B, ($=\exp(-2\pi a/\lambda)$) also produces a monotonic decrease of the reproducing head flux as the recorded wave-length is decreased. Here $a$ is the head-to-tape spacing

$$\text{Factor } C_1\left(\,= [\sin(\pi g^1/\lambda)/(\pi g^1/\lambda)]\left[\frac{5-4(\lambda/g^1)^2}{4-4(\lambda/g^1)^2}\right]\right)$$

is a more complicated expression which accounts for interference effects in the gap region. As the recorded wave-length becomes shorter and approaches the gap length, destructive interference between oppositely magnetized elements of tape occurs with regard to their contributions to the head core flux. This leads to a series of minima in the core flux on further reducing the wave-length. Thus, in order to obtain a continuous wave-length response, it is necessary to use a sufficiently narrow gap so that the first minimum occurs outside the wave-length range of interest.

It is found that the calculated reproduction function of equation 3 agrees well with experimental results. It is also apparent that the losses occurring in recording with separation from the recording head are less severe than the reproduction losses described above. Some idea of the reduction in the reproducing head flux, due to separation loss for recorded elements inside the tape coating, is obtained from the example that 75 per cent of the output at the present limit of broadband recording is due to a coating thickness of only 0·375 microns. The importance of a smooth surface to the tape and heads is clearly shown.

*Reproduction of pulse recording.* In the process of reproducing the sharp tape magnetization reversals that occur in pulse recordings, the objective is to obtain an output voltage spike having the smallest possible time spread. However, in practice the output pulse is widened due to spreading of the magnetization transition of the recording, and due to the finite extent of the reproducing head sensitivity function. In addition, interference from adjacent pulses causes the voltage spike to be shifted in time, which leads to possible errors in detecting the presence or absence of output signals. Normally, the outputs of a multitrack recording are sensed at a time specified by a separate timing track and output pulses between 100 and 50 per cent of maximum are counted as evidence of a recorded '1'. In contrast to analogue recording, it is not necessary to maintain linearity in the reproducing process and the reproducing head voltage pulses are often narrowed electronically to minimize interference effects; this is achieved by the use of filters which compensate for the lowpass filtering effects of the reproducing process.

Applying the reciprocity equation (equation 1) to a recorded step function which is reproduced with a narrow gap head, the output voltage for infinitesimal coating thickness is given by

$$e_x = -n(d\varphi_c/dt)$$

$$= KI_{x\,(\text{max})} \ln\left[\frac{x^2+(a+c)^2}{x^2+a^2}\right] \quad (4)$$

where $K$ is a constant. This is in approximate agreement with the measured voltage pulses using narrow gap heads. Taking account of a small perpendicular magnetization component, and of distortion in the recording process, leads to the familiar asymmetrical shape of the reproduced pulse shown in Fig. 4b. Furthermore, taking account of a finite coating thickness and an effective head-to-tape separation leads to a widening of the reproduced pulse. At present, the use of very narrow reproducing head gap lengths produces little resolution improvement since the recorded transitions are spread out by demagnetization effects in the tape. Again, tapes with very thin coatings and high ratios of $H_c/I_r$ will approach the ideal step function recording.

*Noise in reproduction.* Any reproduced signal which is not part of the original recorded signal is defined here as noise. First, there are a number of unwanted signals arising from imperfections in the tape transport and in the recording and reproducing transducers. If the tape speed is caused to vary, either due to periodic changes in the transport system or due to oscillations set up by the friction between the moving tape and the stationary heads, undesirable changes in signal occur, which are known as '*wow*' and '*flutter*' respectively. Unwanted noise signals may of course be generated by the heads themselves or by the reproducing amplifier. However, the most noticeable noise signals usually originate in the tape itself.

When a demagnetized tape is reproduced, background noise may be detected. This could be due to insufficient demagnetization of the tape by the erasing head, or more fundamentally, to the particulate nature of the recording medium. This latter noise source is due to the randomly-oriented magnetically-saturated domains which constitute the demagnetized tape. The noise voltage thus produced appears as if it were due to a noise magnetization of constant intensity over the whole frequency spectrum and is termed '*white noise*'. When the tape is magnetized, or becomes recorded with a signal, the noise behind the signal increases significantly above the background noise level. This is called '*modulation noise*' and may be 15 dB above the background noise. It is caused by imperfections in the coating, such as surface asperities, as well as voids and agglomerations in the coating. Finally, unwanted signals can also be obtained due to an effect known as '*print through*', which occurs in a wound recorded reel of tape. During storage of a recorded tape, the magnetic fields of the recording penetrate the adjacent layers of tape in the reel and can sometimes produce a low level print or recording which is detectable on reproduction. It is found that this undesirable effect increases with temperature and with the presence of small external fields. The single domain particles of the recording medium have a distribution of shapes and sizes and it is known, that as the volume of such particles decreases, the relaxation times for magnetization change are reduced. In this case the probability of magnetization in a small external field is increased and the printed magnetization level is determined by the field, the ambient temperature and the time of exposure.

*Magnetic Recording Tapes*

Although early developments in magnetic recording were made using flexible metallic tapes and wires as the recording media, the most successful type of recording medium for the last 20 years has consisted of a single thin magnetic coating on a flexible plastic tape. Typically, the plastic tape base is polyvinyl chloride (PVC) or polyethylene terephthalate, e.g. '*mylar*'. Mylar tape is the preferred base material; it has inherent flexibility, immunity to humidity variations, and is highly resistant to stretching and tearing. Furthermore, it can be manufactured with a minimum of surface defects which could cause corresponding defects (dropouts) in the magnetic coating. Almost universally the magnetic coating consists of a dispersion of very small particles of iron oxide ($\gamma Fe_2O_3$) in a plastic binder. Typical tape dimensions are: width 0·25 or 0·5 in., thickness 0·001 to 0·0015 in., length 1200–3600 ft. The tape base is normally about 0·001 in. thick and the coating thickness depends on the application but is about 0·0001 to 0·0005 in.

The iron oxide particles are normally needle-shaped, about 0·6 micron long and 0·1 micron diameter; they occupy about 40 per cent of the coating volume and are oriented with their long axes along the length of the tape. With a continuing emphasis on achieving higher recording densities, the surface smoothness of the coating and its ability to conform closely to the head contours becomes a limiting factor. There is also a resolution advantage to be gained by using even thinner magnetic layers and, to a large extent, the reduction of magnetic material is offset by a higher intrinsic remanent magnetization in the layer. Consequently, higher coercive forces are required to avoid short wave-length losses caused by self-demagnetization effects. Due to these requirements, there has been a return to considering the advantages of metallic magnetic media. However, the metallic tapes now under development consist of a thin metallic layer deposited onto the plastic base material; in this way the physical and magnetic properties of the resulting tape are both optimum.

*Magnetic materials for tape.* From the consideration of the recording, reproducing and storage conditions, it is evident that a highly non-linear remanent magnetization characteristic is required giving a low sensitivity to small external fields. On the other hand, once the applied field magnitude reaches the irreversible magnetization threshold, a high slope remanent magnetization characteristic is required for high recording sensitivity. An array of identical single domain particles could fulfil these requirements. For instance, the switching field of a needle shaped single domain particle can be controlled by its shape, if the switching fields due to other characteristics, such as crystal and strain anisotropy are small. In this case, the preferred magnetization direction is along the length of the particle. When a field is applied opposite to the magnetization direction, no magnetization change occurs while the energy due to the applied field is less than the energy required to rotate the magnetization into the hard direction. When these energies are equal the magnetization rotates completely into the field direction; thus, needle shaped particles can yield the desired non-linear magnetization characteristic. Crystal and strain energies may also be controlled to yield similar characteristics but due to thermal fluctuations the critical fields for switching are normally less stable than the shape anisotropy controlled particles.

In selecting a suitable material for shape anisotropy controlled single domain particles, attention is paid to the size range over which single domain behaviour exists. Outside this range, multidomain and superparamagnetic properties are obtained which reduce the magnatization stability. When the chosen particles are mixed with the plastic binder and spread onto the plastic base material, the aim is to produce complete orientation of the particles, so that a recording field can be applied along their long axes to obtain the same magnetization characteristic in all particles. It is also desirable to produce a uniform dispersion so that the internal fields between particles have a low dispersion and so that noise due to particle clumping is minimized. The extent to which practical particle dispersions fulfil the above requirements is shown in Fig. 8; the needle-shaped iron oxide particles ($\gamma Fe_2O_3$) are typical of present day tape recording media. The saturation magnetization ($I_s$) of such a tape is about 160 gauss and $I_r/I_s = 0.75$ for practical oriented tapes. The coercive force, $H_c = 250$ oe, has a magnitude corresponding to an incoherent magnetization rotation process. Hysteresis loops and anhysteretic magnetization curves, in the direction of particle orientation are shown for this material in Figs. 3 and 5 respectively. Other oxide powders tried in the past for magnetic tapes include small particles of cobalt-doped iron oxide in which crystal anisotropy dominates. Higher coercivities are thereby obtained which reduce the tendency to self-demagnetization at short wave-lengths. However, the large temperature variation of crystal anisotropy produced poor storage stability in this material.

Needle-shaped metal powders, on the other hand, do appear at first sight to offer good tape material characteristics. The single domain size is very small (0.04 micron length) promising low noise characteristics. Tape saturation magnetization and coercivity, on the other hand, are high compared to the oxides; for instance for iron particles $I_s = 680$ gauss, $H_c = 850$ oersted. Thus, high output tapes are possible or alternatively very thin layers may be used. Unfortunately, this latter advantage cannot be fully realized, since coating techniques cannot produce satisfactory layers less than 2 microns thick. Compared to oxides, self-demagnetization effects will not be reduced in iron particles having the above properties. However, higher coercivities have been obtained in cobalt particles where coherent magnetization rotation processes have been observed. Alloy particles of iron-cobalt and cobalt-nickel also show somewhat similar properties indicating at least a three-fold increase in remanent magnetization compared to oxide powders.

Another approach to the manufacture of very thin metallic magnetic layer tapes has been attempted using electrodeposition or electrodeless deposition of the material onto the plastic base material. In this method, the inherent advantage of coating dispersions is lost; that is to say, there is less room for manufacturing error since no averaging out of variations in magnetic properties can take place. Such layers of cobalt-nickel-phosphorus have been used for a number of years on magnetic drums and are now successfully deposited onto mylar base. Using very thin layers of Co-Ni-P or Co-P (say 0.2 micron) the flexible properties of the mylar are not impaired but recording advantages are obtained. All of the coating thickness contributes to the reproducing head signal even for the shortest wavelengths. Also, self-demagnetization and adjacent bit demagnetization effects are reduced for such thin layers. The loss in output due to the use of thin metal films is largely offset by the high intensity of magnetization ($I_s = 900$ gauss) and the reduced losses described. It thus appears that thin metallic film tapes have the potential to replace oxide tapes providing an adequate

FIG. 8. *Horizontally oriented iron-oxide tape particles.* (*Mag. X20,000.*)

degree of quality control can be maintained in their production.

*See also:* Data transmission.

*Bibliography*

DAVIES G. L. (1961) *Magnetic Tape Instrumentation*, New York: McGraw-Hill.
HOAGLAND A. S. (1964) *Digital Magnetic Recording*, New York: Wiley.
MEE C. D. (1964) *The Physics of Magnetic Recording*, Amsterdam: North-Holland.
SPRATT H. G. M. (1964) *Magnetic Tape Recording*, New York: Macmillan.
WINCKEL F. (1960) *Technik der Magnetspeicher*, Berlin: Springer-Verlag.

C. D. MEE

**MAN-MACHINE COMMUNICATION AND ERGONOMICS.** The problem of securing effective communication between man and his tools generically known as 'machines', is as old as technology itself. However, systematic study and analytical approaches to its solution have only recently been initiated as part of the emerging discipline known in U.K. and Western Europe as *ergonomics*. This is a branch of applied science dealing with 'human performance and human factors in work, machine control and equipment design' which emerged under the stimulus of military needs during World War II and later (1946–1950) crystallized as a distinct research area. At the present time it is acquiring recognition as a new professional specialism, a process somewhat farther advanced in the U.S.A. where the titles 'human engineer' and 'human factors specialist' are already widely accepted (Kraft 1962). The British term will be used in this article to cover the latter areas together with engineering psychology and sections of industrial design and industrial engineering.

At a research level ergonomics draws on the pure sciences of anatomy, physiology, psychology, and the professional discipline is closely linked with the older-established ones of mechanical, electrical and industrial engineering. Significant attention is also being devoted to man-machine communication problems within electrical engineering particularly in the U.S.A., as evidenced by the fact that a professional group on Human Factors in Electronics has been formed by the Institute of Electrical and Electronic Engineers and a section of its published proceedings is devoted to the subject.

*Importance of man-machine communication.* While the man-machine communication problem dates from antiquity, its current importance is mainly due to three relatively recent technological advances which have materially changed the nature and scope of the questions facing designers. First came the widespread application of mechanical power to replace human muscles in industrial, agricultural, military and domestic tasks. As a result electric power and internal-combustion engines currently aid human effort in nearly all kinds of work and transportation, under detailed human guidance and control. Some obvious instances are the airplane, agricultural tractor, sensitive drill-press, and industrial sewing-machine, all of which have subjected to ergonomic analysis in attempts to improve the speed and precision of human control (Ashkenas and McRuer 1962; Upton 1961; Corlett 1963; Singleton 1960).

Secondly the development of electrical and radio systems for measurement, communication and remote control has greatly increased the scope and flexibility of methods for getting information to and from human beings in system operation. Instances are the transmission of speech, coded data and visual images from point to point by radio and landline; measurement and remote indication by many kinds of transducers and transmission systems including radar and multiplex telemetry; remote control of machine functions using such devices as pulse-actuated uniselectors (the automatic telephone exchange) and analogue servomechanisms (materials handling and process control). All these have radically altered the man-machine communication problem by permitting arbitrary relocation and centralizing of operating points (Welford 1960; Crossman 1960), as well as greatly improving the display and control facilities available to the designer.

Third, most recent and perhaps ultimately most important is the spreading use of digital computers for all kinds of data-acquisition, storage, retrieval, and processing previously carried out by human beings. These perform routine 'mental' work quicker and more efficiently, but widespread experience since about 1950 has shown that difficult man-machine communication problems must be solved before a computer system can yield its full potential (Licklider 1960). Such 'hardware' developments as the online CRT display and light-pen, and 'software' ones including symbolic assemblers such as Fortran (Backus 1959) for compiling source-programmes written in English-like mnemonic code have been direct responses to this challenge, but there is plenty of room for further advance. On the other hand small-scale on-line computers make it possible to generate displays and interpret operator commands in a very much more flexible way than was previously possible. One instance of this is seen in computer-controlled automatic teaching machines currently being field-tested and another is computer-aided engineering design using visual displays and keyboard input (Sutherland 1965).

Parallelling these major practical developments there have been important theoretical advances in automatic control, communication theory and general cybernetics which besides aiding the system designer and analyst have provided new concepts and quantitative methods for studying man-machine communication. As a result the field is now wide and diverse enough to defeat any attempt at complete coverage within the scope of this article. Therefore two specific areas, vehicle control and man-computer interaction, have been somewhat arbitrarily selected to illustrate the general analysis given in the next section. Extended treatments of the more detailed aspects of display and control design, as well as research methods and system-design principles may be found in the many excellent handbooks of ergonomics and human engineering (Murrell 1965; Chapanis 1959; Woodson and Conover 1964; McCormick 1964; Floyd and Welford 1954) and in the relevant journals (Ergonomics; Human Factors; I.E.E.E. Trans.). Discussions of the social and economic impact of the newer man-machine systems are found under 'automation' (Wiener 1954; Proc. O.E.C.D. 1965).

*The man-machine interface.* Man-machine communication cannot be meaningfully discussed apart from the total man-machine system within which it occurs. The latter may fall into one of many categories according to its purpose and mode of functioning, which must be carefully considered. Most are designed or evolve to meet a practical need, for instance in transportation, manipulation of materials, data-processing, or scientific research. Any system's efficiency must of course be judged by its success in attaining its operating objective or *goal;* this is often not explicitly stated at the time of operation but must exist in the mind of the operator (or his supervisor). Reaching the goal is normally beyond the capacity of the unaided operator and it is for this reason that he enlists the aid of a machine. But to do so entails communicating objectives to the machine, a minimum basic purpose of man-machine communication. Several objectives such as speed, accuracy and economy of means are often sought simultaneously, and overall evaluation of system performance is often difficult because of the lack of a well-defined overall 'objective function'.

In order both to communicate the objective and also supply detailed guidance where the machine lacks sensory inputs or the power of decision the *human operator* manipulates one or more *controlled members* (or *controls* for short) which affect the behaviour of the machine or plant, observing and evaluating the feedback resultant performance by means of displays. Thus a closed-loop dependence or feedback is set up between man and machine, which normally results in more or less rapid attainment of the desired state which may be a discrete endpoint as in landing an aircraft or continuous maintenance of specified conditions as in an electricity distribution system. The flow of information and control may be represented as in the figure. More complex man-machine systems involving team-work, multi-machine operation and supervisory (multiloop) control produce more complicated but not radically different patterns.

The total set of displays and controls through which communication is established between man and machine is known as the *man-machine interface.* This normally includes both components explicitly provided for display and control purposes, such as pointer instruments, printers, handwheels, pushbuttons, keyboards, etc., and also those aspects of machine function which may be directly sensed by its operator, such as the motion of vehicles or sound of machinery. Sometimes control intervention is also possible through informal channels such as direct injection of signals into electric circuits or manipulation of working parts and these must be considered part of the interface.

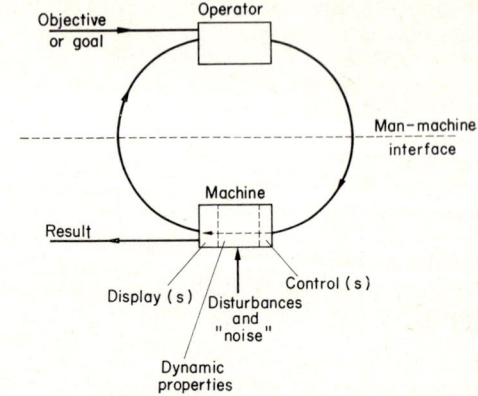

It is the task of the ergonomist or other designer responsible for the man-machine interface to ensure an adequate flow of information in both directions while minimizing the cost of special display and control equipment, and of training or experience needed by the operator. Generally speaking this is achieved by carefully matching the interface to known human capacities and limitations in the following respects: 1) physical display characteristics are matched to human sensory channels, keeping well above threshold and minimizing 'noise'; 2) display coding is adjusted to natural or normally acquired perceptual structures such as visual perspective and familiar letter-number-word sequences, and to human memory capacity; 3) controlled members are made to suit the size, shape, strength and precision of limb-movements of the normal user population; 4) the pattern of control manipulation is selected in conformity with normal or specially acquired adult motor skills such as eye-hand manipulation, typing and speech; 5) immediately displayed responses to operator's control actions (control 'feel', verification) are made to agree with normal human kinaesthetic and other local feedback modes.

An analytical approach to these complex design requirements evidently needs an adequate data-base in sound scientific knowledge of human input and output characteristics. The data should preferably be expressed in terms compatible with those used in other branches of engineering to describe the physical and informational characteristics of hardware components forming the machine side of the interface. While the results of older physiological and psychological studies provided much insight into sensory and motor function, their results often cannot be translated into such terms as quantitative stress-strain relationships, frequency-response curves, information-capacity, noise-level, and so forth. Thus a large part of the current research effort in ergonomics and engineering psychology is devoted to measuring or remeasuring properties of the human operator with these new needs in mind and compiling readily usable design data from the results (see e.g. Meiry 1965; Murrell 1957).

The literature by now contains numerous reports of cases where the analytical approach to man-machine interface design has yielded significant gains both over trial-and-error procedures using mockups and over simple adherence to convention (Murrell and Kingston 1966; Shackel 1962). However, ergonomics is not yet mature enough for standardized design procedures to have emerged and much still depends on individual flair and initiative. In at least some cases, for instance the aircraft altimeter (Rolfe 1965) and machine-tool handwheels (Gibbs 1952) widely used interface components have been shown to have marked disadvantages by comparison with more 'ergonomic' designs but have been retained because users are reluctant to accept new and unfamiliar equipment. It is probably true to say that conservatism is more marked here than in relation to less visible parts of a machine system. For instance motorists may react more strongly to a change in foot-pedal layout than to introduction of front-wheel drive, though the latter has much more effect on overall system performance.

An essential if indirect aspect of interface design is the dynamic response of the machine to control changes since this determines the pattern of display change caused by control action, known in general terms as the *control-display transfer*. Since the operator has limited flexibility of response it largely determines the precision and stability of the closed-loop system. This will be further discussed below.

In most cases disturbances or *noise* arising inside or outside the machine also cause display changes independent of operator action and thus departure from the desired state or goal. The total amount of information flowing through the interface to and from the operator, and hence the severity of the communication problem, depends jointly on these two factors, machine dynamics and noise, and on the desired accuracy of control set by the objective-function. All three vary widely according to the type of system being considered, its environment, and working objectives, but an upper limit is set by the information throughput capacity of the operator (Crossman 1964); when this limit is exceeded either total breakdown results or the objective fails to be attained in one or more respects.

One further general feature of man-machine communication may be noted, viz. the intermittency of connexion between man and machine. Information flows in either direction under control of what might be called an executive program within the operator. He may reject or ignore displayed data at will by ceasing to attend to it, and he may also choose not to make control changes; generally speaking operators are found to adjust their scanning or sampling behaviour adaptively to match the information currently being provided by the various display features, or required for adequate control (Fitts *et al*. 1950; Senders 1964). Thus the physical existence of an interface does not guarantee communication; the operator must also be 'programmed' (trained or experienced) to attend to the right displays at the right time and to use controls with the correct frequency. In extreme cases (e.g. sleep) operators may, so to speak, disconnect themselves while remaining physically present; instances have been reported where they fail to respond to signals while awake, alert, and directly fixating the item in question.

This brief survey of topics related to the man-machine interface should serve to indicate the scope and complexity of the subject. In summary, the factors specifically affecting man-machine communication may be listed as follows in approximate order of importance:

(1) *System objectives*, whether simple or complex, tight or loosely defined, precise or imprecise.

(2) *Machine dynamics*, the pattern, speed and predictability of machine response to control action.

(3) *Noise*, the nature, amount and speed of random or unpredictable disturbance arising in the machine or its environment.

(4) *Fundamental operator capacities and limitations*, of sensory channelling, decision speed and power, limb force and precision, etc.

(5) *Operator skills and abilities*, acquired operator training and experience in general and on the particular system studied.

(6) *Interface design*, the type of displays and controls used, whether digital or analogue, natural or artificial, many or few.
   a) The detailed design of displays and controls.
   b) Display and control coding and display-control compatibility.

For more concrete illustration the next two sections give more specific results on two particular types of man-machine communication currently being studied; these fall at opposite ends of the spectrum of possible systems, the first requiring fast relatively simple response from the operator to analogue display variables, and the second slow complex response to discrete symbolic information. Most others fall somewhere in between.

*Fast analog systems—pilot/aircraft communication*. In this broad class of man-machine system continuous analogue signals are exchanged between man and machine, and the operator's control decisions must be made in 'real time' at a rate independent of his own volition (i.e. under machine pacing). Flying a light aircraft may be taken as the paradigm case. Here the machine is an aircraft with its controls, instrumentation and airfield facilities, and the system objectives have to do with transportation either of the pilot himself or of passengers, materials or equipment (e.g. crop-spraying, aerial photography).

The interface may be readily visualized; displays available to the operator (pilot) fall into five groups; visual contact with the surroundings such as horizon, terrain and clouds, yielding information on attitude, speed, geographical location, etc.; visual instruments including compass, artificial horizon, turn and bank indicator, altimeter, airspeed indicator all of which provide time-continuous one-dimensional analog signals; otolith and semicircular canals in his head which register the aircraft's accelerations in three linear and three angular degrees of freedom; control 'feel' sensed kinaesthetically; and radio, providing intermittent verbal information.

The total display includes some 30–40 distinct 'channels' through which the operator can get data on the machine's behaviour. Clearly he cannot use all of them all the time and eye-fixation recordings (Senders 1963) have shown that he actually devotes different percentages of time to the various visual channels according to his current objective (i.e. manoeuvre). Presumably a similar but unobservable scan-pattern for auditory and proprioceptive channels occurs internally. Many of the channels are redundant, for instance visual contact, altimeter and otolith organs all provide data on height and its time-derivatives. In general the different channels 'transmitting' a given machine variable have different sensitivity, error and 'noise', and their data are combined by the operator on a statistical basis to provide a current best-estimate or inference of its true value. Efficient scanning patterns and methods of combining data-sources are acquired by the operator during training and experience, some of which may utilize a simulator rather than the actual aircraft.

As is typical of most man-machine systems the controls are less numerous than the displays. The latter fall into three groups: continuous position- or force-actuated members such as joystick, rudder-bar, throttle, trim-controls; switch-settings; and a microphone for radio contact, numbering between 5 and 10 in all according to the exact definitions used. The current status of each controlled member can be sensed either visually or kinaesthetically as part of the total display.

The control-display transfer is complex and time-dependent; several of the controls interact to cause changes in several displays. For instance throttle and joystick motion transfer jointly to artificial horizon, altimeter and otolith sensation. A stepwise change applied to a single control such as throttle while holding other controls constant will reveal its transfer to a specific display such as the altimeter by way of the machine dynamics, in terms of a 'weighting function', whose leading characteristics are gain, linearity and 'order' of control. The latter is shown by its time-pattern; a stepwise display response would show zero-order (proportional) control; a ramp response, i.e. continued steady change, would indicate first-order (integral) control and so forth; in each case there will usually be some lag in reaching the final state. By such a test applied to the throttle with constant joystick position, it is found to act as a first-order control of aircraft height and hence of altimeter reading, with small lag. Aircraft controls range up to fourth-order, and some crossed effects are even more complex.

The objectives of the aircraft/pilot system are determined by the nature of the current 'mission', and vary through time with the different phases of a flight. Flying straight and level on a compass-course requirts regulation of altitude, direction, height, speed wieh some penalty attached to integrated error in each degree of freedom. Landing requires only attainment of a given final position at zero velocity. The major unpredictable disturbances in the man-machine loop are due to vertical air currents and wind, though other aircraft, physiological conditions such as anoxia in the pilot, engine faults, obstacles on the ground and so forth may occasionally cause 'noise'.

Much empirical and theoretical study has been devoted to specific aspects of the pilot/aircraft system, but the writer is not aware that a comprehensive man-machine analysis covering all of the areas noted above has yet been attempted. However, sophisticated laboratory and field studies intended to simulate one or two-dimensional joystick control, as in maintaining a desired attitude against disturbances in the roll and pitch axes, have established a 'pilot describing function' (i.e. the pilot's display-control transfer) expressed in conventional frequency-response terms, and summarized in Laplace-transform notation (McRuer and Krendel 1959; McRuer et al. 1965). This can be used in analytical design studies to predict the precision and stability of manual control to be expected with different aircraft handling characteristics (Ashkenas and McRuer 1962) and 'live' studies in actual flying have corroborated the results.

The pilot is found to behave approximately as a linear low-pass filter with a fixed delay (about 0·1 sec) and adaptive phase-lead and lag terms (i.e. differentiation and integration). His gain, lead and lag time-constants adjust automatically to the system being controlled and the nature of the disturbance encountered, the general result being to create a closed-loop (man-machine) system with nearly neutral stability. Error tends to increase with disturbance bandwidth and the feedback is ineffective above about 2 cycles per second. Current research is concerned with multivariable and multiloop control tasks, extending this specialized model of the operator to more general cases.

The visual 'contact' needed for landing presents more difficult problems than these single-variable compensatory tracking tasks performed in flying straight and level. Relatively little is known of the visual pattern-perception and kinetic perspective effects involved, beyond the fact that the centre-of-expansion of the visual field provides an important cue to direction of motion (Gibson and Crooks 1938).

Thus in some but certainly not all respects the aircraft pilot can be considered as a linear continuous communication-channel with bandwidth about 2 cycles per second.

Among other predominantly analogue communication tasks may be listed, control of road and agricultural vehicles, control of industrial process-plant, use of power-tools such as drilling and milling machines, and many scientific data-gathering procedures. In general understanding of man-machine communication in such cases seems now to be firmly based on engineering automatic-control and allied concepts; experimental methods are being refined and definitive results have been obtained in some of the more elementary cases involving single display and control modes and statistically stationary inputs. Further research seems likely to extend the coverage to successively more complex and more general cases.

*Slow digital systems—man-computer interaction in process control.* At the other end of the man-machine communication spectrum are systems where discrete digital information is exchanged with the machine at a relatively slow pace allowing the operator plenty of time for consideration, or at least rest-pauses. Typical interface equipment are keyboards, push-buttons, printers, panel-lights, illuminated signs and so forth. Most commercial and industrial data-processing systems are of this kind as well as scientific and engineering applications of digital computers. While typewriters and desk calculators are more numerous, current interest centres mainly on the more complex area of man-computer interaction, and we will take on-line digital control of industrial or other process plant as a paradigm case.

The 'machine' here includes two components, a plant or process which otherwise could be operated manually in analog fashion, and a computer programmed for the necessary monitoring and adjustment to carry out the routine functions needed to stabilize and optimize the process, i.e. to 'close the loop' around the plant. In most practical cases the computer does not directly adjust controlled members (valves, switches, etc.) on the plant itself but changes the setpoints of analog 'minor-loop' controllers. In a typical oil-refinery application (Anon. 1963) the computer has control of 8 setpoints and scans some 200 transducers reporting temperature flow, pressure, etc.

Communication with the operator takes place in symbolic (alphanumeric) code through the medium of teleprinters and switch-registers. The teleprinter types out messages from the computer concerning the current state of the plant, reporting various fault conditions, 'recommending' certain control policies or specific actions, and/or requesting permission to execute control decisions already taken. The operator exerts control over the data gathering, decision-making and other activities of the program, and hence over the behaviour of the process, through switch-registers and/or a keyboard into which he may enter commands selected from a pre-arranged list using mnemonic or purely arbitrary codes. Usually the details of the command and any accompanying data are verified on some form of visual display before pressing an 'execute' button to cause the information to be entered into the computer.

The control-display transfer, i.e. the computer-plant response to operator commands, takes a combined logical and continuous form. Certain commands cause messages to be printed out indicating the current state of affairs at some point in the plant, but others elicit no overt response and the result may only show up in later values of printed data. Disturbances in plant or surroundings may cause 'spontaneous' messages outside the normal scanning cycle; if these require immediate action warning lights may also appear or hooters sound. But most disturbances are automatically corrected by the machine and the operator only becomes aware of them subsequently through variation of the recorded values of internal control variables.

The operator's main tasks are to decide on current objectives, communicate them to the computer, and monitor the overall results for major deviations. As part of determining objectives he may decide the limits within which the control program shall be permitted to operate the plant. At a quite different level he also performs manipulative activities that cannot be done by automatic equipment, such as lubricating pumps and inserting new chart paper.

The major problem in man-machine communication here is that of coding typewritten messages and command formats. For economy of machine processing and information-storage it is usually necessary for them either to be compressed into short 'mnemonics' which can be interpreted into even shorter instructions by the program, or else simply coded into combinations of digits like telephone numbers. Since operators are prone to make errors of interpretation and execution in dealing with these arbitrary symbolic messages it is usually necessary to provide some form of checking within the program to ensure that commands entered are feasible and safe to execute, or if not, to output some form of query requesting reconsideration.

Apart from coding problems there are certain basic limitations on the rate at which operators can transmit digital information to and from such a digital interface. 25 bits/second may be taken as an absolute upper limit for highly practiced keyboard operation, and rates around 5 bits/second are measured in performance by unpractised subjects. But these rates depend heavily on the type of keyboard and display layout used and on the operator's familiarity with the particular system. Rates as low as 0·1 bit/second may well be more typical than the above, which are maxima attainable under excellent conditions. Thus important benefits may be secured by ergonomic improvements in the design of consoles (Whitfield 1964).

A further significant problem arises in the division of function between man and machine. The strength of the computer lies in its fast reliable fatigue-free logical operations and precise numerical data-processing, and it follows that as far as possible human operators should be relieved of all such tasks. Their particular strength lies in the flexible use of information from numerous sources and in rapid adaptation to changing, even totally new circumstances. Hence the human operator of a computer-based control system should be provided with enough pre-digested data to provide an overall picture of the internal state of the machine permitting complicated heuristic treatment of fault conditions and other non-routine problems. This is hard to achieve, and much more research will be needed to achieve man-computer interface designs that permit full use of human capacities. In the writer's opinion most such designs are currently geared more closely to computer circuitry and internal logical design than to the preferred thought-patterns of their operators, and there is room for ergonomic studies of the various alternative possibilities such as pictorial and kinetic displays.

Finally, mention should be made of the widespread development of program compilers and interpreters designed for easy on-line and off-line programming. These include Fortran for scientific computations, Cobol for commercial data-processing, APT for numerically-controlled machine-tools and many others. They all interface between a programmer and the machine (computer) that he wishes to use, helping to match the developed pattern-perception and generating powers of humans, which rely on large amounts of redundancy, to the logically atomistic internal functioning of computers. Several existing compilers appear to have reached the limit of complexity useful for their specific subject-matter and further progress will depend on developing further specific languages for specific applications. One likely area is engineering design, where already computer logic circuits are being developed with the aid of a specialized program (IBM Corp. 1962).

*Concluding remarks.* In concluding this review it may be said that the field of man-machine communication is at present undergoing rapid development and the state of the art twenty years hence is likely to differ even more from the present than the latter does from twenty years ago. Most rapid progress may be expected in the use of small digital computers as interfaces between the human operator and his mechanically powered equipment. By then probably very few routine monitoring and inner-loop control tasks will be performed by the unaided human, whose activities will consist mainly of overall determination of objectives, supervisory control, fault-diagnosis and optimization.

If certain technical barriers can be overcome, man-machine communication will be much freer than at present. Automatic speech recognizers capable of interpreting the human voice at conversational speeds, and visual (optical) devices for reading imperfect handwriting with the same ease as humans are particularly needed to facilitate the transfer of information from man to machine. In the other direction sophisticated graphic, pictorial and perhaps auditory displays are required capable of conveying complex information to operators in the patterned form most meaningful to human perceptual mechanisms. If these new interface facilities can be developed, the next major need seems to be for compilers able to interpret human commands and statements expressed at a successively higher conceptual level and with less detail than at present. If these are used in conjunction with time-sharing computer systems capable of accepting the output of many operators concurrently in real-time, human beings will finally become able to multiply their problem-solving and decision-making capacity many times over. Thus man-machine communication studies seem likely to play a growing part in the development of future technology.

*See also:* Computers, multiaccess to. Graphical communication. Psychological limiting factors in human performance. Speech recognition, automatic.

*Bibliography*

ANON. (1963) *Computer-controlled F.C.C. Unit sets performance records, Oil and Gas J.* (U.S.A.) Jan.

ASHKENAS I. L. and MCRUER D. T. (1962) *A Theory of handling qualities derived from pilot-vehicle system considerations, Aerospace Engng.* **21**, 83.

BACKUS J. (1959) *Automatic programming: properties and performance of FORTRAN systems I and II*, in *National Physical Laboratory Symposium No. 10, Mechanisation of Thought Processes*, London: H.M. Stationery Office.

CHAPANIS A. (1959) *Research Techniques in Human Engineering*, Baltimore: John Hopkins.

CORLETT E. N. (1963) *Human factors in machine control, Ergonomics* **5**, 217.

CROSSMAN E. R. F. W. (1960) *Automation and Skill*, D.S.I.R. Problems of Progress in Industry, No. 9, London: H.M. Stationery Office.

CROSSMAN E. R. F. W. (1964) *Information Processes in human skill, Brit. Med. Bull.* **20**, 32.

*Ergonomics* (official publication of the Ergonomics Research Society.) London: Taylor and Francis.

FITTS P. M., JONES R. E. and MILTON J. L. (1950) *Eye-movements of pilots during instrument landing approaches, Aeronaut. Engng. Rev.* **9**, 1.

FLOYD W. F. and WELFORD A. T. (Eds.) (1954) *Human Factors in Equipment Design*, London: H. K. Lewis.

GIBBS C. B. (1952) *A new indicator of machine-tool travel, Occupational Psychology* **4**.

GIBSON J. J. and CROOKS L. E. (1938) *A theoretical field analysis of automobile driving, Amer. J. Psychol.* **51**, 453.

*Human Factors* (the journal of the Human Factors Society), New York: Pergamon Press.

I.B.M. Corporation (1962) *General Information Manual: Engineering data-processing for manufacturing industries*, New York: I.B.M. Tech. Pubs.

*I.E.E.E Transactions on Human Factors in Electronics* (publication of the corresponding professional group within the Institute).

KRAFT J. A. (1962) *The 1961 picture of Human Factors research in business and industry in the United States of America, Ergonomics*, **5**, 293.

LICKLIDER J. C. R. (1960) *Man-computer symbiosis, I.R.E. Trans. on Human Factors in Electronics* HFE 1.

MCCORMICK E. J. (1964) *Human Factors Engineering*, New York: McGraw-Hill.

MCRUER D. T. and KRENDEL E. S. (1959) *The human operator as a servosystem element, J. Franklin Institute* **267**, 1.

MCRUER D. T., GRAHAM D., KRENDEL E. S. and REISE-

general conditions. The conclusions of these investigators have tended to concur with those reached by Birmingham and Taylor (1954). The latter state that, for the best performance, the operator's task should be as simple as possible, i.e. he should effectively be required to operate as a simple amplifier over a restricted frequency range—not more than 1 Hz—with a lag corresponding to his reaction time. This can be effected by making the controlled element dynamics as simple as possible, and by modifying the operator's display by adding terms approximating the inverse of the controlled element transfer function. For example, with controlled element dynamics consisting of a simple lag, an appropriate lead is inserted into the error channel so that the loop external to the operator possesses an overall transfer approximating a simple gain. This process is known as *rate-aiding*.

It is necessary to ensure that the power output required of the operator should not be excessive. All controls should be as light and frictionless as possible so as to postpone the onset of fatigue. It should be recognized that fatigue problems will generally be exacerbated by an increase in the bandwidth of the required operator output motion, and that there are physiological constraints on the range of output motion of which operators are capable. The process of reducing the output effort required of the operator is known as *unburdening*.

A considerable amount of effort has been devoted to obtaining mathematical descriptions of the human operator, both from physiological interest, and with a view to the eventual improvement of human operator control system performance through a better understanding of the operator's basic characteristics. One of the initiators of this line of research was Tustin (1947), who used a crude form of spectral analysis—which has nevertheless formed the basis of many subsequent studies—to derive a linear continuous model for the operator's transfer in a gun-aiming task. Tustin proposed a transfer of the form:

$$G(p) = K \frac{(1+pT)}{p} \cdot e^{-3p}$$

where $p$ is the Laplace operator. He coined the term 'remnant' for that part of the operator's output not linearly coherent with the input (the target course). The various forms of models which have subsequently been derived are discussed below.

*Linear continuous models.* In addition to the model proposed by Tustin, described above, many linear continuous representations of human operator dynamics have been derived by other workers, mostly in connexion with the description of pilot's transfer functions. These have been summarized by McRuer and Krendel (1959), who propose a composite model of the form.

$$G(p) = K \frac{(1+pT_L)\cdot e^{-pT_d}}{(1+pT_1)(1+pT_n)} \cdot K_T$$

where $T_d$ represents reaction time delay;
$T_n$ represent neuromuscular lag;
$\frac{1+pT_L}{1+pT_1}$ represents equalization introduced by the human operator as a result of training;
$K_T$ represents a small threshold effect (a gain describing function not directly measurable);
$K$ represents the inherent gain of the operator—it is a parameter particularly sensitive to variations in input and controlled element characteristics.

Krendel and McRuer indicate that there is little point in considering similar models with more leads and lags, because these would be unlikely to effect any material improvement in the fit of the model, so that the extra parameters introduced would be rather arbitrary.

The manner in which the parameters of the above linear continuous model are affected by the characteristics of the input signal, in a simple compensatory task, are exemplified by the results obtained by Elkind (1956). He found that, with a rectangular spectrum extending from near d.c. to 0·16 Hz, $K = 34·5$ dB, $T_d = 0·64$ sec, and $T_n = 28·6$ sec. With an input spectrum of similar form, but extending to 2·4 Hz, the appropriate values were, $K = -0·6$ dB, $T_d = 0·122$ sec, and $T_n = 1·7$ sec.

*Non-linear models.* Models combining essentially the above linear continuous representation with non-linear elements have also been investigated; a notable example is that evolved at Goodyear Aircraft (1952), the chief features of which are shown in Fig. 2. These have been fitted to operator data by means of a direct comparison between model and operator input and output traces.

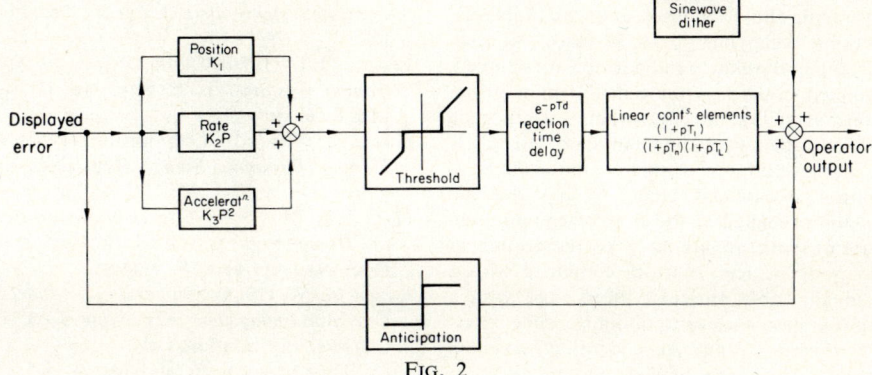

Fig. 2

They are chiefly of use in describing the operator's performance when controlling a system with complex dynamics (e.g. an aircraft), where a simple linear continuous model will often give but a poor fit — sometimes more than half the operator's output power is not accounted for by such a model.

*Sampled data models.* The proposal that the operator acts in a discontinuous fashion was made by Craik (1947, 1948) in 1947. He proposed that the operator sampled his input about twice per second, and then formulated a response which ran to completion before the next sample was taken. Craik's hypothesis was consistent with the phenomenon known as the *psychological refractory period*, which has been the subject of some contention in the psychological literature. Many experiments indicated that an operator appeared to be incapable of responding normally to a second stimulus when this was applied within 0·3 to 0·5 sec of the preceding stimulus, and that the time to respond to the second stimulus was considerably lengthened. However, further evidence suggests that the psychological refractory period may be as short as 100 msec in certain circumstances, so that caution must be exercised in interpreting results published in the literature.

Following Craik's hypothesis, several sampled data models have been proposed and investigated. Bekey (1962) examined a class of models consisting of a sampling action (interval 0·3 to 0·5 sec), followed by a data reconstruction and linear continuous transfer elements. He fitted models in the frequency domain by attempting to reproduce the peaks sometimes observed around 1 5 Hz in the spectra of operator's outputs. Only moderate success was obtained, and this required models incorporating a small pure prediction as part of their continuous transfer elements. Later, Raoult (1962), in a study of models utilizing similar sampling frequencies, concluded that data reconstruction was inadmissible, because it inevitably required a subsequent delay much less than the smallest delay observed.

The deficiencies of these models are due to their rather low sampling frequencies. Results of work at Imperial College, London (Lange 1965) have led to the conclusion that the operator samples his input in a random manner, with sampling intervals ranging from about 80 to 200 msec, and averaging about 130 msec, and with individual sampling actions occupying up to 50 msec. At each sampling 'instant' both velocity and position are sampled, and these sampled values pass to a central computation, occupying one sampling interval, where appropriate hand motion over the succeeding sampling interval is formulated. The overall aim of this computation is to match the output position and velocity to those required by the input (as predicted at the time of computation of the program), with an accuracy corresponding to the specified performance criterion, combined with a constraint on allowable muscular effort, and with a form of output motion such as to minimize some criterion of effort, which is strongly dependent on maximum muscular force. The programmed motion is then executed over the succeeding sampling interval, while a further input sample is processed.

The basic form of the model is that of a random sampling of position and velocity over short periods of time, followed by an essentially 'digital' computation, and adaptive form of output motion. In idealized form, with regular instantaneous sampling, this model can achieve an excellent fit, both in terms of correlation (0·9 between errors) and fine structure of output, to trained operators performing a simple compensatory tracking task.

The simple linear continuous models which have been proposed cannot be regarded as more than gross representations of operator characteristics, but these are nevertheless convenient for many purposes. Sampled data models represent an attempt to achieve a closer simulation of the actual structure of human operator tracking. The model as described in Lange (1965) is conceptually able to account for the great majority of the results reported in the literature relating to visual-manual tracking.

The models so far proposed, as outlined above, do not offer a precise description of the manner in which operator learning and adaptation take place, or of the characteristics of tracking involving several sensory modalities. Further, they do not adequately describe the operator's behaviour when tracking in several dimensions. Work is currently in progress to rectify these deficiencies, notably in the U.S.A, in connexion with the space programme.

*See also:* Control systems, sampled-data. Eye movements. Man-machine communication and ergonomics.

*Bibliography*

BEKEY G. A. (1962) *Sampled Data Models for the Human Operator in a Control System*, Ph.D. Thesis, UCLA, and Space Tech. Labs. Rep. No. 9990–6013-RU-000.

BIRMINGHAM H. V. and TAYLOR F. V. (1954) *A Design Philosophy for Man-Machine Control Systems*, Proc. I.R.E., **42,** No. 12, Dec.

CRAIK J. K. *The Theory of the Human Operator in Control Systems*, Brit. J. Psych., Dec. 1947 arnd Mar. 1948.

ELKIND J. I. (1956) *Characteristics of Simple Manual Control Systems*, Tech. Rep. No. III, Linclon Lab., M.I.T., 6 April.

Goodyear Aircraft Corporation (1952) *Final Report, Human Dynamic Study*, Rep. No. GER-4750, 8 April.

HALL I. A. M. (1958) *Effects of Controlled Element on the Human Pilot*, WADC Tech. Rep. 57–509, ASTIA Doc. No. AD 130979, August.

LANGE G. W. (1965) *Syntheses of a Model of the Human Operator Engaged in a Tracking Task*, Ph.D. Thesis, University of London, Oct.

LI Y. T., YOUNG L. R. and MEIRY J. L. (1965) *Adap-

*tive Functions of Man in Vehicle Control Systems*, IFAC (Teddington) Symposium, Sept.

McRuer D. T. and Krendel E. S. (1959) *The Human Operator as a Servo System Element*, J. Franklin Inst., **267**, No. 5 May, and No. 6 June.

Raoult J. C. (1962) *Étude de l'opérateur human en tant qu'élèment d'un system asservi*, Thesis for Doctor és Sciences Degree, University of Toulouse.

Tustin A. (1947) *The Nature of the Operator's Response in Manual Control and its Implications for Controller Design*, J. Inst. Elec. Eng., Part IIA, May.

G. W. Lange

**MODELS FOR HUMAN MEMORY.** There is no one process in the human that can be called 'the memory'. Usually the word memory means the remembrance of a past event, but in this remembrance many factors are involved. We can specify three different logical classes of operations: one, acquisition, in which the initial perception of the physical stimulus occurs and the physiological representation of that stimulus is placed in a storage system; two, storage, in which the perceived item is retained; three, retrieval, in which the desired information is sought for in the storage system and extracted from it. It is important to note that this classification represents logical distinctions among operations and does not necessarily correspond to different physiological structures.

Most studies of the properties of human memory are aimed at discovering the properties of the storage system. Although behavioural studies of storage must invariably reflect properties of acquisition and retrieval as well, most of what is known today about memory, is in fact, about storage. It seems possible to discriminate among several different types of storage systems in the hur an. These systems differ in their temporal properties, the nature of errors made in recall, and the effect of different types of interfering materials and tasks on later recall. The picture emerging from the research of recent years is of a graded sequence of storage systems, each retaining material for longer time intervals than the one before and each one feeding information into the next.

The first stage in this chain is a *very short term memory store* (VSTM) (which has usually been studied with visual stimulus presentations). Material in this storage appears to be retained for only a short time—approximately 200 milliseconds—as a rather complete sensory image of the stimulus. About 12 through 20 items can be stored in VSTM. They cannot all be recalled, however, because in the time required to speak or write the first few, the others fade away.

Storage in VSTM is affected by presentation of other visual material: the images of new material degrade the images of previous stimulus items. The new presentation can lag behind the original by 50 to 100 milliseconds and still have an interfering effect.

Second in the sequence of storages in a *short term memory store* (STM) which appears to have properties intermediate to those of VSTM and longer-term systems. There is much debate over the temporal properties of this memory system. Some researchers contend that material becomes unavailable after some 20 to 30 seconds. Others believe that time itself has little effect, but that only the presentation of later material destroys the stored representation of earlier material. These researchers believe that time factors affect only the process of acquisition.

Regardless of these differences, it is generally agreed that material in STM is in a transient state and does not last long. Moreover, verbal and textual material appear to be encoded by an acoustical representation, no matter whether the material was originally presented visually or acoustically. Thus, if a subject makes an error in recall, it is likely to be by responding with an item of similar sound to the correct one; a visually presented 'E' is more likely to be recalled as a 'D' than as an 'F'. Not only do errors in recall reflect this property of acoustical encoding, but lists composed of items which sound alike are less likely to be recalled correctly from STM than other types of lists.

At the highest level of storage is a *long term memory store* (LTM). It is difficult, if not impossible, to demonstrate a decrement in the storage of information in LTM; information which seems to have been completely lost from storage may re-appear at some later time, sometimes years after it has been supposedly forgotten. Difficulties in retrieval are to be expected in any system with such a large capacity: some estimates of the storage capacity of LTM place it at $10^{10}$ bits. In systems of this type organization holds the key to retrieval. In a large library, a book out of its proper location might just as well be lost: it will be retrieved only by accident. Yet it would be wrong to say that the book was not in the library. So it is with human memory: irretrievable information might still be in memory.

Information appears to enter VSTM and STM with little or no delay following its presentation. Not so in LTM. Input to this system requires time or repeated presentations of the material. In VSTM, physical overlapping of different stimuli can cause decrements in recall. In STM, acoustically similar material leads to difficulties in recall. In LTM, it is semantically similar material that creates most problems in recall. It is thought that in STM and VSTM the stored representation is destroyed by interfering material, but in LTM interfering material seems only to confuse the path of the recall process.

Popular methods and courses for *memory improvement* often do work because they teach methods of attention and tricks and systems for establishing unusual associations to the material which is to be remembered. Thus they first increase the likelihood that material gets into LTM and then, by establishing unique paths, they increase the likelihood of later recovery.

It seems unlikely that there are not intermediate storage systems between STM and LTM. The gap between these two seems out of line with the difference between VSTM and STM. Clinical evidence of *retrograde amnesia* suggests that there is an intermediate memory with a time duration measured in tens of minutes. But, as yet, no conclusive evidence for intermediate memories has appeared. Indeed, as in much of Psychology, there is little agreement even about the systems described here. Many contemporary researchers do not believe there is any evidence for more than one type of storage system.

Models of the memory process suffer from a lack of knowledge concerning the nature of the stored unit. Earlier attempts to analyse stored material by the amount of information (in bits) required for its specification failed to yield useful results. It is commonly assumed that the basic units of stored information are groupings of more elementary units, but exactly what these so-called 'items' or 'chunks' are and how they relate to the physical properties of the stimulus are completely unanswered questions.

Quite a number of different mechanisms have been proposed to account for various features of data which result from experiments on memory. Recently a number of mathematical models have been suggested to describe different features of these experiments.

One approach is to develop a probability model which depicts the storage system as a *Markov process* with the different memory stores corresponding to the different states of a transition matrix. The probability of a correct retrieval varies with the *state* (storage system) of the stored item and with the method of test. Deterioration of the stored material is described by the transition of items from storage into a null storage system, called the 'forgotten' state. Items cannot be recalled from this state.

A second form of model is more suggestive of a psychological mechanism in its attempt to describe the way items pass among different storage systems. Transition from one memory into another (STM into LTM, say) is accomplished by a sequential servicing device which actually does the transferring. The transfer takes time, however, so that items in the lower order memory form queues waiting for the mechanism to get to them. If the average service time is longer than the average interval between the arrival of new items, it can be seen that a rather long queue might develop. Because the lower order memory is usually a transient storage system, items in a queue may be lost (forgotten) before they can be transferred. Detailed predictions from this model are rather hard to make because the mathematics quickly become very complicated and do not always reduce to manageable solutions. It is clear, however, that the first few items presented will always get through the queue and be serviced; hence, they are very likely to be retrieved later. The last few items presented may be retrieved from the queue even if they have not yet been serviced provided, of course, that their recall was requested before they were forgotten. Thus, this model readily predicts that there should be more errors in the middle of a list than at either end, the typical result found in memory experiments. It is also quite clear that any model of this type predicts severe time dependencies: the probability that an item will be transferred into a more permanent storage system will depend upon its position in the list of items and the rate at which the items are presented.

A third form of model postulates an underlying continuum of strength values for stored items. Each stimulus is assumed to have a representation in memory and each representation has some strength value associated with it. The strength value is simply a real positive number which reflects the overall attributes of the memory trace for that item. For example, in STM, presentation of some item, $i$, causes the STM strength component for $i$ to increase: presentation of other items causes the strength of item $i$ to decrease, usually as an exponential function of the number of other items which have followed the presentation of $i$. Strengths may be assigned to the associations between items as well as to the representations of the items themselves. The memory for individual items and the memory for their order of presentation are represented by separate strength values. Retrieval from memory requires an assessment of the strength value. A item is recognized as having just previously been presented if and only if the strength value of its stored representation is sufficiently great.

The strength model would be trivial, were it not that natural perturbations or noise is assumed to enter into the process. During retrieval, the decision system evaluates the strength of each item. The noise causes the strength values seen by the decision system to be random variables, so the problem of decision becomes one of extracting the true value from the noise. Because of this noise, the decision processes must make mistakes, both of omission (missed retrievals) and of commission (false retrievals). Moreover, the probabilities of making these mistakes can vary with the decision rule used in the retrieval process. In some situations it is better to make false retrievals than to miss retrievals; in other situations false retrievals ought to be avoided at all costs. The power of strength models of memory lies in their ability to suggest a reasonable description of the way observed behaviour changes with changes in the relative importance of the consequences of that behaviour.

These three different types of models are often concerned with different aspects of memory. *Probability models* are most successful in descriptions of the acquisition or learning phase of memory and in describing the effects of repeated presentations of the same stimulus items. *Queuing models* are best for describing the transfer of stored information from one memory system to another, for accounting for some of the idiosyncracies of the end positions in a serial list of items, and for predicting the effects of varying the rates of presentation upon the storage of material. *Strength models* generally describe the retrieval process, along with the accompanying decisions that must be made.

The probability and strength models are the most highly developed at the present time: probability models because they borrow heavily from work done on similar models in mathematical learning theory; strength models because they borrow from work in psychophysics and from communication models of signal detection.

The types of models presented here represent only a portion of current thinking and research on memory. Completely absent from this discussion are studies of the details of storage and work on computer simulation of memory processes. The various models and schemata discussed here do seem to represent the major types of quantitative mathematical thinking in recent years which, in turn, suggests the way that work on memory will progress in the near future.

*See also:* Concept identification—information processing approaches.

*Bibliography*

The five conferences on Learning, remembering, and forgetting held in Princeton, New Jersey (1963—1968), proceedings published by Science and Behavior Books, Inc. (Palo Alto, California, USA) contain the latest researches and models of the memory processes. Most formal models find their way eventually to the *J. Math. Psychology*, and the entire sequence of this journal ought to be examined by the interested reader.

D. A. NORMAN

**NERVE AND MUSCLE, INITIATION AND CONDUCTION OF IMPULSES IN.** From the point of view of its electrical activity, an excitable cell may be looked at as an ionic solution of one composition (the intracellular fluid) enclosed by a cylindrical semipermeable membrane and immersed in a solution of the same total ionic concentration but of another composition (the extracellular fluid).

The *permeability* of the membrane to the various ions is not constant but is a function of the potential difference, $V$, across the membrane. The most important ions to be considered are $Na^+$, $K^+$, and $Cl^-$ which are present in both intra- and extracellular fluid. In comparison with the extracellular concentrations, the intracellular concentrations of $Na^+$ and $Cl^-$ are low and that of $K^+$ is high. This comes about because the cell contains large organic anions to which the cell membrane is impermeable and because at rest, i.e. when the cell is not conducting an impulse, the cell membrane is considerably more permeable to $K^+$ and $Cl^-$ than it is to $Na^+$. Furthermore the intracellular concentration of $Na^+$ ($Na_i$) is kept low with respect to the extracellular concentration ($Na_e$) because it is extruded by an active process which keeps pace with the slow passive entry of $Na^+$. As a first approximation, neglecting the small permeability to $Na^+$ of the membrane, $K^+$ and $Cl^-$ would be distributed according to the *Gibbs-Donnan equilibrium*, such that

$$\frac{K_i}{K_e} = \frac{Cl_e}{Cl_i} = \lambda \quad (1)$$

where $\lambda$ varies from about 20 to 50 in various cells of different species, and a p.d., $V_r$, would exist across the membrane given by

$$V = \frac{RT}{F} \ln \lambda \quad (2)$$

the extracellular fluid being positive with respect to the intracellular fluid. Observed values of $V_r$ range from about 50 to 100 mV. If account is taken of the permeability to $Na^+$ and it is assumed that the active extrusion process is such that the outward transfer of one $Na^+$ ion is accompanied by the simultaneous inward transfer of one $K^+$ ion, then it may be shown that a better approximation than that given in equation 1 is

$$\frac{K_i + bNa_i}{K_e + bNa_e} = \frac{Cl_e}{Cl_i} = \lambda \quad (3)$$

where $b$ is the ratio:

$$\frac{\text{Permeability of the membrane to } Na^+}{\text{Permeability of the membrane to } K^+}.$$

When a *stimulus* is applied to a cell, whatever the nature of the stimulus it ultimately leads to a '*depolarization*' i.e. to a reduction in the absolute magnitude of the p.d., $|V|$, across the cell membrane. If the depolarization is large enough, i.e. if the stimulus is suprathreshold, an *action potential* is generated. By an autocatalytic process the p.d. across the membrane rapidly changes through zero to a value, $V_a$, opposite in sign to that of the p.d., $V_r$, in the resting state. The p.d. then begins to revert to its resting value. In any particular type of cell, $V_a$ and the duration of the action potential are constant but there is variation between types of cell and species of animal. Typical values for $V_a$ are between 30 and 50 mV (inside positive) and the total duration of the action potential is usually between 0.5 and 5 msec.

Action potentials are propagated along cells at a constant speed which depends both on the type of cell and on its diameter. Muscle fibres of 50–100 $\mu$ in diameter conduct at a few metres per sec. Myelinated nerve fibres (in which most of the surface area is insulated from the external solution by a sheath of the fatty material myelin) which are of diameter of 1–20 $\mu$ conduct at 5–120 m/sec and unmyelinated nerve fibres which are of 1 $\mu$ diameter or less conduct at speeds below 3 m/sec. The minimum interval between *impulses* varies between less than 1 msec for the larger myelinated motor nerve fibres which conduct impulses from the spinal cord to skeletal muscle, to a few msec for the slowly conducting unmyelinated fibres which signal for example temperature changes or pain. It is probably only rarely, however, that *in vivo* the frequency of impulses along a nerve fibre exceeds 100/sec.

In the laboratory, action potentials in isolated nerve or muscle fibres are generated by the depolarization of a segment of the cell membrane by means of brief current pulses. *In vivo*, the depolarization is caused in one of two ways (a) a substance is released from the terminal portion of one nerve as a result of the action potential in that nerve; this substance then reacts with a specialized chemosensitive region of the membrane of a second nerve or muscle fibre to produce a change in the permeability of this region to the environmental ions or (b) the terminal region of the nerve fibre is specialized in such a way that the membrane permeability is directly affected by changes for example in temperature, pressure or length, which would have little if any effect on the permeability of the membrane as a whole. The occurrence of the action potential is due to the way in which the permeability of the membrane varies with the p.d. across it. Voltage and current electrodes have been inserted into the interior of the giant *axon* of the squid, a nerve fibre of 0.5 to 1 mm in diameter, and by means of a feed-back amplifier the current flowing in response to voltage step-functions have been recorded. The individual ionic conductances as functions of the p.d. across the membrane have been determined by applying the technique to axons bathed in solutions of different ionic composition.

The results were consistent with the model of the membrane shown in Fig. 1:

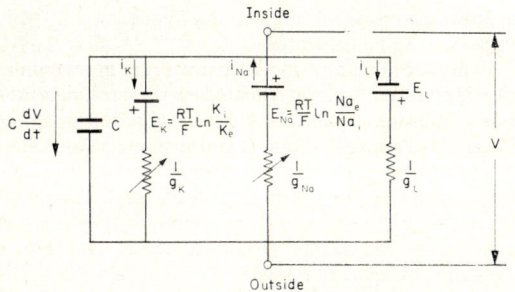

FIG. 1. *V is the potential difference across the membrane (inside-outside), c the membrane capacity of the segment of the membrane, $g_K$, $i_K$ the conductance to $K^+$ and the $K^+$ current, $g_{Na}$, $i_{Na}$ the conductance to $Na^+$ and the $Na^+$ current and $g_l$, $i_l$ the conductance to other ions (mainly $Cl^-$ and their currents. In the resting state $g_K$ and $g_l$ are approximately equal (corresponding to about $0.25$ mmho/cm²) and $g_{Na}$ is negligible. At the peak of the action potential $g_{Na}$ corresponds to about $30$ mmho/cm² and $g_K$ to about $3$ mmho/cm². When $E_K = 75$ mV, $E_l = 55$ mV, $E_{Na} = 55$ mV then $V_r \doteq -65$ mV and $V_a \doteq +40$ mV.*

$C$ and $g_l$ were found to be constant; $g_k$ and $g_{Na}$ were found to be functions both of $V$ and of the time, $t$, after the imposition of a change in $V$.

In general, according to the model, $V$ is given by

$$C\frac{dV}{dt} + g_K(V+E_K) + g_{Na}(V-E_{Na}) + g_l(V+E_l) = 0. \quad (4)$$

This equation has been solved numerically for $V$ as a function of $t$, with initial conditions corresponding to various forms of stimuli, and the solutions have been found to correspond closely to the action potentials actually observed.

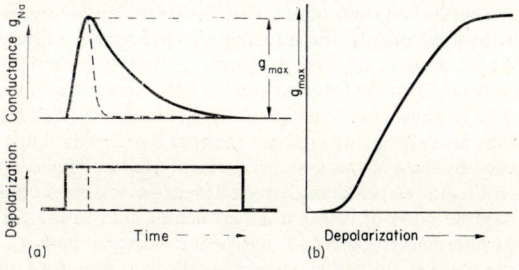

FIG. 2. *Effect of depolarization on Na—conductance of membrane (a) time course of change in $g_{Na}$ (b) relation between peak value of $g_{Na}$ (g max) and amplitude of depolarization.*

The equations defining $g_{Na}(V, t)$ and $g_K(V, t)$ are given by Hodgkin and Huxley (1952), Huxley (1959), Cole (1962) and Noble (1966); the essential features responsible for the form of the action potential are as follows. A sudden reduction in $|V|$ causes a rapid increase in $g_{Na}$ (Fig. 2); reference to Fig. 1 shows that the membrane therefore has an initially negative resistance, depolarization being accompanied by an inward current of $Na^+$. However, at constant depolarization, $g_{Na}$ after reaching a peak reverts to its small resting value within one to a few msec. If the resting potential is restored during the period in which $g_{Na}$ is greater than normal, $g_{Na}$ reverts to its *resting* value almost immediately. Depolarization causes an increase in $g_K$ also (Fig. 3), but only after a significant delay. The inward current of $Na^+$ is therefore followed by an outward current of $K^+$, and the resistance of the membrane becomes positive. The increased value of $g_K$ is maintained for as long as is the depolarization and when the resting

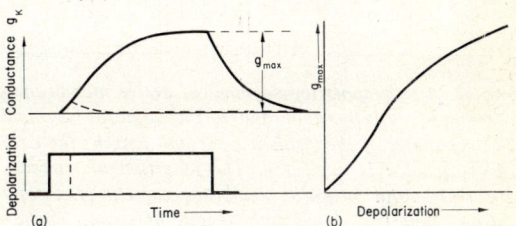

FIG. 3. *Effect of depolarization on K—conductance of membrane (a) time course of change in $g_K$ (b) relation between peak value of $g_K$ (g max) and amplitude of depolarization.*

potential is restored, $g_K$ reverts to its resting value slowly.

A consequence of these properties of $g_{Na}$, and $g_K$ is that when an axon is stimulated say by a brief current pulse which partly discharges the membrane capacity, $g_{Na}$ rises almost instantaneously and $|V|$ is further reduced, the membrane capacity being discharged by an inward $Na^+$ current. This leads to a further increase in $g_{Na}$ and so on; $V$ therefore passes through zero and approaches the value of $E_{Na}$. The time relations are such that before $V$ attains the value of $E_{Na}$, $g_{Na}$ begins to revert to its original value and $g_K$ begins to increase. The membrane potential is therefore rapidly restored to its original value, the membrane capacity being recharged by an outward current of $K^+$. Each action potential evidently involves a loss of intracellular $K^+$ and an equal gain of $Na^+$ but the amounts exchanged are too small to affect the concentrations significantly and the *status quo* is restored by the metabolic 'pump' referred to earlier.

The above description refers to the stiatuion in which the membrane along the whole length of the axon is excited simultaneously. Normally the action potential is generated at one point and is then propagated along the cell. Propagation occurs because the inward ionic current across the active region of the membrane is supplied by an outward current from an adjacent region of the membrane. The outward current discharges the membrane capacity and reduces $|V|$ and hence acts as a stimulus to the initially passive adjacent segment. It may be seen from Fig. 4 that the total outward current across a segment of the membrane is given by

$$i = \frac{1}{r}\frac{\partial^2 V}{\partial x^2} \qquad (5)$$

and ∴ by (4) with an obvious change in notation

$$i = C\frac{\partial V}{\partial t} + g_K(V+E_K) + g_{Na}(V-E_{Na}) + g_l(V-E_l). \qquad (6)$$

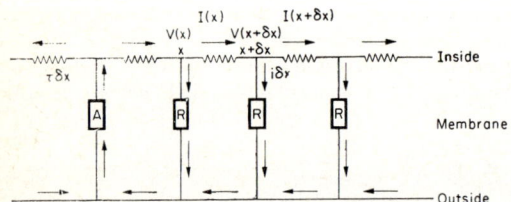

FIG. 4. $A$ represents the segment of active membrane of the length $x$ of the axon and $R$ the adjacent segments. The resistance of the inside is $r$ per unit length, the external resistance is neglected. The longitudinal current is $I$ and the total outward membrane current (i.e. capacitative + ionic) is $i$ per unit length of axon. Then,

$$i = \frac{I(x)-I(x+\delta x)}{\delta x} = -\frac{\partial I}{\partial x} \quad \text{and}$$

$$I = \frac{V(x)-V(x+\delta x)}{r\delta x} = -\frac{1}{r}\frac{\partial V}{\partial x}$$

hence $\quad i = \frac{1}{r}\frac{\partial^2 V}{\partial x^2}.$

The form of the propagated action potential and the speed of conduction should therefore be completely predictable from equations 5 and 6. The resulting non-linear partial differential equation has not been solved; however, if it is assumed that the action potential is conducted with some unspecified uniform speed, $\theta$, then

$$V(x,t) = V(x-\theta t) \quad \text{and} \quad \frac{\partial^2 V}{\partial x^2} = \frac{1}{\theta^2}\frac{\partial^2 V}{\partial t^2}.$$

Equations 5 and 6 may therefore be replaced by the ordinary differential equation

$$\frac{1}{r\theta^2}\frac{d^2 V}{dt^2} = C\frac{dV}{dt} + g_K(V+E_K) + g_{Na}(V-E_{Na}) + g_l(V+E_l). \qquad (7)$$

The numerical solution to equation 7 is in good agreement with the observed form of the propagated action potential and it predicts the observed speed of conduction.

It may be asked why an action potential travelling from left to right, say, along an axon does not re-excite previously active regions to the left. The reasons are that, as previously stated, $g_K$ does not revert to its resting value for some millisec after the resting potential is restored and furthermore $g_{Na}$ is not increased by depolarization unless the membrane has been at the resting potential for the previous one or a few millisec. These features are also reponsible for the limiting frequency with which impulses can be generated.

In muscle fibres and unmyelinated nerve fibres conduction is continuous. In myelinated nerve fibres, regions of the membrane capable of generating action potentials ('nodes of Ranvier') occur at uniform intervals of about 2 mm separated by insulated stretches of core conductor, and conduction is said to be 'saltatory'. The processes in saltatory conduction are essentially the same as in continuous conduction (Frankenhaeuser and Huxley 1964; Frankenhaeuser 1965).

*See also:* Nervous system, role of pulse distribution in information flow. Receptors: relation between the stimuli and the activity in single primary units. Receptors as transducers. Receptors in joints and muscles. Sensory processes.

*Bibliography*

COLE K. S. (1962) *Biophys. J.* **2**, Suppl. 101.
FRANKENHAEUSER B. (1965) *J. Physiol.* (London) **180**, 780.
FRANKENHAEUSER B. and HUXLEY A. F. (1964) *J. Physiol.* (London) **171**, 302.
HODGKIN A. L. and HUXLEY A. F. (1952) *J. Physiol.* (London) **117**, 500.
HUXLEY A. F. (1959) *Ann. N.Y. Acad. Sci.* **81**, 221.
NOBLE D. (1966) *Physiol. Rev.* **46**, 1.

B. L. GINSBORG

**NERVOUS SYSTEM, ROLE OF PULSE DISTRIBUTION IN INFORMATION FLOW.** It is generally believed that the Central Nervous System is responsible for organizing the wide range of complex behaviours seen in man and many other creatures. The problem of how it does this is almost totally unsolved since relatively little is known either about how information is stored in the nervous system or the details of the neural organization that makes the information processing possible. An antecedent of these problems, is that of determining in what form the information is likely to be made available to those parts which are concerned with information processing and storage, in other words what code is used by the nervous system for its internal transmissions. In this latter problem there is at least available a considerable body of relevant experimental data in the form of microelectrode recordings of the electrical activity in the close vicinity of single nerve cells. It is therefore possible to observe the behaviour of those elements which are generally regarded as being the basic building blocks of the system. The dominant characteristic of these records is their appearance as a sequence of well defined spikes standing out above the background electrical noise. The spikes are all essentially the same height so that the information transmitted by the neuron must be coded in the pattern of the time intervals between successive spikes. This pattern itself is very variable. In some neurons, e.g. those innervating muscle stretch receptors, it is extremely regular with a mean interval between spikes that varies inversely with increasing muscle stretch. In others, e.g. auditory nerve neurons it can be very irregular and indeed it appears to be quite random. However, it is not impossible that this randomness may really be the superficial appearance of the coding of a complicated signal. In neurons of the cortex the most striking feature of the spontaneous activity is the tendency to fire in bursts with relatively quieter periods between.

The digital appearance of these signals encourages the view that the spikes might play a role in the nervous system analogous to that of pulses in a digital computer. Available information on neurons indicates that it is quite possible for them to behave as the *or-gates* and *and-gates* from which computers are built up. On this basis the neurons are to be conceived of as devices which perform logical operations on serial trains of pulses, and produce new trains of output pulses as a result. A model of nervous system function on these lines was developed by McCulloch and Pitts in 1943 and elaborated by others since then. In such a model it is necessary for the neurons to be able to detect the non-occurrence of pulses as well as their occurrence. In other words, they must be told at what times pulses can potentially occur before they can extract the bit of information resulting from the detection or non-detection of a spike. It is therefore necessary for the system to have some sort of clock and to operate synchronously—at least locally. Another important requirement of such a digital system is that the information to be transmitted must be organized into something resembling computer words. It is not sufficient to have isolated independent bits arriving at a processing point, information must be provided about their context by other bits in close space or time proximity. The information must therefore be coded into blocks of bits. In the absence of any definite information to the contrary it is possible to imagine that this has been done by the time the information reaches the interior regions of the nervous system, since it will by then have passed through the neural data processing apparatus nearer the periphery. It is then necessary to assume that the coding of the signals entering the peripheral neurones is in some sense more 'natural' to the types of signal entering the system or to attribute a rather elaborate coding function to the transducers themselves. This latter possibility is thought to be unlikely. It seems probable therefore that the randomness of the times of firing of neurons in the auditory nerve is a true randomness and not an artefact caused by a complicated code.

A plausible 'natural' code is one which encodes the intensity of an input as a function of the length of interval between successive pulses. Considerable evidence can be provided in support of the existence of such a code in that recordings from a wide variety of peripheral neurons show increased firing rates in these neurons when the corresponding transducers are activated. Use of such a code again implies the existence of some kind of clock in the neurons which are to read the code or process the information it contains. Furthermore, it is no longer possible to assume that the input impulses arrive at a neuron synchronously since the position of each pulse is now some complicated function of the signal history of its activating inputs. The simple 'and' and 'or' functions proposed above for neurons are therefore not directly applicable for processing such information streams and more complicated neural functions or more complicated neural networks must be postulated.

An alternative form of coding which has the natural properties of the interval length code and the suitability for processing by neurons of the binary synchronous code is one which is based simply on firing rate and not on detailed firing pattern. In this case it is assumed that the input to the neuron is some stimulus intensity, derived either from a sensory transducer element or from the outputs of other neurons, and that the recipient neuron responds by firing at a rate which is a monotonically increasing function of the input intensity. It is not, however, the occurrence of a pulse which is directly affected by the input, so much as the probability of the occurrence of a pulse, hence an output results in which the distribution of pulses is random. A consequence of this mode of operation is that it is only possible for any detection system, neural or otherwise, to obtain a reliable estimate of the signal which was encoded, by examining a large number of interpulse intervals.

In attempting to assess whether any or all of the codes described above is actually used by any part of the nervous system there are three factors which must be considered. The first factor is whether, on the basis of what is known about the workings of neurons it is plausible to assume that they could handle information which has been encoded in any of these ways. The second factor is whether the experimental data from recordings of the time distribution of pulses from neurons is compatible with the existence of any of these codes, and the third consideration is whether an information processing system operating on lines determined by the first two factors would be adequate to handle the amount of information which must be processed by a device with as wide a range of function as the nervous system. Since this is heavily dependent on how the execution of function is related to the method of information processing, about which virtually nothing is known, it is not possible to use this consideration to put any restriction on the type of code which must be used. Indeed, it seems more likely to expect that knowledge of the nature of the code used will be a necessary prerequisite to the solution of the former problem. It therefore rests on the outcome of the first two considerations above as to whether or not a particular code is likely to be used, consequently it is first necessary to review briefly some of the generally accepted properties of nerve cells.

Nerve cells are enclosed by a membrane which normally maintains the inside of the cell at a resting potential of about −70mV relative to the outside. If the potential across some region of the membrane is reduced to the order of −50mV (called threshold potential), that part of the membrane goes temporarily into an unstable state, the transmembrane potential moves rapidly to about +20mV then after a few milliseconds returns to the resting state. The voltage swing of the order of 90mV is the spike detected by the recording electrodes. This voltage swing is generally sufficient to bring about large enough voltage displacements in adjacent regions of the membrane to cause them to exhibit the same behaviour. In this way the transient voltage wave passes over the whole cell surface and in particular it can be transmitted from one extremity of the cell to another. Transmission from one cell to another operates on a different principle. At certain specialized endings on the cell which are in close proximity to other cells the arrival of the voltage pulse releases an amount of chemical substance which has the effect of altering the membrane potential in the closely adjacent regions of the second cell. The alteration may be sufficient to cause the cell to fire as described above, or it may not. In the latter case the voltage returns more or less exponentially to its resting level. In any event, the mechanism allows the recipient cell to monitor the inputs of many cells which may have excitatory or inhibitory effects on it (depending on the sense of the change induced), and to fire on these occasions when the excitatory effect is sufficiently dominant. It is easy to see how the rate of firing of the neuron is therefore a representation of the intensity of the input at the neuron, whether from another neuron or from a suitable transducer which can generate transmembrane voltage changes.

On the basis of the description just given it seems likely that the neuron behaves primarily as a threshold logic element with a short term memory rather than as a simple and-gate or or-gate. Nonetheless, it could behave as a gate if a combination of circumstances obtained. These are, that the increment pulses are large compared with the distance between resting potential and threshold potential, that relatively few inputs converge on each neuron and that they arrive more or less synchronously. There is no obvious mechanism in the neuron which would seem to have the specific function of recognizing a pulse interval code. While implicit clocks exist as the various time constants of the voltage changes, their relation to a pulse-length code seems incidental rather than direct.

Rather more light can be shed on the code problem by examining the many recordings which exist of the firing patterns of neurons. The data from these sources are generally presented in a more or less condensed form, perhaps the most common for spontaneous firing is the interpulse interval histogram. From peripheral neurons where the input during spontaneous activity can plausibly be considered to be some kind of stationary random process these have typical shapes as shown in Fig. 1, which can generally be fitted by something like a gamma function. Such neurons usually show a

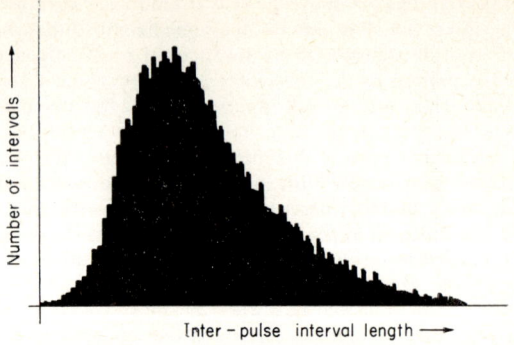

FIG. 1

high degree of independence between successive pulse intervals as measured by their serial correlation coefficient. It is true that low negative correlations are sometimes seen, but these are generally accounted for by assuming that after a short interval between firings the neuron takes longer to recover, and the probability of another short interval is therefore slightly reduced.

A function which expresses the information contained in the interpulse interval histogram in a form which is sometimes more convenient is the renewal density function. It is defined as $h(t) = f(t) \Big/ \int_{t}^{\infty} f(x)\,\mathrm{d}x$ where $f(t)$ is the probability density function of which the pulse interval histogram is assumed to be the observed realization. $h(t)$ is sometimes called the age specific firing rate since $h(t)\,\delta t$ is the probability that the neuron will fire in the interval $t, t+\delta t$ since it last fired. It is of particular interest, therefore, since it is what is postulated to be coded by the rate code. For peripheral neurons of the type mentioned above, responding to a stationary input its form is as in Fig. 2, expressing the fact that after a recovery time during which there is a reduced probability of firing the probability of firing is a constant. The eventual constancy of $h(t)$ for large $t$ is a

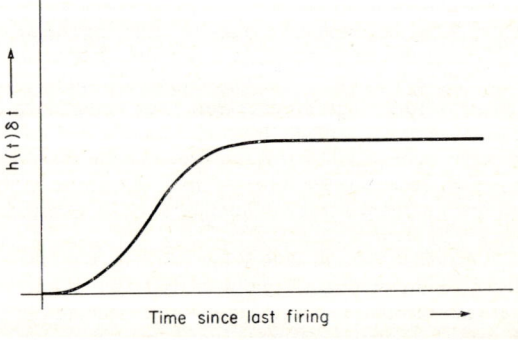

FIG. 2

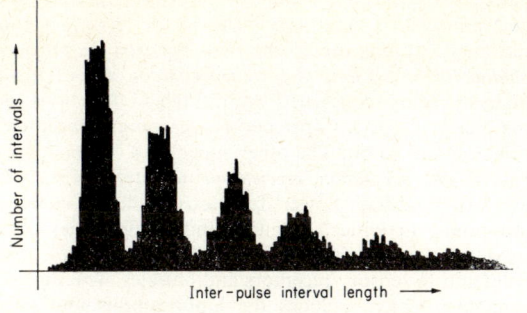

FIG. 3

property of all probability density functions with negative exponential tails and vice versa. Departures from such constancy are most readily observed in neurons which are assumed to be being driven by some external stimulus. In the auditory nerve for example the neurons respond to low frequency tonal stimuli by firing at an increased rate, but also by showing a tendency to lock their firing times to a particular phase of the stimulating sinusoid. This gives an interpulse interval histogram of the form in Fig. 3, and an age specific firing rate of the form in Fig. 4, which provides a good example of a neuron encoding an input intensity as a probability of firing.

The data from neurons responding to a repeated cycle of stimulation is more usually presented as a post-stimulus-time (PST) histogram which gives the number of pulses in a stated interval since some standard time on the stimulus cycle. The most noticeable feature of such records is the speeding up of the firing rate at some point on the cycle. This again is compatible with the view that a rate code is being employed. It is of course not incompatible with the view that some more complicated code is being used since it could be argued that during some parts of the stimulus cycle there might be more information to be coded than at others and the firing rate is speeded up to deal with it. However, since at this level of the nervous system at least, the rate code imposes fewest demands in the way of assumptions about the existence of special encoding mechanisms it is adopted as the most likely possibility unless definite evidence shows it to be unacceptable. Progressing up towards the cortex from the periphery it is generally observed that the mean rate of firing decreases and that the spontaneous rate of firing becomes more erratic. The interpulse interval histograms have a more complicated appearance, having for example more than one mode. The latter finding is of some interest since it implies that there is a preferred time, after a neuron has fired, for it to fire again, which implies, in turn, that there is some periodicity in the input. In some cases such results have been used to infer the existence of local feedback loops.

At the cortex itself the spontaneous firing is relatively slow and tends to occur in bursts. It has been shown that the majority of the records obtained can be described as alternating Poisson processes; in other words, the bursts occur at random with constant mean rate, while within bursts spikes occur at random with a much higher mean rate. Responses to stimuli at cortical and other high levels tend to be of the hard-on/hard-off type and the stimuli which are responded to are usually more or less complicated patterns or combinations of the ones which elicited firing rate increases further down. It appears, therefore, that at higher levels the nervous system may be functioning in a more digital way in that the signals being transmitted are 'pulses' of relatively intense activity separated by periods of inactivity. However, here too the information seems to be coded as a local rate of firing rather than in some way which makes use of the detailed distribution of the pulses in time.

*Conclusions.* It is now necessary to consider again, in the light of the above remarks, the role of pulse distribution in information flow in the nervous system. On the basis of the facts known about the operation of the neuron it seems that the rate code is the one which it would find most natural to handle. The evidence from the records of neurons firing does not provide any conflict with this postulate. Indeed, it lends its support in that considerable progress has been made in fitting the observed distribution of interpulse intervals in peripheral neurons firing at random, to distributions calculated for model neurons whose properties are slightly axiomatised versions of the ones given above. (A comprehensive list of references to this work is contained in Moore *et al.* (1966).)

The notable deficiency of the rate code is its inferior information carrying capability relative to codes which make use of the information contained in the length of each individual interval. In particular, it is not possible to obtain an accurate and instantaneous estimate of the rate of a single neuron. At the higher levels, this is probably unnecessary since the neurons seem to function in a hard-on/hard-off mode so that good resolution of firing rates is not required. Nearer the periphery, however, much finer gradations in rate are observed and while it is possible for external observ-

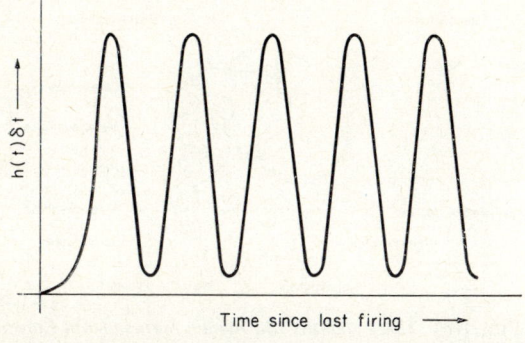

FIG. 4

ers to measure the rate by counting spikes over a long period it does not seem likely that the neuron's time constants would allow it to do the same thing. The only alternative solution is for the higher order neurons to receive inputs from many lower level neurons, all of which are carrying a similar rate signal. The net average rate then seen by the recipient neuron will be relatively free from fluctuations and hence of adequate resolution to carry a finely graded signal. It is reassuring to note that a high degree of convergence of nerve fibres is observed in these regions of the nervous system where such activity would be required. An important consequence of the existence of such a highly redundant system is that it is robust against component failures and insensitive to detailed structural variations, both of which properties would seem to be desirable in the nervous system.

The problem of deciding whether the rate code is so low in information capacity that it could not supply the nervous system with adequate sensory input is complicated by the difficulties in deciding how much sensory input the nervous system wants. Perhaps it is sufficient to note that the results of calculations on the upper bound of information inflow using a pulse distribution sensitive code have prompted the question 'what can it do with it all?'. It therefore seems fair to conclude that the detailed pattern of pulse location in time does not play a central role in information processing in the nervous system.

*See also:* Nerve and muscle, initiation and conduction of impulses in. Neuronal nets. Representation of information about stimuli in populations of receptor units.

*Bibliography*

MOORE J. P., PERKEL D. H. and SEGUNDO J.P. (1966) *Statistical Analysis and Functional Interpretation of Neuronal Spike Data,* Ann. Rev. Phys. **28**, 493.

H. ROSS

## NEURONAL NETS.

*Introduction*

Neuronal nets are aggregates of interacting nerve cells or 'neurons'. Neurons are the basic structural units of animal nervous systems. To survey in any real detail the experimental background involved is of course completely out of the question. The reader is referred to the standard reference on the subject (Handbook of Physiology I, 1959) for authoritative surveys of the subject matter. Here we give only a brief survey.

Figure 1 shows lateral and medial aspects of vertebrate cerebral hemispheres with some of the more prominent features indicated. These features represent constellations of neuronal nets, or 'super nets' whose patterns of interconnexion or 'wiring-diagrams' are determined on a hereditary basis, in the large if not in the small. Among these super nets perhaps the *telencephalon, diencephalon,* and *rhinencephalon* are of most interest, being concerned with 'higher' functions of the nervous system—perception, learning, conceptual thinking and so on. The other super nets, the *mesencephalon, metencephalon, myelencephalon* and *spinal cord,* are concerned with 'lower' functions—reflex behaviour, autonomic activities, attention and so on. They also serve to relay signals to and from the higher super nets, from and to sensory receptors and muscles. The rhinencephalon, which includes the hippocampus and part of the orbital surface of the frontal lobes (see Fig. 1), can be considered to be the *visceral* and *olfactory brain.*

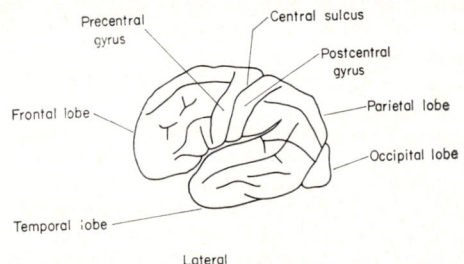

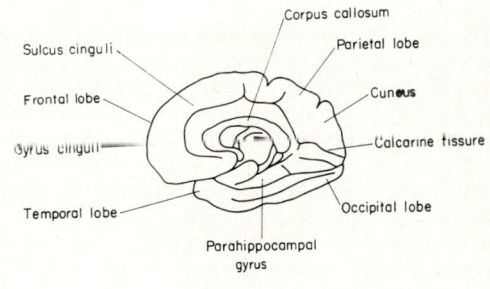

FIG. 1(a) *Cerebral hemispheres (from Ranson and Clarke 1959).*

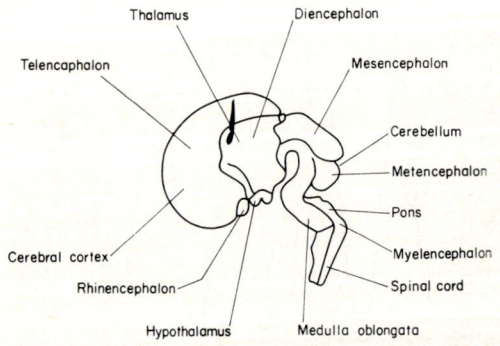

FIG. 1(b) *Three months old human foetus (from Ranson and Clarke 1959).*

It apparently plays an important role in determining the long-term behaviour of animals, since it appears to exert some degree of control over the addressing of signals to the storage centres supposedly located in the telencephalon, (Young 1964). The diencephalon, which includes the neuronal nets of the thalamus and hypothalamus, plays a very important role in the integration of the total activity of the central nervous system (CNS). From thalamic nets develop the retinas and optic nerves for example, and upon such nets converge incoming or 'afferent' paths conveying signals from receptors. It acts as a relay station where afferent signals are processed and sent to the telencephalon. There is also diffusion and spread of signals to other super nets.

What appears to be a very general rule in the anatomy of the nervous system is found in diencephalic interconnexions with the telencephalon, namely that there are two-way interconnexions between nets. For example the medial geniculate connects with the superior temporal gyrus and vice versa, the pulvinar connects with parietal and temporal areas of telencephalic cortex and vice versa. At a lower level there are two-way interconnexions between diencephalic nets and non-specific nets located in the myelencephalon—the reticular formation. This two of three tiered arrangement of neuronal nets is of great importance.

The telencephalon is undoubtedly the most important of the super nets of the nervous system with respect to the execution of higher functions. The *cerebral cortex* is that part of this super net which is especially concerned with such functions. The microstructure of this cortex is heterogeneous and contains a large number of cell types and wiring-diagrams. Grossly speaking there are two types of tissue to be seen—'grey matter' comprising the 'cell bodies' and 'dendrites' of neurons, and 'white matter' comprising the 'axons' or outgoing processes of such neurons. The neurons are arranged in fairly definite layers. There are about five different cell types of which the most important are the 'pyramidal' cells and the 'stellate' cells. Axonal bundles enter the cortex from subjacent white matter generally at a direction normal to the cortical surface. In this way cortical nets are separated into columns normal to its surface. Many of the axon bundles comprising the white matter are corticifugal, running as 'association' fibres to other nets in the ipsilateral hemisphere, or as 'commisural' fibres to corresponding nets in the contralateral hemisphere, or as 'projection' fibres to extracortical nets. Similarly there are corticipetal fibres from such nets and association and commisural fibres from other cortical nets. Figure 2 shows some of these details.

The cerebral cortex does not have a uniform histological structure. There are differences in the distribution of cell types, their number and packing-density. Indeed there is a highly specific selection of cell types and wiring diagrams, at least in the large, with laminar and columnar organization very common. Important cortical nets are the 'projection' cortices—visual, auditory, and somaesthetic, which receive afferent stimuli from peripheral nets, and the motor cortex which transmits signals to peripheral effectors. As far as the microstructure of such nets is concerned, it seems that averages are the only stable histological parameters. D. A. Sholl (1956) has estimated many of these parameters, the more important of which are the number and packing-density of neurons, the mean size and shape of the neuronal membrane—the 'perikaryon', the length and distribution of axons, and the origin and distribution of afferent fibres. As a result of Sholl's calculations it may be estimated that as much as $0{\cdot}1\,\text{mm}^3$ of cortex has its state modified as an immediate result of the activity in a single afferent neuron.

This then is the anatomical substratum upon which physiological aspects must be superimposed. It is evident

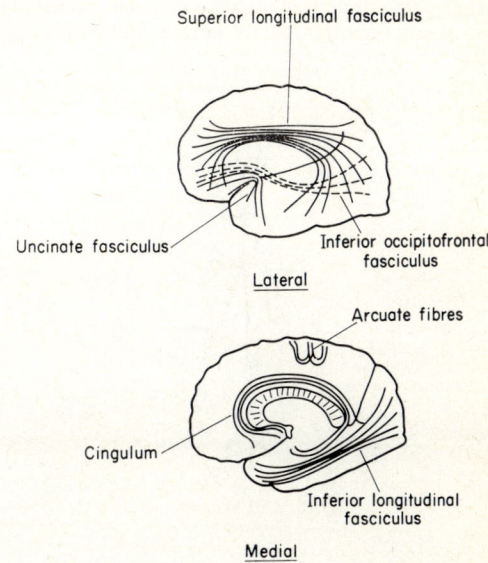

FIG. 2. *Axonal bundles (from Ranson and Clarke 1959).*

that the laminar and columnar organizations of cortical nets, together with the tiered arrangement of super nets coupled everywhere by two-way interconnexions, makes for a very complex system within which the coding, addressing, transmission, storage and retrieval of signals takes place. The investigation of such processes is one of the aims of neurophysiology.

*The Neuron*

Neurons are cells usually not more than 0·1 mm in diameter, which have become specially adapted to processing and transmitting electrical signals within the nervous system. Each neuron comprises a 'soma', together with dendrites, and a single axon, (see Fig. 3). The dendritic complex functions as an antenna, collecting incoming signals and conveying them to the soma while the axon functions as a transmitter, conveying outgoing signals to other neurons and to muscles. Such signals generally have to cross separating gaps between neurons, called 'synapses'. How they do so has been the subject of much recent work (Eccles 1964).

The neuron and its processes are separated by a lipid-protein membrane from the surrounding extracellular medium. The somato-dendritic or 'SD-membrane' of the neuron is very sensitive to incoming signals. In recent years direct studies of the nature of this sensitivity have been carried out via intracellular and extracellular recording by microelectrodes of very small tip diameter, about 1 micron. It has been established that the SD-membrane has a total capacitance of about 3 m$\mu$F and a total conductance of about 1$\mu$mho. The membrane as a whole responds to incoming signals effectively like a parallel RC-circuit with a time constant of about 3 msec. A very important factor in such a response is the

*aptic potentials* or *EPSP's* and hyperpolarizing ones as *inhibitory postsynaptic potentials* or *IPSP's*, since they (respectively) contribute to or detract from the state of excitation built up within the neuronal membrane. Synapses can be either excitatory or else inhibitory.

An equivalent electrical circuit has been inferred for the SD-membrane and associated synaptic regions of neurons in the output or motor side of the nerve trunks in the spinal cord. It should be realized that there are different neuronal types which have varying modes of response to stimuli, and that the output or 'motoneuron' equivalent circuit is not necessarily typical of neuronal responses within the nets of the CNS proper, as distinct from the spinal cord. In particular, dendritic effects certainly influence the way in which excitation is built up within the cell membrane, and probably play an important role in CNS function. The motoneuron equivalent

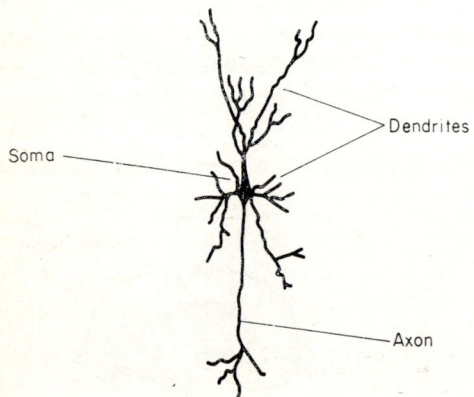

FIG. 3. *A neuron.*

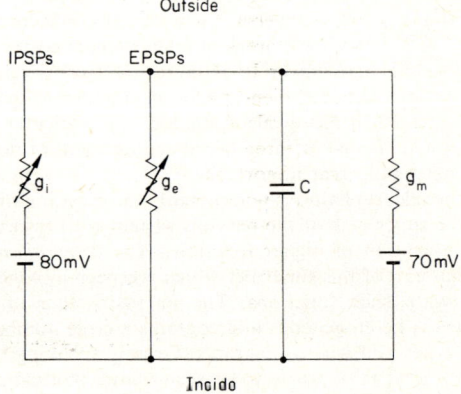

FIG. 4. *Neuronal membrane—an equivalent circuit (from Eccles 1957).*

influence of varying conditions at the synapses. Electron-micrographs show that the neuronal membrane surface is convered by many button-like processes or '*boutons*', which have been identified as the regions of interaction with other neurons. The gaps between such boutons and the cell membrane are the synapses. The physicochemical phenomena involved in synaptic transmission are of great complexity and interest. Roughly speaking, electrical potentials arriving at some synapses induce '*presynaptic potentials*' which liberate certain chemicals or '*transmitter substances*', which appear to migrate across the synapses, causing potential changes in subsynaptic regions of the SD-membrane, called '*postsynaptic potentials*'. The equilibrium or 'resting potential' of the membrane is about $-70$ mV (with respect to some reference electrode), and the postsynaptic potentials act either to depolarize the membrane towards 0 mV, or to hyperpolarize it towards $-80$ mV. When the membrane is sufficiently depolarized a breakdown in its resistance occurs, resulting in a rapid swing in the membrane potential leading to the production of an outgoing impulse from the neuron. Depolarizing postsynaptic potentials are known as *excitatory postsyn-*

circuit is shown in Fig. 4 (Eccles 1957). $G_e$ and $G_i$ are variable conductances composed of hundreds or even thousands of individual synaptic conductances such that the highest observed value for $G_e$ is of the order of 2 $\mu$mhos, that for $G_i$ slightly less. The membrane conductance and capacitance are as previously noted. The resting potential of the membrane is represented by the battery generating a voltage $E_m$ of $-70$ mV, and the potential driving the IPSP's by the battery generating a voltage $E_i$ of $-80$ mV.

Consider first the effects of a single excitatory and a single inhibitory synapse of conductances $g_e$ and $g_i$ respectively, connected to the membrane circuit at time $t = 0$. Following excitation by presynaptic potentials, transmitter substances are released which effectively result in a short-circuiting of subsynaptic SD-membrane regions, so that currents flow which either charge or discharge the membrane, depending upon the nature of the transmitter substance. The chemical nature of transmitter substances, especially that serving inhibition, is still an open question.

It is easily shown that the response is given by the equation

$$e(t) = E_m + \frac{g_i}{g'}(E_i - E_m)\left(1 - \exp\left(\frac{g't}{C}\right)\right) - \frac{g_e}{g'}E_m\left(1 - \exp\left(-\frac{g't}{C}\right)\right) \quad (1)$$

where $g'$ is the total circuit conductance equal to $g_m + g_e + g_i$. After times $t_e$ and $t_i$ both of the order of 1 msec, the presynaptic excitations cease, and the circuit returns to its equilibrium value with a time constant of $g^{-1}C$ secs. If the excitation is solely inhibitory or else excitatory, either $g_e$ or else $g_i$ is zero, and the individual responses are readily obtained. Figure 5 shows some typical responses of the system.

We note that the calculated EPSP's and IPSP's only approximate to those observed *in vivo*. Firstly there is a

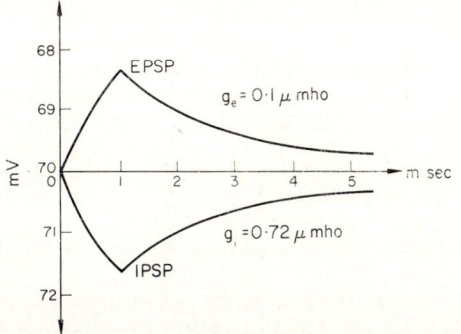

FIG. 5. *Some typical responses of the equivalent circuit.*

delay of about 0·5 msec between the onset of a presynaptic potential and the build-up of a postsynaptic potential. Secondly observed EPSP's usually have time constants longer than 3 msec. It has been suggested that these effects are due to the finite times taken to build up and to remove concentrations of transmitter substance (Eccles 1964, op. cit.). It has also been suggested that the effects are due to the influence of the dendritic complex, non-negligible even in motoneurons, which in effect means that the 'lumped' equivalent circuit of Fig. 4 must be replaced by a 'distributed' circuit (Rall 1959). The resulting electronic effects tend to smear out EPSP's and IPSP's induced in peripheral regions of the dendritic complex so that their form at the soma is somewhat distorted, the onset and rate of decay being slowed down. Figure 6 shows an example of the results of Rall's calculations.

As we have noted the SD-membrane is covered with synapses, so it is continually being charged and discharged. Every change $\partial g_i$ in the total inhibitory synaptic conductance generates a current $(E_i - E_m)\partial g_i$ mA (in the lumped parameter model) charging the membrane, and every change $\partial g_e$ in the total excitatory synaptic conductance generates a current $-E_m\partial g_e$ mA discharging the membrane. When the membrane potential reaches a certain minimum level, the conductance $g_m$ changes suddenly and the result is a rapid change of potential, followed by a slower recovery to the resting potential (usually after a prolonged period of hyperpolarization), when presynaptic potentials again begin to affect the membrane. The phenomenon is complicated in that the sudden potential change, known as the 'action potential' has several components, and is generated at specific sites in the neuronal membrane. In motoneurons it is the initial segment of the axonal membrane—the '*IS-membrane*', which initiates the action potential. Potential changes in the IS-membrane, which has a lower threshold than the SD-membrane for resistive breakdown, elicit even larger changes in the SD-membrane and wipe out the existing potentials there, to produce the fully-fledged action potential.

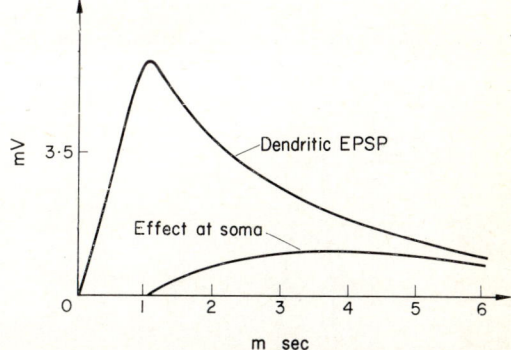

FIG. 6. *The effects of distributed parameters (from Rall 1964).*

We therefore consider an axonal membrane, particularly the IS-membrane. Its equivalent circuit is simply the right-hand side of the circuit shown in Fig. 4. To account for the breakdown of the membrane resistance, the underlying ionic phenomena have to be considered. The basic idea is embodied in the sodium-potassium ion pump postulated by A. L. Hodgkin and A. F. Huxley (1952). In the resting state, the membrane permeability to potassium ions is supposedly much greater than that to sodium ions. When the membrane potential is sufficiently large, an increased permeability to sodium ions is created which if sufficiently greater than the potassium ion permeability, causes a change of membrane potential from the negative potassium potential to the positive sodium potential. Thereafter a recovery period occurs when the membrane returns slowly to its resting potential. An equivalent circuit which accounts for the ionic changes is shown in Fig. 7. $E_K$ the diffusion potential for potassium ions, is given by the *Nernst equation*

$$E_K = 58 \ln \frac{[K]_0}{[K]_i} \quad (2)$$

where $[K]_0$ and $[K]_i$ are respectively the outside and inside concentrations of potassium at the membrane.

A similar equation governs the flow of sodium ions and other species. The resulting membrane current is given by the equation

$$i_m = C\frac{de}{dt} + m^3 h g_{Na}(e - E_{Na}) + n^4 g_K(e - E_K) \quad (3)$$

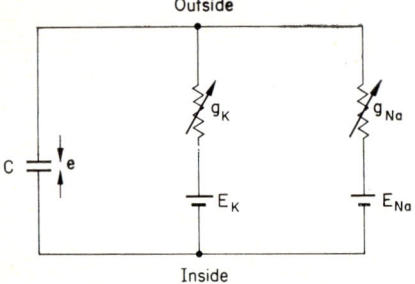

FIG. 7. *IS membrane—an equivalent circuit (from Hodgkin and Huxley 1952).*

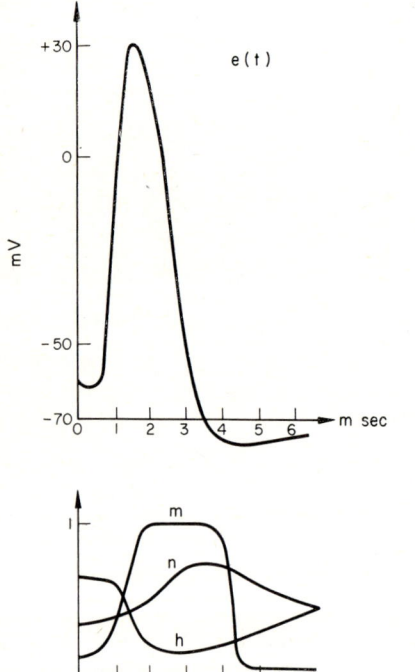

FIG. 8. *Analogue computer solutions of the Hodgkin–Huxley equations (from Fitzhugh 1960).*

where $m$ equals Na activation, $h$—Na inactivation, and $n$—K activation. These variables are dimensionless, varying between 0 and 1, each satisfying an ordinary differential equation involving $e(t)$, $E_m$ and the absolute temperature $T$. The Hodgkin-Huxley model is thus based on four ordinary non-linear differential equations. No general solutions of these equations are known but they have been solved by numerical integration, and by analogue computer simulation. R. Fitzhugh (1960) obtained the solutions shown in Fig. 8 using such a computer. The most notable feature of the solutions is the existence of a threshold for the production of the fully-fledged action potential or 'spike'. Such spikes are produced as a result of the excitation built up in the neuronal membrane and are transmitted by the axon to other cells, propagating without decrement until they reach the terminal arborization of the axon. Because there is a threshold for spike emission, and because the spike propagates without decrement with an amplitude depending only upon local conditions in the axon and independent of stimulus strength, the process was called 'all-or-none' emission (Adrian 1921).

Although there is no direct relationship between spike parameters and the intensities of stimuli acting on the SD-membrane, there is one between the mean rate of spike emission and the stimulus intensity. A number of experimental determinations have been made of this relation (Barron and Matthews 1938; Granit and Renkin 1961; Granit et al. 1963; Verveen 1960; Kernell 1965a, b; Hodgkin 1948; Pecher 1939). Interpretation of the experiments is difficult in that data are taken from widely varying preparations (Frog, Rat, Cat; isolated axon motoneuron, pyramidal neuron; constant stimulating currents, intermittent current pulses), and various secondary effects such as adaptation and accommodation of the SD-membrane to constant stimuli play a role in determining the shape of the rate-intensity curves obtained. Roughly speaking the mean rate of spike-emission is a monotonic increasing function of the quantity $i/i_0$, where $i$ is the intensity of the applied current, and $i_0$ is the 'rheobase', the smallest current which will elicit a spike. In general there is a maximum rate for spike-emission. This occurs because the membrane requires some time to recover its sensitivity after emitting a spike, and for some time after the emission of a spike the membrane is hyperpolarized. The minimum interspike interval is called the 'refractory period'. Figure 9 shows three examples of rate-intensity curves, one linear, one exponential, and one sigmoidal. It seems to be a general finding over a wide range of stimulus intensities, that if the reciprocal of the interval between the first two spikes emitted by a cell is taken as the firing-rate, then the rate-intensity function is sigmoidal. There is indirect evidence supporting such a conclusion in recent observations of correlations between 'post-stimulus time' histograms (PSTH) of spikes emitted by cortical neurons, and the changes of membrane potential recorded on a common microelectrode (Robertson 1966; Cowan 1967).

All these rate-intensity functions represent averages, and there is much variability in the emission of a single spike. The source of this variability may be either entirely outside the cell, e.g. receptor potential fluctuations (Loewenstein 1961), or in synaptic or neuromuscular junctions (Kuno 1964; Fatt and Katz 1952; Adolph 1964), or there may be intrinsic fluctuations in the neuronal membrane itself (Blair and Erlanger 1933; Pecher op. cit.; Hagiwara 1954; Verveen 1961, 1962). Recently Verveen and Derksen (1965, 1966) have shown that the spectrum of the potential fluctuations in the axonal membrane is predominantly of the 1/f type of spectrum found in current-carrying carbon resistors, thin metal films, and semiconductor devices. These particular fluctuations are related to the flux of potassium ions across the membrane. The extension of these results to SD-membrane let alone to neurons *in vivo* is an open problem. However, there is evidence of variability in

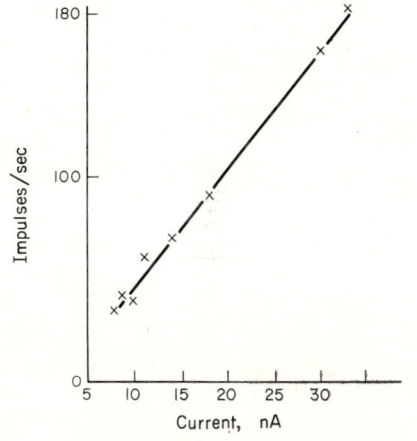

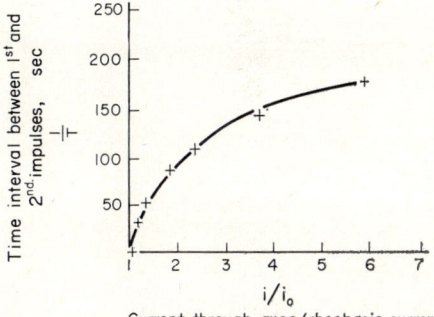

FIG. 9. *Current through axon/rheobasic current (from Verveen 1948).*

the many studies which have been made of the spikes emitted by 'spontaneously' active neurons, and of 'driven' ones in various nets within the CNS, (see for example Rosenblith 1954; Rall and Hunt 1965; Viernstein and Grossman 1961; Rodieck, Y-S. Kiang and Gerstein 1962; Kuffler *et al.* 1957). All these experiments lead to the conclusion that there are numerous sources of variability acting upon the neuronal membrane, some of which are linear in their effect, some non-linear. A statistical description is ultimately required of the neuronal response. The existence of sigmoidal and exponential rate-intensity curves evidently implies the existence of unimodal probability-density functions of spike-emission.

As we have already noted, these rate-intensity curves cover only the first few milliseconds of the neuronal response. The main reason for this is that the neuron 'adapts' to constant stimuli so as to limit the number of spikes it emits. Similarly the neuron 'accommodates' to stimuli in that a gradual increase in stimulus intensity eventually fails to evoke a spike discharge. The time constants of these processes are of the order of tens of milliseconds. Both processes are thought to be due to a slow increase in the threshold for spike emission, brought about by a reaction in the membrane opposing the applied current, tending to re-establish equilibrium.

Many of the concepts we have discussed have been derived from work on motoneurons. For other neuronal types it is certainly true that there are significant departures from motoneuron-like behaviour which are important features of signal processes. We have already cited Rall's work on the dendritic complex. We reiterate that local potential changes in subsynaptic regions of SD-membrane spread electrotonically to the IS-membrane. Clearly the total excitation built-up there may be weighted by a spatial as well as a temporal factor, so that dendritic geometry may well play a very important role in information processing within the CNS. In addition, because of differences in the neuronal membrane, different regions may be in different dielectric states so that current flows continually between them. In peripheral systems dealing with sensory transmission and with the regulation and control of such vital processes as respiration, it appears that many neurons have a 'gain' greater than one, i.e. they emit more spikes than they receive (Young 1961), an effect which is sometimes ascribed to oscillations in the after-potentials which follow spike-emission.

With these reservations in mind we conclude this section, having built up a picture of the neuron as a cell which converts neuronal 'messages' represented within spike patterns into continuous signals, by processes of spatial and temporal summation and integration, and then sends its own 'to whom it may concern' message within its output spike pattern. If, as some neurophysiologists contend, the neuronal message is partly coded in the form of variation of the mean spike-rate or equivalently of the mean interspike interval, then it will be seen that the neuron acts essentially as a pulse-interval modulator, with spike trains of some mean rate serving to carry signals.

*Neuronal Nets*

Such much for the individual neuron. We now turn to neuronal nets proper. We shall look at only three aspects of nets—the responses of single neurons imbedded in a net, the responses of nets inferred from recordings of the activity of large numbers of neurons, known as 'electrocorticograms' or ECoG when such recordings are made from the exposed surface of the brain, and the responses of immense numbers of neurons, inferred from recordings of electrical activity through the scalp, the 'electroencephalogram' or EEG.

*The electroencephalogram.* When gross electrodes (about 1 cm in diameter) are placed on the surface of the scalp and the activity measured either monopolarly or else bipolarly, a fluctuating voltage (about 100 $\mu$V) can be seen. Because of the impedance characteristics of the system and recording apparatus, the recorded voltages are a measure of the electrical activity of supernets seen through a low-pass filter. Thus the EEG is a record of the activity essentially under a monopolar electrode, or else it is the algebraic sum of the activities under bipolar electrodes. Its importance is that it serves as a relatively stable measure of physiological significance.

FIG. 10. *Resting EEG of a normal adult.*

The EEG as a whole is a complex comprising many varying patterns, and is characterized by such statistics as its autocorrelogram, power spectrum, amplitude distribution and envelope amplitude distribution. Figure 10 shows a typical sample of EEG from a normal adult. Figures 11 and 12 show a correlogram and spectrum, and amplitude and envelope amplitude distribution respectively, of typical samples of EEG. It will be seen that there are prominent rhythmic components in some of the samples. These were discovered by H. Berger (1929) who described the EEG as essentially two basic rhythms, the alpha and beta rhythms. The alpha rhythm is usually in the 8–13 cycles per second range when it exists, is prominent in parieto-occipital regions, and disappears in a visually attentive subject. However, a well developed alpha rhythm is a relatively uncommon finding in a normal adult, many samples showing instead, low voltage faster activity, in the frequency band. The beta rhythm is also low voltage fast activity between 18 and 30 cycles per second, and is prominent in precentral and postcentral gyri. It will be seen from Fig. 12 that the EEG spectrum is indeed concentrated in alpha and beta bands. The autocorrelograms do not imply that there is a stable oscillator generating these rhythms, and in fact narrow-band Gaussian noise gives autocorrelograms indistinguishable from EEG (Weiss 1960). In addition the amplitude and envelope amplitude distributions are approximately Gaussian and Rayleigh distributed (Weiss op. cit.; Saunders 1965). These properties are of course also found in narrow-band Gaussian noise.

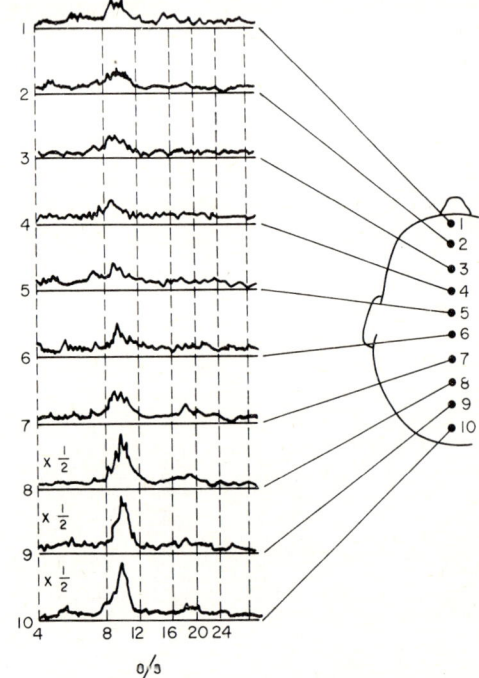

FIG. 11(b). *Spectra of an adult EEG (from Suhara 1963).*

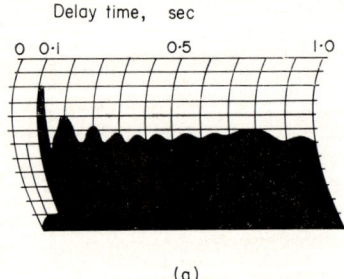

(a)

FIG. 11(a). *Autocorrelogram of resting EEG of normal adult (from Saunders 1965).*

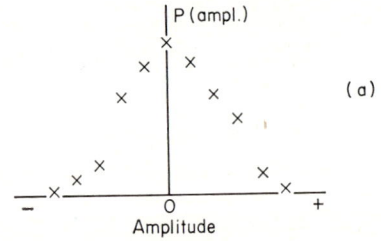

FIG. 12(a) *Probability density of amplitudes of EEG of a normal adult.*

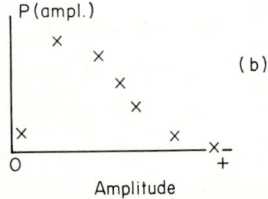

FIG. 12(b). *Probability density of amplitudes of EEG envelope of a normal adult (from Saunders 1965).*

As we shall discuss later, there is evidence that EEG rhythms are generated in the supernets of the diencephalon and telencephalon, under control by myelencephalic signals. Recent work by Walter et al. (1966) suggests that there are at least two different generative processes at work—a process which spreads homolaterally from posterior occipital regions, generating significantly coherent activity in and around the alpha band, and a bioccipital process generating less coherent activity in the same band. The association of these processes with diencephalic nuclei has not been proved. It has been suggested that the beta rhythms are harmonically related to the alpha rhythms or that they are the result of a difference in myelencephalic control signals (Brazier 1960). It is fair to say that the detailed mechanisms underlying the generation of the EEG remain to be discovered. In spite of this lack of understanding, the EEG has proved to be of value as an index of 'physiological state', and an important aid to the diagnosis of pathological conditions in the brain.

terms it might be said that the frequencies found in the analysis of the EEG are the most obvious index of physiological state, although the shape and amplitude of the activity is also of some interest. Figure 15 shows a schematic representation of the frequency spectra associated with different physiological states.

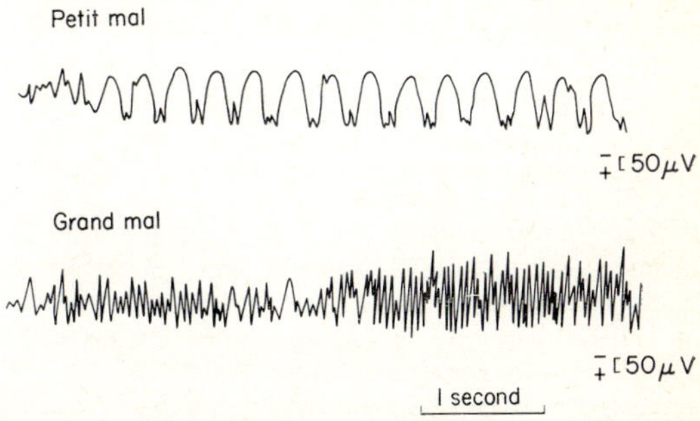

*Electrocorticograms and evoked responses.* So far we have considered only the spontaneous activity of the nervous system. A very important source of knowledge concerning the system is its response to stimuli. Such response may be studied by means of the gross surface electrodes used in electroencephalography, or else smaller extracellular electrodes may be inserted into selected regions of the system, to sample the local responses of neuronal nets. In either case the recorded evoked potentials differ from the spontaneous activity in that

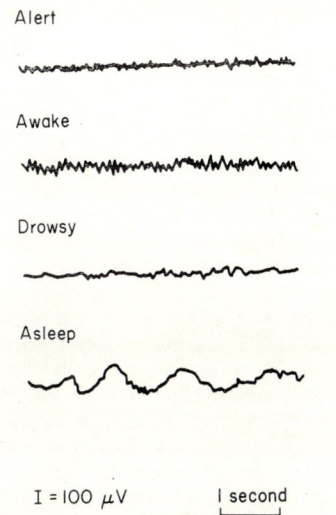

FIG. 13. *Changes in the normal EEG during alertness, drowsiness and sleep (from Brazier 1960).*

Figure 13 shows the sequence of changes in the normal EEG during alertness, drowsiness, and sleep. It will be seen that there is a progressive change from the low voltage fast activity of the alert state, through successive states characterized by higher voltages and lower frequencies, to the 'delta' waves of deep sleep. It will be seen that the waves in all these records are roughly symmetric and could conceivably be generated by linear oscillators. This is not the case with the EEG's typical of pathological conditions such as Epilepsy and other diseases. Figure 14 shows typical patterns found in 'Petit-Mal' and 'Grand-Mal' Epilepsy, the former showing the well known 'Spike-and-Wave' phenomenon, the latter characteristic high-frequency spike activity. In general

FIG. 14. *Abnormal EEG's.*

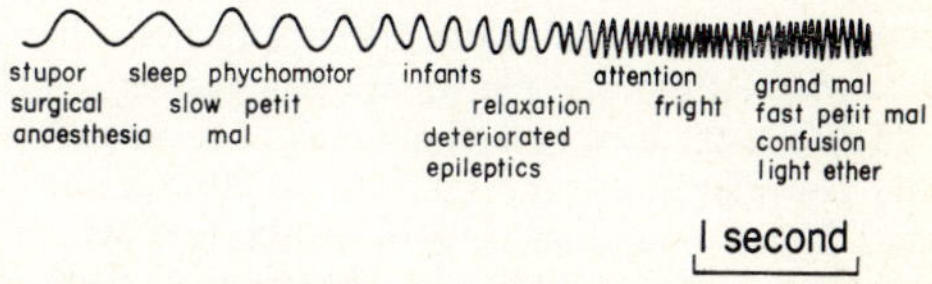

FIG. 15. *The cortical frequency spectrum (from Gibbs and Gibbs 1948).*

they have a definite relationship to the onset of the stimulus, a constant pattern of response and a focus of maximal response in the system. Stimuli may be natural, or else clicks, flashes, and so on; or else stimulating electrodes may be inserted in other neuronal nets to produce signals which in turn stimulate the observed net.

Figure 16 shows a fairly typical record (Brazier 1957) of an evoked potential in the visual cortex of a lightly anaesthetized cat responding to a light flash of 10 $\mu$sec duration. The record is an average over fifty flashes given at 1 msec intervals. According to convention the downward deflexion corresponds to a positive surface potential, the upward one to a negative potential. The biphasic nature of the response, a surface-positive deflexion followed by a longer lasting surface-negative deflexion, is typical of most evoked responses. In addition the surface-negative deflexion is often followed by

FIG. 16. *Evoked potential in the visual cortex of a lightly anaesthetized cat (from Brazier 1960).*

ong-lasting after-effects such as rhythmic activity. According to volume conductor theory the surface-positive deflexion is due to signals from the periphery approaching the cortex—presynaptic excitation, whereas the surface-negative deflexion is due to signals within the visual cortex more-or-less receding from the recording electrode—most probably postsynaptic excitation induced in the dendrites of cortical neurons by presynaptic excitation. Figure 17 shows another typical evoked response (Brazier 1958) to flash in Man. Here there is a noticeable after-discharge phase locked to the flash. Such a record is quite common, the rhythmic after-discharges evidently having some significant functional role. Similar evoked responses are found in all those areas of the cortex which first receive signals from the periphery—the projection areas. There appear to be topological maps from receptor areas through intermediate diencephalic nuclei to these projection areas. So neighbourhood relations on 'receptive-fields' are preserved to the projection areas, and the evoked response is a local response, a change of state in perhaps 1 mm³ of cortex caused by stimulation of some particular set of receptors. However, the receipt of signals from such sources is not restricted to the primary projection areas of the cortex. For example, in somatic-sensory cortex, second and even third receiving areas have been found. Similar considerations apply to the visual and auditory cortices. Finally in some areas the initial biphasic evoked response is followed by a larger and longer-lasting biphasic response, the 'secondary' response. This is much less localized than the primary evoked response, and it is established that it reaches the cortex by a different path (Dempsey *et al.* 1941). The primary response represents activity in thalamo-cortical fibres resulting from the stimulation of thalamic nuclei by signals from peripheral nets. These signals follow the *'classical sensory pathway'* to the contralateral cortex via the lateral division of the medial lemniscus and the ventrolateral nuclei of the thalamus. The secondary response is due to peripheral signals following a different path which does not traverse the thalamus.

In addition to the response evoked by stimulation of receptive fields, there are those evoked by stimulating electrodes placed in different regions of the brain. These responses can be either specific, local responses to the stimulus, or else non-specific generalized responses of supernets appearing as changes in the EEG. In either case they provide valuable information into the nature of the interactions between supernets, particularly the mechanisms responsible for attention. For example Moruzzi and Magoun (1949) discovered that maintenance of the waking state does not depend on inflow along the classical sensory pathway, which would give rise to specific evoked responses, but instead depends on signals in the 'ascending reticular system' comprising nets in both the diencephalon and myelencephalon. Stimulation of this system produces changes in the EEG from slow to fast activity, sometimes over the whole cortex, sometimes only in fronto-parietal nets. Sensory modality is apparently signalled by such an influx. In contrast to this the hippocampus changes from fast to slow activity, as seen in the ECoG (Green and Arduini 1954). Dempsey and Morison (1942) found that slowly repeated stimulation of medial non-specific nuclei in intralaminar nets of the thalamus at rates not too different from that of the animal's own cortical potentials can entrain these rhythms to the stimuli. Such responses are called *'recruiting' responses*. These differ from the *'augmenting' responses* seen on stimulation of other nuclei. Recruiting responses are of long latency, widely distributed over cortical nets, and are predominantly surface-negative. They have the characteristics of dendritic potentials initiated in the upper cortical layers. This surface-negative component is depressed by simultaneous high frequency stimulation of the reticular system. Augmenting responses are local responses of short latency restricted to the projection areas served by the thalamic net which is stimulated, and they are diphasic with an initial surface-positive component. It will be seen that differences exist in evoked potential and ECoG records which are related to the specificity of the nets involved. It seems that alpha and beta rhythms, recruiting responses, and secondary components in the evoked response result from the interaction of nets within the upper five cortical layers with nets of the thalamic, myelencephalic and mesencephalic reticular systems. The primary components of the evoked response together with augmenting responses appear to result from the interaction of nets in middle cortical layers with nets in the ventrolateral nuclei of the thalamus.

Broadly speaking we may assume that there are essentially two different subsets of supernets within the nervous system, one dealing with the classification and encoding of specified stimulus attributes, the other with holistic aspects of the CNS in relation to its environment, i.e. with the general physiological state of the animal. We may term the former subset 'phasic', the latter 'tonic'. There is anatomical evidence for the specificity

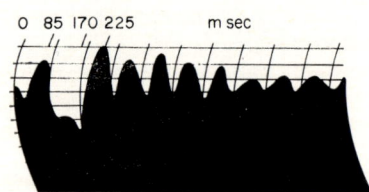

FIG. 17. *Response to flash in man (from Brazier 1960).*

attributed to phasic responses in the topological maps from receptive-fields to projection areas. It has been suggested (Dempsey and Morison op. cit.) that the 'non-specific fibres' (Ramon y Cajal 1894) of unknown origin which terminate in the upper layers of the cortex, may be efferents from reticular nets especially thalamic ones. Brazier (op. cit.) has noted that these fibres could synapse with the dendrites of pyramidal cells in the cortex, and has suggested that such an interaction could give rise to tonic activity. There have been many suggestions that cortical potentials measured by gross and macroelectrodes represent both presynaptic and postsynaptic excitation in the dendrites of pyramidal neurons (see Bremer 1957). The surface-positive components of the evoked response could well be the sum of presynaptic potentials, and the surface-negative components together with the waves of the EEG are equally likely to be summed EPSP's and IPSP's, seen through some kind of low-pass filter. Recent work by M. R. Klee et al. (1965) has shown that there are significant correlations between waves in the EEG and slow membrane transients in single neurons in cortical nets, during the course of spontaneous activity and also during augmenting and recruiting responses. Some light is also shed on this possibility by measurements of the changes in d.c. potentials on the cortical surface (measured with respect to a reference electrode usually placed in a ventricle) associated with evoked potentials, (see O'Leary and Goldring 1959). H. Caspers (1959) has suggested that a 'dynamic balance' exists between EPSP's and IPSP's in dendritic regions of cortical pyramids, which is reflected in both the d.c. potential and the evoked responses. The 'resting' level is supposed to be a state in which on the average, depolarizing effects cancel with hyperpolarizing ones. A positive or negative shift of the d.c. potential increases the average number of units which will respond to an input by a relative increase in either depolarization or hyperpolarization. Caspers concludes that the evoked potentials may represent a modulation of the d.c. potential. It is of interest that W. Grey Walter (1964) has found changes in the EEG—'*E waves*'—with time-constants of about 1 sec which appear to relate the state of human subjects to stimulus contingencies. E-waves appear to be closely related to the cortical d.c. potentials.

Direct stimulation of the cortical surface (Eccles 1951) has led to the suggestion that the observed superficial response, a brief surface-negative wave, corresponds to the focal record of EPSP's induced in the 'Apical' dendrites of pyramidal cells by presynaptic impulses. Experiments on the changes accompanying spreading depression (Leao 1944; Grafstein 1956), and on isolated slabs of undercut cortex (Burns 1957) relating changes in d.c. potentials and evoked potentials caused by direct cortical stimulation, to changes in the firing patterns of individual neurons, all support the conclusion that postsynaptic potentials in dendrites constitute the main component of the EEG and of the evoked responses.

These conclusions are based on experiments with corticipetal fibres. As we have previously noted it seems that for every corticipetal fibre there is a corticifugal one. So we have to consider the possibility of physiological feedback from cortical nets to thalamic, mesencephalic, and myelencephalic ones, and the role it serves in maintaining or modifying the activity of the CNS. Evidence is available concerning corticifugal pathways playing upon the mesencephalic reticular formation. Rossi and Zanchetti (1957) have summarized the anatomical evidence. Descending 'suppressor' effects induced by cortical stimulation (McCulloch et al. 1946) strongly suggest that these cortico-thalamic paths are partly inhibitory in nature, and indeed Hughelin et al. (1960) have shown that the reticular formation is under the restraining action of the cortex. At diencephalic levels Andersen et al. (1964) have demonstrated that stimulation of certain cortical areas causes inhibition in peripheral afferent nets. Calma (1965) has demonstrated a cortical influence, mainly inhibitory, on some of the thalamic relay nuclei in the classical sensory pathway—the ventrobasal and posterior thalamic nuclei. In addition to such 'vertical' circuits, it appears that there are 'lateral' circuits between homologous areas in the two hemispheres. Koella and Ferry (1963) have found that transcortical electrical polarization of one hemisphere interferes with the evoked potentials not only in the polarized ipsilateral cortex, but also in the contralateral one. Within a limited range the changes observed in the contralateral hemisphere were opposite to those in the ipsilateral cortex. Indeed the experiments show that surface-positive polarization decreases the 'arousal' level in the ipsilateral cortex and enhances it in the contralateral cortex, while surface-negative polarization has the opposite effect. This suggests that there are negative-feedback circuits between cortical and mesencephalic nets. Koella and Ferry note that a particular aspect of such a system would be that its output diverges bilaterally to impinge upon two separate effector areas, and that the feedbacks from these two areas converge upon the brainstem and operate through a mixer to exert their combined restraining influence. Figure 18 shows some general features of the postulated system. Because of the mixer (which is just a summing device) such influences can be excitatory or inhibitory. This suggestion is of interest in the light of the findings of Bremer (1958), Hang (1953) and Marsam and Morillo (1963) of both excitatory and inhibitory influences of commisural fibres. Finally we should add that many cases of physiological feedback within nets

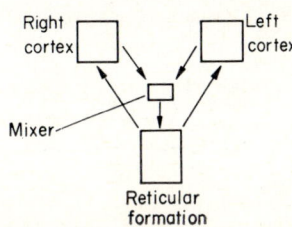

FIG. 18. *Cortico-subcortical circuits (from Koella and Ferry 1963).*

have been discovered. A frequently found pattern is for excitatory cells to synapse via '*recurrent collaterals*' with inhibitory '*interneurons*' which in turn synapse with the excitors. Such circuits have been described in the cerebral cortex (Phillips 1959), in the hippocampus (Kandel et al. 1961), in the ventrobasal complex of the thalamus (Andersen and Eccles 1962), and in the lateral geniculate (Sefton and Burke 1965). Such feedback 'oscillators' have in fact been postulated to provide the basis for the slow rhythms which we have discussed (Andersen and Eccles op. cit.).

This then concludes our survey of the slower potentials of neuronal nets. We have of course looked at only a small fraction of the relevant experimental data, and we have certainly oversimplified. Nevertheless we can surely conclude that there are broadly speaking, tonic and phasic components in the slow potentials, that both presynaptic and postsynaptic excitation in neuronal nets give rise in some way to these potentials, and that the multiplicity of circuits between and within nets is crucial for the maintained functioning of the system.

*Microelectrode recordings and slow potentials.* We now turn to the problem of integrating what we have learned concerning slow potentials with the spike-patterns that can be recorded by extracellular and intracellular microelectrodes. Renshaw et. al (1940) first recorded spikes emitted by neurons within the nets of the cortex, but they could find no correlation between spike-patterns and slow potentials recorded from the hippocampal surface. Li and Jasper (1953) obtained simultaneous records of spike patterns and electrocorticograms (see Fig. 19). Jasper concluded that there was no clear-cut relationship between the two different records. The problem is that there is great variability in the records. The gross electrodes apparently pick-up only coherent activity in a relatively large volume of tissue—about 1 mm³. The microelectrode picks up all the activity in that part of the neuronal membrane which is near the electrode tip. In recent years, developments in the technology of data processing have made it possible to compute statistical measures of the activity sampled by both gross and microelectrodes (see Processing neuroelectric data 1959). In this way correlations can be found between spike patterns and slow potentials. In Section 1 we discussed determinations of rate-intensity curves for isolated neurons, and noted that correlations have been found between PSTH's and mean slow potentials, obtained from records taken with a single microelectrode of the activity

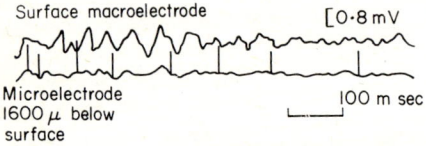

FIG. 19. *Spike patterns and EEG (from Li and Jasper 1953).*

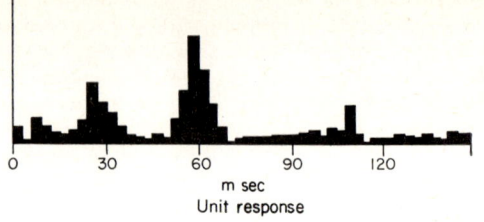

FIG. 20(a). *Unit response.*

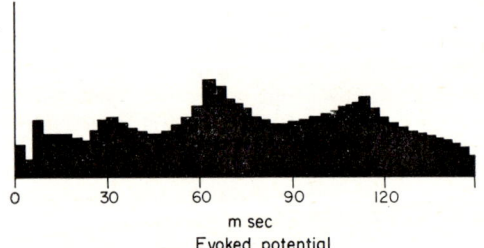

FIG. 20(b). *Evoked potential (from Robertson 1966).*

of a neuron within a cortical net. Figure 20 shows such records with obvious correlation between them. Fox and O'Brien (1965) have obtained somewhat similar results, and because the slow potentials are still recorded even after the observed neuron has been killed, have inferred that the slow potential recorded on the common microelectrode is a close approximation to the evoked response of the net containing the observed neuron. The inference drawn from this is that the frequency distribution of the firing of a single neuron corresponds to the mean evoked response of the net. Such a conclusion implies a very high degree of synchrony within such a net, and it is perhaps doubtful that the postulated relation is generally true. However, Robertson (1966b) has found correlations between the mean firing rate of cortical neurons in unanaesthetized preparations, and the level of surface-positive polarization of the cortical surface, which is known to affect the amplitude of the evoked response (Caspers op. cit.). In addition to these results relating to the evoked response, there is also evidence relating to correlation between oscillations in slow potentials and temporal patterns of neuronal firing known as 'bursts'. In the spinal cord Terzuolo and Gernandt (1956) have found *burst activity* to be coincident with the rising phase of the slow potential. Verzeano and Negishi (1960) have found similar correlations in records from cortical and thalamic neurons. Robertson (1966b op. cit.) has also found correlation between neuronal spike bursts and 'spindles' in the EEG. Verzeano and Negishi's results are also of interest in that working with multiple microelectrodes they found circulating spike activity in just those corticothalamic circuits which are held to be responsible for the tonic components of neuronal activity.

All these different considerations certainly indicated that the slow potentials reflect the postsynaptic effects of afferent input to neuronal nets, and possibly the efferent flow from nets. Experimental results seem to indicate that the mean spike emission rate in neuronal nets is a monotonic function of such parameters of the slow potentials associated with the net, such as amplitude and rate of change. John *et al.* (1964) conditioned animals to respond to periodic stimuli and noted a tendency towards increased correlation between evoked potentials and the conditioning stimulus, and also between evoked potentials in different regions of the CNS. It was suggested that iterated stimulation builds a net which reflects the temporal pattern of previous inputs, i.e. entrainment indicates the influence of afferents on nets; and by such mechanisms a multiple representational system is developed. Since wave-shapes *per se* do not propagate in the manner of impulses, it was suggested that the wave-shapes arising in neuronal nets influence the spatiotemporal patterns of spikes emitted therein, so that the pattern of postsynaptic excitation in nets which receive such spikes reflects the time course of excitation in the initial nets. Thus the evoked potential represents the temporal input to neuronal nets. It may or may not reflect the time course of events related to the outflux from these same nets. It is conjectured that neurons within a net extract the average pattern of influxes by spatial and temporal integration. John *et al.* in fact suggest that the wave-shape itself may be precisely what constitutes functional information for the CNS.

*Functional aspects of nets.* However, we have so far considered only temporal aspects of the firing patterns of neurons related to macropotentials. In recent years much data has been generated in studies of the spatial aspects of neuronal interaction, particularly in the sensory projection systems. Macroelectrodes have of course been used extensively in such studies, but of necessity the fine details are averaged out so that essentially topographical information has been acquired. In this way the gross organization of receptive-fields and the representational systems within the CNS have been elucidated. What emerged from early studies was the concept of a rather static nervous system—a central core wherein all the important processing was carried out, with a well-defined localized representational system in its sensorimotor cortex, connected to its receptors and effectors by transmission lines or cables. The new concept of organization which has emerged from work with microelectrodes is much more dynamic in that even peripheral nets are seen to process signals in a complex fashion selecting, filtering, abstracting, computing, under constant control from more central nets. Indeed hierarchies execute a progressively selective response to stimuli as the map from periphery to centre unfolds.

In the visual system for example, a very detailed hierarchy has been discovered. Early work by Hartline (1935, 1938) and later by Granit (1947) on the retinas and optic nerves of vertebrates had demonstrated the existence of units which responded phasically only to the onset or offset of a stimulus or to both. Such units have become known as '*on*', '*off*', and '*on-off*' units re-

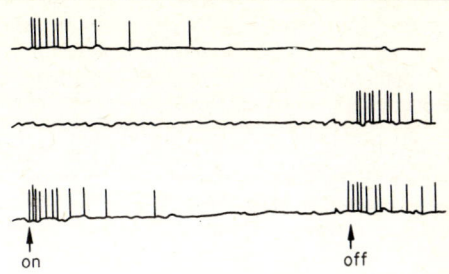

FIG. 21. '*On*', '*Off*', and '*On-Off*' units.

spectively. Figure 21 shows some idealized spike-patterns generated by such units. In addition to these temporal aspects of peripheral discharges Hartline (1940) measured the receptive fields of units in the frog retina. Such fields are relatively large, up to 1 mm diameter at the retinal periphery, smaller towards the centre. Now in a frog's retina there are about $3 \times 10^4$ nerve fibres, and about $1 \times 10^6$ receptor cells. Hartline's results suggest that some kind of spatial convergence must occur, and that a process of spatial summation must occur in retinal units. Barlow (1953) was able to demonstrate such summation. In addition he found that there was decreased sensitivity of '*on-off*' units towards the edges of their receptive-fields. Figure 22 shows the results of one of Barlow's experiments, in which a central and a peripheral spot are used. It will be seen that illumination of both the central and side spots result in a much smaller response than when the central spot is alone illuminated. Barlow attributed this to a process of 'surround inhibition', that is the excitatory centre of the receptive-field of the 'on-off' unit is surrounded by an inhibitory region. This region appeared to interact linearly with the excitatory centre, suggesting spatial summation of both excitatory and inhibitory potentials. It was also noted

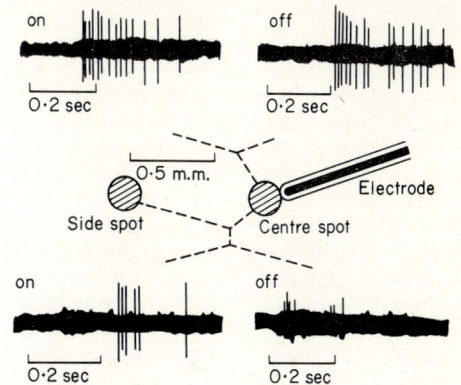

FIG. 22. *Discharge produced by central spot inhibited by side-spot turned on and off with it, top: centre spot alone; bottom: centre and side-spots (from Barlow 1953).*

that 'on-off' units respond to a change in the spatial *pattern* of light, even if there is no change in the total incident light flux. Barlow concluded that there were *overlapping* receptive fields in the retina, each comprising about $2 \times 10^3$ receptors and overlapping with about eighty other fields; that 'on-off' units were more than just 'off' units with an inhibitor mechanism; and on epistemological and teleological grounds that 'on-off' units act precisely to detect the frog's natural prey—flies—so that frog retina as a whole functions like a computer, rejecting unwanted information, and transmitting useful information. The epistemological approach was followed by J. Y. Lettvin *et al.* (1959 who greatly extended the earlier findings, by studying the function of retinal cells in response to light and dark patterns moved in the visual field against different backgrounds. The retinal cells studied were the 'ganglion' cells. It was shown that they comprised five classes: edge detectors, convex edge detectors, changing contrast detectors, dimming detectors, and darkness detectors. The first class evidently corresponds to Hartline's 'on' units, the third class to the 'on-off' units, and the fourth class to the 'off' units. However, the second and fifth classes, the convexity and darkness detectors, have no earlier counterparts. Lettvin *et al.* were able to exhibit a structural correspondence between the different classes and different kinds of ganglion cells, especially concerning dendritic organization. They found that such cells formed five populations uniformly distributed in a retinal layer, with many overlapping receptive-fields. The axons of cells in each class were found to end in separate layers within nets of the central portion of the frog's nervous system, the 'Tectum'. There was a topological map from retina to tectum. Lettvin *et al.* concluded that the main function of the frog retina is to *analyse* stimulus patterns in terms of qualities, and that the intrinsic nature of the retinal units as well as their patterns of interaction is vital for such a task.

Detailed information concerning the nature of interaction mechanisms is provided by the work of Hartline and Ratliff (1957) on the eye of the Horseshoe Crab—*Limulus*. It was found that activity in any one optic nerve fibre could be elicited only by illumination of the receptor unit giving rise to the fibre, i.e. unlike the frog retina there is no spatial summation in the *Limulus* eye. However, the discharge of spikes by any given receptor unit is inhibited by illuminating neighbouring receptor units. Such an interaction was termed *lateral inhibition*. Moreover under steady illumination the inhibition exerted by one unit on another is a linear function of the rate at which the unit emits spikes, (see Fig. 23). The intensity of illumination inhibition falls off with increasing distance between units. Such factors can easily be shown to lead to 'on' and 'on-off' spike bursts. Lateral inhibition appears to be present in the spinal cord where it is known as 'reciprocal inhibition' (Renshaw 1941; Eccles *et al.* 1954), in the vertebrate retinas (Kuffler 1952), in somatic-sensory cortex (Mountcastle 1957), auditory cortex (Katsuki *et al.* 1958; Y-S. Kiang *et al.* 1966) and visual cortex (Hubel and Wiesel 1959, 1962; Baumgartner *et al.* 1959).

*Hubel and Wiesel*'s results are of particular interest since they indicate that contrary to the discoveries of Lettvin *et al.* in frog retinas, interaction properties rather than unit properties *per se* are of primary importance for visual integration. The system studied was that of the cat. It comprises layers of differentially sensitive receptors, the 'rods' and 'cones' innervating a layer of 'bipolar' neurons which in turn synapse with ganglion cells. From here signals proceed up the optic nerve to a diencephalic relay net, the lateral geniculate nucleus, and thence to the visual or 'striate' cortex, located in that region of the occipital pole known as area 17 (see Ranson and Clark 1959; Polyak 1958). Because of the small size of the bipolars, it has not yet been possible to record spikes from them. Electron-micrograms (Pedler 1966) show, however, that between the rods and cones and

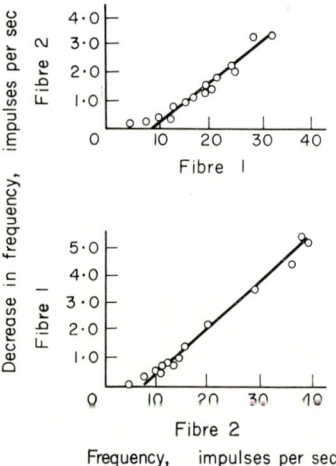

FIG. 23. *Mutual inhibition of two receptor units (from Hartline and Ratliff 1957).*

bipolars there is a regular feltwork of interacting processes—bipolar dendrites, 'horizontal cells' and so forth —making a complicated plexus within which some kind of image sharpening and intensifying probably occurs. The bipolars interact with ganglion cell dendrites and 'amacrine' cells in another plexus which also receives centrifugal fibres from cephalic nets. Figure 24 shows in schematic form some of these details. The ganglion cells are somewhat larger than the bipolars and the spike patterns they emit were recorded by Hubel and Wiesel. Two classes of ganglion cells were found, those with 'on' centres and surround-inhibition, and those with 'off' centres and surround-inhibition. None of the more complicated classes found by Lettvin *et al.* were found in the cat retina. In the lateral geniculate, two similar classes were found usually with pronounced inhibitory surrounds and such that a specific optic nerve fibre excited a maximum response from the cell under observation. A precise topographical representation of retinal fields was found in the geniculate.

In area 17 no cells were found with concentric 'on' or 'off'-centred receptive-fields, but a variety of new classes. In fact the cells seemed to fall into two broad general categories which Hubel and Wiesel called 'simple' and 'complex'. Simple cells have the property that their receptive-fields can be partitioned into excitatory and inhibitory regions, separated by straight lines. Stimuli such as slits, bars, and edges are likely to be the most potent stimuli for such cells. Moreover the stimuli must be of fixed position and orientation in the receptive-field. Complex cells in general cannot be partitioned simply into excitatory and inhibitory regions, and they respond to slits, bars, and edges of constant orientation located anywhere within the receptive-field. Figure 25 shows typical responses from a simple and a complex cell. In neighbouring regions of cortex, in areas 18 and 19, sometimes known as 'secondary visual areas', Hubel and Wiesel found yet another category of cells which they called 'hypercomplex'. These are cells which respond to moving slits, edges, and bars, and to more complicated patterns containing corners, niches, and the like, all with constant orientation. However, the terms 'excitatory' and 'inhibitory' if used to characterize the receptive-fields of hypercomplex cells, must be understood in a more abstract way than hitherto, since the effects of regions do not summate spatially in any simple sense. Fig. 26 shows the response of such a hypercomplex cell.

In addition to these differing cell classes, Hubel and Wiesel found a very important general property of all simple and complex cells, and of almost all hypercomplex cells, namely that cells which are close neighbours almost always have the same receptive-field orientation. Furthermore regions or '*columns*' of constant orientation extend from surface to white matter with walls normal to the cortical layers. Within any one column in area

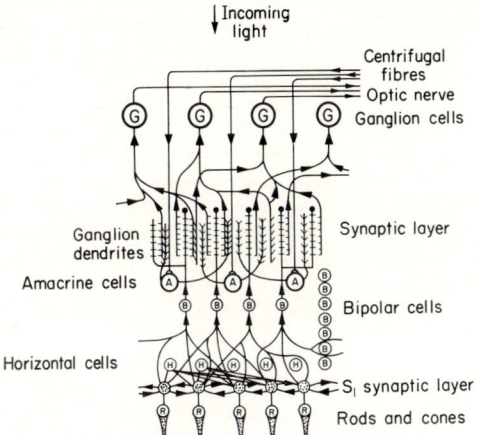

FIG. 24. *Retinal anatomy (from Pedler 1965).*

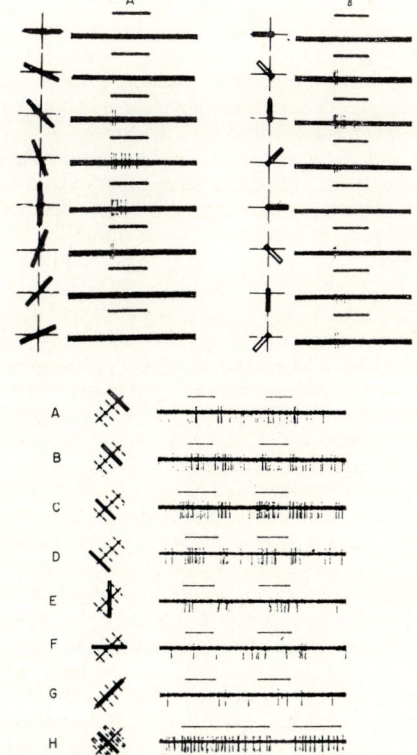

FIG. 25. *A simple and a complex cell (from Hubel and Wiesel 1962).*

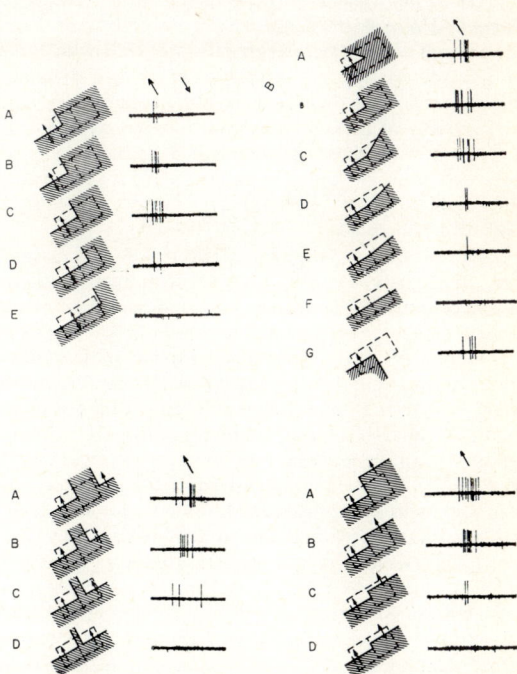

FIG. 26. *A hypercomplex cell (from Hubel and Wiesel 1965).*

17 there are both simple and complex cells, within any column in areas 18 and 19 there are hypercomplex cells of differing orders of complexity. Finally, a given small area of the retina is represented many times in area 17, in columns representing many orientations.

These results are of considerable importance in that they provide us with some insight into the nature of the 'local' mechanisms of functional organization of neuronal nets. There is evidently great convergence onto bipolars and ganglion cells from receptors, leading to overlapping receptive-fields of considerable extent. Although there is no direct evidence of lateral inhibition anywhere within the vertebrate visual system, it is plausible that horizontal and amacrine cells in the retina are responsible for the appearance of surround-inhibition in ganglion receptive-fields. There appears to be an approximately 1:1 map from the ganglionic layer to the lateral geniculate, however, the map from hereon to area 17 is probably many: many since the simplest assumption needed to explain the responses of simple cortical cells is that they act as coincidence detectors of inputs from the lateral geniculate. Similarly complex cortical cells can be considered to be coincidence detectors of inputs from simple cells, and hypercomplex cells as detectors of various combinations of complex cell activity. Sholl's data (op. cit.) suggests that cells which are interconnected tend to be nearest neighbours, and since there appears to be a prominent vertical component in dendritic orientation (Lorente de Nó 1943) there is an anatomical substratum for the columnar organization. Indeed the column emerges as the 'functional unit' of the cortex. To quote Hubel and Wiesel:

'Far from being a mere aggregation of cells with common characteristics, the column emerges as a dynamic unit of function. In the visual areas the columnar system can probably be looked on as a solution to the problem of dealing with three independent variables—two to specify position on the retina and the third for receptive-field orientation—in a structure, the cortex, that is in a sense two-dimensional.'

It is significant that columnar structure was also discovered in somatic-sensory cortex (Mountcastle 1957). Indeed columnar organization may be a feature of many cortical nets.

Hubel and Wiesel's discoveries provide some indication of how stimulus coding takes place in the vertebrate visual system. It is noteworthy that the coding seems to result from analysis of local attributes of stimuli. Nothing definite is said concerning how these attributes are integrated into a holistic representation of the stimulus. Indeed nothing is said concerning how codes for such local attributes modify the maintained activity found in neuronal nets (Kuffler *et al.* op. cit., Burns *et al.* 1962) which is held to be fundamental to the integration of nets. One possible reason for this is that Hubel and Wiesel have worked entirely with animals under barbiturate anaesthesia. As a result many of the observed cells which responded to retinal stimulation were not spontaneously active. Robertson (1965) found that even very low doses of barbiturate reduced the number of spontaneously active cells observed, and generally increased the number of cells which responded to retinal stimulation. Moreover receptive-field organization was greatly altered and stabilized by the anaesthetic. Lilly (1952) recorded with macroelectrodes, the spatial distribution of neocortical activity in anaesthetized animals and found that the effect of anaesthesia was to isolate functional regions from one another in the cortex, to simplify their activity, and to prevent interactions between neighbouring regions. Burns *et al.* working with unanaesthetized preparations could evoke responses only from spontaneously active cells. Most cells gave 'on-off' responses to visual stimuli, superimposed on a background of maintained activity. It was suggested that signals were presented to the visual system as short-lasting deviations from the mean firing rate of cortical cells. Kuffler *et al.* (op. cit.) reached similar conclusions concerning the retina.

*Discussion*

As we have seen, macroscopic studies of neuronal anatomy and physiology lead to the view of the nervous system as a complex of ordered nets arranged in a three-level hierarchy, with many circuits within and between the constellations of neurons we have called supernets. On the average such nets are specific; there are for example well-defined laminar and columnar structures in cortical nets. EEG's, ECoG's, and d.c. potential records indicate that there is an underlying dynamical activity generated within supernets. Feedback inhibition undoubtedly plays a very important role in maintaining the activity which is controlled both by external and internal signals, especially from nets of the lower levels—the reticular systems. The EEG serves as a measure of the general level of the dynamic activity of supernets, the d.c. potentials as measures of the stationary states of such activity, i.e. as long-time averages, and the ECoG and evoked responses as measures of the incoming and outgoing fluxes in nets. There are two broad categories of evoked responses. One is associated with tonic aspects of the nervous system, is related to the gross spontaneous activity, and is probably generated in the same corticothalamic circuits. The other is the modality-specific response associated with phasic aspects of the system, generated in different circuits.

The view of the nervous system which results from microscopic studies of single cells and their interactions, fills in the details necessarily obscured by macroscopic studies. However, there are also significant differences, the resolution of which is a difficult problem. Studies of isolated cells have established the manner in which cells respond to stimuli and emit spikes. In general there is a monotonic relation between the rate of spike-emission and the currents generated in somato-dendritic regions of the neuronal membrane. The role of transmitter substances, of EPSP's and IPSP's, and of ions in determining such responses is becoming known. There are definite relationships between spike-patterns and macropotentials, at least on the average. It is probable that such potentials are the algebraic sums of EPSP's and IPSP's seen through some kind of low-pass filter, and that d.c. potentials reflect the states of balance between EPSP's and IPSP's that constitute the stationary states of the dynamical system. Studies of the interactions between cells and of the phasic responses of cells to patterned stimuli have established that there is a specific organization of columnar nets, maintained by nearest-neighbour interactions, spatial summation and inhibition. There are topological maps between many nets and from receptive-fields. Studies of the effects of anaesthesia indicate that tonic responses may also be present in the cells of 'physiological' animals, although it is not clear that the precise solumnar organization is then completely preserved.

Concerning the neuronal coding of signals, one apparently general operating mode is via pulse rate modulation, so that signals are deviations from steady-state activity. The view that the evoked response sends its signals by modulating the stationary balance between EPSP's and IPSP's comprising the d.c. potentials is consistent with this. However, pulse rate modulation is only one possibility. Receptive field experiments indicate that the specificity of the individual neuronal response is a very important signal. These responses occur as spike bursts, and it is possible that in physiological preparations, variations in such parameters as the frequency of bursts, number of spikes per bursts, together with cell specificity, and response latency all constitute meaningful signals. One view is that almost all changes in the spatio-temporal patterns of firing within neuronal nets convey information. *Per contra* it has been suggested that nets average over incoming fluxes by processes of spatial and temporal summation and integration within cells, plus diffusion between cells, and that the shape of the evoked response—the average pattern of influxes and outfluxes—is the important signal. Certainly receptive-field experiments indicate that signals set up locally within nets are important for detecting and abstracting qualitative features of stimuli. Neither how these features are integrated into a holistic representation of stimuli, nor how such representations are eventually coded and stored, is yet known. The columnar organization which has been discovered points to columns as being the 'functional units' of the nervous system, and it is worth noting that columnar coordination plus orientation, presumably supplied by dendritic geometry, serve to represent a three-dimensional Euclidean manifold.

We conclude this survey of neuronal nets by observing that what we have outlined and probably oversimplified is only one aspect of a much broader vista. We cannot hope to understand how neuronal nets function without knowing how they came to be, and what controls their continued existence, i.e. neurochemistry, genetics, embryology, and so forth. Nor have we looked at the functional or informational aspects of nets, for example learning, recognition, and so forth. It has been said that the great need is for a physiological theory of thought, and that a way must be found to reconcile the phenomena of perceptual generalization, the stability of memory, and the instabilities of attention (Hebb 1949). Perhaps the electrophysiology of neuronal nets will one day help to answer these questions. Certainly the problems will occupy neurophysiologists, mathematicians and others for a very long time. Meanwhile perhaps the most appropriate description of neuronal nets is still that by Sherrington (1940):

'A scheme of lines and nodal points, gathered together at one end into a great ravelled knot, the brain, and at the other trailing off to a sort of stalk, the spinal cord. Imagine activity in this shown by little points of light. Of these some are stationary and flash rhythmically, faster or slower. Others are travelling points, streaming in serial trains at various speed. The rhythmic stationary lights lie at the nodes. The nodes are both goals whither converge, and junctions whence diverge, the lines of travelling lights... (The brain is) an enchanted loom where millions of flashing shuttles weave a dissolving pattern, always a meaningful pattern though never an abiding one; a shifting harmony of sub-patterns.'

*Acknowledgements.* The work embodied in this review was performed with financial support from the U.S. Department of the Navy, Office of Naval Research, Physics Branch, under Contract No. N. 62558–4256, for which support the author is extremely grateful.

The author would also like to express his gratitude to Sir Willis Jackson, F.R.S., Head of the Electrical Engineering Department, Imperial College of Science and Technology, for the warm hospitality he has enjoyed as an Academic Visitor, while this review was written. Many helpful discussions with Mr. N. W. Ellis and Mr. A. D. J. Robertson are gratefully acknowledged. Finally the author would like to thank Mrs. L. M. Talbot and Mrs. B. Broadhurst for the preparation of the manuscript and figures.

*See also:* Attention. Models for human memory.

*Bibliography*

ADOLPH A. R. (1964) *J. Gen. Physiol.* **48**, 297.
ADRIAN E. D. (1914) *J. Physiol.* **47**, 460.
ANDERSON P. and ECCLES J. C. (1962) *Nature*, **196**, 645.
ANDERSON P. and SEARS T. A. (1964) *J. Physiol.* **173**, 459.
BARLOW H. B. (1953) *J. Physiol.* **119**, 69.
BARRON D. H. and MATTHEWS B. H. C. (1938) *J.Physiol.* **92**, 276.
BAUMGARTNER G. and HAKAS P. (1959) *Pflügers Arch.* **270**, 29.
BERGER H. (1929) *Arch. f. Psychiat.* **87**, 527.
BLAIR E. A. and ERLANGER J. (1953) *Amer. J. Physiol.* **106**, 524.
BRAZIER M. A. (1957) *Acta Physiol. Neerlandica*, **6**, 692.
BRAZIER M.A. (1958) *Symposium on Electroencephalography and Higher Nervous Activity*, Academy of Sciences, U.S.S.R.
BRAZIER M. A. (1960) *The Electrical Activity of the Nervous System*, New York: Macmillan.

BREMER F. (1958a) *Physiol. Revs.* **38**, 357.
BREMER F. (1958b) *Proc. Assoc. Res. Nerv. Ment. Dis.* **36**, 424.
BURNS B. D. et al. (1957) *J. Physiol.* **112**, 156.
BURNS B. D., HERON W. and PRITCHARD R. (1962) *J. Neurophysiol.* **25**, 165.
CALMA I. (1965) *Nature*, **205**, 394.
CASPERS H. (1959) *Pflügers Arch.* **269**, 157.
CHANG H. T. (1953) *J. Neurophysiol.* **16**, 133.
COWAN J. D. (1967) In preparation.
DEMPSEY E. W. and MORISON R. S. (1941) *Amer. J. Physiol.* **131**, 718.
DEMPSEY E. W. and MORISON R. S. (1942) *Amer. J. Physiol.* **135**, 293.
ECCLES J.C. (1951) *EEG, Clin. Neurophysiol.* **3**, 449.
ECCLES J. C. (1957) *The Physiology of Nerve Cells*, Baltimore: Johns Hopkins Press.
ECCLES J. C. (1964) *The Physiology of Synapses*, Berlin: Springer.
ECCLES J. C., FATT P. and KOKETSU K. (1954) *J. Physiol.* **126**, 524.
FATT P. and KATZ B. (1952) *J. Physiol.* **117**, 109.
FITZHUGH R. (1960) *J. Gen. Physiol.*, **43**, 867.
FOX S. S. and O'BRIEN J. H. (1965) *Science*, **147**, 888.
GRAFSTEIN B. (1956) *J. Neurophysiol.* **19**, 154.
GRANIT R. (1947) *Sensory Mechanisms of the Retina*, London: Oxford University Press.
GRANIT R. and RENKIN B. (1961) *J. Physiol.* **158**, 461.
GRANIT R., KERNELL D. and SHORTESS G. K. (1963) *J. Physiol.* **169**, 743.
GREEN J. D. and ARDUINI A. (1954) *J. Neurophysiol.* **17**, 533.
HAGIWARA S. (1954) *Japanese J. Physiol.* **4**, 234.
Handbook of Physiology I (1959) *Neurophysiology I*, (Ed. J. Field), Washington, D. C.: American Physiological Society.
HARTLINE H. K. (1935) *Amer J. Physiol.* **113**, 59.
HARTLINE H. K. (1938) *Amer. J. Physiol.* **121**, 400.
HARTLINE H. K. (1940) *Amer. J. Physiol.* **130**, 690.
HARTLINE H. K. and RATLIFF F. (1957) *J. Gen. Physiol.* **40**, 357.
HEBB D. O. (1949) *The Organisation of Behaviour*, London: Chapman and Hall.
HODGKIN A. L. (1948) *J. Physiol.* **107**, 163.
HODGKIN A. L. and HUXLEY A. F. (1952) *J. Physiol.*, **117**, 500.
HUBEL D.H. and WIESEL T. N. (1959) *J. Physiol.* **148**, 574.
HUBEL D. H. and WIESEL T.N. (1962) *J. Physiol.* **160**, 106.
HUGELIN A., DUMONT S. and PAILLAS N. (1960) *EEG Clin. Neurophysiol.* **12**, 797.
JOHN E. R., RUCHKIN D. S. and VILLEGAS J. (1964) *Ann. N.Y. Acad. Sci.* **112**, 362.
KANDEL E. R., SPENCER W. A. and BRINLEY F. J. (1961) *J. Neurophysiol.* **24**, 225.
KATSUKI Y., SUMI T., UCHIYAMA H. and WATANABE T. (1958) *J. Neurophysiol.* **21**, 569.
Y-S KIANG N. (1966) *Discharge Patterns of Single Fibers in the Cat's Auditory Nerve*, Cambridge, Mass.: M.I.T. Press.

KERNELL D. (1965a, b) *Acta Physiol. Scand.* (in press).
KLEE M. R., OFFENLOCH K. and TIGGES J. (1965) *Science*, **147**, 514.
KOELLA W. P. and FERRY A. (1963) *Science*, **142**, 3592, 586.
KUFFLER S. W. (1952) *Cold. Spr. Harbor. Symp. Quant. Biol.* **17**, 281.
KUFFLER S. W., FITZHUGH R. and BARLOW H. B. (1957) *J. Gen. Physiol.* **40**, 683.
KUNO M. (1964) *J. Physiol.* **175**, 81.
LEAO A. A. P. (1944) *J. Neurophysiol.* **7**, 359.
LETTVIN J. Y., MATURANA H. R., MCCULLOCH W. S. and PITTS W. H. (1959) *Proc. I.R.E.*, **47**, 11, 1940.
LI C-L. and JASPER H. (1953) *J. Physiol.* **121**, 117.
LILLY J. C. (1952) in *The Biology of Mental Health and Disease*, New York: Harper.
LOEWENSTEIN W. R. (1961) *Ann. N.Y. Acad. Sci.* **94**, 510.
LORENTE DE NO (1943) (2nd Edn) in *Physiology of the Nervous System* (Ed. J. F. Fulton), Oxford: The University Press.
MARSAM C. A. and MORILLO A. (1963) *Arch. Ital. Biol.* **101**, .
MCCULLOCH W. S., GRAF C. and MAGOUN H. W. (1946) *J. Neurophysiol.* **9**, 127.
MORUZZI G. and MAGOUN H. W. (1949) *EEG Clin. Neurophysiol.* **1**, 455.
MOUNTCASTLE V. B. (1957) *J. Neurophysiol.* **20**, 408.
O'LEARY J. and GOLDRING S. (1959) in *Handbook of Physiology*, op. cit.
PECHER C. (1939) *Arch. int. Physiol.* **49**, 129.
PHILLIPS C. G. (1959) *Quant. J. Exp. Physiol.*, **44**, 1.
POLYAK S. L. (1958) *The Vertebrate Visual System*.
*Processing Neuroelectric Data* (1959) by Communications Biophysics Group of R.L.E. and W. M. Siebert, Cambridge, Mass.: M.I.T. Press
RALL W. (1959) *Exptl. Neurol.*, **1**, 491.
RALL W. and HUNT C. C. (1956) *J. Gen. Physiol.* **39**, 397.
RAMON y CAJAL (1894) *Les Nouvelles Idées sur la Structure du Système Nerveux chez l'homme et chez les Vertebris*, Paris: Rizwald.
RANSON S. W. and CLARK S. L. (1959) *The Anatomy of the Nervous System*.
RENSHAW B. (1941) *J. Neurophysiol.* **4**, 167.
RENSHAW B., FORBES A. and MONSON B. R. (1940) *J. Neurophysiol.* **3**, 74.
ROBERTSON A. D. J. (1965) *Nature*, **205**, 4966, 80.
ROBERTSON A. D. J. (1966a) *Nature* (in press).
ROBERTSON A. D. J. (1966b) In preparation.
RODIECK R. W., KIANG N. Y-S. and GERSTEIN G. L. (1962) *Biophys. J.* **2**, 351.
ROSENBLITH W. A. (1954) *Proc. Symp. Inf. Networks*, P.I. Brooklyn, 223.
ROSSI G. F. and ZANCHETTI A. (1957) *Arch. Ital. Biol.* **115**, 199.
SAUNDERS M. G. (1965) in *Mathematics and Computer Science in Biology and Medicine*, London: H.M. Stationery Office.
SEFTON A. J. and BURKE W. (1965) *Nature*, **205**, 1325.

SHERRINGTON C. S. (1940) *Man on His Nature*, Cambridge: The University Press.
SHOLL D. A. (1956) *The Organization of the Cerebral Cortex*, London: Methuen.
TERZUOLO C. and GERNANDT B. E. (1956) *Amer. J. Physiol.* **186**, 263.
VERVEEN A. A. (1960) in *Structure and Function of the Cerebral Cortex*, (Eds. D. B. Tower and J. P. SCHADE) Amsterdam: Elsevier.
VERVEEN A. A. (1961) Thesis, Amsterdam.
VERVEEN A. A. (1962) *Acta Morphologica Neerlando-Scandinavica* **5**, 79.
VERVEEN A. A. and DERKSEN H. E. (1965) *Kybernetic* **2**, 152.
VERVEEN A. A. and DERKSEN H. E. (1966) *Science*, **151**, 3716, 1388.
VERZEANO M. and NEGISHI K. (1960) *J. Gen. Physiol.* **43**, (Suppl.) 177.
VIERNSTEIN L. J. and GROSSMAN R. G. (1961) in *4th London Symposium on Information Theory*, (Ed. E. C. Cherry) London: Butterworths.
WALTER D. O., RHODES J. M., BROWN D. and ADEY W. R. (1966) *EEG Clin. Neurophysiol.* **20**, 3, 224.
WALTER W. G. (1964) *Arch. f. Psychiat.* **206**, 309.
WEISS T. F. (1960) in *Medical Electronics* (Ed. N. Smyth), London: Illife.
YOUNG A. C. (1960) in *Medical Physiology and Biophysics*, (Eds. T. C. Ruch and J. F. Fulton), London: Saunders.
YOUNG J. Z. (1964) *A Model of the Brain*, Oxford: The University Press.

J. D. COWAN

## NON-NEURAL ELEMENTS IN RECEPTOR SYSTEMS.

This article is concerned with the part played in reception by structures other than the receptor cells themselves and associated neurons. In some receptor systems, notably those concerned with taste and smell, the receptor cells are directly exposed to the external stimulus. In the eye and the ear, on the other hand, the transducer elements are separated from the external event by complex and specialized structures which are themselves essential to the function of these organs as receptors. Still others, those situated in the skin for example, are separated from the external event by structures which are not specialized particularly for transmitting the stimulating energy. Nevertheless, these structures play an important part in determining the space-time distribution of the primary energy through the tissues, and therefore the responses of the receptors. When a group of receptors share a common supporting structure, then the properties of that structure will to a considerable extent determine the over-all patterns of neural activity in such a group.

All the examples cited above are of receptors involved in signalling about events external to the body. There are, however, many others concerned with the internal state of the organism. Once again, non-neural structures may play an important role in determining the properties of these receptors. For example, the labyrinths, which signal about the acceleration of the body, have a complex internal structure involving non-neural elements. Likewise, the response patterns of the various receptor endings in the muscle spindle must be largely determined by the mechanical properties of the intrafusal muscle fibres.

In the rest of this article, three examples of the part played by non-neural elements in receptor systems will be dealt with in detail. Firstly, the way in which the cells immediately surrounding a single receptor can determine many of its characteristic properties will be described. The example taken is the *Pacinian corpuscle*, a mechanically sensitive receptor distributed widely through the higher mammals. Secondly, the way in which a common supporting structure for many different receptor types may effect their properties is examined: this is done in relation to the mechanical properties of skin. Thirdly, the part played by non-nervous elements in the operation of the ear is described as an example of the way the specialized organization of a complex sense organ contributes to its function.

### Mechanics of Pacinian Corpuscle

The main features of the structure of the Pacinian corpuscle are shown in Fig 1. It consists of a single nerve fibre which is surrounded by a series of concentric membranes or lamellae. The innermost lamellae form a closely

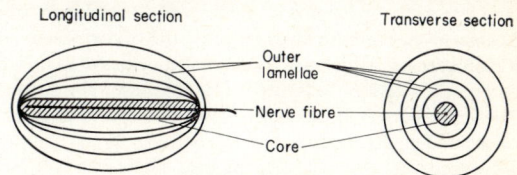

FIG. 1. *The Pacinian corpuscle.*

packed core and are nearly cylindrical in shape, whilst the outer lamellae are separated by fluid filled spaces and are ovoid in shape. There are also a few fine attachments between the adjacent outermost lamellae. The number of clearly separated (outer) lamellae varies a good deal from corpuscle to corpuscle but is typically about 30 (only a few are shown in Fig. 1 for clarity). Similarly, corpuscles vary a good deal in size but are usually about 1 mm long and 6/10 mm in diameter.

The transducer element of the corpuscle is the nerve fibre, and its properties are described elsewhere (see *Receptors as transducer*. Briefly, it responds to mechanical stimuli as follows: the mechanical event causes, across the membrane of the fine nerve terminal, a graded change in electrical potential, the receptor potential. If this is sufficiently large, it initiates a nerve impulse which is propagated along the nerve fibre to the central nervous system.

The corpuscle is usually stimulated experimentally by placing it on a rigid plate with its long axis parallel to the surface of the plate and displacing the farthest point from the plate with a blunt probe. If, under these conditions, a sudden step of displacement is applied, the receptor potential has only a brief duration. It rises to a peak in 1–2 msec and then falls off, approximately exponentially, with a time constant of about 2 msec. Removal of many of the outer lamellae greatly prolongs the receptor potential by reducing its rate of decay. Twelvefold increases in receptor potential duration have been obtained by this means (Loewenstein and Mendelson 1965). The lamellae are therefore responsible for the very brief time-course of the normal receptor potential. This ability of the corpuscle to transmit only the higher frequency components of an appaied displacement to its core has been clearly demonstrated by Hubbard (1958), who measured the displacements of lamellae at different distances from the surface during rapid compressions by means of high speed flash photography. He showed that the time course of the displacement arriving at the core of the receptor was of a similar duration to the receptor potential and varied with changes in the amplitude and velocity of the applied stimulus in qualitatively the same manner as the receptor potential. A detailed mechanical analysis of a model similar to the Pacinian corpuscle has been made by Loewenstein and Skalak (1966).

The Pacinian corpuscle can also be excited by the quick release of a steady displacement—the off response. This response disappears with the removal of the outer lamellae. The mechanical model of Loewenstein and Skalak gives pressure changes after the quick release of a displacement which are similar in time-course to the off receptor potential obtained under these conditions. These pressure changes differ from those on application of a sudden displacement principally in being rotated 90° about the axis of the corpuscle. These changes will therefore be similar to those produced by stimulating the corpuscle from a position a quarter of the way farther round its circumference. Since displacements applied at all points around a corpuscle excite it, then the pressure changes due to the rapid release of a compression would also be expected to do so.

It is clear, therefore, that the characteristic properties of the Pacinian corpuscle—the extremely fast adaptation and the excitatory off response—are primarily due to its mechanical structure and not to the properties of the nerve fibre.

## Skin Mechanics

Many different types of mechanically sensitive receptor endings are situated in or immediately below the skin, which therefore forms the coupling between them and any external event. A certain amount is known about the mechanical properties of the body surface (e.g. von Gierke et al. 1951), but this knowledge has not been applied to the properties of specific receptor systems, although it has been used to help explain the variations in vibratory sensitivity over the human body (Kiedel 1956).

However, the mechanical properties of skin will clearly cause the spatial spread of any stimulus applied to its surface and will therefore play an important role in determining the size of the skin area from which a given receptor may be excited—its 'receptive field'. The time course of the mechanical change which stimulates a receptor ending may also differ from that of the external event initiating it because of its passage through the skin.

The importance of mechanical factors in determining the properties of a receptor system are shown clearly by the sensitive phasic mechanoreceptors of the cat's foot pad (Armett and Hunsperger 1961). If a sudden small step of displacement is applied to the surface of the cat's pad, a wave of mechanical activity spreads out through the pad with a finite velocity (around 10 m/sec). The surface velocity and attenuation of displacement with distance of this wave are qualitatively similar to the changes in threshold and latency seen in the impulse responses of mechanoreceptors at different distances from the stimulus. The time course of the excitability change at the receptors following a step displacement, which takes the form of a heavily damped sinusoid with a half period of the order of 1 msec, is also believed to be largely due to the mechanical properties of the pad. Since there are a group of mechanoreceptors which may be stimulated from the foot pad, its mechanical properties play an important part in determining the patterns of neural activity in this population of receptors.

## The Non-neural Parts of the Ear

*1. The outer ear.* This consists basically of a tube, the external auditory meatus, closed at one end by a flexible membrane, the tympanic membrane or eardrum. It displays resonances, but these are heavily damped. Maximum pressure transfer occurs in man between 3400 and 4000 c/s and is 5 dB down at 2000 c/s and 6000 c/s (Wiener and Ross 1946).

*2. The eardrum.* This completely separates the outer and middle ears and is cone-shaped with its apex pointing inwards. The first of the middle ear bones, the

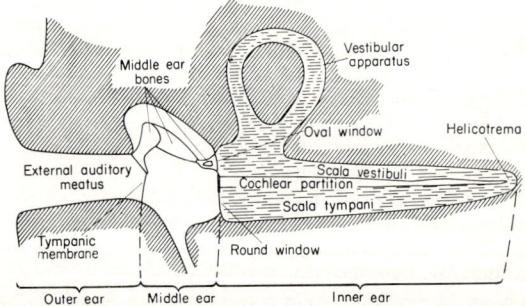

FIG. 2. *Cross-section of human ear.*

malleus, is attached to it. The mode of vibration of the tympanum varies with frequency, but the movements of the malleus produced by it approximate well to those of the air molecules in the outer ear at all frequencies in the auditory range.

*3. The middle ear.* The middle ear acts as an impedence matching device between the air-filled outer ear and the liquid-filled inner ear. This matching is achieved by amplifying the airborne pressure changes at the tympanum. A system of bony levers couples the tympanum to the oval window, a flexible membrane covering part of the base of the liquid-filled cochlea, and amplify the applied force by approximately 1·3 times. The largest increase in pressure is, however, due to the small effective area of the oval window compared with that of the tympanum, the ratio being about 15 : 1. There is therefore an over-all pressure gain between the two of about 26 dB, which goes a long way towards minimizing energy losses from transmission between the air-filled and fluid-filled parts of the ear. There are some frictional losses during this transmission and the system does not transmit all frequencies of vibration equally well. Maximum transmission occurs in man at around 1000 c/s, at which frequency the elastic and mass reactances of the system cancel each other out.

The middle ear is not simply a passive impedance-matching device. By altering the state of small muscles attached to the middle ear bones the stiffness of the transmission system can be quickly altered, and therefore the energy losses at low frequencies greatly increased. This occurs when the ear is exposed to very loud sounds and also during yawning, vocalization and mechanical disturbances of the outer ear.

*4. The cochlea.* The cochlea consists of a fluid-filled tube of roughly circular cross-section which is totally enclosed in bone except for two flexible membranes, the round and oval windows, at its base. The tube is coiled like a snail shell and the central bony core is called the modiolus. It is divided longitudinally into a number of compartments as shown in Fig. 3. The scala vestibuli and tympani are separated by the cochlear partition, except at the apex where they are linked via a small hole, the helicotrema. This partition comprises a bony projection from the modiolus and then a number of membranes and other structures, two of which traverse the tube and are attached to the spiral ligament on the outer edge of the cochlea. These two structures are the basilar membrane and Reissner's membrane. On the basilar membrane lies the organ of Corti, which has a complex structure and includes the hair cells, the transducer elements.

Most of our knowledge of the mechanics of the cochlea has been obtained from the study of those of men and guinea pigs, both of which behave in much the same way, and is due to the researches of one man, Georg von Békésy. Most of his important work has been published in one book, Experiments in Hearing (1960), and the reader is referred to that for details on any points arising out of the following section.

The movements of the cochlear partition, which includes the transducer elements, in response to those of the oval window have been observed and measured in the intact ear. At low frequencies (less than 50 c/s in men) the whole partition vibrates in phase with the applied vibration, with maximal amplitude at the apex, and fluid streaming taking place through the helicotrema. As the frequency of the applied vibration increases, a point of maximum excursion of the cochlear partition appears and this moves towards the base of the cochlea with increasing frequency. Changes in phase also occur along the cochlea at these higher frequencies. These phase changes and the shape of the envelope enclosing the vibrations along the human cochlea for different frequencies are shown in Fig. 4. If the phase changes and relative amplitudes of the vibrations of the cochlear partition are observed at one point, then these change with changing frequency as shown in Fig. 5. These variations in the position of maximum amplitude of vibration of the cochlear partition with changing sound frequency determine the distribution of activity in the nerve fibres from it and thus provide the basis for a neural code for sound frequency depending on the spatial distribution of activity in the auditory nerve fibres.

From the observations described above it has been concluded that vibrations of the oval window set up travelling waves along the cochlear partition. Physical measurements of the stiffness of its various component structures have shown that the stiffest of these is the

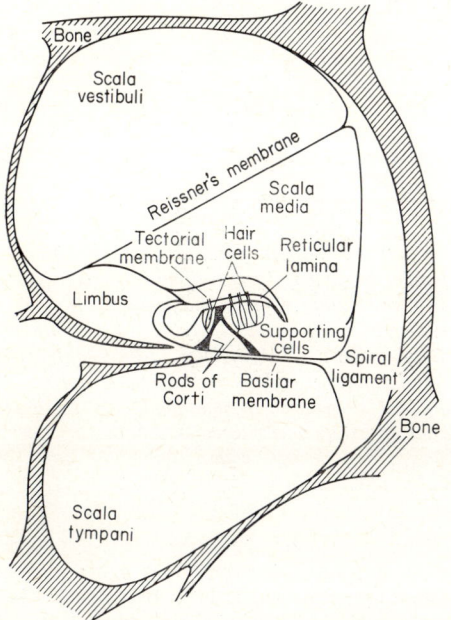

FIG. 3. *Cross-section of second turn of guinea pig cochlea.*

basilar membrane. Moreover, the stiffness of the basilar membrane decreases by 2 orders of magnitude and it becomes wider as one goes from stapes to helicotrema. None of the other parts of the cochlear partition show any variation in stiffness along its length. The only other part which is at all stiff compared with the basilar membrane, is the tectorial membrane, and this is only so in the longitudinal direction, being fairly compliant to side to side or up and down movements.

appreciable stiffness they will all move together. The hairs of the cells, however, pass through the reticular lamina and are embedded in the tectorial membrane. When the cochlear partition is vibrating these must be subjected to considerable shearing forces, both radially (i.e. sideways across the partition) and longitudinally. Since the tectorial membrane is stiff longitudinally, it will tend to shear the hairs at places where the cochlear partition is sharply curved longitudinally, which is in the region between the position of maximum amplitude and the apical limit of vibration, as is clear from Fig. 6, which shows the actual position of the cochlear partition

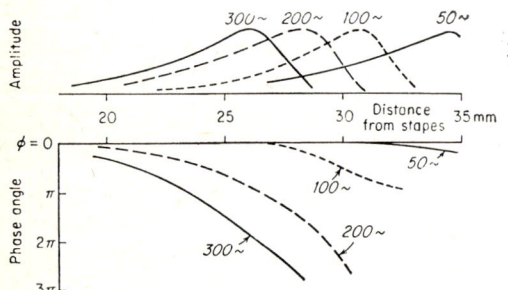

FIG. 4. *Phase changes and relative amplitudes of vibration along the human cochlear partition for 4 low tones. The phase angle is relative to stapedial motion.*

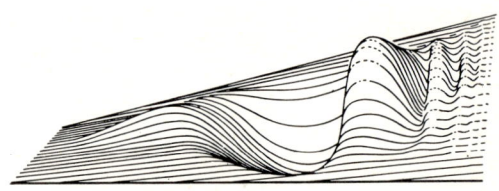

FIG. 6. *Actual displacement pattern of the cochlear partition under the effect of a travelling wave, consisting of a series of alternating mounds and troughs. At every place where displacement occurs there is a curvature in two directions, radial and longitudinal. In the proximal region the radial curvature is dominant; in the distal region the longitudinal curvature is dominant. At the locus of maximal transversal displacement, both curvatures are equal.*

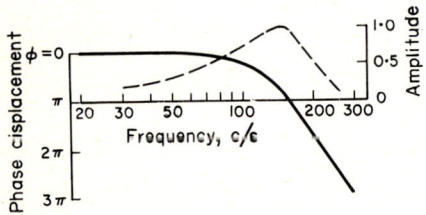

FIG. 5. *Phase displacement (solid line) and relative amplitude (broken line) of vibration for a point on the human cochlear partition 30 mm from the stapes at different frequencies. The phase angle is relative to the stapedial motion.*

Experiments with models and theoretical considerations have shown that it is to the particular form of the basilar membrane that the cochlear partition owes its particular vibratory pattern. Its stiff basal region offers a very high impedance to all but the highest audible tones, whilst the more compliant and wider apical region can be set in motion by relatively low frequency vibrations.

Although the overall pattern of vibrations of the cochlear partition is clear, it is the forces which these cause within the partition itself which must excite the hair cells. The nature of these forces is still speculative, but from the mechanical properties of the various parts of the partition and their arrangement, a certain amount may be deduced. The hair cells are fixed at their top ends to the reticular lamina which is itself fixed to the pillars of Corti and thus to the basilar membrane. Since none of these structures other than the basilar membrane has

(simplified to a ribbon-like form) at one instant during a steady sinusoidal vibration. This figure also shows the curvature across the cochlear partition (radially in a coiled cochlea) during vibration, due to its lateral attachments to the bony shell of the cochlea. This curvature will cause radial shearing of the hairs because the axis of rotation of the reticular lamina (and basilar membrane) is not the same as that of the tectorial membrane. This shearing will be maximal at the point of maximum amplitude of vibration.

5. *Non-neural parts of the ear—summary.* Two important factors seem to be involved in the biological design of the ear. One involves the maximum transference of the stimulus energy to the transducer elements which is achieved in two steps, the first from air to liquid via the middle ear and the second from liquid pressures to mechanical shearing due to the structure of the cochlea. The second is the way in which the mechanical arrangement of the cochlea ensures that, over nearly all of the auditory frequency range, different receptor units will be stimulated optimally at different frequencies. This means that different sound frequencies will give rise to different spatial patterns of neural activity in the auditory nerve fibres.

*Summary*

For the three examples which have been dealt with above a good deal is known about the part played by non-neural elements. These are not the only examples about which we have detailed knowledge, for example a great deal is known about the optical properties of eyes, but there are many systems, including most invertebrate ones, about which very little is known. However, the examples do show the great extent to which changes occurring at receptor endings are due to the interactions of external stimuli with the non-nervous elements linking them to the receptor cells, and the changes in time course and spatial distribution of the stimulating energy between its arrival at the surface of the body and the transducer elements which this involves. These changes are particularly important where they affect a population of receptors, since will they then largely determine the patterns of activity in such a population, patterns from which the animal's central nervous system must extract all its information about the event initiating them.

*See also:* Nerve and muscle, initiation and conduction of impulses in. Receptors as transducers. Receptors in joints and muscles. Receptors, populations of, representation of information about stimuli.

*Bibliography*

ARMETT C. J. and HUNSPERGER R. W. (1961) *Excitation of receptors in the pad of the cat by single and double mechanical pulses,* J. Physiol. **158**, 15.

HUBBARD S. J. (1958) *A study of rapid mechanical events in a mechanoreceptor,* J. Physiol., **141**, 198.

KEIDEL W. D. (1956) *Vibrationsreceptoren; Der Erschüngssinn des Menschen,* Erlangen, Universitätsbund.

LOEWENSTEIN W. R. and MENDELSON M. (1965) *Components of receptor adaptation in a Pacinian corpuscle,* J. Physiol., **177**, 377.

LOEWENSTEIN W. R. and SKALAK R. (1966) *Mechanical transmission in a Pacinian corpuscle, an analysis and a theory,* J. Physiol., **182**, 346.

VON BÉKÉSY G. (1960) *Experiments in Hearing,* New York: McGRAW-Hill.

VON GIERKE H. E. et al. (1951) *Physics of vibrations in living tissues,* J. Applied Physiol., **4**, 886.

WIENER F. M. and ROSS D. A. (1946). *The pressure distribution in the auditory canal in a progressive sound field,* J. Acoust. Soc. Amer., **18**, 401.

B. LYNN

# O

**OPTIMIZATION, AUTOMATIC.** Many schemes for designing or operating technological systems, including those that are automatically controlled, involve describing the possible systems mathematically, choosing a precise measure of effectiveness, and then setting the variables where they give the best possible value of this measure. The final stage of this three step process is known as *optimization*, since the optimum (either maximum or minimum, depending on the context) value is desired. If the synthesis procedures are to be programmed for digital computer, they must be themselves completely automatic in the sense that no human intervention in the computations can be allowed. This article describes optimization methods that can be made suitably automatic. The descriptions being more literary than mathematical, the reader interested in precise details must refer to the original research articles listed in the bibliography.

To optimize a function whose analytic character is either unknown or too complicated to be exploited, one has to gain information on that function by making a number of direct measurements. Using the information accumulated in this process, the experimenter is automatically led to the optimum if the rules of his strategy are appropriate.

If nothing at all can be stated in advance about the behaviour of the objective function, the only way to locate the optimum is by an exhaustive search. Fortunately, less time-consuming techniques are available when certain mild restrictions can be imposed on the objective function. To be definite we assume here that the required optimization is a maximization, and we consider first the case where the objective function $y$ depends on a single variable $x$.

If preliminary study of the problem indicates that in a certain interval ($a < x < b$) there lies a single maximum $x^*$, and if there is no interval of finite length included in ($a, b$) where $y(x)$ is horizontal, then $y$ is said to be *strictly unimodal* in ($a, b$).

After having performed $k$ measurements of that function, let us consider the outcome $y(x_i)$ ($a < x_1 < x_2 < \ldots < x_i < \ldots < x_k < b$). Let $x_j$ be the location of the best point among them; if $y(x)$ is strictly unimodal, and

if $y(x_{j-1}) < y(x_j) > y(x_{j+1})$ then $x_{j-1} < x^* < x_{j+1}$
if $y(x_{j-1}) = y(x_j)$ then $x_{j-1} < x^* < x_j$
if $y(x_j) = y(x_{j+1})$ then $x_j < x < x_{j+1}$.

We are thus led to the conclusion that the interval of uncertainty ($a, b$), initially of length $I_0$, has shrunk to $I_k(I_k = (x_{j+1} - x_{j-1})$ or $(x_j - x_{j-1})$ or $(x_{j+1} - x_j)$). Therefore, the maximum possible interval of uncertainty after $k$ measurements (a length dependent only on the search plan $\mathbf{x}_k$) is

$$I_k(\mathbf{x}_k) = \max_{1 < j < k} (x_{j+1} - x_{j-1})$$

The plan that minimizes $I_k(\mathbf{x}_k)$ is said to be *minimax* and is thus the appropriate strategy for an interval reduction by *simultaneous* search.

If two measurements were very closely spaced, their outcomes might be indistinguishable. It is therefore necessary to constrain the search plan by requiring that a certain minimum distance, or resolution $\varepsilon I_0$, should be maintained between adjacent measurements. This constraint determines the maximum number of distinguishable experiments that can be performed.

If the resolution is known *a priori*, a search plan by *uniform pairs* ($k = 2p$) is minimax; the even-numbered experiments should be located at

$$x_{2h} = \frac{h(\varepsilon+1)I_0}{p+1} \quad (h = 1, 2, \ldots, p)$$

and the odd-numbered ones at

$$x_{2h-1} = x_{2h} - \varepsilon I_0.$$

The remaining interval is $I_{2p} = (\varepsilon+1)I_0/(p+1)$. Usually, the resolution is unknown, and a *uniform* search by an odd number of equally spaced experiments ($k = 2p+1$) will yield an interval of uncertainty slightly shorter than the search by uniform pairs using one less measurement ($I_{2p+1} = I_0/(p+1)$).

When a limited number of experiments may be performed sequentially instead of simultaneously (as in an iterative digital computer program), the interval of uncertainty is reduced in a much more efficient way. If the resolution is known, the sequential minimax *search* plan is to place the first of $k$ experiments at a distance from $a$ equal to

$$x_1 = I_0(F_k+\varepsilon)/F_{k+1}$$

where the *Fibonacci numbers* $F_k$ are given by

$$F_k = (\tau^k - \tau^{-k})/\sqrt{5} \quad (\text{with } \tau = 1.618\ldots)$$

The second experiment should be located symmetrically with respect to the mid-point of ($a, b$), and then the first elimination performed. The remaining interval already contains one measurement, and the search proceeds by placing the following measurement symmetrically to the latter with respect to the mid-point of the remaining interval, and so on, until all $k$ experiments have been expended. The length of the remaining interval is

$$I_k = I_0(1 + \varepsilon F_{k-1})/F_{k+1}$$

If the resolution is unknown *a priori*, another Fibonaccian minimax search plan, discovered by Kiefer, will narrow down the interval of uncertainty to

$$I_k = I_0(1+\epsilon F_{k+1})/F_{k+1}$$

The number of measurements in a sequential plan is usually unknown before the end of the search. We may then use the search by *golden section*, a plan that is not minimax but gives results almost as good as does Fibonacci search. Golden section search is conducted in the same manner as Fibonacci search except that the first experiment is placed at a distance $I_0 \tau^{-1}$ from one end. This distance, which depends on neither the number of experiments nor the resolution $\epsilon$, gives a final interval only about 17 per cent longer than the minimax scheme.

If it is impossible to conduct the search completely sequentially, for, say, lack of time, it is still possible to devise an optimal search plan. This involves grouping the measurements into $x$ blocks of $k$ simultaneous measurements. After each block of $k$ measurements, the interval of uncertainty is reduced, before placing the $k$ measurements of the next block. Avriel and Wilde have shown where to locate the experiments of the minimax *block search* plan. Likewise, the search by *golden blocks* (a generalization of the search by golden section) is used when seeking for a maximum with an indefinite number of blocks of $k$ measurements. To our knowledge, no solution has yet been provided for the important problem of finding the minimax sequential search plan when the result of one experiment is still unknown at the moment the next one has to start.

If the function to be explored is not only strictly unimodal but also differentiable *(differentiable unimodality)*, a sequential search may be considerably accelerated. When this more restrictive assumption is satisfied, proper use of the idea that in the neighbourhood of the optimum $y(x)$ should behave approximately like a parabola, will double the number of significant figures of the estimated value of $x^*$ at each iteration. Specifically, one would start with three experiments and find the parabola

$$y_1 = a_1 x^2 + b_1 x + c_1$$

passing through the experimental points. The abscissa $x_1^*$ of the maximum of this parabola would be the location of the next experiment. Discarding the lowest point of the three initial experiments, one would then fit the parabola $y_2(x)$ passingh through the two best first experiments and $y(x_1^*)$, and so on. This method of *polynomial approximation* is the adaptation to peak-finding of the well-known root-finding method of Newton and Raphson.

*Multivariable optimization.* Let us turn to the case where the objective function depends on two independent variables ($x_1$ and $x_2$). The multivariable optimization techniques can then be demonstrated in geometric terms, and the extension to more than two variables is straightforward.

The powerful sequential search plans described above can be generalized to domain elimination techniques only under a very restrictive assumption. Namely, if along any line drawn through the maximum $(x_1^*, x_2^*)$ the objective function $y(x_1, x_2)$ is strictly unimodal, we say that $y$ has the global property of *strong unimodality*. Consider the projections on the $(x_1, x_2)$ plane of the lines of constant $y$, i.e. the contours of the objective function. Let us choose a point $A$ as 'centre' of the domain of uncertainty. One measurement at $A$ and two more in the vicinity of $A$ will enable us to draw $t_A$, the tangent to the contour on which $A$ lies ($y = y_A$). Moreover, by considering the sign of the difference between $y_A$ and the value of $y$ at an experimental point which is not on $t_A$, we can decide on which side of $t_A$ the maximum must be; the other half domain can thus be discarded safely. A point $B$ is now chosen in the middle of the promising partial domain, and the search proceeds until the domain of uncertainty has been suitably reduced.

More general methods are called for when maximizing a differentiable objective function that is unimodal, but not strictly unimodal. The *sectioning* method (see Friedman and Savage 1947) breaks down the multivariable search into a sequence of unidimensional searches along lines parallel to the axes: the maximum $A$ along a parallel to $Ox_1$, is found; then along the parallel to $Ox_2$ passing through $A$, the maximum $B$ is found, and so on, the direction of search being permuted after each maximum has been located.

A more appealing technique, due to Cauchy, is the *method of steepest ascent* (see Box and Wilson 1951). At the starting point $M_0$ of the search, the first partial derivatives are evaluated, which enables one to locate the gradient $\nabla y$:

$$\nabla y = \left( \frac{\partial y}{\partial x_1}, \frac{\partial y}{\partial x_2} \right).$$

As this vector points in the direction where $y$ is increasing most rapidly in the neighbourhood of $M_0$, it is reasonable to locate the maximum $M_1$ (by unidimensional search) along this line. That maximum $M_1$ is taken as the new starting point, the gradient is located, a new unidimensional search determines the maximum $M_2$ along this line, and so on.

Under extremely favourable conditions, the sectioning method or the gradient method might lead the experimenter quickly to the peak, but these methods have a tendency to oscillate, and the actual attainment of the true peak in principle requires an infinite number of unidimensional searches.

From the point of view of differential geometry, the maximum of $y$ is an elliptic point. Therefore, one should expect, at least in the vicinity of $(x_1^*, x_2^*)$, the contours of $y$ to be very close to ellipses, geometrically similar and concentric to the conic section of Dupin (see Struik 1950) of the maximum. Once the oscillating path described by the lines of search of the gradient method has entered this domain, it is possible to accelerate the search, by taking advantage of a geometrical property of this family of contours: if $M_0$, $M_1$ and $M_2$ are the maxima reached in three successive searches, a last acceleration search along the straight line $M_0 M_2$ will lead the experimenter exactly to the peak. Alternating searches along the gradient and along the acceleration step would allow the location of the centre of a family of $n$-dimensional hyper-ellipsoids (geometrically similar and concentric) to be determined likewise in only $(2n+1)$ unidimensional searches. This parallel tangent (or *PARTAN*) technique of Buehler, Shah, and Kempthorne can be used to optimize unimodal functions whose contours are very different from hyper-ellipsoids. When this is the case, the search is not completed after a fixed number of steps, but must continue until no further improvement of $y$ can be detected.

Let us consider the locus $R$ of points of maximum curvature of the contours. This line may be called the *ridge* of the hill we wish to climb, and it has been observed that the ridges of many objective functions, which naturally lead to the maximum are fairly straight. Instead of following a path oscillating across a ridge (as the path of the unaccelerated gradient method would), one would prefer a technique keeping the successive experiments as close as possible to $R$. In other words, instead of searching in the whole $(x_1, x_2)$-plane, we should try to locate the ridge and then follow it to the peak, by performing a unidimensional search along it. This is the principle of all *ridge-following techniques*, among which are the method of *rotating coordinates* of Rosenbrock, and the *pattern* or *direct* search method of Hooke and Jeeves (a logical improvement, involving acceleration, of the sectioning method).

If a search is prematurely stopped, the most efficient hill climbing technique may fail to locate the maximum, even though the objective function may not improve significantly at each iteration. It is therefore advisable to inquire into the possibility of fitting a quadratic approximation to the objective function in the neighbourhood of the best point obtained so far. If the quadratic form is not negative-definite, which means that the point is not elliptic, the search should be resumed.

As the methods discussed above tend to bring the experimenter near to the optimum in a small number of large steps, very bad outcomes may occasionally be obtained. The application of these techniques to the improvement of performance of large industrial plants is therefore precluded. A slower but more cautious method due to Spendley, Hext, and Himsworth may be used to bring the plant close to its optimal conditions, even when the optimum is slowly drifting in time. Let the domain of possible operation be criss-crossed by three families of equidistant parallel lines, forming a net of equilateral triangles (or simplices), and let us start by performing experiments at the summits of one simplex (points 1, 2, and 3). Let $y(2)$ be the worst outcome; the first rule of the method of *evolutionary operations* (EVOP) is then to make the next experiment at the summit 4, symmetrical to 2 with respect to the line 1–3. If $y(4)$ is larger than either $y(1)$ or $y(3)$, then the first rule is invoked again; otherwise, one uses the second rule, which is to proceed to the point symmetric to the second worst point of the first simplex (instead of that symmetric to the worst point). If a given point is common to a number of successive simplices, i.e.

if the search is circling around this point, it may be the maximum, or else, experimental error may have caused a spuriously high outcome. The third rule is to check that point, and if the result is reproduced, to verify that the point is a maximum by fitting a quadratic function to the results.

Measurement of the gradient at $n$ different points would in principle give enough information for fitting a quadratic approximation to the objective function. To do this would require solving $n^2$ simultaneous linear equations, a formidable task whose rewards do not justify the labour unless the equations have a particularly simple structure. Fletcher and Powell have shown how to adapt the iterated gradient method so that the information accumulated can generate a quadratic approximation efficiently, with never more than $n$ simultaneous equations at a time to solve. Although a gradient is measured at each new point, the next step proceeds along a line chosen to make subsequent computations easy. The best point on the line of search is where a new gradient is measured. Two $n^2$ matrices, corrected at each step, determine how much to deflect the line of search from the gradient. The Fletcher-Powell method is appropriate when gradients, i.e. first derivatives, can be measured easily and accurately. Otherwise, the method of parallel tangents (steep ascent PARTAN), which also has quadratic convergence properties, could be used.

Consider now the problem of minimizing a sum of $n$ squared non-linear functions $\varphi_M(\mathbf{x})$.

$$y(\mathbf{x}) = \sum_{m=1}^{n} \varphi_m^2(\mathbf{x}).$$

This function arises in the *least squares* curve fitting problems of statistics and in control syntheses where the measure of effectiveness is a sum of squared errors. It also occurs when one is solving the $n$ simultaneous equations $\varphi_m(\mathbf{x}) = 0$ ($m = 1, \ldots, n$) by minimizing the sum of squared functions. Each squared function, and consequently the sum, is zero and hence locally minimum at a solution.

Gauss was the first to develop a special technique for minimizing a sum of squares. His procedure involved using the gradients $\nabla \varphi$ of every function at a point to construct a quadratic approximation to $y$ which gives an estimated location of the minimum when its derivatives are set to zero. Since the new point, obtained by solving $n$ linear equations, may be far outside the range of applicability of the approximation, Levenberg modified the method to reduce the dangers of extrapolation. His procedure seeks the point minimizing Gauss' approximation on a circle surrounding the original point. The radius depends on a parameter $\lambda$ which, once chosen, gives $n$ linear equations as does Gauss' procedure. The solution depends therefore on $\lambda$, which can be optimized by a Fibonacci procedure to locate a new point where the gradients can be recalculated for an improved approximation.

Powell has developed a least squares scheme usable when the functions $\varphi_m$, but not their gradients, can be measured directly. The method begins by estimating the first partial derivatives of the $\varphi_m$ by direct perturbation and using them to predict the minimum by Gauss' method. Together with the starting point, this predicted optimum forms a line of search upon which the true minimum is found, say, by Fibonacci search. Values of the $\varphi_m$ at the two points closest to this minimum are used to estimate directional derivatives along the line. These replace the derivatives along one of the coordinate axes. Each iteration replaces a set of $m$ old derivatives with new ones along the most recent line of search until the minimum is found.

Automatic procedures for optimizing functions whose independent variables are constrained to lie within restricted regions are often called 'mathematical programming' methods. Space does not permit discussion of the manifold mathematical programming techniques here.

Automatic optimization developed rapidly when digital computers became available to handle the calculations. As they become more widely known, automatic optimization methods should find wide application to design, control, and statistical problems.

*See also:* Automata, infinite state. Control, hill climbing in. Control, on-off.

*Bibliography*

AVRIEL M. and WILDE D. J. (1966) *Optimal search for a maximum with sequences of simultaneous function evaluations, Management Sci.* (to be published).

BOX G. E. P. (1957) *Evolutionary Operation: A Method for Increasing Industrial Productivity, Appl. Statist.*, **6**, 81.

BOX G. E. P. and WILSON K. B. (1951) *On the experimental attainment of optimum conditions, J. Roy. Stat. Soc.* B**13**, 1.

CAUCHY A. (1847) *Méthode générale pour la résolution des systèmes d'équations simultanées, Compt. rend. Acad. Sci. Paris*, **25**, 536 (Also in *Oeuvres complètes d'Augustin Cauchy* X (Gauthier-Villars, Paris, 1901) 399.

FLETCHER R. and POWELL M. J. D. (1963) *A rapidly convergent descent method for minimization, The Computer J.* **6**, 2, 163.

FRIEDMAN M. and SAVAGE L. S. (1947) *Planning experiments seeking maxima*, in *Selected Techniques of Statistical Analysis* (C. Eisenhart, M. W. Hastay, and W. A. Wallis, Eds.), New York: McGraw-Hill (cited by Shah, Buehler, and Kempthorne).

GAUSS CARL FRIEDRICH (1821) *Werke*, **4** (Gottingen) cited in Davies, 578.

HOOKE R. and JEEVES T. A. (1961) *'Direct search' solution of numerical and statistical problems, J. A. C. M.* **8**, 2, Apr. 212.

KIEFER J. (1953) *Sequential minimax search for a maximum, Proc. Am. Math. Soc.* **4**, 502.

LEVENBERG K. (1944) *A method for the solution of certain nonlinear problems in least squares, Quart. Appl. Math.* **2**, 164.

POWELL M. J. D. (1965) *A method for minimizing a sum of squares of nonlinear functions without calculating derivatives, Computer J.* **8**, 303.

ROSENBROCK H. H. (1960) *An automatic method for finding the greatest or least value of a function, Computer J.* **3**, 3 Oct., 175.

SHAH B. V., BUEHLER, R. J. and KEMPTHORNE O. (1964) *Some algorithms for minimizing a function of several variables, J. Soc. Ind. Appl. Math.*, **12**, 1, March, 74.

SPENDLEY W., HEXT G. R. and HIMSWORTH F. R.. (1962) *Sequential application of simplex designs in optimization and evolutionary operations, Technometrics*, **4**, 4, Nov., 441.

STRUIK D. J. (1950) *Lectures on Classical Differential Geometry*, New York: Addison-Wesley.

WILDE D. J. (1964) *Optimum Seeking Methods*, Englewood Cliffs, N. J.: Prentice-Hall.

WILDE D. J. and BEIGHTLER C. S. (1966) *Foundations of Optimization*, Englewood Cliffs, N. J.: Prentice-Hall.

S. J. WAJC and D. J. WILDE

**OPTIMIZATION OF INDUSTRIAL PROCESSES.**
Modern commercial organizations operating in a competitive economy generally need to employ techniques for optimizing their performance in order to remain in existence. Ideally, these should be directed towards the ultimate optimization of the whole organization as an integrated system, although present-day knowledge and technology are not adequate for the attainment of such an ideal. Instead the trend is to examine subsystems within the organization, with a view to optimizing their individual performance using the available techniques. In this way it is hoped that an aggregate of optimized subsystems will result in a system which is close to the ideal of the overall optimum. This tenet will, of course, only be acceptable provided that the measures used for the assessment of the performance of each subsystem have been correctly related to the overall objectives of the organization as a whole. The problem of selecting the right combination of performance measures is one which should not be underrated, since it cuts across the whole spectrum of activities within an industrial organization. Typical subsystems in such an organization will be concerned, on the one hand, with the optimum choice of product, of method of production, of production capacity, of distribution and sale of product, and on the other with optimum design and operation of the process subject to constraints of safety, economics and engineering practicability. 'Process optimization' is a term which is used to describe optimization of process operation, but includes to a lesser extent optimization of the design. This is because good design implies optimization, but it is nevertheless appropriate to talk of the optimum design of control systems which forms a very important part of process optimization. Broadly speaking, the activities listed above fall mainly in the realms of Operations Research or Engineering,

and it is not uncommon to find little interaction between the respective groups of workers, despite the fact that they often call upon and develop similar mathematical and computational techniques. This is less true now that digital computers are becoming more widely used as tools in such activities. Many of the techniques to be mentioned in the context of engineering process optimization are highly relevant to the other optimization problems found within an industrial organization. The common features emerge when mathematical formalism is used to describe the optimization problems.

The first stage in the optimization of a process is to formulate the operating objectives. For example it may be required to operate the process at maximum profit or to yield a maximum rate of return on capital invested, and these may in turn be related to speed of response, expenditure of energy, consumption of raw materials, overall yield and amount of unwanted by-product. The profit may be an instantaneous profit which varies with time, or more usually it will be a long term profit integrated over a significant period of operation of the plant.

Essentially an industrial process operates on a supply of raw material and produces products according to the policy of the organization. This policy is executed by varying the flow of material and energy to the plant until the operation of the process is satisfactory, i.e. the flow of products satisfies the demand for them in terms of quality, quantity and market value. The energy and material flow rates are called the control variables. The operation of the plant is monitored by a set of measuring instruments which record, for example, temperatures, pressures, flow rates, compositions and other physical and chemical properties, both for the product and for strategic points within the process. A question which naturally arises is which combination of control variables within their permitted range will yield the best plant performance.

It is immediately apparent that an essential feature of process optimization is the influence of time as an independent variable. The process behaviour and the operating objectives are both time dependent, the former through energy conversions, the latter through changing economic factors. The process performance can depend on time in two ways. First there is the manner in which the process responds to its controlled inputs, and secondly there are the random changes which occur within the process, as for example fluctuations in catalyst activity, heat transfer rates, etc. If the influence of random disturbances is small, and the process responds very rapidly to changes in its control variables when compared with changes in the economic factors, the problem is one of steady state optimization. If, on the other hand, internal disturbances are significant, or the process responds at a rate comparable with changes in the economic factors, then the problem is one of dynamic optimization. Dynamic optimization includes steady state optimization, and, as would be expected, is generally much more difficult, if at all possible, to achieve.

The problem can be formulated mathematically by supposing that the operation of the plant on the raw materials and energy supplies can be represented as a set of first-order differential equations with time as the independent variable:

$$\frac{dx_i}{dt} = f_i(x_1 \ldots x_n, u_1 \ldots u_m) \quad i = 1(1)n. \quad (1)$$

These equations can be derived from the physical and chemical laws governing the behaviour of the plant, for example, the laws of conservation of mass, energy, momentum, etc. Such sets of equations are frequently called a mathematical model of the process. **u** is a vector of the independent control variables, **x** is an $n$-dimensional state vector, where $n$ is the number of degrees of freedom of the process. The components of **u** are generally constrained to lie within finite intervals, either separately or jointly. The performance required of the plant is then formulated as a functional of a measurement vector **m** and the control vector **u**, usually it is assumed that **m** is identical to **x**, although in general this would not be the case. Optimization of the process now corresponds to the mathematical problem of determining as a function of time within the specified region of hyperspace which maximizes the functional subject to the differential equation governing the behaviour of the process. Frequently **x** will also be constrained, and this adds further complications to the problem.

Various techniques for complete dynamic optimization are described elsewhere, as for example in the articles on *Dynamic programming* and *Control by maximum principle*, to which reference should be made for further details. Such techniques have as yet found little or no application to real cases of process optimization, and this is perhaps not to be unexpected, when it is apparent that many problems in static optimization yet remain to be solved.

Unfortunately such a methodology has several shortcomings from the point of view of industrial process optimization. First of all there is the assumption that the equations describing the behaviour of the plant can be constructed with sufficient accuracy. This is not usually possible. Secondly, assuming that the process model can be constructed, there are numerous mathematical and computational difficulties associated with the determination of the control function which optimizes the performance function. Finally, a full dynamic optimization is extremely expensive in terms of man-hours of highly trained personnel needed to carry out the exercises, and the powerful computing machinery needed to carry out the computations. Thus, such a study applied to a small subsystem of a large organization, concerned with the optimization of its overall performance in economic terms is quite likely to detract from the overall objective.

If sights are lowered, and only static optimization is attempted, there is more hope of a successful outcome, although considerable problems still remain. In the steady state, the plant is described by equations (1), with derivatives put to zero, i.e.

$$f_i(x_i \ldots x_n, u_i \ldots u_m) = 0 \quad i = 1(1)n. \quad (2)$$

which is a set of algebraic equations. The state and control vectors are still constrained to lie within bounded regions of hyperspace described by further algebraic equations:

$$g_i(x_i \ldots x_n, u_i \ldots u_m) \leq 0. \qquad (3)$$

Finally, the performance of the plant is represented by a scalar function of **x** and **u** in general. The static optimization problem is thus one of finding the extreme value of an algebraic function of several variables which are themselves constrained to lie within or on the bounds of specified regions of a hyperspace. Such problems are generally treated by the methods of a recently developed branch of mathematics called mathematical programming.

Before describing in a little more detail the methods of *mathematical programming*, it should be mentioned that empirical methods of process optimization have been developed to cope with those cases where it is not possible to construct with any degree of certainty the mathematical equations for the process, or where the mathematical form of the performance function and process model are too complicated for explicit treatment. In these cases it is accepted that the process represents a generalized operation in the inputs to the outputs, and trial and error adjustments are made to the inputs until no further improvement can be detected. The methods rely on performing a set of experiments on the process. As the number of experiments is increased, the optimum is located with ever increasing precision. For example, in the case of a univariable process with a unimodal performance function, several sequential search procedures have been devised where information from previous experiments is used to locate the next. At each stage of the optimization part of the feasible region is eliminated. Several well known methods of this kind are the Dichotomous Search, the Fibonacci Search, the Golden Section Search and the Lattice Search. In the case of multivariable processes, the problem is more difficult, so that after each set of local experiments it is necessary to determine where to conduct the next set of experiments in order to obtain an improvement in the performance function. Basically two kinds of strategy have been developed, both of which depend on the most recent linear approximation to the performance function. First there are the *contour tangent elimination* methods which use the local measured tangent to the contour to eliminate part of the feasible region from further consideration. They have much in common with the sequential search methods mentioned above in the case of univariable processes. Unfortunately the methods are adversely affected by experimental errors, and are only usable on strongly unimodal functions. Furthermore, the computational effort becomes large as the number of independent variables is increased. Secondly, there are the well-known methods of *steepest ascent*, which position the new set of experiments in the direction of the local measurement of the gradient of the performance function. Gradient methods are not affected by the limitations of the contour tangent methods, and for this reason they are very popular. Various refinements are usually adopted in practice to accelerate the convergence to the optimum. Generally the refinements are based on the fact that most performance functions display 'ridge' characteristics, so that by searching out a ridge and then following it, the optimum is reached more quickly than would otherwise be the case. A *ridge* is described as the locus of points for which

$$p(x_1 \ldots x_j \ldots x_n) > p(x_1 \ldots x_j \pm \varepsilon \ldots x_n)$$

where $\varepsilon$ is the separation of points for which a change in $p(x)$ can be detected. The optimizing strategy based on variation of parameters one at a time will not be able to proceed beyond a ridge in its search for the optimum. Several more sophisticated methods which are able to follow ridges have been developed, such as the methods of parallel tangents, pattern search, Rosenbrock's rotating co-ordinates and Mugele's method. Of these, Rosenbrock's method has been found most efficient in following curved ridges. As its name implies, in this method the co-ordinate system is rotated so that an axis continually points along the ridge, displacements in the direction of the other axes which are normal to the first are therefore very effective in correcting the estimate of the trend of the ridge. Mugele's method does well on curved ridges, but tends to be slow on straight ridges.

Considering now the more general field of mathematical programming, it is convenient to mention the various techniques which have been developed according to the classes of performance function and constraint function to which they refer. A well known and common type of problem is a linear performance function and a linear constraint function, and the term 'linear programming' is used to describe methods of solution. Most methods employ the simplex approach, or variants thereof, and coupled with the use of digital computers are capable of handling problems in hundreds or thousands of variables.

Basically the *Simplex method* starts by choosing a basis of vectors in $m$ dimensions, where $m$ is the number of inequalities, which is then successively modified until one is found which solves the problem. For iterations in the feasible region the performance function moves towards the optimum, or at most remains constant. Inequality constraints are modified to equations by the introduction of slack variables, e.g. if the inequalities are:

$$g_i(x_1 \ldots x_n) \geq 0, \quad i = 1(1)m,$$

introduce slack variables:

$$x_{n+1} \ldots x_{n+m} \geq 0$$

and write:

$$g_i - x_{n+i} = 0.$$

More generally the non-linear programming problem is to maximize the continuous and differentiable function:

$$p(x_1 \ldots x_n)$$

subject to the inequality constraints:

$$g_i(x_1\ldots x_n) \geqslant 0, \quad i = 1(1)m$$
$$x_j \geqslant 0, \quad j = 1(1)n.$$

Iterative algorithms have been developed of several combinations of assumptions in the functions $p$ and $g$. Most of the algorithms use some variation on a gradient technique to move from an initial point within the feasible region to a new point with improved performance. Several are described in Saaty and Braun (1964), for example:

(i) *Frank and Wolfe's method* is one for solving a concave quadratic optimization problem subject to linear inequalities and $x \geqslant 0$. The algorithm depends on the equivalence between concave programming and the saddle value problem, and uses the Simplex method of linear programming.

(ii) *Rosen's Gradient Projection* method can be applied to problems where the performance and constraint functions are non-linear. The method proceeds iteratively by projecting the gradient of the concave function to be optimized on to the boundary, and re-evaluating the gradient at the end of a suitable displacement on the projection. In the non-linear case projections are made on tangent planes.

(iii) *Carrol's Response Surface Technique* makes use of a linear combination of the performance function and the reciprocal of the constraints, e.g.

$$p(x) + r \sum_{i=1}^{m} \frac{1}{g_i(x)} = P(x, r)$$

where the second term can be interpreted as a penalty for requiring a minimum of $p$ subject to the constraints. By suitably choosing a sequence of $r$'s decreasing to zero and minimizing $P(x, r)$ for each value of $r$, a sequence of values of $x$ is obtained which comes arbitrarily close to the minimum of $p$ as $r \to 0$.

(iv) *Zoutendijk's method* is useful for maximising a quadratic subject to linear constraints. Iterations are made in feasible directions (do not violate constraints) making the smallest angle with the gradient which necessarily points in the direction of maximum increase of performance function at the point. For small steps in the feasible region the procedure converges.

(v) *Kelley's method* of cutting planes is applicable to linear performance function and non-linear constraints. A compact convex set can be circumscribed by a compact convex polyhedron to any desired order of accuracy. A polyhedron is chosen to enclose the feasible region, and linear programming is used to maximize the performance function over the polyhedron. A cutting plane is then passed between the optimizing vertex and the feasible region, and a new polyhedron is obtained. The process is repeated until a solution is obtained to the required order of accuracy.

Many other algorithms have been developed, but space does not permit their inclusion in such a short article.

In such a brief account it has not been possible to consider in detail any particular technique or aspect of process optimization. However, attention has been drawn to the fact that process optimization is usually only a small part within the optimization of a large organization, and as such, should not be allowed to become too obscured in the details of mathematical analysis, some of which are extremely powerful even by modern standards. Little has been said about dynamic optimization beyond referring the reader to relevant articles in the Encyclopaedia, and perhaps the sounding of a cautionary note about its feasibility in the light of some of the difficulties of static optimization, which is, after all, a more manageable subset of dynamic optimization.

*See also:* Control by the maximum principle. Control, hierarchical. Control, on-off. Dynamic programming. Optimization, automatic.

*Bibliography*

WILDE D. J. (1964) *Optimum Seeking Methods*, New York: Prentice Hall.
SAATY T. L. and BRAM J. (1964)*Non-Linear Mathematics*, New York: McGraw-Hill.
ARIS R. (1961) *The Optimal Design of Chemical Reactors*, (A study in dynamic programming) New York: Academic Press.
BOX M. J. (1966) *A Comparison of Several Current Optimisation Methods, and the Use of Transformations in Constrained Problems, The Computer Journal*, **9**, (1) May, 6.
O'GRADY W. P. and ROBERTSON H. H. (1966) *On-Line Steady State Optimisation and Direct Set-Point Adjustment of a Two Pass OXO Synthesis Process*, Third IFAC Congress, Paper 32 E, 23rd June.

A. HAZLERIGG

# P

**PATTERN RECOGNITION.**

*1. Introduction*

This article is a review of pattern recognition, which is defined by engineers as the sorting or classifying of entities (objects, processes, phenomena, etc.) into classes or categories, using measurements made on these entities. This article discusses pattern recognition only when it is performed by machines. It does not discuss human perception and recognition of entities.

The study of pattern recognition encompasses all aspects of the design of machines capable of such recognition tasks. This includes specification of:

(1) The kinds of entities to be classified.
(2) The nature of the environment in which the entities to be recognized are found.
(3) The measurements to be made on the entities.
(4) The rules by which these measurements are used to put class labels on entities.
(5) The criteria by which machine performance is to be judged.

A pattern recognition system is coupled to an 'environment' and consists of a 'measurements section' and a 'classifier' (see Fig. 1). Of these two parts the classifier

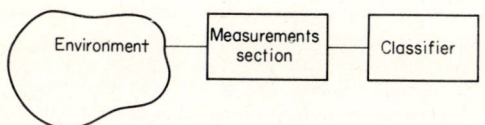

FIG. 1. *A pattern-recognition system.*

is the better understood. Much of the work in pattern recognition has been on classifiers that can 'learn' the rules by which measurements of entities can be used to assign class labels. Not all pattern-recognition systems 'learn.' An example of one that does not learn is the machine that reads magnetic characters on bank cheques.

Broadly speaking, three points of view have been taken toward pattern-recognition problems:
(1) That the similarity between pattern-recognition-machine functions and certain human functions could be exploited by using models of human 'neural nets' as guides for the design of these machines.
(2) That pattern recognition is a statistical problem and that statistical decision theory could be used to design pattern-recognition systems.

(3) That pattern recognition is *not* to be viewed in a rigorously statistical framework, and that only quasi-statistical reasoning should be used.

As work in pattern recognition has progressed, mathematical similarities between the results obtained by taking each point of view have been discovered. Now designers of practical recognition systems may use each or all points of view as these points of view are helpful or appropriate.

Machine pattern-recognition techniques are useful in situations such as the following:
(1) When it is necessary to 'learn' objective rules by which measurements can be used to put class labels on entities. (A pattern-recognition system may or may not have this learning capability.)
(2) If repeated and rapid classification and coding of entities (such as alphabetical characters) into machine-readable form is required.
(3) If a machine—for example, a robot explorer on Venus—is so remote from man that it cannot be easily controlled in its actions and some capability for the machine's taking autonomous action is required.

Implicit in most pattern-recognition system that 'learn' the objective rules for assigning entities to classes are the concepts of interpolation and continuity. The number of samples from which the machine must 'learn' the rules for assigning labels to measurements is generally small with respect to the number of possible samples. Therefore we are forced to assume that we can 'interpolate,' using some notion of continuity, among the samples that the machine has already 'seen' in order to classify samples from entities to be 'seen' in the future. In complex problems the number of samples is too small to characterize completely the various classes of entities. Also, at present it is not economical to store a complete description of all the samples the machine has seen in the past. Much of the work in pattern recognition can be viewed as seeking to find ways to describe the classes of entities as simply as possible, using as few measurements as possible, and to retain sufficient detail to allow the machine to perform acceptably.

Commercial pattern-recognition systems have been developed for reading and sorting bank cheques using magnetic ink characters, and for optical reading of alphanumeric characters for a limited number of type fonts. (Reading rates for optical character readers of up to 1000 characters per second have been achieved.) Systems that function reasonably well on an experimental basis have been developed for classifying electrocardiograms and for classifying limited vocabularies of words spoken by limited numbers of speakers.

Systems presently under development include those for the classification by machine, of blood cells, graphical symbols, hand printed characters, three-dimensional objects, aerial photographs, large vocabularies of words spoken by many speakers, and engineering schematic drawings.

## 2. Definitions

Many of the specialized terms used in machine pattern recognition are anthropomorphic. The implied analogy is understood today to be between *functions* performed by human and machine with no implication that the machine is performing learning and recognition using *means* that are similar to those used by humans.

The following terms, frequently used to discuss machine pattern recognition, are defined as in the technical literature. Where synonymous terms have been used, the synonyms are listed after the primary term.

*Pattern.* The specific description of one observation of an entity used by the classifier to assign a label to the

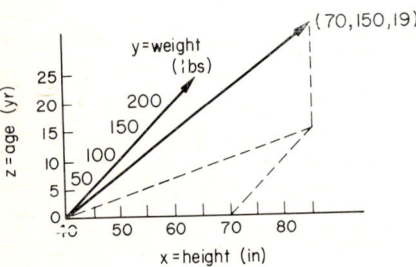

FIG. 2. *Representations of measurements using vectors.*

entity—for example, the height, weight, and age of a man. Each element, such as weight, used in the description constitutes one measurement. These measurements can usefully be viewed as components of a vector or *n*-tuple. Each pattern vector can be uniquely associated with one point in a space having as its coordinate axes the measurements. In Fig. 2 we illustrate this way of representing a pattern. Note that pattern-recognition techniques are primarily useful when the number of measurements is much greater than three.

*Class* (category). The set to which an entity belongs —for example, a class might be all those entities that are labelled as the alphabetical letter *A*, including both upper and lower case letters from different type fonts.

*Training set* (design set, design data). The set of patterns used by the pattern-recognition system to obtain the rules for assigning class labels to patterns.

*Testing set.* The set of patterns used to test the performance of the pattern-recognition machine.

*Learning.* In its most general sense, implies that the classifier's description of each class changes as the classifier 'sees' more patterns out of the training set. Usually improvement in performance of the classifier as it sees more patterns from the training is implied. Learning may imply that the patterns in the training set are seen more than once by the classifier, or it may imply that some function, such as the average pattern within each class, is computed from seeing each pattern in the training set only once. The terms 'adaptive' and 'self organizing' usually denote machine 'learning' in the broad sense. Useful distinctions are between:

*Learning with a teacher* (learning with supervision, learning with performance feedback), in which each pattern in the training set has had associated with it from some 'external' source a label assigning that pattern to a particular class. For a survey of such techniques see Nilsson (1966).

*Learning without a teacher* (learning without supervision, learning without performance feedback, cluster-seeking techniques, mode-seeking techniques, clumping techniques), in which the training set of patterns does *not* have class labels associated with the patterns. Situations in which patterns might not have labels include:

(a) Unknown radio signals buried in noise;
(b) Unlabelled but distinct sub-classes contained within one large labelled class (e.g. lower case *a*'s and upper case *A*'s within the class of all *A*'s).

Techniques are known that can sort a set of unlabelled heterogeneous patterns into subsets such that the patterns in each subset are 'similar,' where the definition of similarity depends on the technique used. For a survey of such techniques see Ball (1965).

*Learning with an unreliable teacher* (bootstrap learning), in which the labels given by the teacher for the patterns in the training set are, with some probability, incorrect.

*Measurement space.* The space in which pattern vectors are defined. Its coordinate axes correspond to the measurements that define the pattern.

## 3. The System Description

Pattern-recognition systems have been described as coupled to an 'environment' and consisting of a 'measurements section' and a 'classifier.' To clarify the nature of a pattern-recognition system we discuss each part, using as an example one possible pattern-recognition system for determining the identity of a person speaking the word 'hello' (see Fig. 3):

(1) The environment consists of:

(a) The entity we wish to recognize. In this case, the person speaking the word 'hello.'
(b) Other entities that obscure the entity to be recognized. These entities might include the noise of machinery in the room, or other people talking.

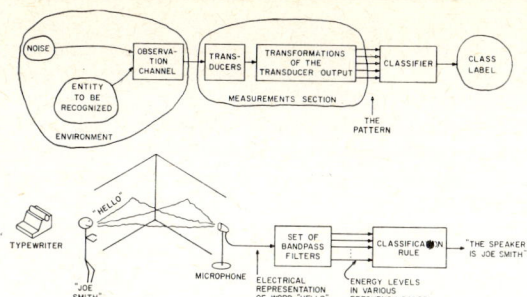

FIG. 3. *A pattern-recognition system.*

(c) The observation 'channel' through which we observe the entity to be classified. The channel in this case is the air between the speaker and the microphone.

(2) The measurements section ('receptor' or 'preprocessing') consists of:

(a) Transducers that convert the machine's 'view' of the entity to be recognized into a type of energy, such as electricity, that can be easily processed. A microphone serves as the transducer here.

(b) Transformations of the transducer output that produce a description of the entity to be classified that make classification by the classifier of the patterns as straightforward as possible. In the example we have used a set of bandpass filters to obtain the energy of the speech waveform in selected frequency bands. This set of energy levels is the pattern that is examined by the classifier.

(3) The classifier (categorizer or discriminator) that transforms the measurements into class labels. In this case the class label would be the identity of the person speaking, i.e. 'Joe Smith.' Note that a different pattern can result each time Joe Smith says 'hello', and so we cannot say that any single pattern is the only one that represents Joe Smith. Therefore the pattern recognition system must contain a complex description of Joe Smith.

Each part of the pattern-recognition system is discussed in more detail below, and various alternative approaches are described.

*A. The environment.* Detailed knowledge of the environment of the entity to be recognized appears essential to the useful solution of a difficult pattern-recognition problem. The environment usually distorts the pattern-recognition system's view of the entity. When the environment is well understood, its distortion of the pattern recognition system's representation of the entity to be recognized can be taken into account when specifying the measurements to be made.

The environmental distortions of the entities and the inherent variability of patterns derived from a given class of entities to be classified leads to the concept of 'within-class' variability. Within-class variability is large or small only in relation to 'between-class' variability. In difficult problems the classes lie sufficiently close to each other to cause overlap between classes, as shown in Fig. 4. (Note that if the statistical model of pattern recognition is used and if the ideal classifier is obtained from an in-

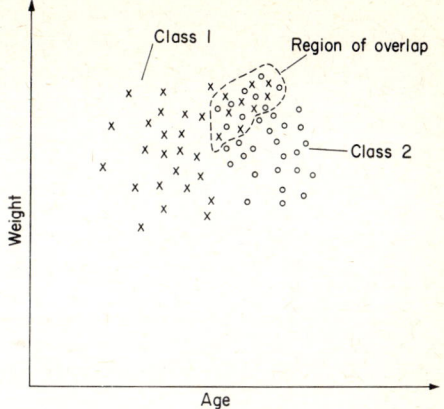

FIG. 4. *Overlap between two classes.*

finite set of training patterns or from *a priori* knowledge, then it can be shown that the amount of overlap between classes cannot be reduced by transformations of the same measurements. It can be reduced only by taking different measurements.)

*B. The measurements.* The measurements section should use the environment's representation of the entity to be classified to produce a pattern that makes it possible for the classifier to distinguish between the classes with the required degree of accuracy. *The obtaining of a good set of measurements from which to make the pattern is usually the most difficult aspect of pattern recognition.* We divide the measurements section into (1) the transducer, and (2) the section for transformation of the output of the transducer into a set of measurements.

*1. The transducer.* Some method is generally necessary to change the form of the environment's representation of the entity to be classified into an electrical signal or other conveniently manipulated signal. Little theory has been developed in pattern recognition specifically to guide the engineer designing the pattern-recognition system in his choice of a particular type of transducer or a specific transducer within a type. Fortunately, the choice of transducers suitable for a particular problem is usually limited, and those available are fairly adequate for the task. Hence, selection by experiment is usually feasible.

Examples of transducers are:

(1) Sound-to-electrical—microphones.
(2) Physiological-to-electrical—electric probes, thermocouples.
(3) Light-to-electrical—TV camera, flying spot scanner.

*2. Transformation of the transducer output.* The procedure for finding good ways to transform the transducer output into measurements that allow the required degree of accuracy in classifying entities can be divided into procedures for:

(1) Specifying a set of possibly good measurements.
(2) Evaluating the 'goodness' of this set of measurements.

*a. Specifying new measurements.* Exhaustive evaluation of *all* possible measurements that can be derived from a given transducer output is, generally, impossible. Therefore, it is desirable to evaluate only measurements that are likely to be good. In some problems one of the following methods may be useful in finding potentially good measurements or in reducing a large set of measurements to a smaller set by combining measurements:

(1) If the transducer output from each class can be assumed to have a multivariate normal probability distribution, then the statistical technique of discriminant analysis leads to those linear combinations of measurements that are most effective in separating pairs of classes. For large numbers (greater than 100 to 200) of measurements, however, the matrices to be manipulated may become impractically large.

(2) If the environment causes changes of certain types in the representation of the entity seen at the transducer input (e.g. the change in position of a letter to be read by an optical character reader) then measurements invariant with respect to these changes should be sought in order to reduce the complexity of the classifier.

(3) If the modes of classes of patterns are known, the differences in the measurements between the modes from different classes are useful; for example, a measurement that detects the tail of the $Q$ (the 'difference' between $Q$ and a super-imposed $O$) is useful. (Class modes can be found by learning-without-a-teacher techniques.)

(4) When any proposed set of measurements can be evaluated for their 'goodness' extremely rapidly, then random search for good measurements can be tried. Experience seems to indicate, however, that such random searches are apt to be inefficient and not as likely to find good measurements as would a more systematic search through measurements proposed by the pattern-recognition-system designer.

In future complex and difficult pattern-recognition problems, it appears that the researcher who is an expert in the field in which the recognition is to be done will continue to play the most important role in specifying new measurements. For him to perform this role successfully in difficult problems, however, computational assistance provided by a (possibly on-line) computer probably is essential. This assistance would speed up the evaluation of new measurements that may occur to him, and so suggest even better measurements.

*b. Evaluating measurements.* The division between the measurements section and the classifier is artificial, but it is made in order to maintain a manageable level of complexity of the overall system. The most desirable goal would be to optimize the overall performance of the entire pattern-recognition system, but it is not known how to do this economically. For this reason, a separate evaluation is sometimes made of the measurements and then the performance of the classifier optimized, given this preselected set of measurements.

Since the goal of a pattern-recognition system is to discriminate between the classes of patterns, measurements that are different for different classes must be considered good. The 'distance' between the measurements obtained from different classes for a given set of measurements is therefore a measure of the goodness of the measurements.

In order to evaluate objectively the 'goodness' of a measurement, specific criteria of 'distance' between classes must be selected. (The selection of the criteria is usually subjective, however.) Four such criteria have been proposed in the literature for problems in which the measurements are numerically valued. These are discussed in Appendix A and references are given to articles discussing them in detail.

No number derived from an objective criterion should be considered to characterize adequately the goodness of the measurements. Somehow the design engineer must balance the information provided by objective criteria of measurement 'goodness' with his own judgment. In evaluating measurements the following almost intuitively obvious guides are useful:

(1) A measurement that has small overlap between the various classes is a good measurement in most instances.

(2) When a given measurement is the only measurement helping to discriminate between two difficult-to-separate classes, it is worth retaining even if it does not help discriminate between any other classes.

(3) Measurements duplicated by other measurements such that little additional information about the classes is gained by retaining them are generally not useful. (It is important to realize that although a measurement may be very powerful taken alone, it may not necessarily be a member of the set of the 'best' measurements when a set of $k$ measurements are used. An example of this would be that set of $k$ measurements that used the best single measurement twice.)

*3. Property lists.* A viewpoint, considered quite different by some, toward the measurements is that each measurement should correspond to a property—for example, the colour of the entity. Each property detector classifies the entity to be recognized as to the presence or absence of a single property. The classifier then classifies the entity based on the list of properties it possesses. The necessity of finding good properties and good measurements from which to obtain good properties remains. The distinction between property lists and previously mentioned ways of obtaining measurements does not appear to be very great.

*C. The classifier.* The classifier embodies the rule that assigns class labels to patterns. In measurement space the classifier can be seen as assigning class labels to *regions* in measurement space, so that each region is associated with one particular class of patterns. In Fig. 5 we show that:

(1) The regions in measurement space associated with one class need not be simply connected—for example, Class 1 is not.

(2) The boundaries between regions may have complicated shapes (although if simple boundaries are adequate, machine complexity and memory requirements are reduced).

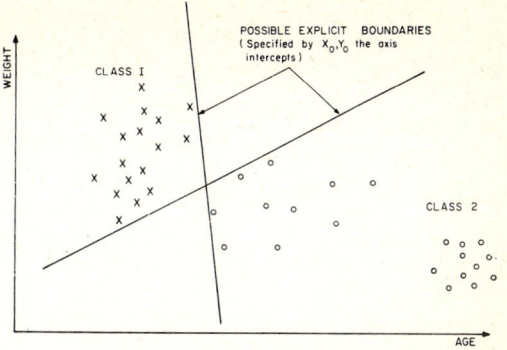

FIG. 6. *A boundary-describing classifier.*

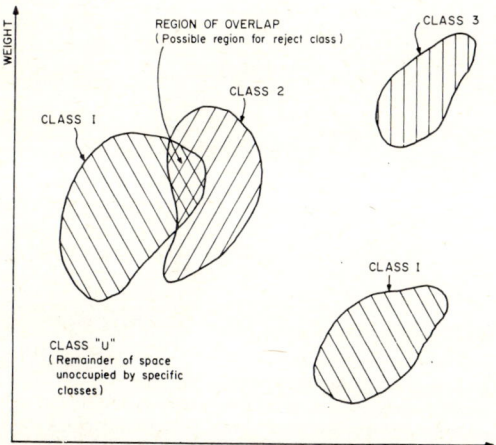

FIG. 5. *Pattern classes in two-dimensional measurement space.*

(3) Some of the space can be assigned to the class of unknown classes (classes not seen before) or to a reject class (as when a distinction between two classes is too ambiguous to warrant definite assignment to either class. A reject class can be useful, for example, in the classification of numbers on bank cheques since an error is much more costly than a reject.).

Two useful dichotomizations of the variety of rules (classifier designs) proposed for assigning labels to patterns are:

(1) 'Boundary describing' vs. 'location describing' classifiers.

(2) Learning vs. non-learning classifiers (see the definition of Learning).

Classifiers are dichotomized into 'boundary-describing' classifiers vs. 'location-describing' classifiers based on the class description that is *explicitly* stored in the computer.

A 'boundary-describing' classifier explicitly stores the parameters describing the boundary positions in measurement space. For example, in the case of two measurements, a boundary-describing classifier might store the coefficients of the equations of a set of straight lines. The goal of this type of classifier is to place these boundaries between classes so that the boundaries in measurement space separate the various classes of patterns from each other. Ideally each region contains only patterns from one class, as shown in Fig. 6.

A 'location-describing' classifier specifies explicitly the 'locations' of each of the classes. It then makes a calculation based on relative class locations in measurement space to determine which regions in measurement space to associate with each class. This calculation can usually be viewed as computing a distance. For example, the location description might be the mean of each class (other kinds of descriptions are shown in Fig. 7), and

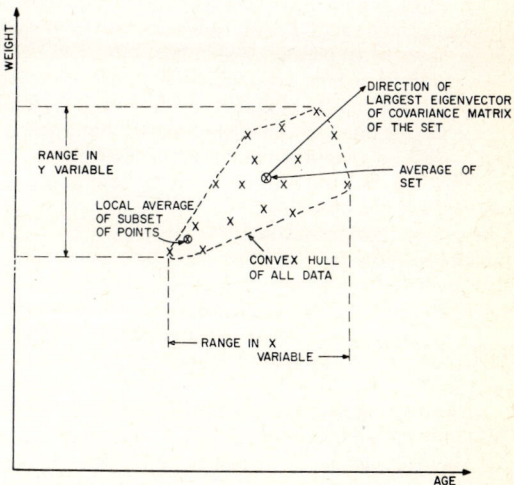

FIG. 7. *Ways to describe a set of data points.*

the calculation, the 'distance' of an unknown pattern from each mean. An unknown pattern would be assigned to that class whose mean was closest to the unknown pattern, as shown in Fig. 8. (Note that quite complicated rules based on individual class characteristics, such as cost of mis-classification or within-class variability, can be used for determining 'closeness.')

The complexity of the descriptions of boundaries or locations varies greatly. Much of the work done on boundary-describing classifiers has involved using linear functions of the measurements. However, since non-linear functions (powers and cross-products, etc.) of some original set of measurements can be used as input to the classifier, then arbitrary polynomial boundaries with variable coefficients can be generated using linear classifier theory. For example, given measurements $X_1$ and $X_2$, we can calculate $X_1^2$, $X_1 X_2$, $X_2^2$, $X_1$, $X_2$, and so construct

$$A_0 + A_1 X_1 + A_2 X_2 + A_3 X_1 X_2 + A_4 X_1^2 + A_5 X_2^2$$

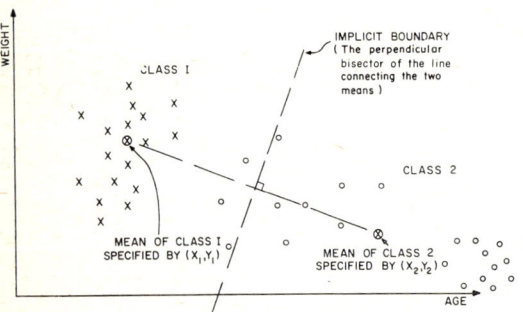

FIG. 8. *A location-describing classifier.*

which is linear in the $A_i$'s. Thus a quadratic boundary in a measurement space $X_1$, $X_2$ can be constructed using linear theory by increasing the number of measurements.

Location-describing classifiers sometimes make the complicated simpler by using a mixture of simple functions (obtained by using learning-without-a-teacher techniques) to obtain a complicated description. The classifier uses several simple location descriptions to describe a single class.

In some pattern-recognition problems particular functional forms for $p(x|i)$ (the class probability density that gives the probability that $x$ will take on specific values given that $x$ is from the $i$th class) can be assumed and the parameters of these densities can be estimated from the patterns of the $j$th class that are in the training set.

In Table 1 the most common existing classifying methods are divided up, using the dichotomies given earlier. In Appendix B the functions of the measurements calculated by the classifiers are listed and detailed discussions of these methods are referred to.

The boundaries or locations used to describe the classes are either 'learned' or directly calculated from the training set. Direct calculation can involve:

(1) Maximization (or minimization) of some function of the training set, as, for example, in a discriminant analysis in which, for two classes, a straight line is determined such that the variation *between* the samples from *different* classes projected onto this straight line is as large as possible relative to the variation *within* the two classes (about the class average) projected onto the same straight line.

Table 1. Types of Classifying Methods*

|  | Location Description | Boundary Description |
|---|---|---|
| Non-learning | (1) "Template" matching (average pattern in each class)<br>(2) Bayes decision theory [parameters of $p(x|i)$ and $p(i)$ in order to compute $p(i|x)$]<br>(3) Nearest neighbour rules (location of all patterns in the training set) | Discriminant analysis (hyperplanes perpendicular to linear discriminant) |
| Learning | (1) Bayes decision theory<br>(a) Using iteratively estimated parameters (need parameters of $p(x|i)$ and $p(i)$).<br>(b) Using $D$ dimensional histograms (cell densities for each of the various classes).<br>(2) Reference point methods using mode seeking or cluster seeking algorithms (reference points plus distance measure). | (1) Linear adaptive threshold logic (hyperplanes perpendicular to weight vector)<br>(2) Iterative adjustment of discriminant functions (coefficients of terms in linear discriminant function). |
| Compound | Compound Classifiers consisting of several applications of a mixture of the above classifiers. | |

* Class descriptions needed are given in parentheses.

(2) Estimation for each class of a statistic, such as the sample mean and covariance matrix, as, for example, in Bayesian decision theory when Gaussian probability densities are assumed.

(3) Calculation of the numerical average of all patterns in each class, as in template matching.

'Learning' the class description can be accomplished by:

(1) 'Error-correcting' training algorithms that modify the boundary position if a pattern from any class is incorrectly classified because of the present location of the boundary, as in much of the work on adaptive threshold logic. In this method a trial boundary position is tried against patterns in the training set and modified so as to reduce the number of errors of misclassification. (In some error-correcting algorithms erratic behaviour will occur if pattern classes overlap.)

(2) Estimation of parameters of probability densities using the patterns in the training set one at a time, usually by proportionate weighting of the previous value of the parameter and some function of the pattern from the training set presently being 'learned', as in the decision theoretic learning techniques.

(3) Relocation of reference points based on evaluation of the description, using a criterion such as minimizing the sum of the squared distances of all of the patterns in each class in the training set from the closest class reference point, as in cluster seeking methods, or using as criterion the number of misclassifications due to poor reference-point location, as in mode-seeking methods. Note that distances are frequently measured from

reference points using a quadratic form $(x-r_i) A(x-r_i)'$, where $x$ is the pattern, '$A$' is a positive definite matrix, and $r_i$ the $i$th reference point. (Cooper (1963) contains a detailed discussion.)

*1. Compound classifiers.* Any of the above classifiers can be applied several times to different measurements made on the same entity to produce a compound classification procedure. Situations where this is advantageous include those in which:

(1) Measurements are made sequentially and it is desirable to reduce the number of measurements made in obtaining the classification. This reduces time and cost required to classify an entity, i.e. only some subset of the total set of measurements is used to reach each classification.

(2) Measurements vary in quality and hence in importance due to a changing environment, e.g. in identifying speakers by the characteristics of their voices, high-frequency measurements on *distant* voices may be of less value than low-frequency measurements, due to greater attenuation of the higher frequencies, while at *short* distances they may be more important. Here the classifier would need to judge the closeness of the speaker and use this information in judging the importance of the measurements.

(3) The entity can be viewed at different times and the classifications at each at these times combined to reach the final classification.

*2. Additional comments.* In utilizing any of the classifiers, the following warnings seem most important:

(1) The training patterns must be typical of the classes they come from in order to provide the classifier with a boundary or location description based on relevant past experience.

(2) The number of samples of each class in the training set must be large enough to provide the classifier with a sufficiently accurate description of each class to obtain adequate recognition of patterns not yet seen (see Allais 1966).

*4. Criteria for Evaluating Pattern-recognition Systems*

These criteria can be split into those evaluating performance and those evaluating cost. All performance criteria involve some notion of the 'amount' of error in classifying patterns. The 'amount' can be specified as:

(1) The number of misclassifications summed over all classes. A useful detailed display shows the number of misclassifications with errors being specified as to the number of patterns from Class i being assigned to Class j in a 'confusion matrix,' as shown in Fig. 9.

(2) Squared error or absolute error or other function of the difference between the correct classification and the system specified classification. It is used when *distance* between the correct answer and the system specified answer is a meaningful concept.

(3) The cost of misclassification. The cost of making one kind of misclassification may be greater than making another. This can be formalized by specifying a loss matrix $L = [l_{ij}]$ where $l_{ij}$ is the loss incurred by labelling a pattern from the $i$th class as a pattern from the $j$th class. (Note that if $L$ is of the form $l_{ii} = 0$, and $l_{ij} = 1$ for $j \neq i$, then the expected loss equals the expected probability of error.)

(4) The number of patterns (i.e. rejects) for which no decision was reached by the system. Generally, the greater the number of rejects the fewer the patterns that will be misclassified; hence a trade-off exists between errors and rejects.

In comparing machine performance with human performance, it is important to take into account the helpful information provided by context used by a human, but not presently used by pattern-recognition machines in most cases. For example, human recognition rates on arbitrary orderings of hand-printed characters in which context was not available to aid recognition were 96.8% correct in one experiment conducted (see Neisser and Weene 1960).

|  | Pattern recognition system classification specified by | | |  |
|---|---|---|---|---|
|  | 1 | 2 | 3 |  |
| Correct classification  1 | 24 | 3 | 6 | Implies 14 patterns from class 2 incorrectly classified as class 3 |
| 2 | 1 | 22 | (14) |
| 3 | 7 | 2 | 28 |

FIG. 9. *A confusion matrix.*

Criteria for evaluating cost include:

(1) Type, amount, and cost of memory required for a satisfactory solution to a recognition problem.

(2) Length of time required, and prorated cost, to process each pattern from the training set, each pattern from the testing set, and each pattern in the final operating system.

*5. Conclusions*

The design of a pattern-recognition system requires the specification of a transducer, a set of measurements, and a classifier. Of these, it is generally felt that the most difficult task lies in specifying a good set of measurements. The more similar (as seen by the transducer) the various classes of patterns, the more important the specification of a powerful set of measurements becomes. For example, making distinctions among a Holstein cow, a rock, and a car requires less subtlety in specifying measurements than making distinctions among a Holstein cow, a Jersey cow, and a Guernsey cow. In the first case it might be expected that many different kinds of measurements would each make classification possible, while in the latter case the measurements would need to be selected with much more care if the classification is to be possible. Obvious as this is, it is easy to forget that

Table A-1. Criteria for Evaluating Measurements

| | Criterion and Reference | Description of Criterion |
|---|---|---|
| (1) | Percentage correct recognition | $\left\{\sum_{g=1}^{G} [N_g - (\# \text{ errors in classifying patterns from } g\text{th class})]\right\} (100/N)$ |
| (2) | Divergence (Marill and Green 1963) | $\int_X \ln\left(\frac{p(\mathbf{x}\mid I)}{p(\mathbf{x}\mid J)}\right) [p(\mathbf{x}\mid I) - p(\mathbf{x}\mid J)] \, d\mathbf{x}$ |
| | (Mahalanobis 1936) | When $p(\mathbf{x}\mid I)$ and $p(\mathbf{x}\mid J)$ are normally distributed $N(\mu_l, K)$, $l = 1, 2$. then divergence $(I, J) = (\mu_I - \mu_J)' K^{-1} (\mu_I - \mu_J)$, the Mahalanobis distance between $N(\mu_I, K)$ and $N(\mu_J, K)$. |
| (3) | Mutual information (Lewis 1962) | $\sum_{g=1}^{G} \int_{X_l} p(g, x_l) \ln [p(x_l \mid g)/p(x_l)] \, dx_l$ assuming independent measurements $\{X_l\}$. |
| (4) | Ratio of 'sums of squares between' to 'sums-of squares within' (Miller 1962) | Select $x^{(1)}$ out of $x_1, \ldots, x_K$ such that<br><br>Trace $W^{-1} B(x^{(1)}) \geq \max_l$ Trace $W^{-1} B(x_l) = (b_{ll}/w_{ll})$<br><br>where Trace $A = \sum_{l=1}^{D} a_{ll}$, $A$ being an arbitrary $D \times D$ matrix.<br><br>Pairs, triples, etc. of measurements can be evaluated by a natural extension of the criterion. |
| | Definitions | $G$ is the number of classes. $N_g$ is the number of patterns in each class.<br><br>$N = \sum_{g=1}^{G} N_g$ is the total number of patterns.<br><br>$x = (x_1 \ldots, x_K)$ is a pattern. $p(x\mid I)$ and $p(x\mid J)$ are the probability densities of the $I$th and $J$th classes. $\mu_I$ and $\mu_J$ are the means of these classes. $K$ is their covariance matrix.<br>$W$ is the pooled, *within*-class sum-of-products matrix with element<br><br>$w_{ij} = \sum_{g=1}^{G} \sum_{k=1}^{N_g} (x_{gik} - \frac{1}{N_g} \sum_{l=1}^{N_g} x_{gil}) \cdot (x_{gjk} - \frac{1}{N_g} \sum_{l=1}^{N_g} x_{gjl})$<br><br>where $x_{gjl}$ is from the $g$th group, and is the $j$th component of the $l$th pattern, and $B$ is the pooled, *between*-class sum-of-products matrix with element<br><br>$b_{ij} = \sum_{g=1}^{G} N_g \left(\frac{1}{N_g} \sum_{l=1}^{N_g} x_{gil} - \frac{1}{N} \sum_{m=1}^{G} \sum_{l=1}^{N_g} x_{mil}\right) \cdot \left(\frac{1}{N_g} \sum_{l=1}^{N_g} x_{gjl} - \frac{1}{N} \sum_{m=1}^{G} \sum_{l=1}^{N_m} x_{mjl}\right)$. |

Table B-1. Functions Computed by Classifiers

| (1) | Template Matching | $\max_i(\mathbf{x} \cdot \mathbf{R}_i) = \sum_{j=1}^{D} x_j r_{ij}$ |
|---|---|---|
| (2) | Decision theory (a) without learning (Blackwell and Girshick 1954) or (Chernoff and Moses 1959) | Minimize $\left\{ \bar{L}(d) = \sum_{g=1}^{G} \int_x L[i, d(\mathbf{x})] p(\mathbf{x} \mid i) p(i) d\mathbf{x} \right\} \bar{L} = (d^*)$. <br><br> If $L(i,j,) = \begin{cases} 0, i = j \\ 1, i \neq j \end{cases}$ (which makes $\bar{L}(d)$ the expected value of the probability of error) <br><br> then, <br> $d^*(\mathbf{x}) = i$ such that $p(\mathbf{x} \mid i)p(i) \geq \max_j p(\mathbf{x} \mid j)p(j)$. |
| | (b) with Learning (Abramson and Braverman 1962) or (Nilsson 1965) | If $p(\mathbf{x} \mid i) = N(\boldsymbol{\mu}_i, K)$, and $p(i) = \dfrac{1}{G}$, all $i$, $i = 1, 2, \ldots, G$, <br><br> then $d^*(\mathbf{x}) = i$ such that <br><br> $(\mathbf{x} - \boldsymbol{\mu}_i) K^{-1} (\mathbf{x} - \boldsymbol{\mu}_i)' = \min_j (\mathbf{x} - \boldsymbol{\mu}_j) K^{-1} (\mathbf{x} - \boldsymbol{\mu}_j)'$ <br><br> If learning is used, then parameters of probability densities must be estimated. |
| (3) | Nearest neighbour (Fix and Hodges 1951) | Unclassified $\mathbf{x}$ classified as $i$th class if $k$ closest patterns [using Euclidean distance $(\|\mathbf{x} - \mathbf{x}_i\|^2)$] in training set are predominantly $i$th class. |
| (4) | Reference point methods (Cooper 1964) | $\mathbf{x}$ assigned to $i$th class if $\mathbf{R}_k$ associated with $i$th class and if <br> $(\mathbf{x} - \mathbf{R}_k) A (\mathbf{x} - \mathbf{R}_k)' \leq \min_j (\mathbf{x} - \mathbf{R}_j) A (\mathbf{x} - \mathbf{R}_j)'$ <br> where $A$ is a positive definite symmetric matrix. |
| (5) | Discriminant Analysis (Anderson 1951) (Sebestyen 1962) | Value of $\mathbf{y} \mathbf{y} \cdot \mathbf{R} = \sum_{j=1}^{D'} y_j r_j = \sum_{j=1}^{D'} f_j(\mathbf{x}) \cdot r$ <br><br> (each class is assigned to a region of values of $\mathbf{y} \cdot \mathbf{R}$) |
| (6) | Adaptive threshold logic. (Hawkins 1961) (Nilsson 1965) | One threshold logic function (TLU), $\mathbf{y} \cdot \mathbf{R} + r_0 \lessgtr 0$ <br><br> (binary decision only). <br><br> Networks of TLU's are used for more difficult decisions. |
| | Definitions | $\mathbf{x}$ and $\mathbf{y}$ are patterns. $\mathbf{R}_i$ is a reference vector. $p(\cdot)$ is a probability density. <br> $d(\mathbf{x})$ is a decision rule that maps $\mathbf{x}$ into the categories. <br> $L(i, d(\mathbf{x}))$ is the loss function. It specifies that loss incurred when $i$ is the correct category and $d(\mathbf{x})$ is the decision made. <br> $\mu_i$ is the mean of the $i$th class, and $K$ is the covariance matrix. |

red-green and yellow-blue channels; these, in combination, evaluate the spectral characteristics of the stimulus, relative to surrounding and preceding stimulus conditions. Each of the foregoing major types of signal, it should be stressed, operates in terms of a polarized, or opponent-pair, process. The intensity signal may increase above a base firing rate to indicate a stronger stimulus, and fall below the base rate as the stimulus intensity decreases (or the reverse may be true), while the base rate, itself, shifts according to surrounding and preceding events in the system. Similarly, a red-green channel may carry a higher impulse rate to indicate increased stimulus wave-length and a lower rate to indicate decreased wave-length (or vice-versa), but again, these changes will be relative to a base firing rate that is sensitive to other events in the system (the same remarks apply to yellow-blue channels). Only under very restricted and precise experimental conditions will such a system evaluate the absolute spectral characteristics of a stimulus (see below).

The perceptual terms, *'adaptation'*, *'contrast'*, and *'constancy'* are beginning to have meaningful analogues in the physiological processes outlined in the foregoing paragraph and much excellent research is being devoted to clarification of these aspects of the visual system. For instance, it is now clear that the output of a cell, if it produces discrete impulses, may not be at all simple. First, nearly all cells (or, perhaps, *all*) exhibit some base rate of spike production (De Valois 1965); this is sometimes called *'spontaneous activity'*, but is probably spontaneous only in the sense that it represents a momentary, neutral-state level. Second, relative to the (variable) base rate, there may be not just higher or lower rates, but bursts of impulses (or bursts of 'silence') related to the onset or offset of a stimulus, or bursts at both the beginning and the end of a stimulus presentation. A variety of firing patterns has been found, leading to the conclusion that great flexibility of signal mode is available in the visual system, even within the limitations of *frequency modulation*. (At present, most of our information concerning cell firing patterns comes from examination of sub-human visual systems.)

The fourth order of visual neurons occurs outside the eye, in the *lateral geniculate bodies;* from these a few fibres go directly to the *motor cortex*, while most go to the *striate cortex* of the *occipital lobes*, the so-called *'visual cortex'*. It is clear, however, that important events in colour vision occur before impulses reach the cortical level; for the latter we have very little data concerning the processing of colour information.

*Definitions of 'response' and 'perception'*. Now we leave the mechanisms of colour vision and turn to colour perception. Throughout the following discussion no precise definitions for the important terms, *'response'* and *'perception'*, have been attempted, but the matter cannot be shirked entirely, even though the definitions to be given are implied rather than overt. Researchers working on colour problems often employ three distinct vocabularies: (1) the physical—for example, wave-length or waveband, spectral energy distribution or wave-length composition, and intensity or energy level; (2) the psychophysical—dominant wave-length, purity, and luminance; and (3) the psychological or perceptual—hue, saturation, and lightness or brightness. The first vocabulary is defined by physical, experimental operations assumed to produce constant results regardless of the observer; the second is defined by operations in which an organism (usually human) is employed as a measuring instrument and in which the results are clearly dependent upon the characteristics of the organism (physical devices may, of course, be calibrated in terms of psychophysical units based upon a *'standard observer'*, the latter being an agreed-upon, statistical entity not representative of any individual organism; photometric units are examples of this kind of standardization); the third is similar to the second, except that stimulus qualities and magnitudes are expressed in terms of the second vocabulary before responses are obtained from the measuring or evaluating organism.

This state of affairs can be confusing to an interested scientist who merely wishes to find out something about colour perception, or the colour vision system, without becoming a specialist. A simple way to view the matter is to conceive of the psychophysical vocabulary as representing a set of *transfer functions* for the visual system. It is then possible to assess the utility of expressing and manipulating stimuli directly in transfer function units during attempts to relate these stimuli to more general system responses (the latter expressed in the psychological or perceptual vocabulary). Nevertheless, it remains true that in colour work physical energies are varied and organisms respond differentially, either by adjusting stimulus conditions until a state of perceptual equality or a just noticeable difference occurs, or by emitting verbal signals such as 'equal', 'brighter', 'greyer', 'different', 'red', 'green', 'neutral', 'I saw it', or 'I saw nothing'.

Thus, the primary independent variables of most colour research are wave-length composition and intensity, but various aspects of these will usually be found expressed in psychophysical units; the primary dependent variables are discriminative responses quantified or ordered through apparatus adjustments or by means of linguistic categories. Whether or not the independent variables are expressed in psychophysical units may be, in a basic sense, irrelevant, so long as the following major fact is not obscured: the wave-length composition and intensity of a given stimulus, though important, never suffice for an accurate prediction of the colour response. Among many other factors that must be considered are: spatial and temporal effects related to the stimulus field (*figure* and *ground)*, figural complexity of the field, retinal angle or size of the elements of the stimulus, angle of incidence of the stimulus at the retina, binocular or monocular stimulus presentation, the state of adaptation of the visual system (in both a long-term and a short-term sense, and with respect to the entire visual system and to parts of it), and matters of organism motivation, attention, conditioning, and expectation.

*Trivariance of colour vision.* The human visual system,

with respect to colour, is a synthesizing device. Receiving energy of mixed frequencies from an object or a light source, it produces a unitary response to the mixed stimulus. A single, narrow waveband of energy that will produce this same response can, with one exception, always be found, provided that (a) the field conditions surrounding the mixed and the elemental stimulus are identical, (b) the elemental stimulus may be mixed with a selected amount of an essentially flat, wideband stimulus (i.e. 'white' light), and (c) the total energy of the elemental stimulus plus 'white' light may be varied. The exception comprises stimuli that evoke purple responses; these often require both long and short wave-lengths in the matching stimulus.

Similarly, a mixture of *any* two (or more) narrow wavebands of visual energy produces a response that may be matched by the response obtained from some single, narrow band (again, with the foregoing exception) plus 'white' light; finding such a waveband is the operation that defines the *dominant wave-length* of the stimulus to be matched. Furthermore, the 'white' component of the stimulus for the matching response may always be replaced by a single, narrow waveband selected for its ability to neutralize or reduce the effectiveness of the other component. The third restriction remains: it must be possible to control the total intensity of the stimulus for the matching response.

It is, therefore, true (within limits to be mentioned presently) that three numbers suffice for the specification of a colour response. Colour *vision* is trivariant; it is a system based on three degrees of freedom. Colour *perception*, on the other hand, cannot generally be organized strictly within the limits of a three-dimensional system; illustrations will be given below.

*Dimensions of the colour response.* The three dimensions of a colour response are often organized in terms of (1) *hue*, a response component that permits definition of the dominant wave-length of the stimulus; (2) *lightness* (if the energy source is a non-radiating object) or *brightness* (if the source is a luminous body), a component related to the intensity of the stimulus, if surrounding conditions are held constant, and (3) *saturation*, a component that expresses the relative effectiveness of the dominant stimulus element with respect to the 'white' part of the stimulus (whether the latter be a wide energy distribution or a narrow, neutralizing waveband).

There exist standard coordinate systems (Hurvich *et al.* 1965) within which the hue and saturation of each possible colour may be located on a plane surface and in which lightness (or brightness) may be expressed on a third axis. In these systems when lightness is varied, the configuration of hues and saturations changes in predictable ways *(Bezold–Brücke effect)*. Furthermore, for fixed lightness values, changes in saturation are associated with shifts in hue *(Abney effect)*, with a few important exceptions. Also, saturation maxima vary with both hue and lightness. It is clear, therefore, that the colour response, when characterized as containing hue, lightness, and saturation components, does not operate on the basis of three completely independent elements. Interactions among parts of the response must always be considered in analysing the colour vision system.

*Transduction capacity o colour system.* How many different states of stimulus energy can this system transduce? For the entire range of spectrally pure lights at average intensity the system yields about 200 different hue responses. As stimulus intensity is increased, the ranges of hue narrow to include only yellows and blues; as intensity is decreased, the hue ranges come to include only reds and greens. At extreme intensities, high or low, no hues and, thus, no saturations, are generated; lightness (or brightness) alone is retained. When the intensity and bandwidth of the stimulus vary, in addition to the effective wave-length, then the visual system is thought to be capable of distinguishing about 10,000,000 different states of the stimulus (Judd 1951). If surrounding or antecedent conditions also vary, an even larger set of responses can occur. (The hue, 'brown', is an example; this is a non-spectral colour associated with a yellow-producing stimulus when the latter is surrounded by a 'neutral' stimulus of considerably greater *luminous intensity*. 'Supersaturated hues', produced by 'complementary' surrounds, or by prior, 'complementary' stimulation, are also examples of the class.) This tremendous capability is not reflected in our everyday descriptions of the world. Evans (1948) noted that just 12 colour terms accounted for 92·4 per cent of the 4416 occasions upon which colour was mentioned in 17 current novels. Moreover, only 7·9 per cent of the colour terms or phrases included modifiers such as 'pale', 'dark', or 'pinkish'. Chapanis (1965) has determined experimentally that average observers can probably employ about 55 colour terms for making unambiguous distinctions between regions of colour space. It is clear that the colour vision system responds in much more varied and precise ways than we are normally capable of describing verbally.

*Spatial and temporal pattern variables in colour.* An additional complication must now be considered. Although, under certain laboratory conditions (i.e. a colour sample of 2° subtense, viewed in a dark surround, and within a specified range of intensities only) colour vision is trivariant, it is, nevertheless, necessary to employ a minimum of six numbers for the specification of a colour stimulus when the conditions of seeing are 'normal' or general. This follows from the fact that the response related to any specific part of the visual field is determined (at least) by the energies reaching the system from that part of the field *and* by the energies from the surroundings of the part. Furthermore, responses both to the part and to the surround are time dependent in the sense that effects of recent stimuli change the character of current responses; this may imply the necessity of six additional quantities for the prediction of a colour response.

Basically the system is an adaptive one; it moves in the direction of null responses to constant stimuli in order that it may be as sensitive as possible to small changes in stimulus energies. Such a system produces acute distinctions between similar stimuli present concurrently or available in rapid sequence, but is not, in general, an accurate measuring or transducing device on an absolute basis (see *Mechanisms of the colour-vision system*). It can be stated categorically that given energies reaching the visual system bear *no* constant relationship to particular hues, lightnesses, or saturations. Nevertheless, when the characteristics of the visual field are known, and some knowledge of the recent history of stimulation is available, it is possible to predict, within limits, the values of the components of the visual response. Such predictions can be made with fair accuracy for a broad range of visual conditions, but the elements of a colour prediction always exist in a matrix of complex relationships.

*Many colours from two wavebands; a spatial effect.* An experimental example may give meaning to some of the foregoing generalizations. Consider two stimulating wavebands, one with a dominant wave-length of 612 nm (reddish orange), the other being average tungsten light with a dominant wave-length of about 585 nm (yellowish). Let these two stimuli be mixed, in varying proportions, in an extended visual field; further, let the same two stimuli occur independently in controlled mixtures in a small subregion of the total field. If we now fix the *maximum* intensities of the four lights at some equal and reasonable level (equivalent to a *luminance* of about 15 *foot-lamberts*, for instance), it will be possible, by adjusting the *relative* intensities of the four lights, to produce, with respect to the subregion (test patch), the entire gamut of hues except, perhaps, a narrow range of purples. It will not, however, be possible to associate all hues with all combinations of brightness and saturation. In fact, saturation will be severely limited for hues in the ranges that include blue, purple-blue, purple, red-purple, and yellow-red, yellow, and yellow-green. Simultaneously, the first of these ranges will tend to be restricted to low, and the second to high, brightness levels. Meanwhile, reds, greens, and blue-greens may be obtained over considerable ranges of brightness and saturation (Wheeler 1963).

The proportions of the two stimuli in the extended field (surround) are important in the experiment just described. When red light predominates in the surround, the relative frequency of hues lying outside the red through yellow range will be highest (with respect to a constant and well-spaced sampling of test patch mixtures under varying conditions of the surround) and blue-greens will occur more often, at the expense of purples and yellows. When red light alone makes up the surround, greens and yellow-greens will occur more frequently, while blues and purples will be minimized. When the tungsten light predominates, blues and purples will occur more frequently, at the expense of greens and yellow-greens. When tungsten light exists alone in the surround, reds, yellows, and yellow-reds will be the principal hues associated with the test patch.

The total intensity of the two stimuli in the surround is also an important element of this experiment *(Helson–Judd effect)*. If equal proportions of red and yellow light are employed at low intensity, some two thirds of the sample of hues in the test patch will be reds, yellows, or yellow-reds. If the surround intensity is set equal to the strongest total intensity of the test patch, then about a third of the hues will fall within the foregoing range, but if the surround intensity is approximately doubled, only about one fifth of the hues will remain in the yellow to red range. The implication of the latter condition is that by appropriate manipulation of the surrounding conditions, at least 80 per cent of a set of mixtures of red and yellow lights can be made to produce hues other than red, yellow, or yellow-red. The saturations and brightnesses of this gamut of hues may be restricted, but they will not be negligible. Given a greater increase in the surround intensity, hues in the red to yellow range may be entirely eliminated as responses to the test patch, but the remainder will be so dark that they can scarcely be identified.

Other pairs of wavebands may be examined in a similar way with somewhat similar results (Judd 1940; Helson 1959; Land 1959). Experiments of this kind provide striking demonstrations of the fact that the physical values of a visual stimulus, examined out of context, are not sufficient for an accurate prediction of the associated colour response.

*A colour response complementary to its stimulus; a temporal effect.* Temporal relationships among components of the stimulus can greatly affect the colour response. Consider the following experiment. Divide a flat disk along a diameter into black and white halves. Near the rim, at the division between halves, make a small aperture. If the disk is 10 inches in diameter, then an aperture half an inch in diameter would be appropriate. Illuminate the disk with some reasonable approximation of daylight and provide means for rotating it over a range of frequencies from 20 through 120 c/s, with the white sector following the aperture. Through the aperture, from behind the disk, project stimuli for red, yellow, blue, green, and purple hues, one at a time, at *luminous intensities* roughly equal to that reflected from the front of the spinning disk. ('Luminous intensity' is an energy measure stated in the psychophysical vocabulary; this takes into account the fact that organisms are not equally sensitive to lights that differ in wave-length.) At one or more frequencies of rotation within the specified range a normal observer (i.e. not colour blind) will report, for each stimulus, a hue that is approximately the *complement* of the hue of the stimulus when the latter is observed directly.

Nothing very mysterious occurs at the critical frequencies. The immediate response to the stimulus waveband is masked by, or mixed with, the response to the 'white' half of the disk cycle, while the strongest, complementary phase of the after-image produced by the stimulus occurs during the dark half of the cycle (Sperling 1960). The latter hue is, in these circumstances, unmixed with the direct, but masked hue of the stimulus, and is perceived as the hue of the aperture. At other frequencies of rotation the report will refer to the direct hue of the stimulus, to a neutral (hueless) light, to a ring of the complementary hue filled by the stimulus hue, or to an alternation between, or superimposition of, the stimulus hue and its complement. In the latter case the perception is of *two*, unmixed hues simultaneously associated with a single light!

Experimental operations of this kind permit sensitive, though indirect, measurements of important temporal characteristics of colour responses to stimuli of varying wavebands. Some investigators, employing these and other means, have produced data suggesting that the action time of the system (interval during which a component of the colour response reaches its maximum value) varies with the intensity of the stimulus and, probably, with its wave-length characteristics; evidence on these points, the latter especially, remains equivocal (Wheeler and LaForce 1967).

The foregoing experiment emphasizes the fact that temporal aspects of the visual stimulus have profound effects upon colour responses. It can be shown, in fact, that under appropriate conditions *(Benham's top)* a 'white' stimulus and the absence of light, combined in certain temporal patterns, may produce the entire gamut of hue responses, though of low saturation (Cohen and Gordon 1949).

*Angle of incidence, subtense, and duration effects.* Other characteristics of the stimulus situation, besides spatial and temporal patterns, have strong effects upon colour responses. Among these are the angle of incidence of the stimulus at the retina, the retinal subtense of the stimulus, and the duration of the stimulus. These by no means exhaust the class of stimulus variables that produces measurable changes in basic states of given colour responses, but they provide insight concerning the variety of conditions that must be taken into account in the study of colour perception.

As the *retinal angle of incidence* of a visual stimulus deviates from the (geometric) normal, hues change *(Stiles–Crawford hue shift effect)*, and the change is related to the wave-length of the stimulus. Short wave-lengths produce greener hues, middle wave-lengths bluer hues, and long wave-lengths redder hues, than in the normal condition. Lightness (or brightness) also changes as a function of angle of incidence *(Stiles–Crawford brightness shift effect)*; it is reduced in magnitude as the deviation from normal increases. This fact, coupled with the finding that the hue gamut tends to reduce to greens and reds as angle of incidence deviates from the normal, should, perhaps, be associated with the earlier statement that stimuli of low intensity produce hue ranges restricted to these same two hues.

Certain effects of *retinal subtense* are of a similar character. Stimuli that impinge upon very small portions of the fovea produce red, green, or hueless colours, but not yellows and blues. This *small field tritanopia* (Hartridge 1945) is not entirely restricted to the foveal area of the retina; evidence exists that colour distinctions are reduced, for stimuli of very small subtense, in more peripheral regions as well. The general conclusion, from data supplied in terms of intensity, angle of incidence, and subtense, is that red and green hues are more easily evoked than are yellow and blue; they have, so to speak, a lower threshold. Much other evidence (see *Mechanisms of the colour-vision system*) supports the view that important characteristics of the visual system differ for these two pairs of responses; so much so, in fact, that colour vision is said to be both trivariant and tetrachromatic (Hurvich 1960).

On the other hand, it has been demonstrated that stimuli of small subtense sometimes produce a more varied range of hues than the wave-length compositions of the stimuli would lead one to expect. For example, a series of red and blue-green colour samples, of only two dominant wave-lengths, but varying in the saturations and lightnesses they produce, when viewed as stimuli of small retinal subtense, may be matched (by normal observers) to a series of samples that span the entire hue gamut (again, with the possible exception of a small range of purples). This *anti-tritanopic conversion* (Karp 1960), at present a rather poorly understood behaviour of the colour vision system, produces effects similar to those of the two-waveband experiment described above and, together with small field tritanopia, serves to remind us of the important fact that colours are not uniquely related to the wave-length and intensity characteristics of their stimuli, but result from much more general and complex relationships in the visual field.

Effects of the *duration of the stimulus*, relative to a given set of retinal receptors, are startling when first observed. If a coloured stimulus image is produced in such a way that no movement of the image occurs on the retina, virtually all hues disappear within a few seconds, followed shortly by the partial or complete disappearance of boundary or outline responses as well (Evans 1963). As noted previously, the visual system rapidly approaches a null response to constant stimuli, and the 'constancy' may be very brief. When adaptation of this kind has occurred with respect to stimuli of given dominant wave-lengths, the system is then extremely sensitive to stimuli of other dominant wave-lengths; so much so, in fact, that stimuli that might usually produce neutral or hueless colours would, under these conditions, produce hues complementary to those of the adapting stimuli.

The colours of *afterimages* are also related to the effects just described, but afterimages are not, themselves, simple phenomena (Judd 1927). A brief, intense stimulus of a specified waveband and restricted subtense, for example, sets off a train of responses that has a quite measurable periodicity with respect to brightness, and that varies systematically in hue and saturation, being at some times so desaturated that no image is perceived, and at others containing either the hue associated with the original stimulus, its complement, or a hue lying between these in the colour circle. The surround of the figure in the afterimage goes through a series of characteristic changes closely related to simultaneous events within the figure itself. Moreover, the surround of the original stimulus figure, and the conditions of observation of the afterimage also produce differences in the response, as do the state of adaptation of the observer and the duration, intensity, and waveband of the stimulus.

Thus, a variety of effects based upon stimulus duration indicate, as do many other data, that responses of the colour vision system must be examined in terms of an entire matrix of events, both external and internal, both past and present, relative to the reacting organism. The everyday view that colour is specified by the wave-length composition and intensity of the light from the stimulus simply does not coincide with experimental results that have been accumulated over the past 200 years.

A bibliography of twelve items is appended. This brief list does not begin to exhaust the class of useful and informative volumes on colour and colour vision, nor does it include references to the thousands of journal articles in the field (references cited in the foregoing discussion are also illustrative rather than exhaustive). It is a miniature library for the reader who wishes to make, with some feeling of completeness, a rapid examination of the topic of colour perception.

*Aknowledgment*

C. J. Burke, B. H. Crawford, G. G. Heath, D. B. Judd, and A. Karp and M. F. Lewis provided extremely helpful criticisms of this article. The author is grateful and has incorporated many of their suggestions. None of these kind readers, however, is responsible for inaccuracies or idiosyncrasies remaining in the final presentation.

*See also:* Perception, stereopsis as an aspect of. Perception, visual.

*Bibliography (in a preferential reading order)*

BURNHAM R. W., HANES R. M. and BARTLESON C. J. (1963) *Color: A Guide to Basic Facts and Concepts*, New York: Wiley.
EVANS R. M. (1948) *An Introduction to Color*, London: Chapman and Hall; New York: Wiley.
LE GRAND Y. (trans. by HUNT R. W. G., WALSH J. W. T. and HUNT F. R. W.) (1957) *Light, Colour, and Vision*, London: Chapman and Hall.
Committee on Colorimetry, Optical Society of America (1953) *The Science of Colour*, New York: Thomas Y. Crowell.
JUDD D. B. (1951) *Color in Business, Science, and Industry*, New York: Wiley.
WRIGHT W. D. (1958) *The Measurement of Colour*, London: Hilger and Watts.
GRAHAM C. H. (Ed.) (1965) *Vision and Visual Perception*, New York: Wiley.
HERING E. (trans. by HURVICH L. M. and JAMESON D.) (1964) *Outlines of a Theory of the Light Sense*, Harvard: The University Press.

SOUTHALL J. P. C. Ed. (1962) *Helmholtz's Treatise on Physiological Optics*, New York: Dover.
(1958) *Visual Problems of Colour*, National Physical Laboratory Symposium No. 8, London: Her Majesty's Stationery Office.
(1960) *Mechanisms of Colour Discrimination*, Proceedings of an International Symposium Sponsored by The International Council of Scientific Unions, Oxford: Pergamon Press.
DE REUCK A. V. S. and KNIGHT J. (Eds.) (1965) *Colour Vision; Physiology and Experimental Psychology*, Ciba Foundation Symposium. London: Churchill.

*References*

CHAPANIS A. (1965) *Color Names for Color Space*, American Scientist, **53**, No. 3, 327.
COHEN J. and GORDON D. A. (1949) *The Prevost-Fechner-Benham Subjective Colors*, Psychological Bulletin, **46**, No. 2, 97.
CRAWFORD B. H. (1965) *Sketch of the Present Position of the Young-Helmholtz Theory of Colour Vision*, in *Colour Vision; Physiology and Experimental Psychology* (De Reuck A. V. S. and Knight J. Eds.) London: Churchill.
DE VALOIS R. L. (1965) *Behavioral and Electrophysiological Studies in Primate Vision*, in *Contributions to Sensory Psychology*, Vol. 1, (W. D. Neff, Ed.) New York: Academic Press.
DE VALOIS R. L. and ABRAMOV I. (1966) *Color Vision*, in *Annual Review of Psychology*, Vol. 17, Palo Alto: Annual Reviews Inc.
EVANS C. R. (1963) *A Comparison of the Behaviour of Geometrical Shapes When Viewed under Conditions of Steady Fixation, and with Apparatus for Producing a Stabilised Retinal Image*, Brit. J. Physiol. Optics, **20**, No. 4, 1.
EVANS R. M. (1948) *An Introduction to Color*, New York: Wiley; London: Chapman & Hall.
HARTRIDGE H. (1945) *The Change from Trichromatic to Dichromatic Vision in the Human Fovea*, Nature, **155**, 657.
HELSON H. (1959) *Adaptation Level Theory*, in *Psychology: a Study of a Science* (S. Koch, Ed.) New York: McGraw-Hill.
HURVICH L. M. (1960) *The Tetrachromatic Scheme*, in *Mechanisms of Colour Discrimination*, International Council of Scientific Unions, Oxford: Pergamon Press.
HURVICH L. M., JAMESON D. and KRANTZ D. H. (1965) *Theoretical Treatments of Selected Visual Problems*, in *Handbook of Mathematical Psychology*, Vol. 3, (Luce, Bush and Galanter Eds.), New York: Wiley.
JUDD D. B. (1927) *A Quantitative investigation of the Purkinje After-Image*, Amer. J. Psychol. **38**, 507.
JUDD D. B. (1940) *Hue, Saturation, and Lightness of Surface Colors with Chromatic Illumination*, J. Res. National Bureau of Standards, **24**, 294.

JUDD D. B. (1951) *Color in Business, Science, and Industry*, New York: Wiley.

KARP A. (1960) *Tritanopia and Two-Colour Image Synthesis, Nature*, **188**, 40.

LAND E. H. (1959) *Color Vision and the Natural Image, Part I Proceedings of the National Academy of Sciences*, U.S.A. **45**, No. 1, 115.

PEDLER C. (1965) *Rods and Cones—a Fresh Approach*, in *Colour Vision; Physiology and Experimental Psychology* (De Reuck A. V. S. and Knight J. Eds.) London: Churchill.

SPERLING G. (1960) *Negative Afterimage without Prior Positive Image, Science*, **131**, 1613.

WHEELER L. (1963) *Color-Matching Responses to Red Light of Varying Luminance and Purity in Complex and Simple Images, J. Opt. Soc. Amer.*, **53**, No. 8, 978.

WHEELER L. and LAFORCE R. C. (1967) *Sustained Bidwell Afterimages: Effects of Disc Rotation Speed, Color-Pulse Chromaticity, and Color-Pulse, Luminance, J. Opt. Soc. Am.* **57**, No. 3, 386.

LAWRENCE WHEELER

**PERCEPTION OF SOUND.** Auditory perception is a mode of behaviour, an active process whereby a listener becomes acquainted with his surroundings and sets himself in specific relationship with his acoustic environment. A significant measure of selectivity in attention is implied. Indeed, it is an important aspect of perceptual behaviour that preferential attention is spontaneously directed to certain groups of sounds; the character (e.g. pitch, regularity, complexity) of these sounds tends to set the perceived character of the total complex of sounds. It is useful to refer to such associated sound groups as *auditory images*, a concept which acquires further significance in a spatial sense.

The active process of setting up a relationship with the environment has the following meaning. If at all possible, sounds are assigned to one or more apparent source locations spatially referred to the listener's position. The ability to achieve this localization is somewhat dependent on prior experience—for example how talkers sound when located near the corner of the room. Similarly, listeners utilize prior experience also to interpret and characterize sounds, relate these to events in the external world and perhaps in turn initiate action, as for example, the spontaneous adjustment of loudness or speed of speech in a noisy or echoic environment. It has been common therefore to describe perceptual activity as referring a sensation to an external cause.

Some of the important basic facts of auditory perception are as follows. Sounds are perceived to have various attributes such as loudness, characteristic temporal features involving pitch, tonality and continuity and other properties, perceptually assigned to their presumed source, such as direction and spatial volume; these latter are, of course, assessments about the auditory environment. Certain of these main effects depend upon binaural interaction, requiring therefore that sounds are presented to both ears of a listener; this is the normal listening situation. Other subjective effects such as fatigue and annoyance resulting from auditory stimulation certainly depend to some degree on the prior set of the listener.

In the normal binaural situation, listeners perceive a sound source as forming a spatially more or less compact *sound image*, or concentration of sound. This need not coincide with the physical source of sound. For example, a listener in a position corresponding to the apex of an isosceles triangle and facing loudspeakers at the two other corners perceives a sound image near the centre of the base line between the loudspeakers when these are driven with identical non-simple audio signals. When the audio signals to each loudspeaker are totally different, two independent images are perceived, located at the site of the physical sources. It follows that simultaneously occurring separate acoustic signals may be perceived as separate images by virtue of their differing apparent source location; if the physical sources coincide, two separate acoustic signals may still be separately identified, even though perhaps with difficulty, by a listener. Thus a listener can selectively attend to one of two separate speech messages presumably with the aid of their different temporal patterns. But while such a mechanism of separation is conceivable, there is little evidence as to the actual brain function involved.

Quite independently of these image effects, it may be observed that a complex of sounds is often perceived as a single totality if at all possible. For a simple example, consider the situation in which a number of separate (say five or more) equal-level tones of different frequencies are simultaneously presented. Listeners are able to isolate and match the pitch of very few, perhaps none, of these component tones. If one more tone is added abruptly, it is separately perceived in isolation against the complex background of other components. Independent matching of its pitch with that of a separately generated reference oscillation (the reference tone and the test signal complex being presented in succession) can be achieved. However, within a few seconds or so of its addition, the added tone apparently merges into the complex background and can no longer be independently isolated or matched with any more ease than any other component.

*Binaural effects.* The main matters are as follows. When identical sounds are presented to the two ears of a listener, a fusion or combination of the acoustic inputs apparently takes place. The resulting fused image is almost invariably reported as intracranial when earphone listening is involved, and extracranial, in the normal situation with external sound sources. It is not known what cues are responsible for the externalization of the image, but changes in the signals differentially presented at the two ears, as the head is rotated, may be assessed for this purpose. If earphones are used, and are moved away from the ears, and perhaps substituted by loudspeakers, the image of wideband binaural signals is reported to become extracranial. Listeners commonly report that the image moves above and behind the head as the loudspeakers are moved further away from the ears. If the loudspeakers are moved forward of the listener to the isosceles triangle arrangement discussed above, the image is reported to move on a sagittal arc down to a final position midway between the sources.

Identical binaural earphone signals generate judgements of a central intracranial image position; if the signal to one ear is removed, the monaural image shifts to the other ear. In earphone listening, a binaural image may be displaced from its perceived central location by introducing either an interaural time delay or an interaural amplitude difference, or both. An interaural time delay (ITD) which causes one aural signal to lead the contralateral signal, has an effect which depends upon the temporal character of the signal. With signals such as speech or wideband noise the image shifts towards the side receiving the earlier signal. The minimum detectable shift requires some 10 $\mu$sec ITD and most of the movement is complete with ITD of 500 $\mu$sec. With single low frequency pure tones, period $T$, the situation is more elaborate; for ITD values corresponding to less than one half period $T/2$ the image is judged to move towards the leading side, but as ITD is increased continuously beyond $T/2$ a transition of attention occurs to an image on the contralateral side which is then tracked in to a judged central position as ITD approaches a value equal to the full sinusoidal period $T$. The magnitude of the maximum displacement perceived is greatly dependent upon circumstance, but for all listeners the extent of image displacement seems to diminish as the sinusoidal frequency is increased. At frequencies above 1500 c/s, little or no image movement with ITD can be detected and results are consistent with the view that extent of judged image displacement is dependent in a simple way on magnitude of ITD, provided that due allowance is made for the human faculty of adapting the scale of subjective estimates according to circumstances. Failure of judged displacement for high pitched tones is thus to be thought of as a limit of resolution effect. If two low frequency tones are both applied binaurally at equal level, two simultaneous images may be perceived; however, listeners spontaneously attend to whichever image happens to be in a position judged nearer centre at the given ITD value. If attention is directed to either tonal component, it is judged as if it occurred alone. The mechanism which operates this selective attention to one or other image is still to be resolved. Further examples will be quoted below.

Otherwise identical binaural signals establish an image which is subject to judged displacement of position due to interaural amplitude difference (IAD) towards the side receiving the louder signal. All signals exhibit this effect. However, the spatial volume of the fused image of wideband continuous signals is invariably reported to increase with IAD, becoming appreciably more diffuse. For this reason while it is possible with suitable signals to balance the image shift due to ITD by an opposing change of IAD, thus 'trading' amplitude difference for time delay, a limited range of IAD is available for valid image-centring experiments of this type. In free field listening, an external image is perceived; its apparent position may be assessed by relative time and amplitude cues at the two ears, but there is presumptive evidence that directional hearing may independently utilize the dynamic acoustic signal changes at the two pinnae resulting from slight head movements. Prior experience presumably brings sophistication in this activity.

Interesting multiple images are perceived with another type of binaural signal commonly met in the usual environment, binaural acoustic transients. In the normal earphone listening situation the listener spontaneously perceives a single dominant impulsive image which is judged to track across the intracranial field, as ITD alters, exactly as for other wideband signals. Careful attention reveals, however, that a number of images, in fact, are perceived to coexist. If the transients are repetitive at a rate exceeding about 50 per second, a variety of tonal images can be perceived; these correspond to harmonics of the fundamental repetition frequency and each image may be displaced by the addition of a suitably phased locked sinusoid of the relevant frequency at one ear, precisely as if that image occurred alone. The dominant images, however, are impulsive, the major image being of medial pitch apparently due to signal components below about 1500 c/s and the secondary image being high pitched, its character largely determined by the signal spectrum at higher frequencies.

If the signal situation presents single transients, A, at one ear and double transients (BC) at the other ear of a listener, two main impulsive images $S_1$ and $S_2$ are perceived. These $S_1$ and $S_2$ images correspond to fusions AB and AC respectively. It appears further, that the $S_1$ image comprises the usual medial pitch (main) image and a high pitched secondary image as discussed above. The $S_2$ image shows both medial and high pitched component images only if the spacing between pulses B and C is relatively large, 4 $\mu$sec or larger. For smaller BC spacing, the listener perceives a medial pitch image $S_1$ which is displaced with ITD, being judged central when the pair AB are simultaneously applied. As ITD increased, delaying A on B, the listener perceives the medial pitched component of image $S_2$, due to AC, and this is tracked across the intracranial field, being judged central when A and C are presented simultaneously. However, the high pitched component of $S_2$ is apparently suppressed, for small BC spacing, due to monaural masking of pulse C by the immediately preceding pulse B, which reduces the effective magnitude of the high pitched components of C. The high pitched $S_2$ image is thus displaced off to one side by the effective IAD thus established.

The physiological correlates of the existence of the high- and medial-pitch images are discussed below, but remarks about monaural masking are warranted here. A signal presented at one ear is judged to be somewhat less loud if another signal (the masker) with some spectral components in common, is simultaneously presented. The signal is said to be masked. It is a monaural effect, in that it certainly occurs as a result of peripheral interaction at each ear alone, probably in the cochlear nerve or its sensory terminations in the inner ear. It is probably related to the fact that once a nerve fibre has transmitted an impulse it is totally refractory for a short period and relatively insensitive for a longer subsequent period. Thus when the transient B of the BC pair discussed above pre-empts some of the neural terminations or connected fibres associated with the region of the cochlea most sensitive to high frequency signals, fewer fibres are then available to respond to the subsequent transient C. Transient waveforms are thought to experience a substantial dispersion in time in the cochlear response which they elicit as they approach the distal (apical) end of the cochlea optimally responsive to lower frequency signals; the BC interval thus becomes greatly increased and less significant for masking effects.

Important *masking phenomena* also occur with binaural listening. When in an earphone experiment speech and wide-band noise of sufficient level are simultaneously presented monaurally to the same ear of a listener, a low level of speech intelligibility can be found. When, however, identical noise is presented to the contralateral ear, simultaneously with ipsilateral noise and speech unaltered from the last experiment, the listener perceives that the noise image moves to a central intracranial position; the important concommittant is that the speech is, in effect, unmasked and its intelligibility immediately rises, perhaps doubling. Accordingly this release-from-masking effect is of great interest. It can be demonstrated for other signals and also when both signal and noise are binaural; as the interaural time delay of the signal is altered its detectability rises appreciably. Effective improvements of some 8 dB are commonly found and much higher figures are sometimes quoted for simpler signals.

Related binaural effects are found in normal environmental listening. The ability of a listener to discriminate in favour of a wanted sound source and against an unwanted source, is significantly improved when the two sources are moved apart spatially, even though held equidistant from the listener.

*Physiological correlates of some perceptual effects.* Sensory terminations of the cochlear nerve which comprises some $3 \times 10^4$ fibres in man, are arrayed along the length of the basilar membrane in the cochlea. Mechanical activity of the membrane in response to wide-band acoustic signals extends along much of the cochlear length although the time-response pattern of mechanical displacement is greatly a function of cochlear locus, as described by the impulse response at the site of interest. Mechanical activity of the membrane initiates local nerve fibre activity in the form of bursts of neural spike potentials (regenerative depolarizations of neuron membrane potentials) probably synchronized with upward (rarefaction) movements of the basilar membrane.

Any given sensory termination of the cochlear nerve is thus thought to be triggered on a probabilistic basis by mechanical events in a corresponding region of the cochlea. Any region of the cochlea is thought to stimulate a group of fibres in the cochlear nerve and the temporal distribution of firing due to a specific stimulus is again thought to be subject to probabilistic effects. The pattern of firing, to an impulsive acoustic transient, of a single fibre and hence a neighbouring group, is most conveniently described by the post stimulus time (PST) *histogram* of neural spikes (i.e. as a function of time after the initiating stimulus). The effect of increasing acoustic stimulus level is to advance and flatten the main peak of the histogram, certainly as seen in the time-average PST of single cochlear nerve units; it is presumed at present that similar effects could be seen in the PST for a single transient, ensemble-averaged over the group of fibres from a given cochlear region.

The perceptual correlates of these propositions are as follows. Binaural images from similar aural signals and thought to arise by interaction of neural activity in fibres originating in generally corresponding regions of the two cochleae, are considered to be affected in two ways by a change of relative interaural signal level. In the case of a binaural acoustic transient stimulus the neural signals in a group of neighbouring fibres from the ear receiving the louder signal are thought to exhibit an effective time advance and an increased spread in time; subsequent interaction with neural activity in a corresponding group of fibres from the other ear would thus indicate a more diffuse image than in the equal level case, with the image displaced towards the louder side. These propositions quantitatively parallel auditory perceptual experience in this situation.

It will be clear that neural activity must be expected to arise in many cochlear regions and further resolution of this activity is required. The main auditory image to which attention seems spontaneously directed, is apparently to be associated with neural activity arising in the medial cochlear region, when wide-band transient signals are used. Secondary images apparently arise from basal region activity.

The character of the main images perceived in both monaural and binaural situations is therefore determined by the neural activity arising in one or more cochlear regions. In the binaural situation the images not only have temporal characteristics but experience displacement of perceived location under influence of interaural factors, in a way which depends upon the general form of the membrane mechanical displacement at the relevant cochlear locus. Selective attention to one or other of these images is possible, with the medial pitched image most readily identified for wide-band acoustic transients. In short, while attention may be directed to one or other of the images, the character (e.g. pitch) of the dominant image determines the main character of the total complex as usually perceived. In this way, it is possible to account for the main multiple image effects and the nature of the relevant binaural perceptual phenomena. It is to be noted that in situations where multiple images simultaneously occur listeners may attend to different images at different times, and this effect confuses some commonly reported observations.

*Intersensory and sensorimotor effects.* The environment perceived by a listener is not normally selectively based on auditory stimuli alone and it is unavoidable that an integrated association of visual tactile and acoustic cues results from an individual's attempts to become acquainted with his surroundings. Not surprisingly therefore, several modalities frequently contribute to a total perception, and indeed this may be significant in communication. For example appreciable improvements in the intelligibility of speech degraded by noise are seen when the listener is permitted to watch the speaker's lips. (This faculty presumably corresponds to the improvement in intelligibility of heavily noise-masked speech which results when prior information is given that the message comprises a given restricted set of words, such as a list of digits.) This example of information presented through one sense assisting the interpretation of stimuli received through another is supplemented by the reverse effect in which contradictory stimuli are received through two sense modalities. A listener's perceived auditory environment may be subjected to a significant spatial displacement by judicious visual cues related to the acoustic source.

Finally, it may be noted that auditory perception is also important to certain human motor activity. It is known that the process of normal human speech production involves some auditory monitoring (for level, rate and intonation) of the speech sounds as they are produced. It has also been argued that the mechanism whereby speech defects such as *stammering* are mediated involves the perceptual apparatus; in short, stammering behaviour is dependent upon the speech perception mechanism at least as much as the speech production mechanism.

*See also:* Cochlear mechanics. Speech perception.

*Bibliography*

BÉKÉSY G. v. (1960) in *Experiments in Hearing* (Ed. E. G. Wever), New York: McGraw-Hill.
CHERRY E. C. and SAYERS B. McA. (1960) *Experiments upon the Total Inhibition of Stammering by External Control* in (Eysenck H. J. Ed.) *Behaviour Therapy and the Neuroses*, Oxford: Pergamon Press.
FLANAGAN J. L. (1965) *Speech Analysis, Synthesis and Perception*, Berlin: Springer-Verlag.
TOOLE F. E. and SAYERS B. McA. (1965) *Inferences of Neural Activity with Binaural Acoustic Images*, J. Acous. Soc. Amer., **38**, 769.

B. McA. SAYERS

## PERCEPTION, STEREOPSIS AS AN ASPECT OF.

*Stereopsis and binocular depth perception.* Stereoscopic depth perception or *stereopsis* is based on the fact that the two-dimensional projections of a three-dimensional object on the left and right retinas differ in their horizontal positions (see Fig. 1). This horizontal shift between corresponding points in the two retinal images is called *retinal disparity*, or just simply *disparity*. The terms *binocular parallax* or *parallax shift* are also used. Wheatstone's discovery of the *stereoscope*, published in 1838, was the first demonstration that disparity gives rise to vivid stereopsis. That disparity *alone* is adequate for stereopsis was demonstrated in 1841 by Dove, who repeated Wheatstone's experiments using exposures too brief for any convergence motion of the eyes to be initiated. In order to obtain stereopsis the stereo images

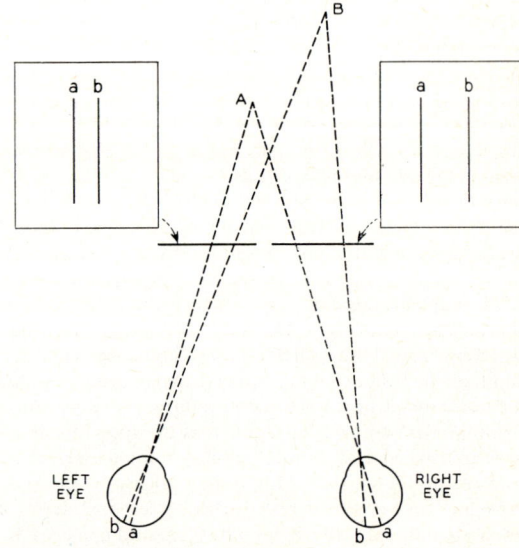

FIG. 1. *Disparity as the basis of stereoscopic depth perception.*

must be brought in rough registration within the critical limits of disparity. The main function of *convergence* and *accommodation* (focusing) is to fixate the eyes at a point in our visual environment and enable the central nervous system to derive a percept of space in a small neighbourhood around the fixation point.

The global process of building up the entire visual space from these local samples of space by successive scanning and convergence motions of the eyes is called *binocular depth perception*. It incorporates the *binocular depth cues* of stereopsis, convergence and correlative accommodation (differential focusing of the two eyes) and integrates them into a global percept of depth. Thus binocular depth perception utilizes both the disparity information derived by the central nervous system and to some extent the *proprioceptive* information on convergence movements and tension changes in extra-ocular muscles.

Contributions to the study of binocular depth perception have been made through investigations of such problems as that of the *horopter* (the surface of space having points which are perceived at the same depth) and the hyperbolic metric of binocular space (Luneburg 1947), nevertheless the emphasis of this account will be on stereopsis.

*Relative and absolute depth.* Stereopsis itself gives us the experience of *relative depth* only. It enables us to rank order the nearness-farness of objects within a region of space around the fixation point. Even the proprioceptive cues are not adequate to localize the *absolute depth* of the fixation point. Absolute depth perception is a result of many *monocular depth cues* which augment the binocular depth cues in intricate ways not yet fully clarified. These monocular depth cues are usually complex familiarity cues which presuppose learning and memory. The most important monocular depth cues are *interposition* (the superposing of near objects on far objects), *linear perspective* (such as converging railroad tracks), *motion parallax* (change of appearance with change of observer's position), *retinal gradient of texture* (decreasing size of texture elements with distance), *shadow patterns* (the light-and-shade relations yielding relief), *apparent size of objects* of known size (which decreases with distance of observer), etc.

*The importance of stereopsis.* The monocular cues together compensate to some extent for the loss of stereopsis. Nevertheless, stereopsis is the most powerful single depth cue.

During the course of evolution, stereopsis emerged from binocular vision after it was made possible by the overlapping of the left and right visual fields and the accompanying complex movements of eye-coordination. Prior to that time the two eyes, placed sideways, received separate views, which together constituted a *panoramic view*. The advantages of depth perception, combined with the development of flexible head motions, probably outweighed the loss of panoramic vision for some animals. With depth perception, spatial location of objects is perceived vividly as an independent sensation, similar to the sensation of colour or brightness, and as such helps in the formation of a useful model of the outside world.

*Disparity and pattern recognition.* The quantification of relationships between disparity and perceived depth has beeen the main activity of researchers for a hundred years. The pioneering work of Panum, Hering, Helmholtz, Hillebrand and Tschermak was primarily aimed at exploring the limits of disparity, particularly of minimum and maximum disparity thresholds under various stimulus conditions. It raised theoretical questions concerning the nature of stereopsis as well. These classical experiments used simple lines or dots as stimuli. More recent experiments with complex stimuli of randomly scattered dots have achieved considerable theoretical and experimental simplifications.

In earlier experiments, the assumption generally made was that disparity is detected and corresponding areas in the left and right fields are found by a process of *recognition*. Thus each image would be evaluated *monocularly* and after the similarity between corresponding projections of the same figures was recognized, their disparity would be measured. These projections may differ, however, in position and shape because of perspective, in brightness because of reflections, and in picture content because of hidden objects which are presented to one eye only. The problem of establishing a correspondence between patterns in the two fields is thus basic. The process of form recognition on which this assumption rests is not clear. It has been demonstrated, however, (Julesz 1960) that for stereopsis no monocular recognition process is necessary. The much simpler process of *cross-correlation* will suffice. This may be shown with stimuli of random-dot stereo images without any depth or familiarity cues except disparity.

FIG. 2. *Random-dot stereo pair. When the two fields are viewed stereoscopically, the centre square appears in front of the background. (A prism in front of one eye greatly facilitates fusion of the stereo pairs. A satisfactory prism can be made of gelatin. In an optically transparent container, tilted by 15 to 20 degrees, a concentrated solution of gelatin is placed until it sets. The flat surface of the container and the hardened top surface of the gelatin form an optical wedge which can be used as a viewing prism.)*

Such a stereo pair is shown in Fig. 2. When viewed monocularly, both fields of Fig. 2 give a homogeneous random impression without any recognizable features. But when viewed stereoscopically, this image pair is vividly perceived in depth, with a centre square in front of its surround. Figure 2 consists of randomly selected picture elements of black and white, and the right and left field are identical except for a centre square which is also identical in the left and right fields but shifted horizontally in one fields as if it were a solid sheet. Figure 3 shows a similar display with three monocularly-invisible rectangles. These rectangles can be regarded as corresponding left and right projections of a rectangular planar surface located in depth when viewed from different angles. When viewed stereoscopically, the upper rectangle is seen in front of the surround, since its disparity is in the direction of the nose. The surround has zero disparity and serves as the reference plane. The lower rectangle, with a disparity in the direction of the temples, is seen behind the surround. The middle rectangle, with a periodic pattern corresponding alternately to temporal or nasal disparity, is ambiguous and can be seen in front or behind at will. Figures 2 and 3 were generated by a computer, since it would have been impractical to generate by hand tens of thousands of brightness elements, with varying constraints for each experiment.

Although these demonstrations prove that stereopsis may occur in the absence of all monocular depth or familiarity cues one might still argue that the observer might shift his attention to some monocular micropatterns in the two fields and try to fuse them. This possibility was explored and eliminated (Julesz 1960) in an experiment removing the diagonal connectivity in the left field of Fig. 2. The stimulus is shown in Fig. 4 where the

FIG 3. *Stereo pair which, when viewed stereoscopically, contains an upper rectangle perceived in front of the surround, a lower rectangle perceived behind the surround, and an ambiguous middle rectangle perceived either in front of or behind the surround.*

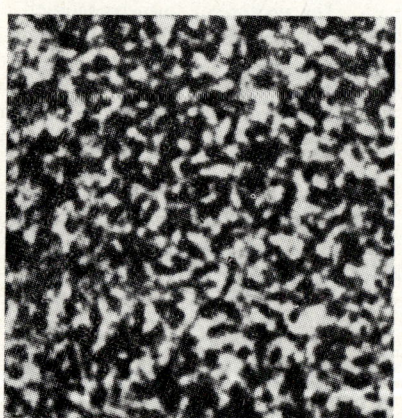

FIG. 4. *Stereo pair identical to that of Fig. 2 except for the fact that in the left field the diagonal connectivity is broken; 84 per cent of the picture elements of the stereo pair are identical. Stereopsis is easy to obtain.*

left and right fields differ only in 16 per cent of their picture elements. Although the two fields look very different monocularly and corresponding micropatterns are also different, they can be easily perceived in depth when viewed stereoscopically. Thus the central nervous system performs the cross-correlation between the picture elements, here 84 per cent identical, and the processes of monocular pattern recognition is unnecessary.

Dove's findings are also valid for random-dot images. Stereopsis can be obtained in very brief *tachistoscopic* exposures of Figs. 2, 3 or 4.

*Quantitative aspects of stereopsis.* Simple line drawings and random-dot stereo images are attempts to use stimuli which are more controllable by the experimenter than real-life pictures. The reasons for using lines and dots are simplicity of production and presumed correspondence to certain neurophysiological processes of feature extraction (edge and slit detectors) in the early stages of central nervous system processing. Advantages of random-dot images include the absence of monocular form cues and the presence of the disparity information in each picture element, since no large areas of uniform brightness, which do not give information on disparity, exist. Several theoretical considerations and practical findings depend on these differences between the stimuli used.

*Minimum disparity for stereopsis.* The smallest disparity which gives rise to a noticeable depth difference is called *stereoscopic acuity*. It is usually measured as the angular separation between two thin wires or two small dots in space at the threshold of differential depth perception. Its value depends on brightness, contrast, visual acuity of the eyes and the separation of the two dots or lines. Stereoscopic acuity is much finer than *visual acuity* (minimum perceivable angular separation between two dots), which is of the order of one minute of arc, but is coarser than *vernier acuity* (minimum perceivable angular separation between the break points of a line), which is of the order of a few seconds of arc. A common value for stereoscopic acuity, $\Delta$, is 20 seconds of arc ($10^{-4}$ radians). If the interpupillary distance $p$ is taken as 6 cm, then the critical distance $d$ for which stereopsis still exists is $d = p/\Delta = 0.06/10^{-4} = 600$ metres. Stereoscopic acuity decreases toward the periphery of the eye, just as visual acuity decreases with peripheral angle. This decrease of acuity is probably due to the increasing separation between retinal *receptive fields* with increasing distance from the centre.

*Maximum disparity for stereopsis.* The maximum disparity for stereopsis (when line drawings are used) depends on whether the perceptual criterion by which it is measured is fusion or depth. The limiting largest disparity which still gives rise to a *single fused* image in depth is called the horizontal dimension of *Panum's fusional area* or *fusion threshold*. The fusion threshold increases from 6 minutes of arc in the centre to 20 minutes of arc at a peripheral angle of 6 degrees of arc. For random-dot stereo images the fusional limits are larger, up to several degrees. For instance, when Fig. 2 is presented in such a way that the horizontal size of the images extends 80 degrees of arc, the maximum fusion threshold is 6 degrees of arc.

For line drawings, outside Panum's fusional area the left and right images break away and are seen as double but stereopsis is still experienced if disparity is less than a critical value. Thus fusion is a special case of stereopsis. This disparity region is called the area of *patent stereopsis* since in spite of the lack of fusion stereopsis occurs unavoidably. Often one of the double images is suppressed, but with care the limits of patent stereopsis can be measured and are about four times larger than fusion thresholds (Ogle 1952). Patent stereopsis is also characterized by a correlation between increased disparity and increased feeling of subjective depth. With further increase of disparity this correlation breaks down as the region of *qualitative stereopsis* is entered and eventually even the sense of depth gradually fades. The doubling of images outside Panum's fusional area was thought by Hering and his followers to be an important depth cue. Indeed, when the eye is fixating at an object, another object much closer seems double and 'crossed,' whereas an object further away from the fixation point appears double and 'uncrossed.' The random-dot stimulus results show that Hering's hypothesis is unnecessary, for, in the absence of monocular images, no double image can exist.

*Vertical disparity.* The horizontal positioning of our eyes has resulted in a directional anisotropy of psychological functions. While horizontal disparity gives rise to stereopsis, vertical disparity does not. When vertical shift is introduced in addition to a horizontal shift, stereoscopic acuity and in general stereoscopic performance decreases. On the other hand, Panum's fusional area is about 6 minutes of arc for vertical disparity too in the centre of the retina. For line drawings at larger vertical disparities the images double; nevertheless at 0.3 degree of arc of vertical disparity the loss in stereoscopic acuity is only 50 per cent. For random-dot images stereopsis disappears for vertical disparities larger than Panum's fusional limits.

When stereo images are retinally stabilized (by close-fitting contact lenses and special projection systems) a *hysteresis effect* takes place which is different for line drawings and random-dot images (Fender and Julesz 1966). It also shows markedly the directional anisotropy for stereopsis. The left and right images have first to be brought together within Panum's fusional area; then they can be shifted horizontally several magnitudes outside Panum's area while fusion is maintained. For random-dot images the fusion takes place at 6 minutes of arc and the break-away disparity is 120 minutes of arc. For line stimuli the break-away disparity is less by a factor of two.

*Perception time.* Stereopsis occurs within a 30 msec exposure if afterimages are erased by uncorrelated successive stimuli. The time delay between stimuli to the two eyes (simultaneity threshold) are correlated with brightness differences between the eyes and result in the *Pulfrich phenomenon*. A pendulum swinging in a front-parallel plane is seen to appear in an elliptical path in depth when viewed binocularly with one eye darkened by a filter.

*view*, may be different processes. The more different the two images are the less easy it is to combine them in a single percept and *binocular rivalry* results. The rules of combination and rivalry were investigated by Levelt (1965), who found that the amount of contour detail in a given image determines its contributions in the binocular

FIG. 5. *Stereo pair identical to that of Fig. 2 except the left field is blurred. In spite of the blurring the two fields will give rise to stereopsis; moreover, the fused image looks sharp (Julesz 1960).*

*Binocular combination and rivalry.* Stereopsis and *binocular combination* of the images, into a single *cyclopean*

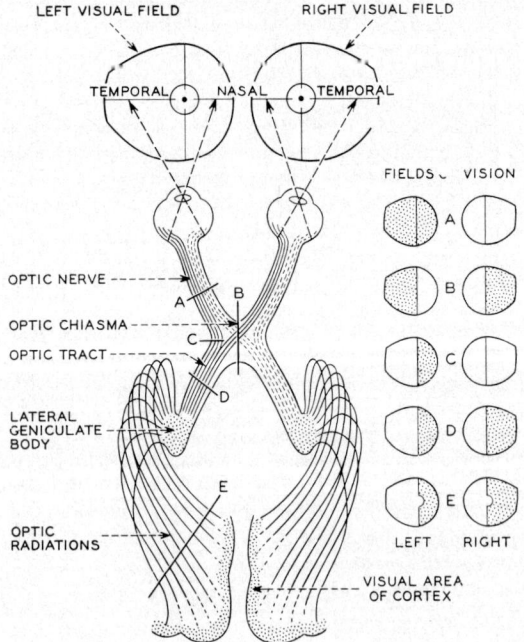

FIG. 6. *The central visual pathways. The shaded areas show the extent of blindness of the visual fields resulting from lesions A, B, C, D, E, (after Fulton).*

percept. Figure 5 shows a stereo image pair with one image blurred. In addition to being perceived in depth, the image seems like the sharp one. Thus the contour-rich channel contributes to the final percept at the expense of the channel with the blurred contours.

*Neurophysiological basis of stereopsis.* The findings that no complex form recognition processes are needed for stereopsis indicate that stereopsis has to occur at some relatively early level of central nervous system. Neurophysiological findings (Hubel and Wiesel 1960) confirm the expectation. It has long been known that the left-half fields of both retinas connect to the left cortical hemisphere, and similarly the right; by the crossing of the optic nerves at the *chiasma*, and by the projecting of the *lateral geniculate nucleus* at Area 17 of the *striate cortex* (see Fig. 6). Hubel and Wiesel investigated the visual system of the cat and spider monkey. They found in the visual cortex neural units which have elongated retinal receptive fields in all possible orientations. The majority of these slit and edge detectors can be driven binocularly by stimulating corresponding receptive fields in the left and right retinas having the same orientation and position. These binocular units have varying monocular dominance, but the most frequent units can be driven equally by both eyes. They also found that pattern deprivation at an early age irreversibly changes the dominance distribution of these binocular units. For instance, if one eye of a newborn kitten receives only diffused light for several weeks, the neural units which were originally binocular become irreversibly monocular units and can be stimulated only by the non-deprived eye.

*See also:* Perception of colour. Perception, visual.

*Bibliography*

JULESZ B. (1960) *Binocular Depth Perception of Computer-Generated Patterns, Bell System Tech. J.*, **39**, 1125.
JULESZ B. (1964) *Binocular Depth Perception without Familiarity Cues, Science*, **145**, 356.
JULESZ B. (1965) *Texture and Visual Perception, Scientific American*, **212**, 38.
LEVELT W. J. M. (1965) *On Binocular Rivalry*, Soesterberg, The Netherlands: Institute for Perception.
OGLE K. N. (1962) *The Optical Space Sense*, in *The Eye*, Vol. IV, (Ed. Davson H.) New York: Academic Press.

B. JULESZ

**PERCEPTION, VISUAL.** *Introduction*. Perception is the link between the outer world and the inner world, between what is commonly called material on the one hand and what has been variously named mind, consciousness, ego, psyche, on the other. We see, hear, smell, we taste, we feel heat and cold, form, size, texture, but of all these varieties of perceptive link, sight is the richest, most precise and least dispensable; it is only the blind who cannot fend for themselves.

What, then, is this visual perception? Assuming the existence of a material world and assuming the existence of mind, sight transmits an image of the former to the latter which receives it and takes cognisance of it. This transmission, reception and cognisance together constitute visual perception. Most of the processes involved in transmission and reception are known; cognisance at present remains largely a mystery. Perhaps the best way to discuss visual perception is to describe, stage by stage, the various links involved.

*The links in the visual pathway*. The first link is radiation, emitted by, or reflected from a material object, transmitted through and refracted by more or less transparent media, to fall as an image upon an array of receptors which are suitably sensitive to the radiation. Our knowledge of the properties of radiation is detailed and profound, and although it cannot be truly said that we know what it is, we know that it is the carrier from object to receptor of the power necessary for visual perception. The amount of power involved is minute, so that for many years this link in visual perception remained a mystery; even the direction of propagation was a matter for argument. Radiation is an electromagnetic disturbance propagated as transverse waves. The range of frequencies responsible for vision is barely an octave and the wave-lengths are short enough (*ca.* $0.5 \mu$) for propagation to be linear and ray-like to a first approximation. Indeed, some ingenuity and close observation are needed to detect the wave nature of light.

The precision of the information derived by a visual perception is primarily due to accurate optical imaging of light on to a sensitive (photosensitive) surface. It would obviously be unpractical to separate the optical imaging system from the photosensitive surface, and so in all organisms which possess a true visual sense they are combined in a single organ, an eye. There are two principal forms of eye which differ rather fundamentally from each other, namely, the simple eye and the compound eye. The words 'simple' and 'compound' are misnomers; the simple eye is the more complex and is, on the whole, the more efficient.

The *simple eye* is optically the equivalent of a photographic camera, a box with a lens system and variable diaphragm in front and a photosensitive surface (the retina) at the back; see Fig. 1. The *compound eye*, in spite

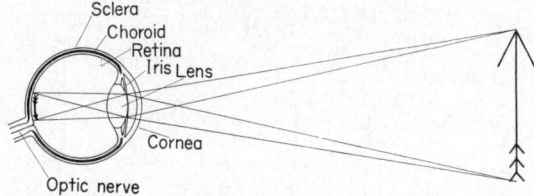

FIG. 1. *Schematic diagram of image formation in eyes of the human type. Note the inversion of the image relative to the object. The outer corneal surface is the main refracting surface; the lens is a fine adjustment for precise focussing. (See also Fig. 3.)*

of its impressive outward array of thousands of lenticular elements, is little more from the point of view of image formation than a bundle of blackened tubes, each with a photosensitive receptor at the inner end, which gives a relatively coarse mosaic-like impression of the outside world. The function of the lenses is to increase the efficiency of piping radiation to the receptors and also, in conjunction with pigment screening between receptors, to avoid 'cross-talk' between neighbouring picture elements; see Fig. 2. A, B, C. At low luminance levels, the pigment has been shown in many cases to recede from between the receptors. If at the same time the receptors are grouped together by lateral nervous interconnexions, there will be a substantial increase in sensitivity, although at the expense of resolution of detail, see Fig. 2 C.

Returning to the simple eye, precise focus is obtained by muscular action on the periphery of one component of the lens system, commonly called the lens, which can be elastically deformed. The lens is under permanent tension from elastic components in a circumferential band of tissue, which flattens the shape to the extent of bringing parallel incident rays to a focus on the retina. The same band of tissue also contains muscular tissue arranged to contract circumferentially. This contraction, usually a reflex action, but also under volitional control, allows the lens to contract radially and expand longitudinally and so to bring divergent incident rays (from a near object) to sharp focus on the retina; see Fig. 3. The action is called accommodation.

Many variations of this scheme exist, both abnormalities and true varieties. The abnormalities, e.g. of length of eyeball, curvature of cornea, etc. produce long or short sightedness; with advancing age the elasticity of the lens diminishes and with it the range of accommodation (*presbyopia*). The true varieties of mechanism include almost every possibility; absence of lens, giving the equivalent of a 'pin-hole' camera (the mollusc *Nautilus*); longitudinally moving lens (many fishes); a sloping retina, giving sharp focus on different distances in different directions (horse).

The photosensitive surface, or retina, is essentially a mosaic of receptor elements, so that perception of the image of the outside world is the result of mental integration from a number of more or less discrete signals, although of much finer grain than in any compound eye. One case is known, *Copilia*, a small marine crustacean, in which the retina has only a single receptor element, the lens being in a state of continual transverse oscillation, which gives a linear scan of the outside world. Since the organism is free-swimming in the sea, it is likely that the scan will be effectively two-dimensional owing to bodily rotation; whether the creature's brain performs time integration into a picture of the outside world is problematical.

In the best eyes, the spacing of the retinal mosaic is nicely adjusted to make full use, but no more, of the resolving power of the lens at its average day-adapted aperture for the median frequency of daylight radiation. The optical quality of the lens system of the eye is also very nearly optimal for the spectral quality of daylight radiation, except in regard to chromatic aberrations. In some way, however, the visual mechanism manages very nearly to disregard or eliminate the disability due to *chromatic aberration*, or, in simple terms, not to perceive the coloured fringes at image edges. How this is achieved is

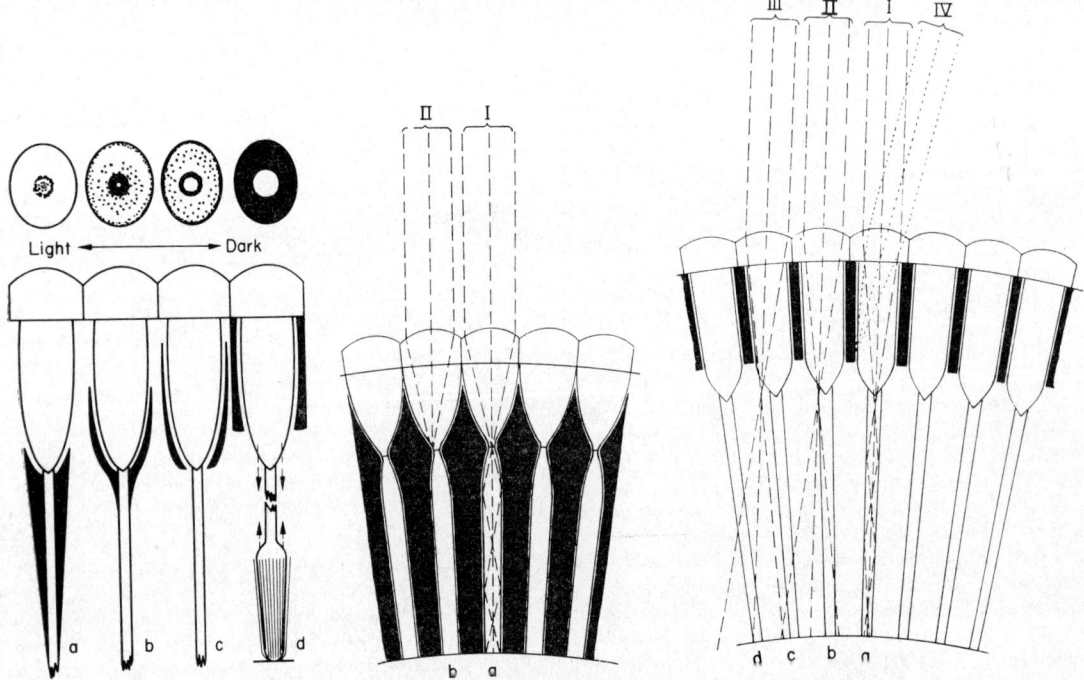

FIG. 2. *Schematic diagrams of image formation in eyes of the compound type. A, pigment location in various states between light and dark adaptation; a, light adapted; b, c, intermediate states; d, dark adapted. Only certain species show pigment migration; in many, the pigment is fixed, or nearly so, in location b or d. B, image formation for pigment location a: maximum efficiency in resolving detail. C, image formation for pigment location d: maximum sensitivity, lower resolving power. Beam I from an object is imaged normally on receptor a; beams II and III from the same object are received by b, c, d, etc.: beam IV from another object at a sufficient angular distance is absorbed before reaching a, b, c, d, etc. (Adapted from Yagi and Koyama 1963.)*

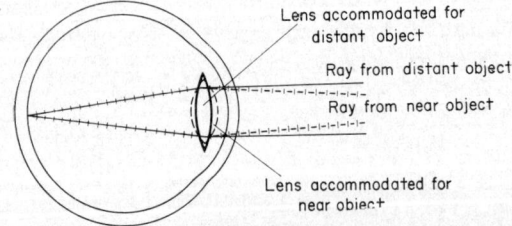

FIG. 3. *Schematic diagram of the mode of accommodation of the human eye.*

not yet fully understood, but it is interestingly parallelled by the experimental fact that the colour components in a television picture can be of a much coarser texture than the black-and-white components without loss of apparent picture quality.

The phenomenon of the Mach bands indicates that the eye also has a mechanism for improving the sharpness of a blurred or out-of-focus image. A small degree of blurring of the image of a sharp edge appears less blurred than it really is; that is, the gradient of luminance across the edge appears steeper. If, however, the width of blurring is large the 'sharpening mechanism', whatever its nature may be, breaks down and produces the appearance of a pair of bands (the Mach bands) instead of a single edge. That this can be a real disadvantage is shown, for instance, by the presbyope, when trying to manage without glasses, tending to count double the true number of coins in his hand.

The previous two paragraphs have discussed aspects of vision in relation to image formation, but at the retina we arrive at the beginning of the next link in perception. The first link ends in an image of the outside world which at its best is very close to the best possible for the daylight band of radiation. The next link is a photochemical reaction. Histological examination of the retina shows that it is a thin but complex layer of tissue containing nerve fibres, nerve ganglia, blood vessels, connective tissue and a highly regular array of cells, unlike any others in the body, the spacing of which corresponds closely to the measured resolving power of the eye; see Fig. 4. All evidence points to these latter cells, the so-called rods and cones of the retina, being the seat of the photochemical link in visual perception. The items of evidence may be enumerated as follows:

(a) the spacing of rods and cones in the central part of the retina corresponds closely to the effective resolving power in the same part; (b) rods and cones can be mechanically isolated from all other retinal components and then shown to contain a photosensitive pigment; (c) electron microscopy has shown clearly that each rod or cone is at one end of a nerve fibre, which is presumed to lead eventually to the brain (the presumption is almost certainty, but the evidence is in a slight degree circumstantial); (d) photosensitivity has recently been found associated with the pigment epithelium behind the rods and cones (Cope 1964) but there are no appropriate nerve connexions to form a perceptive link; (e) in the human retina the cones of the central part and the rods of the remainder are long and thin and the visual effect is a maximum only when the direction of incidence of radiation points accurately down the axes of the cones or rods (the *Stiles-Crawford effect*), there being no other retinal structure to correlate with direction of incidence.

The site of the transformation of absorbed radiant energy into a nerve signal having been thus satisfactorily located, we come to the first real uncertainty as to the exact mechanism involved. In the simpler and more accessible interactions of radiation with matter, such as photoelectric emission or fluorescence, the absorption

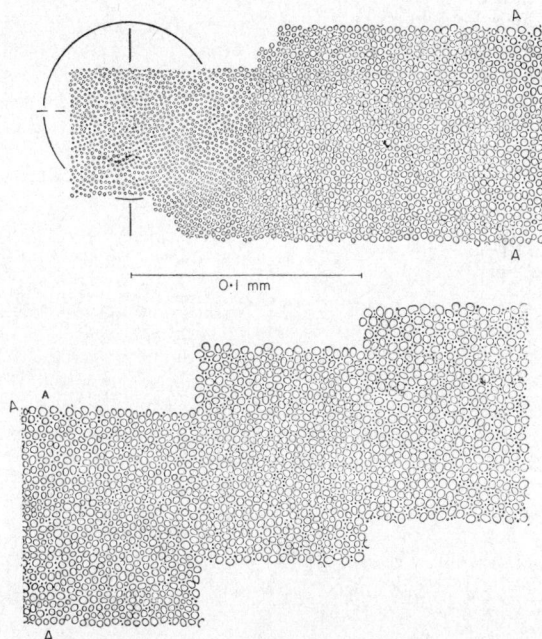

FIG. 4. *Horizontal section through a region of a fixed human retina containing the fovea.*

*The scale refers to the retina in the fixed state; multiply by 1.3 to allow for the shrinkage due to fixation. The centre of the fovea (on the left, top drawing) is defined by the intersection of the three straight lines, or the centre of the circle. The drawing is continued at the same magnification on the next page, with an overlapping indicated by the letters AA.*

*The section has cut through the inner segments of the rods and cones. In the centre of the fovea, the cones are represented by small circles. These become progressively larger as one goes towards the parafovea. In this region the rods, appearing as small circles, are seen in between the broad inner segments of the cones (see especially lower drawing). The first rod is seen in the preparation near the middle of the top drawing, above the right end of the scale. It is situated at a distance from the foveal centre corresponding to 0·13 mm in the living retina. Flat sections such as this are more likely to reveal the presence of rods near the foveal centre than vertical sections, since the latter may fall in between the rods nearest to the centre, and miss them. This may explain why the 'rod-free area' as measured on preparations of the latter kind is sometimes found to have a considerably larger radius than on the present preparation; but the possibility of individual variations from retina to retina must also be borne in mind. (Redrawn from Østerberg, 1935 at a higher magnification (650) and slightly modified. Figure from Pirenne, 1948.)*

of a quantum of radiant energy results in the displacement of an electron from a lower to a higher energy level, or its complete ejection from the material body. The electron can then be collected and detected, or it falls back to a lower energy level and may emit radiation in so doing, again being detected in a fairly direct manner. In the case of the visual system the photosensitive pigments involved are complex and their molecular structure and associations when *in situ* and *in vivo* are largely unknown. We can say little more than that radiant energy is absorbed and a nerve impulse starts on its way to the brain. Even the quantum relations in absorption are still obscure and experiments on minimal (absolute threshold) perception are variously interpreted as indicating the detection of one quantum, or the necessity for a pair of quanta, or no relation to quanta (Pirenne 1962); Scholes 1964).

The nerve impulse having started, somehow, from a rod or cone, there is an extraordinarily complex array of branching and interconnecting nerve elements through which it must find its way to produce an image in the mind which is sufficiently unambiguous to be useful. The simplest condition would be a single, isolated connexion from each receptor element (rod or cone) to a perceptor element in the brain. This is very far indeed from actuality. On closer analysis, it would also seem to be unpractical in many respects. There are two aspects of this analysis, structure and mechanism on the one hand, function on the other. On the structural side, the study of the components of the retina, first by ordinary microscopy, later by electron microscopy, has revealed and continues to reveal the extraordinary complexity of nerve connections which immediately follow the rod or cone (see Figs. 5 to 8). Although this seems far more than is necessary for the basic purpose of transmitting the retinal image to the brain, it serves other purposes. One of the outstanding characteristics of vision is the enormous range of luminous intensities over which it operates efficiently, which may be contrasted with the painful exactitude of exposure required in

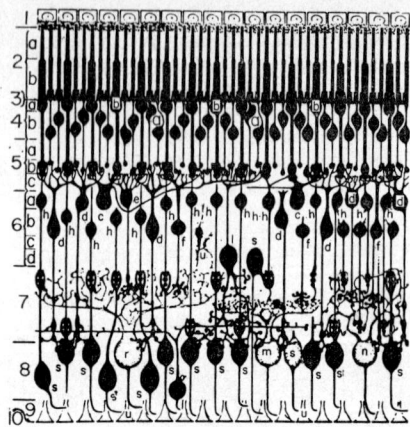

FIG. 6. *Scheme of the structures of the primate retina as revealed by the method of Golgi. The layers and the zones are designated as follows: (1) pigment layer; (2-a) outer zone and (2-b) inner zone of the rod and cone layer; (3) outer limiting membrane; (4-a) outer zone and (4-b) inner zone of the outer nuclear layer; (5-a) outer zone, (5-b) middle zone and (5-c) inner zone of the outer plexiform layer; (6) inner nuclear layer with its four zones; (7) inner plexiform layer; (8) layer of the ganglion cells; (9) layer of the optic nerve fibres; and (10) inner limiting membrane. The nerve cells are designated as follows: (a) rods, (b) cones, (c) horizontal cells, (d, e, f, h) bipolar cells, (i, l) so-called 'amacrine cells', (m, n, o, p, s,) ganglion cells and (u) 'radial fibres' of Müller. In this scheme the nervous elements are reduced to their essentials, with, however, the characteristic features of each variety preserved—the location of the cell bodies, the size, the shape, and the spreading of the dendrites and of the axis cylinders—and with the synaptic contacts presented accurately.*

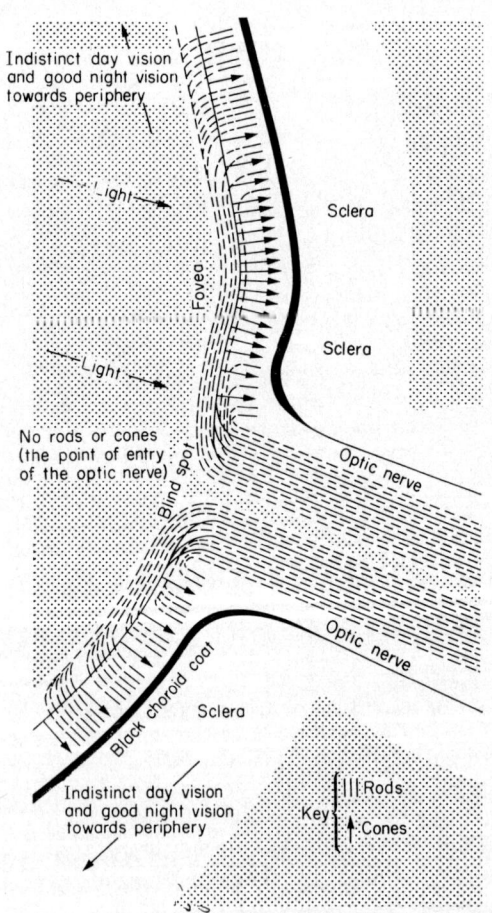

FIG. 5. *Transverse section through the central region of the retina of the human eye (schematic). (Adapted from Ruch 1953.)*

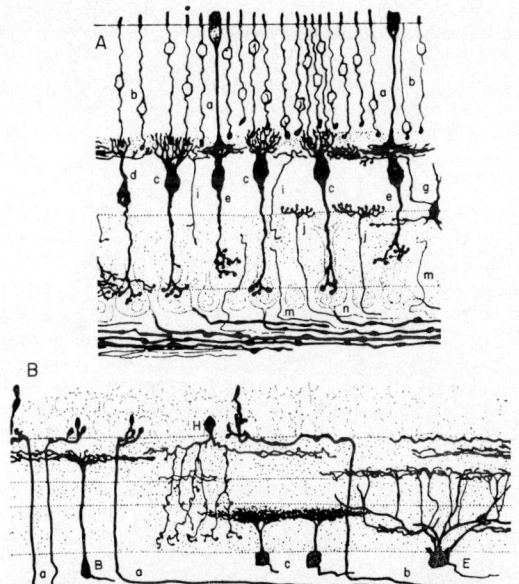

FIG. 7. *A. Retina of the dog showing (a) cone axons; (b) rod axons; (c–e) types of bipolars of which e is Ramón y Cajal's cone bipolar; (m, n) ganglion cells; (i) ascending nerve fibre; and (j) centrifugal fibres. B. Details of structure of ganglion cells (B, C and E) and of connections made by centrifugal fibres (a).*

sensitive pigment by bleaching, but preservation of effective vision during bleaching will be facilitated by plentitude of nerve connexions. Even though the majority of the nerve connexions are blocked by the superfluity of pulses initiated from the receptor, a few are likely to remain available for effecting transmission to the brain.

If the preceding few paragraphs seem unduly vague and full of suppositions, we should ponder upon the magnitude of many of the investigations involved. Sjöstrand, for instance, has mentioned the examination of a single retinal nerve plexus by the cutting of some eighty thousand serial sections, photographing them under the electron microscope, printing as transparencies and finally assembling the transparencies in a pile in correct register to make a model of the original plexus.

It will be difficult from now on to avoid some mention of colour in this discussion of vision, although colour perception forms the subject of a separate article; some overlap is inevitable. All evidence, anatomical, electrophysiological and psychophysical, points to successive stages of combination of the original receptor pulses into groups. Some of this grouping is of a relatively simple sort, probably within the retina, such as that

photography. Some of this adaptability of the visual process is undoubtedly due to association of receptors in even larger groups as the luminous intensity falls. Resolution of detail is sacrificed to sensitivity, which is not, perhaps, an ideal device, but better than a sudden cessation of vision below a moderate minimum intensity.

Another aspect of this complexity of retinal connexions which is less well understood is its possible relation to the characteristics of nerve stimulation and conduction. A stimulus starts the transmission along a nerve of a pulse or wave of change, the exact nature of such change being still uncertain. Following such a pulse, there is a period of recovery before the nerve can again conduct; this ensures unidirectional propagation but may also hinder vision by limiting the rate of pulse transmission to something less than the receptor is capable of initiating. The multiple connexions and alternative paths provided in the retina may have the function of overcoming this hindrance.

The reverse of adaptability to low intensities of light is adaptation to high intensities; both directions of adaptation are necessary. Again, behaviour similar to that of the photographic process would be useless, a mere sensation of dazzling brightness, no contrasts left to make a meaningful image, at intensities above a modest maximum. Most of this adaptation to high intensities will be due to depletion of the concentration of photo-

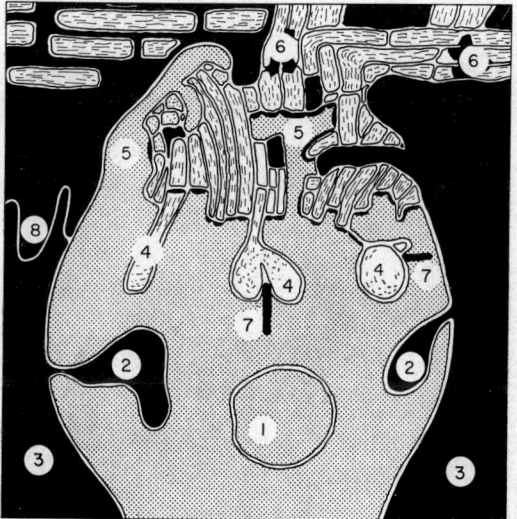

FIG. 8. *Schematic illustration to show the main relationships between a complex receptor pedicle and the neurites of the outer plexiform layer. The pedicle body contains several vacuoles surrounded by double membranes (1). The pedicle itself is enclosed by radial fibre material (3, in black), which sends protrusions (2) into the body of the pedicle. Some bipolar dendrites insert deeply into the pedicle (4) and are in close relationship with the synaptic ribbons or lamellae (7). Basal filaments (5) are thrown up on the inner surface and make many contacts with the neurites in the outer plexiform layer. Normally all the latter (6) run horizontally at right angles to the long axis of the receptor.*

which gives rise to the increasing area of integration of light perception as the general intensity level drops. Another sort of grouping has been postulated (Walraven 1962) to explain the apparently simultaneous occurrence of both the three-component colour mixture phenomena (*Young–Helmholtz*) and the two pairs of opponent colour mechanisms which seem necessary to explain other aspects of colour vision (*Hering*). There is now excellent evidence from physical measurements of spectral adsorption in single cones for the presence of three characteristic colour receptors in the retina, which directly supports the Young–Helmholtz theory. Walraven postulates a scheme of nerve interrelations as shown in Fig. 9 in order to produce the signals for luminosity, red versus green and blue versus yellow, which are demanded by the Hering theory.

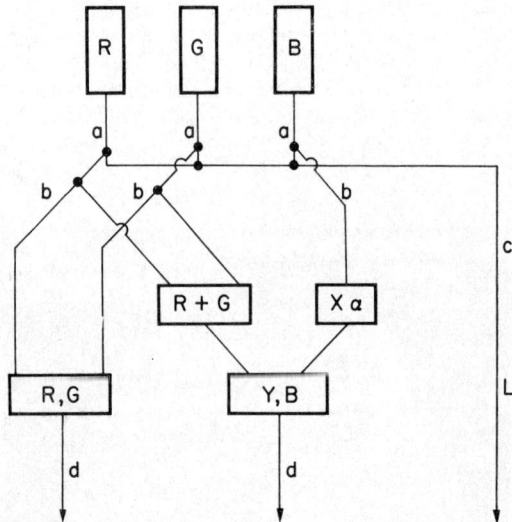

FIG. 9. *A simple symbolic diagram of retinal, or possibly higher, interrelations of nerve pathways from the receptors which explains both the Young-Helmholz trivariance of colour vision and the Hering opponent-colour phenomena of vision, including the apparently independent sense of luminosity. R, G and B are three types of photoreceptor. At level a, R and G are interrelated to give the Hering red-green pair of responses. At level b, R and G combine to give a yellow response, which interrelates with a signal from B to give the Hering yellow-blue pair of responses. Also at level a, proportions of R, G and B are summated to give the luminosity response. (After Walraven 1962.)*

Evidence for yet another form of grouping, probably quite high in the retina-to-brain pathway, is rapidly accumulating from work such as that of Bennet-Clarke and Evans (1963) on fragmentation of the stabilized image. Under most conditions this disappears and reappears in certain units, largely independent of size, which may form the basis of pattern recognition, thereby making this a much more rapid and accurate process than it could otherwise be.

*The end of the visual pathway.* Finally, the last stage in visual perception, the nerve pulses reach the perceptual level of the brain. Here, or hereabouts, they not only present to our consciousness a representation of the outside world, but a selection at least is preserved, some of it for a lifetime. The mechanism of our final perception, as of the storage of impressions, is unknown. Hints of associated chemical changes in the brain cells appear here and there in the literature, and theories based on these are attractively reasonable; it is tempting to postulate stages in chemical change correlated with the finer layering of memory-fleeting, short, medium but temporary, long and permanent. There is at least plenty of space in the brain cells for all degrees of chemical change; even the simplest organic cells known to us are so complex as to be still incompletely analysed. Perhaps one should not emphasize the word 'chemical' too strongly; at the ultimate molecular level there is no clear distinction between things chemical and things physical.

### The Phenomena of Visual Perception

Having sketched the general manner in which visual perception works, it is now desirable to outline the capabilities of vision. It is almost universal for animals to have a pair of eyes and in the human case, perhaps also in others, there is a group of perceptual capabilities in which the two eyes cooperate which may be called the binocular capabilities. The majority of capabilities, however, are not dependent on such cooperation and may be grouped together as the monocular capabilities.

### Units of Measurement

Before embarking on a description of these capabilities it is convenient to define two units of measurement much needed in describing the results of measurement. The first is the unit of retinal illumination, the *troland* (earlier called the photon, but this was discarded owing to confusion with the same word used to denote a quantum of radiation). The troland is defined as the retinal illumination produced by viewing an extended surface of luminance equal to 1 candela per square metre through a pupil of area 1 square millimetre. No allowance is made for absorption by the eye media. It will be noticed that the troland can also be considered as the illumination of the retina from a source of luminous intensity of 1 microcandela situated in the pupil aperture, which is often convenient in calibrating the retinal illumination from an apparatus employing Maxwellian view of the field. A useful conversion table, allowing for the average natural pupil size, is given in le Grand (1957).

The other unit is that of the frequency of the radiation used to stimulate vision. The use of wave-length for this purpose is to be deprecated, although long established, since frequency is the quantity most closely correlated with absorption profiles, photochemical reactions, etc. The matter is discussed in detail by Wald (1965), Szent-Giorgi (1966) and others. Of the two forms of frequency unit, *wave number* is already widely used (number per cm, cm$^{-1}$), although inconveniently large; expressed as mm$^{-1}$ it would be more convenient in magnitude for the visually significant range (400 nm ≡ 2500 mm$^{-1}$, 800 nm ≡ 1250 mm$^{-1}$). The other convenient unit is the *terahertz*, sometimes known as the fresnel, which is the true frequency divided by $10^{12}$ (400 nm ≡ 750 terahertz, 750 nm ≡ 400 terahertz). The terahertz will be used in this article.

## The Monocular Visual Capabilities

*Spectral range of vision.* As already mentioned, the spectral range of radiation effective in vision is short, barely an octave, from about 750 terahertz (400 nm) to about 395 terahertz (760 nm). The limits are not sharply defined; at higher frequencies the media of the human eye begin to absorb strongly and to fluoresce; at lower frequencies the retinal sensitivity is falling rapidly, so that the situation is soon reached wherein the eye is thermally damaged if the radiation is sufficiently intense to be seen. Figure 10 shows the spectral sensitivity of the average, normal eye for the photopic and scotopic states of adaptation.

*Acuity.* Some mention has been made of the *acuity of vision:* under optimum conditions of image formation, fixation, illumination and contrast the resolvable detail reaches the theoretical limit for the median frequency of

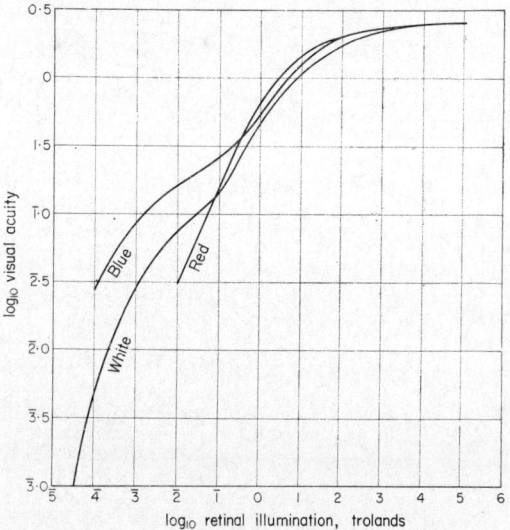

FIG. 11. *The relation between visual acuity and retinal illumination for white, red and blue fields. (After Schlaer et al. 1942; Pirenne and Denton 1952.)*

daylight radiation. Under other conditions of illumination and contrast the resolving power of the eye is less. Resolving power may be measured in various ways: minimum perceptible distance between two points, distance between lines in a grating pattern, width of break in a line or simple character (Landolt C), lateral displacement of two halves of a line or edge, thickness of a line, or size of a spot. Much modern interest centres around grating patterns with sinusoidal variation of luminance, rather than a square-wave variation, owing to the greater simplicity of the basic mathematics when the results are considered according to the theory of transfer functions. Figures 11 and 12 show representative curves of the variation of acuity with field luminance and with pattern contrast.

*Contrast sensitivity.* In the relatively simple case of a uniform object seen against a large uniform background there is a characteristic relationship between the contrast between object and background and the luminance of the background; over a wide range of high and medium luminances, the liminal contrast or *Fechner*

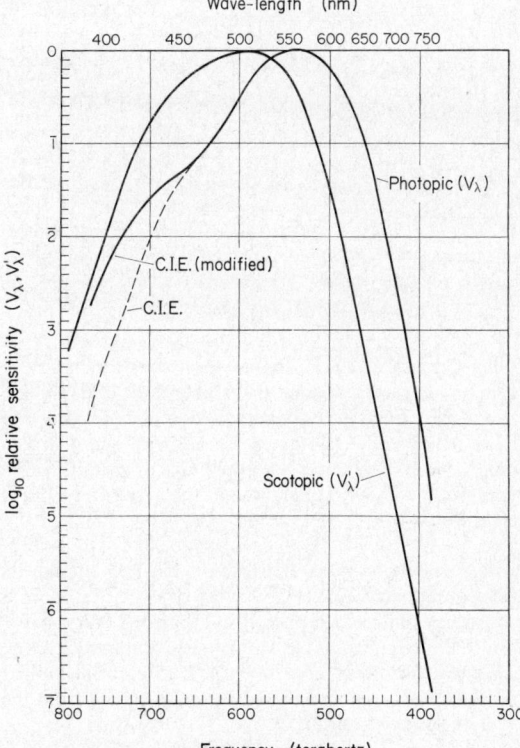

FIG. 10. *Relative spectral sensitivity of the human eye when light-adapted (the photopic state) and when dark-adapted (the scotopic state). (Adapted from CIE Publication 1.1, International Lighting Vocabulary, 1957.)*

fraction $\Delta L/L$ is constant, but it increases rapidly at low levels of luminance. It is generally more useful to express results as liminal brightness increments, or thresholds of luminance difference. The value of threshold for a given background luminance depends on size and shape of object, on the retinal location of its image and on the time period of its exposure. Some representative values are shown by the curves of Fig. 13.

*Stiles–Crawford effect.* The perception of contrast, as of brightness generally, is subject to an interesting and unexpected effect. Whereas in a camera the effective radiation reaching the negative is proportional to the area of the lens aperture, in the human eye this is not so: the outer zones of the pupil aperture appear to be less efficient than the centre. This is because light incident upon the retina with a slight obliquity is less effective in stimulating vision than light incident normally; see Fig. 14

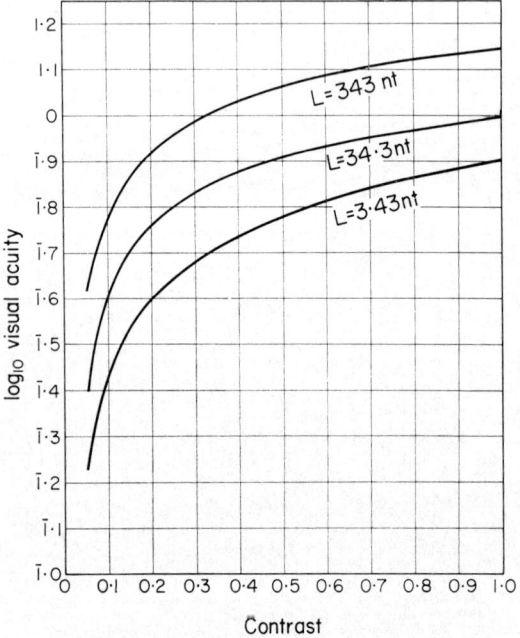

FIG. 12. *The variation of visual acuity with contrast of the test pattern. (After Luckiesh 1944.)*

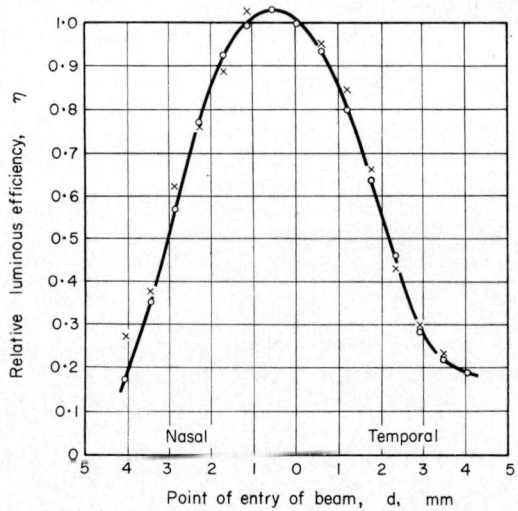

FIG. 14. *The Stiles-Crawford Effect; variation of brightness (apparent luminance) with point of entry of light through the eye pupil.* ⊙ *right eye;* × *left eye. (From Stiles and Crawford 1933.)*

(Stiles–Crawford, 1933). Although the effect has been much investigated during the thirty-odd years which have passed since its discovery, a completely satisfying theory of the effect has not yet been proposed. Perception of colour also varies with the point of entry through the pupil, but this is considered in the article on Colour Perception.

*Integration with area.* If an object is small enough its detection depends on the total flux of radiation from it irrespective of size as is shown in Figure 15 (Weinstein–Arnulf, 1946). The lower the general luminance level, the larger the object area for which integration holds; the integration area also increases with distance from the fovea or fixation point.

*Movement sensitivity.* Although contrast sensitivity falls off as the tested area recedes from the fovea, sensitivity to movement of the object appears to increase. This is at least partly due to the phenomenon of image fading (sometimes known as *Troxler's effect*) in the pa-

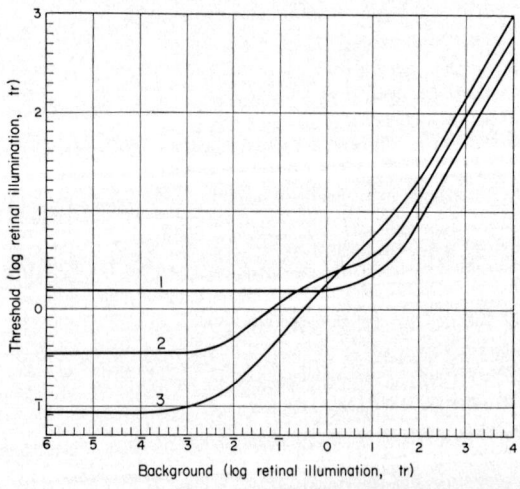

FIG. 13. *The variation of luminance difference threshold with background luminance. Curve 1, fovea; curve 2, 5° from fovea; curve 3, 14° from fovea. Test field diameter, 0·46°; exposure time, 0·05 sec. (After Crawford 1937.)*

rafoveal and peripheral parts of the retina; the image of a static object quickly fades under steady fixation, so that when an object moves there is the appearance of a totally new and vigorous image among the more or less faded details of the static background. Satisfactory quantita-

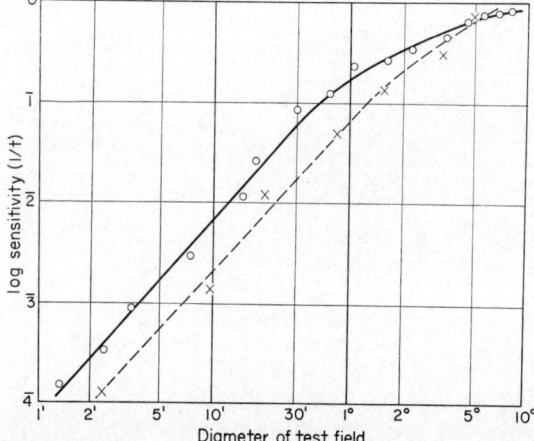

FIG. 15. *The variation of sensitivity (inverse absolute threshold in micronits) with size of test field. Over the linear range, sensitivity is proportional to area of test field (Ricco's Law). (After Weinstein and Arnulf 1946 (circles); Reeves 1917 (crosses).)*

tive measurements of the effect are lacking, but the researches of Barlow and Levick (1965) and others into the mechanism of directional sensitivity to motion of an image are adding substantially to our knowledge of motion perception.

*Flicker sensitivity.* The alternation of higher and lower levels of luminance in any area of the visual field gives rise to a sensation of flicker if the frequency of alternation is below a certain critical value, the critical fusion frequency (cff). Experimental determinations of cff under various conditions of size, colour, intensity and retinal location of field and of the wave-form of the light-dark change have been legion. The cff is also widely used as a criterion of equality of luminance between fields of different colours, but it should be remembered that there are several other criteria and that they all give slightly, but significantly, different results. From the many investigations reported in the literature a few representative results have been selected and are shown in Figs. 16, 17, and 18 (Hecht *et al.* 1933).

*Integration with time.* When a flash of light is sufficiently brief, the visual effect, judged, for example, by the threshold of detection, depends on the total (time × intensity) integral, not on either time or intensity separately *(Bloch's law)*. For the central region of the retina, Bloch's law has been found to hold for times less than 0·1 second if the diameter of the test field is not greater

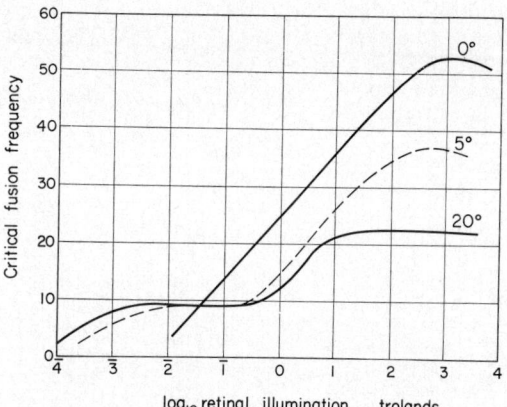

FIG. 16. *Variation of critical flicker frequency with retinal illumination at the fovea and at 5° and 20° from the fovea. (After Hecht et al. 1933.)*

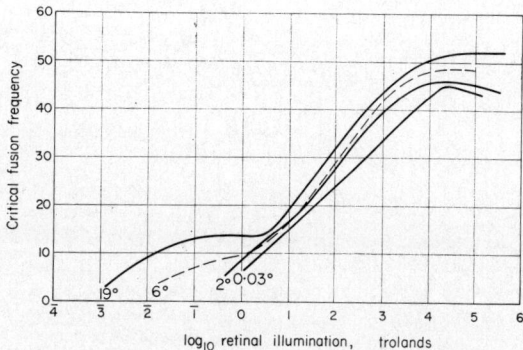

FIG. 17. *Variation of critical flicker frequency with retinal illumination for test fields of diameters 0·03°, 2°, 6° and 19°. (After Hecht et al. 1933.)*

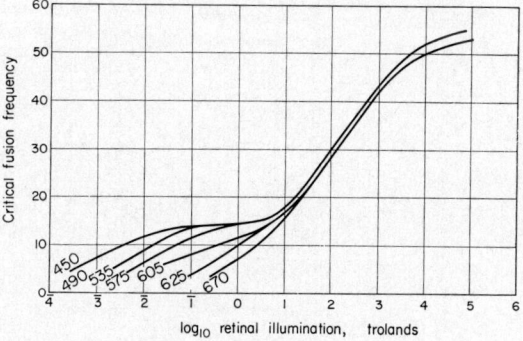

FIG. 18. *Variation of critical flicker frequency with retinal illumination for test fields of different colours. narrow wavebands centred at 667THz (450nm), 612THz (490nm), 561THz (535nm), 522THz (575nm), 496THz (605nm), 480THz (625nm) and 448THz (670nm). (After Hecht et al. 1935.)*

than 2′ and for times less than 0·004 second if the diameter is 1° (Baumgardt and Segal 1946, 1947). For intermediate diameters there correspond intermediate time limits of integration.

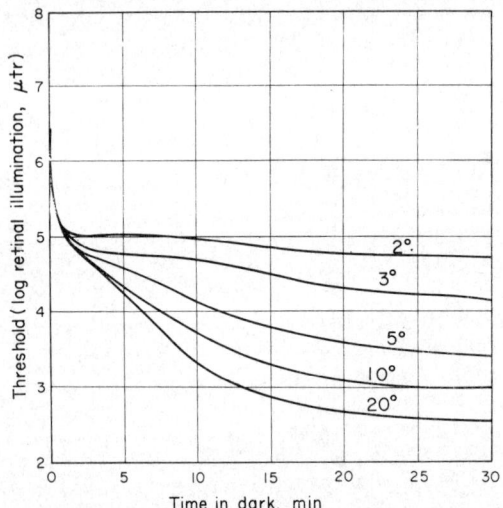

FIG. 19. *Time variation of visual sensitivity during dark adaptation for different sizes of test field. (After Hecht et al. 1935.)*

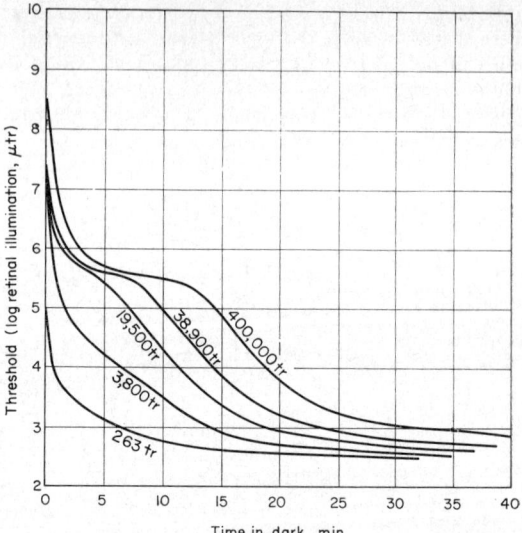

FIG. 20. *Time variation of visual sensitivity during dark-adaptation after different initial intensity levels of light-adaptation. (After Hecht et al. 1937.)*

*Adaptation, temporal.* Whenever the general level of luminance of the field of view changes, the eye takes a finite time to reach an optimum performance at the new level; the process is known as adaptation. Adaptation from dark to light is more rapid than from light to dark, at least in the sense of the eye reaching its optimum capability of seeing, by several orders of magnitude. The interest of experimenters has centred almost entirely on dark adaptation, partly because the length of the process, an hour or more, gives it great practical importance, but also for the two reasons, firstly, that the process reveals very clearly the duplex nature of vision, by 'rods' and by 'cones', and secondly, that the ultimate sensitivity

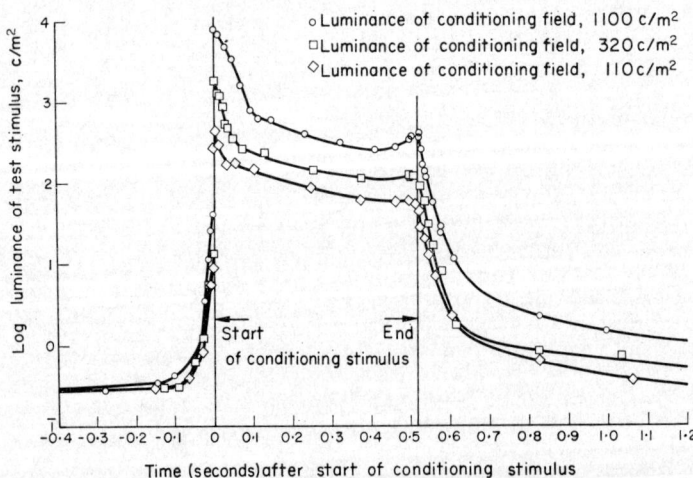

FIG. 21. *Time variation of visual sensitivity during light-adaptation to different intensity levels. Complications due to conductive links between reception and perception are indicated by the rise in threshold before a change in retinal stimulation. (After Crawford 1947.)*

corresponds to stimulation by very few quanta of radiant energy, or even by only one. The course of dark adaptation can be followed under many conditions of size, colour, time of exposure and retinal location of field; Figs. 19 and 20 exhibit some typical results of such measurements (see also Fig. 22).

valent background transformation has been applied to a variety of visual phenomena, including temporal adaptation; see, for example, the curves of Fig. 22 (Crawford 1947). The implication is clear in most cases that the equivalent background is a manifestation of scattered light.

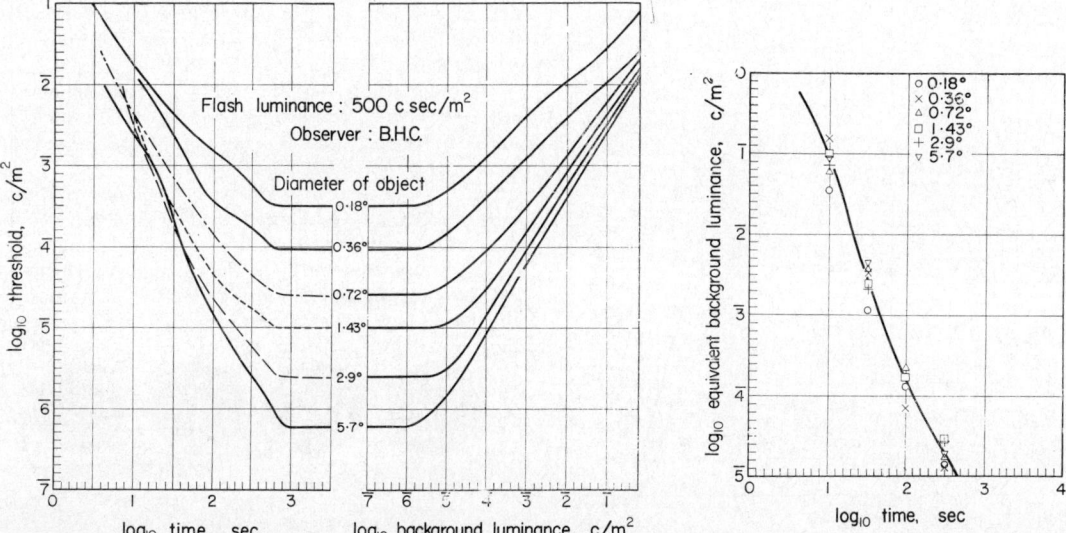

FIG. 22. *An application of the equivalent background principle: the variety of time recovery curves during dark adaptation for different sizes of test field is reduced to a single curve by the equivalent background transformation. (After Crawford 1947.)*

The course of light adaptation, as revealed by measurements of visual sensitivity, is relatively extremely rapid and needs more sophisticated methods of investigation. The aspect of the results which is of special interest is the obvious involvement with links in the perceptive chain at higher levels than the retina. Some measurements are illustrated in Fig. 21 (Crawford 1947).

*Adaptation, spatial.* A light stimulus on part of the retina affects perception of light stimuli by every other part of the retina. The quantitative relationships in effect are most clearly demonstrated in the case of a single stimulus of high intensity and small area; this lowers the sensitivity of other parts of the retina according to a law which holds with some precision over a very wide range, viz. $B_e = kI/\theta^n + B_0$. $I$ is the intensity of illumination at the eye from the stimulus (often referred to as a 'glare source'), $\theta$ is the angle subtended at the eye between glare source and test area, $B_0$ is any uniform luminance which may be present over the test area, and $k$ and $n$ are constants. The quantity $B_e$ is known as the 'equivalent background luminance'; it is that uniform luminance which conditions the eye to the same sensitivity, in the chosen test area, as does the glare source. The experimental evidence shows fairly unequivocally that the part of $B_e$ due to the glare source is essentially the light scattered from the image of the glare source on the retina. The equi-

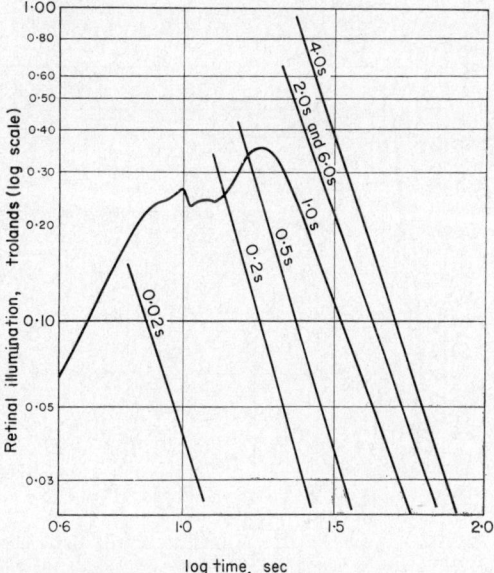

FIG. 23. *Relation between apparent brightness of afterimage, expressed as equivalent retinal illumination, and time after cessation of stimulus for various periods of stimulation. (After Padgham 1957.)*

*After images.* As the name implies, these are images of bright objects which remain visible, though fading, after the original stimulus has ceased. Their exact nature is not known, though many workers have endeavoured to elucidate the rather complicated colour changes which are observed. In two directions, however, some definite knowledge has been gained. Only the true, or positive, after image is considered here; the so-called negative after image is really a phenomenon included under dark adaptation. Figures 23, 24 and 25 show the time variation of apparent intensity of positive after images for the parameters time of exposure, size and colour of initial stimulus (Padgham 1957, 1963).

The other aspect of after images which has led to some definite results in the study of visual perception is the fact that, if the initial stimulus is sufficiently brief, circa 0·001 second, the after image is sharp and stabilized, i.e. absolutely immovable upon the retina (see also the next section). Bennett-Clarke and Evans (1963) have found that such stabilized (after) images exhibit fading in certain unit fragments, the shape and character of which provide very significant clues to the processes of pattern recognition (Fig. 26); at some fairly high level in the per-

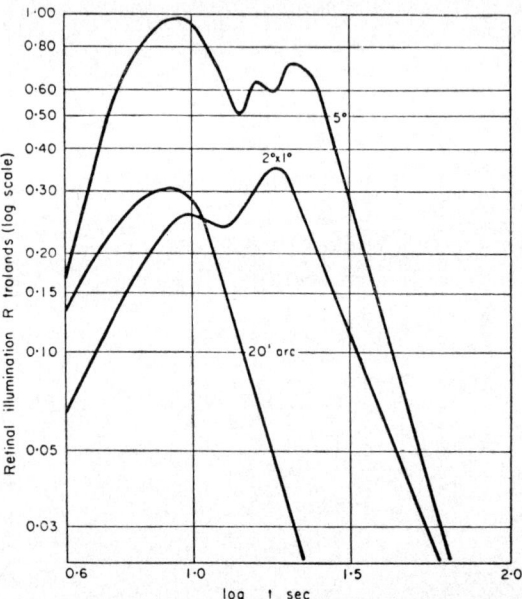

FIG. 24. *Decay curves of after images formed by white light stimuli of different angular size. (Stimuli of colour temperature 2900°K and of retinal illumination $2 \times 10^6$ trolands for 1 sec.) (From Padgham 1963.)*

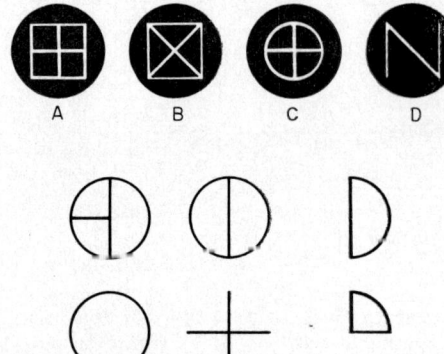

FIG. 26. *Fragmentation of stabilized (after) image: the most frequent patterns from an initial stimulus C. (From Bennett-Clarke and Evans 1963.)*

ceptual chain there appears to be a mechanism for perceiving these unit fragments over a range of size and orientation which would help to explain the facility of character recognition in reading, for instance.

*Stabilized images.* It has been shown that the human eye is in continual slight motion, even though its owner is trying to fixate steadily. This is due to the system of muscles which direct the eye; these act in pairs in opposition, both members of each pair being in balanced tension. It is to be presumed that the state of balance is subject to continual readjustment, also that the eye muscles, like all other muscles, are in continuous micro-tremor, which gives to the eyeball a complex motion of small and minute excursions randomly directed. Although such motion would seem to be inimical to clear vision, the experiments on stabilized visual images show exactly the contrary.

The use of an after image as a stabilized image has already been mentioned. Several other methods have been

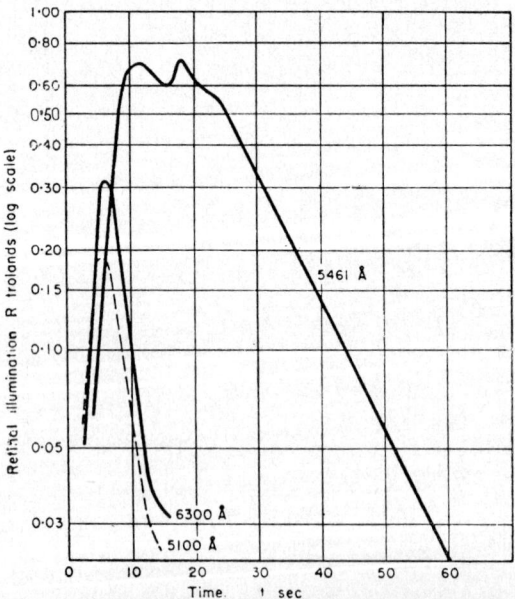

FIG. 25. *Decay curves of after images formed by monochromatic stimuli. (From Padgham 1963.)*

devised which depend on countering the movement of the eyeball with an equal and opposite movement of the apparent position of the object. All these other methods depend upon the attachment of a contact cup to the cornea of the eye. This may carry either a complete object and viewing system (Fig 27), which is a simple arrange-

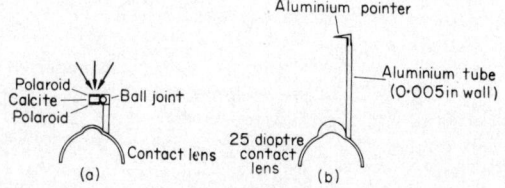

FIG. 27. *Simple form of apparatus for producing stabilized retinal images. (From Ditchburn and Pritchard 1960.)*

ment but of limited application, or it may carry only a light mirror, all the rest of the imaging and stabilizing being done by an external optical system (Fig. 28). It may be noted that no contact cup method is perfect owing to

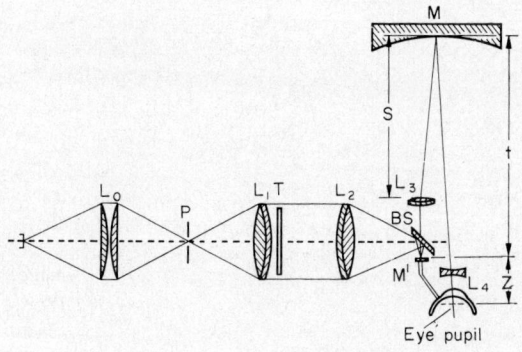

FIG. 28. *Apparatus for producing a stabilized retinal image of any target. T is the target pattern. For full explanation of the optical system, the design of which is critical, see original paper. (From Ditchburn 1963.)*

unavoidable slipping between cup and cornea and all experimental results must be carefully analysed with this point in mind. Nevertheless, the experimental results obtained by many workers are consistent and may be accepted with confidence: they may fairly be described as spectacular. In a well-stabilised image boundaries and contrasts rapidly disappear, reappearing only at relatively long intervals or when the image finally moves upon the retina due to an unusually vigorous jerk of the observer's eye. Tremor is obviously an essential part of effective vision, one more example of a fine natural performance being the result of a number of apparently haphazard approximations.

### The Binocular Visual Capabilities

*Stereoscopy and space perception.* The most obvious of the visual capabilities in which the coordinated perceptions from the two eyes play a decisive part is the stereoscopic perception of relative distances of objects in the field of view. Owing to the lateral separation of the eyes, the retinal images of objects at different distances differ in the two eyes, as indicated in Fig. 29. At some high level in the perceptive chain these disparate images are

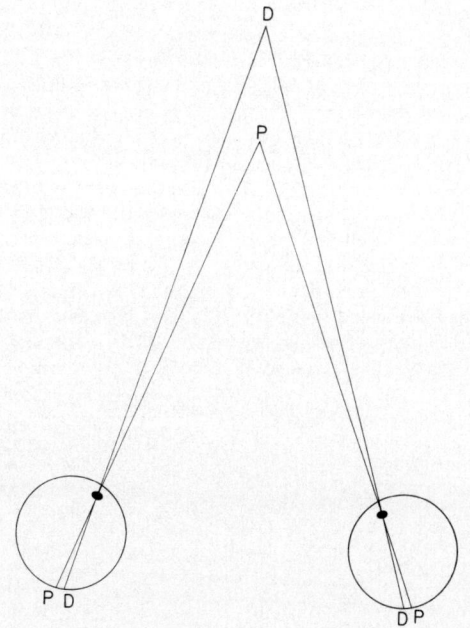

FIG. 29. *Schematic diagram of the basis of stereoscopic perception of distance. Two objects, P and D, at different distances from the observer, are imaged on the two retinae in mutual transposition. In spite of this transposition, only single images of P and D are perceived, but P is perceived as nearer than D. It is possible, however, by supplementary optics, to increase the degree of transposed separation of the images to such an extent that perceptual fusion breaks down, and with it the stereoscopic impression of depth.*

compared, perhaps superposed, and the relative positions of objects in depth are deduced. The whole scheme of depth perception contains more than this, however, and the brain takes account of other depth clues such as focus, probable or typical size of objects, partial screening of some objects by others, perspective regression lines and so on. In the assessment of the truly binocular contribution to depth perception the contributions of these other clues must be carefully allowed for or eliminated.

Stereoscopic depth perception is of great practical service in certain types of rangefinder and, especially, in the plotting of heights and contours from appropriate pairs of aerial photographs, i.e. pairs taken serially with a distance between taking points adequate for the desired sensitivity in height determination. The binocular parallax is given by the formula $p = hx/d^2$ radians, where $h$ is the observer's interpupillary distance, $x$ is the difference in depth between two objects and $d$ is their mean distance from the observer. The smallest detectable parallax, or stereoscopic threshold, is approximately 10 seconds of arc. The corresponding greatest distance of depth perception, taken as the farthest point which can be distinguished from infinity, is 1320 metres.

*Binocular visual summation and independence.* The other binocular capabilities of the eyes are less spectacular than depth perception, but not without interest and practical significance. On the one hand, illumination of one eye, even to a high level, has no effect whatever upon the sensitivity of the other eye (Crawford 1940), and yet the sensitivity of the two eyes working together is greater than that of either eye alone (assuming that both eyes are normal and well-matched). Under static conditions the binocular threshold is about 0·9 of the monocular threshold at the fovea, about 0·8 in the parafovea (8° from the fovea) (Crawford 1940). There is some evidence that the ratio is greater for smaller test areas (Lythgoe and Phillips 1938). It is certainly greater during the course of dark adaptation, about 0·5, reverting to the smaller values when dark adaptation is complete (Fig. 30, adapted from Crawford 1940).

*Binocular alternation. Troxler's effect*, or the fading of a steadily fixated image in the peripheral retina, has been mentioned above, also the devastating effect on the perceived image of stabilization. It is evident that the visual mechanism is subject to fatigue. Under most normal circumstances of vision the two eyes alternate in effective perception. The alternation, at an order of frequency of once per few seconds, is irregular and largely under volitional control. There is substantial overlap of the perceptual periods of the two eyes, so that there is never a black-out, and it is presumably during the overlap periods that binocular depth perception is operative. The alternation is, in fact, only noticeable when there is a marked pattern difference between the retinal images in the two eyes; the insignificant difference between monocular and binocular sensitivity helps to conceal the alternation.

*Binocular asymmetry.* This is fairly common as it affects optical performance and sensitivity; in most cases, the first probably engenders the second, one eye becoming 'dominant', the other 'lazy'. In a more interesting, but very rare, form of asymmetry, one eye has normal colour vision, the other defective. This state might be expected to lead to some elucidation of the colour appearance of the world to colour vision defectives, but in fact has not done so in the few cases reported; the psychological difficulties of description proved insurmountable.

## Illusions, Ambiguities and Incongruities

The differentiation of illusions, ambiguities and incongruities from so-called normal vision is a delicate matter. If visual perception were our only link with the material world, illusions would be non-existent, since all visual appearances would have equal validity; we should only be able to observe, as time went on, that certain appearances were ambiguous. In the case of the illusion shown in Fig. 31, for instance, the lines a b

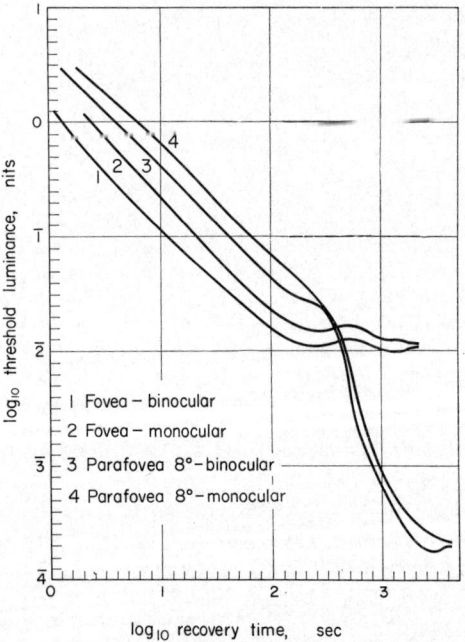

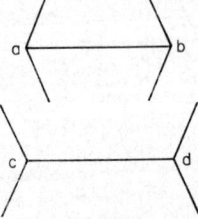

FIG. 30. *Comparison of monocular and binocular recovery of sensitivity during dark-adaptation for one observer with sensibly identical eyes. Note the approximately 2 to 1 ratio of monocular to binocular threshold during dark-adaptation, which diminishes to approximately 1.2 to 1 when dark-adaptation is complete. (After Crawford 1940.)*

FIG. 31. *An optical illusion: the lines ab and cd are actually equal in length, although to most normal observers cd appears the longer (the Müller-Lyer illusion).*

and c d, actually equal in length, but in appearance unequal, might eventually be shown to be equal by juxtaposition of some third object of the same length first with one and then with the other. The ambiguity of Fig. 32 presents a different problem; it is merely a configuration of lines which can be interpreted by analogy in more than one way, but vision alone cannot perceive one

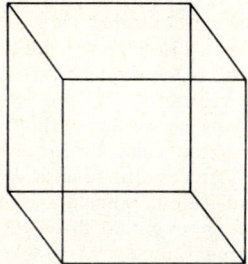

FIG. 32. *An optical ambiguity: most observers can interpret the pattern of lines as a cube viewed obliquely from above, or, with equal ease, from below. Interpretations as various forms of hollow box are added by some observers (the Necker cube).*

way as more real than another. The incongruity of Fig. 33 is different again, being a configuration of lines which cannot be interpreted consistently at all except in parts. It is only the illusion which has two mutually exclusive realities, one perceptual, the other factual.

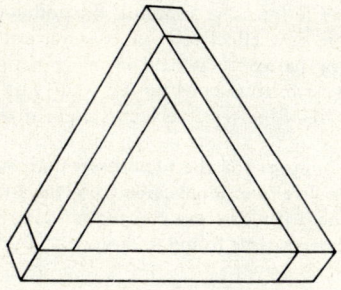

FIG. 33. *An optical incongruity: any one corner of the pattern can be interpreted as a right-angled joint between square section bars, but the whole figure cannot be consistently interpreted.*

### Information Selection

It may be safely asserted that no person, at any time, ever perceives all possible details of the scene in front of him, that is, all the details which the optical and receptive capabilities of his eyes could reveal if he was able to pay attention to them. In other words, there is a high degree of selection in vision, which may be divided under three headings: selection by movement; selection by intrusion; selection by mental attention.

Selection by movement has already been noted in an earlier section, *Movement sensitivity*. Biologically, it can be of extreme importance, drawing attention to the predator approaching with intent to pounce upon its victim, or, contrariwise, to the prey being sought by the hungry predator.

Selection by intrusion is meant to cover those cases in which an object in the field of view is so obtrusive in pattern or contrast that it cannot be passed over, or in which a stimulus to another sense, e.g. a sound, draws attention to a particular visual stimulus. Both forms of intrusion are of fundamental importance in advertising and in signalling, although the latter method is unsuitable for general application in signalling owing to the relatively slow speed of propagation of sound relative to light; if the sound arrives noticeably later than the light it can no longer draw attention to it.

Selection by attention, again, may have great significance in practice as the following example shows. A lecturer quietly draws his coat lapels together so as to conceal his necktie, then asks the audience what colour it is. Although they have been looking at him for, perhaps, half an hour, it is rare indeed that any one of them has perceived the colour of his tie. It is sufficiently obvious that mental attention selects only a very small fraction of the details of the visual field for perception; the art of the conjuror rests heavily on the smallness of this fraction. No exhaustive or quantitative discussion can be given here, but the possible effects of selection should always be borne in mind in the consideration of visual problems, including the enormous variation which can occur both in degree and in kind of visual selection.

*See also:* Perception of colour. Perception, stereopsis as an aspect of.

### Bibliography

BARLOW H. B. and LEVICK W. R. (1965) *J. Physiol.*, **178**, 477.
BAUMGARDT E. and SEGAL J. (1946) *C.R. Soc. Biol.*, **140**, 231.
BAUMGARDT E. and SEGAL J. (1947) *Année Psychol.*, **43**, 54.
BENNETT-CLARKE H. C. and EVANS C. R. (1963) *Nature*, **199**, 1215.
BLOCH A. M. (1885) *C.R. Soc. Biol.*, **37**, 493.
Commission Internationale de l'Éclairage Publication 1.1. International Lighting Vocabulary, 1957.
COPE F. W. (1964) *J. Chem Phys.*, **40**, 2563.
CRAWFORD B. H. (1937), *Proc. Roy. Soc.* B, **123**, 81.
CRAWFORD B. H. (1940) *Proc. Roy. Soc.* B, **128**, 552.
CRAWFORD B. H. (1947) *Proc. Roy. Soc.* B, **134**, 283.
DITCHBURN R. W. and PRITCHARD R. M. (1960) *Quart. J. Exp. Psychol.*, **12**, 26.
DITCHBURN R. W. (1963) *Opt. Acta*, **10**, 325.
GREGORY R. L. (1964) *Nature*, **201**, 1166.
HECHT S. et al. (1933) *J. Gen. Physiol.*, **17**, 237.
HECHT S. et al. (1935) *J. Gen. Physiol.*, **19**, 321.
HECHT S. et al. (1937) *J. Gen. Physiol.*, **20**, 831.
LE GRAND Y. (1957) *Light, Colour and Vision*, (Trans.

by Hunt, Walsh and Hunt) London: Chapman and Hall.
LUCKIESH M. (1944) *Light, Vision and Seeing*, New York: van Nostrand.
LYTHGOE R. J. and PHILLIPS L. R. (1938) *J. Physiol.*, **91**, 427.
MÜLLER-LYER F. C. (1896) *Z. Psychol.*, **9**, 1; **10**, 421.
PADGHAM C. A. (1957) *Opt. Acta*, **4**, 102.
PADGHAM C. A. (1963) *Vision Res.*, **3**, 45.
PEDLER C. (1965) *Proc XIX Int. Congr. Ophthal.*, Delhi, 1962. In press. Also in *Colour Vision: Physiology and Experimental Psychology*, Ciba Foundation Symposium, London: Churchill.
PIRENNE M. H. (1948) *Vision and the Eye*, London: Chapman and Hall.
PIRENNE M. H. and DENTON E. J. (1952) *Nature*, **170**, 1039.
PIRENNE M. H. (1962) *Absolute thresholds and quantum effects* in *The Eye* (Ed. H. Davson) New York: Academic Press.
POLYAK S. (1941) *The Retina*, Chicago: The University Press.
RAMON y CAJAL S. (1894) *Die Retina der Wirbeltiere*, Wiesbaden: Bergmann.
REEVES P. (1917) *Astrophys J.*, **46**, 167; *J. Frank. Inst.*, **184**, 717.
RUCH F. L. (1953) *Psychology and Life*, Chicago: Scott, Foresman and Co.
SCHLAER S. *et al.* (1942) *J. Gen. Physiol.*, **25**, 553.
SCHOLES J. H. (1964) *Nature*, **202**, 572.
STILES W. S. and CRAWFORD B. H. (1933) *Proc. Roy. Soc.*, B, **112**, 428.
THOMAS J. P. (1965) *J. Opt. Soc. Amer.*, **55**, 521. (Source of earlier references to work on Mach bands.)
WALD G. (1965) *Science*, **150**, 1239.
WALRAVEN P. L. (1962) *On the mechanisms of colour vision*, The Netherlands: Institute for Perception RVO-TNO, Soesterberg.
WEINSTEIN C. and ARNULF A. (1946) *Comm. lab. Inst. Opt.*, **2**, 1.
YAGI N. and KOYAMA N. (1963) *The Compound Eye of Lepidoptera*, Tokyo: Maruzen.

B. H. CRAWFORD

**PERCEPTUAL BREAKDOWN WITH STABILIZED IMAGES.** In human beings the eyes are continuously active, this mobility consisting of relatively gross movements under voluntary control, and also of a series of rapid flicks and a fine tremor which the individual is apparently unable to inhibit or modify at will. The complete range of eye movements are discussed in detail elsewhere (see *Eye movements*), but here we may summarize by saying that the larger, voluntary movements have to do with achieving and maintaining foveal fixation, while the function of the involuntry tremor is not yet fully understood.

As a receiver of visual information, the eyes seems to be almost maximally efficient—a single receptor may be excited by a stimulus whose energy has been calculated to be as low as $2 \times 10^{-10}$ ergs. As a collater and interpreter of this information it seems to be doing even better than its basic equipment should permit, for very fine lines can be resolved when the retinal angle subtended by their width is considerably less than that of the smallest single receptor. The question here is simply this; how can a receptor, which may give only an on or off signal, discriminate between two lines of varying thickness, both of which have a smaller diameter than the receptor? The problem is of course insuperable as long as we are dealing with only one receptor. In practice, lines thrown onto the retina involve hundreds and even thousands of receptors, and as Marshall and Talbot pointed out in their classic paper (1942), if one were to include the movements of the image brought about by a rapid, low amplitude tremor of the eye itself, then this 'scanning' would obviously provide extra information through the involvement of an even greater number of receptors. This would seem to suggest that the involuntary eye movements were functional, rather than constituting a kind of 'noise' inevitable in a finely balanced oculomotor system. Proof of this hypothesis might be forthcoming if these fine movements could be inhibited, or controlled for in some way.

Probably the first successful method of compensating for retinal image motion was that of Ditchburn (Ditchburn and Ginsborg 1952). In its simplest form, a pattern was attached to a close-fitting contact lens and a micro-lens provided to bring the pattern into sharp focus on the retina. The stimulus, the contact lens and the eye were now effectively one system, and thus the image of the pattern was held in one position on the back of the eye, thus constituting what was termed a *stabilized retinal image*. One such system is depicted in Fig. 1.

Striking support for the hypothesis that the fine eye movements were functional came from the first observations made with this system, for patterns viewed as stabilized images were found to disappear. Furthermore,

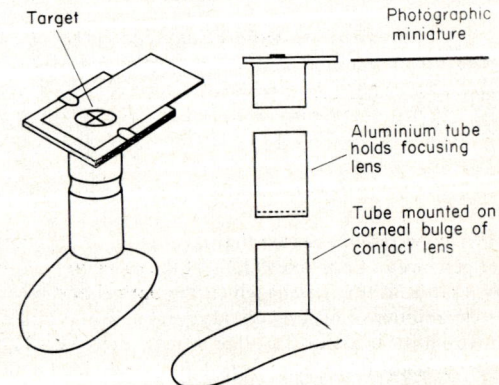

FIG. 1. *A simple system for producing a stabilized retinal image. Eye, lens and pattern move as one and shifts of the image across the retina are, in theory, negated.*

observers were surprised to note that they disappeared frequently *in part*, regenerating sometimes in whole, sometimes in part, and then subsequently fragmenting again. Typical fragmentations when a particular pattern—in this case a circle with an inscribed cross—is viewed are shown in Fig. 2.

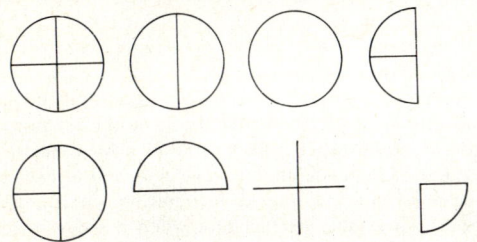

FIG. 2. *Typical fragmentation effects when a pattern (a circle with an inscribed cross) is viewed as a stabilized image. Fragments come and go, with individual straight lines, the most common units involved.*

Now the fading and disappearance of stabilized patterns was not in itself a surprise, and merely seemed to support the hypothesis advanced by Marshall and Talbot. The partial and non-random nature of the disappearance and reappearance was another matter, for it suggested that simple explanations of the loss of perception in terms of retinal fatigue were not really tenable. Some more central process seemed to be involved, for the unitary disappearance of straight lines, curves etc. subtending as much as 5 or 10 degrees of arc implied principles of organization which would seem most unlikely to be retinally determined.

Early experiments sought to confirm the non-random nature of the fragmentation, and to relate the phenomena to current psychological theory. Patterns such as those depicted in Fig. 3 were studied both qualitatively by Pritchard *et al.* (1960) and quantitatively by Evans (1965) with intriguing if somewhat puzzling results. In Pritchard's studies, for example, it was reported that the 'meaningful' line shaped rather like a face was less liable to fragment or disappear than its 'meaningless' analogue. Quantitative studies showed that figures with angles and intersections were more liable to disappear than less jagged, smoother ones. Of all enclosed figures, the circle disappeared least of all, and the most common single fragmenting unit was the straight line. However, apart from a tenuous link with the rather antiquated Gestalt Theory (which drew attention to the ordered discontinuities experienced in the visual world), the odd phenomena noted with stabilized images seemed to add little to help in our understanding of the nature of perception.

At about the time when fragmentation effects were beginning to attract the attention of psychologists, some very striking animal experiments were being performed which were immediately realized as having great significance for perceptual theory, but whose relationship to stabilized image work at first passed unnoticed. The work in question was that of the physiologists D. H. Hubel and T. N. Wiesel (1959, 1962), and it was performed on the visual system of the cat. At the present time microelectrode techniques have become sufficiently refined to permit the recording of signals from individual cell bodies in the brain. Thus one can study the action of selected parts of the visual system in a novel way. Individual cells, as Hubel and Wiesel showed, behave in interesting and revealing ways. One cell, for example, may give sustained bursts of firing when the cat is shown a vertical line, and yet when the same line is shown in a different orientation, it may remain silent. At the same time, another cell in the same area of the brain which had previously not fired when the cat was viewing the vertical line, might now suddenly commence firing at the horizontal stimulus. The implication of these findings is that the cat's visual processing system operates on a classificatory basis—a fact which had been suspected for years but which awaited experimental confirmation.

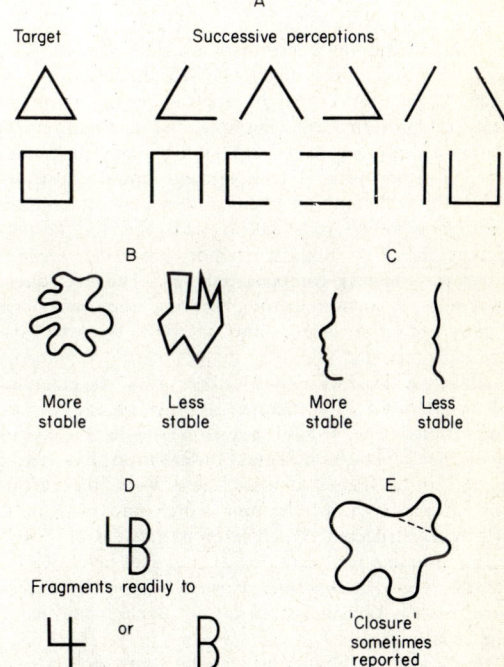

FIG. 3. *Some patterns used in early studies. The phenomena attracted the attention of psychologists and physiologists because of their possible significance to perceptual theory.*

A classificatory system of this sort, in which cells in the cortex each have 'receptive fields' of cells in the retina would be an economical recognition system, and one that might just as well function, possibly with greater complexity, in Man. Gestalt psychology has long been interested in the structural bases of perception which are revealed in the tendency of dots to cluster, or for a series of lines to be seen as a continuous whole. To many this has always seemed to constitute evidence for a classificatory system of perception, and to these and to the Gestalt theorists, the very characteristic fragmentation phenomena of stabilization seemed to have great significance.

In 1963 however, a critical paper by H. B. Barlow (1963) questioned the degree of stabilization achieved by contact lenses. Barlow flashed a brief, but very intense light through a stabilizing system of his own devising in which the 'contact lens' was given extra adhesion through suction bulbs. The flash of light produced an after image, which of course consisted of changes in the state of the retinal cells themselves and was therefore a perfectly stabilized image. Subjects were then able to compare, for the minute or so for which the after image remained visible, its position relative to the image formed by the contact lens optical system. They found that shifts of the latter were occurring relative to the presumably immobile after image, and that these shifts were variable in extent and might be as great as 30 minutes of arc. Barlow justly pointed out that his findings questioned much of the theoretical speculation which had followed the discovery of image fragmentation. Might not the partial reappearances of patterns, for example, be a function of differential contact lens slip along one particular plane? Furthermore, if lens slippage could cause destabilization of contours over as much as 30 minutes of arc, how much justification had one for assuming that the physiological tremor (covering *seconds* of arc) was reliably compensated for? The first question could be answered by observing the behaviour of *patterned after images*, and in 1963 Bennet-Clark and Evans reported that after images of simple patterns —such as the circle with an inscribed cross—fragmented and regenerated in a manner typical of the earlier observations. The second question was less easy to answer, but a curious incidental observation (Evans and Piggins 1963) suggested that there were theoretical ramifications to the whole topic which had not previously been suspected. When large patterns are viewed in dim illumination with head and eyes held steady, but *without any attempt at compensating for the physiological tremor*, typical 'stabilization' phenomena occur quite reliably.

Thus when one now considers the three methods of compensating for retinal image motion (a) steady fixation in poor illumination, (b) partial stabilization with contact lens, and (c) complete stabilization through the use of an after image, it becomes evident that inhibition or cancellation of the effects of the fine tremor is not a necessary condition for the loss of perception and systematic fragmentation.

Current research is taking the approach that the criterion for fragmentation effects to take place, is not that an image should be held in one position on the retina, but rather that information about the pattern and its contours should be restricted in some way.

This restriction may be done in a number of ways, not all of which will require a perfectly stabilized image; for example it has lately been discovered that when patterns are presented briefly (say for one hundredth of a second) on a screen or in a tachistoscope, after repeated, suitably spaced presentations *at the same exposure time*, subjects report the perception of fragments rather than the whole of the pattern, and that these fragments correspond to those reported in orthodox stabilization studies.

Present trends in research seem to suggest that emphasis has shifted away from the study of the phenomenology of stabilization effects and is now concerned with the use of the stabilized image as a tool to explore the workings of the human recognition system. For example, if we take the fact that when a *single* line is viewed as a stabilized image (in the case of the experiments described, as an after image) it may sometimes be seen to vanish as a whole, and sometimes seen to break up into parts. This might be interpreted as indicating the presence of specific cell systems in the retina, sensitive to straight lines and perhaps analogous to the Hubel and Wiesel 'receptive fields'. A model such as that schematically presented in Fig. 4 grows from this assumption and can be simply tested. Figure 5

FIG. 4. *Hypothetical model to illustrate a possible mechanism for unitary and fragmentary action of a single straight line. The vertical dotted line represents a perceptual unit whose component cells fire in unison. A short stabilized line falling as in (a) will either be seen as a unit or vanish as a unit. When overlapping as in (b) it would be expected to fragment. As line length increases, (c), (d) and (e) probability of unitary action should fall, and of fragmentation should rise.*

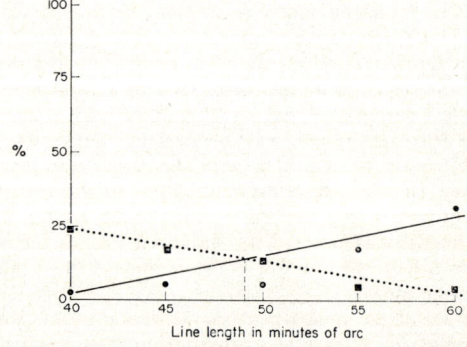

FIG. 5. *Typical result illustrating change in probability of unitary action (dotted line) or fragmentation (solid line) with increase in size of stabilized line. Crossover point of two curves indicates half size of receptive units.*

in fact shows a typical result of such a test; here the data is obtained from foveal positioning of the after images. As can be seen, fragmentation increases in probability as does the length of the stimulus-line, while unitary action falls off. The cross-over point of the lines indicate the presence of 'receptive units' somewhat over one and a half degrees in length. Much larger units have been found in the periphery of the retina, and there appears to be evidence of units specific to curved lines and to various other shapes. It is clear that one of the most interesting roles to which the perfectly stabilized image (after image) may be put, is as a tool for retinal mapping which allows a more basically physiological approach to the problem than is normally feasible with human subjects.

See also: Gestalt psychology. Neuronal nets. Perception, visual.

*Bibliography*

BARLOW H. B. (1963) *Slippage of contact lenses and other artefacts in relation to fading and regeneration of supposedly stable retinal images*, Quart. J. exp. Psychol. **15**, 36.
BENNET-CLARK H. C. and EVANS C. R. (1963) *Fragmentation of patterned targets when viewed as prolonged afterimages*, Nature, **199**, 1215.
DITCHBURN R. W. and GINSBORG B. L. (1952) *Vision with a stabilized retinal image*, Nature, **170**, 36.
EVANS C. R. and PIGGINS D. J. (1963) *A comparison of the behaviour of geometrical shapes when viewed under conditions of steady fixation and, with apparatus for producing a stabilized retinal image*, Brit. J. physiol. Optics, **20**, 1.
EVANS C. R. (1965) *Some studies of pattern perception using a stabilized retinal image*, Brit. J. Psychol. **56**, 2 and 3, 121.
HUBEL D. H. and WIESEL T. N. (1959) *Receptive fields of single neurones in the cat's striate cortex*, J. Physiol. **148**, 574.
HUBEL D. H. and WIESEL T. N. (1962) *Receptive fields, binocular interaction and functional architecture in the cat's visual cortex*, J. Physiol. **160**, 106.
MARSHALL W. H. and TALBOT S. A. (1942) *Recent evidence for neural mechanisms in vision leading to a general theory of sensory acuity*, in Kluver H., *Visual Mechanisms*, Biol. Symp. **7**, 117.
PRITCHARD R. M., HERON W. and HEBB D. O. (1960) *Visual perception approached by the method of stabilized images*, Canad. J. Psychol. **14**, 2, 67.

C. R. EVANS

**PHONETICS, ACOUSTIC.** This is the branch of experimental phonetics which deals specifically with the acoustic description and classification of speech sounds and with the relations between acoustic features and linguistic units. Two principal lines of work in acoustic phonetics may be distinguished: first, the study of the *speech mechanism* as a physical system for generating sounds of different kinds with a view to establishing its modes of operation and its physical constants, and second, the measurement, classification and isolation of *acoustic characteristics* which are correlated with the occurrence of *linguistic units* and which form their realization at the acoustic level.

*The carrier nature of speech.* The speech mechanism, viewed acoustically, is generally thought of as a device for generating a *carrier-wave* (the *larynx tone*) which is modulated in a number of ways by the action of the complex set of cavities to which the generator is coupled. It is necessary therefore to examine the properties of the *glottal wave*, the *source function*, and the properties of the vocal tract, the *system function*, and to derive some notion of the time course of characteristic changes in both of these.

*The source function.* Basically the carrier for speech is provided by the opening and closing action of the *vocal cords* when they are vibrating. The laryngeal muscles approximate the edges of the vocal cords, thus interrupting the flow of expired air from the lungs. This closure withstands a certain rise in pressure on the underside of the cords, depending on the force exerted by the larynx muscles, and when the pressure becomes too great, the cords part, releasing a pulse of increased pressure into the tract above the larynx. The elastic nature of the tissues forming the vocal folds together with suction effects which arise on their underside restore the cords to their closed position and the cycle of movement begins again.

It is difficult to arrive at the exact form of the pulse-wave generated by the larynx. The closest estimates have been obtained by taking high-speed pictures of the cords reflected in a laryngeal mirror and plotting changes in area of the space between the cords. The result is a wave showing pulses of generally triangular form, separated by intervals corresponding to the duration of the closed phase of the vocal cord action. A sample plot obtained in this way is shown in Fig. 1(a). The time relations

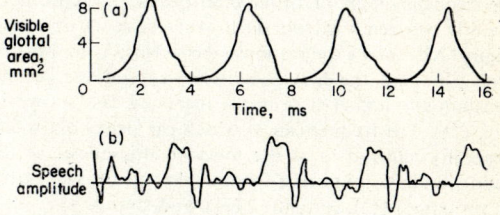

FIG. 1 (a) *Variation in glottal area during the production of a vowel of the type* [a]. (b) *Wave-form of the sound from the speaker's lips during the same period, recorded at a distance of 4″. (From: J. S. Gill, Estimation of larynx-pulse timing during speech, Proc. 4th Int. Cong Acoustics, Copenhagen, 1962.)*

of the open and closed phases of the cord movement vary considerably from speaker to speaker and from one moment to another; the open phase is likely to range from 0·3 to 0·7 of the period of the whole cycle. The period of successive cycles varies continuously during speech; this is one of the factors which distinguish speech from singing. The periodicity or fundamental frequency of the glottal wave is highly correlated with the pitch of the sound heard by the listener. The amplitude of the glottal pulses is correlated with the loudness of the speech for the listener, and variations in the timing and the form of the pulses are correlated with differences in voice quality in the speaker.

*The system function.* The glottal wave is applied to the vocal tract above the larynx, that is to a tube of varying cross-sectional area and about 17 cm in length in the adult male speaker. This tube acts as a transmission path having specific physical properties and coupled to the outside air at the lips and/or at the nostrils. The main effect of transmission along this path, apart from the inevitable loss of energy through absorption, is to change the relative amplitudes of the frequency components which make up the glottal wave. This effect can be seen from the wave-form shown in Fig. 1(b) which is the amplitude curve registered at the mouth of the speaker during the sound which gave rise to the glottal area curve of Fig 1(a). The simplest view of this transformation of the glottal wave is that the vocal tract constitutes a series of *filters* each of which modifies the amplitude of frequencies within a certain band, and effectively introduces an amplitude peak in the spectrum of the complex sound issuing from the mouth. It has been calculated that, if the vocal tract were a cylindrical tube of uniform cross-section, and given a tube length of about 17 cm, the effect of the filters would be to introduce peaks in the sound spectrum at approximately 500, 1500, 2500 and 3500 c.p.s. In these conditions the frequency response of the tract would be given by the curve in Fig. 2(a) and the resulting sound would have the quality of a neutral (central) vowel (ǝ). In fact the cross-sectional area of the tract varies throughout its length and also varies continuously in speech owing to the movement of the body of the tongue. The effect of this is to shift the frequency location of the filter peaks, particularly of the first two, reading from the lowest frequency upwards. Figure 2(b) shows the response curve for a sound of the type [i] where the first peak is lower and the second substantially higher than in the idealized case shown in Fig. 2(a). The frequencies at which the peaks occur are generally referred to as the *formant* frequencies of the sound, and are numbered from the lowest peak upwards as formant 1 (F1), formant 2 (F2) and so on.

This very much simplified account of the acoustic system used in speech must be amplified by adding that the source and system arrangement just described holds good for a large part of the time spent in normal utterance, but provides only for the case in which there is a single source function and that function is periodic. In whispered speech, the source is again at the glottis but now generates random noise instead of periodic pulses. The noise is transmitted through the vocal tract which shapes the noise much in the same way as it shapes the glottal wave in voiced speech. In many consonant sounds, however, either an alternative or a second sound generator is temporarily established at some level in the vocal tract other than the glottis. For sounds

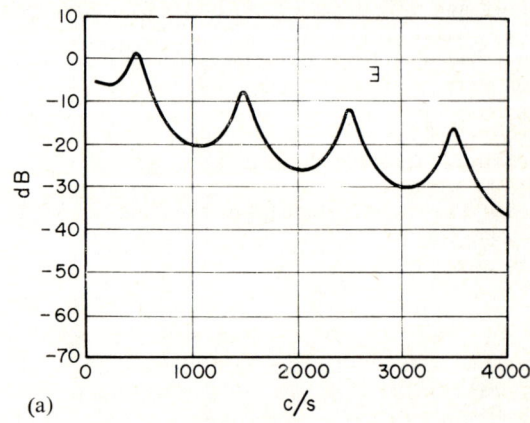

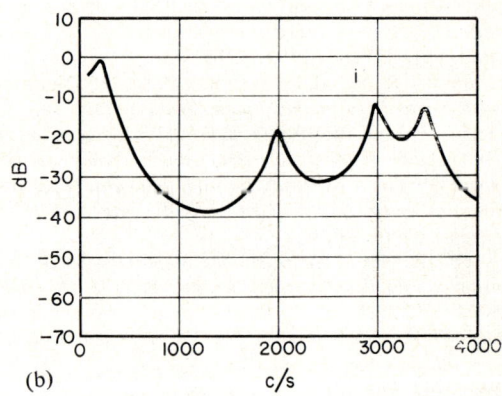

FIG. 2 (a) *Curve showing the transmission characteristics of the idealised vocal tract (viewed as an open cylindrical tube).* (b) *Transmission characteristics of the vocal tract modified to produce a vowel of the type [i]. (From: G. Fant, Acoustic Theory of Speech Production.)*

of the [s]-type, for example, a noise generator at the level of the upper teeth ridge creates turbulence in the airstream; for sounds of the [f]-type, the generator is at the level of the lower lip. In such cases the acoustic mechanism is still that of a sound source coupled to a transmission system, but these sounds differ from the periodic sounds and from each other in the characteristics of the source function and in the point at which the source is coupled to the vocal tract. In the voiced counterparts of such sounds, e.g. [z], [v], there are two sources, the one at the larynx generating a periodic pulse-wave, and the one further forward generating noise.

One further complication is presented by the case in which the vocal tract transmission system is modified by the addition of a branch tube, provided by the opening of the air path through the naso-pharynx. This is the situation during the production of nasal or nasalised sounds in speech. In the simplest terms, the addition of the nasal branch to the transmission system has the effect of broadening the resonances of the vocal tract and of introducing an anti-resonance somewhere in the region of 1200 to 1800 c.p.s.

The speech mechanism viewed as an acoustic generator may therefore consist of one or two sources of sound energy, providing periodic and aperiodic waves, coupled to a single tube or a tube plus a side-branch. Such a mechanism necessarily creates acoustic effects of the greatest complexity, a complexity which is reflected in the time variations of the sound-waves which issue from the speaker's mouth and nose.

*Acoustic analysis of speech sounds.* The method adopted in acoustic phonetics to impose some recognizable order on observations of the speech sound-waves and to provide at the same time a basis for establishing linguistic-acoustic correlations is to make a frequency analysis, usually with the aid of the *sound spectrograph*, a device for carrying out frequency analysis of sounds so as to show the location of the formants and the relative amplitude of the frequency components in the spectrum. In this instrument, a recorded utterance is passed through a set of electronic filters covering the range of frequencies occurring in speech, and the level of acoustic energy in each filter band is registered at succeeding moments during the utterance. The results of the analysis are usually presented in a three-dimensional visible display in which variations in energy level with time are recorded on the horizontal axis, variations with frequency on the vertical axis and the energy differences themselves appear in the darkness of the trace in the recorded pattern. In such a device, time and frequency resolution are interdependent and are determined by the width of the filter bands used. A commonly used instrument offers a choice of two band-widths, 45 and 300 c.p.s. With the first of these settings the frequency resolution makes it possible to record the energy in individual harmonics of the vocal tone, but the time constant of the system is of the order of 20 msec; the second setting will not show separate harmonics except in high notes but will record time changes down to about 4 msec, such as, for example, the amplitude peaks resulting from each opening of the vocal cords.

*Acoustic-linguistic correlations.* Acoustic measurements of speech can be made with respect to fundamental frequency, over-all intensity, spectral distribution of energy and the duration of specific acoustic features. The main purpose of such measurements is to form a basis for correlating acoustic properties with the occurrence of *linguistic units*. A factor of the greatest importance in this connexion is that single linguistic entities are represented at the acoustic level by a scatter of measured values so that correlations can be established only in terms of the range and distribution of the data. Variations in fundamental frequency are correlated with the occurrence of *tone* and *intonation* patterns and also with *stress* and *rhythmic* pattern. Changes in over-all intensity form one correlate of stress and rhythm units but are also correlated with sequential changes in the phonemic string. The principal correlate of the *phonemic sequence*, however, is variation in the spectral distribution of energy and this is one reason for the very widespread use of the sound spectrograph in acoustic phonetic research. The sound spectrogram affords a means of detecting, in the first instance merely by inspection, points in time at which there is a marked change in the location of peaks of acoustic energy or a changeover from periodic to noise source and vice versa. The frequency location of the formants at any instant can be readily seen together with the rapid changes of formant frequency with time *(formant transitions)* which have proved to be important cues for the recognition of certain classes of speech sound by the listener.

One of the major tasks of acoustic phonetics lies in the isolation and specification of acoustic cues which operate in everyday communication by speech. Results already obtained show some of the general lines along which speech recognition works and indicate in particular that the time course of acoustic events, that is not only the duration of given features but also their rate of change, is the vehicle for many of the *oppositions* upon which the linguistic structure depends.

*Bibliography*

FANT G. (1960) *Acoustic Theory of Speech Production*, 's-Gravenhage.
FLANAGAN J. L. (1965) *Speech Analysis, Synthesis and Perception*, Berlin.
FLETCHER H. (1953) *Speech and Hearing in Communication*, Princeton: The University Press.
FRY D. B. (1965) *The Mechanism of Normal Speech*, in *Diseases of the Ear, Nose and Throat* (Eds. W. G. Scott-Brown, J. Ballantyne and J. Groves) (2nd Edn), London.
JOOS M. (1948) *Acoustic Phonetics*, Language *Monograph* 23, Baltimore: Linguistic Society of America.

D. B. FRY

**PHONETICS, ARTICULATORY.** This is the study of the production of speech sounds in terms of the movements of the organs of speech involved. Such study may involve direct visual, proprioceptive, instrumental or radiographic observation. An exhaustive discussion of the physiological bases of articulation may be found in Arnold (1957); the most detailed phonetic treatment is that by Pike (1943).

There are no 'organs of speech' as such: all the organs concerned have other, primary, physiological functions.

The lungs and the nasal passages, and the trachea and pharynx which connect them, are primarily used for respiration; the lips, tongue and teeth are used for chewing, sucking in, and swallowing food and drink; while the pharynx acts as a junction box to keep these two functions from interfering with one another, by means of two valves—an upper one, the soft palate, which can close off either, neither, or both of the mouth and nasal cavities, and a lower one, the epiglottis, which performs the same task for the oesophagus (leading to the stomach) and the trachea. The larynx, the box which contains the so-called vocal cords, not only protects the lungs from the entry of foreign bodies, but also provides a strong air-tight closure to the lung cavity, which facilitates muscular effort by the arms or abdomen.

Almost all speech can be regarded as a modified form of exhalation, the air expelled by the lungs being subjected to some kind of obstruction or interruption before being allowed to leave the body.

The first place where the air-stream, having left the lungs, may encounter an obstruction, is the *Larynx*. This is a box-like structure of cartilage and muscle, and contains two folds of ligament and elastic tissue running horizontally from back to front (the *Vocal cords*), whose position can be varied by the action of the arytenoid cartilages. The opening between the vocal cords is known as the *Glottis*.

The vocal cords may be kept apart (glottis open), or brought together so as to close the air passage completely (glottis closed). They may also be narrowed, as for whispering. When they are brought close together and air is forced between them, they vibrate, producing *Voice*. This, their most important function in speech, is known as *Phonation*.

Leaving the larynx, the expelled air passes into the *Pharynx*. Its further route is then determined by the *Soft palate*, which, as mentioned above, controls entry into the nasal cavity. If the soft palate is lowered, the air is free to pass out through the nose, producing nasal consonants, e.g. [m, n, ŋ], or nasalized vowels, such as the French [ɛ̃, ã], depending on whether or not there is a closure somewhere within the mouth. For all other types of consonant and vowel the soft palate is raised, and the air is channelled through the mouth only.

The most varied and intricate adjustments in the articulation of speech sounds occur within the mouth cavity. The organs here may be divided into two classes: the Passive articulators, whose position is relatively fixed (teeth; alveolar ridge; hard palate; upper jaw), and the Active articulators, which are movable (lips; the various parts of the tongue; soft palate and uvula). (See Fig.).

It is usual, for descriptive purposes, to divide the roof of the mouth into three zones: the *Alveolar ridge*, the ridge of gum which can be clearly felt with the tongue just behind the upper teeth; the *Hard palate*, the bony arch behind it; and, further back still, the *Soft palate* (or *Velum*), mentioned above. Hanging from the end of the soft palate is the *Uvula*, a fleshy appendage.

Of all the organs of speech, the *Tongue* is by far the most flexible and variable. Although physiologically it consists of one mass of flesh showing no obvious superficial divisions, it is useful to be able to describe its position in some detail. For this reason it is conventionally divided into the Back (opposite the soft palate when the tongue is at rest, the highest part in the articulation of *back* vowels such as [u, o]), the Front (opposite the hard palate, and the highest part in the articulation of *front* vowels such as [i, e, y]), and the Blade (the tapering part facing the alveolar ridge). At the end of the blade is the Tip.

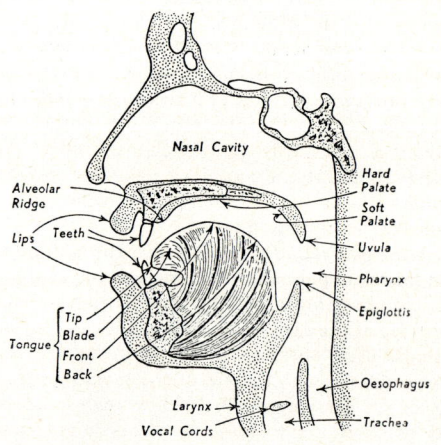

The last organs passed by the air-stream on its outward path through the mouth are the *Lips*. They, too, are highly flexible; they may be spread, narrowed, closed, opened, protruded, and retracted.

An alphabetical listing of the principal phonetic terms descriptive of *Place of articulation* is as follows:

| term | stricture between |
| --- | --- |
| Alveolar | tip or blade of tongue and alveolar ridge |
| Alveolo-palatal | front of tongue and hard palate, also blade of tongue and alveolar ridge |
| Apical* | tip or blade of tongue and upper teeth or alveolar ridge |
| Bilabial | upper and lower lips |
| Dental | tip or blade of tongue and upper teeth |
| Dorsal* | front or back of tongue and hard or soft palate |
| Glottal | left and right vocal cords |
| Interdental | tip or blade of tongue between upper and lower teeth |
| Labial* | upper lip or teeth and lower lip |
| Labio-dental | upper teeth and lower lip |
| Labio-velar | upper and lower lips, also back of tongue and soft palate |

*These are cover terms having hyponyms as follows: Apical = (inter)dental/(palato-, post-)alveolar/ retroflex; Dorsal = (alveolo-)palatal/ velar/ uvular; Labial = bilabial/ labio-dental.

| term | stricture between |
|---|---|
| Palatal | front of tongue and hard palate |
| Palato-alveolar | blade of tongue and alveolar ridge, also front of tongue and hard palate |
| Pharyng(e)al | pharynx wall and root of tongue |
| Post-alveolar | tip or blade of tongue and area immediately behind alveolar ridge |
| Retroflex | inverted tip of tongue and alveolar ridge |
| Uvular | uvula and back of tongue |
| Velar | back of tongue and soft palate. |

Some consonants involve a complete closure somewhere in the mouth—for example English [p, b] (bilabial closure), [t, d] (alveolar closure), [k, g] (velar closure). The soft palate is raised for these sounds, thereby preventing the air escaping through the nose; since it cannot escape through the mouth either, because of the complete closure there, it is entirely obstructed. This obstruction normally lasts only a brief moment, however, before the organs concerned are separated again because of the articulation of the next sound. Consonants of this kind are termed *Plosives* (or alternatively *Stops*).

For other kinds of consonant the obstruction (or *Stricture*) in the mouth is not so complete. Instead of being fully closed, the articulating organs may merely be held closely together—not so closely as to stop the air flow, but closely enough to give rise to *Friction* (air turbulence resulting in a temporally random, aperiodic acoustic component). Thus for English [f, v] there is friction produced by labiodental stricture; for the *th* sounds, [θ, ð], interdental or dental friction; for [s, z], friction between the grooved blade of the tongue and the alveolar ridge; and for the 'shushing' consonants heard in *ash, pleasure* (phonetic symbols [ʃ, ʒ]), palato-alveolar friction. These consonants are termed *Fricatives*.

For *Laterals* (*l*-sounds), the tongue articulates against the roof of the mouth (usually the teeth or the alveolar ridge) in the same way as for plosives, but the side rims of the tongue are not raised to make contact with the upper molars; the air can thus escape over the sides of the tongue and pass round the obstruction. In the case of *Fricative Laterals*, friction is brought about by narrowing between the side rims of the tongue and the molars.

With *Nasals*, as mentioned above, the soft palate is lowered, allowing the air to pass out by way of the nasal cavity; but there is also a complete closure in the mouth, as for plosives—bilabial for [m], alveolar for the English [n], and velar for [ŋ], the English *ng*-sound.

*Rolls* (or *Trills*) are rapid intermittent closures ('taps') made by a flexible active articulator against a firm passive articulator. Examples are [r], the 'trilled *r*' or *Lingual roll* used in Italian, Russian, etc., and the *Uvular roll*, [ʀ], characteristic of some kinds of French. Bilabial and epiglottal rolls may also be encountered. An articulation of a similar nature but involving just a single tap is called a *Flap*, e.g. the [r] used intervocalically for /r/ by some English speakers.

The remaining consonantal types of speech sound are *Frictionless continuants* and *Semivowels*. The former are related in articulation to fricatives, but the stricture between the articulators is so weak that no friction is produced. Thus the labiodental frictionless continuant [v], used in Dutch and in many Indian languages, and as a common variety (usually considered defective) of English /r/, is like a very weak [v]. The /r/ of English *drain* is usually a post-alveolar fricative, but that of *rain* a post-alveolar frictionless continuant. Semivowels are gliding, vowel-like sounds: English *y* and *w* are similar in articulation to the vowels [i] and [u], i.e. they are phonetically VOCOID, although their function in the language is consonantal—like other consonants, they typically occur at syllable margins (*yet, wet*—cf. *bet, set, let*) rather than, like vowels, between consonants. The category of semivowel is thus phonologically oriented. For a discussion of the classification and articulation of vocoids (i.e. semivowels, vowels, diphthongs, etc.), see *Phonetics, auditory*.

Plosives may be *Released* in various ways. The simplest is by the straightforward separation of the articulators involved. The entire plosive then has phases as follows:

(i) *Approach* of the articulators.
(ii) *Hold, Compression*, or *Tenue:* articulators remain together, while the airstream builds up behind the closure.
(iii) *Release* or *(Ex)plosion:* articulators separate.

Plosives may alternatively be released by the lowering of the soft palate, allowing the airstream to escape via the nasal cavity while the primary articulators retain their position (Nasal release, e.g. the [d] in *midnight*); by the conversion of the closure to a partial one, e.g. the lowering of the side rims of the tongue while the tip retains its alveolar contact (Lateral release, e.g. the [d] in *sadly*); or the release may not be audible—either because of the formation of another plosive before the first has been released (the so-called Incomplete plosives, e.g. the [k] in the common pronunciation of *actor*—a feature of English phonetics not usually found in the phonetics of other languages), or because the release is not made at all until after the air compression behind the closure has weakened with the ending of pressure from the lungs (Unreleased or Unexploded plosives, as sometimes in utterance-final *rip, rib*).

A normally released plosive may be characterized by unusually slow separation of the articulators, so that a fricative at the same place of articulation is produced during the release. The resultant sequence of plosive plus homorganic fricative is known as an *Affricate*. Examples are [tʃ, dʒ], the palato-alveolar affricates of English *church, judge*.

There follows an alphabetical listing of the principal phonetic terms descriptive of *Manner of Articulation:*

| | |
|---|---|
| *Affricate* | complete closure, with fricative release |
| *Flap* | single tap |

| | |
|---|---|
| *Fricative* | narrowing causing friction |
| *Frictionless* | |
| *Continuant* | narrowing not causing friction |
| *Lateral* | partial closure |
| *Nasal* | complete closure in the mouth, but soft palate lowered |
| *Plosive* | complete closure, behind which air builds up |
| *Roll* | rapid intermittent closure |
| *Semi-Vowel* | vowel-like articulation |
| *Spirant* | = Fricative |
| *Stop* | = Plosive |
| *Trill* | = Roll |

In English and other Germanic languages (with the exception of Dutch), it is usual for voiceless plosives initial in a stressed syllable to be followed by a brief flow of air, after the release of the plosive but before the onset of phonation for the following vowel. Such plosives are termed *Aspirated*.

A rough phonetic classification of a sound may be achieved by attaching to it a tripartite label defining it in terms of Voicing, Place of articulation, and Manner of articulation. Representative allophones of some English phonemes may thus be classified as follows:

- [t] voiceless alveolar plosive
- [v] voiced labio-dental
- [m] voiced bilabial nasal
- [l] voiced alveolar lateral
- [r] voiced post-alveolar frictionless continuant.

However, it may sometimes be desired to describe some particular [t], say, more precisely by characterizing it also by other features, such as by its manner of release (nasally released, aspirated, etc.): or by the mentioning of *Secondary articulations*. Thus, in addition to the alveolar contact, there may be lip-rounding or *Labialization*, as in the case of the labialized [t] in *twin*, or raising of the front of the tongue towards the hard palate, as in the Palatalized [t] of *tune*. The so-called *dark l* used before consonants in English is a Velarized [l], that is, it has a secondary articulation consisting of the raising of the back of the tongue in the direction of the soft palate. Terms referring to secondary articulations end in *-ized, -ization*.

In some languages Simultaneous articulations (double articulations) occur, e.g. the labiovelar plosives [kp, gb] of certain African languages.

A voiceless/voiced pair such as English [s, z] are distinguished not only by voicing but also by the breath force and muscular effort involved. In fact some English realizations of /z/ are not voiced, although weakly articulated in comparison with realizations of /s/. To account for this feature, [s] is defined as *Fortis* and [z] as *Lenis*. If *dig* is said in isolation, the [d] and [g], while remaining lenis, may be in fact voiceless; they do not nevertheless become identical with [t, k]. In the French word *digue* /dig/, however, the consonants are always fully voiced.

Some sounds are articulated without the use of air passing from the lungs. Examples are the *Ejectives* and *Implosives* used in various languages, which are made with the glottis closed and the airstream (egressive or ingressive respectively) initiated in the pharynx, and the Clicks (e.g. the English paralinguistic 'tut-tut', a voiceless alveolar click) and Reverse clicks made with a velar closure and airstream initiated in the mouth.

The principal disadvantage in the methods of articulatory description outlined above is that they tend to obscure the fact that the organs of speech are in constant movement rather than in a succession of postures. The usual description of phonetic segments should, for an adequate analysis of the articulations involved, be supplemented by a description in terms of phonetic (physiological) parameters.

*Bibliography*

ARNOLD G. E. (1957) *Morphology and physiology of the speech organs*, in (Kaiser L. Ed.) *Manual of Phonetics*, Amsterdam: North-Holland.
GIMSON A. C. (1962) *An Introduction to the Pronunciation of English*, London: Arnold.
PIKE K. L. (1943) *Phonetics. A critical analysis of phonetic theory and a technic for the practical description of sounds*, Ann Arbor: University of Michigan Press.

J. C. WELLS

**PHONETICS, AUDITORY.** This is the study of speech sounds in terms of the subjective impression they bring about in the listener. Although such study is necessarily introspective and individual, it nevertheless constitutes the most accurate way yet known of analysing and classifying vocoids (vowels and vowel-like sounds). It is also the basis for the phonetic-paedagogic technique of ear-training, whereby a person's ability to discriminate and idenfity sound-types may be enormously enhanced.

These two aspects of auditory phonetics are treated separately below. (See also Gimson 1962; Jones 1957.)

*1. Classification of Vocoids*

The classification of vowels and diphthongs must inevitably differ from that of consonant-type sounds. *Consonants* usually involve some kind of narrowing or closure within the mouth; the manner (degree of stricture) and place of articulation can then be pin-pointed without much difficulty. The articulation can be felt proprioceptively by the speaker, and may often be observed visually. In the case of *vocoids*, on the other hand, there is no closure or marked narrowing within the mouth and little proprioceptive sensation of the articulation. It is for these reasons that for the analysis of vocoids the techniques of articulatory phonetics must be supplemented by those of auditory phonetics. A vowel description is normally dependent mainly on auditory judgments of sound relationships, together with a certain amount of articulatory description (notably re lip position). It is, however, customary to describe the results of auditory judgments in articulatory or pseudo-articulatory terms, e.g. 'front' 'close', 'retroflex'. (Vocoids, like consonants, may also be analysed by investigation of the physical nature of the sound involved: see *Phonetics, acoustic*.)

Vocoids may be defined as *median-oral frictionless continuants*, i.e. sounds during which the air escapes over the centre of the tongue without friction in the mouth: see *Phonetics, articulatory*. This sound-type includes almost all *vowels*, *diphthongs* and *semi-vowels*.

In any such sound there is a certain amount of space between the tongue and the roof of the mouth. If this space is reduced by the raising of the tongue, there will come a point when friction is produced. The set of such points is known as the *vowel limit line*. If a prolonged *eee*-sound (symbolized as [i:]) is made, and the body of the tongue pressed progressively closer against the roof of the mouth, the sound will first acquire a 'noise' component, as it becomes a voiced palatal fricative, and then entirely block the flow of air, as it becomes a voiced palatal plosive. Likewise, an *ooo*-sound, [u:], will turn into a kind of velar fricative when 'tightened' by raising the back of the tongue further towards the soft palate. The vowel limit line thus defined is one of the reference points used in vowel description. It is the 'close' extremity of the dimension of classification labelled articulatorily *tongue height*, extending from *CLOSE* (e.g. [i:]) to *OPEN* (e.g. [ɑ:]).

The other principal dimension of vocoid classification is labelled, again articulatorily, *tongue advancement*, extending from *FRONT* (e.g. [i:]) to *BACK* (e.g. [u:]). This is determined by the part of the tongue that is nearest the roof of the mouth, thus determining the relative volumes of the oral and pharyngeal cavities.

Vocoids are unlike most non-vocoid sound types in that they are continuously variable in several dimensions, and do not fall phonetically into discrete categories. It is therefore desirable in their classification to have a set of fixed reference-points in relation to which any given vocoid may be described. It would not be appropriate to use the vowels of any actual language as reference points for this purpose, since allophonic, regional/social, idiolectal and diachronic variation lead to an unstableness that renders them unsuitable; the most satisfactory technique for overcoming this deficiency of actual languages is the system of *cardinal vowels* devised by Daniel Jones (1957). This is a set of sounds chosen arbitrarily as reference points in the continuum of vowel variation; they have been recorded on gramophone records and are regularly taught to any serious student of phonetics (at least in Britain). They thus constitute a fixed and stable set of vowel sounds independent of any actual language.

The first and fifth cardinal vowels, [i] and [ɑ], are articulatorily determined: no. 1, [i], is the closest and frontest vocoid that may be articulated, since anything closer would cross the vowel limit line and become a fricative, while no. 5, [ɑ], is the openest and backest vocoid that may be articulated. Cardinals 2–4, [e, ɛ, a], are intermediate between these two extremes, and are chosen so as to yield a series of auditorily equal intervals between successive cardinal vowels, all remaining maximally peripheral. These auditory intervals are then continued, with the addition of lip-rounding, for the back cardinal vowels nos. 6–8, [ɔ, o, u]. The system thus combines articulatory and auditory features.

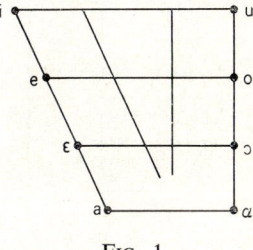

Fig. 1

The familiar vowel diagram (Fig. 1) is based on these eight *primary* cardinal vowels, with the addition of grid lines linking [e–o] and [ɛ–ɔ] and setting off the central area from the peripheral area. The line [e–o] is labelled HALF-CLOSE and the line [ɛ–ɔ] HALF-OPEN; these again are pseudo-articulatory labels for auditorily defined degrees of opening (tongue height).

As has been mentioned, the first five cardinal vowels have spread or neutral *lip position*, while [ɔ] has open lip-rounding and [o, u] close lip-rounding. By altering the lip positions from rounded to spread or vice versa, a second series of cardinal vowels (*secondary cardinals*) is derived; e.g. [y] with the tongue position for [i] but close lip-rounding, [œ] with the tongue position for [ɛ] but open lip-rounding, and [ɯ] with the tongue position for [u] but lips spread. This provides a supplementary set of reference points for the classification of 'front rounded' and 'back unrounded' vowels. A further two additional cardinal vowels may be placed just beneath the limit line half way between cardinals [i] and [u]; these are [ɨ] (unrounded lips) and [ʉ] (rounded).

The cardinal vowel system, although open to various theoretical objections, has proved highly effective in use, enabling vowel qualities to be described surprisingly accurately on the basis of auditory judgments. For example, one common variety of the vowel /ɔ:/ of *saw* in Received Pronunciation might be described as falling midway between cardinals [ɔ] and [o] and having medium-close lip-rounding. Another, American, variant of the same vowel might be described as being one-third of the way from secondary cardinal 5 to primary cardinal 6, with open lip-rounding. The change in the pronunciation of the RP /ʌ/ (as in *cup*) over the last eighty years or so can be shown as in Fig. 2, where it can be seen to have moved from near secondary cardinal 6 towards primary cardinal 4.

Other features which may need to be mentioned in the description of vocoids are as follows:

[1]. *Diphthongization.* Many English vowels, as well as those of many other languages, do not remain constant throughout their duration, but have a *gliding* nature. In the sound [ɔi], as in *boy*, the vowel-sound starts with an auditory impression similar to cardinal 6, but this changes immediately and moves towards the area of cardinals 1 and 2. Articulatorily, it starts with the

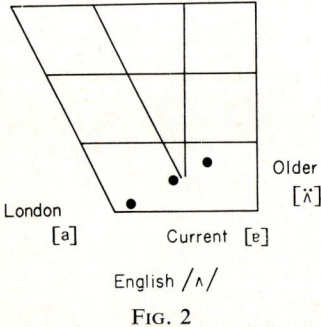

Fig. 2

back of the tongue as the highest part, raised about to half-open, but the part highest becomes progressively fronter and approaches more closely to the roof of the mouth; meanwhile the lips move from open rounding to a spread position. The vowel sounds of the words *say, know, fear*, (in R.P.) are similarly diphthongal; those of *far, law*, and *stir* are, however, 'pure' or monophthongal.

[2]. *Duration.* English vowels vary in duration as a result of a complex network of factors. They fall into two classes, *long* (e.g. the vowels of *bead, bard, bird*, etc.;) and *short* (those of *bid, bed, bud*, etc.). Other factors being constant, long vowels have greater duration than short vowels; but this simple relationship is complicated by many other factors, of which perhaps the most important is the shortening effect of final fortis (voiceless) consonants upon the vowel of a syllable, whereby the vowel of *beat* is considerably shorter in duration than that of *bead*.

[3]. *Tone.* The frequency of vocal cord vibration during the utterance of a vowel-sound affects the pitch which it is perceived as having. In some languages this is exploited as tone, whereby lexical distinctions may be made (e.g. Chinese, Igbo); in perhaps all it is exploited for the purpose of intonation.

[4]. *Nasalization.* Vowels during the articulation of which the soft palate is in the lowered position, allowing the air to escape by way of the nose as well as through the mouth, have a characteristic tamber recognized auditorily but described articulatorily as nasalization. This is an essential feature of certain vowels in some languages (e.g. French), and an incidental (allophonic) feature in others (e.g. the vowel of the English *man*).

[5]. *R-colouring (retroflexion).* The vowel heard in the common American pronunciation of *bird* has a characteristic tamber referred to as *r*-colouring. This auditory effect may be achieved by either of two articulatory means: by inverting or retroflexing of the tongue tip during the vowel, or by the lateral constriction and humping of the tongue.

[6]. *Tenseness and laxness.* Some consider the muscular tension of the tongue and lips during articulation as of importance in determining vowel quality: the vowel of *seat* is said to be *tense* and that of *sit, lax*.

An alphabetic listing of phonetic terms referring to vowels and other vocoids is as follows:

Back     Back of tongue highest, e.g. [ɑ, ɔ, o, u]
Central     Part of tongue between front and back highest, e.g.[ə]
Centralized     Less front, or back, than some norm, e.g. R P. /ɪ/ is centralized from cardinal [e]
Centring     (Diphthong) moving towards a central vowel quality
Close     Tongue near vowel limit line, e.g. [i, u]
Closing     (Diphthong) moving towards a close vowel quality
Diphthongal     Changing, gliding vowel sound
Falling     (Dipthong) with decreasing prominence, e.g. vowel of R.P. *fear*
Front     Front of tongue highest, e.g. [i, e, ɛ, a]
High     = close
Low     = open
Mid     Approximately half-way between close and open
Monophthongal     Of constant, unchanging tamber; non-diphthongal
Nasalized     With soft palate lowered
Open     Tongue far from vowel limit line, e.g. [a, ɑ]
Pure     =monophthongal
*R-coloured, Retroflexed* With *r*-tamber (see above)
Rising     (Diphthong) with increasing prominence, e.g. second vowel of R.P. *happier*

## 2. Ear-training

The cultivation of the auditory memory is an essential part of a phonetician's training and a valuable asset for any linguist. Ear-training exercises enable one to increase one's powers of auditory discrimination: to recognize a greater number of sound-types and to distinguish more readily and more accurately between similar sounds.

To achieve this end, systematic practice is needed in *listening for* sounds. The exercise that has proved valuable in this connexion is the dictation, by a teacher able to pronounce the sounds it is desired to discriminate, of isolated sounds, meaningless syllables and groups of syllables. The learner writes down his impression of these sounds and 'nonsense words' in narrow phonetic transcription. The errors he makes show the features he is failing to discriminate, and the teacher then repeats the original sound-type and the one erroneously perceived, in isolation and in context, drilling the learner until he can hear the distinction correctly. This exercise can be done (a) for the sounds of a given foreign language, e.g. to enable an English pupil to perceive the difference between dental and retroflex, aspirated and unaspirated, plosives in Hindi, which the naive English ear hears as in distinguishable; (b) for the sounds of a foreign language and of the pupil's native language, e.g. to impress on the learner the differences between the French syllable-initial [t], dental and unaspirated, and the English syllable-initial [t], alveolar and aspirated; (c) for training in general phonetics, when the sound-types used may be drawn from any language or none, thus equipping the learner to face the problems set by a language not previously analysed.

It is generally the case that improved auditory discrimination is followed by improved articulatory performance, i.e. a better pronunciation of the foreign language involved—rather than, as the learner tends to suppose, vice versa.

*Bibliography*

GIMSON A. C. (1962) *An Introduction to the Pronounciation of English*, London: Edward Arnold.
JONES D. (1957) (8th Edn) *An Outline of English Phonetics*, Cambridge: Heffer.

J. C. WELLS

**PHONETICS, EXPERIMENTAL.** This is the application of experimental methods to the study of speech sounds and of the relations between these sounds and the language units with which speakers and listeners operate. The purpose is to establish correlations between the occurrence of units such as *phonemes*, *morphemes*, *words* and *sentences* in the linguistic form of the message and the characteristics of the sound sequence, that is the physical form in which the message is transmitted and received. Study of the sound waves of speech cannot be complete without an investigation of the physiological mechanisms used in the generation of the sounds and the field of experimental phonetics therefore includes the movements of the muscles used in speech and the neural control of these muscles.

On the linguistic side, work in experimental phonetics presupposes that a language user has at his disposal a stock of linguistic information and that the features of this stock and the ways in which it is organized and used can be discovered from a study of his overt linguistic behaviour, whether this takes place spontaneously or in an experimental situation. The general method of experimental phonetics therefore is to start from an hypothesis concerning the nature of the language units adopted by the language user for a particular purpose, and to look for recurring features in the physiological activity of speech or in the sound-waves resulting from this activity which are correlated with the occurrence of the language units. The first stage of this search for correlates is observation and analysis of the sound-waves, muscle actions and neural signals of speech and classification of the data obtained. This stage has to be followed by a second in which experimental situations are set up so as to evoke specific behaviour from speakers and listeners with a view to confirming, denying or modifying the form of the correlations and the nature of the hypothetical language units.

Two facts about the correlations between language units and the physiological and acoustic events in speech are basic for all work in experimental phonetics. The first is that any spoken message, viewed at the linguistic level, can be represented as a linear sequence of discrete units. In the realization of the message at the physiological and acoustic levels, discreteness is not preserved; the message is transformed into a continuous flow of physiological activity, or more exactly a complex of several streams of physiological activity, each with its own time course, resulting on the acoustic level in a continuous soundwave.

The second fact follows partly from the first and partly from other considerations. It is that the relations between linguistic units and physiological and acoustic events are always statistical; such is the nature of speech that a one-to-one correlation is never found between the occurrence of a given language unit and the occurrence of a particular feature in the physiological activity or the acoustic output. For example, the occurrence of a given word in the linguistic *string* will be correlated with many variants in physiological pattern and in acoustic output, even in the case of an individual speaker, and with a very much larger number of variants if many speakers are considered; similarly, a wide variety of acoustic inputs may evoke the same word as a response either from one or from many listeners. (The instruction being 'tell me what was that sound'.)

The purpose of physiological and acoustic measurements of speech events, therefore, is to provide information about the range and scatter of observations correlated with a given language unit.

*Physiological activity in speech.* Three main muscle systems are employed in speech: the breathing muscles provide the outgoing stream of air which is the power supply for speech, the laryngeal muscles generate the carrier sound wave of speech, and the muscles of the neck and head perform the movements of articulation. The action of these muscles and the neural impulses which control their action together constitute the physiological aspect of speech.

The nerve impulses in man are not accessible to direct investigation except very rarely in pathological cases where some part of the brain may be open to artificial stimulation resulting in linguistic activity of one kind or another. Generally neural activity has to be inferred from measurements of *action potentials* in the muscles themselves, that is by electro-myography, using either needle or surface electrodes. The action of the breathing muscles has been studied by means of needle electrodes, particularly with the object of establishing the time course of various muscle actions and of correlating data so obtained with patterns of stress and syllabification at the linguistic level.

Other aspects of breathing may be investigated by using a pneumograph to measure changes in the circumference of the thorax and abdomen, a *spirometer* for showing the volume of air inspired or expired, and an air-flow meter to register variations in air-flow during a speech sequence.

The various actions of the larynx during speech, including the act of *phonation*, are difficult to investigate directly by any method that does not interfere grossly with the normal process of speech production. Action potentials in laryngeal muscles have been studied by using needle electrodes. The movements of the vocal cords can be seen reflected in a laryngeal mirror placed at the back of a speaker's mouth and in suitable conditions they can be photographed. Successful X-ray pictures of the larynx can be made only by adopting the technique of *tomography*, that is the focusing of the rays at a selected plane so as to give a sharp sectional image of, for example, the vocal cords and the ventricular folds. This method has been developed to the point where it is possible to make a cinefilm consisting of successive tomograms. All of these methods, save possibly the last, make it impossible for the experimental subject to speak quite normally. One further method, which does not have this disadvantage, is based on the fact that the impedance of the laryngeal structures to a high-frequency electric current is affected by the closing and opening of the vocal cords. The necessary *alternations* can be passed through the larynx with the aid of small surface electrodes and thus the interference with speech is slight, but the technique is at present only a promising one because there are still difficulties in the way of obtaining reliable results.

The articulatory mechanism consists of the cavities above the larynx (the pharynx, naso-pharynx and the mouth) and the muscles which enclose the cavities (the pharyngeal, palatal, tongue and facial muscles). A method of obtaining action potentials from various points in this mechanism, by means of small surface electrodes held on by suction, has been brought to a high degree of reliability.

The most commonly used method of examining the articulatory mechanism is by photography, direct or X-ray, taking single shots with short exposure times or using cinematography. Such records provide a means of establishing the dimensions of the vocal tract during the production of specific sounds or sound sequences and give a basis for the calculation of some of the acoustic properties of the speech mechanism.

*Acoustics of speech.* Acoustic study of speech sounds is essential to experimental phonetics because the sound waves represent the output of the speech generating mechanism and the input to the speech receiving mechanism and they thus provide a medium through which the experimenter can check what is produced by a speaker in response to some instruction and can control signals designed to elicit a specific response from the listener. The sound-wave of any speech sequence is a succession of particle movements whose amplitude varies rapidly with time and, as has been said above, the wave is continuous through a single utterance. The hearing mechanism subjects the continuous wave to some form of frequency analysis and consequently the acoustic study of speech sounds is most often carried out through the use of a *sound spectrograph*, a device for establishing the spectral distribution of sound energy at succeeding moments in time.

One of the primary uses of this information is in the search for acoustic correlates of linguistic features and for acoustic cues used in the recognition of linguistic units. A central difficulty in this work is the statistical nature of the correlations, the fact that there are no acoustic invariants to represent the relatively stable linguistic entities. Not only is there a wide scatter in the values obtained for any acoustic characteristic but there are always several characteristics which may signal the occurrence of a given unit. These acoustic cues may be broadly classed as *frequency cues*, *intensity cues* and *time cues*. For example, the *opposition* between the vowels in the two English words *bought* and *bit* is signalled on the acoustic level by a frequency cue: the second peak in the energy spectrum is in the region of 700–800 c.p.s. for the first vowel and near to 2000 c.p.s. for the second; by an intensity cue: the overall intensity of the first vowel is on average about 7 dB greater than that of the second; and a time cue: the duration of the periodic sound corresponding to the first vowel is on average one and a half times as great as that of the second. All linguistic oppositions are signalled by a plurality of cues in this way and one of the major tasks of experimental phonetics is first to characterize the various cues by looking for patterns in analytical data from speech sounds and then to attempt to evaluate the cues by determining their relative weight for the language user in a given situation. The second part of this task requires that acoustic characteristics, that is the cue values, should be controlled experimentally and varied systematically so that their effects may be measured. The most efficient way of doing this is to employ *speech synthesis*.

*Use of speech synthesis.* The normal method of speech synthesis is to use electronic circuits to generate speech-like sound sequences in which acoustic features (the cues) can be varied independently and over some considerable range. The responses of language users to sets of stimuli produced in this way afford a means of measuring the relative effects of the acoustic cues in a given context. Taking the example given above, the opposition between the vowels of *bought* and *bit*, it would be possible to synthesize versions of the sounds in which the second spectral peak ranged from 700 to 2000 c.p.s., the relative intensity of the sounds varied over a range of 0–10 dB, and their relative duration over a range of ratios from 1 : 1 to 1 : 2. Such synthetic stimuli would be arranged in listening tests and groups of listeners asked to register, for each test item, whether he recognized *bought* or *bit*. From the distribution of votes it is possible to obtain information about the weight given to the various acoustic cues and about their interaction.

The use of synthesized sounds also makes it possible to measure the capacity for distinguishing between sounds, as distinct from the ability to place them in linguistic categories, and in this way to gain some insight into language functioning at a level where the subject is himself unaware of its operation. This is one of the most valuable, as well as being one of the most difficult, tasks undertaken by experimental phonetics.

*See also:* Phonetics, acoustic.

*Bibliography*

COOPER F. S. (1965) *Instrumental methods for research in phonetics*, Proc. 5th Int. Cong. Phon. Sci., 142 (Basel).
FRY D. B. (1961) *Linguistic theory and experimental research*, Trans. Philol. Soc. 1960, 13, Oxford: The University Press.
FRY D. B. (1963) *Coding and decoding in speech*, in *Signs, Signals and Symbols* (Ed. Stella E. Mason) 65, London.
LADEFOGED P. (1962) *Sub-glottal activity during speech*, Proc. 4th Int. Cong. Phon. Sci., 73, The Hague.
LIBERMAN A. M. (1957) *Some results of research on speech perception*, J. acoust. Soc. Amer., **29**, 117.
PENFIELD W. and ROBERTS L. (1959) *Speech and Brain-Mechanisms*, Princeton: The University Press.

D. B. FRY

**PHONOLOGY: CONTRAST AND OPPOSITION.**
*Phonetic and phonological relevance.* There are two aspects of human speech. On the one hand, it is a physical phenomenon analysable and describable with reference to general articulatory and acoustic categories, which being determined by man's sound producing and receiving mechanisms are not restricted in their validity, but are applicable to all languages. This is the *phonetic* aspect. On the other hand, the spoken medium of a language constitutes a network of relations between elements within it. These relations characterize the particular language, they are its *phonological* component. Some of them may be common to groups of languages and a few are universal (see below). Elements of sound are thus connected with general concepts that lie outside the language under description, and they also form an internal system of dependencies. The general framework provides the phonetic material, the substance that enters into the *formal relations* (Sapir 1925).

The spoken medium of a language may be compared to a house. It is possible to use the same kinds of material to build houses of widely differing lay-out. But the construction proceeds according to a plan. In the blue-print the various parts of the house are seen in relation to each other; it considers the relative sizes of the rooms, stair-cases, walls etc. It determines the final shape of the house, it shows its underlying structure, which is present in every part of it. Everything is linked with everything else. The vocal elements of a language form such a house; general phonetics provides the material, phonology the blue-print, the structural relations.

Two segments in two different languages may be the same phonetically, but occupy different places in the respective structures. For instance, English has both aspirated and unaspirated plosives (see *Phonetics, articulatory*), but in any environment it can be predicted whether a plosive will be aspirated or unaspirated: the unaspirated ones follow *s* immediately within the same word, e.g. the *p* in **spa : k** *spark*, the *k* in **ska :** *scar*, while various degrees of aspiration—depending on whether they are pre- or post-vocalic, accented or unaccented—characterize the others, e.g. the *ph* in **pha : k** *park;* the *kh* in **kha :** *car*. Segments which are phonetically the same as these occur in Urdu, but here it is no longer possible to infer from general rules which will occur in a given environment; thus, they stand in a different relation to each other, i.e. they are phonologically different, e.g. *p* and *k* occur in the same environment as *ph* and *kh* in ʼpaniʼwater', ʹphaʧʌk 'gate'; ʹkaɣoz 'paper', ʹkhana "eat".

Another, similar example is provided by fronted and retracted velar plosives ($\underline{k}$ and $\underset{+}{k}$ respectively) in English and French. In both languages the difference in place of articulation is governed by general rules, which are, however, not the same. In English, $\underset{+}{k}$ precedes but does not follow high front vowels, whereas in French it also follows them: $\underset{+}{k}$**i :** *key*, **ku : l** *cool*, **wi :** $\underline{k}$ *week;* $\underset{+}{k}$**i** *qui*, **ku** *cou*, **fli**$\underset{+}{k}$ *flic*.

These two examples not only show that phonetic sameness in two languages may conceal a phonological difference, but also that phonetic features enter the structural matrix in two different ways: either they are predictable on the basis of contextual rules, or they are not predictable. In the latter case they are *distinctive*, in the former they are *redundant*.

*Contrast and opposition.* Among the formal relations we must distinguish between *contrasts* and *oppositions*. Phonological segments can be joined to form sequences only according to a limited number of patterns. So word initial **pr-** and **tr-** are possible in English, but not **pt-**, or **tp-**. The items are ordered in any language into groups such that fewer restrictions are imposed on external combinations than on internal ones. In English words, for example, many more clusters occur *between* the classes of stops/fricatives and of nasals/laterals than *within* each of these. These classes are in *contrast*. Contrast thus refers to combinatorial possibilities, to sequential arrangements. The members within the groups form a series of *oppositions*. As contrastive classes are defined by sequence they are based on purely abstract relations, not on phonetic substance, but the relations between individual elements, i.e. oppositions, are largely associated with distinctive phonetic features. It is at this point that *some* of the 'material' enters the structural network, namely the *distinctive* phonetic components; all the *redundant* ones can subsequently be inferred from context rules.

But oppositions can only be expressed in this concrete way if all the elements symbolized in the same fashion have a common phonetic denominator statable in the terms provided by general phonetics. If there is no such common phonetic feature the oppositions are abstract relations. The terms *fortis* and *lenis* refer to oppositions such as *p–b*, *t–d*, *k–g* in English, where no single phonetic feature can be found that distinguishes *all* of *p, t, k*, from *all* of *b, d, g*. Reference to force of articulation or something similar is too vague to be of any real phonetic value. *fortis* and *lenis* are therefore not phonetic terms, but express the abstract relationship between the elements concerned, which are given phonetic exponents, such as glottalisation, devoicing, aspiration, length of preceding vowel, *in contextual rules*. The oppositions between nasal and oral or stop and non-stop, on the other hand, are concrete and have real phonetic relevance in English.

The following simple reflection will reveal the need to distinguish the two kinds of structural relations (opposition and contrast). If in a given language segments (defined according to their distinctive phonetic specifications, i.e. according to the oppositions in which they are involved), could be combined in any way at all in a language, this language would have no phonological pattern. The demands on the human brain would obviously be enormous. As the resources of our memory are limited we must assume that the child can only learn, and the adult only master, his native language, if there is a high degree of regularity. Furthermore, it is only on the basis of this assumption that *inherent* combinative structures can be separated from *alien* ones, a differentiation any speaker of any language is able to make. If the combinations of elements are only restricted in number without being regularized nothing is gained, because the child still has to learn, and the adult to remember, every existing combination as a unique item, outside any general pattern, and the distinction between native and foreign is still impossible to make. The greatest degree of efficiency is reached when there are two groups of componentially specified elements such that (a) the combinations *between* the groups are very little restricted and (b) fairly high strict and regular limitations are imposed on combinatorial possibilities *within* the groups, the degree of restriction depends on the particular language in both cases, but is always lower in the former than in the latter. These two groups have been well known for hundreds, if not thousands, of years under the names of *vowels* and *consonants*. It follows from the above assumption of a simplicity criterion underlying all language that these two groups, V and C, must be universals, and as they are defined by sequence they form a universal contrast. We call that class consonants that contains stops, which can never function as vowels (O'Connor and Trim 1953; Arnold 1955/6).

This implies that the opposition between stop and non-stop must also be common to all languages and must enter into their structural relations in some way or other. There are languages without fricatives (e.g. Hawaiian, which has only two constrictives, namely the stops *p* and *k*), but no languages without stops. *Stop* and *non-stop* are universal distinctive phonetic features, all languages possess them. In some languages any segment is either the one or the other; in others one group of segments are both stop *and* non-stop (i.e. the two features alternate according to fixed rules) while a second group are either stop *or* non-stop. English represents the first type, and Spanish is an example of the second. In Spanish, as in many other languages, voiced stops interchange with voiced fricatives: voiced stops occur word-initially and after nasals, voiced fricatives between vowels, **'donde** *donde*, **'laðo** *lado*; **'bomba** *bomba*, **'kaβo** *cabo*; **'gaŋga** *ganga*, **'aɣo** *hago*. On the other hand, voiceless stops and voiceless fricatives are not related in this way in Spanish, since they are always separate.

That the phonetic features stop and non-stop are basic in all languages is demonstrated by another linguistic fact. The first sound sequence a child acquires after the babbling stage contains a stop and an open vowel, i.e. it contrasts complete closure with complete opening. The two features thus play an important role in the acquisition and functioning of language (Jakobson and Halle 1956).

On exactly the same principle of sequential arrangement as in the case of C and V some languages distinguish between different classes among consonants: they are again determined by the ways in which they combine with each other and with vowels. In English *h, j, w* can only *precede* a vowel and enter into very few pre-vocalic combinations within the same morpheme. Only *h, t, d, k, θ, s* occur before *w*: *which, twist, dwell, quench, thwart, swim*. *gw* is only found in special items, such as proper names, e.g. *Gwendolin*. ð, *z* + *w* are possible between vowels, and in these cases ð, *z* are post-vocalic *w* is pre-vocalic so that the sequences do not form real clusters. *ju* in *news, mews, fuse, argue, hue*, etc. is a single vowel, not CV because *Cj* can only be followed by *u*.

*m, n* (nasals) and *l, r* (liquids) form another group in English because they combine more freely with the remaining consonants than among themselves — the only sequences within this class are *post*-vocalic liquid + nasal *(film, firm, fern)* —, and also because they are always nearer the vowel than is any accompanying consonant. *sm-, sn-, sl-, ʃr-* are possible *(small, snore, slim, shrub)*, but not *ms-, ns-, ls-, rʃ-*. Similarly *post*-vocalic nasals and liquids occur *before* stops and fricatives *(lamp, dent, tense, belt, else, twelve, smirk, earth, scarf)*. In *bottle, button, cable, happen*, etc. we have V + lateral consonant *(l)* and V + nasal consonant *(m, n)* the vowel being obligatorily deleted in certain cases, and optional in others.

*Phonological contrasts—differences between languages.* Languages differ markedly with regard to phonological contrasts, and these divergencies fall into two categories: either (a) groups of languages have the same *general* classes of elements and only differ in *details* of clustering, in *details* of restrictions between and within the classes, or (b) the languages differ in the extent to which consonants can be grouped on the basis of phonological contrasts—in some languages, indeed, no such grouping is possible.

(a) On the same basis as English, Serbo-Croat observes the same general distinction between nasals and liquids and between stops and fricatives, but not all the clusters are common to both languages *fl-*, *ʃr-* are only known in English, *pt-*, *tk-*, *tm-*, *mr-* and many others only in Serbo-Croat.

The contrast between vowels and consonants belongs to all languages, but the possible combinations of these are nevertheless individually different. Some languages, e.g. Arabic, do not allow vowels in word-initial position, others have no post-vocalic consonants. Japanese is an example of the latter type, although this is not always obvious from the *phonetic* facts, because a vowel may be followed by a nasal element, the so-called 'syllabic nasal of Japanese', which can have a number of different realizations including contoids $(n, m, ŋ, ɴ, ũ, ɣ̃)$, but always functions as a vowel (for vocoid/contoid and vowel/consonant, cf. Pike (1943)). Furthermore, there are in Japanese long stops and fricatives, which also seem to contradict the statement, but they have the same quantity as C+V in the rhythmic pattern of Japanese and so *behave* as if they represented a stop or fricative followed by a vowel. The structure of the language allowed the Japanese armed forces in the Second World War to use a syllabary-keyboard Morse sender for radio telegraphy which was designed so as to send out the vowel signal before the consonant signal. This can be done without causing serious misunderstandings only if the language does not permit more than one position for the consonant in relation to the vowel.

(b) If a language has no consonant clusters and if either no consonants occur post-vocalically or those which do are the same as those which occur pre-vocalically, there cannot be a consonant contrast, so that all C's are on the same level and are only contrasted with with all V's. Most languages of the Polynesian group have this very simple structure. Japanese provides a further example, though the phonetic *substance* again sometimes conceals the phonological structure, since *i* and *u* are often voiceless between voiceless consonants and may even be dropped altogether thus producing sequences that look like CC: *hitori* → *çtori*, *hukimasita* → *Φu̥kimaʃta*. Other linguistic facts however, show quite conclusively that Japanese does not allow *phonological* consonant sequences: for instance, the English word **a:sks** *a:sks* is perceived as a string of five 'syllables'. If the structure of the language demands that every consonant should be followed by a vowel, and if a long vowel counts as two, then *asks* must be heard as containing five vowels. The phonological shape of Japanese loan-words from European languages, e.g. *bisuketto* (biscuit), *kiroguramu* (kilogram), *doriburusuru* (to dribble), shows the same underlying formal relations.

Whenever two languages differ in combinatory patterns, borrowings from the one into the other undergo substitutions according to the phonological structure of the recipient language, and these points of divergence in form also raise problems in foreign language learning. A few more examples will illustrate this phenomenon.

Finnish does not permit consonant clusters in word initial position (and it has no voiced stops), so the Swedish words *strand* and *skräddare* were borrowed as *ranta* and *räätäli*. In English the consonant sequence *ts* is most commonly associated with word final *t* + plural marker. The loan-words *tsetse* and *Tsar* thus exhibit structural peculiarities, and pronunciations like '*tsetsi* and *tsa:* are certainly odd in that they are un-English, because they lie outside any regular patterning. It is therefore not surprising to hear the naturalised forms '*tetsi* and *za:* This also explains the difficulties English learners of German have with the German affricate *ts*, which can occur initially and even enter into clusters, and is thus structurally different from English *ts:* thus **tsvai** *zwei*, **tsvantsik** *zwanzig* are often rendered as **svai**, '**svantsik**.

*Phonological oppositions—differences between languages.* Languages differ, however, not only in contrastive relations, but also in respect of the oppositions they observe. Whereas vocoids function as vowels universally, not all languages have vocalic liquids $l̩$ and $r̩$ (i.e. liquids functioning as vowels), as in Czech, where the liquids become vocalic when preceded by a consonant and not followed by a vowel. The words *śkrtl* ʃkrtl 'scrapped', **trval** *trval* 'lasted' are di-vocalic, *rval* **rval** 'tore', *zlo* **zlo** 'evil' mono-vocalic.

All vowel oppositions between vocoids involve differences of tongue height. In some languages these may be the only existing ones, e.g. Adyge has three vowels (low, mid, high) and non-distinctive variations front-back, rounded-unrounded according to context. This type is, however, rather rare. Tongue height is usually combined *distinctively* with the dimensions front-back and/or rounded-unrounded. The simplest arrangement of this kind has three vowels $i-u-a$ (e.g. classical Arabic, Tagalog). In German, French, and Dutch there are, in addition to degrees of opening, the oppositions between front unrounded, back rounded and front rounded, while in Bulgarian, Roumanian and Ukrainian we find front unrounded, back rounded and back unrounded.

Just as in the case of contrasts, differences of oppositions in two languages cause linguistic interference in borrowings and in foreign language learning. French *y*, as opposed to *i* and *u*, has been taken into English as *ju* for centuries (cf. *resume*, *issue*, *argument*) and still presents difficulties to English learners of French today. Russian speakers of French and German replace the front rounded vowels by front unrounded ones. German and French learners of English have to acquire an unfamiliar opposition between the flat fricatives θ, ð (as in *think*, *then*) and the grooved fricatives, *s*, *z* (as in *sink*, *zen*) and consequently often substitute *s*, *z* for θ, ð.

*Phonology and syntax*. The network of phonological contrasts and oppositions, although devoid of meaning by itself, carries the meaningful patterns of a language, and is closely related to the syntax, by which it is partially conditioned, i.e. some phonological relations depend on and can be predicted from syntactic structures. The following example illustrates this.

The nasal consonants of the English words *sin* and *sing* seem to form an opposition expressible as a distinctive difference in place of articulation, namely dorsal versus non-dorsal, which would parallel the relations among English stop consonants. But this parallelism is deceptive because the spelling, the history of the language and words like *anger—anchor*, *fender—enter* tell us that *sing* and *sink* must form the same correspondence as *hand* and *ant*. In both pairs, therefore, a nasal consonant is followed by a lenis or a fortis stop, and the distinctive feature of articulation point is attributed to the sequence of segments, not to the individual elements separately. (Distinctive features thus attributed to more than one segment are enclosed in braces {}.) Thus, using '+' and '−' to show the presence and absence of a following feature, we can represent the final pairs of segments in *sing* as {N(asal) S(top)-fortis} + dorsal in *sink* as {N S+fortis}+dorsal, in *hand* as {N S-fortis}-dorsal and in *ant* as {N S+fortis}-dorsal. In the context {N S-fortis}+dorsal S-fortis is retained if it occurs within a morpheme, before the comparative and superlative endings -*er* and -*est* or before the suffixes -*ate*, -*ation*; it is deleted in all other cases. This means that a knowledge of the grammatical structure and function of the words concerned allows us to predict when the pronunciation of the *phonological* sequence {N S-fortis}+dorsal is ŋ or ŋg *phonetically*. The above rule, which is based on English morphology, accounts for all the following possibilities: *anger* -ŋg-, *angle* -ŋg-; *longer*, *longest* -ŋg-; *elongate* -ŋg-, *prolongation* -ŋg-; *sing*, -*er*, -*ing*, -ŋ-, *long*, -*ish*, *len* -*gth* -ŋ-.

The nasals in *sin* and *sing* do not therefore form an opposition, but are contrastively different; and only the underlying structural relations reveal this fact, the gross phonetic substance being misleading. The phonetic signal is, however, uniquely determined by grammatical rules from the phonological specification. It now also becomes clear why ŋ cannot occur word initially, whereas *m* and *n* can. ŋ is different from *m* and *n*, in that phonologically it is a nasal followed by a stop, and this kind of cluster is barred from pre-vocalic position by the structural laws of English. Furthermore, the functional status of ŋ explains the absence of long vowels before it — there are only a very few consonant clusters which can occur after long vowels and only a limited number of long vowels are possible in this position (e.g. *find*, *old*, *pint*).

The above example demonstrates the difference between the formal ralations of constrasts/oppositions and phonetic substance. It shows that phonetic substance does not enter the structural framework in one lump, so to speak, but rather in portions. The phonological specification {N S-fortis}+dorsal is not devoid of phonetic information, but it is not a full signal yet; all the remaining phonetic features must be added by grammatical and contextual rules. If we concentrate our attention on the *gross* phonetic data instead of the network of formal relations and the *gradual* introduction of phonetic features the linguistic facts cannot be explained adequately (cf. also the Japanese examples above). The example also illustrates the necessity of linking phonology with syntax, without which a great deal of generality would be lost.

*See also:* Linguistic form: transformational theory. Phonetics, articulatory. Phonetics, auditory.

*Bibliography*

ARNOLD G. F. (1955/56) *A Phonological Approach to Vowel, Consonant and Syllable in Modern French*, Lingua, **5**, 253.
JAKOBSON R. and HALLE M. (1956) *Fundamentals of Language*, The Hague.
O'CONNOR J. D. and TRIM J. L. M. (1953) *Vowel, Consonant, and Syllable — A Phonological Definition*, Word, **9**, 103.
PIKE K. L. (1943) *Phonetics*, Ann Arbor.
SAPIR E. (1925) *Sound Patterns in Language*, Language, **1**, 37.

K. KOHLER

**PHONOLOGY: DISTINCTIVE FEATURES.** The concept of distinctive features arose in connexion with the classification of phonemes according to their phonetic quality. It is evident that the description of the phoneme as 'oppositive, relative et negative' (de Saussure) is no more than partial. Phonemes are realized phonetically, and therefore have some relation to the physical phenomenon of speech. Their realization can, to some extent, be described in terms of positive characteristics, articulatory or acoustic; such characteristics constitute *phonetic quality*.

It is further evident that the relationship between items in a phoneme system as regards phonetic quality is not the same for each item; there are greater and lesser degrees of resemblance between phonemes. Hence a qualitative description of the phonemes of a language must treat them, not as forming a single system, but rather as falling into several systems within the overall phoneme inventory. The degree of resemblance of one phoneme to another can then be represented in the description by the extent to which they share membership within the various systems and subsystems.

The concept of phonetic resemblance between phonemes implies a splitting up of their phonetic quality into combinations of phonetic characteristics, such that they are regarded as sharing some characteristics, while differing in others. The phonetic quality of a phoneme is thus seen as a complex of various features, each of which differentiates the phoneme in question from other phonemes in the total system. It is to such characteristics that the term 'distinctive feature' has been applied.

The first comprehensive account of the analysis of phonemes by features is to be found in Trubetskoy's *Grundzüge der Phonologie*. Each phoneme is seen as having a corresponding 'phonic image'—presumably abstracted from its actual realisations in speech. The 'phonic image' has various qualitative characteristics; some of these contrast with the characteristics of other phonic images, and are therefore phonologically relevant, while others have no such distinctive function, and therefore no relevance in phonology. The phoneme is regarded as composed of those characteristics which are phonologically relevant.

The distinctive characteristics of a phoneme are isolated by considering the oppositions between that phoneme and every other phoneme in the system. Oppositions can themselves be classified in various ways, according to their relations with other oppositions of the system, and the relation of the phoneme pairs involved to each other. The combination of features shared by two phonemes in opposition may be unique to the phonemes concerned: in this case the opposition is termed bilateral. Multilateral oppositions, on the other hand, are those in which the shared features serve as a basis of comparison for other phoneme pairs. Thus the opposition between English /t/ and /d/ is bilateral, the common features of alveolarity and plosive articulation not being found together in any other English phoneme; whereas the opposition of /t/ and /k/ is multilateral, since the shared features of plosion and voicelessness are also found in the oppositions of /p/ to /t/, and /p/ to /k/. A bilateral opposition implies a binary choice on the part of the listener; a multilateral opposition does not.

The extension of the differentiating feature of an opposition may also be used as a criterion for classification: an opposition whose differentiating feature is used to distinguish between other phoneme pairs is termed proportional, as against isolated oppositions, whose distinguishing features are not found elsewhere in the system. Thus the English opposition of /t/ and /d/ is proportional, because the differentiating factor of voice also serves to distinguish /p/ from /b/ and /k/ from /g/.

A further classification hinges on the type of distinction involved in the opposition. If the contrast is between the presence of a feature and its absence (e.g. voicing as opposed to voicelessness), the opposition is privative: if the difference involves the presence of a feature to a greater or lesser degree (e.g. vowel systems with three or more degrees of openness), the opposition is gradual: and if the contrast is between two different, and equally positive, features (e.g. English /p/ as opposed to /k/), the opposition is termed equipollent. These latter characterizations are largely a matter of viewpoint; voicelessness, for instance, can equally well be regarded as a positive characteristic. The decisive factor in this classification is the occurrence or non-occurrence of a distinguishing feature where the opposition in question is neutralized.

The status of an opposition as privative or gradual depends similarly on its place in the total system: if a differentiation of degree serves to distinguish more than two phonemes, having the same features in common, and is therefore employed in more than two degrees, the oppositions in question are gradual.

Two phonemes whose opposition is at the same time bilateral, proportional, and subject to neutralization are regarded especially closely related. The degree of relationship between phonemes is thus expressed in terms of the character of the opposition between them, which in its turn is derived from the functioning of the system as a whole.

The distinctions between phonemes in opposition are described exclusively in articulatory terms: this, however, does not mean that the features attributed to a phoneme are actually present as articulations whenever that phoneme is realized in speech. The features are abstract, phonological entities; their correlation with phoneme realization is not discussed by Trubetskoy. Hence the basis for the distinction between relevant and non-relevant features is largely intuitive, or dictated by the requirement of economy in the description of the phoneme system as a whole. The difference between English /b/ and /v/ concerns both manner of articulation (plosive as opposed to fricative) and place (bilabial as opposed to labiodental); the treatment of the former difference as distinctive and the latter as redundant is based on overall pattern congruity rather than any hypothesis about the recognition of these phonemes by the listener. The only criteria adduced as capable of supporting a given feature analysis are those of linguistic function—in particular, possibilities of neutralization.

The treatment of differing degrees of resemblance between phonemes in terms of shared and differentiating features was further elaborated by Jakobson and Halle, in *Preliminaries to Speech Analysis* (1952) and *Fundamentals of Language* (1956). Their descriptive framework diverges in several respects from that of Trubetskoy. In the system propounded in *Preliminaries*, the distinctive features perform essentially the same function as the features postulated by Trubetskoy. They differ firstly in being acoustically defined, i.e. they are viewed not as phonological abstractions, but as characteristics observable in the acoustic speech spectrum—observable, moreover, at successive points in time, corresponding to the sequential occurrence of the phonemes which they constitute.

The acoustic features which are termed distinctive, from among the general mass of acoustic features, are those whose function in language is to differentiate morphemes. Other linguistic functions are performed by various other acoustic features, which are characterized as follows:

*Configurational features* signal the boundaries of grammatical units.

*Expressive features* signal the emotional attitude of the speaker.

*Redundant features* (those having none of the functions listed above) serve to signal the presence of certain other sound features, which have linguistic function.

The distinctive features are further divided into *inherent* and *prosodic features*, the prosodic features requiring for their acoustic definition the comparison of points in a time series. Features of stress and tone are of this type. The inherent features may be defined qualitatively, without reference to successive points in time. Only the latter features are fully described.

Since distinctive features are acoustically defined, their isolation from the data of speech is not primarily dependent on relations within particular language systems. The hypothesis is put forward that the acoustic features used distinctively in languages are relatively few in number, and that a descriptive apparatus comprising these features can handle the phonological aspect of any language: in other words, the distinctive features are universal properties of language. The precise acoustic realisation of any feature must vary from one language to another: such variation, being predictable upon identification of the language, is regarded as redundant.

While it is claimed that no language makes use of more than the specified distinctive features, it is not postulated that every language employs the complete set. Since some of the features are defined in terms of absolute characteristics (the vocalic and consonantal features, for example), cases may presumably arise in which these features must be regarded as present, with or without distinctive function. It seems, therefore, that there remains a possibility of choice in dealing with particular languages, as to which of the universal set of features shall be taken as distinctive, and which as redundant. Here, considerations of economy in description and pattern congruity (the exploitation of proportional oppositions) are paramount. It is therefore possible, within the distinctive feature framework, to give alternative phonological descriptions of the same language material.

A further innovation in the feature system of Jakobson and Halle is that all choices made by the listener in the recognition of a sound are assumed to be binary, i.e. that all sound differences are due to either the presence of an acoustic feature in contrast with its absence elsewhere, or differences in the degree to which a feature is present in different segments. This means that the multilateral oppositions of Trubetskoy have no correlate in the distinctive feature system. The single threefold choice between English /p/, /t/ and /k/ is broken down into a sequence of two choices—firstly between /k/ and /p, t/, and secondly between /p/ and /t/—the distinctions in the two choices being attributed to different acoustic features.

Greater difficulty is caused by the oppositions which in Trubetskoy's terms are both multilateral and gradual, i.e. where a contrast is postulated between more than two points on a single dimension. This situation appears to arise in the case of only one feature; the solutions advanced will be discussed together with the specification of the feature concerned.

The original specification of the distinctive features is to be found in *Preliminaries to Speech Analysis;* this account was later modified in some details, and a second, partial list is given in *Fundamentals of Language*. Application of the framework in the description of particular languages has given rise to further modifications; but these are of a minor character, and do not affect the general appearance of the system.

The distinctive features and specifications given in *Fundamentals of Language* are as follows:

*Sonority features*—utilizing the amount and concentration of energy in the spectrum and in time.

I Vocalic/non-vocalic:

Acoustic description:
presence v. absence of a sharply defined formant structure.

Articulatory correlate:
primary excitation at the glottis, combined with a free passage through the vocal tract.

II Consonantal/non-consonantal:

Acoustic description:
low, v. high, total energy.

Articulatory correlate:
presence v. absence of an obstruction in the vocal tract.

(These two features yield a preliminary, fourfold classification of sounds into consonants, vowels, liquids and glides. Consonants are both consonantal and non-vocalic, corresponding to the articulatory class of obstruents. Vowels have the opposite feature combination, being vocalic and non-consonantal. Liquids are marked by the presence of both vocalic and consonantal features, while in glides both features are negative.)

III Compact/diffuse:

Acoustic description:
higher, v. lower, concentration of energy in a relatively narrow, central region of the spectrum.

Articulatory correlate:
higher, v. lower, ratio of the volume of the cavity in front of the primary stricture to the cavity behind the stricture.

(This feature applies to both consonants and vowels. It differentiates back dorsal consonants (compact) from front apicals and labials (diffuse), and serves also to distinguish open from close vowels. It is frequently the case that vowel systems make use of more than two degrees of openness; such systems are dealt with in various ways. In a system using three degrees of openness, the mid term may be regarded as both compact and diffuse simultaneously, as compared to the extreme terms; or the feature itself may be stated as two features —compact/non-compact and diffuse/non-diffuse. The mid vowel is then characterized as negative with regard to both features. Systems using four degrees of openness will be handled by the second of these alternatives.)

IV Tense/lax:
  Acoustic description:
    higher, v. lower, total amount of energy in conjunction with greater v. smaller spread of energy in the spectrum and in time.
  Articulatory correlate:
    greater, v. smaller, deformation of the vocal tract away from the neutral position.

(This is taken as the differentiating feature between English /p, t, k/ (tense) and /b, d, g/ (lax). Tension is chosen rather than voicing, or aspiration, on the grounds that the tense/lax opposition is the only one to be found in every position where the two plosive series contrast—voicing, for instance, may be absent from /b, d, g/ in word-initial position. It appears then that despite references in the exposition of the distinctive feature system to the listener's activity in the speech situation, the function of a characteristic of the acoustic spectrum as regards recognition is not of prime importance in deciding whether it should be taken as the acoustic correlate of a distinctive feature.)

V Voiced/voiceless:
  Acoustic description:
    presence, v. absence, of periodic low-frequency excitation.
  Articulatory correlate:
    vibration v. non-vibration of the vocal cords.

VI Nasal/oral:
  Acoustic description:
    spread of the acoustic energy over wider, v. narrower, frequency regions, by a reduction in the intensity of certain formants and the introduction of additional formants.
  Articulatory correlate:
    use v. non-use of the nasal resonator.

VII Discontinuous/continuant:
  Acoustic description:
    silence, followed and/or preceded by spread of energy over a wide frequency region, v. absence of abrupt transition between sound and silence.
  Articulatory correlate:
    plosive v. fricative articulation in consonants; in liquids, flapped or trilled articulation as opposed to continuant liquids such as laterals.

VIII Strident/mellow:
  Acoustic description:
    higher v. lower intensity noise.
  Articulatory correlate:
    rough-edged v. smooth-edged; rough-edged sounds are distinguished by a supplementary obstruction creating edge effects at the point of articulation.

(The distinction appears to correspond to the phonetic distinction between sibilant and non-sibilant fricatives, e.g. between English /s, ʃ/ and /f, θ/. It also serves to differentiate plosives (mellow) from affricates (strident); the triple distinction between plosive, affricate and fricative is then handled by the application of features VII and VIII.)

IX Checked/unchecked:
  Acoustic description:
    higher rate of discharge of energy within a reduced time-span, v. lower rate of energy discharge over a longer interval.
  Articulatory correlate:
    use of glottalic pressure v. use of the lung air-stream mechanism.

*Tonality features*—involving the extremes of the frequency spectrum.

X Grave/acute:
  Acoustic description:
    concentration of energy in the lower, v. upper, spectral region.
  Articulatory correlate:
    peripheral v. medial articulation, e.g. the distinction of labials and velars (grave) as against alveolars and palatals (acute).

(This feature, coupled with feature III, can then differentiate between four places of articulation in the mouth. It distinguishes also between front and back vowels, the former being acute, the latter grave.)

XI Flat/plain:
  Acoustic description:
    flat phonemes are characterized by a downward shift or weakening of some of their upper frequency components.
  Articulatory correlate:
    decrease in the back or front orifice of the mouth resonator (i.e. labialization or pharyngalization), with concomitant velarization expanding the mouth resonator.

(The acoustic correlates of labialization and pharyngalization are regarded as equivalent. The argument for this equation rests on the grounds of complementary distribution and phonetic similarity: in this instance, however, complementary distribution is between language systems, rather than between environments within a single language. In other words, a language may make distinctive use of either labialization or pharyngalization; the use of one precludes the use of the other. The similarity between them lies in the appearance of the acoustic spectrum of sounds to which these features are attributed.)

XII Sharp/plain:
  Acoustic description:
    sharp phonemes are characterized by an upward shift of some of their upper frequency components.

Articulatory correlate:
> widening of the back orifice of the mouth resonator; concomitant palatalization restricts the mouth cavity.

As is apparent from the feature specification given above, the relationship between phonological features and their acoustic representation is seen as extremely simple—a 1:1 correlation, in fact. Acoustic features are presumed to occur in bundles, each bundle corresponding to a phoneme; utterances are seen as actual strings of feature-bundles, corresponding in sequence to the phoneme strings abstracted from them. Segmentation of the acoustic material is regarded not as a process of abstraction, but as a matter of locating the changeover in time from one feature-bundle to another.

This raises the question of the criteria used for selecting certain attributes of the speech spectrum as having distinctive function. It might well be possible to select characteristics of the speech wave such as to fulfil the requirement of sequential occurrence in time; but this in itself would not entail their having any function in the speech situation. The same applies to the criterion proposed in 'Preliminaries to Speech Analysis', that for an acoustic feature to be distinctive, it must occur in all realizations of the phoneme to which it is attributed. It does not follow from the application of either of these criteria that the features selected would have any function, apart from that of fulfilling the criteria by which the selection was made. Before the distinctive features can be recognized as functional, it must be shown that the criteria by which they are selected from the acoustic data are motivated in some way.

The selection of acoustic characteristics, if it is other than arbitrary, must reflect a correspondence between these features and something which is utilized by the listener in the speech situation, i.e. the features must function as perceptual cues for phoneme recognition. No evidence is adduced for any such function, in spite of frequent reference in the exposition of the theory to the activity of the listener. The results of experimental work on speech perception give no indication that the phoneme sequence is reflected in the temporal order of occurrence of recognition cues. Nor is there any evidence for the assumption that the cues for recognition of a particular phoneme are the same in all its environments.

It appears, then, that any equation of the acoustic distinctive features with perceptual cues would prove untenable; that the correlation of acoustic data with distinctive features is no less complex than that between acoustic data and phonemes; and that the justification for the use of a distinctive feature framework in phonology—if any empirical justification is sought—must be that the degrees of relationship between sounds which are implied by this form of description are reflected in their linguistic function.

Further modifications in the distinctive feature framework have resulted from its incorporation into the theory of transformational grammar. The phonological component of a transformational grammar, as expounded by Halle ('On the Bases of Phonology', 1964), operates with features of two kinds, phonemic and phonetic.

*Phonemic features*, selected from the universal set of about 15, are posited to differentiate morphemes—the original function of features. They have no direct association with the acoustic characteristics of speech. Any feature whose value for a particular segment is predictable, on phonological or morphophonemic grounds, is left unspecified, so that for some segments, the specification of their content is incomplete.

From these are derived the *phonetic features*, which relate directly to the acoustic speech signal. The derivation involves the specification of unspecified phonemic features, and a statement of feature changes in the phonetic form of morphemes to correspond to conditioned variations from the base form in contextual realization. The phonological rules embodying the derivation account for both phonological and morphophonemic conditioning.

The phonemic features, then, appear as logically prior to the phonetic features. Since the former, though still regarded as universals, are not directly associated with the acoustic signal, they can presumably no longer be considered as acoustic features; since they are posited solely to distinguish between linguistic forms, their justification must be on phonological grounds. Halle indeed points out that the classification of segments entailed by a distinctive feature analysis almost always corresponds to the classification required for economical statement of phonological and morphophonemic processes. This correspondence is claimed as evidence of close correlation between the phonological and the acoustic levels of language: however, since no convincing exposition of the distinctive features as direct acoustic correlates has yet been made, it would appear that the suitability of the framework for phonological statements springs from the use of covert phonological criteria in its establishment, i.e. the acoustic criteria of Jakobson have been abandoned in favour of the functional criteria of Trubetskoy.

This reversal is not explicit, but rather implied in the logical priority of phonemic over phonetic features. Hence the distinctive features of transformational theory are still overtly defined in acoustic terms: a procedure which serves to mask the phonological grounds upon which they actually rest.

*See also:* Linguistic form: transformational theory.

*Bibliography*

HALLE M. (1964) *On the Bases of Phonology* in (J. J. Fodor and J. A. Katz) *The Structure of Language.*

JAKOBSON R., FANT C. G. M. and HALLE M. (1952) *Preliminaries to Speech Analysis*, M.I.T. Acoustics Laboratory Technical Report No. 13.

JAKOBSON R. and HALLE M. (1956) *Fundamentals of Language*, 's-Gravenhage.

TRUBETSKOY N. S. (1939) *Grundzüge der Phonologie.*

E. M. HIGGINBOTTOM

**PHONOLOGY: PHONEMES AND BROAD TRANSCRIPTION.** A question that is often asked in connexion with Phonological Contrast and Phonological Opposition is: How can they be recognized, how can they be discovered in the *phonetic* data? As phonological structures partly depend on syntax and as all contrasts and even some oppositions are purely abstract relations the question is unanswerable. This state of affairs raises serious problems for investigators of unknown languages, since all that is open to analysis in the initial stages is phonetic material so that the first approach leads through substance, under which all the relevant structures, grammatical and phonological are 'hidden'. Similar difficulties arise in foreign language teaching where basic sound distinctions have to be dealt with at the outset when the student has very little or no knowledge of the syntax and when a discussion of abstract relations would be of no help, but would only cause confusion.

In order to overcome this problem linguists have imposed a number of very heavy restrictions on spoken language, which enable them to provide a preliminary systematization of it on the basis of *phonetic substance*. As syntactically determined phonological relations cannot be inferred from phonetic substance alone the first principle advocated for linguistic fieldwork is the separation of the levels of grammar and phonology. In keeping with this postulate the presence or absence of voice in the dental fricatives of the English words *thy* and *thigh*, for example, is considered distinctive, although a closer examination shows that in word initial position voiced dental fricatives are restricted to, and voiceless ones barred from, pronouns and adverbs *(they, them, their, this, that, the, there, then, thither;* but: *thick, thin, thank)*. The laryngeal feature (the presence or absence of voice) of a word-initial dental fricative can therefore be inferred from the word's grammatical class by a rule, and is thus not phonologically distinctive (if, that is, it is held that a feature must be *either* predictable from the grammatical structure, *or* phonologically distinctive, but not both; there is disagreement among linguists as to whether this is a necessary restriction; in this article it is taken to be necessary). But this statement presupposes a fairly detailed knowledge of the internal structure of the language as a whole, which is not given in the initial stages of an investigation or of teaching so that the other interpretation is the only possible one. As it loses a great deal of generality, however, it must be corrected later when the necessary grammatical information is available.

*The identification of phonetic segments as 'same' or 'different'.* When a phonological analysis can only rely on phonetic substance the distinction between abstract and concrete must be abolished, so that all relations are expressed in terms of concrete features occurring in phonetically specified segments in the speech chain. The two guiding principles are *complementary distribution* and *phonetic similarity*. It is assumed that certain phonetic segments can occur in the *same* phonetic context: that, e.g. the English words *pea, me, sea* all contain the same vowel, which is only true on a crude phonetic level. It is impossible to define the notion of sameness with regard to *phonetic* context, since the investigator's ability to perceive phonetic distinctions depends on his training and experience. Once it has been established which contexts are phonetically the 'same', however, segments will be found that have no environments in common. They complement each other, and are said to be in complementary distribution. The strongly aspirated stops in English *pay, Tay, cay* and the weakly aspirated or glottalised ones in *ape, eight, ache* behave in this way. To decide whether the stops are complementary in *pay* and *ape* rather than in *pay* and *eight* the principle of phonetic similarity is evoked, which means that those segments are grouped together that have most features in common, and are separated from the others. The consonants in *pay* and *eight* are distinguished as to place of articulation, the ones in *pay* and *ape* are not: the former differ in distinctive features, the latter in redundant ones. This postulate can only be applied if the phonological oppositions are concrete; it cannot handle abstract relations such as *fortis* and *lenis*. It is true that the difference between *p–b, t–d, k–g* has been treated as a concrete opposition by most linguists (usually as completely voiceless versus partially voiceless), but this is only possible if features like glottalization are ignored. Furthermore, the principle can only deal successfully with oppositions that are concrete *and* positive. The stops in English *pall, call, tall* are not distinguished *phonologically* as labial, velar and alveolar, although these are their *phonetic* values, but rather as labial, dorsal and non-dorsal. In certain accents the alveolar stop of *Tay*, the post-alveolar one of *tray* and the glottal stop in *eight* are thus the same phonological entity, although the stops in *Tay* and *eight* have only one *positive* feature in common, namely that they are both stops, which would also apply to *ape* and *eight*. In a case like this the principle of *pattern congruity* is brought in. As the plosives in both *pay–cay* and *ape–ache* are differentiated as labial and dorsal, the stop in *Tay* must bear the same relation to the first pair as the stop in *eight* does to the second, i.e. they must be identified.

*Phoneme and allophone; phonemics and phonology.* Phonetic segments which have been established on the basis of phonetic similarity and pattern congruity as being in complementary distribution are said to represent the same *phoneme*, to be *allophones* of the same phoneme. Thus [t] (alveolar), [t̪] (post-alveolar) and [?] (glottal) are allophones of the /t/-phoneme in some kinds of English. (If they are to be set-off from normal orthography, phonemic notations are put between slants /.../, while allophonic notations, or purely phonetic ones, are put between square brackets [...].) The discipline that studies the occurrence of allophones and the patterns of phoneme combinations is called *phonemics. Whereas *phonology* uncovers the structural relations of the spoken medium from within the language and shows how the phonetic substance enters this matrix in a series of steps leading to the actual signal the approach of *phonemics* is reversed; it takes the signal as the starting point and states the distribution of fully specified elements, in which all the phonetic features are treated together. Phonology requires that the phonetic output should be uniquely determined by a network of contrasts and oppositions and a set of rules, phonemics, on the other hand, also assumes that the formal units follow unambiguously from the substance. This assumption of bi-uniqueness leads to the concepts of the phoneme and the allophone and has important consequences for the analysis, as may be seen from the following examples.

Scottish English, like all other accents of Standard English, observes the oppositions *p–b*, *t–d*, *k–g*, but at word junctions before lenis constrictives only lenis stops occur. We thus find **blagbord** *blackboard* by the side of **blak** *black*. In a phonemic interpretation, *blackboard* contains the /g/-phoneme, *black* the /k/-phoneme so that the two words are dissociated from each other, although a single contextual rule could produce *g* from *k*. German affords another example of the same type. The uninflected words *bunt* and *rund* are both pronounced with *t*, but the inflected form *bunte* has *t*, whereas *runde* has *d*. In phonemic terms *rund* ends in the /t/-phoneme, *runde* contains the /d/-phoneme. But since all lenis constrictives become fortis in word final position a general rule would suffice to derive the *t* of *rund* from a base with *d*. Here a phonetic difference represents the same phonological entity, but phonemics cannot handle this, because of the very heavy restrictions imposed by bi-uniqueness.

The English words *impression* and *promotion*, on the other hand, would get the same fricative phoneme /ʃ/, although *impression* is related to *impress*, *promotion* to *promote* and a simple rule

$$s, t \text{ in context } -jV \rightarrow ʃ$$

(i.e. *s, t* become *ʃ* when immediately followed by *j* and a vowel) connects the members of each pair. In this case one signal stands for an underlying phonological opposition, but phonemic bi-uniqueness again prevents this solution.

A phonemic analysis of English postulates an opposition *ʃ–ʒ*. The lenis fricative /ʒ/, however, either occurs in modern loan-words from French *(mirage, garage)* or goes back to -ʒjV as in *seize – seizure, please–pleasure, measure, fuse–fusion, lesion*. Its occurrence can thus be inferred from rules and consequently it does not enter into a phonological opposition with *ʃ*.

It has been argued at great length whether the palatal and velar fricatives in German are separate phonemes or not. Their distribution can be covered by rules, which seems to suggest that they are allophonic variants. The palatal fricative is found in word initial position *(Chemie* ce′mi:*)*—provided the Ch-spelling is not rendered as *k*—after front vowels and diphthongs ending in a front element *(mich* **miç**, *Tücher* ′**ty : çer**, *Löcher* ′**løçər**, *Teich* **taiç**, *euch* **oiç)** and after consonants *(Milch* **milç**, *manch* **manç**, *durch* **durç)**. The velar fricative occurs in all other cases *(doch* **dox**, *lachen* ′**laxən**, *Buch* **bu : x**, *auch* **aux)**. There are, however, two words, *Kuchen* ′**ku : xən** 'cake' and *Kuhchen* ′**ku : çən** 'little cow', which differ only in one segment—namely *x*/*ç*—and thus form a *minimal pair* indicating a phonemic distinction. *rauchen* ′**rauxən** 'to smoke', *Frauchen* ′**frauçən** 'little woman' point to the same conclusion. This contradiction can easily be resolved by including the grammar into the phonology. *Kuhchen* and *Frauchen* are diminutives formed from *Kuh* and *Frau*, and the diminutive ending is always *-çən*, no matter what precedes; it behaves like words with initial 'Ch'.

Some linguists have strictly adhered to the concepts of parallel and complementary distribution and called *ç* and *x* different phonemes. Others have allowed the grammatical considerations to intervene. As this part of German grammar and phonology is well known and far beyond the initial stages of investigation and as the facts can easily be presented to learners without causing confusion there is absolutely no necessity for a separation of levels in this case. This is an example of a *procedural* postulate being turned into a *theoretical* issue.

*Systematic transcriptions.* Apart from being useful in language teaching and linguistic field work the phonemic principle finds a practical application in making *systematic transcriptions*, i.e. transcriptions that are based on some sort of linguistic analysis, as opposed to impressionistic ones, which refer sound to general phonetic categories directly (Abercrombie 1964).

An economical graphic representation of structural relations can evidently not reflect the gradual introduction of phonetic features into the matrix of phonological contrasts and oppositions. What is required is a list of symbols that can indicate the sequential arrangements in phonology and at the same time incorporate all the phonetic features thought necessary in the various parts of the string. This inevitably leads us to adopt the phoneme as the basic unit for systematic transcriptions which are economical and allow sentences to be written and read ease. It follows that these transcriptions must be alphabetic, and as the Roman alphabet is the one that is most widely used among literate people it is the obvious one to adopt, expanded by diacritics, diagraphs and new shapes, as outlined in the Principles of the International Phonetic Association (1949).

The most elementary transcription that can be made on these principles uses one symbol per phoneme. It is called a *phonemic* or *broad transcription*, and requires a set of conventions that add all the missing phonetic features to allow a reader to turn it into speech. If some of these conventions relating to contextual variants, i.e. to allophones, are introduced into the text the transcription becomes *allophonic*. Various degrees of allophonicness are possible depending on the amount of information that is transferred from the conventions to the text. As noted above phonemic notations are put between

/ /, and allophonic ones between [ ], if they have to be set off from orthography.

*See also:* Phonetics, articulatory. Phonetics, auditory. Writing.

*Bibliography*

ABERCROMBIE D. (1964) *English Phonetic Texts*, London.
CHOMSKY N. (1964) *Current Issues in Linguistic Theory*, Janua Linguarum, The Hague.
The Principles of the International Phonetic Association (1949), London.

K. KOHLER

**PHONOLOGY: PROSODIC FEATURES.** The phonetic features characterizing different sounds, or sound sequences, are generally described under two headings—phonemic, and prosodic. *Prosodic features*, in contrast with features characterizing phonemes, are considered not as inherent characteristics of any particular sound, but rather as superimposed on a sound or sequence of sounds without affecting their inherent quality. The features most generally classed as prosodic are *length*, *stress* and *pitch*, corresponding to the duration of sounds, their force, and in the case of voiced sounds, the voice-pitch with which they are produced.

Any auditory stimulus, to be perceived at all, must have a certain force and duration, and produce some impression of pitch in the hearer; so that these attributes are present to some degree in any utterance. Whether they are linguistically relevant or not depends on the use made of them by particular languages: whether variations in length, stress or pitch are used to convey differences of meaning.

The prosodic features are regarded as correlating with duration of an articulation in the case of length, muscular force of utterance in the case of stress, and rate of vibration of the vocal cords in the case of pitch; also with the physical dimensions of time, intensity and frequency. In fact, the correlation of the linguistic features with articulatory and physical characteristics is far from simple. The complexity of the relation is increased in many cases by the tendency of languages to employ these attributes in conjunction, rather than singly—to realize a given distinction by a combination of differences in several attributes, wherever this is possible without prejudice to other distinctions; so that word accent, for instance, may be realized by a combination of increased force with increased duration of the accented syllable.

There is general agreement on the use of some kind of two-fold classification of phonetic characteristics: about the criteria to be used in this classification, and the membership of the resulting classes, there is some variation.

Jones (1950) describes sounds in terms of four attributes—length, stress, pitch and tamber. Under the heading of *tamber* he places characteristics such as manner and place of articulation, nasality, secondary articulations, etc. The first three attributes are distinguished from tamber in that they are capable of functioning expressively, i.e. of conveying emphasis, contrast or emotional attitudes of the speaker, as opposed to differentiation of lexical or grammatical items. The term 'prosodic features', however, is not applied to them in expressive function, but only when they serve to distinguish linguistic items—a function which they share with differences of tamber.

Trubetskoy (Grundzüge der Phonologie) compares prosodic features of speech to the characteristics of a melody—variations in the pitch, loudness and duration of a note, or group of notes. This would seem to entail the pre-eminence of syntagmatic contrast (variations in an attribute at different points in a sound sequence) as opposed to paradigmatic contrast (the relation between features substitutable for each other in the same environment), for the recognition of prosodic oppositions. Jakobson and Halle (1956) also use the necessity of syntagmatic comparison as a criterion in the differentiation between *inherent* and *prosodic distinctive features*.

Bloomfield (1933) draws a distinction between *basic articulations* and *modifications*, in which the basic articulation of a sound seems to correspond roughly to the primary stricture. Secondary articulations are included among modifications, along with length, stress and pitch. The articulatory distinction is not altogether rigorous, and seems to reflect a phonological criterion, in that those features are classed as modifications which are most commonly used as secondary phonemes (i.e. differentiating between morpheme sequences as opposed to individual morphemes). The expressive use of these features is again not considered a linguistic function.

Pike (1947) distinguishes between, in his terms, *segmental* and *suprasegmental features* on acoustic grounds: suprasegmental features relate to quantitative differences in the wave form of a sound, i.e. differences which do not alter the basic wave shape. This assumes a simple correlation between length and duration, stress and amplitude, and pitch and frequency.

The distinction drawn by Malmberg (1954) is a corollary of Trubetskoy's description of prosodic features as pertaining to neither consonants nor vowels as such, but to syllables or syllable parts. Prosodic features are defined as differentiating phonological units larger than phonemes—units which, following Trubetskoy, he terms *prosodemes*. These units are set up simply as a frame for the description of prosodic contrasts: they are not necessarily appropriate for other purposes, such as the statement of phoneme distribution. This criterion distinguishes prosodic features as extensive, i.e. best described with reference to sound sequences rather than single sounds.

The criterion of extensiveness is also employed in American structural phonology, to distinguish segmental from suprasegmental phonemes, the latter comprising distinctions of stress and pitch. The terms 'segmental' and 'suprasegmental' correspond roughly in their application to the terms 'phonemic' and 'prosodic'.

While the potential expressive function of length, stress and pitch may be taken as a criterion distinguishing them from other phonetic features, it is usually only when they serve to convey lexical or grammatical distinctions that the term, 'prosodic' is applied to them. Trubetskoy also distinguishes *demarcative* from *prosodic features*, applying the latter term only to features having distinctive function, i.e. differentiating one unit from another, as opposed to marking unit boundaries. If, for instance, stress in a given language has only demarcative function, he would not consider it a prosodic feature of that language. Jakobson and Halle follow him in this, distinguishing prosodic distinctive features from configurational features, and applying the latter term to features with demarcative function.

Physical definitions of prosodic or suprasegmental features, like that of Pike, presuppose a 1 : 1 correlation between linguistic features and physical dimensions. Work on the recognition of distinctions of length, stress and pitch has shown that this supposition is untenable. Pitch differences, for instance, are perceptible in voiceless sounds, in spite of the absence of vocal cord vibration or of a fundamental frequency component. The perception of stress variation appears to correlate with variation not only of intensity, but also of the frequency and duration of sounds. A complex correlation is, indeed, to be expected, since in the process of articulation which produces the physical signal, a change in the state of one organ cannot but affect the state of other parts of the articulatory mechanism.

The auditory criterion proposed by Jakobson and Halle, namely the necessity of syntagmatic comparison for the recognition of prosodic distinctions, certainly characterizes length, stress and pitch as prosodic. However, this criterion is not sufficiently exclusive; in particular, syntagmatic comparison has been shown to play a considerable part in the recognition of distinctions in vowel quality. Possibly relative acoustic judgments are involved in the recognition of any sound distinctions where the articulatory differences are along a single dimension; though recognition of variations in length, stress and pitch might be marked by the predominance of relative over absolute auditory judgments.

The criterion of extension, though sometimes stated as entailing an extended realization of the features in question, is phonological rather than phonetic. Phonetically it is impossible to delimit the span over which a feature occurs, or has influence: successive articulatory movements merge into one another without interruption, each influencing the adjacent stretches of the utterance; so that no distinction can be drawn on the phonetic level between features realized between boundaries of any type, and features extending across those boundaries—phonetically, no boundaries can be found. Phonoliogcally, however, a distinction can be made on the grounds of possibilities of choice. If, in a phoneme sequence, it is possible to make as many significant choices of pitch as there are phonemes, each choice being made independently of the others, then pitch must be considered a feature of individual phonemes. If, however, the pitch to be assigned to one phoneme is predictable from that assigned to another, there being only one significant choice of pitch within the phoneme sequence, then the sequence itself may be considered as a unit for the statement of pitch distinctions, and pitch may be termed an extensive feature. Extensive features comprise not only length, stress and pitch; features such as palatalization, nasalization or retroflexion, to mention only a few, may also in some cases be statable with reference to phoneme sequences.

Significant differences of length, stress and pitch may take a variety of forms, postulating different types of phonological statement, and having various functions. Variations in pitch may have the typical function of phoneme distinctions—differentiation of words, both as distinct lexical items and as different derivatives of a single root. The term '*tone language*' is applied to languages using pitch in this way.

Tone languages fall into two types, according to the unit of tone distinctions: in some cases, e.g. Chinese, there is a choice of tone on each syllable; in others, a single choice on each word, e.g. some Norwegian and Swedish dialects. In the latter case, the tone marks word accent, in parallel fashion to the stress accent of English words. A single syllable of the word is marked as prominent by a certain tone; the pitch of other syllables in the word is then predictable from the accentual tone. *Accentual tone* differs from *accentual stress*, however, in that words may be distinguished not only by the position of the tone in the word, but usually also by the type of tone used, i.e. the pitch contrasts may be both syntagmatic and paradigmatic. In languages using several tone distinctions, the differences are not always purely of pitch, but are frequently reinforced by differences of voice quality—breathiness, glottality, etc.

Pitch variation in non-tonal languages has other functions—among them the differentiation of grammatical structures. This use of pitch is known as *intonation*—a term also applied to pitch differences having expressive function. The unit of intonation is again posited on the grounds of possibility of independent choice of pitch in a given sequence. The intonation unit is generally found to correspond with a grammatical unit of some kind—clause, phrase, etc.—but not to any one of these exclusively.

Languages may use both a tone system and an intonational system simultaneously; in such cases, the intonation is realized largely by modifications in the word or syllable tones. This situation is exemplified in several West African languages.

Description of the two remaining prosodic features, length and stress, is more problematical, owing to the frequent difficulty of isolating one from the other. Stress distinctions, in particular, are commonly realized at least partially by variations in length, and clear cases of length and stress functioning simultaneously as independent, extensive features are lacking. The status of length as an extensive feature, except when coupled with stress, is dubious: length distinctions in most languages seem to be adequately describable as phonemic (attributed to consonants or vowels according to the language), rather than as characterizing any sequence. Length variation of the type found in Norwegian, however, where long vowels are followed by consonants of relatively short duration, and vice versa, might be held to postulate a supra-phonemic unit of length, since the consonantal variation is entirely dependent on the length of the preceding vowel.

Where length variations relate only to vowels, and affect every vowel (and every syllabic) in the system, the extraction of length variation as a syllable property may yield a simpler description. This is Trubetskoy's procedure, exemplified by his treatment of Czech; however, he links this syllabic feature with word-accentual stress, regarding both as manifestations, on the word and syllable respectively, of a single phonetic feature. The two uses of this feature then parallel the syllabic and accentual uses of pitch. He therefore postulates two distinctive prosodic characteristics of the syllable, or syllable part—*register* (corresponding to pitch) and *intensity*. These are paralleled by the two types of word accent.

If length of the type found in Czech is not taken as a form of stress, then there exists no use of stress corresponding to the syllabic use of tone. Stress is, however, widely used in word accentuation, i.e. one syllable in the word is made prominent by strong stress, the degrees of stress on other syllables being predictable from their position relative to the prominent syllable. Word stress may be free or bound, i.e. the prominent syllable may vary in position from word to word, as in English, or may be fixed at a given place—initial, final, penultimate, etc.—as in Hungarian or Polish. In the latter case, stress placement cannot function distinctively, but only as a marker of word boundaries.

It is probable that word accentuation, whether attributed to stress or tone, is almost always marked in fact by a combination of attributes, tonally accented syllables having increased length and stress in addition to the tonal distinction, and stressed syllables providing potential locations for pitch choices in intonation. Tonal accent differs from stress accent in that whereas tonal accent may distinguish words both by positioning of the tone and by its type, stress accent can vary only in position. Some instances of variation in stress type as well as position are cited by Jones; but in all cases, there seems to be a concomitant variation in pitch, so that these instances may equally be regarded as tonal accentuation.

Patterns of stress, like pitch patterns, may pertain to sequences longer than the word. It seems doubtful, however, whether such patterns are found, with distinctive function, except in combination with intonational systems. They do, however, function demarcatively, as signals of grammatical boundaries of various ranks.

Many of the distinctive manifestations of stress and pitch have simultaneous demarcative functions; since whenever variations in an attribute are statable with reference to a grammatical unit, they are by definition demarcative of that unit. Free accentuation, then, is demarcative of the word, in addition to its distinctive function; though it marks rather the number of words in a given utterance than their boundaries. Demarcation of this type is sometimes termed *culminative*, as opposed to the marking of boundaries, which is termed *delimitative*. Likewise features such as palatalization, vowel harmony, dissimilation, etc., if describable with reference to a grammatical unit, are demarcative of that unit.

Longer patterns of stress and intonation, while not coinciding with any one grammatical unit to the exclusion of other types, nevertheless generally coincide with grammatical units of some kind, in particular sequences, so that they too may be regarded as having a demarcative function. Such patterns frequently resemble patterns of word accent, in that a single choice of a culminative syllable determines to a considerable extent the variation possible on other syllables. Where this culminative syllable has a fixed position in the total pattern, its function is delimitative. Strong stress in French, for instance, is bound to the final syllable of each stress unit—the end of a stress unit serving to mark a grammatical boundary.

Prosodic features, and extensive features in general, are not the only means of demarcation to be found. Allophonic variation and phoneme distribution, where these are stated with reference to a unit such as the word, must also be regarded as having demarcative function. As a factor differentiating length, stress and pitch from other features, demarcative function is even less effective than extension.

It does not appear, then, that any absolute distinction can be drawn between the features generally termed prosodic, and other phonetic features. A relative distinction, however, may be more feasible: with regard to auditory recognition, the rôle of syntagmatic comparison and relative judgements may be larger in the perception of length, stress and pitch distinctions than in distinctions involving other features; and with regard to function, the prosodic features may be more frequently used than other features to differentiate units larger than the morpheme.

*Bibliography*

BLOOMFIELD L. (1933) *Language*.
JAKOBSON R. and HALLE M. (1956) *Fundamentals of Language*, s'Gravenhage.
JONES D. (1950) *The Phoneme*, Cambridge: The University Press.
MALMBERG B. (1954) *La Phonétique*, Paris.
PIKE K. (1947) *Phonemics*, Ann Arbor.
TRUBETSKOY N.S. (1939) *Grundzüge der Phonologie*.

E. M. HIGGINBOTTOM

**PROBLEM SOLVING.** *On definitions.* Problem solving is a general term used to describe certain forms of behaviour. Like its cousin terms—recognizing, learning, communicating, etc.—it is compounded not only from features of actual behaviour, but from notions of the structure of environments, hypothesized internal structure of the problem solver, and the functions served by the behaviour. It is an empirical term, having meaning prior to any theory of problem solving. However, it cannot be defined precisely outside of a theory. Rather, it appears to be best explained by example (again, like its cousins). Several instances are advanced that surely involve problem solving. Attention is directed to various essential features, but without claiming that these characterize the term adequately.

Consider the following situations as problematic:

(1) You arrive at a river bank, which you want to cross; however, neither bridge nor boat is in sight.

(2) Mary is twice as old as Ann was when Mary was as old as Ann is now. If Mary is 24 years old, how old is Ann?

(3) You are to play chess against an opponent with whom you are evenly matched.

(4) You are a scientist; an experiment of yours has just failed, although apparently methodologically satisfactory. What do you do next?

The essential features of these situations seem to be three. First, the problem solver wants some environmental situation other than the existing one; he has a definite goal or difficulty. Second, the problem solver cannot attain the goal immediately. More precisely, he doesn't know how to attain it. Situations do not present problems where the way is clear, and only time or effort is required to reach the goal, e.g. there is a bridge in sight and all one has to do is walk to it. Third, the problem solver must engage in relevant behaviour. Weeping in the face of the uncrossed river is not problem solving. That one can think of circumstances where it is, as a woman inducing a male by-passer to help, only shows the paradigmatic nature of the definition.

Thus, problem solving involves deliberate, extended use of information processing. It is contrasted with *recognizing;* the latter referring to situations producing an immediate correct response. It is distinguished from the simple use of past *learning*, by sufficient novelty in the environment so that past learning must be supplemented by additional constructive activity. Problem solving is taken to be a variety of *thinking*, but not all of it; clarity of goal seems to distinguish it from much other activity that one would call thinking. Finally, problem solving does not necessarily cover all of *creativity;* to assert it does, implies a (perhaps true) reductionist theory that the processes underlying problem solving are also adequate to explain creativity.

We have tried to clarify the term by relating it to the usage of similar terms. More precision requires a theory of problem solving. Of prime importance in any such theory is its *sufficiency*—its demonstration of how it is possible for problem solving to occur. The theory sketched below derives from recent work in constructing computer programs that solve problems, as well as studies of the problem solving behaviour of intelligent humans. The tasks that have been studied are very much in the centre of the paradigm: problems of a rather neat and formal kind, such as examples (2) and (3). Although one would wish for additional evidence from more 'open' problems, such as (1) and (4), the theory is the only one so far that provides any demonstrations of sufficiency for non-trivial problems.

*Information processing theory of problem solving.* The gross anatomy of a problem solver consists of 1) a goal structure; 2) an internal representation of the problem; 3) a collection of methods; 4) a collection of evaluations; and 5) a memory of information that may be relevant. The executive structure involves a basic cycle of selecting a method, applying it and evaluating the result. This much in the way of search (trial and error) is forced because the problem solver does not know exactly how to proceed. In the course of this cycle, the goal structure is modified; applying methods generally leads to establishing of subgoals. Similarly, information generated by the methods is (or may be) useful later in the problem, sometimes in applying the method, sometimes in quite different ways. More rarely, modifications of the problem representation occur, including the (perhaps implicit) initial selection of an internal representation.

The scheme above is almost vacuous unless the parts are specified, and to these we now turn. However, this vacuity seems to be a necessary concomitant of generality.

*Goal structure.* A goal is a symbolic structure that represents to the problem solver what is desired (it may provide much other information as well). Operationally, 'representation' means only that the goal can function as information, along with the objects of the problem, both to be the method selection process and the evaluation process. The goal structure is a hierarchy, a subgoal corresponding to the attainment of some part or aspect of the supergoal. In problem solving programs the hierarchy is almost always an AND-OR tree: to each goal belongs either a disjunction of subgoals, any one of which would attain the supergoal; or a conjunction of subgoals, all of which must be attained.

*Representation.* Although a problem must be represented *somehow*, almost nothing is known about what representations are possible, nor how a good representation can be chosen. Almost all the problems that have been investigated in detail, have required a representation with a 'problem space' that contains both the initial problem situation and the desired one. The other points in the space represent potentially intermediate situations. The possibilities for problem solving in this space are represented by a set of admissible operators that permit new situations to be obtained from ones already obtained. In addition, the situations themselves are structured and describable, permitting sundry direct diagnoses and comparisons. Problem solving with such a representation becomes a search in a space whose paths must be constructed. Good examples can be found in *theorem proving* (see *Theorem proving by machine*). In games the objects are boards, the operators are legal moves; in theorem proving, the objects are theorems, the operators rules of inference.

Auxiliary representations often arise as *models* of the true situation. An example is the diagram of a geometry theorem, which provides a new representation that is subject to very different operations—i.e. direct measurement of angles, lengths, areas, etc. Again, although a few examples have been studied, little is known about how models are discovered or what full range of functions they satisfy.

*Methods.* A method is a scheme (or program) for behaviour that may contribute to progress in solving a problem. Operationally, it must be a symbolic structure that can be interpreted by the problem solver as a (conditional) sequence either of manipulations of objects (in the internal representation) or of subgoals to be attained. Methods can be as specific as a complete program, e.g. a program for matrix inversion. However, since the problem solver characteristically lacks knowledge of how to proceed or of the details of the problem, methods of wide generality are of greatest interest. Four will be mentioned here; they encompass almost all methods that have been demonstrated on computers, and they are used extensively in human problem solving behaviour.

*Generate and test.* The method provides some systematic way of constructing a sequence of candidates for the solution; they are produced one by one, each being tested to see if it should be kept. The system may be cascaded, so that the generated objects are passed through a sequence of tests. Almost always this method is used at the lowest level in a problem solver, e.g. the moves of the Queen are tried in order; each theorem on a theorem list is considered in order.

*Heuristic search.* Radiating outward from the given situation, new ones can be constructed, by means of the admissible operations. Each new situation becomes the input for another stage of generation. Thus the search tree tends to grow exponentially. But, the search is pruned and guided by the application of various *heuristics* (aids to discovery) at each branch point, e.g. situations that are too complex may be abandoned. If the heuristics are good, the search converges; if poor, it blows up. This method is at the heart of almost all problem solving computer programs.

*Means-ends analysis.* Although a variation of heuristic search, this method requires special treatment. If situations can be described, then the operations can be described in terms of the differences between their inputs and outputs. The description of the difference between the given situation and the desired situation can be used to select an appropriate operator; namely, one that reduces this difference. This is the familiar attempt to relate means to the ends to be attained; it results in labelling operators (the means) by their 'functions.' For example, in chess moves are called 'attacks,' 'defences,' 'blocks,' etc.

Means-ends analysis has been investigated in several computer programs; and evidence for its generality exists. It seems to characterize a vast amount of human problem solving, not only in formal tasks, but in everyday reasoning.

*Matching.* There may exist a *form* of the solution; that is, a symbolic object that already partially corresponds with the desired solution, but which has some missing parts. Then the missing parts may be determined by matching the form to structures already in the environment. This is an extremely powerful technique, since it involves a search only over the subparts of a situation (as they are put into correspondence), rather than through the whole space of situations. Matching accounts for much of the power of present day theorem provers (but not game players, which have not yet been able to incorporate it). In computer programs the missing parts of the forms are almost always represented by variables, so matching is achieved by substitution. However, in one variation, which might be called *guided growth*, the solution is constructed *ab initio* step by step, the existing situation guiding each step. This technique has accounted for the success of programs that induct relations, such as 'What are the blanks in A, B, C, B, C, D, –, –?'

*Planning.* A plan is a sequence of operations and/or goals that provides a guide to obtaining the desired situation. It differs from a method only in being constructed for the occasion; and hence being of little generality. The plan itself must be constructed by some problem solving mechanism, generally involving a 'planning space,' which is a simplification or abstraction of the original problem space. The mathematician, when he 'proceeds formally,' ignoring all questions of existence and uniqueness, is planning in this sense. In the simplified space, problem solving is easier.

Planning is ubiquitous in human problem solving, both spontaneously and in various formalized ways (such as planning a trip). Many programs exist that carry out problem solving in a specified planning space, e.g. airline scheduling programs. Indeed, some degree of abstraction is hard to avoid! However, little is yet known about how problem solvers develop their own planning spaces, given only the original, fully detailed problem.

*Evaluation.* Problem solvers have a vast collection of specific information they use to evaluate results. A chess player knows that Bishop and Knight are about even, but two Bishops are better than two Knights in an end game. In the context of problem solving programs, considerable work has gone into the study of evaluations, usually expressed as weighted sums of features. Much additional work has been done on the evaluation of alternatives, especially risky ones, by humans. It is not possible to summarize the results; except to note that several strands of evidence indicate that human evaluation functions may not be very sophisticated.

*Relevant information.* The role of auxiliary information can be critical—for example, a problem is readily solved if you happen to know the answer (there is a bridge around the bend). It is not known what role large stores of information play in good problem solving. No problem solving programs exist yet that make use of large stores, and hence illuminate the possibilities. It has been hypothesized, however, that what distinguishes mastery in a field is primarily an extensive data base so that 'no problem is new for the master.'

*Fundamental processing requirements.* Problem solving, as described above, implies a substantial capability for symbolic manipulation (see *Symbol manipulation by digital computer*). This means the ability to read, write, store, retrieve, and interpret (in the sense used in programming) symbolic structures. The underlying processing systems are fundamentally serial in nature, although perhaps with parallel detection or recognition capabilities. In turn this implies there is a limited immediate memory. These characteristics appear to affect the nature of the problem solving process, but no adequate formulation of the interrelations yet exists.

The above description of problem solving has been termed a theory. It is certainly not a formalized, closed system. However, it takes a stand on the essential nature of problem solving that is at variance with at least three other views: (1) The *Gestalt view* takes the organization of the perceptual field, with its sudden restructuring (as in ambiguous figures), as the appropriate root metaphor for problem solving. Problem solving need not be extended in time and need not involve search (trial and error); rather, the requirements of the problem situation and the appropriately receptive organism combine to organize the problem solver to 'see,' with great clarity, the solution. (2) In *Freudian psychology* the locus of most of the problem solving is the unconscious (technically, the preconscious). Extensive combinatorial activity is supposed to take place there, only the highly selected products emerging into consciousness. (3) Finally, classical *S-R psychology* has been loath to admit the kind of active manipulative and constructive ability that permeates the theory described above. Complex behaviour is to arise simply from a chaining together of simple S-R links. *Mediational links* (links whose stimulus and response are both entirely internal to the organism) are now admitted, but they go only a short way toward the full complexity demanded by the theory set forth here. These other viewpoints have taken as starting points different concerns than the theory presented; none of them as yet provides any demonstrations of sufficiency.

*See also:* Symbol manipulation by digital computer. Theorem proving by machine.

*Bibliography*

BOBROW D. G. (1964) *A question-answering system for high school algebra word problems, Proceedings Fall Joint Computer Conference*, **26**, 591, New York: Spartan Press.

DEGROOT A. (1965) *Thought and Choice in Chess*, The Hague: Mouton.

FEIGENBAUM E. and FELDMAN J. (Eds.) (1963) *Computers and Thought*, New York: McGraw-Hill. This provides a collection of most of the important early papers on problem solving programs, as well as an extensive bibliography.

KUBIE L. S. (1958) *Neurotic Distortion of the Creative Process*, Kansas: The University Press. For Freudian view.

NEWELL A. and ERNST G. (1965) *The search for generality*, (E. W. Kalenich Ed.) *Proceedings IFIP Congress*, **65**, 17, New York: Spartan Press.

POLYA G. (1945) *How to Solve it*, Princeton: The University Press. On heuristic; a classic.

REITMAN W. R. (1965) *Cognition and Thought*, New York: Wiley.

SIMON H. and KOTOVSKY K. (1963) *Human acquisition of concepts for sequential patterns*, Psychological Review, **70**, no. 6, 534.

STAATS A. W. and STAATS C. K. (1963) *Complex Human Behavior*, New York: Holt, Rinehart and Winston. For S-R view.

WERTHEIMER M. (1945) *Productive Thinking*, New York: Harper and Row. For Gestalt view.

A. NEWELL

**PROSTHETIC LIMBS.** The first record of an artificial limb being worn dates back to 500 B.C. It was not until the nineteenth century, however, that artificial limb design became at all sophisticated. Although one firm in Great Britain was making artificial legs at the turn of the century, prosthetic limbs were not produced in quantity until the end of the First World War. Work progressed steadily for the next forty years until, in about 1960, a sudden increase in the number of congenitally deformed children caused research and development to gather momentum. This increase in the number of congenitally deformed children occurred as a result of the mother taking certain drugs during the early weeks of pregnancy. The deformities took a variety of forms, many of the children having neither arms nor legs.

There are many countries throughout the world working in the field of artificial limbs. Of these, Canada, Germany, Great Britain, Russia, Scandinavia and the United States are the main centres of activity.

The field of prosthetic limbs may be divided into two groups, lower-extremity and upper-extremity, which may be subdivided into body-powered and externally-powered prostheses. However, before examining these subdivisions, it must be pointed out that any limb is satisfactory only if it is acceptable to the patient. However elegant a limb may be as a piece of engineering, a patient may still reject it for psychological reasons. Therefore, it is important to consider carefully the mental attitude of the amputee at all stages of design and development.

*Lower-extremity prostheses.* Although artificial legs were being made before artificial arms the overall progress has, perhaps, been less spectacular, due to more limitations. Legs have always been body-powered, the wearer having to produce the energy himself in order to make any movements. Due to the large power-consumption required during walking and running it is unlikely that artificial legs will ever be totally powered from an external source. It is possible, however, that power-assisted walking may be introduced, and work is progressing along these lines.

The original 'peg' legs were rigid from the site of amputation, whether above or below the knee, to the ground. Once the articulated leg had been introduced with hinges at the knee and ankle, progress was towards two main objectives. The first was to produce a leg which enabled the amputee to have a natural gait, and the second was to reduce to a minimum the harness needed to attach the leg to the amputee's body.

To surmount the first problem it was necessary to obtain detailed information about the gaits of normal human beings. Careful study was carried out using a variety of techniques, and the resulting data was analysed. From these results it was possible to obtain a criterion of performance, and to design legs to fulfil this criterion. This has been achieved by introducing damping at the knee and ankle joints, using various hydraulic devices. This method has proved satisfactory for low frequency movement, and gives the amputee a natural and steady gait. However, the problem of walking quickly, or of running, has yet to be solved.

The second objective, of minimizing the harness, has also largely been solved. Initially, it was necessary to have a waist belt and various other straps in order to hold the leg firmly onto the stump. However, a method has been developed for producing a total-bearing suction-socket which holds the limb in place by means of a close-fitting socket which bears on the stump. The advantages of these are greater comfort, due to the relieving of high-pressure points in the socket, and a greater freedom of movement, due to the removal of restrictive harnesses.

*Upper-extremity prostheses.* Artificial arms are in many ways both more important and more difficult to design than artificial legs. The loss of one or both arms is to the sufferer, largely a loss of his independence in his private life, whereas a leg amputee's disability is only an inconvenience. The human being's natural desire is to be able to look after himself, and his loss of ability to dress himself, to attend to his own toilet, and so on, can be the cause of acute unhappiness and embarrassment. Accordingly, much effort has been expended on the design of arm and hand prostheses.

The human arm has seven degrees of freedom from the shoulder to the wrist (see Fig. I), quite apart from the unique versatility of the hand. To attempt to reproduce each movement and its related power output with an artificial device is not at present possible, and compromises are constantly being made.

Conventionally, artificial limbs are powered and controlled by the wearer by means of a harness and Bowden

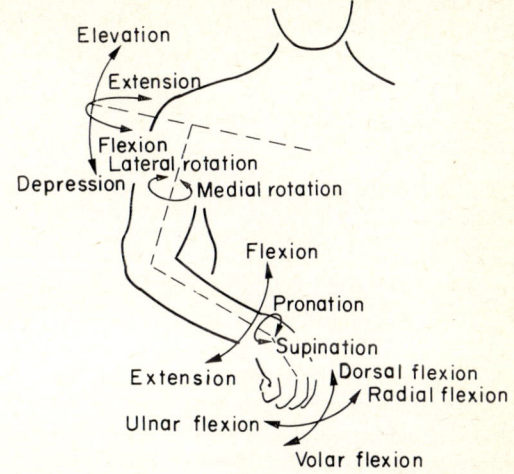

Fig. 1

cable (see Fig. 2). This harness not only restricts the natural movement of the body but also limits the positions in space where a prosthesis may be operated successfully, due to the Bowden cable becoming slack. To overcome these problems attempts have been made to take an output direct from the muscle by means of *cineplasty*. Here a tunnel is made through the skin and the muscle so that a suitable attachment can be made to the muscle by passing a rod through the tunnel (see Fig. 3). This rod is attached to the Bowden cable. However, the method has now been rejected for a variety of reasons, such as hygiene and discomfort.

The idea of powering a prosthesis from an external source is attractive for a variety of reasons. First, it enables the wearer to conserve his strength for other movements; second, he is not limited in the positions in which he may use his prosthesis successfully; third, more power can often be made available from an external source than from the body. The first attempts were made by Alderson and Vaduz, independently, at powering hands from electrical sources. However, neither successfully produced hands which could be fitted to patients. Later, in 1956, work began on pneumatically-powered arms. Over the succeeding years development has continued in both fields, and there are now several

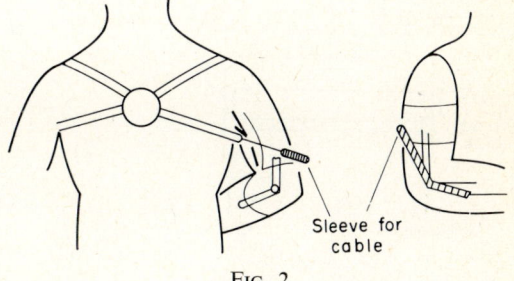

Fig. 2

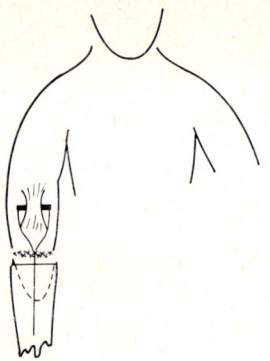

Fig. 3

teams around the world working on externally powered prostheses.

The pneumatically powered arms use carbon-dioxide as a power source. It is stored in liquid form, but is used at a working pressure of about 100 psi. There are a variety of single-piston and double-piston motors in use. Of the single-piston motors, some are 'spring-return' whilst others are 'double-acting'. The double-acting motors being developed are of the differential-area variety. These allow a maximum saving of gas to be achieved by using the same gas for both the power/exhaust stroke, when it acts at high-pressure on the small side of the piston, and the return stroke, when it acts at high pressure on both sides of the piston, the large side then being dominant. Outputs are taken from the motors in a variety of ways. Bowden cables, linkages, and direct drives are all commonly used. Figure 4 shows a differential-area wrist-rotator.

Electrically powered arms are still largely in the development stage. Many cells exist which are both safe and rechargeable, but no one cell is used universally because there has been such rapid progress in the field caused by the various space programmes. The motors used are servomotors, which drive the prostheses through gear-trains.

The design of suitable terminal devices has always been a complex problem. The human hand is unique n nature, and attempts to copy its performance mechanically have always ended in indifferent results. As with the arm, compromises must be made, and an order of priority of movements established. The common system with body-powered prostheses is to supply the amputee with a variety of terminal devices which are suitable for specialized tasks, and which he may attach to the artificial wrist by a locking device. The desirability of having only one terminal device has led to various designs of split-hooks, which have proved very versatile. Unfortunately, these are cosmetically unsatisfactory, and attempts have been made, unsuccessfully, to achieve the performances of a split-hook with a terminal device which resembles a hand more closely. No satisfactory solution has been found, however, which is universally acceptable.

One of the largest problems in both body-powered and externally-powered arms is that of control. Each pair of movements, such as elbow extension and flexion, must have a separate control site which is completely independent of other movements. As indicated above, the cable-operated arm uses a harness which acts as a single large control site. If this harness is linked to a splithook, or other terminal device, as is common, movement of, say, the elbow has to be achieved either by using the other arm, or by a 'flick' from the shoulder which swings the forearm to the desired position, where it is locked.

In the case of an externally powered prosthesis the control site has to be large enough to accommodate only a control valve or switch. Thus, it is easier to find more control sites on the body for an externally-powered than for a body-powered prosthesis. However, it is at present impossible to find enough independent sites to control a full range of movements for both arms of a bilateral amputee. Typical sites which may be used are the shoulders, the chest and the waist, the last two needing harness to cause a valve to open when, say, the chest expands. It is also possible to make use of the toes, if the legs are insufficiently developed to enable a child to walk.

For the amputee who has lost a limb through an accident, it is sometimes possible to control a limb myoelectrically. The success of this form of control depends on the availability of strong muscles above the point amputation, since it is the signal reaching these muscles from the central nervous system which is used as a control signal. One of the present limitations of this system is the necessity for a pair of muscles to control one movement. For instance, an above elbow amputee requires more movements in his prosthesis than a below-elbow amputee, but has less muscles available for myoelectric control. This problem may be surmounted in the near future by the use of implants. By implanting amplifiers or transmitters in the muscle it may be possible to receive a more localized signal from a part of a muscle than is possible at present. If this can be achieved, the number of available control sites will be greatly increased, giving a wider range of possible movements. It will also reduce the number of limitations at present encountered with myoelectric control.

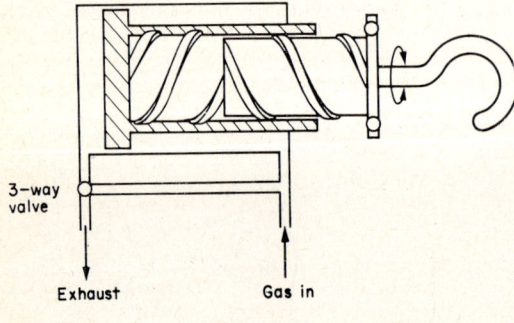

Fig. 4

Although the field of limb prosthetics is long-established, research into the use of externally-powered prostheses is in its infancy. Future work is likely to include (1) development in the motors used (2) refinement of the controls and control systems (3) examination of different power sources as they become available (4) further work in the use of implants. This list is, however, far from exhaustive, and further developments in other related and unrelated fields of technology should certainly enlarge the number of directions in which research and development will continue in this field.

*Bibliography*

BATTYE C. K. *et al.* (1955) *The Use of Myo-electric currents in the operation of Prostheses, J. Bone Surg.*
BOTTOMLEY A. H. and COWELL T. K. (1964) *An artifical hand controlled by the nerves*, New Scientist.
(Aug. 1965) *J. Bone Joint Surg.*
KLOPSTEG and WILSON (Eds.) (1954) *Human Limbs and their Substitutes* (Available from National Central Library), New York: McGraw-Hill.
PAUL I. (1961) *An investigation of compact power sources for externally powered prosthetic and orthopaedic devices*, M.S. Thesis, M.I.T.
(Oct. 1965) *Proceedings of Symposium on Powered Prostheses*, Roehampton.
TOMOVIC R. (1960) *Human hand as a feed-back system*, IFAC Conference in Moscow 1960; Automatic and Remote Control, London: Butterworths.
TOMOVIC R. and BONI G. (1962) *An adaptive artifical hand*, Trans I.R.E.

N. D. RING

**PSEUDONOISE SEQUENCES.** Periodic binary sequences with impulse-like autocorrelation functions have various pseudonoise characteristics which lead to the following applications:

1. simulation of noise in a repeatable manner (Kramer 1965);
2. synchronization of telemetry codes (Barker 1953; Gilbert 1960; Stiffler 1962);
3. improving the power content of radar signals without deterioration of their resolving power (Siebert 1956; Stewart and Westerfield 1959);
4. ranging techniques in radar and telemetry (Bartee and Wood 1963; Weiss and Gorenstein 1962);
5. generation of harmonic spectra (Ingram *et al.* 1966);
6. measurement of system transfer functions (Berson 1962; Corran and Cummins 1962);
7. communication signal multiplexing (Judge 1962; Suran and Marolf 1964);
8. design of telephone switching networks (G.E.C. 1966).

They are also important in statistics in the guise of cyclic balanced incomplete block designs (Mann 1949).

The concepts of binary pseudonoise sequences, integer difference sets and cyclic symmetric balanced incomplete block designs are introduced and the problems of the existence of these three entities are shown to be equivalent. The two latter problems have been studied extensively in the past and one purpose of this paper is to bring these earlier studies to the attention of those interested in pseudonoise sequences. It is not intended to give rigorous proofs of all the theorems as these may be found elsewhere.

Two classes of pseudonoise sequences, known as maximal length and quadratic residue, are particularly useful, the first being easily generated, by means of feedback shift registers (Elspas 1959), and the second being more numerous than any other known class. Properties of these two classes are discussed in some detail. Other classes are defined and a list of sequences is given.

*Problem 1.* In general we shall be concerned with periodic sequences whose elements belong to a finite field (Dickson 1958), $GF(p)$, of $p$ elements, where $p$ is a prime. We shall take the elements of the field to be $0, 1, 2, \ldots, p-1$, with addition and multiplication performed modulo $p$. Modulo $p$ addition and subtraction will be denoted by $\oplus$ and $\ominus$.

A sequence, $\ldots a_0, a_1, \ldots, a_r, \ldots, a_{v-1}, \ldots$, or more briefly $\{a_r\}$, is said to have *period* $v$ if $v$ is the smallest integer such that $a_r = a_{r+v}$ for all $r$.

Following Zierler (1959), we define the *autocorrelation function*, $A_s$, of a sequence $\{a_r\}$ with respect to a mapping $\eta$ of the elements of $\{a_r\}$ into the complex numbers by

$$A_s = \Sigma_r \eta(a_r)[\eta(a_{r+s})]^*, \quad s = 0, 1, \ldots, v-1,$$

where * denotes complex conjugate and $\Sigma_r$ denotes $\Sigma_{r=0}^{r=v-1}$.

If the elements of $\{a_r\}$ belong to the finite field $GF(p)$ we will take

$$\eta(a_r) = \gamma^{a_r},$$

where $\gamma$ is a primitive complex $p$th root of unity, e.g. $\gamma = \exp(2\pi i/p)$. We then have as the autocorrelation function of $\{a_r\}$,

$$A_s = \Sigma_r \gamma^{a_r} \gamma^{\ominus a_{r+s}} = \Sigma_r \gamma^{a_r \ominus a_{r+s}}. \tag{1}$$

It will be noticed that in the case of binary sequences this definition gives the same value for $A_s$ as that obtained by the following, more familiar, definition (Golomb 1964). Define the binary sequence $\{\hat{a}_r\}$ as a sequence of $\pm 1$, related to $\{a_r\}$ by $\hat{a}_r = (-1)^{a_r}$; then we will have from equation 1,

$$A_s = \Sigma_r \hat{a}_r \hat{a}_{r+s}, \tag{2}$$

since in this case $\gamma = -1$.

We now define a sequence $\{a_r\}$ to be *pseudonoise*, with respect to the mapping $\eta$, if $A_s = A$, a constant, for $s = 1, 2, 3, \ldots, v-1$.

*Example 1.*
If $\{a_r\} = \ldots 1001110 \ldots$
then $A_0 = 7$ and $A_s = -1$ for $s = 1, 2, \ldots, 6$, using equation 1.

Problem I – for what values of $v$ do binary pseudonoise sequences exist?

*Problem II.* A set of $k$ distinct integers $(d_1, d_2, \ldots, d_k)$ modulo an integer $v$ is called an integer difference set (Ryser 1963), $D$, if every integer $b \not\equiv 0 \pmod{v}$ can be expressed in exactly $\lambda$ ways in the form $d_i - d_j \equiv b \pmod{v}$, where $d_i, d_j$ belong to $D$.

Example 2.

If $D = (0, 3, 4, 5)$ with modulus 7,

then
$$\left.\begin{array}{l}1 \equiv 4-3 \equiv 5-4 \\ 2 \equiv 5-3 \equiv 0-5 \\ 3 \equiv 3-0 \equiv 0-4 \\ 4 \equiv 0-3 \equiv 4-0 \\ 5 \equiv 3-5 \equiv 5-0 \\ 6 \equiv 3-4 \equiv 4-5\end{array}\right\} \text{ modulo } 7$$

so that $\lambda = 2$.

Problem II – for what values of $v$ do integer difference sets exist?

*Problem III.* A symmetric balanced incomplete block design $(v, k, \lambda)$ is an arrangement of $v$ objects into $v$ sets in such a way that

(i) every set contains exactly $k$ objects
(ii) every object occurs in exactly $k$ sets
(iii) every pair of objects is contained in exactly $\lambda$ sets.

The design may be illustrated by an object-set incidence matrix $M = (m_{ij})$, where $m_{ij} = 1$ if object $i$ is contained in set $j$, and $m_{ij} = 0$ otherwise.

The design is said to be cyclic if $M$ can be made cyclic (circulant, Aitken 1942) by suitable renumbering of the sets and objects.

Example 3.

|       | $S_0$ | $S_1$ | $S_2$ | $S_3$ | $S_4$ | $S_5$ | $S_6$ |
|-------|-------|-------|-------|-------|-------|-------|-------|
| $0_0$ | 1     | 0     | 0     | 1     | 1     | 1     | 0     |
| $0_1$ | 0     | 1     | 0     | 0     | 1     | 1     | 1     |
| $0_2$ | 1     | 0     | 1     | 0     | 0     | 1     | 1     |
| $0_3$ | 1     | 1     | 0     | 1     | 0     | 0     | 1     |
| $0_4$ | 1     | 1     | 1     | 0     | 1     | 0     | 0     |
| $0_5$ | 0     | 1     | 1     | 1     | 0     | 1     | 0     |
| $0_6$ | 0     | 0     | 1     | 1     | 1     | 0     | 1     |

with $v = 7$, $k = 4$, $\lambda = 2$.

Problem III – for what values of $v$ do such cyclic designs exist?

*Necessary conditions for solutions to the above problems to exist.*

*Problem I.* Let $k$ be the number of $a_r$, $0 \le r \le v-1$, for which $a_r = 1$ in $\{a_r\}$, $\{a_r\}$ being pseudonoise and binary. Summing equation 1 over all values of $s$ we obtain

$$\begin{aligned}\Sigma_s A_s &= \Sigma_s \Sigma_r (-1)^{a_r}(-1)^{a_{r+s}} \\ &= \Sigma_r (-1)^{a_r} \Sigma_s (-1)^{a_{r+s}} \\ &= \Sigma_r (-1)^{a_r}[k(-1)^1 + (v-k)(-1)^0] \\ &= (v-2k)\Sigma_r (-1)^{a_r} \\ &= (2k-v)^2.\end{aligned}$$

The left hand side is equal to $A_0 + A_1 + \ldots + A_{v-1} = v + A(v-1)$.

Thus
$$v + A(v-1) = (2k-v)^2. \tag{3}$$

Let $n_1$ be the number of groups of consecutive ones in one period of $\{a_r\}$,

e.g. if $\{a_r\} = \ldots 100110101110 \ldots$

then $n_1 = 4$.

Since $\{a_r\}$ is periodic, the number of groups of consecutive zeros is also $n_1$.

By definition
$$A_1 = A = \Sigma_r (-1)^{a_r}(-1)^{a_{r+1}}$$

and this sum is equal to the number of places in which $\{a_r\}$ and $\{a_{r+1}\}$ agree in each period less the number of places in which they disagree.

So $A = v - 2$ (number of disagreements). Since $\{a_r\}$ and $\{a_{r+1}\}$ differ by one position they will disagree only at the first element of each group (of ones and zeros) in $\{a_r\}$,

e.g. if $\{a_r\} = \ldots 100110101110 \ldots$

$\{a_{r+1}\} = \ldots 001101011101 \ldots$

d-d-dddd—dd

where $d$ denotes disagreement.

Hence $A = v - 2$ (number of groups, of zeros and ones, in one period of $\{a_r\}$)

$$= v - 4n_1. \tag{4}$$

Elimination of $A$ from equations 3 and 4 gives

$$(k - n_1)(v - 1) = k(k - 1) \tag{5}$$

which may be written as

$$\lambda(v - 1) = k(k - 1), \tag{6a}$$

where

$$\lambda = k - n_1.$$

Thus a necessary condition for a binary sequence to be pseudonoise is that its parameters satisfy equation 6a. However, this condition is not sufficient. For example, no binary pseudonoise sequence exists with parameters $v = 16$, $k = 6$, $n_1 = 4$.

*Problem II.* The total number of non-zero differences between the $k$ elements of a difference set is $k(k-1)$.

The number of distinct non-zero integers $b$, modulo $v$ is $v - 1$, and since each appears as a difference $\lambda$ times we have

$$\lambda(v - 1) = k(k - 1). \tag{6b}$$

Again this is a necessary but not sufficient condition for an integer difference set to exist.

*Problem III.* Given a cyclic symmetric balanced incomplete block design $(v, k, \lambda)$ we will count all pairs of objects containing object $0_0$, say, in two ways:
(a) the pair of objects $0_0, 0_j, j = 1, 2, \ldots, v-1$, occurs in $\lambda$ sets for each $j$ so that the total number of such pairs is $\lambda(v-1)$, (b) in each set in which object $0_0$ occurs it is counted $k-1$ times, once with each other object in the set, and it occurs in $k$ sets and is therefore counted $k(k-1)$ times.

Hence $\qquad \lambda(v-1) = k(k-1).$ \hfill (6c)

That this condition is not sufficient is illustrated by the following object-set incidence matrix, whose parameters satisfy equation 6c but which cannot be made cyclic by any permutation of the rows or columns.

```
0 1 1 1 | 1 0 0 0 | 1 0 0 0 | 1 0 0 0
1 0 1 1 | 0 1 0 0 | 0 1 0 0 | 0 1 0 0
1 1 0 1 | 0 0 1 0 | 0 0 1 0 | 0 0 1 0
1 1 1 0 | 0 0 0 1 | 0 0 0 1 | 0 0 0 1
--------+---------+---------+--------
1 0 0 0 | 0 1 1 1 | 1 0 0 0 | 1 0 0 0
0 1 0 0 | 1 0 1 1 | 0 1 0 0 | 0 1 0 0
0 0 1 0 | 1 1 0 1 | 0 0 1 0 | 0 0 1 0
0 0 0 1 | 1 1 1 0 | 0 0 0 1 | 0 0 0 1
--------+---------+---------+--------
1 0 0 0 | 1 0 0 0 | 0 1 1 1 | 1 0 0 0
0 1 0 0 | 0 1 0 0 | 1 0 1 1 | 0 1 0 0
0 0 1 0 | 0 0 1 0 | 1 1 0 1 | 0 0 1 0
0 0 0 1 | 0 0 0 1 | 1 1 1 0 | 0 0 0 1
--------+---------+---------+--------
1 0 0 0 | 1 0 0 0 | 1 0 0 0 | 0 1 1 1
0 1 0 0 | 0 1 0 0 | 0 1 0 0 | 1 0 1 1
0 0 1 0 | 0 0 1 0 | 0 0 1 0 | 1 1 0 1
0 0 0 1 | 0 0 0 1 | 0 0 0 1 | 1 1 1 0
```

*Note*—for each of these problems there are trivial solutions for all $v$ with $k = 0, 1, v-1$ and $v$, and $\lambda = 0, 0, v-2$ and $v$ respectively; these will be ignored. Also it follows fairly readily from the definitions that if a solution exists for parameters $(v, k, \lambda)$ then there is a corresponding solution with parameters $(v, v-k, v-2k+\lambda)$. This solution is the complement of the original solution obtained by

I replacing $\{a_r\}$ by $\{\bar{a}_r\}$, where $\bar{a}_r = a_r \oplus 1$.
II forming $\bar{D}$, where $\bar{D}$ consists of just those integers, modulo $v$, which are not in $D$
III forming $\bar{M}$ where $\overline{m_{ij}} = m_{ij} \oplus 1$.

Thus where convenient we may assume that $2 \leq k \leq v/2$.

*Equivalence of the three problems,* 'I $\leftrightarrow$ II $\leftrightarrow$ III'. We now show that these three existence problems are equivalent, i.e. if a solution for any one of them is found then there are corresponding solutions for the other two.

'I $\Rightarrow$ II'. Suppose $\{a_r\}$ is a binary $(0, 1)$ pseudonoise sequence having period $v$ and $k$ ones in any one period. Then $\Sigma_r(-1)^{a_r}(-1)^{a_{r+s}} = A$ is constant for $s = 1, 2, \ldots, v-1$. Define $m_s$ to be the number of places, in each period, in which $\{a_r\}$ and $\{a_{r+s}\}$ have a one in common, i.e. $a_r = a_{r+s} = 1$ for $m_s$ values of $r$, $0 \leq r \leq v-1$. Then $\{a_r\}$ and $\{a_{r+s}\}$ differ in $2(k-m_s)$ places and have zero in common in $v-m_s-2(k-m_s)$ places. This is easily seen by rearranging the terms of the sequences so that they may be compared as follows:

$$\overbrace{1\ldots1}^{m_s}\ \overbrace{1\ldots\ldots1}^{k-m_s}\ \overbrace{0\ldots\ldots0}^{k-m_s}\ \overbrace{0\ldots\ldots\ldots0}^{v-m_s-2(k-m_s)}$$
$$1\ldots1\ \ 0\ldots\ldots0\ \ 1\ldots\ldots1\ \ 0\ldots\ldots\ldots0$$

Thus $\quad A = m_s(1)^0 + 2(k-m_s)(-1)^1 + (v-2k+m_s)(-1)^0$
$\qquad\quad = v - 4k + 4m_s.$

Since $A$, $v$ and $k$ are fixed $m_s$ is constant, $m$ say, for $s = 1, 2, \ldots, v-1$. So for each non-zero $s$ there are exactly $m$ integers $r$ such that $a_r = a_{r+s} = 1$.
Hence the integers $r$, for which $a_r = 1$, form a difference set modulo $v$. Compare examples 1 and 2.

'II $\Rightarrow$ III'. Given a difference set $D = (d_1, d_2, \ldots, d_k)$ modulo $v$, with parameter $\lambda$, arrange $v$ objects in $v$ sets as follows:

put objects

| $d_1$ | $d_2$ | --- $d_k$ | into set 0 |
| $d_1+1$ | $d_2+1$ | --- $d_k+1$ | into set 1 |
| --- | --- | --- | |
| $d_1+v-1$ | $d_2+v-1$ | --- $d_k+v-1$ | into set $v-1$. |

Then each set contains $k$ objects and, since each column of this $v \times k$ array consists of the integers 0 to $v-1$, each object is contained in $k$ sets.

Now consider a pair of objects $a$ and $b$, say. Since $D$ is a difference set

$$a - b \equiv d_i - d_j \pmod{v} \text{ in exactly } \lambda \text{ ways.}$$

For each of these $\lambda$ ways, integer $a$ will occur in the $i$th column of the array above and integer $b$ in the $j$th column, in each case in the $(a-d_i-1)$th $[\equiv (b-d_j-1)$th] row.

Thus each pair of objects appears in exactly $\lambda$ sets and the above arrangement is a solution to III. Compare Examples 2 and 3.

'III $\Rightarrow$ I'. Assume a cyclic $(v, k, \lambda)$ design. Consider the first row of the incidence matrix to be a binary sequence, then the other rows are all cyclic shifts of it. It will be sufficient to show that each pair of rows has exactly $\lambda$ ones in common, and this follows immediately since, from the symmetry of the design, each pair of sets has exactly $\lambda$ objects in common.

*Sampling of pseudonoise sequences.* Given $\{a_r\} = \ldots a_0, a_1, \ldots, a_{v-1}, \ldots$, not necessarily pseudonoise, form $\{b_r\} = \ldots b_0, b_1, \ldots, b_{v-1}, \ldots$, where $b_r = a_{fr}$. Thus $\{b_r\}$ consists of every $f$th term of $\{a_r\}$. We call $f$ a *sampler* of $\{a_r\}$. If $f$ and $v$ are relatively prime, i.e. $(f, v) = 1$, then $\{a_r\}$ and $\{b_r\}$ have the same period and $\{b_r\}$ is a rearrangement of $\{a_r\}$.

*Theorem 1.* If $A_s$ is the autocorrelation function of $\{a_r\}$ (not necessarily pseudonoise) and $B_s$ is the autocorrelation function of $\{b_r\}$, where $b_r = a_{fr}$ and $f$ is relatively prime to $v$, the period of $\{a_r\}$, then

$$B_s = A_{fs}, \quad \text{for all } s.$$

In other words, the autocorrelation function of the sequence obtained by sampling is the same as the sampled autocorrelation function of the sampled sequence.

*Proof.* Using equation 1

$$B_s = \sum_r (-1)^{b_r \Theta b_{r+s}}$$
$$= \sum_r (-1)^{a_{fr} \Theta a_{fr+fs}}.$$

Now $(f, v) = 1$ and thus the values, modulo $v$, taken by $fr$ are a permutation of those taken by $r (r = 0, 1, \ldots, v-1)$.
Hence

$$B_s = \sum_r (-1)^{a_r \Theta a_{r+fs}}$$
$$= A_{fs}.$$

*Corollary.* If $\{a_r\}$ is pseudonoise and $(f, v) = 1$, then $\{b_r\} = \{a_{fr}\}$ is pseudonoise with the same parameters as $\{a_r\}$.

Thus from a pseudonoise sequence of period $v$ it may be possible to form others with the same period by sampling,

e.g. if $\{a_r\} = \ldots 1110100 \ldots$
then $\{a_{2r}\} = \ldots 1110100 \ldots$
and $\{a_{3r}\} = \ldots 1001011 \ldots$

We will return to consider the sampling of particular sequences later.

*Multipliers of difference sets* (Mann 1965). *Theorem 2.* Let $D = (d_1, d_2, \ldots, d_k)$ be a difference set with modulus $v$, and put $E = (td_1, td_2, \ldots, td_k)$. Then $E$ is a difference set with modulus $v$ if $(t, v) = 1$.

*Proof.* In $D$ we have, for any non-zero integer $b$,

$$b \equiv d_i - d_j \pmod{v} \text{ in } \lambda \text{ ways}.$$

Since $(t, v) = 1$, as $b$ varies from 1 to $v-1$, $tb \pmod{v}$ varies from 1 to $v-1$ in some order.
Thus

$$tb \equiv td_i - td_j \pmod{v} \text{ in } \lambda \text{ ways, for all } tb \not\equiv 0,$$

i.e. for all $b \not\equiv 0$.

Thus $E$ is a difference set,
e.g. if $D = (1, 2, 3, 5)$ with modulus 7, $\lambda = 2$ and $t = 4$
then $E = (4, 1, 5, 6)$ which may be verified to be a difference set modulo 7 having $\lambda = 2$.

*Definition.* Given a difference set $D = (d_1, d_2, \ldots, d_k)$ modulo $v$, then $t$ is said to be a *multiplier* of $D$ if there exists an integer $s$ such that

$$(td_1, td_2, \ldots, td_k) = (d_1+s, d_2+s, \ldots, d_k+s),$$

i.e. multiplication by $t$ leaves the difference set unchanged apart, perhaps, from a constant added to all elements.

Note that it is not implied that $td_1 = d_1+s$, $td_2 = d_2+s$, etc.,
e.g. in the example above $s = 3$.

*Relationship between samplers and multipliers.* *Theorem 3.* If $\{a_r\}$ is the binary pseudonoise sequence corresponding to a difference set $D$ and $t$ is a multiplier of $D$, then $f \equiv 1/t \pmod{v}$ as a sampler of $\{a_r\}$ leaves the sequence unchanged apart, perhaps, from a cyclic shift.

*Proof.* If $D = (d_1, d_2, \ldots, d_k)$, then $t$ is such that $(td_1, td_2, \ldots, td_k) = (d_1+s, d_2+s, \ldots, d_k+s)$. The sequence $\{a_r\}$ corresponding to $D$ is given by $a_r = 1$ if and only if $r = d_i$, $d_i$ in $D$.

Sampling $\{a_r\}$ with $f \equiv 1/t$ we get $\{b_r\}$, where $b_r = a_{r/t}$.

Thus $b_r = 1$ if and only if $r/t \equiv d_j$, $d_j$ in $D$
i.e. if and only if $r \equiv td_j$,
i.e. if and only if $r - s \equiv td_j - s$,

and since $t$ is a multiplier there exists a $d_i$ in $D$ such that

$$d_i \equiv td_j - s.$$

Hence $b_r = 1$ if and only if $r - s \equiv d_i$
and so $b_r = a_{r-s}$.

Thus $\{a_{r/t}\}$ is the same as $\{a_r\}$ with a cyclic shift of $s$.

*Known classes of pseudonoise sequences. Quadratic residue* (Lehmer 1953). An integer $\mu$ is said to be a primitive root of a prime $v$ if $1 = \mu^0, \mu^1, \mu^2, \ldots, \mu^{v-2}$ are all distinct modulo $v$, see Vinogradov (1955). Thus every non-zero integer (mod $v$) can be expressed as a power of $\mu$. Notice that $\mu^{v-1} \equiv 1$, since otherwise we get a contradiction,
e.g. 3 is a primitive root of 7 since the first six powers of 3 (mod 7) are 1, 3, 2, 6, 4, 5. Vinogradov (1955) gives a list of primitive roots for all primes up to 4000.

*Definition.* Define a modulo $v$ quadratic residue sequence as follows:

$\hat{a}_r = (-1)^t$, where $r \equiv \mu^t \pmod{v}$ and $\mu$ is a primitive root of $v$.

Thus $\hat{a}_r = 1$ if $r$ is a square, modulo $v$, and $\hat{a}_r = -1$ otherwise, i.e. $\hat{a}_r = 1$ for $r = 1, \mu^2, \mu^4, \ldots, \mu^{(v-1)/2}$. For the moment we leave $\hat{a}_0$ undefined. Note that, not counting $r = 0$, the number of $r$ for which $\hat{a}_r = 1$ is equal to the number for for which $\hat{a}_r = -1$. Also the sequence obtained in this way is independent of the primitive root of $v$ which is chosen, e.g. if $v = 7$, with $\mu = 3$, then $\mu^2 \equiv 2 \pmod{7}$ and the powers of $\mu^2$ are 1, 2, 4 giving the sequence $\ldots \hat{a}_0 110100 \ldots$ We will now investigate the conditions for a quadratic residue sequence to be pseudonoise.

*Lemma.* If $\{\hat{a}_r\}$ is a modulo $v$ quadratic residue sequence, then for $r, s \not\equiv 0 \mod v$,

$$\hat{a}_r \hat{a}_s = \hat{a}_{rs}.$$

*Proof.* Let $\mu$ be a primitive root of $v$, then there exist integers $t$, $u$, such that $r \equiv \mu^t$, $s \equiv \mu^u$ (mod $v$).

Then $\hat{a}_r = (-1)^t$, $\hat{a}_s = (-1)^u$

so that $\hat{a}_r \hat{a}_s = (-1)^{t+u}$.

Now $rs \equiv \mu^{t+u}$

so that $\hat{a}_{rs} = (-1)^{t+u}$.

Hence $\hat{a}_r \hat{a}_s = \hat{a}_{rs}$.

*Theorem 4.* A binary quadratic residue sequence is pseudonoise if and only if its period $v \equiv 3$ (mod 4), i.e. $v$ is of the form $4K-1$.

*Proof.* Using equation 2 for the autocorrelation function we have

$$A_s = \Sigma_r \hat{a}_r \hat{a}_{r+s} = \hat{a}_0 \hat{a}_s + \hat{a}_{-s} \hat{a}_0 + \sum_{\substack{r=1 \\ r \neq v-s}}^{v-1} \hat{a}_r \hat{a}_{r+s}, \quad s \neq 0.$$

Since $v$ is prime, for each non-zero integer $r$, modulo $v$, there exists an integer $r^{-1}$ such that $rr^{-1} \equiv 1 \pmod{v}$, (Birkhoff and Maclane 1965).
Thus $\hat{a}_{r+s} = \hat{a}_{r+rr^{-1}s} = \hat{a}_r \hat{a}_{1+sr^{-1}}$, by the lemma.
Hence

$$A_s = \hat{a}_0(\hat{a}_s + \hat{a}_{-s}) + \sum_{\substack{r=1 \\ r \neq v-s}}^{v-1} \hat{a}_r^2 \hat{a}_{1+sr^{-1}}$$

$$= \hat{a}_0 \hat{a}_s(\hat{a}_1 + \hat{a}_{-1}) + \sum_{\substack{r=1 \\ r \neq v-s}}^{v-1} \hat{a}_{1+sr^{-1}}, \text{ since } \hat{a}_r^2 = 1, \text{ for all } r \neq 0.$$

As $r$ runs through the integers $0, 1, \ldots, v-1$, omitting $0, -s$, $r^{-1}$ runs through the integers $0, 1, \ldots, v-1$, omitting $0, -s^{-1}$ so that $1+sr^{-1}$ runs through the integers $0, 1, \ldots, v-1$, omitting $1, 0$. So

$$A_s = \hat{a}_0 \hat{a}_s(\hat{a}_1 + \hat{a}_{-1}) + \sum_{r=2}^{v-1} \hat{a}_r$$

$$= \hat{a}_0 \hat{a}_s(\hat{a}_1 + \hat{a}_{-1}) - \hat{a}_1 + \sum_{r=1}^{v-1} \hat{a}_r.$$

Since just half of $\hat{a}_r$ ($r = 1, 2, \ldots, v-1$) are $+1$ and the other half are $-1$,

$$\sum_{r=1}^{v-1} \hat{a}_r = 0.$$

Hence

$$A_s = \hat{a}_0 \hat{a}_s(\hat{a}_1 + \hat{a}_{-1}) - \hat{a}_1. \quad (7)$$

If $\{\hat{a}_r\}$ is to be binary, $\hat{a}_0 = \pm 1$ and the sequence can be pseudonoise only if $A_s$ is independent of $s$. Thus we require $\hat{a}_1 = -\hat{a}_{-1}$.
Now $\mu^{v-1} \equiv 1$, and by taking square roots
$\mu^{(v-1)/2} \equiv -1$, since it cannot be $+1$ by the definition of $\mu$. So $\hat{a}_{-1} = (-1)^{(v-1)/2}$ and $\hat{a}_1 = 1$.
Only if $(v-1)/2$ is odd will we have $\hat{a}_{-1} = -1$ as required; hence $v$ must be of the form $4K-1$.

In this case

$$A_s = -\hat{a}_1 = -1 \text{ for all } s \neq 0 \bmod v.$$

Note that this result is independent of the value of $\hat{a}_0$. If the binary condition is removed we have:

*Theorem 5.* Quadratic residue sequences are pseudonoise for all odd primes $v$ if $\hat{a}_0 = 0$.

*Proof.* Putting $\hat{a}_0 = 0$ in equation 7 gives

$$A_s = -\hat{a}_1 = -1.$$

See Belevitch (1965).
The two theorems above may be summarized in the following table.

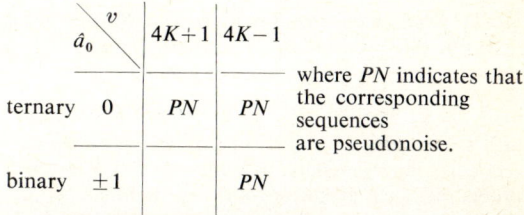

where $PN$ indicates that the corresponding sequences are pseudonoise.

*Theorem 6.* (a) The modulo $v$ quadratic residue sequence of period $v = 4K-1$ with $\hat{a}_0 = +1$ is the reverse of the negative of the same sequence with $\hat{a}_0 = -1$,

i.e. $\hat{a}_r = -\hat{a}_{-r}$, $r \not\equiv 0 \pmod{v}$.

(b) The modulo $v$ quadratic residue sequence of period $v = 4K+1$ with $\hat{a}_0 = 0$ is a 'palindrome',

i.e. $\hat{a}_r = \hat{a}_{-r}$, for all $r$.

*Theorem 7.* If a modulo $v$ quadratic residue pseudonoise sequence is sampled with $f$, $f \not\equiv 0 \bmod v$, then:
(a) if $v = 4K-1$ the original sequence is obtained if $f$ is a quadratic residue (a square) modulo $v$, and the reverse sequence is obtained if $f$ is a non-quadratic residue, modulo $v$, (b) if $v = 4K+1$ ($\hat{a}_0 = 0$) the original sequence is obtained for all $f$.
These two theorems are readily proved from the definitions above.

*Biquadratic residue sequences* (Lehmer 1953). A modulo $v$ biquadratic residue sequence, $\{\hat{a}_r\}$, is defined for a prime $v$ and non-zero $r$ by

$\hat{a}_r = 1$ if $r$ is a power of $\mu^4$, modulo $v$,

$\hat{a}_r = -1$ otherwise,

($\hat{a}_0$ is undefined for the moment),

where $\mu$ is a primitive root of $v$.
It can be shown that only two cases of binary pseudonoise sequences arise, and these are

(a)      $\hat{a}_0 = -1$, $v$ of the form $4(2K+1)^2 + 1$
(b)      $\hat{a}_0 = +1$, $v$ of the form $4(2K+1)^2 + 9$.

*Octic residue sequences* (Lehmer 1953). A modulo $v$ octic residue sequence, $\{\hat{a}_r\}$, is defined for prime $v$ and non-zero $r$ by

$\hat{a}_r = 1$ if $r$ is a power of $\mu^8$, modulo $v$,

$\hat{a}_r = -1$ otherwise,

($\hat{a}_0$ is undefined for the moment),

where $\mu$ is a primitive root of $v$.

Again it can be shown that only two cases arise for which $\{\hat{a}_r\}$ is binary and pseudonoise, and these are
(a) $\hat{a}_0 = -1$, $v$ simultaneously of the forms $8(2K+1)^2+1$ and $64(2L+1)^2+9$,
(b) $\hat{a}_0 = +1$, $v$ simultaneously of the forms $8(2K+1)^2+49$ and $256L^2+441$.

*Twin prime sequences* (Stanton and Sprott 1958; Titsworth 1963). Given $p$ and $q$ primes, with $p+2 = q$ and $\mu$ a common primitive root of $p$ and $q$, then

$$1, \mu, \mu^2, \ldots, \mu^{(p^2-3)/2}; 0, q, 2q, \ldots, (p-1)q,$$

form a difference set, modulo $pq$, from which the corresponding binary pseudonoise sequence may be derived. (Proofs that such primitive roots can be found are not known to the author, but presumably such proofs do exist.)

Alternatively, define $\{\hat{a}_r\}$, $\{\hat{b}_r\}$ to be quadratic residue sequences (obviously not both pseudonoise) with periods $p$ and $q$ respectively. The twin prime sequence $\{\hat{c}_r\}$ is defined by

$\hat{c}_r = \hat{a}_r \hat{b}_r$ for $r \not\equiv 0 \bmod p$ or $\bmod q$,

$\hat{c}_r = +1$ whenever $r \equiv 0 \bmod q$,

$\hat{c}_r = -1$ whenever $r \equiv 0 \bmod p$, but $r \not\equiv 0 \bmod q$.

Then $\{\hat{c}_r\}$ is pseudonoise.

*Example.* Take $p = 3$, $q = 5$ and the common primitive root $\mu = 2$. Then the difference set defined above is

$$1, 2, 4, 8; \quad 0, 5, 10$$

giving the sequence

$$\ldots + + + - + + - - + - + - - - - \ldots$$

which is pseudonoise with parameters $v = 15$, $k = 7$, $\lambda = 3$.

Alternatively, using the quadratic residue sequences

$$\{\hat{a}_r\} = \ldots \hat{a}_0 + - \ldots$$
$$\{\hat{b}_r\} = \ldots \hat{b}_0 + - - + \ldots$$

$\hat{c}_r = +1$ for $r \equiv 0 \pmod{5}$

$\hat{c}_r = -1$ for $r \equiv 0 \pmod{3}$, but $r \not\equiv 0 \pmod{5}$

$\hat{c}_r = \hat{a}_r \hat{b}_r$ otherwise.

Thus we obtain the sequence

$$\{\hat{c}_r\} = \ldots + + + - + + - - + - + - - - - \ldots$$

as above.

*Hall sequences* (Hall 1956). Binary pseudonoise sequences of this type exist for periods $v$ of the form $4K^2+27$ and prime. They are defined as follows: choose a primitive root $\mu$ of $v$ such that if $3 \equiv \mu^t \pmod{v}$, then $t \equiv 1 \pmod{6}$, $\{\hat{a}_r\}$ is then defined by

$\hat{a}_r = +1$ if $r \equiv \mu^s \pmod{v}$ where $s \equiv 0, 1$ or $3 \pmod{6}$,
$\hat{a}_r = -1$ otherwise. (Proofs that such primitive roots can be found are not known to the author, but presumably such proofs do exist.)

*Example.* A suitable value for $v$ is 31, which has 3 as a primitive root. Now $\hat{a}_r = 1$ if $r \equiv 3^t \pmod{31}$, where $t \equiv 0, 1$ or $3 \pmod{6}$,
i.e.

| 0 | 6 | 12 | 18 | 24 | | 1 | 16 | 8 | 4 | 2 |
|---|---|----|----|----|---|---|----|---|---|---|
| $t = 1$ | 7 | 13 | 19 | 25, so that $r =$ | 3 | 17 | 24 | 12 | 6 |
| 3 | 9 | 15 | 21 | 27 | | | 27 | 29 | 30 | 15 | 23 |

i.e. $\hat{a}_r = 1$ for $r = 1, 2, 3, 4, 6, 8, 12, 15, 16, 17, 23, 24, 27, 29, 30$.

*Maximal length sequences (m-sequences).* A polynomial $\phi(x)$, with coefficients in $GF(p)$ is *primitive* (Peterson 1961), (has maximal period (Elspas 1959)), over $GF(p)$ if the smallest non-zero integer $e$ such that $\phi(x)$ divides $x^e \ominus 1$ is $e = p^n - 1$, where $n$ is the degree of $\phi(x)$. The division is performed modulo $p$. See Table 1 for a list of some primitive polynomials.

*Binary m-sequences.* Define $\phi(x) = x^n \ominus [\alpha_{n-1} x^{n-1} \oplus \alpha_{n-2} x^{n-2} \oplus \ldots \oplus \alpha_0]$, $\alpha_i = 0$ or 1, to be a primitive polynomial over $GF(2)$. Define the sequence $\{a_i\}$, over $GF(2)$, recursively by

$$a_{n+i} = \alpha_{n-1} a_{n+i-1} \oplus \alpha_{n-2} a_{n+i-2} \oplus \ldots \oplus \alpha_0 a_i, \quad (8)$$

where $a_0, a_1, \ldots, a_{n-1}$ are arbitrary elements of $GF(2)$ (but not all zero). Note that by (ii) below, the initial $n$-tuple is arbitrary since all non-zero $n$-tuples will be generated.

Alternatively, if we define the vectors

$$\mathbf{x}_0 = \begin{pmatrix} a_{n-1} \\ a_{n-2} \\ \vdots \\ a_0 \end{pmatrix}, \quad \mathbf{x}_1 = \begin{pmatrix} a_n \\ a_{n-1} \\ \vdots \\ a_1 \end{pmatrix}, \ldots \mathbf{x}_r = \begin{pmatrix} a_{n+r-1} \\ a_{n+r-2} \\ \vdots \\ a_r \end{pmatrix}, \ldots$$

then the recurrence relation may be written in the form

$$\mathbf{x}_{r+1} = T\mathbf{x}_r,$$

where $T = \begin{pmatrix} \alpha_{n-1} & \alpha_{n-2} & ---- & \alpha_0 \\ 1 & 0 & ---- & 0 \\ 0 & 1 & ---- & 0 \\ \vdots & & \ddots & \vdots \\ 0 & 0 & --- 0 & 1 & 0 \end{pmatrix}$, with addition modulo 2.

The generation of these sequences with feedback shift registers is described by Elspas (1959). Some well known properties of such sequences $\{a_r\}$ are

(i) the period, $v$, is $2^n - 1$;

*Table 1. Primitive Polynomials over GF(p).*

The following table gives the coefficients of the polynomials in the form $x^n \ominus [\alpha_{n-1} x^{n-1} \oplus \ldots \oplus \alpha_0]$.

| $p$ | $n$ | $\alpha_6$ | $\alpha_5$ | $\alpha_4$ | $\alpha_3$ | $\alpha_2$ | $\alpha_1$ | $\alpha_0$ |
|---|---|---|---|---|---|---|---|---|
| 2 | 3 | | | | | 0 | 1 | 1 |
|   | 4 | | | | 0 | 0 | 1 | 1 |
|   | 5 | | | 0 | 0 | 1 | 0 | 1 |
|   | 6 | | 0 | 0 | 0 | 0 | 1 | 1 |
|   | 7 | 0 | 0 | 0 | 1 | 0 | 0 | 1 |
| 3 | 3 | | | | | 0 | 1 | 2 |
|   | 4 | | | | 0 | 0 | 2 | 1 |
|   | 5 | | | 0 | 0 | 0 | 1 | 2 |
| 5 | 3 | | | | | 0 | 2 | 3 |
|   | 4 | | | | 0 | 4 | 3 | 3 |
| 7 | 3 | | | | | 0 | 4 | 5 |
| 11 | 3 | | | | | 0 | 10 | 7 |
| 13 | 3 | | | | | 0 | 12 | 7 |
| 17 | 3 | | | | | 0 | 16 | 14 |
| 19 | 3 | | | | | 0 | 18 | 15 |
| 23 | 3 | | | | | 0 | 22 | 20 |
| 29 | 3 | | | | | 0 | 28 | 18 |
| 31 | 3 | | | | | 0 | 30 | 17 |

(ii) each non-zero $n$-tuple appears exactly once in each period;
(iii) the number of ones in each period is $2^{n-1}$, the number of zeros $2^{n-1} - 1$;
(iv) the Shift and Subtract property which states that for all $s \not\equiv 0 \pmod{v}$ there exists an integer $w$ such that
$$a_r \ominus a_{r+s} = a_{r+w}, \text{ for all } r.$$

This is often called the Shift and Add property in the binary case, since there $\ominus$ and $\oplus$ are equivalent. We prefer the former name since the Shift and Add property does not generalize, without modification, to the non-binary case.

*Theorem 8.* The $m$-sequence $\{a_r\}$ defined above is pseudonoise.

*Proof.* We have, by equation 1
$$A_s = \Sigma_r (-1)^{a_r \ominus a_{r+s}},$$
whence, by (iv) above, we get for $s \not\equiv 0$
$$A_s = \Sigma_r (-1)^{a_{r+w}}$$
$$= \Sigma_r (-1)^{a_r}$$
$$= (\text{no. of zeros}) - (\text{no. of ones})$$
$$= -1, s = 1, 2, \ldots, 2^n - 2, \text{ by (iii)}.$$

Further properties:

(v) if a binary $m$-sequence is sampled with $f$ equal to a power of 2, then the same sequence results
(vi) sampling $\{a_r\}$ with each $f$ in turn, $(f, 2^n - 1) = 1$, $1 \leq f \leq 2^n - 2$, will produce all binary $m$-sequences of period $2^n - 1$ (each exactly $n$ times) and no others.

Note: the number of different $m$-sequences of period $2^n - 1$ is $n^{-1} \phi(2^n - 1)$, where $\phi(m)$ is the Euler totient function denoting the number of integers less than and relatively prime to the integer $m$.

Sampling with $f$ corresponds to replacing the generating polynomial $\phi(x)$ by $\psi(x)$ where the roots of $\psi(x) = 0$ are the $f$th powers of the roots of $\phi(x) = 0$. If $(f, v) = 1$ then $\psi(x)$ is primitive. Example. $x^4 \ominus (x \oplus 1)$ is primitive over $GF(2)$.

Using equation 8 we have
$$a_{4+i} = 0 \cdot a_{3+i} \oplus 0 \cdot a_{2+i} \oplus 1 \cdot a_{1+i} \oplus 1 \cdot a_i.$$

Put $a_0 = a_1 = a_2 = a_3 = 1$
then $\{a_r\} = \ldots 111100010011010 \ldots$
To illustrate property (iv) consider $\{a_r\} \ominus \{a_{r+1}\}$

$\phantom{\ominus}$ 111100010011010
$\ominus$ 111000100110101

000100110101111; the difference is $\{a_{r+4}\}$.

Sampling with $f = 1, 2, 4$ or 8 we get
$\ldots 111100010011010 \ldots$

Sampling with $f = 7, 14, 13$ or 11 we get
$\ldots 010110010001111 \ldots$

These sequences correspond to the two fourth degree primitive polynomials $x^4 \ominus (x \oplus 1)$ and $x^4 \ominus (x^3 \oplus 1)$. Note that $\frac{1}{4} \phi(15) = 8/4 = 2$.

*$m$-sequences over general $GF(p)$.* Again we require a primitive polynomial, but over $GF(p)$, i.e.
$$\phi(x) = x^n \ominus [\alpha_{n-1} x^{n-1} \oplus \alpha_{n-2} x^{n-2} \oplus \ldots \oplus \alpha_0]$$
is to be primitive, and the $\alpha_i$ are to belong to the finite field $GF(p)$ of $p$ elements.
The $m$-sequence $\{a_r\}$ is defined over $GF(p)$ by
$$a_{n+i} = \alpha_{n-1} a_{n+i-1} \oplus \alpha_{n-2} a_{n+i-2} \oplus \ldots \oplus \alpha_0 a_i.$$

The matrix T is defined as before, remembering that now addition is carried out modulo $p$.
Properties (i) to (vi) for the binary case become

(i)′ the period, $v$, is $p^n-1$;
(ii)′ each non-zero $n$-tuple appears exactly once in each period;
(iii)′ the number of occurrences of each non-zero element in each period is $p^{n-1}$, the number of zeros is $p^{n-1}-1$;
(iv)′ the Shift and Subtract property which states that for all $s \not\equiv 0 \pmod{v}$ there exists an integer $w$ such that
$$a_r \ominus a_{r+s} = a_{r+w} \quad \text{for all } r.$$
(v)′ if a $p$-nary $m$-sequence is sampled with $f$ equal to a power of $p$ then same sequence results;
(vi)′ sampling $\{a_r\}$ with each $f$ in turn, $(f, p^n-1) = 1$, $1 \leq f \leq p^n-2$, will produce all $p$-nary $m$-sequences of period $p^n-1$ (each $n$ times) and no others. Note that the number of different $m$-sequences of period $p^n-1$ is $n^{-1}\phi(p^n-1)$.

Since, from (ii)′, each non-zero $n$-tuple appears exactly once in each period, if the sequence contains the $n$-tuple $(a_i, a_{i+1}, \ldots, a_{i+n-1})$ it also will contain $(ba_i, ba_{i+1}, \ldots, ba_{i+n-1})$ for each non-zero integer, $b$, of $GF(p)$. Since the generating recurrence relation is linear the term following $(ba_i, ba_{i+1}, \ldots, ba_{i+n-1})$ will be $ba_{i+n}$. Hence each period of the $p$-nary $m$-sequence is made up of $p-1$ 'blocks' each of length $(p^n-1)/p-1$ and each 'block' is a constant integral multiple, $\beta$ say, of the previous 'block'. Clearly, $\beta$ must be a primitive root of $p$.

*Theorem 9.* The $p$-nary $m$-sequence defined above is pseudonoise.

*Proof.* Let $\gamma$ be a primitive complex $p$th root of unity. Then using equation 1 we have, for $s \neq 0$,

$$A_s = \Sigma_r \gamma^{a_r \ominus a_{r+s}}$$
$$= \Sigma_r \gamma^{a_{r+w}}, \text{ for some } w, \text{ by (iv)}',$$
$$= \Sigma_r \gamma^{a_r}$$
$$= (p^{n-1}-1)\gamma^0 + p^{n-1}(\gamma^1 + \gamma^2 + \ldots + \gamma^{p-1}), \text{ by (iii)}',$$
$$= -1 + p^{n-1}\frac{(1-\gamma^p)}{1-\gamma}$$
$$= -1, \text{ since } \gamma \neq 1 \text{ and } \gamma^p = 1.$$

*Theorem 10.* If in the $p$-nary $m$-sequence $\{a_r\}$ of period $p^n-1$, defined above, we replace the non-zero terms by zero and the zero terms by one, then the resulting binary sequence has period $(p^n-1)/p-1$ and is pseudonoise.

*Proof.* That the period is $(p^n-1)/p-1$ follows from the 'block' structure of the $p$-nary sequence. The pseudonoise property will follow from the ensuing discussion. An alternative proof follows from the Corollary to Theorem 12 of Zierler (1959).

Theorem 10 also holds for binary sequences derived from $q$-nary $m$-sequences, defined over a general Galois field, $GF(q)$.

*Finite projective geometry* (Carmichael 1937). A finite projective plane $\pi$ is a finite collection of points and lines such that

(a) any two points uniquely determine a line
(b) any two lines uniquely determine a point
(c) the plane contains at least four non-collinear points.

Note the similarity with symmetric balanced incomplete block designs.

Given a finite field $GF(p)$ such a plane may be constructed as follows.
Represent a point, $X$, by the 3-vector

$$\mathbf{x} = \begin{pmatrix} x_1 \\ x_2 \\ x_3 \end{pmatrix},$$

where the coordinates belong to $GF(p)$, and are not all zero, and two points $X$ and $X'$, are the same if $x_1'/x_1 = x_2'/x_2 = x_3'/x_3$. The number of non-zero 3-vectors is clearly $p^3-1$ and thus there are $(p^3-1)/p-1$ distinct points.

A line, $L$, represented by $\begin{pmatrix} l_1 \\ l_2 \\ l_3 \end{pmatrix}$ is given by the equation

$$l_1 x_1 \oplus l_2 x_2 \oplus l_3 x_3 = 0,$$

i.e. $(l_1, l_2, l_3) \begin{pmatrix} x_1 \\ x_2 \\ x_3 \end{pmatrix} = \mathbf{l}^t . \mathbf{x} = 0.$

$l_1, l_2, l_3$ belong to $GF(p)$ and are not all zero. Two lines $l$ and $l'$ are the same if $l_1'/l_1 = l_2'/l_2 = l_3'/l_3$. Hence the number of distinct lines is also $(p^3-1)/p-1$. The points on the line joining $X$ and $Y$ are given by $a\mathbf{x} + b\mathbf{y}$, where $a$ and $b$ belong to $GF(p)$ and are not both zero. Thus the number of distinct points on the line $(\mathbf{x}, \mathbf{y})$, and hence on any line, is equal to the number of pairs $(a, b)$, of elements of $GF(p)$, such that all ratios $a/b$ are different. The distinct ratios are

$$0/1, \ 1/1, \ 2/1, \ \ldots, (p-1)/1, \ 1/0.$$

Hence the number of points on each line is $(p^2-1)/p-1$. Similarly the number of lines through each point is $(p^2-1)/p-1$.

A finite projective geometry of $n-1$ dimensions may be constructed in a similar manner by representing each point and each hyperplane by an $n$-vector of elements of $GF(p)$. A hyperplane $H$, represented by $\begin{pmatrix} h_1 \\ h_2 \\ . \\ . \\ . \\ h_n \end{pmatrix}$ is a space of $n-2$ dimensions with equation

$$\mathbf{h}^t . \mathbf{x} = 0.$$

It is not difficult to show that this geometry has the following properties:

(i) the total number of points is $(p^n-1)/p-1$;
(ii) the total number of hyperplanes is $(p^n-1)/p-1$;
(iii) any hyperplane contains $(p^{n-1}-1)/p-1$ points;
(iv) any point has $(p^{n-1}-1)/p-1$ hyperplanes passing through it;
(v) any two hyperplanes intersect in a space of $n-3$ dimensions which contains $(p^{n-2}-1)/p-1$ points.

Returning to the $p$-nary $m$-sequence $\{a_r\}$ of period $p^n-1$ we see that the first $(p^n-1)p-1$ $n$-tuples may be taken to represent all the points of an $n-1$ dimensional projective geometry.

Consider the hyperplane $H_0$ given by $x_1 = 0$, i.e.
$$1.x_1 \oplus 0.x_2 \oplus 0.x_3 \oplus \ldots \oplus 0.x_n = 0.$$

This hyperplane contains just those points whose first coordinate is zero.

We now construct the point-hyperplane incidence matrix, $M$, for this geometry, the rows representing the hyperplanes and the columns the points. We take as the points

$$\mathbf{x}_0 = (a_{n-1}, a_{n-2}, \ldots, a_0)^t$$
$$\mathbf{x}_1 = (a_n, a_{n-1}, \ldots, a_1)^t$$
etc.

Then row one, corresponding to $H_0$, contains ones in just those columns corresponding to the points with zero first coordinate, i.e. corresponding to the positions of the zeros in the first 'block' of $\{a_r\}$. There will be $(p^n-1)/p-1$ values of $i$ for which point

$$\mathbf{x}_i = (a_{n+i-1}, \ldots, a_i)^t \text{ lies on } H_0.$$

Now $T\mathbf{x}_i = \mathbf{x}_{i+1}$ for all $i$,
where
$$T = \begin{pmatrix} \alpha_{n-1} & \alpha_{n-2} & - & - & - & \alpha_0 \\ 1 & 0 & - & - & - & 0 \\ 0 & 1 & - & - & - & 0 \\ & & \cdot & & & \\ & & & \cdot & & \\ & & & & \cdot & \\ \cdot & & & - & - & 0 & 1 & 0 \end{pmatrix}$$

Thus if $\mathbf{x}_i$ lies on the hyperplane $H_0$, whose equation is
$$\mathbf{h}^t\mathbf{x} = 0,$$
then $T\mathbf{x}_i$ lies on the hyperplane, $H_1$ say, whose equation is
$$\mathbf{h}^t.T^{-1}\mathbf{x} = 0.$$

This is easily seen by substituting $T\mathbf{x}_i$ for $\mathbf{x}$. Hence if $\mathbf{x}$ lies on $H_0$ then $\mathbf{x}_{i+1}$ lies on the hyperplane $H_1$ with coordinates $\mathbf{h}^t T^{-1}$. Similarly the point $\mathbf{x}_{i+2}$ lies on the hyperplane, $H_2$, with coordinates $\mathbf{h}^t T^{-2}$, etc. Continuing this process we obtain a cyclic incidence matrix, each row containing $(p^{n-1}-1)/p-1$ ones.

But we known from the geometry that any pair of hyperplanes intersect in an $n-3$ dimensional space containing $(p^{n-2}-1)/p-1$ points and thus any pair of rows of $M$ have $(p^{n-2}-1)/p-1$ ones in common. Hence $M$ is the incidence matrix of a symmetric balanced incomplete block design with parameters

$$v = \frac{p^n-1}{p-1}, \quad k = \frac{p^{n-1}-1}{p-1}, \quad \lambda = \frac{p^{n-2}-1}{p-1}.$$

It follows that the binary sequence defined in Theorem 10 is pseudonoise.

As an example of Theorems 9 and 10 consider the $m$-sequence over $GF(3)$ generated by the primitive polynomial
$$x^3 \ominus (x \oplus 2)$$

The sequence is defined by
$$a_{3+i} = 0.a_{2+i} \oplus 1.a_{1+i} \oplus 2.a_i$$
and
$$T = \begin{pmatrix} 0 & 1 & 2 \\ 1 & 0 & 0 \\ 0 & 1 & 0 \end{pmatrix}, \quad T^{-1} = \begin{pmatrix} 0 & 1 & 0 \\ 0 & 0 & 1 \\ 2 & 0 & 1 \end{pmatrix}.$$

Taking $a_0 = 0$, $a_1 = 0$, $a_2 = 1$ we obtain
$$\{a_r\} = \ldots 001012112011100202122210222 \ldots$$
which may be verified to be pseudonoise with $A_s = -1$, $s = 1, 2, \ldots, 12$. The points of the finite projective plane, given by the first thirteen 3-tuples are:

$$\mathbf{x}_0 = \begin{pmatrix} 1 \\ 0 \\ 0 \end{pmatrix}, \mathbf{x}_1 = \begin{pmatrix} 0 \\ 1 \\ 0 \end{pmatrix}, \mathbf{x}_2 = \begin{pmatrix} 1 \\ 0 \\ 1 \end{pmatrix}, \mathbf{x}_3 = \begin{pmatrix} 2 \\ 1 \\ 0 \end{pmatrix}, \mathbf{x}_4 = \begin{pmatrix} 1 \\ 2 \\ 1 \end{pmatrix},$$

$$\mathbf{x}_5 = \begin{pmatrix} 1 \\ 1 \\ 2 \end{pmatrix}, \mathbf{x}_6 = \begin{pmatrix} 2 \\ 1 \\ 1 \end{pmatrix}, \mathbf{x}_7 = \begin{pmatrix} 0 \\ 2 \\ 1 \end{pmatrix}, \mathbf{x}_8 = \begin{pmatrix} 1 \\ 0 \\ 2 \end{pmatrix}, \mathbf{x}_9 = \begin{pmatrix} 1 \\ 1 \\ 0 \end{pmatrix},$$

$$\mathbf{x}_{10} = \begin{pmatrix} 1 \\ 1 \\ 1 \end{pmatrix}, \mathbf{x}_{11} = \begin{pmatrix} 0 \\ 1 \\ 1 \end{pmatrix}, \mathbf{x}_{12} = \begin{pmatrix} 0 \\ 0 \\ 1 \end{pmatrix}.$$

The points $\mathbf{x}_1, \mathbf{x}_7, \mathbf{x}_{11}, \mathbf{x}_{12}$ all lie on the hyperplane (line)
$$H_0: 1.x_1 \oplus 0_0 x_2 \oplus 0.x_3 = 0, \text{ i.e. } \mathbf{h} = \begin{pmatrix} 1 \\ 0 \\ 0 \end{pmatrix}.$$

The points $\mathbf{x}_2, \mathbf{x}_8, \mathbf{x}_{12}, \mathbf{x}_0$ all lie on
$$H_1: \mathbf{h}^t T^{-1} = (100)\begin{pmatrix} 0 & 1 & 0 \\ 0 & 0 & 1 \\ 2 & 0 & 1 \end{pmatrix} = (010)$$

The points $\mathbf{x}_3, \mathbf{x}_9, \mathbf{x}_0, \mathbf{x}_1$ all lie on
$$H_2: \mathbf{h}^t T^{-2} = (010)\begin{pmatrix} 0 & 1 & 0 \\ 0 & 0 & 1 \\ 2 & 0 & 1 \end{pmatrix} = (001)$$

etc.

## Table 2.

Known binary sequences with $n_1 \leq 32$ are listed. Only one sequence of each type is given, the remainder being obtainable by sampling and complementing.

### Quadratic residue sequences

| $v$ | Values of $r$ for which $a_r = 1$ | No. of Seqs |
|---|---|---|
| 7 | as binary $m$-sequence | 4 |
| 11 | 1, 3, 4, 5, 9 | 4 |
| 19 | 1, 4, 5, 6, 7, 9, 11, 16, 17 | 4 |
| 23 | 1, 2, 3, 4, 6, 8, 9, 12, 13, 16, 18 | 4 |
| 31 | 1, 2, 4, 5, 7, 8, 9, 10, 14, 16, 18, 19, 20, 25, 28 | 4 |
| 43 | 1, 4, 6, 9, 10, 11, 13, 14, 15, 16, 17, 21, 23, 24, 25, 31, 35, 36, 38, 40, 41 | 4 |
| 47 | 1, 2, 3, 4, 6, 7, 8, 9, 12, 14, 16, 17, 18, 21, 24, 25, 27, 28, 32, 34, 36, 37, 42 | 4 |
| 59 | 1, 3, 4, 5, 7, 9, 12, 15, 16, 17, 19, 20, 21, 22, 25, 26, 27, 28, 29, 35, 36, 41, 45, 46, 48, 49, 51, 53, 57 | 4 |
| 67 | 1, 4, 6, 9, 10, 14, 15, 16, 17, 19, 21, 22, 23, 24, 25, 26, 29, 33, 35, 36, 37, 39, 40, 47, 49, 54, 55, 56, 59, 60, 62, 64, 65 | 4 |
| 71 | 1, 2, 3, 4, 5, 6, 8, 9, 10, 12, 15, 16, 18, 19, 20, 24, 25, 27, 29, 30, 32, 36, 37, 38, 40, 43, 45, 48, 49, 50, 54, 57, 58, 60, 64 | 4 |
| 79 | 1, 2, 4, 5, 8, 9, 10, 11, 13, 16, 18, 19, 20, 21, 22, 23, 25, 26, 31, 32, 36, 38, 40, 42, 44, 45, 46, 49, 50, 51, 52, 55, 62, 64, 65, 67, 72, 73, 76 | 4 |
| 83 | 1, 3, 4, 7, 9, 10, 11, 12, 16, 17, 21, 23, 25, 26, 27, 28, 29, 30, 31, 33, 36, 37, 38, 40, 41, 44, 48, 49, 51, 59, 61, 63, 64, 65, 68, 69, 70, 75, 77, 78, 81 | 4 |
| 103 | 1, 2, 4, 7, 8, 9, 13, 14, 15, 16, 17, 18, 19, 23, 25, 26, 28, 29, 30, 32, 33, 34, 36, 38, 41, 46, 49, 50, 52, 55, 56, 58, 59, 60, 61, 63, 64, 66, 68, 72, 76, 79, 81, 82, 83, 91, 92, 93, 97, 98, 100 | 4 |
| 107 | 1, 3, 4, 9, 10, 11, 12, 13, 14, 16, 19, 23, 25, 27, 29, 30, 33, 34, 35, 36, 37, 39, 40, 41, 42, 44, 47, 48, 49, 52, 53, 56, 57, 61, 62, 64, 69, 75, 76, 79, 81, 83, 85, 86, 87, 89, 90, 92, 99, 100, 101, 102, 105 | 4 |
| 127 | 1, 2, 4, 8, 9, 11, 13, 15, 16, 17, 18, 19, 21, 22, 25, 26, 30, 31, 32, 34, 35, 36, 37, 38, 41, 42, 44, 47, 49, 50, 52, 60, 61, 62, 64, 68, 69, 70, 71, 72, 73, 74, 76, 79, 81, 82, 84, 87, 88, 94, 98, 99, 100, 103, 104, 107, 113, 115, 117, 120, 121, 122, 124 | 4 |

## Biquadratic residue sequences

| $v$ | Values of $r$ for which $a_r = 1$ | No. of Seqs |
|---|---|---|
| 13 | 0, 1, 3, 9 | 8 |
| 37 | 1, 7, 9, 10, 12, 16, 26, 33, 34 | 8 |
| 101 | 1, 3, 10, 13, 16, 19, 36, 40, 41, 44, 48, 49, 59, 63, 69, 77, 78, 79, 80, 85, 90, 91, 93, 95, 97 | 8 |
| 109 | 0, 1, 3, 5, 7, 9, 15, 16, 21, 22, 25, 26, 27, 35, 38, 45, 48, 49, 63, 66, 73, 75, 78, 80, 81, 89, 97, 105 | 8 |

## Octic residue sequences

| $v$ | Values of $r$ for which $a_r = 1$ | No. of Seqs |
|---|---|---|
| 73 | 1, 2, 4, 8, 16, 32, 37, 55, 64 | 16 |

## Twin prime sequences

| $v$ | Values of $r$ for which $a_r = 1$ | No. of Seqs |
|---|---|---|
| 15 | as binary m-sequence | 4 |
| 35 | 1, 3, 4, 5, 9, 10, 11, 12, 13, 15, 16, 17, 20, 25, 27, 29, 30, 33 | 4 |

## Hall sequences

| $v$ | Values of $r$ for which $a_r = 1$ | No. of Seqs |
|---|---|---|
| 31 | as binary $m$-sequence | 12 |
| 43 | 1, 2, 3, 4, 5, 8, 11, 12, 16, 19, 20, 21, 22, 27, 32, 33, 35, 37, 39, 41, 42 | 12 |
| 127 | 1, 2, 3, 4, 5, 6, 7, 8, 10, 12, 14, 16, 19, 20, 23, 24, 25, 27, 28, 32, 33, 38, 40, 46, 47, 48, 50, 51, 54, 56, 57, 61, 63, 64, 65, 66, 67, 73, 75, 76, 77, 80, 87, 89, 92, 94, 95, 96, 97, 100, 101, 102, 107, 108, 111, 112, 114, 117, 119, 122, 123, 125, 126 | 12 |

## Binary m-sequences

| $v$ | Values of $r$ for which $a_r = 1$ | No. of Seqs |
|---|---|---|
| 7 | 1, 2, 4 | 4 |
| 15 | 1, 2, 3, 5, 6, 9, 11 | 4 |
| 31 | 1, 2, 5, 7, 8, 10, 11, 12, 13, 15, 17, 21, 24, 25, 26 | 12 |
| 63 | 1, 2, 3, 4, 5, 6, 12, 17, 18, 22, 24, 27, 28, 29, 30, 32, 36, 37, 38, 41, 44, 46, 47, 49, 50, 51, 53, 54, 57, 58, 60, 62 | 12 |
| 127 | 1, 2, 3, 4, 5, 6, 7, 12, 13, 14, 16, 17, 18, 19, 22, 24, 25, 28, 31, 38, 42, 45, 46, 50, 52, 53, 54, 56, 58, 59, 61, 62, 68, 69, 72, 73, 75, 77, 80, 81, 82, 85, 86, 87, 88, 90, 91, 93, 98, 100, 102, 104, 105, 106, 107, 108, 110, 113, 115, 119, 120, 122, 123, 124 | 36 |

*Binary sequences derived from q-nary m-sequences*

| $v$ | $q$ | $n$ | Values of $r$ for which $a_r = 1$ | No. of Seqs |
|---|---|---|---|---|
| 21 | 4 | 3 | 0, 1, 4, 14, 16 | 4 |
| 85 | 4 | 4 | 0, 1, 2, 4, 7, 8, 14, 16, 17, 23, 27, 28, 32, 34, 43, 46, 51, 54, 56, 64, 68 | 16 |
| 73 | 8 | 3 | as octic residue sequence | 16 |
| 273 | 16 | 3 | 0, 1, 3, 7, 15, 31, 63, 90, 116, 127, 136, 181, 194, 204, 233, 238, 255 | 24 |
| 1057 | 32 | 3 | 1, 5, 13, 29, 52, 61, 107, 125, 136, 217, 253, 275, 296, 336, 346, 437, 450, 509, 526, 553, 595, 675, 695, 700, 752, 790, 877, 903, 922, 988, 1021, 1055, 1056 | 120 |
| 13 | 3 | 3 | as biquadratic residue sequence | 8 |
| 40 | 3 | 4 | 0, 1, 2, 4, 5, 8, 13, 14, 17, 19, 24, 26, 34 | 8 |
| 121 | 3 | 5 | 1, 3, 4, 7, 9, 11, 12, 13, 21, 25, 27, 33, 34, 36, 39, 44, 55, 63, 64, 67, 68, 70, 71, 75, 80, 81, 82, 83, 85, 89, 92, 99, 102, 103, 104, 108, 109, 115, 117, 119, | 44 |
| 91 | 9 | 3 | 0, 1, 3, 9, 27, 49, 56, 61, 77, 81 | 24 |
| 757 | 27 | 3 | 1, 7, 25, 41, 79, 127, 171, 218, 241, 308, 385, 402, 407, 443, 453, 464, 468, 503, 517, 576, 606, 639, 651, 658, 671, 727, 755, 756 | 168 |
| 31 | 5 | 3 | 0, 1, 3, 8, 12, 18 | 20 |
| 156 | 5 | 4 | 0, 2, 11, 18, 21, 22, 27, 29, 32, 36, 39, 42, 44, 56, 70, 71, 75, 86, 87, 93, 95, 96, 109, 118, 122, 137, 142, 148, 150, 154, 155 | 24 |
| 651 | 25 | 3 | 1, 31, 43, 56, 78, 106, 112, 117, 127, 165, 179, 205, 269, 277, 296, 300, 320, 337, 366, 402, 420, 496, 505, 512, 649, 650 | 120 |
| 57 | 7 | 3 | 0, 1, 3, 13, 32, 36, 43, 52 | 24 |
| 133 | 11 | 3 | 0, 1, 3, 12, 20, 34, 38, 81, 88, 94, 104, 109 | 72 |
| 183 | 13 | 3 | 0, 1, 3, 16, 23, 28, 42, 76, 82, 86, 119, 137, 154, 175 | 80 |
| 307 | 17 | 3 | 0, 1, 3, 30, 37, 50, 55, 76, 98, 117, 129, 133, 157, 189, 199, 222, 293, 299 | 204 |
| 381 | 19 | 3 | 0, 1, 3, 12, 17, 65, 75, 94, 117, 124, 132, 145, 163, 167, 200, 271, 297, 303, 337, 357 | 168 |
| 553 | 23 | 3 | 0, 1, 3, 17, 36, 42, 64, 93, 131, 149, 161, 193, 204, 219, 227, 264, 273, 313, 400, 448, 452, 472, 479 | 312 |
| 871 | 29 | 3 | 0, 1, 3, 12, 22, 53, 76, 81, 121, 203, 219, 268, 286, 311, 315, 347, 373, 381, 466, 540, 595, 634, 651, 697, 711, 735, 741, 748, 768, 783 | 528 |
| 993 | 31 | 3 | 0, 1, 3, 17, 72, 77, 103, 130, 152, 165, 222, 250, 262, 286, 318, 368, 419, 429, 458, 462, 473, 492, 510, 557, 599, 767, 792, 812, 833, 871, 879, 987 | 440 |

Other Sequences (Hall 1956)

| $v$ | Values of $r$ for which $a_r = 1$ | No. of Seqs |
|---|---|---|
| 63 | 0, 1, 2, 3, 4, 5, 6, 8, 9, 10, 12, 16, 17, 18, 20, 23, 24, 27, 29, 32, 33, 34, 36, 40, 43, 45, 46, 48, 53, 54, 58 | 12 |
| 121 | 1, 3, 4, 5, 9, 12, 13, 14, 15, 16, 17, 22, 23, 27, 32, 34, 36, 39, 42, 45, 46, 48, 51, 64, 66, 69, 71, 77, 81, 82, 85, 86, 88, 92, 96, 102, 108, 109, 110, 117 | 44 |
| 121 | 1, 3, 4, 7, 8, 9, 12, 21, 24, 25, 26, 27, 34, 36, 40, 43, 49, 63, 64, 68, 70, 71, 72, 75, 78, 81, 82, 83, 89, 92, 94, 95, 97, 102, 104, 108, 112, 113, 118, 120 | 44 |
| 121 | 1, 3, 4, 5, 7, 9, 12, 14, 15, 17, 21, 27, 32, 36, 38, 42, 45, 46, 51, 53, 58, 63, 67, 68, 76, 79, 80, 81, 82, 83, 96, 100, 103, 106, 107, 108, 114, 115, 116, 119 | 44 |
| 133 | 1, 4, 5, 14, 16, 19, 20, 21, 25, 38, 54, 56, 57, 64, 66, 70, 76, 80, 83, 84, 91, 93, 95, 98, 100, 101, 105, 106, 114, 123, 125, 126, 131 | 72 |

Hence the incidence matrix, $M$, is

$$\begin{array}{c|cccccccccccccc}
 & X_0 & X_1 & X_2 & X_3 & & & & & & & & & & X_{12} \\
\hline
H_0 & 0 & 1 & 0 & 0 & 0 & 0 & 0 & 1 & 0 & 0 & 0 & 1 & 1 \\
H_1 & 1 & 0 & 1 & 0 & 0 & 0 & 0 & 0 & 1 & 0 & 0 & 0 & 1 \\
H_2 & 1 & 1 & 0 & 1 & 0 & 0 & 0 & 0 & 0 & 1 & 0 & 0 & 0 \\
H_3 & 0 & 1 & 1 & 0 & 1 & 0 & 0 & 0 & 0 & 0 & 1 & 0 & 0 \\
H_4 & 0 & 0 & 1 & 1 & 0 & 1 & 0 & 0 & 0 & 0 & 0 & 1 & 0 \\
H_5 & 0 & 0 & 0 & 1 & 1 & 0 & 1 & 0 & 0 & 0 & 0 & 0 & 1 \\
H_6 & 1 & 0 & 0 & 0 & 1 & 1 & 0 & 1 & 0 & 0 & 0 & 0 & 0 \\
H_7 & 0 & 1 & 0 & 0 & 0 & 1 & 1 & 0 & 1 & 0 & 0 & 0 & 0 \\
H_8 & 0 & 0 & 1 & 0 & 0 & 0 & 1 & 1 & 0 & 1 & 0 & 0 & 0 \\
H_9 & 0 & 0 & 0 & 1 & 0 & 0 & 0 & 1 & 1 & 0 & 1 & 0 & 0 \\
H_{10} & 0 & 0 & 0 & 0 & 1 & 0 & 0 & 0 & 1 & 1 & 0 & 1 & 0 \\
H_{11} & 0 & 0 & 0 & 0 & 0 & 1 & 0 & 0 & 0 & 1 & 1 & 0 & 1 \\
H_{12} & 1 & 0 & 0 & 0 & 0 & 0 & 1 & 0 & 0 & 0 & 1 & 1 & 0 \\
\end{array}$$

and so the binary sequence

....0100000100011....

obtained as described in Theorem 10 is pseudonoise.

*Acknowledgement.* The author would like to thank Dr. P. R. Bryant for most helpful discussions, Mr. F. W. Parker for preparing programs to produce primitive polynomials and sequences and The General Electric Company Limited for permission to reproduce this article.

*See also:* Telecommunication, global.

*Bibliography*

AITKEN A. C. (1942) *Determinants and Matrices*, Edinburgh: Oliver and Boyd.
BARKER R. H. (1953) *Group synchronisation of binary digital systems*, Communication Theory (Ed. W. Jackson), London: Butterworths.
BARTEE T. C. and WOOD P. E. (1963) *Coding for tracking radar ranging*, M.I.T. Lincoln Lab. technical report No. TR-318, June.
BELEVITCH V. (1965) *Conference networks and Hadamard matrices*, Symposium on Network Theory at Cranfield, September.
BERSON B. F. (1962) *Impulse response of linear systems using correlation and direct measurement*, AD281770, August.
BIRKHOFF G. and MACLANE S. (1965) *A Survey of Modern Algebra*, New York: Macmillan.
CARMICHAEL R. D. (1937) *Groups of Finite Order*, New York: The Athenaeum Press.
CORRAN E. R. and CUMMINS J. D. (1962) *Binary codes with impulse autocorrelation functions for dynamic experiments*, Report No. AEEW-R210, September, Control and Instrumentation Division, A.E.E., Winfrith, Dorset.
DICKSON L. E. (1958) *Linear Groups*, New York: Dover.
ELSPAS B. (1959) *Theory of autonomous linear sequential networks*, Trans I.R.E., Vol. CT-6, March, 45.
G.E.C. Electronic exchange at Leamington Spa (1966) *G.E.C. Telecommunications*, No. 34, January.
GILBERT E. N. (1960) *Synchronisation of binary messages*, Trans. I.R.E., Vol. IT-6, September, 470.
GOLOMB S. W. (1964) *Digital Communication*, New York: Prentice-Hall.
HALL M. Jr. (1956) *A survey of difference sets*, Proc. Amer. Math. Soc., **7**, 975.
INGRAM D.G.W. *et al.* (1966) *Digital techniques in carrier frequency generation*, Proc. I.E.E., **113**, No. 2, 243, February.

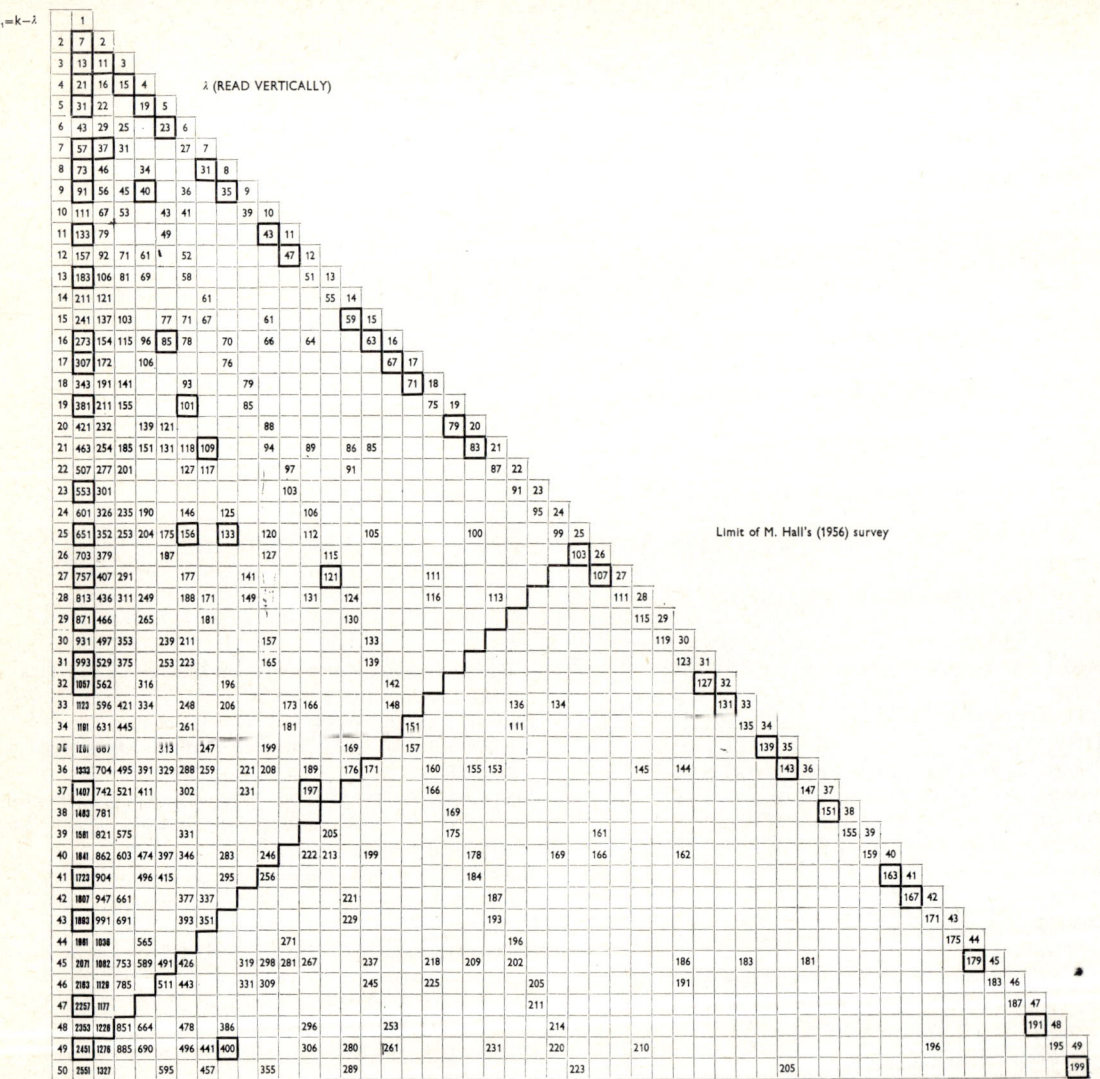

Table 3. Values of v for which pseudonoise sequences may exist. Sequences are known for the outlined values of v. Note: the off-peak auto-correlation $A = v - 4n_1$.

Judge W. J. (1962) *Multiplexing using quasi orthogonal binary functions*, Trans. A.I.E.E., Pt. 1, (Communication and Electronics), May, 81.

Kramer C. (1965) *A low frequency pseudo random noise generator*, Electronic Engineering, **37,** No. 449, July, 465.

Lehmer E. (1953) *On residue difference sets*, Can. J. Math., **5,** 425.

Mann H. B. (1949) *Analysis and Design of Experiments*, New York: Dover.

Mann H. B. (1965) *Addition Theorems*, Interscience tracks in pure and applied mathematics, No. 18, New York: Interscience.

Peterson W. W. (1961) *Error Correcting Codes*, Cambridge, Mass.: M.I.T. Press; New York: Wiley.

Ryser H. J. (1963) *Combinatorial mathematics*, Carus Mathematical Monographs No. 14, New York: Math. Assn. of America, Wiley.

Siebert W. (1956) *A radar detection philosophy*, Trans. I.R.E. Vol. IT—2, September 204.

Stanton R. G. and Sprott D. A. (1958) *A family of difference sets*, Can. J. Math., **10,** 73.

Stewart J. L. and Westerfield E. C. (1959) *A theory of active sonar detection*, Proc. I.R.E., **47,** 872.

Stiffler J. J. (1962) *Synchronisation of telemetry codes*, Trans. I.R.E., Vol. SET-8, June, 112.

Suran J. J. and Marolf R. A. (1964) *Integrated circuits and integrated systems*, Proc. I.E.E.E., **52,** No. 12, December, 1661.

Titsworth R. C. (1963) *Optimal and minimax sequences*, Proc. of International Telemetering Conference, London.

Vinogradov I. M. (1955) *An Introduction to the Theory of Numbers*, Oxford: Pergamon Press.

Weiss E. and Gorenstein D. (1962) *An acquirable code*, AD281751, July.

Zierler N. (1959) *Linear recurring sequences*, J. Soc. Ind. Appl. Math., **7,** No. 1, March, 31.

D. Everett

## PSEUDORANDOM BINARY SIGNALS, USE OF, IN CORRELATION ANALYSIS OF DYNAMIC SYSTEMS.

*1. Dynamic Description of Linearized Systems*

One of the fundamental ways of describing the dynamic behaviour of a system, either linear or assumed linear for small variations of variables about mean operating conditions, is the use of a weighting function relating output to past values of input. The equation of a linearized system may be written as a convolution integral

$$y(t) = \int_0^\infty w(r)x(t-r)\,dr$$

where $y(t)$ is the output of the system at time $t$; $x(t-r)$ is the input to the system at a time $r$ previous to present time $t$, and $w(r)$ is a weighting function representing the relative effect of the input at time $r$ previous to the present.

The function $w(r)$ is also called the *impulse response* of the system. If the input $x(t)$ is taken as a perfect unit impulse at time zero

$$x(t) = \delta(t)$$

then the convolution integral simplifies to give

$$y(t) = \int_0^\infty w(r)\delta(t-r)\,dr = w(t).$$

In most practical cases, even if a true impulse could be applied to the system, the actual output would not strictly correspond to $w(t)$ because the system would undoubtedly enter a non-linear region of behaviour. The impulse response is the Fourier transform of the frequency response function of a system so that

$$w(t) = \int_{-\infty}^{\infty} F(\dot{\gamma}\omega)e^{\dot{\gamma}\omega t}\,dw$$

and

$$F(\dot{\gamma}\omega) = \int_{-\infty}^{\infty} w(t)e^{\dot{\gamma}\omega t}\,dt.$$

It is thus possible to obtain the frequency characteristics of a system without the necessity of experimental testing with a range of sine wave signals, if a satisfactory method of obtaining the weighting function is available.

*2. Correlation Analysis of Dynamic Systems*

Correlation analysis is a method which enables the linearized system impulse response to be obtained without the need for applying actual impulse test signals. The method depends on the equivalence between two relations: that between input and output; and that between the input signal auto-correlation function and the input/output cross-correlation function.

The cross-correlation function for two signals $x(t)$, $y(t)$ is defined by

$$\varphi_{xy}(s) = \lim_{T\to\infty} \frac{1}{2T}\int_{-T}^{T} y(t)x(t-s)\,dt$$

where the variable $s$ is the displacement, or lag, between the two signals. A similar definition holds for auto-correlation function. In practice, estimates of the infinite average correlation functions, based on averaging over finite time $T$, have to be used.

On multiplying the direct relation on both sides by the input signal delayed by lag $s$, $x(t-s)$, integrating with respect to time, and averaging, the relation between correlation functions is obtained

$$\varphi_{xy}(s) = \int_0^\infty w(r)\varphi_{xx}(s-r)\,dr.$$

This is of exactly the same form as the direct relation. Thus, if a signal whose auto-correlation function is an impulse,

$$\varphi_{xx}(s) = \delta(s)$$

is used as the input to the system, then the cross-correlation function between input and output

$$\varphi_{xy}(s) = \int_0^\infty w(r)\delta(s-r)\,dr = w(s)$$

will give the impulse response function.

A particular advantage of correlation analysis is that it may be carried out using known test perturbations added to the normally occurring input without the latter causing errors so long as the correlation between normal input and test perturbations may be taken as negligible. The direct relation for this case may be written

$$y(t) = \int_0^\infty w(r)x(t-r)\,dr + n(t)$$

where $x(t)$ is the test signal, while $n(t)$ represents output variations due to other input signals, and to process and measurement noise. Then correlation with a delayed test perturbation gives

$$\Phi_{xy}(s) = \int_0^\infty w(r)\varphi_{xx}(s-r)\,dr + \varphi_{xn}(s).$$

If the test signal $x(t)$ is uncorrelated with the output signal $n(t)$, then $\varphi_{xn}(s)=0$, and the correlation equation reduces to the simple form

$$\varphi_{xy}(s) = \int_0^\infty w(r)\varphi_{xx}(s-r)\,dr$$

which includes no term depending on $n(t)$.

One type of signal which has the required impulse form of auto-correlation function is a random disturbance with its power evenly distributed over all frequencies—white noise. A random test signal also ensures that the correlation with other input signals will be zero. However, certain practical difficulties are found when attempts are made to apply correlation analysis using white noise.

These difficulties are not due simply to the impossibility of obtaining true white noise, with power at frequencies extending to infinity, because approximate white noise, with a substantially flat power spectrum over a wide range, can be generated. They arise partly because correlation, involving multiplication of signals and integration over a range of displacements between signals, is inaccurate in analog form, and time consuming in digital form. Even when this is overcome there remains the worst hazard, caused by the same randomness of the signal that makes it so desirable from its auto-correlation property. This is the difficulty of reliably estimating the cross-correlation function from reasonable amounts of data, because the variance of the estimates is inversely proportional to the length of data used.

There are alternative random signals such as the *Random telegraph signal* (which takes only two values changing from one to another at intervals which are random with a Poisson distribution) or the Discrete Interval *Random binary signal*, (where the changes between the two values are at randomly selected intervals which are multiples of a basic time interval). These can reduce the problems of test signal generation and correlation computation, but they still retain the difficulty of obtaining reliable estimates of cross-correlations from small amounts of data.

## 3. The Advantages of Pseudorandom Binary Sequences in Correlation Analysis

Pseudorandom binary sequences are sequences whose elements take either of two possible values (which as input sequences may be taken as 1, −1, but which in theoretical analysis are conveniently taken as 0, 1), the distribution of these values being in a manner which appears random over a short length of the sequence. The sequences have certain properties similar to those of a true random binary sequence, but are actually deterministic and periodic.

The main properties are:
a) In a period $N$ of the sequence, 0's and 1's occur as nearly as possible in equal numbers;
b) The normalized auto-correlation, which may be defined over a period $N$ to give the same value as over an infinite sequence, has only two values, one for zero lag, and another for lags 1 to $N-1$. Obviously the auto-correlation function has period $N$. If the element values are taken as $\pm 1$, the auto-correlation values are 1 at the peak and $-\dfrac{1}{N}$ off peak.

The two main families of such sequences are
I. *m*-sequences, which exist for all $N = 2^n - 1$ ($n$ being any positive integer), and are maximum length sequences obtainable from a linear feedback shift register of $n$ stages;
II. *QR*-sequences, which exist for all prime $N = 4k-1$ ($k$ being a positive integer) and are obtained from consideration of quadratic residues modulo $N$.

Full details of these and other sequences appear elsewhere in the Encyclopaedia.

The use of PRBS has the following practical advantages:
a) The sequences are readily generated, either by feed-

back shift registers, or by simple computer programs. Delayed versions are also easily generated.
b) In applying test perturbations it is necessary only to switch between two values.
c) Correlation is reduced to addition and subtraction of output measurements, according to the sign of the test signal perturbation, instead of requiring multiplication and integration.
d) The estimates of cross-correlation from one whole period $N$ have no random contribution from the test signal. In the absence of process or measurement noise, estimates from any sequence of $N$ intervals will be exact.

### 4. Correlation Analysis Using PRBS

It is convenient, when using PRBS with a basic interval of $\lambda$, to use a discrete (or sampled data) version of the various equations and definitions, using the same basic interval. We may then write (1) to (3):
(1) The system equation

$$Y_t = \sum_{r=0}^{P-1} W_r X_{t-r} + n_t$$

where $Y_t$, $X_t$, and the noise $n_t$ are values at time $t$, and $W_r$ is the weighting coefficient for the effect at time $r$ ago. Note that $W_r$ corresponds to $\lambda w(r\lambda)$ in the continuous case. $P$ terms appear in the sum, where $P\lambda = T_s$, the system settling time. Values of $W_s$, $s > P$, are assumed equal to zero.
(2) Correlation functions

$$R_{xy}(s) = \frac{1}{N} \sum_{r=0}^{P-1} Y_t X_{t-s}.$$

This is defined over a finite number of terms where $N$ is the period of the PRBS, and so $N > P$.
(3) Correlation equation

$$R_{xy}(s) = \sum_{r=0}^{P-1} W_r R_{xx}(s-r) + R_{xn}(s).$$

The test signal $X_t$ may be taken as a PRBS with amplitude $a$ and period $N$. Hence its estimated auto-correlation function $R_{xx}(s)$, defined over $N$ terms is the same as its true auto-correlation function $\varphi_{xx}(s)$, defined over an infinite range. In discrete form, this can be written

$$\varphi_{xx}(s) = a^2 \frac{(N+1)\delta_s - 1}{N} \quad (s \bmod N).$$

That part of the output signal which is unknown, $n_t$, may be taken as a constant together with a random term, of variance $\sigma_n^2$.

$$n_t = \bar{n} + \xi_t.$$

This means that the cross-correlation between $X_t$ and $n_t$ is not zero, but has expected value

$$E\{R_{xn}(s)\} = E\left\{\frac{1}{N} \sum_{t=0}^{N-1} n_t X_{t-s}\right\}$$

$$= \frac{1}{N} \sum_{t=0}^{N-1} \bar{n} X_{t-s} = \frac{a\bar{n}}{N}$$

and a variance

$$\sigma^2 = E\{R^2_{xn}(s)\} - (E\{R_{xn}(s)\})^2 = E\left\{\left(\frac{1}{N} \sum_{t=0}^{N-1} \xi_t X_{t-s}\right)^2\right\}$$

$$= \frac{1}{N^2} \sum_{t=0}^{N-1} \sum_{u=0}^{N-1} E\{\xi_t \xi_u\} X_{t-s} X_{u-s}$$

$$= \frac{1}{N^2} \sum_{t=0}^{N-1} \sum_{u=0}^{N-1} \varphi_{\xi\xi}(t-u) X_{t-s} X_{u-s}$$

*Estimate variance.* If the original process and measurement noise is of bandwidth greater than $1/\lambda$, then the sampled noise $\xi$ has an apparent bandwidth of $1/\lambda$, with individual samples independent of one another. The noise auto-correlation function can therefore be approximated by

$$\varphi_{\zeta\zeta}(u) = \sigma_n^2 \delta_u.$$

A slightly longer argument is needed when the original noise is of bandwidth smaller than $1/\lambda$, since the individual samples are no longer uncorrelated. However, quantitatively, the result is little different.

Using the noise auto-correlation approximation given above, the estimate variance becomes

$$\sigma^2 = \sigma_n^2 \frac{1}{N^2} \sum_{s=0}^{N-1} \sum_{t=0}^{N-1} \delta_{t-u} X_{t-s} X_{u-s} = \sigma_n^2 \frac{1}{N^2} \sum_{t=0}^{N-1} X_{t-s}^2$$

$$= \frac{\sigma_N^2 a^2}{N}.$$

For correlated noise the variance is somewhat less. Note that this result is independent of $u$, the lag for which the estimate is being made.

*Estimate bias.* The expected value of the cross-correlation function $R_{xy}(s)$ is given by

$$E\{R_{xy}(s)\} = \sum_{r=0}^{N-1} W_r \varphi_{xx}(s-r) + E\{R_{xn}(s)\}$$

$$= \sum_{r=0}^{N-1} W_r a^2 \frac{[(N+1)\delta_{s-r} - 1]}{N} + \frac{a\bar{n}}{N}$$

$$= \frac{N+1}{N} a^2 W_s - \frac{a^2}{N} \sum_{r=0}^{N-1} W_r + \frac{a\bar{n}}{N}.$$

The first term shows the desired component proportional to the weighting coefficient. The remaining terms give a bias, one term being due to the imperfect approximation to the ideal input auto-correlation function, and the other due to the 'noise' present in the system.

The actual estimates also include a random noise component. If this were not so, if would be possible to compensate for the bias, by subtracting the value of the estimate of $R_{xy}(N-1)$ from the remaining estimates, since we assume that the impulse response is negligible at such a lag so that $W_{N-1} = 0$. The estimates for $s > P$ where $W_s$ is zero, will be scattered about the bias value. It is therefore convenient to take an average over the last third or half of the $N$ estimated values in order to correct for the bias.

Computationally better procedures can be devised if we are to estimate $P$ weighting coefficients from $N$ measurements. This is best analysed by considering the covariance matrix of the estimates. The analysis given here is, however, quite adequate.

## 5. Choice of Parameters

The main parameters of the PRBS method are the amplitude of the applied test signal $a$, the basic interval time $\lambda$, and the total sequence time $N\lambda$. The system settling time $T_s$ must be less than $N\lambda$ for the theory to hold. The method can give no information about system effects with time constants less than $\lambda$. Thus it is desirable that:

i) the test signal amplitude be small, to avoid undue disturbance of the operation of the process.

ii) the basic interval $\lambda$ be small, to give good resolution on the impulse response.

iii) the summation time $N\lambda$ be close to $T_s$ in order to have rapid determination of changes in the dynamic characteristics. Unfortunately these requirements are opposed to those for reliability of estimates, and a compromise must be sought.

It is possible to define a 'signal to noise' ratio for the estimates, dividing the average value of the weighting coefficient estimates over lag $T_s$ by the standard deviation of an estimate. The average coefficient estimate is

$$\bar{R}_{xy} = \frac{1}{P}\sum R_{xy}(s) \simeq \frac{\lambda}{T_s}\sum a^2 W_s = \frac{a^2 g \lambda}{T_s}.$$

Hence the 'signal to noise' ratio is

$$\bar{R}_{xy/\sigma} = \frac{a^2 g \lambda}{T_s} \bigg/ \frac{a\sigma_N}{\sqrt{N}} = \frac{ag\lambda\sqrt{N}}{\sigma_N T_s}.$$

This may be written

$$\frac{\bar{R}_{xy}}{\sigma} = \frac{ag}{\sigma_N}\sqrt{\frac{\lambda}{T_s}}\sqrt{\frac{N\lambda}{T_s}}.$$

The term $\dfrac{ag}{\sigma_N}\sqrt{\dfrac{\lambda}{T_s}}$ may be called the '*disturbance ratio*' since it is proportional to the ratio of the standard deviation of the output due to the test signal, and the standard deviation of the output due to measurement and process noise. The term $\dfrac{N\lambda}{T_s} = \dfrac{N}{P}$ may be called the 'experimentation time ratio', since it is the ratio of the summation time to the settling time.

It will be seen that within limits, the value of $\lambda$ itself is not important. If the allowed disturbance ratio is fixed, then we may choose a smaller $\lambda$ and a larger $a$, or vice versa. If the experimentation time is fixed, we may use a smaller $\lambda$ and a larger $N$.

Improvement of the impulse response estimates can come either by increasing the disturbance ratio (if not by reducing the noise level, then by increasing the test signal amplitude, or by increasing $\lambda$), or else by increasing the experimentation time.

Where the impulse response estimates are being used to obtain another parameter of the system, these considerations may be modified. If the parameter sought is the gain $g$, then the expected value is the sum of the ordinates $W_s$, and the variance is $T_s/\lambda = P$ times the variance of the individual estimates. Thus, a 'signal to noise' ratio is

$$\frac{\sum R_{xy}(s)}{\sqrt{\frac{T_s}{\lambda}}\sigma} = a^2 g \bigg/ \sqrt{\frac{T_s}{\lambda}}\frac{a\sigma_N}{\sqrt{N}} = \frac{ag}{\sigma_N}\sqrt{\frac{N\lambda}{T_s}}$$

$$= \frac{ag}{\sigma_N}\sqrt{\frac{\lambda}{T_s}}\sqrt{\frac{N\lambda}{T_s}}\sqrt{\frac{T_s}{\lambda}}.$$

In this case, with disturbance ratio and experimentation time fixed, improvement can be obtained using larger basic intervals.

## 6. Extension to Multiple Input Systems

Systems in which a number of inputs affect a particular output can be described by an extension of the method used for the single input case, as the sum of a number of convolution integrals

$$y(t) = \sum_{j=1}^{c}\int_0^{\infty} w_j(r)x_j(t-r)\,dr$$

where the $c$ weighting functions $w_j(r)$ represent the relative effect of the $c$ inputs $X_j$ at time $r$ previous to the present.

If the correlation between the output and the input signal is considered, then

$$\varphi_{x_k y}(s) = \sum_{j=1}^{c}\int_0^{\infty} w_j(r)\varphi_{x_k x_j}(s-r)\,dr.$$

In order to have a method of reasonable simplicity for use, it is desirable that these equations reduce to

$$\varphi_{x_k y}(s) = \text{const.}\times W_k(s)$$

so that the $c$ weighting functions can be found directly from the cross-correlation functions. Thus, input signals are sought with the properties

a) $\quad\varphi_{x_k y_k}(s) = \delta_s$

b) $\quad\varphi_{x_k x_j}(s) = 0$

at least for $s < T_s$, the maximum settling time within the system.

One possible set of input signals with these properties is obtained by modifying the original pseudorandom binary sequence by changing the sign of successive elements according to the different rows of a Hadamard matrix. The orthogonality of these rows leads to the required conditions on the cross-correlation functions. Although the auto-correlation functions of the new sequences are not as close to the desired form as that of a PRBS, they are nevertheless satisfactory for the method to be used.

For example, for four inputs, using the standard form of the Hadamard Matrix with elements denoted by +, −

$$\begin{bmatrix} + & + & + & + \\ + & - & + & - \\ + & + & - & - \\ + & - & - & + \end{bmatrix}$$

and the PRBS of period 7 [+ + + − − + −], the resulting sequences are

[+ + + − − + − + + + − − + − + + + − − + − + + +
− − + −]

[+ − + + − − − − + − − + + + + − + + − − − −
+ − − + + +]

[+ + − + − + + − + + + + + − − − + − + − − +
− − − − − +]

[+ − − − − + + + − + − + + − + + + + + − − −
+ − + − −]

It may be noted that the first sequence is the original sequence repeated four times; the second sequence has period 14, and the third and fourth sequences are of period 28. Also, the fourth sequence is the third shifted by 7 intervals. The cross-correlations will be identically zero, except between the 3rd and 4th where peaks will arise at ±7 intervals. These will not introduce errors if the weighting functions are negligible before 7 intervals as would be assumed in the single channel case.

The auto-correlation functions of the new sequences have spikes at intervals of 7 or 14 (including negative spikes, since the sequences have second halves of periods, the negative of first halves). In between these spikes the value will be ±1 or 0, so that there will be little effect from these terms.

As the Hadamard matrices are of order $4q$, while the PRBS are of period $4K-1$, it is necessary to take sequences of length $4q(4K-1)$ in order for the cross-correlation properties to hold. Thus this method is in practice limited to a small number of inputs if rapid determination of the weighting functions is required.

*See also:* Control, identification techniques for. Pseudonoise sequences.

P. A. N. BRIGGS

## PSYCHOLOGICAL LIMITING FACTORS IN HUMAN PERFORMANCE.

The performance limits which are reported in the literature have usually been established by asking the human operator to function in highly restricted and correspondingly artificial situations. The best-known example is the reaction time experiment in which the interval between the appearance of a stimulus and the initiation of the response is recorded. A consensus of the result obtained is shown below.

| Sensory mode | Reaction time (seconds) |
|---|---|
| Vision | 0·18 |
| Hearing | 0·16 |
| Touch | 0·15 |

This is superficially attractive and unambiguous as the measure of the shortest interval during which the human operator can transmit information but, in fact, it has little theoretical or practical importance. There are many variables which effect the value obtained apart from the sensory mode used. They include learning, age, sex, limb action, stimulus intensity and also the subject's attitude or set. This latter is of critical importance since the human operator in a time constrained situation always tries to optimize his behaviour by anticipation. In a reaction time experiment the subject has to predict the onset of the stimulus as best he can from the instructions and attitude of the experimenter, the appearance of the apparatus and his past experience of the situation. Extrapolation to real behaviour is dubious for the same reason, a series of events will normally be more complex but at the same time better structured and high-speed skills are a function of anticipatory ability rather than of sudden fast response.

Complexity in that it can be quantified by the range of alternative stimulus/response combinations is incorporated into the description of reaction-times by Hicks Law, which states that:

$$R.T. \text{ (Seconds)} = K \log_{10}(n+1)$$

where $n$ is the number of equiprobable alternatives and $K$ is a constant between 0·5 and 0·65.

Skilled performance normally implies also a graded response, that is, the controlled build-up and restriction of the muscular activity, this characteristic also is absent from the reaction time situation. It can be incorporated in experimental studies by the use of the *continuous tracking* situation in which the response of the operator is intended to nullify the effects of some external disturbance. The general *transfer function* can be expressed in the form

$$G_p(s) = \frac{Ke^{-ts}(T_L s + 1)}{(T_N s + 1)(T_I s + 1)}$$

where

| | | |
|---|---|---|
| Neuromuscular time lag | $T_N$ has range | 0·10 to 0·16 sec; |
| Lead time constant | $T_L$ has range | 0·25 to 2·5 sec; |
| Lag time constant | $T_I$ has range | 5 to 20 sec. |

This notation is used by Fogel (1963) who summarizes the results of many experiments in this field. The above parameters vary not only between subjects and between experimental situations but also within subjects depending on the instructions given and the levels of motivation, learning and fatigue. In addition there are non-linearities due to sudden changes of strategy, the '*indifference threshold*' (errors below which are ignored by the subject) and the '*range effect*' (small errors are usually overcorrected, large errors are undercorrected).

There are complications also due to the '*psychological refractory period*'. This term is used to describe the characteristic of behaviour in which the human operator appears to be incapable of initiating more than one response within about half a second, much longer than would be expected from a knowledge of his simple reaction time. This is evidenced in the continuous tracking situation by the essentially quantized nature of output. That is the human operator appears to respond, even when a continuous response would be optimal, by a series of discrete reactions with a frequency of about two per second. This phenomenon has been studied mainly in discrete stimulus/response experiments (Welford 1952). He suggests, in essence, that it may be due to each response requiring two reaction times, one between the external stimulus and the response and one during which the accuracy of the response is checked. This concept has some validity if the meaning is interpreted carefully. Manifestly it does not mean that the human operator can only cope at one instant with a problem having only one degree of freedom. Rather it suggests that the operator can only, at one time, deal with one item or set of data on a conceptually unitary theme and moreover that it takes time to switch between concepts. This 'shift of attention' time seems to be about 0·2 sec. It has also been suggested, although it is by no means proved, that the human operator deals with input information in quanta of about 0·1 sec duration.

The capacity of the sense organs appears to be several orders greater than that of the data handling mechanisms so that all inputs involve filtering or selection of sensed data. Looked at the other way the sense organs rarely act as the information bottle-neck. Even in cases in which data from different directions and distances have to be rapidly assimilated the limiting factor is usually in the perceptual organization of data.

This is a function of the size of the direct access store. As with computers it is convenient to separate the storage or memory system into two parts. The long-term memory which uses elaborate coding systems and for which, although the cross referencing system is highly efficient, some decoding has to take place before data are made available at the conscious level and the short-term memory or literal store where organization and manipulation of data from the sense organs and from the long-term store takes place.

The long-term store has no limit which is of any significance, the short-term store appears to be very small, not more than 30 bits. There is no general agreement about how to measure this capacity and indeed whether it is best measured in bits or items since the capacity in bits seems to decrease for small alphabets, that is, when the information per item is less than two or three bits (Crossman 1961). The principle of regarding the human operator as an information channel has led to two distinct lines of research in pursuit of limits. One is the maximum information which can be transmitted in one stimulus-response unit (bits/item), the other the maximum information which can be transmitted in unit time (bits/second). Experiments on the former are summarized by Garner (1962). Studies of discrimination of pitch, loudness and brightness indicate that about 2·2 bits/item is the limit, others on hue and pointers on lines (analogous to dial reading) indicate about 3·2 bits/item and in the case of discriminating angles a result of more than 4 bits/item has been obtained. These results prompt Garner to make the ingenious suggestion that there is a fundamental channel capacity of about 2·2 bits but this can be increased by adding 'perceptual anchors', that is, cues such that additional one-bit choices are possible before the final discrimination. There is also evidence that adding stimulus dimensions can increase the transmitted information.

The many studies on maximum rates are summarized by Luce (1960). The highly practised technique of speech reception would appear to be a natural candidate for the highest rate. Results calculated vary depending on assumptions made about information content per letter or per word, but, when due account is taken of the many kinds of redundancy an answer of between 10 and 20 bits per second emerges. Typing is in the same range, so also is piano playing. Speed of movements with certain assumptions about measuring accuracy in information terms indicates a rate of 10–12 bits/second.

The wide spread of results obtained have been attributed to two factors, the alphabet size and the coding methods used; for small alphabets the limit is set by the motor performance, for large alphabets the sheer range of stimuli and responses sets the limit and it is only for medium sized alphabets that a true information limit is being measured. On coding problems it has been suggested that the maximum rates of 10–15 bits/second can only be achieved by using imitation codes which have been highly *overlearned* in childhood (e.g. correspondence in space), and that arbitrary codes (e.g. symbols) will often reduce the rate, even after long learning periods, to about 5 bits/second.

It is tempting to conclude that the size and versatility of the human brain is such that there are no real psychological limits of performance. The apparent limits noted in many experiments are essentially imposed by the artificiality of the experimental situation or the lack of practice allowed within it. Given that he must cope regularly with a given situation the human operator will either change the situation so that any specific limitations are avoided or he will develop new performance strategies which enable him to break through an apparent performance ceiling. The skills developed in relation to high speed performance are an excellent illustration of this phenomenon. The flexibility of mental performance is such that there is an inherent slowness relative to the behaviour of lower animals and some aspects of the physical world, particularly when it is modified by engineering devices. To avoid the apparent limitations of this slowness the human operator has developed a range of strategies such as anticipatory behaviour of several distinct kinds, grouping of items so that information can be dealt with in larger units, input and output buffer stores so that decision making is not restricted to real time operation and so on.

Thus the technologist interested in matching his system to the human operator will perhaps serve his and the users' interests best by concerning himself not so much with the possible limits of human performance but with designing mechanisms flexible enough to provide the user with sufficient scope to exercise his tremendous abilities to devise new performance strategies.

*See also:* Man-machine communication and ergonomics. Man-machine in control systems.

*Bibliography*

CROSSMAN E. R. F. W. (1961) *Information and Serial Order in Human Immediate Memory*, in *Information Theory*, (Cherry C. Ed.) London: Butterworths.
FOGEL L. J. (1963) *Biotechnology: Concepts and Applications*, New York: Prentice-Hall.
GARNER W. R. (1962) *Uncertainty and Structure as Psychological Concepts*, New York: Wiley.
LUCE R. D. (Ed.) (1960) *Developments in Mathematical Psychology*, Illinois: Glencoe Free Press.
WELFORD A. T. (1952) *The 'psychological refractory period' and the timing of high-speed performance, A review and a theory*, Brit. J. Psych. 43, 1, 1.

W. T. SINGLETON

**PSYCHOLOGICAL LINGUISTICS: PSYCHOLINGUISTIC STUDIES OF SYNTAX.** Much of the recent impetus to experimentation (and re-evaluation of earlier data) in the psychology of language was provided by Chomsky's attempt to formulate a revealing theory of linguistic structure and a descriptively adequate grammar of English based upon this theory (Chomsky 1957). The organization of the later versions of the theory of *transformational grammar* (Katz and Postal 1964; Chomsky 1965) is shown in Fig. 1.

A descriptively adequate grammar should provide an explicit characterization of the sets and subsets of formal objects which constitute a language. Some of these sets (e.g. the set of distinctive features, the set of grammatical formatives, the set of semantic markers) are finite, but many of the most interesting sets (e.g. the set of sentences, the set of noun phrases, the set of direct objects) contain an infinite number of members. A *grammar*, then needs to be a recursive rule-system which enumerates the sentences of a language and displays the structural elements of each enumerated sentence. Grammars of this nature mark a return to pretaxonomic conceptions of linguistic inquiry and thus (by definition) make an empirical claim of 'psychological reality' for the objects (the structural descriptions) which they enumerate. It seems necessary that a claim of 'psychological reality' must also be entered for the specific rules which inter-relate units to produce full structural descriptions. (Chomsky (1965) argues that *'evaluation metrics'* for strongly equivalent grammars are essential, pre-determined decision-procedures whereby, for instance, the child 'chooses' a *single* grammar which is

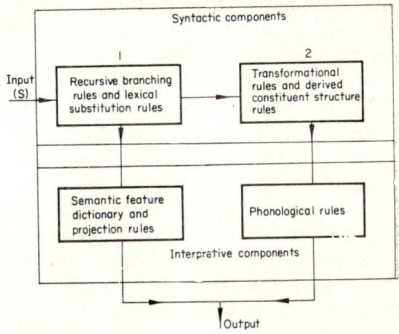

FIG. 1. *The full structural description, phonological, syntactic and semantic, of an arbitrary sentence.*

compatible with the data he has heard.) By describing the type/token structure of verbal discourse these studies provide a framework within which further questions of psychological interest may meaningfully be asked. Thus some of the important (and largely unrealized) goals of *psycholinguistic theory* include: 1) The explanation of how the structural descriptions specified by grammars are encoded into and decoded from utterances; 2) the statement of how their representations are stored in and retrieved from 'memory'; 3) the development of linguistic complexity and 'importance' measures appropriate to different psychological tasks. Grammars *per se* provide *no* information concerning how these goals are to be achieved (although they usually provide counter-examples to the mechanisms which have been suggested!). Clearly, however, the statement of *what* must be done in verbal communication precedes the statement of *how* it is done (i.e. it is both traditional and useful to distinguish between knowledge and the manner of realization of that knowledge).

*Storage and retrieval of structural descriptions.* It seems reasonable to assume that the 'objects' which a perceptual model must recover and store in memory correspond to the *'deep structure'* of utterances as characterized by the first syntactic component. It is this part of the output of the syntactic component (see Fig. 1) which is interpreted semantically (e.g. in order to disambiguate 'fair' in the sentence 'The woman was fair in her treatment of the workers' the deep structure rules must associate 'fair' with 'treatment' not directly with 'woman'). (Cf. the discussion of such problems in Rubenstein (1965) and Katz and Postal (1964).) Furthermore, the deep structure uniquely specifies the transformational operations which will be carried out by the second syntactic component in the course of producing a phonologically interpretable 'surface structure'.

Savin and Perchonock (1965) studied the recall of sentences followed by unrelated strings of words. They were able to show that the amount of *'memory space'* taken up by various sentence types (as indexed by the number of unrelated words remembered subsequent to correct sentence recall) does correspond to the length of their deep structure representations. Mehler (1963) has shown that various syntactic features such as 'passive', 'negative', 'question' (which in the more recent developments of grammatical theory are used to 'trigger' re-ordering and deletion transformations) may be forgotten independently of the strings assigned to categories which represent grammatical relations such as 'subject', 'object', 'main verb', etc. Grammatical relations (defined over sub-trees generated by the deep-structure component) are clearly vital to semantic interpretation and can furthermore be assigned 'importance' measures. Thus Blumenthal (1966) demonstrated that nouns acting as logical subjects ('Gloves were made by *tailors*'), a category which relates to the entire sentence, are more effective prompts to correct recall than nouns which are only involved in adverbial phrases modifying the main verb of the sentence ('Gloves were made by *hand*').

*Models of the decoding process.* How is this 'deep structure' recovered by the perceptual system? Miller and Chomsky (1963) suggest that a two-stage device is involved in the processing of syntactic information. They propose that the first component of the model (operating within the known drastic limitations of short-term memory) assigns a preliminary analysis of the surface structure of the sentence. This information is the input to the second component (stored in long-term memory) which uses the resources of a transformational grammar to recover the underlying phrase-markers. (An algorithm, conceived as a psychological hypothesis not as an exercise in artificial intelligence, which simulates the assignment of surface structure is described by Thorne *et al.* (1965). Their model avoids many of the psychologically untenable assumptions of previous automatic parsers.) A 'division of labour' of this nature may be supported by such facts as:

1) Some subjects are capable of accurately 'shadowing' sentential material with an extremely short time delay. Afterwards, however, they have very little idea of what the passage was about. With longer time delays the material is usually understood. This seems to show the *psychological* independence of the phonologically interpreted surface structure and the semantically interpreted deep structure.

2) Studies of the integrity of perceptual units show that extraneous clicks heard while attending to sentences are subjectively displaced to the major derived constituent boundaries of the sentences (Garrett *et al.* 1966).

3) At fast rates of presentation, sentences presented in phrase-structure units are learned in considerably fewer trials than sentences broken into arbitrary units (Wales 1964). Some idea of this effect can be obtained by considering Fig. 2.

| | |
|---|---|
| Yesterday | Yesterday I |
| I noticed | noticed that the young |
| that the young girl | girl in the next |
| in the next room | room was |
| was reading | reading a |
| a book | book about |
| about chess | chess with great |
| with great care | care |

FIG. 2

However, Thorne *et al.* (1965) point out, in connexion with the operation of their programme, that 'it is not necessary to describe the surface structure of a sentence fully in order to reconstruct its deep structure'. The problem, clearly, is to find the deep structure as quickly as possible. Little is yet known concerning the organization of this component of a perceptual model. It seems unlikely, though, that 'analysis by synthesis' techniques (even after a preliminary analysis has reduced the space that must be exhaustively searched) could match the speed of human processing.

*Measures of syntactic complexity.* Various measures of *syntactic complexity* have been proposed and discussed (see Miller and Chomsky 1963). The most widely studied have been 'degree of nesting and self-embedding', 'depth of postponed symbols', 'node to terminal node ratio', and 'number of transformational steps used in the mapping of deep into surface structures'. As measures of complexity relative to perceptual and production tasks, these metrics have the drawback that they often involve the assumption that the operations which must be carried out by psychological performance models have a one-to-one correspondence to the operations whereby grammars generate structural descriptions (i.e. the measures presuppose a commitment to relatively 'pure' analysis by synthesis procedures). The fact that some of these metrics interact in complex ways (e.g. the transformation which converts 'Look up the number' into 'Look the number up' decreases the node/terminal node ratio of the derived tree) produces awkward problems in the analysis of experimental data which bear upon the validity of the measures. It is known, however, that iterated self-embedded structures will eventually exceed the processing capacity of any perceptual model with a finite memory, and Miller and Isard (1964) have shown that the human capacity to deal with these structures is very severely limited. Studies of a fairly wide range of tasks (including learning, reading, conversion of one sentence type into another, decision-making with respect to truth or falsity of sentences) have indicated that transformational complexity correlates well with behavioural difficulty (as indexed by such standard measures as number of trials to criterion, time taken to perform the task, number type of errors, etc.). Important results demonstrating some kind of psychological additivity for performing transformational operations have been obtained (see

Miller and McKeen 1964). Many of these results were demonstrated, however, for a rather narrow range of syntactic types (the optional, singulary transformations described in Chomsky (1957), especially passives, negatives, questions, and their combinations). One of the central problems here is that it is not easy to tell from many of the published experiments whether the psychological difficulty observed is due to the structural description of the material being difficult to recover, difficult to store, or difficult to retrieve and output (or worse, some combination of all three). Presumably there are different psychological limitations on these separate aspects of performance and presumably in each case the grammar is involved in radically different ways. Another problem is that of preventing the subject from formulating *ad hoc* 'rules' which allow him to perform the particular experimental task quite efficiently but which, perhaps, throw little light on normal processing skills.

*Models of the encoding process*. One almost totally neglected area has been the development of formal models of the speaker, devices which will map 'thoughts' onto the base structures of the syntactic component. The difficulties involved are obviously formidable—no coherent account of the structure of human thought is available. Certain related problems (e.g. the explication of paraphrase, analyticity, and contradiction; the representation of lexical entries by complex feature matrices) are being investigated within the framework of transformational grammar. Lakoff (1964) has studied some implications of a production system which takes advantage of the (perhaps quite limited) correspondences between the dual representations of features which may have both a syntactic and a semantic interpretation, (such notions include 'subject', 'predicate', 'animate', 'abstract') and which maps semantic features fairly directly into a variety of base strings. Several of the question-answering devices that have been proposed in the artificial intelligence literature suggest interesting psychological hypotheses (although these schemes usually operate with a very restricted syntax).

When production models are available it should be possible to test aspects of their psychological validity by seeing if their output can simulate, in a natural fashion, the wide variety of *hesitation phenomena* (false starts, retracings, repetitions, filled and unfilled pauses, etc.) that occur in normal speech. Various distributional studies have been published which show that different kinds of hesitation phenomena reflect different types of encoding problems. The face validity of such studies is reflected in the fact that the frequency of pauses, etc. varies with the (intuitive) level of cognitive complexity of the encoding task.

Hesitation pauses occur at word boundaries. They are rarely found at syllable or morpheme boundaries. (The whole word is usually repeated when this does occur.) Pauses are relatively frequent prior to major lexical categories (especially nouns). The bilateral predictability of the specific item subsequent to a pause is usually low, although *form-class* membership is often highly predictable following pauses (see Tannenbaum *et al.* 1965). Pauses are infrequent within some constituent structures (e.g. between the members of a verb-adverb or an intensifier-adverb phrase, between an auxiliary and an infinitive). The interpretation of data in this field is difficult because of the problems of distinguishing between 'stylistic' and emphatic pauses, juncture pauses, and true non-fluency. Boomer (1965) offers a useful methodological and theoretical critique of much of the literature. Evidence is presented which seems to show that, in many cases, hesitations occur subsequent to the decision as to which phrase type will be produced and prior to a set of lexical choices being made.

*See also:* Linguistic form: generative grammar. Linguistic form: transformational theory.

*Bibliography*

BLUMENTHAL A. L. (1966) *Prompted recall of sentences*, J. Verbal Learning and Verbal Behavior (in press).
BOOMER D. (1965) *Hesitation and grammatical encoding*, Language and Speech, **8**, 148.
CHOMSKY N. (1957) *Syntactic Structures*, (Janua Linguarum, Series Minor, 4) The Hague: Mouton.
CHOMSKY N. (1965) *Aspects of the Theory of Syntax*, Cambridge, Mass.: M.I.T. Press.
GARRETT M., BEVER T. and FODOR J. A. (1966) *The active use of grammar in speech perception*, Perception and Psychophysics, **1**, 30.
KATZ J. J. and POSTAL P. M. (1964) *An Integrated Theory of Linguistic Descriptions*, Cambridge, Mass.: M.I.T. Press.
LAKOFF G. (1964) *Toward Generative Semantics*, Mimeo, Machine Translation Group, M.I.T.
MEHLER J. (1963) *Some effects of grammatical transformations on the recall of English sentences*, J. Verbal Learning and Verbal Behavior, **2**, 346.
MILLER G. A. and CHOMSKY N. (1963) *Finitary models of language users*, in (LUCE R. D., BUSH R. and GALANTER E. Eds.) Handbook of Mathematical Psychology, Vol. 2, New York: Wiley.
MILLER G. A. and ISARD S. (1964) *Free recall of self-embedded English sentences*, Information and Control, **7**, 292.
MILLER G. A. and McKEAN K. O. (1964) *A chronometric study of some relations between sentences*, Quart. J. Experim. Psychol. **16**, 297.
RUBENSTEIN H. (1965) *Problems in automatic word disambiguation*, Paper presented to Conference on Computer-related Semantic Research (Las Vegas, December, 1965).
SAVIN H. B. and PERCHONOCK E. (1965) *Grammatical structure and the immediate recall of English sentences*, J. Verbal Learning and Verbal Behaviour, **4**, 348.
TANNENBAUM P. H., WILLIAMS F. and HILLIER C. S. (1965) *Word Predictability in the Environment of Hesitations*, J. Verbal Learning and Verbal Behavior, **4**, 134.

THORNE J. P., DEWAR H., WHITFIELD H. and BRATLEY P. (1965) *A model for the perception of syntactic structure*, Mimeo, University of Edinburgh, English Language Research Unit.

WALES R. J. (1964) *Problems of repetition in verbal learning*, Paper read to the meeting of the British Psychological Society (London, December 1964).

J. C. MARSHALL

## PSYCHOLOGICAL LINGUISTICS: PSYCHOLOGICAL ASPECTS OF SEMANTIC STRUCTURE.

Theories of *natural languages* are *rulesystems* which pair '*meanings*' with their physical representations as *acoustic signals*. An essential part of a theory of language must accordingly be a semantic theory which provides an account of the conceptual structure of *lexical items* and their concatenations. Such an account should explicate the relatively clear semantic 'intuitions' of native speakers concerning the relationships between various n-tuples of words in their language. These relationships include synonymity (ILL-SICK), various forms of antonymy (MAN-WOMAN; WIDE-NARROW; RED-BLUE-GREEN-YELLOW; LION-TIGER), the notions of superordinate (ARTIFACT to TABLE), subordinate (FEAR to EMOTION) and proper part (MANE to LION). Katz and Fodor (1963) have suggested a formalism for dictionary entries which is capable of representing such information. This work is updated in Katz (1966). Briefly, it is proposed that lexical items be characterized by a set of *syntactic markers*, *semantic markers* ('atomic' conceptual elements) and *selection restrictions* (the function of which is to exclude anomalous word combinations within major *grammatical constituents*, i.e. to mark HOT IDEA as deviant whilst permitting HOT SOUP). Figure 1 illustrates (in a highly tentative and simplified form) the entries for MAN and COLD (each in one sense only); in these entries syntactic markers are not parenthesized, semantic markers are enclosed in round brackets, and selection restrictions (SR) are enclosed in diamonds.

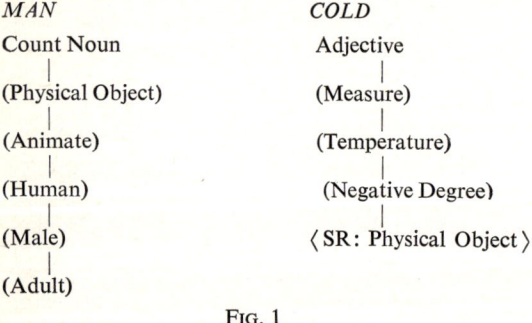

FIG. 1

The investigations of linguistic performance which reflect structure of this nature most directly are studies of 'free'—association. Free-association tests are usually given with instructions stressing the necessity of responding as quickly as possible (and forbidding the repetition of the stimulus word). It seems reasonable to suppose that the manipulation of lexical information takes time and that therefore the most frequently given responses will form minimal *syntactic* and semantic *contrasts* with the stimulus items. We thus find, in general, that *paradigmatic responses* (i.e. items which closely match the intrinsic syntactic and semantic features of the stimulus, e.g., MAN →WOMAN, COLD → HOT, LION → TIGER) occur more frequently than *syntagmatic responses* (i.e. items from a different syntactic class but which meet the selection restrictions of the stimulus word, e.g. MAN → TALL, COLD → SNOW, LION → ROAR). Within the class of paradigmatic responses we find that superordinates (e.g. EAGLE → BIRD, LION → ANIMAL) occur much more frequently than proper part responses (e.g. EAGLE → WING, LION → MANE). It is obviously easier to retrieve a word corresponding to a marker already contained in the original stimulus. Paradigmatic responses which involve the change of a single marker are usually more frequent than associations in which two or more markers are changed. (e.g. the two most frequent associations to MAN are WOMAN and BOY; the two next most frequent associations are WOMEN and GIRL). This strong tendency to change a single marker is shown most clearly in associations to adjectives where the occurrence of polar contrasts (COLD-HOT, HIGH-LOW, DEEP-SHALLOW) has often been noted. Examples of this nature, however, suggest a further generalization. One would expect that the lexical entry for WET is highly similar to the entry for COLD (differing, perhaps, only in that WET contains the marker 'Humidity' where COLD contains 'Temperature'). Whilst WET does occur as an association to COLD the overwhelmingly preponderent association is COLD → HOT. Consider also the highly similar entries for DEEP and HIGH (Fig. 2).

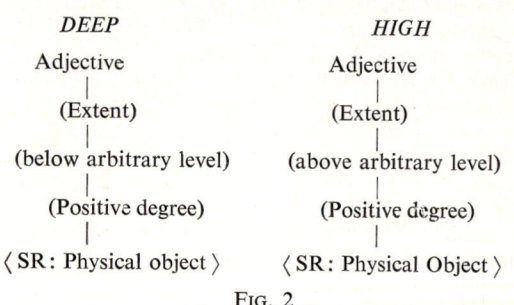

FIG. 2

Again, whilst DEEP and HIGH do elicit each other as free-associations, the predominant or primary associations are DEEP → SHALLOW and HIGH → LOW. It seems, then, that it is much easier to change what might be called a 'directional' marker (positive degree to negative degree, or vice-versa) than to change a 'substantive' marker in a free-association task. (Associational data concerning all the examples which have been discussed so far will be found in Palermo and Jenkins, 1964: College student norms.) A class of antonymous adjectives of particular interest is the class of pairs which have a *marked* and *unmarked* member. Examples include HIGH-LOW, FAR-NEAR, GOOD-BAD. In each of these pairs the first item is the primary or unmarked member and hence occurs in such semantically neutral questions as 'How high is the building?', 'How far is the garage', 'Was the movie good?'. (To ask such questions with the marked adjective implies either that one has a special motive for asking or that one already partially knows the answer.) Lakoff (1965) and Greenberg (1966) contain interesting recent discussions of the notion of markedness. This distinction seems to be reflected, under time pressure, in associational studies. If subjects are asked, without being given a stimulus item, to produce all the pairs of antonymous adjectives they can think of, they normally produce them in the order unmarked-marked (e.g. they say DEEP-SHALLOW not SHALLOW-DEEP). Deese (1964), however, studied the primary associations to adjectives in the usual manner (i.e. with one adjective being given as the stimulus). The data he presents suggests rather strongly that, whilst the associations FAR→NEAR, NEAR→FAR, HIGH→LOW, LOW→HIGH, etc. are the predominant ones, more subjects produce the antonym responses Marked→Unmarked (e.g. LOW→HIGH) than produce Unmarked→Marked (e.g. HIGH→LOW). It seems, then, that in the absence of a context it is easier to retrieve unmarked lexical items and that given a marked item in an association experiment it is easier to retrieve the related unmarked item than vice-versa. Greenberg (1966) has studied the relationship of the marked-unmarked distinction for syntactic features to word-association. He argues that, in general, singular nouns should elicit singular nouns and plural nouns plurals as associations but that plurals should elicit the unmarked category 'singular' more often than singulars elicit the marked category 'plural'. In like fashion, base adjectives should elicit base adjectives and comparative adjectives elicit comparatives but again the association COMPARATIVE ADJECTIVE→BASE ADJECTIVE should occur much more frequently than the association BASE ADJECTIVE→COMPARATIVE ADJECTIVE. A similar argument is put forward for the associative relations between the infinitive and the present participle forms of verbs. Greenberg shows that all these structural predictions are fully born out by the Palermo-Jenkins norms. A further syntactic example concerning verbs might also be mentioned. It is usually argued that the present tense is unmarked (with respect to the marked tense *past*). Here, too, the Palermo-Jenkins norms show, as predicted, that the association WAS→IS occurs much more frequently than the association IS→WAS.

Some studies have been reported in which direct latency measures have been taken for different types of association. Thus the data of Siipola, Walker and Kolb (1955) show that, when the instructions stress time pressure fairly forcibly, most subjects can produce antonym responses much more quickly than they produce syntagmatic (in this case ADJECTIVE→NOUN) responses. To change a single semantic marker and produce the appropriate phonological realization is thus faster than retrieving an essentially new word which meets the selection restriction of the stimulus. Likewise, Karwoski and Schachter (1948) showed that antonym responses were faster than superordinate responses which, in turn, were faster than subordinate responses. These results, too, are predictable from a theory of lexical organization which displays 'atomic' structure.

Disruption of the retrieval of the internal structure of lexical entries can be observed in the paraphasic naming errors produced by certain types of neurological patient. For example, Kinsbourne and Warrington (1964) studied a patient who was unable to select the correct member from the set of colour antonyms. Although no perceptual defect was discovered which could explain this the patient consistently confused RED, GREEN, BLUE, YELLOW, etc. when asked to name either blocks or ordinary objects of these colours. The total instability of the links between sets of semantic markers and their appropriate phonological realizations was further shown by the patient's inability to acquire new associations to colour words in a standard paired-associate learning task. The remarkable specificity of this particular syndrome is indicated by the fact that performance with the words BLACK, WHITE and GREY was *not* impaired. Marshall and Newcombe (1966) studied a case of fairly gross dyslexic impairment in which semantic errors predominated. The patient would read BUSH as 'tree', LARGE as 'long', SHORT as 'small' etc. In this case the specificity of the syndrome is shown by the fact that the patient did not make 'directional' antonym errors with, e.g. adjectives (i.e. he did not change the marker 'positive degree' to 'negative degree' or vice-versa). Only a small number of 'substantive' markers were confused. The precise study of the breakdown of language functions is potentially capable of throwing much light on the mechanisms which subserve linguistic behaviour. Jakobson (1964) has proposed an interesting preliminary typology of aphasic defects which distinguishes clearly between 'serial order' and 'parallel' (specific retrieval) disabilities on all levels of linguistic organization.

Little is yet known concerning complexity measures for semantic structure, although the general problem of assessing 'conceptual complexity' is of major importance. A useful approach to this problem will be found in Wallace (1961). Wallace tentatively proposes that the complexity of folk taxonomies of the type studied in '*componential analysis*' (i.e. semantic sub-systems such as status and kinship terminologies which are acquired without special training by all members of a speech-community) can always be expressed in a space of six binary dimensions. Kinship terms in different cultures are considered and it is shown that the complexity of kinship terminology does not increase as a function of the technological complexity of societies. (See also, in this connexion, the proposals by Katz (1966) for determining the semantic categories of a language.)

*See also:* Semantics: context and collocation. Semantics: introduction. Linguistic form: paradigmatic. Semantics: field theories. Linguistic form: syntagmatic. Linguistic form: transformational theory.

*Bibliography*

DEESE J. (1964) *The associative structure of some common English adjectives, Journal of Verbal learning and Verbal behaviour,* **3,** 347.

GREENBERG J. H. (1966) *Language Universals,* in *Current Trends in Linguistics,* Vol. 3, (Ed. T. A. Sebeok), The Hague: Mouton.

JAKOBSON R. (1964) *Towards a linguistic typology of aphasic impairments,* in *Disorders of Language: Ciba Foundation Symposium,* (Eds. A.V.S. deReuck and M. O'Connor) London: Churchill.

KARWOSKI T. F. and SCHACHTER J. (1948) *Psychological studies in semantics, J. Soc. Psychol.,* **28,** 103.

KATZ J. J. (1966) *The Philosophy of Language,* New York: Harper and Row.

KATZ J. J. and FODOR J. A. (1963) *The structure of a semantic theory, Language* **39,** 170.

KINSBOURNE M. and WARRINGTON E. K. (1964) *Observations on colour agnosia, J. Neurol. Neurosurg. Psychiat.,* **27,** 296.

LAKOFF G. (1965) *On the nature of syntactic irregularity,* Report No. NSF-16, The Computation Laboratory, Harvard University.

MARSHALL J. C. and NEWCOMBE F. (1966) *Syntactic and Semantic Errors in Paralexia, Neuropsychologia,* **4,** 169.

PALERMO D. S. and JENKINS J. J. (1964) *Word Association Norms,* Minneapolis: University of Minnesota Press.

SIIPOLA E., WALKER W. N. and KOLB D. (1955) *Task attitudes in word association, projective and non-projective, Personality,* **23,** 441.

WALLACE A. F. C. (1961) *On being just complicated enough, Proc. Nat. Acad. Sci.,* **47,** 458.

J. C. MARSHALL

## PSYCHOLOGICAL LINGUISTICS: THEORIES OF LEARNING IN RELATION TO LANGUAGE.

Learning theory is a generic term covering a large number of significant alternatives (cf. Estes *et al.* 1954). Since several of the more recent approaches are discussed elsewhere, this paper will concern itself with particular explanatory problems which language raises for these theories. These problems are associated with the structural aspects of language; and may be crudely divided into those which refer to attempts to explain the initial acquisition of language by the child, and those which refer to the subsequent learning of particular instances as mediating processes.

The characteristic feature of *linguistic structures* is that they are hierarchically organized, one within the next higher structure and so on. A paragraph is composed of sentences, sentences of phrases, phrases of words, words of morphemes, etc. In speaking or writing we have to deal with relations between these at all the different *levels* of the hierarchy, both horizontally and vertically. Recently, American linguists, notably Chomsky (1959, 1965), have pointed out with great clarity and forcefulness the importance of this hierarchical organization for psychological theories of speech perception, language learning; in general for any theory of language use.

Psychological theories have been suggested which exhibit a parallelism with these structures in that they are theories of the hierarchical organization of behaviour. They are at present mainly attempts to construct a theory of language behaviour, and as such are fairly restricted. However, there have been attempts to generalize the notions originally stemming from linguistics to other aspects of *serial* behaviour; principally the work of Miller, Galanter and Pribram (1960). In this, the authors suppose all such behaviour to be guided internally by hierarchically organized 'Plans'; the lowest levels of the Plan corresponding to simple motor adjustments while the higher levels may correspond to long-term plans sustained over varying periods of time. Using these notions (which are similar to those current in several different information-processing models for simulating various aspects of human behaviour) the authors cover a wide range of psychological phenomena— from hypnotism to memorizing. We shall return to these ideas below.

This approach to serial behaviour was antedated by about ten years by Lashley (1951). In this celebrated paper, Lashley discussed various interpretations and explanations of language behaviour and other sustained serial behaviour which were dependent on the classical learning theory notions of stimulus, response, and reinforcement, generalization and transfer. He pointed to a number of serious difficulties inherent in complex behaviour of this type, which learning theory could not get around: the rapidity and comparative ease with which a child learns a language, the exceptionally complex motor sequence involved in producing speech which occurs far faster than any sort of neurophysiological correlate of reinforced associations could account for, the ability we all have to understand and produce strings of words never previously associated, and various systematic errors in speech production such as spoonerisms. Lashley concluded by marking down the problem of serial order as a crucial one for psychology. Since the old formalism of stimulus-response association breaks down completely when applied to Lashley's various examples, a new formalism must be found which does not lose the value of the S-R formalism, viz. that it provides a mechanism for taking the organism through time without recourse to vitalistic notions. There are two main reasons why the S-R explanations will not do.

(1) They provide essentially linear explanations for behaviour sequences which are clearly non-linear.

(2) They are firmly and immodifiably deterministic

in a curious way—events in the past, and *only* events in the past determine present events.

These objections may be clarified with examples. The choice of words in sentences by a speaker provides innumerable instances of a given choice being dependent on a word or words yet to come. (The fact that it is not, or not always, the other way round, i.e. the choice of the particular word determining succeeding words—is patently obvious, but spoonerisms provide an empirical demonstration of this.) However, if point (2) above is to be satisfied, then point (1) must be violated. That is, if my choice of the adjective 'green' in the phrase 'green apples' depends on the fact that I am going to talk about apples and not oranges, then I can treat 'green apples' as a unit and still retain a deterministic approach. But this entails proscribing associations between aspects of stimuli and between aspects of responses at different levels of integration. These, and many other, difficulties all point to the need for a psychological theory of serial behaviour which reflects the hierarchical organization of low-level units into higher-level units to be found in linguistic data.

What proposals have been forthcoming with reference to this complex of problems? A number of the recent alternatives are reviewed and discussed in Lyons and Wales (1966). As will probably be evident from the foregoing, one of the major points of contention is the form in which the problem for explanation is initially conceived. Thus the kind of theorizing against which Lashley argued started from an attempt to conceptualise the process of behaviour in terms based directly on observable behaviour, whereas most attempts to formalize an alternative have concentrated on trying to characterize the internal structures which would enable the organism to behave in the manner observed. One of the most fundamental distinctions that has been suggested is that between the organisms '*competence*' and '*performance*' (cf. Chomsky 1965). A theory of competence purports to be a principled account of the knowledge of the language that an idealized speaker-listener would need to have internalised in order for him to be able to understand and produce any of the infinite possible sentences in his language. It attempts to account for his 'intuitions' concerning the language, and to 'project' a finite corpus of *utterances* to a set of *rules* which assign *structural descriptions* to the infinite potential of sentences in the language. A theory of performance would account for the way in which we put this linguistic capacity to use, and indicate the limitations of the mechanism which expresses our competence.

For reasons of space and simplicity let us indicate with a non-linguistic hierarchy some of the issues involved in drawing this kind of distinction. Consider a double-alternation sequence, e.g. AA BB AA BB AA etc. Let us list some experimental findings with reference to the recognition of a double alternation given a predictive procedure with knowledge of results.

(i) Human subjects may recognize the correct sequence either as units of AA BB, or AB BA (or trivially the inverse of these)—when they are aware of the iteration it is usually AA BB.

(ii) We may train subjects with one of two procedures (suggested by Dr. A. R. Jonckheere) (a) the subjects 'correct' responses may be determined by the experimenter's predetermined sequence (b) the subjects' 'correct' response may be the opposite of the subjects' own response the trial before last, even if on that trial the subject had been 'incorrect'.

(iii) When Wales compared adults and children on the number of trials to correctly recognize a double alternation using these two training procedures, the adults were faster on system (a) whereas the children were quicker on system (b).

To return to our competence–performance distinction, we may indicate a number of levels of description. First we may suppose that we can specify two (at least) alternative *phrase structure 'grammars'*. Thus

$$
\begin{aligned}
(1)\ & S \to CDS & (2)\ & S \to EFS \\
& \phantom{S} \to CD & & \phantom{S} \to EF \\
& C \to AA & & E \to AB \\
& D \to BB & & F \to BA
\end{aligned}
$$
and

Both of these could be used to describe 'behaviourally' identical strings of symbols.

If we are concerned to evaluate our 'grammars' with respect to the subjects' 'intuition' of the organization of the double-alternation (say AA/BB) we would select 'grammar' (1) as a correct description of the subjects' 'competence'. We might, however, wish to go further and attempt to specify what kind of mechanism would enable the subject to perform so as to be able to recognize the hierarchical patterning in a sequence such as ... AABBA ... We would, in such an account of performance, wish to indicate what limitations would be imposed by, e.g. such factors as rate of presentation of the sequence. Further, for a complete account of performance we would need to be able to indicate how a child learned to recognize such a sequence and how the mechanism developed with age and experience. That this is, however, a somewhat trivial example—by comparison with natural language problems—is shown by the fact that a child producing two-word utterances is already involved in a much more complex state of affairs.

*Psychological reality of linguistic description* One of the most difficult areas in attempting to relate competence and performance is concerned with whether it is appropriate to speak of linguistic rules as being 'psychologically real' or whether we should only claim psychological reality for *linguistic units* (which have been shown to be basic perceptual units). This issue needs to be taken much further. It is worth noting that there is a distinction that might offer a useful parallel. When we have a *descriptively adequate grammar*, the rules are said to characterize our intuition in that they give an explicit description of the knowledge that would be necessary for us to understand and speak the language. The adequacy of the grammar may be evaluated by judging whether the rules are consistent with the intuitions which are available to us through introspection and experiment. However, it is clear, we can distinguish between that intuitive knowledge which is available to us in the above ways and that which is necessary and sufficient (but may not be available) for us to be language users. A similar distinction with respect to human knowledge of logical operations is drawn by Beth and Piaget (1961). That which is psychologically real and available they call 'psychological' knowledge, that which is necessary for adequate description 'epistemological'. Beth and Piaget state, first, that the object of psychological study is not 'behaviour' but 'conduct'—and this includes 'awareness' and the study of the conditions that determine 'becoming aware'. The process of becoming aware may offer specially useful opportunities for introspection. (Notice that one becomes aware particularly when obstacles are encountered and are being overcome.) Secondly, they state that, so far as logical structures are concerned we have to suppose: (a) that the subject constructs them and they are in this sense 'in him', (b) that the subject can, at some point, become aware of them, *as if* he discovered them.

There are, obviously, many degrees of awareness and only a psychologist/epistemologist/linguist will normally attempt to provide any explicit description of these structures. The distinction Beth and Piaget draw between (metaphorical homunculi) 'sujet psychologique' (S.P.) and 'sujet epistémique (S.E. conceived as expressing what is common to all subjects at the same level of development) rests on (a) awareness and (b) role, i.e. S.P. has a functional role, S.E. has a constructive role, is the *source* of cognitive structures. The structures, in so far as S.E. is conceived as building them, obviously have psychological reality. It is the status of the descriptions which is in doubt—and the issue seems to be how well they fit the structures in S.E. How do we find out? S.P. cannot always tell us. S.E. cannot ever tell us. This seems to reduce to attempts to make S.P. more aware, i.e. to extend his awareness of S.E. As Chomsky has said (1965: 24) 'it may be necessary to guide and draw out the speaker's intuition in perhaps fairly subtle ways before we can determine what is the actual character of his knowledge of his language or of anything else'.

Thus we have: (1) Necessary and sufficient knowledge for given performance. (2) Subjects' awareness of that knowledge. (3) Description of that knowledge. Both (1) and (3) might be described as intuition. It is of course to (1) that (3) must correspond. However, if we are concerned with psychological reality we will be also concerned with (2): and only with respect to (2) will we be in a position to claim that those features which exhibit psychological reality are in fact features of the individual rather than merely features of the descriptive model, i.e. rules.

If notions of hierarchical organization and the psychological reality of grammatical description cause problems when the relevant information has already been internalised, then so much more so does the question of how the knowledge is internalised in the first place. What has to be accounted for is not only how a mechanism develops which can handle related hierarchies. Also necessary is a description of how a child abstracts the relevant regularities which are unobservable in the physical speech signals, and how it selects from the infinite number of possible competing hypotheses that which is the correct specification of the language being learned. Because of these apparently insuperable obstacles to language learning, which nevertheless normally proceeds with remarkable uniformity and speed, Chomsky (1965) (cf. also Smith and Miller 1966), has argued for the necessity of certain innate predispositions which enable a child to select (from its linguistic environment) the appropriate features necessary to learning a language (cf. Shepard (1964) for a lucid discussion of related problems in the prestructuring of possible perceptual experience). A certain amount of correlative evidence for the biological basis of language has been presented by Lenneberg (1964). His argument includes reference to (i) the existence of linguistic universals (ii) the relatively invariant recorded history of human language (iii) the likelihood of a 'critical period' for the start and development of language in the child (iv) the fact that language acquisition cannot be accelerated by specific teaching (v) unique organic correlates of language behaviour in man (cf. these arguments with the work of the ethologists Lorenz, Tinbergen, Thorpe etc., on the hierarchical structure of 'instincts'). The nature of the universals would be crucial with reference to what needs to be claimed for these inherited predispositions.

When Lashley expounded the problem of serial order, he described the issue as one of a search for the 'syntax of action'; for 'generalized schemata' which impose order on the specific constituent acts of a piece of behaviour. The notions of Miller, Galanter and Pribram—developed in the conclusion of Miller and Chomsky (1963)—purport to do just this. An organism has a variety of plans for various activities at his disposal: some acquired through experience, some inborn. Some plans may be 'put aside' while one is executed, that is, we may generate subgoals and goals. Intentions, goals and other troublesome notions are described as the residue of a plan; the postponed or unfinished part of the plan. Perhaps it would be fair to say that such theories were primarily motivated by the need to develop an alternative to the S—R formalisms which might deal adequately with such complicated behaviour sequences as speech production or perception. To date it is not clear whether they have demonstrated very much beyond the fact of their construction—which is merely to indicate that many problems which these theories have elucidated are still with us (cf. Marshall's articles for an indication of what such attempts have managed to achieve.)

Finally it is worth drawing attention to the work of Hansen and Rodgers (1965) in which, given the definition of elements within one level of a hierarchy, they have been able to apply certain implications of the one-element stimulus sampling model by way of optimizing learning of initial reading. This suggests that more sophisticated forms of S-R theory may provide useful quantitative predictions of learning in limited situations.

The author is grateful to R. N. Campbell, M. C. Donaldson, J. C. Marshall and J. P. Thorne for their help with some of the issues discussed.

*See also:* Linguistic form: algebraic linguistics. Linguistic form: generative grammar. Linguistic form: system and structure. Linguistic form: transformational theory.

*Bibliography*

BETH E. V. and PIAGET J. (1961) *Epistémologie mathématique et psychologie*, Paris: Presses Universitaires de France.
CHOMSKY N. (1959) *A review of Verbal Behaviour* by B. F. Skinner (1957) *Language*, **35**, 26.
CHOMSKY N. (1965) *Aspects of the Theory of Syntax*, Cambridge, Mass: M.I.T. Press.
ESTES W. K. *et al.* (1954) *Modern Learning Theory*, New York: Crofts.
HANSEN D. and RODGERS T. (1965) *An exploration of psycholinguistic units in initial reading*, Tech. Rep. No. 74; Institute for Mathematical Studies in Social Sciences, Stanford University.
LASHLEY K. S. (1951) *The problem of serial order in behavior*, in (L. A. Jeffress Ed.), *Cerebral Mechanisms in Behavior*, New York: Wiley.
LENNEBERG E. H. (1964) *The capacity for language acquisition*, in (J. A. Fodor and J. J. Katz Eds.) *The Structure of Language*, Englewood Cliffs, N. J.: Prentice Hall.
LYONS J. and WALES R. J. (Eds.) *Psycholinguistic Papers* Edinburgh: The University Press.
MILLER G. A. and CHOMSKY N. (1963) *Finitary models of language users*, in (D. Luce, R. Bush and E. Galanter Eds.), *Handbook of Mathematical Psychology*, Vol. 2, New York: Wiley.
MILLER G. A., GALANTER E. and PRIBRAM K. (1960) *Plans and the Structure of Behavior*, New York: Holt.
SHEPARD R. N. (1964) *A review of Computers and thought* (E. Feigenbaum and J. Feldman Eds.) *Behavioral Science*, **9**, 57.
SMITH F. and MILLER G. A. (Eds.) (1966) *The Genetics of Language*, Cambridge, Mass.: M.I.T. Press.

R. J. WALES

**PSYCHOLOGY, USE OF MODELS (LEARNING).** Models are symbolic structures that correspond to and represent salient features of real systems. From a theoretical point of view, it does not matter very much whether the model is stated in the abstract, as a set of mathematical equations, or whether it is embodied in a computer program or a tangible artifact like Uttley's (1956) conditional probability machine. In practice, however, one form may be far more convenient than another. Since the equations for complex biological systems are commonly intractable, there is a reasonable bias in favour of computer simulation and hardware. But it is sometimes possible to gain mathematical elegance in statements about the class of models or in a statistical treatment of the system. Thus numerous workers have simulated the behaviour of networks of finite automata (any of which is an idealized and maximally simplified model of a real neuron), McCulloch and Pitts (1943) proved the fundamental theorem that any unambiguous statement could be computed by a network of this sort (an abstract logical proof to do with the class of models), and Cowan is currently developing a statistical theory of the activity in these networks.

If a model is only used in a descriptive fashion its form is unrestricted. But the majority of models are constructed as vehicles for posing and testing hypotheses about a real system, or for explaining how it works. In either case, it is necessary to guard against the fallacy of 'nominalism' (that a stone falls because it has the property of 'heaviness') or, in general, the fallacy of confusing the attachment of a label (the name for a definitive property of a class of observables) with the provision of a causal explanation. (Deutch (1957) provides experimentally oriented discussion of the issue.) Such a confusion is impossible if a model is *reducible* to units of an already established type; for example, if we have already established the calibre of a 'computing unit' and we aim to explain the phenomenon of 'learning', then the requirement that any learning model may be reduced to (or assembled from) a collection of computing units by the application of well defined composition rules, guarantees that no special 'learning property' has been slipped into the model unawares; if the model can be identified with reality, then it genuinely does explain learning in terms of computation (in general, in terms of the basic units and the assembly rules).

*Reduction type of models.* We shall insist upon *reducibility* and will categorize models according to the units that are deemed irreducible or atomic constituents. Two sorts of unit are particularly common and lead to '*computational*' and '*cybernetic*' *models*. These are:

(I) A 'finite automaton', that computes an output as some definite function of its input and its present states, and
(II) A 'control unit' that is designed to achieve a particular goal.

Some typical cases of the 'computational' model unit in (I) are:

(1) A linear operator, such as the matrix representing interactions between the excitation of several nerve tracts, in Reichart's (1962) model for lateral inhibition in Lemullus eye.

(2) A 'threshold logic' unit that operates at discrete instants to produce a binary output of value 1 (at this instant) if and only if the weighted sum of its binary input variables exceeds some threshold value. Units of this sort feature in various learning models such as

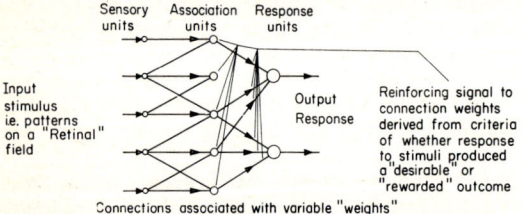

FIG. 1. *Threshold logic unit.*

Rosenblatt's (1961) 'Perceptron' and Widrow's (1962) 'Adaline' networks; in each case the (input multiplying) weights are altered in a manner that depends upon previous values of the input and output variables, and usually a 'reward' or 'reinforcement' signal, as in Fig. 1.

(3) A conditional propability unit, which estimates the proportional conjoint occurrence of binary events or inputs, $A$, $B$, to produce an output signifying $A$ if

tion, when the unit becomes a communication channel in the sense of Shannon (Shannon and Weaver).

Some typical cases of the 'cybernetic' unit in (II) are:

(1) Homeostatic systems, of the sort discussed by Ashby (1960, 1964), as in Fig. 2.

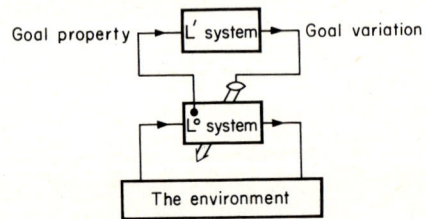

FIG. 3. *Hierarchical adaptive control system.*

(2) Hierarchically organized adaptive control systems of the type shown in Fig. 3, and using a functionally equivalent convention, in Fig 4. (The higher level or $L^1$ control system in Fig. 3 selects the goal of the lower level or $L^0$ control system; in Fig. 4 the $L^1$ control system selects from a set of $L^0$ control systems with given goals. In either case, if the structure is realized in some malle-

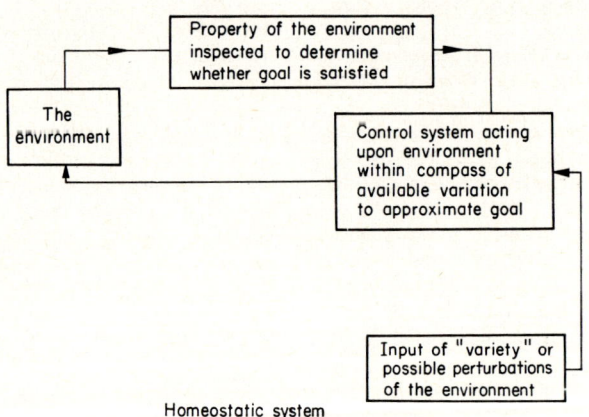

FIG. 2. *Homeostatic system.*

either $A$ occurs *or* $B$ occurs *and* the estimated probability $p(A/B)$ exceeds some definite value. Such components appear in the models of Uttley (1956), Maron (1962), Steinbuch (1961) and Pask (1963).

(4) Any subroutine in a computer program (in particular, in a simulated 'artificial intelligence') that computes some definite function (that multiplies, adds, or autocorrelates input signals). Selfridge's 'Pandemonium' (1958) Fiegenbaum's 'associative' memory programme (1963) and some of Minsky and Paperts automata are built from these units.

(5) The limiting case in which 'computation' is reduced to a one to one correspondence or identity transforma-

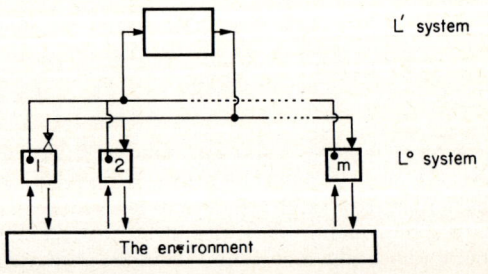

FIG. 4. *Hierarchical adaptive control system.*

able fabric so that the result of an $L^1$ action is retained an '$L^1$ selection' is '$L^0$ learning'.)

(3) The TOTE (or 'Test, Operate, Test, Exit') units that Miller, Gallanter and Pribram (1960) regard as the building blocks for *mentation*. TOTE units may be sequentially concatenated in the manner of Fig. 5. Any

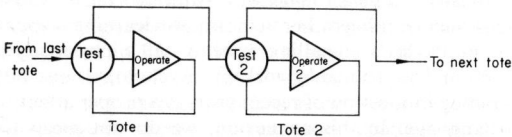

FIG. 5. *Test, operate, test, exit units.*

TOTE unit is a program for a control system; it tests for whether or not a goal is achieved, operates to achieve this goal until the test is affirmative and finally 'exits' to engage the next TOTE unit. Within such a system, learning gives rise to the sort of higher level organization indicated by Fig. 6.

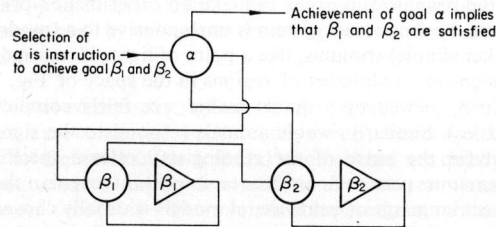

FIG. 6. *Higher level organization, achieving two goals.*

(4) A subroutine in an 'Artificial Intelligence' program, such as Andrea's 'Stella' program (1964) and (1960) Newell, Shaw and Simon's 'General Problem Solver', which either aims for goals or constructs goals.

The composition rules for assembling comutation and control units into hierarchies of learning (as above) or command (as in attention models (Sokolov 1960)) have been stated implicitly by the constructions used for Figs. 1–6. (Arbib (1965), Mesarovic (1963) and Rosen (1958) discuss the matter in a rigorous fashion.) But these are not causal principles which say why an aggregate of control systems should be more stable or more likely to survive (in evolution) than the separate entities.

Some causal principle is needed, of course, and one principle (peculiarly applicable for cybernetic models) has recently received a deal of attention. It appears, as Von Foerster (1960) has stressed, that natural systems are characterized by the fact that configurations with highly correlated activity are relatively stable; that they have some energetic advantage over others. Crudely, this amounts to a principle of cooperation; a pair of systems can gain more (of food, of energy, of **stability**) if they act jointly than either can gain by acting alone.

More precisely the measures (of certain relevant) composition rules are superadditive rather than additive in form. Structures appear to mediate the communication between systems that is a prerequisite for their cooperative interaction.

*Probabilistic and deterministic models.* Either computational or cybernetic models can be deterministic or probabilistic. Thus, Lettvin, Matturana, McCulloch and Pitts (1959) have advanced and validated a deterministic model for visual perception in the frog. The computing elements are real neurons, the network is their detailed connexion. The system 'computes' in the sense that it filters or analyses five distinct coordinates of the frog's visual world. The intensity of stimulation corresponding to each of these attributes is represented (for each retinal field) on one of five layers in the frog's colliculus, as in Fig. 7. At the other extreme, the Perceptron model, mentioned a moment ago, is designed according to the premise that, providing the network has a certain laminar topology, its detailed connexion pattern is irrelevant, (hence, the actual connexions from layer to layer in a

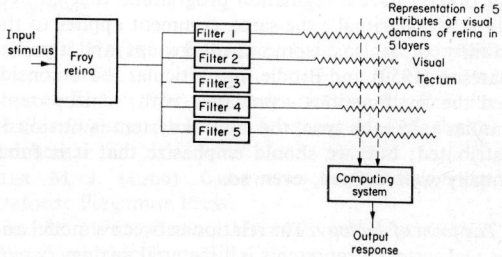

FIG. 7.

Perceptron are selected from a random number table). Between these extremities there are structures like R. L. Beurle's (1956) and Farley and Clarke's (1962) models for the activity in a part of the mammalian cortex. The computing units are idealized but fairly elaborate representations of real neurons; their connexion is determined by random selection within the constraints imposed by statistical data gleaned from histological examination of dendritic distributions in the real cortex; the behaviour of the model is interpreted statistically. So far as cybernetic models are concerned, the goal state may be probabilistically rather than deterministically

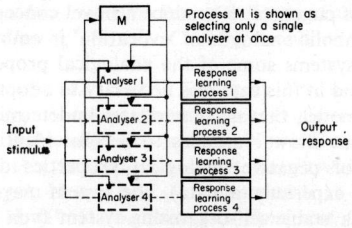

FIG. 8.

Gorn S. (1961) *The treatment of ambiguity and paradox in mechanical languages, Recursive Function Theory, Proc Symp. Pure Maths.* **5,** Providence, R. I.: American Mathematical Society.

Harmon L. D. (1962) *Studies with Artificial Neurones, 1. Properties and Function of an Artificial Neurone, Kybernetik* 1, **3,** 89.

Helson H. (1964) *Adaption-Level Theory,* New York; Harper and Row.

Hilgard E. H. (1958) *Theories of Learning,* London: Methuen.

Hull C. L. (1952) *A Behaviour System,* New Haven, Conn.: Yale University Press.

Klix F. (1964) *Proc. Symposium on Cybernetics Problems in Psychology,* Humboldt University, D. D. R. Berlin.

Koestler *The Creature Act,* London: Hutchinson.

Laefgrew L. in *Biological Prototypes and Synthetic Systems.*

Lettvin, Matturana, McCollough and Pitts (1959) *What the Frog's Eye Tells the Frog's Brain, Proc. Inst. Radio Engineers,* Nov.

Luce D., Bush R. and Gallanter E. (1963) *Handbook of Mathematical Psychology,* New York: Wiley.

Maldonado H. (1963) *The Visual Attack Learning System in Octopus Vulgaris, J. Theoret. Biol.* **5**, 470.

Maron H. E. (1962) *The Design Principles for an Intelligent Machine, International Symposium on Information,* Inst. Radio Engineers, Trans. in *Inf. Theory,* **II,** 8, No. 5.

McCullough W. S. and Pitts W. (1943) *A Logical Calculus of the Ideas Immanent in Nervous Activity, Bull. Math. Biophysics,* **5,** 115.

McCullough W. S. (1965) *Embodiments of Mind,* Cambridge, Mass.: M.I.T. Press.

Mesarovic M. (Ed.) (1963) in *Views on General System Theory,* New York: Wiley.

Miller G. A., Galanter E. and Pribram K. (1960) *Plans, and Structure of Behaviour,* New York: Henry Holt.

Napalkov A. *Systematics in the Working of the Brain and Some Problems in Cybernetics, Proc. 3rd International Congress of Cybernetics.*

Newell G. (1960) *Intelligent Learning in the General Problem Solver,* in *Self-Organising Systems,* (Eds. Yovitts and Cameron), Oxford: Pergamon Press.

Pask G. (1959) *Physical Analogues to the Growth of a Concept,* in (A. Uttley Ed.) *Mechanisation of Thought Processes,* London: H. M. Stationery Office.

Pask G. (1963) *Statistical Computation and Statistical Automata,* in (K. Steinbuch and S. W. Wagner Eds.), *Nevere Ergennisse der Kybernetik,* Oldenbourg.

Pask G. *Man as a System that Needs to Learn,* in (S. Beer, P. H. George and D. Stewart Eds.), *Advances in Cybernetics,* New York: Academic Press.

Pask G. *Advances in Computers,* **5.**

Rappaport and Vayda *Ritual Regulation of the Environmental Relations of the Tsombega,* New York: Columbia University Press (in press).

Reichart W. (1962) *Symposium on Information Processing in Nervous Systems,* Leyden.

Rosen R. (1958) *The Representation of Biological Systems from the Standpoint of the Theory of Categories, Bull Math. Biophysics,* **20,** 317.

Rosenblatt F. (1961) *Principles of Neurodynamics, Perceptrons and the Theory of Brain Mechanisms,* Cornell Aeronautical Lab. Report. No. VG-1196-G-8.

Selfridge O. (1958) *Pandemonium, Mechanisation of Thought Processes,* London: H. M. Stationery Office.

Shannon C. and Weaver W. *Mathematical Theory of Communication,* Illinois: The University Press.

Skinner B. F. (1961) *Teaching Machines, Scientific American,* Nov.

Sokolov E. N. (1960) *Neuronal models and the orienting reflex,* in *The Central Nervous System and Behaviour,* (Brazier M. A. Ed.), Macy.

Steinbuch R. (1961) *Learning matrices, Kybernetik,* **36.**

Sutherland N. S. (1964) *The Learning of Discrimination by Animals,* in *Endeavour,* **23,** No. 90, Sept.

Taylor (1963) *Proc. 1st I.F.A.C., Conf.,* Basle, London: Butterworths.

Tolman E. C. (1951) *A Psychological Model,* in *Toward a General Theory of Action,* (Ed. Parsons and Shils), Harvard: The University Press.

Uttley A. M. (1956) *Conditional Probability Machines and Conditioned Reflexes, Automata Studies,* (Ed. Shannon and McCarthy), Princeton: The University Press.

Von Foerster H. (1960) *Self-organizing systems and their environments,* in *Self-Organizing Systems* (Yovits and Cameron Eds.), Oxford: Pergamon Press.

Von Foerster H. 'Biologie' in *Biological Prototypes and Synthetic Systems,* (Eds. F. E. Berward and M. R. Kane.)

Vygotsky L. in *Thought and Language,* New York: Wiley.

Walter W. G. (1953) *The Living Brain,* London: Duckworth.

Widrow B. (1962) *Information Storage in a Network of Adaline Neurones,* in *Self-Organising Systems,* New York: Spartan Press.

Winograd and Cowan (1963) *Reliable Computation in the Presence of Noise,* Cambridge, Mass.: M.I.T. Press.

Young J. Z. *A Model of the Brain,* Oxford: The University Press.

G. Pask

**RANDOM SIGNALS AND NOISE.** 'Random signal' might be thought a contradiction in terms. On any particular occasion, the sender of a message intends to be definite, and hopes that the recipient will equally be left in no doubt. However, one particular signal conveys information only to the extent that other signals were possible, and it is this variety which lends itself to statistical description and to the use of the word 'random'. Indeed, the greater the variety available, the richer the code or language, and the apparatus of communication must allow for all possibilities. A set of possible signals forms a class known as an *ensemble*, each member of which has (once we have dissociated our minds from a particular occasion) a certain probability of occurrence. Noise, the name given to unwanted random effects, may be discussed in exactly the same mathematical terms. The only difference is that a signal may have an artificial meaning attached to it whilst a noise does not.

A discrete signal may consist of a single symbol, such as a letter chosen from an ensemble of 26 letters, or it may consist of a stream of such symbols. Conceptually, a stream may be treated as one grand composite choice, but for practical analysis, the finer subdivision is the more useful. The set of probabilities for a symbol may, as in natural language, be context-dependent yet at the same time be independent of absolute position in the stream. For example, the probability of the letter $u$, in English, is influenced by whether the previous letter was $q$, but the probability of $u$ as the tenth letter on the page is not different on different pages. Under these circumstances, a process is said to be *stationary*. Strictly the definition can apply only to infinitely long streams and is mathematically expressed by saying that the process is stationary if the *ensemble of streams* is unchanged by shifting any number of places to the right or left. In the shift, most of the individual streams which go to make up the ensemble will change (exceptions would be periodic sequences) but the ensemble, or whole collection, would be unaltered. If, in addition, any one stream is typical of the whole ensemble, in the sense that every permissible sequence of symbols will be encountered sooner or later, the process is said to be *ergodic*. (In stricter terms, an ergodic ensemble is stationary, but has no smaller stationary sub-set, except for trivial sub-sets with zero probability.) As an illustration, a signal having a 50–50 chance of being entirely in English or entirely in French would be stationary but non-ergodic. Nearly all the elementary theory of random signals and noise is effectively restricted to stationary ergodic processes.

In a 'purely random process' as defined by Min Chen Wang and Uhlenbeck (1945), successive symbols in the stream are statistically independent. This is the simplest case, but in the next more complicated process, we must define transition probabilities from one symbol to the next, like the probability of finding the letter $u$ after the occurrence of $q$. Let us denote by $P$ the probability that the $n$th symbol in a stream is $s_n$ when all preceding symbols ($s_{n-1}$, $s_{n-2}$, etc.) are known. Using the notation prob $(a \mid b)$ to mean the conditional probability of $a$ when $b$ is given, we have by definition

$$P = \text{prob}\,(s_n \mid s_{n-1},\, s_{n-2},\, \ldots).$$

If this is equal to

$$\text{prob}\,(s_n \mid s_{n-1})$$

the process is a discrete *Markoff process*; if $P$ is equal to prob $(s_n)$ unconditionally, the process is 'purely random'. In a Markoff chain, prediction of the next or any future symbol is not assisted by knowledge of other than the most recently available symbol. Furthermore, the probability of the stream as a whole takes the simplified form

$$\begin{aligned}\text{prob}\,(s_1, s_2, s_3 \ldots) &= \text{prob}\,(s_1) \\ &\times \text{prob}\,(s_2 \mid s_1) \\ &\times \text{prob}\,(s_3 \mid s_2) \\ &\times \text{etc.}\end{aligned}$$

In an infinitely long stream, the first factor never occurs, and it is clear that the amount of choice, or information, associated with each symbol in a Markoff chain is governed solely by first-order transition probabilities. In more complicated processes, higher order transition probabilities have to be considered.

Signals do not always consist of discrete symbols. For example, in many control applications we have to deal with continuously varying parameters like the height of water in a reservoir. The statistical ideas are basically similar. To describe continuously varying time-functions we need the concept of a continuous distribution of probability. Thus, if the time-function $u(t)$ can at any instant take any value of a continuous range, we must use a continuous function $p(u)$ to describe the *density* of $u$ in the ensemble. If we normalize to unity the integral of $p(u)$ with respect to $u$, we are simply saying that, by definition, the probability of finding $u$ between two values, $u$ and $u+\Delta u$, is $p(u)\,\Delta u$. If we confine attention to ergodic processes, a simpler interpretation can be given. As $u$ is stationary, $p(u)\,\Delta u$ is independent of $t$ and it represents the proportion of time $u$ spends between the two levels, $u$ and $u+\Delta u$. The contrast between these different ways of regarding $p(u)$ is brought out by the different expressions which can be used for the average value of $u$. The *ensemble average*, which must always be

energy, nervous impulses; these then convey the information as a digital code. At what point in the chain of structural elements and transfer processes which this involves does the actual energy transduction take place, and what is the mechanism of the transduction? Are the answers to these two questions in any way common to sensory information channels of different modality and in different species? It must be admitted at once that, despite our already large and ever-increasing experimentally-derived knowledge about receptor processes, these questions can be answered at best only tentatively at the present time.

*Components of the receptor unit.* The structural and functional components of receptor units vary considerably in specificity, sensitivity, location and morphological complexity. For detailed information about some

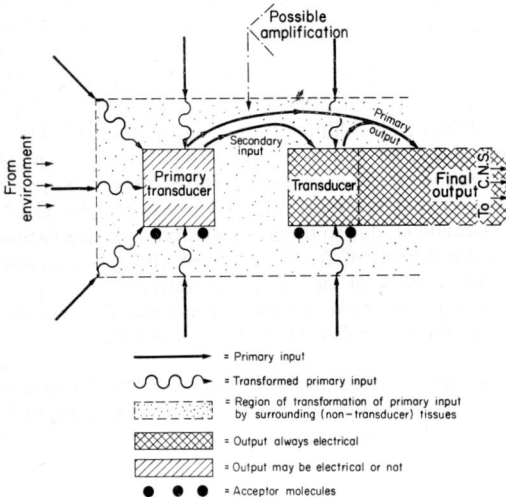

FIG. 1. *Components of a receptor unit. N.B. All types of receptor units do not have all the components included in the diagram. Conversely, components present in some receptor units (e.g. sensitizing or inhibitory efferents) are omitted.*

of these the reader is referred to standard physiology and histology textbooks and to the several reviews and proceedings of symposia on the subject (Gray 1959; Davis 1961; (Biological receptor. ...; Cold Spring Harbour. ...)). The diagram in Fig. 1 attempts to represent the features of a 'generalized' biological transducing system such as is thought to occur in a receptor unit.

The primary input to the system is the environmental energy which constitutes the stimulus to the receptor. It is theoretically measurable in physical units although this measurement may be difficult to make in practice. A receptor unit is usually specifically sensitive to one type of input energy—either mechanical, chemical, thermal, or electromagnetic—and its specificity is frequently further restricted to a particular range, or other property, of the energy within one of these broad categories. The receptor unit is normally virtually insensitive to types of environmental energy other than that of its specific stimulus, provided that the input of these is not so large as to be grossly unphysiological. Some receptors are known, however, which have a high specificity for more than one type of energy; others have a relatively low specificity for several types.

The final output of all receptor units is in the peripheral process of the afferent neuron, which is electrically excitable. In some types of unit there is one such nerve fibre serving each receptor, in others several receptors may be served by one fibre. The function of the nerve fibre is to transmit non-decremental electrical impulses; it is these impulses, set up in a sensory nerve fibre by the transducer component of the receptor(s) it serves, which convey information about the environment to the spinal cord and brain. Since the impulses in any nerve fibre are all of equal size, the quantitation of information in a single channel is possible only by frequency modulation, and the frequency of impulses in one fibre may vary from zero to several hundred per second. Some receptor units, such as those which carry information about the degree of stretch of a muscle, are in constant activity and signal both steady states and rates of change of state of the environmental input; other units, such as touch receptors, signal only changes of state.

In many receptors, a specialized terminal portion of the receptor neuron forms a single stage transducer component on which the primary input of environmental energy acts directly. The transducer mechanism in one such receptor, the Pacinian corpuscle, is described in some detail below. In other types of receptor, the transducer may have more than one component. When this is so, the primary transducer element commonly consists of a receptor cell, such as that found in taste buds or certain mechanoreceptors. The sensory cell may be preceded, or indeed its place in the receptor chain may be taken by, acceptor molecules as in many receptors which respond to electromagnetic stimuli. When the primary transducer element consists of a receptor cell its output, which is frequently electrical but may be chemical in some receptors, forms the secondary input to the neuronal component of the receptor. Amplification of the secondary input may take place in a two-stage transducer system, as with auditory receptors. Whether the transducer is single-stage or multi-stage, the primary output is always a local electrical response which acts upon the receptor nerve fibre.

In the majority of receptors the primary input undergoes some degree of transformation before reaching the transducer component and the structures responsible for this transformation are often extremely complex in both morphology and function. Furthermore, the transfer functions from one component to the next throughout the receptor chain may be complicated by sensitization and inhibition resulting from the feed-back action of efferent neurons.

*The sensory nerve fibre.* Not only is it the function of the transducer to 'trigger off' electrical impulses but, as already pointed out, the transducer element may be a specialized part of the nerve fibre in which the impulse is initiated and transmitted. Comparison of the structures of these two regions of the same cell and the chemical and electrical events occurring in them has contributed greatly to our understanding of the transducer mechanism. Before going on to discuss the transducer it is necessary, therefore, to consider briefly the mechanism of the impulse in the sensory nerve fibre (see *Nerve and muscle, initiation and conduction of impulses in*).

A nerve fibre consists of a hollow tube bounded by a high impedance membrane. The axoplasm inside the membrane and the extracellular fluid outside it have different electrolyte compositions; there is a high $Na^+$ gradient directed inwards across the membrane and a high $K^+$ gradient directed outwards. The $K^+$ gradient and the semipermeable properties of the membrane result in a potential difference, the membrane potential, existing across it in the 'resting' (non-conducting) nerve fibre. In mammals, this potential is of the order of 90 mV, the inside being negative to the outside. During an impulse, the resting membrane potential is reversed, the inside of the fibre becoming some 30 mV positive to the outside. This transient change in potential is brought about by the fact that, for a brief time, $Na^+$ ions are able to pass into and $K^+$ ions out of the fibre; the $Na^+$ permeability change is rapid and that of $K^+$ is delayed. The permeability of the membrane to $Na^+$ and $K^+$ varies with the value of the membrane potential in a graded but reversible manner, provided that the latter does not fall below a certain limit. A propagated impulse is initiated, however, whenever the membrane potential falls below the critical threshold value, usually by about 10 per cent of the resting potential.

In a medullated nerve fibre—that is, one in which the axon is surrounded by a myelin sheath which is interrupted at regular intervals along its length by nodes of Ranvier—impulse conduction is saltatory. This suggests that $Na^+$ can only enter the fibre at the nodes of Ranvier, the myelinated internodes being depolarized by local circuit action. When such a fibre conducts an impulse, therefore, the suggested sequence of events is that as the membrane at each node is depolarized below the threshold for impulse initiation, current flows into it from the next node. This node in turn thus becomes depolarized and the cycle is repeated along the fibre. The initial depolarization at the peripheral end of a receptor nerve fibre, which leads to this regenerative conduction, is brought about by the electrical activity of the transducer.

*The mechanism of the transducer. Experimental investigation.* Experimentation on the transducer mechanism, using the techniques of electrophysiology, is only possible under certain conditions. The desirable requirements for an experimental preparation from which quantitative information can be obtained about a receptor unit (other than that relating primary input to final output) include:

(1) The receptor unit must be of the type in which only one receptor ending is served by one discrete nerve fibre.

(2) It must be possible to record the electrical activity of both the nerve fibre (impulse) and the transducer output. This normally means either recording with external electrodes very close to the transducer membrane, or placing a microelectrode near to or through it.

(3) The stimulus to the receptor unit must be completely controllable and measurable.

(4) Factors other than the actual stimulus which might affect the input-output relations of the receptor unit must be controlled as far as possible. These factors include not only obvious ones such as temperature, pH, vibration etc., but also the transforming or distorting action of surrounding tissues on the energy reaching the transducer, the influence of nearby receptor units, and any feedback activity of efferent neurons.

(5) An obvious way to investigate a single receptor unit in isolation under controlled conditions is to carry out the experiment *in vitro*. To do this the size of the receptor, its location, and the nature of the surrounding tissues must permit microdissection of the receptor and the nerve fibre serving it.

(6) It is desirable to be able to effect controlled changes in the composition of the extracellular fluid in the immediate vicinity of the transducer component, particularly in respect to its ionic make-up, and to introduce pharmacologically active agents.

It would be too much to expect that any one biological system would fulfil all the above requirements. As it is, our knowledge of the transducer mechanism is based to a great extent on a relatively few receptors which lend themselves, at least in part, to experimentation. Among these, the receptors which respond to mechanical stimuli predominate.

*The Pacinian corpuscle.* One mechanoreceptor which has been the subject of extensive research and has proved to be particularly rewarding is the Pacinian corpuscle. Touch receptors of this type are found in the mesentery of the domestic cat; their function at this site is a matter of controversy but is not relevant to their use for investigations of the transducer mechanism. The end-organs consist of the terminal portions of single medullated nerve fibres enclosed up to a point between the first and second nodes of Ranvier by a large number of concentric lamellae of connective tissue (Fig. 2a). The mechanical energy of the stimulus deforms these lamellae and undergoes transformation by them before reaching the transducer region of the nerve fibre, which lies in the central core of the corpuscle. It is probable that the storage and filtering of energy by the lamellated capsule can account for the rapid adaptation of the receptor to a sustained stimulus. At the point of entry to the central core the nerve fibre loses its myelin sheath and the terminal, unmyelinated region has certain structural characteristics which distinguish it from the rest of the fibre. These include its elliptical cross-section, the absence of a Schwann cell sheath, and the presence of large numbers of mitochondria massed within the nerve fibre membrane.

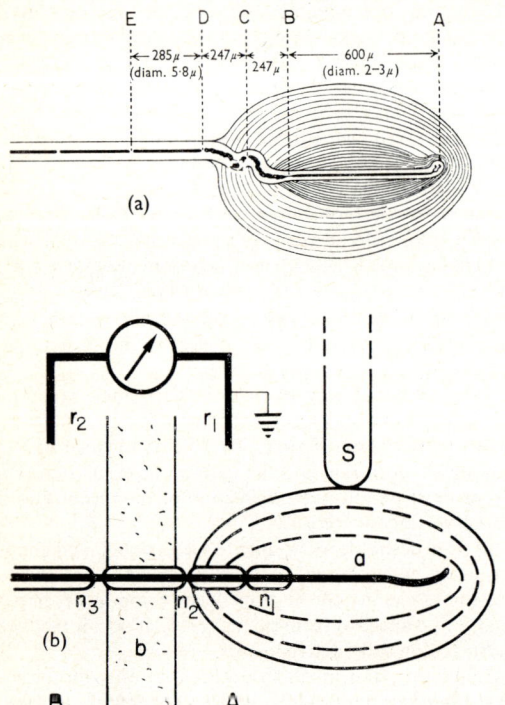

FIG. 2. *The Pacinian corpuscle.* (a) *Diagram of a typical corpuscle. A-B, central core with non-myelinated nerve fibre terminal. The nerve fibre is myelinated beyond point B; C, first node of Ranvier which is inside the lamellated capsule; D, E, second and third nodes of Ranvier which are outside the capsule (slightly modified from Quilliam and Sato, 1955).* (b) *Method of recording the electrical activity of a corpuscle. a, non-myelinated nerve fibre terminal; $n_1$, $n_2$, $n_3$, nodes of Ranvier; b, high resistance barrier separating one pool of conducting fluid (A) from the other (B); $r_1$, $r_2$, recording electrodes; s, mechanical stimulator operated by piezoelectric crystal.*

A Pacinian corpuscle, together with its axon, can be isolated by microdissection, removed from the animal and set up *in vitro* in a manner such that it can be stimulated with controlled mechanical pulses and the resulting electrical activity recorded. One method of doing this which has been used extensively by Gray (1959) and his co-workers, is shown in Fig. 2b. The corpuscle lies in one pool of conducting fluid, the nerve fibre passes through a high resistance barrier which encloses it between the second and third nodes of Ranvier, and the remainder of the fibre lies in another pool of conducting fluid. When the nerve membrane is depolarized,

even at a point some distance from the barrier, the fibre acts like an electric cable, current flows through the high resistance of the barrier, and can be recorded between two electrodes, one dipping into each of the pools. The flow of current resulting from mechanical stimulation of the corpuscle can be divided into three phases. The second of these, in order of time, is due to depolarizations of the nerve membrane at the first and second nodes of Ranvier, both of which are on the peripheral side of the recording barrier. The third phase is due to depolarization at the third and subsequent nodes on the central side of the barrier. Both of these phases are of an all-or-none character and are due to the propagated impulse passing along the fibre. The first phase of the response is a local potential change which occurs across the membrane of the non-myelinated terminal; this is the receptor potential which is the primary output of the transducer in this receptor. The

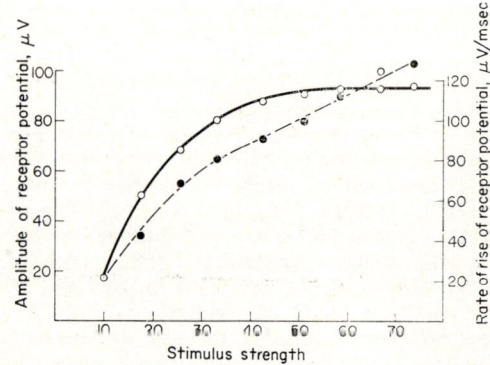

FIG. 3. *The relationship between two parameters of the receptor potential in a Pacinian corpuscle and the strength of the mechanical stimulus.*

○──────○ *amplitude of receptor potential ($\mu V$);*
●┈┈┈┈┈● *rate of rise of receptor potential ($\mu V/msec$).*
*The stimulus strength (abscissa) is plotted as relative displacements at the surface of the corpuscle, when stimulated as in Fig. 2b (replotted from Gray 1959).*

impulse activity can be abolished with procaine in a concentration which does not appreciably affect the receptor potential, thus enabling the parameters of the latter to be studied in detail and related to the parameters of the stimulus (Fig. 3) (Gray and Sato 1953). Elaborations of this technique have further enabled Gray and his co-workers to investigate the dependence on $Na^+$ (Fig. 4) (Diamond *et al.* 1958) and temperature coefficients (Inman and Peruzzi 1961) of the receptor potential and to compare these and its maximum amplitude and site of origin with those of the impulse which it generates (Diamond *et al.* 1956). In another method of recording the receptor potential of the Pacinian corpuscle the concentric connective tissue lamellae are removed by microdissection. The activity of the ending is then recorded by means of one or more microelectrodes placed in contact with the non-myelinated terminal membrane. Using this technique, Loewenstein (1959) and his co-workers, have shown that the removal of the non-nervous structures does not impair the transducer action and that the transducer proper appears to be the membrane of the non-myelinated nerve terminal. Furthermore, the total receptor potential is built up statistically from the activity of functionally independent transducer sites which are scattered all over this membrane.

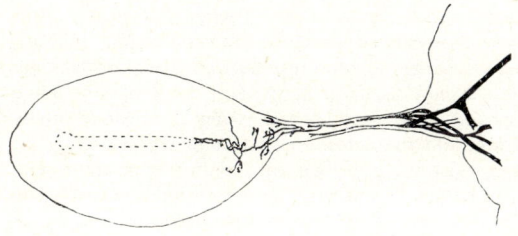

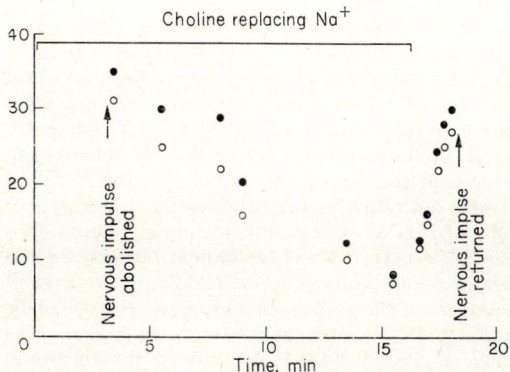

FIG. 4. *The dependence on $Na^+$ of the receptor potential in a Pacinian corpuscle. The ionic composition of fluid in the region of the central core was controlled by perfusing the intracorpuscular capillary bed during the experiment. (top) the capillary bed of a Pacinian corpuscle revealed by injecting indian ink. (bottom) two parameters of the receptor potential during perfusion.* ○ *amplitude ($\mu V$);* ● *rate of rise ($\mu V/msec$). During the time indicated by the line, $Na^+$ in the perfusing fluid was replaced by* $choline^+$ *(both from Diamond, Gray and Inman 1958).*

*General conclusions on the transducer mechanism.* It would obviously be quite unjustified to base any general theories about the transducer process on the experimental results obtained from work on one receptor. It is not possible, in an article of this type, to discuss in detail our knowledge of the transducer processes in all the receptors which have been studied; attention has therefore been focused on the Pacinian corpuscle in the previous section. Many of the facts relating to the activity of the Pacinian corpuscle have been shown to be true in some other receptors, and postulated with a fair degree of certainty for others. It seems reasonable, therefore, to consider the basic principles of transducer action for receptors in general, bearing in mind that some receptors may not conform to all of them.

The site of transduction is the cell membrane either of a specialized terminal portion of the sensory nerve fibre or of a receptor cell which precedes the neuronal component of the receptor. The effect of the incident energy on this membrane is to cause an increase in permeability to one or more ionic species. Ions then move down their electrochemical gradients causing a transfer of charge which results in a local, non-regenerative potential difference across the membrane. This potential is a linear function of the strength of the primary stimulus and persists as long as the energy of the latter continues to reach the transducer. The local potential initiates nerve impulses in the electrically excitable membrane of the receptor nerve fibre, either directly or through an intermediate mechanism, and the pattern of these is determined by the parameters of the local potential. Some confusion of terminology exists regarding the local potential. The potential directly responsible for the excitatory depolarization of the nerve fibre membrane, which triggers impulse activity (the 'primary output' of Fig. 1) is called the *generator potential*. The potential developed across the transducer membrane resulting directly from the stimulus is called the *receptor potential*. In a receptor such as the Pacinian corpuscle these are clearly one and the same and either term is applicable. When the local potential initiates an impulse directly it is always due to a depolarization of the transducer membrane, since this is the only way in which it can serve as a current 'sink' for the current 'source' of the excitable membrane. When the local potential is the first stage of a multi-stage transducer mechanism, however, and does not initiate the impulse directly it may equally well be due to a hyperpolarization. In fact, it is conceivable that the activation of the transducer membrane in such a case may not lead to an electrical response at all but to the production of some other 'secondary input', such as a chemical transmitter.

The mechanism whereby a specific form of incident energy causes a permeability change in the transducer membrane is not known. The membrane is morphologically specialized in many receptors and tends to be electrically inexcitable. Furthermore, the membrane processes underlying the receptor and generator potentials differ from those underlying the impulse in both temperature dependence and sensitivity to drugs, in addition to those properties already mentioned. It seems possible that the energy of the stimulus may bring about localized changes in the structure of the membranes, involving reorientation of their lipid and protein components and facilitating diffusion across them (Lucy 1964). Alternatively, the transducer membrane of a particular receptor may have a characteristic molecular arrangement, the permeability change resulting from a specific stimulus being caused by alteration of intermolecular forces. Such speculations as these are entirely unjustified at the present time. It is possible, however, that the current widespread research into the structure and ultrastructure of biological membranes, both 'real' and 'artificial', may give them substance.

*See also:* Cochlear mechanics. Nerve and muscle, initiation and conduction of impulses in. Non-neural elements in receptor systems.

*Bibliography*

Biological Receptor Mechanisms (1962) Symp. Soc. exp. Biol., **16**.
Cold Spring Harbor Symposia on Quantitative Biology (1965) **30**.
DAVIS H. (1961) *Some Principles of Sensory Receptor Action*, Physiol. Rev., **41**, 391.
DIAMOND J., GRAY J. A. B. and INMAN D. R. (1958) *The Relationship Between Receptor Potentials and Sodium Ion Concentration*, J. Physiol., **142**, 382.
DIAMOND J., GRAY J. A. B. and SATO M. (1956) *The Site of Initiation of Impulses in Pacinian Corpuscles*, J. Physiol., **133**, 54.
GRAY J. A. B. (1959) *Mechanical Into Electrical Energy in Certain Mechanoreceptors*, Progr. Biophys., **9**, 285.
GRAY J.A.B. and SATO M. (1953) *Properties of the Receptor Potential in Pacinian Corpuscles*, J. Physiol., **122**, 610.
INMAN D. R. and PERUZZI P. (1961) *The Effects of Temperature on the Responses of Pacinian Corpuscles*, J. Physiol., **155**, 280.
LOEWENSTEIN W. R. (1959) *The Generation of Electric Activity in a Nerve Ending*, Ann. N.Y. Acad. Sci., **81**, 367.
LUCY J. A. (1964) *Globular Lipid Micelles and Cell Membranes*, J. Theoret. Biol., **7**, 360.

D. R. INMAN

**RECEPTORS IN JOINTS AND MUSCLES.** *A priori*, it might be expected that the central nervous system exerts its delicate control over the position and movement of limbs partly on the basis of the feedback of mechanical information from receptors in joints and voluntary muscles. Such receptors do indeed exist in profusion. They have been intensively studied by histologists and by electrophysiologists, but without as yet obtaining a full understanding of their role in the body.

*Joint receptors.* The capsules which surround joints are supplied by afferent (sensory) nerve fibres of all sizes. In the knee joint of the cat, which has been the most intensively investigated (Gardner 1950; Skoglund 1956), the relatively few fibres of over $10 \mu$ diameter are thought to terminate in the joint ligaments in Golgi type endings which are similar to those in tendons (see below). The numerous fibres of $5$–$10 \mu$ diameter terminate largely in the Ruffini type endings in the joint capsule. These endings are about $100 \mu$ in diameter and consist of a network of fine fibres surrounded by a thin sheath. In addition, the thickly encapsulated ending called the Pacinian Corpuscle may be found lying close to joint capsules and a few small modified corpuscles with a thinner capsule may be found in the joint capsule itself; these corpuscles are all also supplied by medium sized fibres. The many smaller afferent fibres appear to terminate as free nerve endings spread over an appreciable area of the joint capsule without a definite sense ending.

The behaviour of these various endings has been studied by recording the discharge set up in single afferent nerve fibres on moving the joint, using standard electrophysiological methods. The Pacinian corpuscles, like those elsewhere in the body, are very rapidly adapting and discharge only during actual movement of the joint. They do not discharge at all while the joint is held at a constant angle. They are also extremely sensitive to vibration, and the detection of ground vibration may be their function rather than the monitoring of movement. The smaller afferent fibres have not been extensively studied, but are more likely to supply pain receptors than those involved in signalling the mechanical state of the joint. The Golgi and the Ruffini endings are, however, undoubtedly important mechanoreceptors. Both give a steady discharge when the joint is held at a constant position, though that of the Ruffini endings may also be influenced by the contraction of neighbouring muscles deforming the joint capsule. Both types of ending discharge impulses over only a part of the range of movement of the joint and there is an optimum position, different for each individual ending, at which the discharge is of highest frequency. Commonly, the optimum position is near full flexion or extension of the joint, but some endings have optimum positions in the middle of the range of movement so that as the joint is progressively rotated the discharge first increases and then decreases again. The Ruffini endings, like the Golgi endings, are sensitive to the dynamic stimulus of movement of the joint over and above their response to its actual position. As the joint is rotated towards the optimum position of a Ruffini ending its discharge is greater at any length than it would be in the absence of movement; conversely, the rotation of the joint away from the optimum position reduces its discharge further. These responses to angular velocity take some 10 sec to disappear after the joint is held in a constant position. It seems likely that appropriate combination of the information from the Golgi and Ruffini endings and the Pacinian corpuscles could provide a measure of both the position and the angular velocity of any joint; for this a knowledge of muscle contraction might also be required, because it alters the response of the Ruffini endings. Such computations should be well within the power of the central nervous system.

The reflex effects on the spinal cord of the joint receptors has been investigated by stimulating the joint nerves electrically or by rotating joints. The responses found on the presumed excitation of the fibres from the Golgi and Ruffini endings have been small and inconstant. The smaller afferents excite the flexor reflex, which is the ubiquitous response to a nociceptive (painful) stimulus.

More significantly, weak electrical stimulation of joint nerves leads to large evoked potentials in both the cerebral and cerebellar cortices, indicating that numerous nerve cells have been activated there. This all suggests that the information provided by the joint receptors is utilized mainly at the higher levels of the nervous system, rather than for reflex control by the spinal cord. In accordance with this, human experiments have shown (Merton 1964) that the conscious sensation of the position of a limb is derived almost entirely from joint receptors. This was demonstrated by selectively anaesthetizing the nerves to a finger joint, while leaving untouched the nerves to the muscles moving the joint; this nearly abolished position sense. Classically, it had always been intuitively supposed that the numerous receptors in muscle (see below) were primarily concerned with signalling conscious 'muscle sense'. With the direct demonstration that it is the joint receptors which are responsible for sensation the muscle receptors are shown to be largely concerned with the subconscious, automatic, control of movement and posture.

*Muscle receptors.* The importance of muscle receptors to the central nervous system may be judged from the fact that a typical muscle has as many medium to large afferent fibres as it has ordinary motor nerve fibres; in addition, there are numerous small motor fibres supplying the muscle spindles exclusively. The two main types of sensory structure in voluntary muscle are the Golgi tendon organ and the muscle spindle. There are also numerous free nerve endings derived from small medullated fibres and from non-medullated fibres. Electrophysiological recording suggests that these free endings are largely pain receptors and that they do not signal the mechanical state of the muscle; they will not be considered further here.

The essential difference between the muscle spindle and the Golgi tendon organ lies in their anatomical position with respect to the ordinary striated muscle fibres. As illustrated in Fig. 1A the spindle lies in parallel with the main muscle fibres, whereas the Golgi tendon organ lies in series with them. Both kinds of ending are stretch receptors, in that impulses are initiated in their afferent fibre when the muscle containing them is passively stretched. But when the muscle contracts actively they behave quite differently. The strain on the spindle is then partly relieved because of yield in the tendon so that the discharge of the ending decreases; In contrast, the strain on the tendon organ increases during contraction, with a consequent acceleration of its discharge (Fig. 1B). The spindle may be thought of as signalling the length of the muscle and the tendon organ as signalling the tension in it; from the control point of view these two signals are completely different though both are derived from 'stretch receptors'.

There is little further to say about the Golgi tendon organ. It is derived from a large medullated nerve fibre (10–20 $\mu$ diameter, group Ib) which breaks up into a series of fine sprays which run between the bundles of collagen fibres at the musculo-tendinous junction. It may be up to 1 mm long. It is found both at the origin and at the insertion of a muscle. It adapts very slowly to a maintained stimulus. It responds to the absolute value of the tension and is little influenced by rate of change of tension *per se*. The discharge rate increases approximately linearly with the tension in the muscle. However, a given tension produced by active contraction of the muscle may have rather more excitatory action than the same tension produced by passive stretch. In the body, muscles with their normal attachments probably cannot be stretched far enough to produce appreciable passive tension, so that functionally the Golgi tendon organ may be looked upon as a simple linear recorder of contractile tension.

The structure of the muscle spindle has proved to be extremely complicated, and agreement has still not been reached on several points of detail. It consists essentially of a bundle of specialized muscle fibres upon and around which are found a variety of nerve endings. A single muscle spindle may be supplied by up to 25 separate nerve fibres! The intrafusal (i.e. spindle) muscle fibres are of smaller diameter than the ordinary extrafusal muscle fibres, but are equally clearly cross-striated. The intrafusal fibres may be up to 10 mm long. The central half of the intrafusal bundle is surrounded by fluid contained in a definite capsule. It is this central swelling which gives the muscle spindle its fusiform shape and hence its name. The intrafusal fibres are of two different

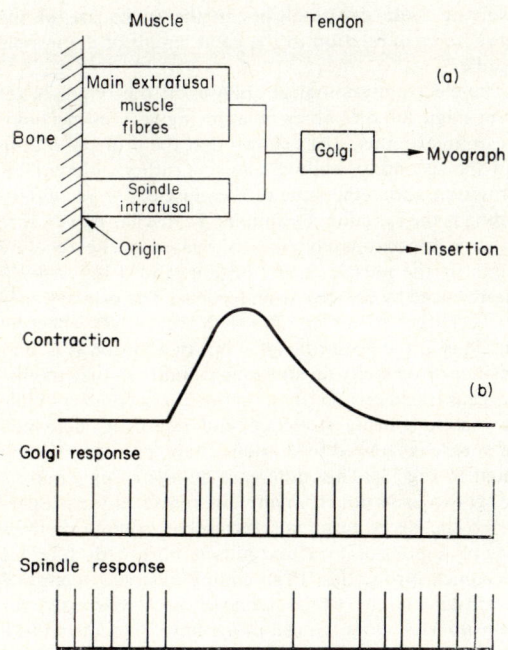

FIG. 1. *A. The relative positions in a muscle of the muscle fibres, the muscle spindle and the Golgi tendon organ. B. Diagrammatic representation of the discharges of a Golgi tendon organ and a muscle spindle occurring during a brief muscle contraction.*

kinds (Boyd 1962). These are the nuclear-bag fibres which are characterized by a conglomeration of nuclei along their central 300 $\mu$, and the nuclear-chain fibres which here have only a single row of nuclei, lying as it were on a 'chain' rather than in a 'bag'. The nuclear-bag fibres are longer and of greater diameter than are the nuclear-chain fibres. Both kinds of fibre are poorly striated in their central 300 $\mu$ or so, and it is therefore likely that this region of the fibres is only weakly contractile. Typically, there may be 2 nuclear-bag fibres and 4 nuclear-chain fibres in a spindle, though the actual numbers of each vary greatly in different muscles and in different species.

There are two histologically distinct kinds of afferent (sensory) ending within the spindle; they are called the primary or annulo-spiral ending and the secondary or flower-spray ending. The primary ending lies in the central 300 $\mu$ of the spindle and is supplied by a large medullated nerve fibre (12–20 $\mu$ diameter, group Ia) which branches in the spindle to terminate in a series of spirals round each one of both the nuclear-bag and the nuclear-chain intrafusal muscle fibres. The secondary ending lies to one side of the primary ending and is supplied by a medium-sized medullated fibre (4–12 $\mu$ diameter, group II) which terminates in spirals and sprays. These terminations, in contrast to those of the primary ending, lie predominantly on the nuclear-chain fibres. A spindle always contains a single primary ending, but there may be up to four secondary endings, or none at all. Figure 2 is a simplified diagram of the general structure of a muscle spindle.

The spindle is also supplied by medullated motor fibres, which at their point of entry to the spindle are of small diameter (1–5 $\mu$). Individual motor fibres may end in either a discrete 'plate' ending somewhat similar to those of the ordinary motor fibres on the extrafusal muscle fibres, or they may end in a diffuse 'trail' or 'network' type ending somewhat similar to those found in certain amphibian and avian muscles. The 'plate' endings are usually found further from the centre of the spindle than are the trail endings, and neither kind is found in the central 300 $\mu$ where the primary afferent ending lies. It seems to be generally agreed that the two types of motor ending are derived from different nerve fibres. It is not yet agreed whether both types of intrafusal muscle fibre regularly have both types of motor ending upon them; however, 'plate' endings seem to be commoner on nuclear-bag fibres and 'trail' endings on nuclear-chain fibres. Nor is it yet certain whether the two distinct kinds of intrafusal muscle fibre are regularly supplied by separate nerve fibres (irrespective of the structure of their termination), or whether both nuclear-bag and nuclear-chain intrafusal fibres are regularly supplied by branches of a single motor fibre. These points are crucial for understanding the internal mechanism of the spindle, but unfortunately they are currently the subject of a spirited controversy (Andrew 1966; Granit 1966; Matthews 1964). The basic difficulty in resolving these questions lies in the small size of the nerve fibres in relation to the great length of the muscle spindle.

The electrophysiological analysis of the impulses set up in single afferent fibres on applying various mechanical stimuli to muscle has shown that the primary ending and the secondary ending transmit rather different information about the state of the muscle. The secondary ending is the functionally simpler. It discharges at a rate which is approximately linearly related to the absolute length of the muscle at any instant, and it is relatively uninfluenced by velocity stimuli *per se*. The primary ending discharges at similar rates to the secondary when the muscle is at a constant length; but in addition it is very sensitive to velocity on dynamic stimuli, so that its discharge is much greater than that of the secondary while the muscle is being stretched, and relatively less when the muscle is allowed to shorten. These points are illustrated in Fig. 3. This difference in their behaviour is thought to arise not from any differences in the properties of the nerve terminals themselves, but from their lying on regions of intrafusal muscle fibre with different mechanical properties. If an ending lies on a region of intrafusal muscle which behaves less 'viscously' to extension than does the rest of the fibre, then the ending will be relatively overstretched during the dynamic phase of stretching in relation to the constant stretch applied to it when the muscle is maintained at a fixed length. The difference between the behaviour of the primary and the secondary endings would be adequately explained if the primary lay on a region with low viscosity

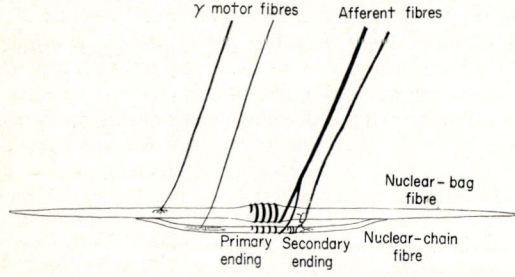

FIG. 2. *Considerably simplified diagram of the structure of a muscle spindle. See text for further description of actual structure. (Not to scale.)*

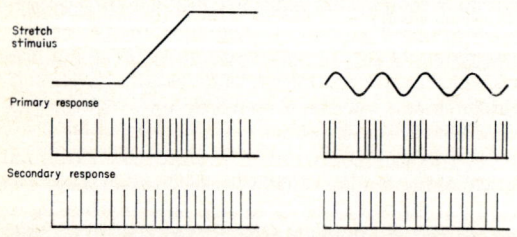

FIG. 3. *The different responses of the primary and the secondary afferent endings of the muscle spindle to mechanical stimuli containing a velocity component.*

while the secondary did not do so. This would be quite possible in the light of the histological findings, but the matter has not yet been investigated experimentally.

In the frog, the motor fibres to the muscle spindles are branches of the motor nerve fibres to the extrafusal muscle fibres. In the mammal, such an arrangement occurs occasionally but the majority of the motor fibres to spindles (fusimotor fibres) are quite separate from the ordinary motor fibres. These exclusively fusimotor fibres are of smaller diameter (2–8 $\mu$) in the main nerve trunk than are the ordinary or $\alpha$ motor fibres (10–20 $\mu$). The fusimotor fibres are often called $\gamma$ (gamma) motor fibres on the basis of their size, because sometime ago medullated nerve fibres were classified in order of descending size as $\alpha$, $\beta$, $\gamma$, $\delta$, (it may be noted, however, that this classification is not applied systematically to all nerve fibres). Quite recently, the fusimotor fibres have been classified into two functionally distinct groups by means of their action on the primary ending. Stimulation of either kind of fusimotor fibre excites the primary ending when the muscle is at a constant length. Some fibres, the dynamic fusimotor fibres, have the additional action of sensitising the primary ending to a velocity stimulus, causing it to be yet more dynamically sensitive than normal. Other fibres, the static fusimotor fibres, tend to decrease the normal dynamic sensitivity of the primary ending while still powerfully exciting it. The secondary afferent ending is excited by stimulation of the static fibres only, and it is not excited by stimulation of the dynamic fibres. The excitation of the afferent endings by fusimotor stimulation when the muscle is at a constant length is thought to depend upon the contraction of the intrafusal fibres stretching the sensory endings. The regions of intrafusal fibre upon which the endings lie are generally less well striated than the rest of the fibre, and so might be expected to contract less strongly. In consequence, the uneven contraction of the fibre would stretch these regions with deformation of the endings. The velocity sensitizing action of the dynamic fusimotor fibre on the primary ending may well be mediated by a change in 'viscosity' of the contracting intrafusal fibre. But, the internal mechanism of the spindle and the structural background for the classification of fusimotor fibres into static and dynamic types remains obscure, partly because of the present disagreement about the detailed arrangement of the motor innervation of the spindle. The main function of the fusimotor fibres is also obscure. They may serve primarily to control the sensitivity of the spindle as a measuring instrument (for example by altering the ratio of direct to derivative response), but it is likely that they also play a part in biassing the reflex 'servo-mechanism' by means of which it has been postulated that the length of a muscle is maintained (Merton 1965). This and related questions are considered on other pages. Here, it may merely be emphasized that the receptors in muscle potentially provide the central nervous system with information on the tension within the muscle (from the tendon organ), its length (from the spindle secondary ending), and its velocity of shortening (by combining the signals from the spindle primary and secondary endings). The length and velocity signals, however, are so dependent upon the amount of fusimotor activity that they could only be interpreted unequivocally in the light of such knowledge. It is very possible that the central nervous system never breaks the information down into such conceptually simple components, but utilizes it in some more sophisticated manner. The joint receptors would seem to provide an adequate measure of the position and angular velocity of all parts of a limb, uncomplicated by the degree of fusimotor activity.

*See also:* Control, stability and. Nerve and muscle, initiation and conduction of impulses in. Receptors: relation between the activity and the stimuli in single primary units.

*Bibliography*

ANDREW B. L. (Ed.) (1966) *Control and Innervation of Skeletal Muscle*, Dundee: Thomson & Co.
BOYD I. A. (1962) *The structure and innervation of the nuclear bag muscle fibre system and the nuclear chain muscle fibre system in mammalian muscle spindles*, Phil. Trans. Roy. Soc. B, **245**, 81.
GARDNER E. (1950) *Physiology of movable joints*, Physiol. Rev. **30**, 127.
GRANIT R. (Ed.) (1966) Nobel Symposium 1. *Muscular afferents and motor control*, Uppsala: Almqvist and Wiksell.
MATTHEWS P. B. C. (1964) *Muscle spindles and their motor control*, Physiol. Rev. **44**, 219.
MERTON P. A. (1964) *Human position sense and sense of effort*, Symp. Soc. exp. Biol. **18**, 387.
SKOGLUND C. R. (1956) *Anatomical and physiological studies of knee joint innervation in the cat*, Acta physiol. scand. **36**, Suppl. 124.

P. B. C. MATTHEWS

**RECEPTORS: RELATION BETWEEN THE STIMULI AND THE ACTIVITY IN SINGLE PRIMARY UNITS.** Information from the receptors enters the central nervous system in the form of nerve impulses (action potentials) and in any individual afferent fibre the only variables are the presence or absence of an impulse and the interval between impulses. The initiation of impulses at the receptors by transducer action has been dealt with in the article *Receptors as transducers*. In the present section two important aspects of the properties of afferent units (defined as the afferent nerve fibre and its associated receptor) will be considered. *First*, the relation between the frequency of discharge in individual afferent fibres and the physical stimulus to the receptor, and *second* qualitative differences among afferent units that contribute to the discrimination achieved by the sensory system at the level of the primary event, in the sequence that forms part of the analytical sensory system. For a recent review see 'Touch, Heat and Pain', Ciba Symposium.

*1. Relation of afferent discharge to the stimulus.* One of the commonest transducing systems converts mechanical energy to nerve impulses and the general term 'mechanoreceptors' covers this category of unit. At the onset of mechanical deformation there is an interval during the application of the stimulus when the frequency of discharge—the interval between impulses, rises steeply. The threshold for discharge of an impulse may depend on both the extent of the movement—its amplitude, and the rate of change of position—the slope. At low slopes the threshold amplitude is highest and falls as the slope increases to reach some final minimal value. Because of this relation there are afferent units which may fail to be excited by relatively large deformations if the rate of change of position is sufficiently low. The failure may be related to the processes of activation and inactivation of ionic carriers in the membrane, both of the transducer element in the receptor and of the terminal impulse generating part of the afferent axon. The mechanical linkage of the deformation to the nerve element in the transducer may also play a part, as in the Pacinian corpuscle (Loewenstein and Skalak 1966), where only rapid transients are transmitted to the nerve terminal in the core of the receptor.

At threshold displacement an afferent unit will respond with only one impulse. Stronger stimulation will cause more impulses to be discharged but another important property of the afferent unit determines the frequency and persistence of this discharge—this is the *rate of adaptation*. Some mechanoreceptors (e.g. Pacinian corpuscles) respond with only a single impulse or a short burst of 2 or 3 impulses when stimulated with a single mechanical pulse, whereas others continue to respond with a continued stream of action potentials, e.g. 'secondary' receptors in the mammalian muscle spindles (Matthews 1964). The former are termed 'rapidly-adapting' and the latter 'slowly-adapting' and each class, under normal conditions, maintains a consistent response. There are intermediate types of unit in which the discharge persists but only for a short time. The duration of the discharge is also stimulus-amplitude dependent and at low intensities or small displacements the slowly-adapting mechanoreceptors may respond with only a short burst of action potentials. The rapidly-adapting units, on the other hand, will not, even at large deformations, continue to discharge.

During a steadily *maintained* deformation of the receptor, that is with a constant load, the frequency of discharge depends on two factors, a) the rate of adaptation of the afferent unit and b) the amplitude of displacement. The rapidly-adapting units are excited only when the deformation is changing—that is they are *movement detectors* since they respond only during movement. The slowly-adapting units continue to discharge during a steadily maintained deformation. Immediately after the displacement has reached a steady value the frequency of discharge from these latter units declines, and the rate at which this occurs gives some indication of the rate of adaptation of the afferent unit. The mechanism of this initial decline is not fully understood but includes at least two components—viscoelastic changes in the mechanical linkage of the deformation to the transducer and changes in the membrane of the receptor itself. Evidence for the former comes from Loewenstein and Skalak's work and for the latter from Hodgkin's experiments on crab axon. In these experiments Hodgkin (1948) showed that during a steadily applied current the frequency of discharge of impulses declined slowly during maintenance of the stimulus.

*Accurate detection of displacement.* The adapted frequency of discharge of a slowly-adapting afferent unit may be very exactly related to the amplitude of the displacement or load on the receptor, as found by Matthews in 1933 for the muscle spindle receptors and very recently by Werner and Mountcastle (1965), for a slowly-adapting cutaneous receptor. The latter work, in which the mechanical deformation of the receptor was very exactly controlled by a feedback system, established that the relation between the adapted frequency of discharge and the deformation of the receptor obeyed a power law function $R = K \cdot S^n$ where $R$ is the mean number of impulses per response, $K$ is a constant of proportionality and $S$ is the stimulus intensity measured as the net skin indentation, over a wide range of deformations, from 100 $\mu$ to 1mm. The exponents ranged from 0·3 to 1·2 for the cutaneous slowly-adapting receptors in the cat and was almost exactly 1 for slowly-adapting receptors in the hairless skin of the hand of the monkey. The slowly-adapting receptors are, therefore, very well suited to the function of transmitting information to the central nervous system about steady deformations in the periphery, e.g. the muscle spindles in somatic muscles, the slowly-adapting joint receptors and the slowly-adapting cutaneous receptors in both hairless and hairy skin. The rapidly-adapting mechanoreceptors on the other hand cannot provide exact information about the amplitude of mechanical stimulation since they display a high degree of rate of change of position sensitivity. They may, on the other hand, be particularly effective in indicating the presence of movement and possibly also the rate of change of the stimulus. Because they adapt rapidly they can give no information about steady deformations.

*Vibration.* In many psychological and psychophysical experiments the mechanical stimulus used often has a vibratory character, rather than a steady displacement which is more often used by physiologists. The electrophysiological response of mechanoreceptors to vibratory stimulation has only recently been studied at all extensively. Some units are capable of following high frequencies of stimulation—as high as 600 per sec. At frequencies as high as this the rapidly-adapting Pacinian corpuscle will fire an impulse for every oscillation of the tip of the mechanical stimulator (Hunt 1961). At still higher frequencies the response is phase-locked to the stimulus but may now appear only with alternate displacements of the probe and at even higher frequencies still this relationship may come down to 1 to 3 or even lower. At these frequencies of vibratory stimulation the amplitude of movement is important as well as the rate of adaptation of the afferent receptor. It is likely that the ability to follow very high frequencies of mechanical stimulation depends on rapid adaptation of the receptor. The slowly-adapting mechanoreceptors in the skin will also display a phase-locked, one to one response, at low frequencies of stimulation, but as the frequency of the oscillation increases the afferent discharge no longer follows a one to one relation to the displacement. Instead impulses drop out although the remaining impulses continue to be phase-locked. The slowly-adapting units therefore have a type of response which is similar to that of the rapidly-adapting units with the one important difference that they are unable to follow frequencies of oscillation at such high rates as the latter. These properties of the mechanoreceptors may be important factors to be considered in the design of experiments using vibratory stimuli, since unless standardized conditions are used (particularly as regards frequency), the afferent input in apparently identical experiments may be very different. For example, vibration at 50 or 60 cycles/second will be 'followed' by both slowly and rapidly-adapting cutaneous afferent units, whereas at 600 cycles/second only the rapidly-adapting will follow, and at lower frequencies only the slowly-adapting units will be excited.

In this connexion it is necessary to specify exactly the conditions of mechanical stimulation. A *constant stimulus* in neurophysiological experiments usually means the steady application of a constant deformation, whereas for the psychologist it may mean the constant application of a vibrating stimulus. In terms of the discharge in a population of primary afferent units the two stimuli will provoke entirely different patterns of impulse discharge.

*Spontaneous activity.* The degree of ongoing activity in afferent fibres is determined by the excitability of the receptor, its rate of adaptation and the physical conditions surrounding it. The rigorous control of experimental conditions necessary to obtain highly standardized conditions is rarely met in more normal circumstances. Even in carefully controlled systems the afferent units may discharge impulses, usually at low frequencies, in the absence of an applied stimulus. In some situations it is not possible to avoid suprathreshold stimuli. Elaborate precautions may fail to prevent excitation of mechanoreceptors. Vibrations transmitted through the floor and experimental table, or air-borne vibrations, may set-up a discharge from Pacinian corpuscles. The slowly-adapting receptors are more likely to carry a resting discharge because of deformations of the tissues in which they lie. Joint receptors are a special case since their sensitivity is dependent on the angle of the joint and at a characteristic angle any individual afferent fibre will carry a steady stream of impulses (Skoglund 1956). The statolith receptors in the vestibular apparatus are similar. The primary and secondary muscle spindle receptors may also carry a continuous discharge. This discharge although continuous cannot properly be called 'spontaneous', since it can be directly related to the normal stimulus for the receptors.

Thermoreceptors will also carry a steady discharge of impulses under constant thermal conditions, depending on the temperature and the characteristics of the particular afferent unit. Some cutaneous receptors may carry a spontaneous discharge and several categories exist; rapidly-adapting hair follicle afferent units with a discharge at the heart rate, due to deformation transmitted from arterial vessels; slowly-adapting dermal receptors discharging steadily at frequencies of 5 to 20/sec. The precise stimulus for the latter may be small distortions in the skin. The slowly-adapting epidermal receptors, on the other hand, rarely carry a resting discharge in the absence of an applied stimulus (Iggo 1963), presumably because they are effectively insulated by their structure from mechanical strains transmitted through the skin.

The existence of 'spontaneous' (i.e. arising in the absence of an applied stimulus or detectable distortion) activity can thus be questioned, although the presence of background discharge may be an important physiological property of the afferent units (see Granit 1955).

*2. Selective sensitivity.* Afferent units are characterized by differences in sensitivity to different forms of energy change or stimuli. There are two main categories of cutaneous unit—*mechanoreceptors* and *thermoreceptors* and a third class—*chemoreceptors* are found in special regions such as the tongue (taste receptors), olfactory mucosa, viscera (acid/alkali receptors) and blood vessels (oxygen concentration detectors). For each category the receptors display a maximum sensitivity to the appropriate form of energy change, but the sensitivity is not absolute, e.g. mechanoreceptors can be excited by a temperature change (usually a fall), and by chemicals; thermal afferent units and chemoreceptors can be excited by sufficiently vigorous mechanical deformation. In general, the site of action of any stimulus is uncertain, but for each class of unit the transducer action is presumably directed towards the energy change to which the receptor is most sensitive. The terminal element of the Pacinian corpuscle, for example, converts a mechanical stimulus to a current flow (Loewenstein and Skalak 1966). The additional, lower, sensitivity of an afferent unit to other forms of energy may be associated with the transducer, or may arise in the non-myelinated or myelinated pre-terminal nerve-ending or in the elements linking the transducer element to surrounding structures.

Within each main category of receptors further subdivisions or subclasses can be recognized, and in some instances the structure of the receptor element is known. A full list of these subclasses in mammals alone would run to sixty or more and only some examples will be cited here. The cutaneous *mechanoreceptors* include rapidly-adapting hair follicle afferent units, Types D, G and T (Iggo 1966) with differences related to the structure of the hair follicle, sensitivity to mechanical displacement, density of innervation and number of hairs in a sensory unit. In some situations it is possible to obtain selective excitation of one or another class of these units but multiple recording has established that in some situations movement of a single hair may excite all three categories of hair follicle afferent unit. Nevertheless, for any particular hair one of them displays the greatest sensitivity. The other rapidly-adapting units are Pacinian corpuscles (Hunt 1961), which have a high vibration sensitivity—these form a very small proportion of the total population. The glabrous (non-hair) skin is also richly supplied with rapidly-adapting units (Iggo 1963).

The other main class of cutaneous mechanoreceptor adapt slowly, and some of them (slowly-adapting Type II—dermal receptor of cat and monkey (Iggo 1963)) carry a persistent discharge in the absence of an applied stimulus. The other slowly-adapting units present in hairy skin ('touch corpuscle' slowly-adapting Type I units) are normally silent, and will maintain discharge for minutes or longer when stimulated mechanically. The receptors have a distinctive structure and thus refute the idea that there are no organized receptors in hairy skin. In glabrous skin of the hands and feet there are also two kinds of slowly-adapting unit and their mechanical sensitivity is also related to the morphology of the skin.

In special regions, such as the face, where the cutaneous innervation is much richer than elsewhere, the receptor population may have different characteristics from elsewhere on the body surface. For example, there are slowly-adapting receptors associated with the vibrissae—these have a directional sensitivity, and there are also other hairs innervated by axons that run only to a single tactile hair with slowly-adapting receptors. Other special skin regions contain fewer classes of receptors, e.g. the skin of the rabbit's ear contains only hair follicle receptors, Types D and G are present but the skin of the ear appears to have no slowly-adapting units.

The *thermoreceptors* form a distinct class of afferent unit, on the basis of their differential sensitivity, and both static and dynamic temperature sensitivity. Two main subclasses exist—those excited by a fall of temperature, the most common kind, and those excited by a rise in temperature. The characteristic features of a thermoreceptor are 1) a steady discharge of impulses at a constant temperature, 2) frequency rise on sudden cooling, 3) no response or sudden warning if the afferent unit is silent, or an inhibition of a resting discharge and 4) no response to 'non-painful' mechanical stimulation (or at least a considerably higher threshold than sensitive mechanoreceptors). Finally, the thermal sensitivity should be not less than the sensitivity of temperature sense in man. Afferent units with these properties exist in the skin of man and other animals.

The greater part of the body surface in the cat, rabbit or rat has thermoreceptors with non-myelinated afferent fibres, a most unexpected discovery, whereas in the primates (monkey, baboon) many of the units have myelinated axons (Iggo 1964). The skin of the head has more specialized thermoreceptors, i.e. the axons are myelinated, in the dog and cat, and the tongue is richly supplied with myelinated thermoreceptors (Hensel and Zotterman 1951).

*3. Significance of fibre diameter.* So far the myelinated cutaneous fibres have been mentioned in most detail. There are, in addition, very numerous non-myelinated axons in cutaneous nerves. These axons are slowly-conducting, less than 2·5 m/sec and very fine (Gasser 1955). They were once regarded as a population of nociceptors but there is now clear evidence that they include diverse units, some with high mechanical (Iggo 1960) some with a high thermal sensitivity (Hensel *et al.* 1960) as well as others excited by damaging or noxious stimulation. The full significance of this new work has not been established.

The diameter of the afferent fibres influences the afferent unit in two ways: a) by determining the conduction velocity, hence the time taken for an impulse to travel from the receptor to the central nervous system and b) by limiting the frequency at which impulses can be conducted in succession. The non-myelinated axons in mammals range from 0·1 $\mu$ in the olfactory tract to a maximum of about 1 $\mu$ in peripheral nerves. At larger diameters than 1 $\mu$ a myelin sheath is present and the largest myelinated axon have diameters up to 20 $\mu$ (conduction velocity up to 120 m/sec).

The maximum frequency of discharge in these large units is as high as 1500 impulses/sec compared with about 100/sec for the non-myelinated units. The information carried by the former is therefore much greater. The larger number of fine fibres (4 to 5 times in some cutaneous nerves) may offset this advantage of the large fibres to some extent but can do nothing to alter their greater conduction velocity, e.g. 1 sec is required for an impulse to travel one metre in an average non-myelinated fibre compared with 8 msec for the largest myelinated axons.

In *summary* it can be seen that there is a quantitative relation between stimulation of receptors and the discharge of impulses in afferent nerve fibres. The relation depends on 1) the sensitivity of the receptors to the appropriate stimulus, 2) the rate of adaptation of the afferent unit, which determines the persistence of the response, 3) the differential sensitivity of the afferent unit. All receptor systems are specialized and any receptor is most highly sensitive to mechanical, thermal or chemical stimuli. A fourth factor—the diameter of the afferent fibre determines the maximal frequency of impulses and the conduction time in any afferent unit. The thicker the fibre the higher the maximal frequency and the higher the velocity.

*See also:* Nerve and muscle, initiation and conduction of impulses in. Receptors in joints and muscles.

*Bibliography*

Ciba Foundation Symposium (1966) *Touch, Heat and Pain*, (Eds. A. V. S. de Reuck and J. Knight) London: Churchill.

Gasser H. S. (1955) *J. gen. Physiol.* **38**, No. 5, 709.
Granit R. (1955) *Receptors and Sensory Perception*, New Haven: Yale University Press.
Hensel H., Iggo A. and Witt I. (1960) *J. Physiol.* **153**, 113.
Hensel H. and Zotterman Y. (1951) *Acta physiol. scand.* **23**, 291.
Hodgkin A. L. (1948) *J. Physiol.* **107**, 165.
Hunt C. C. (1961) *J. Physiol.* **155**, 175.
Iggo A. (1960) *J. Physiol.* **152**, 337.
Iggo A. (1963) *Acta neuroveg.* **24**, 1, 225.
Iggo A. (1964) *Nature* (London), **204**, 481.
Iggo A. (1966) Ciba Fdn. Symp. *Touch, Heat and Pain*, (A. V. S. de Reuck and J. Knight Eds.) London: Churchill.
Loewenstein W. R. and Skalak R. (1966) *J. Physiol.* **182**, 346.
Matthews B. H. C. (1933) *J. Physiol.* **78**, 1.
Matthews P. B. C. (1964) *Physiol. Rev.* **44**, No. 2, 219.
Skoglund S. (1956) *Acta physiol. scand.* Suppl. 124, **36**, 1.
Werner G. and Mountcastle V. B. (1965) *J. Neurophysiol.* **28**, 359.

A. Iggo

## RECEPTORS: REPRESENTATION OF INFORMATION ABOUT STIMULI IN POPULATIONS.

*Introduction.* One may describe *stimuli* which affect our senses either in terms of the physical parameters required to define them, or in terms of the sensations they evoke. Thus a particular musical note may be defined by its frequency, amplitude, and overtone content, or described subjectively as having a certain pitch, loudness and timbre. Because these two types of description often correspond with each other, as they do in this example, it is tempting to assume that information relating to each stimulus parameter is somehow extracted separately by the sense organs, represented separately in the discharge from the receptor population, and kept separately represented through the *C.N.S.* until it reaches consciousness. In other words, it is often assumed that simple relationships exist between the parameters one requires to describe the nervous activity associated with a sensory response (type of receptor active, frequency of firing, number of fibres active etc.) and the physical parameters of the stimulus. This is very often not the case. To take a simple example, there are no receptors in the eye which respond specifically to the light of wave-length 590 m$\mu$, which we would normally describe subjectively as the colour yellow. The sensation of yellow is evoked when receptors which are most sensitive to red light, and other receptors most sensitive to green light, are responding simultaneously. In other words the subjective statement 'x is yellow' or the objective statement 'x is 590 m$\mu$' are represented in the retinal discharge as 'x is a particular combination of red and green'. The purpose of the present article is to try to analyse some of the ways in which information relating to stimulus parameters, objectively defined, is represented in the responses obtained from populations of receptors.

*The single receptor unit.* The discharge of a single receptor consists of a sequence of action potentials, which can be related to the magnitude of a particular physical stimulus, and the way this changes with time. Two stimulus parameters, magnitude and time, are thus represented in the impulse sequence, and this might be thought likely to cause ambiguity between the two. If for example the C.N.S. measures magnitude by averaging the discharge frequency over a period of time, then if the stimulus magnitude changes rapidly with time successive averages can no longer be performed, and information relating to time and magnitude will become confused. In practice such confusions are avoided. Receptors such as the *chemoreceptors* of the carotid sinus, which respond to the very slowly changing blood $CO_2$ concentration, give steady discharges whose frequency is a simple function of concentration. Such receptors are known as *tonic* receptors. The sensitive *mechanoreceptors* of the cat's pad, however, respond to rapid mechanical deformation of the pad surface by producing a single action potential, after which there is no sustained discharge. Such receptors, responding only to events in time, are said to be *phasic*. In the former case it is true to say that the magnitude of the stimulus is represented as impulse frequency, while in the latter case the magnitude of the stimulus is not represented in the discharge at all, and only the temporal sequence of events at the unit is represented in the sequence of action potentials. Many receptor discharges contain both tonic and phasic components. *Stretch receptors* in the frog's skin, for example, respond to change in length with a burst of impulses (phasic response) which settles down to a steady discharge whose frequency is a simple function of the degree of extension of the receptor (tonic response). The question: 'does impulse frequency represent stimulus magnitude, or does impulse interval represent time interval?' is one which can only be answered by the C.N.S. Indeed, the C.N.S. may choose to use the same information in different ways at different times; thus, visually, one can follow events in time up to 50/second, or one can match the brightnesses of two surfaces to within 1 per cent, but one cannot do both at the same time.

*Populations of receptors.* While a single receptor responds only to stimuli at a point, an organized array of receptors opens up the possibility of using the spatial pattern of the response to obtain additional information about the stimulus. The sources of this additional information can be divided, for discussion purposes, into two types.

a) Information resulting from the fact that more than one type of receptor is available.

b) Information resulting from the relation of the spatial distribution of receptors to the spatial distribution of the stimulus.

*Mixed receptor assemblies (a).* In many sense organs the receptors are not all of one type. In the human eye, for example, there are 'rods' with extremely high sensitivity, and 'cones' with relatively lower sensitivity, and the cones may be subdivided into three classes depending on the part of the spectrum to which they are maximally responsive. *Colour* (which may be defined objectively as the distribution of intensity with respect to wave-length of a source of light) is represented in the retinal response as the extent to which each of the three types of cone is responding. As each cone responds to light over a range of wave-lengths, the response of any one cone to monochromatic light is a function both of intensity and 'nearness of the stimulus wave-length to the wave-length which stimulates that cone most effectively'. Each of the other two kinds of cone will be responding differently to the same stimulus, though in the same kind of way. Thus, although information relating

four types of chemical: 'salt', 'sweet', 'acid' and 'bitter'. Electrical recordings from individual sensory nerve fibres have shown that this simple picture is an oversimplification. While some fibres respond only to chemicals which normally evoke the sensation of 'salt', other fibres respond both to 'salt' and 'acid', and sometimes to 'bitter' chemicals as well. It thus becomes extremely difficult to relate the frequency of firing of each receptor to any particular attribute of the stimulating molecule. This is not, however, to say that information relating to chemical nature is not coded in terms of the type of unit responding, it is just that this code is very complex. While this complexity is a source of confusion to the experimenter, it is unlikely to cause embarrassment to

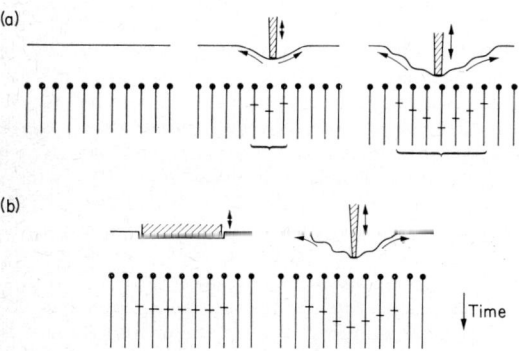

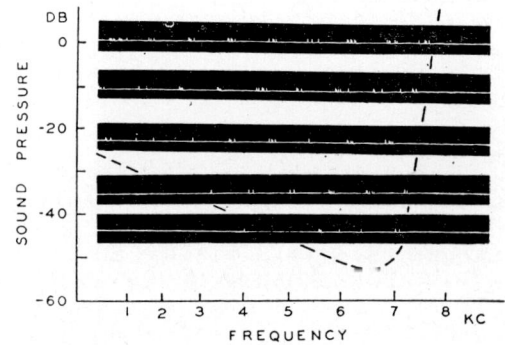

FIG. 2. *Representation of frequency and amplitude in the set of responses given by a single auditory nerve fibre to a series of tone pips. The response of a single cell contains ambiguous information relating to both stimulus parameters.* (From I. Tasaki (1954) *J. Neurophysiol.* **17**.)

FIG. 1. *Types of representation in a system of mechanoreceptors. (a) Representation of stimulus amplitude by the number of fibres active. (b) Complex representation of stimulus amplitude and area by number of fibres active and impulse timing.*

to intensity is not distinguished from information relating to wave-length in the responses of single cones, it is possible for the C.N.S. to extract this information separately by, for example, taking the sums and differences of the responses obtained from cones of different types. Such a system, unlike a spectrophotometer, is liable to supply ambiguous information—it is impossible, for example, to distinguish subjectively between a spectral yellow and an equal mixture of green and red light—but it does provide a basis for distinguishing between wave-lengths less than 3 m$\mu$ apart over most of the visible spectrum, as well as between many hundreds of complex wave-length combinations.

A somewhat similar system to that concerned in colour vision occurs in the sense of *taste*. On the basis of subjective experiments it was found possible to classify chemicals which give rise to taste into four types—depending on the sensation evoked and the type of 'papilla' (collection of taste buds) stimulated by them. It was postulated that four types of chemoreceptor are present in the tongue, each sensitive to one of these

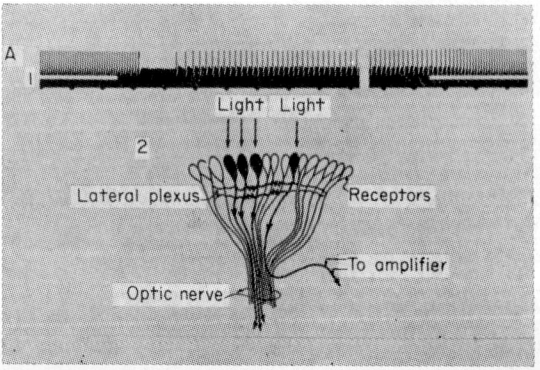

FIG. 3. *Lateral inhibition in the eye of Limulus. The trace at top shows the inhibitory effect on the discharge of a single illuminated ommatidium when adjacent ommatidia are illuminated simultaneously (this is indicated by blackening of the stimulus trace).* (From F. Ratliff, W. H. Miller, and H. K. Hartline (1958) *Ann. New York Acad. Sci.* **74**.)

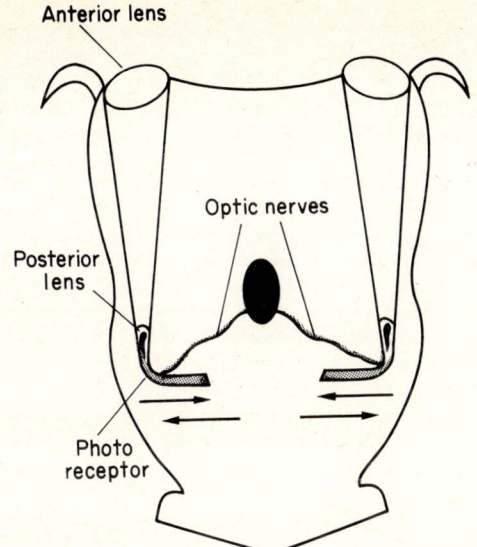

FIG. 4. *Scanning eye of the crustacean Copilia. The single receptor unit moves to-and-fro across each image plane at a rate of 0.5 cycles per second. (From R. L. Gregory (1966) Eye and Brain.)*

the brain, which is less interested in performing a chemical analysis than in obtaining a potentially resolvable pattern of useful information.

In the senses both of taste and *smell*, it is found that some fibres have different thresholds with respect to chemical concentration, even though they respond to the same kinds of chemical substance. This means that the magnitude of the stimulus (in this case its concentration) may be represented in the response of the population by the number of fibres active, as well as by the rate of discharge of each receptor. A similar type of representation occurs when a stimulus is not distributed uniformly through a population of receptors with similar thresholds. A good example of this is seen in the system of mechanoreceptors in the cat's pad (see Fig. 1). A brief mechanical stimulus applied at a point sets up a travelling wave in the pad, whose amplitude decays with distance (see *Non-neural elements in receptor systems*). At a certain distance from the stimulus, the displacement of the pad surface becomes too small to excite the underlying receptors—the greater the amplitude of the stimulus, the larger is the area over which receptors are excited. The magnitude of the stimulus is thus represented in the response from the population by the number of active units, and as these particular receptors normally fire once only to each stimulus, this is the *only* way magnitude is represented.

In certain sense organs where extremely high sensitivity is required, there may be an advantage in having many receptors all responding in an identical manner. Certain fishes with an electrical sense are sensitive to external electrical fields of $0.15$ $\mu V/cm$, a field strength corresponding to a current of $0.001-0.003$ $\mu\mu A$ in each receptor. Machin has calculated that this current is 200 times smaller than the noise current in each receptor, and that for the C.N.S. to obtain a signal to noise ratio of unity from the receptor discharges, the responses from $200^2$, i.e. 40,000 receptors would have to be correlated simultaneously.

*Spatial representation of information (b)*. In many sense organs the receptors are arranged in a two-dimensional array. The simplest example is the skin itself, where receptors responding to mechanical and thermal stimuli are present as a two-dimensional matrix over virtually the whole body surface. In this case the spatial distribution of active units does represent the spatial distribution of the stimulus, but as we have already seen, other stimulus parameters, such as magnitude, may affect this simple spatial distribution of activity. This picture is further complicated by the way the stimulus spreads in time as well as in space. For example, a strong mechanical stimulus applied at a point may stimulate receptors over the same area as a much weaker stimulus applied over a larger area; whereas in the latter case all the receptors will fire simultaneously, in the former the receptors nearest to the point of stimulation will fire earlier than those further away from it. Hence the two types of response are still potentially resolvable, even though the receptors now relate stimulus magnitude to response area, and stimulus area to response timing in a complex overlapping way. This example serves to emphasize the general point that no parameter of the response pattern is reserved exclusively for the use of any particular parameter of the stimulus pattern.

The ear and the eye are both sense organs in which the spatial distribution of receptor activity is of great importance. The cochlea of the ear contains a virtually one-dimensional array of receptors. This array, the *organ of Corti*, is only four receptor cells wide, but many thousands of cells long, extending the full length of the basilar membrane. Sounds of different frequencies cause the basilar membrane to vibrate with different amplitudes at different positions along its length (see *Non-neural elements in receptor systems*). Because there is coupling between the basilar membrane and the mechanoreceptive cells of the organ of Corti, cells in one position on the receptor array respond to notes of a different frequency from cells in other parts of the array. This representation of pitch as distance along the population of the position of maximum response is not as simple as it appears. Tasaki showed that, while cells in one position have their lowest threshold for notes of a particular frequency, at intensities above threshold the cells responded to a range of frequencies (chiefly frequencies below the threshold frequency, see Fig. 2). Thus both amplitude and frequency are represented in the spatial dimension of the responding region, and the rate of firing of each receptor shows a similar dual dependence. As with the other receptor systems so far mentioned, it is probably a matter of indifference to the brain in what form the information relating to pitch and intensity reaches it. The function of the cochlea is to provide a resolvable *pattern* of neural activity, rather than to perform a complete analysis in terms of sound frequency and intensity. An orchestral conductor has neither time nor need to perform such an analysis to spot a wrong note in a stimulus pattern as complex as a symphony.

In the eye, for a change, the spatial distribution of receptor activity has a precise geometrical relationship with the stimulus. The optical system of the eye forms an image on the two-dimensional retina, and the distribution of receptor activity in the retina corresponds to the distribution of illumination, in two dimensions, in the environment. The same statement can be made with some reservations about the compound eyes of insects and other arthropods, where each facet (ommatidium) receives light from only a small part of the environment. The visual receptors of the compound eye of the Horseshoe Crab, *Limulus*, have been studied in detail by Hartline and others. Each receptor responds to the onset of illumination by producing a discharge containing both tonic and phasic components, so that the light intensity of a particular part of the field of view is represented as discharge frequency, while changes of intensity with time are emphasized by transient increases or decreases of discharge frequency. Besides having phasic receptors which emphasize intensity changes with respect to time in their representation of the stimulus, this eye also possesses a system for emphasizing changes in intensity with respect to space (see Fig. 3). When two adjacent receptors are simultaneously illuminated, the discharge from each is reduced in frequency, compared with the frequencies when the two ommatidia are illuminated separately; this phenomenon, known as *lateral inhibition*, is caused by each cell having inhibitory connexions onto adjacent cells. The effect of lateral inhibition is to emphasize edge contrasts in spatial patterns—cells responding to a lighter part of the environment will respond with higher discharge frequencies when they are adjacent to cells responding weakly to a darker part of the environment, than when both they and their neighbours are inhibiting each other in the middle of a light area. Lateral inhibition, as an aid to the neural sharpening of spatial contours, has been postulated in other sense organs including the ear, and also in the vertebrate C.N.S. itself. The roles of phasic receptors and of lateral inhibition have been discussed by Barlow in connexion with information compression in the nervous system.

In one eye, that of the copepod crustacean *Copilia*, spatial information about the environment is not represented as a spatial pattern of impulse activity, but as a temporal pattern. This eye contains only one receptor unit, but this receptor moves relative to the image—oscillating across the optical axis of the lens several times per second, and thus scanning part of the environment (see Fig. 4). Scanning, the translation of physical differences in space into neural differences in time, has an important role in the human senses of both sight and touch. When we speak of the texture of a surface we are referring to variations in space, but these are nearly always determined by our fingers as variations in time.

*Conclusions.* The patterns of sensory nervous activity associated with stimuli are not usually resolvable into simple components which bear direct relationships with any of the stimulus parameters. It is often naive to expect simple transfer functions between stimulus and response parameters. The concern of the C.N.S. is very often to distinguish between complex patterns, rather than to analyse them in detail, and the role of the sense organs is to provide such patterns of information. The C.N.S. is often able, from this information, to reconstruct with precision many features of the stimulus; but it is much more usual for the C.N.S. to relate the neural pattern directly to the stimulus—to say that a fish tastes fishy—rather than to analyse the stimulus and reconstruct it afterwards.

*See also:* Perception of colour. Receptors in joints and muscles.

*Bibliography*

BARLOW H. B. (1961) *The Coding of Sensory Messages*, in *Current Problems in Animal Behaviour*, (Eds. W. H. Thorpe and O. L. Zangwill), Cambridge: The University Press.

BEAMENT J. W. L. (Ed.) (1962) *Biological Receptor Mechanisms*, Symposium XVI of the Society for Experimental Biology, Cambridge: The University Press.

FIELD J. (Ed.) (1959) *Handbook of Physiology*, Section I, Vol. I, Washington D.C.: American Physiological Society.

GRAY J. A. B. (1962) *Coding in Systems of Primary Receptor Neurons*, in Symp. Soc. Exp. Biol. XVI, Cambridge: The University Press.

GREGORY R. L. (1966) *Eye and Brain*, London: World University Library/Weidenfield and Nicolson.

RUCK T. C. and FULTON J. F. (1960) *Medical Physiology and Biophysics*, Section IV, *Sensory Functions of the Nervous System*, London: Saunders.

M. F. LAND

**RELATIONS BETWEEN LANGUAGES: INTRODUCTION.** If, with Wilhelm von Humboldt, we are to consider that each language is a specific interpretation of the world by a speech-community, an instrument whereby 'reality' is rendered assimilable for the human mind, then the comparative study of languages must of necessity be a universal undertaking. The aspect of language most accessible to such a study is form and it is in fact mainly the formal structures of languages that have been the subject matter of comparison, statements concerning linguistic relationship being based upon observable similarities systematically studied.

Such systematic comparison requires in the first instance a choice of items to be compared and these must themselves be the product of previous linguistic analytsis. In other words similarities can only be made expliciti-analytically in the form of limited statements made separately for the levels of phonology, morphology, lexis etc. Comparison therefore presupposes compatible descriptive analyses of the languages concerned, the units selected for comparison being set up by the linguist for his own purposes.

The outcome of any linguistic comparison will be conditioned by the items selected and the criteria applied. Although, *a priori*, any items are eligible for comparison, some will give better results than others in that these will be corroborated by additional material, the evidence being cumulative. Again, since all languages share certain basic characteristics or universals such as the two facets *meaning* and *form*, the two sets of minimal functional unit, *phoneme* (of which each language has a limited set, ranging from about 15 to 50 for the languages of the world) and *morpheme*, and perhaps even such broadly defined classes as *noun* and *verb*, any number of languages may in theory be the object of simultaneous comparison. In practice, however, the investigator is usually less concerned with features shared by all languages than with similarities between particular languages or groups of languages or, which in point of fact often amounts to the same thing since languages are profitably classed on the basis of shared characteristics, he is interested in the distribution of certain specific features. Independent yet equally valid classifications may, however, be arrived at depending upon whether such features are selected on the basis of one or the other of two fundamentally different methods of linguistic comparison, historical or genetic comparison and synchronic or typological comparison.

*Typological comparison* deals with the different types of structural patterning in languages at all levels of analysis. Priority has long been given to the morphological organization of languages and, in the Prague tradition, to the structures of phonological systems whereas, more recently, content systems have also been compared. As opposed to historical comparison, generally accepted procedures and techniques have been only partly evolved, and there exist almost as many structural relationships between languages as actual comparisons that have been made, languages being classed as structurally similar or 'related' depending upon the criteria applied. So far, the statements obtained for the different levels of analysis have only partially been integrated. A study of the relationship between grammatical categories (classes) and their exponents (segments) appears however to be universally applicable and to provide a means of linking through morphology the syntactical and phonological levels (see *Relations between languages: Typological and areal classifications*).

The classification will also vary depending upon whether diachronic considerations are taken into account or not. Chinese, for example, the prototype of isolating languages, is believed to have once been inflectional whereas French and Latin, although genetically directly connected, are structurally hardly of the same type. Structural patternings are by no means constant and are as much subject to change as individual words or morphemes. Yet considerations of this sort are marginal to typological comparison which is by definition synchronic. (This may be a reaction against the views of the 19th century in which different types of morphological structure were given an historical interpretation and considered to represent successive stages in the evolution of language.)

Although, fundamentally, typological similarities are independent of the distribution of languages in space, structural features are sometimes found to extend over limited geographical or cultural areas linking otherwise unconnected neighbouring languages (cf., for example the distribution of retroflex consonants in India, or the European languages with a suffixed article). Such *linguistic areas* often cut right across genetic boundaries, comprising languages which differ widely both in structure and provenance, and the linking features, secondary and extraneous in origin, are clearly due to contact and a certain amount of bilingualism, although substratum influences cannot in principle be ruled out. In contrast with purely structural relationships convergence phenomena of this type, although studied synchronically and structurally, are not without genuine historical implications and these *areal groupings* (alliances des langues, Sprachbünde; see *Relations between languages: typological and areal classifications*) may be thought of as the synchronic counterpart of the genetic groupings (language families) established chiefly on the basis of material correspondences.

*Historical comparison* is only concerned with similarity of grammatical structure insofar as this is accompanied by corresponding items in the stock of morphemes of the languages compared, that is by morphemes which are similar in form and meaning. In historical comparison explicit procedures based on theoretical postulates have been developed which serve to systematize and correlate the findings from the various levels or systems analysed. This so-called *comparative method* is a means of establishing sets of corresponding features in different languages via comparable items. The series E(nglish) *stone* : G(erman) *stein*, E *bone* : G *bein*, E *home* : G *heim*, E *tame* : G *zahm*, E *tide* : G *(ge-)zeit*, E *to* : G *zu* will suffice to illustrate the cardinal operation, namely the equation in different languages of similar sequences of segments (phonemes) provided that such sequences carry identical or similar meanings, and the abstracting from them of sets of correspondences which prove to be constant for genetically related languages; in our case E *ou* : G *ai*, E *t* : G *ts*. Although 'similar' in this context remains undefined it follows from the examples given above that strictly phonetic similarity is outweighed—there is a G *t* and there is an E *ai*—by the requirement of simultaneous similarity on the meaning side as well. (If this were ignored the outcome would simply be a typological comparison of the two phonemic systems.) Such agreement in both form and meaning

of a large number of lexical and grammatical morphemes (cf. also such sets as E *good—better—best*: G *gut—besser—(der) beste;* E *drink—drank—drunk:* G *trinken—trank—(ge-)trunken*) in a set of languages, extending throughout their recorded histories, will lead to the hypothesis of an actual historical relationship between them, and the following additional observations may result in the assumption of original identity, that is a *parent language* from which they have all developed:
1. There are a relatively large number of 'similar' words in certain groupings of languages as compared to others, and this in spite of the fundamentally arbitrary nature of the relationship between the form of a word and its meaning, in any language (i.e. the fact that E *knife* is called *messer* in G, *couteau* in F, ..).
2. Phonetic change within the history of any particular language is regular (i.e. OldE *ūre* becomes ModE *our*, OE *thū* > E *thou*, OE *hūs* > E *house*, OE *mūs* > *mouse*,..).
3. Finally, the further that one goes back in the history of related languages the more alike the items compared become: cf. E *mouse* : L *mūs* and OE *mūs* : L *mūs* 'mouse.

The regular correspondences between comparable segments can thus be explained as the result of different but equally regular sound changes in the development of the respective languages, and the observation, drawn from the history of individual languages, that phonetic change is regular has been turned into a theoretical postulate and extended to cover their prehistory as well. This postulate that the same rules or 'laws' govern the history and the prehistory of languages alike, and the theory of the regularity of such laws (i.e. their validity without exception within a given framework) made historical comparison a science and provided a definite means of testing the validity of individual equations. It also supplied a hypothetical explanation for the historical relationship of the languages so related, namely their descent from a common ancestor and by applying the appropriate sound laws in reverse order and direction this parent language, or something like it, could even be 'reconstructed'. (See *Relations between languages; comparative philology*). In this context 'relationship' therefore implies actual contact and an initially common history of the languages in question, whence the term historical comparison.

Regular correspondences between segments resulting from regular phonetic change are found to occur in three different situations:

1. between successive forms of 'the same word' at different stages in the history of one and the same language (see *Comparative philology*);
2. between corresponding words in related languages, inherited from the same common ancestor (cognates) (see *Comparative philology*);
3. between borrowed words which have come into a language and their underlying forms in the source language (see *Loanwords*).

These more subtle distinctions can only emerge as the result of a thorough analysis, since similar items will exhibit regular correspondences whether they be inherited or borrowed. Such an analysis can, of course, be of great importance for the investigation of the prehistoric relationships between peoples, being often the only source of information available. A number of groups of genetically related languages or *language families* have been established on the basis of historical comparison, some with clearcut membership like Semitic, Finno-Ugrian, Indo-European, others less clearly defined.

*Summary.* 'Relationship' is a concept vague enough to be open to different interpretations and it has in fact been used in different ways:

1. For purely *structural* relationships or similarities between languages.
2. With factual and *historical* implications, referring to actual contact between languages at some point in the past. Here two subdivisions can be made according to whether the relationship is:

   (a) *genetic*, i.e. results from the *divergence* of an original unit (found in *language families*, due to loss of contact among the members).
   (b) *areal*, i.e. the result of contiguity producing *convergence (bilingualism, lingua franca, loans*, and *areal affinities*).

It should be noted that the difference between (a) and (b) is fundamental as well as chronological. It is *chronological* since what is considered to be due to inheritance may in fact be an early case of borrowing for which the direction of the borrowing can no longer be determined, it is *fundamental,* because the similarities in a linguistic area are of a different nature (grammatical and lexical *calques*) from the ones in a language family although the concept of a parent language does not in principle imply complete homogeneity for we are only able to reconstruct similarities and not differences and lack of evidence for these is no proof of their non-existence.

*Bibliography*

BAZELL C. E. (1958) *Linguistic Typology* (Inaugural Lecture, London).
COHEN M. and MEILLET A. (1952) (2nd Edn) *Les langues du monde.*
ELLIS J. (1966) *Towards a General Comparative Linguistics.*
HUMBOLDT W. v. (1836) *Über die Verschiedenheit des menschlichen Sprachbaues und ihren Einfluss auf die geistige Entwickelung des Menschengeschlechts.*
LEWY E. (1964) (2nd Edn) *Der Bau der europäischen Sprachen.*
SAPIR E. (1921) *Language.*
WEISGERBER. L. (1951) *Die Wiedergeburt des vergleichenden Sprachstudiums, Lexis*, 2, 3.

T. BYNON

## RELATIONS BETWEEN LANGUAGES: BILINGUALISM.

Bilingualism arises when two or more languages are used alternately by the same speaker, whether these languages are as diverse as Nootka (an Amerindian language) and Nupe (a Nigerian language) or as closely related as the 'dialects' of neighbouring villages; and whether their speakers have knowledge of only a few lexical items of one of the languages or native-like command of both systems.

It would be possible to subdivide what is here termed simply bilingualism along a number of parameters, e.g. into:

(i) bilingualism proper *versus* multilingualism—that is, according to the number of languages spoken.

(ii) *diglossia*—that is, where the two or more languages spoken are varieties of the same language, e.g. Classical and Colloquial Arabic.

(iii) native *versus* non-native bilingualism—that is, where there are two 'first' languages (mother tongues) as opposed to one first language and one second language acquired appreciably later.

(iv) reciprocal *versus* non-reciprocal bilingualism—that is, where language A is used or understood by speakers of language B but not vice versa.

In general, however, the basic problems, particularly the linguistic ones, are comparable in all cases, and can be treated as a compounding of the problems inherent in bilingualism proper. These and other possible distinctions will be ignored henceforth.

The effects of bilingualism are treated under three headings:

(a) linguistic—viz. the effect on the languages;
(b) psychological—viz. the effect on the individual bilingual speakers;
(c) social—viz. the effect on the bilingual community.

Most attention will be paid to the first of these.

*a) Linguistic effects of bilingualism.* When two languages are spoken by the same individual it is usual for patterns peculiar to one language to be transferred unconsciously into the patterns of the other, (those of the first language normally being taken over into the second), and so to produce divergence from the norm of the second language. This phenomenon of *Interference* operates at a number of linguistic levels simultaneously. For simplicity they will be treated separately under the headings 'phonic' (covering both phonemic and phonetic), 'grammatical' and 'lexical'.

*(i) Interference at the phonic level.* In order to make the burden of assimilating a second language tolerable, identification by the speaker of interlinguistic units is inevitable. Thus, despite the difference of aspiration between English and French /p/, both are treated, on the basis of gross similarity as somehow the 'same'. Interference at the phonic level arises when a bilingual identifies a phoneme (it might be better to deal in terms of distinctive features rather than phonemes; the underlying principle, however, remains unchanged) in one language, system A, with a phoneme in his other language, system B, and subjects this phoneme $/x/_A$ to the rules applicable to $/x/_B$. There are three possible results of such interference:

(1) mere mispronunciation—one phoneme in each language is bi-uniquely interpreted in terms of another.
(2) *dephonemicization*—giving rise to confusion, when $/x/_A$ is interpreted as both $/x/_B$ and $/y/_B$.
(3) unnoticed *hypercorrection*—when $/x/_A$ is interpreted now as $/x/_B$ now as $/y/_B$.

All three cases may be exemplified from Hausa and Nupe where a native Hausa speaker

(1) interprets Nupe /gb/ as Hausa /'b/
(2) interprets Nupe /kp/ and /kw/ as Hausa /kw/
(3) interprets Nupe /k/ as Hausa /k/ and /k'/.

Diachronically interference may even lead to change in the phonemic system of a language. For instance, Bulgarian influence is often held responsible for the presence of the central vowels /ă/ and /ĭ/, and the palatalised/non-palatalised consonantal contrast in Rumanian. An example of total phonetic and partial phonemic interference is provided by Latin as spoken by English people. Space prohibits further exemplification but, clearly, interference is not limited to individual segmental phones: consonant combinations, stress, intonation and linear non-parallelism also need to be taken into account.

*(ii) Interference at the grammatical level.* Contrary to the traditional belief that the 'grammatical systems of two languages are impenetrable to each other' we have three basic possibilities in terms of which most, if not all, phenomena of grammatical interference can be explained:

(1) The direct transfer, borrowing, of morphemes from one language to another;
(2) the transfer of grammatical relationships of one language to the morphemes of another;
(3) the interlingual equation of specific morphemes and subsequent remodelling of the function of $\{x\}_A$ with reference to $\{y\}_B$.

With (1) it is difficult to draw the line between lexis and grammar; the following, however, would appear to be unambiguously grammatical: On the model of the English plural in -s German has adopted -s as the pluraliser for most foreign borrowings, as, e.g. 'die Sputniks', even though two other forms were available and occasionally used: either the learned Russian form 'Sputniki' or the usual form for German words ending in -ik 'Sputniken'.

(2) is typified by mistakes of word-order, as in the French speaker's perennial English: 'he speaks very well German', but more delicately we can again set up a tripartite division:

(i) mere grammatical incorrectness with unambiguous retention of the meaning, e.g. 'I like the Doctor, she has such a nice beard', where 'she' is substituted for 'he' by a speaker of a language which makes no such distinction (in this case, Hungarian).

(ii) grammatical incorrectness resulting in ambiguity or misinformation, e.g. a Hindi speaker's omission of the article in 'she came in the morning' was interpreted as 'she came in mourning'.

(iii) the imposition of unneeded distinctions which, while not 'incorrect', may be noticeably superfluous, e.g. the monotonous use by an English speaker of the word-order Subject-Verb-Object in Russian where this is not necessary. (Russian shews the subject–object relationship by case inflection, with merely a favoured sequence S–V–O.)

(3) is a little more complicated: after equating ${x}_A$ with ${y}_B$ the value or function of ${y}_B$ is reduced or extended by analogy with the other functions or values of ${x}_A$, e.g. a Nupe speaker will say 'I came because I saw him' to mean 'I came in order to see him', while for 'I came because I saw him' he says 'I came because that I saw him', on analogy with the constructions in his own language.

(iii) *Interference at the lexical level.* This is the most obvious and also the most deeply affected aspect of language interference and has been treated more exhaustively than any other. It can be disposed of summarily under three headings:

(1) *Loan-words*, viz. direct borrowing or transfer of a word from language A into language B, e.g.

| English sputnik | from Russian |
| raison d'être | from French |
| ketchup | from Chinese |
| taboo | from Polynesian etc. |

Note that such items may or may not be completely assimilated into the language either phonically or grammatically. Thus 'raison d'être' may be phonically assimilated [reizn dɛtr] or left as an exotic intruder [Rɛzɔ̃ dɛtR]; 'sputnik' may be grammatically assimilated and given the plural 'sputniks' or left as an interloper with the affected plural 'sputniki'.

(2) *Loan-translation*, viz. the translation of individual morphemes of language A into their nearest equivalent in language B, e.g. English 'skyscraper' has served as a contact model for:

| French | gratte-ciel |
| Italian | grattacielo |
| Spanish | rascacielos |
| Russian | n'eboskr'op etc. |

A special form of this phenomenon is '*loan-rendition*' where the morphemes of language A, instead of being translated literally, are given approximate equivalents in the receiving language B, for instance:

| German | Wolkenkratzer | — cloud scratcher |
| Arabic | nāṭeḥat saḥāben | — cloud butter etc. |

(3) *Loan-extension*, viz. the extension of the meaning f a particular lexical item in language B on analogy with the wider meaning or polysemy of the equivalent lexical item in language A, e.g. English 'introduce' has given the meaning of 'introduce someone to someone else' to the forms

| French | introduire |
| Italian | introdurre |
| Portuguese | introduzir |

within the last few decades.

Further types and examples of interference at all the above linguistic levels could be multiplied: no mention has been made of 'semantic' interference, interference in the written language, features favouring or inhibiting interference such as the functional load of (phonemic) contrasts and systemic gaps in one language as opposed to another, nor of the possibilities now of measuring the degree of interference of control of two systems. For all these and other problems the reader is referred to the bibliography, and especially the bibliography in Weinreich's 'Languages in Contact'.

*(b) Psychological effects of bilingualism.* The linguistic effects of bilingualism can be described with a fair degree of objectivity. Unfortunately there is no corresponding consensus on the various psychological aspects of bilingualism, and all that can be done here is sketch the problems. First there is the question of the nature of the bilingualism, viz. whether a bilingual has two discrete systems where, say, the concept 'cat' is related to the word /kat/, and the different concept French 'chat' is related to the word /ʃa/, or whether there is a single conceptual system where 'cat = chat' but with different realizations determined by the situational context. Intuitively one would expect there to be a combination of the two possibilities with a tendency for each to predominate in turn in different sectors of the vocabulary: for instance where cultural differences make equation of concepts more or less arbitrary. Whether, however, it will ever be possible unambiguously to determine such a distinction, and also incorporate differences implicit in the mode of learning a second language (for instance the relation of the 'sign' to the 'concept' is likely to be radically different if one has learnt a language in a detextualized situation, viz. from a book rather than in society) depends on developments in psychology rather than linguistics.

Allied to this we have the psycho-social problem of the acculturation of the bilingual. There would appear to be four possibilities:

(1) where the bilingual has complete mastery of both languages and adapts himself fully to both situations and coexistent cultures. This is probably a rare attainment.

(2) where only the primary culture is retained as an operative system of values and the bilingual remains uncommitted to the second culture.

(3) where two cultures are merged and the individual makes a synthesis of the two.

(4) where neither culture is preserved and there is resultant aculturalism: a depressingly frequent phenomenon in rapidly colonialised territories.

Probably partially dependent on the nature of the bilingualism is the ability of the individual to acquire a number of languages and to switch from one code to the other in the requisite circumstances. Although relative proficiency is fairly easily quantifiable, no results yet obtained would seem to allow us to form useful hypotheses on the nature of the resultant systems. More surprisingly we are also still unable to state definitively whether early (infant) exposure to two languages results in greater mastery of them and more facility in code-switching than exposure in childhood or even adult life. It does seem clear, however, that bilingualism has little if any effect on the intelligence of the speaker; and that any retardative effect in the general, non-linguistic, development of the child is overcome by mid-adolescence. There are still insufficient data to judge the differences on ability of the mode of learning, viz. one parent speaks language A the other language B *versus* both speaking both languages alternate days, etc. Comparative studies which should give us information on this are rarely of cases where an individual has been *equally* exposed to both languages, and are therefore not reliable. Similarly there is no evidence at all for some of the claims made for the deleterious/ameliorative effect of bilingualism on the individual's character.

*(c) Social effects of bilingualism.* The social effects of bilingualism can be studied from the overlapping points of view of culture, as above, politics and education, for all of which the most important factor will originally be the functional role of the different languages in the community.

Language function may be subdivided as 'official'—the legally sanctioned major language, used for politics, education, international communications, etc., e.g. English in Ghana; 'group'—a minority language used within the territorial limits of an official language, usually by an ethnic minority. E.g. Tiv in Northern Nigeria; 'wider communication'—use of a non-official language for international trade, etc., a kind of lingua franca. E.g. Hausa in West Africa; 'literary'—a non-official language used primarily for literary purposes. E.g. Provençal; 'religious' a (non-official) language used primarily for religious purposes. E.g. Latin in catholic Western Europe; 'technical'—use of a language for access to international technical literature. E.g. Russian in the U.S.A.

Educationally multilingualism raises a number of problems whose nature can only be hinted at here.

(i) The relative proficiency of children in the language of instruction, for some of whom it will be the first, for others the second or even subsequent language; and the psychological effects of this situation.

(ii) The availability of teaching materials in non-official languages.

(iii) The need for the second language and the uses to which it will be put: hence the motivation for learning it.

(iv) The availability of bilingual teachers.

(v) The prestige differential between the languages to which the children are exposed.

(vi) Culture clash.

These clearly overlap with political problems such as:

(i) The feelings of minority groups and nationalist pride.

(ii) Wider (international) communication problems.

(iii) Problems of internal communication.

(iv) The problem of providing a homogeneous education.

These aspects of the situation, however, remove us from the realm of linguistics, and for further discussion the reader is again referred to the bibliography.

*See also:* Semantic change.

*Bibliography*

DARCY N. T. (1963) *Bilingualism and the measurement of intelligence, J. Gen. Psychol.*
FERGUSON C. A. (1959) *Diglossia, Word.*
FRIES C. C. and K. L. PIKE (1949) *Coexistent Phonemic Systems, Language.*
HARRIS Z. S. (1954) *Transfer Grammar, I.J.A.L.*
HAUGEN E. (1953) *The Norwegian language in America: A study in bilingual behaviour,* 2 Vols., Philadelphia: University of Pennsylvania Press.
*Proceedings of the CCTA/CSA Symposium on Multilingualism* (1962) Brazzaville, Publication No. 87.
RICE F. A. (Ed.) (1962) *Study of the role of second languages in Asia, Africa and Latin America,* Washington, D.C.: Center for Applied Linguistics of the Modern Language Association of America.
VILDOMEC V. (1963) *Multilingualism,* Leyden: Sythoff.
WEINREICH U. (1953) *Languages in Contact,* New York: Linguistic Circle of New York.
WEINREICH U. (1957) *On the description of phonic interference, Word.*

N. V. SMITH

**RELATIONS BETWEEN LANGUAGES: COMPARATIVE PHILOLOGY.** 1. The comparative method. 2. The genetic hypothesis. 3. The regularity of phonetic change. 4. Historical comparison and historical linguistics. 5. The status of 'starred' forms.

In spite of the fact that the relationship between the form of a word and its meaning is arbitrary for each language, when languages are compared a larger number of shared 'similar' words are found to result from some comparisons than from others. Groupings of languages on the basis of such shared 'similar' forms are further substantiated by regular correspondences between the equated forms, including elements of grammatical structure. The traditional language families, such as Caucasian, Finno-Ugrian, Semitic, Bantu, Indo-European etc., were set up on the grounds of such similarities which had for long been observed.

*1. The comparative method.* Regular relationships between forms are established and tested by the so-called comparative method which consists in the following series of operations: (1) the corresponding segments within formally and semantically 'similar' words in different languages are compared and sets of correspondences established for them.

For the sake of convenience examples in illustration of the behaviour of language families in general will be chiefly drawn from well-known Indo-European languages. The first ten cardinal numbers have been chosen because they form part of a set and their similarity is less likely to be due to chance than similarity between isolated lexical items; as numerals they have the additional advantage of not posing any problems as to meaning.

The relationships between corresponding segments which are established as a result of this first operation are found to be constant or 'regular' for languages within the same family. (2) Each correspondence series is now given an identifying 'label' for the purpose of reference. This is done by taking one of the segments and preceding it with an asterisk and, in the interests of economy, that segment is selected which is present in the majority of languages compared. Where a clear majority is not apparent (as, for instance, in the case of the first vowel in 9 or the first consonant in 4) a label will usually emerge from the examination of the evidence provided by additional languages. In other cases a label may have to be chosen from completely outside the series in order to avoid overlap. Thus, since the sym-

|    | *G(reek)* | *L(atin)* | *S(anskrit)* | *Go(thic)* |
|----|---|---|---|---|
| 1  | heĩs, (oínōs)¹ | ūnus | ékas | ains |
| 2  | dýō | duo | dvá | twai |
| 3  | treĩs | trēs | tráyas | threis (ei = /ī/) |
| 4  | téttares | quattuor | catváras | fidwor |
| 5  | pénte | quīnque | páñca | fimf |
| 6  | héks | sex | saṣ- | sáihs (ai = /e/) |
| 7  | heptá | septem | saptá | sibun |
| 8  | oktṓ | octō | aṣṭá | ahtau |
| 9  | en-néa | novem | náva | niun |
| 10 | déka | decem | dáśa | táihun |

¹ The 'one' employed on dice.

|    | *Akkadian* | *Hebrew* | *Arabic* | *Japanese* |
|----|---|---|---|---|
| 1  | ištēn | ʾeḥād | ʾaḥad | hito |
| 2  | šina | šənayim | ʾitnāni | futa |
| 3  | šalāšat | šəlōšā | talāt₁at | mi |
| 4  | erbet | ʾarbāʿā | ʾarbaʿat | yo |
| 5  | hamšat | ḥămiššā | hamsat | itsu |
| 6  | šeššet | šiššā | sittat | mu |
| 7  | sebet | šibʿā | sabʿat | nana |
| 8  | samāne (fem.) | šəmōnā | tamāniyat | ya |
| 9  | tišīt | tišʿā | tisʿat | kokono |
| 0  | ešeret | ʿăśārā | ʿašarat | tō |

It is immediately apparent from the table that these eight languages can be divided into two groups: Greek, Latin, Sanskrit and Gothic (Indo-European) opposed to Akkadian, Hebrew and Arabic (Semitic), with Japanese lying outside both. (These dead languages have been chosen because they show the similarities more clearly than the corresponding living languages; cf. section 2.) For corresponding segments in the Indo-European group, compare:

in 2 and 10, the initial consonants: G d L d S d Go t
in 6 and 7, the initial consonants:   h  s  s
in 10 and 7, the first vowels:        e  e  a  i, e

Similar series could of course be set up for the Semitic examples.

bols *e *o *a have already been used for the series:

5, 6, 7, 10      *e for    G e   L e   S a   Go e, i
8                *o for    o     o     a     a
(on other evidence *a for  a     a     a     a

the symbol *a cannot be chosen on the basis of 7, 9, 10 (second vowels) in order to label G a L e S a Go u where, quite apart from the difference in the vowel series, a vowel followed by a nasal corresponds in some languages to just the vowel in others. It can in fact be shown that this particular vowel series is restricted to the environment of a nasal and further analysis assimilates them to a starred nasal as its allophones in this position. The same type of analysis also applies to the series 3 *t t t th* and 8 *t t t t* where Go *t* is a variant of $*t$ in the context $*k$. Devices of this sort are necessary in order to avoid duplication of symbols and show why it is not sufficient to give a label automatically to every set of correspondences.

(3) Finally, strings of labels can now be used to summarize the correspondence series in complete words; such forms are preceded by an asterisk (**treyes* '3', *\*dekm* '10') and are known as '*starred forms*'.

*2. The genetic hypothesis.* The technique described above as a sequence of more or less mechanical operations obviously implies the assumption that there is a relationship between the languages compared. But since no one of the languages is either identical with or basically closer to the sum of starred forms representing their possible common denominator, no one of them can itself represent the source from which the others derive, although they all point to the existence of such a common source symbolized in the labels. The labels are then taken to 'represent' the segments of this lost source, a once existent ancestor '*reconstructed*' by means of the comparative method. By definition a group of languages which have evolved from a common ancestor is a *language family*, the parent language either being documented (such as the spoken Latin underlying the Romance languages) or merely postulated from comparative evidence (such as Proto-Semitic, Proto-Indo-European etc.). It is assumed that the different languages have developed regularly from their common ancestor and will therefore exhibit regular correspondences. Yet it must not be forgotten that the process by which the 'reconstructed' forms were reached was determined by the principles of simplicity and economy and may or may not parallel actual historical developments, and it was also assumed that the subsequent evolution of each language was undisturbed and in isolation. All of this demands that we adopt an attitude of reserve towards the 'reconstructed' forms. They certainly imply the existence of underlying words in a parent language but they are *not* these words themselves nor do their structural patterns necessarily render the structure of the original underlying words.

The model traditionally used to illustrate and explain the evolution of a language family is the genealogical or family tree (see below), an original unity branching off by successive splits into separate and more and more differentiated units, each branching representing loss of contact and subsequent divergent development. This model is essentially based upon the observation that the further back that one goes in time the more alike the forms compared become, a fact which is easily demonstrated by for example substituting French, Hindi and English for Latin, Sanskrit and Gothic in the table and comparing the forms *un deux trois quatre* .. and *ek do tin car* .. with the English. It will be noted that the establishing of correspondence series proves much more difficult and yields less clear cut patterns in this latter case.

The Latin forms not only are closer to their Sanskrit and Gothic etc. equivalents, but also contain *in nuce* all the relevant features of the Romance languages just as Gothic in the same way summarizes the essentials of Germanic. This is to say that when the comparative method is applied to the Romance languages, the reconstructed forms will yield something very close to Latin (which is, of course, historically their ancestor) and Latin is therefore commonly taken to serve as the

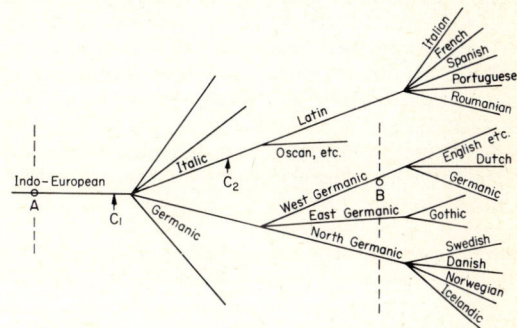

representative of the whole Romance subfamily. Gothic is used in the same way with regard to Germanic although historically it is not the ancestor, and the same is the case for Sanskrit with regard to Hindi, Bengali etc.

The model does, however, convey a false image of linguistic evolution in that it assumes that languages no longer influence each other once they have separated and that maximum differentiation (dialects) is confined to the final stage of a historical development, assumptions both of which are equally untenable. Yet it is still perfectly valid as a model of the linguist's method when he compares forms, successively reconstructing their ancestors by working downwards from fork to fork as if the branches had each really developed in complete isolation, and it also shows upon what grounds inherited words (for example A in the diagram) can be separated out from loanwords (B in the diagram). An item like A may be expected to exist in all or most of the branches, having participated in all their respective developments. The distribution of B on the other hand is likely to be defective and, in the unlikely event of its having spread into all the branches, it will still have escaped the changes that took place between the levels of A and B and therefore lack the features characteristic of these (see *Loans, loanwords)*. All those comparable items on the other hand that are found to exist in all or most of the branches and which exhibit the expected regular sets of correspondences can be ascribed to the parent language.

*3. The regularity of phonetic change.* The family tree model is methodologically adequate for yet another reason. This is the observation arrived at empirically that languages change in a regular way at least as far as their phonological systems are concerned and that such change can be stated in the form of rules which, for a particular language and within a definite period of time, apply to every segment irrespective of the meaning, frequency or grammatical status of the word or morpheme in which it occurs. Thus, for example, Old English $\bar{u}$ became at a certain period Modern English *ou* (OE *hūs* > MdE *house*, *mūs* > *mouse*, *thū* > *thou* etc.). The rule had, however, ceased to be operative by the time that L *mūtus* was borrowed into English and its $\bar{u}$ was not changed to *ou* but rather to $\bar{u}$ [ju:] and this makes it a member of another series which includes such examples as L *acūtus* > E *acute*, L *fūmus* > E *fume(s)*, etc., with L $\bar{u}$ > E $\bar{u}$ [ju:]. Between the two changes there was a definite lapse of time and the rules must therefore be stated in their correct chronological order. If all such rules for all the members of a language family are collected together and ordered they will, ideally, make it possible to predict from underlying forms the different outcomes in related languages. Correspondences between forms in related languages are then necessarily regular because they result from regular changes applied to common underlying forms, and this situation is symbolized in the family tree.

The fact of fundamental importance which has made historical comparison a science, is that such empirical observations have been turned into a theoretical postulate, namely that of the regularity of phonetic change, and thus provide a means of testing individual comparisons against the appropriate rules. If such rules are to be of general application 'exceptions' cannot be tolerated and must somehow be accounted for by means of additional or subordinate rules. Some changes are in fact found to be restricted to specific contexts only such as I-E *$t$ > Germanic $t$ in the context $s$-, $k$-, etc., but > $th$ in all other cases, such context-sensitive rules describing independent developments of originally allophonic variations (cf. section 1). Other 'exceptions' are due to the analogical influence of semantically or grammatically close forms, as for example the German adverbial genitive *des Nachts* formed on the pattern of its semantic opposite *des Tags* which as a masculine quite 'correctly' has an *-s* in the genitive whereas the feminine *die Nacht* should not rightly have one. In other circumstances the analogy may be due to a close syntagmatic relationship, such as the case of Latin *(eorum) deum* which was replaced by *(eorum) deorum* under the influence of the pronoun, in which the *r*-forms are inherited.

As regular phonetic development also applies in general to borrowed words and since there is on purely formal intralinguistic grounds no means of deciding whether for example $C^1$ and $C^2$ in the diagram are inherited or borrowed (we may for instance happen to know the extralinguistic history of $C^1$ but how are we to know that $C^2$ came in at the point indicated when it is only found in the left hand branch, for it may have come in in exactly the same way as $C^1$ and for some reason or other been lost in the right hand branch) the notion of a parent language becomes relative to some extent. Where then are we to draw the line between early loans and inherited words? What really matters in fact in what we call a 'language family' is mutual intercomprehensibility between the ancestors of a group of languages previous to their subsequent divergent development (split). How close this 'original' contact was, that is to say what was the actual degree of uniformity within the parent language, remains unknown since, although we are capable of reconstructing similarities, we have no means of assessing any contemporary differences. This is not a refutation of the linguistic concept of the language family but simply a more realistic view of the actual historical situation. As a linguistic concept the language family is established on the basis of regular corre- spondence series resulting from regular sound shifts in common lexical and grammatical elements.

*4. Historical comparison and historical linguistics.* It has been argued that the comparative method does not imply true (i.e. structural) comparison and that it should, in fact, be termed the historical method since the essential relationship between the members of a language family is a historical one and since the method employed by the linguist is exactly the same whether genetically related languages or different stages in the history of one and the same language are being compared. The decision as to whether we are to treat any particular comparison as applying to different languages or to different stages of the same language, whether it is for example better to derive language X from language Y or both from language Z is very much a question of simplicity of statement. In a case where the reconstructed language Z is identical or almost identical with Y it is more economical to derive X directly from Y rather than both from Z. This is a purely linguistic decision designed to provide an answer on the question of whether X and Y are different languages or not and does not require that any extra-linguistic criteria such as continuity of population in the same place, etc. be taken into account. It is therefore largely a matter of choice whether one is to consider historical linguistics as a special case within historical comparison or historical comparison as a special instance of historical linguistics. Both also are faced with the same theoretical problems which, in spite of their historical precedence, have resulted in their being treated somewhat as the stepchildren of modern linguistics. For the method taken over from the 19th century of tracing the development of individual items right throughout their history, from say Indo-European to Gothic, clashes with the actual grammatical systems operating in the languages at any one time. A statement of the type 'I-E *$t$ > Go $th$ in all environments except after $s$-, $k$- etc. where > t' tends to obscure the synchronic situation in Gothic. For, although *$t$ is a phoneme for I-E, its reflexes $th$ and $t$ in Gothic are not allophones of the same phoneme since for Gothic /th/ [þ] is an independent phoneme, and [t] (historically-speaking an allophone of I-E *t) is synchronically now one of the allophones of Gothic /t/ which itself continues I-E *$d$. There is, then, no one-to-one relationship between the two phonological systems, and the historical development can only be understood as a replacement of one complete system by another or, rather, as a continuous reorganization of the system in order to counteract losses of distinctive oppositions resulting from sound change.

5. *The status of reconstructed forms.* For each member of a language family the parent language may be treated as its particular ancestor, the reconstructed forms being treated as if they represented the earliest documented stage of its history. This does not only provide a means of tracing the history of a language back into prehistoric periods and possibly relating it to archeological and prehistoric findings but it is also important for an understanding of many points of its structure. The comparative method as described in many handbooks leaves the impression that historical comparison consists largely in reconstructing as many items as possible of the lost lexicon of the parent language and, since the actual number of related words found in all or the majority of the member languages is quite small, the achievements of such comparison have rightly been questioned. Yet the fact is sometimes forgotten that the uniformity of a language family, say I-E, largely rests upon and was discovered as a result of the striking similarity in the morphological structure of its members. Franz Bopp's classical book, which in 1816 definitively created Indo-European, bears the significant title: 'On the system of conjugations of the Sanskrit language compared to Greek, Latin, Persian and Germanic' which means that the whole proof of the genetic relationship of these languages was from the very outset based on *comparative morphology*. Compare, for example:

|  | S | G | L | Lith | Go | Hitt |
|---|---|---|---|---|---|---|
| *es-mi (I am) | ásmi | eimí | sum | esmî |  | ešmi |
| *es-(s)i (you are) | ási | essí, ẽi | es | esî | is |  |
| *es-ti (he is) | ásti | estí | est | estî | ist | ešzi |
| *s-enti (they are) | sánti | entí | sunt |  | sind | ašanzi |

The alternation *es- in the singular, *s- in the plural is matched by such forms as:

*stē-, *dō- in the singular, and *stə-, *də- in the plural:

(I stand) G hí-stā-mi, (we stand) hí-stă-men, and
(I give)  G dí-dō-mi, (we give)  dí-dŏ-men,  cf.
(I give)  S dá-dā-mi, (we give)  da-d-más

and by E *sing : sung, bite : bit, write : written*, etc.

In all these cases a root allomorph with full vocalism in the singular of the present tense alternates with an allomorph with reduced vocalism in the present plural or the past tense, according to the same principle (ablaut). From the rules of ablaut and from the appropriate sound laws for the languages concerned all their various forms become predictable. From the reconstructed forms an 'Indo-European grammar' can then be set up which often has the capacity of explaining grammatical forms in the individual languages which, from a purely synchronic point of view, are 'irregular' (that is to say unanalysable and unmotivated from the point of view of productive patterns). Such plurals as E *oxen, children* are synchronically isolated in English. What is for them a plural suffix (*-en* and *-r-+-en*) is historically the stem formant and 'the same *n*' as in L *leo, leonis* (stem *leon*-), L *strabō, strabōnis* (stem *strabon*-) and 'the same *s*' (changed into *-r*-) as in L *genus, generis* (stem *genos*-), S *janas, janasas* (stem *janas*-). That is to say, in Germanic the inherited forms have been given a new functional interpretation, after the loss of various case endings and of the *s*-stems as a separate class. Examples of such plurals are much commoner in German (*Lamm – Lämmer, Rind – Rinder, Kind – Kinder*), especially the *n*-forms (*Ochse – Ochsen, Mühle – Mühlen, Republik – Republiken* etc.) though here too they are no longer productive.

Corresponding grammatical forms in related languages agree largely in the *composition* and *distribution* of their morphemes and allomorphs, that is to say in their *morphological structure*. Thus, when Hittite was discovered at the beginning of the century, it was classed as an Indo-European language on the grounds of its morphological structure, especially the characteristic distribution of certain allomorphs, rather than on the grounds of specific lexical equations, these being rare and often ambiguous. Similarity of morphological structure appears to be essential for the definition of a language family and for the establishment of its membership, and in extreme cases may even outweigh the absence of corresponding lexical items. If a definition of the term '*parent language*' is to be attempted, it should be somewhat along the following lines: a parent language is an abstract representation of a stage in the development of the members of a language family by which the similarities which exist between them in historical times can be e x p l a i n e d.

*See also:* Relations between languages: introduction.

*Bibliography*

BLOOMFIELD L. (1934) *Language*.
GUTHRIE M. (1953) *The Bantu Languages of Western Equatorial Africa*, (Handbook of African Languages).
HOENIGSWALD H. M. (1950) *The principal step in comparative grammar, Language*, **26,** 357.
LEHMANN W. P. (1962) *Historical Linguistics: An Introduction*.
MARTINET A. (1955) *Économie des changements phonétiques*.
MEILLET A. (1937) (8th Edn) *Introduction à l'étude comparative des langues indo-européennes*.
MOSCATI S. *et al.* (1964) *An Introduction to the Comparative Study of the Semitic Languages*, (Porta Linguarum Orientalium N.S.VI.).
PEDERSEN H. (1962) (2nd Edn) *The Discovery of Language*, in *Linguistic Science in the Nineteenth Century*, (Trans. by J. W. Spargo).

T. BYNON

## RELATIONS BETWEEN LANGUAGES: LINGUA FRANCA.

A lingua franca is any language which is used as a means of communication among people whose native languages are mutually unintelligible; whether this lingua franca is the native language of either of the two people or a 'neutral' third language.

Clearly a lingua franca only arises in conditions of bilingualism, is susceptible to all the 'interference' typical of bilingual situations, and can best be described in the light of the general language background. The present article will give first a review of the different kind of linguistic phenomena subsumed under the general heading of lingua franca, with an account of the linguistic characteristics of the various types; and secondly a note on the policy to be adopted with regard to linguae francae, especially with the problem of language standardization.

Writings on bilingualism have left us with a plethora of terminology for the results of linguistic contact, and it may be helpful to explicate the following in addition to lingua franca: creole, pidgin, trade language, contact language, vehicular language, international language, auxiliary language, artificial language and marginal language, as all of them, given our initial definition, may *also* be linguae francae. Indeed this role is in many cases the origin of the term for the language, and in some cases for the origin of the language itself.

A *creole* is a language which has arisen from the mixture of two other languages, and in its new state has become the mother-tongue of at least one community. Clearly as all languages shew traces, usually fairly considerable traces, of external linguistic influence, all languages could, strictly speaking, be called creoles. Typically, however, this term is reserved for the case where, as a result of trading, a dominant culture language has imposed a large amount of its vocabulary onto the grammatical framework of a minority language spoken by an 'underdeveloped' or 'primitive' people. For instance, in the Caribbean there are a number of creoles based on French, English, Dutch and Spanish/Portuguese, all of which appear to have a relatively homogeneous substrate (possibly manifesting an African background) but which are all mutually unintelligible with each other and with the respective standard languages despite their structural similarities. In the extreme case we may speak of the '*relexification*' of the substrate: i.e. the replacement of the original vocabulary by that of the new language; or, to a less degree, of the '*restructuring*' of the new language, i.e. the replacement of the grammar of the new language by that of the substrate original.

Creoles normally arise via a process of pidginization. (Note that the speakers of a 'creole' are not necessarily 'creoles' in the ethnic sense of this term.) In the early stages of contact of the kind described in the preceding paragraph, a form of language arises which is used *merely* for trade or some other severely restricted function, and is the first language or mother tongue of no group at all. When such a form of language is markedly closer to one of the two or more natural languages from which it has sprung it is known as a 'pidginized' language; when it is indeterminate to which language the new form is closer it is known as a '*pidgin*'. (This distinction is not always clearly kept to in the literature).

Creoles and pidgins are linguae francae which have obviously arisen from the fusion of two or more natural languages, the former being a more advanced version (complete with native speakers) of the latter. Equally frequently, however, we find the case of a trade language being used in such situations: that is, a language which is native to one group asserts itself at the expense of the other(s), and is used virtually exclusively for commerce and trade both by native speakers of the language and by other groups, or even by these other groups among themselves. An obvious example is Hausa which, native to a large part of Northern Nigeria, is used as a lingua franca for trade etc. throughout a wide area of the Western Sudan in both the situations cited. Marginally, if at all, distinct from trade languages are contact or vehicular languages: that is, any languages which are used, however intermittently, in contact situations. These two terms would seem to be useful merely in that they provide a neutral designation potentially subsuming all other types without any further implications as to functions or status. It should be noted in passing that the language types mentioned in this paragraph are, of course, subject to the same kind of interference as that which elsewhere has given rise to both creoles and pidgins. The extent of this interference is merely less.

As a special case of a natural language being 'taken over' by non-native speakers in specific situations—cf. trade language above—we have *international languages*, i.e. languages which, by virtue of their large number of native speakers, cultural dominance and, usually, geographical spread, have become media of communication in all spheres among national groups. (*Ipso facto* also among individuals and units smaller than the 'nation', but this is incidental to their 'international' function and definition.) The outstanding example of an international lingua franca is English, used not only in the 'English-speaking world' but also throughout a large part of Asia and Africa as a medium for telecommunications, diplomatic activity and education, as well as the more obvious commercial activities. Typically all international aviation communication is effected through the medium of English.

An international language of another kind—again a special case of the preceding—would be a scholarly language used for cross-linguistic communication. Thus Latin in the European Middle-Ages was used as the medium of expression by all educated people irrespective of their native language, both when dealing with someone from a different linguistic group in general, and for all scholarship even within a homogeneous (obviously non-Latin) linguistic group. Similarly today Classical Arabic is used among nationals of the different Arab countries whose individual colloquial Arabic 'dialects' are in many cases mutually unintelligible. Note that English is currently both an international lingua franca, as defined above, and also a scholarly lingua franca in much the same way that Latin used to be and Arabic still is; though with the added advantage that the range of usage, even within 'scholarship', is much wider for the former than for the two latter.

Different in kind from any of the preceding is the group consisting of auxiliary, artificial and marginal languages. An *auxiliary language* is one which has been intentionally fostered in parallel usage with a native language to act as a lingua franca. Such an auxiliary may be a natural language, e.g. the obligatory learning of Russian by all language groups in the U.S.S.R.; or it may more commonly refer to a devised language typified by Esperanto, and pruned of the linguistic irregularity inherent in all natural languages, in order to make it easier of acquisition and use by a heterogeneous mass of speakers, and less subject to the interference common to all bilingual situations. (Note that there are now some native speakers of Esperanto, so it is presumably becoming a 'natural' language.) An auxiliary language may be, and Esperanto for instance, is an *artificial language*, although this latter term is frequently also applied to the invention of non-verbal *semiotic* systems, and accordingly lies outside the scope of this article. Finally we must mention the development of *marginal languages* in certain situations: for instance the 'household' languages used between masters and servants in some Asian and African countries. The distinctness of this category is itself marginal, merging as it does with pidgins on the one hand and artificial languages on the other.

Mention has been made intermittently above of the phenomenon of interference in these languages; and in some cases the actual distinctions between the different types of lingua franca are based on the degree of interference in them. For general treatment of interference the reader is referred to 'Bilingualism'; here a few notes on the most typical results of interference in linguae francae must suffice. Basically all interference in contact situations of the kind described leads to simplification of the system in general, of the *morphological* system in particular. Thus English, when used as a lingua franca, tends to lose redundant distinctions ('redundant' in the sense that ambiguity is normally excluded by the context or co-text) of the he/she, who/which, walk/walked variety (so too may some English based creoles even when these are no longer linguae francae); Hausa, as spoken by non-natives for trading purposes, loses the $-n/-r$ gender distinction in the genitive, and the majority of its irregular plurals, etc. Clearly this tendency is not universal: syntactic patterns often flourish at the expense of morphology, giving rise to structures in the lingua franca not found in the standard; scholarly linguae francae by their nature retain a complexity alien to their non-scholarly rivals, e.g. Classical Arabic beside the colloquial forms, and so on. (In case misunderstanding should arise, it should be emphasized that 'simplification' in any absolute sense can only be applied to such languages as pidgins which are *always* secondary, viz. have *no* native speakers. In all cases where a language has native speakers it is possibly safest to posit equal overall complexity for all languages, but obviously with the possibility of localized simplification, e.g. in morphology, at the expense of complication in the syntax.) In view of the foregoing it should perhaps be stressed that we are referring here to the properties and complexities of the language system, and not to the performance of the individual speakers using a given lingua franca. There is, of course, a continuum of performing ability in a lingua franca as in any second language, ranging from native or native-like fluency on the one hand, to the extreme of a restricted code, exemplified by marginal household languages or the English of foreign air-pilots, on the other.

We turn now to the non-linguistic aspects of linguae francae: specifically the political, cultural and educational attitudes and policies in regard to them. The problems inherent in any bilingual situation have been sketched elsewhere and appertain very largely to linguae francae too. Thus a lingua franca has a special, rather powerful, functional role in the national community, being the normal medium for all 'official' affairs; it has obvious advantages in the field of education, and in many cases it avoids the odium of ethnocentricity (cf. for all these cases the use of English in West Africa). This, however, presupposes that the lingua franca is an international language; the problem is somewhat different if it is a creole. In this case the one language which is universally comprehensible may simultaneously be the only one which has no large body of written material, few highly qualified native speakers, and perhaps worst of all, zero prestige. (The incipient literature for certain pidgins and creoles is still negligible.) It is customary to hear creoles denigrated as being 'not real languages', 'impure dialects', 'degenerate', 'ugly' and so on, with the result that not only are people ashamed to use them, but that there is active opposition to any official attempt to extend their use; even where their distance from the standard is so great as to render learning the latter a major undertaking.

This leads us finally to the problem of *language standardization*. Normally language standardization is thought of only with regard to the so-called standard languages, viz. specific dialects sanctioned by socially superior usage, an academy, etc.; it is, however, equally applicable to any language. Following Ray we may view standardization from the angle of: (i) linguistic efficiency: covering writing facility as well as orthography and, as far as this may be possible, grammar; (ii) linguistic rationality: (a) in time, e.g. the avoidance of archaisms; (b) in place, e.g. the avoidance of dialectalisms; (c) in scope, e.g. the standardization of inter-related terminology and usage; (iii) linguistic policy: subdivided into the *development* of a standard and its subsequent *promotion*. The application of these processes will obviously be the same in kind if not in degree for the lingua franca as for any other language; the real problem still consisting in deciding whether it is necessary to standardize and, if it is, carrying out the standardization. Ideally it would be advantageous if English could be universally standardized to obviate the interfering differences between Indian and W. African as opposed to British English. Practically it seems inevitable that distinct varieties of English will arise and set their own standards—as in America. Provided these standards are kept to, and further deviation is halted so that the lingua franca still *is* a lingua franca, the process would seem harmless.

*Bibliography*

COHEN M. (1956) *Pour une sociologie du langage*, Paris: Albin Michel.
HYMES D. H. (1964) *Language and Culture in Society*, New York: Harper and Row.
MEILLET A. (1913) *Aperçu d'une histoire de la langue grecque* (Part 3), Paris: Hachette.
*Proceedings of the CCTA/CSA Symposium on Multilingualism* (1962) Brazzaville, Publication No. 87.
RAY P. S. (1964) *Language Standardization*, The Hague: Mouton – Janua Linguarum, 29.
RICE F. A. (Ed.) (1962) *Study of the role of second languages in Asia, Africa and Latin America*, Washington, D.C.: Center for Applied Linguistics of the Modern Language Association of America.
SAMARIN W. (1955) *Sango, An African Lingua Franca*, Word.
SPENCER J. (Ed.) (1963) *Language in Africa, Papers of the Leverhulme Conference on Universities and the Language Problems of Tropical Africa*, Cambridge: The University Press.

N. V. SMITH

**RELATIONS BETWEEN LANGUAGES: LOANS AND LOANWORDS.** *Loans.* 'Borrowing' between languages takes place most frequently at the level of the word.

*Loanwords* are words which have been taken over by one language from another language and they represent only one phenomenon in the wider context of languages in contact (see *Typological and areal classifications*, *Bilingualism*).
Experience shows that words often travel along with the objects that they represent (e.g. *coffee*, *tea*, *banana*, *bicycle*, etc.) and are introduced into speech-communities at the same time as the objects themselves. From this point their development may follow one or other of two possible lines: a loanword may either carry over into the receiving language features or patterns of the source language and because of this, appear foreign; or it may be completely assimilated into the systems and patterns of the receiving language and thus become virtually indistinguishable from a native word.
The possibility of *detecting loanwords* in a language is therefore restricted and depends largely upon extralinguistic information or historical and comparative evidence rather than upon intralinguistic criteria. From a strictly synchronic and monosystemic viewpoint the setting up of a separate category of loans is even, in fact, undesirable as it does not conform to the principle of the fundamentally systemic character of language. A word should either be considered as belonging to a language and consequently as participating in its system, or as not belonging to it. A less rigorous attitude however will often prove more economical and words of foreign origin may be treated separately from the system of the language on the basis of the low frequency and non-productivity of their patterns. It is only on such a basis that a purely *synchronic* criterion for the detection of loanwords in a language, namely that of *partial integration* into its grammatical system, can be established.

Partial *phonological* integration is found in such English words as *restaurant* and *garage* when the former is pronounced with a final nasalized vowel [ã:] and the latter with a final [ʒ], since nasalized vowels and final |ʒ| do not belong to the primary, i.e. native, phonological system of English. Pronunciations like [ˈgærɪdʒ, ˈgæra:dʒ] and [ˈrestərənt] on the other hand show the same words completely assimilated into English by the replacement of the foreign elements by the nearest English equivalents.

*Morphological* integration is incomplete in such plurals as English *data*, *cacti* and German *Kommata*, *Atlanten*, as opposed to complete integration in the cases of English *indexes*, *atlasses*, and German *die Teenager* (without plural suffix, matching such native words in *-er* as *Lehrer*, *Pfarrer*, *Maler*, etc., where the plural has the same form as the singular). Its assimilation into German is also apparent from its phonological structure, /ˈti:netʃər/, which replaces English |ˈti:neɪdʒə|. French *un pull*, German *Pulli* on the other hand have completely freed themselves from the original form *pullover* and have developed independently in both languages.

The degree of *semantic* integration of a loanword will largely depend upon whether it will fit easily into the structure of the semantic fields of the receiving language's lexicon. This is a relatively simple matter in the case of words for newly introduced objects, but it is more complicated when they conflict in some way with concepts already present in the language when they are likely to cause a reshuffling or even the loss of established words. Thus, for example, in German *(der) Teenager* has replaced the unpopular *Backfisch* ('teenage girl') but at the same time forfeited part of its original meaning to suit the German field structure. It would also appear that loanwords are less likely to enter the more closely knit linguistic fields and the more tightly structured word classes; thus nouns, which everywhere form an open class, are the most frequently subject to borrowing, whereas this is much less common in the case of adjectives and verbs and extremely rare in the case of conjunctions and pronouns, these latter forming closed classes.

There are also differences in behaviour between languages, some for instance proving more resistant to loans than others. Thus English has been very open to borrowing (cf. such Germanic—Romance doublets as *deep : profound, sweat : perspiration, writing : script, kingly : royal*, etc.) whereas Modern Hebrew has, like German, a strong tendency to create its new words from its own stock of morphemes.

Borrowing is very often accompanied by a change in meaning; compare, for example, German *Pudding* (for any sort of thick custard), German and French *smoking* (for evening dress), Berber dialect [*'ṭṭakksi*] (for any small car), or French *un kodak* (for 'camera' in general) with their originals.

Nor are there any absolute criteria for the detection of loanwords *diachronically*. In favourable cases, two or more sets of regular correspondences may be established for a pair of languages on the basis of two or more sets of corresponding words. In the case of genetically unrelated languages, these could represent two distinct layers of loans or loans from two different sources, whereas for genetically related languages they would most likely represent jointly inherited words (cognates) as opposed to loanwords (cf., for example, Latin *pater*: English *father*, L *ped- (pēs, pedis)* : E *foot*, L *mūs* : E *mouse*, L *sūs* : E *sow* against L *mūtus* : E *mute*, L *fūmus* : E *fume(s)*, L *planta* : *plant*, L *parentes* : E *parents*, with the two sets of correspondences, L *p t ū* : E *f th ou* in the case of cognates, and L *p t ū* : E *p t ū* in the case of loans in which latter class the greater phonetic similarity of the segments reflects borrowing and not common inheritance).

In less favourable circumstances we may have to have recourse to other criteria such as the geographical distribution of a word. Taking our examples once more from Latin and English, although the equation L *piscis* : E *fish* conforms to the established correspondences for forms inherited from Indo-European (I-E *\*p* : L *p* : E *f*), the word is not likely to be inherited for distributional reasons. For it is only found in Romance, Germanic, Irish, Polish and Russian, and is therefore likely to have spread from a centre in Europe, like the word for 'sea', L *mare*, German *Meer* etc., which is restricted to the same area. Whether *\*piscis* is in fact an innovation (a possible etymology is to connect it with *\*ap-* 'water') or borrowed from a non-Indo-European language is unlikely to be resolved. Other Indo-European languages have other words for 'fish'. In many cases in fact a clearcut decision as to whether a particular word is inherited or borrowed is not possible, especially for early loans (see *Comparative philology*).

Borrowings at a level lower than that of the word are hardly ever direct. If a foreign suffix happens to become productive in a language it has usually been abstracted from morphologically transparent loanwords, as in the case of English *-er* from Latin *-ārius*, through such forms as *molinarius* > *miller*, .., previous to being suffixed to native words (> *reader, teacher*). Complete phrases or idioms may, on the other hand, be borrowed, e.g. *comme il faut, a priori, abracadabra*, etc.

Rather a special case is constituted by such words as *telephone, thermometer, dipsomania*, etc., for, although the morphemes have been taken from Latin and Greek and the construction usually conforms to the patterns of these languages, the words themselves are deliberate recent formations of science or technology.

Apart from the borrowing of words complete in their form and content, there are other more subtle types of borrowing as for example when the meaning of an inherited native word has been shifted or extended to carry the meaning of a foreign word. Thus, with the introduction of Christianity, such Germanic words as *God, heaven, hell, sin . . .* were 'stripped of their heathen connotations' and used to convey the Christian concepts attached to the forms *deus, caelum, infernum* and *peccata*. In such cases the meaning of a native word is patterned entirely on the source *(loanshifts)*. If the pattern in the source language is morphologically complex but analysable it may be imitated in the receiving language, employing semantically matching items from its own stock of morphemes. The meaning of the new formation is, of course, the same as that of the underlying form. Such *loan translations* or *calques* were also very common in early bible translations and were employed to introduce new concepts. Examples are OldEnglish *al-weldend* for *omni-potens*, both second members being participles of verbs meaning 'to rule', later replaced by *al-mighty* following a more productive pattern in English. Another such calque is OE *arm-* or *mild-heort-nesse* from L *misericord-ia*, later replaced in English by *pity, mercy*, yet retained in German *Barm-herz-ig-keit*. More recent examples of calques are F *chemin de fer*, G *Eisen-bahn*, ModGreek *sidēró-dromos*, Swed. *järn-väg* 'railway'; or German *Fernsprecher* besides *Telephon*, *Zu-fall* 'accident' (L *ad+cadere*), *Wolken-kratzer* from *sky-scraper*, etc.

Complete idioms are also often calqued on foreign patterns, for example, *faire la cour* led to *den Hof machen*.

Finally, once a loanword has been detected, an attempt will be made to trace it back to its *origin*. In this operation extralinguistic information is often the most important source, and the history of the word is virtually inseparable from the history of the object or concept to which it refers.

On purely linguistic grounds it is principally a matter of finding for foreign features a meaningful indigenous context. Nasalized vowels in European languages may, for instance, suggest a French origin. On the grammatical level, that language will be considered to be the source which can account for the morphological structure of the word. *Teenager*, for instance, is only analysable in English, *Blitz-ab-leit-er* in German, *fin de siècle* in French. In a word like *apricot*, Dutch *abrikoos*, Span. *albaricoque*, Arab. *al-barquq*, the *al-* makes sense (as the prefixed article) in Arabic alone, and the forms without the *−l−* are therefore likely to be younger. The rest of the word is only analysable in Latin: *prae-cocium*, from *prae-cox* 'early ripe', originally applied to an early ripening variety of peach (Prunus armeniaca L.). The etymology of a loanword is thus the indispensable guide to its origin.

## Bibliography

HENDERSON E. J. A. (1951) *The phonology of loanwords in some South-East Asian languages*, Trans. Philol. Soc. 131.
HOCKETT C. F. (1964) *A Course in Modern Linguistics*.
WEINREICH U. (1953) *Languages in Contact*.

T. BYNON

**RELATIONS BETWEEN LANGUAGES: SEMANTIC CHANGE.** Although the pioneers of modern *semantics* tended to define their field as the study of *'meaning'* or 'signification' their approach reflected the contemporary conception of linguistics as an historical discipline: what interested them was not so much the nature of 'meaning' itself as the investigation and classification of *changes* in meaning. In so far as the intelligent ordering of materials is a prerequisite of any coherent description or analysis, the aim was praiseworthy. No one system of classification has, however, ever won anything approaching general acceptance by scholars. Only a brief summary of certain systems can be given here (for a fuller account, cf. S. Ullmann's survey (1957)).

The early 'logico-rhetorical' classifications of A. Darmesteter, H. Paul and M. Bréal were largely based on the 'figures of speech' distinguished by the rhetoricians of classical antiquity, although Bréal at least also discussed some of the social factors involved in semantic change. The main categories distinguished by these scholars were 'restriction of meaning' (e.g. Old English *mete* 'food' > English *meat*), 'extensions of sense' (e.g. Middle English *dogge* 'dog of particular breed' > English *dog*, Latin *panarium* 'bread-basket' > French *panier* 'basket') and 'transfer of sense', embracing all changes which were not covered by the other two categories, with sub-divisions taken straight from the terminology of rhetoric: 'metaphor', 'hyperbole', 'catachresis', 'metonymy', etc. In various forms, this basically simple scheme is still frequently used, mainly, but by no means exclusively, by non-linguists. Although comprehensive and simple, it is almost completely valueless as a tool of linguistic analysis. Its *a priori* categories are purely logical or rhetorical, and their application leads to a purely formal arrangement of material which sheds no light whatever on the linguistic, social or psychological conditions underlying the changes which it classifies.

Dissatisfaction with the 'logico-rhetorical' classifications led to the formulation of a variety of schemes laying greater stress on the *causes* of semantic change. Antoine Meillet distinguished (i) changes due to *linguistic* causes (e.g. the negative value acquired by French words such as *personne*, *rien* and *jamais* through their use in combination with *ne*), (ii) changes due to *historical* causes (covering cases such as those of the words *booking-office* or *pen*, where changes in the referent has not been parallelled by changes in terminology), and above all, (iii) changes due to *social* causes, e.g. 'specialization of sense' within the usage of particular social groups (Latin *mutare*, Old French *muer* 'to change' > French *muer* 'to moult') and 'extension of sense' through the passage of a term from the usage of a particular group to that of the whole speech-community (the nautical sense of Late Latin *adripare* giving way to the general sense of French *arriver*). Meillet's scheme was not intended to be comprehensive; he admitted the legitimacy and necessity of other approaches, such as that of his contemporary W. Wundt, who applied to semantics theories of association developed by the psychologists of his time. This study of the psychological factors involved has been pursued from a variety of viewpoints. Hans Sperber, for instance, while refusing to attempt any explicit scheme of classification, drew attention to the importance of emotive factors, stressing not so much the 'emotional charge' of particular words as that attaching to whole spheres of thought: thus, the soldier releases some of his pent-up emotion about battle, weapons and death by extending military terms to other spheres (*expansion*) or by introducing non-military ones into the military sphere (*attraction*). The influence of Freudian ideas is also manifest in Sperber's analysis of euphemism, which he ascribes to regard for the feelings of others, or in psychoanalytic terms, to the working of 'inner censorship'.

In so far as they are both concerned with explaining and classifying semantic changes in terms of their underlying causes, Meillet's and Sperber's schemes may be described as *causal* classifications as opposed to the *typological* ones of Darmesteter, Paul and Bréal, in which the type of change is the basis of the classification. All the schemes so far proposed can be reduced to these two basic types or to their combination in an *eclectic* classification.

The classification scheme at present enjoying the widest degree of general acceptance is that proposed by S. Ullmann in *The Principles of Semantics* and elsewhere, which, although it belongs to the *causal* group, differs from those of Meillet and Sperber in being concerned not with ultimate causes but with the more immediate psychological and linguistic background to the changes, or, as Ullmann (1957) puts it, with 'the general functional and structural background, a kind of matrix in which the semantic innovation takes shape, under the impact of efficient causes'. Having first isolated 'changes due to linguistic conservatism' (cases such as those of *booking-office*, where changes in the referent have not involved changes in the 'name'), Ullmann proceeds to class other changes on the basis of associations of (a) similarity and (b) contiguity, first at the level of the 'sense' and then at the level of the 'name', ending up with a category of 'composite transfers' where there appear to have been associations at both levels. Ullmann's classification has the virtues of simplicity, elegance and comprehensiveness, bringing together as it does within one unified scheme changes originating at the levels of both 'form' and 'sense'. It is not, however, without its defects: It focusses attention on relatively superficial associations and sheds little light on other factors such as social borrowing and changes in the expressive force of words. However, in so far as no unitary system of classification can simultaneously take into account all the complex factors involved in the production of semantic change, the criticism is an unfair one: the search for a perfect unitary system of classification is a hopeless one, and the arrangement of data can and should vary, as different criteria are applied in order to illuminate different facets of the phenomenon of semantic change. A more fundamental objection is that, like the other classifications discussed, Ullmann's scheme tends to produce an 'atomistic' picture of semantic change, focussing attention on aspects of the development of individual words where modern linguistics constantly stresses the fact that a language is a structure or series of structures of interdependent elements.

Although the nature of linguistic structures can only be established by synchronic analyses, attempts have been made, *inter alia* by Ullmann himself, to introduce the structural viewpoint into diachronic semantics. In theory, the idea is simple: the history of a given term will be studied through the comparison of its position within the language-system at different periods, i.e. through the combination of synchronic and diachronic perspectives. In practice, however, the application of the procedure raises a variety of problems. A 'language-system' at any given period shows wide variations at social and regional levels. Society, like language, is also constantly evolving, and the language-system cannot be considered in isolation from the relevant aspects of that evolution. Finally, there are different ways of assessing the 'oppositions' and 'associations' which determine the synchronic value of a given term, i.e. constitute its 'semantic field'.

There have been two main approaches, the '*conceptual*' and the '*morpho-semantic*', or to use other terms, an approach based on the level of 'content' only, as opposed to one which takes into account both the levels of 'content' and those of form or 'expression'. Both appear to afford valid insights into semantic processes. The case of Latin *coxa* 'hip' > French *cuisse*, Italian *coscia* 'thigh' provides an illustration of both approaches. If we consider the case in purely 'atomistic' terms, we can only note that the name of one part of the body (the hip) has come to be applied to another, adjacent part (the thigh), from which, furthermore, it is not sharply divided: the change of sense will therefore be considered in terms of 'contiguity of sense' based on the physical contiguity of the referents. If we consider the history of the word in terms of its relationship to other lexical items in the same semantic sphere, our conclusions will be quite different. From the 'morpho-semantic' point of view, the change will appear, not as the result of physical or semantic contiguity, but rather of a chain-reaction sparked off by changes affecting the word *femur*. Phonetic and morphological changes produced homonymy between *femur* 'thigh' and *fimus* 'manure' and as a result of this unfortunate association, *femur* was discarded in favour of its neighbour in the 'field', *coxa*. The place of the latter was filled by the borrowing of the Germanic term *hanka* (> French *hanche*, Italian, Spanish *anca* 'hip'). On the other hand, if we approach the problem from the point of view of 'content' alone, we can make the equally valid point that in terms of 'units of content' which are in opposition to each other, there has been *no* change: the number of units of 'content' involved remains the same, and their relationships to each other remain the same — the changes at the 'expression' level are structurally irrelevant. Applying the same viewpoint to the case of the Romance replacements of Latin *patruus* 'paternal uncle' and *avunculus* 'maternal uncle', it becomes clear that it is structurally irrelevant that the French word *oncle* is the phonetic continuant of one of these terms, whereas Italian *zio*, Spanish and Portuguese *tio* are derived from variants of a Greek loanword. What is significant is that in each case there has been a 'semantic re-structuring' through the loss of an opposition between the two lines of descent, and, further, through the extension of the single term (whatever its source) to cover not only blood relationships but also relationships by marriage. In this, as in other modifications in the terminology of kinship from Latin to Romance (cf. the parallel development of the terms for 'aunt' and 'cousin'), changes in the semantic structure of the 'field' of kinship may be largely seen as the consequence of changes in the underlying social organization which rendered superfluous the continued notation at the linguistic level of such oppositions as that between the paternal and maternal lines.

A case which can be considered in purely linguistic terms is that of the demonstratives in the Romance languages. The system of the Latin demonstratives distinguished (i) proximity to the speaker (*hic, haec, hoc*), (ii) proximity to the person addressed (*iste, ista, istud*), and (iii) distance from either (*ille, illa, illud*). In most of the Romance languages, this tripartite structure of the demonstrative has been preserved, although in no case do all the terms derive directly from the corresponding Classical Latin ones (in Spanish, for instance, the forms *este, ese* and *aquel* derive respectively from *iste, ipse* and a reinforced form of *ille*, only the latter occupying the same place in the system as it had in Latin). In Old French and Rheto-Romance, on the other hand, the tripartite opposition gave way to a dual one distinguishing only proximity to, and distance from, the speaker, as in the Germanic languages (cf. English *this/that*, German *dieser/jener*). In certain cases, therefore, the comparison of successive synchronic states, considered in terms of related units of 'content', will bring out clearly shifts in semantic structure.

Valuable as it may be in certain cases, it is questionable whether this approach can be applied on a large scale. Trier's '*field*' *theory*, for instance (see *Semantics: field theories*) depends on the highly questionable assumption that for all the speakers of a given language, meanings are structured as interdependent elements within conceptual spheres or fields which divide up and articulate the whole of experience without overlapping, like the pieces of a mosaic. This view of meaning-structure does not do justice either to the complexity of associations between words at the phonetic and syntactic levels or to the existence of different 'styles' or 'registers' within the usage of the individual, not to mention lexical variations within social, regional or occupational groups. In any case, in so far as 'contents' can be satisfactorily approached only through the study of 'forms', the 'conceptual' approach should therefore be considered rather as an extension of the 'morpho-semantic' one, as a process of abstraction which in appropriate cases affords supplementary insights. Although the semanticist is interested in 'meaning', modern methods would seem to demand that he work upward from 'forms' to 'meanings' rather than the other way round.

Because of the existence of synonymy on the one hand and of homonymy on the other, the relationships between the two levels cannot be dealt with in terms of one-for-one correspondences, i.e. the number of meaningful 'forms' does not correspond to the number of 'contents' or 'meanings'. The introduction into a language of a new 'form' (mainly through borrowing) may have a variety of different consequences. It may involve the introduction of a new meaning (e.g. *chocolate* and *Schadenfreude*, to quote borrowings of rather different types). It may result in the re-structuring of a 'content' expressed by an existing term, as when the introduction into English of the word *spirit* resulted in a sub-division of the semantic 'range' of the term *ghost* (for a survival of the earlier, more inclusive sense of this word, cf. the expression 'the Holy Ghost'). Finally, it may simply be added to the range of 'forms' expressing a given 'content'. The existence of synonyms or near synonyms is, however, in itself a factor in semantic differentiation: the change in the meaning of Middle English *deor* 'wild animal' to *deer* in its present sense was surely conditioned not only by the fact that the deer was for the huntsman the beast *par excellence*, but that synonyms such as *beast* and *animal* had been borrowed into the language from French.

The close study of the semantic, formal and contextual associations of a term within a language at different periods can certainly add much to our knowledge of the factors which have conditioned changes in its meaning. This knowledge will still, however, be largely about the 'how' rather than the 'why' of specific changes. The fact that particular changes have occurred must frequently be attributed to factors which lie outside the range of linguistics considered as an objective study of language structures. Historical semantics therefore seems doomed to remain an 'impure' discipline drawing on materials gleaned from psychology and socio-cultural history. Some changes arise out of shifts within a language itself, others are conditioned by unpredictable and extralinguistic factors such as changes in fashions, prestige and social organization within the speech-community which uses the language. Similarly, the high rate of lexical replacement affecting words referring to, say, sexual matters, illness and death cannot be explained in linguistic terms. Such words are not *linguistically* peculiar in any way: the 'emotive charge' which attaches to them is a purely psychological phenomenon. This remains true whether one continues to regard 'meanings' in terms of 'concepts' or of 'uses' or 'functions'.

*Bibliography*

Coseriu E. (1964) *Pour une sémantique diachronique structurale*, Travaux de Linguistique et de Littérature, **2**, 139, Strasbourg.
Cremona J. (1951) *Historical Semantics and the Classification of Semantic Changes*, Hispanic Studies in Honour of I. González Llubera, Oxford.
Stern G. (1931) *Meaning and Change of Meaning*, Göthenburg.
Ullmann S. (1957) (2nd Edn) *Principles of Semantics*, Glasgow-Oxford.
Ullmann S. (1962) *Semantics: An Introduction to the Science of Meaning*, Oxford.

N. C. W. Spence

**RELATIONS BETWEEN LANGUAGES: TYPOLOGICAL AND AREAL CLASSIFICATIONS.** Traditionally there have been three bases for the classification of languages: the *genetic*—according to the 'genealogical' relationship among the languages; the *typological*—according to the structural characteristics of the languages; and the *areal*—according to the geographical location of the languages. In fact these three classifications are not comparables. The so-called genetic classification is in reality no more than an hypothesis of historical relationship, based on the evidence of the other two modes of classification, which alone can really claim to be rigorous. In other words only the typological and areal methods provide formal criteria for grouping languages together, and it is only these which will be treated here. The genetic hypothesis is discussed elsewhere in the volume.

Areal and typological classifications are normally, and most usefully, made interdependently. The areal aspect is reasonably self-explanatory: languages are grouped together because they are all spoken within one geographical area, for instance, Europe, India, on the Mediterranean coast-line, etc. Then on top of this linguistically somewhat arbitrary delimitation is imposed a typological classification. The rest of this article will be devoted to a review of the nature and problems of typological analysis.

Criteria for a classificatory typology may be divided into the lexical and the structural. The first of these is generally considered the concern and indeed the prerogative of genealogical classification: regular phonological correspondences among words of the 'same' meaning in different languages are taken to be evidence for the genetic relationship of these languages. In fact, sound correspondences are as much a 'structural' feature as any of the others, but in view of their special status in comparative historical work will not be further mentioned.

Structural criteria proper may themselves be subdivided into (i) phonological and (ii) grammatical. The possibility of there being systematic semantic correspondences across languages is in no way denied by this dichotomy, it is merely that there has been developed no semantic theory as yet which is capable of dealing with them. It is also obvious that no criterion or set of criteria from a single level is to be taken in isolation. Multiple cross-classification is essential, and divisions are made here only to simplify and exemplify.

*(i) Phonological criteria.* Before exemplifying the kind of phonological criteria used in classifying languages, it should be emphasized that while these criteria may be relevant and sufficient to shew structural affinities among languages within a strictly determined geographical area, they are relatively unuseful in building up a general typology of language, because of the overall lack of agreement among linguists as to the basic elements with which one is dealing. Accordingly the following selection, while perhaps sufficiently general to provide some kind of very rudimentary classification in some strictly defined areas would need to be widely extended, or have certain irrelevant items omitted, if used in other particular areas. (Irrelevant because every language in the group would be alike in respect of one feature, e.g. all the Romance languages are non-tonal (intonational) and have no vowel harmony.) Whether general or particular it would need to be refined and extended, and also combined with other, putatively grammatical, selections to provide any really valuable insights.

(a) The presence or absence of *lexical tone:* distinguishing the tonal, most of the languages of West Africa, the Sino-Tibetan languages and Amerindian languages, from the intonational, most Indo-European languages with the exception of border-line cases such as Swedish and Serbo-Croat. Clearly all languages use pitch in some way: a tone language is one where pitch differences are systematically distinctive at the rank of word or morpheme; an intonational language is one where pitch differences are systematically distinctive *only* at the ranks above word: —group or clause. Many languages combine both tone and intonation, here they would be described as tonal.

(b) The presence or absence of *distinctive stress:* separating stressless (i.e. syllable-timed) languages such as French or Hindi, from the stressed languages such as English or Russian. It should be noted that stress is very frequently, but not necessarily, correlated with tonal distinctions in those languages which are tonal, e.g. a number of the languages of West Africa.

(c) The presence or absence of *vowel harmony:* distinguishing Turkish, the Finno-Ugric and some of the West African languages from, say, the vast majority of Indo-European languages. In languages with vowel harmony a word (or comparable unit) can contain vowels only from a specific subset of the total vowel inventory of the language, the quality of the initial vowel determining this subset for all subsequent vowels. For instance, at its strictest, if the first vowel of the word is front rounded, all subsequent vowels will be front rounded, and no back or unrounded vowel will appear until after a word boundary.

(d) The occurrence of particular distinctive sounds, e.g. the labio-velars [kp] and [gb] in a large number of West African languages and no others; retroflex consonants in Indian and some other S.E.Asian languages; front rounded vowels in a number of Indo-European languages, e.g. French, German and Dutch, but excluding most dialects of English; back unrounded vowels in Korean and a number of the languages of S.E.Asia, and so on.

(e) The occurrence of certain sound sequences, i.e the *canonical form* of items in different languages. Thus all words have the structure CV (CVCV...) in many W. African languages with no possibility of consonant clusters at all of the type found in English: (str-, pl-, -mpst) etc. or Russian: (psk-, mst-) etc. Likewise the relative complexity and constituency of such clusters could be made into a more delicate differentiating criterion for English and Russian.

(f) The make-up of the different phonological systems operating at different places in structure, e.g. the possibility or otherwise of all initial consonants also occurring medially and/or finally. For instance in English /r/ and /h/ occur only syllable initially and [ŋ] only syllable finally, whereas all other consonants may occur either initially or finally. (/r/ of course may be post-consonantal but this is irrelevant here as it must still immediately precede a vowel.) In a number of languages of S.E. Asia and of Africa widely differing systems of consonants operate at initial *versus* non-initial position.

*(ii) Grammatical criteria.* The usual distinction into morphology and syntax would seem to be relevant to the localization of a structural differentiation of languages, but with the past lack of adequate syntactic descriptions this aspect has been largely ignored and the traditional grammatical typologies depend mainly on morphology alone. Mention will be made below to one possible basis of typology in syntax, otherwise the normal schema with its limitations will be followed.

One of the earliest and best formalizations of morphological classification was presented by *Sapir* with his three intercrossing parameters of 'conceptual type', 'technique' and 'degree of synthesis'. On the supposition that all languages have to express 'radical concepts' and 'relational ideas', but that 'derivational', and 'mixed relational' concepts may both be present, both absent or either one present, Sapir devised a four-term conceptual system comparing: (a) simple pure-relational languages with no affixation or internal change, e.g. Chinese; (b) complex pure-relational languages, like (a) but with affixal possibilities, e.g. Turkish; (c) simple mixed-relational languages with syntactic relations 'in necessary connexion with concepts ... of concrete significance' but no further affixation; and (d) complex mixed-relational languages like (c) but with marked affixal possibilities. The second parameter—the technique of modifying the radical element—comprised the terms: (i) *agglutinative*, where all modifications are expressed affixally and each affix can be unambiguously ascribed a single meaning or function, e.g. Turkish. (ii) *fusional*, where modifications are typically expressed by the fusion of two morphemes, only one of which may be segmentally identifiable, e.g. English in such examples as 'depth' from 'deep' (in contrast to the agglutinative 'goodness' from 'good'). This is somewhat difficult to distinguish from: (iii) *symbolic*, where modification is typified by reduplication, changes in vowel quality and quantity, and in stress and pitch, e.g. as in Arabic and Shilluk; (iv) *isolating*, typified by the absence of all affixes and modification of the radical element, e.g. Annamese and Chinese. The last parameter—degree of synthesis—is much easier to segment (a tripartite division is usually set up) although, as with all the other divisions, the distinctions are relative and actually form a cline. The three terms used were: *analytic*, *synthetic* and *polysynthetic*, languages being ranged on the scale according to the average number of morphemes in the word (taken as the minimal free form), analytic being supposed to have just one, the others correspondingly more. Chinese would again come at one end of the spectrum (analytic), a number of Amerindian languages at the other (polysynthetic).

Clearly Sapir's division is too cumbersome and subjective to be very useful, but it represents the apogee of traditional 'morphological' classification, from which most others were deviations, or of which they were unformalized precursors. 'Polysynthetic' soon died a natural deaths and there remained a somewhat hybridized scale comprising *agglutinative*, *isolating* and *inflexional* (this last roughly parallel to fusional and symbolic), with *analytic* or *synthetic* tagged on as makeweights.

A more convincing scale which is overtly comparable to the preceding, yet which largely avoids another drawback in Sapir's—namely, that the terms in the systems are not mutually exclusive—was provided by *Bazell*. Most classifications fell down to a greater or less extent because of the difficulty in setting up segments and classes by reference to which one can classify the languages concerned (e.g. in Latin, is 'puellarum' to be analysed as puell+arum', 'puella+rum' or 'puell+a+rum', and what is the status of the medial 'a'?). It was precisely this problem of analysis which Bazell made the basis of his typology. In other words languages will be classified according as they present difficulties of: (a) segmentation, e.g. the inflexional languages exemplified by Latin or Classical Arabic; (b) class determination e.g. the isolating languages, exemplified again by Chinese and, to a less degree, English; or (c) present no obvious conflict as between segmentation and class determination at all—for instance the agglutinative languages exemplified by Turkish. Thus in case (a) the simplest classes, in themselves quite easily divisible, have no clear or simple segmental realizations; in case (b) the simplest, easily recognizable, segments have no immediately obvious, unambiguous class membership, whilst in case (c) there is, optimally, a clear one to one correlation between classes and segments.

This more abstract 'problem classification' is clearly superior to the item-oriented traditional schema. It is still, however, morphological and could be usefully supplemented by a syntactic typology. One way of effecting this suggests itself in the light of recent developments in transformational-generative grammar. If, as seems probable, the deep-structure of all languages is broadly similar, whereas the surface structure, as generated by the transformational rule cycle, is cross-linguistically disparate, this would imply that the surface domain of language is the most suitable focus for comparative typological statement. Clearly, a marked difference in the phrase structure would, by virtue of its rarity, provide a highly significant comparative measure, but with most phrase-structure differences being apparently minor and most transformational ones being extreme, the most fruitful basis for comparative typological statement would appear to reside in a comparison of the transformational rules necessary to map the deep structure into surface structure.

The preceding gives some very sketchy indications of the criteria for classifying language similarity. Any inferences which can be made as to the causes of such similarity lie, strictly, outside the scope of this article. It should be emphasized in closing, however, that aside from the unlikely hypothesis that all similarity is due to chance, the only apparently tenable explanation is that there has been *contact* among languages displaying linguistic similarity. Without historical evidence of the kind available for Latin and the Romance languages (and which is not generally available even for the whole of Indo-European), however, it would appear to be impossible to pontificate in any way on the nature of this contact: borrowing, drift, and genetic relationship are merely different aspects of the same phenomenon.

*See also*: Language varieties: language and dialect. Bilingualism. Lingua franca.

*Bibliography*

BAZELL C.E. (1958) *Linguistic Typology*, Inaugural Lecture, London: School of Oriental and African Studies, University of London.
EMENEAU M. B. (1956) *India as a linguistic area, Language*.
HENDERSON E. J. A. (1965) *Topography of certain phonetic and morphological characteristics of South East Asian Languages, Lingua* 15: Indo-Pacific Linguistic Studies II.
JAKOBSON R. (1938) *Sur la théorie des affinités phonologiques entre les langues*, Actes du 4ᵉ Congrès international de linguistes (Copenhagen, 1936), Munksgaard, Copenhagen.
LAMB S. M. (1959) *Some proposals for linguistic taxonomy, Anthropological Linguistics*.

MEILLET A. and COHEN M. (1952) *Les langues du monde*, Paris: Centre National de la Recherche Scientifique.
SAPIR E. (1921) *Language*, New York: Harcourt Brace.
SEBEOK T. A. (1950) The meaning of 'Ural-Altaic', *Lingua*.
TROUBETZKOY N. S. (1939) *Gedanken über das Indogermanenproblem, Acta Linguistica*.
WOLFF H. (1959) *Subsystem Typologies and areal linguistics, Anthropological Linguistics*.

N. V. SMITH

# RELIABLE COMPUTATION WITH UNRELIABLE ELEMENTS.

*Introduction.* Computers contain many modules and connexions. We call these *elements*. Networks of these elements, known as *modular nets* are required to execute long sequences of precise calculations at high speeds and with high levels of reliability. In analogue computers, physical quantities are represented by voltages, currents, and the like, and precision is limited by noise present in the elements. In digital computers, physical quantities are represented by numbers, and arbitrarily high precision may be obtained by increasing the number of digits used in the representation. However, such an increase of precision is obtained at the cost of decreased reliability; the longer the digital expansion, the greater is the expected number of errors in calculation caused by malfunctions or failures of computing elements. For example, the overloading of electrical networks may cause short-circuiting and the breakdown of valves or transistors; or the contacts of a relay network may stick occasionally, or there may be power failures. In addition elements may be old or may have suffered radiation damage, and connexions may be faulty—dry-joints, mistakes in wiring, shorting and open-circuiting—all may contribute to the overall unreliability of the system. These various sources of error are called *faults*.

In general, faults may be divided into two classes: *malfunctions*, which produce transient errors, and *failures*, which produce stationary errors. Associated with this classification are differing definitions of *reliability*. For transient errors a reliability measure used is the probability of net malfunction, when given the probability of malfunction of modules and connexions. For stationary errors, the measure used is the expected lifetime to failure, given the mean lifetime of modules. The problem of reliable system design is to find system designs for operation at any required level of reliability, given unreliable elements. More exactly consider a certain computing automaton A, (see Fig. 1). Let $N$ be the number of modules in A and let $t_i$ be the number of times the $i$th module $(i = 1, 2, \ldots, N)$ influences any single output from A. Let $\sum_i t_i$ be finite, equal to $Q$, i.e. there may be circuits within A but their effect is of finite duration. Let $p_m$ be the probability of any single module malfunctioning, and let $P_A$ be the probability that the automaton malfunctions. It is evident that

$$P_A \leq 1 - (1 - p_m)^Q. \qquad (1)$$

So for fixed values of $p_m$ there is an upper bound on $P_A$. Similar considerations apply for connexion errors and failures.

The problem is to make the upper bound on $P_A$ as small as possible. In case $p_m$ is fixed, this means that another automaton A' must be designed which will compute the same functions as A, and which will also contain mechanisms for limiting errors. There are several ways of doing this. A' may incorporate a *fault-detection and location* mechanism coupled to a procedure for the removal and replacement of faulty elements. Or A' may be designed so that faults have little or no effect on the computations executed within the automaton, i.e. *fault-masking* mechanisms may be incorporated. Yet another possibility is to make A' adaptive; faulty elements have progressively less influence in the automaton than correctly functioning ones.

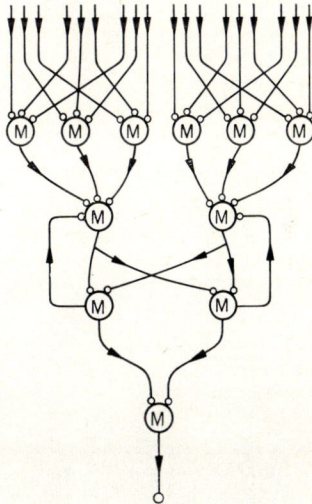

FIG. 1. *An automaton A.*

*Fault-masking of transient errors.* We consider first the case of malfunctions resulting from transient errors. We distinguish between *contact nets* (c-nets) and *gating nets* (g-nets). The basic difference between these nets is that in the former, the output of each module uniquely specifies the input, whereas in the latter this is not the case. So relay switching circuits are c-nets, whereas modular nets comprising NOR-gates are g-nets.

To mask the effects of transient errors a basic principle of design is almost always utilized, that of replication of identical elements, i.e. *redundancy*. So more elements are used in the design of A' than in A, and the extra elements are used to provide repetitions of the operations executed in A. Consider for example, an idealized relay whose malfunctions consist of the failure of its contacts to open or close when signalled to do so by the current flowing in the coil. When the relay is energized, the contact is closed with probability $\alpha$, open with probability $1-\alpha$. When the relay is not energized, the contact is closed with probability $\beta$, open with probability $1-\beta$. If $\alpha > \beta$, the contact is called a 'make-contact', if $\alpha < \beta$, a 'break-contact'. In general, to preserve closure of a c-net (i.e. to guarantee that at least one essential contact is closed) we need only to construct a *parallel c-net*, and conversely to preserve an open circuit we need a *series c-net*. Thus replacing the single relay with associated make-contact (see Fig. 2) by a relay-net with an associated series-parallel c-net (see Fig. 3) produces a large improvement in reliability. For if each of the contacts $x_1$, $x_2$, $x_3$, $x_4$ has the probability $p_c$ of being closed the probability of the c-net being closed is

$$h(p_c) = 1-(1-P_c^2)^2 = 2p_c^2 - p_c^4. \quad (2)$$

A plot of $h(p_c)$ is shown in Fig. 4. Clearly if $\alpha < 0.618 < \beta$ we will have a better relay in respect of closure than

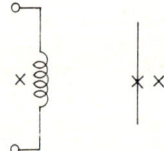

Fig. 2. *Single relay $X$ with make contact $x$.*

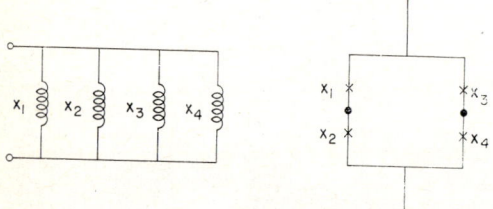

Fig. 3. *Series–parallel net.*

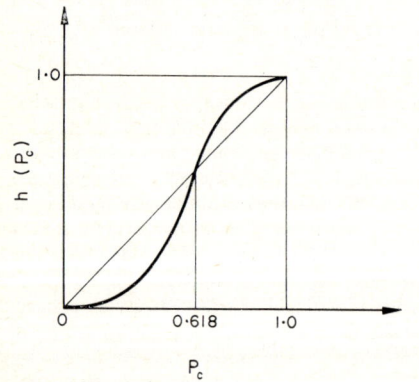

Fig. 4. $h(P_c)$ — *the probability of closure of a four-contact net as a function of the closure probability $P_c$.*

a single relay system. For example, if $1-\alpha = \beta = 0.01$ the series-parallel c-net makes errors when the coils are energized, with probability $3.96 \times 10^{-4}$, and when the coils are not energized with probability $2 \times 10^{-4}$.

In general many multi-contact relay nets have this property characterized by a polynomial of the form:

$$h(p_c) = \sum_{n=0}^{m} \gamma_n p_c^m (1-p_c)^{m-n} \quad (3)$$

where $m$ is the number of contacts in the net, and $\gamma_n$ is the number of ways in which a subset of $n$ contacts can be selected so that if these are closed and the remaining contacts open, the total net is closed. Such c-nets are sometimes called 'Hammock nets' after E. F. Moore and C. E. Shannon (1956). Extensions and refinements of this work have been carried forward by R. E. Barlow and F. Proschan (1965).

In g-nets, fault-masking of transient errors via redundancy is used both at the system level and at the elementary level. The simplest example (attributed to J. von Neumann 1952) is the *triplication* of an entire g-net

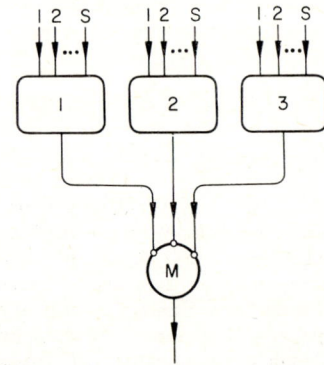

Fig. 5. *A triplicated g-net, plus majority organ M.*

(see Fig. 5) followed by a vote-taker or 'majority organ'. This module computes the function such that if at least two g-nets give similar outputs, then so does the majority organ. The majority organ is therefore said to be single error-insensitive. The probability of net malfunction may be calculated, assuming independence of the malfunctions in g-nets and in the majority organ. Let $p_m$ be the probability of malfunction of each g-net, and $\delta$ that of the majority organ. Then the probability of at least two of the g-nets being in error is

$$\gamma = 3p_m^2(1-p_m) + p_m^3$$
$$= 3p_m^2 - 2p_m^3 \quad (4)$$

and the probability of system malfunction (in case there are no connexion errors) is

$$P(\delta, p_m) = (1-\delta) \cdot \gamma + \delta \cdot (1-\gamma)$$
$$= \delta + (1-2\delta) \cdot (3p_m^2 - 2p_m^3). \quad (5)$$

The graph of this function $P(\delta, p_m)$ is shown in Fig. 6 for a fixed value of $\delta$. It can be shown that by suitably modifying the redundant net (that is by using two layers of majority organs, one of which is triplicated), and by iterating the nets themselves, that the stationary value $P(\delta, p_m) = P_0$ will be reached, provided that $\delta < 7.3 \times 10^{-3}$. For example, an error-level of $P = 2 \times 10^{-2}$ can be reached and maintained in such a system if $\delta \leq 4.1 \times 10^{-3}$ and $p_m < 0.5$. Unfortunately, such a design requires the use of a very large number of modules. In fact if $\tau$ is the longest chain of logical operators to be executed by the net, then about $3^\tau$ modules are required. Consequently the procedure is impracticable for all but a small range of values of $\tau$.

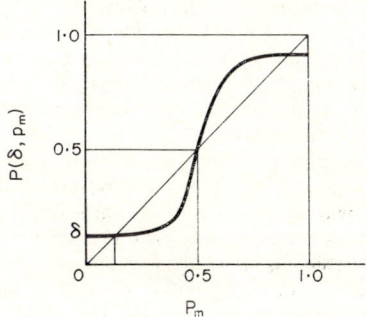

FIG. 6. *Probability of malfunction of triplicated g-net plus majority organ.*

However, it is also possible to control malfunctions within g-nets themselves by the use of redundant elements rather than redundant g-nets *per se*. It is known that nets which can execute arbitrary logical functions may be composed from 'universal' logical elements, and that *mutatis mutandis* the majority organ is universal in this sense. So any Boolean function may be computed by g-nets comprising only majority organs. The technique of replicating elements (introduced by von Neumann op. cit.), known as 'multiplexing', entails the replacing of all single connexions in g-nets by groups of connexions, known as 'bundles', and replacing all modules in the g-nets by aggregates of similar modules (see Fig. 7).

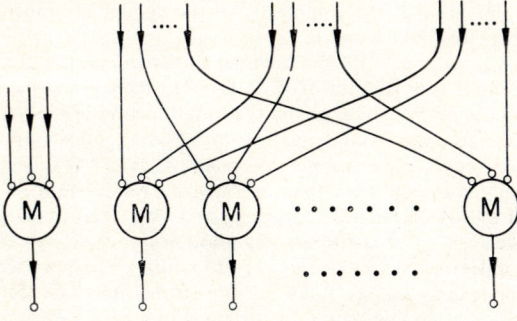

FIG. 7. *Multiplexing.*

It can be shown, with suitable randomization of the input and output bundles to and from aggregates, and in the absence of malfunctions, that these g-nets approximate the function computed by a single majority organ, sometimes called the 'quorum function' (Moore and Shannon op. cit.). However, in the presence of malfunctions, an error-controlling net is needed to maintain the approximation. It was shown by von Neumann that the net shown in Fig. 8 will control transient errors. The redundancy created by multiplexing is used in a certain *coding* of the signal patterns in the net. The details of this coding are as follows:

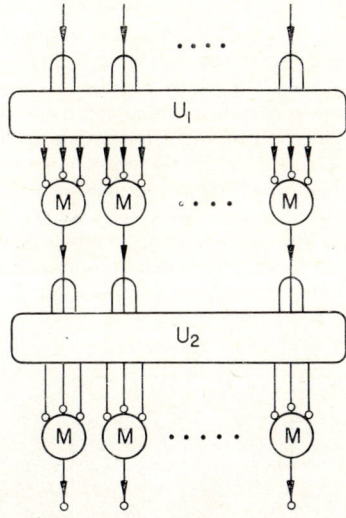

FIG. 8. *An error-controlling net.*

each bundle consists of $n$ connexions, each of which carries a binary impulse (signal or no signal). So there are $2^n$ distinct signal patterns in the bundle ranging from $(111\ldots1)$ to $(000\ldots0)$. If no malfunctions were to occur, these extremes would be the only ones to be found in the bundles. Let the number of ones in any pattern be $x$, and let there be a fiduciary level $\partial$, set so that $x\varepsilon[(1-\partial)n, n]$ represents the presence of a signal '1', $x\varepsilon[0, \partial n]$ represents the absence of a signal '0', and any intermediate level of excitation $x\varepsilon(\partial n, (1-\partial)n)$ represents the occurrence of a malfunction '$m$'. The design problem is now transformed into the problem of maintaining levels of excitation throughout the multiplexed net sufficiently close to $x = n$ and $x = 0$. Von Neumann showed that the g-net of Fig. 8 had only two stable states of excitation, corresponding to the required extrema. So this g-net has the property that with probability close to one, any input bundle whose level of excitation is close to one of these extrema, gives rise to an output bundle whose level of signal excitation is even closer to the extremum in question. The function of the box labelled U in Fig. 8 is to maintain the statistical independence of the inputs to the next layer of majority organs, and it executes a suitable permutation of its inputs sufficient to maintain such independence. Under these conditions if $\alpha n$ of the inputs are excited, the probability that any majority organ is excited is

$$\alpha' = 3\alpha^2 - 2\alpha^3 = g(\alpha). \qquad (6)$$

For sufficiently large $n$ it is highly probable that approximately $\alpha n$ outputs will be excited. Figure 9 shows the graph of $g(\alpha)$. It will be seen that only the levels $g(\alpha)$ equal to 0 or 1 are stable, and so they represent the asymptotic behaviour of this net for any initial excitation $\alpha \neq 0.5$. This net is clearly error-controlling in the sense that any excitation corresponding to malfunctions of some majority organs will be 'restored' by iteration of the operation, to a final excitation corresponding to 0 or 1. For this reason von Neumann called such nets 'restoring organs'. The whole process is analogous to the use of certain circuits in actual automata for amplification of signals rather than for gating or detection.

Equation 6 is true on the assumption that the restoring organ is not itself subject to malfunctions. It can be shown that if malfunctions are assumed to occur with some positive probability $p_m$ in all elements of the redundant g-net, then there exists an optimum fiduciary level $\partial_{\text{opt}}$, so that for sufficiently large $n$, the probability

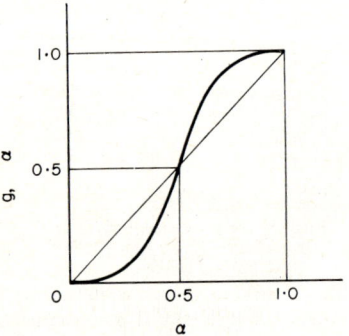

FIG. 9. *Behaviour of the restoring organ.*

of malfunction of the entire redundant g-net $P(n, p_m)$ can be made lower than any given fidelity level $\delta$. For example when $p_m < 1.07 \times 10^{-2}$, $\partial_{\text{opt}} = 7 \times 10^{-2}$,

$$P(n, p_m) = (1/\sqrt{(2\pi k)}) \cdot \exp.(-k^2/2) \qquad (7)$$

where $k = 0.062 \sqrt{n}$. Table 1 gives some numbers for this formula in case $p_m = 5 \times 10^{-3}$. It will be seen that a redundancy of $n$ greater than a thousand is required before $P(n, p_m) < p_m$. Such a design is therefore not very practicable, and indeed these results concerning net and element replication should be seen as no more than proofs of the existence theorem, that reliable automata may be constructed from nets of unreliable elements.

It should be noted that the elements comprising such automata are all majority organs, which are 'simple' in the sense that they compute functions of only three variables. (Certain other universal elements can be used, e.g. the 'Sheffer-stroke' organ—not $(x$ and $y)$—which is even simpler.) If more 'complex' elements are used that compute functions of an indefinitely large number of variables, a rather different existence theorem can be proved, where the levels of reliability required for the synthesis of reliable automata can be minimized (Winograd and Cowan 1963). The basis for this theorem is to be found in the theory of error-correcting codes (Petersen 1961). These codes are rules for transforming from one set of symbols to another. Thus if $x_1 x_2 \ldots x_k$ is a message to be transmitted through, say, a noisy communication channel, what is in fact transmitted is the symbol sequence $X_1 X_2 \ldots X_n$ where $X_\beta = e_\beta(x_1 x_2 \ldots x_k)$, $\beta = 1, 2, \ldots n; k < n$. The function $e_\beta$ is called an 'encoding function'. In general any $X_\beta$ is a function of many $x_\alpha, \alpha = 1, 2, \ldots, k$; and any $x_\alpha$ is thus represented in many of the $X_\beta$. It is this multiple representation of message digits which allows messages to be recovered from signal sequences distorted by channel noise. To do this a 'decoding function' operates at the receiver, according to the transformation $x_\alpha = d_\alpha(X'_1, X'_2, \ldots, X'_n)$, where $X'_\beta$ is a (possibly) distorted version of $X_\beta$. It will be seen that there are essentially two parameters associated with such a coding system, the ratio $n/k$ which is a measure of the redundancy in the code, and the complexity inherent in the coding functions, which we can relate to the range of variables over which the functions $e_\beta$ and $d_\alpha$ operate. The probability of error in decoding, $P_e$, averaged over a certain ensemble of codes that map long sequences of messages into long sequences of signals, has been related to the redundancy $n/k$, and to the channel noise, in a famous theorem (Shannon 1948). It is proved that noisy communication channels can be described by a certain number, the 'channel capacity' which specifies the minimum redundancy required, for any level of reliable communication over the channel. Thus if $C$ is the channel capacity and $R$ the 'rate' of transmission of information over the channel—the reciprocal of redundancy—then on the average for the specified ensemble of codes

$$P_e \doteqdot \exp_2(-n(C-R)). \qquad (8)$$

In principle then, arbitrarily small error-rates $(P_e \to 0)$ can be obtained provided $R < C$, i.e. $k < nC$, by using sufficiently long sequences (increasing both $k$ and $n$) so that the ratio $k/n$ remains constant. This does imply, however, that the complexity of the coding equipment increases with $k$ and $n$.

Consider now the modular net shown in Fig. 1. Equation 1 tells us that for fixed values of $p_m$ there is an upper bound on $P_A$, the probability of malfunction of the net. To make this bound small we proceed as follows. We consider $k$ copies of the design for $A$, rather than one copy, although the copies may operate on different sets of inputs or on different programs. We then replace each set of $k$ corresponding modules and associated connexions by an aggregate of $n$ modules with associated connexions via the following transformation. Let each set of $k$ modules compute the functions

$$f_{i\alpha}(x_i), (i = 1, 2, \ldots, N; \quad \alpha = 1, 2, \ldots, k)$$

where $x_i = x_1 x_2 \ldots x_s$ represents the set of input connexions to the $i$th module of A. Then the functions computed by the $n$ corresponding modules of the redundant automaton A′ are given by

$$f'_{i\beta} = e_\beta \begin{bmatrix} f_{i1}(d'_1(X'_{1n}), d'_1(X'_{2n}), \ldots, d'_1(X'_{sn})), \\ f_{i2}(d'_2(X'_{1n}), d'_2(X'_{2n}), \ldots, d'_2(X'_{sn})), \\ \ldots\ldots\ldots\ldots\ldots\ldots\ldots\ldots\ldots\ldots \\ f_{ik}(d'_k(X'_{1n}), d'_k(X'_{2n}), \ldots, d'_k(X'_{sn})) \end{bmatrix} \quad (9)$$

where the decoding function $d'_\alpha$ equals $d_\alpha$ if $X'$ is not an external input, and equals the identity function otherwise. Thus the $k$ modules that compute the functions $f_{i\alpha}(x_i)$ are replaced by $n$ modules that compute the functions $f'_{i\beta}(X'_{1n}, X'_{2n}, \ldots X'_{sn})$ where $X'_{sn}$ represents $n$ copies of the $s$th input to the corresponding $i$th module of A, i.e. a (possibly) noisy bundle. Figure 10 gives an

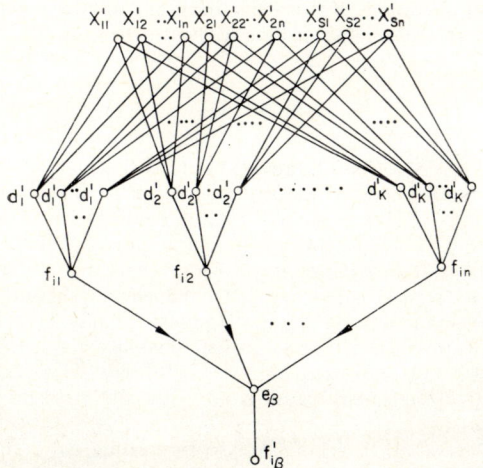

FIG. 10. *Structure of the function $f'_{i\beta}$.*

indication of what is meant. It will be seen that each of the functions $f'_{i\beta}$ operates on at most $ns$ input variables whereas each of the $f_{i\alpha}$ operates on only $s$ input variables. So each of the modules that execute the functions $f'_{i\beta}$ is at most $n$ times more complicated than those which execute the functions $f_{i\alpha}$. What is gained by this increased complexity is that each module of A′ *decodes all its inputs and so corrects errors in modules feeding directly into it, executes its requisite function, and then encodes this function for transmission to the next aggregate of modules.* Since an $(n, k)$ code is obviously embedded in A′ so that the structure of A′ is isomorphic to that of A, equations 1 and 8 can be combined to give a formula relating $P_{A'}$, the probability that A′ malfunctions, to $P_e$, the average error-probability, for sufficiently large $n$ and $k$, of $(n, k)$ codes. That is

$$P_{A'} \leq 1 - (1 - \exp_2(n(C-R)))^Q. \quad (10)$$

Equation 10 implies that the upper bound on $P_{A'}$ may be made to approach 0, for fixed $p_m$ and $Q$, by increasing $n$ so that the ratio of $n$ to $k$ is held constant, providing that the modules used in A′ have a 'computation capacity' greater than $k/n$. It can also be proved that if the numbers of errors of interconnexion is not too great, then they also can be controlled by the use of modular redundancy embodied in error-correcting codes. If each connexion of the automaton A′ is improper with probability $p_w$, and if $p_w \log(1/1-p_w) < (C-R)$, then with probability close to 1, A′ may still be made to function with arbitrarily high reliability. The quantity $(C-R)$ thus defines an ensemble of possible patterns of interconnexion over which A′ may function reliably. If $C-R$ is small this ensemble has few members, and interconnexions must be made with high precision. If $C-R$ is large, however, the corresponding ensemble has many members so that interconnexions may be made imprecisely, the resulting errors being controlled by the error-correcting codes embedded in A′.

This particular solution to the problem of synthesizing reliable automata from unreliable elements differs radically from von Neumann's. In his construction redundancy was introduced locally, each module being replaced by $n$ similar copies. This corresponds to the use of an $(n, 1)$ error-correcting code, with associated coding equipment constructed from the simplest modules. In the newer construction, redundancy is introduced non-locally over an aggregate of $k$ modules, using an $(n, k)$ error-correcting code, with the associated (complex) coding equipment contained in the $n$ complex modules that comprise the redundant aggregates. In a certain sense this construction represents the other extreme to von Neumann's solution, where complexity is minimized at the cost of redundancy to obtain small error-rates. In this case redundancy is minimized at the cost of complexity. However, it is a crucial requirement of the construction that modular malfunctions do not become more probable with increased modular complexity. This is not a requirement that can be met by present technological methods of module fabrication, and so neither of these designs represents a practical method for obtaining very high levels of reliable computation. For fixed levels, however, some application of the coding technique seems feasible. Indeed J. G. Tryon (1962) has utilized what is essentially a (4,1) code for single error correction.

Evidently suitable combinations of the two techniques of transient error control, multiplexing and coding, may lead to practical solutions to the reliability problem. Given modules of fixed complexity a certain amount of non-local coding may be possible, resulting in a lowered error-rate for certain aggregates of modules. If still lower error-rates are required, there will be some level at which further use of codes will require more complex modules than are available. Such modules would have to be constructed from the (less complex) ones available, in which case (since the number of the less complex modules required increases rapidly with $ns$), there will be a level where the outputs of the complex modules are statistically independent of the inputs ($C = 0$). This suggests a scheme in which coding is applied at the lowest elementary level of organization until complexity or channel capacity is used up, whence multiplexing is then applied *to the already coded aggregates*. It seems reasonable to expect that this method will result in efficient designs for controlling transient errors, in the sense that for given hardware and fidelity requirements, some kind of minimum redundancy design will result. W. H. Pierce (1964a, b; 1965) has in fact produced results consistent with these ideas, and many of the bounds in his work are to be expected of the composite designs.

*Control of stationary errors.* In case the errors in A are stationary, resulting from permanent failures of its elements, the techniques discussed in Section 2 do not provide complete answers to the reliability problem, which now becomes the problem of designing an automaton $A'$ whose expected lifetime to failure is arbitrarily longer than the expected lifetime to failure of any of its elements. (In certain cases the problem is that of designing integrated circuit configurations so as to increase the yield of usable circuits resulting from a given manufacturing process.)

An important technique recently discovered uses 'adaptive' majority organs (Pierce 1962). A basic defect in the multiplexing technique (and indeed in the error-correcting coding technique) is that as far as stationary errors are concerned, since some inputs to majority organs may be permanently in error, a consistently reliable minority may be outvoted by a consistently unreliable majority. Such a limitation may be overcome by the generalized majority organ shown in

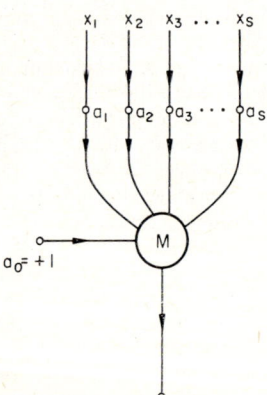

FIG. 11. *Generalized majority organ.*

Fig. 11. This module is a 'linear threshold element with variable weights'. It computes the quorum function:

$$f(x_i) = \text{sign} \left( a_0 + \sum_{i=1}^{s} a_i x_i \right) \quad (11)$$

all inputs $x_i$ taking the values $+1$ or $-1$. If input errors are statistically independent the vote-weights $a_i$ can be chosen so that the output is the digit most likely to be correct, on the assumption that what is required of the module is the reliable computation of the quorum function on $x_i$. If the error probability of the $i$th input is $p_{w,i}$ then the weights $a_i$ that give such an output are:

$$a_0 = \ln \left( \frac{a \text{ priori probability of } +1}{a \text{ priori probability of } -1} \right) \quad (12)$$

$$a_i = \ln \left( \frac{1 - p_{w,i}}{p_{w,i}} \right).$$

If any input is completely random then $p_{w,i} = 0.5$ and $a_i = 0$, otherwise $a_i$ increases monotonically as $p_{w,i}$ approaches 0 or 1. The required vote-weight settings may be obtained by comparing the inputs $x_i$ with the output $y_i = f(x_i)$ of the module, and counting the number of coincidences between the values. Thus in a cycle of $M$ operations, if $P_i$ is the number of coincidences and and $Q_i$ the number of disagreements, then the settings

$$a_i = \ln \left( \frac{P_i}{Q_i} \right) \quad (13)$$

will give equation 12. Provided suitable limits are placed on the possible values of the $a_i$, it can be shown that automatic setting of these weights controlled by feedback from the output can be used to optimize the vote-weights. If errors have the further property that they are catastrophic, i.e. that they tend to influence neighbouring elements in adverse ways, a modified technique can be used in which a threshold of unreliability $\gamma$ is set, so that if $P_i/Q_i$ ever exceeds $\gamma$, $a_i$ is set to zero. A practical way of implementing this is to couple the $\gamma$ system to fuses.

Several other techniques exist for dealing with stationary errors, which generally comprise a combination of fault-detection and location (a special case of fault-masking) with either a replacement mechanism, or a mechanism which switches redundant aggregates of unused components (or freshly serviced components) into the system, upon receipt of a signal from the fault-locating system (Lofgren 1962; Griesmer *et al.* 1962).

*Acknowledgements.* The work embodied in this review was performed with financial support from the U.S. Department of the Navy, Office of Naval Research, Physics Branch, under Contract No. N62558-4256, for which support the author is extremely grateful.

The author would also like to express his gratitude to Sir Willis Jackson, F.R.S., Head of the Electrical Engineering Department, Imperial College of Science and Technology, for the warm hospitality he has enjoyed as an Academic Visitor, while this review was written. Finally the author would like to thank Mrs. L. M. Talbot and Mrs. B. Broadhurst for the preparation of the manuscript and figures.

*See also:* Error correcting codes.

*Bibliography*

BARLOW R. E. and PROSCHAN F. (1965) *Mathematical Theory of Reliability*, New York: Wiley.

GRIESMER J. H., MILLER R. E. and ROTH J. P. (1962) *Redundancy Techniques in Computing Systems*, (Eds. R. H. WILCOX and W. C MANN) Washington, D. C.: Spartan Books.

LOFGREN L. (1962) *Biological Prototypes and Synthetic Systems*, (Eds. E. BERNARD and M. KARE) New York: Plenum Press.

MOORE E. F. and SHANNON C. E. (1956) *J. Franklin Inst.*, **262**, 191, 281.

PETERSEN W. W. (1961) *Error-Correcting Codes*, Cambridge, Mass.: M.I.T. Press.

PIERCE W. H. (1962) *Redundancy Techniques in Computing Systems*, (Eds. R. H. WILCOX and W. C. MANN) Washington, D. C.: Spartan Books.

PIERCE W. H. (1964a) *J. Franklin Inst.* **277**, 55.

PIERCE W. H. (1964b) *Information and Control*, **7**, 340.

PIERCE W. H. (1965) *Failure-Tolerant Computer Design*, New York: Academic Press.

SHANNON C. E. and WEAVER W. (1949) *Mathematical Theory of Communication*, Illinois: The University Press.

TRYON J. G. (1962) *Redundancy Techniques in Computing Systems* (Eds. R. H. WILCOX and W. C. MANN), Washington, D.C.: Spartan Books.

VON NEUMANN J. (1956) *Automata Studies* (Eds. C. E. SHANNON and J. MCCARTHY), Princeton: The University Press.

WINOGRAD S. and COWAN J. D. (1963) *Reliable Computation in the Presence of Noise*, Cambridge, Mass.: M.I.T. Press.

J. D. COWAN

# S

**SCIENTIFIC DOCUMENTATION.** The first scientific journal began publication in 1665 and the first journal devoted exclusively to abstracts appeared in 1714. Now, it is credibly estimated that about thirty-five thousand scientific and technical journals are currently published in the world, carrying between them one to two million papers a year of various worth, and some two to three thousand abstracts journals producing about eight million abstracts a year. Other carriers of scientific information include a large and expanding report literature, reviews, conference proceedings and symposia, theses, patents, textbooks and data compilations of various sorts. There is evidence that the primary literature is increasing exponentially, doubling in from ten to fifteen years.

It is clearly no longer possible for a scientist to scan every journal which may carry material relevant to his interests: without the use of retrieval devices, ranging in sophistication from a simple author index to a multiple access computer, it is also impossible to search the existing body of literature for information on a specific topic. It is convenient therefore to consider the handling of scientific information in two parts, the first including the origination and dissemination of information via primary and secondary publications, and the second the storage and retrieval of information as the need for it arises, whether the need be for a specific fact, a description of a process or device, or a broad survey of a particular topic.

Originally the working scientist would cover his day-to-day needs for current awareness information by subscribing to the few journals which he felt he needed to see on a regular basis. Nowadays the more common practice is for the scientist to instruct his library to acquire and circulate to him such journals as he feels he needs to see, and such others as they may acquire and judge worthy of his attention. Since this approach nowadays is liable to flood the scientist with an embarassingly large number of titles attempts have been made to relieve him of the necessity of scanning this large number of journals. This is often done by the publication, either by a commercial organization, or a learned society, or on a smaller scale by the scientist's librarian, of lists of titles of papers to be found in selected current journals. An example is *Current Contents to Space, Electronic and Physical Sciences* (Philadelphia: Institute for Scientific Information) which is simply a collection of photocopies of the contents pages of about six hundred research journals. About 125,000 articles are listed yearly and there is only a brief time lag between the publication of the journal and its inclusion in *Current Contents*. A 'tear-sheet' service which will supply on request the original articles torn from the journals is also offered to subscribers. Another example is *Current Papers in Physics* a bi-monthly publication consisting of lists of titles of papers in a large number (over 800) of physics journals, classified by the main subject headings used in *Physics Abstracts*. Each item listed in this service is subsequently abstracted in *Physics Abstracts*.

Another approach to the dissemination of information aims to provide the individual scientist with only those items which appear to be of potential interest to him. The IBM Corporation have done much pioneering work in this direction, mainly for scientists within their own organization. Basically their selective dissemination of information (*SDI*) works as follows: a 'personal profile' is made up of the 'Key-words' that can be used to describe the scientist's interests. (As an example, one man's interests were described by the following words: arithmetic, coding, compilers, computers, computing, data processing, input, language, mathematics, multi-programming, output, processing, programming, programs routines, sequence, sortings, systems, tapes.) Each scientist's profile is punched on cards and recorded on magnetic tape. As documents are received by the information service, they are indexed with a list of keywords describing the subject matter on the document. These document keywords are also stored on magnetic tape. Batches of document keywords are then compared with the personal profiles of the scientists by a computer, and where a sufficient degree of matching is noticed, a message is printed, giving details and an abstract of the document, and addressed to the scientist whose profile suggests he is likely to be interested. This notification is printed on a punched card and the person receiving it can indicate by pushing out prescored holes in the card whether he has already seen the document or not, and would or would not like to. These feed-back cards are then returned to the computer, which can analyse the record to determine what proportion of really relevant material the user is receiving. It is then possible to adjust the individual scientist's profile, so that he receives more material or less material, by adjusting either the number of matches required in comparing document key-words with his profile, or by modifying his profile. Such a system depends for its success largely on the skill with which the individual personal profiles are composed and keywords allocated to the documents, and the degree to which the users' inevitably changing interests can be catered for. A badly constructed profile can either overwhelm the scientist with minimally useful documents, or at the other extreme starve him of information of which he should be aware. Although an SDI system of this type is in a sense only a formalisation of the manner in which many librarians have long been accustomed to operate, the servicing of a large number of scientific users, or the handling by this means of a large intake of documents, is only made feasible by the use of computers; the labour involved in manual matching of profiles would be so great as to be prohibitive.

Abstracts journals are used for both current awareness and retrospective searching. However, their increasing bulk renders them yearly less useful as current awareness devices. As an example, *Physics Abstracts* in 1961 published 20,287 abstracts of items selected from 405 journals, and by 1965 annual output had increased to 36,000 abstracts from journals.

In using abstracts for retrospective searching, there are also increasing difficulties. Indexing is an intellectual process and the greater the degree of specialization in a scientific discipline, the greater the indexing effort required to ensure adequate retrieval of the material indexed. Indexing is a time-consuming process, and the adequate indexing of increasing amounts of material means either the employment of an uneconomic number of indexers (who may not always be readily available) or a greater time lag between publication of the original article and its abstraction.

A tendency is becoming evident towards the operation of an abstracting or indexing service as part of an integrated service offering a Current Awareness facility, a formal abstracting publication and the facility for computerized searches on specific topics. One of the most ambitious examples of this type of organic service in scientific documentation is the National Library of Medicine's MEDLARS (Medical literature analysis and retrieval system). Before the introduction of this system much time and effort was spent on compiling the almost comprehensive periodical index, *Index Medicus* (which does not carry abstracts, but only classified titles), listing around 146,000 items a year. The Index is now recorded on magnetic tape using the same amount of input effort but giving the additional facilities of being able to produce recurring bibliographies in special fields of medicine, and of performing 'one-off' demand searches on questions of considerable complexity. The printing of *Index Medicus* is done on a specially developed output device, Graphic Arts Composing Equipment (GRACE), a device which takes the information from the tapes and composes the pages of *Index Medicus* on film which is then sent to the printer for plate-making, printing and binding. Copies of the MEDLARS tapes are being made available to several centres throughout the world, enabling local searches of the medical literature to be made. In Britain the University of Newcastle upon Tyne is being operated for an experimental period, under Government grant, as a MEDLARS 'station', in co-operation with the National Lending Library.

*Chemical Abstracts* is also part of a system which produces a current awareness tool, *Chemical Titles*, a formal abstracts service with various types of index, and on-request searches by computer of the machine-stored indexes. Complete runs of *Chemical Abstracts* are now also available on microfilm.

Microfilm, which has been used for many years in libraries where space is at a premium, is becoming an increasingly important medium for the storage and dissemination of information. (Microfilm has been objected to on grounds of difficulty of reading and the expense and difficulty of producing life-size hard copy: however, a number of *viewers* now available (e.g. Lodestar and Filmac) produce hard copy at the touch of a button at economic rates.) All United States government research reports are now produced on microfiche—a sheet of film, $6'' \times 4''$, containing the negative images of up to 40 pages of text. This documentary form is cheap to produce and mail. Microfilm is also an important medium in some of the equipment which has been developed for information retrieval systems. In the File-Search system, sold by FMA Incorporated, documents are recorded on 35 mm film, up to 6400 pages being stored in one magazine. Indexing words indicating the content of the document are also recorded along the edge of the film, coded in a series of square 'bits', which can be scanned by the retrieval unit of the system by photoelectric sensing, at a rate of one minute per magazine. The search is initiated by punching in a card the codes corresponding to the terms of the search request. This card is then inserted into the scanning device which searches the film until the requisite codes are found, halts the film transport and produces the document as an image on a screen, a hard copy or a one-to-one film copy. One major advantage of a retrieval system based on microfilm is that the result of a search produces facsimile copies of the documents, and not a list of numbers or titles which necessitates delay while the library finds the original.

Many of the more recent developments in scientific documentation have their origin in the United States where the value of scientific information seems to be more clearly recognized and the difficulties posed by its expansion to be felt more acutely than in some other countries. In the Report of the President's Science Advisory Committee, 'Science, government and information' (better known as the 'Weinberg Report'), the establishment of specialized information centres was said to be 'a major key in the rationalisation of the transmission and handling of scientific information'. A specialized information centre is defined as an organization which 'makes it its business to know everything that is being published in a special field ... collates and reviews the data, and provides its subscribers with regularly issued compilations, critical reviews, specialized bibliographies and other such tools'. The operations of such centres may be illustrated by briefly describing one such which has been functioning in the United States since 1961. AGED (Advisory Group on Electron Devices) is the main information centre for government work in the electronics field. It advises the Department of Defence on research and development in electronics and its output is available to government agencies and government contractors. Its input includes all forms of reports —government laboratory, contract, technical intelligence and so on—periodicals and proceedings, conference reports and symposia, reports of visits to contractors' plants, catalogues and other trade literature. 3000 reports are added annually to an existing holding of about 15,000. Information is supplied in response to specific questions, and is also actively disseminated to companies working in the field. Among the publications issued are annual state-of-the-art reports, special device lists, project books abstracting all terminated and current AGED projects (available to government agencies only), project briefs summarizing projects and contract awards, monthly status reports on projects dealing with advanced electron device technology, and long-range programme recommendations. Cost of the information function alone is estimated at only 0·2 per cent of the value of research and development work covered. Depending on how a specialized information centre is defined, there are between 200 and 1000 currently operating in the United States. Their establishment and operation is naturally facilitated by the great part played by the Federal Government in the sponsoring, control and financing of research.

The greater availability of computers in the United States has had considerable influence on development of new documentation techniques. An early application of computers was the development of the Keyword-in-Context (KWIC) index, which can be produced with a minimum of human effort, and which is based on the use of significant words within the titles of papers as indexing keywords. It is far more effective as a retrieval device than the crudeness of its compilation would suggest, and there are indications that the continued use of titles for providing indexing terms is affecting the producers of scientific information, in that titles of published papers are becoming more meaningful.

Another example of the application of computers to documentation is a production by the Institute for Scientific Information of the citation index. A citation index is essentially a list of journal articles and their accompanying citations to the literature, the citations being distributed and arranged alphabetically by the cited author, so that it is possible to find where any given reference has been cited in the collection of papers covered by the index. This is similar to the well-known method of taking a known relevant paper and looking up its references, except that the citation index allows the user to move forward in time as well as backwards. In 1965 the *Science Citation Index* covered the entire contents of 1147 journal titles, a total of 235,801 papers in all fields of science. 60,492 patents were also covered. Using this index it is possible to take any one of more than two million papers and find out the author, title and reference of any paper in the journals covered, which cited it in 1965. The *Science Citation Index* is published quarterly, with annual cumulations. Its publication is a speedy operation, the annual cumulation appearing usually in March or April of the following year. Coupled with the index is a form of SDI, known as the Automatic Subject Citation Alert (ASCA). To use this service a scientist selects a number of papers on the subject in which he is interested, and notifies the Institute for Scientific Information of his choices. Thereafter he is notified weekly, by computer print-out, whenever and where in the journals covered by the service any of his selected papers are cited. In addition to specialized papers, he may also use as 'profile items' an author's name, a USA patent specification number, or even a particular organization, in the publication of whose staff members he may be interested. Such a service, it is obvious, would be entirely impracticable by any means other than computer processing.

Perhaps the most interesting investigation on the use of computers in documentation, since it gives us a glimpse into future possibilities, is that being done by the Technical Information Project under the direction of Dr. M. M. Kessler at the Massachusetts Institute of Technology. A 'library' of the authors, titles, and bibliographies of 50,000 papers from 24 physics journals is stored in the computer of the Time Sharing System provided by the MAC project at MIT. The system consists of an IBM 7094 computer at a remote location, with teletype consoles available in the library, and at 96 other locations in MIT. The consoles are connected to the computer by telephone lines. The library information and programs are stored on magnetic disks and are available at all times. The user types his requests on the teletype console and the results of the search are transmitted back to him at his remote station in a matter of a few seconds. A maximum of thirty users may consult the system simultaneously. A set of programs are available which allow the user to 'browse' through the journals, looking for particular authors, or keywords in titles. Other programs permit citation tracing and bibliographic coupling (i.e. finding groups of papers having a number of citations in common). Much of the appeal of this prototype system is in the direct interaction between the user and his literature without the intervention of documentary middle-men.

One of the greatest problems in documentation, although not always realized, is the question of the actual availability of documents. There are many systems for the provision of references which may be relevant to the users' needs, but a reference is only the indication of the existence of a document and is not the document itself. It is clearly uneconomic for any library to hold all published material in case it may at some future time be requested to supply a given document. In Britain this problem is answered by the existence of the National Lending Library. The NLL, which began operation in 1961, is a vast loan collection of scientific journals and selected scientific books. It is currently acquiring 22,000 journal titles, and has 4000 more on order. Its acquisition policy is controlled simply on the basis that should a given title be requested and be found not already to be in stock it will be ordered, and the acquisition of that title is then continued until the demise of the journal. It also acquires all openly available United States Government research reports, and reports of the United Kingdom Atomic Energy Authority. Through its numerous agents throughout the country, it receives requests for specified items and issues the requested material on postal loan to the demanders. It is also responsible for a number of cover-to-cover translations of Soviet journals. Its importance to the British scientific community may be appreciated from the fact that in 1965 it made 286,693 postal loans.

Much of the foregoing may suggest that the application, of modern technological developments to the problems of scientific documentation has solved or is solving many of these problems. It must be appreciated that this is not an accurate picture. There is a great deal of evidence to support the view that many working scientists do not appreciate the importance of literature, or realize the quantity of information which is available to them, and of those who do realize its importance a large number are not equipped by their training fully to exploit the information available to them. It is also true that many working scientists do not enjoy adequate information services or library facilities. Although the picture, happily, is changing a great many organizations both academic and industrial still do not realize the importance of a dynamic information acquiring and dissemination service to their research and development effort.

*See also:* Information storage and retrieval.

*Bibliography*

ADAMS S. (1965) *MEDLARS: performance, problems, possibilities*, Bulletin of the Medical Library Association, **53**, 139.
COBLANS H. (1966) *Use of mechanised methods in documentation work*, London: Aslib.
KESSLER M. M. (1965) *The M.I.T. Technical Information Project*, Physics Today, **18**, 28, March.
LUHN H. P. (1961) *Selective dissemination of new scientific information with the aid of electronic processing equipment*, American Documentation, **12**, 131.
MARTYN J. (1965) *An examination of citation indexes*, Aslib Proceedings, **17**, 184, June.
PRICE D. J. DE S. (1963) *Little Science, Big Science*, New York.
U.S. President's Science Advisory Committee (1963) *Science, Government and information: the responsibilities of the technical community and the Government in the transfer of information*, Washington. (Report of the Panel on Science Information. Chairman ALVIN M. WEINBERG.)

H. EAST and J. MARTYN

**SEMANTICS: INTRODUCTION.** Semantics, as a branch of general linguistics, investigates *meaning* or *signification* in languages. The term 'semantics', since its invention in 1900 as a translation of M. Bréal's 'la sémantique', has been used in various fields on the borders of linguistics; for example, in linguistic philosophy and psycholinguistics. It has also received widely different interpretations within linguistics. J. R. Firth (1957), for whom the whole task of linguistic description was to make 'statements of meaning', appeared to equate semantics with the entire field of linguistic study. S. Ullmann (1959, 1962), in two well-known textbooks of semantics, recognizes no clear division between semantics and stylistics, including in the former the emotive, imitative, and figurative uses of language which come to the fore in the study of literature. A narrower and more clear-cut conception of semantics limits its scope to the field of what is called (according to the philosophical standpoint) '*denotative*', '*cognitive*', or '*conceptual*' meaning, i.e. the study of the significatory property of language, and the interrelations of words, sentences, etc. on the basis of this property. Semantics thus narrowly understood is the subject of this article. It includes the study of meaning relations such as synonymy and paraphrase, logical inclusion and exclusion (e.g. the relation of *dog* to *animal* and *dog* to *human* respectively); also the explication of logical relations between sentences, of analycity and contradiction, semantic inacceptability (e.g. the 'nonsensical' character of 'Is that square round?'), and, marginally, the explanation of how utterances which are literally nonsensical (e.g. 'Life's but a walking shadow') nevertheless receive an interpretation by metaphorical transference, etc. Of course, any given semantic theory may consider only a selection of these within its goals.

*History.* It is convenient to trace the history of semantics within the present century in terms of three philosophical trends, which we may name *mentalism* (or conceptualism), *contextualism, and formalism.* These are placed in order of their historical ascendancy, although there is much chronological overlap. De Saussure, who first advocated a synchronic, structural approach to semantics (in *Cours de Linguistique Générale* published posthumously in 1916), may be considered the dominant representative of the first trend. His notion of 'valeur', whereby a term is held to derive its meaning from its place relative to other terms in the language, prepared the way for important European developments which earned the title 'structural semantics'. By 'structural semantics' is understood the study of interrelations of meaning based on the assumption that differences of meaning are discrete, and are dependent on relative contrasts within the language system. Most successful studies on this pattern (notably by the German exponents of the 'semantic field' theory and the Danish glossematicians), were in limited areas of meaning (kinship, colours, military ranks, etc.) which lend themselves to analysis in terms of elementary notions of semantic contrast.

Saussurian structural semantics is at least tacitly *mentalistic*, since what it sets out to study is the relationships between the 'concepts' or mental entities expressed by words in a given language. The case against such an approach was put by J. R. Firth in 1930 as follows: 'If we regard language as 'expressive' or 'communicative' we imply that it is an instrument of inner mental states. And as we know so little of inner mental states, even by the most careful introspection, the language problem becomes more mysterious the more we try to explain it by referring it to inner mental happenings which are not observable. By regarding words as acts, events, habits, we limit our inquiry to what is objective in the group life of our fellows.' Firth's notion of *context of situation*, and L. Bloomfield's (1933) views on meaning despite profound differences, can be brought together as representing the *contextualist* approach to semantics. Bloomfield defined the meaning of a linguistic form as 'the situation in which the speaker utters it and the response which it calls forth in the hearer'. Since no object of human cognition can be excluded from the situations which prompt people to utter speech, he pessimistically concluded that success in semantics presupposes an accurate scientific description of everything in the universe. Firth's more optimistic proposal for semantic analysis through the study of items within contexts on various levels was founded on the hope that the linguist's description of the universe can be limited to those factors which relevantly correlate with linguistic behaviour.

Contextualism goes hand in hand with a relativistic approach to the semantic comparison of languages. If a speaker learns the use of a word by its manipulation in actual situations, then meanings in different languages must be bound to cultural and physical environment. This view, expounded by the anthropologist B. Malinowski in Britain (Ogden and Richards 1923), was re-expressed in America in the writings of B. L. Whorf (Carroll 1956), who argued the incomparability of the *Weltbild* of different languages more on the grounds of their radical differences in grammatical or lexical structure. Whereas it is easy, from a conceptualist point of view, to assume certain aspects of meaning (e.g. logical operations such as negation and quantification) to be universal properties of the human mind, a contextualist will assume disparity until shown otherwise.

As forms of language are not generally absolutely predictable from their context, nor their context from them, contextualism favours a probabilistic as opposed to deterministic method of analysis. It leads to a disregard for the concerns of structural semantics—discrete contrasts of meaning—and a concentration on the formal distribution of linguistic forms within utterances and the relations of utterances (discourses) to their 'socio-physical setting'. Synonymy, if identified with equivalence of formal distribution, becomes an unusable concept: even apparent synonyms like *oculist* and *eye-doctor* are not individually substitutable for one another in a sentence like 'Oculist is another word for eye-doctor'. Antonymy and other semantic relationships are similarly ignored as unreal or beyond the scope of scientific description. 'Contextualist semantics' might indeed be regarded as a contradiction in terms, as the underlying postulate of semantics, that language is a significatory system, appears irretrievably mentalistic.

*Formalism* in semantics, as in general linguistics as a whole, is the position of those who seek to explain a person's mastery of his native language in terms of abstract, mechanically applied, quasi-mathematical rules or formulae. It might be regarded as a return to mentalism, except that its rules and symbols need not entail the assertion of corresponding psychological states or entities, such as 'concepts'. Moreover, a formalist theory of semantics, although concerned with linguistic ability rather than actual performance, may be held falsifiable by behavioural tests (for example, paraphrase tests, in which subjects are invited to produce, or judge, sentences said to 'express the same thing in different words').

Formalist semantics relies, at least implicitly, upon the philosophical distinction between *meaning* and *reference* (or, with slightly different implications, between *intension* and *extension*). Thus 'my favourite film-star' and 'the woman who played Cleopatra' may, in a given case, refer to the same person. The linguist, however, will not be interested in this connexion: he will be interested in showing how, for example, (a) 'the film-star I like best' is synonymous with (b) 'my favourite film-star'. This connexion in itself will entail certain facts about reference and truth value: for instance, that (a) will always have the same reference as (b), provided the circumstances of their utterance are the same; and that any true statement containing (a) will remain true if (b) is substituted for (a).

Since recent progress and renewed interest in semantics have been in the spirit of formalism, the remainder of this account will be written from a formalist viewpoint.

*Sentence meaning and word meaning.* The study of meaning has in the past pursued two largely independent courses, concentrating on either the sentence or the word as the unit of semantic statement. The study of sentence meaning, i.e. of the logical structure and affinities of sentences, has until very recently been something that linguistics has been content to leave to philosophy. Philosophy, through the development of symbolic logic, has made rapid advances in this field since 1900. The 'formal logic' which has evolved, however, deviates from the 'natural logic' of natural languages, since it has been expressly devised to overcome what logicians consider the disadvantages of natural languages as logical systems. (The use of the term 'semantics' in philosophy is at variance with its use in linguistics, being in contrast to 'syntax', which corresponds roughly to 'logical meaning' in this present context, and may therefore be *included* in semantics in the linguist's sense.)

Within linguistics, in contrast, semantic analysis has been traditionally concerned with word meanings ('word' is used somewhat inaccurately here, since in formal linguistic accounts it is usually replaced by either 'morpheme' or 'lexeme'). In European structural semantics, in fact, it has often been assumed that semantics consists solely in studying the 'structure of the vocabulary' of a language.

The descriptive study of word meanings has reached a sophisticated pitch in the anthropologically inspired *componential analysis* of kinship terms, colour terms, etc. by F. G. Lounsbury (1962), W. H. Goodenough

(1956), H. C. Conklin and others in the U.S.A. Componential analysis may be characterized as the formalistic equivalent of 'structural semantics' in the European tradition. It is founded on the notions of semantic likeness and contrast, as intuitively revealed in proportions such as this:

|    | man   | is to *woman* |
|----|-------|---------------|
| as | ram   | is to *ewe*   |
| as | drake | is to *duck*. |

From this tabulation it is possible to abstract a dimension of meaning, that of sex, and to distinguish on that dimension the contrastive components 'male' and 'female'. It is convenient to represent the dimension by a capital letter—S = 'sex'—and the components by different subscripts—$S_1$ = 'male', $S_2$ = 'female'. As an example of componential analysis, we might analyse the most important kinship terms of English (a far easier task than Lounsbury's work on primitive kinship systems) in terms of the three dimensions of generation, collaterality, and sex:

| Generation | | Collaterality | Sex |
|---|---|---|---|
| $G_{+2}$ | 2nd ascending generation | $C_0$ linear kin | $S_1$ male |
| $G_{+1}$ | 1st ascending generation | $C_1$ collateral kin (1st degree) | $S_2$ female |
| $G_0$ | same generation | $C_2$ collateral kin (beyond 1st degree) | |
| $G_{-1}$ | 1st descending generation | | |
| $G_{-2}$ | 2nd descending generation | | |

It is obvious that the sex distinction runs through most of the basic kinship terminology of English: *uncle/aunt, brother/sister*, etc. We shall be content, therefore, to specify formulae illustrating the other two dimensions:

$G_{+2}$, $C_0$ *grandparent*
$G_{+1}$, $C_0$ *parent*
$G_{-1}$, $C_0$ *child*
$G_{-2}$, $C_0$ *grandchild*
$G_{+2}$, $C_1$ *gt.-aunt/-uncle*
$G_{+1}$, $C_1$ *aunt/uncle*
$G_0$, $C_1$ *brother/sister*
$G_{-1}$, $C_1$ *nephew/niece*
$G_{-2}$, $C_1$ *gt.-nephew/-niece*
$C_2$ *cousin*

Whether this is an adequate analysis, or the best possible analysis, is not at issue: it is presented simply as a specimen. Many sophistications of componential analysis are possible; at present, we may note that in its elementary form it provides a characterization of basic meaning relations. *Antonymy* is the relation between components in a dual opposition, as between 'male' $S_1$ and 'female' $S_2$. *Logical inclusion* is the relation of the meaning of one term $x$ to that of another $y$ where the componential definition of $y$ contains all the components in that of $x$. $G_{+1}$, $C_0$ *parent*, for example, logically includes $G_{+1}$, $C_0$, $S$ *father*. *Logical exclusion*, on the other hand, obtains between meanings which contrast with respect to at least one dimension: in fact between any pair of terms taken from the above table. *Synonymy* and *polysemy* (multiple meaning) are not meaning relations, but rather conditions obtaining between form and meaning: the former is the case where two or more forms have the 'same meaning' (i.e. share the same componential definition), and the latter the case where two or more meanings share the same form. It is obvious, for example, that *child* is not solely a kinship term, and that it needs a second definition at least, to describe the sense in which it contrasts with *adult*.

That the description of lexical meanings and sentence meanings are closely connected scarcely needs exemplification. We are able, for instance, to predict semantic relations between sentences on the basis of relationships between lexical meanings within them. For the following three statements about kinship it is specified that $y_1$ logically *includes* $y_2$, and logically *excludes* $y_3$:

A. $p$ is a $y_1$ of $q$  EXAMPLE: $p$ is a grandchild of $q$
B. $p$ is a $y_2$ of $q$  EXAMPLE: $p$ is a grandson of $q$
C. $p$ is a $y_3$ of $q$  EXAMPLE: $p$ is an aunt of $q$

Given that $p$ and $q$ are constants, it will always be the case that if B. is true, A. is also true; and that if A. or B. is true, C. is false.

Only very recently have linguists turned seriously to the problem of '*combinatorial semantics*', i.e. of how to derive the meaning of a sentence from the meanings of the words or morphemes of which it is composed. The naïvest theory of combinatorial semantics holds that the meaning of a sentence is simply the sum of the meanings of its component parts. This is inadequate not only because the meanings of some words (logical words such as *not*) must be stated in the form of rules applicable to whole sentences, but because in many cases sentences made up of the same constituents do not have the same meaning: 'My wife wants a new dog'; 'My new wife wants a dog'; 'My new dog wants a wife'; etc. Further, sentences which contrast in word meaning may be synonymous: 'The pencil is in this box' and 'This box contains the pencil'. The first two of these objections may be met by certain modifications or additions to the 'whole-is-sum-of-parts' theory just mentioned: for example, by saying that differences in grammatical structure in themselves imply differences of meaning. The third objection, however, is more troublesome. Somehow, combinatorial semantics has to indicate the difference between the overt, grammatical structure of a sentence, and its covert, logical structure, so that two sentences of diverse grammatical structure and lexical content can be shown to have the same meaning. In the given example, it has to show that 'is in' and 'contains' are converse relations, which we might represent $\vec{R}$, $\overleftarrow{R}$, such that 'The pencil is in this box' and 'This box contains the pencil', written $x \vec{R} y$ and $y \overleftarrow{R} x$

respectively, are shown to have the same logical structure.

The contrast between 'grammatical structure' and 'logical structure' drawn here may be explained in different ways. Within certain general linguistic theories, it is possible to treat many distinctions between overt ('grammatical') and underlying ('logical') relationships (e.g. between the 'real' and 'logical' subjects of a passive sentence) as questions of grammar alone. Less amenable to grammatical handling are those cases (*x contains y/y is in x; x owns y/y belongs to x; x is y's parent/y is x's child*, etc.) in which logical equivalence is signalled lexically. At least in these cases, it seems necessary to entertain a notion of logical structure beyond the 'deepest' of grammatical analyses. Moreover, the relationship of elements, on the logical or semantic level of structure, is independent of the superficial ordering of grammatical elements: this fact is conveyed in the arrow notation ($x \vec{R} y, y \overleftarrow{R} x$) used above to represent converses.

*The delimitation of semantics.* The relation of semantics to grammar, a topic which has been much discussed recently, can be approached not only from the structural viewpoint, but from that of units and of classes. Although it has been found necessary to distinguish between grammatical and semantic structure above, a certain dependence of semantics upon grammar has been assumed, in that meaning has been discussed with reference to grammatical units: morpheme, lexeme, word, sentence. A more radical separation of the levels of grammar and semantics is entailed if semantic statements are made in terms of units set up specifically for that purpose, e.g. 'component' or 'sememe', 'statement' or 'proposition'. The latter approach has three advantages over the former: (a) the two types of semantic analysis we have discussed, componential analysis and logical analysis, cannot be restricted to the particular grammatical units of word and sentence respectively. Beyond the scope of componential analysis are words defined by equation with an expression having implications of logical structure, or containing logical elements like *not*: 'phlatelist' = 'person who collects stamps'; 'blind' = 'who/which cannot see'; etc. Conversely, componential analysis often applies to larger units than the word: the relationship between *male frog* and *female frog* is exactly parallel to that between *man* and *woman, duck* and *drake*, etc. (b) In many cases a word or a morpheme has no meaning except as part of a larger expression. Idioms such as *green fingers* defy rules of combinatorial semantics, for their meanings cannot be deduced from the meanings of their parts. (c) Stretches of language convenient for semantic statement sometimes fail to coincide with any grammatically isolable unit. Above we noticed a semantic relationship between the verb *contain* and the grammatically arbitrary sequence *is in*. Idioms often clash with grammatical segmentation (*not cricket, put up with*, etc.) and may even be grammatically discontinuous (*let* [somebody] *down; give* [somebody] *short shrift*, etc.).

In comparing grammatical and semantic features of classification (i.e. the relation between components of meaning and grammatical classes such as 'singular'/'plural'; 'masculine'/'feminine'), attention tends to fall on the overlaps between these two fields of study, rather than on their divergences. Complete overlap of classification raises the problem of whether a feature should be identified in grammar, in semantics, or in both. This question arises with many classes set up to account for selection restrictions: for example, classes of human, non-human, animate, non-animate, concrete and abstract nouns, and corresponding classes of verbs which are capable of occurring in a 'Subject-Verb' or 'Verb-Object' relationship with these nouns (Chomsky 1965). Selection restrictions are usually considered part of grammar, being akin to grammatical concord and agreement rules, and yet the effect of disregarding them is often felt to be semantic:

*Care was written on his face
*And finally John happened.
*The hills danced.

The oddness of these sentences stems from a 'wrong' selection of verb after an abstract, a personal, and an inanimate noun respectively. The selection entails, however, a semantic incompatibility: the sentences are literally nonsensical, and are interpretable only figuratively, through exercise of the imagination. The difficulty of drawing a line between grammar and semantics seems to become more evident as work on both progresses. One hopes that its solution will ultimately lie in the demonstration that a particular fact of language is more economically accounted for in grammar than in semantics, or vice versa.

The delimitation of semantics in other directions is also vague. The boundary between denotative meaning and connotative or stylistic meaning is notoriously uncertain in some cases. How far, for example, can cognitive meaning go in the explication of terms like *thug, quack,* or *blackguard?* How far are these words merely expressions of a speaker's emotions or attitudes? Likewise the distinction between meaning and reference alluded to earlier, although theoretically essential to semantic study, is difficult to apply in individual cases. Should, for instance, the oddity of the sentence 'Elephants have eighty legs' be considered a matter of language (i.e. of semantics) or a matter of zoological fact? These indeterminacies do not, however, effect the practicability of research in semantics; indeed, it is only through further research that the issues involved in delimitation can be understood, and criteria devised for determining the limits of semantic study.

*See also:* Relations between languages: semantic change.

*Bibliography*

BLOOMFIELD L. (1933) *Language*, New York: Holt, Rinehart and Winston.
CARROLL J. B. (Ed.) (1956) *Language, Thought and Real*

*ity: Selected Writings of Benjamin Lee Whorf*, Cambridge, Mass.

CHOMSKY N. (1965) *Aspects of the Theory of Syntax*, Cambridge, Mass.

FIRTH J. R. (1935) *The Technique of Semantics*, Trans. Philol. Soc., reprinted in *Papers in Linguistics 1934–1951*, Oxford (1957).

FIRTH J. R. (1964) *Speech*, in *The Tongues of Men and Speech*, Oxford.

GOODENOUGH W. (1956) *Componential analysis and the study of meaning*, Language, **32**, 195.

KATZ J. J. and FODOR J. A. (1963) *The structure of a semantic theory*, Language, **39**, 170.

LOUNSBURY F. G. (1964) *The structural analysis of kinship semantics*, in *Proc. 9th Intern. Congr. Ling.* (Ed. H. G. Lunt), 1073, The Hague.

LYONS J. (1963) *Structural Semantics*, Publ. Philol. Soc., **20**, Oxford.

OGDEN C. K. and RICHARDS I. A. (1923) *The Meaning of Meaning*, London.

ULLMAN S (1959) (2nd Edn) *The Principles of Semantics*, Glasgow.–Oxford; (1962) *Semantics: an Introduction to the Science of Meaning*, Oxford.

WEINREICH U. (1963) *On the semantic structure of language*, in *Universals of Language* (Ed. J. H. Greenberg), 114, Cambridge, Mass.

WEINREICH U. (1966) *Explorations in semantic theory*, in *Current Trends in Linguistics*, (Ed. T. A. Sebeok), 3, Bloomington, Indiana.

G. N. LEECH

## SEMANTICS: CONTEXT AND COLLOCATION.

In ordinary parlance, the term '*context*' is applied primarily to the written language, the context of a word being the phrase or sentence in which it occurs, that of a phrase, a passage of indeterminate length immediately preceding and following it. The term is also applied to the spoken language, although in most cases, the reference is to a speech which has also been recorded in writing. The context as a linguistic 'environment' cannot, however, be dissociated entirely from a wider, more inclusive 'context': the relation of the utterance to a particular situation in a particular culture. This wider view of context underlies the use of such expressions as 'in the context of the discussions', 'the cultural context', and so forth.

It is difficult to generalize about the use of the term by linguists because of the differences in terminology and approach between different schools. Most scholars, while doubtless more aware than laymen of the existence of different types of context, do not explicitly distinguish between them, and still apply the word both to immediate linguistic environments and to wider environments. Other linguists, on the other hand, use the term in a specialized sense which can be fully appreciated only within the framework of their particular theories of linguistic analysis. The following discussion of the British school's use of the terms 'collocation' and 'context (of situation)' will therefore not attempt to go into the finer points made by individual members of the school.

The concept of '*collocation*' was first introduced into linguistics by the late J. R. Firth. For the latter, the 'collocation' of words were the *lexical* environments in which they occurred, the '...word accompaniment, the other word-material in which they are most commonly or most characteristically embedded'. 'Collocation' deals with patterns of word-association at the formal level, but not in terms of the grammatical categories to which the words belong (studied at a different level of analysis), nor in terms of the 'wider context' in which they are used (again handled at a different level of analysis, that of 'context of situation' – *vide infra*). To quote an example given by Firth, *dark* frequently '*collocates*' with *night*, and vice versa. This obviously does not mean that collocations such as *bright night* cannot occur, but because of its lesser frequency of occurrence, the latter combination stands out more in an utterance than the more typical one. The use of these combinations is obviously related to referential and situational factors, but these relations are not part of the collocation as such, although reference to the 'context of situation' will be made where appropriate: distinctions between different 'styles' or 'registers', for instance, can hardly be made without reference to situation.

The primary object of the study of collocations is, however, to establish the '*collocational ranges*' of words, considered as *lexical items*. The use of some words, such as the English articles, is restricted only by the grammatical patterns of the language. At the other extreme, there are words which occur only in a very limited number of collocations or even in one alone (e.g. *kith and kin*). In other cases, we find habitual collocations (e.g. *to have green fingers, to have one over the eight*) whose meaning is not deducible from the meaning of their individual elements, but must be learned separately: such collocations are usually called '*idioms*'. Between the unrestricted (and therefore uninformative) 'collocability' of *the, a, if, but* and such words, and the extraordinarily restricted one of, say, *kith* or *betwixt*, there is an infinity of gradations. All but those words with unrestricted collocability would appear to have a collocational range which is peculiar to them. Further, in the speech of individuals, variations in the use of collocations are incomparably more numerous than variations at the grammatical level. The study of collocations therefore extends into the field of stylistics as well as linguistics. It is, however, possible to set up for given words at a particular period the 'ranges' of collocation which are typical of usage and of the various styles which can be distinguished within it (Robins cites among current clichés the house-agent's *desirable residence* and the journalist's *inside information*). In the historical study of a language, the comparison of collocational ranges in texts from different periods will shed light not only on the language and style of the individual authors concerned, but on changes in the general patterns of word-use from one period to another (cf. J. R. Firth's 'The Technique of Semantics', *Transactions of the Philological Society*, 1935).

Firth's distinction between 'collocation' and '*context*

*of situation*' removes much of the ambiguity inherent in the use of the term 'context' to refer both to linguistic environments and to the extralinguistic patterns to which linguistic utterances are related. This is not to say that the concept of 'context of situation', as developed by Firth, is beyond criticism. The utterance is related to the situation in which it is articulated by bringing into the statement of '*meaning*' the participants in the utterance and their behaviour, non-verbal as well as verbal, the effects of their verbal action, and the 'objects' to which reference is made. As has been pointed out elsewhere (see *Meaning and reference*), the precise relationship between the *individual* elements of the utterance and the extralinguistic patterns is not precisely analysed, nor is it clearly brought out how 'typical' elements in the context of situation are to be distinguished from those which are unique to it. Recent work by members of the British school (cf. particularly the publications of M. A. K. Halliday and R. M. W. Dixon) has gone some way towards meeting such objections through the development of more sophisticated techniques of analysis. The main point to be retained, however, is that 'context' and '*contextual meaning*' have more precisely demarcated senses in the work of British structuralists than in that of most other linguists, because of the limited currency outside the British Isles of the distinction between collocation and context.

Another problem, that of the relationship between 'meaning' and 'context', has thus been mainly discussed within a frame of reference in which 'context' includes both linguistic and extralinguistic relations. A number of linguists and philosophers (including H. Walpole, an American, J. Kurylowicz, a Pole, and L. Hjelmslev, the leader of the Danish school of glossematicists) have denied that words have meaning independently of context: cf. Hjelmslev's remark that 'In absolute isolation no sign has any meaning; any sign-meaning arises in context, by which we mean a situational context or explicit context'. Other scholars maintain that words have 'basic' meanings which are independent of context, and 'secondary', 'occasional' or 'contextual' meanings which attach to them only in specific linguistic or extralinguistic 'contexts'. This distinction between 'basic' and 'contextual' or 'secondary' meanings can be combined (as by T. Slama-Cazacu and S. Ullmann) with a recognition of the importance of 'context': for these scholars, in language, words are always used in contexts, and their rather abstract 'basic' meaning is 'individualized' and enriched by use in 'concrete' contexts.

These various attitudes are all open to some criticism. The use of the term 'basic' is unfortunate in so far as it suggests that secondary or 'contextual' meanings stand in a relation of dependence to 'basic' ones; the fact that in many cases the 'secondary' meaning can be shown to be *historically* a later development is irrelevant to the functioning of the language at the synchronic level, and the 'contextual' meaning cannot justifiably be considered synchronically as arising out of the 'basic' meaning by a form of osmosis from the context. The meaning of *green* in such phrases as *green with envy, to have green fingers* and *a green youth* is just as much determined by 'rules of use' as its meaning in the combinations *green paint* or *a green coat*. The difference between the meanings of *green* in the two groups is therefore a difference in frequency of occurrence, a quantitative rather than a qualitative one: the 'basic' meaning of *green*, as well as its 'secondary' ones, can only be established on the basis of abstraction from 'contexts' (in the terms used by the British school, 'collocations and contexts'). 'Basic' meaning, in addition to being related to what is in the last resort frequency of occurrence and to etymological priority, has also been defined in terms of the 'common core of meaning' underlying the various uses of a word. In so far as it can be determined at all, this 'common denominator' of all the meanings of a given form appears to shed little light on how words are used in language (cf. Paul Ziff's definition of *good* as 'answering to certain interests'). If the distinction between 'basic', 'ordinary' or 'normal' and 'contextual' or 'secondary' meanings is to be made at all, it should be on the basis of relative frequencies of occurrence—which means occurrence in spoken and written texts.

This is not to maintain that the isolated word is 'meaningless' or even that its meaning is 'vague'. The position is rather that is has a range of specific 'meaning-possibilities' which we can illustrate by reference to typical collocations and contexts: the vagueness lies not in the possible meanings themselves but in the choice between them. In so far as words are not used in isolation in language, the whole debate is a somewhat academic one. If meaning is to be profitably discussed, it must surely be in terms of the use and function of words in typical utterances and situations.

*Bibliography*

DIXON R. M. W. (1964) *On formal and contextual meaning*, Acta Linguistica, Budapest, **14,** 23.
DIXON R. M.W. (1965) *What is Language? A New Approach to Linguistic Description*, London.
FIRTH J. R. (1935) *The techniques of semantics*, Trans. Philol. Soc., 36.
FIRTH J. R. (1957) *A Synopsis of Linguistic Theory, 1930–1955*, in *Studies in Linguistic Analysis*, Oxford: The University Press.
HALLIDAY M. A. K. (1961) *Categories of the theory of grammar*, Word, **17,** 241.
SLAMA-CAZACU T. (1961) *Langage et Contexte*, The Hague.
ULLMAN S. (1962) *Semantics: An Introduction to the Science of Meaning*, Oxford: The University Press.

N. C. W. SPENCE

**SEMANTICS: FIELD THEORIES.** The principal tenet of twentieth-century linguistics is that a language constitutes a system (or series of sub-systems) of interdependent elements: the value and function of the individual element are therefore determined by its relations to the other elements within the system. Only slightly less dominant has been the view that linguistics, as a science, must be based on rigorously objective methods and criteria. This second principle of structural linguistics has, however, acted as something of a brake to progress in the investigation of *semantic* or *lexical structures* because, while it is comparatively easy to analyse the phonetic and grammatical structures of a language in an objective way, it is extremely difficult to satisfy this criterion when studying *meaning*. It has, in any case, been felt by some (particularly American) linguists that meaning is insufficiently 'structured' to be analysed in the same way as other levels of language.

Nevertheless, there have been a number of attempts, particularly in Germany, where there has never been the same prejudice against the discussion of meaning in terms of 'concepts', to apply the structural approach to semantics also. Common to all these approaches is the view that the *vocabulary* of a language is not a mere agglomeration of unrelated and independent items, but is organized. Precisely how, and to what extent it is organized, are questions which have been answered in different ways by the various scholars who have investigated the problem. Almost all have made use of the term *'field'* to describe the networks of associations and oppositions within which words and their meanings are organized, but there is great variation in the type and scope of the 'fields' envisaged. A basic distinction can, however, be made between two main types, 'semantic' or 'conceptual' theories, which view the field as being based on oppositions at the level of meaning or 'content' alone, and *'morpho-semantic'* theories, which take into account associations at the level of 'form' as well as at that of 'content'.

Both these approaches are outlined in that seminal work, the *Cours de Linguistique générale*, published in 1916 on the basis of courses of lectures given between 1906 and 1911 by the great Swiss linguist, F. de Saussure. Saussure presented the meaning of a linguistic sign as a *'value'* determined by its oppositions to the 'values' of related signs, pointing out, for instance, that the 'value' of French *boeuf* and *mouton* differed from that of English *beef* and *mutton* because, unlike the latter, they were not opposed to terms relating to live animals. Here the emphasis is on relations between *signifiés* or 'meanings'. Later in the *Cours de Linguistique générale*, and specifically with regard to vocabulary, he also outlined a rather different approach, centred on the individual sign and the various associations into which it entered at the level both of the *signifié* and of the *significant* or 'form'. In illustration, he presented the word *enseignement* as being at the centre of a series of different associations: at the purely semantic level, with words such as *éducation, apprentissage*; at the semantic and formal levels, with the verb *enseigner* and its paradigms; at the morphological level, with other nouns in *-ment*; and at the purely formal level, with other words ending in *-ment* (*clément, justement*, etc.). Viewed in this way, the vocabulary appears as a network of complex and overlapping associations. This particular approach, which Saussure did little more than suggest, was developed by his disciple, C. Bally, and others.

This is not to say that Saussure's suggestions were the sole inspiration of the field approach. As early as 1910, R. M. Meyer was studying the structure of terms relating to military rank and showing that each term within this 'semantic system' derived its value from its position within a co-ordinated whole. Work in other disciplines (the development of Gestalt psychology, for instance) helped to create interest in a structural approach. More important, perhaps, was L. Weisgerber's revival and development in the 1920's of the ideas of the German Romantic, W. von Humboldt, who a century before had already seen a language as an 'organically organized totality'. Illustrating his hypothesis, *inter alia*, by examples from colour and kinship terms, Weisgerber sought to show that a language shaped not only the conceptual thinking of its speakers, but their perception and interpretation of the world of reality.

The ideas of Humboldt and Weisgerber, on the one hand, and those of Saussure, on the other, appear to have been the principal inspiration of the most influential of the field theories so far put forward, that of J. Trier. In his book on intellectual terms in German (*Der deutsche Wortschatz im Sinnbezirk des Verstandes*), published in 1931, and in a number of later articles, Trier portrayed the vocabulary of a language as being organized in fields in which the different elements define and delimit each other without overlapping, like the pieces of a mosaic. Further, the fields themselves are seen as fitting together in the same way, so that the whole vocabulary—or rather the conceptual structures on which it rests—constitutes an articulated whole, without gaps and without overlapping. This attribution of complete order and coherence to the semantic structure of a language is the weakest point in Trier's theory, going far beyond the inferences which could be drawn from his illuminating study of a particular field.

According to Trier, the 'field' of Middle High German terms was in about 1200 A.D. organized round three key terms, *kunst*, *list* and *wîsheit*. In about 1300 A.D., the key terms were *kunst*, *wizzen* and *wîsheit*. The change, however, goes far beyond the substitution of one term (*wizzen*) for another (*list*): there has been a re-organization of the whole internal structure of the field in the intervening period. Around 1200, the term *kunst* was applied to courtly skills, and *list* to non-courtly ones—but some branches of knowledge could not be appraised without reference to the social status of the person whose skill was involved. Skill at arms was a *kunst* in a knight, but only a *list* in a man-at-arms. The gulf between the courtly and the non-courtly was, however, transcended at a higher level, since the term *wîsheit* embraced all forms of knowledge, material, spiritual and religious.

The social and synthetic characteristics of the field thus constituted had by 1300 A.D. given way to a structure of a more objective and analytic type. The term *kunst* was applied to certain of the higher branches of knowledge, and *wizzen* to technical skills and abilities and to knowledge in general, but without the earlier 'social' connotation. Further, *wîsheit* was no longer used as a synthetic term, but was applied only to spiritual and religious wisdom. The content of, and relations between, the three key words are therefore quite different from those of *kunst*, *list* and *wîsheit* in 1200. The field has been totally re-organized, reflecting, as Trier sees it, the disintegration of the earlier 'catholic' conception of knowledge and its replacement by a more analytic one.

Although Trier's analysis has been criticized on various grounds, it is clear that his approach to the study of individual fields or sectors of the vocabulary is of considerable significance to linguistics. It does, however, raise many problems. It is clear that semantic structures are not directly comparable, as Trier tends to infer, to phonemic and grammatical ones. Whereas a speaker of a given language cannot 'know' it without having mastered the latter, he seldom knows (according to Jespersen's estimate) more than a tenth of the total vocabulary of his mother tongue. The infinite variations between the vocabularies of individual speakers (and therefore between the number of elements which can enter into oppositions), the existence of specialized terminologies, regional variations, different 'styles' or 'registers'—all these are largely ignored by Trier. Trier also disregards the complex associations entered into by words not only at the formal level, but at that of the 'collocation' (see *Context and collocation*), which can hardly be ignored in the consideration of meaning. Finally, Trier's view of the field as a structure of concepts rather than of words raises methodological difficulties.

It therefore seems clear that structural patternings of meaning are both more complex and looser than Trier maintains. The different 'registers' and specialized terminologies constitute 'sub-systems' which co-exist within the usage of a given speech-community, and indeed within the usage of a given individual: these 'subsystems' do not form one fully integrated structure, but rather a series of structures which, although they overlap, must surely be studied independently, as 'restricted languages', in order to establish the nature of their particular patterns. Even the study of structural patterning in non-technical, standard usage presents some problems, because of the extreme variations between the vocabulary of different individuals. Uniformity of structures, i.e. supra-individual structures rather than individual structuring, is therefore most likely to be sought and found in 'basic' sectors of the vocabulary.

The examples so far chosen to demonstrate the existence of clear-cut semantic structures (colour and kinship terms, words referring to grades and ranks, etc.) are not equally convincing. It is obviously true, for instance, that the mark *good* will mean something different on a scale which distinguishes three levels *(poor, satisfactory, good)* than on one which adds a further two grades *(very good* and *excellent)*. In so far as both these scales are *set up* to function as self-contained systems with fixed values, their structures are not directly comparable with the semantic structure of the same terms as they function in ordinary language, i.e. within an 'open' and somewhat looser structure, in which the relative positions of, say, *poor*, *good* and *excellent* are clear, but those of *brilliant* and *outstanding*, relative to *excellent*, are not. The terminology of ranks within a hierarchy constitutes a self-contained system, but its linguistic patterning appears merely to reflect the rigidity of a social structure—the hierarchy itself.

One of the most promising areas for the application of the field approach would seem to lie in the comparison of the ways in which aspects of external reality are lexically 'divided up' in different languages, since this permits correlations between invariables (natural phenomena) and sets of variables (the lexical items in the different languages). The linguistic structuring of the colour spectrum, for instance, has been extensively studied, with illuminating results. In comparing the sectors of vocabulary referring to weather, topography, flora and fauna, greater regard has to be paid to environmental differences, but similar, if less spectacular, differences between lexical structures can be shown to exist, even where the phenomena to which they refer are directly comparable: for instance, whereas English distinguishes *grass*, *herb* and *weed*, French has only one generic term, *herbe*, supplemented adjectivally in combinations such as *herbes potagères*, *fines herbes*, *mauvaises herbes*, while French distinguishes *fleuve* and *rivière* where English has only the word *river*.

Two recent theories have been largely motivated by the desire, praiseworthy in itself, for a more 'objective' conception of, and approach to, semantic fields. In attempting to establish fields on the basis of the *sociological* significance of their constituent elements, G. Matoré (1953) does not, however, appear to have found a more satisfactory approach. It is never very clear whether Matoré is relating lexical items to society or vice versa: he speaks on the one hand of starting from the study of vocabulary to explain a society, and on the other of establishing his 'notional fields' on the basis of the analysis of a society. It is difficult to see how the 'sociological significance' of lexical items is established, or, if it is, in what way such items can be seen as constituting an integrated structure. In any case, fields which are presented as 'characterizing a given state of society' have little scientific validity as *linguistic* structures, since sociological and linguistic structures, although interrelated, cannot be equated. The approach suggested by J. Lyons (1963) is much more rigorous in its methodology, and is concerned with *linguistic* structures. In seeking to avoid positing the existence of concepts, Lyons proposes to define the meaning of a word in terms of its 'meaning-relations' to other words in the same 'lexical sub-system', as the 'meeting-point' of a series of 'functions'. In spite of the solid merits of his analysis, it is debatable whether Lyons through his substitution of 'meaning-relations' for oppositions between 'meanings' has provided linguists with what they have been seeking, a truly 'objective' approach to the study of meaning-structures. The meaning of the word *wet*, say, can be defined in terms of its 'meaning-relations' (for instance, that to its antonym *dry*), but it is not demonstrated that the procedure is a purely 'objective' one, since the meaning-relations themselves (e.g. the antonymy of *wet* and *dry*) appear to be established on the basis of 'unscientifically' demonstrated, prior knowledge of the meanings of the words in question, i.e. of what is to be defined.

The 'morpho-semantic' approach differs from those discussed above in that its starting-point is not a 'conceptual sphere' or a sector of the vocabulary seen as functioning as an integrated 'sub-system', but an individual word and its various associations, including those with other words outside its normal semantic environment, either in set phrases or at the purely formal level. The 'semantic' and 'morpho-semantic' approaches can complement each other. Considered 'atomistically', without reference to related terms, the semantic change represented by Latin *coxa* 'hip' > French *cuisse*, Italian *coscia* 'thigh' appears to be merely the result of a shift produced by the physical contiguity of the referents and the absence of any sharp dividing line between them. However, as W. von Wartburg has pointed out, if we take into account the relationship of *coxa* to its neighbours in the field and their formal associations, the change can plausibly be shown to be the result of a chain-reaction first affecting not *coxa*, but *femur* 'thigh'. Because phonetic and morphological changes in Vulgar Latin had produced homonymy between *fimus* 'manure' and *femur*, the latter was replaced by its semantic 'neighbour' *coxa*, the place of which was filled by borrowing the term *hanka* (> French *hanche*, Italian *anca*) from Germanic. On the other hand, if we consider the change purely in terms of the semantic oppositions involved, we may make the equally valid observation that there has been no change in the internal structure of the 'field' concerned: all that has happened is that some *forms* have been substituted for others.

Because of the existence of homonymy and synonymy, the relationships between the levels of 'form' and 'meaning' cannot be dealt with in terms of one-for-one correspondences, or without reference to *both* levels. This does not mean that there is no place for an approach which considers a field as a network of 'units of content'—indeed, by forcing one to consider only the bare essentials, such a procedure can afford valuable insights into semantic structure. It would, however, seem both practically and methodologically advisable that this stage should be reached by a process of progressive abstraction from the observable forms of language.

There have been a number of other field theories of more modest scope, several of them arising out of controversy between Trier and his German colleagues. For G. Ipsen, the field was a lexical group linked by tangible morphological as well as semantic marks: the Latin names of metals thus formed a field following their conversion into colour adjectives in such combinations as *argentum aes* 'Silver Age'. The 'elemental meaning-fields' distinguished by W. Porzig are also limited, but in a less arbitrary manner: they consist merely of 'inherent' combinations between verb and noun (e.g. *see—eye, bark—dog*) or more rarely, between adjectives and noun (*blond—hair*). The combinations are 'inherent', however, not in nature but in a given language at a specific period: The Modern German *fahren* 'implies' vehicular transportation, whereas Middle High German *varen*, from which it derives, applied also to travel on foot. Without ceasing to study his own 'elemental' fields, Porzig has now accepted Trier's approach in analysis at a different level.

As a group, field theories have in common only the fact that (to a lesser or greater extent) they stress the interdependence of lexical items instead of treating them as independent units. Although lexical structures are clearly not as uniform and coherent as scholars such as Trier have maintained, and various theoretical and practical problems still have to be solved, the field approach has established itself as an indispensable tool of modern semanticists. Because of the complexity of the relations between the elements of the vocabulary, it seems likely that a satisfactory analysis of lexical structures will have to operate on a number of levels.

*See also:* Linguistic form: paradigmatic. Relations between languages: semantic change.

*Bibliography*

COSERIU E. (1964) *Pour une sémantique diachronique structurale*, in *Travaux de Linguistique et de Littérature*, **2**, 139.
DUCHÁČEK O. (1960) *Les champs linguistiques*, *Philologica Pragensia*, **3**, 22.
GUIRAUD P. (1956) *Les champs morpho-sémantiques*, *Bull. de la Société de Linguistique de Paris*, **52**, 265.
LYONS J. (1963) *Structural Semantics: An Analysis of Part of the Vocabulary of Plato*, Oxford.
MATORÉ G. (1953) *La Méthode en Lexicologie, Domaine français*, Paris.
ÖHMAN S. (1951) *Wortinhalt und Weltbild*, Stockholm.
ÖHMAN S. (1953) *Theories of the 'Linguistic Field'*, *Word*, **9**, 123.
TRIER J. (1931) *Der deutsche Wortschatz im Sinnbezirk des Verstandes. Die Geschichte eines Sprachlichen Feldes*, I, *Von der Anfängen bis zum Beginn des 13ten Jahrhunderts*, Heidelberg.
ULLMANN S. (1957) (2nd Edn) *Principles of Semantics*, Glasgow-Oxford.
ULLMAN S. (1962) *Semantics: An Introduction to the Science of Meaning*, Oxford.

N. C. W. SPENCE

**SEMANTICS: MEANING AND REFERENCE.** In their attempts to analyse meaning, philosophers and linguists have since classical times been grappling with the problems raised by the relationship between language, thought and external reality: Aristotle, for instance, already saw the word as a *symbol* for a *thing*. A language is a system of signs or symbols which can at certain levels be studied largely as a self-contained structure, but at the *semantic level*, correlations with extralinguistic patterns have to be taken into account. The *meaning* of utterances involves not only the signs themselves, but *inter alia* what they refer to. This is of course clearest where the *referent* (the 'object' referred to) belongs to the class of tangible, physical phenomena. In their discussions of the nature of the linguistic sign, many theorists have therefore distinguished three elements of meaning. The best-known of such tri-partite analyses is probably that of Ogden and Richards (1936) as it is schematized in their 'basic triangle':

THOUGHT OR REFERENCE

CORRECT            ADEQUATE
Symbolizes          Refers to
(a causal relation)     (other causal relations)

SYMBOL        REFERENT
Stands for
(an imputed relation)
*The 'basic triangle' of Ogden and Richards*

Here the 'thought or reference' (in other terminologies = 'meaning', 'sense' or 'content') is placed in direct causal relationships with both the 'symbol' (the 'form' or 'name') and the 'referent', while 'symbol' and 'referent' are merely joined in an 'imputed relation' ('symbol' *stands for* 'referent'). This analysis of sign function has been criticized by Ullmann on the grounds that the 'referent', the extralinguistic feature or event as such, clearly lies outside the province of the linguist; the latter's attention must therefore be concentrated on the relation between 'symbol' and 'thought or reference', or, as Ullmann prefers to put it, between '*name*' and '*sense*'. This view needs to be qualified in so far as the 'sense' of the word includes its range of reference to extralinguistic phenomena. Ullmann does attempt to counter this objection by noting that the linguistically relevant features of the 'referent' will be included in the analysis as they form part of the 'sense', but this merely confirms that referential functions cannot in fact be excluded from the analysis of meaning.

The tradition in which Ogden-Richards and Ullmann have worked has, however, been under fire for some time because of its reliance on 'thoughts', 'senses' or 'concepts' posited as separate entities. Such entities are felt to be too 'metaphysical' to be of any use to modern linguistics, as a science based on objective criteria and procedures. The study of meaning in America has, for instance, been profoundly influenced by the views of Leonard Bloomfield, expressed in his book, *Language* (London, 1933). In order to avoid recourse to entities which he considered to be inaccessible to scientific analysis, he proposed to relate observables (the forms of language) directly to other observables. The meaning of a term thus became in behaviourist terms 'the situation in which the speaker utters it and the response which it calls forth in the observer' (*op. cit.*, p. 19). Meaning was even more closely related to extralinguistic criteria by Bloomfield's further suggestion that the meaning of a word should be defined in terms of some other science, saying, for example, that the ordinary meaning of the English word *salt* is 'sodium chloride' (NaCl) (*ibid.*, p. 139), and that terms such as *love, friend, kind, hate*, relating to social behaviour, could be defined in terms of ethnology, folklore and sociology provided these studies had reached a perfection and accuracy undreamed of today (*ibid.*, p. 280). These 'definitions' no longer have anything to do with the behaviourist definition in terms of stimulus and response, and it is difficult to see what relevance they have to the meaningful use of words in language: the shift from definitions based on the social sciences to ones drawn from the natural sciences (at least in the case of terms referring to physical phenomena) is clearly inappropriate. In attempting to avoid positing such entities as 'thoughts' or 'concepts', Bloomfield ended up by equating wherever possible 'meaning' and 'referent'—indeed by excluding 'meaning' since all we are left with in cases such as that of the word *salt* is the observable 'form' of the sign and the 'referent' to which it relates. The meaning of 'concrete' terms is thus placed outside language in the scientific analysis of external reality, while that of 'abstracts' and relational words cannot be satisfactorily catered for within his scheme because of the alleged inadequacies of the social sciences. Since all words have meaning, although the latter may not include a referential function, Bloomfield is exaggerating the dichotomy between words which do refer to tangible phenomena and those which do not have a 'referent' of this type. As will be seen, this distinction poses real problems since, on the one hand, all language signs are in a sense equally 'abstract', but on the other their meanings are not equally dependent on correlation with extralinguistic objects, events or patterns.

The relationship between 'form' and 'referent' appears to have been more satisfactorily conceived by the American philosopher Charles Morris. Like Bloomfield, he aimed at objectivity but without oversimplifying the complex nature of the sign function and without appealing, as Bloomfield did, to the natural sciences for definitions rather than to the more appropriate human sciences. As Morris sees it, the sign vehicle (a linguistic 'form') itself is simply one object, and its denotation of other objects resides solely in the fact that there are rules of use which correlate the two objects (*Foundations of the Theory of Signs*, p. 24). The 'meaning' of the sign (although Morris avoids the use of this term because of its imprecision) is neither equated with the 'referent' nor presented as a 'thought' or 'image', but as part of a network of social conventions which convert the 'forms' of spoken or written language from noises or marks into actual 'signs'. Bloomfield's difficulty about the meaning of 'abstracts' disappears since, as Morris puts it, 'while every sign has a designatum ['meaning'], not every sign has a denotatum' (*ibid.*, p. 5).

Although Morris' conception of the sign is presented in referential terms, this does not in his view make meaning 'private' or 'subjective'. There may be subjective aspects of the process of communication through language signs

—aspects which one speaker experiences and others do not—but this does not mean that meanings are subjective. They must be *inter-subjective*, or the signs could not function as signs, in fact would not *be* signs. In order to break down the complexity of the sign function, Morris further distinguishes three aspects of it—the syntactic, the semantic and the pragmatic—based on three elements involved in the sign situation: the sign itself, the referent and those who produce and react to the sign. The syntactic aspect considers only the relation of sign to sign, the semantic that between sign and referent and the pragmatic, the relations between all three, the latter aspect being usually understood as the actual behaviour of organisms in their use of the sign system. Morris' analysis is rather abstract, but a number of his points appear to be valid, in particular the need to consider a language at the semantic level not only as a formal system but as a system which is correlated to objects in the world of reality through rules of use which are not subjective but social and which cannot be equated either with the 'forms' of the signs themselves or with the objects which they denote.

The correlation of the sign-system (language) with the extralinguistic world through the concept of the use or function of the signs poses a number of problems. For the American structuralist, G. L. Trager, meaning can only be satisfactorily treated within the framework of '*metalinguistics*', a field covering the interrelationship of the different cultural systems (including language) that a society possesses: 'The full statement of the point-by-point and pattern-by-pattern relations between language and any other cultural systems will contain all the 'meanings' of the linguistic forms, and will constitute the metalinguistics of that culture.' How this programme is to be translated into practice remains somewhat obscure. A similar but more pragmatic approach is favoured by the British School, using the '*context of situation*' technique developed by B. Malinowski and J. R. Firth in the 1930's. Maintaining with some justification that the normal meaningful unit of language is not the individual sign or word but the 'utterance', they attempt to state the meaning of the latter by relating it to the *situation* or environment in which it is produced—or could be produced. This involves reference to the persons involved in the utterance, their non-verbal as well as their verbal behaviour, the 'objects' to which reference is made and the effects of the verbal action. Because the emphasis is on the 'total utterance' in its relation to the 'total situation', this procedure does not lead to the sort of 'point-by-point', 'pattern-by-pattern' correlation visualized by Trager, nor is it always very clear where the line is to be drawn between features which must be related to general cultural patterns and those which relate to particular individuals in a particular situation. In order to have general validity, the relevant 'social' features must be abstracted from the particular 'contexts'. This process of abstraction from the particular to the 'typical' must be carried still further in, say, a dictionary, where the unit described is no longer the utterance but the word. The dictionary entry can merely summarize schematically the uses or functions of the word (including its referential functions, if any) in 'typical' collocations (see *Context and collocation*) or 'contexts of situation'. This, however, represents such a watering-down of the 'context of situation' approach as to come very close to the long-standing practice of traditional descriptive lexicographers.

Although the 'total' meaning of a particular utterance cannot perhaps be apprehended outside its 'context of situation', the 'general' meaning of an utterance such as 'Is it raining?' may be said to be independent of the particular contexts in which it is used. Some scholars therefore resort to context only as a means of removing ambiguity about the meaning of utterances considered in isolation, the purpose being to treat language without unnecessary reference to extralinguistic factors. The role played by referential relations to patterns outside language remains important even in a scheme which proposes to deal with meanings as far as possible in this way. As D. Bolinger (1965) points out in his observations on Katz and Fodor's 'The Structure of a Semantic Theory', the semantic 'markers' and 'distinguishers' on which the latter wish to base their analysis of meaning ('male' – 'female', 'abstract' – 'concrete', etc.) are determined in terms of non-linguistic data.

It must, however, also be borne in mind that the relationship between language and external phenomena is a complex one. Each language focusses attention on different aspects of 'reality', and its sign-system itself helps to classify and order the infinite variety of phenomena in a systematic way—a way which will differ from one language to another, so that our perception of the world of immediate experience is not only ordered by language but to some extent at least moulded by it (an obvious example is the variety of ways in which the colour spectrum is divided up in different languages, although the physical phenomena involved are the same). Reference is therefore in some degree a factor which is determined by the language system as well as one which determines meaning. Even in the case of words which have concrete referents, meanings are based on the structures existing within the language-system. It will be seen that the way in which meaning functions in language is complex. Some clarification may result from the application of distinctions such as those proposed by Morris between the 'syntactic' and 'semantic' aspects of meaning or by R. M. W. Dixon between 'internal' and 'external' meaning (the former being based on correlations within the patterns of language, the latter on correlations between a language-pattern and a non-language pattern). The treatment of reference will still pose problems. It would, however, seem reasonable to maintain that the referential function of a word, where it has one, should not be considered as belonging to a special category, but merely as one of the functions which it performs in the utterances and contexts in which it occurs.

*Bibliography*

BOLINGER D. (1965) *The Atomization of Meaning*, *Language*, **41**, 555.
DIXON R. M. W. (1965) *What is Language?: A New Approach to Linguistic Description*, London.
HALLIDAY M. A. K. (1961) *Categories of the Theory of Grammar*, *Word*, **17**, 241.
KATZ J. J. and FODOR J. (1963) *The Structure of a Semantic Theory*, *Language*, **39**, 170.
MORRIS C. W. (1938) *Foundations of the Theory of Signs*, International Encyclopedia of Unified Science, Vol. 1, No. 2, Chicago: The University Press.
MORRIS C. W. (1946) *Signs, Language and Behaviour*, New York.
OGDEN C. K. and RICHARDS I. A. (1936) (4th Edn) *The Meaning of Meaning*, London.
ROBINS R. H. (1952) *A Problem in the Statement of Meaning*, *Lingua*, **3**, 121.
ROBINS R. H. (1964) *General Linguistics: An Introductory Survey*, London.
TRAGER G. L. (1949) *The Field of Linguistics*, S.I.L. Occasional Papers, No. 1.
ULLMANN S. (1963) *Semantics: An Introduction to the Science of Meaning*, Oxford.

N. C. W. SPENCE

**SEMANTICS: SIGN AND SYMBOL.** *Sign* and *symbol* are among the many terms which are used in different ways by different linguists. The more inclusive term is certainly *sign:* anything which 'stands for' or 'directs attention to' something other than itself can be included in the general category of signs. A word is therefore often described as a 'sign' and a language as a 'sign system'. Since, however, the sign thus defined covers a wide range of phenomena, different types of sign may be distinguished, including 'symbols' and, less frequently, 'signals'. Ogden and Richards (1923), for instance, defined 'symbols' as 'those signs which m en use to communicate with one another and as instruments of thought'. For them, and for most linguists who make the distinction between 'sign' and 'symbol', all symbols are signs, but not all signs are symbols. We will on the basis of our previous experience associate a blush with embarrassment or smoke with the presence of fire: the blush may therefore be said to be a sign of embarrassment, or the smoke a sign of fire. In such cases, however, the association is based on a natural or causal relation, and is not, as in those signs used in communication, a *conventional* one. The relation, for instance, between the sound-group [faiə] and the phenomenon to which it refers exists in virtue of a convention valid only for English-speakers: witness the equally 'conventional' function of *ignis* in Latin, of *feu* in French, of *fuego* in Spanish, and so forth. Although language is by far the most complex and important system of symbols or 'conventional' signs, many non-linguistic phenomena also function as symbols in so far as they stand for something else in virtue of social conventions: traffic lights, road signs and stereotyped gestures, to cite only a few examples, come into this category.

Such things as photographs, portraits, recordings and maps have also been classed as 'signs' on the grounds that they refer to something other than themselves, but clearly they belong neither to the class of 'natural' signs nor to that of 'symbols' used in communication. Signs which are similar to what they denote have been described by Charles Morris as '*iconic*' (from the Greek εικον 'image'), but clearly not all 'iconic' signs have the same type of function: a picture, although it may well be said to express or communicate something, does not do so on the basis of social (other than artistic) conventions. A road sign or a pictogram (such as an Egyptian hieroglyph), on the other hand, may have 'iconic' form, but its use is 'conventional', and its function, communication: on the basis of the earlier distinction, it will therefore rank as an 'iconic' *symbol* as opposed to an 'iconic' *sign*.

A distinction on these lines between *signs* and *symbols* is, however, far from essential to linguistics, since linguists are in practice exclusively concerned with systems of communication. One of the founders of modern linguistics, F. de Saussure, visualized the creation of a science (*sémiologie* or '*semiology*') devoted to the study of signs—but its field was to be that of signs 'used in society', i.e. primarily that of 'conventional' signs (or symbols) used in communication. Although the 'theory of signs' which philosophers (among them C. Morris and E. Cassirer) have sought to develop is more inclusive in its general approach, it is also above all concerned with 'conventional' signs (or symbols) and the way in which signs function. Within linguistics, certainly, little or no ambiguity arises out of the frequent and continuing use of the term 'sign' rather than 'symbol' when referring to 'conventional' signs. The focus of interest is on differences between those signs which are used in human communication and on the nature of the sign function. Within this frame of reference, the term 'symbol' can be, and is, used in more restricted senses, i.e. applied only to *certain* of the 'conventional' signs, according to criteria which may vary from one scholar to another. The most noteworthy of these distinctions is possibly that first made by Cassirer between 'symbols' and 'signals'. To quote an example given by Stern, the exclamation *oh!* uttered when a person bangs his head against a door is a sign of pain, but not the *name* of pain, in the way that *table* is the sign and name of an object. A sign of this 'expressive' type can therefore be termed a 'signal' in order to distinguish it from those which have a more specific referential function. The category of 'signals', as Stern sees it, covers interjections (words like *hell* being either 'signals' or 'symbols', depending on the way in which they are used), expressive gestures, and linguistic devices such as stress, length, and intonation used to communicate emotion rather than intellectual content.

The precise demarcation between 'signals' and 'symbols' is a matter for debate, but the distinction is one of those which may be made within the body of signs used in communication. Other, more important differences can also be distinguished. Signs may be seen as constituting systems, but systems of greatly varying coherence and complexity: the use made of 'conventional' gestures (if we except artificially devised systems such as that used by 'tick-tack' men) is restricted and conforms to no coherent pattern, while traffic lights constitute a restricted but rigidly patterned, closed system. A language, on the other hand, is a highly complex system (or series of systems) exhibiting a high, if less rigid, degree of patterning at various levels. A further, important difference which may be distinguished between signs is their degree of 'conventionality'. Mathematical symbols, the dots and dashes of morse, and most alphabets are sign-systems whose elements are purely conventional. Road signs, on the other hand, constitute a 'mixed' system in that some (e.g. the 'No entry' sign) are purely conventional, while others, through their (admittedly stylised) representation of the phenomena to which they refer, are 'iconic'. Some scripts, e.g. Egyptian hieroglyphs and Chinese ideograms, were largely 'iconic' in origin, but as they evolved, the element of pure conventionality increased (the Chinese script can now be regarded as purely conventional, since the 'representational' value of the characters is minimal).

A spoken language is a system consisting exclusively or almost exclusively of purely conventional signs, since its acoustic basis limits the possibility of 'direct' relations between signs and their referents to the range of acoustic phenomena. It was one of the tenets of F. de Saussure, for instance, that language was a system of '*arbitrary*' (i.e. purely conventional) and 'unmotivated' signs. This question of the arbitrariness of the linguistic sign has given rise to heated discussion, much of it at cross-purposes because of differing interpretations of the terms 'arbitrary' and 'unmotivated'. It has been pointed out, for instance, that for the speaker of a given language, the relation between the sign and what it refers to is not 'arbitrary', but 'necessary'. This does not, however, alter the fact that the relation itself is not normally based on any 'natural' link between the two elements, but is conventional. Onomatopoeic words have often been held to be 'naturally' motivated signs. The degree of conventionality of even onomatopoeic words is, however, considerable: the acoustic phenomena at the basis of onomatopoeic words are represented in a stylised way, so that what is commonly considered to be purely onomatopoeic in one language will not necessarily be recognized by the speakers of another: a test conducted by A. Sauvageot showed that French-speakers unfamiliar with the Finno-Ugric languages were unable to identify with even a fair degree of accuracy the onomatopoeic elements of those languages. The relative conventionality of even onomatopoeic words may be illustrated by an example chosen from more closely related languages: the crowing of the rooster is represented in English by *cock-a-doodle-doo*, in French by *cocorico* and in German by *kikeriki*.

'Arbitrariness' or 'conventionality' therefore remains the essential characteristic of the 'social' sign. The sign function of a word such as *cuckoo* does not depend on its undoubtedly onomatopoeic—and therefore 'iconic'—form, which may be seen as supplementary to the sign function proper. Conventionality does not, however, exclude *motivation*. As we have seen, the motivation can be 'natural' only when the sign refers to something which is either itself an acoustic phenomenon (a *splash*, a *boom*, a *crack*, etc.) or can be characterized in acoustic terms (as when the call of the cuckoo motivates the name of the bird itself). 'Linguistic' motivation, which plays a more important rôle, is based not on any direct similarity between the sign and the thing to which it refers, but on the relations of the sign itself to other signs within the system. We may thus say that the sign *mark*, for instance, is 'arbitrary', but that *marker*, *marked*, *unmarked*, *pockmark*, *watermark*, and so forth, are 'motivated' relative to it. Linguistic motivation exists in all languages, but its rôle varies in importance from one language to another, and indeed within the same language (e.g. while the relation of *mark* and *marked* is formally motivated, that of, say, *go* and *went* is not). On the basis of the relative importance of linguistic motivation, typological distinctions have been made between 'lexically unmotivated' languages, such as French, in which the conventionality of the sign is accentuated by the relative lack of formal motivation, and 'lexically motivated' ones, such as German, in which semantic links are more frequently reinforced by formal associations (cf. German *Wort* 'word', *Wörterbuch* 'dictionary', *Wortkunde* 'lexicology', *Sprichwort* 'proverb', *Zeitwort* 'verb', etc.). A rather different, and more debatable type of linguistic motivation has been distinguished in the form of the link between the different senses of a given form: according to this view, *bed* in 'the bed of a river', 'a bed of roses' may be seen as motivated by the more usual application of the word.

The study of the linguistic motivation of signs within a given language-system illuminates certain characteristics of the structure of that particular system of signs. Through the creation of a network of formally and semantically related forms, 'internal', linguistic motivation would appear to make the system easier to assimilate. The functioning of the system does not, however, in any way depend on the existence of these internal motivations. The latter are a guide to the interpretation and memorization of the signs, but not a guide upon which we can rely: we have to learn the conventions which govern the use of motivated forms also. The existence of a motivated pattern of the type *sow—sower*, *sell—seller*, *buy—buyer* and *cart—carter* does not permit us to infer, for instance, that the sense of *duster* is 'someone who dusts', nor that a *draper* is someone who drapes. The subordination of linguistic motivation to the conventions which govern the use of a given form can be illustrated historically by the semantic differentiation which affects formally and semantically related forms (cf. the development of *undertake* and *undertaker*). In language at least, motivation must be subordinated to conventionality, since a rigidly motivated system would be an ossified one, and language must constitute a system of signs which is free to adapt to change.

*See also*: Writing.

*Bibliography*

GUIRAUD P. (1955) *La sémantique*, Paris.
MORRIS C. (1938) *Foundations of the Theory of Signs, International Encyclopedia of Unified Science*, Vol. 1, No. 2, Chicago.
MORRIS C. (1946) *Signs, Language and Behavior*, New York.
OGDEN C. K. and RICHARDS I. A. (1936) (4th Edn) *The Meaning of Meaning*, London.
SPANG-HANSSEN H. (1954) *Recent Theories on the Nature of the Language Sign*, Copenhagen.
STERN G. (1931) *Meaning and Change of Meaning*, Gothenburg.
ULLMANN S. (1957) (2nd Edn) *The Principles of Semantics*, Glasgow–Oxford.
ULLMANN S. (1962) *Semantics: Introduction to the Science of Meaning*, Oxford.

N. C. W. SPENCE

## SENSORY DISCRIMINATION, MEASUREMENT OF.

### 1. Introduction

Whether measures of sensory discrimination are used to study the sensory systems themselves or as dependent variables indicating changes in other systems, it is always useful and sometimes essential to understand how the measures used relate to the underlying sensory mechanisms. The theory of sensory discrimination will be briefly outlined here, and the main procedures giving sensory measures will be presented and discussed.

In psychophysics the term 'stimulus' is used to refer to a controlled physical situation, one aspect of which may take different values on a physical dimension. Thus a completely black screen may be presented to a subject. A faint circle of light of constant area is then projected for a fixed short duration on to the screen and its intensity is increased by equal increments on successive trials, starting from zero, until the subject sees it. The light flash varies only in its luminance, $I$ (see the Glossary of Symbols), and the luminances $I_1, I_2, I_3 \ldots$ of the flashes presented on trials 1, 2, 3 ... define the corresponding stimuli. The stimulus intensity the subject first sees may be taken as an estimate of his *absolute threshold*.

Much of the theory of sensory discrimination owes its origin to Fechner's book 'Elemente der Psychophysik', first published in 1860 (Fechner 1966), which presented both a coherent theory of discrimination and methods for studying it. Fechner assumed that a physical stimulus of sufficient intensity produces an effect on the body, i.e. the receptors and the nervous system, which in turn produces an effect in the mind, 'sensation'. Sensation is measurable, its magnitude being a continuous function of stimulus intensity. When a sensation or a difference between sensations is sufficiently large it will become conscious, leading to a judgment which the subject can report. Fechner used 'threshold' to mean 'the point at which a stimulus or stimulus difference becomes noticeable'. The stimulus first became detectable at the 'absolute threshold'; the 'differential threshold' was the 'just noticeable difference' (j.n.d.) between the sensations caused by two stimuli.

In this account the threshold should have the same value each time it is determined, but in practice subjects show great variability in their responses to near-threshold stimuli. Fechner attributed this to 'irregular chance fluctuations... Some of [which] are inherent in the operations, others are based on the subjective nature of the interpretations of compared magnitudes'. Thus even though two stimuli produced a sensation difference less than the 'just noticeable difference' subjects might report detecting it on a proportion of trials: 'Let us assume that the difference between two weights ... is so small that it falls below the point where it can be consciously recognized ... simultaneously with the difference which we are trying to apprehend, there are at work random effects which would on the average make the judgment come out equally often in favour of one or the other. The difference creates an additional tendency to throw the judgment in one direction ... by summation with the other influences. The level of probability ... depends on the size of the difference.' Thus the stimulus difference exactly producing the just noticeable difference in sensation could only be estimated, and statistical analysis of repeated observations was required for that.

### 2. Theory of Sensory Discrimination

Fechner's main ideas provided the starting-point for the modern theory of sensory discrimination, though his mentalistic superstructure, which at no point has contributed to the useful development of theory, has been discarded. The theory that has emerged from the work of Cattell (1893), Thurstone (1948), Swets *et. al.* (1961), Blackwell (1963), and many others, rests on two main assumptions: (a) sensory judgments require the signal produced by the stimulus to be discriminated from noise arising from physical and biological sources; (b) faced with ambiguous sensory messages the subject makes decisions in keeping with the tenets of statistical decision theory. Many variant or alternative theories have been proposed (Swets *et. al.* 1961; Luce 1963) but the account which will be outlined here is that which has proved most widely applicable.

If a stimulus is to be perceived it must produce some effect in the nervous system. Thus a light flash may excite retinal receptors, which in turn cause firing in the optic nerve and higher visual pathways. The magnitude of the neural effect produced at some level will determine what response the subject selects; this magnitude can be represented on a central dimension, $E$, the 'decision axis'.

The decision made here will result in an overt response. The series of neurophysiological events leading from presentation of the stimulus to performance of the response can be divided into three parts.

(i) *The afferent system.* Presentation of a stimulus on trial $i$ leads to the production of a central effect, $E_i$. There is evidence that excitation of the sensory receptors will not necessarily ensure a positive response, and that the threshold decision is made centrally, in vision, for example, at or beyond the point at which the messages from the two eyes come together (Treisman 1966). Fechner's 'chance fluctuations' arise from variability in the stimulus and in the afferent system. Thus if a light flash of nominally constant intensity $I_S$ is presented repeatedly, the $E$ values produced will vary. These fluctuations can be attributed to: (a) the irreducible physical variability of the stimulus, e.g. the quantum variability of light; (b) the spontaneous production of sensory messages, due to impulses arising in the absence of stimulation, or from the spontaneous decomposition of visual pigment, or entering the afferent path from sources other than the receptors; (c) variation in the efficiency with which the neural pathways transmit the sensory messages entering them. Consequently, the central effects produced by repeated presentation of a given stimulus can be represented by a conditional probability density function on $E$. Figure 1 shows two distributions, $f(E|I_N)$

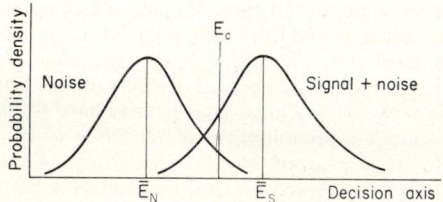

FIG. 1. *The central distributions produced by repeated presentation of $I_N$, the 'standard' or background stimulus, or $I_S$, the 'signal + noise'.*

with mean $\bar{E}_N$ produced by repeated presentation of $I_N$ (the 'standard' or background stimulus used in many experiments, whose value may be zero or greater) and $f(E|I_S)$, with mean $\bar{E}_S$, produced by $I_S$ (the 'signal' of intensity greater than $I_N$). The occurrence of 'noise' has two consequences: central effects are produced even when a stimulus of zero intensity is given, and there is a dispersion of the effects of any given stimulus. These central distributions may be taken to be approximately normal, and with approximately constant standard deviations, $\sigma_E$.

(ii) *The response system.* If on trial $i$ the central effect $E_i$ is produced, and the subject may only respond 'Yes' (Y), indicating that the signal, $I_S$ was presented, or 'No' (N), indicating that $I_N$ was given, then, since $E_i$ might have been produced by either stimulus, the response selection system is in the same position as a statistician who must choose between two hypotheses on the basis of a single observation. The 'noise' distribution (which might describe the effects of an unilluminated or uniformly illuminated screen) would correspond to a 'null hypothesis', the 'signal + noise' distribution (produced when a light flash increases the total intensity to $I_S$) would correspond to the 'experimental hypothesis'. Statistical decision theory prescribes an optimal strategy for choosing the response: (a) select a criterion, $\beta$; (b) on trial $i$ calculate the likelihood ratio corresponding to $E_i$; $1(E_i) = f(E_i|I_S)/f(E_i|I_N)$; (c) if $1(E_i) > \beta$ give the response 'Y', if $1(E_i) \leq \beta$ give the response N.

The decision procedure can be applied to any monotonic function of likelihood ratio, such as $E$, and it would be simpler to suppose that the subject operates directly on $E$, using a criterion $E_c$, where $\beta = 1(E_c)$, than that he computes the likelihood ratio corresponding to each value of $E$ before making a decision. There are a number of alternative prescriptions for selecting an optimal criterion. The two most frequently applied are: (a) The *maximum expected value criterion* takes account of the *a priori* probabilities of the signal and the noise, $P(I_S)$ and $P(I_N)$, and the values of the pay-offs, attaching to the different types of performances: $v(N|I_N)$—the value of responding $N$ on a trial on which $I_N$ was presented, etc. The critical likelihood ratio, $\beta$, is then given

by $\beta = \left(\dfrac{P(I_N)}{P(I_S)}\right)\left(\dfrac{v(N|I_N)-v(Y|I_N)}{v(Y|I_S)-v(N|I_S)}\right)$ (1)

(b) The *Neyman-Pearson criterion* depends on the probability of responding Y when $I_N$ is presented, $P(Y|I_N)$, which is also known as the false positive rate (FPR). It corresponds to the probability of rejecting the null hypothesis when it is correct. An acceptable limiting false positive rate FPR $= \varepsilon$ is defined, and the criterion is then the likelihood ratio such that $P(Y|I_N) = \varepsilon$. To apply the Neyman-Pearson criterion, the subject must be able to assess his FPR and vary $E_c$ accordingly until FPR $= \varepsilon$. This should be a well-learned skill, since daily life affords many opportunities to make near-threshold sensory judgments which can later be confirmed or refuted: words heard indistinctly may be repeated, objects seen in a glance or at a distance may be re-examined; and it has been shown experimentally that subjects can produce a required FPR (Swets *et al.* 1961). To apply the maximum expected value criterion the subject must know: (a) $P(I_S)$ and $P(I_N)$ and (b) the pay-off values and costs attaching to the different possible performances in order to calculate $\beta$; and (c) the form of the 'noise' distribution, and (d) the form of the 'signal + noise' distribution, in order to determine $1(E_i)$ or to find the value of $E_c$ such that $\beta = 1(E_c)$, in order to apply the criterion. But all this prior knowledge is not always available to the subject; in some procedures not even the experimenter knows the exact stimulus values which will be used until the experiment is concluded. Again, in some procedures (e.g. the Method of Limits) $P(I_S) = 1$ but the threshold is not greatly lowered thereby, as equation 1 would require. It has been shown that variation in the *a priori* probabilities and stated monetary pay-off values may cause the subject's criterion to vary in the direction though not to the full extent which would be implied by equation 1. But this is equally compatible with the assumption that in these cases $\varepsilon$ may vary as a function of the *a priori* probabilities and pay-off values. Thus the Neyman-Pearson criterion appears the more *parsimonious* and the more plausible of the two, and it is assumed in the present account.

The decision axis is sometimes defined in terms of the logarithm of likelihood ratio, but this has the disadvantage that if more than one 'signal' is used a separate axis must be defined for each, whereas any number can be represented on E.

'Noise' may arise in the response system: it would be represented by instability in the criterion. But as in practice any contribution from this source cannot be distinguished from the sensory noise, it is usually not separately considered.

*(iii) The effect of instructions.* We have described how the afferent and response systems may operate when performing a set task. It is obvious that further and complex mechanisms are present which adjust these systems to perform appropriately, interpreting the instuctions, selecting the required afferent channel and set of responses, computing the criterion. We are fortunate that in the normal human subject these mechanisms usually operate so well that his performance is limited only by the discrimination system, so that for present purposes we may ignore them.

The account given here describes how the information in the experimenter's choice of stimulus magnitudes is transmitted to the subject's responses. This transmission is limited by the sensory noise, whose effect is summarized by the conditional probability density function on $E$ which corresponds to any stimulus magnitude. This suggests that a 'sensory discrimination task' may be defined as any experimental procedure in which the subjects' performance is limited only by this sensory noise; his performance in such a task will provide measures which are more or less directly related to the parameters of the underlying sensory discrimination system. In the next section we shall present some of the more important sensory discrimination tasks, describe the measures that can be obtained from them, and consider how they relate to the parameters of the underlying mechanisms. The model has been presented as a functional schema of the operations underlying the selection of discriminative responses to stimuli. Any acceptable model of behaviour must be consistent with what is known of the underlying physiology or in principle capable of being related to it. The mechanisms which select the discriminative responses cannot yet be identified at the neurophysiological level, but for the most part the sense organs and afferent pathways which receive and convey the sensory information are known, and we can suppose that the spontaneous discharges and variability of the nerve messages observed in them correspond to the sensory noise in the model. But as yet only tentative steps have been taken in relating $\sigma_E$, as estimated from performance in sensory discrimination tasks, to the physical and sensory noise (Treisman 1966).

## 3. Measures of Discrimination

The prime measure of discrimination, the 'threshold' has suffered from the double usage given to the term by Fechner, who applied it both to the 'sensation' and to the stimulus giving rise to it. In the first sense the differential threshold was the 'just noticeable difference' in sensation and as such completely fixed. In the second, it was the difference in magnitude between two stimuli that would just produce this j.n.d. of sensation. This double use was based on the assumption that sensation was a continuous function of stimulus magnitude, that one could be measured in terms of the other. However, Fechner found that, because of the variation produced by 'chance fluctuations', the effect of a given stimulus difference was not fixed. Observations had to be repeated many times, and a statistic derived from the resulting data was used to estimate the subject's stimulus threshold, which in turn corresponded to the sensation threshold. We shall use 'threshold' only as a measure defined in terms of the subject's responses.

Many experimental designs, in many modifications, have been developed for the sensory discrimination task. Most of them derive from the traditional three designs described by Fechner. We shall briefly outline some of the more important of these designs, and consider how the statistics derived from them relate to the parameters of the model. In any psychological experiment a great many precautions are necessary; effects on the subject's performance of any knowledge he may have of the experimenter's expectations, or of variations in his state due to fatigue, loss of interest or other factors must be controlled or allowed for and preliminary experimentation to find suitable values of the independent variables is almost always necessary. However, this will not be discussed in detail here (Thurstone 1948; Guilford 1954; Woodworth and Schlosberg 1955).

A sensory discrimination task consists of a series of similar trials, on each of which a stimulus presentation is given to the subject and a response obtained from him. Among the ways in which designs differ are: (a) a stimulus presentation may consist of 0, 1, 2, or more stimulus values; (b) if two stimuli are presented on each trial, one of them may be identified as a standard or background stimulus $(I_N)$, present on each trial, and the other as a comparison stimulus, or their different identity may be kept from the subject; (c) the stimulus values used may come from a set of 0, 1, 2, or more; (d) the comparison stimuli may be presented in random order on successive trials, or in some systematic order which may take account of the subject's responses; (e) responses may be chosen from a finite set greater than one, or the number may be unrestricted. The set of stimulus values used in a given design will be denoted by $S'$, and the set of responses by $R'$. $S'_N$ is the number of elements in $S'$, and $R'_N$ the number in $R'$.

'Feedback' is sometimes given to the subject, as the information that his response has been 'right' or 'wrong', and monetary rewards or costs may be attached to the different types of performance.

*1. Designs with $S'_N > 2$ and random ordering.* Random order is often chosen in order to avoid, or to some extent to average out, biases in the subject's responses resulting from the immediately preceding pattern of stimuli and responses.

*1.1.* The design traditionally known as the *Method of Constant Stimuli* (MCS) may be used to determine the incremental or absolute threshold. $S' = \{I_N, I_1, I_2 \ldots I_k\}$ with usually $5 \leqslant k \leqslant 10$; $I_N < I_1$; for the incremental threshold $I_N > 0$, for the absolute threshold $I_N = 0$; the stimuli are usually (though not necessarily) equally-spaced, except that $(I_1 - I_N)$ may differ from the other intervals. On each trial $I_N$ is presented, identified as the standard or background stimulus, together with a comparison stimulus. The comparison stimuli may include one of the same magnitude as $I_N$. They are presented in random order on successive trials, usually equally often. $R' = \{Y, N\}$. The instructions for the incremental threshold require the subject to report on each trial whether or not he has detected an increment to $I_N$, and for the absolute threshold he reports detection of a stimulus.

In an experiment using this design to determine the incremental threshold the subject might be continuously presented with a 1000 c/s tone at 50 dB SPL ($I_N$). For a half-second interval on each trial the intensity of the tone would increase, the increment coming from a set which includes zero. With the zero increment the intensity of the comparison stimulus would also be $I_N$, and this would be known as a 'blank trial'. When the absolute threshold is determined, $I_N$ might correspond to the presentation of a screen reflecting no light, and the comparison stimuli would be produced by projecting light flashes on to the screen at intensities such that the subject only sometimes reports detecting them. On blank trials no light flashes would be projected.

With this design it is found that the probability of responding 'Yes', $P(Y)$, increases with the intensity of the comparison stimulus; this relation is known as the psychometric function, and it is usually well fitted by a normal ogive. This is best fitted by probit analysis (Finney 1952). This is shown in the lower half of Fig. 2, in which three comparison stimulus values, $I_N$, $I_{0.50}$ (the stimulus intensity which is found to give $P(Y) = 0.50$), and $I_{0.84}$ are shown. The range spanned by the psychometric function, from its lower to its upper asymptote, is sometimes known as the 'zone of transition'. The upper half of the figure illustrates the explanation of this result provided by the statistical decision model. It shows the probability density functions on the central decision axis corresponding to these three stimuli, with mean values of $\bar{E}_N$, $\bar{E}_{0.50}$ and $\bar{E}_{0.84}$, and the response criterion $E_c$. Since the decision rule applied by the response system is: 'If $E_i > E_c$ respond $Y$; if $E_i \leqslant E_c$ respond $N$', it follows that $P(Y)$ for any stimulus is given by the proportion of the corresponding central distribution lying to the right of $E_c$. Thus $P(Y|I_N)$ is the small proportion of the distribution centred on $\bar{E}_N$ which lies to the right of $E_c$. As the stimulus values increase above $I_N$, the corresponding normal central distributions will increasingly exceed $E_c$, so that the values of $P(Y)$ generated will be described by the normal cumulative distribution function. This rests on the assumption that the central distributions are normal, $\sigma_E$ is constant, and the

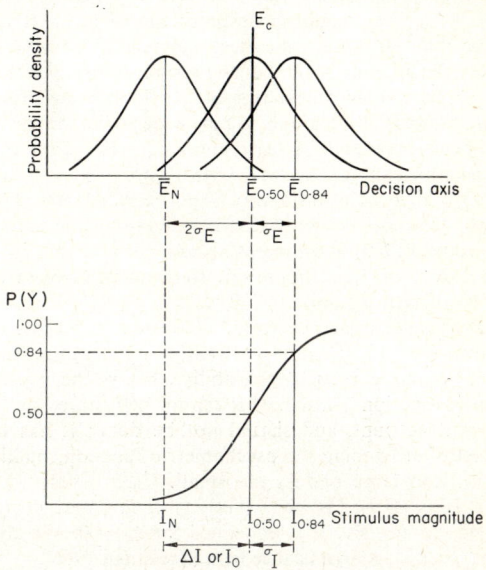

FIG. 2. *The lower half of the figure shows the psychometric function relating $P(Y)$ to the intensity of the comparison stimuli, when the MCS is used to determine the incremental or absolute threshold. The upper half shows the distributions on the decision axis corresponding to three stimuli, $I_N$, $I_{0.50}$ and $I_{0.84}$.*

relation between $E$ and $I$, $E = f(I)$, is linear. This last assumption is certainly not usually true, but for the small range of stimulus values used in sensory discrimination tasks it is an acceptable approximation. It can also be shown that $\sigma_E$ must increase with $E$, producing positive skew (Thurstone 1948), but in most cases the effect is so small that it is lost in the experimental error.

Since $E_c$ is chosen to give the acceptable limiting false positive rate $\varepsilon$, we can write $E_c = \bar{E}_N + z\sigma_E$, where $z$ is the standardized normal deviate which cuts off a tail of the normal curve equal in area to $\varepsilon$. Thus we should expect $P(Y|I_N) = \varepsilon$. We can see that $I_{0.50}$ is the stimulus whose mean central effect coincides with $E_c$, so that half the area of its central distribution lies to the right of the response criterion. Since the psychometric function is a normal ogive, the stimulus $I_{0.84}$ lies one standard deviation ($\sigma_I$) above $I_{0.50}$. Correspondingly 0.84 of the area of the distribution centred on $\bar{E}_{0.84}$ must lie to the right of $\bar{E}_{0.50} = E_c$, so that, since the distribution is normal, $\bar{E}_{0.84} - E_c = \sigma_E$.

Certain of the statistics which can be derived from such data estimate parameters of the model or are simply related to them. (a) $\Delta I = I_{0.50} - I_N$ would usually be taken as the incremental threshold in this design. Figure 2 shows that $\Delta I(I_0)$ corresponds to $z\sigma_E$, the product of two parameters, one expressing the effect of physical and biological noise in the afferent system, and the other the preferred response criterion. The threshold is sometimes defined in terms of a value of $P(Y) \neq 0.50$, but this would have a very similar interpretation; thus $\Delta I' = I_{0.84} - I_N$ would correspond to $(z+1)\sigma_E$. It follows that $\Delta I$ is not the best measure if we wish to study the afferent system, or the response system, alone.
(b) $\sigma_I$, the standard deviation of the psychometric function, depends on $\sigma_E$ alone, as can be seen from the correspondence between $I_{0.84} - I_{0.50}$ and $\bar{E}_{0.84} - \bar{E}_{0.50}$, and thus gives a measure of the total sensory noise.
(c) $C = \Delta I/\sigma_I$. This ratio, which may be called the *Crozier ratio*, tends to be constant for different values of $I_N$ (Blackwell 1963). It estimates $z\sigma_E/\sigma_E = z$ and thus gives a measure of the response criterion independent of the effect of sensory noise.

$P(Y)$ is sometimes corrected for false positives by the formula $P'(Y) = [P(Y) - P(Y|I_N)]/[1 - P(Y|I_N)]$, where $P'(Y)$ is the 'corrected' probability, before the psychometric function is fitted. This cannot be justified on the present account, and should not be done; it has the effect of steepening the psychometric function, making $\Delta I(I_0)$ too large and $\sigma_I$ too small.
(d) $W = \Delta I/I_N$, is the *Weber fraction*, and corresponds to $z\sigma_E/\bar{E}_N$. It is undefined for $I_N = 0$. We shall not discuss its significance here (Treisman 1966).
(e) FPR $= P(Y|I_N)$. The false positive rate estimates $\varepsilon$. Since $\varepsilon$ determines $z$, which is estimated by $C$, these two measures should agree if the model is consistent. Figure 3 shows the results of a comparison of this sort. An auditory intensity incremental threshold was determined, using the MCS, and FPR was given by the positive responses on blank trials. The false positive rate predicted by the value of $C$ for each subject, FPR|$C$, was taken as the area of the tail of the normal curve cut off by $C$, regarding the latter as a standardized normal deviate. FPR|$C$ is plotted against FPR in Fig. 3, which shows the values obtained lie about the straight line corresponding to FPR|$C$ = FPR.
(f) $I_N$ and the comparison stimuli may sometimes differ in more than one way. For example, the comparison stimuli might be pure tone increments of varying intensity added to a continuous background of white noise. In such a case it would seem plausible that $\sigma_E$ might be similar for the different combinations of white noise and tone, but have a different value for the white noise background ($I_N$) alone. If $\sigma_S$ is the former value and $\sigma_N$ the latter, it would then be of interest to estimate them separately. In this case $\sigma_I$ would correspond to $\sigma_S$, and $\Delta I$ to $z\sigma_N$. The standardized normal deviate corresponding to FPR, $z$(FPR), is an estimate of $z$, so that $\Delta I/z$(FPR) would correspond to $\sigma_N$. A difficulty is that a large number of observations is needed to give an accurate estimate of FPR.

Fechner placed the origin of his scale of sensation at the absolute threshold. Sensory scaling will not be discussed here (Stevens 1960; Treisman 1964a, 1965) but it is of interest that if we are concerned with the relation $E = f(I)$, the present account suggests three possible locations for the origin of the $E$ scale. (a) We may, as is usually done, take it to correspond to the absolute threshold, $I_0$, in which case we place it at $E_e = \bar{E}_N + z\sigma_E$; (b) we may place it at the $E$ value obtaining in the absence of any external stimulation, i.e. at $\bar{E}_N$. (c) The distribution centred on $\bar{E}_N$ represents the central effects of

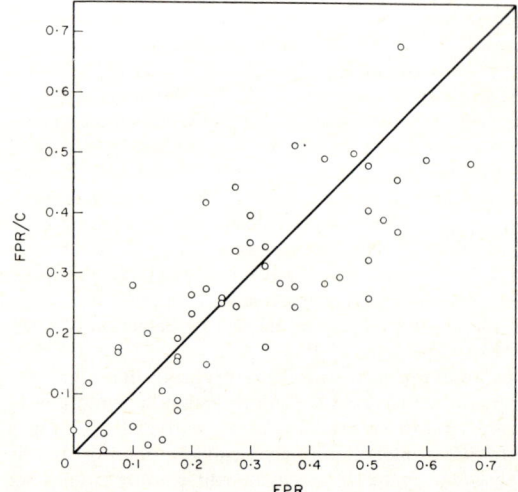

FIG. 3. *False positive rates predicted from C (FPR/C) plotted against the obtained false positive rate (FPR) for 31 subjects.*

the spontaneous activity and its variable transmission by the afferent system, in the absence of external stimulation. It is from this biological activity, simulating the effect of physical stimulation, that the comparison stimuli have to be distinguished. We can represent this spontaneous activity by the level of stimulation, $I_n$, which would produce the equivalent mean central effect if there were no biological noise. We could then write $E = f(I + I_n)$; when $I = 0$ we would have $\bar{E}_N = f(I_n)$, and we might wish to make the origin of the $E$ scale correspond to $f(-I_n + I_n) = f(0)$, the central effect in the absence of any physical or biological input. For example, the 'dark light', $I_n$, which is equivalent to the biological noise at the absolute threshold for light intensity is approximately 400–1000 quanta/sec deg². This might be partly produced by spontaneous decomposition of molecules of visual pigment or similar events indistinguishable from those consequent on the absorption of quanta of light. The origin of the $E$ scale might then be placed at the point corresponding to the absence of decompositions from either source.

*1.2.* In the *Method of Constant Stimulus Differences*, used to determine the differential threshold, the comparison stimuli are placed symmetrically about $I_N$: $S' = \{I_{-k} \ldots I_{-1}, I_N, I_1 \ldots I_k\}$, with $k > 2$ usually, $I_N > I_0, R' = \{G, D, L\}$. On each trial two stimuli are presented, one being identified as the standard $I_N$, the other being a comparison stimulus, and the instructions require the subject to report whether the latter is 'Greater' or 'Less' than the standard, or whether he is 'Doubtful'; or some other intermediate category of response, such as 'Equal', may be used.

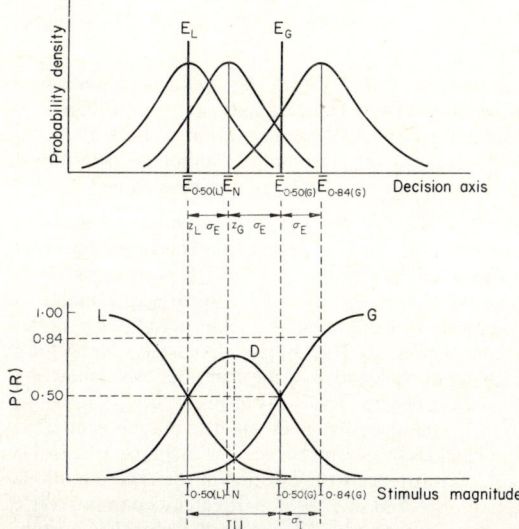

FIG. 4. *The method of constant stimulus differences applied to determining the differential threshold. The lower half of the figure shows the psychometric functions for three categories of response, and some corresponding central distributions are shown above.*

To choose between three responses two criteria are needed, as shown in the upper part of Fig. 4. The criteria are $E_G = \bar{E}_N + z_G \sigma_E$ and $E_L = \bar{E}_N - z_L \sigma_E$, where $z_G$ and $z_L$ are constants which may be regarded as standardized normal deviates and which need not be equal. On trial $i$ the response system must compare $E_i$ with these criteria; if $E_i > E_G$ the subject responds G; for $E_L < E_i \leq E_G$ he responds D, and for $E_i \leq E_L$ he responds L. We will then get the G and L normal ogives and the D curve shown in Fig. 4. The mean central effect of $I_{0.50(L)}$, the stimulus for which $P(L) = 0.50$, corresponds to $E_L$ and the mean effect of $I_{0.50(G)}$ similarly corresponds to $E_G$. $I_{0.50(L)}$ is sometimes known as the 'lower limen' (LL) and $I_{0.50(G)}$ as the 'upper limen' (UL).

This design gives similar measures to those described above. (a) The Interval of Uncertainty (IU) is defined by $\mathrm{IU} = I_{0.50(G)} - I_{0.50(L)}$. The difference threshold is often taken as $\Delta I = \mathrm{IU}/2$. We see that IU will correspond to $(z_G + z_L)\sigma_E = 2\bar{z}\sigma_E$, if we define $\bar{z} = (z_G + z_L)/2$, and $\Delta I$ will then correspond to $\bar{z}\sigma_E$. (b) $\sigma_I$ will correspond to $\sigma_E$. Theoretically it should be greater when determined from the G ogive than from the L curve, but the difference is too small to demonstrate experimentally. The terms 'threshold', '*limen*', 'j.n.d.', and sometimes $\Delta I$ have been used more or less interchangeably, and have not always been applied to the same statistic. (However we shall restrict $\Delta I$ to the definitions given.) The use of IU/2 as a 'threshold' measure has been criticised on the grounds that it is readily affected by the attitude and temperament of the subject, and minor variations in the instructions, and some workers have defined the threshold in terms of $\sigma_I$ instead. The contribution of $(z_G + z_L)$, as well as $\sigma_E$, to $\Delta I$ probably explains its variability. It seems that if we wish to study the afferent system alone, $\sigma_I$ will usually be the more useful measure. In analysing the data Fechner shared out D responses between the two extreme categories before determining the slope of the resulting psychometric function; this flattens the curve, making $\sigma_I$ overestimate $\sigma_E$, and is thus undesirable.

The term '*sensitivity*' is sometimes used, usually being defined as the reciprocal of $\Delta I$, or of $\sigma_I$, or some related measure; Fechner used $h = 1/2^{\frac{1}{2}}\sigma_I$. There is no apparent advantage in this transformation, which gives measures corresponding to the reciprocal of $z\sigma_E$ or $\sigma_E$. (c) If we are interested in the response criteria alone, the Crozier ratio $C = \mathrm{IU}/2\sigma_I$, which will correspond to $\bar{z}$, may be useful.

(d) $W$ may be taken as $\Delta I/I_N$ or $\sigma_I/I_N$, corresponding to $\bar{z}\sigma_E/\bar{E}_N$ or $\sigma_E/\bar{E}_N$, depending on the definition of the threshold preferred. The choice does not seem to affect the relation found between $W$ and $I_N$ as the latter varies (the Weber function), in keeping with the assumption that $\bar{z}$ tends to be constant for a given subject, as implied by Crozier's law.

(e) The *Point of Subjective Equality (PSE)* is the stimulus value at which the L and G ogives intersect. It corresponds to $\bar{E}_N + (z_G - z_L)\sigma_E/2$.

(f) The Constant Error (CE) is given by $\mathrm{CE} = \mathrm{PSE} - I_N$ and will correspond to $(z_G - z_L)\sigma_E/2$. Thus it reflects any asymmetry in the two criteria. It has been used in studying the effects of features of the experimental design such as the order in which the two stimuli are presented and the time interval between them. It might be better to separate effects on sensory noise from those on the criteria used. An index of the latter might be defined as Criterion Asymmetry (CA) = $2\mathrm{CE}/\sigma_I$, which would correspond to $(z_G - z_L)$.

(g) No FPR can be calculated, but $P(G|I_N)$ and $P(L|I_N)$ are analogous measures, though they have not been studied. Thus it should be possible to predict $P(G|I_N)$ from $(I_{0.50(G)} - I_N)/\sigma_I$ in the same way that FPR may be predicted from $C$ (see Fig. 3).

*1.3.* The design given above may be employed with $R' = \{G, L\}$. The subject may be instructed to guess when seriously uncertain about his responses. An advantage of this design is that all responses now determine a single ogive, as in 1.1, thus $\sigma_I$ is determined more reliably, but fewer measures are obtained. We suppose that the subject employs only one criterion, $E_c$, at or near $\bar{E}_N$. The relation between the model and the data obtained, plotted as $P(G)$, is then similar to that shown in Fig. 2 for the incremental threshold, except that $I_N$ will now be at or near $I_{0.50(G)}$.

In this design (a) $\sigma_I$ or a related measure, determined by $\sigma_E$ alone, is taken as the 'threshold'. (b) $W = \sigma_I/I_N$. (c) PSE $= I_{0.50(G)}$ and will correspond to $E_c$. (d) CE $=$ PSE$-I_N$ and will correspond to $E_c-\bar{E}_N$.

*1.4.* The two designs for determining the differential threshold (1.2 and 1.3) may be modified so that the subject does not know on each trial which of the two stimuli is the standard, the order in which they are given and any other relevant cues being randomized. Thus he might be asked to report whether the second of a pair of weights is more or less heavy than the first; when the second is a comparison stimulus the response G would be recorded as G; when it is in fact the standard, G would be recorded as L.

The model for this design will differ from the account given above only in the definition of the decision axis. Thus if design 1.2 is modified in this way, the decision axis in Fig. 4 must be re-defined. On any trial $i$ on which two stimuli are compared two central effects are produced, $E_{i(1)}$, the input from the weight presented first, say, and $E_{i(2)}$, the input from the weight given second. We suppose that the subject takes the difference between these two inputs, $D_i = E_{i(2)} - E_{i(1)}$, and uses the dimension, $D$, on which these differences are recorded, as the decision axis. Then, if the comparison and standard weights are both of magnitude $I_N$ the distribution of differences on the $D$ dimension will be normal and will have its mean at $(\bar{E}_N - \bar{E}_N) = 0$, and the 'Greater' and 'Less' criteria will be determined in relation to this mean and will be given by $D_G = z_G \sigma_D$ and $D_L = -z_L \sigma_D$. The mean of the distribution of the differences when $I_j$ is compared with $I_N$ will be $(\bar{E}_N - \bar{E}_j)$ when $I_j$ is given first, and $(\bar{E}_j - \bar{E}_N)$ when $I_j$ is given second. If on trial $i$, $D_i = (E_{i(2)} - E_{i(1)}) > D_G$ the subject will report that the weight given second is 'Greater'. Thus the normal central distributions on the $D$ decision axis will determine normal ogive psychometric functions as in the unmodified design. One difference is that $\sigma_D$ is greater than $\sigma_E$. If the central effects of the two stimuli are uncorrelated $\sigma_D = 2^{\frac{1}{2}}\sigma_E$, with correspondingly flatter psychometric functions. Since $I_N$ is not identified to the subject it also follows that the effects of any difference between $z_G$ and $z_L$ will be averaged out, so that non-zero values of CE will arise only from sampling error.

*1.5.* Designs 1.2 and 1.3 may also be modified by omitting the standard stimulus on each trial; this is the *Method of Single Stimuli* (MSS). Thus we might have $S' = \{I_{-k} \ldots I_N \ldots I_k\}$ and $R' = \{G, D, L\}$; on each trial a single stimulus, taken from $S'$ in random order, is presented to the subject. He is instructed to compare it with a standard, which may have been presented previously or named, and to report appropriately. Figure 4 would apply in this case too, and the same measures would be given as by the corresponding MCS design.

We assume that presenting the standard stimulus on each trial serves only to ensure that appropriate values of $E_G$ and $E_L$ are maintained; since $\sigma_I$ depends on the variability of the central effects of the comparison stimuli and not on that of the standard, it should not be affected by the omission of the standard. This is borne out by experiment: the values of $\sigma_I$ given by the MCS and the MSS are very similar, but IU tends to be larger in the latter procedure, suggesting that in the absence of frequent presentations of $I_N$, $z_G$ and $z_L$ are chosen larger.

*2. Designs with $S'_N = 2$, $R'_N$ finite, and random or invariant ordering.* These designs can be considered restricted versions of those in section 1. Because of the small stimulus set 'thresholds' cannot be determined, but some measures of interest can be obtained.

*2.1.* $S' = \{I_N, I_S\}$; $R' = \{Y, N\}$; the subject is asked to report whether he has detected $I_S$. This might be a flash of light near the absolute threshold. It is presented in the same way on every trial, no comparison stimulus of magnitude $I_N$ being used. A background $I_N$, e.g. a dark screen, is present. This simple design may be useful in studying the behaviour of the criterion. We assume that $E_c$ is set in relation to $E_N$, as in Fig. 1, and $P(Y)$ is then given by the proportion of the distribution centred on $\bar{E}_S$ which lies to the right of $E_c$. The main measure is then $P(Y|I_S)$; this reflects the position of the criterion in relation to $\bar{E}_S$. The effects of particular conditions on $E_c$ can then be found by calculating $P(Y)$ for the appropriate subsets of responses. Thus Howarth and Bulmer (1956) studied the effect of previous responses on a present response by comparing $P(Y|Y)$, $P(Y|YY)$, the $P(Y)$ following a $Y$ on the previous trial, or following a run of two $Y$'s, etc. They found that $P(Y|YYY) > P(Y|YY) > P(Y|Y) > P(Y|N)$; apparently the choice of $Y$ on one trial lowered $E_c$ on the next, while the choice of $N$ raised it. The extent of these shifts is better represented by the standardized normal deviates corresponding to the probabilities: $z(Y|YYY)$, $z(Y|YY)$, etc.; these give $(\bar{E}_S - E_c)/\sigma_S$ for the corresponding conditions.

*2.2.* $S' = \{I_N, I_S\}$, $I_S > I_N$; $R' = \{1, 2\}$; a similar simple design uses two stimulus values, given so that $I_N$ is not identified to the subject, as in design 1.4. This is achieved by presenting both stimuli on each trial, but in a randomly varying order in time or space. The subject must report whether, for example, the light flash was given in the first or second of two indicated temporal intervals, or of two locations on a screen. The proportion of the responses given which name the location of the signal correctly, P(C), is recorded. This is known as the *Forced Choice Procedure* (FCP).

This procedure is illustrated in Fig. 5; in the lower half of the figure two distributions on the $E$-axis are shown, corresponding to $I_N$ and $I_S$; the $E$-axis is shown scaled in $\sigma_E$ units, with $\bar{E}_N = 0$. We suppose that on each trial the response system records the values of $E$ in each of the two intervals, and takes their difference. If on trial $i$ the difference $E_{i(2)} - E_{i(1)}$ is positive the subject responds '2'; if however $E_{i(1)} > E_{i(2)}$ he responds '1'. (We assume there is no bias to one or the other response.) Then $P(C)$ is the probability that $E_{i(S)}$, the central input from $I_S$ on trial $i$, will be greater than $E_{i(N)}$, giving a positive difference, $D_i = E_{i(S)} - E_{i(N)}$, and thus determining a correct response. The distribution of $D_i$ is shown

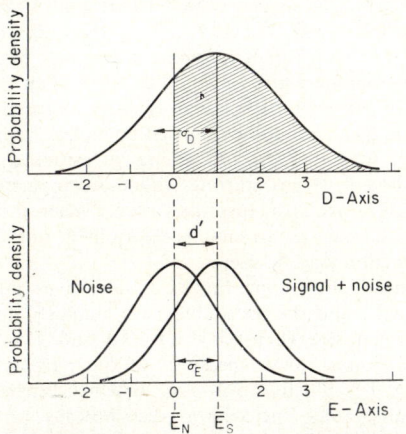

FIG. 5. *The Forced Choice Procedure: the central distributions on the E-axis corresponding to $I_S$ and $I_N$ are shown. In this case $d' = (\bar{E}_S - \bar{E}_N)/\sigma_E = 1$. The distribution of the differences between the central effects of $I_S$ and $I_N$ on each trial is shown above. $P(C)$ corresponds to the proportion of positive differences, shown shaded. Both axes are scaled in units of $\sigma_E$.*

in the upper half of Fig. 5; it is also normal, with mean $\bar{E}_S - \bar{E}_N$) and if the two inputs on each trial are uncorrelated its standard deviation is $\sigma_D = 2^{\frac{1}{2}}\sigma_E$. $P(C)$ is then the proportion of the distribution to the right of zero.

$P(C)$ can be used to determine the difference between the means of the two distributions on the $E$-axis, with $\sigma_E$ as unit; this is defined as $d' = (\bar{E}_S - \bar{E}_N)/\sigma_E$. The standardized deviate corresponding to $P(C)$, $z(C) = [(\bar{E}_S - \bar{E}_N) - 0]/\sigma_D = (\bar{E}_S - \bar{E}_N)/2^{\frac{1}{2}}\sigma_E$, therefore $d' = 2^{\frac{1}{2}}z(C)$. $d'$ is comparable to $C$ ($C$ corresponds to $(E_c - \bar{E}_N)/\sigma_E = z$): each is a standardized measure of a deviation from $\bar{E}_N$. $C$ is the more generally meaningful, since $E_c$ is selected by the subject and may be characteristic of him, whereas $I_S$ is chosen arbitrarily by the experimenter. $d'$ may be used to study the effects of different conditions, using a single value of $I_S$.

The FCP may be used with more than two intervals or locations on each trial; in this case we assume the subject reports the stimulus to be in the interval in which the largest central effect is recorded.

2.3. *The Yes-No Procedure* (YNP) has $S' = \{I_N, I_S\}$, $R' = \{Y, N\}$. The subject reports whether or not he can detect the signal which may be, for example, a pure tone of short duration and constant intensity presented in white noise. On each trial the white noise background ($I_N$) is present; on some trials, in random order with probability $P(I_S)$, the pure tone ($I_S$) is added, on others it is omitted ($I_N$). The subject's responses are analysed separately for the two comparison stimuli, giving $P(Y|I_S)$ and $P(Y|I_N)$.

Two or more series of responses are obtained, the conditions being varied so as to induce the subject to use different response criteria in each. This may be done by varying $P(I_S)$ for the different series, or by attaching monetary values and costs to the different types of performance and changing these, or trained subjects may simply be asked to use 'strict', 'medium' or 'lax' criteria. $P(Y|I_S)$ and $P(Y|I_N)$ are then determined for each series.

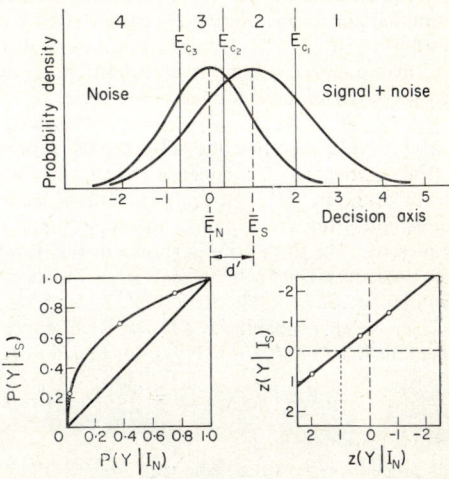

FIG. 6. *The Yes-No and Rating Procedures: the upper graph shows the distributions on the decision axis corresponding to $I_S$ and $I_N$ for $d' = 1$ and $\sigma_S/\sigma_N = 4/3$. The axis is scaled in units of $\sigma_N$, with $\bar{E}_N = 0$. The responses in RP are shown between their respective criteria. The lower left graph shows the resulting ROC curve when $P(Y|I_S)$ is plotted against $P(Y|I_N)$, and the lower right graph gives the straight line obtained when the corresponding standardized normal deviates are plotted.*

Figure 6 shows the central distributions corresponding to $I_S$ and $I_N$, together with three alternative criteria, $E_{c_1}$, $E_{c_2}$ and $E_{c_3}$. For each criterion, $P(Y|I_S)$ and $P(Y|I_N)$ is given by the proportion of the corresponding distribution to the right of the criterion. As the criterion used shifts to the left both these probabilities increase, and if we plot $P(Y|I_S)$ against $P(Y|I_N)$ we get a curve such as that shown in the lower left graph, known as a Receiving Operating Characteristic (ROC) curve. This allows us to compare $\sigma_S$, the standard deviation of the 'signal + noise' distribution, and $\sigma_N$, the standard deviation of the 'noise' distribution. Figure 6 shows the curve given for $d' = 1$, $\sigma_S/\sigma_N = 4/3$. The ROC curve is asymmetrical; when $\sigma_S/\sigma_N = 1$ it is symmetrical. In the lower right graph the standardized normal deviates $z(Y|I_S)$ and $z(Y|I_N)$ are plotted instead of the corresponding probabilities. The straight line given has the equation

$$z(Y|I_S) = (\sigma_N/\sigma_S)(z(Y|I_N) - d') \qquad (2)$$

The measures given by this procedure are (a) $d' = (\bar{E}_S - \bar{E}_N)/\sigma_N$, the standardized deviation of the signal mean from the noise mean. It is given by the intercept on the $z(Y|I_N)$ axis. (b) $\sigma_S/\sigma_N$ is the reciprocal of the slope of the line. (c) The values of $z(Y|I_N)$ locate the response criteria as standardized deviations from $\bar{E}_N$. The likelihood ratio corresponding to each criterion ($\beta$) is given by the ratio of the ordinates of the normal distribution at $z(Y|I_S)$ and $z(Y|I_N)$.

2.4. By requiring the subject to use more than one criterion simultaneously the *Rating Procedure* (RP) makes more efficient use of each response, and thus avoids the need to manipulate instructions or conditions in order to alter the criterion used for successive series of trials. $S' = \{I_N, I_S\}$; $R' = \{1, 2 \ldots k\}$, $R'_N > 2$. The design is similar to YNP except that the subject must report on each trial his degree of confidence that $I_S$ was given, using, for example, $R' = \{1, 2, 3, 4\}$ with '4' meaning 'signal definitely not given' and '1' meaning 'signal definitely present'. The three criteria shown in Fig. 6 would then be used simultaneously on each trial. The decision rule would be: If $E_i > E_{c_1}$, $R_i = 1$; if $E_{c_2} < E_i \leq E_{c_1}$, $R_i = 2$, etc. The probabilities for the ROC curve are given by: for $E_{c_1}$, $P(Y|I_S) = P(1|I_S)$; for $E_{c_2}$, $P(Y|I_S) = P(1|I_S) + P(2|I_S)$; for $E_{c_3}$ $P(Y|I_S) = \sum_{k=1}^{3} P(r_k|I_S)$, $r_k E R'$. $P(Y|I_N)$ is found similarly.

This procedure gives the same measures as YNP. As $d'$ depends on the value of $I_S$ chosen by the experimenter its use as a general measure of sensitivity is restricted, comparisons across conditions or between experiments requiring the same value of $I_S$; changes in $d'$ are then likely to reflect changes in $\sigma_N$. In that this procedure gives a good estimate of $\sigma_S/\sigma_N$, while MCS gives $\sigma_I$ which corresponds to $\sigma_S$, the two procedures are complementary.

3. *Designs with $S'_N > 2$, and an order of presentation which takes account of the subject's responses.* 3.1. If the absolute threshold for a circle of light was a single fixed value, the simplest way to find it would be to start with the circle of light clearly visible and then decrease the intensity in small steps until the subject reported that it had just disappeared: the intensity at that point would be the absolute threshold. This idea led to the development of the *Method of Limits* (ML), a procedure which has been used to determine absolute, incremental and differential thresholds, in designs that parallel most of those in section 1. We shall consider its application to the differential threshold.

$S' = \{I_{-k} \ldots I_N \ldots I_k\}$; the stimuli are usually equally spaced; not all the stimuli available to the experimenter will necessarily be used in any single experiment, and the stimuli used are not used equally often. $R' = \{G, D, L\}$. On each trial two stimuli are given, one identified as $I_N$, and the other a comparison stimulus. The latter are taken in order and fall into runs, descending runs starting with stimuli which evoke the response G, and ascending runs starting with stimuli giving L. Thus a descending run might have $I_6$ as comparison stimulus on the first trial and evoke G; successive stimuli would then be given in sequence until the response changed, for example $I_5$: G, $I_4$: G, $I_3$: G, $I_2$: D. The sequence would then stop (other stopping rules may be used), and the stopping point, $I_2$, would be taken as an estimate of the 'upper limen' (sometimes $(I_3 + I_2)/2$ is used). This descending run would be followed by an ascending run, starting, say, at $I_{-5}$, and giving an estimate of the 'lower limen'. (Runs starting with the comparison stimulus at $I_N$ are also sometimes used.) When the absolute or incremental threshold is determined, runs in only one direction may be used.

The mean of the upper limen estimates gives the upper limen, UL, and the ascending runs similarly give the lower limen, LL. Then $IU = UL - LL$ and $\Delta I = IU/2$. The relation of these measures to the parameters of the model is illustrated in Fig. 7, which represents a descending run. The central distributions produced by the presentation of $I_N$ (dashed lines), $I_2, I_3, I_4$ or $I_5$ are shown. If $I_5$ is the first stimulus presented, then the probability that $I_5$ will be the stopping point on this run, $P(I_5 = UL)$, will be given by the area of the corresponding central distribution to the left of $E_G$ (shown shaded), $p_5$, which is the probability of a response other than G when this stimulus is presented. Similarly $P(I_4 = UL)$ on this run is given by $P(I_4 = UL) = p_4(1 - p_5)$. If the run does not end at this stimulus it may end at $I_3$: $P(I_3 = UL) = p_3(1 - p_4)(1 - p_5)$; and $P(I_2 = UL) = p_2(1 - p_3)(1 - p_4)(1 - p_5)$. It is apparent that it is not necessary or even likely that the UL determined in this way will coincide with $I_{0.50(G)}$ as determined by MCS. $P(I_2 = UL)$, for instance, will be greater if the run starts at $I_4$ rather than at $I_5$, and it will be greater if larger step sizes are used, e.g. if the run starts at $I_4$ and the step interval is two, $P(I_2 = UL) = p_2(1 - p_4)$. It depends also on the size of $\sigma_E$, and may be markedly affected by any tendency for series of similar responses to cause systematic changes in $E_G$, since stimulus order is not random. Considering all these factors except the last, Brown and Cane (1959) showed that, for a sufficiently distant starting point $(I_{0.50(G)} + 3\sigma_I)$, and step size $= \sigma_I$, we would get $UL = I_{0.50(G)} - 0.27\sigma_I$, and for step size $0.50\sigma_I$, $UL = I_{0.50(G)} + 0.24\sigma_I$.

Although the IU and $\Delta I$ given by the ML are related to the same parameters as the similar measures given by MCS, they are likely to be biased to unknown and possibly serious extents in any experiment. $SD_L$, the standard deviation of the set of estimates of UL (or LL) given by the descending (or ascending) runs, tends to be proportional to $\sigma_I$ but to underestimate it. $C = \Delta I/SD_L$

will not be a good estimate of $\bar{z}$, but it may demonstrate Crozier's law. PSE = (UL+LL)/2 and CE = PSE$-I_N$ are particularly unsatisfactory since they will depend not only on the asymmetry of the subject's criteria but also on the distances of the run starting points from $z_G$ and $z_L$. Starting points are usually randomly varied to reduce the tendency for the subject to show fixed patterns of response, but the mean starting points are unlikely to be symmetrically placed about the criteria. No FPR can be determined.

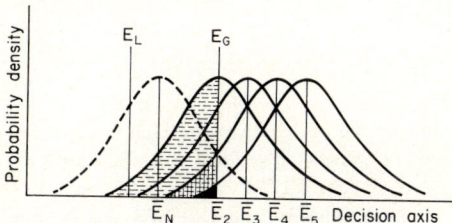

FIG. 7. *The Method of Limits*: the central distributions corresponding to $I_N$ (dashed lines), $I_2, I_3, I_4$ and $I_5$. The shaded portions of the curves, to the left of $E_G$, give the probability of a response other than G for each stimulus.

The ML has little to recommend it save its speed and simplicity, and its acceptability to subjects; but these considerations may make it a preferred method when a quick and rough measure is all that is needed. A particular danger is the temptation to the experimenter to try to speed the experiment by using large steps where he does not expect to find a threshold, and small ones where he does. This may be an appropriate strategy when searching for a needle in a haystack, but applied to the threshold it can lead to totally invalid results.

3.2. A procedure which makes more efficient use of the subject's responses is the *Staircase Method* (SM), which can be used to determine absolute and incremental thresholds. The underlying idea is that if following the response 'Yes' we present the subject with a weaker stimulus, and following 'No' we present him with a stronger stimulus, a record of the stimuli used will oscillate about $I_{0.50}$.

Stimuli are drawn from $S' = \{I_N, I_1, I_2 \ldots I_k\}$ in accordance with the subject's responses. $R' = \{Y, N\}$. On each trial $I_N$ and a comparison stimulus are presented, and the subject reports whether he detects an increment (for the absolute threshold $I_N = 0$, and he reports detecting the stimulus). The 'staircase' obtained depends on the stimulus presentation rule used by the experimenter. The basic rule is: If on trial $i$ stimulus $I_j$ is given and evokes the response $R_i = Y$, then on trial $(i+1)$ present $I_{j-1}$; if $R_i = N$, then on trial $(i+1)$ present $I_{j+1}$. The sort of record given is shown in Fig. 8: '1' represents a positive and '0' a negative response by the subject. If we define a 'run' as a sequence of responses of constant direction, terminating in a change of response, the record shows 6 runs, their end-points occurring on trials 2, 6, 7, 11, 12, and 13.

The mean of the run end-points provides a good estimate of $I_{0.50}$; for the record in Fig. 8, this gives $I_{0.50} = I_9$, as shown by the arrow. Two precautions are important in this method: (a) the starting point of the staircase should be near $I_{0.50}$, to avoid bias in the final estimate of $I_{0.50}$. Therefore a preliminary staircase of 6 or 8 runs is recorded, using a step size of $0.5\,\sigma_I$ to $\sigma_I$ if an estimate of $\sigma_I$ is available, and $I_{0.50}$ is then estimated. Using this estimate as the starting point and halv-

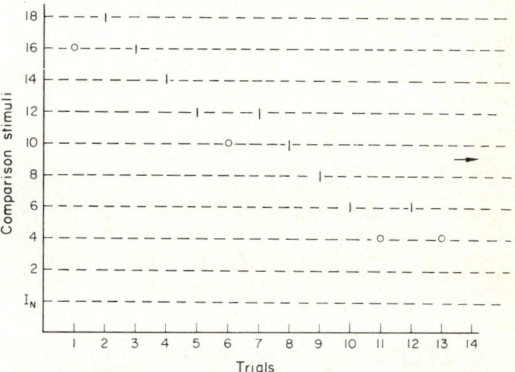

FIG. 8. *Staircase method*: A protocol given by the rule: if on trial $i$, $R_i \mid I_j = Y$, present: $I_{j-1}$; if $R_i \mid I_j = N$, present $I_{j+1}$. Here the step interval $= 2$, '1' represents a positive response, and '0' a negative response.

ing the step size an experimental staircase of, say, 20 or more runs (an even number is preferable) can then be obtained and the final value of $I_{0.50}$ estimated from this (a suitable step size should not give runs much longer than 3–4 responses). (b) If a single staircase is determined the stimulus presentation rule may become evident to the subject, which will affect his responses; also any tendency to produce patterns of response, such as YNYN..., or to avoid long runs will give spurious results. These difficulties can be met by determining two staircases simultaneously in random alternation: trials are allotted to the two staircases by a random procedure and on each trial the stimulus given is determined by the response on the previous trial of that staircase. Figure 9 illustrates this: staircase A is determined on the randomly selected ringed trials, and B on the unringed trials. A shows three runs, with end-points on trials 19, 25 and 26; B shows three runs, with end-points at 18, 27 and 28.

The mean of the run end-points gives a good estimate of $I_{0.50}$, the stimulus whose mean central effect corresponds to $E_e$. We then have $\Delta I = I_{0.50} - I_N$, for the increment threshold, or $I_0 = I_{0.50}$ for the absolute threshold. We can calculate $W$ but not $\sigma_I$, $C$ or FPR. An advantage over other procedures is that the record gives an indication of any drifts or shifts in $E_e$ during the course of the experiment.

3.3. The '*Transformed Response Staircase Method*' (**TRSM**) (Wetherill and Levitt 1965) is an improved procedure giving more information. If instead of alternating between two staircases, each of which estimates $I_{0.50}$, we alternate between two staircases which estimate, say, $I_{0.7071}$ and $I_{0.2929}$ respectively, these values will bracket $I_{0.50}$ and their difference will give a measure of $\sigma_I$. The design is similar to the SM, except for the stim-

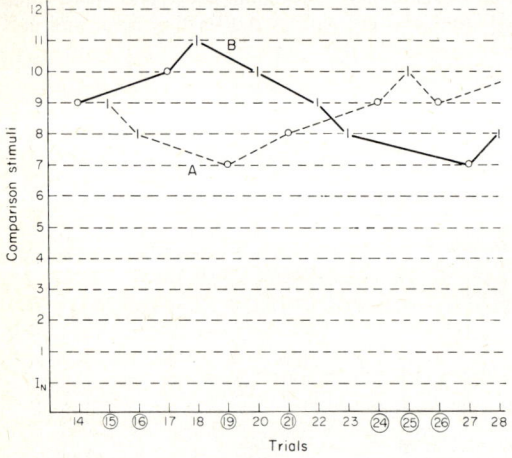

FIG. 9. *Double Staircase Method: Trials are randomly allotted to two staircases; in this case staircase A is determined on the ringed trials, and B on the unringed trials.*

ulus presentation rule. If $P(Y|I_{0.7071}) = 0.7071$, then $P(YY|I_{0.7071}) = 0.50$. Therefore if the record moves down only when two positive responses are evoked in succession by a given stimulus value, and moves up for other patterns of response, it will oscillate about $I_{0.7071}$. The stimulus presentation rule for $I_{0.7071}$ is therefore: If two presentations of $I_j$ give the response sequence YY, present $I_{j-1}$ on the next trial; if one presentation of $I_j$ gives N or two presentations give YN, present $I_{j+1}$ on the next trial. Similarly for $I_{0.2929}$ we would have: For NN, present $I_{j+1}$; for Y or NY, present $I_{j-1}$. Figure 10 shows part of a staircase to determine $I_{0.7071}$; there are 4 runs, with end-points on trials 5, 6, 10 and 16. In the full design, starting points for the two staircases would be estimated from a short preliminary series, and the experiment proper would alternate randomly between the two staircases. (With the appropriate rules, other pairs of points, such as 0.794 and 0.206 or 0.8409 and 0.1591 can also be found.)

The means of the run end-points for the two staircases give $I_{0.7071}$ and $I_{0.2929}$. Then $I_{0.50} = (I_{0.7071} + I_{0.2929})/2$. For the absolute threshold $I_0 = I_{0.50}$, and for the incremental threshold $\Delta I = I_{0.50} - I_N$. If we use $R' = \{G, L\}$, with comparison stimuli lying above and below $I_N$, then PSE = $I_{0.50}$, and CE = PSE $- I_N$ will correspond to $E_c - \bar{E}_N$. We also have $\sigma_I = (I_{0.7071} - I_{0.2929})/1.09$, which corresponds to $\sigma_E$, $C = \Delta I/\sigma_I$ corresponding to $z$, and $W = \Delta I/I_N$. The two staircases will not only show

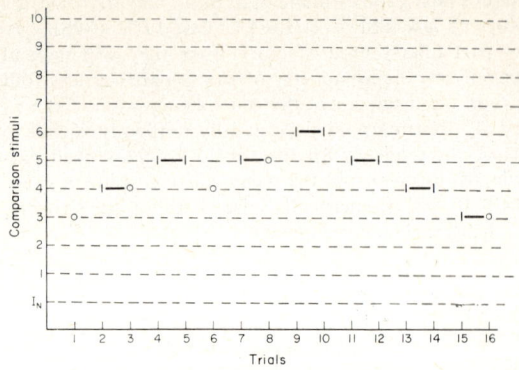

FIG. 10. *Part of a staircase to determine $I_{0.7071}$. The rule is: After 11, present $I_{j-1}$; after 0 or 10, present $I_{j+1}$.*

any drifts in $E_c$ during the course of a session but will also reflect changes in $\sigma_E$.

4. $S'_N = 0$ or 1; $R'_N$ is unlimited. 4.1 In the *Method of Reproduction* (MR) (Method of Adjustment, Method of Average Error) $S' = \{I_N\}$, the standard stimulus is presented on each trial, and the instructions require the subject to adjust the intensity of a variable stimulus to equality with $I_N$ each time. The intensity at which it is left is taken as the subject's response. In this way a distribution of reproduction stimulus intensities is obtained which can be fitted by a normal density function: $f(I_j|I_N)$ is then the probability density that $I_j$ will occur as a reproduction of $I_N$. This distribution is shown in the lower half of Fig. 11, and the upper half shows its derivation from the model. We assume that the response

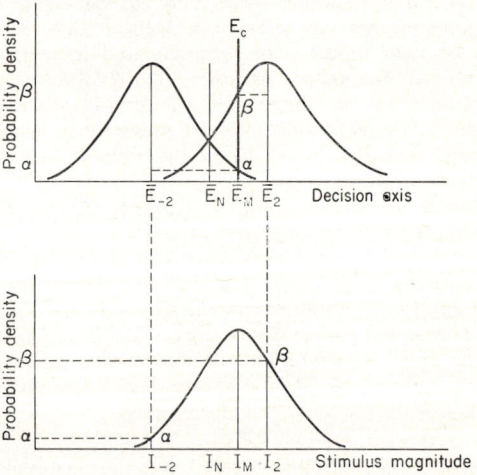

FIG. 11. *The Method of Reproduction: the distribution of reproductions given below is related to the distributions on the Decision Axis. Distributions correspondings to $I_{-2}$ and $I_2$ are shown.*

system employs a criterion, $E_c$, at or near $\bar{E}_N$, and on each trial applies the decision rule: Terminate trial $i$ when the variable stimulus produces a central effect $E_i$ such that $E_i = E_c$. Then the probability density that when the variable stimulus is adjusted to the intensity $I_j$ the subject will make this his reproduction is given by $f(E_c | I_j)$. Thus in the figure $f(E_c | I_2) = \beta$, and therefore $f(I_2 | I_N) = \beta$; similarly $f(E_c | I_{-2}) = f(I_{-2} | I_N) = \alpha$.

We see that the distribution of reproductions will reflect the central distributions, provided $E = f(I)$ is approximately linear and $\sigma_E$ approximately constant, and provided all the stimulus intensities in the range used are examined equally often, a condition which it is very difficult to ensure is exactly met. The threshold is taken as the standard deviation of the reproductions, $\sigma_I$ or some related measure; $\sigma_I$ corresponds to $\sigma_E$ but may include variability due to the motor effectors. Since values of $\sigma_I$ given by MCS and MR may be very similar the effector system variability may be relatively unimportant. The mean of the reproductions, $I_M$, is taken as the PSE; it is the stimulus whose mean central effect coincides with $E_c$, and therefore $CE = PSE - I_N$ corresponds to $E_c - \bar{E}_N$. $W = \sigma_I / I_N$ and there is no $C$.

4.2. The *Method of Production* (MP) is similar save that $S' = \emptyset$: no standard stimulus is presented on each trial. The instructions require the subject to produce a stimulus intensity equal to a named standard, or to one given before the production trials are embarked on. We suppose that the response system selects a criterion, $E_c$, and proceeds as before, and the same measures are given. With this procedure $\sigma_I$ may be slightly larger than with MR, possibly due to greater instability of the criterion, and the absolute value of CE tends to be greater.

### 4. Conclusion

Measures of sensory discrimination may be used as dependent variables in a variety of problems, such as investigating nutritional effects on dark adaptation or the neurological integrity of a sensory system, or they may be used to study the sensory discrimination mechanisms or the perceptual systems themselves, their interrelations as shown by the positive or negative interactions which occur between stimuli in the same or different modalities (Treisman 1963, 1964b), Weber's law and the other sensory laws which they give rise to, or sensory scaling, as it concerns the $E$ axis. In every case, to interpret the evidence correctly it is most important to understand how the experimental design used and the measures derived from it may relate to the underlying sensory discrimination mechanisms.

### Glossary of Symbols

$\beta$: the critical likelihood ratio.
$C$: the Crozier ratio; $C = \Delta I / \sigma_I$ or $IU/2\sigma_I$.
$CA$: the Criterion Asymmetry, given by $CA = 2CE/\sigma_I$.
$CE$: the Constant Error; $CE = PSE - I_N$.
$\Delta I$: the differential or incremental threshold; $\Delta I = IU/2$ or $\Delta I = I_{0.50} - I_N, I_N > I_0$.
$d'$: $(\bar{E}_S - \bar{E}_N)/\sigma_N$.
$D$: the response 'Doubtful'
$D_i$: the difference between the central effects of two stimuli given on trial $i$.
$\varepsilon$: an acceptable limiting false positive rate.
$E$: the dimension representing the magnitude of the central effect of a stimulus used in selecting the response; the 'decision axis'.
$E_c$: the response criterion, the $E$ value used in selecting responses, for the response $Y$.
$E_G$: the response criterion for $G$.
$E_i$: the magnitude of the central effect produced on trial $i$.
$\bar{E}_j$: the mean central effect of stimulus $I_j$.
$E_L$: the response criterion for $L$.
$\bar{E}_M$: the mean central effect of $I_M$.
$\bar{E}_N$: the mean central effect of $I_N$; the mean of the 'noise' distribution.
$\bar{E}_S$: the mean central effect of $I_S$; the mean of the 'signal + noise' distribution.
$\bar{E}_{0.50}$: the mean central effect of $I_{0.50}$.
$FCP$: Forced Choice Procedure.
$f(E | I_j)$: the probability density function on $E$ given that stimulus $I_j$ is presented.
$f(E_i | I_j)$: the probability density of $E_i$ when $I_i$ is presented.
$f(I_j | I_N)$: the probability density that $I_j$ will occur as a reproduction of $I_N$.
$FPR$: the false positive rate; $P(Y | I_N)$.
$G$: the response 'Greater'.
$I$: a physical dimension of intensity or magnitude, such as luminance, weight, or temporal duration.
$I_j$: a given stimulus magnitude.
$I_n$: the physical stimulus intensity which would be equivalent in its mean effect to the spontaneously arising sensory noise.
$I_M$: the mean of the productions or reproductions of a standard stimulus.
$I_N$: the intensity of the 'standard' or background stimulus, of intensity zero or greater, giving rise to the 'noise' distribution.
$I_S$: the stimulus intensity serving as 'signal + noise' in a given experiment.
$IU$: the interval of uncertainty; the range between the stimuli giving $P(G) = 0.50$ and $P(L) = 0.50$ when three categories of response are used.
$I_0$: the absolute threshold; $I_0 = I_{0.50}, I_N = 0$.
$I_{0.50}$: the stimulus magnitude such that $P(Y | I_{0.50}) = 0.50$.
$I_{0.50(G)}$: the stimulus magnitude such that $P(G | I_{0.50(G)}) = 0.50$.
$I_{0.84}$: the stimulus magnitude such that $P(Y | I_{0.84}) = 0.84$.
$l(E_i)$: the likelihood ratio for $E_i$: $l(E_i) = f(E_i | I_S)/f(E_i | I_N)$.
$L$: the response 'Less'.

LL: the lower limen; $I_{0.50(L)}$, or the analogous measure for ML.
MCS: Method of Constant Stimuli.
ML: Method of Limits.
MP: Method of Production.
MR: Method of Reproduction.
MSS: Method of Single Stimuli.
$N$: the response 'No'.
$P(C)$: the proportion of the responses which name the location of the stimulus correctly, in the FCP.
$P(I_j)$: the *a priori* probability that $I_j$ will be presented.
$P(I_j=UL)$: the probability that $I_j$ will be the stopping point of a descending ML run.
$p_j$: the probability that $I_j$ will evoke $D$ or $L$.
$P(R)$: the probability of the response $R$.
$P(R \mid I_j)$: the probability of the response $R$ on trials on which $I_j$ is presented.
$P(R \mid R)$: the probability of $R$ given the response $R$ was made on the preceding trial.
$P(R \mid RR)$: $P(R)$ following a run of two $R$'s.
PSE: the Point of Subjective Equality; the point at which the $G$ and $L$ ogives intersect.
$R$: a given response, which may be defined as, e.g. $Y, N$ or $D$.
$R'$: the set of responses allowed in a given experimental design.
$R_i$: the response on trial $i$.
$R'_N$: the number of elements in $R'$.
RP: Rating Procedure.
$\sigma_D$: the standard deviation of the distribution of the differences between the central effects of two stimuli.
$\sigma_E$: the standard deviation of the distribution on $E$ produced by repeated presentation of a given stimulus.
$\sigma_I$: the standard deviation of the psychometric function.
$\sigma_N$: the value of $\sigma_E$ for the central distribution produced by $I_N$.
$\sigma_S$: the value of $\sigma_E$ for the central distribution produced by a comparison stimulus $I_S$.
$S'$: the set of stimulus values used in a given experimental design.
$SD_L$: the standard deviation of a set of estimates of UL (or of LL) obtained by ML.
SM: Staircase Method.
$S'_N$: the number of elements in $S'$.
TRSM: Transformed Response Staircase Method.
UL: the upper limen; $I_{0.50(G)}$, or the analogous measure for ML.
$v(R \mid I_j)$: the value or cost attaching to the response $R$ when $I_j$ is presented.
$W$: the Weber fraction; $W = \Delta I / I_N$, or $W = \sigma_I / I_N$.
$Y$: the response 'Yes'.
YNP: Yes-No Procedure.
$z$: the standardized normal deviate cutting off a tail of the normal distribution equal in area to $\varepsilon$.
$\bar{z}$: $(z_G + z_L)/2$.
$z(C)$: the standardized normal deviate corresponding to $P(C)$.
$z(FPR)$: the standardized normal deviate corresponding to FPR.
$z_G$: the constant determining the response criterion $E_G = \bar{E}_N + z_G \sigma_E$.
$z_L$: the constant determining the response criterion $E = \bar{E}_N - z_L \sigma_E$.
$z(R \mid I_j)$: the standardized normal deviate corresponding to $P(R \mid I_j)$.

*See also:* Hearing. Sensory processes. Simulation of traffic problems using chain code random generators.

*Bibliography*

BLACKWELL H. R. (1963) *Neural theories of simple visual discriminations*, J. Opt. Soc. Amer. **53**, 129.
BROWN J. and CANE V. R. (1959) *An analysis of the limiting method*, Brit. J. Stat. Psychol. **12**, 119.
CATTELL J. M. (1893) *On errors of observation*. Amer. J. Psychol., **5**, 285.
FECHNER G.T.(1966) *Elements of psychophysics*, Vol. I. (Trans. H. E. ADLER) New York: Holt, Rinehart and Winston.
FINNEY D. J. (1952) (2nd Edn) *Probit Analysis*, Cambridge: The University Press.
GUILFORD J. P. (1954) (2nd Edn) *Psychometric Methods*, New York: McGraw-Hill.
HOWARTH C. I. and BULMER M. G. (1956) *Non-random sequences in visual threshold experiments*, Quart. J. Exper. Psychol., **8**, 163.
LUCE R. D. (1963) *Detection and recognition*, in (LUCE R. D., BUSH R. R. and GALANTER E. Eds.) *Handbook of Mathematical Psychology*, Vol. 1, New York: Wiley.
STEVENS S. S. (1960) *The psychophysics of sensory function*, Amer. Scient. **48**, 226.
SWETS J. A., TANNER W. P. and BIRDSALL T. G. (1961) *Decision processes in perception*, Psychol. Rev. **68**, 301.
THURSTONE L. L. (1948) *Psychophysical methods*, in (T. G. ANDREWS Ed.), *Methods of Psychology*, New York: Wiley.
TREISMAN M. (1963) *Auditory unmasking*, J. Acoust. Soc. Amer. **35**, 1256.
TREISMAN M. (1964a) *Sensory scaling and the psychophysical law*, Quart. J. Exper. Psychol. **16**, 11.
TREISMAN M. (1964b) *The effect of one stimulus on the threshold for another: an application of signal detectability theory*, Brit. J. Stat. Psychol. **17**, 15.
TREISMAN M. (1965) *Signal detection theory and Crozier's law: derivation of a new sensory scaling procedure*, J. Math. Psychol. **2**, 205.
TREISMAN M. (1966) *A statistical decision model for sensory discrimination which predicts Weber's law and other sensory laws: some results of a computer simulation*, Perc. and Psychophys. **1**, 203.

WOODWORTH R. S. and SCHLOSBERG H. (1955) *Experimental Psychology*, London: Methuen.
WETHERILL G. B. and LEVITT H. (1965) Sequential estimation of points on a psychometric function, *Brit. J. Math. Stat. Psychol.* **18**, 1.

M. TREISMAN

## SENSORY PROCESSES.

### Sensory Discrimination

Many sensory systems depend on a spatial distribution of receptors as their primary analytic tool. This arrangement may reflect the analysis of a true external spatially-organized situation as in vision or touch, or a pseudo-spatial situation such as hearing where the receptor position reflects some non-spatial dimension of the signal such as frequency. Ideally the analytic process would be sufficiently sharp that each receptor in the array would respond only to the corresponding element in the signal pattern. For various reasons this is not achieved. The lack of precision is in part due to the physical limitations of the media, e.g. the failure of the lens system of the eye to form an image free from fringes, the spread of the mechanical wave of deformation when the skin is touched. Other limitations may arise from conflicting physiological requirements; thus, the Helmholtzian ear, constructed of resonators sufficiently sharply tuned to realize the degree of frequency discrimination achieved by the whole auditory system, would be quite unable to meet the transient response requirements needed for other aspects of auditory performance.

As a result of these shortcomings and conflicts, a 'point stimulus' produces a neural response which involves a considerable number of receptors and their associated nerve fibres, and this active array overlaps that produced by the next adjacent discriminable stimulus. This overlap may be very considerable. In the auditory nerve, for example, 98% of the fibres activated by two adjacent just discriminable tones may be the same (Fig. 1).

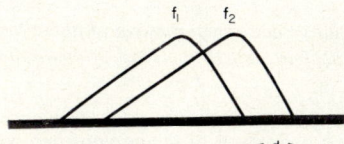

FIG. 1. *The overlap in the array of fibres stimulated by each of two just distinguishable tones, $f_1$, $f_2$, is very considerable. The difference 'd' may be as small as 2% of the total number activated by $f_1$ or $f_2$.*

Although the primary fibre array carries the necessary information about the stimulus in so far as each of the two discriminable stimuli gives rise to a unique pattern of activity, this information is not in a form readily utilizable by the nervous system. Since the receptor discharge rate is usually a direct monotonic function of the stimulus strength, the activity in the fibre array can be represented as in Fig. 2a where the height of each line represents the discharge rate of that particular fibre. Clearly, such a code is unsuitable for transmission through neural channels. The introduction of a quite small amount of noise into the system in the form of random

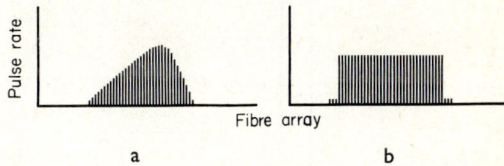

FIG. 2. *Diagram to illustrate the transformation of sensory information along the nervous pathway. (a) Response of an array of sensory fibres to a given stimulus. The height of each line represents the rate of impulse discharge in a fibre or small group of fibres. (b) Corresponding response of a group of fibres at a higher level in the nervous system to the same stimulus.*

pulses could completely blur the distinction between the positions of the maxima of overlapping response envelopes, and similarly with the positions of the borders of the active arrays.

The sensory nervous system appears to solve this problem uniformly, in all modalities, by sharpening the edges of the active array, so that the distinction between activity and inactivity is more clear cut; fibres then tend to be either 'hard-on' or completely inactive apart from background activity (Fig. 2b). This transformation is brought about by the system of regularly arranged excitatory and inhibitory interconnexions between adjacent members of the array which occurs at the cell stations along all sensory pathways.

The mechanism of such a transformation was studied by Allanson & Whitfield in the auditory pathway. The fibres of the auditory nerve divide very regularly as they enter the cochlear nucleus, and each sends a terminal to several hundred cells. The distributions of adjacent fibres overlap to give the convergence/divergence network illustrated diagrammatically in Fig. 3a. If the synaptic terminals were uniformly excitatory the effect of this network would, in general, be simply to spread the activity even more widely in the output of the distribution. However, inhibitory processes also occur in the nucleus, probably through the interpolation of inhibitory internuncial cells (Fig. 3b). There will thus be a complete inhibitory network, corresponding to the excitatory one of Fig. 3a, though the convergence factor may be different. When analysed quantitatively, it is found that the effect of such a network is to suppress completely those inputs which fail to reach a certain very low firing rate, but to produce a large and almost uniform output rate in those channels whose inputs exceed this critical value. This input/output transformation is represented by the curve of Fig. 4. The effect of such a transform is to convert the 'humped' pulse rate distribution pattern in the primary array into a 'square' output distribution (Fig. 2). This has the clear advantage that the edge of the activity is now well defined so that a small shift in its position

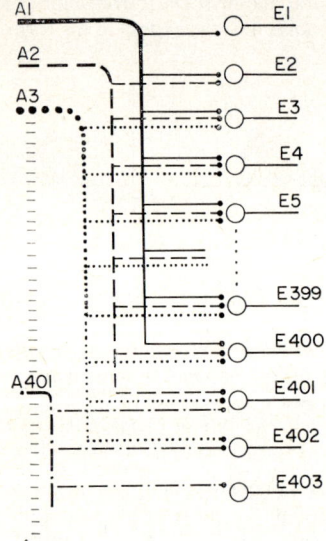

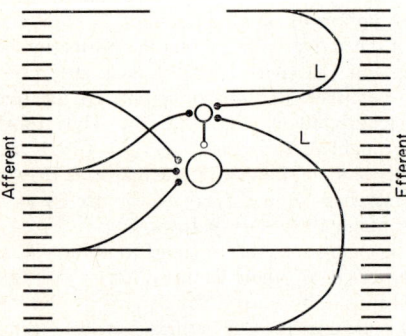

FIG. 3. (a) *Diagrammatic representation of the distribution of adjacent auditory nerve fibres to cells of the cochlear nucleus. Only three out of the several hundred branches of each fibre are actually shown.* (b) *The formation of an inhibitory network by means of an inhibitory internuncial (small neuron). Only one inhibitory afferent and three excitatory afferents are shown. There will of course be a complete array of each, as in (a). The fibres marked L represent collateral inhibitory pathways.* (Whitfield, Allanson and Whitfield).

can be detected in the presence of noise. The nervous system appears well-adapted for detecting such boundaries between activity and inactivity. Although the main effect of such a network is to produce an output which is either zero, or else has some finite value nearly independent of the input rate, it is found that within a certain range of relative excitatory/inhibitory conver-

gence the network exhibits a tendency for the output to fall when the input rises above a certain rather high value (Fig. 4 dotted curve). This leads to a 'double-hump' in the output distribution (Fig. 5 dotted curve), which even further accentuates the position of the edges in comparison with the rest of the active array. That this situation exists in real sensory systems is emphasized by the common occurrence of a non-monotonic relationship between stimulus intensity and fibre discharge-

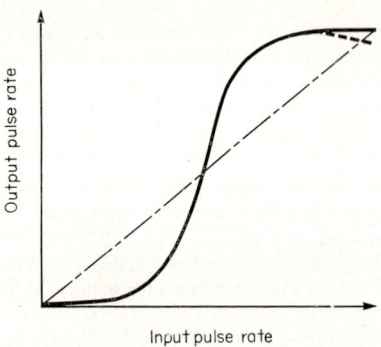

FIG. 4. *The input/output relation for pulse rates in the cochlear nucleus. The straight (chain) line represents what the relation would be if the transform were linear.*

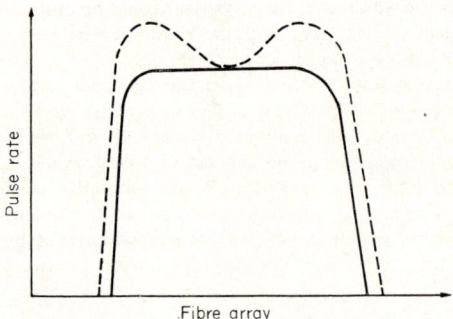

FIG. 5. *Relative activity in a group of fibres for moderate stimuli (full line) and very strong stimuli (dashed line) (cf. Fig. 2(b)).*

rate in the higher levels of the nervous pathway. As has been stated, the relationship between discharge-rate and stimulus intensity in a primary sensory fibre is monotonic and commonly sigmoid (Fig. 6a). The relationship for higher levels is shown by the two examples in Fig. 6b, one from the output of the cochlear nucleus, and the other at a still higher level, the inferior colliculus.

So far we have been considering the discrimination of two stimuli presented successively, and shown how these are distinguished by small changes in the position of the boundaries between active and inactive groups of fibres, even though the bulk of the fibres activated may be identical in the two cases. We must now consider the situation when two stimuli are presented simultaneously. Suppose we consider two stimuli which are far enough apart that each activates an array of primary fibres such that there is a 20% overlap between the two arrays (Fig. 7). If these two stimuli are presented simultaneously, and the primary pattern undergoes the squaring transformation considered above, then clearly the output will consist of a single block of active fibres—a signal which would be indistinguishable from that produced by a single intense stimulus centre somewhere between the two which we are considering. Experiment shows,

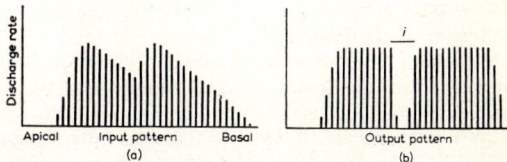

FIG. 7. (a) The discharge pattern in the array of auditory nerve fibres when two tonal stimuli are presented simultaneously. (b) Inhibition of certain fibres (i) in the output array preserves the identify of the two blocks of activity

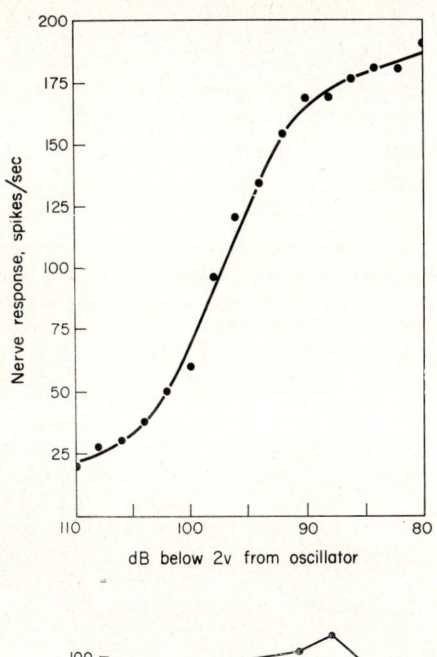

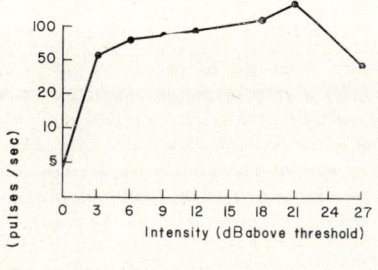

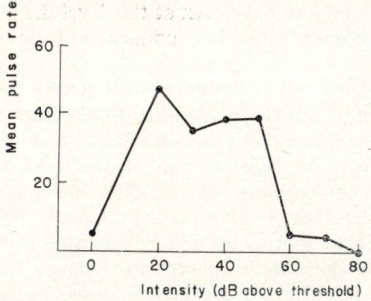

FIG. 6. (a) Sigmoid relationship between stimulus strength and fibre discharge rate (cell at root of auditory nerve). This shape is typical of a sensory nerve fibre. (b) Non-monotonic relationship between stimulus strength and response rate, from higher levels in the sensory system. Above: trapezoid body; Below: inferior colliculus. (Constructed from data of Galambos and Davis, Hilali and Whitfield, Hind et al.)

however, that this does not happen. If we examine the behaviour of a fibre f′ in the output array (corresponding to f in the input array) we find that it responds when stimulus (a) is presented alone and responds likewise when stimulus (b) is presented alone. However, when both stimuli are presented together, the response is reduced or absent. This '*mutual inhibition*' is illustrated by an example from the auditory system in Fig. 8. The effect is me-

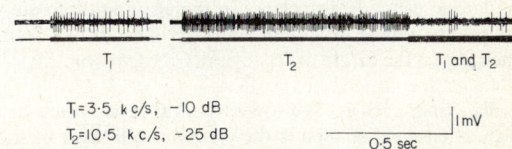

FIG. 8. Mutual inhibition. The unit responds to tone $T_1$ when presented alone, and to $T_2$ when presented alone. When $T_1$ and $T_2$ are presented simultaneously the response is almost completely inhibited.

diated by lateral inhibitory fibres of the type shown diagrammatically in Fig. 3b. The two blocks of active fibres do *not* coalesce when the two stimuli are simultaneously presented, and the separate identity of the two responses is preserved.

Although examples in the above description have been drawn from the auditory system, the same principles seem to obtain in sensory systems in general. They are certainly applicable to the visual and somatic systems, where similar lateral interconnexions between adjacent channels are histologically manifest, and where similar sharpening of the edges of activity can be shown to occur. Such contrast phenomena have been especially studied in the visual system.

*Neural Extraction of Stimulus Pattern*

There are two problems involved in the attempt to generalize the role of sensory systems in extracting features of different complexity from the stimulus situation. Firstly, in many modalities, of which taste and smell are good examples, it is impossible to define what is meant by a pattern, since there is no objective way of describing the relationships between individual stimuli. The most that can be done is to group the stimuli in various ways, according as they appear to resemble, or not resemble, one another.

Most work on pattern recognition has, therefore, been carried out on the senses of sight, hearing and touch, where it is possible to make some attempt at relating one pattern with another. Even here there are inter-modal difficulties. Clearly a chequerboard is a more complex visual pattern than a single point of light, and a spoken word more complex than a pure tone, but how to compare the complexity of the appearance of a chequerboard with that of the sound of the word 'chequerboard'? It will be necessary therefore to deal with each system separately, but nevertheless we shall find in each system that neurophysiological investigation confirms the prediction that patterns of increasing complexity are extracted at higher and higher neural levels, rather than all appearing in parallel at the highest level.

Another difficulty in endeavouring to pin-down the occurrence of particular degrees of complexity to particular neural levels is that even within one modality the appropriate level varies from species to species. Thus the frog and the pigeon have direction-sensitive units in the retina, whereas in the cat these are not found lower than the lateral geniculate nucleus. In the ensuing discussion the results, unless otherwise stated, will be drawn from one species, the cat, in order to assist comparison.

*The visual system.* The lowest neural level which has been extensively studied is the ganglion cell layer of the retina. Since these cells effectively form the output terminals of the retina, a great deal of neural interaction between the signals from individual receptor elements has already taken place by this stage. We begin to see, in the ganglion cell response, one of the fundamental organization patterns of the spatial senses, that is the concentric inhibitory/excitatory field shown in Fig. 9. The centre of the receptive area may be excitatory and the surround inhibitory or vice versa. In the former case, for example, a white patch introduced over the central region of the receptive field causes the ganglion cell to fire, whereas it inhibits firing when in the surrounding area. This organization is evidently an elaboration of the lateral inhibition effect between receptor outputs described under stimulus discrimination.

Since the surround is larger than the central area, a large white spot covering the whole region produces a much smaller neuronal response than a smaller spot covering only the central region. The effect of individual elements of the surrounding area is cumulative—excitation of only a minor part of the surround is insufficient to completely antagonize excitation of the centre. Thus a small highly convex stimulus shape (Fig. 10a) may give a larger response than an area with a straight boundary

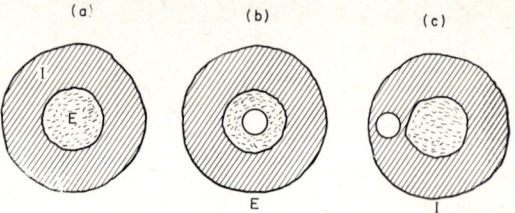

FIG. 9. *(a) Organization of the field of a retinal ganglion cell: E, excitatory area; I, inhibitory area. (b) A white disk near the centre of the field produces a discharge in the nerve fibre. (c) The same stimulus near the periphery inhibits the discharge.*

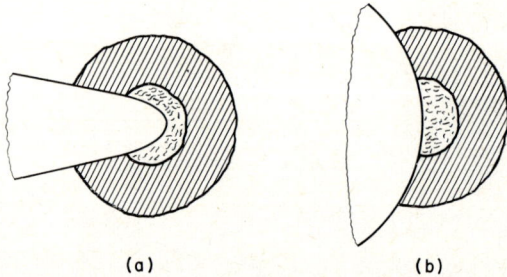

FIG. 10. *(a) A narrow convex object placed across the field produces a nerve discharge, since it covers a relatively large part of the excitatory region and only a small proportion of the inhibitory region. (b) An object of large radius does not produce a discharge, because it influences a sufficiently large part of the inhibitory area to entirely annul the excitation from the centre.*

(b). We therefore have even at this level the possibility of shape discrimination in a rudimentary form.

*Lateral geniculate.* Lateral geniculate cells respond to diffuse light, but the predominant organization is one like that of the retinal ganglion cells, so that a given cell has its receptive field arranged in the form of an on-centre and an inhibitory surround or vice versa; the two forms are present in about equal numbers. The central response area appears to be more restricted at the lateral geniculate than at the lower retinal level, the largest spot which will give a maximal response being smaller than that which is optimal for a ganglion cell fibre.

Many of these units respond more strongly to stimuli moving across their fields, than to stationary stimuli, or even to changes in ambient illumination. The response may be asymmetrical, in the sense that the response to an object approaching the centre differs from that when the same object is leaving it. The fields are, nevertheless, radially symmetrical, so that, for example, a right/left traverse gives a response not significantly different from that to a left/right traverse. In this they differ from units on the visual cortex. It is to be noted, however, that Kozak, Rodieck and Bishop found a few units in the geniculate which were directionally sensitive, so that the distinction may not be absolutely clear cut.

*Visual cortex.* The units of the primary visual cortex do not respond significantly to general illumination of the retina, but respond to restricted spots of light, both stationary and moving. Examination of the receptive fields reveals adjacent excitatory and inhibitory regions, as at lower levels, but these are no longer concentric. They are organized so that the response is not to a spot on a contrasting background, but rather to a straight-line edge. The precise position of this edge in the visual field is not critical, but its *orientation* is highly important. Thus a given unit may respond to a vertical boundary (Fig. 11), but not to a similar horizontal or diagonal

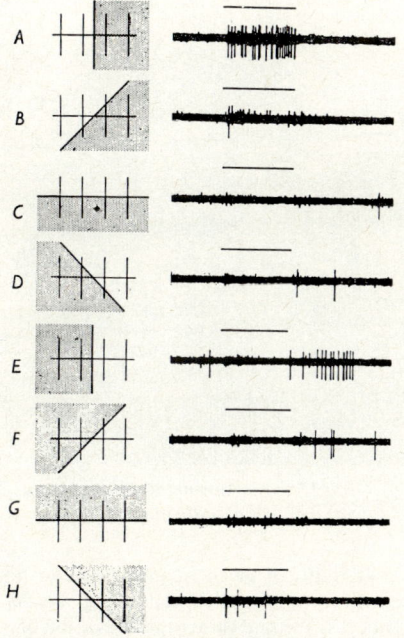

FIG. 11. *Neuron in primary visual cortex which responds to a vertical edge, but not to a horizontal or diagonal edge. Note that it responds to presentation of the stimulus when the left-hand half of the field is illuminated (A), but to its withdrawal when the right-hand half is illuminated (E).*

boundary. Units are found in this region for which the adequate stimulus is a light or a dark bar (Fig. 12). Again the position of the bar in the receptive field is not critical, but a slight change of the orientation of the bar within that field abolishes the response. As with light-spots at the geniculate, a moving stimulus often produces a larger response than a stationary one, but at the cortex such movements are strongly directional, one direction of movement producing a large response, while movement in the opposite direction gives no response or even inhibition (Fig. 13).

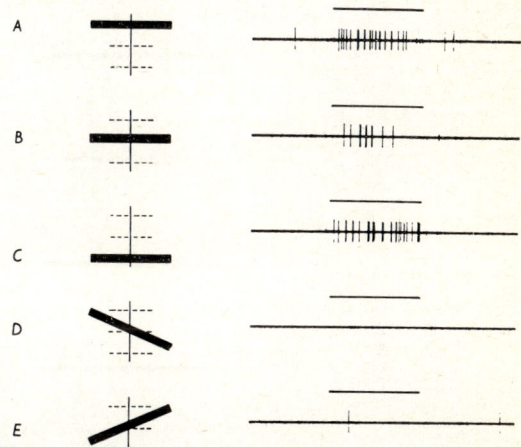

FIG. 12. *Neuron in visual cortex which responds to a dark horizontal bar, irrespective of its exact position in the field (ABC). It fails to respond to the same bar placed diagonally across the field (DE).*

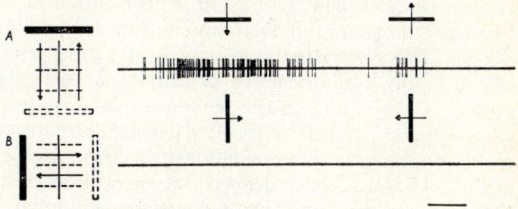

FIG. 13. *Unit in primary visual cortex responding strongly to downward movement of a horizontal bar, but much less to upward movement of the bar (A). It does not respond at all to movement of a vertical bar (B). Time bar=1 sec.*

In the primary visual cortex (area 17), these 'complex' units are in a minority compared with the 'simple' units responding to lights-spots. However, in the secondary visual area (area 18) they predominate, making up 90–95% of the population. 'Simple' units are no longer found here, the remaining 5–10% being now what Hubel and Wiesel term 'hypercomplex'. These represent a still higher degree of specificity of response pattern. The 'complex' unit responds to an edge or a bar, provided it is correctly oriented and/or moving in the correct direction. The 'hypercomplex' unit requires the bar to have the appropriate length, or the edge to be terminated at the correct point to form a corner (Fig. 14). Although there are comparatively few such units in area 18, they form a majority (60%) of units in the tertiary visual area (area 19).

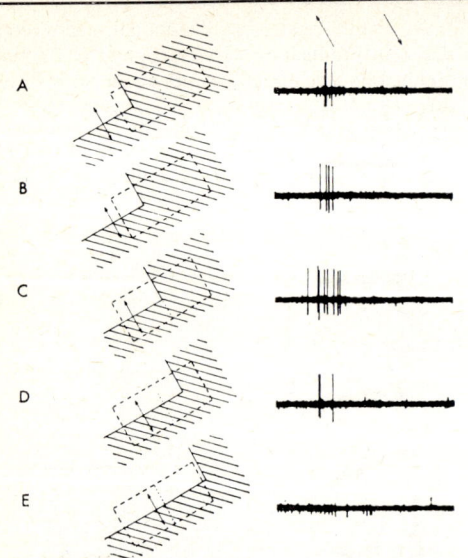

Fig. 14. *'Hypercomplex' unit which responds preferentially to an edge limited at the correct point (C) by a second edge at right angles to the first.*

*The auditory system.* The basilar membrane (see *Cochlear mechanics*) can be regarded as responding to two aspects of sound stimuli—their distribution in the frequency domain, and their distribution in the time domain. These two aspects are, in general terms, represented in the auditory nerve as activity in particular groups of fibres, and as the temporal relationships of nerve impulses, respectively. After passage through the cochlear nucleus, the representation of frequency by fibre position becomes better defined (see *Sensory discrimination*). A complex sound wave, containing a number of frequency components, now gives rise to a number of groups of active fibres in the total array (Fig. 15).

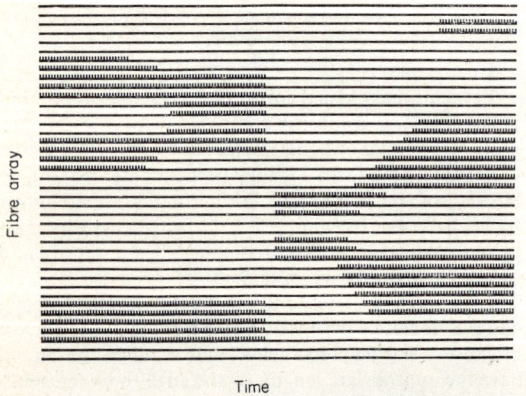

Fig. 15. *The representation of the frequency components of a complex sound in terms of nerve impulse discharge in the array of fibres in the auditory pathway.*

Considerable neurophysiological effort has been expended, over the years, in trying to locate neurons somewhere in the auditory system which would respond only to some particular discriminable stimulus frequency and not to any other, but such attempts have failed; all neurons respond over quite wide bands of frequency—sometimes several octaves. At one time the auditory cortex was assigned this discriminatory role, but detailed investigation has failed to support the hypothesis. Furthermore, behavioural tests show that in the cat, and probably in man, normal frequency discrimination persists after bilateral destruction of the whole temporal cortex. Animal experiments indeed suggest that frequency discrimination is complete at the level of the inferior colliculus.

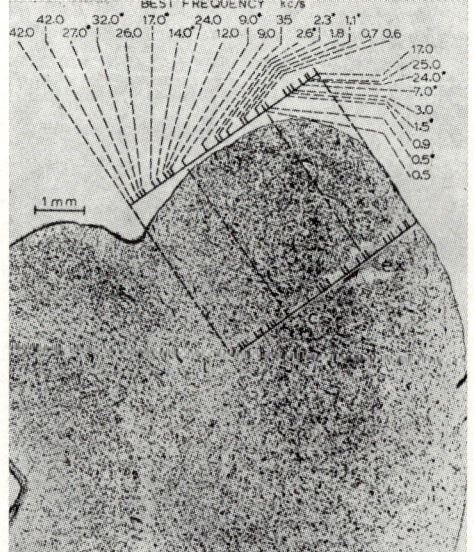

Fig. 16. *Orderly arrangement of frequency in the inferior colliculus.*

For a stimulus of given frequency we do not, then, find anywhere a uniquely responding single cell or groups of cells. We find rather the activation of a unique *combination* of adjacent elements, most of the individual elements being also activated by one or other of many alternative stimuli. Since the ultimate result of a sensory stimulus is generally to participate in a motor response, and since this latter itself involves a complex activity pattern, it is clearly reasonable to set up a polyneuronal correspondence between the two patterns, rather than to funnel all stimuli through highly specialized bottlenecks.

An anatomical orderliness of the channels in terms of frequency (tonotopicity) is preserved as far up the system as the inferior colliculus (Fig. 16), so that the grouped activity referred to above is a spatial, as well as a functional pattern. Figure 17 shows the speech spectrogram of a number of vowel sounds and the way these are characterized by particular positions of the formant frequencies. Comparison with Fig. 15 suggests an analogous process in the nervous system for the recognition of such vowel sounds. Many neurons, even at lower levels, respond better to impulsive stimuli than they do to steady tones. This probably reflects the time dependent

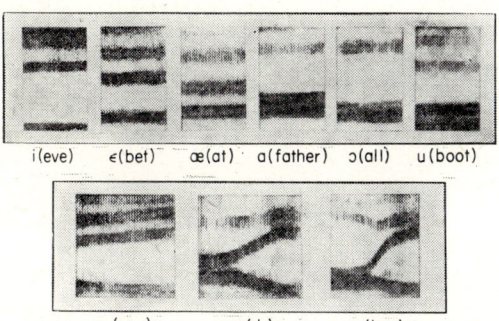

FIG. 17. *Spectrograms of the characteristic formant frequencies of some vowel sounds. The vertical axis represents frequency, and the darkness of the trace represents the intensity of the particular frequency component.*

properties of the basilar membrane referred to earlier. However, at the auditory cortex we find the temporal aspects of stimuli becoming especially important. Although, behaviourally, the auditory cortex is not essential for frequency discrimination, it *is* necessary for the discrimination of temporal patterns of sound. Thus in the bilateral absence of auditory cortex, the tone sequence ABA cannot be distinguished from the sequence BAB.

Experiments on single cortical neurons support the behavioural findings. Large numbers of neurons in the primary auditory cortex will not respond to steady tones at all, or do so only insecurely. They respond readily, on the other hand, to frequency-modulated tones, e.g. tones which change their frequency at a rate of, say, 1/2 octave/sec (Fig. 18). Many of these units are di-

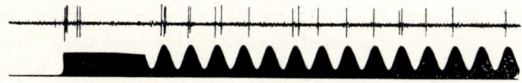

FIG. 18. *Cortical neuron which does not respond to a steady tone after the initial onset, but responds continuously when the tone is sinusoidally frequency modulated. The signal trace is amplitude modulated to represent the presence or absence of frequency modulation in the stimulus.*

rectionally oriented, i.e. they respond when the frequency is rising, but not when it is falling through the same region, or vice versa (Fig. 19). The particular frequency passed through is not crucial, the adequate stimulus being a sufficient frequency excursion in the appropriate direction. Some 30% of units in the primary auditory cortex will not respond even to frequency-modulated tones, though they will respond to 'noises' such as a 'rattle'. Such units presumably represent an even higher complexity of organization. Some of these units will for example respond to a combination of a steady and a frequency-modulated tone (Fig. 20). In many other cases, however, the critical parameters of the complex stimulus remain undetermined. Responses to direction of frequency change, as discussed above, could presumably be involved in the recognition of consonant vowel combinations such as that of the sound 'bee' (Fig. 21).

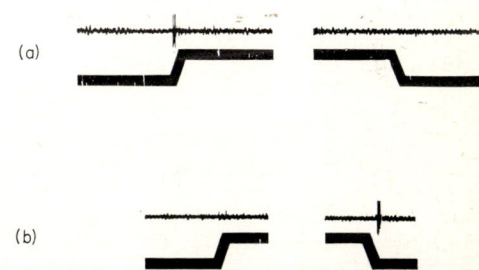

FIG. 19. *(a) Neuron in primary auditory cortex which responds when the stimulus frequency rises by about 10%, but not when it falls through the identical frequency range. (b) Neuron responding to a fall of frequency, but not to a rise.*

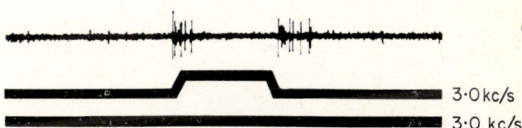

FIG. 20. *The horizontal lines represent continuous tones of 3·0 kc/s and 3·8 kc/s, respectively. The frequency of the 3·0 kc/s tone rises about 10% and then falls again as shown by the signal trace. The cortical response only occurs during the change. There is no response to the change in the absence of the 3·8 kc/s tone.*

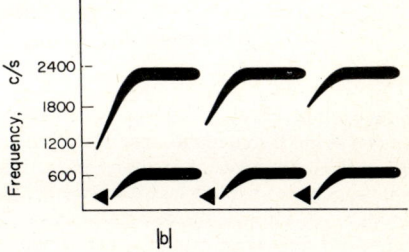

FIG. 21. *Diagrammatic representation of the movement of the formant frequencies during the phoneme 'bee'.*

It is noteworthy, and perhaps surprising, that there do not appear to be any units in the auditory system which respond preferentially to harmonic combinations of tones. It seems that the subjective properties of, say, the octave or the fifth are due to their effect on the mechanics of the inner ear, and are not related to any special properties of the nervous system for responding to such combinations.

*Somatic system.* In the somatic system we have to consider, broadly, four sources of stimuli, those subserving cutaneous touch, those subserving deep pressure on the tissues, those subserving pain and noxious stimuli, and those concerned with proprioceptive information such as joint and limb position. For obvious reasons, the first and last are much more amenable to the study of pattern than are the other two. The receptive fields for units responding to noxious stimuli seem, for example, to be very large, and may cover a quarter or more of the body surface. We shall therefore consider here only the analysis of 'discriminative touch' and of proprioception. Although signals subserving both these modalities run along the same neural pathways from periphery to cortex, they nevertheless remain quite distinct, and a primary cortical neuron which responds to one is only very exceptionally influenced by the other.

The receptive fields for touch, as determined at the thalamic or primary cortical levels, have a formal similarity to those in the visual system—that is to say a limited excitatory area with an annular inhibitory surround (Fig. 22). Steady stimulation of the excitatory area

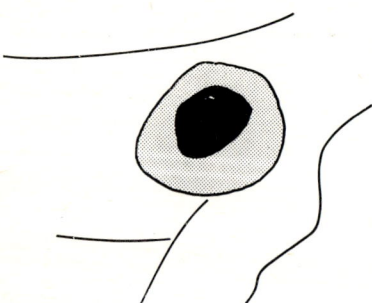

FIG. 22. *An excitatory area (black) with an inhibitory surround for cutaneous touch receptors on the skin of the shoulder.*

produces an initial rapid discharge, which declines after one or two seconds to a maintained steady rate of about a third of the initial value. Simultaneous stimulation of the inhibitory region suppresses the discharge. The effects of stimuli moving across the receptive field have unfortunately not been investigated, so far as the author is aware. Primary cortical units responding to joint position show essentially similar patterns in that movement of the joint induces a discharge which settles down to some lower value when the joint becomes stationary. Some units discharge during extension of a joint, while others behave reciprocally (Fig. 23), discharging during flexion and ceasing to discharge during extension.

Although there is evidence that the primary cortical neurons respond differentially to movement of a joint in the direction of flexion and of extension, no examples are known of units which respond completely specifically to direction of movement and not to absolute position. It should be emphasized however that only the primary somatic cortex has been examined. By analogy with vision, one might expect to find neurons specific for shape and motion in the 'higher order' areas of the cortex.

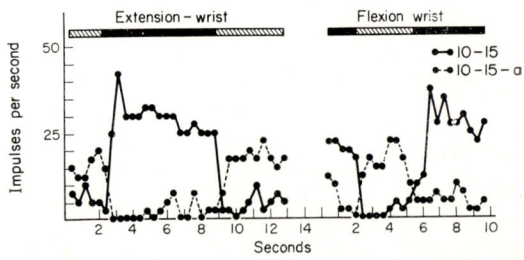

FIG. 23. *Reciprocal firing by two different units in the primary somatic cortex to extension and flexion of the wrist.*

*Anatomical relationship of channels.* In each of the modalities that we have been discussing, there appears to be a very well-maintained anatomical orderliness discernible between functionally adjacent channels. At the lower levels of each system, this orderliness is related to the point discrimination of the system and so we find fibres arranged in the order in which they leave the retina, the basilar membrane or the skin surface. This is evidently the most economical arrangement to permit the excitatory/inhibitory interactions between adjacent channels which assist such discriminations. At the level of the primary cortex, this arrangement begins to break down, as other more complex patterns have to be extracted. Although remnants of the original spatial pattern remain on the gross scale, this pattern is less apparent when the fine mosaic is examined. This mosaic consists of a large number of vertical columns of cells, each column forming a functional group containing the necessary elements to extract a particular pattern from a particular receptor area. However, the exigencies of this pattern extraction mean that adjacent columns will no longer be arranged in the order in which the inputs left the periphery. This reorganization seems to have gone furthest in the primary auditory cortex, where little frequency relationship remains between adjacent columns, and least far in the primary somatic cortex, where the body surface is still apparently represented in a fairly orderly way. Stages of the process can be seen by comparing the primary, secondary, and tertiary visual cortices, where the adjacent cell columns become less and less related to adjacent points in the visual field as the patterns to which they respond become more complex.

It is hazardous in the present fragmentary state of our knowledge to attempt to draw parallels, or to generalize in any detail about neural mechanisms of pattern extraction between modalities. Nevertheless, the diverse and fragmentary observations which have been made do not contradict the general idea of an increased degree of complexity being extracted at higher neural levels than at lower. The lowest levels of neural integration (b, Fig. 24), seem to be concerned with the discrimination and separation of the static elements of a pattern,

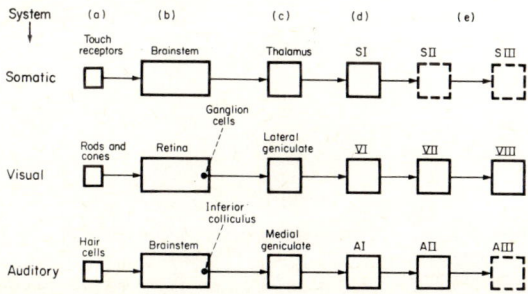

FIG. 24. *Diagram to illustrate the homology between anatomical structures in different modalities. Regions not considered in the text are shown dotted.*

whether it be a truly spatial one, or, say, the frequency components of a complex tone. At the thalamic level (c) we begin to find responses to the relation *between* stimuli in space and time becoming an important parameter, and in the primary sensory cortex (c) orientation becomes crucial (that is to say, the slope of a line is signalled independently of its precise location, and the direction of change of pitch is signalled irrespective of the precise frequency). At still 'higher' cortical levels, only the visual system has so far been examined, but it is evident that here still more complex parameters of visual stimuli are extracted.

In making these generalizations it must be emphasized that the levels at which various degrees of complexity are reached are not clear cut. Thus, when we say that orientation is extracted at the primary cortical level, this only means that a large proportion of neurons at this level are concerned with this parameter; a smaller number at both higher and lower levels may also so respond.

It must also be pointed out that in more primitive animals complex parameters tend to be extracted at lower neural levels, albeit more crudely. As the nervous system becomes more developed in higher forms, the refinement with which particular parameters can be extracted increases, but at the same time the mechanism 'retreats' to higher neural levels.

## Centrifugal Control of Signal Strength

Centrifugal connexions paralleling the classical sensory afferent pathways appear to exist for many, if not all, sensory modalities. Such connexions have for example been described between the mid-brain and the retina, between the cerebral cortex and the somatosensory nuclei, and amongst almost all levels of the auditory system. It is this latter system which has been most studied anatomically and from which most of our knowledge of possible functions for such pathways derives.

The first such pathway to be anatomically defined was the olivo-cochlear bundle (tract of Rasmussen) which originates in cell groups of the superior olive, and terminates in the inner ear; it is now known, in fact, to terminate in direct relation to the hair-cell receptors. Held, as early as 1893, had drawn attention to the presence of 'recurrent' fibres entering the cochlear nucleus, without being able to define their origin, and Lorente de Nó, sixty years later, described another such pathway. It was again Rasmussen who demonstrated that the source of most of these fibres is either in the superior olivo or in the nuclei of the lateral lemniscus, both of which are cell groups of the ascending auditory pathway. Rasmussen, and Desmedt and his associates, have demonstrated, by histological and stimulation methods, centrifugal connexions between the temporal cortex, the medial geniculate body, the inferior colliculus and lower brain stem centres. A summary of these centrifugal pathways is given in Fig. 25.

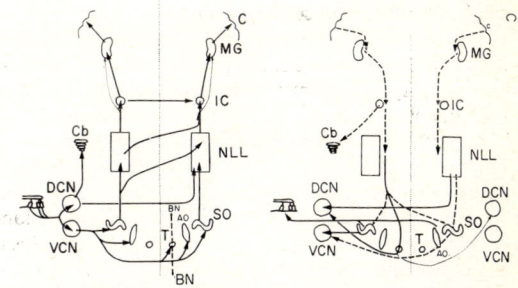

FIG. 25. *Summary of ascending and descending pathways of the auditory system. DCN, VCN, dorsal and ventral cochlear nuclei; SO, AO, superior olivary nuclei; NLL, nuclei of lateral lemniscus; IC, inferior colliculus; MG, medial geniculate body; C, cortex; Cb, cerebellum.*

An early clue to the possible function of these pathways was provided in 1955 by Hernandez-Peon and Scherrer, and by Galambos and his associates, who reported that the electrical evoked potentials at various neural levels in response to a sound stimulus could change when the animal became habituated to the sound, or was made by conditioning procedures to attend to it (Fig. 26). Later experimenters got rather variable results

are now becoming apparent as the details of the control mechanisms are being elucidated.

In 1956 a direct relationship between activity in a centrifugal pathway and the size of the afferent response was demonstrated by Galambos, who showed that electrical stimulation of the olivo-cochlear bundle resulted in a reduction of the whole-nerve response of the auditory nerve to clicks. Desmedt later showed, too, that stimulation of a point in the brain stem near the ventral nucleus of the lateral lemniscus reduced the evoked click response in the contra-lateral cochlear nucleus.

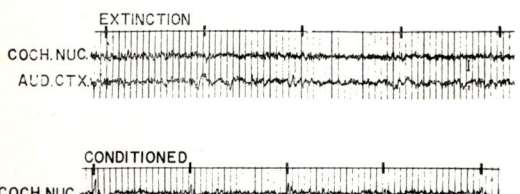

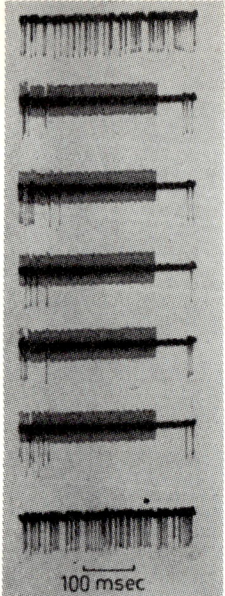

FIG. 26. *Above: EEG records showing lack of response to clicks (top line) at the auditory cortex and the cochlear nucleus, after habituation to the stimulus. Below: return of the click responses at these sites after the animal was conditioned to attend*

FIG. 27. *Top and bottom traces: response of an auditory nerve fibre to a sound stimulus. Centre traces: suppression of this response by stimulation of the olivo-cochlear bundle (indicated by block of short diphasic spikes).*

in similar experiments, but nevertheless confirmed the general proposition that the behavioural state of the animal can affect the sensory responses at quite peripheral neural levels. The reasons for the variable results

Single-unit studies by Fex, have confirmed that reduction of activity in auditory nerve fibres follows stimulation of the olivo-cochlear bundle (Fig. 27). The fibres of this centrifugal bundle terminate in large granulated endings (NE2) in the base of the hair-cells in close juxtaposition to the afferent terminals (NE1) (Fig. 28). It is presumably here that the inhibitory interaction takes place. Activation of the olivo-cochlear bundle does not reduce the cochlear microphonic potential—if anything it enhances it. Although considerable exprimentation has been carried out on the pharmacology of these terminals, the mechanism of the inhibition is at present not understood.

Another section of the centrifugal pathway which has been studied at the single neural unit level is that originating in the superior olivo and terminating in the ventral cochlear nucleus. Comis and Whitfield showed that stimulation of the medial part of the lateral olivary nucleus can lower the threshold to sound of neurons in the cochlear nucleus by as much as 15 dB (Fig. 29). Thus, in contrast to the olivo-cochlear bundle, activation of this pathway enhances the response to peripheral stimulation. Experiments with local application of drugs to the appropriate neurons of the cochlear nucleus suggest that this excitatory pathway is cholinergic.

Since, as has been stated above, stimulation of some regions of the brain stem is capable of reducing the gross response in the cochlear nucleus, it appears that there are both excitatory and inhibitory pathways reaching the nucleus from higher levels, and this may account for the variable results obtained in behavioural experiments under different conditions. This dual system does not however extend to the periphery, where, so far, only inhibitory effects have been found.

The feedback loops, as far as they have been defined, appear to be quite complex. The olivo-cochlear bundle takes origin from the olivary nuclei of both sides. However, according to Rasmussen, the afferents reaching both the cell groups involved come from the same ear to which the centrifugal bundle projects. The loop involving the ventral cochlear nucleus and the lateral superior olivary nucleus appears also to be confined to one side of the system. However, inputs from both ears reach the lemniscal nuclei, and recurrent pathways from these descend to reach the olivary and cochlear nuclei of both sides. It is not known whether, in the crossing and recrossing, individual loops remain predominantly connected with one side or whether, as seems more probable, there is complete interaction between the feedback systems of the two ears. Certainly, the observation of Fex that fibres in the olivo-cochlear bundle can be activated by sounds delivered to the *opposite* ear requires some such interaction.

Both the unit studies, that on the auditory nerve and that on the cochlear nucleus, have shown that the latency of onset of the effect of centrifugal stimulation is of the order of some tens of milliseconds and that the effect persists for a like time after termination of the stimulus. This suggests that there is considerable temporal integration of the activity in the pathway, and that the feedback loops control the general level of activity

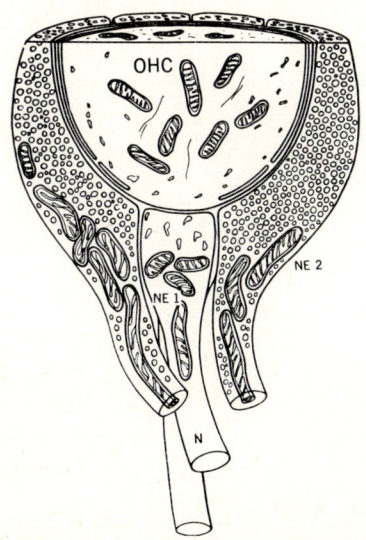

FIG. 28. *Termination of centripetal (NE1) and centrifugal (NE2) nerve fibres on the base of an outer hair cell (OHC).*

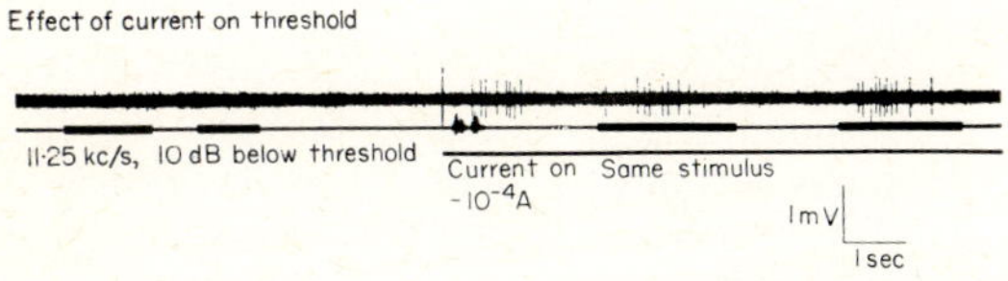

FIG. 29. *Unit in the central cochlear nucleus sensitive to a tone of 11·25 kc/s. It does not normally respond when this tone is presented at an intensity of 10 dB below threshold, but responds to the same stimulus when the superior olivo is stimulated by current.*

in the afferent channels, rather than, for example, influencing the actual distribution of individual pulse intervals.

The results of experiments so far, indicate the existence of a dual gating mechanism which can either increase or decrease the through-put of activity from the peripheral receptors to the higher centres, and possibly from the afferent brain-stem nuclei directly to effector mechanisms.

How discrete these controls are is not yet known. We do not know if they are capable of suppressing the response to one aspect of the stimulus while enhancing

another, or whether they act simply as an overall 'volume-control'. The number of fibres in the olivo-cochlear bundle (cat) is very small (some 500) compared with the number of afferent fibres in the auditory nerve (about 40,000) so that the control cannot be very detailed. On the other hand, the constraints on the afferent system imposed by the mechanics of the basilar membrane (see *Cochlear mechanics*) mean that there are nothing like 40,000 independent afferent channels, so that the discrepancy is not as the ratio of the figures would suggest. The experiments of Fex do indicate, rather tentatively, that there is some segregation of efferent fibres according to sound frequency, and that these fibres reach the appropriate point of the cochlea.

The auditory system is the only one in which, so far, the centrifugal system has been shown to extend right out to the peripheral receptor itself. However, even here, the demonstration has been a matter of some difficulty owing to the fineness of the fibres involved, and more refined electron microscopy may perhaps show similar arrangements in some other sensory systems.

*See also:* Cochlear mechanics. Hearing. Perception, visual. Sensory discrimination, measurement of.

I. C. WHITFIELD

**SIMILARITY.** Much mental activity takes the form of detecting similarities and differences between events. Such activity can broadly be called pattern recognition. It is the exercise of determining that event A is more like event B than it is like event C. This is the process involved when we detect that a letter is a letter X and not a letter Y, or that the word CAT is not the word DOG, or that we are looking at a photograph of an aeroplane, or that little George is more like his Aunt than he is like his Grandpa. It is essentially involved when we make an electromagnetic analogy for a dynamic mechanical system, or when we match the right algorithm to the problem we wish to solve.

Consideration of this list shows that the decision that A is more like B than like C is not absolute. This is clear in the example about George and his Aunt and Grandpa, for although his Mother might think he is more like his Aunt, his Father might well think he is more like his Grandpa. Both would be right, for the decision depends on their different points of view. The two decisions do not contradict one another, since they are essentially two different decisions each being a function both of the discriminator and of the things being discriminated. What is obviously true in the case of little George is true of every case of 'is A more like B than C', for this question cannot be asked in isolation, but only when A, B and C are considered in context. The decision is dependent on this context.

All that follows is much concerned with this rather odd phenomenon, which is considered from three points of view, which might seem to be quite different, but in the end, in their proper context, will be found to be very alike. The first approach is about systems.

*Systems approach.* Most of the data that interest man are about systems, or the interaction between systems. They can relate to influences acting on systems, to internal events occurring within the system as a result, or to the influence the system has on other systems. Always the data must compare or contrast one situation with another. In this context data are any entities or concepts which show if situations or experiences are the same, or, if not, specify their differences. Let us define a set of symbols as a set of entities of such nature that a certain system can distinguish any one from all the rest. A set of such symbols call a language. It will be noticed that this set of definitions directly implies the existence of a certain system, and indeed included this system. This is fundamental; the idea of a symbol is meaningless unless one also includes the system. This shows the role of context.

To say that a system can distinguish between input patterns either means it is aware of the difference, or that a second system can tell that the input patterns cause different internal or output patterns in the first system. The second system can only do this if the input and output patterns of the first, and the internal state patterns of the first, are in fact input symbols of the second. In passing note that this raises matters of philosophy that cannot be lightly dismissed. At a simple level it might be argued that it is sufficient to say that a system can distinguish between input patterns if these produce differing patterns within it. But in the last resort this means very little. A man examining the system might come to any one of very many different conclusions about the system, depending upon the sensitivity and kinds of detecting system he uses. Further it is not possible to discover anything about a system without altering it at least in some degree. To assume a detecting system does not resolve the dilemma—it moves it up a stage. To make the chain conceptually sound one has to assume the existence of some self-aware system that knows that the response to the symbols is different. This leaves the difficult problem of what is meant by awareness unanswered.

What then is a pattern? What is meant by likeness? We have noted that two patterns which would be judged very like in one context would be judged as quite unlike in another. However, starting from a few extra definitions one can build up an idea of pattern, and likeness between patterns which on the one hand is mathematically precise, and on the other hand is consistent with intuitive ideas. It is possible to have symbols which are built up of more elementary symbols. For example, associated with a machine with 10 input wires, each of which could have a potential on it or not there would be 20 elementary symbols. The machine might be able to recognize combinations of these and so distinguish 1024 'built-up' symbols, each of which we will call a pattern. Any sub-symbol using less than all of the elementary symbols we shall call a '*mark*'. A mark in one pattern might be itself a pattern made of more elementary marks. It should be noted that marks can only make a pattern if each one bears some relation to at least one other such as, for example, a spatial relation. One can define a symbol P (a pattern) which contains a symbol Q (a mark) as being of higher rank than Q. If system A divides a sub-language T of a system B into sets, $S_1$ of symbols containing no other symbols, $S_2$ of symbols containing one or more of $S_1$, $S_3$ of symbols containing one or more of $S_2$, and so on, then one can define these sets as being of symbols of steadily higher rank. If two patterns have a common mark as part, one can define them as *alike*.

One can also define sub-rank within rank if one says that the highest sub-rank symbol of two symbols of equal rank is that which contains most marks of one rank less. One can make similar definitions of sub-sub-rank.

The following formula, based on the above conceptions can be used to give a mathematical definition of likeness.

If the ranks of two patterns are $R_1$, $R_2$, and that of the the common marks are $R_a$, $R_b$, etc. the degree of likeness can be defined as

$$L = \frac{R_a}{R_1+R_2-2R_a} + \frac{R_b}{R_1+R_2-2R_b} \text{ etc.}$$

This also gives a definition of 'X is more like Y than Z is like Y'. Where patterns are the same this formula gives a likeness of $\infty$, where they are quite unlike it gives a likeness of 0. The formula fit in with intuitive ideas of likeness. Very like things have major sub-patterns in common and only differ in small points of detail. Very unlike patterns only have small points of detail in common.

It will be noted although the likeness so defined is quite definite provided the systems A and B are both defined, it is not independent of context. The calculated ranking scores of symbols of B will depend greatly on which sublanguage of B is taken, and this will affect the likeness score. This is also consistent with intuitive ideas. The estimated likeness of two patterns depends both on the observer system (A)—be it man or machine—and on the context, (A, B and environment), because different observer systems do in fact use different sub-languages of the patterns.

*Decision logics approach.* The second approach is via the ideas connected with decision logics. As an introduction to this note that at the most trivial level one observes an event or not. A great deal of our decision experience has to do with cyclic events such as the swing of a pendulum, or the state of an electron in a ground state hydrogen atom or the spin of an electron. The essence of such cyclic events is that they keep returning to an 'identical' state, yet it cannot be said that the 'identical' states are identical in every sense, for if they were they would not be in any way distinguishable, and therefore could not be in a sequence. The difference between them is, of course, their position in a sequence. This leads to the idea of ordered sets of observations and to the ideas of dimensions. Once we have got this far, it is a small extension to get to the idea of distinguishable and known dimensions.

Two adjacent members in an ordered set of events are clearly very much alike—and the further they are apart in the set, the more different they are.

The next step is to consider 'macro' observations, emanating from more than one event. If the events stimulating a macro-observation are all of different dimensions then clearly it can be categorised by the events themselves. The difference between two observations then depends on the total number of different events in them. This leads to the representation in which observations are considered as vertices of a hypercube. Consider the three-dimensional cube shown in Fig. 1. This three-dimensional set-up allows eight different

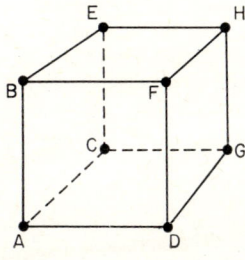

Fig. 1

observations. Observations at the ends of an edge are 'one' apart, at the ends of a diagonal of a square 'two' apart, and at the ends of a diagonal of a cube 'three' apart.

The next situation, although it is extremely familiar, is one where complications set in. Consider two observations each consisting of two events, but each chosen from the same two dimensions, as shown in Fig. 2. Clearly the observations are different, and clearly it is not right to call the difference the sum of the differences in the two dimensions for this would falsely imply that two observations that differed by a place in each dimension differed by as much as two events two units apart in one dimension. A somewhat complex argument, out of place here, leads to the pythagorean difference measure with which we are familiar (the root of the sum of the squares of the differences). Given information spaces of more than one dimension we have the added complication of which we all have experience. In the three-dimensional space we know well one can clearly have a set of axes which are not at right angles—dimensions which are not independent. Given such dimensions it is necessary to carry out a transformation to find the closeness of two points—the similarity between two observations.

So far in this decision-logics approach the similarity between two macro-observations has been a definite

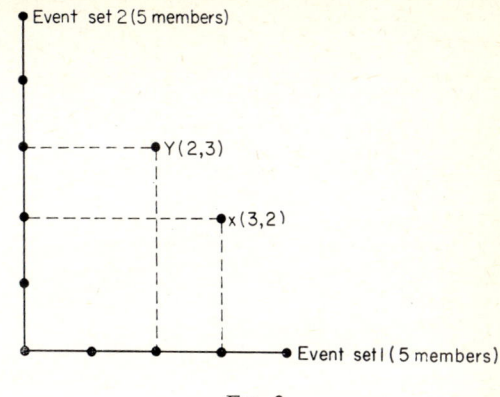

Fig. 2

quantity, giving no chance for one observer to disagree with another. Now consider the situation in which an observation consists of a number of events within one ordered set, such as the four member set in Fig. 3. All the two event observations are shown. No meaning, in this kind of observation, can be assigned to the situation which would be represented in the figure by two coincident crosses. Such an observation would be indistinguishable from one containing just one event. There are therefore six different observations of the two cross kind. Given one way of 'looking' at this set of observations, all six are independent. They could be represented as the six points adjacent to the origin in a six-dimensional hypercube. In Fig. 4, then (c) is as much like (a) as (d). Yet clearly there are ways of looking at the figure which would say that (c) is the more like (a) and ways which would say no, (d) is the more like (a).

In this six-dimensioned hypercube model, there are understood constraints. Only six of the $2^6$ vertices of the hypercube are occupied. The observing machine refuses to 'know' about the remainder.

It can be seen that with this kind of multi-event observation there is no 'right' representation or 'right' hypercube model. For example, as an alternative to the

|   |   |   |   |     |
|---|---|---|---|-----|
| × | × | − | − | (a) |
| × | − | × | − | (b) |
| × | − | − | × | (c) |
| − | × | × | − | (d) |
| − | × | − | × | (e) |
| − | − | × | × | (f) |

Fig. 3

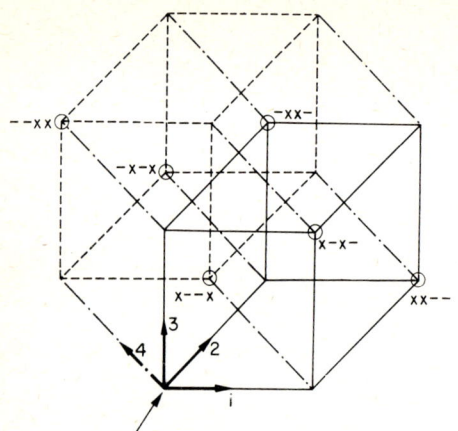

Fig. 4

six-dimensioned model, the observations could be represented by the four-dimensioned model shown in Fig 4, where the patterns are represented as points (circled) in four-dimensional space; this indicates just one way of looking at the various observations. Only a few of the available points in the four-dimensional cube are occupied by patterns—in other words there are a number of

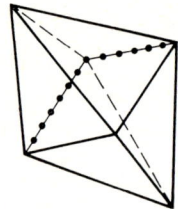

Fig. 5

constraints operating—and the allowable points are all on the vertices of a three-dimensional figure, actually the octohedron shown in Fig. 5.

In this figure it can be seen that the patterns are not all equidistant. This is not so with the three-dimensional case shown in Fig. 6, where it can be seen that in a similar representation a, b, c, lie on an equilateral triangle.

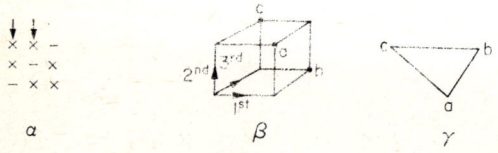

Fig. 6

If on looking at it one way one considers an observation to be made up of two measures, measure a and measure b, the patterns of Fig. 6α can be represented as shown in Fig. 7α. The figure represents all the patterns of Fig. 6α twice, and can therefore be folded along a diagonal as shown in Fig. 7β. This representation no longer makes patterns a, b, c of Fig. 6α all equidistant —equally alike. It implies a hierarchical kind of constraint, since the dimensions a, b of Fig. 7 do not correspond to simple events, whilst the folding of 7α to make 7β is also an extra step.

It can be seen that in general likeness cannot be judged simply by distance apart in a hypercube, but rather by distances apart in a complex, hierarchical dimensional structure, subject to constraints imposed by the recognition device.

*Self-aware approach.* In the last approach assume that a 'recognition' device has a set of 'terminal' states, of which it is 'aware'. The effect of any detectable event is to change one state into another. If one keeps to the idea that an 'observation' is a set of events, two identical 'observations' will take a given state to the same other state, although the paths might be quite different.

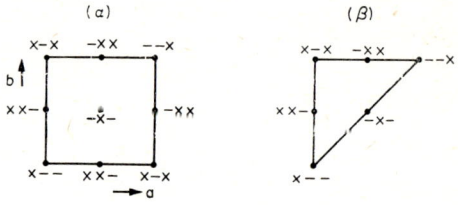

Fig. 7

According to this concept the identity of two observations is a function of the state in which the stimulus finds the system, and the state in which it leaves it. In this way it has a slight analogy with the idea of Potential Difference (P.D.) between two points in electrical theory. One can define the potential at a point as the P.D. between it and a hypothetical ground state. In an analogous way one can define an observation as the state it leads to from a hypothetical ground starting point. Similar observations will lead to similar states, that is to states that can be reached from one another by a small number of 'events'. In a simple scheme, likeness can be defined as the shortest event path between end states. A more sophisticated scheme would take into account the number of different event routes. But in either case the likeness of two stimuli depends not only on the stimuli, but also on the recognition system, and on the state of that system at the start of the observation.

A system of $n$ states (Fig. J. here), every one of which is directly connected to every other is a fully connected $n$ node graph. It is equivalent to a simplex in $(n-1)$

space. Thus a fully connected four node graph is equivalent to the tetrahedron shown in Fig. 8.

For a recognition system of this sort, every set of events is exactly like one of the twelve possible events. In Fig. 8b the (A D) direct link has been removed.

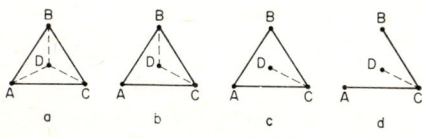

FIG. 8

States A and D are now two events apart but there are two equal shortest routes that lead from one to the other. Figs. 8c and d show two further stages of removing links. In the example shown in Fig. 8d, A, B and D are mutually 2 apart but C is only 1 from any of the other three states.

The most important recognition systems, living systems, develop by a process of evolution.

In an evolved recognition system containing a very large number of states there can be groups of states so richly interconnected that they are easily readable from

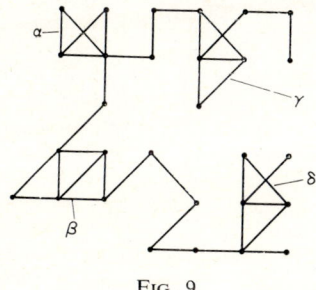

FIG. 9

each other. That is to say the graph consists of a number of strongly connected areas.

This sort of thing is illustrated in Fig. 9. Clusters of states $\alpha$, $\beta$, $\gamma$ and $\delta$ represent distinguishable classes of similar states.

Evidence is very strong that living recognition systems develop a hierarchical state system. Looked at in the broad sense their state graphs will be found to contain a number of closely connected 'areas'. Closer inspection of these areas shows that they consist of closely connected areas loosely connected to each other. Study in further detail shows similar sub-structures. Such a system matches our description of the universe. We find loosely connected tight knots of stars, or galaxies. Galaxies contain solar-planet systems. This hierarchy continues right down to atomic nuclei.

In the recognition system, starting from the large primary clusters, which may be looked upon as 'concepts',

one works right down to the minor groups. To get from a 'neutral' state into one of the major clumps the system must make a major observation, whereas an isolated event in general leaves the state of the system within a clump.

It is of some importance to note that noise—a sequence of 'random' events—is unlikely to lead to a state outside a really tightly connected state clump. To get from one clump to another a very special sequence of events is needed.

Recognition systems having in their state graphs hierarchies of 'knotted' nodes clearly have many of the properties of living recognition systems. They tend to group observations into classes, they take little notice of random events, what they 'see' depends as much on their starting state as on the stimuli they receive, and different recognition systems will disagree heavily about the relative likenesses of the members of a set of complex stimuli.

They thus 'see' the universe as a hierarchical pattern system having a great deal in common with that which arises in the systems approach, earlier in this article.

Within a state graph one can have many independent chains of connectivity. Each of these chains produces an ordered set of the kind discussed in the second part of the article (Decision logics approach).

It can be seen that the state graph concept is a very general one. It can represent the kinds of response pattern in a recognition system that could deduce pattern stimuli of all the kinds discussed. Furthermore it implies that judgement of similarity between two sets of stimuli is as much a function of the recognition system as of the stimuli themselves.

*See also:* Concept formation by artificial intelligence. Learning machines: a unified view. Pattern recognition. Speech.

E. A. NEWMAN

**SIMULATION OF TRAFFIC PROBLEMS USING CHAIN-CODE RANDOM GENERATORS.** *Introduction.* Problems associated with traffic take many forms. The study of such problems is frequently difficult or impossible using conventional mathematical techniques. Simulation is a valuable alternative. While simulation using a digital computer, the 'software' approach, has received considerable attention in recent years, (see for example Tocher 1963), special-purpose digital simulators have been neglected. The use of chain-codes to generate random arrivals offers attractive possibilities for this 'hardware' approach. This article compares and contrasts the two techniques and provides some details of recent work with a road-traffic simulator by way of illustration. While road-traffic simulation receives principal attention, the application of the techniques described to other fields should be readily apparent.

*Complexity of traffic problems.* Traffic problems range from the operation of docks and harbours and the organization of coal mining operations, to the queueing problems associated with post-office counter work and the waiting-room of a doctor.

Problems comprising random arrival at a single-server with uniform service time may be treated using comparatively conventional mathematical techniques. The *Pollaczek–Khintchine formula* (Saaty 1961) may be used for example in the analysis of queueing systems which have an input with a Poisson distribution to a single server with an arbitrary service-time.

However, situations such as those which occur at a road-traffic intersection are in general more complex. Several queues of traffic build up as vehicles arrive. Adams (1936) has shown that for an isolated intersection, the arrival of vehicles is random with a

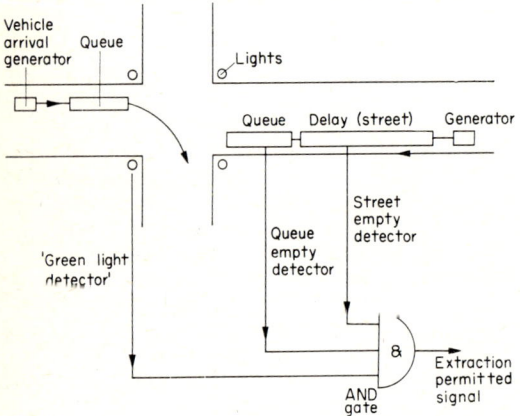

FIG. 1. *Illustration of simple right-turning situation.*

Poisson distribution. At intersections with traffic lights extraction for straight-on traffic occurs during the green period. The rate of extraction is a function of driver reaction time and vehicle performance. For turning traffic, however, the situation is more complicated. Successful extraction depends on right-of-way (a green signal) and at the same time a gap in the opposing traffic stream, itself random, which is sufficient to permit a safe manoeuvre. The turning traffic and the straight-on traffic are assumed to be in separate queues. This situation is illustrated in Fig. 1. Often, however, both classes of vehicle are mixed in a common queue. While in some circumstances average arrival rates remain substantially constant, the case of flow increasing to a peak and later falling away at the conclusion of a rush-hour period is common.

The mathematical analysis for a complete intersection with perhaps eight streams of conflicting traffic, possibly without the benefit of traffic light control, is formidable indeed. It postulates a situation with multiple random arrivals and their interaction in a complicated fashion. Such a process while stochastic is probably non-linear, and may be non-stationary. The position for multiple intersections is correspondingly more difficult. For the study of such situations some form of simulation approach is the only practical technique.

Inevitably simplifications will be necessary. Typically each element in the situation will be regarded as identical in characteristics, so that, for example, it may be represented by a single piece of information, perhaps a single pulse. Such simplification is a feature of all simulation work and need not detract from its value.

*Software and hardware simulation.* Two types of simulation are possible. One is the use of an appropriate computer program prepared for a large general-purpose machine. This is the so-called software-simulation approach. Using this technique pseudo-random arrivals are generated for each of the input channels. For most general-purpose machines library routines are available to provide distributions suitable for the particular traffic situation under consideration. In the case of road-traffic, for example, a Poisson distribution is appropriate. This corresponds to a negative exponential distribution for the gaps between successive arrivals.

Interaction of the various elements appearing at the input channels of a traffic situation is achieved through the application of logical rules defining the behaviour of the elements of the situation, e.g. traffic-light operation. In order to retain some relation to real-time operation, the program must allow for delays in the system. Thus in the case of road-traffic, provision must be made for acceptance gaps and driver reaction times. The representation of the passage of a vehicle along a street might be achieved by the addition of a digit into a register for each time epoch of operation. When the contents of a register attain a prearranged value the vehicle is deemed to have arrived at the end of the street. Detection of an empty street for an opposing stream provides the acceptance gap for a turning vehicle in the situation of Fig. 1.

Such software simulation has immediate attractions. The use of *autocodes* minimizes the time taken in program preparation. With care a versatile program may be constructed for use with a variety of individual situations. For example see (Bone *et al.* 1964). Such programs may require substantial amounts of computer time for their execution unless the simulation is very much simplified. Where multiple queues occur the sequential generation of random arrivals for each channel reduces the overall speed of operation substantially. This becomes serious if extensive experiments are necessary. Sometimes experiments involving direct-digital-control of traffic situations may be required. Typically this involves the connexion of a small process-control computer and peripheral equipment to the simulation. This presents difficulties if the general-purpose machine is used for bureau service.

The approach via a special-purpose machine offers advantages if the machine can be built with minimum hardware. Such a proposal looks hopeful at first sight. Queue counters and delays, i.e. shift registers, are readily provided using flip-flop stages with suitable interconnexions. Elements such as AND, OR and NOT (or NOR) may be used for the logical operations governing extraction from queues, detection of empty streets, traffic-light operation and the like. With each epoch the the state of the overall simulation is advanced by one time interval, i.e. operation is parallel. In consequence speeds may be high.

However, the foregoing presupposes that parallel generation of a possible random arrival in each input channel can occur at every epoch of machine operation. The use of conventional techniques to achieve this result requires substantial equipment. The exploitation of the properties of chain-codes, described briefly in the next section, effects considerable economy. The realization, with limited equipment, of a set of random generators operating in parallel is the distinctive feature of the traffic simulator described below.

*Chain-codes.* Linear sequential networks have been systematised by Huffman (1956) and Elspas (1959). Such sequences for the binary case have been considered by Heath and Gribble (1960) and Heath (1961). These sequences bear the name of chain-codes. A chain-code may be defined as follows: if a sequence of $2^n$ or less binary digits are arranged such that any $n$ adjacent digits designate the position of those digits uniquely, then the sequence is a chain-code.

For example in the case of $n = 4$, a complete code of 16 digits might be

1111010110010000/111101

where any pattern of four adjacent digits, for example 1101, will appear only once. Since the number of permutations of $n$ binary digits is $2^n$, this is the maximum length of any chain-code. While in many cases codes may be less than $2^n$ digits long, in practice codes of length $2^n - 1$ digits may be generated readily using only shift register stages and modulo-two adders. The significance of the term chain-code is seen if a sequence is joined in

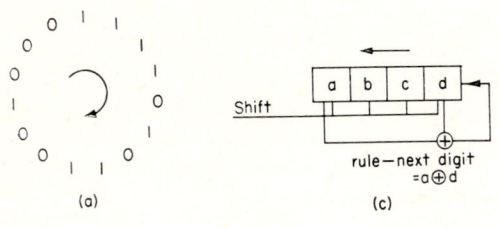

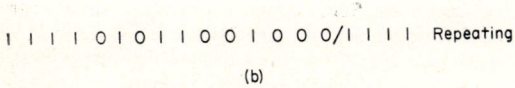

Fig. 2. *A simple chain code.*

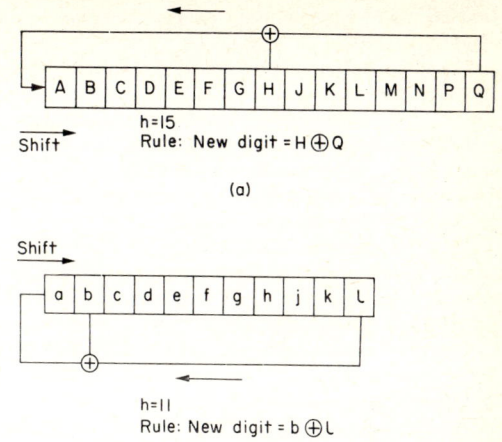

Fig. 3. *Examples of longer chain codes.*

cyclic form as in Fig. 2a. Here the total length is $2^n - 1$ digits.

Codes of length $2^n - 1$ are called chain-codes of maximal length or m-sequences. A maximal-length code of length $2^n - 1 = 15$ where $n = 4$ is shown in Fig. 2b. Such a code may be generated by the circuit shown in Fig. 2c. It is seen that it differs from the full code only by the omission of 0000 pattern. It should be noted that this circuit is extremely economical in components requiring only four flip-flop stages and a single modulo-two adder. With each application of shift a fresh pattern comprising the previous values of $b$, $c$ and $d$ and a new digit $a \oplus d$ is produced ($\oplus$ signifies modulo-two addition). Such a code may be started at any point by the imposition of the digit pattern corresponding to that point. The full code will be attained in every case. This means that repeatable codes are readily available.

Suitable values of $n$ and appropriate pick-off positions for the modulo-two adders result in $m$-sequence of considerable length. For example if $n = 15$ then the code of maximum length is $2^n - 1 = 2^{15} - 1 = 32767$ digits. The code can be attained with the simple pick-off shown in Fig. 3a. Similarly $n = 11$ with a suitable pick-off arrangement yields a maximal-length code of $2^{11} - 1 = 2047$ digits. This is illustrated in Fig. 3b.

In a full length code of $2^n$ digits there are $2^{n-1}$ ones and $2^{n-1}$ zeros. For a code of length $2^n - 1$ the number of zeros is one short since the $n$ zeros pattern is not present. The nearest contains $n - 1$ zeros and a single one. With a long chain-code, apart from local non-randomness, due to an all ones starting pattern for example, random appearance of 0 or 1 at any particular stage would appear probable. If tests for randomness were shown to be satisfied, then since the series is deterministic and repeatable, the term pseudo-random could be applied.

Extensive tests for randomness using a digital computer program to simulate the operation of the logica arrangements of Figs. 3a and 3b have been carried out by Redshaw (1961). They included,

(i) A test for the number of digits in the complete code.

(ii) A test to determine the number of ones and zeros.

(iii) A serial test to count the number of 00, 01, 10 and 11 pairs in the complete code.

(iv) A 'poker' test to count the number of ones in every group of four adjacent digits.

The results showed, apart from small discrepancies caused by the missing zero, the same relative frequencies for the sequence of heads and tails expected from the repeated tossing of a coin, i.e. a Poisson distribution. However, the sequence obtained with $n = 11$ or $n = 15$ is limited in length, and local non-randomness occurs in the region of the all ones pattern.

Hence the chain-code generators discussed above were incorporated in a single random-arrival generator. A basic arrangement is shown in Fig. 4. The effect of taking an output dependent upon half-addition between the two generators is to produce a chain-code with an overall length of

$$(2^{15}-1)(2^{11}-1) = 67,074,049$$

digits before repeating.

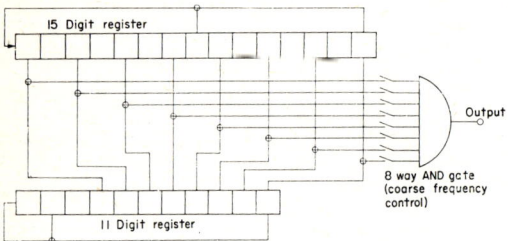

FIG. 4. *Block diagram of basic random generator.*

In addition, the technique minimizes local non-randomness and permits a wide range of flow rates. Figure 4 shows the arrangements for varying the flow rate. Since the output at any stage of either generator may be 1 or 0 with equal probability, and an output occurs for every shift pulse at basic clock rate, the avarage rate of output pulses, 1's, is half the clock rate.

For a modulo-two adder the four permutations of 1 and 0 result in two outputs of 1 and two of 0. Hence with only a single modulo-two adder connected to the AND gate of Fig. 4 and the remainder of its inputs set to 1, a flow rate equal to half the clock rate is achieved. In general the chance of an output 1 from the AND gate will be $(\frac{1}{2})^m$ where $m$ is the number of half-adders in circuit. With eight half adders available as shown in Fig. 4, eight basic rates are possible.

Provision for fine frequency control is also made. This is illustrated in Fig. 5. Any desired number up to and including 11111 (decimal 31) may be set up in a register. Pick-offs from the chain-code generator insert at every epoch a random five-digit binary number into a second register. This number will take values with equal probability in the range 0 to 11111. The numbers in the two registers are compared using appropriate logic. Only when the random number is less than the number set into the five-digit register can an output pulse appear. Suppose for example the number set up is 10111 (decimal 23), then the flow rate is reduced to the value:

original flow rate x 22/31

Successful tests for randomness have been carried out on the output of the random generator. They included,

(i) A frequency test to test the frequency of pulses appearing per unit time against the theoretical value.

(ii) A test to check for correlation in the length of intervals between successive pulses.

(iii) A test for exponential distribution of gap length.

(iv) A bunching test for randomicity.

(v) A chi-squared test.

One important feature is that the pattern of output pulses is repeatable starting at any point. As a result

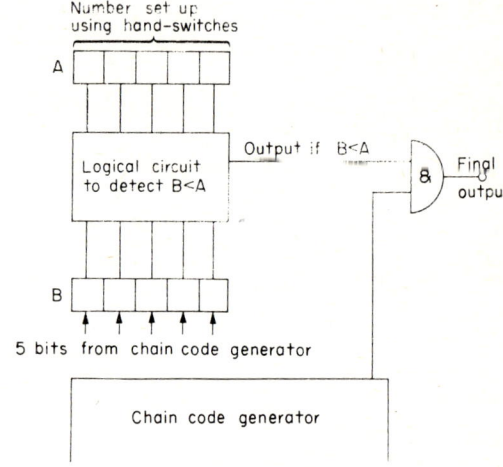

FIG. 5. *Fine control of output frequency.*

experiments may be repeated readily. This is valuable as a check against possible error in a simulation.

*The Manchester digital traffic simulator.* The main features of a road-traffic simulator incorporating the items described in the sections above are illustrated in Fig. 6. This special-purpose machine has been used for extensive experiments concerned with traffic behaviour at intersections. Some design features and preliminary experiments are described in Hartley and Green (1965). Experiments involving the on-line control of the model by means of a process-control computer situated at some distance have also been performed (Green *et al.* 1967).

One fruitful area of study concerns the short-term simulation of certain aspects of machine operation using a general-purpose digital computer. Using this technique the desirability of the incorporation of extra facilities in the model have been investigated. The technique has also been used in preliminary studies relating to the formulation of policies of direct-digital-control (Green and Hartley (1966)).

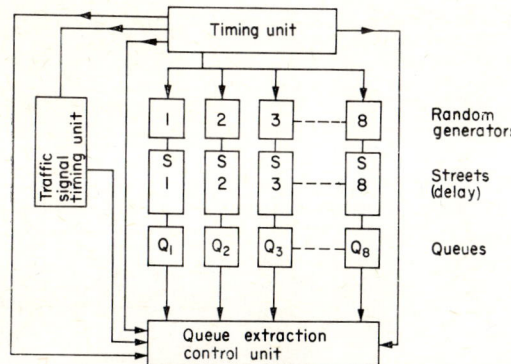

FIG. 6. *Schematic diagram of the complete road traffic simulator.*

*See also:* Pseudonoise sequences. Pseudorandom binary signals, use of in correlation analysis of dynamic systems.

*Bibliography*

ADAMS W. F. (1936) *Road Traffic Considered as a Random Series*, J. Inst. Civ. Engrs. **4**, 121.
BONE A. J., MARTIN B. V. and HARVEY T. N. (1964) *The Selection of a Cycle Length for Fixed Time Traffic Signals*, Research Report No. R64-09, Systems Laboratory, Department of Civil Engineering, Massachusetts Institute of Technology, Cambridge, Mass, April.
ELSPAS B. (1959) *The Theory of Autonomous Linear Sequential Networks*, Trans. I.R.E. CT-6, 45.
GREEN D. H. and HARTLEY M. G. (1966) *The Simulation of Simple Traffic Control Policies for a Signalised Intersection*, Opl. Res. Q. **17**, 263.
GREEN D. H., HARTLEY M. G. and FOULK P. W. (1967) *On-line Control of Simulated Traffic Intersections*, Second Convention on Advances in Computer Control. U.K.A.C. April.
HARTLEY M. G. and GREEN D. H. (1965) *Study of Intersection Problems by Simulation on a Special Purpose Computer*, Traffic Engineering and Control, July, **7**, 3, 219.
HEATH F. G. (1961) *Digital Codes and Converters*, Ph.D. Thesis, Manchester.
HEATH F. G. and GRIBBLE M. W. (1960) *Chain-Codes and their Electronic Applications*, I.E.E., Monograph 392 M, July.
HUFFMAN D. A. (1956) *The Synthesis of Linear Sequential Coding Networks*, in (C. Cherry Ed.) *Information Theory*, London: Butterworths.
REDSHAW S. (1961) *A Repeatable Random Pulse Generator Using Chain-codes*, M.Sc. Tech. Thesis, Manchester.
SAATY T. L. (1961) *Elements of Queueing Theory*, New York: McGraw-Hill.
TOCHER K. D. (1963) *The Art of Simulation*, London: English University Press.

M. G. HARTLEY

## SORTING TECHNIQUES.

### *1. Introduction*

Most computer applications fall into one of three categories: simulation, calculation and data processing. Most of the latter type are concerned with the ordering of items of information, whether alphabetic or numeric. Systems programs (software, e.g. compilers, assemblers, operating systems) can be thought of as high level data processing programs in that they spend much of their time manipulating and searching data structures, whether in core memory or on magnetic tape or disk. The methodology for ordering information, which has a direct bearing on the efficiency (hence, economy) of the overall system, has been a subject of keen study and testing for some time. It should be noted that there are two basic types of 'data rearrangement'—Sorting and Merging.

*Sorting* can be defined as the ordering (in a pre-arranged hierarchial sequence) of arbitrarily or randomly situated items of information. If the information is numeric, the new order is numerically ascending or descending; if alphabetic, it is alphabetically ascending (A, B, C, D ———) or descending (Z, Y, X, W ———). If the information contains other characters (e.g. + — * / , £) these must be assigned some hierarchy (Douglas 1959).

*Merging* is the act of combining two or more ordered (i.e. already sorted) sequences of information into one ordered sequence.

### *2. Basic Fundamentals and Definitions*

A complete set of information is called a *file*. For example, if a company has two factories it would probably store its payroll information in two files, most likely on magnetic tape. There is no restriction on the size of a file—it may take part of one reel of tape or may comprise several reels. All the information for an employee (e.g. name, age, tax code, employee number, years of service, etc.) is grouped together into one *record* of information. Thus, if a company has 500 employees its payroll file would contain 500 records. This information is sorted with respect to a particular item of information, called a *key*. Thus, the payroll file might be sorted alphabetically (if the key item is employee name) or numerically (if the key is employee number). It should be noted that *all* the information in the record is moved when sorting with respect to the key, not just the key itself. Usually, in an internal storage sort, the *addresses* of the records are shifted until the comparison of keys has been completed (i.e. the core storage address of the initial item of information in the record). The final stage is simply a shifting of the records into their sorted sequence according to the addresses. Since most sorts involve more records than can be held in core at one time the information is brought in in *segments*, each being sorted into *strings*. These are then merged in a subsequent phase, or *pass*, into the final sorted sequence. Magnetic 'work tapes' are used to store the strings until they are needed for intermediate and final merge passes.

### 3. Sorting Methods

Most mathematical methods of sorting fall into one of two main types: (A) digital sorting and (B) merge sorting.

A. *Digital sorting*. (1). The basic digital sort, employed by punched card mechanical sorters, uses successive digits (or characters) in the key, starting at the most significant digit. For numeric keys and information sorted on magnetic tape, this would involve examining each key and placing the information into one of ten intermediate piles according to the most significant digit, then inputting this information and storing it according to the next digit, etc, etc. This is called *radix sorting* (Gotlieb 1963).

(2). Another simple sort method is to search the list of $N$ items (or keys) until the largest is found, then stored. Then the largest of the $N-1$ remaining items are searched until the largest is found, then stored immediately below, etc. This process is continued until the file is exhausted. The number of machine comparisons is $N(N-1)/2$. This method is sometimes known as *selection sorting*.

(3). The method of *interchanging pairs* is often used (Grabbe *et al.*). It consists of examining the $N$ items two at a time. That is, items 1 and 2, 2 and 3, 3 and 4, ....., $N-1$ and $N$ are compared, interchanging where necessary. The process is repeated until no interchanges occur. The number of machine comparisons, in the worst case, is $N(N-1)$. The upper bound on the number of exchanges is $N(N-1)/2$.

For example consider the arbitrary sequence of 8 single-digit items: 4, 9, 3, 2, 7, 5, 1, 6. Using the method above the intermediate stages are:

| (1) | (2) | (3) | (4) | (5) | (6) | (7) |
|---|---|---|---|---|---|---|
| 4 | 4 | 3 | 2 | 2 | 2 | 1 |
| 9 | 3 | 2 | 3 | 3 | 1 | 2 |
| 3 | 2 | 4 | 4 | 1 | 3 | 3 |
| 2 | 7 | 5 | 1 | 4 | 4 | 4 |
| 7 | 5 | 1 | 5 | 5 | 5 | 5 |
| 5 | 1 | 6 | 6 | 6 | 6 | 6 |
| 1 | 6 | 7 | 7 | 7 | 7 | 7 |
| 6 | 9 | 9 | 9 | 9 | 9 | 9 |

This involved 42 compares and 16 exchanges.

B. *Merge sorting*. The process of merge sorting requires more storage than the previous methods ($2N$ locations for $N$ items) but the number of machine operations is significantly less. Pairs of keys are examined in turn; within each pair the smaller key is placed first. After the first pass the group of $N$ items consists of $N/2$ strings, each of length *two*. Next, pairs of strings are merged and sorted to produce $N/4$ strings, each of length *four*. The process continues until a single string of length $N$ is produced by a final merge pass. Since any number $N$ can be said to be bounded by two successive integral powers of 2 (that is, $2^{K-1} < N \leq 2^K$) this method can readily be seen to require $K$ passes (or $NK = N \log_2 N$ comparisons).

Using this method to sort the above sequence we observe the following stages:

| (1) | (2) | (3) | (4) |
|---|---|---|---|
| 4 | 4 | 2 | 1 |
| 9 | 9 | 3 | 2 |
| 3 | 2 | 4 | 3 |
| 2 | 3 | 9 | 4 |
| 7 | 5 | 1 | 5 |
| 5 | 7 | 5 | 6 |
| 1 | 1 | 7 | 7 |
| 6 | 6 | 6 | 9 |

A generalization of this method is to compare $P$ keys on each pass (rather than 2) yielding $N/P$ strings after the first pass, $N/P^2$ after the second, etc. The number of passes, $K$, is then $\log_p N$ rather than $\log_2 N$.

### 4. Merging

We have seen that when the information file to be sorted is stored on several magnetic tapes, a sort proceeds in three stages. First, groups of records on one tape are brought into internal high speed core, sorted by whatever method is employed, and written out onto intermediate tapes. Thus, strings of sorted data are produced. In the second stage, which usually requires several passes, these strings are merged to produce a single sorted tape. This process is repeated for all the tapes which make up the file. In the final stage the various tapes, each one already in sequence, are collated to produce a single multi-reel sorted file. The second stage, where the strings of a single tape are gradually combined to produce a sequenced tape, is accomplished by some kind of merge process. Merge methodology, like sort methodology, is an integral part of the overall sort process.

A standard 3-way merge requires six tape units to be completely automatic. This is illustrated in the figure. (The numbers represent ordered strings on the original tape.) First, the strings are distributed onto three work tapes A, B and C. The initial strings on each tape are input to core, merged, then output as a single string on work tape D. The second strings on each tape are input, merged, then output to tape E. In a similar manner the next merged string is put on tape F. This process is repeated until the new intermediate tapes D, E and F, contain $N/3$ sorted strings instead of the original $N$. The output tapes (D, E, F) now become input to the next pass, the input tapes (A, B, C) become output and a new pass begins. At the end of this pass, tapes D, E and F contain $N/9$ sorted strings. The total number of passes required to merge $N$ strings is $\log_3 N$. In general, where $2P$ tape units are available, the number of passes in a $P$-way merge is $\log_p N$. $P$ is said to be the *order* of the merge.

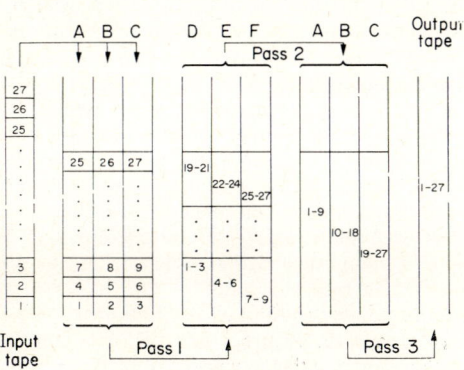

In a low order merge the key comparison time is less than that needed to read records. Sort speed, then, is *tape limited*, i.e. determined by tape reading speed. It is particularly important to keep tapes moving to optimize efficiency. When tape speed is high and the order of the merge is high the sort may become *process limited*, i.e. determined by basic arithmetical and transfer times (sometimes termed *compute-bound*). For a given machine and peripherals, then, the sort will be fastest, or optimized, when process and tape speeds are balanced. When tapes can be read backward some economy in tape rewind can be achieved.

### 5. Method Evaluation

Formulae have been developed for estimating sort time for given computer and data parameters. Procedures using these estimates are used to compare the efficiency of various sorting techniques. These formulae and procedures, described in (Hall 1963), are very lengthy and complex but should be used to determine optimum combinations of sorting method for a given computer and data (i.e. internal CPU times, tape speeds, number of input data records, lengths of keys, etc.).

Finally, a glossary of sorting and merging terms was provided for the ACM Sort Symposium, held in Princeton, New Jersey, U.S.A. November 29–30, 1962 (Hall 1963, Glossary).

*See also:* Symbol manipulation by digital computer.

*Bibliography*

DOUGLAS A. S. (1959) *Techniques for the Recording of, and Reference to, Data in a Computer*, Comp. J. No. 2, 1.
GOTLIEB C. C. (1963) *Sorting on Computers*, Communications of the ACM (May), 194.
GRABBE, RAMO and WOOLDRIDGE, *Handbook of Automation, Computation and Control*, Vol. 2, 145.
HALL M. H. (1963) *A Method of Comparing the Time Requirements of Sorting Methods*, Communications of the ACM (May), 259.
*A Glossary of Sorting and Merging Terms* in Hall (1963), 281.

L. K. GRODMAN

**SPEECH.** The pseudo-couple speech and language are separable as vehicle and code. Theories connecting speech and language are topics of linguistics. In treating speech on a pre-linguistic level, this article employs linguistic terminology as a matter of convenience.

The natural medium of speech is acoustic. In its acoustic form, speech as an object of study is well understood in the sense that it is possible to identify the physical features of speech that correlate highly with perception and to trace the origins of these features to movements and shapes of the human speech organs.

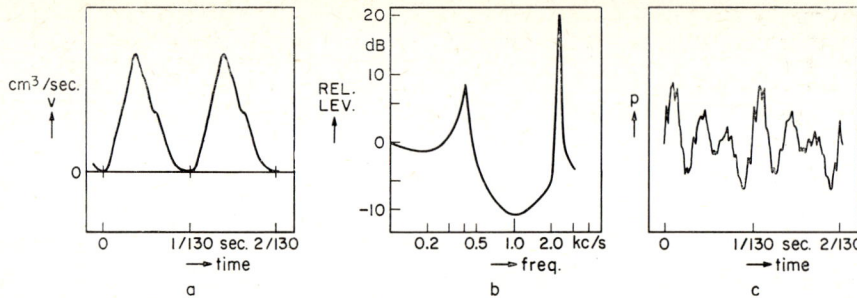

FIG. 1. *Representative acoustic functions in speech. Panel (a) displays two cycles of air flow at the level of the vocal cords. As the abscissa indicates, the period of each cycle is approximately 1/130 second. The ordinate is volume velocity in cubic centimetres per second on an arbitrary scale. Panel (b) is a transfer function characteristic of the vowel /i/. It includes the two lowest resonant frequencies of the mouth and effects of higher resonances and radiation impedance. Panel (c) displays two cycles of a radiated pressure wave of /i/. The three panels are not computationally related.*

Transmitted through air, speech is best described as a pressure wave, a sample facsimile of which is shown as $s(t)$ in Fig. 1c. Inspection of the segment reveals that the waveform appears to be nearly periodic and that it appears to be mainly the sum of three oscillations. Since the slowest component has a period equal to 1/130 second, its frequency is 130 cycles per second (c/s). This component corresponds to what is often called pitch. The two higher components, which oscillate perhaps 3 and 17 times within one pitch period and therefore are near 400 and 2200 c/s in frequency, represent formants that largely determine the phonetic value of the segment, the vowel /i/. (Phonetic symbols appearing in this article either have a phonetic value suggested unambiguously by English pronunciation or are identified in Fig. 2.)

The foregoing inspection of a signal in the time domain amounts to a rough spectral analysis implying that the fine structure of the spectrum consists approximately of a series of discrete harmonically related frequencies and that the shape, or envelope, of the spectrum is peaked twice above the fundamental frequency. Because phonetic values in speech typically last less than 0·15 second, it is most useful to perform running short-term spectral analysis, i.e. to transform $s(t)$ into $S(t,f)$. This type of analysis, which is illustrated in Fig. 2, is of major importance in acoustic phonetics.

The time-domain speech pressure wave often exhibits randomness rather than periodicity. This aperiodicity turns up in the spectrum as continuous rather than discrete fine structure. Spectral envelope again largely determines phonetic value. Aperiodicity is represented in Fig. 2 by open circles. As Fig. 2 illustrates, phonetic units may consist of periodic, aperiodic, or both spectral fine-structure components. Momentary cessation of audible sound may also have critical phonetic value.

Formally decomposed into envelope and fine-structure factors, $S(t, f)$ may be expressed as $S(t, f) = E(t,f)F(t,f)$ Since it is practical to approximate these factors physically, this form of decomposition is the basis of important methods of speech synthesis and of relatively economical speech transmission. The latter application is possible because, as Fig. 2 suggests, $S(t,f)$ is a function changing in time much more slowly than $s(t)$.

Communication theory helps quantify the transmission requirements of $s(t)$ and $S(t, f)$. Experiment has shown that although the spectrum of $s(t)$ extends naturally higher than 10,000 c/s, the lower 3500 c/s at a signal-to-noise ratio of 30 dB is sufficient to retain nearly complete intelligibility. This reduced signal may be represented by a sampled and quantized signal of about 35,000 bits per second. At the cost of eliminating secondary features of speech that underlie naturalness and speaker identity, phonetic symbols might replace speech and be transmitted at a rate of perhaps 40 bits per second. It has been shown that transmitting forms of $S(t, f)$ may be accomplished satisfactorily for some purposes at a rate of 2000 bits per second.

Another interpretation of $S(t, f)$ bears on the physiology of speech. Figure 3 first identifies the relevant speech organs and their acoustic products.

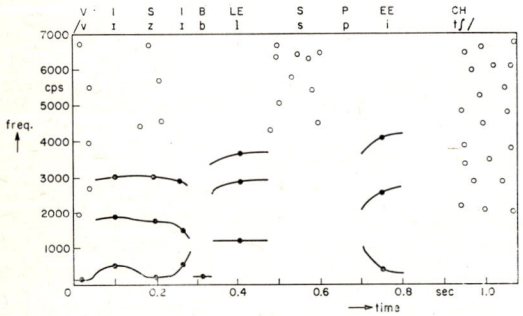

FIG. 2. *A schematic spectrogram of the phrase 'visible speech'. Time runs on the abscissa and frequency on the ordinate. Solid lines with filled circles indicate the locations of formants in the spectra of periodic components of the speech signal. Empty circles indicate location of aperiodic components in the spectrum.*

The chest region is a gas pump power supply, the output of which is, acoustically, a static pressure. The larynx is the source of periodic oscillation, i.e. of voice in a narrow sense. The vocal cords within the larynx generate voice by vibrating like lips in the mouthpiece of a wind instrument. Figure 1a depicts two cycles of air flow past the vocal cords. The waveform, which, as shown, is usually triangular, resembles the waveform of the variation of area between the vocal cords. Flow may be reduced to zero for longer fractions of the period than what is pictured; in fact, longer fractions occur in good singing voices. Incomplete closure, on the other hand, causes breathy voice.

In a second mode of activity, the vocal cords form a constriction that sets the air flowing past into aperiodic turbulence. This mode has significance in speech in whispering, when all spectral fine structure is aperiodic, and in the typically aperiodic phonetic unit /h/. In a third mode, the vocal cords remain wide enough apart so as not to vibrate and not to impede the static pressure originating in the chest.

Most phonetic differentiation occurs in the mouth (including the pharynx) and nose, where the mobile structures are the jaw, lips, pharyngeal walls, tongue, and

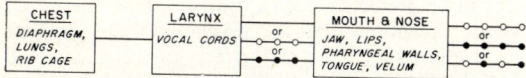

FIG. 3. *A schematic block diagram of the moving structures producing human speech. The acoustic output of the chest is static pressure. The output of the larynx may be either static pressure (simple line), aperiodic oscillation (empty circles), or nearly periodic oscillation (filled circles). The speech-significant output of the mouth and nose, what is radiated as speech, may be periodic, aperiodic, or both.*

velum. The mouth, as an acoustic tube, almost always is a significant resonator in speech and may simultaneously be a source of sound.

In vowels, the tube is essentially closed at one end by the vocal cords and is open only at the lips. To produce characteristic vowel formants, the speaker assumes appropriate configurations of his vocal tract. The tube actually resonates at a large number of frequencies, but it has been demonstrated that the lowest two, which always lie below 3000 c/s, determine the phonetic value of most vowels. For example, in men, formants near 300 and 2300 c/s produce /i/. Because the vocal tracts of women and children are shorter than those of men, their typical formants are somewhat higher. Figure 1b depicts the shape of the transfer function that largely determines formant location.

The mouth generates phonetically significant sound either by stopping and suddenly releasing air, as in the typical /t/; by setting air into turbulence in a constrictive gap, as in /s/; or by vibration of an organ, as in trilled /r/. When the velum is lowered, the nose, as another acoustic tube, is coupled to the mouth. Air flow is completely diverted to the nose in a phonetic unit such as /m/ or partially diverted in the linguistically significant nasalization of vowels in many languages. The three types of phonetic units are represented in the output of the mouth and nose in Fig. 3. In the pathological condition known as cleft palate, structural abnormality prevents the decoupling of nose and mouth. It must be furthermore noted that any shaping and activity of the vocal organs produces a predictable acoustic result. The reverse is not true, for, as the ventriloquist demonstrates, an acoustic signal possessing stable phonetic value may be produced by alternate physiological means.

Now $S(t, f)$ may otherwise be decomposed into the product of the source factor $G(f, t)$ and a transfer factor $H(f, t)$, i.e. $S(t, f) = G(t, f)H(t, f)$. In other words, the spectrum of the speech wave is the product of the spectrum of the source, such as the vocal cords, and the spectral transfer function determined by the resonances of the mouth and nose and by radiation effects. Alternatively analysed in the time domain, the speech wave $s(t)$ may be considered to be the result of the convolution of the source function and the impulse response of the transfer function. Figure 1 combines the time-domain and frequency-domain representations.

The second and far less accessible physiological level of speech production is the neuromuscular. That the speech-producing muscles are in neurally mediated feedback loops suggests that momentary regulation of muscular activity is not required. Nervous system control of speech may be organized in units as long as or longer than minimal phonetic units. Plain evidence is the coordinated behaviour of the articulators anticipating succeeding phonetic units. Although adequate hearing is necessary for the acquisition of normal speech, the mature speaker does not need auditory feedback to speak accurately. It is possible to train deaf persons to speak serviceably.

Ultimate control of speech and language resides in the left hemisphere of the brain. This is true of most people, right or left handed. What the right hemisphere does for speech and language is not established. Even in the brain, speech and language appear to be separable, since, after brain injury, disturbance of articulation may occur without aphasia. One theory joins speech and language in the postero-superior sections of the left temporal lobe. Damage there results in impaired discrimination of phonetic units. Language consequently suffers, as in effect, the vehicle speech is distorted beyond recognition.

*See also:* Phonetics, auditory. Speech perception.

*Bibliography*

CHERRY C. (1957) *On Human Communication*, New York: Wiley; London: Chapman and Hall.
FANT G. (1960) *Acoustic Theory of Speech Production*, The Hague: Mouton and Co.

FLANAGAN J. L. (1965) *Speech Analysis, Synthesis and Perception*, New York: Academic Press; Berlin: Springer-Verlag.

FLETCHER H. (1953) *Speech and Hearing in Communication*, New York: Van Nostrand.

MALMBERG B. (1963) *Structural Linguistics and Human Communication*, New York: Academic Press.

MILLER G. A. (1951) *Language and Communication*, New York: McGraw-Hill. (Paperback edition published by McGraw-Hill, 1963.)

SAPORTA S. (Ed.) (1961) *Psycholinguistics*, New York: Holt, Rinehart and Winston.

N. GUTTMAN

**SPEECH PERCEPTION.** Early investigations of Speech perception aimed at discovering the properties of telephony channels that enabled the transmission of intelligible speech. These experiments were undertaken for an engineering purpose, to compress telephone bandwidth, and focussed primarily upon waveform distortions and speech statistics rather than perceptual mechanisms. Subsequently the focus of interest changed to (1) Psychophysical experiments with speech stimuli. (2) Correlations of particular acoustic cues with particular linguistic responses. (3) Attempts to define 'units' of speech perception. (4) Formulations of the role of context in identification tasks. (5) Theories of the mechanism underlying the performance in recognizing spoken language.

*1. The psychophysics of speech.* A number of experiments have been done at the Bell Telephone Laboratories and elsewhere aimed at specifying the precision required in speech processing circuits—chiefly telephony schemes that analyse the speech into a small number of important parameters and resynthesize it into something approaching the original, at the receiving end. These experiments measure differential sensitivity—sensitivity to changes in the value of the speech parameters, and predict with some success the quantising noise tolerable in digital transmission of the speech parameters. Some typical findings are that formant-frequency discrimination is worse than pure-tone discrimination, the differential threshold being about five per cent of the absolute value; for voice pitch, however, discrimination is if anything better than for pure tones at the same frequency because a voice contains information about the repetition frequency of the waveform throughout its spectrum.

These psychophysical experiments and the quality judgements with which they agree consider speech independent of its role as a mode of communication. While on the stimulus side there is some overlap between factors contributing to intelligibility and factors contributing to naturalness, behaviourally, the two types of assessment of communications are relatively independent. There has been little success in predicting facts about judgements of quality or naturalness from assumptions about the process of recognition. There may even be a physiological basis for this separation. There is some evidence that short-term memory for speech is better when the stimulus is presented to the ear contralateral to the cerebral hemisphere dominant for language and the reverse appears to hold for short tunes; possibly non-identification skills for speech sounds are under less control from the language dominant hemisphere. It has also been shown that learning of semi-speech sounds is worse than learning of either non-speech or acceptable speech sounds, and this suggests an ambiguous processing of the hybrid stimuli.

Another application of psychophysical techniques to non-linguistic properties of speech is in subjective scaling. Here a subject is asked to assign numerical values to stimuli which vary along some dimension with a simple physical correlate. In the case of speech, loudness, effort, rate and some attitudes conveyed by simple intonation contours have been scaled. Scaling experiments usually show the 'subjective magnitudes' to be power functions of the physical magnitudes; although the actual exponents vary from subject to subject this variation is usually smaller than that due to the specific attribute being scaled, and so the results are meaningful for experimental comparisons. Exactly what a 'psychological magnitude' is, is of course a completely open question.

It can be predicted from a general '*Motor theory*' of speech perception that the psychophysical exponent with a given subject on the speech loudness scale will be more like his exponent for vocal effort than his exponent for loudness of pure tones. This theory holds that speech is perceived with reference to the articulations of the listener required to produce the heard sounds, and for loudness this involves an implicit assessment of vocal effort. The prediction is not confirmed in some experiments; however, this negative result does not preclude another type of relationship between perception and articulation. Judgements and the perceptual experiences upon which they depend achieve information about real states and events through interrelationships of *cues* which are individually unreliable. In some cases it is possibie to assess the individual cues in isolation. Thus we can expect two types of result in the scaling of attributes of a complex sound, attitude towards the 'object' and attitude towards the stimulus at the subject's sensory receptors, or a particular attribute of it. Depending upon the particular experimental arrangement and instructions a subject might perform either way. Thus, *loudness*, where there is a particular need for accurate judgements of intensity in a simple dimensional manner because of the physical correlate of distance, is an unfair test of the theory. In the case of identifying speech sounds, individual physical cues such as frequencies of the speech formants are unreliable, and there is no doubt that complex relationships of the individual cues are used in achieving perceptual evaluation of the articulations. Whether or not the listener's own articulations are relevant to these judgements is a different question, much more difficult to prove.

Subjective scaling has also been used for assessing speech defects and transmission quality of telephone circuits. The purpose of this type of experiment is to isolate the important physical variables and to provide a quantitative relationship between them and the subjective ratings of acceptability and unacceptability.

2. *Stimulus correlates of linguistic responses.* Experiments in this class form the largest group of experiments upon speech perception. Although some investigators have used selective distortions such as tape-cutting, filtering and masking, the most direct access to the cues used in distinguishing possible utterances is speech synthesis. A large number of the experiments have been done at Haskins Laboratories with the Pattern Playback synthesizer. This device sums a phase-free Fourier series where the temporal variations of the amplitude coefficients are obtained optically from schematised drawings of a frequency-time-amplitude spectrum. As the experimental results are particular statistical facts about perceptual responses, they are not given in detail, but an example is provided in Fig. 1.

Some general conclusions can be drawn from these experiments, though; only a broad and non-unique specification can be given for the acoustic correlates of a given phoneme, greater precision requiring regard for context as the example of Fig. 1 shows. This suggests that the term 'acoustic correlates of a phoneme' is not meaningless, as some linguists would say, but that a phoneme can be represented by a set of articulatory

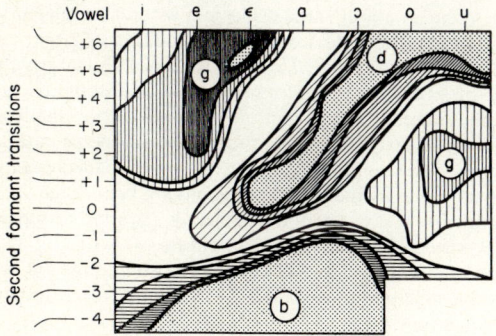

FIG. 1. *Some cues for the stop-consonants /b, d, g/. The dependent variable, frequency of response, is coded as darkness of hatching. One independent variable is the vowel with which the consonant is paired in the synthesized vowel-consonant pairs; this amounts to, chiefly, the frequency of the second-formant in the vowel, and can thus be represented continuously on the abscissa. The ordinate is the direction and magnitude of the second formant transition relative to the vowel, in multiples of 120 c/s. Other cues than the one illustrated play a part, such as the centre-frequency of the stop burst before a transition. It is typical of stimulus-response relationships in speech perception that the pattern of /d, g/ optimal cues reverses between vowels /ε/ and /u/. For vowel /i/, with high second formant, further cues are required to give a dominant /d/ response. (By permission from Liberman et al. (1954) Psychol. Monog., 68, 8.)*

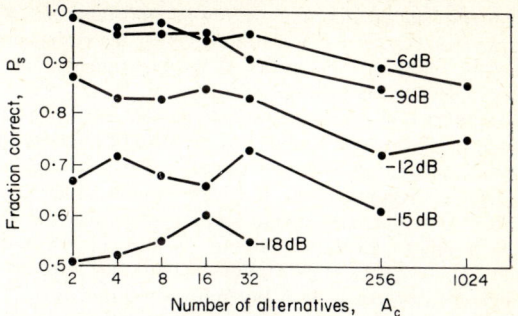

FIG. 2. *The data of Miller, Heise and Lichten are plotted in terms of the 'discriminant rule', showing the required drop in the estimated sensitivity parameter P(s) for large vocabularies. (After Stowe A. N., Harris W. P., and Hampton D. B. with permission.)*

'target values' approached but rarely reached or held for any length of time in real speech. Practically this works for English, but because phonemic descriptions of a language are not unique, and because languages exist where allophones of some phonemes are not simply influenced by continuity with adjacent segments, this use of the term 'phoneme' for articulatory and perceptual segments is a loose one. But it is a useful one, especially in English where only a few phonemes have a variable place of articulation.

In discussing cues and perceptual errors the term 'feature' is also useful, in a sense wider than the linguists' 'distinctive feature' though not unrelated to it. For example, the cues which differentiate /p, t, k/ overlap with those that distinguish /b, d, g/ /f, s, χ/, and /m, n, ŋ/. The between-group distinction is one of manner of articulation and the within-group distinction one of place, a classification long used in articulatory phonetics. In perceptual confusion tests and in everyday life, multifeature errors are rare, except when there is a high bias for the particular wrong response. An unemployed man might mistake 'coal' for 'dole', but a more likely error would be 'toll' or 'goal'.

A quite general finding in the discrimination of speech sounds that can be ordered on a continuum (as in Fig. 1) is that, with naive subjects, the differential sensitivity function closely follows the phonemic labelling function: that is to say, sensitivity to acoustic differences on the continuum is greater between the areas usually associated with linguistic categories than within these areas. This 'phoneme boundary' is not an artefact of the differential threshold procedure used. It suggests that only the relevant discriminations are learned by the individual who is required merely to identify speech sounds. Further training would be required for perception of the stimuli as psychophysically continuous rather than linguistically discrete, and this is part of the training of auditory phonetics.

Experiments have also been done on non-segmental distinctions such as stress. Here it is found that pitch changes, lengthening of some vowels, and precision of articulation can act as cues, although judgements depend heavily upon the framework of the experimental subject's own expectancies.

Some of the results of these perceptual experiments could in principle be obtained by an acoustic analysis of sounds spoken to order by subjects; but this implies perceptual acceptance by the experimenter, and only him, that the spoken sounds were what he asked for. This is only a logical difficulty but it is also possible that there will be quirks of perception such that the most obvious acoustic correlate is not most important perceptually. Only a perceptual synthesis experiment can arrive at the simplest and most economical description of the cues used and any linguistic relevance of instrumental studies must depend upon some measure of perceptual validation.

*3. Units of perception.* Although it is not tautologous to show that various levels of category employed in structural linguistics are reflected in perceptual performances, these demonstrations say very little about the performances themselves. The value of 'perceptual unit' studies lies therefore in the relation of the particular conditions of perceiving to the apparent 'chunk' size on different occasions. This is not an old-fashioned perceptual structuralism in the image of a modern linguistic analysis, but a means of approaching the mechanism of recognition by examining its processing span.

One way to define a perceptual '*chunk*' is to say that it corresponds to the length of symbol string in the symbolic representation of an utterance, over which decision is habitually suspended and often revised in the light of subsequent perceptual evidence. But this definition is experimentally unmanageable and may lead to rather different estimates of chunks for different subjects. A more practical way is to reflect the continuity or the 'busy-ness' of the perceptual process at different points in an utterance. This has been done by superimposing an irrelevant click on a sentence and asking subjects to locate it on a written transcription. Typically it is found that clicks are subjectively displaced from their actual location towards major syntactic breaks in the sentence. This could be just a response bias, but in addition subjects display improved discrimination of location near the syntactic boundaries. Several experiments support the importance of grammatical constraints in the perception of continuous speech. The grammatical 'units' yielded by this procedure are thus probably units of understanding rather than primary recognition, and so the results do not support any concept of time-quantisation in auditory perception. However they do support a strong involvement of selective attention in speech perception.

Another procedure for identifying perceptual chunks requires interruption of speech at various positions and rates. It can be argued that interruption by switching speech from ear to ear in the middle of 'chunks' will prevent half the necessary information reaching the recognizer, and intelligibility will be low; with longer samples some chunks will be correctly recognized; with smaller samples each unit stands a higher chance of recognition, and thus intelligibility will be higher at faster and slower interruption rates. However, if the perceptual chunking is conceived as tied to the structure of the speech it yields wrong predictions. The above argument only applies when there is a difference in the amount of constraint operating between the sub-parts of the acoustic correlate of the unit, and the external constraints of units upon one another. With equal internal and external constraints there will be no result at all. With high internal and low external constraint interruption in mid-unit will be deleterious. Experiments show that the loss in intelligibility for speech switched from ear to ear is greatest when a switch occurs at a rate of about one per syllable. Thus if the perceptual units are related to the structure of the speech, they must correspond to either whole syllables, or the consonant clusters where syllables meet. The relative internal constraint is probably higher for consonant clusters, but interruption in the consonant clusters, when the action of the switch is tied to the speech, is no more deleterious than interruption in vowels.

The possibility remains that perceptual quantization is related not to stimulus structure but to some free running internal clock. If this is the case there are not many implications of 'perceptual units' for study of the perception of speech. There is some evidence, however, that the dip in intelligibility for speech switched from ear to ear at about three cycles per second, is related to lag in the mechanism controlling switching of attention. When noise is alternated with the speech, frequent switching of attention is discouraged and the dramatic dip in the intelligibility function becomes more shallow, shifting slightly upwards towards the phoneme rate in speech. The magnitude of these intelligibility decrements is partly due to the experiments having been done with shadowing tasks, where the subject is required to repeat back speech continuously. But effects of switching also appear in simple identification tasks so the results are not due solely to interactions of switching with response organization.

*4. Quantitative formulations of context.* It has been shown that adequate representation and recognition of a phoneme may require some acoustic context. Acoustic context may even be important at a supra-segmental level; it has been found that words excised from fluent speech were more intelligible given a recording of preceding context than when a transcription of that context was given. This interesting finding has not been explained: it may lie in uncertainty in the subject about the tempo of the speech or uncertainty about the vowel system of the speaker, or merely in a general 'surprise' factor. Uncertainty about the speaker's vowel system is a strong possiblity, because other experiments have shown vowel identifications to depend heavily upon this—a perceptual constancy analagous to the dependence of visual size judgements upon distance information.

However, the main role of context is to restrict alternatives rather than to correct acoustic cues; the restriction is both syntactic and semantic. Chiefly context operates to limit the response uncertainty; in a monitoring task, where subjects have to say 'yes' if a certain word turns up, the performance is not affected by the number of other words that may appear. It appears that this restriction in the number of possible or likely responses operates both in perception of continuous speech and experimental tasks where single words are identified. Accordingly the latter task is used more often because it offers more experimental control. In both cases, one equation which provides a good prediction of accuracy as a function of context is the 'discriminant rule':

$$P(c) = P(s)^n \quad \text{where} \quad n = \log_2 N.$$

$N$ is the vocabulary size for which the articulation score, $P(c)$ is to be predicted; $P(s)$ is the probability of a correct response among two alternatives under the same stimulus conditions. The mathematical form does not require that the stimuli be structured in $\log_2 N$ dimensions or that any dimensions they have should be binary, as it is only a formal law dependent for confirmation upon the rough manner in which context operates. Other quantitative formulations exist for the effect of vocabulary size in the psychophysical literature on detection and recognition, but this formula has two advantages. It is simple, and it only agrees with experimental data up to a vocabulary size of 32. For larger vocabulary sizes, subjects could not possibly have all the responses equally available. The discriminant rule shows the required drop in the index of discriminability for large vocabularies.

5. *Models of the recognition mechanism.* A scientific goal is to provide theories that explain data in areas outside those where the theory was originally formulated. In psychology this is still rather an ideal than a reality, so it is to the credit of the Motor Theory that it even generates the predictions discussed earlier under the psychophysics of speech. The relationship of theory to data on speech perception is still tenuous, so arguments of biological economy and logical arguments have their place. The current version of the Motor Theory, which has a long history in phonetic speculation, was introduced to explain the relative simplicity of perceptual-articulatory relationships given the relative complexity of perceptual-acoustic relationships. This evidence is substantial and supports a weak form of the Motor Theory to the extent that speech perception is effectively articulation perception; no evidence yet exists to support the stronger form of the theory, that recapitulatory involvement of the neural commands to the articulators is necessary for speech recognition by the mature perceiver. Evidence from some speech pathologies does not support the ability to speak a given utterance as a necessary condition for recognizing it. Experiments with learning of frequency transposed speech by adults have been inconclusive: no large difference emerged between subjects who learned by hearing their own voices distorted and those who learned with a similar amount of experience of other voices distorted. It is possible that being able to speak assists the child's perceptual learning, but a case has been reported of speech comprehension by a child unable to speak. The statistical properties of utterances alone could serve as the basis of learning; also a more direct 'passive filter' recognition mechanism has advantages in the adult organism in that it is rapid (only slow readers mouth words) and does not preclude simultaneous input and output.

Some of these difficulties are avoided by an 'active' or analysis-by-synthesis theory, which postulates not motor involvement, but matching of input preliminarily recognized at the feature level, with a symbolic representation generated by the same rules as used in speech production. Analysis-by-synthesis still faces the difficulty that a completely active system cannot recognize items for which it is not prepared, without the additional postulate of a perfect memory and infinite time available. With this modification such a system could recognize items by matching all the possible symbolic representations in order of probability. To give a realistic performance, some passive, filter-like element is required to say in what respects the input and a particular matching representation differed and so to hasten matching with a representation which is correct. Why then incorporate the analysis-by-synthesis mechanism at all? It may have a special function in learning and in difficult discriminations, as a number of writers have suggested.

A weaker form of 'active' theory is a 'pre-set filter' theory suggested for phenomena of selective attention. It proposes that the input paths for immediately relevant features are selectively facilitated. This view predicts that accuracy for expected items will be greater than for unexpected items even when possible response biasing has been subtracted out.

An extreme view of the remaining model, the '*passive*' *model* proposes a fixed set of input analysers that send a representation of the stimulus to decision units dispersed in the nervous system; the scale of unit depends upon the task given, but in general it will be in control of a word response. The unit whose characteristics agree most closely with the stimulus representation generally fires, although the system must be noisy. On this model, thresholds of certain units can be non-selectively lowered if they control responses to important or probable stimuli. This type of threshold-lowering leads, of course, to the important item being a frequent wrong response —a response bias. This model is like some projected electronic speech recognizers.

The 'passive' theory differs from the 'active' theories in its prediction about the way context affects performance. The element of 'preparedness' implies that context restricts the number of possible stimuli, while the passive model invokes only response uncertainty in explaining how context works. For example, among all the words in the language, common words tend to be most intelligible; but this 'word-frequency effect' has been shown to be purely a bias—a tendency to emit frequent words as responses, right or wrong. Considering apart very common words like 'the', 'and', 'to' there is no evidence that sequential probabilities of stimulus features are different in common words from uncommon words, so it is not surprising that true sensitivity is no higher for common words, although some psychologists have in the past believed it was. In the case of limitation of vocabulary size a parallel result is found; in general, restricting the vocabulary before a stimulus word is given is no more advantageous than restricting it after the stimulus, thus accuracy depends upon the number of response alternatives rather than stimulus alternatives. These results were obtained using noise masking; but, with a different stimulus, speeded speech, some effects of stimulus set restriction over and above response set restriction have been found with small vocabularies. These results suggest that a 'pre-set filter' type of recognition mechanism may exist in the human perceiver, but that its operation is not exclusive, and is probably not as general as is the case of the 'passive' type of analysis.

The models mentioned are very simple models for the recognition process only. It would be elegant if all the classes of experiment discussed could be integrated in one theoretical framework, but, as in other areas of psychology it is only profitable to apply models to fairly limited aspects of the total performance.

*See also:* Statistics of language: introduction. Perception of sound Phonetics, auditory. Speech. Speech synthesis.

*Bibliography*

BROADBENT D. E. (1958) *Perception and Communication*, Oxford: Pergamon Press.
BRUNSWICK E. (1955) *Perception and the Representative Design of Psychological Experiments*, Berkeley: University of Calif. Press.
FISCHER–JØRGENSEN E. (1959) *What can the New Techniques of Acoustic Phonetics contribute to Linguistics? Proc. VIII Int. Cong. Linguists*, Oslo: The University Press.
FLANAGAN J. L. (1965) *Speech Analysis, Synthesis and Perception*, Berlin: Springer.
GARNER W. R. (1962) *Uncertainty and Structure as Psychological Concepts*, New York: Wiley.
HUGGINS W. H. (1964) *Distortion of the temporal pattern of speech*, J. Acoust. Soc. Amer., **36**, 1055.
LANE H. L. (1965) *The Motor Theory of Speech Perception: a Critical Review*, Psychol. Rev., **72**, 275.
LIBERMAN A. M. (1957) *Some results of research on speech perception*, J. Acoust. Soc. Amer., **29**, 117.
LICKLIDER J. C. R. and MILLER G. A. (1951) *The perception of speech*, in (Stevens S. S. Ed.) *Handbook of Experimental Psychology*, New York: Wiley.
LUCE R. D. (1963) *Detection and Recognition*, in (Luce R. D., Bush R. R. and Galanter E. Eds.) *Handbook of Mathematical Psychology*, Vol 1, New York: Wiley.
MILLER G. A., HEISE G. A. and LICHTEN W. (1951) *The intelligibility of speech as a function of the context of the test materials*, J. Exp. Psychol., **41**, 329.
MILLER G. A. and CHOMSKY N. *Finitary models of language users*, in *Handbook of Mathematical Psychology* Vol II.
MILLER G. A. and NICELY P. E. (1955) *An analysis of perceptual confusions among some English consonants*, J. Acoust. Soc. Amer., **27**, 338.
*Proceedings of the Symposium on Models for the Perception of Speech and Visual Form*, Boston, (1964) To be published by M.I.T. Press.
STOWE A. N., HARRIS W. P. and HAMPTON D. B. (1963) *Signal and context components of word-recognition behaviour*, J. Acoust. Soc. Amer., **35**, 639.

M. P. HAGGARD

**SPEECH RECOGNITION, AUTOMATIC.** *Abstract.* Automatic spech recognition is a task for a machine. The appropriate machine to perform the task has not yet been constructed. Some reasons for this apparent failure are briefly touched on, and the author then considers the disturbances and constraints on the speech signal which it is desired to recognize, and goes on to an outline of the structure implied by the constraints. A description of this structure is a pre-requisite of speech recognition—for two reasons; first to describe general speech structure in terms which allow knowledge of it to be built into the machine as an aid to recognition; secondly to allow a good enough description of the input signal to be made for it to lead to a minimum set of recognition possibilities which includes the likely alternatives. An outline is drawn of a hypothetical machine which might be built to recognize a fairly unrestricted speech input. This comprises a basic recognizer, working on short segments of acoustic waveform only, onto which may be added further structures to use knowledge of speaker characteristics, speech statistics, syntax rules, and semantics as an aid to the recognition process. A distinction is drawn between speech recognition in a general sense, and the immediate commercial possibilities. For the latter restrictions will be necessary, both on the range of speakers and the vocabulary. Also emphasis must be placed on means of error correction, and procedures for training the speaker to become more recognizable. Future progress will not be compromised by this strategem providing the base is kept broad enough to allow progressive removal of all restrictions as knowledge, techniques, and demand improve.

*Introduction.* The specification of a machine to "recognize" speech has been the goal of intensive research for more than two decades. Thus far, success has eluded those engaged in the work, and the chief reason has its roots in the fact that what is being attempted is the automation of a human process which is by no means understood (see *Speech perception*). A second important reason lies in the need to specify the machine's task within the limitations of the machine, which include storage size and feasibility. It seems clear that the task is exceedingly complex, and requires abilities within the general field of artificial intelligence the automation of any one of which would be difficult enough. The immediate goal of current automatic speech recognition research is to define a recognition process with sufficient economy to allow the building of a machine which is able to achieve a useful recognition performance at a competitive price.

It is not the aim of this section to survey past work on automatic speech recognition; the reader will find this well covered by part I of Lindgren's series on the machine recognition of human language (1965). Nor is it intended as a manual of automatic speech recognition research; the course books from the University of Michigan summer course (1963) are a help in that direction. The intention is to view the various aspects of the problem in their proper relation, partly to provide a framework for further study, and partly to lead to the description of a hypothetical recognizer, embodying many of the functions believed necessary for automatic speech recognition in the full sense, in order that research priorities may be viewed in terms of what constitutes a 'basic' recognizer, and what may be added later.

*The problem.* First we must consider a little of the background to the problem, starting with the transcription of spoken utterances by humans. To produce an accurate written record of the linguistically significant characteristics of an utterance requires skill and training. If the language structure of the utterance is unknown many more detailed characteristics may need to be noted than if the language is well understood. This is because the discriminably different characteristics which *might* be significant, in the unknown language, have all to be recorded, whereas only those *known* to be significant in the fully described language need be recorded. Groups of sounds which are significantly different from other groups are called phonemes, and two sounds only fall into the same phoneme category if the difference between them never distinguishes two words in the language—hence the need to be given more information about an unknown language than the sounds produced in a selection of utterances if it is to be analysed. It will also be noted that a language must be specified before talking about phonemes, since the phoneme structure is specific to the language. Much early work on Automatic Speech Recognition (ASR) ignored the fact that the definition of phonemes does not lead readily to their identification on acoustic criteria alone. It was assumed that there were, in the acoustic waveform, invariant data groupings bearing a one to one relation with the phonemes of the language, and that simple matching procedures would recover the underlying phoneme string, and hence the word the talker intended to communicate. One result of work to date has been to show that this assumption is not true, even for one speaker. Knowledge of the context, and of the overall structure of the language, is frequently needed, even by humans, in order to recognize unambiguously.

The problem is thus seen to be threefold: (1) it is necessary to arrive at a self-consistent description of language in all its aspects: (2) information must be used to arrive at economical procedures for relating meaningful units (words, or groups of words) to acoustic signals: (3) these procedures, and all the necessary reference information, must then be 'packed' into a machine in such a way that not only can it be built, but also—if the aim is commercial—so that its performance is worth the price. The description of language is a difficult and unsolved problem, and becomes — in ASR work — the feature extraction problem. The features of the input signal, on which recognition is based, and the features of the language structure which are stored for use in assisting the recognition process, are the descriptors of the language. Inappropriate descriptions of language have hindered ASR research for many years. The achievement of sufficient economy in the recognition process, given a good set of features, is also a big problem—though perhaps one that need not be considered until uneconomical recognition has been achieved, if that should prove easier. Economy would seem to require an ability to generalize from incomplete data, an ability to adapt to a changing environment, an ability to abstract from large amounts of data, an ability to retrieve information with minimum cost, an ability to use to advantage the constraints of the environment, and an ability to profit from mistakes and successes. Figure 1 attempts to relate, in a simplified form, the characteristics of speech, the ASR machine, and its task.

All this defines a formidable problem set, requiring a great deal of interdisciplinary research. Two approaches to a solution are possible. One aims to erode the problem over the course of time by tackling small sections and by attempting to be completely general, the other involves attempts to solve the whole problem at once, but for an artificially restricted language. The former seems more scientific, but the latter more attractive as a commercial proposition where investment must be justified in terms of hope for an early profit. In fact both approaches have their limitations, and both have their advantages. In practice, of course, it may be difficult to distinguish one from the other—in any case they may be used in combination—but they are, nevertheless, distinct philosophies. Thus attempts towards grammars that generate all allowable sentences in a language, and only these, are just as much ASR research as attempts to build a machine to recognize ten digits for a number of selected talkers. A great deal more ASR research is going on, therefore, than a count of machines in progress might indicate. On the other side of the coin, ASR may be considered, in a sense, as one goal which provides a 'raison d'etre' for research into problems quite general to the field of artificial intelligence and the simulation of behaviour.

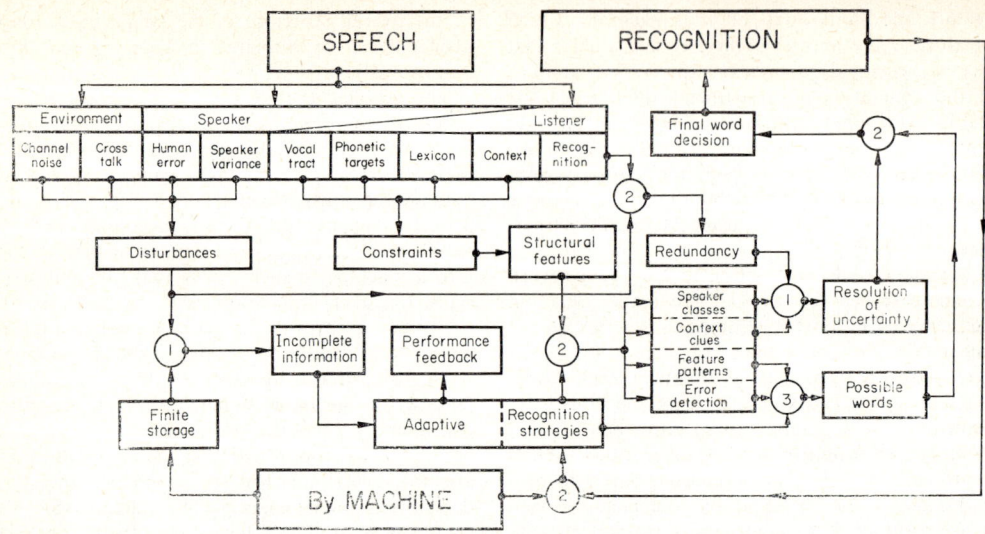

Fig. 1. *The ASR problem.*

*Speech.* Speech implies a speaker, a listener, and a common environment which includes the transmission channel for the speech signal. This signal is subject to various sorts of noise, distortion, variation, and error. These disturbances degrade the information in the signal. The signal is also subject to constraints due to the speaker's physiology, intention, and previous linguistic experience—which includes his previous experience of the listener. Some of these constraints are particular to the individual speaker, some will reflect characteristics of speakers in general. The listener recognizes the signal, and what he recognizes will depend on his linguistic experience, his knowledge of the speaker—which may be acquired during reception of the signal—and the context. That this process can resist quite severe disturbances is evidence of redundancy in the signal with respect to the listener's recognition process.

*Disturbances:* the first disturbance to be considered is channel noise, which comprises reduction of information by added noise, by attenuation of the signal, or by distortion of the signal due to the nature of the transmission path. Then there is cross-talk, which can lead to a problem known, in the most severe form, as the cocktail-party problem. The effect on recognition performance for human listeners is considerable, for the competing noise has the same general form as the signal. Next there is simple error in the generating process, sounds—even words and phrases—never intended by the speaker being uttered by mistake. Finally, there is a great deal of speaker variation. Even the same speaker attempting an identical series of utterances will produce signals which differ noticeably from utterance to utterance, and the words he utters in isolation will be different to those he utters as part of connected speech. Between different speakers there can be considerable variation. For example, the data groupings pertaining to the vowels and fricatives of one speaker are very likely to overlap those for different vowels and fricatives for other speakers. Speakers may also use the same vowel categories in different ways because they have different accents.

*Constraints:* as hinted at in the introductory paragraph, the constraints on the signal can only be fully determined by a precise knowledge of the individual speaker: but, by the same token, identification of the speaker allows more detailed knowledge of the constraints to be used to aid the recognition process. There are still well defined constraints on the signal even when the speaker is unknown, however, and there are also clues in the signal concerning speaker characteristics which should permit some degree of speaker identification *(vide infra)*, and hence the more detailed determination of the constraints. At the most general level there are constraints on the signal due to the nature of the generator, the human vocal apparatus. In addition to the static acoustic constraints on the signal as a consequence of the resonant properties of the vocal tract in a given configuration (see *Speech synthesis*), there are dynamic and neurological constraints. These parts of the tract have inertia and particular forms of attachment, and the messages which activate movement have limitations. Thus the rate at which changes can occur, and the possible configurations, are limited in a manner quite general to human speakers. Constraints at a less general level result from the acquired articulatory habits of speakers, and depend on the language learned as well as more particular factors. In attempting an utterance, the speaker will be aiming at a series of phonetic targets, and this in a particular way depending on his acquired articulatory habits, which are difficult to break. A further constraint on his speech is the speaker's vocabulary, or lexicon. Speakers of the same language, even the same dialect, will use different vocabularies. The last set of constraints are contextual. Some are due to the syntax and semantics of particular utterances, some are situational in that the topic of conversation, and what the speaker and listener know about each other, restrict the likely use of the vocabulary. They range from quite general rules about how utterances may be constructed from lexical items, and what is meaningful, to quite particular restrictions on what is likely to be talked about next, and what interpretation should be placed on what was said a few moments ago in the light of what is said now.

*Redundancy:* the redundancy is embodied in all aspects of speech and results from the constraints which exist. Certain signal component structures are not used because of the generative and phonetic target constraints, and certain recognition possibilities may be ruled out on grounds of lexical, syntactic, and semantic constraints. The redundancy can be increased by selectively restricting the lexicon, and imposing stricter rules on the construction of utterances from lexical items.

*Structural features and the recognition machine.* In talking about structural features we are talking about cues for recognition, and about information concerning language structure which must be stored in a recognition machine. It is therefore necessary to discuss structural features with one eye on speech and the other on the ASR machine that we wish to build. The structure reflects the constraints on the speech, and the structural features are appropriate descriptors for the structure. The more restrictive the constraints, the less will be the variety of the structure, and the fewer and more general the structural features. Whatever level of description is aimed at, the primary evidence for the recognition of a particular utterance must come from the acoustic signal. However useful and easy it is to describe utterances in terms of non-acoustical features it does not help ASR if these cannot, ultimately, be related to the acoustic signal—albeit using knowledge of general language structure.

There are two ways of arriving at a description of the structure—analytic and synthetic, and two ways of formulating the description—segmental and parametric. The analytic determination of structure depends on the analysis and classification of data from signals exhibiting the structure; the synthetic approach depends on setting up models of the structure to form the basis of synthesis, and testing the predictive power and performance of these models with respect to reality. The difference between the segmental and parametric formulations is that the former divides the signal with respect to time, using multi-dimensional descriptors, whereas the latter considers temporal variations in unidimensional descriptors. In general the two will be strongly related, for the segmental descriptors may be compounded from the parameters. Also, if recognition of meaningful units is required, then, at some stage in the recognition process, segmentation must be implicit at least, if not explicit. The smallest segment normally considered in the study of language is at the level of phonemes, though so-called machine phonemes used in some recognition schemes are (or were) of considerably shorter duration than the corresponding phonemes. In building a word recognizer, there is no necessity to consider segments below the word level—a point which seems to escape some and obsess others. In building a speech recognizer the recognition unit, and thus the maximum requirement for segmentation, is likely to vary to as long as a sentence or two. As Miller has pointed out (1962) there is no reason to assume a fixed decision unit for human recognition, quite the reverse in fact.

For parametric formulation either continuously varying parameters, or two-state parameters may be used. The former are found on the analytic side in formant-tracking, and pitch tracking, for example, and on the synthetic side there is Lawrence's Parametric Artificial Talker (and its successors) which produces reasonably natural and intelligible speech on the basis of eight slowly and continuously varying parameters (Antony and Lawrence 1962). The two-state parameter approach arose as a consequence of the fact that the (segmental) phonemes could be dichotomised in a number of ways, at least on the basis of an articulatory description. Jakobson, Fant, and Halle (1961) proposed a complete set of such dichotomies which coded the phonemes in binary terms. The features which formed the basis of the dichotomies they termed distinctive features, and each consisted of a pair comprising the opposition of two polar qualities of the same category, or the opposition between presence and absence of a certain quality. A concurrent bundle of distinctive features defined a phoneme. Being based on articulatory considerations the original distinctive features are difficult to relate to the acoustic signal, but the idea that speech may be described in terms of a small number of primitive characteristics switching on and off, and bearing a certain order relationship to one another, lies behind several approaches to ASR, and the engineer, free from linguistic inhibitions, but (hopefully) with some linguistic knowledge, looks for acoustic features which may be detected as present or absent, and which bear a useful relation to the speaker's intention. There are other schemes which attempt to recognize phonemic segments, but they inevitably run into what is termed the 'segmentation problem' (*vide infra*) since it is less reasonable to ask speakers to utter isolated phonemes than to ask them to utter isolated words. In practice, of course, a segmentation problem of some sort will be encountered whenever an attempt is made to recognize units which represent sub-divisions of the input, but meaning and grammar may be able to assist the process of segmenting words in connected speech.

Shearme, Holmes, and Mattingly (1965) have developed a procedure for synthesizing speech from a set of rules. Although a parametric synthesizer with 'continuously' varying parameters is used, the procedure accepts a phonemically segmented input, the rules taking care of continuity. This supports the view that the two approaches are strongly related, in fact both are probably necessary to a complete description of speech. However, if phonemic recognition is the aim of an engineer, it seems probable that must achieve the necessary segmentation by rules which are, in some sense, the inverse of those used by the workers quoted, rather than by any sampling technique operating on the input.

It is convenient, and possibly more general, to say that particular configurations of, and or changes in, and/or sequences of changes in the parameters constitute an event in speech and that these events are the features that an ASR engineer wishes to detect. The relation between such events and human perception has been investigated systematically, using synthetic speech, at the Haskins laboratory, and many papers describing the classic work, and results, are available. They have added extensively to our knowledge concerning the essential structure of speech. Like all work on synthetic speech, it is open to the criticism that the fact that certain parameter variations induce a certain perceptual effect does not prove that these variations are either necessary, or sufficient, for recognition. The evidence is, nevertheless, convincing. Liberman (1957) nominates 'as important cues' such events as spectral quality of sounds at constant constriction, spectral quality in transient sound—at or near the time of maximum constriction, transitional events in the parameters—indicating movement of the articulators, and events characteristic of the introduction of the nasal passage. In general, work on the synthetic approach to the determination of structure has emphasized the importance of human perception, and cues found to pre-dispose a listener to hearing a particular sound have been assumed to be cues to look for in order to give the machine power to make the same recognition.

On the analytic side surprisingly few data have been published which are concerned with the representative sampling of the acoustics of utterances. Wells (1963) has made a study of the formants of British English vowels, Lehiste (1962) has published a study of allophonic variations in (1, r, w, y, h) and included whispered speech, Strevens (1960) has investigated the spectra of fricative sounds, and Green (1958) has made an extensive study of second formant transitions. These are a sample of the more recent and informative.

So far attention has been focussed on the structural features associated with direct measurement on the acoustic signal, and with the associated problem of segmentation or sampling. This has also introduced the problem of approach and formulation. It is now possible, as further structural features are considered, to begin considering the bones of a hypothetical recognition machine, which we should like to build, to operate and recognize using these features. It is intended that this outline should be as general as possible. More specific detail of the suggested operation appears in Hill (1966). Figure 2 gives a block diagram of the machine.

The first part of the machine is concerned with the detection of the acoustic events in the speech signal, events such as those investigated at the Haskins laboratory, which we shall now call *Primitive Acoustic Features* or *PAF*'s. Knowledge of the statistics of the *PAF*'s may be used to monitor and modify the output of the PAF detector, and this knowledge may be kept up-to-date by on-line statistical estimation, combined with error statistics fed back from the results of successful recognition. Besides providing evidence directly concerned with identifying the utterances, these PAF's should provide evidence for *speaker identification*.

Some very successful speaker identification has been achieved by examining contour spectrograms (where intensity is given by contour lines, rather than marking density, allowing greater dynamic range and therefore finer detail), but, apart from Kersta (1962), very little has been published. Other approaches have been tried including an attempt to match, point by point, the array from a quantized spectrogram. Features found useful for speaker identification at the acoustic level comprise characteristic shapes of formant transitions, overall energy distribution, fricative energy distribution, and location of higher formants. At other levels there

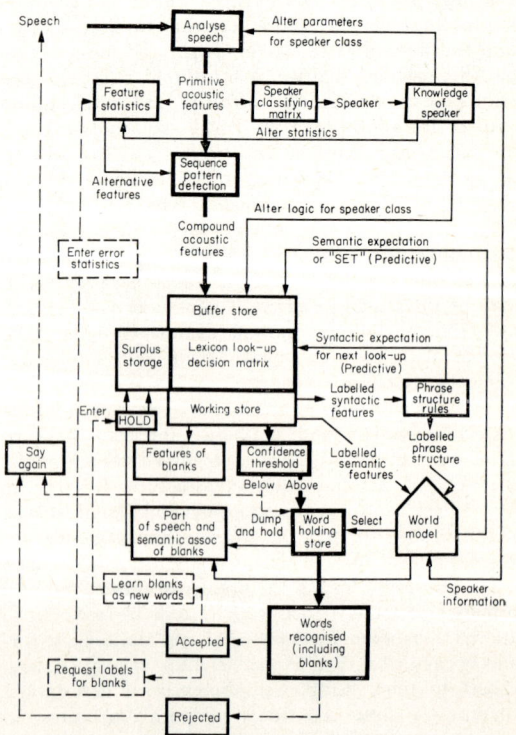

FIG. 2. *A hypothetical ASR machine.*

are equally important clues to speaker identity, and though the problem has not been tackled specifically for ASR, manuscripts have been identified as having been written by particular people on the basis of the words used, the things talked about, and the constructions used. Identification of the speaker, or even the speaker category, could allow the known characteristics of the appropriate category to be used as an aid to recognition, and could include modification of the PAF statistics and detection parameters, changes in the lexicon and lexicon 'look-up' procedure, and even modification to the parts of the machine concerned with context and construction of utterances.

The next class of features and operations is concerned with the sequence of the PAF's. The incorporation of time clues has proved a constant hindrance to ASR schemes and has frequently become mixed up with the segmentation problem and lost, or forgotten. The order information concerning the acoustic cues in the speech stream must be used explicitly. If a time sequence of events is to be recognized, and the sequence is not completely free from noise and disturbance, then—unless the order information is entirely irrelevant—it is self-defeating to attempt recognition by matching the sequence event by event against a reference sequence even on the same time scale. The omission or insertion of one event, or the failure to establish an absolute time reference, ruins the entire matching procedure. If the sequence ABCD is expected, and the B gets lost, the sequential features A–C, A–D, and C–D are still preserved, whereas a straight match without sequence detection would find very little correspondence. The problem arises analogously in other matching procedures—for instance the frequency scale is allowed to obtrude into the matching procedure for categorizing spectral energy distribution. In every case it is a matter of relativizing the information and determining what characteristics are important. Almost no work has been done on the sequential features of words. The determination and use of sequential pattern structure—or 'grammar'—of the PAF's represents an important and virtually unexplored ASR problem, although the analogous problem of detecting, specifying, and utilising essential connectivity in optical pattern recognition has been recognized, and a start made on investigation. Thus, in the hypothetical machine, the second main stage is the detection of important sequential patterns, which we can call *Compound Acoustic Features* or *CAF*'s, which incorporate all necessary order cues for recognition.

It is now convenient to consider, briefly, the features describing the action of the vocal apparatus. There has been a recent upsurge of interest in this topic, for some workers feel that utterances may be more usefully and/or easily described in terms of articulatory descriptors than in terms of acoustic descriptors. Although this may lead to a better understanding of speech, and therefore benefit the ASR effort indirectly—especially in aiding the design of the PAF detector—it would seem as difficult to relate physiological descriptors to the acoustic signal as to recognize the acoustic signal directly. To an engineer building a machine it seems more important to have acoustic descriptions of vocal tract constraints than physiological descriptions of utterances. The necessary descriptors are those used for speech synthesis (*vide supra*, also see *Speech synthesis*).

The descriptors for the lexicon fall into several categories—statistical, syntactic, and semantic. First there is a straight specification of the words in the lexicon. Then there are the frequency of usage of those words, the probability distributions of the recognition features associated with the words at the acoustic level, and perhaps the transition probabilities from word to word. Also the words may be associated with a relatively small number of parts of speech (syntactic features) and they have meaning (semantic features). Thus, in the hypothetical machine, the selection of words for output is complicated. Initial selection would be on the basis of the acoustic signal, aided by knowledge of the speaker, knowledge of the rules for connecting strings of words (grammar), and knowledge of what was being talked about. The last two would be predictive in nature, and would involve estimation of the phrase structure and appreciation of meaning respectively—which brings the discussion to the question of contextual features.

Contextual features are the descriptors of the rules governing the allowable sequences of words which will constitute *grammatical*, *meaningful*, and *relevant* utterances. There are two major ways of looking at the grammar, or syntax, of a language—either in terms of a phrase structure grammar, or in terms of a transformational grammar. The former is analytic, in the sense that observed data is taken as it stands, but still has to be fitted to a modelling of the presumed rules of the language syntax, and there is a predictive element in it. The latter is much more closely synthetic, for the syntax of the utterance is described in terms of the transformations required to produce the utterance from a *kernel sentence*. Though the transformational approach can lead to more accurate, less ambiguous, descriptions of the syntax of an utterance, it seems much less suitable for direct use in an ASR scheme since there is the problem of deciding what the kernel sentence is. In a typical application of phrase structure techniques to ASR the string of sound elements in an utterance is used, in conjunction with the lexicon, to produce possible strings of words, and with each word is associated the part(s) of speech into which the word can be categorized. The resultant labelled strings of parts of speech are then compared with general schema of phrase structures and the impossibilities eliminated. The phrase structure is then mapped back onto the strings of possible words to select the actual words recognized. Some ambiguity may still remain (for example writing/righting) which can only be resolved on semantic grounds. The development of semantic descriptors, and their application to a machine, represent the biggest problem of all, for they are the descriptors of the world we live in. Work is in progress to develop word association networks, but these would seem to avoid the problem of discriminating against inadmissible associations, and barely to touch the problem of meaning. Some idea of the likely difficulties may be gained by considering the fact that a thesaurus frequently shows strong association, in some sense, between a word and its direct opposite.

In the diagram of the machine (Fig. 2) the selective effect of phrase structure constraints and semantic constraints on the output string of words from the lexicon look-up is indicated. The 'Word holding store' contains the possible strings of words. It seem that two sorts of decision would lead to a positive output from the lexicon look-up to the holding store. A confidence threshold would be necessary for each decision, and one decision would recognize part of the input data with sufficient confidence to say that it was this or that word(s) in the vocabulary. The other decision would reject recognition of part of the input data with sufficient confidence to say that it did not relate to any word in the vocabulary, and might therefore be a new word to be learnt. If neither threshold were exceeded, then a partial output (recognition possibilities up to that point in the input data) would be required to inform the talker where the difficulty lay, with a request to repeat from there. From time to time output-proper would occur, and would depend for length on semantic or syntactic considerations. Acceptance would cause any blanks to be learnt as new words, and the machine would need to request labels of some sort. Perhaps labelling could consist of spelling the new word. Acceptance would also stimulate the feed-back of disparities between the input data and the data expected for particular recognition decisions in the form of error statistics. Rejection would merely elicit a request for repetition, and it would be up to the speaker whether to proceed on a word by word basis, rephrase the utterance, or merely repeat.

All this seems highly speculative, but with a machine recognizing a vocabulary of real size, it represents the type of operation that is probably necessary, including the automatic assimilation of new words. On the question of selection according to syntactic and semantic considerations it would be necessary to start at a very primitive level. By way of illustration, consider a simple ASR machine accepting strings of words in the form (number, operator, number). Syntactic constraints would then inhibit the recognition of an operator as the last item, while semantic knowledge would allow the machine to reject the recognition of 'zero' as the last item if the operator happened to be 'divide by'.

*Summary:* an attempt has been made to indicate the general lines of a machine we should like to build to recognize speech, in the hope that, however tentative, ambiguous, and ill-defined the general scheme may be, it will at least give an idea of the complexity of the machine required to recognize a large vocabulary, spoken by speakers who differ significantly and use connected speech to converse with the machine. It is also hoped that it has helped to indicate the relation between the various aspects of research work necessary for ASR. The core of the machine comprises the analyser, the sequence detector, and the word recognition matrix, with an output requiring verification. A first task could be to build, or simulate, these parts for a restricted vocabulary to demonstrate feasibility and investigate the problems encountered. Since sequence detection, and decision cannot proceed without input data, the analyser must necessarily be the immediate goal. The other parts of the machine are more speculative and indicate the general lines of research for some years to come, though progress is already being made, with phrase structure grammars in suitably restricted cases.

*Conclusions.* The description of language is a difficult and unsolved problem as far as ASR is concerned, and descriptions of insufficient generality have been the downfall of schemes in the past. The first problem in ASR research is to determine how to describe the speech signal in terms relevant to recognition, and in terms which show sufficient similarity between utterances intended to represent the same word, despite variation between speakers. This involves research into relative measures for spectral, timing, and sequence cues, including means for adjustment for different speakers. Approaches at the physiological level may lead to a better understanding of speech, and hence aid in the formulation of these descriptions, but physiological parameters are unlikely to enter explicitly into the recognition process unless they are measured directly. As a longer term project, means for using syntactic and sematic constraints must be found, though restricting the machine's 'language' could allow simple use to made of such constraints even now. This restriction of the language is likely to form the basis of any immediate commercial approach to ASR, and probably means starting with a 25 word vocabulary, accepting only 60 per cent of the population, and putting some emphasis on means of error correction, external to the machine, by means of immediate feed-back—to the speaker—of the word(s) recognized. It is also probable that, at first, it will be the speaker who adapts to the machine, rather than the other way round. Procedures for helping the speaker to become more 'recognizable' must also be investigated, and could include the use of 'preferred' versions of the vocabulary words being used as the recognition feed-back. At the same time, if future progress is not to be compromised, the base must be kept broad enough to allow progressive removal of all restrictions as knowledge, techniques, and demand improve.

*See also:* Character recognition. Phonetics. Phonology. Speech perception.

*Bibliography*

ANTONY J. and LAWRENCE W. (1962) *A resonance analogue speech synthesiser, Proceedings of the Fourth Int. Congr. on Acoustics*, Copenhagen, Amsterdam: Elsevier.

GREEN P. S. (1958) *Consonant-vowel transitions, a spectrographic study*, Studia Linguistica, **12**, 57.

HILL D. R. (1966) *Automatic speech recognition—a problem for machine intelligence*, Machine Intelligence *I*, Edinburgh: Oliver & Boyd.

JAKOBSON R., FANT C. G. M. and HALLE M. (1961) *Preliminaries to Speech Analysis*, Cambridge, Mass.: MIT Press.

KERSTA L. G. (1962) *Voiceprint identification*, Nature, **196**, 1253.

LEHISTE I. (1962) *Acoustical characteristics of selected English consonants*, ASTIA Report AD 282 765.

LIBERMAN A. M. (1957) *Some results of research on speech perception*, J. Acoust. Soc. Amer., **29** (1).

LINDGREN N. (1965) *Machine recognition of human language, Pt. I* I.E.E.E. Spectrum 2, (3), March.

MILLER G. A. (1962) *Decision units in the perception of speech* I.R.E. Trans. on Information Theory IT-8 (2), Feb.

SHEARME J. N., HOLMES J. N. and MATTINGLEY I. (1965) *Speech synthesis by rule*, (Lang. Speech, 7 (3), July-Sept).

STREVENS P. (1960) *Spectra of fricative noises in human speech*, Lang. Speech **3** (1), Jan.-March.

UNIVERSITY OF MICHIGAN (1963) *Automatic speech recognition*, University of Michigan Engineering Summer Conference, Report No. 6310 (two Vols.).

WELLS J. C. (1963) *A study of the formants of British English*, Progress Report of the Phonetics Laboratory, University College, London, July.

D. R. HILL

**SPEECH SYNTHESIS.** This has attracted the interest of three disciplines. Linguists desire rigorous methods of relating systems of descriptive categories to the substance of language and rigorous methods for the initial establishment of these categories. Psychologists are interested in isolating the psychological and physiological mechanisms underlying speech production and speech perception. Engineers wish to improve the efficiency of speech communication by transmitting only the important parameters of speech rather than the whole waveform; they also wish to provide two-way speech communication between man and machine.

The synthesis of speech has two distinguishable but related aspects; the static aspect consists of approximating speech sounds in isolation with some kind of vocal tract model. The dynamic aspect consists of achieving a good approximation to the continuity of real speech: selecting as a function of time from the infinity of possible static configurations of the vocal tract.

*1. Vocal tract models.* The chief problem in synthesizing speech sounds is the selection of a small set of parameters that do justice to the sounds occurring in a given language. These follow indirectly from the analytical model of the vocal tract adopted; this may be more or less comprehensive but always has two parts, an excitation or source function, and a transfer or system function. Specification of the excitation function requires information about the location of the energy source exciting the tract and its waveform or spectrum. For voiced sounds it is located at the vocal cords or glottis, *G* in Fig. 1, and is quasi-periodic with audible harmonics up to about 4000 c/s. For other sounds it has a continuous spectrum and is either *impulsive* as in *stop sounds* like /p, t, k/ or *random* as in *fricatives* /s, f/. Combinations occur as in voiced stops /b, d, g/ and *voiced fricatives* /z, v/. From comparisons of the calculated transfer function and actual speech spectra the source spectrum when random is assumed to be spectrally flat. The spectral slope for the quasi-periodic excitation appears to vary between about 12 and 9 decibels per octave.

The transfer function of a network like that schematized in Fig. 1 depends upon four classes of factor; (a) the

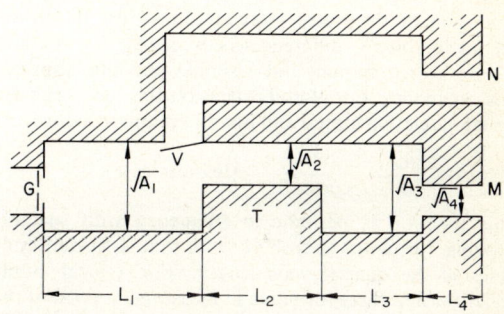

FIG. 1. *Schematic representation of the vocal tract, including the four tube approximation for vowel articulation. G = Glottis. M = Mouth opening. N = nostrils. V = velum. T = Tongue.*

glottal impedance, which varies as the vocal cords are open or closed. This factor causes jitter in the transfer function synchronous with vocal cord vibration but this appears to be of little perceptual importance. Chiefly it affects the transfer function of stop and fricative sounds as these are usually made with open glottis. (b) The velar impedance; this varies with the opening of the velar flap, *V* in the figure, which connects the oral and nasal cavities. When the velum is open there is some radiation at the nostrils with a characteristic nasal formant, and zeros, sometimes called antiformants or antiresonances, are introduced in the oral radiation spectrum. (c) The place of excitation; if this is other than at the glottis—and for stops and fricatives it is well forward in the tract—zeros occur in the transfer function due to shunting resonance in the back cavities. (d) The vocal tract configuration; this is the most important factor in determining the transfer function, having most degrees of freedom that are perceptually distinct. The transfer function of a true vocal tract depends upon series and shunt impedances at all points between the glottis and the mouth and nostril openings. These impedances depend upon the inertance of the air in the tract and its compressibility as well as viscous friction and absorption at the cavity wall. The impedances are calculated by considering these factors as constants and the cross-sectional area at each point up the tract midline as a variable. However, it is possible to lump these impedances as in the four-tube representation of the oral cavities in Fig. 1. Close agreement with obtained speech spectra can then be achieved without an astronomical number of calculations. Further simplification is possible: not all parameters $A_1 \ldots A_4$, $L_1 \ldots L_4$ are free. The tract length, $L_1+L_2+L_3+L_4$ is a constant, and a function of the speaker's age and sex. For characterizing vowels, three dimensions are adequate; (1) the size of the tongue constriction, $A_2$ (2) its distance from the glottis $L_1+L_2/2$, (3) the degree of lip-rounding, (a decreasing function of $A_4$ and increasing function of $L_4$). This is the three-dimensional vowel classification long used by phoneticians. In the resting configuration of the vocal tract employed for the vowel /ɜ/ (as in 'bird'), differences between $A_1$, $A_2$, $A_3$, and $A_4$ are near minimum and a simple one-tube approximation applies. For glottal excitation this has a transfer function relating glottal and mouth volume velocities of:

$$\frac{u_m}{u_g} = \frac{1}{\cosh \gamma L} \qquad \text{(lossless case)}.$$

This function is periodic in frequency with spectral maxima, formants, at $\cosh \gamma L = 0$, that is, at odd multiples of the quarter wave-length. For typical adult males the first three formants in measured spectra of the /ɜ/ vowel are at $F_1 = 500$ c/s, $F_2 = 1500$ c/s, $F_3 = 2500$ c/s. In vowels requiring the four-tube approximation the couplings of the elemental sections require more complicated forms. There is, in fact, an infinite series of formants of which only the first three are usually specified in speech synthesis. $F_4$ and $F_5$ can be heard in vowels with high $F_2$ and $F_3$, but although they vary within and over individual speakers they generally enter a synthesis scheme only in the form of a correction factor.

*2. Synthesizers.* There exists, then, systematic theory relating articulations to speech waves; how are the dependencies reflected in actual synthesizers? So far the transfer function has been characterized simply by spectral maxima and minima. In general this is an adequate picture; the equations for the four-tube approximation that give the formant frequencies also give the relative amplitudes and bandwidths of the formants, and the phase responses follow simply. That such a specification of speech would be adequate was foreseen by Helmholtz, who realized that the amplitude spectrum of speech carried the information whereby possible utterances are distinguished. A synthesizer must, then, create a realistic amplitude spectrum.

The simplest electrical synthesizer is the *Vocoder* or spectrum simulator. In this instrument the output of a noise or pulse generator, or both, is fed to a bank of band-pass filters in the usual speech spectrum, 200–3500 c/s, being amplitude modulated at either the input or output of each filter by an appropriately varying control signal. As the number of spectral channels is increased the degree of precision of approximation increases. Moderately good speech can be transmitted with as few as ten channels but a good spectral shape requires over twice this number. However, the information rate of the combined control signals becomes correspondingly large; the inputs to the synthesizer have to be derived from an analysing network that determines the spectral amplitudes. The analyser also decides whether the speech is currently voiced or unvoiced, and if voiced, tracks the voice pitch. The vocoder is thus an analysis-resynthesis telephone and is the prototype device for extreme compression of telephone bandwidth. Although very intelligible, it is unnatural for at least three reasons; the importance of each factor is not exactly known. (1) Fine structure of the amplitude spectrum is lost, and (2) phase relationships are incorrect; these two factors are important at low frequencies. (3) The pitch tracking is often inaccurate and may also exhibit a lack of cycle-to-cycle fluctuation in period that is characteristic of normal speech. A so-called 'voice-excited-vocoder' avoids these disadvantages by transmitting a base-band intact up to 800 or 900 c/s. Vocoder circuits for higher frequencies are excited by a non-linear distortion of this waveform and the resulting speech quality is extremely good.

Another spectrum synthesizer, but one which avoids the vocoder's disadvantages in a more economical way, is the terminal analogue or formant synthesizer. This represents the spectrum as three resonances with variable tuning and has been used in two versions. A series connexion avoids the need to specify formant amplitudes in vowel sounds, but cannot render many consonant sounds accurately. A parallel arrangement with variable formant amplitudes requires the specification of these three extra parameters but regains some of the flexibility of the vocoder and achieves a good approximation to most consonants, even nasals. The parallel formant synthesizer takes advantage of the lower perceptual discriminability of spectral zeros in simulating these sounds with a theoretically inadequate set of parameters. A vocoder-like broad high-frequency band is also useful in representing the stops and fricatives.

Both series and parallel formant synthesizers are 'terminal' — analogues not models of the vocal tract. Formants depend principally upon different cavities in different configurations and are not therefore articulatory parameters. The true model of the vocal tract is the transmission-line analogue used to test acoustic theory of speech production. In this type of synthesizer the glottis-to-mouth length is divided into about twenty serial cross-sections and the configuration of cross-sectional area as a function of distance from the glottis is closely approximated by varying the impedances in each section. Such an analogue is therefore suitable for testing detailed hypotheses about articulations and their relationship to the speech waveform. This type of vocal tract is sometimes called a dynamic analogue, but it is in fact difficult to operate in the dynamic aspect because of the large number of parameters requiring specification. The control data are difficult to come by, requiring measurements from X-ray photographs. However, as was seen from the adequacy of the four-tube approximation to the vocal tract, there must be considerable interdependence among the twenty or so control signals for the system function of this type of analogue. One aim of research is to provide rules for specifying the twenty cross-sectional area values from a smaller set of parameters. The adequacy of formant synthesizers does not render this effort superfluous, because the transmission line analogue has the advantage that excitation can be applied other than at the glottis. Because of this type of fundamental resemblance to the speech mechanism, this sort of synthesizer offers, ultimately, the best parametric description of speech.

Up until the mid-twentieth century, when electronic-control of electrical synthesizers became feasible, acoustical models, or physiological models as they would now be called, were the chief tool in acoustic phonetic investigations. But the difficulties of control rendered these models completely unsuitable for continuous synthesis, and even the synthesis of isolated sounds was limited by the lack of proper materials for the cavity walls. Interest in these models has been revived as appropriate synthetic materials are now available for constructing them. The control of these models raises questions about the musculature controlling articulatory movements, which has received little study.

There are schemes for synthesizing speech other than vocal tract analogues. Many methods exist for exploiting redundancy remaining in the set of signals specifying spectral amplitudes for a channel vocoder. Two successful examples are; transmitting the frequency of spectral peaks only, and scanning the spectrum repeatedly, coding it as a six-term Fourier series. These and many other schemes exploit the same spectral redundancy that the formant synthesizer depends upon, in a more *ad hoc* fashion. Another example of this strategy, though not related to the vocoder principle is the use of a small set of orthogonal exponentially damped sinusoids which can, with specification of amplitude and phase of each be added together to achieve close correspondence to the waveform for every pitch period. Yet another type of synthesis stores prerecorded phoneme elements and produces continuous speech by fading them into one another. This does not mean that true formant transitions are unimportant, merely that they are sometimes adequately specified by the beginning and end of the transition—like the apparent movement effect well known in visual perception. No reference has been made to synthesis by computer as a method on its own, as any system that can be described mathematically can be simulated by computer and this is frequently done in initial phases of research.

Because there are so many different methods of synthesizing speech which can, with correct control, result in intelligible, even natural sounding speech, criteria of intelligibility and quality are appropriate only as engineering evaluations and are only worthwhile as tests of the models involved in the synthesis procedure at a very coarse level.

In this discussion of vocal tract models the excitation function has been comparatively neglected, reflecting the distribution of research effort. In communication, parameters of glottal excitation convey individual situational, syntactic and semantic information which serve to resolve ambiguities above the level of speech segments. This is true for languages like English which are not tone languages; had more of the research in speech synthesis and perception been done on other languages a different emphasis might have resulted. Even in English these non-segmental aspects play an important part in real communication. The glottis has many parameters of variation which are perceptually differentiable, although not all individuals can manipulate their glottis to realise them. Models have been made of the glottis to relate movements of the larynx musculature to the output volume velocity wave shape which excites the tract, and some progress has been made in relating these physiological parameters to scales and categories of voice quality.

Usually speech is synthesized without close attention to the excitation waveform which, for voiced speech, may be triangular, sawtooth, or a pulse train with low duty cycle. The differences in phase and amplitude spectrum between these alternatives are generally obscured by the greater perceptual importance of the transfer function. For high quality synthesis it is possible to reproduce the first and most important zero in the source spectrum which, for a roughly triangular waveshape, falls near 700 c/s in many adult male speakers. Of glottal articulation parameters, only accurate pitch tracking is likely to meet an important need for transmitting non-segmental information in the case of English. However, linguistically, an understanding of the relationship of movements of the larynx musculature to the glottal waveshape and voice quality is valuable, as languages exist where such variables are of phonological relevance.

*3. The control problem.* Any optimizing approach to a model of the speech process creates problems in acquiring and handling control data. A synthesizer can be controlled in three chief ways. Firstly, the data can be extracted simultaneously from natural speech as in the vocoder; it is also possible to use physiological data from electromyographic or mechanical transducers on a speaking subject, and some success has been achieved by using such non-waveform data in the machine recognition of speech. The second control method requires the extraction by hand of parameter values from an acoustic or physiological analysis, involving a certain degree of interpretation and adaptation to the synthesizer by the human operator. This method is laborious, but probably the best one for acquiring detailed knowledge of speech production and perception.

Thirdly, the continuous parameters can be derived from a string of input symbols—phoneme commands—by two sets of rules, one for the steady state articulations for each phoneme and one for the dynamic aspect of the articulations. Each of the possible control methods has its own advantages but *synthesis by rule* has the widest theoretical and practical implications. Some linguistic theorists require the subject matter of linguistics to

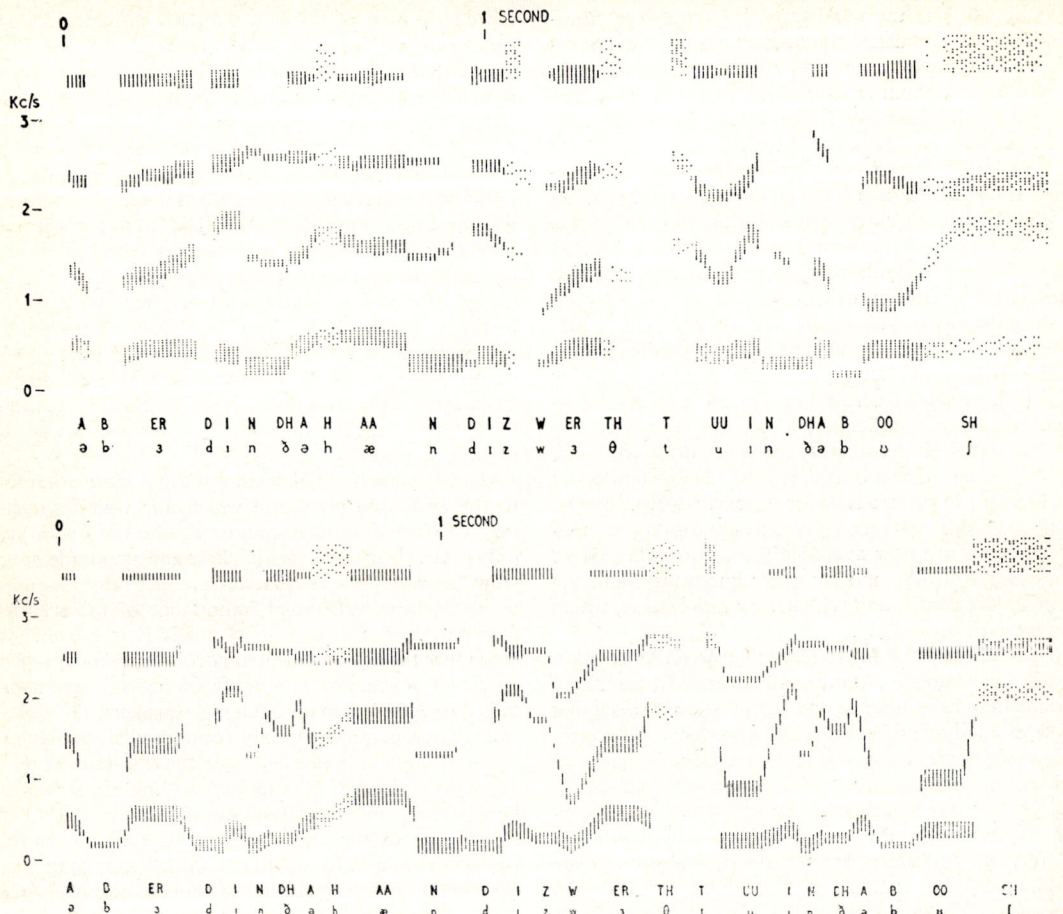

Fig. 2. Schematic spectrograms of the sentence "A bird in the hand is worth two in the bush." (a) Synthesized copy of a natural utterance (b) Synthesized by rule. (After Holmes, J. N., Mattingly I. G. and Shearme J. N. with permission.)

stop at the distinctive feature matrix output by the phonological component of the generative grammar. Below the features level the realization of form in substance is in terms of continuous parameters rather than discrete categories, but lawfulness exists, and its description and explanation must be part of any comprehensive science of language.

Synthesis by rule exploits this lawfulness. Most of the rules for steady state and dynamic aspects of articulation derive directly from experiments done at the Haskins Laboratories on the cues for recognition of different phonemes. Several programs have been written for continuous synthesis. Holmes, Mattingly and Shearme use a table of specifications of parameter values for English phonemes as steady-states (stop consonants are considered multi-element phonemes) and of transition characteristics upon which simple rules operate. Their synthesizer has nine parameters: frequencies and amplitudes of three formants, pitch, voiced-voiceless distinc-

tion and amplitude in a broad high-frequency band. The characteristics entered in the table for each phoneme for determining the transition are: duration of transition within the element; duration of transition within adjacent element; two quantities determining respectively the contributions of the given element and the adjacent one to the value of the parameter in which transition is being computed, at the element 'boundary'. For a given pair of adjacent elements the table entries controlling the transitions in all parameters are determined by an ingenious device: the phonemes are ranked in a hierarchy of influence upon neighbouring phonemes with, for example, the stop consonants high and the vowels low on the list; the dominant element is the one whose table entries control the nature of the transition.

The results of this procedure and other schemes for synthesis by rule are highly intelligible, and not too unnatural. The transitions computed by the procedure are straight lines rather than curves in parameter values as suggested by spectrographic analysis of real speech, but this is probably of minor importance. In early versions of Holmes, Mattingly and Shearme's procedure, many of the transitions were too abrupt but this reflects on the particular table values chosen, which are easily changed rather than on the procedure as a whole. Its overall success gives support to the idea of the articulatory exponents of a phoneme being a set of ideal 'target' values rarely reached or held in the smooth continuum of speech. Programs for synthesis by rule are models of the dynamic aspect of speech production representing the response of the articulators, with their neural and mechanical inertia, to impulse inputs from the speech motor areas of the brain. Speech synthesis by rule is thus of interest to psychology and physiology as well as a comprehensive linguistics.

An important part of good rule synthesis is the prosody—expounded by pitch and timing variations. A generative phonology provides a schematic output for these characteristics of speech from lexical specification and grammatical structure. It is probable that realistic values of voice pitch as a function of time can be derived from these discrete levels by simple one-parameter transition rules similar to those described above for segmental information. Because synthesis by rule embodies a model of both the steady-state and dynamic aspects of speech it exploits maximally the redundancy of speech and is therefore the most extreme form of speech data expansion scheme possible.

4. *Analysis-by-synthesis*. One use of speech synthesis is in speech analysis: in any science synthesis and analysis techniques complement one another. A model is useful as an analytical tool in that events can be analysed in terms of the categories or parameters of the model by synthesizing a representation of the events. This procedure can involve a greater or lesser degree of participation by the human investigator: in an automated version it offers an economical way of analysing complex events like speech, where, for example, the instantaneous spectrum depends upon what is being said, who is saying it, and how. The cyclical application of rules for these three classes of factor would require extremely complex decision logic in any passive type of analysis. In analysis by synthesis the rules are applied as in a generative grammar and all possible outputs are generated for matching with the input to be analysed. The output of the analyser is the set of synthesis parameter values that gives best fit to the events under examination, by, for example, minimizing a weighted r.m.s. error. Although a valuable tool for precise analyses, the analysis-by-synthesis procedure only economizes on computing space at the expense of computing time. Without additional passive analysers to direct the generation of synthetic representations it is too slow to be considered seriously as a model of the process of human recognition and has certain disadvantages in the analysis of continuous speech.

Because of rapid development there are considerable gaps in both fact and theory about the synthesis of speech. The subject is interdisciplinary and abstruse, and the scientific and commercial advantages are only long-term. Thus many problems have gone unanswered. While what has been documented is on a firm scientific basis, there is also a large semi-empirical lore about the microstructure of speech waveforms and spectra because of the laborious analyses required. The same is true of conclusions about the perceptual importance of certain parameters where simple judgements of adequacy have been the rule rather than elaborate behavioural experiments.

*See also:* Phonetics, acoustic. Linguistic form: generative grammar. Speech perception. Speech. Statistics of language: introduction.

*Bibliography*

FANT C. G. M. (1960) *Acoustic Theory of Speech Production*, The Hague: Mouton.
FLANAGAN J. L. (1965) *Speech Analysis, Synthesis, and Perception*, Berlin: Springer.
HOLMES J. N., MATTINGLY I. G. and SHEARME J. N. (1964) *Speech Synthesis by Rule, Lang. Speech.* 7, 127.
LAWRENCE W. (1953) *The synthesis of speech from signals which have a low information rate*, in *Communication Theory*, London: Butterworths.
LIBERMAN A. M., INGEMANN F., LISKER L., DELATTRE P. C. and COOPER F. S. (1959) *Minimal rules for synthesizing speech, J. Acoust. Soc. Amer.*, 31, 1490.
STEVENS K. N. (1960) *Towards a model for speech recognition, J. Acoust. Soc. Amer.*, 32, 47.

M. P. HAGGARD

**STACKS.** The term 'Stack' is used by digital computer programmers to describe a storage element into which items of information may be inserted, and from which items may be extracted (and thereby removed), according to the following rule: of the items present in the stack at any time, only the last one inserted can be extracted. This rule is often expressed concisely as 'last in, first out.' The terms '*push-down store*', '*cellar*' and '*pile*' are sometimes used as synonyms for 'stack'. The item in the stack which is currently available for extraction is referred to as the 'exposed' or 'top' item. When inserting a new item in a stack (and thus creating a new exposed item), or extracting the exposed item, the programmer does not have to specify and address, since the location of the exposed item is implicit in the stack mechanism.

A stack may be either 'programmed' or organized by hardware. In either case, it is likely to consist, physically of a set of consecutively-addressed locations with an associated 'Pointer', i.e. a register containing the address of the exposed item, or of a location adjacent to it. The 'last in, first out' rule is enforced by causing the address in the Pointer register to be suitably modified as each 'insert' or 'extract' operation is performed. Figure 1 illustrates the mechanism of a typical stack, which (a) initially contains items (in order of insertion) A, B, C, D; (b) has one item (necessarily D) extracted; and then (c) has another item, E, inserted.

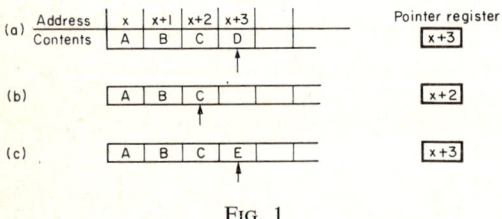

FIG. 1

Figure 1 shows how, when an item is extracted or inserted, the contents of the Pointer register are respectively decremented or augmented (vice-versa if the stack expands through *decreasing* addresses) by a quantity, in this case 1, which corresponds to the number of physical locations occupied by an item. The items in the stack may vary in size, in which case this quantity depends on the type of operation, and on the size of the item previously or subsequently exposed. The capacity of a stack will usually depend on purely physical considerations, i.e. on the number of store locations provided to hold it.

Frequently a stack may have a built-in 'functional' property which is of greater significance to the programmer than the stack mechanism itself, in the sense that the programmer inserts information in the stack so that it may be operated on by the functions associated with the stack, rather than merely to utilise the 'last in, first out' feature. The wide variety of functional properties which may be associated with stacks, and the way they exploit this feature, is illustrated by the following examples:

*(a) A 'subroutine link' stack*. This is used in the following way: when a subroutine is called, the link (return address), with other information which has to be restored when the subroutine ends, is inserted in this stack. At the end of the subroutine, this information will constitute the exposed item (since any items inserted by subsequent subroutine calls should by then have been removed) and is extracted, simultaneously causing the link to overwrite the sequence control register—so returning control to the point at which the subroutine was called—and the other information to be restored to the appropriate registers.

The advantages of this arrangement are that, since the link is not stored in any location connected with the subroutine or the calling program, subroutines may be 'nested' to virtually any depth (depending on the capacity of the stack), and may be recursive, i.e. they may call themselves.

*(b) A 'temporary storage' stack*. Like the subroutine link stack described above, this one is intimately connected with subroutine calls. Its function is to allocate to each subroutine, every time it is called, a temporary block of working storage of the requisite size, i.e. a set of consecutive locations, usually in the main store of the computer, which are made available to the subroutine for its own private use, and are effectively 'wiped out' when the subroutine ends. Each such block constitutes an item in the stack; the exposed item is the block corresponding to the current subroutine. The Stack Pointer designates the first location of the exposed item, and is only modified when the current subroutine ends or when a new subroutine is called (these events correspond, respectively, to the extraction or insertion of an item); meanwhile it is available for use by the subroutine as the 'base address' for the block.

The size of any item inserted in this stack is of paramount importance, since the stack mechanism must know it in order to modify the stack pointer. This size is generally supplied as a parameter by the subroutine.

This arrangement of temporary storage in a stack makes it easier for subroutines which require working storage to be nested and entered recursively, in much the same way as the subroutine link stack described above. If a computer system includes both types of stack, they may be more or less independent (so that subroutines which require no 'working space' need not make an insertion in the temporary storage stack); alternatively, they may be so closely related as to form effectively a single Stack—for instance, the link for a subroutine might always be stored in the first location of its block of temporary storage.

*(c) An 'arithmetic' stack*. Besides inserting and extracting stack items, the programmer can treat them as numerical quantities and specify various types of arithmetic operation to be performed on them. These operations may use one or more operands from the stack—for example a 'Negate' operation could simply extract the exposed item, change its sign, and re-insert it, while 'Add' and 'Multiply' operations could extract two items, and re-insert their sum or product. The programmer does not have to specify addresses when calling for these operations to be performed.

In a typical arithmetic stack, the basic item size will correspond to the 'word length' of the computer. The stack may be capable of operating on items of different types, e.g. fixed-point and floating-point numbers, and 'logical' quantities, and on quantities which occupy multiples of the basic item size, e.g. double-length numbers. The modifications to the stack pointer register implicit in all these operations—which in general remove the operands from the stack and replace them by the result(s)—are performed automatically by the stack mechanism.

The value of an arithmetic stack arises from the way it can exploit the so-called '*Reverse Polish*' notation. In this notation, invented by Lukasiewicz in 1920 (see references given by Hamblin (1962)), arithmetic operators are written after, rather than between, their operands, thus:

| | | | |
|---|---|---|---|
| | $a+b$ | becomes | $ab+$ |
| | $a-b$ | becomes | $ab-$ |
| | $a \times b$ | becomes | $ab \times$ |
| | $a/b$ | becomes | $ab/$ |

Using this notation, it is possible to write complete algebraic formulae in an unambiguous form without brackets, thus:

$$(a+b)c/(d-e) \text{ becomes } ab+c \times de-/$$

Assuming the existence of an arithmetic stack, if a term of the form '$a$' is interpreted as 'insert quantity $a$ in the stack' and the symbols $+$, $-$, $\times$, $/$ cause the corresponding arithmetic operations to take place in the stack, then the last formula, and any similar expression, can be processed from left to right as a 'program' in its own right, thus:

| Instruction | Subsequent contents of Stack (items separated by commas) |
|---|---|
| $a$ | $a$ |
| $b$ | $a, b$ |
| $+$ | $a+b$ |
| $c$ | $a+b, c$ |
| $\times$ | $(a+b)c$ |
| $d$ | $(a+b)c, d$ |
| $e$ | $(a+b)c, d, e$ |
| $-$ | $(a+b)c, d-e$ |
| $/$ | $(a+b)c/(d-e)$ |

The advantages of basing a computer instruction code on an arithmetic stack in this way are threefold:

(i) The ease with which algebraic formulae can be converted, mentally, into Reverse Polish notation, correspondingly eases the task of converting the solutions of numerical problems into computer programs.

(ii) In the 'program', given above, no addresses are involved except those associated with the operands $a, b, c, d, e$. There is no need to address 'intermediate' storage, and the programmer is less concerned with the allocation of facilities and registers which may or may not be available at a particular point in the program. Also, a program written in such a code can be expected to occupy a minimal amount of store, because it uses fewer addresses.

(iii) The translation of algebraic formulae into Reverse Polish can also be easily programmed (Burroughs Corp. 1961; Hamblin 1962; Samelson and Bauer 1960). This means that a well-designed instruction code of this type will facilitate the efficient translation and execution of programs written in high-level languages.

## Computers with Built-in Stacks

*KDF9* (Davis 1960; Haley 1962). The design of KDF9 followed some of the lines suggested by Hamblin (1957). Besides a conventional main store unit, capable of holding up to 32,768 (48-bit) words, and fifteen high-speed 48-bit indexing registers ('Q-stores'), it includes a high-speed arithmetic stack (known as the 'Nesting Store' or 'Nest') with a capacity of sixteen words, and a high-speed subroutine link stack (the 'subroutine jump nesting store') which can hold up to sixteen instruction addresses. To achieve economy in instruction space, instructions occupy one, two or three consecutive 8-bit 'syllables', according to their function. 8-bit instructions specify arithmetic operations in the Nest, while 16-bit and 24-bit instructions are used for transferring information between the nest and the main store, for sequence changes, for transferring information between the nest and individual Q-stores, and for other 'housekeeping' tasks, including

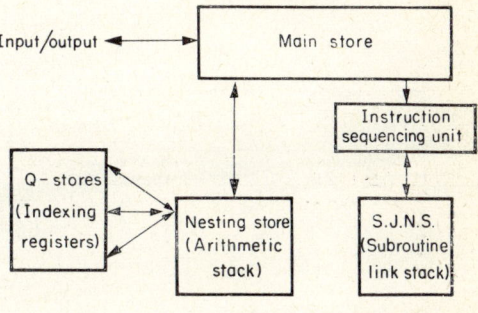

FIG. 2

Input and Output. Figure 2 presents a simplified picture of the system.

The emphasis in the design of KDF9 is on simplicity and economy in coding, and on speed and efficiency in execution of programs. The capacity of the nest is adequate for most applications, though the Compilers which translate programs written in high-level languages, such as ALGOL, have to ensure that the instruction sequences they generate never cause this capacity to be exceeded.

*B5000* (Barton 1961; Burroughs Corp. 1961). Like the KDF9, the B5000 has a 32,768 (48-bit) word main store, but there the similarity ends. There is one stack which combines all the three functions—subroutine link, temporary storage, and arithmetic—described previously. In order to provide this facility, the arithmetic stack, like the temporary storage stack (which incorporates the subroutine link stack), has to be subroutine-oriented, in the sense that each subroutine, when called, is provided with a 'new' arithmetic stack, separated from the previous one by the subroutine's temporary storage area; this area actually includes part of the previous arithmetic stack so that parameters left therein by the calling program are accessible to the subroutine.

Two fast-access registers, 'A' and 'B', hold the exposed item of the current arithmetic stack and its neighbour, though occasionally one (A) or both of these registers are unoccupied, when the exposed item is either in B, or in the main store, respectively. Apart from the items in A and B, the entire stack is contained in the main store.

The stack has two pointers, one of which, held in a register 'S', indicates the location in store of the next item of the current arithmetic stack after the item in B, or of the exposed item if B is empty. The other pointer, held in a register 'F', points to the location in the current temporary storage area which separates the parameters provided by the calling program from the working space of the called subroutine. F's contents may be used as a 'base address'. The temporary storage area also contains the link for the subroutine, the value (+1) to which S must be reset at the end of the subroutine, and the value to which F must be reset. Figure 3 illustrates the contents of the stack locations associated with the

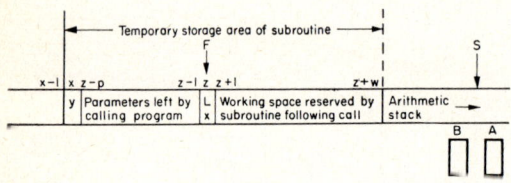

FIG. 3

current subroutine. The results of subroutines are generally left in B.

Instructions each occupy one 12-bit syllable. Indirect addressing is used exclusively—the exposed arithmetic item may be used for indexing. The B5000 was designed primarily for the processing of programs written in high-level languages, particularly those which, like ALGOL, depend on the use of subroutines which may be nested and called recursively. All the features of the stack, including its virtually unlimited size, are designed to make translation easier and execution more straightforward.

In the B8500 (McCullough et al. 1965), a recently-announced descendant of the B5000, the arithmetic and temporary storage stacks are separate, and items in the latter may be used for indexing. Instructions may be from 6 to 24 bits in length.

The disadvantage of keeping a stack in the main store is that it may lead to increased demands on the store, and hence inefficiency. The inclusion of the A and B registers in the B5000 helps to reduce demands on the store. An interesting design is that of the Japanese E.T.L. Mk. 6 computer (Takahashi et al. 1962) in which a 64-word fast-access memory is provided to hold the most recently inserted items of the stack, whose total capacity is 480 words.

## Uses of Programmed Stacks

The literature of programming is rich in applications of programmed stacks, particularly in the execution of programs translated from high-level languages. Randell and Russell (1964) give examples, and also a comprehensive list of references.

Any list-scanning process in which some priority rule directs that certain items from the list have to be held in abeyance awaiting the incidence of other types of item, is likely to require the use of a stack. An interesting and important application is the translation of orthodox algebraic formulae into Reverse Polish notation; the paper by Samelson and Bauer (1960) focussed attention on the way a stack can be used for formula translation, and how the resulting program can exploit another (arithmetic) stack. As a final example, the process for converting the formula

$$(a+b)c/(d-e)$$

cited earlier is illustrated. The formula is scanned from left to right, operators being inserted in, and extracted (discarding brackets) from, a stack as required:

| Input symbol | Operator stack | Output |
| --- | --- | --- |
| ( | ( | |
| a | ( | a |
| + | (, + | |
| b | (, + | b |
| ) | | + |
| × (inserted) | × | |
| c | × | c |
| / | / | × |
| ( | /, ( | |
| d | /, ( | d |
| − | /, (, − | |
| e | /, (, − | e |
| ) | | − / |

This example follows the rules prescribed by Hamblin (1962). Another procedure is described by Burroughs Corp. (1961).

*See also:* Fixed stores and control by microprogram.

### Bibliography

BARTON R. S. (1961) *A new approach to the functional design of a digital computer*, Proc. WJCC, 393. New York: A.C.M.

Burroughs Corporation (1961) *The Descriptor—a definition of the B5000 Information Processing System*, Detroit.

DAVIS G. M. (1960) *The English Electric KDF9 Computer System*, Comp. Bull. **4**, 3, 119.
HALEY A. C. D. (1962) *The KDF9 Computer System*, Proc. FJCC, 108. Washington D. C.: Spartan Books.
HAMBLIN C. L. (1957) *Computer languages*, Australian J. Sci. **20**, 5, 135.
HAMBLIN C. L. (1962) *Translation to and from Polish notation*, Comp. J. **5**, 3, 210.
MCCULLOUGH J. D. et al. (1965) *A design for a multiple user multiprocessing system*, Proc. FJCC, 611, Washington, D. C.: Spartan Books.
RANDELL B. and RUSSEL L. J. (1964) *ALGOL 60 implementation*, New York: Academic Press.
SAMELSON K. and BAUER F. L. (1960) *Sequential formula translation*, Comm. A.C.M. **3**, 2, 76.
TAKAHASHI S. et al. (1962) *Systems design of the E.T.L. Mk. 6 Computer*, Proc. IFIP Congress 62, 690, Amsterdam: North-Holland.

M. R. WETHERFIELD

## STATISTICS OF LANGUAGE: INTRODUCTION

*1*

Language is a conventional symbolic activity whose main function is to help us to think and to influence the behaviour of others without too much effort. It originated by a masterpiece of opportunism and gave the mouth a new function, apart from eating, fighting, and loving. If soup had been the only food, we might not have been able to speak, since the flexibility of the mouth and the variety of speech sounds, might have been too restricted. Although the arms can be used for communication, as in semaphore, they are heavy and inefficient, as compared with the mouth, for communication at close quarters. Mastication led to *homo sapiens*.

The principle of economy applied not merely in the selection of the organ for communication but to some extent in the details of its use. For example, the front of the mouth is used much more than the back, at least in English (Denes 1963) and presumably this is because the front of the mouth is easier to manipulate than the back, owing to the nature of mastication, just as the mouth is easier to move than the arms. A principle of economy is apparent in other linguistic statistics; for example, very frequent words tend to be short. A conscious use of the principle was made in the design of the Morse code, in 1832, in which the most frequent letters have short codes, $E$ = dot, $T$ = dash, $A$ = (dot, dash), etc. Similarly, in the International Teleprinter five-unit alphabet, invented (soon after the invention of Braille) by Weber and Gauss in 1833, and named after Baudot by them, the frequent letters contain few 'marks', thus $E$ = (mark, space, space, space, space) or (1, 0, 0, 0, 0), $T$ = (0, 0, 0, 0, 1), whereas $X$ = (1, 0, 1, 1, 1). (See, for example, Smith, 1960.) Here the economy is in the use of electric current instead of time. It is interesting to note that Bacon anticipated the five-unit code by over two hundred years, as well as anticipating the binary notation for numbers, in his 'biliteral' cipher or cryptographic system (Bacon 1605; see, for example, Friedman 1957). Bacon's code, $A$ = 00000, $B$ = 00001, $C$ = 00010, ..., was economical in that it was easy to memorize. Napier (1617), twelve years later, provided probably the first use of the binary system for calculation. Cryptology has perhaps had far more influence on history than is commonly realized. The ancient Chinese cult of the *I Ching* also uses the binary system but for divination rather than calculation.

Letter frequencies were used in the design of the typewriter keyboard about 1870.

The study of language statistics has a variety of applications and potential applications, and is an interesting branch of linguistics in its own right. The part of linguistics that at present has least to do with statistics is the study of syntactic structures (see, for example, Chomsky 1965; Bach 1964), but even here statistics have some relevance. For example, in the U.S. 'It's I' is correct, whereas in England 'It's me' is correct and 'It's I' is priggish. The notion of 'degrees of grammaticalness' has been discussed (see, for example, Chomsky 1965; Cohen 1965), but not, as far as is known, in relation to probability of occurrence of a particular structure. In problems of semantics, the statistical aspects are more obvious, since the main criterion for including a word in a dictionary is its frequency of use. The frequency depends of course on the topic, and this is why specialized dictionaries are useful. The justification for the use of abbreviations also depends on frequency of use and on the principle of economy. The same principle applies to artificial languages such as those used in mathematics and computer programming: the principle of economy justifies the use of new definitions in mathematics, and of subroutines and other 'procedures' in programming. The statistics of programming languages should be relevent for the design of compilers, and for the choice of hardware. Computers have expensive multiplying equipment because multiplication is a frequent operation. It may be noted that there is a sharp distinction between syntax and semantics for programming languages (see, for example, Woodger 1960, Section 1), although there is not for natural languages.

Language can be talked, thought, written, printed, expressed in shorthand, Morse code, Braille, teleprinter code, and, in the Canary Islands, even whistled (Classe 1957). Each of these codings can be analysed statistically in numerous ways, but only a few will be discussed in this article.

When a language is taught, the student's memory should not be burdened with unusual words, unless they happen to be important (Horn 1926). An example of an important but not very common word, mentioned by Thorndike and Lorge (1944), is 'poison', and other examples are 'warning', 'flammable', and 'explosive'. As in all other decision problems, what matters is the mathematical expection of the utility. But it is easier to measure the frequency of occurrence of a word than its utility, and numerous frequency counts have been made. Some of them will be cited below.

As Bodmer (1944) remarks, the frequencies of words are less relevant for learning to speak than for learning to understand. For speaking, it is wise to start with a basic vocabulary in terms of which nearly all ideas can be expressed, even if somewhat deviously. For reading or listening, obviously the frequencies of occurrence are vital.

Another application for word frequency counts is for a description of style and for the discrimination of authorship, as in Yule (1944), Herdan (1956), Mosteller and Wallace (1963), Morton (1965) and Särndal (1967). Especially useful for this purpose are the frequent variant words, such as 'on' and 'upon', when either will fit the context, or, in Greek, ἵνα, ὡς and ὅπως, all meaning 'in order that' (Good 1965d). The distribution of sentence length has also been found to be reasonably effective for author discrimination for some pairs of authors. (Sherman 1893; Yule 1938; Williams 1939/40; Wake 1957; Herdan 1960; Mosteller and Wallace 1963; Morton 1965).

There are some pitfalls in the analysis of authorship by statistical methods: an author can vary his style with time, the frequencies of pairs of words can be correlated, and so fail to give independent evidence; and, in some cases, especially in correspondence, an author might delegate varying amounts of the composition to a variety of secretaries. There are some studies of the chronology of an author's work by means of his statistical variability. A few of these studies are mentioned in Section 5.

In the analysis of style, the statistical methods can be either Bayesian or non-Bayesian. If they are Bayesian then they depend very much on the estimation of probabilities. (See, for example, Mosteller and Wallace 1963, and, for a work on probability-estimation, Good 1965b, 1966a.) The same is true when linguistic statistics are used for information retrieval. Instead of using unweighted index terms as in classical methods of information retrieval, the index terms can be given weights depending on their probabilities of occurring in a context of a given kind (Luhn 1957). Bar-Hillel (1957) suggested that the 'significance' of a word in a document should be measured by the ratio of the relative frequency of the word in the document to that in the language in general. Good (1958b, 1959b) suggested independently that the larger context should not be as broad as general English: it might, for example, be the English that occurs in papers on electronics. One argument for so restricting the generality of the English is that it leads to a greater degree of statistical independence of the index terms. This is useful when applying Bayes' theorem in order to estimate the probability that a document is relevant to a particular request (Good 1958b, 1965a; Maron and Kuhns 1960; Maron 1961; Edmundson 1963). Even so, many index terms would be too closely correlated, and consequently it is desirable to separate words into clumps or groups. Then a clump can be regarded as a single index term. Another application of clump-finding is for the production of a thesaurus, or, more generally, for approximately dendroidal classification as in taxonomy. The clumping can be done intuitively or statistically. The theory and application of clump-finding has been called 'botryology', from the combining form botry, from βότρυς, a cluster of grapes. See Good (1958a,

1959b, 1962b, 1962c, 1965b, 1965c), Sokal and Sneath (1963) (not concerned with language statistics), and Meetham (1963). Most of these papers are concerned, among other topics, with information retrieval and mechanical translation, and list many other relevant references.

The brain is, among other things, an information-retrieval system, and the frequencies of words are relevant to several other experiments on the psychology of recall, reasoning, and sentence construction. (See, for example, Miller 1951.) It is often easier, especially when we are not wide awake, to think of or recognize a word that, as a successor of the previous word or words, has a high probability, than to think of or recognize a word that makes sense in the context. This shows that there is at least some truth in Freud's contention that every slip of the tongue has an explanation (Freud 1904). It is the price paid for the efficiency of the association mechanism. A hypothetical neurophysiological explanation of the mechanism can be given in terms of the cell assembly theory (Hebb 1949; Milner 1957), especially in the subassembly form (Good 1965a, 1966b). In Good (1965a) some formulae are suggested for the strengths of the associations between assemblies in terms of mutual information and extensions of it. In the application to language these measures depend of course on linguistic statistics. This is not an article on neurophysiology, and these references will have to suffice as an indication that linguistic statistics are likely to have a crucial status, both in future comprehensive theories of brain functioning, and in experimental psychology.

Another application of linguistic statistics, lying largely in the future, is to linguistic philosophy, in relation to definitions of words. Putting the matter succinctly, if $p_i$ is the credibility (logical probability) that an object, $O$, has quality $Q_i$, then the credibility that $O$ is a cow is $f(p_1, p_2, \ldots)$, where the specification of the function $f$ is the task of the rigorous dictionary maker (who does not yet exist). The function $f$ depends on the word to be defined. See Good (1965a), for further details and references.

In a similar spirit, a word 'type' (see next paragraph) in speech must be identified with a clump of speech sounds. The rigorous specification of these clumps is an unsolved statistical problem closely related to the problem of automatic speech recognition.

*2*

A printed linguistic text is a finite sequence or string of symbols or characters (tokens) each of which belongs to a *(generalized) alphabet*, that is, to a finite set of symbols (types) consisting of letters, punctuation, and spaces. The words 'token' and 'type' are conveniently used in this manner in other contexts, for example, to distinguish words of a dictionary (types) from words (tokens) of running text. A fruitful analogy is to compare 'type' with 'species' and 'token' with 'animal', or 'type' with 'genus' and 'token' with 'species': see Section 4.

The 1-plets, 2-plets, ... of the sequence are called

and $\delta$ is therefore a natural measure of dependence in the population contingency table ($p_{ij}$), quadratic in the $p_{ij}$'s. We have just seen that, in a sampled contingency table, the expected chi-squared bulge per character is equal to $\delta$, and is therefore approximately equal to $W_1$.

The minimum value $\delta$ occurs when $p_{ij} = p_{i.}.p_{.j}$, and then $\delta = 0$. In the case $p_{i.} = p_{.i}$, as in linguistic texts, the maximum value of $\delta$ occurs when $p_{ij} = p_{i.}.\delta_i^j$ ($\delta_i^j$ being Kronecker's delta) and then $\delta = t$. So $0 \leq \delta/t \leq 1$, and $\delta/t$ is a good population index of dependence or contingency, with ($\chi^2$ bulge)/($Nt$) as a natural estimator. Similarly, the maximum value of $W_1$ is $-\Sigma p_{i.} \log p_{i.}$ (when $p_{i.} = p_{.i}$), and the corresponding measure of dependence is $W_1/$(entropy per character), which lies between 0 and 1.

If it is felt that rare characters should have little weight, then $\varrho_2 - 2\varrho + 1$, where $\varrho_2$ is the digraph repeat rate, might be preferred to $\delta/t$, as a measure of digraphic cohesion, since it can be proved that $0 \leq \varrho_2 - 2\varrho + 1 \leq 1$. But $W_1/t$ already gives little weight to rare digraphs, and so needs no modification on this account.

Suppose we were interested in the diphonemic cohesion of a language, and that, in error, we had 'overcategorized', that is, we had split up the domain of definition of a phonemic type unnecessarily, into two types $i_1$ and $i_2$. By 'unnecessarily' we mean that the association factor of $i_1$ with $j$ is equal to that of $i_2$ with $j$, for each $j$. The effect would be that our contingency table would have an extra row and column. Then the population parameters $\varrho_2 - 2\varrho + 1$ and $\delta$ would be changed, but $W_1$ and $W_1/$(entropy per phoneme) would be invariant. This shows the superiority of these logarithmic parameters over the 'quadratic' parameters, and the author conjectures that this invariance fixes the definitions of these measures of cohesion or contingency effectively uniquely.

Some of the above theory extends to polygraphs. Suppose, for example, poly $= m+1$, and denote the polygraph type ($i_1, i_2, \ldots, i_m$) by $\mathbf{i}$, and ($i_1, i_2, \ldots, i_m, j$) by ($\mathbf{i}, j$), where $j$ is a symbol of the alphabet. Given two fully specified Markov chains of order $m$, let $H$ and $G$ be the corresponding simple statistical hypotheses. Then $P(j|\mathbf{i}, H)$ and $P(j|\mathbf{i}, G)$ will have known values, where $j$ is a symbol of the alphabet and the comma here represents logical conjunction. If a string of language has a polygraph frequency count ($n_{\mathbf{i},j}$), then the log-factor in favour of $H$ as against $G$ is

$$W(H/G:(n_{\mathbf{i}j})) = A + \sum_{\mathbf{i},j} n_{\mathbf{i}j} \log \frac{P(j|\mathbf{i}, H)}{P(j|\mathbf{i}, G)},$$

where $A$ denotes the sum of $m$ log-factors arising from the first $m$ symbols of the string. The expected log-factor per symbol, if the string is long, is

$$\sum_{\mathbf{i}j} P(\mathbf{i}, j | H) \log \frac{P(j|\mathbf{i},H)}{P(j|\mathbf{i},G)},$$

if $H$ is true. This theory is relevant to the automatic discrimination between two languages, or two dialects of the same language.

If we have decided to adopt a Markov model, but have not decided on its order, then an appropriate procedure is to decide on the degree of Markovity by making use of the likelihood-ratio statistic for Markov chains. For details, see Bartlett (1951), Hoel (1954), Good (1957a), Goodman (1958), Billingsley (1961).

A Bayesian measure of $m$th order Markovity, for a fully specified stochastic process, can be defined as

$$W_m = \triangledown^2 E_{m+1} = E_{m+1} - 2E_m + E_{m-1},$$

where

$$E_m = \begin{cases} \Sigma p_{i_1 \ldots i_m} \log (t^m p_{i_1 \ldots i_m}) & (m \geq 0), \\ 0 & \text{if } m = 0 \text{ or } -1. \end{cases}$$

(The second differences here are similar in origin to those that occur in the statistics mentioned in some of the references just cited.) $\triangledown E_{m+1}$ is the expected weight of evidence per symbol, in favour of Markovity of order $m$ as against Markovity of order $-1$, $N^{-1}W(M_m/M_{-1})$, and hence $W_{m+1}$ is $N^{-1}W(M_m/M_{m-1})$, the *extra* weight of evidence per symbol when the $m$th order transition probabilities are taken into account, given that all lower orders have already been allowed for. Of course $W_m$ is a particular case of

$$\triangledown E_{m+1} - \triangledown E_{n+1} = N^{-1}W(M_m/M_n).$$

It is clear from its interpretation that $0 \leq W_m \leq \log t$, and it can be proved, by reference to the 'teleprinter problem' (Good 1946) that $W$ can be made arbitrarily close to $\log t$. Thus $W_m$ can be 'normalized' by taking $t$ as the base of the logarithms.

If we were trying to select an alphabet of $t$ phonemes, for fixed $t$, it seems reasonable to minimize the expected weight of evidence per symbol, that is, to minimize

$$W_0 + W_1 + W_2 + \ldots = \lim_{m \to \infty} \triangledown E_m.$$

This comes to the same as maximizing the rate of transmission of information per symbol.

It would be possible to suggest similar criteria in terms of the quadratic 'psi-squared' statistic, used in the serial test for flat-randomness (Good 1953), but it would not be as compelling as the Bayesian or information-theory criterion.

It might be possible to arrive iteratively at the optimal phoneme alphabet, starting with a preliminary categorization obtained subjectively or botryologically. The botryological method would be to start with a *large* alphabet of atomic sounds and to reduce the size of the alphabet by putting the sounds into clumps. This would require a measure of the relatedness of each pair ($i, j$) of sound types (cf. Shephard 1962; Needham 1963; Good 1965c; and references therein). This measure could again be either subjective, or perhaps defined as

$$|\Sigma_k p_{ik} I(i:k) - \Sigma_k p_{jk} I(j:k)|,$$

where $k$ runs through the large alphabet, and $I(i:k)$ is the mutual information, $\log (P(i, k)/(P(i)P(k)))$.

The automatic categorization of atomic sound types might not be necessary for languages that are well known, but it might be useful for new primitive languages, including those which some investigators suspect are used by dolphins and whales. Even for familiar languages the problem arises in relation to diphthongs, and in the selection of 'molecular' sound types for optimal stenotyping or discrete speech transmission. The point can be exemplified by analogy with Braille.

*Braille* has an enlarged alphabet consisting of the ordinary alphabet of 26 letters, a spacer, the words *and*, *for*, *of*, *the*, *with*, and the digraphs *ch*, *gh*, *sh*, *th*, *wh*, *ed*, *er*, *ou*, and *ow*. What principles should be used for the optimal selection of an alphabet of $t$ symbols, where $t$ is specified in advance? (For Braille, $t = 41$.) This problem is the one for which Bernard Shaw bequeathed funds in 1950. Two competing principles suggest themselves:

(i) Maximize the rate of transmission of information per symbol;

(ii) Maximize the rate of transmission of information per symbol without loss of any information. The second of these two principles is the one that was used approximately and intuitively by Louis Braille, but, for continuous speech this would be impossible, and the first principle is presumably the right one.

The above discussion is related to the technique of maximizing entropy, or of minimizing expected weight of evidence, in the formulation of hypotheses, especially in connexion with multidimensional population contingency tables. See Good (1963a, 1965b, and 1966a), where further references will be found, especially to E.T. Jaynes (although Jaynes was not concerned with contingency tables). The theory is highly relevant to the sampling of polygraphs, because most samples of polygraphs cannot be made large enough for any naive frequency estimation of probabilities to be adequate.

Even when sampling word digraphs (or 'diwords'), the sample can hardly ever be fully adequate, and this leads to the problem of estimating the probabilities corresponding to empty or nearly empty cells in ordinary large two-dimensional contingency tables. For methods of doing this, see Good (1956, 1965b). It is usually necessary to categorize the words into clumps in order to contract the size of the contingency table. This can be done either by subjective judgement, with the aid of a thesaurus, or by botryology.

In these contingency-table problems, one is concerned with the estimation of probabilities of events that have never occurred, a problem that is familiar in ordinary life; in fact most probability estimation is of this kind. There is no single technique that will solve all such problems, but the device of maximizing entropy, that is, of minimizing expected weight of evidence, that is, of maximizing the degree of independence assumed, comes close to being a unifying principle. By itself it allows only for given probabilities, not for samples. A suggestion made in Good (1963a), for allowing for the finiteness of samples, is to maximize some linear combination of entropy and log-likelihood. For a two-dimensional contingency table, for example, this leads to the suggestion of selecting the $p_{ij}$'s so as to maximize an expression of the form

$$\frac{1}{N} \Sigma n_{ij} \log p_{ij} - \lambda \Sigma p_{ij} \log p_i$$

subject to the constraints

$$\Sigma_i p_{ij} = n_i/N, \; \Sigma_i p_{ij} = n_{.j}/N.$$

(Perhaps $\lambda = 1$ is the most natural value to take.) This leads to an estimate of $p_{ij}$ lying between $n_{ij}''/N$ and $n_{i.} n_{.j}/N^2$, as it should. The method can be regarded as using an initial density proportional to $e^{\lambda X}$ where $X$ is the entropy. Perhaps a linear combination of these densities would be theoretically better, but the calculations would be difficult (cf. Good 1965b, 1967).

The theory for general contingency tables applies to those that arise from Markov chains with only minor modifications. (Cf. Goodman 1955; Dawson and Good 1957.) The theory is therefore useful for discussing the usual statistical model of language. But it is interesting to prove that language cannot be exactly a Markov process. In order to prove this, we shall make use of the repeat rate for polygraphs.

Consider an ergodic Markov process of order 1. (To say that it is ergodic means that, as time proceeds, the probabilities of the various states or characters tend to values mathematically independent of the initial state.) Then

$$\varrho_n = \sum_{i_1, \ldots, i_n} (p_{i_1} q_{i_1 i_2} \cdots q_{i_{n-1} i_n})^2,$$

where $(q_{ij})$ is the transition probability matrix and $(p_i)$ is the vector of stationary monographic probabilities. Hence

$$\varrho_n = \Sigma \pi_{i_1} \varkappa_{i_1 i_2} \cdots \varkappa_{i_{n-1} i_n}$$

where

$$\pi_i = p_i^2, \; \varkappa_{ij} = q_{ij}^2.$$

Hence

$\varrho_n$ = sum of components of the vector $\boldsymbol{\pi}' \mathbf{K}^{n-1}$ where $\boldsymbol{\pi}$ is the column vector $(\pi_i)$ and $\mathbf{K} = (\varkappa_{ij})$. Therefore $\varrho_{n+1}/\varrho_n \to$ the largest eigenvalue of $\mathbf{K}$ when $n \to \infty$, and this is not equal to 1.

Now $\varrho_{n+1}/\varrho_n$ is the conditional probability, given that two $n$-graphs have so far repeated, that the next monograph will also repeat. But, by *scientific induction*, this conditional probability tends to 1. (The form of scientific induction used here is that, if one has had a long run of 'successes', the next 'trial' will be a success with probability tending to 1. Scientific induction was shown to follow from the axioms of logical probability by Keynes (1921) and, with a slight improvement, by Jeffreys 1939/61.) Since this is a contradiction, it follows that language cannot be a Markov process of order 1. But a Markov process of any (finite) order, $m$, can be regarded as one of order 1, by defining a 'character' in an enlarged alphabet as an $m$-graph in the original alphabet, and the successor, in the string, of this character as the $m$-graph having an $(m-1)$-graph overlap with the previous $m$-graph (cf. Good 1946; de Bruijn 1946; Bartlett 1951). Therefore language cannot be a Markov process of any (finite) order. (Markov processes are usually of finite order by definition, although a Markov process of infinite order *can* be defined as one in which the past has less and less influence as it becomes more and more remote.)

The above proof looks like legerdemain until one realizes that, if two texts agree for long enough, it becomes more and more probable that they are replicas of the same message, and even that the garble rate is negligible!

*Frequencies of frequencies and the species problem.* Suppose that a random sample is drawn from an infinite population of animals of various species, or word tokens from a printed text. For example, consider Yule's sample of nouns in Macaulay's essay on Bacon (Yule 1944, Table 4.4, p. 63; repeated in Good, 1953, p. 260). The number of tokens, that is, the sample size, was $N = 8045$, and the number of distinct words (word types) in the sample was $S = 2048$. Let $v_r$ be the number of types each of which was represented $r$ times. It can be called the *frequency of the frequency, r*. The following table gives some of the values of the frequencies of the frequencies. (In this table, where a range is given for $r$, the total of the corresponding $v_r$'s is given.)

| $r$ | $v_r$ | $r$ | $v_r$ | $r$ | $v_r$ |
|---|---|---|---|---|---|
| 1 | 990 | 11 | 24 | 41 | 1 |
| 2 | 367 | 12 | 19 | 45 | 2 |
| 3 | 173 | 13 | 10 | 48 | 1 |
| 4 | 112 | 14 | 10 | 57 | 1 |
| 5 | 72 | 15 | 13 | 58 | 1 |
| 6 | 47 | 16–20 | 31 | 65 | 1 |
| 7 | 41 | 21–25 | 15 | 76 | 1 |
| 8 | 31 | 26–30 | 16 | 81 | 1 |
| 9 | 34 | 31–35 | 6 | 89 | 1 |
| 10 | 17 | 36–40 | 9 | 255 | 1 |

It is typical of sampling from a very large number of categories, whether or not it is strict multinomial sampling, that there are many rare categories not represented in the sample, and that $v_1$ is quite large. As a matter of fact, provided that $v_1$ is large, a good estimate of the probability that the very next token sampled will belong to a new type (species) is $v_1/N$, if the sampling is multinomial. (For a proof, see Good 1953.) There is a similar formula for the total population coverage of all the word types that have so far occurred at least $r$ times. It is also possible to make an estimate of the number of new types that will occur in another sample of size $\lambda N$, if $\lambda$ is not too large, say $\lambda < 5$ (Good and Toulmin 1956). The estimate is

$$\lambda v_1 - \lambda^2 v_2 + \lambda^3 v_3 - \ldots$$

if $\lambda < 1$. If $1 < \lambda < 5$, this formula can be made usable by transforming the series, such as by Euler's or Shank's method of summation. An estimate of the population probability of a type represented $r$ times in the sample is

$$\frac{r^*}{N} = \frac{(r+1)v'_{r+1}}{Nv'_r},$$

where $(v'_r)$ is a smoothing of $(v_r)$, and $r^*$ can be regarded as an adjusted value of $r$. (This formula has been ascribed, with some justification, to Turing and Good.) Methods of smoothing are given in Good (1953). Sometimes simple analytic smoothings can be found.

The theory also provides estimates of the entropy per word, including an approximately unbiased estimate. If the entropy per letter is wanted, then it is necessary to treat words of each length separately and to combine the results in an appropriate manner.

It is hardly necessary to point out that this theory is essential for any one who wishes to compile a dictionary in a rational manner.

Let $p_i$ be the population frequency of the $i$th commonest word of the language. It sometimes happens that $p_i$ is roughly proportional to a negative power of $i$, and also that $v'_r$ is roughly proportional to a negative power of $r$. Such laws are often described as Zipf laws, since Zipf did much to popularize them, although J. B. Estoup, M. Joos, G. Dewey, and E. V. Condon were also involved; see especially Estoup (1916). One modification mentioned by Zipf (1949) is to take the expectation of $v_r$ as proportional to $(r^2 - 1/4)^{-1}$. The inverse power law also often applies to incomes, when it is known as the *Pareto law*, and a reasonable explanation of it was given by Champernowne (1953), another one being given by Whittle and Wold (1957). The inverse power law also applies to the distribution of species in genera, when it is known as the *Willis law* (Willis 1922; Mandelbrot 1956). The *Zipf law* is unreliable but it is often enough a good approximation to demand an explanation. Zipf thought it could be explained by a 'principle of least effort', but his explanation was not quantitative enough to carry much weight. The first quantitative explanation of it was given by Mandelbrot (1953) in terms of some simple notions from information theory that were not available to Zipf. See also Mandelbrot (1957a, b; 1961), Good (1957c, 1961a, 1962a). Rider (1965). There follows an account, in the author's own words, of Mandelbrot's explanation, followed by a modification of it, which the author thinks is an improvement, and which leads to a modification of Zipf's law.

Let $f(i)$ be the amount of effort to extract the $i$th commonest word from memory. Then the expected amount of information per unit of effort is

$$-(\Sigma p_i \log p_i)/(\Sigma f(i)p_i).$$

It is now assumed that the language has evolved in such a way that this quantity is (approximately) maximized, subject to the constraint $\Sigma p_i = 1$. It follows, from Lagrange's method of undetermined multipliers, that $p_i$ is proportional to $\exp(-b_1 f(i))$, where $b_1$ is a constant. Mandelbrot reasonably assumes that $f(i)$ is proportional to log $(i+a)$, for some small positive constant, $a$. This implies that $p_i$ is proportional to $(i+a)^{-b}$, for some constant $b$, and this is the inverse power law modified slightly by the presence of the constant $a$.

The idea behind the logarithmic formula for $f(i)$ is, roughly speaking, that the number of words that can be recalled from 'store', by the closing of $n$ relays of a fully specified kind, goes up exponentially with $n$.

The modification of this argument that the author suggests is that, for large values of $i$, we should allow, not only for the effort in recalling the $i$th commonest word, but for the effort of learning it in the first place. Otherwise the cost per usage of the millionth commonest word would be only about double that of the thousandth. The 'overhead' in learning the word should be divided by the frequency with which it is used, in order to share out the overhead amongst all its usages. This leads to the assumption that $f(i)$ is proportional to an expression of the form

$$(1+\varepsilon p_i^{-1})\log(i+a),$$

if the effort required to learn a word is proportional to the effort required to use it. Here $\varepsilon$ is a very small positive constant. Then we get an equation of the form

$$p_i = c(i+a)^{-b(1+\varepsilon p_i^{-1})}.$$

A first approximation to the solution of this equation is of course

$$p_i = c(i+a)^{-b},$$

and a second approximation is

$$p_i = c(i+a)^{-b\{1+\varepsilon c^{-1}(i+a)^b\}}.$$

Apart from anything else, the second approximation has the merit that $\Sigma p_i$ converges, even if $b < 1$. This removes an objection made by Yule (1944) to Zipf's law in its original forms.

With the help of the equation

$$\mathcal{E}(v_r) = \binom{N}{r}\sum_i p_i^r(1-p_i)^{N-r}$$

(Good 1953) we can infer that, for small values of $r$, $v_r'$ is approximately proportional to $\Gamma(r-b^{-1})/\Gamma(r+1)$. Given a sample, we can decide values for the parameters of the law from the $p_i$'s, for small values of $i$, these being estimable with little sampling error, and can then check whether the above formula for $v_r'$ provides an adequate smoothing of the frequencies of the frequencies for small values of $r$. If not, the Zipf law is refuted for that particular sample.

Certainly the Zipf law is not always a good approximation. It has been found, for example, that, for two samples of words, including the sample of nouns mentioned above, a better smoothing is provided by the formula $Ae^{-\varepsilon r}/(r+r^2)$, and curiously enough this formula also seems to be better than Fisher's logarithmic series for several of the biological samples given by Williams (1944). (See Greenwood and Yule 1920; Corbet et al. 1943; Kendall 1948.) These authors mention only the logarithmic series.

Belonogov (1962) took a sample of nearly 100,000 words of printed commercial Russian, and found that the following law held both for complete words and for stems:

$$p_i = e^{-c(i-1)^k} - e^{-ci^k},$$

where $c = 0.05357$, $k = 0.4464$ for complete (fully inflected) words, and $c = 0.07057$, $k = 0.4844$ for stems. He states further that a law of the same form holds for Roumanian, and bases this on some statistics assembled by L. A. Novak.

A law of yet another form was found to give a good approximation by Belevitch (1959). A generalization of Zipf's law is considered by Matula (1965).

There is scope for someone to assemble all the statistics together, to examine them critically, and to see which laws apply and under what circumstances and with what accuracy. As Herdan (1960), says, it is really misleading to use the word 'law'. Perhaps simply 'distribution' would be better.

A verification of the 'least effort' or 'economic' explanation of Zipf's law can be obtained indirectly by applying a similar argument to Pitman's shorthand (see Good 1957b). The proportion of symbols (tokens) in Pitman's shorthand that have $i$ 'strokes' is close to $2^{-i}$ according to a frequency count given by Herdan (1956). This is consistent with the very natural hypothesis that the effort required to write a symbol is roughly proportional to the number of strokes. Herdan (1953) argued that Pitman's shorthand has an optimal property, but claimed that it maximizes the expected amount of information per word. This is correct if it is known in advance that the expected number of strokes per word is 2; but it is better to say that the expected amount of information per stroke is maximized, without specifying the mean number of strokes per word. This *implies* that the mean number of strokes per word must be 2. It may be noted that Herdan and Mandelbrot almost simultaneously attacked problems of explaining observed linguistic frequency distributions by using Shannon's measure of information. (See also Herdan 1960; Good 1957b.)

The above analysis assumes that all strokes in Pitman's shorthand take the same time or effort to write. A full study of optimization should allow for the times taken to write each stroke, and for whether the strokes are easily distinguishable. Also the problem of the optimal size of 'alphabet' is difficult since the overhead cost of learning the alphabet ought to be taken into account for large alphabets. If we were prepared to ignore this overhead we would have a separate symbol for each word in the language, and would not mind if these symbols were selected at random, provided that they were quick to write and readily distinguishable.

The optimal design of an alphabet or of a vocabulary minimizes the expected cost of communication, for a given amount of communication. It would be necessary to allow for:

(i) the rate of transmission of information;
(ii) the cost of learning the alphabet or vocabulary;
(iii) the cost of the errors arising out of confusion of

symbols that are not adequately distinct (see Zachrisson 1965);

(iv) historical facts whiche influnce (i), (ii), and (iii);

(v) generality of communication; for example, it is useful if the alphabets used for various languages are the same or similar;

(vi) (in the case of an ordinary alphabet) the relationship of the alphabet to phonemes;

(vii) the cost of compiling dictionaries, and of making reference to them when the vocabulary is too large to be completely learned;

(viii) the cost of asking for explanations of terms;

(ix) the cost of errors arising from guessing meanings when dictionaries are not available or one is not willing to refer to one, or one is unwilling to ask for an explanation.

Statistical data are relevant to all nine of these aspects.

*A property of letter and phoneme frequencies.* Some years ago the author noticed a property of letter monograph frequencies that appears to hold for many languages, and has recently checked that it applies also to phonemes. He can think of no explanation for it, economic or otherwise, but the effort in pronouncing phonemes must be very relevant. The observation is that the monograph frequencies seem to be well approximated by breaking up the unit interval at random into $t$ parts, where $t$ is the number of characters in the 'alphabet'. Whitworth (1901) proves that, if the $t$ parts are arranged in order of magnitude, beginning with the least, their respective expectations are

$$\frac{1}{t^2},\ \frac{1}{t}\left(\frac{1}{t}+\frac{1}{t-1}\right),\ \frac{1}{t}\left(\frac{1}{t}+\frac{1}{t-1}+\frac{1}{t-2}\right),\ \text{etc.}$$

These expectations are given in permillages in the second columns of each of the following two tables ($t = 26$, for letters; $t = 32$ for phonemes, but the 'alphabet' size for English phonemes is not always taken as 32, for example, Denes (1963) had $t = 44$). The population frequencies for letters and phonemes are taken respectively from Pratt (1939) and Roberts (1965).

*Letter and phoneme frequencies in decreasing order, compared with the random division of the unit interval*

| | | | |
|---|---|---|---|
| 131 | 148 | 25 | 26 |
| 105 | 110 | 25 | 23 |
| 82 | 91 | 20 | 22 |
| 80 | 77 | 20 | 18 |
| 71 | 68 | 20 | 16 |
| 68 | 60 | 15 | 14 |
| 63 | 54 | 14 | 12 |
| 61 | 48 | 9 | 10 |
| 53 | 44 | 4 | 8 |
| 38 | 39 | 1·7 | 6 |
| 34 | 36 | 1·3 | $4\frac{1}{2}$ |
| 29 | 32 | 1·2 | 3 |
| 28 | 29 | 0·8 | $1\frac{1}{2}$ |
| 118 | 126 | 20 | 21 |
| 93 | 95 | 19 | 19 |
| 70 | 80 | 19 | 18 |
| 68 | 69 | 17 | 16 |
| 66 | 62 | 16 | 14 |
| 63 | 55 | 16 | 14 |
| 47 | 50 | 16 | 12 |
| 46 | 46 | 15 | 10 |
| 45 | 42 | 9 | 9 |
| 39 | 39 | 9 | 8 |
| 33 | 36 | 7 | 6 |
| 30 | 32 | $6\frac{1}{2}$ | 5 |
| 26 | 30 | $4\frac{1}{2}$ | 4 |
| 26 | 28 | 4 | 3 |
| 25 | 25 | $3\frac{1}{2}$ | 2 |
| 23 | 23 | $\frac{1}{2}$ | 1 |

The discrepancies are small and must be well within the probable errors when an interval is dissected randomly (see Moran 1947/53). The language samples also have their statistical errors; for example, Pratt used a sample of only 1000 words.

4

*Sources of statistics of language.* In this final section is mentioned a somewhat haphazard selection of publications where linguistic statistics may be found. Bibliographies on the subject are given by Akhmanova *et al.* (1963), Herdan (1956, 1960, 1962) and by Guiraud, Whatmough *et al.* (1954), which contains some 1700 titles. Herdan (1960), mentions that a supplement to Guiraud, Whatmough *et al.* (1954) is to be edited by the Comité International Permanent de Linguistes. See also Galland (1945), Saccho (1951), and Stumpers (1953/60).

Numerous statistical tables on a variety of linguistic topics are given in Herdan's books, and in Guiraud (1959), and Zipf (1949). These books, and Akhmanova *et al.* (1963), also discuss theoretical aspects in some detail.

For word-frequency statistics, see, for example: Eldridge (1911), who used a sample of over 40,000 words (tokens) of American newspaper English; Horn (1926), who used a sample of over 5,000,000 words from correspondence, and listed the 10,000 commonest words (types) with their frequencies; Zipf (1932), who gave the frequencies of the frequencies for Eldridge's sample of English, and also for some samples of Chinese and Latin; Pratt (1939), who lists words that occurred at least five times in a sample of 10,000 words of 'normal text'; Gaines (1939/56), who lists the 100 commonest words, with their frequencies, based on a sample of 242,432 words taken from numerous authors and newspapers by F.R. Fraprie; Yule (1944), who gives the frequencies of frequencies for nouns used by various authors; Thorndike and Lorge (1944), who list the 30,000 most frequent words, with some information concerning their frequencies, based on a sample of about 18,000,000 words of published texts; and Eaton (1961), who, for English, French, German and Spanish, lists vocabulary according to the 'first thousand concepts', the 'second thousand concepts', ..., the 'sixth thousand concepts', and the first half of the 'seventh thousand concepts'. Belonogov (1962) states a distribution law for Russian and Roumanian, as mentioned in Section 4, but does not give the data on which the law is based. See also Belevitch (1959) and Barnard (1955), who calculates word entropies for four Western languages. (Shannon 1951, had estimated the entropy *per letter* of printed English as one bit.)

Sentence lengths and frequencies of common words have both been listed for use in the diagnosis of authorship, the latter being apparently more likely to be effective. Some references were given in Section 1.

For putting some of Plato's works in chronological order, Kalusch (1904) made use of the 32 pentabits consisting of the final five syllable lengths (long or short) or quantities, of sentences, such as ∪∪−−∪. This work was put on a sound statistical basis by Cox and Brandwood (1959). Malone (1778) had already suggested the use of statistical methods for chronological ordering.

Pratt (1939), gives the frequencies of letters (monographs) for English, French, Spanish, and German; and, for English, initial and final letters of words, doubled letters, digraphs, trigraphs, and letter patterns. Gaines (1939/56), gives monograph frequencies for English, German, French, Italian, Spanish, and Portuguese. Markov (1913) gives data for vowel-consonant dibits of Pushkin.

Among the publications giving phoneme statistics are: Dewey (1926), Zipf (1929), Berry (1953), Denes (1963), Hultzén, Allen, and Miron (1964), Roberts (1965), and Delattre (1965). These all give statistics concerning English and, in addition, Delattre deals with French, German and Spanish, and Zipf with these languages, and also with Russian, Czech, Bulgarian, Hungarian, Swedish, Italian, Greek, and Latin. Some of the recent publications among these give transition probabilities, or, what comes to the same, diphoneme counts, along with the phoneme counts. Berry and Denes used spoken English, whereas most of the other writers inferred their results from printed texts. For example, Roberts based his results on the word frequency counts of Horn (1926).

Statistics concerning various types of shorthand are given by Herdan (1953).

Ross (1950) applied statistical methods to philological problems, for example, for assessing the evidence of the relationship of languages. Among other statistical tables, he lists which of 74 philological features are present in each of nine languages.

*See also*: Computational linguistics: introduction. Information storage and retrieval. Linguistic form: algebraic linguistics. Linguistic form: generative grammar. Statistics of language: structure of written English words.

*Bibliography*

AKHMANOVA O. S., MEL'CHUK I. A., FRUMKINA R. M. and PADUCHEVA E. V. (1963) *Exact methods in linguistic research*, (trans. by D. G. Hays and D. V. Mohr) Berkeley and Los Angeles: University of California Press.

ALBERTI, LEON BATTISTA (c. 1470) *Trattati in cifra*, (available in the Vatican library).

ANON. (1966) *Towards a cashless society*, Financial Times (London, 2nd August, 1966).

BACH E. (1964) *An Introduction to Transformational Grammars*, New York: Holt, Rinehart, and Winston.

BACON, FRANCIS (1605) *The Twoo Bookes of Francis Bacon of the Proficience and Advancement of Learning*, London.

BAR-HILLEL Y. (1957) *A logician's reaction to recent theorizing on information search systems*, American Documentation, **8**, 101.

BARNARD G. A., III (1955) *Statistical calculation of word entropies for four Western languages*, I.R.E. Trans. **IT-1**, 49.

BARTLETT M. S. (1951) *The frequency goodness of fit test for probability chains*, Proc. Cambridge Phil. Soc. **47**, 86.

BELEVITCH V. (1959) *On the statistical laws of linguistic distributions*, Ann. Soc. Sci. Bruxelles Ser. I, **73**, 310.

BELONOGOV G. G. (1962) *On some statistical regularities in written Russian*, Vopr. Jazykoznanija **7**, 100. (In Russian.)

BERRY J. (1953) *Some statistical aspects of conversational speech*, in Communication Theory (Ed. Willis Jackson) 392, London: Butterworths.

BILLINGSLEY P. (1961) *Statistical Inference for Markov Processes*, Chicago: The University Press.

BODMER F. (1944) *The Loom of Language*, London: Allen and Unwin.

CHAMPERNOWNE D. G. (1953) *A model for income distribution*, Econ. J. **63**, 318.

CHOMSKY N. (1965) *Aspects of the Theory of Syntax*, Cambridge, Mass.: M.I.T. Press.

CLASSE A. (1957) *The whistled language of la Gomera*, Scient. Amer. **196**, 111.

COHEN L. J. (1965) *On a concept of degree of grammaticalness*, Logique et Analyse, **30**, 141.

CORBET A. S., FISHER R. A. and WILLIAMS C. B. (1943) *The relation between the number of species and the number of individuals in a random sample of an animal population*, J. Animal Ecol. **12**, 42.

COX D. R. and BRANDWOOD L. (1959) *On a discriminatory problem connected with the works of Plato*, J. Roy. Statist. Soc. B, **21**, 195.

DAWSON R. B. and GOOD I. J. (1957) *Exact Markov probabilities from oriented linear graphs*, Annals Math. Statist. **28**, 946.

DE BRUIJN N. G. (1946) *A combinatorial problem*, Nederl. Akad. Wetensch. Proc. **49**, 758 = Indagationes Math. **8**, 461.

DELATTRE P. (1965) *Comparing the phonetic features*

of English, French, German, and Spanish, London, Toronto, Wellington, and Sydney: Harrap.

Denes P. B. (1959) *The design and operation of the mechanical speech recognizer at University College, London*, J. Brit. Inst. Radio Engrs., **19**, 219.

Denes P. B. (1963) *On the statistics of spoken English*, J. Acoust. Soc. Am., **35**, 892.

Dewey G. (1923) *Relativ frequency of English speech sounds*, Cambridge, Mass.: Harvard University Press, Harvard studies in education, Vol. 4.

Dreyfus-Graf J. (1950) *Sonograph and sound-mechanics*, J. Acoust. Soc. Am. **22**, 731.

Dudley H. and Balashek S. (1958) *Automatic recognition of phonetic patterns in speech*, J. Acoust. Soc. Am. **30**, 721.

Eaton H. S. (1961) *An English–French–German–Spanish word frequency dictionary, a correlation of the first six thousand words in four single-language frequency lists*, New York: Dover.

Edmundson H. P. (1963) *A statistician's view of linguistic models and language-data processing*, in *Natural language and the computer* (Ed. P. L. Garvin), 151, New York: McGraw-Hill.

Eldridge R. C. (1911) *Six thousand common English words*, Buffalo: The Clements Press.

Estoup J. B. (1916) (4th Edn) *Gammes sténographiques*, Paris.

Fréchet M. (1931) *Recherches théoriques modernes sur le calcul des probabilités*, **2** (Théories des événements en chaine dans le cas d'un nombre fini d'états possibles), Paris: Gauthier-Villars.

Freud S. (1904) *The Psychopathology of Everyday Life*, New York: International.

Friedman W. F. (1922) *The index of coincidence and its applications in cryptography*, Geneva, Illinois: Riverbank Laboratories. Available at the Library of Congress.

Friedman W. F. (1964) *Cryptology*, Enc. Brit. **6**, 844.

Friedman W. F. and E. S. (1957) *The Shakespearean ciphers examined*, Cambridge: The University Press.

Gaines H. F. (1939/56) *Cryptanalysis: a Study of Ciphers and their Solution*, New York: Dover.

Galland J. S. (1945) *An Historical and Analytical Bibliography of the Literature of Cryptology*, Northwestern University Studies in the Humanities, 10; Evanston.

Good I. J. (1946) *Normal recurring decimals*, J. London Math. Soc. **21**, 167. (The 'teleprinter problem'.)

Good I. J. (1950) *Probability and the Weighing of Evidence*, London: Griffin; New York: Hafner.

Good I. J. (1953) *The serial test and other tests for randomness*, Proc. Cambridge Phil. Soc. **49**, 276.

Good I. J. (1956) *On the estimation of small frequencies in contingency tables*, J. Roy. Statist. Soc. B, **18**, 113.

Good I. J. (1957a) *The likelihood ratio test for Markoff chains*, Biometrika **42**, 531; **44**, 301.

Good I. J. (1957b) *Review of Herdan's Language as choice and chance*, J. Roy. Statist. Soc. A, **120**, 89.

Good I. J. (1957c) *Distribution of word frequencies*, Nature, **179**, 595.

Good I. J. (1958a) *How much science can you have at your fingertips?*, IBM J. Res. Dev., **2**, 282.

Good I. J. (1958b) *Speculations concerning information retrieval*, Res. Rep. RC-78, Dec. 10, 1958, Yorktown Heights: IBM Research Center.

Good I. J. (1959a) *Private communication to D. L. Richards of the Post Office Research Station*, 14th May, 1959.

Good I. J. (1959b) *Contribution to the discussion of the Theoretical Panel, International Conference on Scientific Information* (1958), Proceedings, Washington, D.C., 1404 and 1406.

Good I. J. (1961a) *Review of a paper by Mandelbrot*, Math. Rev. **22**, 1838.

Good I. J. (1961b) *The frequency count of a Markov chain and the transition to continuous time*, Annals Math. Statist., **32**, 41.

Good I. J. (1962a) *Review of a paper by H. A. Simon*, Math. Rev. **24**, 111.

Good I. J. (1962b) *Botryological speculations*, in *The scientist speculates* (Eds. Good, Mayne, and Maynard Smith), 120, London: Heinemann; New York: Basic Books; German tr., Düsseldorf: Econ-Verlag.

Good I. J. (1962c) *Discussion of a paper by Sparck Jones*, in *1961 International conf. on machine translation of languages and applied language analysis*, 434, London: H. M. Stationery Office.

Good I. J. (1963a) *Maximum entropy for hypothesis formulation, especially for multidimensional contingency tables*, Annals Math. Statist. **34**, 911.

Good I. J. (1963b) *Quadratics in Markov-chain frequencies, and the binary chain of order 2*, J. Roy. Statist. Soc. B, **25**, 383.

Good I. J. (1965a) *Speculations concerning the first ultraintelligent machine*, Advances in Computers, **6**, 31.

Good I. J. (1965b) *The estimation of probabilities: an essay on modern Bayesian methods*, Cambridge, Mass.: M.I.T. Press.

Good I. J. (1965c) *Categorization of classification*, in *Mathematics and Computer Science in Biology and Medicine*, London: H.M. Stationery Office.

Good I. J. (1965d) *Contribution to the discussion of a paper by Morton*, J. Roy. Statist. Soc. A, **128**, 225, corrigenda, p. 623.

Good I. J. (1966a) *How to estimate probabilities*, J. Institute of Math. and its Applications, **2**, 364.

Good I. J. (1966b) *The function of speculation in science exemplified by the subassembly theory of mind*, Theoria to Theory, **1**, 28.

Good I. J. and Toulmin G. H. (1967) *Coding theorems and weight of evidence* (to be published).

Good I. J. and Toulmin G. H. (1956) *The number of new species, and the increase of population coverage, when a sample is increased* Biometrika **43**, 45.

Good I. J. (1967) *A Bayesian significance test for multinomial distributions*. J. Roy. Statist. Soc. Ser. B, (to be published).

Goodman L. A. (1955) *On the statistical analysis of Markov chains*, Annals Math. Statist. **26**, 771.

GOODMAN L. A. (1958) *Simplified run tests and likelihood ratio tests for Markoff chains*, Biometrika, **45**, 181.

GREENWOOD M. and YULE G. U. (1920) *An inquiry into the nature of frequency distributions representative of multiple happenings with particular reference to the occurrence of multiple attacks of disease or of repeated accidents*, J. Roy. Statist. Soc. **83**, 255.

GREGORY R. L. (1966) *Eye and Brain: the Psychology of Seeing*, London: Weidenfeld and Nicolson.

GUIRAUD P. (1959) *Problèmes et méthodes de la statistique linguistique*, Dordrecht: Reidel.

GUIRAUD P., WHATMOUGH J., HOUCHIN T. D., PUHVEL J. and WATKINS C. W. (1954) *Bibliographie critique de la statistique linguistique*, Utrecht: Éditions Spectrum.

HEBB D. O. (1949) *Organization of Behaviour*, New York: Wiley.

HERDAN G. (1953) *Language in the light of the theory of information*, Metron **17**, 1.

HERDAN G. (1956) *Language as Choice and Chance*, Gröningen: Noordhoff.

HERDAN G. (1960) *Type-token Mathematics*, 's-Gravenhage: Mouton.

HERDAN G. (1962) *The Calculus of Linguistic Observations*, 's-Gravenhage: Mouton.

HOEL P. G. (1954) *A test for Markov chains*, Biometrika, **41**, 430.

HORN E. (1926) *A Basic Writing Vocabulary: 10,000 Words most Commonly Used in Writing*, University of Iowa monographs on eduction, No. 4, Iowa City.

HOSTINSKY B. (1931) *Méthodes générales du calcul des probabilités*, Paris: Gauthier-Villars.

HULTZÉN L. S., ALLEN J. H. D. Jr. and MIRON M. S. (1964) *Tables of Transitional Frequencies of English Phonemes*, Urbana: University of Illinois Press.

JAKOBSON R., FANT G. and HALLE M. (1952) *The Preliminaries to Speech Analysis*, Cambridge, Mass.: M.I.T. Press.

JAKOBSON R. and HALLE M. (1956) *Fundamentals of Language*, 's-Gravenhage: Mouton.

JEFFREYS SIR HAROLD (1939/61) *Theory of Probability*, Oxford: Clarendon Press.

KALUSCH W. (1904) *Zur Chronologie der platonischen Dialoge*, Wiener Studien **26**, 190.

KENDALL D. G. (1948) *On some modes of popluation growth leading to Fisher's logarithmic series distribution*, Biometrika **35**, 6.

KEYNES J. M. (1921) *A Treatise on Probability*, London: Macmillan.

KIRSCH R. A. (1964) *Computer interpretation of English text and picture patterns*, I.E.E.E. Trans. Elec. Computers, **EC-13**, 363.

KULLBACK S., KUPPERMAN M. and KU H. H. (1962) *An application of information theory to contingency tables*, J. Res. Nat. Bur. Stand., B, **66B**, 217.

LINDGREN N. (1965) *Machine recognition of human language*, I.E.E.E. Spectrum, March, 114; April, 44; May, 104.

LUHN H. P. (1957) *A statistical approach to mechanical encoding and searching of literature information*, IBM J. Res. Dev. **1**, 309.

MALONE E. (1778) *An attempt to ascertain the order in which the plays attributed to Shakespeare were written*.

MANDELBROT B. (1953) *An informational theory of the statistical structure of language*, in Communication Theory (Ed. Willis Jackson), 486, London: Butterworths.

MANDELBROT B. (1956) *On the language of taxonomy: an outline of a 'thermostatistical' theory of systems of categories with Willis (natural) structure*, in Communication Theory (Ed. Colin Cherry), 135, London: Butterworths.

MANDELBROT B. (1957a) *Linguistique statistique macroscopique*, in Logique, langage et théorie de l'information (Eds. Apostel, Mandelbrot, and Morf), Paris: Presses Universitaires de France.

MANDELBROT B. (1957b) *Théorie mathématique de la loi d'Estoup-Zipf*, Paris: Inst. de Statistique de l'Univ.

MANDELBROT B. (1961) *On the theory of word frequencies and on related Markovian models of discourse*, in Structure of Language and its Mathematical Aspects, (Proc. Symp. Appl. Math., Vol. 12; Ed. R. Jakobson) 190, Providence: Amer. Math. Soc.

MARKOV A. A. (1913) *An example of a statistical investigation of the text of 'Eugen Onegin' illustrating the connection of trials in a chain*, Bulletin de l'Academie Impériale des Sciences de St. Petérsburg, **7**, 153. (In Russian.)

MARKOV A. A. (1924) (4th Edn) *Probability Calculus*, Moscow. (In Russian.)

MARON M. E. (1961) *Automatic indexing: an experimental inquiry*, J. Assoc. Comp. Mach. **8**, 404.

MARON M. E. and KUHNS J. L. (1960) *On relevance, probabilistic indexing, and information retrieval*, J. Assoc. Comp. Mach. **7**, 216.

MARTIN T. B. et al. (1964) *Speech recognition by feature-abstraction techniques*, Tech. Doc. Rep. No. AL TDR, 64, AF Avionics Lab., Wright-Patterson AF Base.

MATULA M. (1965) *Zur Frage der Häufigkeitsverteilung der Worte*, I, Comment. Math. Univ. Carolinae, **6**, 213.

MEETHAM A. R. (1964) *Probabilistic pairs and groups of words in a text*, Language and Speech, **7**, 98.

MILLER G. A. (1951) *Speech and language*, in Handbook of experimental psychology (Ed. S. S. Stevens) 789, New York: Wiley.

MILNER P. M. (1957) *The cell assembly: Mark II*, Psychol. Rev. **64**, 242.

MORAN P. A. P. (1947/53) *The random division of an interval*, J. Roy. Statist. Soc. Supplt. **9** (1947), 92; ser. B, **13**, 141; **15**, 77.

MORTON A. Q. (1965) *The authorship of the Pauline epistles: a scientific approach*, J. Roy. Statist. Soc. A, **128**, 169.

MOSTELLER F. and WALLACE D. (1963) *Inference in an authorship problem*, J. Am. Statist. Ass., **58**, 275.

NAPIER T. (1617) *Rabdologiæ, seu Numerationis per*

*Virgulas, Libri duo: Cum Appendice de expeditissimo Multiplicationis promptuario*, Edinburgh: Hart.

NEEDHAM R. M. (1963) *A method of using computers in information classification*, in *Information Processing, 1962* (Ed. C. Popplewell), 284, Amsterdam: North-Holland.

PATNAIK P. B. (1949) *The non-central $\chi^2$ and F- distributions*, Biometrika **36**, 202, esp. p. 217.

PRATT F. (1939) *Secret and Urgent: the Story of Codes and Ciphers*, Indianapolis.

RIDER P. R. (1965) *The zeta distribution*, in *Classical and Contagious Discrete Distributions* (Ed. G. P. Patil), 443, Oxford: Pergamon Press.

ROBERTS A. H. (1965) *A Statistical Linguistic Analysis of American English*, London, The Hague, Paris: Mouton.

Ross A. S. C. (1950) *Philological probability problems*, J. Roy. Statist. Soc. B, **12**, 19 (with discussion).

SACCHO L. (1951) *Manuel de cryptographie* (French Edn by J. Bres, from the Italian), Paris: Payot.

SÄRNDAL C. E. (1967) *On deciding cases of disputed authorship*, Appl. Statist. (to be published).

SHANNON C. E. (1951) *Prediction and entropy of printed English*, Bell Syst. Tech. J., **30**, 50.

SHANNON C. E. and WEAVER W. (1949) *The Mathematical Theory of Communication*, Urbana: University of Illinois.

SHEPHARD R. N. (1962) *The analysis of proximities. multidimensional scaling with an unknown distance function*, Psychometrika **27**, 125 and 219.

SHERMAN L. A. (1893) *Analysis of Literature*, Boston.

SINKOV A. (1940) *Cryptography and Cryptanalysis*, (Chapter XIV of *Mathematical recreations and essays*, by W. W. Rouse Ball and H. S. M. Coxeter), London: Macmillan.

SMITH F. W. (1960) *Teletypewriter*, in *McGraw-Hill Enc. of Sc. and Tech.* **13**, 453.

SMITH L. D. (1943/55) *Cryptography: the Science of Secret Writing*, New York: Dover.

SOKAL R. R. and SNEATH P. H. A. (1963) *Numerical Taxonomy*, London: Freeman.

STUMPERS F. L. H. M. (1953/60) *A bibliography of information theory (Communication theory—Cybernetics)*, I.R.E. Trans. Information Theory, PGIT-2 (November, 1953); IT-1, 31; IT-3, 150; IT-6, 25.

THORNDIKE E. L. and LORGE I. (1944) *The Teacher's Word Book of 30,000 Words*, New York: Columbia University.

WAKE W. C. (1957) *Sentence-length distributions of Greek authors*, J. Royal Statist. Soc. **120**, 331.

WELCH B. L. (1939) *Note on discriminant functions*, Biometrika, **31**, 218.

WHITTLE P. and WOLD H. O. A. (1957) *A model explaining the Pareto distribution of wealth*, Econometrica J. of Econ. Soc. **25**, 591.

WHITWORTH W. A. (1901) *Choice and Chance*, Cambridge: Deighton and Bell.

WILKS S. S. (1938) *The large-sample distribution of the likelihood-ratio for testing composite hypotheses*, Annals Math. Statist. **9**, 60.

WILKS S. S. (1962) *Mathematical Statistics*, New York: Wiley.

WILLIAMS C. B. (1939/40) *A note on the statistical analysis of sentence length as a criterion of literary style*, Biometrika **31**, 356.

WILLIAMS C. B. (1944) *Some applications of the logarithmic series and the index of diversity to ecological problems*, J. ecol. **32**, 1.

WILLIAMS C. B. (1946) *Yule's 'Characteristic' and the 'Index of diversity'*, Nature, **157**, 482.

WILLIS J. C. (1922) *Age and Area*, Cambridge: The University Press.

WIREN J. and STUBBS H. L. (1956) *Electronic binary selection system for phoneme classification*, J. Acoust. Soc. Am. **28**, 1082.

WOODGER M. (1960) *An introduction to Algol 60*, Computer J. **3**, 67.

YULE G. U. (1938) *On sentence-length as a statistical characteristic of style in prose: with application to two cases of disputed authorship*, Biometrika **30**, 363.

YULE G. U. (1944) *The Statistical Study of Literary Vocabulary*, Cambridge: The University Press.

ZACHRISSON B. (1965) *Studies in the Legibility of Printed Text*, Stockholm: Almqvist and Wiksell.

ZIPF G. K. (1929) *Relative frequency as a determinant of phonetic change*, in *Harvard Studies in Classical Philology*, **40**, 1.

ZIPF G. K. (1932) *Selected Studies of the Principle of Relative Frequency in Language*, Cambridge, Mass.

ZIPF G. K. (1949) *Human Behaviour and the Principle of Least Effort*, Cambridge, Mass.: Addison-Wesley.

I. J. GOOD

**STATISTICS OF LANGUAGE: STRUCTURE OF WRITTEN ENGLISH WORDS.** We define a *written English word* (or simply *word*) to be a punctuation-free lexed entry in any one of the standard American or British dictionaries of English words, or the written inflected form of such an entry, said words considered as an abstract concatenation of letter symbols. (This definition excludes abbreviations and contractions. One of the problems of the field is the substitution of a descriptive definition of *word* in place of the above taxonomic definition (cf. Chomsky 1964).) The *interword space*, or *blank*, is denoted ♯. It is convenient to assume that each word is preceded and followed by an occurrence of ♯. The letter *e* in the contexts *e* ♯, *es* ♯ is called a *final e*, denoted *e*, and is defined to be a *consonant*. All other occurrences of *e* are defined as *vowels*, as are the letters *a, i, o, u, y* in any context. The remaining letters of the alphabet are defined as *consonants*. The *blank consonant*, Ø, is a symbol adjoined to the set of consonants as a marker to permit formal simplifications.

A concatenation of consonants is called a *consonant string* and a concatenation of vowels is called a *vowel string*. With these conventions, every word can be written in the form $w^n = C_1 V_1 C_2 \ldots C_n V_n C_{n+1}$ where the $C$ are consonant strings and the $V$ vowel strings and where $C_1$ and $C_{n+1}$ may be Ø; $w^n$ is an *n* vowel string word. Thus ate (at) is a one vowel string word by these definitions.

Certain notions having to do with the structure of words can only be defined relative to a fixed word corpus. It will usually turn out that a small number of obsolete, foreign, and incorrect (e.g. misprinted) word forms will appear in any sufficiently large corpus chosen in some natural way. These forms act as a source of noise in investigations of the structure of words in the corpus. In order to provide a uniform and simple method for reducing the effect due to these and other less easily recognized noise sources, a cut-off frequency parameter $v$ is introduced which depends on the corpus and also on the particular structural property under examination and which replaces the corpus by a smaller corpus according to the following scheme: if a given structural property partitions the given corpus then each of the partitioning subsets which contains fewer than $v$ members is removed from the corpus. If the original corpus is denoted by K then the resulting depleted corpus can be denoted $K_v$. In order to describe as much of K as possible it is desirable to choose the least $v$ that will lead to reasonably simple structural characterizations. For given structural properties it is often possible to formalize this procedure by the introduction of standard statistical techniques. For many interesting structures relative to the corpus of lexed words in the Shorter Oxford English Dictionary it is enough to choose $v = 4$. (Cf. Dolby and Resnikoff 1964, 1964a.)

*Structure of consonant and vowel strings.* The foundation of the study of written English words is the investigation of the structure of the one-vowel-string words, $w^1(K) = \{C_1VC_2 \text{ in } K\}$. If the corpus K is sufficiently large, then the lists of initial consonant strings and final consonant strings of words in $w^1(K)$ are relatively stable with respect to considerable variation in the size of K and to small changes in $v$. For example, there is one word *(fnese)* with $C_1 = fn$ in The Shorter Oxford Dictionary, but only two such *(fnese* and *fnast)* in the corpus of lexed words in the *Merriam-Webster New International Dictionary*, 2nd edition (1924), which has more than three times as many words. This stability permits the definition of structural initial and final consonant strings of English without regard to a particular cut-off parameter and corpus, by examination of the consonant strings obtained from a lattice of corpora ordered by inclusion. In such a manner the original taxonomic information appears in a form amenable to the inductive step whose object is a descriptive definition.

The vowel string $V$ of one-vowel-string words in an arbitrary corpus has a more complex structure because its properties depend on the presence of a final $e$. Let $x_4$ be the corpus of lexed words in The Shorter Oxford Dictionary with $v = 4$. If $V$ is fixed and $w^1(x_4)$ is partitioned according to the presence or absence of $e$ as a function of $v$, denote the number of words in $w^1(x_4)$ with by $\varrho_+(V)$, the number without $e$ by $\varrho_-(V)$, and put $\varrho(V) = \varrho_+(V)^2 + \varrho_-(V)^2$. Then, after some technical adjustments concerning $y$ in word initial position and the cumulative effects of the application of the various cut-off parameters, a statistically significant gap appears between $\varrho(ey) = 509$ and $\varrho(ay) = 1697$, i.e. $\varrho(V) \leq 509$ or $\varrho(V) \geq 1697$ for all vowel strings $V$. If v denotes the set of $V$ such that $\varrho(V) \geq 1697$, then

(1) the vowels, $a, e, i, o, u, y$ belong to v;
(2) no vowel string with more than two letters belongs to v;
(3) if $V'V''$ is a string of two distinct vowels but not *ei* or *ie*, and if $V'V''$ belongs to v, then $V''V'$ does *not* belong to v. Furthermore, $\varrho(ei) = 1700$ and $\varrho(ie) = 2036$; these traditionally troublesome vowel pairs lie close to each other.
(4) in a standard dialect, indicated e.g. by dictionary phonemic representations, those $V'V''$ in v are one syllable vowel strings, whereas those (in words in $x_4$) not in v are two syllable vowel strings.

Examples of this asymmetry of vowel pairs are: *straight/giant, fraught/dual, coin/pion*. The elements of v are called *admissible* vowel strings.

If B (respectively E) denotes the set of initial (respectively final) non-blank consonant strings for words in $w^1(x_4)$, then the $C_2$ string in the two-vowel-string words $w^2(x) = \{C_1C_2VC_3 \text{ in } x\}$ can be *decomposed* in at least one way as $C_2 = C_2'C_2''$ with $C_2' \varepsilon E \cup \{\emptyset\}$ and $C_2'' \varepsilon B \cup \{\emptyset\}$, with only the exceptions $C_2 \varepsilon \{nct, vr, vv\}$. There are structural reasons for these exceptions: an elided $e$ from the strings *nce, ve* in the first two cases, and a consonantal doubling process having to do with the spelling of inflected forms (cf. *infra*), but application of the cut-off parameter $v = 4$ relative to this partition of internal $C$ strings will replace $w^2(x)$ by $w^2(x_4)$, and every internal $C$ string in the latter set has at least one decomposition of the form described. A similar result holds for each internal $C$ string in an $n$ vowel string word. It follows that an $n$ vowel string word $W$ (in some appropriate $K_v$) can be written as a concatenation $W = W_1W_2\ldots W_n$ where each $W_i$ is a string of the form $C_1VC_2$ with $C_1 \varepsilon B \cup \{\emptyset\}$, $C_2 \varepsilon E \cup \{\emptyset\}$, and $V \varepsilon v$. The $w_i$ are not necessarily in $w^1(x_4)$ or any other corpus, e.g. $W_2 = ceive$ for $W = receive$ leads to a decomposition of the type described, but *ceive* is not a word. It is possible that the decomposition of $W$ is not uniquely determined, e.g. $re\emptyset - place$ and $rep - lace$ for *replace*. However, unique decompositions are of special importance, cf. *infra*.

*Identification of affixes.* The decomposition of internal consonant strings described above suggests a simple formal definition for one-vowel-string affixes contained in two vowel string words (Resnikoff and Dolby 1965). Let $P$ be a fixed letter string and let $\text{CLS}(P/C'')$ denote the subset of $w^2(x_4) = \{C_1VC_2VC_3 \text{ in } x_4\}$ such that $PC'' = C_1VC_2$. Say that $\text{CLS}(P/C'')$ is *admissible* if it contains more than three words. Then $P$ is a *prefix* relative to $w^2(x_4)$ if there are at least two admissible classes of the form $\text{CLS}(P/C'')$ such that $C'' \varepsilon B$, and, if $C' \neq \emptyset$, such that $C' - C''$ is the unique decomposition of the string $C'C''$, while if $C' = \emptyset$, such that $C'' \varepsilon E$.

There is a similar definition for a *suffix*. The set union of the collection of prefixes and suffixes is the set of *affixes*. Affixes can be defined relative to collections of $n$ vowel string words in a similar way; indeed, multi-vowel string affixes can be defined only with respect to collections of words with more than two vowel strings. Note that the inflectional *-s* and the *-le*, which do not contain vowels, can be found in the one vowel string words.

There are certain letter strings which intuition suggests are primarily attached to suffixes of the form *VC* with *C* a one letter string. An example is *-ist*. These cannot possibly be obtained from the definition given above but are given by an analogous definition which specifies that the string being defined be preceded by a suffix in the above sense.

An examination of $w^2(x_4)$ or any other comprehensive corpus shows that there are more than three words of the form $aC'C''C'''VC$ with $C' = C''$ (and $C'''$ possibly blank) if $C' \varepsilon \{b, c, d, f, g, l, n, p, r, s, t\}$, although only *ac-*, *ad-*, and *al-* are prefixes in the sense of the above definition. This, together with the fact that $C'C''$ B if $C' = C''$, suggests a finer description of the initial *a-* prefixes: there are three of them, *a-*, *ad-* (whose existence is assured by the previous arguments without use of the *add-* sequence), and *a( )-*, the latter being a *transformational* prefix defined by the property that

$$a(\ )C' = aC'C', \text{ unless } C'\varepsilon\{k, q\};$$

$$a(\ )k = ack \text{ and } a(\ )q = acq.$$

Thus the representations: *acclaim*↔*a( )-claim*, *affix*↔*a( )-fix*, *appear*↔*a( )-pear*, *attack*↔*a( )-tack*, etc., while *achieve* is an instance of *a- chieve*, not of * *ac-heive*, and *alike* an instance of *a-like*, not of * *al-ike*. The introduction of the transformational prefix results in a description of the data which is both more comprehensive and more error free. Similar arguments apply for the prefixes *en-*, *in-*, *un-*.

An analogous process occurs for certain uffixes. Perhaps the best known instance is the doubling of the final consonant in the gerund and participial forms of certain verbs *(vide infra)*.

It is important to distinguish the problem of determining those letter strings which *can* function as affixes, as discussed above, from the very different problem of deciding whether a letter string that *can* function as an affix *is* so functioning in a particular word. This is of special importance when a word contains both a prefix and a suffix. For example, *reading* contains the prefix *re-* and the suffix *-ing*. It must be understood that the question refers only to *structural* affixes, defined as above or by other formal means, and that the verbal term *function* is meant in a structural sense, rather than in an etymological sense. The latter point of view can lead to the assignment of roles to the various letter strings different from those obtained by structural methods, which is a reflection of the different nature of the problems considered in etymological studies (see for example Bloomfield 1933).

There is a simple algorithm which works well although it is not perfect. Let $W = PLS$ be a word containing more than one admissible vowel string, with $P$ a prefix or Ø and $S$ a suffix or Ø, and $L$ the remaining string of letters. $P - LS$ and $PL - S$ are the prefixed and suffixed decompositions associated with $W$. Put $\pi(W)$ (respectively $\sigma(W)$) = the number of admissible vowel strings in $LS$ (respectively $PL$). Then $P$ is a prefix in the context $W$ if $\pi(W) \leq \sigma(W)$ and $L$ begins with Ø or with a $C\varepsilon$B; $S$ is a *suffix in the context W* if $\pi(W) > \sigma(W)$ and $L$ ends with Ø or with a $C\varepsilon$E. For example, $W$ = reading; $P = re, L = ad, S = ing.$ $2 = \pi(W) > \sigma(W) = 1$, since *ea* is admissible. Then *-ing* is a suffix in the context *reading*. The algorithm cannot be iteratively applied to the subsequence *read* because it has just one admissible vowel string. An example for which this technique contradicts intuition is *deadeye*; in general, there are serious problems with compound words.

*Allocation of words to parts of speech*. It has always been known that certain suffixes determine the parts-of-speech class of words they terminate. This is a special case of the more general phenomenon of the determination of the parts of speech class of a word by the structural features of the word. Denote by w the set of words in $w^1(x_4)$ which have an admissible vowel string. A word in w is *standard* if it has no functional status designation in the dictionary sources, and is *dialectal* if it has either the status designation *dialectal* or *local*. It is *Thorndike-Lorge* if it appears in Parts I or II of Thorndike and Lorge (1944). The table describes some properties of the parts of speech of words in w. The fourth column gives the rounded products of the entries in the first two columns.

*Percentage of words allocated by rule which are allocated likewise by lexicographer.*

| w | Noun or Adjective | Verb | (Noun or Adj) and (Verb) | x |
|---|---|---|---|---|
| w | 95.2% | 80.0% | 76.0% | 76.2% |
| Standard and Dialectal | 96.3 | 85.4 | 82.2 | 82.2 |
| Standard | 96.9 | 86.2 | 84.2 | 83.5 |
| Thorndike-Lorge | 98.2 | 91.8 | 90.2 | 90.1 |

From the hypothesis that all words in w have *((Noun or Adjective) and Verb)* as their part of speech class, the above percentages can be interpreted as leading to estimates of the probability that lexicographers will find and list the parts of speech if they are multiplied by the text frequency of usage of the word. If these probabilities were independent, the percentages given in the third column should be the same as those in the fourth column, the product of the numbers in the first two columns. There is evidently a remarkable agreement, which supports the hypothesis in a striking way. Further, it is not true that almost all words belong to the parts of speech class *((Noun* or *Adjective)* and *Verb)*; only about 14 per cent of the words in x are so classified and a large fraction of these already belong to w.

*Progress and applications.* Even the limited knowledge of the structure of words that is available today is sufficient for many applications to both theoretical questions and practical problems. Among these are the nature of the relation between written and spoken forms and the description of certain aspects of English grammar. The application of word structure to the study of book indexes, abstracts and the formal synthesis of dictionary definitions are areas currently under cultivation and there is every reason to hope that the automatic construction of satisfactory back of the book indexes will be achieved by the end of the current decade. Other areas where progress has been made are:

*Inflection of verbs:* Apart from the *inflection* of the irregular verbs, the occasional doubling of the final consonant in the gerund and participial forms of verbs ending with a single vowel followed by a single consonant is the greatest single problem, e.g. *stop → stopping, stopped, deter → deterring, deterred,* but *water → watering, watered.* The algorithm: *double the final consonant unless there is a suffix in context* is highly accurate and can be effectively implemented in terms of the methods already described. Comparison with the well known phonemic stress pattern rule leads to a partial determination of the stress pattern from graphemic structural information.

*Syllable count:* The number of *syllables* in a word is closely approximated by the number of admissible vowel strings in the word. A much more accurate estimate of the number of phonemic syllables as a function of the number of admissible vowel strings results from a study of the role of affixes and compounding elements. Internal instances of *e* which act as if they were *e* e.g. in *houseboat,* are of special importance. When restricted to standard words in x, an error rate of the order of 3 per cent is compatible with a simple algorithm.

*Hyphenation:* It is likely that the hyphenation problem is the first linguistic problem whose solution has had a direct practical impact on industry. For applications to composition the critical fact is that the need to right-justify lines of printed matter by hyphenation is subordinate to justification by interword spacing. Consequently an accurate hyphenation algorithm that will fail to provide a relatively large proportion of the possible hyphenation positions can still lead to tighter and more accurate line composition than is normally produced by trained compositors. An elementary algorithm will provide 50 per cent of the possible hyphenations with a text frequency error rate less than 1 per cent. Increasing the proportion of hyphenations obtained must be done at the expense of accuracy or of the implementing equipment, or both, although it is possible to maintain error rates of less than 2 per cent and obtain more than 75 per cent of the possible hyphenations using a reasonably compact algorithm. The resulting performance is better than that of human compositors. The major techniques needed are those which give access to the structure of the one syllable words and affixes.

*See also:* Writing.

*Bibliography*

BLOCH B. (1946) *English verb inflection, Language,* **22.**
BLOOMFIELD L. (1933) *Language,* New York.
CHOMSKY N. (1964) *Current Issues in Linguistic Theory,* 's-Gravenhage.
CHOMSKY N. (1957) *Syntactic Structures,* 's-Gravenhage.
DOLBY J. L. and RESNIKOFF H. L. (1964) *On the structure of written English words, Language,* **40.**
DOLBY J. L. and RESNIKOFF H. L. (1964a) *The English word speculum,* Sunnyvale.
RESNIKOFF H. L. and DOLBY J. L. (1965) *The nature of affixing in written English, Mech. Trans.,* **8.**
THORNDIKE E. L. and LORGE I. (1944) *The teacher's word book of 30,000 words,* New York.

J. L. DOLBY and H. L. RESNIKOFF

**SUBSCRIBER'S TELEPHONE SET, DESIGN CONSIDERATIONS OF.** *1. Introduction.* Most of the problems encountered in the design of subscribers' telephone apparatus arise from two basic causes. The first is that the attenuation in the connexion between two subscribers may vary over an enormous range, from virtually zero on a short connexion to a maximum of about 40 dB on a long connexion via a number of switching points. The designer's problem, therefore, is to achieve sufficient sensitivity for the worst connexion, without making reception excessively loud on short connexions. There are sound practical objections to giving the subscriber any form of manually operated volume control (for example, because of the enhanced risk of crosstalk if it is incorrectly used), and any control introduced must be automatic in operation.

The second difficulty arises because the local line, for economic reasons, consists only of two wires and not of four, and this pair of wires has to be shared by both the incoming and the outgoing signals. In the simplest form of telephone set, the transmitter and receiver might be connected in parallel to the line, and such an arrangement is in fact reasonably satisfactory in telephone sets of low sensitivity intended only for use on short connexions. The speech power output of the transmitter is then dissipated equally in the near-end receiver, the distant-end receiver, and the distant-end transmitter, (assuming these to be of roughly equal impedance). There is no control of sidetone, and the talker hears his own voice in his receiver at the same level as he hears his respondent. Over longer connexions, however, conditions are much less satisfactory. If the receiver sensitivity is high enough to hear the distant-end over (say) a 40 dB connexion, then the sidetone (being 40 dB louder than this) will be excessive, and the telephone set will be unpleasant to use.

Sidetone can be controlled by the conventional *hybrid-transformer* arrangement, using a balancing network of

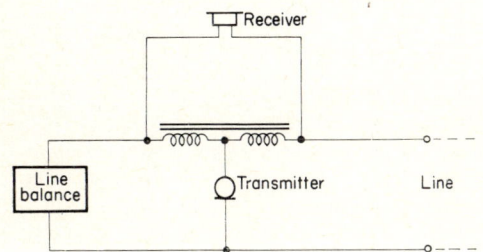

FIG. 1. *Simplified anti-sidetone telephone circuit.*

the same electrical impedance as the line, as shown in simplified form in Fig. 1. On sending, the transmitter power is dissipated equally in the line and in the balance, but not in the receiver; and on receiving, the power from the distant end is dissipated in the receiver and the transmitter but not in the balance (Spencer 1956). Figure 2 shows in more practical form the basic transmission circuit of an actual telephone set (the B.P.O. 300-type) but with the dial and switch-hook contacts omitted for simplicity. The blocking capacitor C is necessary to ensure that the whole of the d.c. line current flows

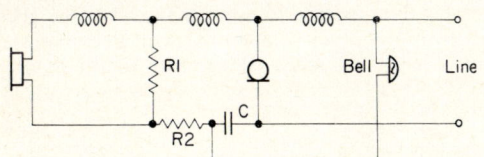

FIG. 2. *Basic transmission circuit of 300-type telephone.*

through the carbon transmitter and that none is wasted in the balance or in the receiver. The impedance of the bell to speech frequencies is so high that its presence may be ignored. The line balance is made up of components R1, R2 and C, of which resistor R2 forms part of the dial spark quench circuit.

However, as will be seen, the designer's problem is to decide exactly what the electrical impedance of the balance network shall be, since the impedance of the line as seen from telephone set can vary over a wide range according to the length of the local line and to what is connected to it through the local exchange.

*2. Standard of transmission.* An essential requirement in the planning of a national telephone network is that the transmission loss between any two subscribers in the network shall always be within limits such that a reasonable minimum standard of communication is maintained. In the British Post Office telephone system this minimum standard corresponds in sensitivity (assessed by loudness against a high-quality reference system) to 6 dB loss introduced into a one-metre air path; in this context a one-metre air path implies monaural listening to a talker at a distance of one metre in echo-free surroundings. The evolution of this transmission standard has been discussed elsewhere in some detail (Swaffield and Richards 1958). It will suffice to say that it was defined physically some thirty years ago by a telephone connexion, each end of which consisted of a Telephone No. 162 connected by 2·56 miles of local line of 10 lb/mile cable (of 450 ohms loop resistance) to a 50-volt non-ballast exchange bridge, with a 27 dB attenuator, representing losses in junctions and trunks, including switching and mismatch losses, inserted between the two bridges. In more recent years other combinations of telephone set, local line and feeding bridge have been rated to find the limiting local lines which give the same performance as the standard. For example, with the type-300 telephone the permitted line limit became 660 ohms of $6\frac{1}{2}$ lb cable for 50-volt non-ballast exchanges, and with the type-700 telephone, which is substantially more sensitive than the type-300 both on sending and receiving, the line limit has become 1000 ohms or $6\frac{1}{2}$ lb cable.

*3. Transmission assessments.* When a new or improved telephone set is introduced, its transmission performance must be assessed in order to determine the length of local line over which it will give the same minimum performance as the standard. This is done in the British Post Office System by two-way conversational tests in which the proposed new local telephone circuit is compared with the standard circuit. In one form of test, the pairs of subjects are asked to solve pictorial puzzles over the telephone circuit as a means of stimulating a balanced conversation, and on completion they are asked to indicate in which of the categories 'excellent', 'good', 'fair', 'poor', 'bad' the call should be placed. The tests are made in the presence of average ambient noise (weighted, at 50 dB above the threshold of audibility), and with a non-reactive attenuator (representing the transmission loss of the trunks and junctions) inserted between the two local telephone circuits. By allocating scores of 4, 3, 2, 1, 0 respectively to these categories the performance, in terms of the mean opinion score from a large number of subjects, is obtained over a wide range of attenuator settings for both the pair of telephones under test and the pair of standards. By interpolation the setting to give a transmission performance equal to standard can be obtained. (It is of interest to note that a connexion with standard local circuits at each end and an attenuator setting of 19 dB corresponds to approximately 90 per cent of subjects expressing opinions of fair or better than fair.)

The number of comparisons required between the new

telephone and the standard for the assembly of local-line-planning data is in fact so great that they cannot all be made by time-consuming conversational-opinion testing methods. The effects of changes in the line, transmission bridge or transmitter feeding current can be estimated sufficiently well by means of subjective loudness tests or objective measurements. Of the former the loudness balancing tests used by the CCITT for specifying the sensitivity of local telephone circuits for international telephony (Williams 1964) is one example. The ratings are here expressed relative to a high quality reference system and are termed reference equivalents. Objective measurements include pure tone tests where, in the case of smoothly varying changes in sensitivity/frequency characteristics such as changes due to different line conditions with unloaded cables, the speech-transmission loss is substantially equivalent to the arithmetic mean of the pure tone loss at 500, 1000, 2000 and 3000 c/s. Alternatively speech stimulus, reproduced from magnetic tape recordings, may be used, and the speech-transmission loss derived from a single measurement of speech voltage. With these two objective methods, allowance must also be made for the feeding current effect—the effect that the magnitude of the line current has on the output of the carbon transmitter, and on any regulator provided in the telephone.

*4. Need for regulation of sensitivity in modern high-efficiency telephone sets.* When two subscribers, each having very short lines to the same exchange, are connected together, the overall sensitivity of the connexion can be as much as 40 dB more than the minimum permissible. The possible range of sensitivity is illustrated in Fig. 3 together with some data on subjects' sensitivity preferences. These data, which are based on

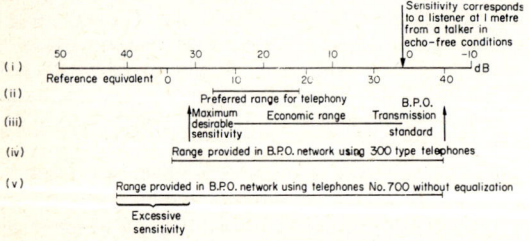

FIG. 3. *Telephone sensitivity ranges.*

experiments carried out at the Post Office Engineering Research Station, show quite good agreement with earlier work in Germany (Strecker and Von Susani). With the British Post Office type-300 set the maximum desirable sensitivity of about 31 dB relative to a metre air path is already exceeded by some 2 dB, and any further increase in sensitivity would be an embarrassment on short connexions. However, the need existed for a telephone set of higher efficiency, to enable longer (or lighter-gauge) subscribers' lines to be used without degradation of performance, and the target set by the requirements of the network was for a local line limit equivalent to 1000 ohms of $6\frac{1}{2}$ lb cable.

This target has been met in the B.P.O. type-700 set (first introduced in 1959), the enhanced performance being obtained by the use of a new receiver of rocking-armature design (Roberton 1956), employing modern

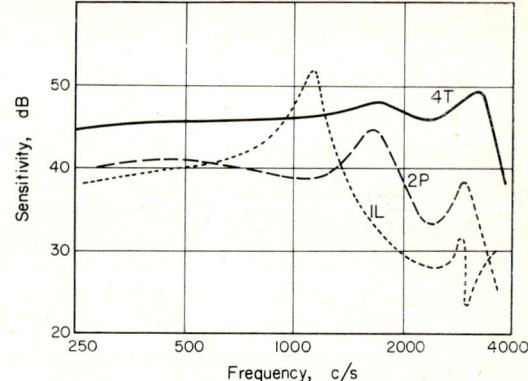

FIG. 4. *Sensitivity of British P.O. receiver insets 1L, 2P and 4T in decibels relative to 1 dyne/cm² per √(mW) available power.*

magnetic materials and embodying acoustic equalization; by the introduction of a new carbon transmitter (the Transmitter Inset No. 16); and by the use of a more efficient closed-core transformer in the anti-sidetone circuit (Spencer and Wilson 1956). Figure 4 shows the sensitivity/frequency response of the rocking-armature receiver type 4T, compared with earlier receivers types 2P and 1L. Figure 5 and 6 show the construction of the carbon-granule transmitter inset No. 16, and its sensitivity/frequency response. As with all carbon transmitters it exhibits some falling-off in sensitivity at low

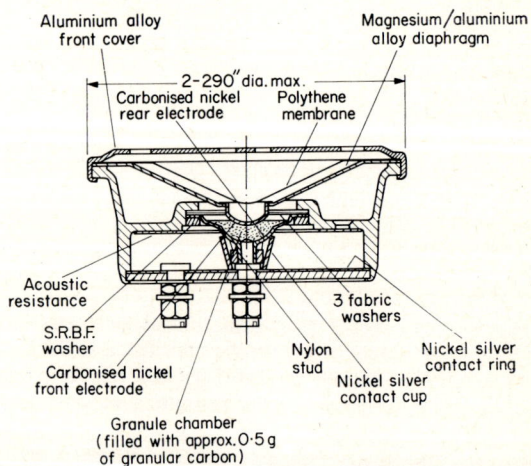

FIG. 5. *Carbon granule transmitter inset (G.P.O. No. 16).*

sound pressures, but this 'amplitude distortion' is much less marked than in earlier designs of transmitter.

With telephone sets of this sensitivity the received level on a short connexion would, if uncontrolled, be as much as 10 dB greater than that generally acceptable, the line current is increased, the loss is inserted progressively (by providing a.c. shunt paths across the transmitter and receiver) and on a zero line, with a line current of 90–100 mA, the loss inserted amounts to 6 dB on sending and 4 dB on receiving.

Figure 7 shows the complete transmission circuit of the type-700 set, with the regulator enclosed for clarity within a chain-dotted rectangle. Basically the regulator is a variable-loss network, of low d.c. resistance, inserted in series with the transmitter, with connexions to two other points (P1 and P2) in the transmission circuit. The variable elements consist of small selenium rectifiers, the resistance of which in the forward direction falls rapidly when a voltage is applied. The control voltage is derived from resistor R1 which consists actually of a small tungsten-filament lamp, advantage being taken of its sharply-rising resistance/current characteristic to obtain a greatly-increased voltage for biasing the rectifiers on a short line.

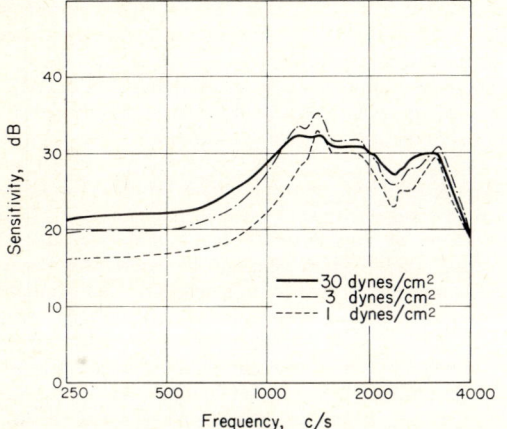

FIG. 6. *Sensitivity of British P.O. transmitter inset No. 16 in handset, in decibels relative to 1 mV/dyne/cm² across matched load.*

and the type-700 set therefore contains a sensitivity regulator which automatically reduces the sensitivity in both the sending and the receiving directions when the set is used on a short line (Williams and Wilson 1959). This it does by sensing the magnitude of the d.c. line current. Thus, if the line current is less than about 50 mA (corresponding to a line resistance of about 500 ohms) the regulator is inoperative and no loss is imposed. As

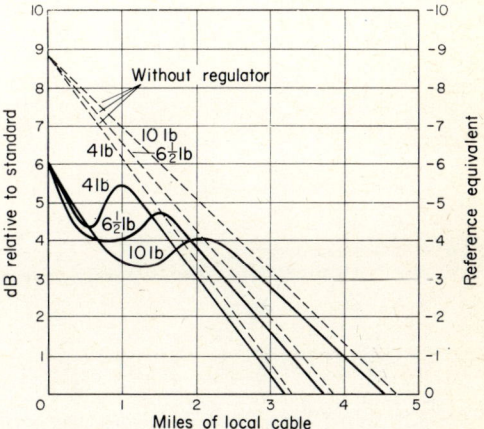

FIG. 8. *Sending performance of 700-type telephone (broken lines show effect of disconnecting regulator).*

Figures 8 and 9 show the sending and receiving ratings of the type-700 telephone expressed in terms of decibels relative to the values for the standard reference circuit, which consists of 3·7 miles of 6½ cable (of loop resistance 1000 ohms). The effect of the regulator in limiting the sensitivity on short lines is clearly evident. Typical transmission planning limits for this telephone set, for a 50 volt, 200+200 ohm relay, transmission bridge for the three conductor gauges in common use are as follows:

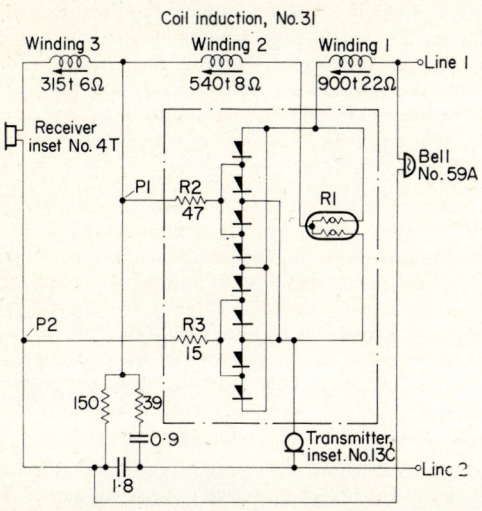

FIG. 7. *Transmission circuit of telephone No. 706.*

| Cable lb/mile | Miles | Loop Resistance |
|---|---|---|
| 4 | 2·8 | 1250 ohms |
| 6½ | 3·7 | 1000 ohms |
| 10 | 4·7 | 830 ohms |

## 5. Impedance matching and the reduction of sidetone.

As mentioned briefly in section 1, the complete control of sidetone by a hybrid circuit employing a line-impe-

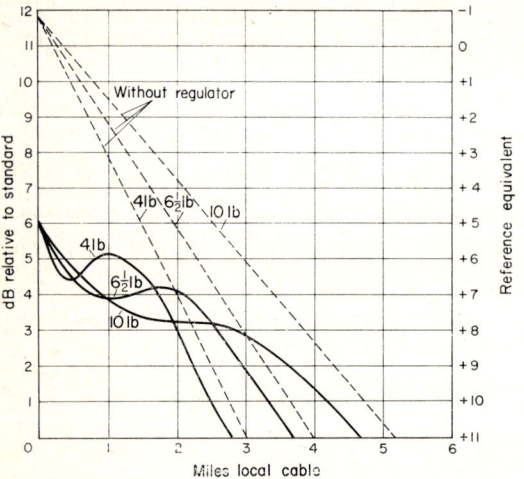

FIG. 9. *Receiving performance of 700-type telephone.*

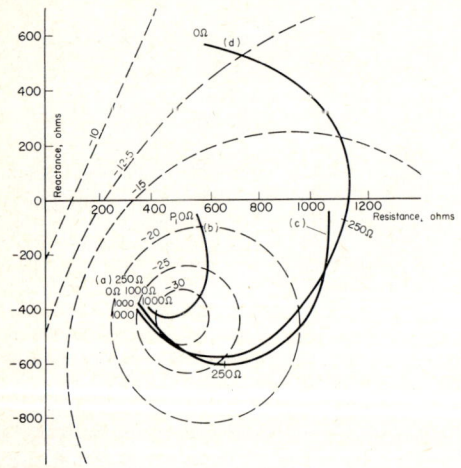

FIG. 10. *Impedance at line terminals of a subscriber's set (at 2000 c/s). With a Stone-type transmission bridge and subscriber's line of $6\frac{1}{2}$ lb/mile cable connected to (a) unloaded junction, (b) amplified junction, (c) loaded junction, and (d) local call to 300-type telephone on zero line. The figures on circles represent sidetone attenuation in decibels relative to the p.d. across a 200-ohm receiver when the transmitter e.m.f. is 1 volt.*

dance balance network requires a precise knowledge of the line impedance, and this is in itself a variable quantity depending upon the length and routing of the connexion. Figure 10 illustrates typical variations of impedance with the line conditions.

The type-700 circuit was designed for the best electrical sidetone attenuation possible on the longer lines using a conventional telephone transmission circuit. A study of Fig. 10 reveals that this necessitates somewhat higher sidetone levels on the short lines. This figure shows, in full line, the curves of impedance expressed as $R$ and $X$ 'seen' from the line terminals of a subscriber's installation looking towards the exchange, for local calls (d), and for several classes of junction circuit, (a), (b) and (c) outgoing from the exchange with typical subscribers' cables of $6\frac{1}{2}$ lb/mile conductor weight, varying from 0 to 1000 ohms resistance (0–3·7 miles). The values shown are for one type of exchange transmission bridge (Stone) and at one frequency only, and are indicative of the large range of impedances to be catered for insidetone balancing. The constant-sidetone circles show the sidetone attenuation of an experimental 700-type circuit for a balance point at $510-j430$ ohms. A change of balance circuit so that the point occurred say, at $P_1$ would result in an electrical sidetone performance more constant with line length, but would give a worse performance on the longer lines. The way out of the dilemma was to balance as shown, and to provide additional sidetone attenuation on the shorter lines by means of the sensitivity regulator.

Ideally, in order to avoid reflection losses, the electrical impedance of the telephone set should match that of the line, but here again the difficulty arises of deciding just what is that impedance. If the local line is long, its impedance will approach that of the characteristic impedance of the cable, and this probably represents the best impedance to choose for matching the set. However, in the telephone sets currently in use no attempt has been made to provide such matching, and the main design consideration has been to secure the best power transfer to the line; reflections have been ignored. With the growth of world-wide communications the possibility of a reflected signal from the distant end, with a substantial transmission delay, becomes more serious, and designers are now paying attention to the desirability of making the impedance of the set resemble more closely that of the line.

In present telephone sets, the received power is dissipated in the receiver (which is highly inductive), the transformer, and the transmitter (which is resistive), and it is not surprising therefore to find that the impedance of the set as a whole has a large positive angle. For example, the impedance of the type-700 telephone, with the regulator out of action, is of the order of $750+j100$ ohms at 2000 c/s. The effect of the regulator on short lines is to provide a resistive shunt, bringing the impedance down to $200+j100$ ohms on a zero line.

The line-matching desideratum requires that the impedance of the line should have a negative angle. The characteristic impedance of typical gauges of cable used in local lines is as follows:

| Conductor weight lb/mile | Characteristic impedance at 1600 c/s |
|---|---|
| 4 | 750 ohms, $-45°$ |
| $6\frac{1}{2}$ | 600 ohms, $-44°$ |
| 10 | 480 ohms, $-43°$ |
| 20 | 350 ohms, $-42°$ |

It is probable that the impedance required to match the local line cannot be realized in telephone sets of present-day design without incurring the penalty of reduced transmission performance. It may, however, well prove practicable in future sets embodying semiconductor devices. Such sets have already been designed experimentally, but have not yet been fully tried in the field.

6. *Applications of voice-operated switching.* The use of semiconductor devices within subscribers' apparatus opens up various possibilities of obtaining improved performance. An obvious application is in the telephone set for the hard-of-hearing (Lowe 1960), employing a 20 dB amplifying stage mounted in the handset and connected in the receiver circuit. However, if the full gain is used while the receiver is not held against the ear, the acoustic output from the receiver which is picked up by the transmitter can be enough to cause the set to 'howl', particularly if the set is being used on a short line and the sidetone is therefore considerable. One way of overcoming this is to provide a further circuit which rectifies the signal output from the transmitter and uses the control voltage thus derived to insert a loss in the receiver path.

With loud-speaking telephone sets this problem becomes more acute. The voice of the distant-end talker issues from the loudspeaker at fair volume, and is picked up, with the addition of room reverberation, by the microphone. Even if the anti-sidetone circuit were efficient enough to avoid 'howling', the distant-end talker would still be disconcerted by the cathedral-like reverberations of his own voice which came back to his receiver. The solution is to provide a highly-developed form of voice-operated switching, in which a loss of (say) 25 dB is shifted from send to receive path according to whether the user is talking or listening. Since there will always be a signal simultaneously in both paths—via the hybrid into the receive path on sending, and via the air path from the loudspeaker to the microphone on receiving—the decision as to whether the set should be switched to sending or receiving has to be made by a comparator, which compares the relative magnitudes of the signals in the two paths.

The change back from 'receive' to 'send' must not take place too quickly on the cessation of the receiver signals, until the room reverberation has died away, or the distant-end talker will receive a disconcerting burst of noise after each of his words. On the other hand, hangover must not be excessive, or the initial speech sounds in to-and-fro conversation will be clipped. The switching may be arranged either so that the set remains switched in one direction until it is caused to change by the next signal, or it may be arranged always to revert to 'receive' in the absence of any sent signal.

It should be noted that *complete* switching from one path to the other, such as might be accomplished by a relay, is very noticeable to the users and makes the set unpleasant to use. It also greatly increases the difficulty of the listener in 'breaking' in while the other end is talking.

Figure 11 shows in block schematic form the British Post Office Loudspeaking Telephone No. 4.

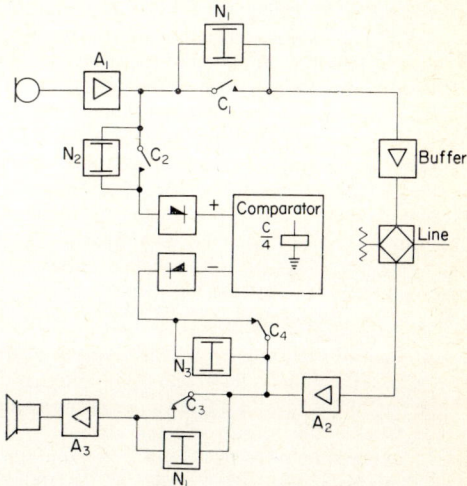

FIG. 11. *Block schematic diagram of loudspeaking telephone set employing voice-operating switching in 'send' and 'receive' paths (B.P.O. loudspeaking telephone No. 4).*

7. *Acknowledgements.* The author gratefully acknowledges the help received from his colleagues in the compilation of this paper, and thanks the Engineer-in-Chief of the British Post Office for permission to make use of the information contained therein.

*See also:* Speech perception.

*Bibliography*

LOWE W. T. (1960) *A New Telephone for Deaf Subscribers—Handset No. 4, P.O. Elect. Engrs. J.* **53**, 24.
ROBERTON J. S. P. (1956) *The Rocking Armature Receiver, P.O. Elect. Engnrs. J.* **49**, 40.
SPENCER H. J. C. (1956) *Some Principles of Anti-Side-Tone Telephone Circuits', P.O. Elect. Engnrs. J,* **48**, 208.
SPENCER H. J. C. and WILSON F. A. (1956) *The New 700-Type Telephone, P.O. Electr. Engnrs. J.* **49**, 69.
STRECKER F. and VON SUSANI G. *Investigations of the most Suitable Range of Reference Equivalent in Tele-*

phone Operating, *Elektrische Nachrichten Technik*, **19**, 241.
SWAFFIELD J. and RICHARDS D. L. (1958) *Rating of Speech Links and Performance of Telephone Networks*, Proc. I.E.E., Paper No. 2666, June **106B**.
WILLIAMS H. (1964) *Overall survey of transmission performance planning*, Proc. I.E.E., **111**.
WILLIAMS F. E. and WILSON F. A. (1959) *Design of an Automatic Sensitivity Control for a new Subscriber's Telephone Set*, Proc. I.E.E., **106 B**, 361.

F. E. WILLIAMS

## SWITCHING AND CONTROL IN TELEPHONY.

*1. Direct dialled switching.* Telephone switching is the process of automatically connecting an inlet to an outlet in a flexible manner. In the simplest concept—direct dialled switching—the selection of the path through the switches to establish a connexion is under the direct control of signals sent from the caller's dial.

There are various types of electromechanical switches: 2-motion, crossbar, uniselector, etc. The first two are the common types. The 2-motion switch has 100 metallic contacts in 10 (vertical) by 10 (horizontal) array. A wiper contact (the inlet), moved by the dialled pulses, makes contact with any one of the 100 switch contacts (the outlets) in one of two modes:

    (a) Stepped vertically by a dialled digit to a particular row of 10 contacts, then searching automatically over the horizontal row for a free outlet in the group to the next switch rank (group selector action),

    or (b) Stepped both vertically and horizontally by dialled digits to a particular contact of the 100 (final selector action).

In the 4-digit, 10,000 line exchange Fig. 1, the incoming subscriber's line is connected to a 1st group selector wiper contact via a concentrator switch. The 1st group selector outlets are trunked to 2nd group selectors, the outlets of which are trunked to final selectors. Each outlet of the final selector group is connected to a subscriber's line. The 1st group selector, stepped by the first dialled digit, defines the 1000th group of called lines. The 2nd group selector, stepped by the second digit, defines the 100th group. The final selector, stepped vertically by the third, and horizontally by the fourth (and final) digit, connects to the particular called line. The system is thus step-by-step.

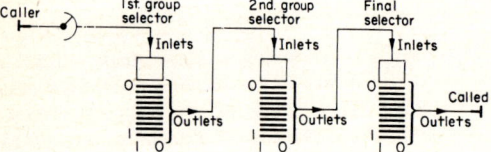

FIG. 1. *Principle of direct dialled switching.*

Due to the single inlet (the wiper contact), a 2-motion switch carries only one call at a time. Exchange switching (or selection) however, requires a number of inlets to have access to a number of outlets. Such a coordinate arrangement is achieved by multiplying the contact banks of a number of switches together. For example, 10 selectors may have their banks multipled together to allow any one of 10 inlets to connect to any one of 100 outlets (Fig. 2).

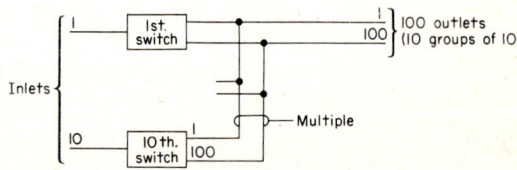

FIG. 2. *2-motion selectors arranged to give access to 100 outlets from any one of 10 inlets.*

A typical crossbar switch has 10 inlets and 10 outlets in array, Fig. 3, giving 100 crosspoint contacts. Each inlet bar has crosspoint access to all the 10 outlet bars and operation of a crosspoint switches an inlet bar to an outlet bar. Thus any one of 10 inlets may have access to 10 outlets and may connect to any one.

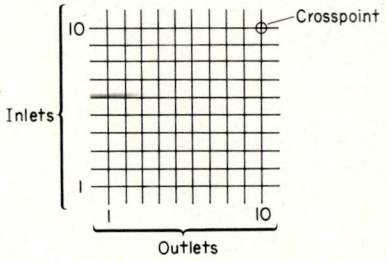

FIG. 3. *Principle of crossbar switch.*

Crossbar switches can be arranged to function in direct dialled mode. As a group selector, the dialled digit marks the particular inlet bar, which can be switched automatically at one of the 10 crosspoints available to it to switch to a free outlet bar of the 10. As a final selector, dialled digits mark a particular inlet and a particular crosspoint, to switch the inlet bar to a particular outlet. More usually however, crossbar switches are used in indirect switching systems.

A 10 by 10 crossbar switch can carry 10 calls at a time, but gives a choice of only 10 different situations. The 10 by 10 2-motion switch, carrying one call at a time, gives a choice of 100 situations. To achieve selection to any one of 100 outlets in crossbar, it is necessary to use another stage of switches in series with the first. This produces a primary-secondary trunking pattern, the secondary stage consisting of 10 switches. Each of the outlets from the primary switch is connected to a different secondary switch, and each secondary switch has 10 outlets (Fig. 4).

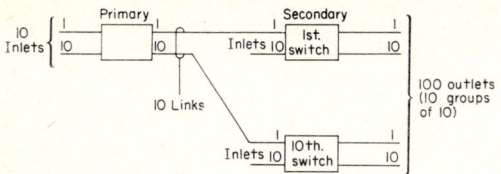

FIG. 4. *Crossbar link network having 10 inlets and 100 outlets.*

2. *Indirect dialled systems.* It is often impracticable to adopt direct dialled switching techniques. Subscriber trunk dialling requires that each subscriber has a unique national number, dialled by all callers regardless of their location in the national network. The national number is made up of an area code plus the subscriber's local number. Incoming traffic to the subscriber is routed over the network in various routings, depending on the location of the caller and the availability of line plant. The fixed area code thus implies that routing should be flexible and divorced from the numbering. Similarly, in international subscriber dialling with a unique country code for each country, the international routing should be divorced from the country code numbering. Routing divorced from numbering necessitates indirect dialled switching techniques, and that the exchange be common controlled.

In addition to common control to deal with area (and country) codes, some switching techniques require common control for the selection of a local number connexion through the exchange, this selection being divorced from the local numbering. For example, in the crossbar arrangement Fig. 4, it will be seen that most of the inlets on the secondary switches are not used. This could be overcome by arranging that both the primary and secondary switches have their outlets multiplied, the otherwise unused inlets of the secondary switches being connected to other primary switches. Figure 5 shows such an array giving 100 inlets and 100 outlets, but configurations used in practice may depart from this decimal form. Switching is performed by selection of one of the connexions between the primary and secondary (a link) and selection of a group of outlets which

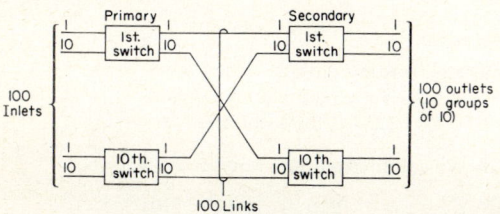

FIG. 5. *Crossbar link network having 100 inlets and 100 outlets.*

has a free trunk. Memory of the links and trunks that are free to pass the call is thus required, which memory, and the selection processes, require common control of switching.

3. *Common control switching techniques.* As in these techniques the dialled information does not operate the switches directly, an interface (a register) is necessary between the dial and the switchblock (Fig. 6). The register receives, and stores, the dialled digits, which gives opportunity for the common control to manipulate the received information in any desired manner to achieve switching.

Consider a dialled long distance call, the national number consisting of an area code plus the local number. On receipt of the area code, the register refers to a translator, which gives the register information to convert the received area code into different routing instructions to enable the call to be routed from the exchange over any desired group of outgoing circuits to the next exchange. The marker, which receives the translated

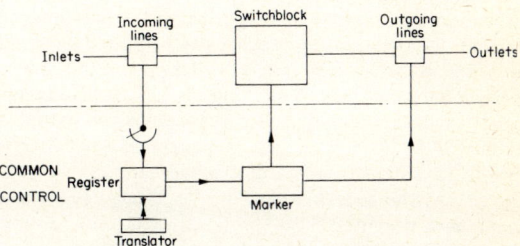

FIG. 6. *Principle of common control switching.*

information from the register, is responsible for choosing the free junction to the next exchange, and for selecting a suitable path through the switchblock to connect the incoming line to the selected outgoing line. In some common control systems, the translation is associated with the marker instead of with the register.

Similarly, in an international exchange, the translator operates on the received country code to route the call out in the desired direction.

The called subscriber's local number received from the dial is stored in the register, and is subsequently sent (non-translated) to a register in the destination exchange, a sender being associated with the originating register for this purpose. The digital information sent forward is transmitted direct to the junction taken, or via the connexion established through the switchblock to the junction, depending upon the detail of the switching system.

On a local call, and at the destination exchange of a long distance call, the register receives the called subscriber's local number only. The common control equipment operates on this information in any desired manner to establish a connexion through the switchblock to connect the incoming line to the called subscriber's line.

The common control equipment is concerned with call set-up only, and is not required in circuit during the conversation period. After a call set-up, the common equipment is released from that call and made available for other calls.

The register provision will depend upon the traffic load, there being many (typically hundreds) in a large busy exchange. Ideally, one translator and one marker per exchange is the requirement (with suitable reserve arrangements), but this would depend upon the speed of operation (typically 0·5 sec) of these devices in performing their functions.

It is a clear requirement that common control switching systems should have fast operating switchblocks as selection takes place after the dialled digits are received, and not at the same time as in direct dialled systems. Otherwise a caller would experience significant delays (post dialling delay) between completion of dialling and receipt of ring tone which indicates the end of complete selection.

4. *Electronic switching systems.* Electronic switching systems are fast operating and invariably common controlled. Of the two approaches studied to date—time division multiplex and space switching of the speech path connexion—space switching appears to have acceptance at the present time, for reasons of compatibility with existing space switched exchanges in a network in particular. Step-by-step and crossbar are examples of space switching techniques in the electromechanical field, and present spaced switched electronic systems may be likened to crossbar switching principles.

A main interest in space switched electronic exchanges is the type of crosspoint device (hot cathode tube, cold cathode tube, semiconductor, sealed reed relay, etc.). The present preferred approach favours a reed relay crosspoint for reasons of cost, reliability, and high on-to-off impedance ratio.

Figure 7 shows a simplified block diagram of a typical space switched electronic telephone system. The

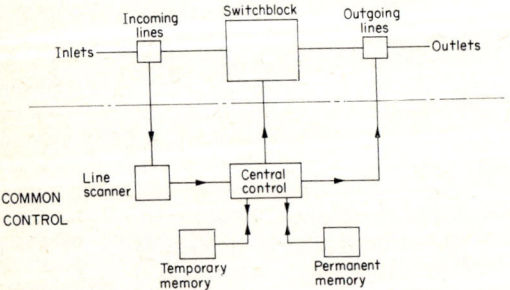

FIG. 7. *Principle of typical electronic switching system.*

similarity to Fig.6 will be noted. The central control controls the selection of the connexion through the switchblock, and in this respect incorporates the function of a marker. The central control uses two memories to perform its function:

(a) a temporary memory which includes the call supervision and register functions,

and (b) a permanent memory which determines the way in which a call has to be processed, and gives translation facilities.

Calls are set up and released by scanning the state (e.g. calling, dialling, release, etc.) of the line, the information relative to a particular call being progressively changed as a result of new conditions from the line scan. This information is stored in the temporary memory, which thus has record of the state of a call, and could have memory of all the calls that are in being in the system.

The permanent memory gives programmed information to determine the action to be taken on a call (e.g. class of service which entitles subscribers to certain features, but may prohibit others). The permanent memory, in conjuction with the central control, thus gives the facility of stored program control. Instructions are written into the memory as how to deal with any eventuality that may arise in establishing connexions, which means that the system is extremely flexible. It offers possibility of setting up various control sequences by changing the program information in the memory.

5. *Numbering scheme.* Subscribers have three unique numbers: (a) local, (b) national, and (c) international. (b) consists of (a) preceded by an area code. (c) consists of (b) preceded by a country code.

A country is divided up into a number of numbering areas for national subscriber trunk dialling, each area being identified by a code. This code serves to route the call over the network. Similarly, each country is given a country code for international subscriber dialling, which code serves to route the call over the world network to a destination country. Both the area and country codes also serve to give call charging information to an originating point.

The national number is prefixed by a trunk access code which serves to distinguish between a national trunk call and others. An international call is distinguished by an international access code prefix. Access codes serve to condition the switching equipment to deal with the appropriate type call.

A typical national number is:

[0·21·643 1234]

where    0 is the national trunk access code,
          21 is the national area code,
and    643 1234 is the local number.

A typical international number is:

[010·44·21·643 1234]

where    010 is the international access code,
          44 is the country code,

and the remainder is the national number (the national trunk access code being omitted on international dialled calls).

Omitting the access codes, the international number should not exceed 11 digits, and the national number should not exceed 11-$N$ digits, where $N$ is the number of digits in the country code.

6. *Routing control.* While communication is necessary between all exchanges in a network, it is clearly uneconomic to achieve this by full interconnexion of the exchanges with line plant. Due to community of interest, situations arise where provision of a direct group of circuits between two exchanges is justified. Where direct groups are not provided, the situation is met with a system of transit switching.

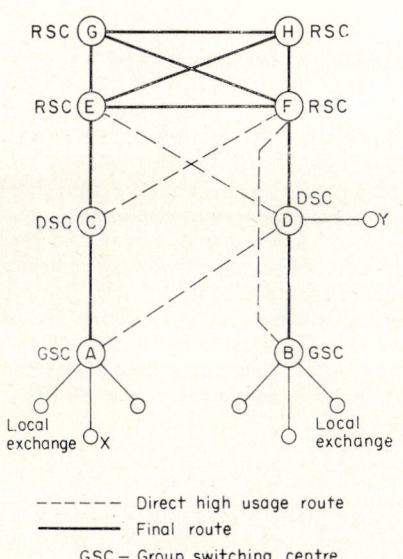

FIG. 8. *Routing plan.*

Figure 8 shows a typical long distance routing pattern for a national network. A number of *GSC's* are subordinate to a *DSC*, and a number of DSC's are subordinate to a *RSC*. The hierarchical order of routing is GSC–DSC–RSC, and the RSC's, which are relatively few, are fully interconnected. The GSC is the first concentration point for long distance traffic, and the local exchanges are directly connected to their parent GSC. DSC's and RSC's may also function as GSCs in certain relations (e.g. when they are the long distance destination exchange on a particular call), and local exchanges may be directly connected to them.

Direct routes (shown typically in Fig 8.) may be provided between any two long distance exchanges. The circuit provision in a direct group may be full (meeting the busy hour traffic requirement), or partial (meeting part of the busy hour traffic), the latter being the more usual for economic reasons.

All the long distance exchanges are connected by means of a final (overflow) route network, the circuit provision being such that traffic can be carried with a low call loss due to insufficient circuits. Each long distance exchange has the facility to alternate route a call from a direct route (where provided) to the final route, should the direct group be congested. The routing of the traffic is controlled by the receipt of the area code at a long distance exchange.

Assume a long distance call from local exchange X to local exchange Y (area code 21). The trunk access code ensures that all the dialled information (except the access code which is dealt with at the local exchange) is received by the long distance exchange GSC(A). Receipt of the area code 21 at GSC(A) causes GSC(A) to attempt to route the call over the direct route to DSC(D) as the first choice. Should no free circuit be available, GSC(A) alternate routes to DSC(C) over the final route network, by sending the area code 21 to DSC(C). As no direct route is provided between DSC(C) and DSC(D), the call is transit switched at DSC(C) to RSC(E) and the area code 21 is retransmitted from GSC(A) to RSC(E). RSC(E) attempts to route the call on the direct route RSC(E) to DSC(D), or, should a free circuit not be available, alternate routes via RSC(F). GSC(A) sends the area code 21 to RSC(F) in the latter case. GSC(A) transmits the called subscriber's local number to DSC(D) when this is reached.

To avoid 'run round' of routings, rules of routing are provided for:

(a) The cross over from one RSC area to another RSC area can be made at any level in each hierarchy (e.g. GSC(A)–DSC(D), DSC(D)–RSC(E), etc.)
(b) The routing pattern of outgoing traffic through a home RSC must be in ascending order of SC's (e.g. GSC–DSC–RSC).
(c) The routing pattern of incoming traffic through a foreign RSC must be in descending order of SC's (e.g. RSC–DSC–GSC).

Thus a call GSC(A) to RSC(F) would be routed via DSC(C), or via DSC(C) and RSC(E), but would not be routed via DSC(D).

World routing is on the same principle, except that a GSC would be an interface exchange between the international and a national network. The DSC would be a collecting point for a number of countries, and the RSC would be a collecting point for a large area of the world. The routing in this case is controlled by the country code.

7. *Signalling control.* The setting up and release of calls on a network is controlled by signalling systems between exchanges. Figure 9 shows the general arrangement of a typical signalling concept. The so-called supervisory signalling (seize, answer, release, etc.) is

performed by means of a per-line signalling system, d.c. or voice frequency (v.f.) depending upon the type of line plant (audio or h.f.). The call set-up signalling is performed by a fast, coded, 2-out-of-5 multifrequency (2/5MF) signalling system, equipped with the common equipment registers. The particular two frequencies compounded denotes the digit value. Fast number signalling in association with fast switching is a firm requirement for common control systems to minimize post dialling delays.

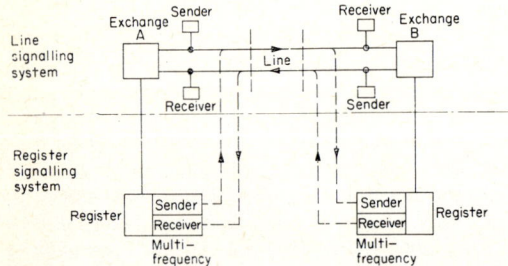

Fig. 9. *General arrangement of line and register signalling systems.*

Figure 10 shows the principle of control of the transmission of the number signalling for call set-up over a typical routing. All the called national numbers are transmitted from the local exchange to the GSC (except the trunk access code) and stored in the originating register. GSC commences to route the call out on receipt

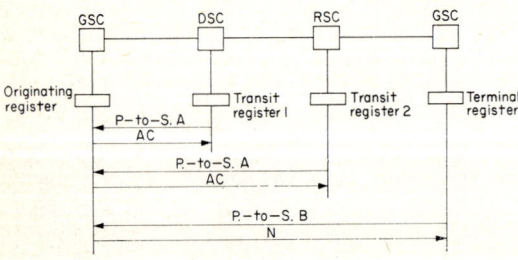

Fig. 10. *Control of transmission of digital information.*

of the area code. When seized, transit register 1 sends back a proceed-to-send signal A to evoke the sending of the area code (AC) from the originating register. Selection is made at the DSC and transit register 1 releases. Another proceed-to-send signal A is sent back from transit register 2 to evoke the sending of AC again from the originating register. Selection is made at RSC, and transit register 2 releases. A proceed-to-send signal B (different from A) is sent back from the terminal register to evoke the sending of the called subscriber's local number (SN) from the originating register. The called local number is now stored in the terminal register of the destination long distance exchange and the originating register releases. The destination long distance exchange then proceeds to set the call up to the called subscriber over the local network.

*See also:* Inland trunk systems. Local networks. Telecommunication, economy in. Telecommunication, global. Telecommunication system planning, international.

*Bibliography*

ATKINSON J. (1952) *Telephony*, Vol. 2, London: Pitman.
*No. 1 Electronic Switching System* (1964) *Bell System Tech. J.* **43**, No. 5, Part 2, Sept.
Subscriber Trunk Dialling (1959) *Post Office Electr. Engrs J.* **51**, Part 4, Jan.
WELCH S. (1962) *The Signalling Problems Associated with Register Controlled Automatic Telephone Exchanges*, Proc. I.E.E. **109**, Part B, Nov.

S. WELCH

**SYMBOL MANIPULATION BY DIGITAL COMPUTER.** *1. Introduction.* In many areas of current interest to computer science, data are represented most naturally by symbolic, rather than numeric, quantities. In order to use modern digital computers in these areas, one must let numeric quantities in the computer represent symbolic quantities of the problem. List processing and other sets of techniques for symbol manipulation provide convenient frameworks for encoding symbolic items into the basic language of the computer and manipulating the resulting structures (Green 1961; Wilkes 1964).

The following are typical examples of computer applications that require the manipulation of non-numeric quantities.

(*a*) *Linguistic data processing* (see Computational linguistics, Machine translation, Information retrieval). Linguistic data consist of symbolic structures: alphabetic characters are strung into words, and words and punctuation are structured into phrases and sentences. These structures satisfy grammatical rules that may themselves be represented by symbolic quantities.

(*b*) *Mathematical manipulation* (see Algebraic manipulation). Symbolic differentiation, simplification of algebraic expressions, and closed form solutions of integrals all involve the representation and manipulation of complex symbolic quantities.

(*c*) *Picture processing.* In computer-aided design and pattern-recognition research a symbolic description of the picture, rather than a direct mapping of the visual image, is generally the most convenient representation of the data.

(*d*) *Artificial intelligence.* Computer programs that play games, solve problems, or simulate aspects of human behaviour, must all manipulate symbolic data structures.

*2. Data forms.* The programmer with a symbol-oriented problem to solve must establish a correspondence between features of the data for his problem and features of symbolic data structures that can be manipulated in a computer. A *list structure* is the form of symbolic structure most convenient for representing data from a wide variety of problem situations; however, *strings*, *binary trees*, or other data forms may be more useful in certain situations.

The most common forms of symbolic data may be defined as follows:

*List.* Any sequence of elements, with the following special property: Associated in the computer's memory with each element of the list is the sequencing information needed to locate the succeeding element.

*List structure.* A list, any element of which may be either a member of a well-defined set of 'basic' elements (i.e. ones that are not themselves lists) or, recursively, a list structure.

*String.* A variable-length sequence of elements from a well-defined set of basic elements. String elements are stored sequentially in computer memory and therefore do not contain internal explicit sequencing information.

*Binary tree.* An ordered pair, each element of which may itself be an ordered pair, and so on to any finite depth.

*3. Data representations.* Each data form has both an external and an internal representation. The external representation is the notation used by a computer programmer when he describes items of data. The internal representation is the actual arrangement of information in the computer. The precise forms of these representations are determined by the particular programming formalism and computer used. The representations described below are typical and are illustrated by examples in the figures. (In the figure we represent graphically a memory unit by a rectangle and the address of a unit by an arrow. The address-arrow represents a 'pointer' from the unit containing the address to another unit. If part of a unit contains a unique numeric code for a basic element, the diagram shows the element itself.)

*A. List structure. External representation.* A sequence of list-structure elements separated by commas and enclosed in parentheses.

*Internal representation.* A chain of units of computer memory, each divided into two equal halves, and all linked together as follows: The left half of each unit contains an element of the list structure, and the right half contains a pointer to the remainder of the structure. A special symbol denoted by '\' marks the end of each list. The address of the first unit identifies the entire structure.

*B. Binary tree. External representation.* A pair of binary tree elements, enclosed in parentheses and separated by a period.

*Internal representation.* A memory unit that contains the two tree elements in its two halves.

Note that the internal representation of a binary tree is more general than that of a list structure. However, list structures are more commonly used because of their more convenient external representations.

*C. String. External representation.* A sequence of elements enclosed in quotation marks.

*Internal representations.* A sequence of consecutive memory units containing unique codes for the elements in the string. A special symbol denoted here by '?' is used to mark the end of the string.

**4.** *List processing.* The term 'list processing' denotes a collection of processes for manipulating list structures. These processes are usually embedded in a uniform controlling formalism called a '*list-processing language.*' The elementary list-processing processes derive their efficiency from the nature of the internal representation of a list structure. The language provides a convenient framework for using the elementary processes.

Consider the elementary process of inserting an element into a list. Suppose an 'X' is to be inserted immediately after the 'B' in the list (A, B, C, D). The internal representation for this list is as follows: (Greek letters identify the memory units used in the list. The entire list is identified by the address $\alpha$ of its first unit.)

The first step in making the insertion is to obtain an unused cell $\varepsilon$. We place 'X' in the left half of $\varepsilon$, and in the right half we place a pointer to $\gamma$, the cell after the cell containing 'B'.

The insertion is completed by replacing the pointer $\gamma$ by $\varepsilon$ in the right half of the cell containing 'B'.

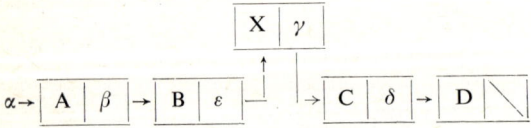

Suppose we now wish to delete the element 'C' from the list (A, B, X, C, D) diagrammed above. We merely replace the pointer from the cell preceding the element 'C' with a pointer to the cell containing the next element after the 'C'. In this case, we replace $\gamma$ by $\delta$ to obtain

Note that the cell $\gamma$ containing 'C' in its left half is no longer part of the list that starts at $\alpha$, and therefore may be removed from this list and used for other purposes.

The principal advantage of list (or tree) processing over other forms of data representation and manipulation is the fact, just illustrated, that data structures may be significantly modified by changing a few pointers. It is never necessary to copy or move large blocks of information to 'make room' for additions.

**5.** *String processing.* The string data form is more convenient than the list-structure form for certain applications. In most linguistic problems, for example, the flexibility offered by lists for building multi-level structures is not needed, and the computer memory space that would be used by list pointers is needed for actual text data. Although not as convenient as the list-structure form for insertions and deletions, the string form is more compact and simplifies certain other processes such as the scanning of a long sequence in search of a particular subsequence.

**6.** *Maintenance of free storage.* Dynamic changes in the amount of memory needed to store data and temporary results in the course of running a program are characteristic of symbol-manipulation processes. Memory cells are drawn from or returned to a pool of unused cells. Most systems keep track of these cells by maintaining a list, called the *available space list* (ASL), of all cells not being used. As data structures grow or shrink, the symbol-manipulation system transfers memory cells between the ASL and the active data.

The problem of deciding when to return cells to the ASL can be complex, especially in list-processing systems that allow a single sublist to be simultaneously an element of several higher level list structures. For example, consider the two list structures $x$ = (A, (B, C), D) and $y$ = (E, (B, C), F). Suppose all computations involving structure $x$ have been completed, but $y$ is still needed for future processing. If the internal representations are

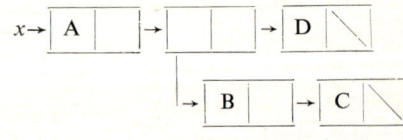

and

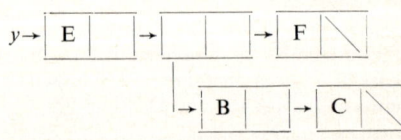

then all five cells of the $x$ list structure may be returned to the ASL. However, if $x$ and $y$ have a common sublist, i.e. if the internal representation is

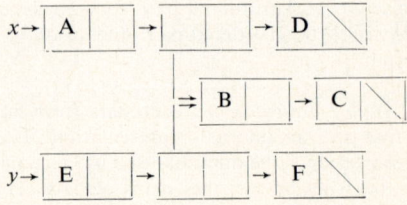

then the cells containing 'B' and 'C' are still needed (by $y$) and may not be made 'available' for other uses. This dilemma may be avoided either by prohibiting the use of common sublists, or by requiring the programmer to keep track of the structures his program creates and to issue 'erase' commands to return cells to available space when necessary.

The *garbage collection* scheme is another solution to the problem of maintaining and updating the pool of available space. In systems employing this solution cells that are no longer needed are simply ignored, and new cells are taken from the ASL until the ASL is exhausted. At that time, processing halts and a *garbage collector* sweeps through memory. The garbage collector starts with a specified set of base cells (such as the program, active registers, and current temporary results), and marks all cells in memory that can be reached by any chain from any base cell. All *other* memory cells cannot possibly be references in future computation and therefore may immediately be chained together to form a new ASL.

Still another storage maintenance technique is the *reference count* method (Weizenbaum 1963). Here a count is associated with each sublist, indicating how many times it is referenced by different list-structure locations. When this count becomes zero, the sublist is immediately (and automatically) returned to the ASL.

7. *Programming formalisms* (Bobrow and Raphael 1964). The formalisms available to the programmer for describing symbol-manipulation processes determine the convenience of using those processes on a computer. These formalisms may be contained in programming languages specifically designed for symbol manipulation, or they may be parts of more general programming languages.

A. *Low-level list processing*. Low-level list-processing languages, such as IPL-V (Newell 1963) and L[6] (Knowlton 1966), require the programmer to specify in a precise manner the operations desired upon symbols and cell pointers. Cells are generally removed from the ASL by the system whenever the programmer gives a 'copy' or 'insert' command, and returned in response to an 'erase' or 'delete' command. Programs consist of sequences of basic instructions.

For example, consider the problem of searching a list to see whether it contains a particular symbol. The program for conducting this search in a low-level language typically would have access to a cell $y$ containing the test symbol, and another cell $x$ containing a pointer to the list being searched. The program would resemble the following programme TEST:

TEST    Set $w := $ contents of $y$;

LOOP    If $x$ points to an 'end of list' symbol, go to DOES-NOT;
         Set $z := $ contents of cell pointed to by $x$;
         If $z = w$, go to DOES;
         Advance pointer $x$;
         Go to LOOP;

DOES-NOT    Set answer: $=$ NO;
               Go to CLEAN-UP;

DOES    Set answer $:=$ YES;

CLEAN-UP    Erase $w$;
               Erase $z$;
               End.

B. *Function-oriented formalism*. Each program in a function-oriented higher-level language such as LISP (McCarthy *et al.* 1962) defines a symbolic-valued function of symbolic data. Programs may be defined recursively. Storage allocation and other bookkeeping chores are handled automatically by the system. The function Member that tests whether a symbol named $y$ is an element of a list named $x$ may be defined as follows:

$$\text{Member } (y, x) \equiv [\textit{if } \text{Empty } (x) \textit{ then } \text{'No'}$$
$$\textit{else if } \text{Equal } (y, \text{First-Element } (x))$$
$$\textit{then } \text{'Yes'}$$
$$\textit{else } \text{Member } (y, \text{Rest } (x))]$$

where Empty, Equal, First-Element, and Rest are elementary functions built into the system. (Rest $(x)$ is the list obtained by deleting the first element from the ist $x$.)

C. *String-processing languages*. The pattern-matching rule is the most important feature of several string-processing languages (Yngve 1963; Farber *et al.* 1964). This kind of program statement declares that a particular string is to be searched in order to identify substrings that satisfy specified conditions. Substrings thus identified may be labelled for future processing. In addition, the success or failure of the identification process determines which program statement will be executed next. For example, one program statement might be the following (appropriately abbreviated): 'In the string named $x$, find the symbols 'ABC' followed by any sequence of symbols—call that sequence $y$—followed by an occurrence of the string named $z$. If successful, reverse the order of substrings $y$ and $z$ in $x$. If unsuccessful, go to statement FAILED.' If the original strings were

$$z = \text{'DEFG'}$$
and    $x = $ 'XXABCSEPARATEDEFGHI'

then execution of the above program statement would result in the following string-name assignments:

$$x = \text{'XXABCDEFGSEPARATEHI'}$$
and    $y = $ 'SEPARATE'.

8. *Summary*. List structures, strings, and binary trees are symbolic data forms that can be used to represent non-numeric information from a variety of problem domains. Computational efficiency and ease of problem representation help determine the choice of a symbolic data form. List-processing languages and other forma-

lisms for symbol manipulation provide several levels of convenience and flexibility for describing symbol-manipulation processes in a digital computer.

*See also:* Algebraic manipulation using lists. Computational linguistics: introduction. Computational linguistics: machine translation. Information storage and retrieval. Timetabling.

*Bibliography*

BOBROW D. G. and RAPHAEL B. (1964) *A Comparison of List-Processing Computer Languages, Comm. ACM* **7, 4,** April.

FARBER D. J. *et al.* (1964) *SNOBOL, a String Manipulation Language, J. ACM 11.* **1,** January.

GREEN B. F. (1961) *Computer Languages for Symbol Manipulation, IRE Trans. HFE-2,* **1,** March.

KNOWLTON D. C. (1966) *BTL Low-Level Linked List Language, Comm. ACM,* August.

MCCARTHY J. *et al.* (1962) *LISP 1·5 Programmer's Manual,* Cambridge, Mass.: M.I.T. Press.

NEWELL A. (Ed.) (1963) *Information Processing Language-V Manual,* Englewood Cliffs, N. J.: Prentice-Hall.

WEIZENBAUM J. (1963) *Symmetric List Processor, Comm. ACM 6,* **9,** September.

WILKES M. V. (1964) *Lists and Why They are Useful, ACM Proc. 19th Nat'l. Conf. P-64, F.* **1,** August.

YNGVE V. H. (1963) *COMIT, Comm. ACM 6,* **3,** March.

B. RAPHAEL

# T

## TELECOMMUNICATION, ECONOMY IN.

### 1. Introduction

*The statistical theory of communication.* Modern communication theory is characterized by the principle that signals, as well as noise, can properly be described only in terms of probabilities and Shannon (1949) has shown that the most efficient communication can be achieved only if the statistical properties of the ensemble of signals are identical with the corresponding properties of the channel. Elementary signal analysis has not been superseded, i.e. a signal will pass through a channel only insofar as its spectrum and range of amplitude are accepted by the channel; and, if the signal is either strictly time-limited and approximately band-limited or strictly band-limited and approximately time-limited, it can be represented in terms of two functionally independent variables per unit time and per unit bandwidth (Fano 1961).

Thus, if the signal $x(t)$ is limited to a bandwidth $W$ Hz it can be defined over a period of $T$ seconds by $2WT$ data. Any orthogonal functions may be used, but it is often convenient to take the set of ordinates $1/2W$ seconds apart, which will be called Nyquist samples.

According to the statistical theory, if signal and noise are independent ergodic ensembles, the average *rate of transfer of information* through a noisy channel is:

$$R = H(x) - H_y(x) \qquad (1)$$

where $x$ and $y$ are the (multidimensional) input to the channel and corrupt final output respectively; $H(x)$ and $H_y(x)$ are the *entropy of the input* and the *equivocation*. If the system is continuous, these are not necessarily bounded or invariant, but the rate $R$ and the channel capacity $C$ are fixed and finite, if properly defined. The set of values $x_1, \ldots x_n$ and $y_1, \ldots y_n$ represented by $x$ and $y$ may be the Nyquist samples over a period $T$ (so that $n = 2TW$ if the bandwidth is $W$).

Then, from Shannon:

$$R = \frac{1}{T} \int\int_{-\infty}^{\infty} p(x, y) \log_2 \frac{p(x, y)}{p(x)p(y)} \, dx \, dy. \qquad (2)$$

where $p(x)$, $p(y)$ and $p(x, y)$ are the multidimensional probability density distributions.

The *capacity of the channel* is simply the highest rate which can be achieved by any signal ensemble $p(x)$ for fixed conditional probabilities $p_x(y)$ and ordinarily with a constraint such as a power limit:

$$C = \lim_{T \to \infty} \max_{p(x)} \frac{1}{T} \int\int_{-\infty}^{\infty} p(x, y) \log_2 \frac{p(x, y)}{p(x)p(y)} \, dx \, dy. \qquad (3)$$

Note that signal ensembles other than those which give the maximum value are redundant with respect to the channel with the given properties.

Similarly, if $u$ is the original message and a fidelity criterion applies to an approximation $v$, the entropy of the message source, $R_s$, is the minimum transmission rate of any system with fixed $p(u)$ which satisfies the fidelity criterion, i.e.

$$R_s = \min_{p_u(v)} \frac{1}{T} \int\int_{-\infty}^{\infty} p(u, v) \log_2 \frac{p(u, v)}{p(u)p(v)} \, du \, dv. \qquad (4)$$

The message $u$ may be encoded into $x$ in order to match the channel, but if further degradation is to be arbitrarily small it is necessary that: $R_s \leq R \leq C$.

*Sensory perception.* Many systems of telecommunication are extensions of the human senses and, by analogy with communication between machines, data should be selected for transmission in such a way that thorough compatibility with sensory characteristics can be achieved. Because not enough is known about these characteristics, conventional systems are designed to make available all of the data in the original message, e.g. the waveform of a sound, or the luminance of every element in a picture (but not continuously). Since the data are also usually encoded singly, channel capacities of up to about $2 \times 10^5$ bits per second are needed for sound and about $6 \times 10^7$ for television, yet it has been estimated that information reaches the cortex through eye or ear at not more than 100 bits per second (Pierce and Karlin 1957; Sziklai 1956). Even if regarded as a channel, the ear is reported to have a capacity of only about $10^4$ bits per second (Jacobson 1951), and the eye between $10^5$ and $10^9$ bits per second (Budrikis 1964; Jacobson 1951; Kelly 1962).

Thus it appears that conventional signals for human communication contain both statistical redundancy, with respect to practical channels, and perceptual redundancy, with respect to the senses. It may be that these are one and the same, since there is evidence that the mechanism of perception is statistical (Cherry 1953), but current work distinguishes between them.

### 2. Practical Codes for Economical Communication

Already, methods have been found for sending through available channels signals which would have too high a data rate with straightforward coding. In addition, some simple processes for making economies have been in use for many years. Examples are, in roughly chronological order:

1. The Morse code—for reducing transmission time by statistically matching the source to the channel.
2. Multiplex voice and signalling; frequency division multiplex.
3. Scanning and line interlace in television, which approach a match between the image and human vision.
4. Spectrum interlace in colour television (Dome 1950).
5. Compatible stereo-sound broadcasting.
6. Amplitude companding in telephony; Lincompex.
7. Time assignment speech interpolation (TASI (Bullington and Fraser 1959))—an adaptive time multiplex.
8. Piccolo—a multitone telegraph which uses very efficient modulation and detection (Robin et al. 1963).
9. Telemetry from space vehicles—some efficient methods have been reported, in particular run-coding for data and visual images (Blasbalg and van Berkom 1962; Kortman 1966).

### 3. Experimental Methods

There have been very many different proposals for improving telecommunication by efficient coding according to the principles of information theory (as summarized by Oliver (1952)). Some examples of the methods are outlined here, in an order which corresponds roughly to the degree of departure from conventional practice.

*1. Analysis-synthesis.* Techniques in this category are the most important for recoding speech. Various systems, generally known as *vocoders*, have been described by, among others, Dudley (1940), Halsey and Swaffield (1948), Flanagan (1956), Schroeder and David (1960), Crystal (1960), Schroeder (1962), David et al. (1962), Tierney et al. (1964) and Gold (1965). They are effective because the sounds of speech, though complex, change slowly.

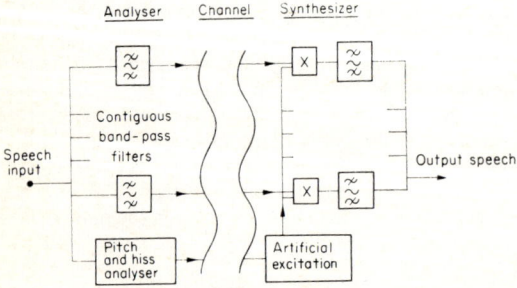

FIG. 1. *Spectrum-channel vocoder.*

In the simplest system (Fig. 1) the speech signal from the microphone is analysed to give measures of the energy in from 8 to 25 contiguous bands in the spectrum and an economical description of the excitation (whether the sound is voiced or not, and the larynx pitch if it is voiced). These data are transmitted and speech is synthesized at the receiver by an artificial source of excitation whose spectrum is shaped under the control of the received signal. Intelligible speech can be sent in this way through a band of about 500 Hz in an ordinary telephone channel, but better quality can be obtained at the cost of increasing the bandwidth to about 1000 Hz if a narrow band from the original speech is transmitted to provide excitation (David et al. 1962).

Since speech sounds typically occupy only a few narrow bands in the spectrum, which are called *formants*, still more economical transmission is possible if two or three of these are encoded in place of a large number of spectrum channels (Flanagan 1956; Steinberg and French 1953). Recent work suggests that a combination of formant encoding and parallel channel vocoding gives better results than either alone (Gold 1965; Swaffield 1965).

An alternative to spectrum analysis is a running measurement of the autocorrelation function, $\varphi(\tau)$, of the signal $s(t)$:

$$\varphi(\tau) = E[s(t) \cdot s(t-\tau)]. \qquad (5)$$

An autocorrelation vocoder takes the form shown in Fig. 2 (from Schroeder) and although the realization

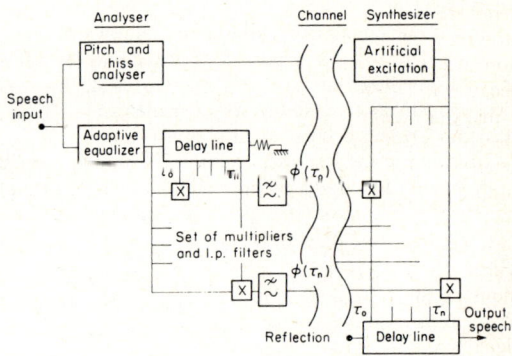

FIG. 2. *Autocorrelation vocoder.*

is different from the channel vocoder, there is a theoretical equivalence because the autocorrelation function and the power spectrum are a Fourier transform pair. The vocoder described by Schroeder required a transmission bandwidth of about 540 Hz and offered speech quality at least equal to the best channel vocoders with the same bandwidth.

Multiplexing of vocoder signals has been studied by Golden et al. (1964), who describe a 1·4 kHz frequency multiplex system for a voice excited vocoder, and by Campanella et al. (1962), who describe analog and digital transmission for a formant encoder requiring either 140 Hz bandwidth or 1000 bits per second and discuss the effects of transmission errors.

*2. Frequency transformation.* Under this heading are included a system for encoding speech, described by

Gabor (1947), and a class of schemes for encoding visual images, proposed by Cherry and Gouriet (1953).

In Gabor's encoder, a record of a speech signal moves with a velocity $v$ which would give correct reproduction with a stationary sensor, but which is scanned by a sensor moving in the same direction with velocity $u$. All frequencies would be transformed in the ratio

$$k = \frac{v-u}{v} \qquad (6)$$

if the process continued indefinitely, but Gabor has shown that if several sensors are used in sequence, one at a time, intelligible speech can be recovered from the output of the sensors by reversing the process, for ratios of up to about $1/6$.

Cherry and Gouriet have pointed out that the energy in the spectrum of television signals decreases sharply with increasing frequency, but that the high frequencies are essential for resolving detail, the edges and contours in pictures. The simplest of their proposed schemes would use negative feedback of the modulus differential of the picture signal to control the velocity of the line scan. Sharp transitions would be scanned more slowly than simply organized regions (which are of almost uniform luminance) and severe band-limiting of the output signal would destroy only faint detail. However, in Beddoes' (1961) experimental investigation acceptable picture quality could not be obtained because of excess phase shift in the feedback loop and a marked vulnerability to noise. The original authors also discussed equalisation of transition times and extensions to two-dimensional and multiple-frame encoding.

*3. Spectrum interlace.* A system for halving the bandwidth of monochrome television signals has been demonstrated by Howson and Bell (1960) in which the frequencies of the components of the upper half of the signal spectrum are changed until they fall in the band of the lower half. This is made possible by the line-harmonic structure of the spectrum, but nevertheless the recovered pictures contained a faint spurious pattern.

*4. Element run coding.* This technique is useful for signals which have a particular statistical property: elements having the same value occur in runs of varying length. Each run can be encoded by generating a single representation of the value and a separate code to give the number of repetitions. Coding is economical if there are more data per run in the original signal than in the coded version, on average.

Both picture signals and telemetry signals lend themselves to run coding, taking as elements the Nyquist samples, and several studies have been reported which differ chiefly in the method for detecting runs and in the codes used for the run lengths.

Michel (1958) and others (Capon 1959; Truehaft 1953), discuss only two-level signals and Gouriet (1957)

and Wyle *et al.* (1961) consider only quantized signals. In these, a change of level begins a new run. Other discriminants may be used (e.g. Julesz 1959) but a poor compromise is likely between picture quality and the proportion of runs caused by noise and insignificant detail unless an inferential decision strategy, such as that proposed by Kubba (1963), is employed.

The common value of the elements in a run can be coded in a conventional way, but since the distribution, $P(r)$, of run-lengths, $r$, is generally closely exponential a statistically matched code is required if the average data rate is not greatly to exceed:

$$H_p = - \sum_r P(r) \log_2 P(r) \quad \text{bits per run.} \qquad (7)$$

Suitable codes, requiring complex equipment, have been described by Schreiber (1958), Michel (1958) and Knight *et al.* (1964) and a simpler alternative has been discussed by Cherry *et al.* (1963) in which extra runs automatically impose restriction to a set of about four standard lengths. Experiments by the writer (Vieri 1966), and Robinson (in prep.) have shown that although artificial restriction increases the data rate needed in run coding, it improves picture quality.

*5. Two-band schemes.* The human eye is critical of the relative values of luminance over simply organized regions of a picture and it is sensitive to the positions of edges and boundaries in detailed regions, but not there to errors of luminance. Consequently, several investigators have described schemes in which the low frequency components of a picture signal are transmitted conventionally but the high frequencies are represented coarsely and the few data needed are efficiently coded, by run coding for example. Schreiber *et al.* (1959) have demonstrated the most complete system, but similar schemes have been described in Graham (1958), Kretzmer (1956) and Vieri (1966).

*6. Two-dimensional picture coding.* It is widely believed that the basic region in efficient picture coding should be multi-element and two-dimensional, but conventional scanning imposes difficulties. However, Gabor and Hill (1961) obtained good results with an experimental scheme in which alternate lines were omitted from the scan, being reconstructed with the condition that the continuity of edges and contours should be preserved. Extensions of contour interpolation were studied, but the schemes suffer the disadvantage of a real loss of resolution.

Huang and Tretiak (1965) have reported simulations by digital computer of several fidelity-preserving two-dimensional codes for pictures, including a development of Schreiber's 'synthetic highs'.

*7. Prediction.* The principle of predictive coding is simple (Fig. 3) but known prediction functions are of little use. Schemes of linear prediction for television have been proposed, in which the prediction function:

$$x_p(t) = \sum_{i=1}^{n} a_i x(t - i/2W) \qquad (8)$$

where the $a_i$ are constant coefficients, $W$ is the bandwidth of the signal $x(t)$ and $n/2W$ is the memory of the predictor. The schemes differ principally in the extent of the data storage—Fukushima and Ando (1964) use only part of a television line, Cunningham (1954) and others (Corradetti 1959; Graham 1958) use a number of lines and Harrison (1952) and Seyler (1960) suggest using several frames. Harrison's work is most fully reported; power savings of up to about 15 dB were achieved.

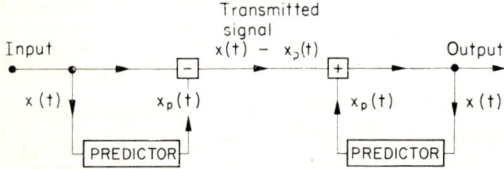

FIG. 3. *Predictive coding.*

*8. Queue storage.* Most of the schemes which have been described in paragraphs 4, 5 and 7 reduce the *average* number of data required to convey a message with the desired fidelity, but the sequence of data may be irregular, with a high maximum rate. The rate of transmission may be made uniform if the data are passed through a queue or buffer store. Errors may occur with a store of finite capacity but can be prevented if, when the store threatens to overflow, the strategy for selecting data from the input is altered so that fewer data are taken—and conversely if the store approaches emptiness (Robinson (in prep.)).

*9. Holograms.* Recently it has been widely surmized that holograms may prove to be efficient codes for visual images. There is little evidence for this, but Akhtar (1965) has carried out experiments with a hologram technique for economically coding two-tone images.

*10. Others.* Other economical coding processes are known, mostly variants of established methods, but two principles for economy in television deserve comment: multiple interlace and improved coarse quantization. The first takes further advantage of the insensitivity to flicker of the fovea in ways which have been described by, among several others, Haantjes and de Vrijer (1951), Teer (1959) and Deutsch and Balaban (1964). In the second, the spurious and objectionable contours which appear in pictures produced from a coarsely quantized television signal are prevented by adding pseudo-random perturbations to the signal before quantization and subtracting them afterwards. Roberts (1962) has devised a coding scheme which uses this principle and Thompson (1966) reports further improvement of picture quality if the perturbation has a periodic component derived from the scanning frequencies.

## 4. Conclusion

*Fidelity.* Despite the widespread interest in economical coding and decoding systems for aural and visual messages, no complete standard form for comparing systems has emerged. The channel capacity requirements are usually not difficult to estimate, but the subjective quality is rarely given a useful measure. However, reliable standards can be achieved—the input to a system can be compared with the final output and degraded in a separate path in a reproducible standard way until the two are subjectively equivalent. The measure of lost fidelity thus obtained will be more accurate if the two changes in the message appear similar.

For example, Newell and Geddes (1962) have compared television pictures from signals which have been through coding and decoding processes with those from signals which have been band-limited and 'crispened'. But, since the perturbations in pictures due to imperfect coding resemble noise rather than the effects of band-limiting, Vieri (1966) has compared reduced-data pictures with pictures from the same source which have been degraded by additive random noise and Pearson (1965) has used the same method for predicting the effect of channel noise on pictures produced from a run-coded signal.

*Progress.* Chief among the problems of economical communication is the difficulty of making machines to imitate human cognitive processes. Intelligible sounds and visual messages are statistically different from the noise-like processes which alone can convey information efficiently through typical channels, besides being perceptually redundant, but it is thought that a simpler and more nearly random system can be obtained by encoding the type and disposition in messages of perceptually significant features. It may be practical to achieve the desired result automatically with an encoder which adapts its coding transformation by measuring the statistics of the message but, although the principle has been applied in a simple case by Blasbalg and van Blerkom (1962), full realization is unlikely in the foreseeable future. However, increasing effort is being devoted to the problems of pattern recognition and to the allied problems of detecting and encoding the various characteristics of speech and pictures and substantial economies in communication may arise if this work is successful.

*See also:* Communication theory. Data transmission. Speech perception.

## Bibliography

AKHTAR S. A-uD. (1965) *Video bandwidth compression using hologram technique*, M.Sc. Thesis, Univ. of Brit. Columbia, Aug.

BEDDOES M. P. (1961) *Experiments with a slope-feedback coder for television compression*, Trans. I.R.E., BC-7, no. 2, 12, March.

BLASBALG H. and VAN BLERKOM R. (1962) *Message compression*, Trans. I.R.E., SET-8, no. 3, 228, Sept.

BUDRIKIS Z. L. (1964) *On the channel capacity of the human sense of vision*, Proc. I.R.E.E. Aust., April, 228.

BULLINGTON K. and FRASER J. M. (1959) *Engineering aspects of TASI*, Bell Syst. Tech. J, **38**, 353, March.

CAMPANELLA S. J., COULTER D. C. and IRONS R. (1962) *Influence of transmission error on formant coded compressed speech signals*, J. Audio Eng. Soc., **10**, 149, Apr.

CAPON J. (1959) *A probabilistic model for run-length coding of pictures*, Trans. I.R.E. IT-5, no. 4, 157, Dec.

CHERRY E. C. (1953) *Some experiments on the recognition of speech, with one and with two ears*, J. Acoust. Soc. Am., **25**, no. 5, 975, Sept.

CHERRY E. C. and GOURIET G. G. (1953) *Some possibilities for the compression of television signals by recoding*, Proc. I.E.E. **100**, pt. III, 9.

CHERRY E. C., KUBBA M. H., PEARSON D. E. and BARTON M. P. (1963) *An experimental study of the possible bandwidth compression of visual image signals*, Proc. I.E.E.E, **51**, no. 11, 1507, Nov.

CORRADETTI M. (1959) *Planar prediction*, M.I.T. Res. Lab. Electronics, QPR 55, 110.

CRYSTAL T. H. (1960) *An autocorrelation vocoder*, M.Sc. Thesis, Mass. Inst. Tech., June.

CUNNINGHAM J. E. (1959) *Picture processing*, M.I.T. Res. Lab. Electronics, QPR 54, 138.

DAVID E. E., SCHROEDER M. R., LOGAN B. F. and PRESTIGIACOMO A. J. (1962) *Voice-excited vocoders for practical speech bandwidth reduction*, Trans. I.R.E. IT-8, S101–S105.

DEUTSCH S. and BALABAN P. (1964) *Pseudo-random dot scan TV systems*, Poly. Inst. Brooklyn, Report PIBMRI 1256-65, Dec.

DOME R. B. (1950) *Frequency interlace colour television*, Electronics, **23**, 70, Sept.

DUDLEY H. (1940) *The carrier nature of speech*, Bell Syst. Tech. J, **19**, 4, 495, Oct.

FANO R. M. (1961) *Transmission of Information*, Cambridge, Mass.: MIT Press; New York: Wiley.

FLANAGAN J. L. (1956) *Automatic extraction of formant frequencies from continuous speech*, J. Acoust. Soc. Am., **28**, no. 1, 110, Jan.

FUKUSHIMA K. and ANDO H. (1964) *Television band compression by multimode interpolation*, J.I.E.C.E. Japan, **47**, no. 1, 55, Jan.

GABOR D. (1947) *New possibilities in speech transmission*, J.I.E.E. **94**, pt. III, 369, Nov.

GABOR D. and HILL P. C. J. (1961) *Television band compression by contour interpolation*, Proc. I.E.E. **108**, pt. B, no. 39, 303.

GOLD B. (1965) *Techniques for speech bandwidth compression using combinations of channel vocoders and formant vocoders*, J. Acoust. Soc. Am., **38**, no. 1, 2, July.

GOLDEN R. M., MACLEAN D. J. and PRESTIGIACOMO A. J. (1964) *Frequency multiplex system for a 10-spectrum-channel voice-excited vocoder*, J. Acoust. Soc. Am., **36**, no. 10, 1962, Oct.

GOURIET G. G. (1957) *Bandwidth compression of a television signal*, Proc. I.E.E. **104**, pt. B, 265, May.

GRAHAM R. E. (1958) *Communication theory applied to television coding*, Bell Syst. Monograph no. 3096.

GRAHAM R. E. (1958) *Predictive quantising of TV signals*, I.R.E. Wescon Record, **2**, pt. 4, 147, Aug.

HAANTJES J. and DE VRIJER F. W. (1951) *Flicker in television pictures*, Wireless Engr., **28**, 40, Feb.

HALSEY R. J. and SWAFFIELD J. (1948) *Analysis-synthesis telephony, with special reference to vocoders*, J.I.E.E. **95**, pt. III, 391, Sept.

HARRISON C. W. (1952) *Experiments with linear prediction in television*, Bell Sys. Tech. J. **31**, 764, July.

HOWSON E. A. and BELL D. A. (1960) *Reduction of television bandwidth by frequency interlace*, J. Brit. I.R.E, **20**, no. 2, 127.

HUANG T. S. and TRETIAK O. J. (1965) *Research in picture processing, Optical and Electro-Optical Information Processing*, (J. T. Tippett et al. Eds.), Cambridge, Mass.: M.I.T. Press.

JACOBSON H. (1951) *The information capacity of the human eye*, Science, **113**, 292, March.

JACOBSON H. (1951) *Information and the human ear*, J. Acoust. Soc. Am., **23**, 463, July.

JULESZ B. (1959) *A method of coding signals based on edge detection*, Bell Syst. Tech. J. **38**, 1001, July.

KELLY D. H. (1962) *Information capacity of a single retinal channel*, Trans. I.R.E. IT-8, no. 3, 221 Apr.

KNIGHT J. M., FADELY J. K., RAGA G. L. and KING B. C. (1964) *Digital TV—Shrinking bulky bandwidths*, Electronics, **37**, no. 31, 77, Dec.

KORTMAN C. M. (1966) *Redundancy reduction—a practical method of data compression*, Lockheed Missile and Space Co., Report 5-12-66-2, May.

KRETZMER E. R. (1956) *Reduced alphabet representation of television signals*, I.R.E. Conv. Record, **4**, pt. 4, 140.

KUBBA M. H. (1963) *Automatic picture detail detection in the presence of random noise*, Proc. I.E.E.E. **51**, no. 11, 1518, Nov.

MICHEL W. S. (1958) *Statistical encoding for text and picture communication*, Trans. A.I.E.E. **77**, 33, March.

NEWELL G. F. and GEDDES W. K. E. (1962) *Tests of three systems of bandwidth compression for television signals*, Proc. I.E.E. **109**, pt. B, 311.

OLIVER B. M. (1952) *Efficient coding*, Bell Syst. Tech. J. **31**, 724, July.

PEARSON D. E. (1965) *Fidelity criteria for visual image transmission over noisy communication channels*, Ph. D. Thesis, Univ. of London.

PIERCE J. R. and KARLIN J. E. (1957) *Reading rates and the information rate of the human channel*, Bell Syst. Tech. J. **36**, no. 2, 497, March.

ROBERTS L. G. (1962) *Picture coding using pseudo-random noise*, Trans. I.R.E. IT-8, no. 2, 145, Feb.

ROBIN H. K., BAYLEY D., MURRAY T. L. and RALPHS J.D. (1963) *Multitone signalling system employing quenched resonators for use on noisy radio-teleprinter circuits*, Proc. I.E.E. **110**, no. 9, 1554, Sep.

ROBINSON A. H. *Automatic digital encoding for bandwidth reduction in visual image transmission*, Ph. D. Thesis, Univ. of London (in preparation).

SCHREIBER E. W. and KNAPP C. F. (1958) *Television bandwidth reduction by digital coding*, I.R.E. Conv. Record, **6**, pt. 4, 88.

SCHREIBER W. F., KNAPP C. F. and KAY N. D. (1959) *Synthetic highs—an experimental bandwidth reduction system*, J. Soc. Mot. Pic. Tel. Engrs., **68**, 525, Aug.

SCHROEDER M. R. (1962) *Correlation techniques for speech bandwidth compression*, J. Acoust. Soc. Am., **10**, no. 2, 163, April.

SEYLER A. J. (1960) *Channel capacity of television relay links*, Fortschritte der Hochfrequenztechnik, **5**, 263.

SHANNON C. E. and WEAVER W. (1949) *The Mathematical Theory of Communication*, Illinois: The University Press.

STEINBERG and FRENCH (1953) U.S. Pat. No. 2, 635, 146.

SWAFFIELD J. (1965) *Speech compression*, J.I.E.E. **11**, 172, May.

SZIKLAI G. C. (1956) *Some studies in the speed of visual perception*, Trans. I.R.E. IT-2, Symposium Rep., 125, Sept.

TEER K. (1959) *Investigations into redundancy and possible bandwidth compression in television transmission*, Philips Res. Rep., **14**, no. 6, 501.

THOMPSON J. E. and SPARKES J. J. (1967) *A pseudo-random quantiser for television signals*, Proc. I.E.E.E. **55**, No 3.

TIERNEY J., GOLD B., SFERRINO V., DUMANIAN J. A. and AHO E. (1964) *Channel vocoder with digital pitch extractor*, J. Acoust. Soc. Am., **36**, 1901.

TRUEHAFT M. A. (1953) *Description of a system for transmission of line drawings with bandwidth-time compression*, Poly. Inst. Brooklyn, Report R-339-53, PIB 274, Sept.

VIERI B. J. (1966) *Experiments with a scheme of data reduction for television signals*, Ph.D. Thesis, Univ. of London.

WYLE H., ERB T. and BANOW R. (1961) *Reduced time facsimile transmission by digital coding*, Trans. I.R.E. CS-9, no. 3, 215, Sept.

B. J. VIERI

**TELECOMMUNICATION, GLOBAL.** Until the first transatlantic telegraph cable was completed in 1866, it was impossible to communicate across an ocean in less time than it took to make the journey. Early signalling speeds were very low—only a few code elements (bits)/sec—and, by comparison, it was possible in 1964 to transmit data via a satellite at nearly a million bits/sec, equivalent to sending the contents of the Bible in 40 seconds; even greater speeds are possible today. By 1902 *telegraph cables* spanned all the oceans; new ones of increased capacity were laid until 1928, old ones renewed as late as 1956.

Marconi's historic transatlantic radio transmission in 1901 presented the first challenge to cable supremacy; a radio-telegraph service (16 kHz) was opened in 1908 and the first radio-telephone (60 kHz) in 1927. High-frequency (h.f.) radio services (10–30 MHz) started in 1928 and global communication depended on these and the telegraph cables until the first transatlantic telephone cable (TAT–1) was completed in 1956. While h.f. radio provided invaluable service it depends on reflections from ionized layers and suffers fading as these change with sunlight and, especially, sunspot activity; this requires the use of technical operators on the circuits, which often become unusable. Moreover, the range of suitable frequencies is restricted and the spectrum soon became overcrowded. Nevertheless h.f. radio still has important applications; up to four telephone circuits, sub-divided for telegraphs as required, can be transmitted on a single carrier frequency and refinements in terminal equipment continue.

*Radio systems* using tropospheric forward-scatter at frequencies *around 1000 MHz*, with frequency modulation and space and/or frequency diversity, can provide wide transmission bands over distances of a few hundred miles. For transoceanic systems there are now repeatered cables, i.e. with amplifiers at intervals, and communication satellites. Such major systems can, within limits of overall propagation time, be interconnected and extended by land systems either permanently or via switching centres, to form global circuits.

*Ocean telephone cables.* The modern concept of long-distance communication is to provide a wide transmission band—up to 10 MHz or more over land—and to assemble the required services within this band by frequency translation (see also *Inland trunk systems*). The means for doing this in a comparatively modest way, together with negative-feedback line amplifiers of adequate quality, existed by the mid-1930's. Reliability considerations, however, did not then justify placing amplifiers on the ocean bed at depths of several miles, where replacement is very expensive. By 1952 conditions were ripe for a joint American-British investigation into the practicability of a transatlantic cable, both countries then having comparatively short systems in service. Agreement was reached on the basis of extreme measures to ensure reliability for some 20 years.

Whereas, in telegraph cables, signal currents return via the armour wires and sea water, it is necessary for high-frequency transmission to add a low-loss return conductor, usually coaxial with the centre wire. Apart from this, higher grade materials and better manufacturing standards and control, the cable used for TAT-1 (Fig. 1) differed little from telegraph cable. Because

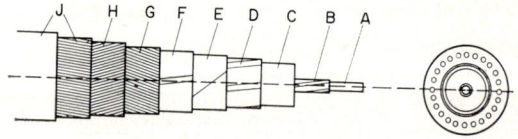

FIG 1. *Armoured Submarine Telephone Cable—Deep-Water Type. A, Centre conductor (Cu); B, 3 surround tapes (Cu); C, Polythene to 0·62 in dia; D, 6 return tapes (Cu); E, Teredo tape (Cu); F, Telconax tape; G, Cutched jute; H, 24 armour wires. (h.t. steel); J, Impregnated jute to 1.21 in dia. Shallow water cable similar but with larger mild steel armour wires.*

conventional deep-sea cable, with its high-tensile steel, helical armour wires, twists under tension it is impracticable to carry out involved operations when laying the repeaters. To overcome this American repeaters, of small diameter, flexible and armoured and laid as part of the cable, were used for the Atlantic crossing to Newfoundland; because of physical limitations these could provide only unidirectional amplification and, so, required two cables. British repeaters, rigid, 10 ft long and 10.5 in. in diameter but providing both-way amplification, were used for the shallow section to the Canadian Mainland. The Atlantic section provided bandwidths of 144 kHz, used for 36 and, later, 48 high-grade telephone circuits. Each cable includes 51 three-stage valve repeaters with 65 dB gain and energized by a d.c. line current of 0·23 A from constant-current generators, series-aiding at the two ends, the voltage being about 2+2 kV.

More ocean cable systems were subsequently laid across the Atlantic and Pacific (Fig. 2):

(a) American two-cable systems, as TAT-1.

(b) British single-cable systems with rigid repeaters made possible by a revolutionary type of deep-sea cable ('lightweight' or 'armourless', Fig. 3) with the strength member at the centre and torsionally balanced. These provide:

were used for the British Commonwealth system (1961–7).

(c) American single-cable systems essentially similar to (b) and providing bandwidths of 384 kHz (128 circuits) over 4000 nm with nearly 200 repeaters and feed voltages 5+5 kV.

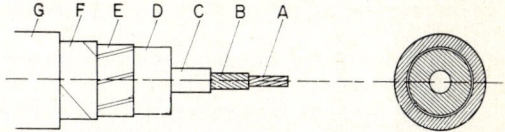

FIG. 3. *British MkI Lightweight Submarine Telephone Cable. A, Die-formed strands, LH lay (h.t. steel); B, Steel wires, RH lay (h.t. steel); C, Longitudinal tape, box-seamed (Cu); D, Polythene to 0·99 in dia.; E, 6 Return tapes (Al)· F, Cotton tapes with corrosion inhibitor; G, Polythene sheath to 1·28 in dia.*

*Armoured cable is used in shallow water.*

There have been a number of cable faults, nearly all due to trawlers, but the reliability of the electronic equipment has been exceptional—one fault in more than

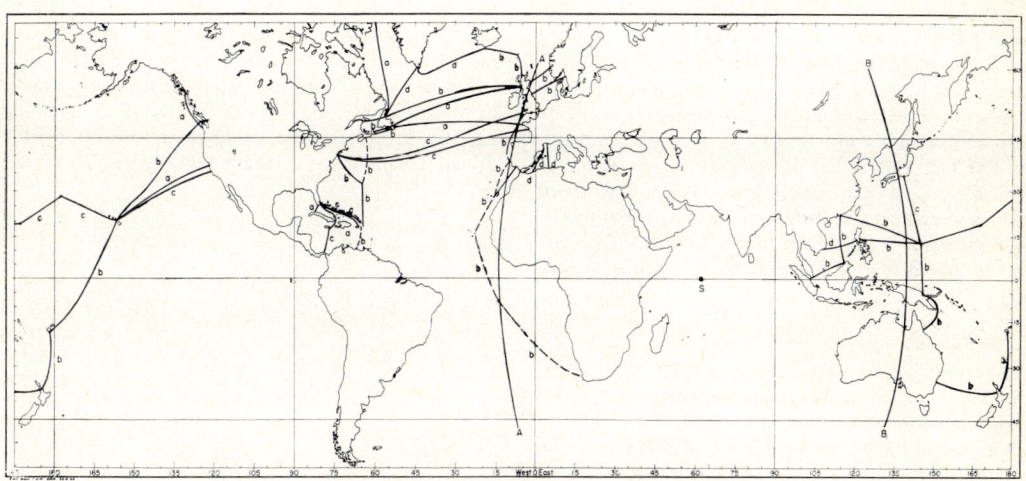

FIG 2. *Ocean Telephone Cables and Satellite Coverage.*

(a) *American 2-cable;*
(b) *British single-cable;*
(c) *American single-cable;*
(d) *Others.*
} see text

*Dotted—under construction or agreed; AA—BB Coverage limits for geostatic satellite S, 5° aerial elevation (Shown at 62° E).*

(i) bandwidths of 240 kHz (80 circuits) over 3000 nautical miles (nm) and

(ii) in a later version, bandwidths of 480 kHz over 2000 nm.

In each case the maximum number of repeaters is about 120 requiring feed voltages 6·5+6·5 kV. These systems

$8 \times 10^9$ component-hours for the British system. All reasonable performance objectives can be met. Between London and Sydney for example, the frequency response is within half the limits recommended by the international consultative body (CCITT) and the standard deviation of overall loss is less than 1 dB; the propagation time is about 130 ms. Introduction of cable service commonly doubles the traffic on a route. In 1963, operator dialling was introduced on Atlantic cables, e.g. a London operator can dial subscribers in major American and Canadian cities; cable service to Australia was opened the same year on the same basis. Subscriber dialling is still some years away.

The history of land communication shows that system costs increase roughly as the cube root of the total bandwidth provided and that more sophisticated systems become economic as requirements increase. Global systems show much the same pattern and, as demand increases, it is highly desirable to provide single systems of greater capacity rather than to multiplicate smaller ones.

All existing ocean systems use thermionic valves and one further valve system is available, a British 360-circuit system, which will be used between South Africa and Portugal for service in 1968. A 640-circuit transistor system has been developed for use in the North Sea and is being adapted for ocean use; it will be used to extend the South Africa cable to Britain and elsewhere. In America a 720-circuit transistor system is available and will be first used between Florida and St. Thomas (Virgin Is.); in Britain a 1400-circuit system is under development; using 1·5 in. lightweight cable and 8 nm repeater spacing it will span some 4000 nm and provide transmission bands of over 4 MHz in each direction.

On a few ocean cables Time Assignment Speech Interpolation (TASI) equipment has been used to approximately double the traffic capacity; this takes advantage of the fact that a circuit does not carry speech in both directions at the same time. Using high speed electronic switching and a control circuit, a channel is seized only when a subscriber starts to speak; this arrangement operates only when nearly all circuits are engaged.

*Communication satellites.* Using American launch vehicles, satellites can be placed in any desired orbit, equatorial, polar or inclined, circular or elliptical. Orbit time is proportional to (semi-major axis)$^{3/2}$ and for a circular orbit at 22,300 miles altitude it is synchronous with that of the Earth's rotation; if the orbit is also equatorial, the satellite is geostatic, though there are always small perturbations. Such satellites have obvious attractions for communications; there are no problems of tracking, transfer or Doppler effect such as occur with lower orbits and three satellites could provide a complete global system. The disadvantages relative to lower orbits are the lower payload, high path loss, 260 ms propagation time between earth stations and long (up to 70 min) eclipses.

A number of experimental satellites have been placed in orbit by the U.S. National Aeronautical and Space Administration; Echo I, a passive reflector in the form of a 100 ft-diameter balloon, in 1960; Telstar I and Relay I, the first satellites with active equipment (transponders), in 1962; Telstar II and Syncom II, the first successful near-synchronous satellite, in 1963; Relay II and Syncom III, in 1964. To operate with these fully-steerable earth stations were built, two with 85 ft-aperture horns under radomes and one, at Goonhilly Downs, Cornwall, an open 85 ft—aperture paraboloid.

Arrangements for the establishment and operation of a satellite system were set up, following the enactment of the U.S. Communications Satellite Act in 1962. This led to the creation, in 1963, of the Communications Satellite Corporation (COMSAT) to 'provide a satellite system and to hire channels to U.S. common carriers and other authorized bodies, foreign and domestic, and to operate earth stations in the United States'. Satellites so provided are owned by the signatories to a Special Agreement, at present 54, in proportion to their investment; the largest investors are U.S.A. through COMSAT ($> 50\%$), Great Britain (about 8 per cent), France and Germany (about 6 per cent each). The consortium is known as INTELSAT and the controlling body, each member of which must represent at least 1.5 per cent ownership, is the Interim Communication Satellite Corporation (ICSC); this plans to provide a full global system—the 'basic phase'—in 1968. It functions until 1969, when permanent arrangements will be agreed.

INTELSAT I (Early Bird), the first geostatic satellite (Fig. 4) was the first product of these arrangements; it weighs 85 lbs and is spin-stabilized parallel to the Earth's axis; 6000 n-on-p solar cells provide a 45W power supply. There are separate transponders, each 25 MHz bandwidth, for E-W and W-E transmissions, 'up' carrier frequencies being in the 6 GHz band and 'down' frequencies in the 4 GHz band. These feed a

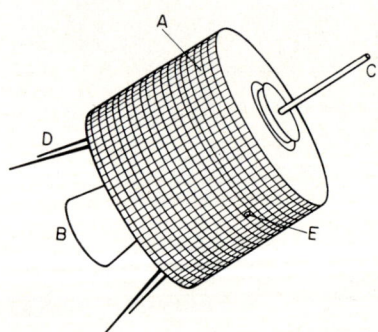

FIG. 4. *INTELSAT I (Early Bird) Satellite. A, 6000 n-p silicon solar cells; B, Apogee motor nozzle; C, Communication aerial system; D, VHF telemetry aerials; E, Radial $H_2O_2$ jets (axial jets in base).*
*Cylinder, $28\frac{1}{2}$ in. dia.; 23 in. high.*

common travelling-wave-tube output stage, the transmitting aerial being circularly symmetrical with an effective radiated power (ERP) of 6 watts. Longitudinal drift (say $0.05°$/day) can be corrected as required by gas jets operated via a v.h.f. telemetry system. Earth station aerials use either programme-control, auto-follow or both. 240 telephone circuits or a television circuit can be provided between one pair of stations only, using frequency modulation.

The CCITT has provisionally agreed that up to 150 ms one-way propagation time is wholly acceptable and that more than 400 ms is normally unacceptable; above 150 ms an increasing proportion of conversations is unsatisfactory. Following a study of user reaction to calls via INTELSAT I, it has been agreed that the delay is acceptable to most users and that the basic phase satellites will be geostatic; extensions, however, will be limited to 300 ms overall. Two-hop satellite links are thus inadmissible but a single-hop connexion between Britain, and Australia is practicable (Fig. 2).

Two geostatic satellites (INTELSAT II), of greater capacity than INTELSAT I, were placed over the Atlantic (6°W) and the Pacific (173°E) in 1966–7. INTELSAT III for the basic phase will have greater ERP, partly achieved by effective attitude stabilization of the aerial and will provide some 1200 circuits; the expected life is 5 years.

The radio frequencies suitable for satellites are about 1–10 GHz and two 500 MHz bands each have been allocated for upward and downward transmission; each band should ultimately provide 5000–10,000 telephone circuits, or their equivalent, per satellite. Because the same frequencies are also used for terrestrial systems, the permitted flux density at the earth is very low ($-152$ dBW/m$^2$ in a 4 kHz band) but with a path attenuation of almost 200 dB, even this figure is not reached at present. Cosmic noise, received at an earth station with the signal, corresponds to only a few °K and to take full advantage of this it is necessary to use a very-low-noise amplifier as well as a highly-efficient aerial. The figure-of-merit of a receiving station is the aerial gain (relative to isotropic) to noise-temperature ratio ($G/T$) and any shortcoming can be compensated only by taking, and paying for, greater power from the satellite. The ICSC requires that earth station performance should normally be based on an 85 ft-diameter aperture at 50 per cent efficiency and an overall system noise temperature of 50°K at 5° elevation ($G/T = 40.7$ dB at 4 GHz). Smaller-aperture stations may be admitted—typically based on a 42 ft aperture at 55 per cent efficiency and 100°K ($G/T = 32$ dB)—the power required from the satellite being correspondingly increased.

INTELSAT II satellites are the first to be capable of working between more than two earth stations, i.e. with multiple access, in which facility resides the outstanding advantage of satellites. The basic phase is expected to give access to some 50 earth stations, some working to more than one satellite.

*The future.* Global traffic will undoubtedly continue to increase rapidly and both cables and satellites will have their parts to play. The cost of cable systems is well established and the cost of the larger systems can be predicted with confidence; the present high cost of satellite circuits can be expected to fall substantially as systems increase in capacity and construction costs decrease. Cable costs are nearly proportional to distance; satellite costs are independent of distance, thus giving them an inherent advantage at long range. Over a half of all global traffic is across the North Atlantic and there is an estimated need for perhaps 1000 circuits by 1970. On this basis there should be scope in the mid-1970's for an Atlantic satellite having a capacity of some thousands of telephone circuits or their equivalent. At this capacity and distance it should have a clear economic advantage over large-capacity cables. A satellite system at lower altitude may eventually be necessary for tandem connexions.

Other potential uses for satellites are mobile services to and between ships and aircraft including navigation aids, television broadcasting and national television distribution. All but the last involve problems of high satellite power and earth station aerial size to varying degrees, but general purpose satellites which provide all or some of these services or integrate them with normal fixed communication services, are a possibility for the future.

*See also:* Data transmission. Telecommunication system planning, international. Pseudonoise sequences.

*Bibliography*

*Anglo-Canadian Transatlantic Telephone Cable (CANTAT)* (1963) *Proc, I.E.E.,* **110,** 1115 (7 papers).
*Bell Laboratories Record,* April 1963. (Special Telstar Issue).
CLINCH C. E. E. (1960) *Time Assignment Speech Interpolation (TASI)*, Post Office Electrical Engineers J. **53,** 197.
GARRAT T. G. R. M. (1950) *One Hundred Years of Submarine Cables,* London: H.M.S.O.
GATLAND K. W. (Ed.) (1964) *Telecommunications Satellites,* London: Iliffe.
HALSEY R. J. (1964) *British Commonwealth Ocean Cables, I.E.E.E, Trans. COM-12* No. **3,** 6.
*Satellite Communications* (1964) Cmnd 2436, London: H.M.S.O.
*The SD Submarine Cable System* (1964) *Bell Syst. Tech. J.,* **43** No. 4, Part 1, 1155 (11 papers).
*Symposium on the Transatlantic Telephone Cable* (1957) *Proc. I.E.E.,* **104**B Suppl 4 (11 papers).

R. J. HALSEY

## TELECOMMUNICATION SYSTEM PLANNING, INTERNATIONAL.

### 1. Introduction

The planning of international telecommunications systems resolves itself into laying down rules for the interchange of information. The information consists of two types, analogue and digital. Examples of the first type are speech, music and television signals, and of the second, telegraphy and data, in the modern context. The rules mentioned must evidently cover the physical means of conveying the information so that systems will interwork and not interfere; and also the technical limits and tolerances allowable so that a satisfactory service, for instance, of speech, can be operated.

The present practical means of conveying information are by radio, land-line, or submarine cable and the International Regulations and Recommendations relating to them are drawn up at conferences of the International Telecommunication Union which is the Special Agency recognized by the United Nations as the responsible body in the field of telecommunications.

The International Regulations are documented as follows:
The Telephone Regulations; The Telegraph Regulations; The Radio Regulations.
They are mandatory and are annexed to the International Telecommunication Convention, the Union's basic instrument, which is signed as a Treaty. In being mandatory the Regulations differ from the Recommendations.

The Telephone Regulations deal with such matters as the composition and use of the system, directories, classes of calls, booking and establishment of calls, programme transmissions, tariffs and charging, accounting, and the general function of the technical organizations which will be mentioned later.

The Telegraph Regulations cover similar ground in respect of telegraph signals, the alphabet to be used, languages, counting of words, routing and transmission, interruptions to traffic, delivery, transmission, press telegrams, phototelegraph service, accounting, archives.

The Radio Regulations cover wider ground. The following are some of the subjects dealt with — general and special rules for the assignment of frequencies for broadcasting, aeronautical, maritime, mobile, beacon, and fixed services; notification of frequencies; measures against interference; administrative provisions; working conditions in mobile services (frequencies, power, etc.) distress, alarm, urgency, and safety; priorities, etc., of radio telegrams.

The I.T.U. has two technical organizations which are responsible for recommendations which, while not mandatory are widely adopted, thus ensuring the interworking of systems, including quality of service and maintenance. These two organisations are:

(a) International Consultative Committee for Telephony and Telegraphy (CCITT) which deals with (i) quality of service on telephone, telegraph, broadcast and television transmission, and a number of other communications, (ii) the technical design parameters of land line and submarine cable systems to ensure interworking to satisfactory standards.

(b) International Consultative Committee for Radio (CCIR) which, *inter alia*, issues technical recommendations regarding the design parameters for radio systems to ensure interworking to satisfactory standards.

This article considers the technical aspects of planning ni some detail. It covers speech, telegraph, and television circuits. The factors affecting the planning of these circuits are interlinked to some extent and it will be convenient to start with speech as the predominant user of the communication networks.

## 2. Speech Channels

*2.1. General.* In planning the transmission performance of telephone connexions, different problems arise according to the class of connexion being considered. The classes range from purely local connexions within a telephone exchange area to world-wide connexions involving tandem switching of several links, inland, submarine and in the near future, satellite. The performance of very short connexions depends mainly upon the subscribers' telephone sets, the interconnecting lines generally adding little degradation. The longest connexions, however, are limited in performance by such factors as loss, which may be subject to random variations, noise, bandwidth restriction, attenuation/frequency distortion, delay distortion, long propagation time, echo and mutilation by echo suppressors. Furthermore, many circuits over expensive line plant make use of speech-channel economy devices and compandors, etc., and each of these is liable to introduce its quota of degradation.

All these factors have to be taken into consideration in planning, but unfortunately it is very difficult to find a common additive unit to express the overall effect of such diverse factors. Also, the effects of different factors are highly interdependent, e.g. a given level of noise at the listener is more important on high-loss connexions than on those of low loss; on the other hand, modest quantities of non-linear distortion or noise introduced at the speaking end may be important on low-loss connexions, but be hardly noticeable when loss is high. The most informative procedure is to determine the percentage of calls that reach a certain standard of excellence, taking account of all the factors present.

The most important of these factors are introduced in paras. 2.2.1 to 2.2.4.

*2.2. Major factors affecting transmission planning.*
*2.2.1. Circuit loss – reference equivalents.* Communication by speech between individuals evolved naturally in a medium consisting of only a few feet of air, but with the introduction of the telephone the distance restriction was removed – worldwide connexions will no doubt soon be comparatively commonplace. It may, however, reasonably be assumed that the nearer the telephone speech link resembles a direct air path a few feet long, the more acceptable will be the result. Ordinary commercial telephony, however, imposes certain restrictions which make even the best connexions rather crude imitations of a direct air path. A fundamental restriction is listening monaurally with an earphone, while economic restrictions affect bandwidth and noise, etc. Fortunately, the human senses are very adaptable and acceptable results are possible despite these restrictions. In fact, if the received signal is sufficiently loud, considerable but not unlimited liberties can be taken.

Loudness of received speech is of paramount importance in planning, not only because adequate loudness is necessary for successful communication but because an extremely wide range of received loudness is inescapable. Also, some of the restrictions referred to can be mitigated to a certain extent by an increase of loudness above that normally associated with a natural direct air path.

Loudness of received speech is a function of (a) the vocal level of the talker and his manner of holding the telephone handset, and (b) the overall air-air acoustic loss of the telephone connexion. The former is largely outside the control of the telephone administration, and a range of $\pm 10$ dB must be accepted; the latter is clearly within the responsibility of the telephone administration, and a method of specifying and measuring a quantity analogous to air-air loss is necessary. The quantity is termed 'reference equivalent', and it is measured by comparing the loudness of the speech signal over a specified reference system with the signal received over the connexion under test. Numerically, the reference equivalent is the attenuation, or gain, that has to be inserted in the reference circuit so that it is subjectively equal in loudness to the test circuit.

For example, the air path connecting a talker and a listener separated by 1 metre has a reference equivalent of 33 dB. The reference equivalent preferred by normal users, listening on a telephone receiver to speech from a linear microphone, is about 21 dB less than this, say 12 dB. The presence of distortion due to the currently used carbon microphone causes users to prefer even lower values of reference equivalent, say 3 or 4 dB.

An arbitrary sub-division of the reference system enables reference equivalent values to be allocated separately to the sending and receiving directions of the local telephone circuit, i.e. the combination of the subscriber's set, subscriber's line and exchange feeding bridge. This enables the reference equivalent of a complete telephone connexion to be specified as the sum of a sending reference equivalent, a receiving reference equivalent and the loss of the circuit connecting individual send and receive parts.

To illustrate the application of reference equivalents to international circuits it is convenient at this stage to introduce the concept of Hypothetical Reference Circuits (h.r.c.) which simplify the specification of, amongst other things, the loss in terms of reference equivalent for circuits of different lengths. Each h.r.c. has a specified length (typically 2500 km) and a specified number of stages of frequency translation. Figure 1 shows three typical circuits. The values of $x_s$ and $x_r$, the send and receive

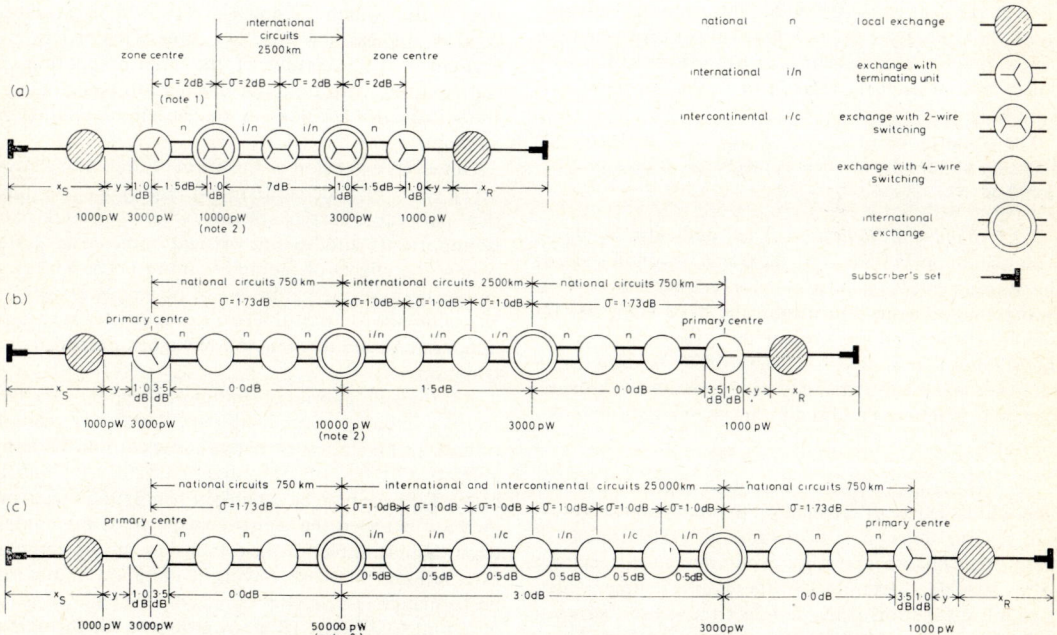

FIG. 1. *Hypothetical connexions of national, international and intercontinental circuits. (a) Old plan for 2500 km; (b) new plan for 2500 km; (c) new plan for 25000 km.*

(1 – variation of loss with time s shown thus: $|\leftarrow \sigma = 2\text{dB} \rightarrow|$ in (a) the two international circuits are assumed to have a normal distribution with a standard deviation $\sigma = 2$dB for the individual circuits. Three international circuits could be interconnected only if the individual standard deviations $\sigma < 1.5$dB. 2 – noise power at all points is considered constant except at international switching points where standard deviations $\sigma = 0$, $\sigma = 3$dB, $\sigma = 5$dB have been taken. 3 – the points to which the various sources of noise have been referred are appropriate to transmission in the direction from left to right.)

reference equivalents respectively, vary with the length of the subscriber's local line, while $y$ depends on the distance of the local exchange from the zone or primary centre. Maximum values of $x_s$ and $x_r$ for modern telephone sets, are 12 and 3 dB respectively; a corresponding value for $y$ is 6·5 dB.

In the case of international connexions a maximum of 40 dB (4·6 Np) reference equivalent is recommended with all interconnexions on a two-wire basis. In order to ensure some uniformity in the distribution of sensitivity between sending and receiving directions of each channel end, the overall limit was sub-divided into 18·2 dB (2·1 Np) for sending, 13·0 dB (1·5 Np) for receiving and 6·9 dB (0·8 Np) for the international line, leaving 1·9 dB (0·2 Np) for switching and other miscellaneous losses. This aspect is discussed further in section 2.4.

*2.2.2. Circuit noise.* Circuit noise arises from the presence of unwanted signals in the speech path. A given level of circuit noise at the listener's ear will have an effect upon conversational performance of a connexion according to the level of the received speech signals. For example, noise at a level of $-60$ dBmp measured at the input of a local telephone circuit, which has a received reference equivalent of 0 dB (quite a typical value), would raise the percentage of unsatisfactory calls from 16 to 28 per cent when the overall reference equivalent is 36 dB, but only from 0·7 to about 1·0 per cent when the overall reference equivalent is 21 dB. (dBmp indicates a power level in decibels, relative to 1 mW, psophometrically weighted.)

The importance of noise in regard to performance planning of speech channels is discussed in detail in section 2.3.

*2.2.3. Bandwidth limitation.* The bandwidth available is another important factor in the transmission of speech; the modern recommendations for commercial speech enforce the necessity to transmit the band from 300 Hz to 3400 Hz, and all modern carrier systems are built to this standard. If a link in a chain of connexions has a narrower bandwidth this causes a penalty or 'impairment' which must be allowed for in assessing the loss of a connexion.

*2.2.4. Other degradations.* To obtain an overall assessment of the degree of satisfaction that telephone connexions give to users, it is necessary to take account of many other factors which, for economic reasons, cannot be made perfect. Examples of these are sidetone, which is mainly a function of the design of the subscriber's set, and echo, which is important on long connexions. Thus, for connexions having a long delay time echo suppressors may be needed, and these have undesirable secondary effects. Further factors are introduced by the desire to obtain the utmost economic advantages from a system; an example is the use of compandors to mitigate the effect of high levels of circuit noise.

*2.3. Noise. 2.3.1. General noise objectives.* Many years ago, the CCIF – now CCITT – recommended that the line loss observed at the end of an international telephone circuit should be sufficiently low, and more particularly, so low, that the psophometric e.m.f. induced in the line by external disturbances from neighbouring electric traction and power lines, or by repeater station noise, should be less than 5 mV in an open-wire line or 2 mV in a cable circuit. Since international circuits are generally on cable and operate with 7 dB loss two-wire to two-wire, this voltage is equivalent, at the input of the circuit, which is taken as the zero relative point, to a psophometric power of approximately 8000 pW ($-51$ dBmOp). (dBmOp indicates a power level in decibels relative to 1 mW at a zero relative level point, psophometrically weighted.)

Subsequent development of multichannel carrier working showed the need to design intermediate repeaters and terminal translating equipment so that European countries could provide plant which would ensure that circuits that transit those countres would meet the CCIF recommendations. These objectives were based on the concept of hypothetical reference circuits described earlier in this article. The objective for a 2500 km circuit on a coaxial-cable carrier system was a psophometric noise power of 10,000 pW ($-50$ dBmOp) at a point of zero relative level, it being understood that this limit would not be exceeded for more than 1 per cent of the time during which the noise level would be expected to be at its highest, e.g. the busy hour. This proviso took account of the variation of the intermodulation-noise contribution with time, the calculation being based on statistical considerations in the design of multichannel amplifiers.

However, extension of this form of design objective to other types of wideband system, especially to symmetrical-pair cable carrier systems (where crosstalk babble is important) and to line-of-sight radio-relay systems (where the effects of fading are important), led to difficulties because the variations of noise power with time characteristic of the different systems were statistically different and could not be combined or subdivided in any common way.

A far reaching series of studies was begun by the CCIF in 1954, in co-operation with the CCIR, on the formulation of general noise objectives which would be applicable to all types of transmission system by line and radio. These were to be capable of being subdivided for allocation between the constituent parts of the complete circuit and suitable for the establishment of a composite international network having a common standard of performance. These studies led, through the formation of a joint CCITT-CCIR study group, to the formulation of the general noise objectives for carrier-transmission system design (C.C.I.T.T. Recommendation G 222).

These recommendations were based on the requirements of the communication signals to be carried (telephone speech, telephone signalling and voice-frequency telegraphy) and are consistent with the characteristics of carrier-cable systems and line-of-sight radio-relay systems. In principle they also apply to analogous systems such as tropospheric-scatter radio links and communication-satellite links, but the special characteristics of these transmission paths necessitate some modifications to the general objectives.

*2.3.2. General noise objectives for 2500 km hypothetical reference circuits.* The general noise objectives for 2500 km hypothetical reference circuits on cable and line-of-sight radio-relay systems have three main aspects:

(a) An hourly mean requirement – 'the mean psophometric noise power during any hour shall not exceed 10,000 pW (−50 dBmOp)'. The period to be taken would be, for a cable system, any busy hour; for a radio-relay system, any hour during a season when fading would be expected to be severe.

(b) One-minute mean requirement – 'the mean psophometric noise power over one minute shall not exceed 10,000 pW (−50dBmOp) for more than 20 per cent of any month or 50,000 pW (−43 dBmOp) for more than 0·1 per cent of any month'. This requirement is essentially to cover the fading characteristics of radio-relay links; it may be assumed that any cable system meeting the requirement of (a) will meet this requirement. The integrating period of one minute was chosen as being comparable to the duration of a telephone call and was convenient for the study of the effects of high noise levels on telephone conversation. It is not greatly different from the durations characterising radio fading, which are typically measured in seconds and tens of seconds.

(c) 5 ms mean requirement – 'the unweighted noise power, measured with an integrating time of 5 ms, shall not exceed $10^6$ pW (−30 dBmOp) for more than 0·01 per cent (4·3 min) of any month'. This percentage of time is considered to be a satisfactory objective for telephony signalling or for 50 baud voice-frequency telegraphy using frequency modulation, but a somewhat higher standard, i.e. a smaller percentage of the time, would be preferred for amplitude-modulated voice-frequency telegraphy.

The integrating time was chosen at 5 ms as being comparable with the duration of the elementary signals in 50 baud voice-frequency telegraphy (20 ms) or telephone signalling (35 ms) on the assumption that the high levels of noise could occur as isolated large-amplitude impulses, each of which could result in an element error. Such impulses are not found to be typical of radio or line propagation, and this clause might therefore seem to be inappropriate for a design objective. However, practical links are found to generate such noise impulses, probably from external sources such as power-switching operations, and it is useful to have established a limit which should not be exceeded in a practical circuit.

The hourly mean and one-minute mean noise-power objectives can be shared between terminal translating equipments and the wideband equipment on the assumption that 2500 pW is allocated between all the modulation stages in the hypothetical reference circuit and 7500 pW is allocated to the 2500 km of high-frequency line or radio system. This latter allocation can be subdivided along the route, giving 3 pW/km as the average rate of generation of noise along the length of the cable or radio path.

*2.3.3. Design objectives in respect of noise.* Guiding principles for the design of plant from the aspect of noise have been formulated, and may be summarized as follows:

Overland plant. Overland plant cannot be expected to provide higher standards for a minority of circuits (very long circuits would represent a small fraction of a typical wideband system); selection of somewhat better channels may be possible in some instances, and the target for a long inland section could be set at 1–2 pW/km, the normal 3 pW/km being accepted where unavoidable and where the length of overland plant is not great.

Submarine cables. Submarine-cable systems may be designed so that the desired noise objective is achieved either without the use of compandors on the channels or on the assumption that compandors will be used on some or all of the channels.

A submarine-cable system designed for use without compandors to permit the unrestricted use of telephony, v.f. telegraphy and data transmission should have a noise performance not worse than 1 pW/km, averaged over all channels in one direction of transmission at a time. The worst channel performance should not exceed 3 pW/km (hourly mean only is considered at the present time).

The use of compandors on some, if not all, channels of a submarine-cable system can be foreseen, perhaps to allow for changes taking place during the life of the system (repairs, ageing etc.), or where it has not been possible to achieve a very close equalisation of the cable loss/frequency characteristic. A general rule is under study by the CCITT to limit the uncompandored noise on any channel at any time in the life of the system to a value which would permit the longest circuits to be used for speech with a single terminal compandor or for a tolerant form of voice-frequency telegraphy.

Considering possible extensions of ocean cables and their interconnexion either under normal or emergency operating conditions, it seems highly desirable that the range of performance standards adopted should not be too wide, particularly if restrictions on the routing of voice-frequency telegraph-bearer circuits follow.

Communication satellites. Communication-satellite systems using active satellites are under consideration so that the majority of intercontinental connexions may be made with no more than one satellite link; a worldwide connexion should involve no more than three (generally two) such links. Naturally, the great-circle distance between the two earth stations could have any value up to the effective span of the link (perhaps 7500 km), and the noise performance cannot be expressed in pW/km as for conventional overland systems. It seems necessary to work within the framework of the hypothetical worldwide connexion and to consider noise on a per-circuit basis. The CCIR recommendation for the hypothetical reference circuit comprising a single satellite link allows 10,000 pW ($-50$ dBmO) mean in any hour and 80,000 pW ($-41$ dBmO) one-minute mean for not more than 0·2 per cent of any month; frequency-translating-equipment noise is excluded from these values. This performance is primarily to meet telephone speech and signalling requirements; voice-frequency telegraphy and data-transmission needs are under consideration.

Present indications are that the variation of noise power with time will follow a somewhat lower and flatter distribution curve with f.m. satellite transmission than with line-of-sight transmission. It should therefore be possible to meet a specification for short-term noise which is very similar to that in the general noise objectives. This should not impose any restriction on the use of satellite channels for voice-frequency telegraphy.

*2.4. Mean power of a channel.* Taking account of statistics of speech-level measurements, signalling and exchange tones, and an assumed distribution of voice-frequency telegraph bearer circuits (perhaps one per supergroup), a conventional value has been chosen for the mean power per channel in a multichannel system during the busy hour. The value taken is 32 $\mu$W ($-15$ dBmO). Experience supports the choice of this value so far as inland wideband systems are concerned. However, intercontinental ocean-cable systems of small capacity seem to attract traffic different from that on inland wideband systems; in particular, in the high proportion of voice-frequency telegraph bearer circuits and the use of speech channel economy equipment. A higher value of mean power per channel has to be assumed for such systems.

*2.5. Very long circuits* (2500 km to 25000 km or more). It will be seen from Fig. 1c that worldwide connexions will involve the interconnexion of national circuits, international circuits conforming to the 2500 km hypothetical-reference-circuit design standards, and very long international and intercontinental circuits. The latter may be provided by means of ocean-cable links, extended on overland plant and, in the future, by communication satellites or combinations of these means. Certain special standards may therefore be necessary for such very long connexions.

*2.5.1. Transmission performance.* Before considering the performance of very long multicircuit connexions that are just in the process of developing, it is desirable to note for comparison the performance of shorter connexions that have been in general use for some time.

Figure 1a shows a typical international connexion set up in accordance with the old CCITT transmission plan. When this plan was introduced, the sending and receiving reference equivalents of subscribers' sets on limiting subscribers' lines ($x_s$ and $x_r$, see Fig. 1a) were typically 9 dB and 4 dB, respectively, and so the reference equivalents of the national ends would be 17·5 dB sending and 12·5 dB receiving, for a value of $y$ (see Fig. 1a) of 6 dB. These values would have been just within the limits recommended by the CCITT of 18·2 and 13·0 dB, respectively. Developments in telephone receivers would have enabled the receiving reference equivalent to be dramatically reduced, e.g. by 6 dB, but in practice some of this improvement has been transferred to sending by changing the ratio of the induction-coil transformer; it has proved much more difficult to increase the sensitivity of telephone microphones, particularly at the lower feeding currents now common with lighter-gauge conductors. Consequently, present-day telephone sets have evolved gradually, and so their reference equivalents on limiting lines are perhaps 11 dB sending and 2 dB receiving; the limiting lines have also been increased from, say 500 $\Omega$ to 1 k$\Omega$ resistance to absorb the improvement attributable indirectly to the modern receiver. This change has been recognized by the CCITT in recommending that, under the new CCITT switching and transmission plan (Section 2.6), the national reference equivalents for sending and receiving should differ by about 9 dB, instead of 5 dB as formerly.

As a fair basis for comparison, the old CCITT plan will be considered here in association with telephone sets of current type, i.e. the situation immediately before implementation of the new plan. Thus, in Fig. 1a the following values would apply for $y = 6$ dB, $x_s = 11$ dB and $x_r = 2$ dB:

National sending reference equivalent = 19·5 dB (18·2)
National receiving reference equivalent = 10·5 dB (13·0)
Nominal overall reference equivalent = 39 dB (40)

The figures in parentheses are the CCITT (old plan) recommended limits.

Figure 1b shows a 2500 km connexion set up in accordance with the new CCITT transmission plan, which was expected to reduce overall equivalents by about 4 dB. The recommended maximum national reference equivalents are 20·8 dB for sending and 12·2 dB for receiving and are calculated to and from the four-wire ends of the international circuit. These maxima are to be respected for 95% of actual connexions.

Again taking $x_s = 11$ dB, $y = 6$ dB and $x_r = 2$ dB, the reference equivalents obtained under the new plan would be as follows:

National sending reference equivalent = 21·5 dB (20·8)
National receiving reference equivalent = 12·5 dB (12·2)
Nominal overall reference equivalent = 34·5 dB.

The figures in parentheses are the CCITT (new plan) recommended limits, and are intended to apply for 95 per cent of calls. It is expected, however, that they will apply for 97·5 per cent of calls. The quoted overall reference equivalent (34·5 dB) might be expected to be complied with in well over 99 per cent of actual calls.

The extension of the new CCITT plan to very long connexions of 25,000 km is illustrated in Fig. 1c. In this case, the nominal overall reference equivalent for the previously quoted values of $x'_sy$ and $x_r$ would be 37 dB, and this is likely to be complied with in about 99 per cent of actual calls.

2.6. *Proposed new CCITT switching and transmission plan.* World-wide telephone traffic in the future may be routed over five or more international circuits switched together in tandem. In addition, in order to reach the most remote local telephone exchange, each terminal country can add, typically, four national circuits, of which three will very likely be four-wire amplified trunk circuits and one an unamplified two-wire junction circuit. The worldwide transmission plan must therefore permit up to about twelve independently maintained low-loss amplified circuits to be connected together with a good chance of satisfactory transmission as regards transmission loss, stability, propagation time, echo, attenuation/frequency distortion, noise and crosstalk.

In order to achieve this aim, the circuits must be connected together with four-wire switching apparatus (or equivalent), and accordingly the CCITT has recommended that:

(a) international transit centres in the future should use four-wire switching apparatus.

(b) international centres (i.e. where national circuits are connected to international circuits) should use four-wire switching or its equivalent (e.g. two-wire pad switching). Four-wire switching is preferred.

An important advantage conferred by four-wire switching is that exchange losses due to wiring and apparatus can be readily absorbed in the line-up of the individual circuits, and thus these losses do not contribute to the overall loss of the connexion.

One example of the new plan is illustrated in Fig. 2; various aspects are discussed in the following Sections.

2.6.1. *Nominal transmission loss between the two-wire points of a complete connexion.* The nominal transmission loss between the two-wire points of a complete connexion should not be less than $4+0.5$ NdB, where N is the number of individually maintained national and international circuits. This loss is achieved in practice by operating the international circuits at 0·5 dB nominal loss between the four-wire switching points cud by recommending that the national extension circuits have a nominal loss of not less than $2+0.5n$ dB, where $n$ is the number of national amplified trunk circuits.

(One method of adding national trunk circuits is according to the formula $3.5+0n$ dB, i.e. a nominal loss that is not a function of the number of trunk circuits. This is acceptable provided that no more than three trunk circuits are needed. If more than three are required, the loss must be increased at not less than 0·5 dB per additional circuit.)

The 0·5 dB per international circuit unfortunately increases the nominal transmission loss of the more complicated connexions, but is necessary to ensure their sta-

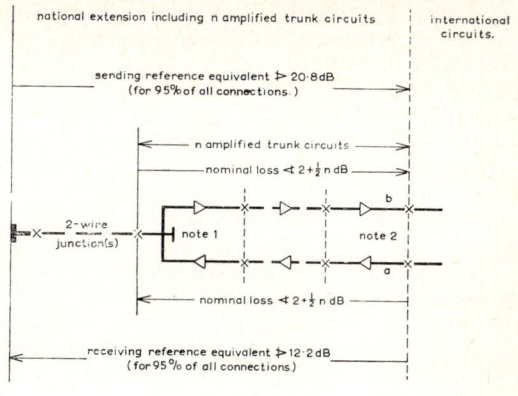

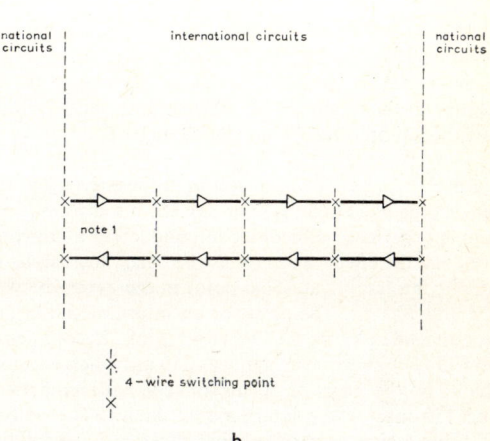

FIG. 2. *Principal provisions of the new CCITT transmission and switching plan.* (a) National circuits. (1 — nominal balance return loss not less than 6dB. 2 — the transmission losses can be allocated as administrations choose, provided that the sum of the nominal losses around the loop from point a to point b (i.e. the ends of the international circuit) has a mean value not less than $10+n$dB. The permitted variations may also be summed in a similar manner, giving a total allowance of $\sqrt{(6.25+4n)}$dB for the standard deviation ).

(b) International circuits. (nominal transmission loss between 4-wire switching points is 0.5dB).

bility. The routing plan will limit the number of international circuits connected in tandem to five. There is no maximum loss specified for the national extension circuits, but administrations must comply with the recommendations concerning the national sending and receiving reference equivalents.

2.6.2. *Balance return loss.* The balance return loss of the two-wire/four-wire terminating unit affects both the stability and the echo in telephone connexions.

*Stability.* As a target for the future, the balance return loss (in the speaking condition at any frequency in the range 300–3400 Hz) presented at the two-wire point is recommended to be not less than 6 dB mean with a standard deviation of 2·5 dB. During the setting up of a call, the conditions are such that, either the four-wire path is not yet established and so there can be no risk of instability, or the stability margin is increased by connecting an impedance across the two-wire point (or attenuator pads in the four-wire path) e.g. while awaiting an answer. Details are left to the individual administrations.

Echo. The CCITT is studying how best the echo-return loss might be measured and specified. Until a recommendation is made, the echo-return loss is assumed to have a mean value of not less than 11 dB with a standard deviation of 3 dB expressed as a weighted mean power ratio over the band 500–2500 Hz.

*2.6.3. Variation of transmission loss.* The mean transmission loss of international circuits at the reference frequency is recommended to be not greater than $\pm 0.5$ dB relative to the nominal transmission loss. The standard deviation should not be greater than 1 dB.

*2.6.4. Propagation time and echo.* If the one-way propagation time of a circuit is long, say 150 ms or more, some people experience difficulties in conducting a conversation, and the effect worsens as the delay increases, becoming intolerable at some point in the range between 250 and 700 ms. The limit for an international circuit, recommended by the CCITT (Red Book, Recommendation G 114) many years ago was 250 ms which was to be shared on the basis of 50 ms for each national network and 150 ms for the international circuit. The velocity of propagation of various types of plant is approximately as follows:

| | |
|---|---|
| Loaded cable | 10000 miles/s |
| High-velocity cable | 120000 miles/s |
| Radio-relay link | 186000 miles/s. |

The effect of propagation time is assuming increasing importance as the worldwide network of communications expands, and tests are at present being conducted to obtain more information on the subject. If echo is present with such long delay times, the combined effect may be very disturbing, although this is dependent to a large extent on the efficiency of the echo-suppressor. The latest recommendation for connexions is that up to 150 ms one-way propagation time is unreservedly acceptable, 150–400 ms is provisionally acceptable, and above 400 ms is provisionally unacceptable.

### 3. Telegraph Channels

*3.1 Summary of rules for Telex and Gentex.* The telegraphy-transmission standards are the same for Telex (subscribers' service) and for Gentex (switched intercommunication between national networks for the forwarding of telegrams), since both services use teleprinters having similar characteristics. Telegraph-transmission limits are based on the study of telegraph distortion, i.e. the degree of departure from the ideal in the timing of a binary transition after its restitution by a telegraph relay at a terminal or intermediate point. Between voice-frequency terminal stations it is customary to measure telegraph distortion on a synchronous basis. Between Telex exchanges it is convenient to make distortion measurements of teleprinter start-stop signals.

For international switched networks and point-to-point circuits, the CCITT has laid down the planning limits (C.C.I.T.T. Red Book, Recommendation R57) shown in the table for the permissible degree of distortion when telegraph channels are connected in tandem.

*CCITT Planning Limits for Telegraph Channels in Tandem*

| Number of channels in tandem within the trunk circuit (i.e. excluding the local section at each end) | The limit of distortion on reversals at the modulation rate employed for adjustment shall be equivalent to the following values at 50 bauds | Limit of the degree of isochronous distortion on standardized text | Limit of the degree of inherent start-stop distortion in service on standardized text |
|---|---|---|---|
| | % | % | % |
| 1 | 4 | 10 | 8 |
| 2 | 7 | 18 | 13 |
| 3 | 10 | 24 | 17 |
| 4 | 12 | 28 | 21 |
| 5 | — | — | 25 |

The values in the table are valid whether the telegraph channels are amplitude- or frequency-modulated.

To allow for the source distortion of the teleprinter transmitter in service, the gross start-stop distortion, measured at the exchange end of the local section, must not exceed 10 percent (C.C.I.T.T. Red Book, Recommendation S3).

If these limits are observed, correct reception should be ensured, provided that the net margin of the receiving teleprinter, measured from the exchange over the local section of line, is not less than 35 per cent (C.C.I.T.T. Red Book, Recommendation S3).

In order that the permissible distortions shall be equitably shared within national networks and on international circuits, the CCITT has further recommended (C.C.I.T.T. Red. Book, Recommendation R 58) that

(a) at the point of exit from the national network the gross start-stop distortion shall not exceed 22 per cent;

(b) the start-stop distortion of the international circuit shall not exceed 13 per cent; this is the equivalent of a circuit made up of two voice-frequency links.

The telegraph distortion of a channel varies in a random manner and is therefore capable of statistical analysis. The degrees of distortion quoted are the maximum values measured during a period of time, which the CCITT has recommended (C.C.I.T.T. Red Book, Recommendation R5) should be 30s, split up into two equal periods for the measurement of early and late distortion, respectively.

*3.2. Situation on very long channels.* From some viewpoints it would be convenient on very long telegraph channels to use the standardized types of voice-frequency telegraph systems with channels spaced at 120 Hz intervals, carrying 50 baud start-stop teleprinter transmission in the usual way, since a large proportion of national telegraph networks are based upon this type of equipment. Then, provided that the telegraph channels perform to the CCITT recommendations, they can be regarded as ordinary links in the communication plan. The recommendation for the performance of a standard voice-frequency telegraph channel is that, in service, the isochronous distortion should not exceed 10 per cent, which includes some allowance for deterioration between routine adjustments. (Isochronous distortion is the ratio, expressed as a percentage, to the unit interval of the maximum measured difference, irrespective of sign, between the actual and theoretical intervals separating any two significant instants of modulation (or of restitution), these instants being not necessarily consecutive.) Analysis of this requirement leads to the conclusion that, for f.m. systems, the minimum signal/random-noise ratio in the telegraph channel should be 28 dB. The corresponding value for a.m. systems, tone-on to random noise, would be 34 dB, but it is unlikely that a.m. systems would be used.

The mean power in a speech-bandwidth channel carrying a voice-frequency telegraph system should not be greater than $-10$ dBmO and that the limit for noise in the same band should be $-43$ dBmOp.

On the assumption that the noise is uniformly distributed with respect to frequency and that the effective bandwidth of the telegraph channel is 80 Hz, these limiting conditions will produce, in a 24-channel f.m. voice-frequency telegraph system, a channel signal/noise ratio of 32·5 dB, providing a margin of 4·5 dB to cater for possible transmission variations. The corresponding signal/noise ratio for a.m. voice-frequency telegraphy would be 35·5 dB, leaving a margin of 1·5 dB.

The rapid growth of traffic that usually follows the provision of new long-distance circuits makes it very desirable to increase the modulation-rate/bandwidth ratio of telegraph channels to increase the traffic capacity, but this cannot be done without taking additional measures to compensate for the higher distortion that results. The two obvious ways of increasing the capacity are by using a greater number of narrower channels or increasing the modulation rate on channels of standard bandwidth.

In either case the increased distortion will make it necessary to use regenerators to ensure satisfactory connexions between national telegraph networks. In addition, time-division multiplexing will have to be used to take advantage of higher modulation rates, and although this appears to be the more complicated arrangement, it has the advantage that it can be applied to individual channels as traffic increases. The retention of channels of standard bandwidth makes it possible to meet occasional special demands for communication at modulation rates somewhat above the normal value but over a restricted number of channels in tandem; this is not possible if the narrower-channel method is adopted.

With t.d.m. synchronous operation over a long-distance link, the modulation rate required is $41\,^1/_7$ bauds per teleprinter circuit, a 6-unit character length being used instead of the $7\frac{1}{2}$ units used in start-stop operation. For an element error rate of the order of 1 in $10^6$, a two-channel synchronous t.d.m. system with an aggregate modulation rate of $82\,^2/_7$ bauds requires a signal/noise ratio of 17 dB in a standard f.m. voice-frequency telegraph channel. Hence there is a considerable margin over the expected noise whilst doubling the capacity. Such a system is in use on transalantic cable routes.

The use of a regenerator specially designed to compensate for the effects of severe bandwidth restriction will increase the capacity of synchronous operation further, and experimental equipment has demonstrated the possibility of carrying three teleprinter transmissions with an aggregate modulation rate of $123\,^3/_7$ bauds, but a signal/noise ratio of 32 dB is needed. This corresponds to a psophometric measurement on the bearer circuit of $-41$ dBmOp, which is very near the limit provided by speech circuits planned for a noise level of $-43$ dB mOp, but it should be possible to select circuits having lower-than-average noise to give a margin for variation in service.

## 4. Television Channels

*4.1. General.* Performance objectives for television channels are detailed in Recommendations drawn up by the CCIR/CCITT Joint Study Group for the Transmission of Television (CMTT), and in respect of monochrome transmissions over long distances, the Recommendations (J61) have been available for several years. Problems associated with the transmission of colour-television signals, however, are at present under study by the CMTT, and preliminary proposals have been

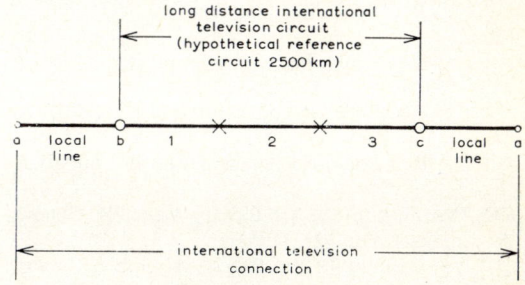

FIG. 3. *International television connexion.*

published. (C.C.I.R. Documents of the Xth Plenary Assembly).

*4.2. Hypothetical reference circuits.* The recommendations for long-distance transmissions are specified in terms of an international hypothetical reference circuit (bc, Fig. 3) comprising a chain of national and international and international coaxial-cable or radio-relay links and having an overall length between video terminal points of 2500 km. There are two intermediate video points dividing the circuit into three sections of equal length, and the three sections are assumed to be lined up individually and then interconnected without overall adjustment, correction, standards conversion or synchronizing pulse regeneration.

The Recommendations detail the requirements at the video-interconnexion points in respect of impedance, signal polarity and amplitude, and the overall transmission performance in respect of gain, noise, line time non-linearity and linear waveform distortion for 405-, 525-, 625- and 819-line systems.

As these Recommendations are extremely detailed and technical, the reader is referred to the current CCITT documents. The requirements for channels have to be built in to the specification for the means of providing the channels, that is land lines, submarine cables, carrier systems, and radio links. All that is necessary to say in the present article is that the parameters described for speech, telegraphy and television are not incompatible as regards system design.

*Acknowledgements.* Acknowledgements are made to the Senior Director of Engineering of the General Post Office for permission to publish information contained in this paper and to The Institution of Electrical Engineers for permission to quote extracts from the Proceedings IEE Vol. 111.

*See also:* Inland trunk systems. Telecommunication, global.

*Bibliography*

C.C.I.T.T. Recommendation G222, New Delhi, (1960).
C.C.I.T.T. Red Book, Recommendation G114, (1960), **111**, 11.
C.C.I.T.T. Red Book, Recommendation R57, (1960) **7**, 46.
C.C.I.T.T. Red Book, Recommendation S3, (1960) **7**, 79.
C.C.I.T.T. Red Book, Recommendation R58, (1960) **7**, 48.
C.C.I.T.T. Red Book, Recommendation R5, (1960) **7**, 14.
C.C.I.T.T. Red Book, Recommendation J61, (1960) **3**, 285.
CCIR Document of the Xth Plenary Assembly, Geneva, Recommendation 421, (1963).
CCIR Document of the Xth Plenary Assembly, Geneva, Report 316, (1963).

H. WILLIAMS

**THEOREM-PROVING BY MACHINE.** A *theorem-proving problem* has the general form:

$$\text{prove that B follows from } A_1, \ldots, A_n \quad (1)$$

where $A_1, \ldots, A_n$ and B are *statements* about some *subject-matter*.

When the statements involved are expressed in a certain formalism (to be described below) the general problem (1) becomes a completely precise combinatorial problem whose solution, if it exists, can be computed out automatically. This solution will be a correct proof (in a perfectly satisfactory sense) of the statement B from the assumptions (axioms, postulates) $A_1, \ldots, A_n$. If B does *not* follow from the given assumptions, then there is no correct proof of B from them, and in this case the computation will usually continue indefinitely without reaching a stop condition. It can in fact be shown (Church 1936) that there does not exist an algorithm which will correctly handle *all* problems of the form (1), including the correct detection of the cases having no solution as being such.

It is known, from over half a century of investigations in mathematical logic and the foundations of mathematics, especially of set theory, that all statements ever likely to be uttered in the context of problems of the form (1) can be adequately expressed within the formalism known as the (*first-order*) *predicate calculus*, a simple version of which will now be described.

A *statement* is either an *atomic statement* (*atom*) or else a *boolean combination* of (simpler) statements, i.e. either a *negation*, $\neg S$, a *conjunction* $(S_1 \wedge \ldots \wedge S_n)$, a *disjunction* $(S_1 \vee \ldots \vee S_n)$, a *conditional* $(S_1 \Rightarrow S_2)$ or a *biconditional* $(S_1 \equiv S_2)$ of one, two or more statements. An *atom* is an expression consisting of a *relation symbol of degree n*, followed (if $n > 0$) by a parenthesized list of $n$ *terms*. A *term* is either a *variable* or else an expression consisting of a *function symbol of degree n* followed (if $n > 0$) by a parenthesized list of $n$ terms.

The *subject-matter* of the statements is assumed to be fixed in the following way: a non-empty set D (the so-called *universe of discourse*) is assumed to have been specified; each relation symbol $R$ of degree $n$ is taken to denote a relation **R** of degree $n$ over D, i.e. a function from $D^n$ to the set of truth values: {*true, false*}, and each function symbol $f$ of degree $n$ is taken to denote a function **f** from $D^n$ to D.

A statement S is then *true* if and only if, no matter what elements of D the variables in S are taken to denote, the truth value **S** denoted by S under following recursive characterization of *denoting* for compound expressions, is *true*: variables, function symbols and relation symbols denote what they are taken to denote; a term $t$ consisting of a function symbol $f$ followed by $n > 0$ terms $t_1, \ldots, t_n$ denotes that element $t$ of D which is the value, for the elements $t_1, \ldots, t_n$ as arguments, of the function **f** which $f$ denotes; an atom $R(t_1, \ldots, t_n)$ denotes that truth value which is the value of the relation **R** the for arguments $t_1, \ldots, t_n$; a boolean combination of statements $S_1, \ldots, S_n$ denotes the value of the corresponding boolean function for the truth values $\mathbf{S}_1, \ldots, \mathbf{S}_n$ as arguments.

With these explanations, it is possible to define B follows from $A_1, \ldots, A_n$ thus: no matter how the subject matter of $A_1, \ldots, A_n$, B is fixed in the manner explained above, the statement $(A_1 \wedge \ldots \wedge A_n \vee \neg B)$ is false. Intuitively: B *must* be true if $A_1, \ldots, A_n$ are all true.

In view of the preceding definition, we can therefore suppose that the general problem (1) is given in the standard form;

$$\text{prove that S is unsatisfiable} \qquad (2)$$

where S is any statement in the formalism, and where by *S is unsatisfiable* we mean that there is no interpretation of S which satisfies S, i.e. that for all possible choices of a non-empty set D as universe of discourse, and all possible denotations in and over D for the function symbols and relations symbols appearing in S, S is false.

D may be any non-empty set whatsoever, of no matter how high a cardinality. Thus to show that S is unsatisfiable is, on the face of it, to establish a claim of enormous sweep. Nevertheless it suffices (Skolem 1928, 1929; Herbrand 1930; Gödel 1930) to show that there is no interpretation of S in which D is the set H of (at most countably many) *terms* constructible from the variables and function symbols which actually occur in S; in which each function symbol *f* is taken to denote the function **f** whose value, for the terms $t_1, \ldots, t_n$ as arguments, is the *term* $f(t_1, \ldots, t_n)$; and in which each relation symbol is given a denotation in the following way: enumerate, in some fashion, without repetitions, the atoms $R(t_1, \ldots, t_n)$ where $R$ is a relation symbol occurring in S and $t_1, \ldots, t_n$ are in H:

$$L_1, L_2, \ldots, ; \qquad (3)$$

next, enumerate, in some fashion, without repetitions, the (at most countably many) *instances of S over H*, i.e. all statements obtainable from S by substituting a term from H for (each occurrence of) each variable in S:

$$S_1, S_2, \ldots, ; \qquad (4)$$

and finally, choose a sequence of truth values:

$$V_1, V_2, \ldots, ; \qquad (5)$$

and take the atom $L_i$ to denote the truth value $V_i$, $i = 1, 2, \ldots$.

Since each $S_j$ in (4) is merely a boolean combination of atoms occurring in (3), any assignment (5) will determine a truth value as the denotation of each $S_j$ in (4). Hence, if there is an assignment (5) under which no $S_j$ is false, it will, together with H as the domain of discourse and the functions chosen as already explained, be an interpretation of S which satisfies S. On the other hand, it can be shown that if none of the assignments (5) makes each $S_j$ in (4) true, then there must be a *finite* set $K$ of instances of S which is truth-functionally unsatisfiable, i.e. for any assignment of truth values to the finitely many atoms which occur in members of $K$, at least one member of $K$ is false. In this case it is clear that there can be no satisfying interpretation of S at all, since any such would provide an assignment of truth values which would satisfy $K$, which is impossible.

The upshot of the discussion is this: S is unsatisfiable if and only if there is some finite truth-functionally unsatisfiable set of instances of S over its 'Herbrand universe' H as defined above. This principle, sometimes called *the fundamental theorem of logic*, underlies, in one or another form, all automatic theorem-proving procedures.

The procedure of generating, given S, a sequence (4) of instances thereof over its Herbrand universe, and of periodically testing the first $k$ of them for truth-functional unsatisfiability, for larger and larger values of $k$, will surely find a finite truth-functionally unsatisfiable set of instances of S if one exists. This procedure is easily mechanized and constitutes the simplest and earliest of the mechanical theorem-proving procedures. It is, however, grossly more inefficient than such procedures need be, requiring, in general, an extremely long sequence of instances to be generated before a finite truth-functionally unsatisfiable set is detected, scattered sparsely throughout the sequence.

More efficient procedures may be designed by taking advantage of the following observations.

Any set $K$ of instances of S can be obtained by performing a *substitution* $\theta$ on a set C of *variants* of S. A variant of S is simply an expression exactly like S up to within the actual choices of letters for the variables. A substitution is an operation of replacing, simultaneously, each of a list $V_1, \ldots, V_m$ of distinct variables by the corresponding member of a list of (not necessarily distinct) terms $T_1, \ldots, T_m$, throughout each expression in the given set. We can then write: $K = C\theta$.

The problem is then to find C and $\theta$ so that $K$ will be truth-functionally unsatisfiable.

Now, whether or not $K$ is truth-functionally unsatisfiable depends entirely on the way in which $\theta$ carries distinct atoms into the same atom or, as we shall say, on the *partition* P induced by $\theta$ on the set of atoms which occur in members of C. This partition is determined by the rule that the atoms X, Y are in the same class of the partition if and only if $X\theta = Y\theta$. If C is *truth-functionally unsatisfiable modulo P* (i.e. if any assignment of truth values in which atoms in the same class of P are assigned the same truth value makes at least one member of C false) then clearly $K = C\theta$ will be truth-functionally unsatisfiable, and conversely.

The various partitions of the atoms which occur in members of C can be investigated to see whether there are any which are *deadly*, i.e. modulo which C is truth-functionally unsatisfiable. If there are no deadly partitions of these atoms then there can be no substitution $\theta$ such that $C\theta$ is truth-functionally unsatisfiable, and conversely. But if P (say) is deadly, the question arises whether P is also *unifiable*, i.e. whether there is a substitution $\theta$ which determines it, i.e. *which carries each class of P into a singleton*. This question can be settled, for any partition P, by applying to P the following *unification algorithm* (Robinson 1965, 1966) which computes such a $\theta$ if one exists, and detects that there is none if there is none. The unification algorithm is very simple to mechanize and is very fast, even when P is large, and goes as follows, given P as input:

*Step 1.* Put $k = 0$, and $P_0 = P$. Go to step 2.

*Step 2.* Given $P_k$, *stop* if each class in $P_k$ is a singleton. Otherwise, take any pair of atoms from some class of $P_k$ which is not a singleton and, scanning each atom from left to right, locate the first symbol position at which they differ. Let $V_k$, $U_k$ be the two subexpressions which begin there, one in each atom. Go to step 3.

*Step 3.* If neither $V_k$ nor $U_k$ is a variable, or if one is a variable that occurs in the other, *stop*. Otherwise at least one, say, $V_k$, is a variable: get $P_{k+1}$ by putting $U_k$ for $V_k$ throughout $P_k$, add 1 to $k$, and return to step 2.

If this process stops in step 2, the required substitution is easily found by comparing $P$ with the final $P_k$. If it stops in step 3, no such substitution exists. Note that the process must eventually stop, since a variable, $V_k$, is eliminated before each return to step 2, and $P_0$ contains only finitely many variables. When (if not before) all variables have been eliminated, the stop condition of step 3 will apply if the stop condition of step 2 does not.

The procedures suggested by these considerations consist of taking, given S, successively larger sets $C$ of variants of S, and seeking, for each $C$, a partition of its atoms which is *both* unifiable *and* deadly (Prawitz 1960; Davis 1963). To enumerate the partitions of one sort, testing whether any is of the other sort, is a theoretically possible but practically inefficient procedure, since there are in general very many partitions of either sort which are not of the other sort.

Further improvements arise if, as may be done without loss of generality, S is taken to be a conjunction of *clauses*. A clause is a disjunction of distinct *literals*, no one of which is the negation of any other. A literal is an atom or the negation of an atom. Since the order of disjuncts is immaterial, a clause may be regarded simply as the *set* of its literals. Then C may be taken to be a set of variants of clauses in S (Davis 1963; Robinson 1966). Also, S may now be taken to be the *set* of its clauses.

Advantage may be taken of the fact that $C$ is a set of clauses by, in effect, replacing *global* analysis with *local* analysis of the partitions. This is done by means of the of the ideas of *clashes* and their *resolution*. A *clash* is a set $\{A_1, \ldots, A_n, B\}$ of clauses in which $B$ has at least $n > 0$ literals $L_1, \ldots, L_n$, and, for each $i$, $1 \leq i \leq n$, $A_i$ contains $\bar{L}_i$ (if $L_i$ is an atom M, $\bar{L}_i$ is $\neg$M; if $L_i$ is $\neg$M, $\bar{L}_i$ is M; in either case $\bar{L}_i$ is the *complement* of $L_i$) but not the complement of any other literal in B, nor the complement of any literal in A·, $1 \leq j \leq n$. The *resolvent* $[A_1, \ldots, A_n, B]$ of the clash $\{A_1, \ldots, A_n, B\}$ is then the clause:

$$(A_1 - \{\bar{L}_1\}) \cup \ldots \cup (A_n - \{\bar{L}_n\}) \cup (B - \{L_1, \ldots, L_n\}). \quad (6)$$

More generally, if P is a unifiable partition of the atoms in a set $N$ of clauses, if $\theta$ is the substitution computed for P by the unification algorithm, and if $N\theta$ is a clash, then the resolvent of $N\theta$ is said to be a resolvent of $N$.

Then a mechanical proof-procedure of the following kind may be used: given S, put $S_0 = S$; then, given $S_k$, let $S_{k+1}$ be $S_k$ together with all resolvents of sets of variants of clauses in $S_k$. It can be shown (Robinson 1965, 1966) that if S is unsatisfiable then, for some $k$, one of the clauses in $S_k$ is empty.

Within this general *resolution* procedure, many efficient variations are possible, such as: resolving only clashes for which $n=1$, such that not both $A_1$ and B are in $T \subset S$, where T is some fixed, *satisfiable* subset of S (Wos *et al.* 1965); or resolving only *maximal resolvable* sets of variants, i.e. sets $N$ such that for no $M$ and $\theta$ is $N \subset M$, and $M\theta$ a clash. Further variations may be developed by exploiting the following equality for resolvents:

$$[A_1, \ldots, A_n, B] = [A_{i_1}, [A_{i_2}, \ldots [A_{i_n}, B] \ldots]] \quad (7)$$

where $i_1, i_2, \ldots, i_n$ is any permutation of $1, 2, \ldots, n$. In particular (7) shows that maximal resolvents can be obtained as the last members of maximal chains of minimal resolvents, a fact which may be used to advantage in computing maximal resolvents.

Examples of theorems proved by these methods are given in the literature cited below, and in the further literature cited therein. It is clear that, while there are many improvements still to be discovered in these methods, they are already capable of handling quite non-trivial theorem-proving problems, and constitute a most attractive and potentially fruitful field for research in non-numerical computing.

*See also:* Problem solving. Unsolvable problems.

*Bibliography*

CHURCH A. (1936) *A note on the Entscheidungsproblem*, J. Symbolic Logic, **1**, 40. Correction, *Ibid.*, 101.

DAVIS M. (1963) *Eliminating the irrelevant from mechanical proofs*, Proceedings of Symposia in Applied Mathematics, American Mathematical Society, **15**, 15.

GÖDEL K. (1930) *Die Vollständigkeit der Axiome des logischen Functionenkalküls*, Monatshefte für Mathematik und Physik, **37**, 349.

HERBRAND J. (1930) *Recherches sur la theorie de le demonstration*, Travaux de la Societe des Sciences et des Lettres de Varsovie, Classes III sciences mathematiques et physiques, No. 33.

PRAWITZ D. (1960) *An improved proof procedure*, Theoria, **26**, 102.

ROBINSON J. A. (1965) *A machine-oriented logic based on the resolution principle*, J. Assoc. Comput. Mach. **12**, 23.

ROBINSON J. A. (1966) *A review of automatic theorem-proving*, Proceedings of Symposia in Applied Mathematics, American Mathematical Society, **19**.

SKOLEM T. (1928) *Über die mathematische Logik*, Norsk matematisk tidskrift, **10**, 125.

SKOLEM T. (1929) *Über einige Grundlagenfragen der Mathematik*, Skrifter utgitt av Det Norske Videnskaps-

*Academi i Oslo*, I. *Matematisk-naturvidenskapelig klasse 1929*, No. 4.

Wos L., ROBINSON G. and CARSON D. (1965) *Efficiency and completeness of the set of support strategy in theorem-proving*, J. Assoc. Comput. Mach. 12, 536.

J. A. ROBINSON

**TIMETABLING.** The purpose of timetabling is to make the maximum use of limited resources. The need for this is apparent in many situations, in the factory to prevent expensive machinery from lying idle or in the school where the talents of the staff should be fully used. The factory situation can be tackled by relatively simple scheduling techniques to achieve a fairly high efficiency.

In the academic timetable however, the complete satisfaction of the curriculum is the aim and as a result more complex methods are needed for its solution. It is in this area therefore that most of the work on automatic timetabling has been concentrated.

*Academic timetables.* The problem of timetabling may be tackled in two ways depending upon the type of school or college. In a specialized school where the number of pupils rarely exceeds a thousand the curriculum for each class or pupil is decided in detail first and the timetable is constructed to meet these requirements. In colleges and increasingly in comprehensive schools, where a much wider range of subjects is offered, the timetable is constructed on the basis of probable student requirements. The students are then free to choose their course within the limits of the timetable, and subject to the restrictions on the number of student places in each course.

*The large scale problem.* The problems of timetable construction and allocation of students to courses for the large college timetable have been successfully tackled by Holz (1963) at the Massachusetts Institute of Technology. The method used assumed the course structure found in most American Universities. In each subject several independent courses are given, so that the total number of courses offered is large. Ideally it should be possible to take any course with any other course, but in practice this can rarely be achieved. In order to make the choice as wide as possible each course can be repeated at a different time. It may also be necessary to cater for large numbers of students and to split the course into several classes taking place at the same time. The distribution of periods is done by allocating time-patterns to a course, for example one requiring three periods could be allocated the time-pattern Monday, Wednesday and Friday, 9.00 a.m.–10.00 a.m. The week, then, is split into definite time-patterns not all of which are independent. Thus two courses with different time-patterns could still clash with each other.

The requirements of each course are given as the number of classes, together with possible instructors and time-patterns listed in order of preference. At each step in the compilation the best available time-patterns and instructors are allocated. If there are not sufficient instructors available without causing a clash the requirement remains unsatisfied and is marked appropriately. Thus the final timetables may not contain all the required classes. In a large college this does not make the timetable useless since it is prepared on the basis of probable, rather than actual, student selections.

*Student scheduling.* The separate process of scheduling students to classes in the compiled timetable is also described in the GASP manual (Holz 1963). The method used is quite simple. Each student selects several courses and these selections are entered into the program. Initially the selection for a student is checked to see if it is compatible with the timetable; if not, the student cannot be scheduled and a message to this effect is printed. The next stage is to compute a workable schedule; the 'value' of the schedule is computed to determine whether it is a good one or not. Output occurs if the schedule is acceptable; if not a new schedule is computed and tested. A limit is imposed on the number of schedules tried, and when this limit is reached the best schedule computed is printed. Each schedule is considered only on its own merits without reference to any other student's schedule. Thus if a student is scheduled badly and fills the last available place in a class this step cannot be retraced.

A slightly different approach to this problem has been made by Sherman (1958) at Purdue University, where the number of students is about twenty thousand. With this number the time to schedule each student is of major importance. The method used aims to schedule each student as quickly as possible by reducing the number of schedules tried before a satisfactory one is found. This can be achieved by ordering the classes so that the most difficult class to fit occurs first in the student selection. Several factors can be brought in to this ordering process. The most obvious one is the number of classes available to the course. Clearly if only one class is available then the student can either be fitted into this class or not, so that rejection occurs very early. Another factor taken into account by this program is the distribution of students within the classes. By keeping the numbers fairly even fewer classes reach their full capacity, and thus late registrants can be fitted into the timetable more easily.

*The school timetable.* The structure of the school timetable differs markedly from the large college timetable, the requirements are generally much more specific and all of them must be satisfied. Because of these restrictions it is not possible to use the methods of the large timetable, for example time-patterns cannot be defined in advance. Accordingly the construction methods are based on fixed requirements with each period in the week treated independently.

*The difficulties of construction.* In order to appreciate the reasoning behind the methods that have been attempted it is necessary to see some of the difficulties inherent in the school timetable problem. Most of these difficulties can be shown by an example. Consider the trivial school consisting of four masters, A, B, C, & D, four classes 1, 2, 3 & 4 and a week containing four periods. The requirements of a timetable to be constructed are that each master shall teach each class for one period in the week. A solution is shown in Fig. 1 which is only

|  | Period | | | |
|---|---|---|---|---|
| Class | 1 | 2 | 3 | 4 |
| 1 | A | B | C | D |
| 2 | D | C | B | A |
| 3 | B | A | D | C |
| 4 | C | D | A | B |

FIG. 1. *Class timetable showing the masters teaching at each period.*

one of many possible solutions, thus there is the problem of choosing the best solution from among the possible solutions. In this simple example it would be feasible to enumerate all the solutions and leave the user to pick the most appropriate one. However, for a school of a more realistic size neither enumeration nor assessment are practicable.

*Existence of a solution.* The second problem is more intractable. It is clearly possible to have a set of requirements for which there is no solution. The simple cases of this where a master is required to teach more periods than there are in the week can be detected very easily. It is possible, however, with more complex requirements for example when two or more classes are taught by one master, that these simple checks may be satisfied but no solution is possible. An example of a such a set of requirements for the simple school is shown in Fig. 2.

| Classes | Master | Number of periods |
|---|---|---|
| 4 | B | 4 |
| 1,2 | C | 2 |
| 2,3 | D | 2 |
| 1,3 | A | 2 |

FIG. 2. *Example of incompatible requirements.*

The proof that a solution exists is only of academic interest unless it also provides the solution. It is more important to know that a solution does not exist since this can be used at any stage during the construction of the timetable to determine whether the partial timetable is compatible with the remaining requirements. The difficulty of proving that a solution does not exist may be judged by the fact that the only method that does this completely is restricted to the simple requirements involving one master and one class.

*Reducing the number of possible solutions.* The problem of choosing a solution from many possible ones is alleviated in two ways. Firstly the complexities in the timetable requirements have the effect of restricting the number of solutions, (they may as in the example of Fig. 2 reduce the number of solutions to zero). Besides these restrictions, caused by grouping classes together, there are limitations imposed on the position of entries in the timetable, for example double periods may not span a break and lessons dependent upon television have to take place at a fixed time. The other restriction on the number of solutions is imposed by the user's criteria. The user may request that periods in a particular subject are distributed throughout the week or that the staff free periods are distributed to include a free afternoon.

*Specification of the requirements.* The formulation of the requirements for an automated method is a complex procedure. Not only must the curriculum be defined in terms of the master teaching each class, but in order to satisfy the user's criteria it is necessary to define for example which subjects must be distributed throughout the week. This problem is currently being tackled in the hopes that a common form of specification may be used for many different types of school.

*Method of construction—the basic technique.* The methods to be described all use the same process for recording the state of the timetable. First, there is the timetable itself which may be either the timetable for each master showing which class is taught or the timetable for each class showing the master teaching. These timetables are clearly interchangeable but in some situations one may be preferable to the other; if storage permits both are useful. The other records that are kept are two arrays of binary digits, showing the availability of masters and classes. The masters availability array has elements $m_{ij} = 1$ if master $i$ is available at time $j$, and 0 otherwise. The class availability array is similar.

*Making an entry in the timetable.* The possible periods for a given requirement may be found by doing a logical 'and' between the appropriate rows of the availability arrays. Examples of the availability arrays after successively satisfying the first three requirements of Fig. 2 are shown in Figs. 3a, 3b and 3c, the final requirement can obviously not be satisfied.

The required period for the entry in the timetable must be chosen from the available periods. It is in the choice of period that the methods differ. The theoretical method chooses a period such that the partial solution is compatible with the remaining requirements while the hand method attempts to satisfy the user's criteria and may create an incompatible partial timetable, an example of this is shown in Fig. 4 where an attempt was being made to compile a timetable similar to Fig. 1.

*Solution by calculation.* An early method, proposed by Appleby, Blake and Newman (1961), attempts to calculate the best position for each entry before inserting it in the timetable. The method makes use of two parameters for each requirement:

(i) $P-N$, The difference between the number of possible positions for this requirement and the number of periods required.

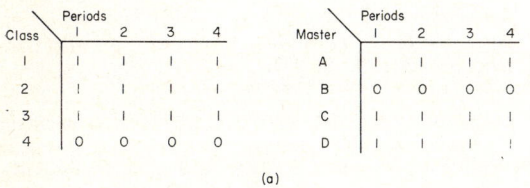

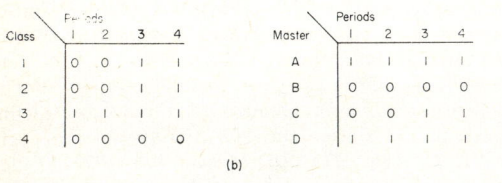

FIG. 3. *Availability arrays for both masters and classes after successively satisfying the first 3 requirements of Fig. 2.*

FIG. 4. *Partial timetable incompatible with the remaining requirements.*

(ii) $M-C$, The difference between the number of masters and classes required for those requirements where parameter (i) is zero.

If $P-N$ is negative for any requirement then the partial timetable so far created is not a possible solution. For positive values the requirement with the lowest value of $P-N$ is chosen for insertion. Although $P-N$ may be positive for each individual requirement a group of requirements involving the same master or class may have a negative value of $P-N$. Accordingly this parameter is also calculated for selected groups of requirements thus extending the portion of the availability arrays inspected.

The second parameter is only used when $P-N$ is zero for every class concerned. The requirement to be inserted is then chosen so that $M-C$ remains positive.

Using this method a fairly complex timetable for 26 classes and 35 masters in a 35 period week was constructed using the ACE computer at the National Physical Laboratory in $1\frac{1}{2}$ hours. The main disadvantage of the method is that it is only possible to recover from an incompatible partial timetable by returning to an arbitrary point in the compilation.

*A theoretical method.* Another possible method (Gotlieb 1962; Csima and Gotlieb 1964) is a theoretical extension of the previous method for a limited class of problem. The problem considered was restricted to requirements involving only one master and one class, and reduced in size by compiling the timetable for each day rather than for the whole week at once. In this way it becomes feasible to test all possibilities of master and class groups instead of a few specific groups as in the previous method. Thus the complete availability arrays are inspected.

The advantage of this method is that it determines whether a solution is possible at every stage of the compilation. However, it succeeds by considering only the simple requirements involving one master and one class and ignoring the complex requirements which appear to be the major difficulty in most practical timetables. A further drawback is the length of time taken to produce a timetable. A very simple problem involving nine masters, nine classes and nine periods where each master taught each class took 1·8 minutes on an IBM 7090 computer.

*The hand method.* The method evolved over the years for compiling school timetables by hand is described by Lewis (1963). The method has been adapted for use on a computer by Berghius, Van Der Heiden and Bakker (1964) and Barraclough (1965). The fundamental difference of this approach is the possibility of recovery from an incompatible partial timetable by interchanging entries rather than by returning to some previous stage and recompiling by a different route.

The construction of the timetable is started by inserting any entries which have to take place at a specific time such as T.V. lessons or games. The most difficult requirements involving several masters and classes being available at the same time are entered next. Finally the simple requirements involving only one master and class are attempted. During this stage of the programme entries may be interchanged to free a master or class for the current requirement.

Three methods of interchanging entries have been used to satisfy the simple requirement that master $i$ should meet class $j$ for one single period. The first possibility is to make an interchange within the timetable for master $i$ such that master $i$ is freed for one of the available periods, for class $j$. If such an interchange can be found then the requirement can be satisfied and no other entry is rejected. The second possibility is to apply this type of interchange to the class timetable. Finally when neither of these interchanges is possible an attempt is made to change the available digits for master $i$ by making any possible interchange even though it does not lead immediately to the insertion of a new entry. Throughout these attempts records have to be kept of the interchanges made in order to prevent cycling.

The time taken on a Pegasus computer for a one form entry Grammar School was 13 minutes.

Two further methods have been suggested, Network Flow Analysis and Integer Linear Programming. Both these methods are designed for tackling a variety of problems and of necessity must treat the timetable problem in a general way, this generality would appear to enlarge the problem to a size outside the scope of most current computers, or restrict the type of timetable that can be tackled.

*Summary.* The problem of timetable construction is essentially a large combinatorial problem. The emphasis in the methods tried has therefore been to reduce the size of the problem by dealing with the particular rather than with the general. With the advent of very fast computers and stores of 2 or 3 million words it may be possible to attempt general methods of construction.

At the present time the method that appears most promising and has had most extensive trials is the hand method. Increasing emphasis has been placed on the user's criteria when selecting the position of the entries in the timetable. The hope is that usable and economically justifiable timetables will be constructed in the near future.

*See also:* Symbol manipulation by digital computer.

*Bibliography*

APPLEBY J. S., BLAKE D. V. and NEWMAN E. A. (1961) *Techniques for Producing School Timetables on a Computer and their Application to other Scheduling Problems, Comput. J.,* **3,** 237.

BARRACLOUGH E. D. (1965) *The application of a digital Computer to the Construction of Timetables, Comput. J.,* **8,** No. 2, July, 136.

BERGHIUS J., VAN DER HEIDEN A. J. and BAKKER R. (1964) *The Preparation of School Timetables by Electronic Computer, BIT,* **4,** 106.

CSIMA J. and GOTLIEB C. C. (1964) *Test on a Computer Method for Constructing School Timetables, Comm. A.C.M.,* **7,** 160.

GOTLIEB C. C. (1963) *The Construction of Class-Teacher Timetables,* 1962, Proceedings of the I.F.I.P. Congress, p. 73, Amsterdam: North-Holland.

HOLZ R. E. (1963) *The Gasp Manual,* June 1963; available through the author, R. E. Holz, Associate Registrar, Massachusetts Institute of Technology, Cambridge, Mass.

LEWIS C. F. (1963) *The School Timetable,* Cambridge: The University Press.

SHERMAN G. R. (1958) *The Sequential Method of Scheduling Students,* Computer Research Report, Purdue Research Foundation, September 1958.

E. D. BARRACLOUGH

# U

**UNSOLVABLE PROBLEMS.** A general problem, expressed in terms of parameters which may vary, is said to be *(effectively) unsolvable* if there is no general effective procedure which produces a solution whenever provided with particular values for the parameters. Usually it suffices to consider the restricted class of *decision problems*, problems whether or not certain properties hold of parameter values. If a decision problem is unsolvable, the parametrized assertion which expresses it is often said to be *(effectively) undecidable*, though this term is often reserved for problems concerning membership of certain sets of formalised sentences *(decidable, undecidable theories);* the two terms 'undecidable' 'unsolvable' are often used as synonyms.

One familiar example of an unsolvable decision problem is the *halting problem* for Turing machines (see *Automata, infinite-state)*, which will be used here briefly to illustrate the concepts and methods involved.

Effective decision procedures must have the property of producing definite decisions for all parameter values. Such procedures should be distinguished from *partial decision procedures* which may be guaranteed to produce a decision only when the assertions to be decided are true. There is a partial decision procedure for the halting problem, but no effective decision procedure which terminates for all parameter values, and it is this fact which justifies the assertion that the problem is unsolvable.

It is important to appreciate that those decision problems for which solvability is in question are general parametrized problems, and to discover, for any particular problem, just which parameters are to be taken as variable in order for the unsolvability result to apply (this is often not immediately obvious from the way in which the problem is stated). Thus the general halting problem involves two parameters, ranging over Turing machines and initial tape configurations respectively. In the halting problem for a universal machine, whose unsolvability actually implies the unsolvability of the general halting problem, the number of parameters is reduced to one by fixing the value of the Turing machine parameter. However, not all parameters may be fixed, since a decision problem without parameters is invariably solvable. Of two individuals, one asserting that a particular Turing machine computation terminates, the other that it does not, one will be correct. What is claimed is that the correct individual has no effective method whereby he could always be correct, and that if he did try to use some effective procedure, there would be some computation for which he would predict incorrectly. This situation is further complicated by the fact that the correctness of a particular prediction may be *formally undecidable*, in that a more or less straightforward formalized version of it may not be provable within some standard deductive system for mathematics. This is to be expected, if one reflects that otherwise a method of searching through the theorems of the deductive system would constitute a decision method for this class of problem. For this reason, there is some confusion between the notions of unsolvability and formal undecidability. However, no examples of formally undecidable propositions are known which are of practical importance to mathematics, although this possibility is still open.

In order to demonstrate the unsolvability of the halting problem, one shows, in the first instance, that no Turing machine may be used as a general method for deciding the question. The following sketch illustrates a crucial point in the argument.

Given an alphabet $a$ containing, among others, the symbols 0, 1, #, a Turing machine T is said to start 'behind' a word w over $a$ if the initial tape for T consists of a sequence of squares containing the symbols of w in order, with only blank squares to either side of it, and if T is started in some standard internal state with reading head over the leftmost square of the sequence representing w. We can show that there is no machine T', and no method of coding machines T as words g(T) over $a$ so that T', when started behind g(T) # t, eventually halts either with 0 under the read head if T would not eventually halt when started behind t, or with 1 under the read head if this computation would eventually halt. From such a machine, it is not difficult to devise a machine T'', with the property that T'', started behind g(T), halts if and only if T fails to halt when started behind g(T). One would proceed by adding a 'prologue' to the specifications of T' to transform g(T) into a configuration g(T) # g(T), and an 'epilogue' to force the computation to continue indefinitely if 1 would finally be under the read head in T' 's computation. However, no T'' fully satisfying these conditions could exist, for after T'' has been started behind g(T''), the computation halts if and only if it does not halt. This contradiction forces the conclusion that there is no Turing machine satisfying the conditions required for T'', and hence no Turing machine T'.

More general versions of this result may be obtained, which allow for more general ways of coding Turing machines T and initial tapes t into initial tapes for T'. For a wide variety of individual cases one can show that no Turing machine T' exists which can be used to solve the halting problem, and which satisfies the constraints involved.

The step from such results, in this case the non-existence of various machines which might be used to solve a particular problem, to the general assertion that the particular problem is therefore effectively unsolvable rests on the assumption usually known as *Church*'s *thesis*. This proposal is often used to justify general investigations (e.g. in recursive function theory) into the properties of effective computing or decision procedures which do not assume any one specific rigorous model for these notions. In practice this is primarily a methodological consideration and the results obtained may be translated straightforwardly into results concerning any of the specific models available. There is a variety of such models, some principal ones being those associated with *(general) recursive functions*, *Herbrand–Gödel systems*, *Markov algorithms*, *Turing machines* and expressions in the *lambda-calculus of Church*. With each of these models may be associated a rigorous mathematical concept, of 'computable function' on the (non-negative) integers, relative in each case (except the first) to some method of encoding integers as parameters for the procedures, and of interpreting their results as integers. Church's thesis proposes that the mathematical concept is, in each case, coextensive with the intuitive concept of 'effectively computable function' on the integers. The evidence for accepting this proposal, which is clearly not susceptible to rigorous proof or disproof, is strong. Each notion defines precisely the same class of functions on the integers *(the recursive functions)*; no intuitively acceptable extensions of this class have been found; and there are well-developed techniques for translating intuitively acceptable descriptions of computable functions into expressions in the formalisms which can be regarded as computing those functions. This principle may be readily extended to functions defined on non-numerical entities, e.g. on words from an alphabet. The technique involved is that of *Gödel-numbering*. A Gödel-numbering is a coding or words, say, as integers, with the property that there are effective methods for obtaining a code for a word (its Gödel-number), of deciding whether an integer is a Gödel-number and if so, of which word. A function from words to words, is then effectively computable if the corresponding function from Gödel-numbers to Gödel-numbers is effectively computable, and Church's thesis may be applied to characterize such functions.

Finally there is an obvious correspondence between effectively decidable propositions, and effectively computable two-valued functions, so that Church's thesis is again applicable. A decision problem is effectively solvable if, and only if, the set of Gödel-numbers of parameters for which the proposition in question holds forms a *recursive set* of integers, a set whose characteristic function is recursive.

Unsolvability results are usually obtained by reduction to problems previously known to be unsolvable. If a proposition $P(p)$, with parameter $p$, is known to be undecidable, to show that some other proposition $P'(p')$ is also undecidable can be achieved by describing an effective method for obtaining a parameter $g(p)$ for $P'$ from each parameter $p$ for $P$, with the property that $P(p)$ holds if and only if $P'(g(p))$ holds, for each $p$. Then $P'(p')$ must be undecidable. Otherwise, a decision method for $P(p)$ would be obtained by applying the decision method for $P'$ to $g(p)$. (However, problems can be devised for which such a method would not suffice, though no uncontrived examples of this phenomenon are known).

Problems concerning simple combinatorial systems provide a useful repertoire for obtaining results in mathematical linguistics and related areas. A number of results apply to a variety of classes of transformatorial systems, systems characterized by rules for the successive transformation of words selected from some class (usually the class of all words over some finite alphabet). Some unsolvable problems for such classes are the following:

(We use the notations $w \to {}_S w'$ to indicate that $w'$ follows from $w$ according to some rule of $S$, and $w \Rightarrow {}_S w'$ to indicate that $w'$ follows from $w$ according to some sequence of such rules. $S$ is said to halt from $w$ on $w'$ if $w \Rightarrow {}_S w'$, and if no rule of $S$ is applicable to $w'$. The notes accompanying each problem indicate which parameters may be fixed without affecting the unsolvability results considered.)

*1) Halting problem:* $S$ halts from $w$ (either $S$ or $w$ may be fixed, $S$ as a 'universal' system, $w$ arbitrarily).
*2)* $S$ halts from every $w$.
*3)* $S$ halts from no $w$.
*4) Derivability problem.* $w \Rightarrow {}_S w'$ (any one or two parameters may be fixed at suitable, not necessarily arbitrary, values; in particular, $S$, $w'$ may be fixed with $S$ as a 'universal' system.)
*5) Strong equivalence problem.* For all $w$, if either $S$ or $S'$ halt from $w$, they both halt on the same word. ($S$ may be fixed arbitrarily.)
*6) Weak equivalence problem:* For all $w$, if both $S$ and $S'$ halt from $w$, they halt on the same word. ($S$ may be fixed as any system which halts from every word.)

Some classes of systems $S$ for which (1)–(6) are undecidable are:

A) *Turing machines:* each regarded as a set of rules for transformation of *Post words* which describe successive configurations of tapes and internal states.

B) *Semi-Thue systems:* (Chomsky Type 0 Grammars) each specified by a set $(w_i, w'_i)$, $1 \le i \le n$, of word pairs. Permissible transformations are given by

$$w w_i w' \to {}_S w w'_i w'$$

for arbitrary words $w$, $w'$.

C) *Markov algorithms:* as (B) with the added restriction that no $w_j$, for $j < i$, be a subword of $w w_i w'$.

D) *Tag systems:* each specified by a set $(s_i, w'_i)$ $1 \le i \le n$, of symbol-word pairs, and an integer $B > 0$. Permissible transformations are given by

$$s_i t_2 t_3 \ldots t_B w \to {}_S w w'_i$$

for arbitrary words $w$, and symbols $t_2 \ldots t$ ($B$ may be fixed at any value $\ge 2$).

E) *Lag Systems:* each specified by a set $(w_i, w'_i)$ $1 \le i \le n$, of word pairs. Permissible transformations are given by

$$w_i w \to {}_S w' w w_i'$$

for arbitrary $w$, where $w'$ results from $w_i$ by deleting the first symbol. (The constraint can be added that each $w_i$ be at most 2 symbols in length).

F) *Normal systems:* each specified by a sequence $(w_i, w_i')$, $1 \leq i \leq n$, of word pairs. Permissible transformations are given by

$$w_i w \to {}_S w w_i'$$

for arbitrary $w$.

The classes (D), (E), (F) may be restricted *to monogenic systems*, systems for which at most one rule of $S$ is applicable in any immediate transformation.

The halting and derivability problems are not always linked. Thus the class of Chomsky Type 1 grammars has a solvable derivability problem, but an unsolvable halting problem. On the other hand the class of *Thue systems*, semi-Thue systems in which all rules are reversible, has a solvable halting problem (trivially), but an unsolvable derivability problem *(the word problem for semigroups;* the analogous *word problem for groups* is also unsolvable).

A basic unsolvable decision problem which does not fit into the above scheme is the *Post correspondence problem*. There is no effective method, given two sequences of words $(w_1, w_2, \ldots w_n)$ $(w_1', w_2', \ldots w_n')$ of deciding whether there exists an integer $k > 0$ and indices $i_1, i_2, \ldots, i_k$ such that

$$w_{i_1} w_{i_2} \ldots w_{i_k} = w_{i_1}' w_{i_2}' \ldots w_{i_k}'$$

Rabin and Scott have applied this result to a problem in automata theory; it is undecidable whether two two-tape finite automata have an acceptable pair of tapes in common. The result has also been applied successfully to problems of phrase structure grammars. A useful variant of the problem has been established by Greibach.

The status of a number of problems concerning phrase structure grammars is given in the table, taken from Landweber.

*Decision Problems of Various grammars*

D   indicates that there exists an algorithm for deciding this question for this class of grammars.

U   indicates that no algorithm exists for deciding this question for this class of grammars.

T   indicates that this question is true for all grammars in this class.

?   indicates that we do not yet know about the existence or non-existence of an algorithm for deciding this question for this class of grammars.

Following each question, and included in parentheses, is the formal representation of the question. Note that if the question involves two grammars, they are of the same type.

| Question | Class of Grammars | | | |
|---|---|---|---|---|
| | Type 3 | Type 2 | Type 1 | Type 0 |
| Is the language generated by a grammar empty? ($L_G = 0$) | D | D | U | U |
| Is the language generated by a grammar infinite? ($L_G$ infinite) | D | D | U | U |
| Is the language generated by a grammar equal to all strings of terminal characters? ($L_G = V_T{}^*$) | D | U | U | U |
| Do two grammars generate the same language? ($L_{G_1} = L_{G_2}$) | D | U | U | U |
| For two grammars, is the language of one included in the language of the other? ($L_{G_1} \subseteq L_{G_2}$) | D | U | U | U |
| Is the language common to two grammars empty? ($L_{G_1} \cap L_{G_2} = 0$) | D | U | U | U |
| Is the language common to two grammars the same type as the grammars? ($L_{G_1} \cap L_{G_2}$ language of same type) | T | U | T | T |
| Is the complement of the language generated by a grammar the same type as the grammar? ($V_T{}^* - L_G$ language of same type) | T | U | ? | U |
| For any strings $\phi, \psi$, can $\psi$ be derived from $\phi$ in a grammar? ($\phi \Rightarrow \psi$) | D | D | D | U |
| For any strings $\phi, \psi$, can some string including $\psi$ be derived from $\phi$ in a grammar? ($\phi \stackrel{*}{\Rightarrow} \psi$) | D | D | U | U |
| Is there a sentence in the language of a grammar that can be derived in more than one way in the grammar? ($G$ ambiguous) | D | U | U | U |
| For a grammar, does there exist an unambiguous grammar of the same type that generates the same language? | T | ? | ? | T |

*See also:* Algorithms for processing algorithms. Automata, finite-state. Automata, infinite-state. Linguistic form: generative grammar. Theorem proving by machine.

*Bibliography*

DAVIS M. (1958) *Computability and Unsolvability*, New York: McGraw-Hill.
HERMES H. (1965) *Enumerability, Decidability, Computability*, Berlin: Springer-Verlag.
KLEENE S. C. (1952) *Introduction to Metamathematics*, Princeton: Van Nostrand.

Hao Wang (1963) *Tag Systems and Lag Systems*, Math. Annalen, **152**, 63.
Greibach S. A. (1963) *The Undecidability of the Ambiguity Problem for Minimal Linear Grammars. Information and Control*, **6**, 119.
Landweber P. S. (1964) *Decision Problems of Phrase-Structure Grammars, I.E.E.E. Transactions on Electronic Computers*, EC-13, 354.
Rabin M. and Scott D. (1959) *Finite Automata and Their Decision Problems, I.B.M. J. Res. and Dev.* **3**, 114.

D. M. R. Park

# W

## WRITING

### 1. Introduction

Part of our linguistic communication is by graphic means, and part of our communication by graphic means is linguistic: this intersection is the domain of writing. Within this domain, from the point of view of linguistics, the centre is occupied by natural written language, that is, by writing (however produced, whether by hand or mechanically) involving a particular natural language (English, French, Japanese, etc.) and its institutionalized *writing-system*. The rest of graphic communication lies outside this domain and is excluded from this brief survey, along with the relation of writing to the less important linguistic media, whether visual or not and whether derived from writing or not (e.g. gesture systems, tactile communication, transmission codes, spectrographic display of speech, etc.). Also excluded are certain important areas within the domain of writing, such as interlingual symbol systems like mathematics or technical notations like linguistic transcriptions—though these share many of the features of the writing-systems which occupy the centre of writing, and must be embraced by any total theory of writing.

### 2. Graphological Theory

Modern linguistics established itself as a science with the investigation of the phonological and phonetic structure of speech. By reaction against the preoccupation of philology with written texts, and the popular identification of language with writing, there was a tendency instead to identify language with speech. This led some linguists to elevate into linguistic theory another popular notion, that writing is the record/representation/'mirror' of speech, historically derivative, and in some way a substitute for the real thing. By these linguists the study of writing, though recognized as a study in itself, was excluded from linguistics, or grudgingly included insofar as writing yielded phonological information.

Nonetheless the development of linguistic theory has proceeded as much in association with written language, in the philological tradition, as with spoken, not because the two are identical in all respects, but because both are language, with the same fundamental communicative function, semantic content, grammatical structure, and realization relation; it is only the realizations that are in distinct media—the substances of 'air' and 'ink', to use Uldall's apt terms. The two media are physically quite different; but each is linguistically patterned substance, and because of this the patterns of 'ink' call for investigation in their own right no less than those of 'air', as many linguists have seen. Unfortunately the investigation of the *graphological* and *graphetic structure* of writing has lagged behind the corresponding investigation of speech, so that some of the terminology in this survey must risk being novel.

On the view adopted here, the relations between sound and symbol which dominate many accounts of writing, take a secondary place. This is not to deny their very great importance in many descriptive and practical respects; but it is to deny that the primary function of writing-systems is to give phonological information.

### 3. Written Language

The two media are complementary in use: we do no-use speech in writing-situations, or writing in speeche situations. Since they fulfil different functions, it is to be expected that different varieties of language will be associated with them. This is always the case in literate societies, though for highly literate people, whose language use and language views are dominated by their literacy, the fact is often obscured by the permeation of the spoken with the written variety and by the ease with which they can switch between the two media.

The differences in grammar and vocabulary between spoken and written language cannot be explored here, but their existence may be further suggested in three ways. First, the language of literacy is always a language of wider communication. It can be a different natural language from the regional spoken language (e.g. Latin in medieval Europe, English in much of modern Africa), or an educated variety of the same language (e.g. Standard English, a more or less uniform language of literacy, in Britain, the U.S.A., Australia etc., or Standard German), but in traditional societies it will be narrow in register (literary, legal, religious) and archaic (e.g. Arabic, Thai, modern Greek katharévousa). Gross disparity between the spoken and the written languages of a society is usually only compatible with minority literacy (e.g. Sinhalese in Ceylon); majority literacy requires a very wide register range in the written language, for administration, science, journalism, education, fiction, commerce, publicity etc., not available in traditional written languages. Secondly, the resources and constraints of the two media differ. Writing does not 'fail to represent' phonological components of speech such as intonation/tone or rhythm, which are part of the spoken grammar, any more than speech 'fails to represent' graphological components of writing like punctuation or capitalization, which are part of written grammar. And the same applies to paralinguistic features such as loudness in the one or size in the other. Thirdly, amongst other situational differences, the recipient in the speech-situation, as well as sharing in the concomitant activity, is attending to the language while it is being produced; in writing he is not. The final product in writing is highly 'drafted'; the language is organized on a larger scale and in finer detail. Though the recipients are given as little evidence of the drafting process as possible, they are given the same opportunity for overall survey of the material as the writer enjoyed. Inevitably the language used draws on special resources of vocabulary and grammar, and of cohesion and arrangement.

These differences at the lexico-grammatical level are quite independent of the relations between graphology and phonology, that is, the relations between the writing-system of a language and its phonology.

### 4. A Graphological Framework

The full description of the graphology of a language requires:
(a) the description of the graphology itself in terms of its own structure; (b) the relation of it to the grammar; (c) the relation of it to the phonology. Such descriptions must await the return of linguists' attention to 'ink', equipped with the gains made during their preoccupation with 'air' and their recent advances in grammar.

The graphology of English is dominated by one highly standardized writing-system which we will call 't.o.' (from 'traditional orthography'). T.o. is a member of the most developed family of writing-systems, the Latin alphabetic family. In sketching the graphological structure of t.o. (in its printed prose variety) we shall use ten groups of features, mentioning other writing systems and kinds of writing by way of illustration.

*(i) Colour contrast.* T.o. operates with a simple two-colour contrast between an unpatterned (but not unbounded) background substance and a patterned foreground substance. These may be referred to as the *substrate* and the *constrate* respectively. All writing-systems operate with this simple contrast, though it may be achieved physically by three-dimensional means (e.g. relief or intaglio carving; impressions made in soft clay, typical of ancient cuneiform writing, or in wax). Substrate and constrate materials show great variety: stone, leather, birchbark, paper, etc.; inks, chalks, photo-chemicals, etc.

*(ii) Orientation.* In t.o. the linear sequence of language is established on a horizontal *axis*, in a constant left-to-right *direction*, with continuity in the next line below, or downward *lining* ( ⇌ ). Most of the possible variations on these three features can be found in the history of writing, though vertical axis with upward direction is very rare ( ↑ ). All existing writing-systems are uni-directional. Bi-directional writing ( ⇌ or ↕, known as '*boustrophedon*') is found in a number of ancient writing-systems as a transitional phase; the reversed units in alternate lines are a graphological complication which does not suit developed literacy.

*(iii) Disposition.* Non-continuous text in t.o. is disposed in short stretches 'punctuated' by means of layout, as in titling, headlines, notices, advertisements, etc. Continuous text is disposed in paragraphs punctuated by means of special marks.

*(iv) Graphological layering.* Leaving aside the important larger units of organization (volume, chapter, section, etc.), we can break paragraphs down into sentences, sentences into words, words into letters. In order to describe the graphology in terms of its own structure, this familiar hierarchy must be filled out and formalized to form the basis of a graphological rank scale (cf. Halliday *et al.* 1964).

Sentences do not overflow paragraph boundaries; nor do colons operate across sentence boundaries, or commas across colons. A paragraph consists either of an integral number of sentences or of one co-extensive sentence. Similarly, a sentence-unit (to give it a graphological name distinct from that of the grammatical unit) consists of either two or more colon-units or of one co-extensive colon-unit. Thus between the familiar 'sentence' and 'word' we have colon-unit, semi-colon unit and comma-unit, the sentence-marker (full-point) taking precedence over the colon-marker, the colon-marker over the semi-colon-marker, and the semi-colon-marker over the comma-marker.

We can follow the same pattern down through 'word' to 'letter'. The comma-unit is constituted by one or more units bounded by word-space, and this, the word-space-unit, is in turn constituted by one or more units bounded by hyphen, hyphen-units. As before, the higher marker takes precedence over the lower where they coincide, and a word-space-unit consisting of a single hyphen-unit (the majority, of course) will have no hyphen-marker (except in special grammatical circumstances). An item like 'grape-juice' (one 'word' or two?) can be written as two word-space-units, GRAPE JUICE, or as one word-space-unit with a further choice of two hyphen-units, or one, GRAPE-JUICE, GRAPEJUICE. We are constantly making such graphological-grammatical choices in writing English today. Finally, to account for the alternation of (groups of) consonant- and vowel-letters, we have a graphological syllable-unit constituted by one or more letters.

Units at the same level in the hierarchy can only occur consecutively; they cannot occur within each other. (In this sentence, for example, all the comma-units, of which there are eight, are, graphologically, on a par with each other, though the grammatical items they coincide with are far from being on a par.) Hence at any given boundary, only one unit at each appropriate level in the hierarchy can be terminating (or beginning), so that only the boundary of the highest unit need be overtly marked. In other words, the units of the hierarchy are 'non-nesting', so their markers are 'non-bunching'; fullstops, colons, commas don't occur next to each other. But there are also punctuation-units which are 'hierarchy free', in that they can occur within any of the hierarchical ones. These are 'parenthesis' and 'quote', which are nesting, and whose markers, occurring in reciprocal pairs, can bunch when the boundaries of nested units coincide, as in the sentence, 'The witness: "I replied, 'Not likely.'"'

The complexity of the description only reflects the complexity of the system, which lies in the depth of graphological layering available and in the variable relation between punctuation-units and grammatical units. The importance of the punctuation system as a graphological resource can be judged by its universality (with variants) amongst European writing-systems, and its adoption into other writing-systems (e.g. modern Hebrew, Urdu). Its standardization in Europe and its expansion elsewhere are closely connected with the advent and spread of printing. As far as t.o. is concerned, our punctuation-system is neither theoretically nor fully dealt with in our present grammars or in our practical guides for printers and authors. Though responded to, in reading, by large numbers of literates, it is mastered in writing by far fewer, the core of whom are concerned with the production of writing, in the form of print, for the public eye.

*(v) Graphemic composition.* The lowest units in the hierarchy are the graphemes, sequential units with no sequential structure of their own (cf. phonemes and morphemes in the phonology and grammar respectively). In t.o. these fall into four main classes: alphabetic (the letters), numeric (the figures), punctuational, and conventional (ampersand, pound and dollar signs, asterisk, arithmetical operators etc.). Linguistically, the most important class is the alphabet of 26 letters which carry the morphemic sequence. These are combinative in contrast to the graphemes of punctuation and convention, but not freely combinative like the figures. Their combinations are determined by the grammar of the language working through the graphological rules which govern the structure of graphological syllables (g-syllable = syllable-unit) and the combination of these into graphological words (g-word = hyphen-unit).

The usual typological classification of writing-systems is by their morpheme-carrying graphemes, with which the following sub-section is concerned.

*(vi) Graphomorphemic typology* (including graphology-phonology relationship). Writing, like speech, can be viewed as a sequence of 'surface' morphemes. In t.o. these morphemes are realized by sequences of letters, usually constituting one or two g-syllables, occasionally more than two (e.g. *banana, Canada*), occasionally less than one (e.g. *s* in *tens, th* in *tenth,* cf. *tenths*). Grammatical morphemes, as opposed to lexical ones, are graphologically short: ten of the commonest are: -*s,* -*ed, a, he, in, is, it, of, and, the.* Most g-words are polymorphemic, and of those that are not, many yield formative g-syllables which are familiar as morphemes: e.g. *y* in *happy, carry,* cf. *filthy, lazy; er* in *gather, murder, Spenser,* cf. *stoker, sterner, fitter.* Parallel statements can be made about the phonological realizations of morphemes.

The written morpheme sequence is in one-to-one correspondence with the spoken. The consequent matching of the graphological and phonological syllables is very close, though on the surface one can point to g-words like *evening* (the noun), *every, medicine, history, mystery,* which tend to have only two syllables in pronunciation. The matching of internal syllable structures (the general structural formula $(C_i)V(C_j)$ holds good for both g-syllables and ph-syllables), is more complicated, and is often misunderstood as simple 'graphophonemics', i.e. the statement of correspondences between phonemes and symbols consisting of one or more letters, like the symbols in *s t ea l th*. But morphemic relations must be taken into account in both the phonology and the graphology before this part of the graphophonology of English becomes clear: thus *steal/stealth, sign/signature, mystery/mysterious, victory/victorious, burglary/burglarious, electric/electrician/electricity, photography/photograph/photo.*

To say that the graphophonology of t.o. can be carried down below the morpheme is to classify t.o. as a phonological writing-system: the graphemic sequence yields information about the phonological structure of the syllables which realize the morphemes in speech.

The same can be said of nearly all existing writing-systems, though the syllabic information varies considerably according to the morphemic and phonological structure of different languages and the way in which borrowed writing-systems have been adapted to them. Alphabetic writing-systems like t.o. exhibit the whole of the syllabic structure by at least an equal number of graphemes, in some cases with a quite simple pattern of grapheme-to-phoneme correspondences, e.g. Finnish, Serbo-Croat. The grapheme inventory rarely exceeds the phoneme inventory, though it may fall short of it as in English. (Historically, The Alphabet, of Semitic origin, consisted of 22 consonant letters, and was adapted to ancient Greek to produce the first fully alphabetic writing-system complete with vowel letters (c. 900–800 B.C.). All alphabetic writing-systems, including our own, derive from this common source, the Latin alphabet being the form of writing in which printing from movable types was invented in Europe in the mid fifteenth century. The letters, in their shapes, names, phonological values and alphabetical positions, preserve features of considerable antiquity, yet serve as the basis of much modern documentation.)

Other phonological writing-systems may be alphabetic insofar as their graphemes correspond to single phonemes and not to sequences of phonemes, but may give only partial phonological information (e.g. Hebrew and Arabic, based on the 22-letter alphabet, typically contain no vowel indications); or they may give full or partial information but with graphemes corresponding to syllable-constituents larger than the phoneme (typically

CV graphemes, as in Amharic or Japanese kana writing). The latter group is classified, somewhat loosely, as syllabic, and their inventories of roughly between 50 and 500 graphemes are larger than those of alphabetic writing-systems.

Writing, however, began non-phonologically (Egypt, Mesopotamia c. 3000 B.C., China c. 1500 B.C.), and phonological and non-phonological graphemes jostle each other throughout its early history. Only one fully non-phonological writing-system has survived, that of Chinese, in which, broadly, each morpheme has its own grapheme ('character'). The grapheme inventory, therefore, runs into thousands. Two points to note are that Chinese is a monosyllabic tone language, and that it breaks down into a number of mutually unintelligible major dialects; character writing simply ignores tone (a source of non-linear complication in phonological writing-systems for tone languages) and at the same time provides a common written language in the absence of a common spoken language.

The above typology, though standard, is really a graphophonological one. Other typological dimensions include the purely graphological (e.g. number of graphemes, combinative and non-combinative classes) and, more importantly, the graphological-grammatical (e.g. graphological 'make-up' of morphemes, differences between lexical and grammatical morphemes, graphological marking of grammatical unit boundaries).

*(vii) Differentiation resources*. Stretches of alphabetic text in t.o. can occur contrastively in upper or lower case (capitals or small letters): both of these can occur in roman or italic: both of these again in plain or bold. The three contrasts can also be applied to numeric text. Upper-case letters are further subdivided into big and small 'caps'. These contrasts are an important resource of printed text. Their exploitation varies from register to register, and many details of their use are determined by printers' and publishers' house-styles. They are not universal: Hebrew, for example, lacks our case- and italics-contrasts; but like other non-European writing-systems, it is rich in differentiation resources of it own deriving, like ours, in their printed form, from manuscript tradition.

*(viii) Capitalization*. One use of differentiated shapes which must be distinguished from differentiation proper is capitalization, whereby, in lower-case text, the first letter of certain words, determined by the grammar, is given contrastive shape, identical with big caps. The reverse does not happen in upper-case text. Nor does capitalization apply to non-alphabetic g-words: a lower-case acronym like 'l.e.a.' (local education authority) is is capitalized if sentence-initial, whereas '007' is never capitalized.

Capitalization is used in most alphabetic writing-systems, including newly designed ones. Its use with word-classes (as opposed to its use in graphological layering at the beginnings of g-sentences) varies to a certain extent (contrast English and German nouns, for example).

*(ix) Graphetics*. We have now arrived at the actual graphic shapes by which the graphemes are realized in print. The 26 members of the alphabet have each a number of systematic allographs (different shapes of the same letter) to suit the purposes of differentiation. The allographs of any one grapheme have a family likeness—at least in the eyes of those familiar with the system. Physically the shapes offer many discrepancies. The case-contrast differences are partly a consequence of the systematic difference between the two cases: lower case is a four-line script having ascenders and descenders (contrast lower-case Russian); upper case is a two-line script, level along the top and bottom.

The difference between grapheme and grapheme is not necessarily one of body shape: it may be one of diacritical marking; or there may be no difference at the graphetic level, as when the same graph realizes both figure 1 and letter *1*, or zero and letter *o*, or full-stop and abbreviation-point, or hyphen and the word-break sign used at the end of a line.

So far we have dealt only with the *system* of contrastive shapes which is found in printed English. A further step is required to deal with the actual physical shapes in which the system is realized in print, and a further step still to cope with the multiplicity of printers' typefaces. Parallel to this field, the field of typography, is the field of handwriting analysis. Here the interesting features are individual as well as institutional: Vachek (1964) stresses the depersonalizing nature of print.

The term *script* has been used above of a linguistic family (or sub-family) of graphs. There is no necessary connexion between a script and a writing-system. Thus Chinese script was adapted to the syllabic kana writing used, along with non-phonological character writing, for Japanese; the Serbo-Croat writing system is written in two distinct scripts, cyrillic and roman; cuneiform script was used for a great variety of ancient writing-systems. There are, of course, close historical connexions between scripts and writing-systems.

*(x) Flexibility*. Phonological writing is more adaptable than non-phonological writing. Small grapheme-inventories lend themselves to printing more easily than large. Differentiation resources (which can be further multiplied), highly flexible layering and sign-posting devices, scope for the open-ended invention and manipulation of conventional signs, enable Latin alphabetic printing to be the most highly organized and most adaptable of all writing.

The ten groups of features just used in sketching the graphological structure of t.o. are not fully systematic, general or exhaustive. In a stricter presentation, the first three, i.e. colour contrast, orientation and disposition, would belong under graphetics. As to generality, capitalization, as such, cannot appear in a writing-system which lacks a case-contrast; but from earliest antiquity proper nouns have received special graphological distinguishers in a number of writing-systems. Finally, an important further group of features is that of abbreviatory devices. Their role in t.o.

cannot be overlooked: it is not merely that they have become a regular source of word-formation in English (e.g. acronyms like *okay, k.o., low.,* or *Nato, laser, hi-fi,* or in *BBC-2 TV, M & B, P. C. Smith*), but they play an especially important role in technical language of all kinds. More generally, the use of abbreviatory letters (see Malkiel 1965) and figures has been crucial to the development of scientific and mathematical discourse.

(A good description of t.o. will be found in Francis 1958.)

### 5. General Graphetics

The area to be covered by this term is very wide and can be divided into static and dynamic graphetics. Though linguistics must eventually provide the theoretical framework, it has made little advance in it on its own account (but see Ray 1963).

The substrate determines the kind of constrate and enters into considerations of corrigibility, reproducibility, portability, durability, storage, access etc. Until recently writing was always stored in a form that was immediately readable; microfilm and electronic storage have introduced reading-instruments in addition to the historical writing-instruments.

The graphic shape of the constrate is always lineal, exploiting configurations of lines, not of solids or lines of different densities, though varying thickness is of great importance in calligraphy and type-design. The lineal patterns occupy the centre of the writing-line, and detached lines or dots usually lie outside them, above or below. In the traditional scripts the shapes tend to be non-systematic, both internally in that they do not use their graphic components economically, and externally, in that changes in graphic substance do not correlate with changes at any other linguistic level. On the other hand, some scripts do show graphic economy and structural systematicness, and this is especially true of shorthands. Punctuation marks are generally graphically simple.

On the dynamic side, graphetics is concerned with the production and reception of writing. Both these aspects can be broken down into their physical and their organizational components. We can study the physical movements made in writing and in reading, and we can study their rate and continuity, and the relevant concomitant behaviour, as a clue to the linguistic organization that is going on. When the study is taken this far dynamic graphetics and dynamic phonetics can be seen to be converging together on the central problem of how we produce and receive language. But it is clear that the organization involved in the composition and comprehension of sustained written language is very different from that involved in the utterance and apprehension of spontaneous spoken language.

At the receptive end (perceptual graphetics), most study has been done by psychologists, in connexion with the reading of print, in order to measure either reading skill or legibility. Reading has received far more attention than its complementary skill, writing, and the methods used are very much the same as those used in assessing legibility. Eye-movements have been much investigated: they break down into saccadic movements, by which the eye moves in jerks along the line of writing focusing at the intervening fixations, return-sweeps, by which the eyes take up the beginning of a new line, and regressions, by which the eyes go back to check up. Activity of the vocal cords during reading has been investigated electromyographically and has been found to increase with slower reading, resulting either from a more difficult text or from a less legible one, e.g. third carbon copy (Edfeldt 1959).

### 6. Literacy

Language (or perhaps 'linguacy') is normally first acquired in the medium of speech (articulacy) without formal instruction. Once the control of language is consolidated, it can be (and in our kind of culture usually is) extended to a second medium, that of writing (literacy), by instruction in the first year or two of formal education (beginning in the U.K. at 5, U.S.A. at 6, U.S.S.R. at 7). It does not appear that literacy can be acquired in the spontaneous way in which articulacy is acquired. Abnormally it may be acquired, by instruction, without antecedent articulacy as in pathological cases such as deaf-mutes whose initial linguacy may be in a visual-gestural or tactile medium.

Literacy, like articulacy, is only acquired once. Thereafter, literacy (as the use of written language, not just of writing), may be extended indefinitely within the mother-tongue and its institutionalized writing-system; formal education depends upon this continuous development. It may also be extended indefinitely beyond the mother-tongue. In crude terms of writing-systems, it may be extended either to the writing-systems of other languages (bi-literacy), or to other writing-systems for the same language (bi-systemacy).

Bi-literacy constitutes an important element in all second language learning that is not purely oral; it has been the form traditionally taken by our modern language teaching, stemming from our classical language teaching and the era of Latin literacy. Courses in Russian or German for scientists exploit this kind of language learning with a clearer view of their linguistic goal.

Bi-systemacy may be either an addition to standard literacy, as with shorthand, or it may be the route by which standard literacy is reached. In contemporary China a latin alphabetic writing-system is being used for initial literacy teaching, with the result that Chinese character, a formidable writing-system in which to acquire literacy initially, is mastered more quickly as an extension of literacy.

Literacy is not always first acquired in the mother-tongue, which may be unwritten, or which, though written, may lack the status of some language of wider communication used as a language of education, such as English in Ghana etc., French in Brittany, Russian in many of the smaller language communities in the U.S.S.R., and so on. Or the mother-tongue may have appropriate status, but be written in a writing-system less easy to acquire than that of some other available language. Urdu speakers in Pakistan, for instance, may become literate first in English (a language of instruction in primary schools), before extending their literacy to bi-literacy in Urdu (Arabic script). Or bi-literacy may be acquired from the start in a bilingual situation.

Literacy can be acquired in one mode, viz. in reading, without the complementary mode of writing. In certain circumstances this is unavoidable, if writing-materials are not available; in others it may represent an acceptable goal of literacy teaching, where the need is only to read the Bible or simple administrative matter, and writing skill can be minimal. This one-sided literacy was, by and large, the goal of the nineteenth century educators, and the flavour of it survives in the use of the word 'reading' in Anglo-American primary education today. It is not an adequate goal in a technologically developed society: advancing literacy requires a proportionate skill in writing. In higher education, for instance, the failure to handle written language in writing may be a good indication of failure to handle it in reading.

Finally, literacy may be acquired in some minimal, pre-'take-off' form, or not at all. This may be despite exposure to literacy teaching—the established approaches to 'backward readers' and dyslexics in Anglo-American education are psychologically and neurologically orientated, not linguistically—or it may be the result of the absence of literacy teaching. This last has been the case with the vast majority of mankind throughout history, but the picture is changing. The move from manuscript culture to print culture initiated the change from minority to majority literacy in Europe. This change is now taking place in the world literacy profile, interlocking with economic development.

The literacy and technology forged in Europe in the last five centuries go hand in hand. As on the economic side, the gap between developed and underdeveloped in literacy is hard to close: while the percentage of illiterates in the world fell between 1950 and 1962, the absolute number increased. It stands now at between 700 and 1000 million. National literacy campaigns, with international co-ordination by UNESCO, are found in every developing country at adult and primary level. But the developed countries, too, have much re-thinking to do on their own account, both in the field of advanced literacy, i.e. secondary and higher education, and in the initial production of literates. It is worth noting that television courses for adult illiterates are not confined to emerging countries such as Nigeria, but have been used in Southern Italy and in parts of the U.S.A.

## 7. Evolution

The history of writing and its cultural transmission have been deeply studied, but the same cannot be said of the history of written language or of literacy. The beginnings of writing lie in the adaptation of pictorial graphics, with clumsy materials, to formulaic and highly restricted linguistic ends. The story ever since has been one of continuously increasing range and facility. If we look upon writing as the oldest form of telecommunication, it is worth noting that the growth of electrical and electronic means of telecommunication (some transmitting speech, some writing) has been accompanied by the growth of universal literacy and a vast increase in the amount of writing. There is little point in speculating about the future of writing until its effects on linguistic evolution and its place in cultural development have been more thoroughly explored.

## 8. Study and Applications

Many long-established fields of study and of practical application concerned with writing may find a valuable unifying source of theory in linguistics. Graphetic analysis, for example, enters into typography, the design of character-recognition machines, the forensic study of handwriting, the psychobiological study of handwriting (familiar, especially in the U.S.A., under the name of 'graphology'), and into the specialized disciplines of the historical study of handwriting (palaeography, papyrology; archaeological decipherment, etc.), where dynamic graphetics throws light on the changes which graphic shapes undergo in the course of time (e.g. influence of the quill pen, the steel pen, and now the ball-point pen). Literacy teaching and language teaching have been mentioned in this article; a related field is that of language standardization, concerned with the reform and design of writing-systems and the development of written languages. Many other fields, particularly documentation and information retrieval, are dealt with specially in this Encyclopaedia.

*See also:* Semantics: sign and symbol.

*Bibliography*

N.B. The useful convention of using diamond brackets to indicate graphological notation (for which italics suffice in this article) will be found in some of the following works.

BOLINGER D. L. (1946) *Visual morphemes, Language,* **22,** 333.
DIRINGER D. (1949) *The Alphabet: a key to the history of mankind,* London: Hutchinson.
DIRINGER D. (1962) *Writing,* Ancient Peoples and Places Series No. 25, London: Thames and Hudson.
DOLBY J. L. and RESNIKOFF H. L. (1964). *On the structure of written English words, Language,* **40,** 167.
EDFELDT A. W. (1959) *Silent Speech and Silent Reading,* Stockholm.
FRANCIS W. N. (1958) *The Structure of American English,* New York: Ronald Press.

GELB I. J. (1963) *A Study of Writing*, Chicago: The University Press.
GLEASON H. A. JR. (1961) *An Introduction to Descriptive Linguistics*, New York: Holt, Rinehart and Winston.
HALLIDAY M. A. K., MCINTOSH A. and STREVENS P. (1964) *The Linguistic Sciences and Language Teaching*, Longmans' Linguistics Library, London: Longmans, Green.
MALKIEL Y. (1965) *Secondary uses of letters in language*, Romance Philology, XIX, 1 (= *Journal of Typographic Research*, I. 1., (1967), 96).
MCINTOSH A. (1956) *The analysis of written Middle English*, Trans. Philol. Soc., 26.
MCLAUGHLIN J. C. (1963) *A Graphemic-phonemic Study of a Middle English Manuscript*, The Hague: Mouton.
MCLUHAN M. (1962) *The Gutenberg galaxy: the making of typographic man*, London: Routledge and Kegan Paul.
RAY P. S. (1963) *Language standardization: studies in prescriptive linguistics*, Janua Linguarum Series Minor no. XXIX, The Hague: Mouton.

RICE F. A. (Ed.) (1962) *Study of the role of second languages in Asia, Africa and Latin America*, Washington D.C.: Center for Applied Linguistics.
SMALLEY W. A. et al. (1964) *Orthography studies: articles on new writing systems*, United Bible Societies Helps for translators Series no. 6 (London: United Bible Societies, with North-Holland Publishing Co., Amsterdam)
ULDALL H. J. (1944) *Speech and writing*, Acta Linguistica, **4**, 11.
WEIR R. H. and VENEZKY R. (1965) *Rules to aid in the teaching of reading*, Cooperative Research Project no. 2584, California: Stanford University, mimeographed.
VACHEK J. (1964) *Written language and printed language*, in *A Prague School reader in linguistics*, comp. Vachek J., U.S.A.: Bloomington: University of Indiana Press.
ZACHRISSON B. (1965) *Studies in the legibility of printed text*, Stockholm: Almqvist and Wiksell.

J. MOUNTFORD

# INDEX/GLOSSARY

*(M) = term mentioned, not explained*
*(G) = term defined in this Index/Glossary*

**Aberration, chromatic:** *see* Perception, visual  374
**Ablaut:** *see* Relations between languages: comparative philology (M)  475
**Abney effect:** *see* Perception of colour  361
**Absolute judgement:** *see* Information theory in psychological measurement  233
— **threshold:** *see* Sensory discrimination, measurement of  512
**ACCENT (1).** When a syllable is *accented* (bears the *accent*), it is more prominent than the surrounding syllables because it is louder and/or longer and/or higher in pitch than they are. *See:* Phonology: prosodic features  411; Linguistic form: transformational theory (M)  280
**Accent (2):** *see* Language varieties: language and dialect  250
**Accent, word:** *see* Phonology: prosodic features (M)  411
**Accentual stress:** *see* Phonology: prosodic features  412
— **tone:** *see* Phonology: prosodic features  412
**Acceptability:** *see* Adaptive control theory  4
**Access to computers:** *see* Computers, multiaccess to  63
**ACCOMMODATION.** Any adjustment of the sensitivity of the visual system, e.g. as a result of changes in brightness of the field seen. The term applies also if the adjustment relates only to part of the field seen. *See:* Eye movements  176; Perception, stereopsis as an aspect of  368
**ACCOMMODATION BY A NEURON.** A reduction in response of a nerve to a persistent stimulus. Contrast with Adaptation (G) *See:* Neuronal nets  320
**ACCUMULATOR.** Device that (1) holds a number indefinitely and (2) adds to it any number subsequently presented to it, retaining the total. (Sometimes, the number in the device is called the accumulator.)
**Acoustic:** *see* Phonology: distinctive features (M)  404; Semantics: sign and symbol (M)  510
— **categories:** *see* Phonology: contrast and opposition (M)  401
— **characteristics of linguistic units:** *see* Phonetics, acoustic  391
— **features:** *see* Phonetics, acoustic (M)  391
— **features, compound:** *see* Speech recognition, automatic  557
— **features, primitive:** *see* Speech recognition, automatic  556
— **level:** *see* Phonetics, acoustic (M)  391
**ACOUSTIC PHONETICS.** An *acoustic description* of a speech sound is a description of the physical characteristics of the sound-wave itself, rather than of the activity of the speaker's vocal organs, as in an *articulatory* description, or of the impression made on the hearer, as in an *auditory* description of it. *Acoustic phonetics* is the branch of phonetics concerned with the acoustic study of speech sounds. *See:* Phonetics, acoustic  391
— **signals:** *see* Psychological linguistics: psychological aspects of semantic structure  442
**Acoustics of speech:** *see* Phonetics, experimental  400
**ACTION POTENTIAL.** A sequence of changes in the potential difference across a cell wall lasting usually between 0·5 and 5 m sec, during which the potential difference changes from *resting potential*, (50 to 100 mV) through zero to about 30 to 50 mV in the opposite direction and then back again. *See:* Nerve and muscle, initiation and conduction of impulses in  314; Neuronal nets  320
**ACTIVE DEVICE.** One which has its own source of power, for the generation of signals (e.g. a transformer). H. Williams.
— **theory:** *see* Speech perception  551
**Activity, burst:** *see* Neuronal nets  330
—, **fast:** *see* Fast activity (G)
—, **physiological, in speech:** *see* Phonetics, experimental  399
—, **reverberating:** *see* Reverberating activity (G)
**ACTIVITY, SPONTANEOUS.** Action potentials arising in a nerve fibre, in the absence of an applied stimulus or detectable distortion of the tissue, under normal physiological conditions; sometimes called *noise* (of the fibre). *See* Receptors: relation between the stimuli and the activity in single primary units  363
**Acuity of vision:** *see* Perception, visual  379
—, **stereoscopic:** *see* Perception, stereopsis as an aspect of  371
—, **vernier:** *see* Perception, stereopsis as an aspect of  371
—, **visual:** *see* Perception, stereopsis as an aspect of  371
**Adapt level:** *see* Adaptive threshold elements  11
**ADAPTATION.** Change in behaviour of an animal, one of its subsystems, or one of *its afferent units*, in the sense of *self-optimization* to a *stationary* input signal. For example, a change in response which favours survival. *See:* Perception, visual  373; Receptors: relation between the stimuli and the activity in single primary units  464
**Adaptation, Bootstrap:** *see* Adaptive threshold elements  11

**ADAPTATION BY A NEURON.** In an experimental nerve preparation, with constant stimulus or repetitive stimuli, the rate of neural impulse production falls to a steady value after an initial strong response. *See:* Neuronal nets 320
—, **spatial:** *see* Perception, visual 383
—, **temporal:** *see* Perception, visual 382
—, **visual:** *see* Perception, visual 373
— **with data repeating:** *see* Adaptive threshold elements 11
— **without data repeating:** *see* Adaptive threshold elements 11
**Adapted:** *see* Adaptive control theory 4
**Adaption:** *see* Perception of colour 360
 — **-automaton:** *see* Adaptive control theory 6
**Adaptive:** *see* Adaptive control theory 1
— **behaviour:** *see* Adaptive control theory 1
— **behaviour, evaluation of:** *see* Adaptive control theory 1
**ADAPTIVE CONTROL.** The control of a *process* in a changing *environment* by a controller which continually optimizes the performance function of the process. *See:* Adaptive control theory 1; Control: basic elements 91; Control by hybrid computers 92; Control by model reference 107; Optimization, automatic 342
**ADAPTIVE CONTROL SYSTEM.** A system of control, capable of producing optimum performance of a plant or other device even while the environment is changing. *See:* Control: basic elements 91
— **Control Theory** 1
— **controller:** *see* Adaptive control theory 1; Control: basic elements 91
**ADAPTIVE MACHINE OR SYSTEM.** A machine or system designed to operate with input signals which are generally almost *stationary*, but which change from time to time. The system changes its *state* to match these changes in its input signals, in order that its performance may improve; that is, its outputs for any particular set of inputs may approach the desired set of outputs, which are collectively called the *goal*. *See:* Learning machines: a unified view 261
**ADAPTIVE THRESHOLD ELEMENT.** An adaptive module whose internal structure includes a set of adjustable *weights*, one for each component of any multiple input: the output depends on whether the sum of each component-times-its-weight exceeds a fixed quantity, the *threshold*. *See:* Adaptive threshold elements 9
**Adaptive Threshold Elements** 9
**ADDRESS.** A position in a store of a computer, usually described in terms of the number of units (e.g. words) from a reference address.
**ADDRESSING.** Instructing a read-write system to read or write at a particular address of a store.
**Advancement, tongue:** *See* Phonetics, auditory 397
**AFFERENT NERVE.** A sensory nerve. Its function is to carry signals from a receptor towards or into the *central nervous system*. *See:* Nerve (G)

**AFFERENT PATHWAY. CENTRIPETAL PATHWAY.** A nerve path in which signals are carried in a direction from the periphery towards the centre. Opposite of *centrifugal* pathway.
**AFFERENT SYSTEM.** A set of afferent nerves, all excited by the same stimulus modality, e.g. range of energy spectrum. *See:* Sensory discrimination, measurement of 512
**AFFERENT UNIT.** An afferent nerve and its associated receptor.
**Affinities, areal:** *see* Relations between languages: introduction 470
**AFFIX.** If a word can be *segmented* into more than one *morpheme*, of which one is a *root*, any morpheme which is not a root is an *affix*. Affixes are classified as prefixes, suffixes or infixes according to whether they occur before the root, after it, or inside it. *See:* Grammar (structural) 189; Statistics of language: structure of written English words 581
—, **inflectional:** *see* Inflection, inflectional affix (G); Grammar (structural) 189
**Affixes, derivational:** *see* Grammar (structural) 189
**Affricate:** *see* Phonetics, articulatory 395; Phonology: distinctive features 407
**AFTER-IMAGE.** The state of the retina and the perceptive system whereby a subject continues to see traces of an image which has been removed from the retina. *See:* Eye movements 176; Perceptual breakdown with stabilized images 390; Perception, visual 384
**Ageing:** *see* Homeostasis in the single cell 218
**AGGLUTINATIVE.** A language is classified *typologically* as *agglutinative* (as opposed to *fusional*, *isolating*, or (sometimes) *polysynthetic*) if the dominant pattern of word-structure is for each word to consist of several *morphemes*, in addition to the *stem*, and for there to be a separate string of *phonemes* (in the *phonological representation* of the word) corresponding to each of these morphemes. *See:* Relations between languages: typological and areal classifications 487
**Agreement rules:** *see* Semantics: introduction (M) 499
**Aircraft, control of, as two non-interacting systems:** *see* Control of aircraft as two non-interacting systems 128
— **/pilot communication:** *see* Man-machine communication and ergonomics 303
**Air-flow meter:** *see* Phonetics, experimental 400
**Alarm concentration systems:** *see* Local networks 288
**Algebraic linguistics:** *see* Linguistics form: algebraic linguistics 270; Linguistic form: generative grammar (M) 272
— **manipulation:** *see* Algebraic manipulation using lists 12
— **Manipulation Using Lists** 12
**Algol 60:** *see* Linguistic form: algebraic linguistics 270
**ALGORITHM.** A set of rules for finding the solution of a mathematical or logical problem in a finite number of steps; a computer program, considered

apart from the data input; a scheme or strategy for performing some specified act of data processing.

**ALGORITHMIC LANGUAGE.** A programming language convenient for expressing a computing precedure step by step, a procedure oriented language, e.g. Algol, Cobol, Fortran. *See:* Algorithms for processing algorithms 15

**Algorithms for Processing Algorithms** 15

—, **Markov:** *see* Unsolvable problems 624

**All-or-none emission:** *see* Neuronal nets 324

**ALLO-.** The *allophones* of a *phoneme* are the *phones* belonging to it, which are either *conditioned* by their *environments* or in *free variation;* likewise the *allographs* of a *grapheme* are the *graphs* belonging to it. This terminology presupposes a model of language in which the relation between *levels of representation* is one of class-membership rather than of *realization. See:* Writing (for *allograph*) 627; Grammar (structural) (for *allomorph*) 187; Phonology: phonemes and broad transcription (for *allophone*) 409

**Allomorph:** *see* Relations between languages: comparative philogy (M) 475

**Allomorphs, suppletive:** *see* Grammar (structural) 189

**Allophones:** *see* Grammar (structural) (M) 186; Phonetics, articulatory (M) 393; Relations between languages: comparative philology (M) 475; Writing (M) 627

**Allophonic variants:** *see* Phonology: phonemes and broad transcription (M) 409

**ALPHA RHYTHM.** Oscillations in an *electroencephalogram* with a frequency between 8 and 13 cycles per second. *See:* Neuronal nets 320

**Alphabetic transcriptions:** *see* Phonology: phonemes and broad transcription (M) 409

— **writing systems:** *see* Writing (M) 627

**ALPHANUMERIC SYMBOLS.** The letters of the alphabet (26 or 52) and the ten numerals, in printed or written form.

**Alternate adjustments, hill climbing by:** *see* Control, hill climbing in 117

**Alternation, binocular:** *see* Perception, visual 386

**Alveolar:** *see* Phonetics, articulatory; 394 Phonology: phonemes and broad transcription (M) 409

— **ridge:** *see* Phonetics, articulatory 394

**Alveolo-palatal:** *see* Phonetics, articulatory 394

**Ambiguities:** *see* Perception, visual 386

**Ambiguity, syntactic:** *see* Linguistic form: transformational theory (M) 280

**AMNESIA, RETROGRADE.** Loss of memory of some of the events close to but preceding some kind of shock, e.g. concussion.

**Amoeboid movement:** *see* Homeostasis in the single cell 217

**Amplitude, signal:** *see* Signal (G)

**ANALOG COMPUTER.** A computing system whose input, output and internal signals are mainly analog signals.

**ANALOG SIGNAL.** A signal whose magnitude contains the vital information, which may correspond to any real number, such as angular position or voltage. *See:* Data transmission 159

**ANALOG-DIGITAL CONVERTER (ADC).** A module whose output signal is digital, its input being analog.

**Analyser, language:** *see* Fact retrieval 180

**ANALYSIS.** The process in *machine translation* of identifying grammatical patterns in a *text* to be translated is analysis; it can be used as a basis for synthesis. *See:* Computational linguistics: machine translation 51

—, **-by-synthesis:** *see* Speech synthesis 563

—, **componential:** *see* Semantics: introduction 500

—, **correlation:** *see* Correlation analysis (G)

—, **correlation, of dynamic systems, using pseudorandom binary signals:** *see* Pseudorandom binary signals, use of, in correlation analysis of dynamic systems 433

—, **deep grammatical:** *see* Semantics: introduction (M) 499

—, **distributional:** *see* Semantics: introduction (M) 499

—, **means-end:** *see* Problem solving 415

—, **phase plane:** *see* Control, on-off 137

—, **predictive:** *see* Computational linguistics: machine translation 53

—, **sensitivity:** *see* Control, sensitivity and 147

—, **slot-filler:** *see* Grammar (structural) 198

—, **spectral, running short term:** *see* Running short term spectral analysis (G)

—, **synchronic:** *see* Relations between languages: semantic change (M) 484

—, **tagmemic:** *see* Grammar (structural) 198

**ANALYTIC.** An *analytic* language is an *isolating* one. *See:* Relations between languages: typological and areal classifications 486

**Anatomical relationship of channels:** *see* Sensory processes 532

**AND-GATE.** A *module* with a single output lead and two or more input leads. The output lead is active if and only if all the input leads are simultaneously active.

**Animal Exploratory Behaviour** 18

— **Learning** 21; *see also:* Learning in animals (G)

— **Motivation** 24

—, **state of:** *see* State of an animal (G)

**Antitritanopic conversion:** *see* Perception of colour 363

**APERTURE CARD.** A card in which holes may be punched in any of several thousand positions. In a set of aperture cards each card may be allocated to an attribute and each aperture position to a document (item of information). The presence of a hole in a particular card therefore indicates that the corresponding document has this particular attribute. *See:* Information storage and retrieval 223

**Apical:** *see* Phonetics, articulatory 394

**Applicational-generative model:** *see* Linguistic form: generative grammar (M) 272

**Approach, conceptual:** *see* Relations between languages: semantic change 484

—, **contextualist:** *see* Semantics: introduction 500

**Approach, morphosemantic:** *see* Relations between languages: semantic change 484
—, **structural:** *see* Semantics: introduction (M) 499; semantics: field theories (M) 504
—, **synchronic:** *see* Semantics: introduction (M) 499
**ARBITRARY.** A linguistic *sign* is arbitrary if the relation between its *form* (1) and its *content* or *function* is conventional, i.e. if the sign is not *iconic* but *symbolic*. Though arbitrary, a sign may be *motivated*. *See:* Semantics: sign and symbol 510; Relations between languages: introduction (M) 470; Relations between languages: comparative philology (M) 475
**Area integration with:** *see* Perception, visual 380
—, **local:** *see* Local networks 284
**AREAL.** A classification of languages according to their geographical locations is an *areal*, as opposed to a *structural* or a *genetic*, classification. *See:* Relations between languages: typological and areal classifications 486
— **affinities:** *see* Relations between languages: introduction 470
— **classifications:** *see* Relations between languages: typological and areal classifications 486
— **groupings:** *see* Relations between languages: introduction 470
**Areas, linguistic:** *see* Relations between languages: introduction 470
**Arithmetic stack:** *see* Stacks 564
**ARITHMETIC UNIT.** A set of modules in a digital computer for performing the instructions add, subtract, multiply, divide, shift (multiply or divide by powers of two). It may also carry out logical instructions (AND, OR etc.) and special instructions connected with the recording of signals.
**Arrangement, item and:** *see* Grammar (structural) 192
**Articulacy:** *see* Writing (M) 627
**ARTICULATION.** *Articulation* is the physical activity involved in producing speech sounds, or, more specifically, the activity of the organs in the *vocal tract* above the larynx. An *articulatory description* of a speech sound is one which defines the *place* and *manner of articulation*, and other characteristics of the articulation required to produce the sound in question, rather than defining the physical characteristics of the sound-wave itself, as in an *acoustic* description of the same sound, or the impression made on the hearer, as in an *auditory* description of it. *Articulatory phonetics* is the branch of *phonetics* concerned with the articulatory study of speech sounds. *See:* Phonetics, articulatory 393; Phonetics, auditory (M) 396
—, **manner of:** *see* Manner of articulation (G); Phonetics, articulatory 395
—, **mode of:** *see* Manner of articulation (G)
—, **place of:** *see* Place of articulation (G); Phonetics, articulatory 394; Phonology: contrast and opposition (M) 401; Phonology: distinctive features 404
**Articulations, basic:** *see* Phonology, prosodic features 411
—, **secondary:** *see* Phonetics, articulatory 396

**Articulatory:** *see* Phonology: distinctive features (M) 404
— **categories:** *see* Phonology: contrast and opposition (M) 401
— **phonetics:** *see* Phonetics, articulatory 393; Phonetics, auditory (M) 396
**Artificial intelligence, concept formation by:** *see* Concept formation by artificial intelligence 76
**ARTIFICIAL LANGUAGE (1).** A *language system* is *artificial* if it has never had any native speakers: otherwise it is *natural*. *See:* Relations between languages: lingua franca 480
**ARTIFICIAL LANGUAGE (2).** Any *system* (1) of non-verbal *signs*. *See:* Statistics of language: introduction (M) 567
**Aspirated:** *see* Phonetics, articulatory 396
— **plosives:** *see* Phonology: contrast and opposition (M) 401
— **stops:** *see* Phonology: phonemes and broad transcription (M) 409
**Aspiration:** *see* Phonology: contrast and opposition (M) 401; Phonology: distinctive features (M) 404; Relations between languages: bilingualism (M) 473
**Assembly, conditional, of macro-instructions:** *See* Assembly languages 27
**ASSEMBLY LANGUAGE.** A very simple language, closely similar to the machine language, for writing instructions to a computer. One instruction in the assembly language produces, on translation, a single instruction in the machine language. *See:* Assembly language 26
— **Languages** 26
**ASSEMBLY PROGRAM.** A program which assembles parts of a program, allocating storage and providing cross-references; and which may translate them for example from the assembly language into the machine language. *See:* Assembly languages 26
**ASSOCIATION.** An *association* or *opposition*, is the *paradigmatic* relation between two (or more) *items* which can *substitute* for one another. *See:* Relations between languages: semantic change 484; Semantics: field theories (M) 504
**ASSOCIATION FACTOR.** A numerical measure of degree of association. If the occurrence of any event (e.g. the occurrence of a word in a printed sentence) influences the number of occurrences of another event (e.g. another word), the two events are said to be associated. *See:* Information storage and retrieval 223
— **fibres:** *see* Axonal bundles or fibres (G); Semantics: field theories (M) 504
**ASSOCIATIVE.** In algebras, obeying the rule exemplified below:

$$(A+B)+C = A+(B+C)$$
$$(A \times B) \times C = A \times (B \times C)$$

Both $+$ and $\times$ are then called associative operators. *See:* Linguistic form: system and structure (M) 278. *See also:* Commutative (G); Distributive (G)
**Asymmetry, binocular:** *see* Perception, visual 386

**Atlas, dialect:** *see* Language varieties: language and dialect 243

**Atomic statement:** *see* Statement (G)

**Attention** 28

**ATTRIBUTE.** An *attribute* of a *subordinate construction* is one which unlike the *head* is not *substitutable* for the whole construction. *See:* Grammar (structural) 186

**Auditory images:** *see* Perception of sound 365

**AUDITORY PHONETICS.** An *auditory description* of a speech sound is a description of the auditory impression it makes on the hearer, rather than of the activity of the speaker's vocal organs *(articulatory)* or of the physical characteristics of the sound-wave itself *(acoustic)*. *Auditory phonetics* is the branch of *phonetics* concerned with the auditory study of speech sounds. *See:* Phonetics, auditory 396

— **system:** *see* Sensory processes 530

— **theory:** *see* Hearing 211

**Augmented text:** *see* Computational linguistics: machine translation 53

**Augmenting responses:** *see* Neuronal nets 328

**AUTOCODE.** An easily memorized programming language with simple imput and output instructions, often sacrificing some of the computer's flexibility and speed.

**AUTOCORRELATION.** The correlation of a signal (usually analog) with a shifted copy of the same signal, generally most marked for small shifts. *Autocorrelation coefficient.* A measure of autocorrelation, when the signal is a magnitude $(\bar{x}+x)$ having a long-term average $\bar{x}$, i.e. produced by a stationary process. If the shifted copy has the value $(\bar{x}+x')$, the autocorrelation coefficient is defined as $\sum xx'/\sum x^2$. *Autocorrelation function.* The dependence of autocorrelation upon shift, indicating the rapidity with which changes occur. *See:* Random signals and noise 453

**Automata:** *see* Linguistic form: generative grammar (M) 273

—, **finite:** *see* Linguistic form: generative grammar (M) 273

—, **Finite-State** 32

—, **Infinite-State** 35

—, **linear-bounded:** *see* Linguistic form: generative grammar (M) 273

—, **self-reproducing:** *see* Automata, infinite-state 38

— **theory, effectiveness in:** *see* Automata, infinite-state 36

**Automatic dictionary:** *see* Computational linguistics: introduction (M) 49

— **language processing:** *see* Computational linguistics: introduction 49

**AUTOMATIC MACHINE.** A machine whose *state* is fixed (or which has a fixed program); that is, it has a definite output for any particular input. *See:* Learning machines; a unified view 261

— **optimization:** *see* Optimization, automatic 342

— **systems:** *see* Computational linguistics: introduction (M) 49

**Automatic typographic composition:** *See* Computational linguistics: introduction 49

**AUTOMATON.** A machine which may both produce an output and change its *state* on receipt of certain inputs. *See:* Automata, finite-state 32; Automata, infinite state 35

—, **adaption:** *see* Adaptive control theory 5

**Autonomous motion:** *see* Control, on-off 137

— **states:** *see* Control, on-off 137

**AUTONOMOUS SYSTEM.** A *control system* with no input. If $y$ is a system variable, its behaviour is represented by the differential equation

$$f(D) \cdot y = 0$$

where $f(D)$ is any function of the differential operator d/d$t$. Autonomous systems are mathematical abstractions, useful in the design of real systems. *Non-autonomous system.* A control system with an input. Behaviour within it is represented by $f(D) \cdot y = g(t)$, where $g(t)$, representing the input varying with time, is called a *forcing function*. *See:* Control, stability and 149 P.A.N. Briggs

**Auxiliary language:** *see* Relations between languages: lingua franca 480

**Available space list (ASL):** *see* Symbol manipulation by digital computer 596

**Avoidance learning:** *see* Animal motivation 24

**Axis:** *see* Writing 628

—, **decision:** *see* Decision axis (G)

—, **visual:** *see* Visual axis (G)

**AXON.** Thread-like process on a nerve cell body along which signals go out. *See:* Neuronal nets 320

**AXONAL BUNDLES OR FIBRES.** When passing out from the cortical surface they are called *corticofugal*, and are sub-classified as *association fibres* if they run to other neuronal nets in the same *(ipsilateral)* hemisphere of the cerebrum; *commisural fibres* if they run to corresponding nets in the other *(contralateral)* hemisphere; and *projection fibres* if they run to neuronal nets outside the cortex. *See:* Neuronal nets 320

**AZIMUTH.** Direction in a horizontal plane, 0° azimuth being directly ahead.

**Back:** *see* Phonetics, auditory 397; Phonology: contrast and opposition 401

**Background, structural:** *see* Relations between languages: semantic change 484

**Backus normal form:** *see* Linguistic form: algebraic linguistics 270

**BANDWIDTH.** A measure of the limitations of an analog *communication channel*. A frequency band between $A$ and $A+W$ cycles per second has a bandwidth $W$. By means of it not more than $2W$ independent signal values per second can be transmitted. The *capacity* of the channel in this ideal case is $2W$. In a noisy channel where $P/N$ is the ratio of signal power to noise power, the capacity = $W \log (1+P/N)$. *See:* Communication theory 46

**Bandwidth compression:** *see* Telecommunication, economy in 599
—, **spectral:** *see* Spectral bandwidth (G).
**Bang-bang control:** *see* Control, on-off 136
**BASE COMPONENT.** The *base* is the *component* (1) of a *transformational-generative grammar* which *generates deep structures*, which are then assigned meanings in the *semantic component* and, after being converted to *surface structures* by the *transformational component*, are assigned *phonetic representations* in the *phonological component*. *See:* Linguistic form: transformational theory 281
**BASE RULE.** A *base rule* is a *rewrite rule*, in the *base component* of a *transformational-generative grammar*, which is applied before the rules which attach *representations* of particular *lexical items* to the *phrase-marker*. *See:* Linguistic form: transformational theory 281
**Baseball:** *see* Fact retrieval 180
**Basic articulations:** *see* Phonology: prosodic features 411
— **elements of control:** *see* Control: basic elements 89
**Batch processing of requests:** *see* Information storage and retrieval 229
**Bayes' theorem.** Let there be any number of mutually exclusive hypotheses $H_1, H_2, \ldots H_i, \ldots$, and let their probabilities of being true be $p(H_i)$ etc. Now suppose an event $E$ occurs which strengthens some of the hypotheses and weakens others. For each hypothesis $H_i$ it must be possible to calculate that an event occurring at random would be the event $E$, the probability being represented by $p(E/H_i)$.
Bayes' theorem states that

$$p(H_i/E) = \frac{p(E/H_i)p(H_i)}{\sum_i p(E/H_i)p(H_i)}.$$

In other words the new probability of truth of $H_i$ after the event $E$ can be calculated in terms of probabilities that were known before the event $E_k$ occurred. (In practice it is fairly satisfactory to assume to begin with that $p(H_1) = p(H_2) = \ldots p(H_i) = \ldots$ and, of course, that $\sum p(H_i) = 1$.)
**Bayesian decision theory:** *see* Pattern recognition 354
**Bazell:** *see* Relations between languages: typological and areal classifications 486
**BEHAVIOUR.** The response (output) of a system (animal or mechanical) to a particular set of stimuli (input signals).
—, **adaptive:** *see* Adaptive control theory 1
—, **adaptive, evaluation of:** *see* Adaptive control theory 1
—, **animal exploratory:** *see* Animal exploratory behaviour 18
—, **conceptual:** *see* Conceptual behaviour 84
—, **conceptual, determiners of:** *see* Conceptual behaviour 85
— **pattern, projection of:** *see* Projecting a behaviour pattern (G).
— **sequences, non-linear:** *see* Psychological linguistics:
theories of learning in relation to language (M) 444
**Behaviourism:** *see* Gestalt psychology 185
**Benham's top:** *see* Perception of colour 363
**BERNOULLI'S THEOREM.** The probability of $r$ events in $n$ trials, when each event has the probability $p$, is $Pn(r) = {}^nC_r p^r (1-p)^{n-r}$.
The binomial coefficients emerge in considering the number of ways of obtaining $r$ events in $n$ trials. When $n$ is large we expect $np$ events within a small *practical* range of error $E$, i.e. the probability that the number of events is between $n(p \pm E) \to 1$ as $n \to \infty$.
**BERNOULLI SEQUENCE.** A random process. *See:* Process (G).
**Bezold-Brucke effect:** *see* Perception of colour 361
**Bias, estimate:** *see* Pseudorandom binary signals, use of ... 435
**BIBLIOGRAPHIC COUPLING.** An association between two documents, established when they are found to have in common a high proportion of *keywords, descriptors, citations* or other simple indications of what they are concerned with.
**Bilabial:** *see* Phonetics, articulatory 394
**Bilateral oppositions:** *see* Phonology: distinctive features (M) 404
**Bilingual:** *see* Writing (M) 627
**Bilingualism:** *see* Relations between languages: bilingualism 473; Relations between languages: introduction 470; Relations between languages: lingua franca (M) 480
**Billet lengths, control of:** *see* Control by hybrid computers 95
**Binary IC:** *see* Grammar (structural) 195
— **matrix:** *see* Matrix (G).
— **searching:** *see* Information storage and retrieval 230
**BINARY SEGMENTATION.** *Binary segmentation* is the principle that *(syntagmatic)* analysis of a text proceeds by a succession of cuts, each of which divides a single item *(constitute)* into two items (its *immediate constituents)*; exceptions are made, by those who accept this principle, for situations in which it is necessary to cut an item into three (or more) immediate constituents. This principle—associated particularly with the *structuralist* approach—also excludes 'unary' branching, in which an item is said to have a single immediate constituent. *See:* Grammar (structural) 186
—, **signal, random:** Pseudorandom binary signals, use of... 433
— **symmetric channel:** *see* Error correcting codes 173
**BINARY TREE.** An *ordered pair*, each element of which may itself be an ordered pair, and so on to any finite *depth*.
*See also:* Tree (G); Symbol manipulation by digital computer 594
**Binit, parity:** *see* Error correcting codes 174
**Binocular alternation:** *see* Perception, visual 386
— **asymmetry:** *see* Perception, visual 386

**Binocular combination:** *see* Perception, stereopsis as an aspect of 372
— **depth cues:** *see* Perception, stereopsis as an aspect of 368
— **depth perception:** *see* Perception, stereopsis as an aspect of 368
— **parallax:** *see* Perception, stereopsis as an aspect of 368
— **rivalry:** *see* Perception, stereopsis as an aspect of 372
— **vision summation and independence:** *see* Perception, visual 386
— **visual capabilities:** *see* Perception, visual 385
**BIONICS.** The application to engineering design of knowledge derived from the study of living systems.
**Bipolar cells:** *see* Perception of colour.
**BIT (BINIT).** The unit of information. A digit in binary notation having the value 0 or 1. (Contraction of 'binary digit'.) *See:* Communication theory 46
**BLACK BOX.** Any system whose only features of interest are its inputs and outputs and the relations between them.
**Blast furnace, control of:** *see* Control by hybrid computers 95
**Bloch's law:** *see* Perception, visual 381
**Block coding:** *see* Error correcting codes, 173
**Block search:** *see* Optimization, automatic 343
**Blocks, golden:** *see* Optimization, automatic 343
**Bode diagrams:** *see* Control, stability and 150
**Bodies, lateral geniculate:** *see* Lateral geniculate bodies (G).
**Body, cell:** *see* Soma (G).
**Boolean discriminant functions:** *see* Character recognition 42
**BOOLEAN FUNCTIONS OF STATEMENTS.** Any of the following, if A, B are two statements implying 'A is true' and 'B is true'.

| | | |
|---|---|---|
| negation | $(\bar{A})$ | not A (A is false) |
| conjunction | $(A \cup B)$ | A or B (or both, are true) |
| disjunction | $(A \cap B)$ | A and B (are both true) |
| conditional | $(A \Rightarrow B)$ | A if B |
| biconditional | $(A \equiv B)$ | A, B are equivalent |

*See also:* Logic element (G).
**BOOLEAN LATTICE.** All the different Boolean functions of $n$ statements or sets ($2^{2^n}$ in number) arranged in a standard order.
**Bootstrap adaptation:** *see* Adaptive threshold elements 11
**Borrowing:** *see* Relations between languages: bilingualism (M) 473
**Bose-Chaudhuri-Hoquenghem codes:** *see* Error correcting codes 174
**BOTRYOLOGY.** The technology of separating interconnected objects (such as words, animal types, examination candidates) into groups. *See:* Statistics of language: introduction 567

**Bound, Elias-Shannon-Gallager:** *see* Error correcting codes 174
**BOUND FORM.** A *bound form* is a *form* (3) or *item*, which must always be accompanied by other forms; therefore, unlike *free forms*, it cannot be used on its own as a complete *utterance* (2). *See:* Grammar (structural).
—, **Gilbert:** *see* Error correcting codes 174
—, **Hamming:** *see* Error correcting codes 173
—, **root:** *see* Grammar (structural) 189
**Boundary-value problem, two-point:** *see* Control by the maximum principle 105
**Boustrophedon:** *see* Writing 628
**Boutons:** *see* Neuronal nets 322
**Box, black:** *see* Black box (G).
— **diagram:** *see* Grammar (structural) (M) 186
**Braille:** *see* Statistics of language: introduction 567
**Brain, olfactory:** *see* Neuronal nets 320
—, **visceral:** *see* Neuronal nets, 320
**Breakdown, perceptual, with stabilized images:** *see* Perceptual breakdown with stabilized images 388
**Brightness:** *see* Perception of colour 363
— **shift effect, Stiles-Crawford:** *see* Perception of colour 363
**BROAD PHONETIC TRANSCRIPTION.** A *broad phonetic transcription* is a transcription which needs only a small number of symbols compared with a *narrow transcription*, since it lets some symbols represent a number of different sounds, whereas the narrow transcription has a different symbol for each distinguishable sound. The broad transcription does not necessarily give less phonetic information than the narrow one, however, since in many cases only one of the sounds represented by a given symbol is possible in a given *environment;* thus, any system of broad transcription is appropriate only for one language, whose *phonemes* it reflects, and it must be accompanied by a set of rules specifying how the symbols are to be interpreted phonetically in different environments. *See:* Phonology: phonemes and broad transcription 409
**Broadcast services, carrier-wired:** *see* Local networks 288
**BUFFER STORE.** A store into which information is temporarily put, when it is being transferred from one storage device to another. The usual reason for doing this is a difference in speed of data flow required by the initial and final devices. Thus a worthwhile buffer store must be cheap to operate even at the lower of the two speeds. To *buffer* data is to transmit data via a buffer store. *Buffering* is using a buffer store. *See:* Computer operating systems 60
**Buffering techniques:** *see* Computer operating systems 60
**Bundles, axonal:** *see* Axonal bundles or fibres (G).
**BUNDLING.** *Bundling* is the situation where several *isoglosses* more or less coincide geographically. *See:* Language varieties: language and dialect 243
**BURST.** Sequence of *action potentials*.
— **activity:** *see* Neuronal nets 330
**Bytes:** *see* Information theory in psychological measurement 233

**Cables, telegraph:** *see* Telecommunication, global 604
**CALCULUS OF VARIATIONS.** A branch of mathematics concerned with obtaining functional relationships (between variables) which optimize a criterion function of these variables, subject to constraint equations between the variables. The method utilizes the effects of small variations in each functional relationship. *See:* Control by the maximum principle 101; Dynamic programming 168
**CALL.** An instruction to a computer to use a specific piece of program (e.g. a *subroutine* prepared by the programmer) or a specific *facility* (e.g. to multiply a number by itself) built in by the engineers and designers. *See:* Algorithms for processing algorithms 15
**Calques:** *see* Relations between languages: loans and loanwords 482; Language varieties: register (M) 251
**Cancer:** *see* Homeostasis in the single cell 219
**CANONIC VARIABLES.** A set of variables used in an expression of the basic rules, e.g. about the *state* of a system.
**Canonical form:** *see* Relations between languages: typological and areal classifications 486
**Capabilities, binocular visual:** *see* Perception, visual 385
**Capacity of the channel:** *see* Telecommunication, economy in 599
— **of a communication channel:** *see* Bandwidth (G).
—, **strong generative:** *see* Linguistic form: generative grammar 272
—, **transduction:** *see* Transduction capacity (G).
—, **weak generative:** *see* Weak generative capacity (G); Linguistic form: generative grammar 272
**Card:** *see* Information storage and retrieval 223
—, **aperture:** *see* Aperture card (G); Information storage and retrieval 224
—, **edge notched:** *see* Information storage and retrieval 224
**CARDINAL VOWEL.** A set of eight primary and eight secondary *vowel-sounds* have been selected as fixed standards by comparison with which any vowel sound can be defined *phonetically*. These sixteen *cardinal vowels* have been precisely defined with reference to their *articulation*, and examples of them are available on gramophone records. *See:* Phonetics, auditory 397
**Cardinals, secondary:** *see* Phonetics, auditory 397
**CARRIER WAVE.** Wave, ideally of constant frequency, upon which modulations of amplitude, frequency or phase can be superposed so that signals may be carried a t the velocity of the wave.
— **wired broadcast services:** *see* Local networks 288
**Carrol's response surface technique:** *see* Optimization of industrial processes 348
**Case:** *see* Grammar (structural) (M) 186
**Categories, acoustic:** *see* Phonology: contrast and opposition (M) 401
—, **descriptive:** *see* Grammar (structural) 204
—, **grammatical:** *see* Semantics: context and collocation (M) 503
**Categories, lexical:** *see* Linguistic form: transformational theory (M) 280; Psychological linguistics: psycholinguistic studies of syntax (M) 439
—, **specific:** *see* Grammar (structural) 204
—, **theoretical:** *see* Grammar (structural) 204
**Category:** *see* Grammar (structural) 204
— **features:** *see* Linguistic form: transformational theory 281
**CATEGORY SYMBOL.** A *string* of symbols *generated* by a *transformational generative grammar* is a *category symbol*, a *complex symbol*, a *formative*, or a set of category and/or complex symbols (a *complex string*). A category symbol is one which is defined as part of the basic vocabulary of symbols introduced by the rules of the grammar, and category symbols can generally be identified with *classes* (1) rather than *functions* (2). *See:* Linguistic form: transformational theory 281
**CATHODE-RAY TUBE (CRT).** An electronic device, similar in construction to a television tube, by whose screen a spot of light is emitted as the result of bombardment of a phosphor by electrons. The position of the spot on the screen is controlled by two electronic deflecting devices (producing electric or magnetic fields) within the tube.
**Cell body:** *see* Soma (G).
**Cellar:** *see* Stacks 563
**Cells, bipolar:** *see* Perception of colour 359
—, **horizontal:** *see* Perception of colour 359
**Cement manufacture, control of:** *see* Control by hybrid computers 99
**CENTRAL.** Occurring near the *centre* of the central nervous system (e.g. at or beyond the point at which signals from the two eyes come together).
—: *see* Phonetics, auditory 398
**CENTRAL NERVOUS SYSTEM (CNS).** The spinal cord and the brain.
**Centralized:** *see* Phonetics, auditory 398
**CENTRE.** The region (usually not precisely specifiable) in the *central nervous system* where an incoming signal becomes an outgoing signal.
**CENTRE OF EXPANSION.** (Of the visual field.) The point from which all fixed objects appear to radiate when approached by an observer, defining the direction of this motion. *See:* Man-machine communication and ergonomics 301
—, **respiratory:** *see* Respiratory centre (G).
**CENTRIFUGAL.** Relating to the nerve paths in which signals are carried in a direction from the centre towards the periphery; opposite in direction to *afferent*, *centripetal*.
— **pathways:** *see* Sensory processes 533
**Centring:** *see* Phonetics, auditory 398
**CENTRIPETAL.** Towards the centre from the periphery.
**CEREBELLUM.** Separable part of the brain, nearest the spine.
**CEREBRUM.** Separable part of the brain, the fore brain. *See:* Cortex (G)
**Cerebral cortex:** *see* Neuronal nets 321
**Chain:** *see* Grammar (structural) 186

**CHAIN CODE.** A sequence of binary digits with period $2^n$ or less: the entire sequence can be developed from any sub-sequence of $n$ digits, according to a rule or formula. *m-sequence.* A chain code of length $2^n-1$ omitting only the pattern of $n$ zeros. *See:* Pseudo-noise sequences 419; Pseudorandom binary signals, use of... 433 P.A.N. Briggs
— **·code random generators, use of in simulation of traffic problems:** *see* Simulation of traffic problems using chain-code random generators 539
**Chained transfer:** *see* Computer peripherals and their control 60
**Change, phonetic:** *see* Relations between languages: comparative philology 475
**Changes, sound:** *see* Relations between languages: introduction (M) 470
**Channel, binary symmetric:** *see* Error correcting codes 173
—, **capacity of:** *see* Telecommunication, economy in 599
—, **communication:** *see* Communication channel (G).
—, **communication, capacity of:** *see* Bandwidth (G).
—, **telephone speech:** *see* Data transmission 160
**Channels, anatomical relationship of:** *see* Sensory processes 532
**CHARACTER.** One of a set of elements used in building up a *signal.* Capable of representation in various ways (e.g. $A = a = \cdot - = 00100001$) and therefore a convenient basis for abstract discussion. *See:* Character recognition 41. *See also:* Alphanumeric symbols (G).
— **Recognition** 41
**Characteristics, acoustic, of linguistic units:** *see* Phonetics, acoustic 391
—, **universal:** *see* Linguistic form: transformational theory (M) 280
**Characterization, explicit:** *see* Psychological linguistics: psycholinguistic studies of syntax (M) 439
—, **phonetic:** *see* Linguistic form: transformational theory (M) 280
**CHECK-SUM.** In the transfer of data to a computer, the sum of all the units of data in a section of the transfer. The computer is instructed to add the units of data as it stores them, compare their sum with the check-sum, and give a failure signal if they fail to agree. The whole sequence of operations is a *sum-check*. *See also:* Parity check (G).
**CHEMORECEPTOR.** A receptor which initiates nerve impulses in response to chemical changes *See:* Receptors: relation between the stimuli and the activity in single primary units 463; Receptors: representation of information about stimuli in populations 467
**Chi-squared test:** *see* Statistics of language: introduction 571
**Chiasma:** *see* Perception, stereopsis as an aspect of 372
**Choice responses:** *see* Information theory in psychological measurement 234
**Chomsky:** *see* Linguistic form: paradigmatic (M) 273
**Chromatic aberration:** *see* Perception, visual 374

**Chunks:** *see* Information theory in psychological measurement 233; Speech perception 550
**Church, Lambda-calculus of:** *see* Unsolvable problems 624
**Church's thesis:** *see* Automata, infinite-state 36; Unsolvable problems 624
**Cineplasty:** *see* Prosthetic limbs 417
**Circuit, integrated:** *see* Integrated circuit (G).
—, **junction:** *see* Local networks 284
—, **neural:** *see* Reverberating activity (G).
**CITATION INDEX.** A list of journal articles and their accompanying citations to literature, arranged alphabetically by cited author. *See:* Scientific documentation 496
**Citations, use of:** *see* Information storage and retrieval 228
**CLASS.** A *class* in linguistics is a set of *items*, and is distinguished from a *function*, which is a particular *syntagmatic* relation to other items. Thus a given item is always a member of the same *class* or classes, whereas it only has a particular *function* when it occurs in a larger *environment*. In *transformational-generative grammar* a symbol representing a class is known as a *category-symbol*. *See:* Grammar (structural) 186; Linguistic form: paradigmatic 273; Linguistic form: syntagmatic (M) 276; Linguistic form: transformational theory (M) 280; Relations between languages: introduction (M) 470; Relations between languages: typological and areal classifications (M) 486; Semantics: introduction (M) 499
— **-cleavage:** *see* Grammar (structural) 201
—, **closed:** *see* Closed class (G); Grammar (structural) 201; Relations between languages: loans and loanwords (M) 482
—, **open:** *see* Open class (G). Relations between languages: loans and loanwords 482; Grammar (structural) 201
—, **paradigmatic:** *see* Linguistic form: paradigmatic 273
—, **substitution:** *see* Grammar (structural) 200; Linguistic form: generative grammar 273; Substitution class (G).
**Classes:** *see* Linguistic form: syntagmatic (M) 276
**Classical sensory pathway:** *see* Neuronal nets 328
**CLASSIFICATION.** The assignment of documents or other items to defined classes. It is often convenient to avoid enumerating a large number of classes by introducing a set of *descriptors*, any combination of which defines a class.
—, **genetic:** *see* Genetic classification (G).
—, **multidimensional:** *see* Dimensional (G).
—, **system:** *see* System (G).
—, **typological:** *see* Typological classification (G). Relations between languages: semantic change (M) 484; Writing (M) 627
**Classifications, typological and areal:** *see* Relations between languages: typological and areal classifications 486
**Classifying:** *see* Linguistic form: paradigmatic (M) 273
**Clause:** *see* Relations between languages: typological and areal classifications (M) 486

**Clicks:** *see* Phonetics, articulatory (M)   393
—, **reverse:** *see* Phonetics, articulatory (M)   393
**Climbing, hill, by alternate adjustments:** *see* Control, hill climbing in   117
—, **hill, by gradient method:** *see* Control, hill climbing in   117
**Cline.** A *cline* is a scale which forms the basis for classifying a specified set of objects; any member of this set can be assigned a place on the scale, but any choice of a single criterion by which items could be assigned to a small number of discrete sets would be arbitrary and unmotivated. *See:* Language varieties: register   251; Grammar (structural) (M)   186; Relations between languages: typological and areal classifications (M)   486
**Clock rate.** The number of bits per second, describing the rate at which signals reach any point in a communication channel.
**Close:** *see* Phonetics, auditory   397
**CLOSSED CLASS.** *Classes* are *open* or *closed;* a closed class has a definable and relatively small membership, whereas an open class has not. *See:* Grammar (structural) 186; Relations between languages: loans and loanwords (M)   482
— **loop.** *See:* Feedback control. Contrast with *open loop control.*
— **loop adaptive controller:** *see* Adaptive control theory   2
**Closing:** *see* Phonetics, auditory   398
**Cochlea:** *see* Non-neural elements in receptor systems   339; Cochlear mechanics   44
**Cochlear Mechanics**   44
**CODE** (1). The *language-systems* comprising a *communication-matrix* are either *languages* (3) or different *dialects* (1); in the first case they are called *codes,* in the second *subcodes. See:* Language varieties: language and dialect   243
**CODE** (2). A set of rules for expressing *data* in terms of members of a set of *characters. See:* Error correcting codes   173
—, **chain:** *see* Chain code (G). Pseudonoise sequences   419; Pseudorandom binary signals, use of...   433
—, **cyclic linear:** *see* Error correcting codes   174
—, **elaborated:** *see* Language varieties: register (M)   251
—, **Golay:** *see* Error correcting codes   173
—, **order:** *see* Order code (G)
— **rate:** *see* Error correcting   173
— **residue:** *see* Error correcting codes   175
—, **restricted:** *see* Relations between languages: lingua franca (M)   480; Language varieties: register (M)   251
—, **sphere-packed:** *see* Error correcting codes   173
—, **systematic:** *see* Error correcting codes   174
**Codes, Bose-Chaudhuri-Hoquenghem:** *see* Error correcting codes   174
—, **error correcting:** *see* Error correcting codes   173
—, **group:** *see* Error correcting codes   174
—, **Hamming:** *see* Information space   222
—, **linear:** *see* Error correcting codes   174

**Codes, linear group:** *see* Information space   222
—, **parity-check:** *see* Error correcting codes   174
**CODING.** The assigning of numbers to information, or alternatively, the conversion of information from one number-scheme to another. *See:* Information space.
—, **block:** *see* Error correcting codes   173
—, **convolutional:** *see* Error correcting codes   175
**Coefficient, autocorrelation:** *see* Autocorrelation (G)
—, **correlation:** *see* Correlation coefficient (G)
**Cognitive complexity:** *see* Psychological linguistics: psycholinguistic studies of syntax (M)   439
— **meaning:** *see* Semantics: introduction   499
**Collaterals, recurrent:** *see* Neuronal nets   330
**Collection of garbage:** *see* Symbol manipulation by digital computer   597
**Colligate:** *see* Grammar (structural)   199
**COLLIGATION.** When two *grammatical items* occur together in a specified *syntagmatic* relation, they are said to *colligate,* and the combination is a *colligation* (as opposed to a *collocation*). *See:* Linguistic form: system and structure   279; Grammar (structural)   199; also Linguistic form: syntagmatic   278
**Collocate:** *see* Semantics: context and collocation   503
**COLLOCATION:** When two *lexical items* occur together in a specified syntagmatic relation they are said to *collocate,* and the combination is called a *collocation* (as opposed to a *colligation*). A particular item's *collocations* are the lexical *environments* in which it can occur. *See:* Semantics: context and collocation   503; Linguistic form: syntagmatic   278; Grammar (structural) (M)   186; Language varieties: register (M)   251; Semantics: field theories (M)   506; Semantics: meaning and reference   509
**Collocational ranges:** *see* Semantics: context and collocation   503
**Colour:** *see* Receptors: representation of information about stimuli in populations   468
— **perception:** *see* Perception of colour   358
**Colour-vision system, mechanisms of:** *see* Perception of colour   362
**COLUMN.** Aggregate of nerve fibres in any part of the *central nervous system. See:* Neuronal nets   320
**Columns of constant orientation:** *see* Neuronal nets   333
**Combination, binocular:** *see* Perception, stereopsis as an aspect of   372
**COMBINATORIAL MATHEMATICS.** The mathematical study of combinations (e.g. binomial theorem), similarities, and logic; introduced by G. W. Leibnitz in 1666.
**COMBINATORIAL SEMANTICS.** *Combinatorial semantics* studies the ways in which the meaning of a sentence as a whole is related to the meanings of its parts. *See:* Semantics: introduction   501
**COMMAND.** A signal to the operating system which manipulates a computer's resources or environment, e.g. the system programs, peripheral machines, file stores or the plant being controlled.
**COMMAND LANGUAGE.** An extra set of instructions

and syntax rules, necessary when a computer operating system (software) is in control. *See:* Computer operating systems 58

**Commisural fibres:** *see* Axonal bundles or fibres (G)

**Common control switching:** *see* Switching and control in telephony 591

**Communication, aircraft/pilot:** *see* Man-machine communication and ergonomics 303

**COMMUNICATION CHANNEL.** The mechanism which governs the transmission of a signal between the sender and the receiver. *Noisy communication channel.* Any communication channel such that the symbol received is not always identical with the symbol sent. *See:* Communication theory 46

— **channel, capacity of:** *see* Bandwidth (G)
— **channel, noisy:** *see* Communication channel (G)
—, **graphical:** *see* Graphical communication 207
—, **man-machine:** *see* Man-machine communication and ergonomics 301

**COMMUNICATION MATRIX.** The members of any given *language community* use different *varieties* of language *(registers)* in different *situations*, and different members may use different *dialects* (1); moreover, all or most of the members may be able to use two or more different *languages* (3), each in a different set of situations. All these varieties and languages taken together comprise a *communication matrix*. Different dialects and different languages within a communication matrix are called *subcodes* and *codes* respectively. *See:* Language varieties: language and dialect 243

— Theory 46

**Community, language:** *see* Language community (G); Language varieties: language and dialect 243

**COMMUTATIVE.** In algebras, obeying the rule exemplified below:
$A + B = B + A$
$A \times B = B \times A$
Both $+$ and $\times$ are then called commutative operators. *See also:* Associative (G); Distributive (G)

**COMMUTE.** *Commutation* is contrasted in linguistics with *permutation;* the two together are sometimes taken to exhaust the possible relations among linguistic *items* or *classes*. A *commutes* with B if A can occur in an *environment* where B can also occur, i.e. where A and B are mutually *substitutable*. *See:* Grammar (structural) 186

**Compact features:** *see* Linguistic form: transformational theory 283

**Comparative method:** *see* Relations between languages: introduction 470; Relations between languages: comparative philology 475

— **morphology:** *see* Relations between languages: comparative philology 475

— **philology:** *see* Relations between languages: comparative philology 475

**Comparison, historical:** *see* Relations between languages: introduction 470

—, **typological:** *see* Relations between languages: introduction 470

**COMPATIBLE.** If two modules are compatible the output signals of one of them are of suitable form to be used as input for the other, or in some sense one module may be replaced by the other

**Compensatory task:** *See* Man-machine in control systems 307

**COMPETENCE.** Linguistic *competence* is contrasted with linguistic *performance;* competence is a native speaker's largely unconscious knowledge of a *language-system* whereas performance is the way in which he exploits this knowledge. *See:* Linguistic form: system and structure 278; Psychological linguistics: theories of learning in relation to language 444

**COMPILE.** To translate, by computer, programs from the programming language into the computer language.

**COMPILER.** A program which puts a computer into the *state* for compiling. *See:* Algorithms for processing algorithms 15

**COMPLEMENTARY DISTRIBUTION.** If one *item* never occurs in the *environments* in which another item can occur, and vice versa, those two items are said to be in *complementary distribution*. For two *phones* to be assigned to the same *phoneme*, as its *allophones*, they must be in complementary distribution and/or in *free variation*. *See:* Phonology: phonemes and broad transcription 409; Phonology: distinctive features (M) 404

**Complex string:** *see* Linguistic form: transformational theory 281

**COMPLEX SYMBOL.** *Complex symbols* (C.S.) are the sets of symbols introduced by *strict subcategorization rules* and *selectional rules* in a *transformational generative grammar*. Each C.S. consists of a set of *features (subcategorization features* and *selectional features)* and is attached to a *category symbol* to which a representation of a particular *lexical item* is later to be attached; the C.S. gives information on the *environment* of the category symbol, so that only lexical items compatible with that environment will be attached to it. *See:* Linguistic form: transformational theory 281; Linguistic form: generative grammar (M) 272

**Complexity, cognitive:** *see* Psychological linguistics: psycholinguistic studies of syntax (M) 439

—, **syntactic:** *see* Psychological linguistics: psycholinguistic studies of syntax 441

**COMPONENT (1).** The whole of a *transformational-generative grammar* (3) is divided into *components* (1), corresponding roughly to *levels of representation;* four components are the *base component*, the *semantic component*, the *transformational component* and the *phonological component*. *See:* Linguistic form: transformational theory 280; Computational linguistics: introduction 50

**COMPONENT (2).** In some cases, *segments* can be treated as bundles of *features* or *components* (2) which can combine more or less freely with each other so that a small number of components in combination form a relatively large number of different segmental *items*. In particular, it is sometimes possible to analyse the meaning of lexical items (usually words) into components *(semantic markers)*; this is called *componential analysis*. See: Phonological: contrast and opposition 401; Semantics: introduction 499

**Component (3):** *see* Vector (G)
**Component (4):** *see* Module (G)
—, **base:** *see* Base component (G). Linguistic form: transformational theory 281
—, **phonological:** *see* Phonology: contrast and opposition 401; Phonology: distinctive features (M) 404
—, **semantic:** *see* Linguistic form: transformational theory (M) 280
—, **syntactic:** *see* Psychological linguistics: psycholinguistic studies of syntax (M) 439
—, **transformational:** *see* Linguistic form: transformational theory 282; Grammar (structural) (M) 186
**Componential analysis:** *see* Semantics: introduction 500
**Components of linguistic systems:** *see* Computational linguistics: introduction 50
— **of a vector:** *see* Vector product (G)
**COMPOSITION.** A *description* of a linguistic *item* may involve specifying two kinds of information about it: its *composition* (or *morphology* (2)), i.e. the items of which it is *composed*, and their *syntagmatic relations*; and its *distribution* (or *syntax* (3), in a restricted sense), i.e. the *environments* in which it can occur. See: Grammar (structural) 186
—, **typographic, automatic:** *see* Computational linguistics: introduction 49
**Compound acoustic features (CAF's):** *see* Speech recognition, automatic 557
— **eye:** *see* Perception, visual 373
**COMPREHENSION (TASKS).** Tasks in experimental psychology designed to study the subject's ability to process relations between concepts. See: Concept identification—information processing approaches 83
**Compression:** See Phonetics, articulatory (M) 393
—, **bandwidth:** See Telecommunication, economy in 599
**Computation, formal:** See Formal computation (G)
—, **reliable, with unreliable elements:** See Reliable computation with unreliable elements 489
**Computational Linguistics: introduction** 49
— **Linguistics: machine translation** 51
— **models:** See Psychology, use of models (learning) 447
**COMPUTER.** A system whose *state* can be set by manipulation or by a special input signal (a program), to perform elaborate computations on its input data without further human intervention. An *analog computer* operates with analog signals whose magnitude contains the vital information. A *digital computer* operates with digital signals, which are finite combinations of a finite number of digits.
— **control, off-line:** See Control by hybrid computers 95
— **control, on-line closed-loop:** See Control by hybrid computers 97

**Computer, digital, symbol manipulation by:** See Symbol manipulation by digital computer 594
— **Language Design Requirements** 54
— **language, syntax of:** See Computer language design requirements 55
— **linked to controllers:** See Control by hybrid computers 95
— **linked to sensing devices:** See Control by hybrid computers 97
— **Operating Systems** 57
—, **parallel:** See Parallel computer (G)
— **Peripherals and their Control** 58
—, **sequential:** *see* Sequential computer (G).
— **Simulation of Human Thought Processes** 60
**Computers, access to:** *see* Computers, multiaccess to 64
—, **hybrid, control by:** *see* Control by hybrid computers 92
—, **Multiaccess to** 63
—, **Stochastic** 66
**Concentration alarm systems,** *see* Local networks 288
**CONCEPT.** A rule for classifying objects by examining their descriptions (Church 1958). See: Concept formation by artificial intelligence 76; Relations between languages: bilingualism (M) 473
**CONCEPT FORMATION.** The assignment by human beings of discriminably different stimuli to the same response category. See: Concept formation by artificial intelligence 76; Concept identification—information processing approaches 80; Conceptual behaviour 84
A more inductive definition: The discovery by subjects of experimentally or naturally assigned regularities in categorization of multidimensional stimulus objects or situations (E.R.F.W. Crossman: Information theory in psychological measurement).
— **Formation by Artificial Intelligence** 76
— **Identification—Information Processing Approaches** 80
**CONCEPT LEARNER.** A system whose input can be any object in the universe and whose output is the member of the *organizing set*, i.e. the *concept*, to which the object belongs. See: Concept formation by artificial intelligence 76
— **learning, informational variables in:** *see* Conceptual behaviour 86
**Conception, normative:** *see* Language varieties: register (M) 251
—, **prescriptive:** *see* Language varieties: register (M) 251
**Concepts, multivariate:** *see* Multivariate concepts (G)
**Conceptual approach:** *see* Relations between languages: semantic change 484
— **Behaviour** 84
— **behaviour, determiners of:** *see* Conceptual behaviour 85
— **meaning:** *see* Semantics: introduction 499
— **theories:** *see* Semantics: field theories (M) 504
**Conceptualism:** *see* Semantics: introduction (M) 499

**Conceptualization, rote:** *see* Concept identification—information processing approaches 80; Rote conceptualization (G)

**CONCORD.** *Concord* is a *selection relation* between *items* in a given *syntagmatic* relation to each other; there is a rule which specifies that they must both belong to the same class, or they must belong to classes which can be equated in some way (as when a singular noun is in concord with a singular verb). This selection may be seen as directed (one item selects the other) or reciprocal (each selects the other) or mutual (some earlier choice predetermines the choice of the class of both items). Concord is a different kind of selection relation from *government*. *See:* Grammar (structural) 203; Linguistic form: syntagmatic (M) 276; Linguistic form: paradigmatic 273

— **rules:** *see* Semantics: introduction (M) 499

**CONCORDANCE.** A file, each of whose entries is the transcription of an utterance, and is filed under some lexical item or syntactic feature. D. G. Hays. *See:* Computational linguistics: introduction 50

**Conditional assembly of macro-instructions:** *see* Assembly languages 27

**CONDITIONAL PROBABILITY.** Let $x$ be the proposition that the next person to telephone a certain number will be aged between 10 and 16. Let $P(x)$ represent the probability, in general, that $x$ will turn out to be true. Let $y$ be the proposition that today is a school holiday. Let $z$ be the proposition that a particular person aged between 10 and 16 is at home at the given telephone number. Then the probability that $x$ will turn out to be true, given $y$, can be written $P(x/y)$; and the probability that $x$ will turn out to be true, given $y$ and $z$ can be written $P(x/y, z)$. These two probabilities are called conditional probabilities and they are likely in the example to differ from each other and from $P(x)$. The propositions $y$ and $z$ are said to be *constraints* on the proposition $x$.

**CONDITIONAL PROBABILITY DENSITY.** In models of sensory discrimination, the probability of a particular *E*-value, given a particular stimulus. (An *E*-value is a standard measurement representing the neural effect of a signal.) *See:* Sensory discrimination, measurement of 513

**CONDITIONING.** An *item* may have a number of different *realizations*, each occurring in a different set of *environments*; these realizations are then said to be *conditioned* by the environments in which they occur. (They are *phonologically*, *lexically* or *grammatically* conditioned according to whether the environment is described in phonological, lexical or grammatical terms.) If the item is seen as a *class*, of which the different realizations are members, and if the item is a minimal *segment* on its own *level of representation*, then the item itself is a *-eme* (e.g. *phoneme, morpheme*) and its conditioned members are *allo-*'s (e.g. *allophones, allomorphs*). *See:* Phonology: phonemes and broad transcription 409; Grammar (structural) 188

**Conditions of Hadamard:** *see* Control, sensitivity and 147

**Conduction of impulses in nerve and muscle:** *see* Nerve and muscle, initiation and conduction of impulses in 314

—, **saltatory:** *see* Saltatory conduction (G).

—, **saltatory impulse,** *see* Medullated nerve fibre (G).

**Cones:** *see* Perception of colour 359

**Configurational features:** *see* Phonology: distinctive features 405

**Congruity, pattern:** *see* Phonology: phonemes and broad transcription 409

**CONNOTATION.** Linguistic *signs* may be classified as *connotative* (or *expressive*) or *denotative* (or *referential*) according to whether their meaning is intellectual or emotive. *See:* Semantics: introduction 499

**Connotative meaning:** *see* Semantics: introduction (M) 499

**CONSONANT (1), CONSONANT SOUND.** Speech sounds can be classified as either *consonant-sounds* (*contoids*) or *vowel-sounds* (*vocoids*); this is a *phonetic* distinction, as opposed to that between *consonants* (2) and *vowels* (2), which is *phonological*. *See:* Phonetics: articulatory 393; Phonology: distinctive features 406; Phonetics, acoustic (M) 391; Phonetics, auditory 396; Phonology: contrast and opposition 401; Phonology: prosodic features 411

**CONSONANT (2).** In most (or all) languages *segmental phonemes* can be classified as *consonants* (2) or *vowels* (2), these two classes being distinguished by the *distribution* of their members; there may also be some phonemes which are neither consonants nor vowels, and for which a third or fourth class has to be set up. The name '*consonant*' will be given to the class whose members tend to be *realised* as *contoids*, and the name '*vowel*' to that whose members tend to be realised as *vocoids*. *See:* Phonology: contrast and opposition 401; Statistics of language: structure of written English words (M) 567; Writing 627

— **string:** *see* Statistics of language: structure of written English words (M) 567

**Consonantal:** *see* Phonology: distinctive features (M) 404

— **features:** *see* Linguistic form: transformational theory 283

**Constancy:** *see* Perception of colour 360

**Constant orientation, columns of:** *see* Neuronal nets 333

— **stimulus:** *see* Receptors: relation between the stimuli and the activity in single primary units 465

— **stimulus differences, method of:** *see* Sensory discrimination, measurement of 517

**CONSTITUENCY.** If one *item* is *segmented* into a number of other, smaller items, the latter are the *constituents* of the former—more precisely, they are its *immediate constituents* (IC's). If these can be segmented, their IC's are also constituents of the first item, but are its *mediate constituents*, as are all their constituents down to their *ultimate constituents*. This *syntagmatic* relation of whole to part and part to whole is *constituency;* but an item's 'constituency' can mean its *composition*. Any *construction* (1) defines a set of *classes* whose members can combine, as *constituents*, to form larger items, which are the *constitutes* in the construction concerned, though they may also occur as constituents in other constructions. Some schools of linguistic theory stipulate that constituency is subject to the principle of *binary segmentation*, i.e. that no constitute can have more than two immediate constituents (apart from a number of exceptional kinds of constitute). *See:* Linguistic form: syntagmatic 276; Grammar (structural) 193

—, **layer:** *see* Grammar (structural) 198

— **relations:** *see* Linguistic form: syntagmatic 277

**Constituent:** *see* Linguistic form: syntagmatic 276; Linguistic form: transformational theory 280; Linguistic form: paradigmatic 274

**Constituent, discontinuous:** *see* Grammar (structural) 195

**Constituent, grammatical:** *see* Psychological linguistics: psychological aspects of semantic structure 442

—, **immediate:** *see* Immediate constituent (G). Grammar (structural) 194; Linguistic form: syntagmatic 277; Linguistic form: system and structure (M) 278

—, **mediate:** *see* Mediate constituent (G). Linguistic form: Syntagmatic 277

—, **string:** *see* String constituent (G). Grammar (structural) 199

—, **ultimate:** *see* Ultimate constituent (G). Grammar (structural) 194; Linguistic form: syntagmatic 277

**Constitute:** *see* Grammar (structural) 193; Linguistic form: syntagmatic 277

**Constitutes, endocentric:** *see* Grammar (structural) 196

—, **exocentric:** *see* Grammar (structural) 196

—, **paratactic:** *see* Grammar (structural) (M) 186

—, **subordinate:** *see* Grammar (structural) 196

**Constraint:** *see* Conditional probability (G).

**CONSTRATE.** Writing, seen as *substance*, consists of marks (the *constrate*) made on some background material (the *substrate* (2)). *See:* Writing 628

**Constrictives:** *see* Phonology: contrast and opposition (M) 401

**CONSTRUCTION (1).** *Items* whose *constituents*, or more specifically *immediate constituents*, are similarly related to each other *syntagmatically* can be grouped together into *classes* called *constructions* (1); or the term 'construction' can be applied to the syntagmatic relations among the constituents and between the constituents and the *constitute*, i.e. to the internal relations defining the class, rather than to the class itself. Constructions can be classified as either *endocentric (coordinate* or *subordinate)* or *exocentric*. *See* Grammar (structural) 193; Linguistic form: syntagmatic (M) 276

**CONSTRUCTION (2).** Any linguistic *item* (or more specifically any *grammatical item*) which can be seg-

mented into smaller items on the same *level of representation*, and is therefore a *constitute*, can be referred to as a *construction* (2).

**Construction, endocentric:** *see* Endocentric construction (G).

—, **Thesaurus:** *see* Information storage and retrieval 227

**Consultation, dictionary:** *see* Computational linguistics: machine translation 53

**CONTACT.** Two languages are in *contact* when either (or each) is known, to some extent, to the speakers of the other.

*See:* Relations between languages: comparative philology (M) 475; Relations between languages: introduction (M) 470; Relations between languages: lingua franca 480; Relations between languages: loans and loanwords (M) 482

— **language:** *see* Relations between languages: lingua franca 480

— **net:** *see* Modular net (G).

**CONTENT.** A linguistic sign is considered to have two parts: a *form* (1) or *signifiant* and a *content* or *signifié*. The sign's *content* is its *meaning*, whereas its *form* is its audible or visible shape. *See:* Semantics: meaning and reference 508; Relations between languages: loans and loanwords (M) 482; Relations between languages: semantic change (M) 484; Semantics: field theories (M) 504;

— **systems:** *see* Relations between languages: introduction (M) 470

**CONTEXT (1), CONTEXT OF SITUATION.** For any given *formal item* (or any set of formal items) it should be possible to specify the circumstances under which it would be appropriate to use it; these circumstances abstracted from the situations in which it is or could be used constitute a *context (of situation)*. This term may or may not include the specifically linguistic *environments* in which the item can occur, as well as the non-linguistic situations in which it can occur. *See:* Semantics: context and collocation 503; Semantics: meaning and reference 509; Linguistic form: paradigmatic (M) 273

**CONTEXT (2).** The symbols on either side of a given string of symbols constitute its *context* (2). *See:* Statistics of language: structure of written English words (M) 581

**CONTEXT (3).** The entire environment of a symbol, including other symbols, the system for recognizing them, and the language from which they are all selected. *See:* Similarity 535

**CONTEXT-FREE.** A *context-free rule* is one which applies in any *context* (2), i.e. in any linguistic *environment*. If the rule is a *rewrite rule*, it provides for the replacement of a specified string of symbols wherever it occurs, i.e. irrespective of the symbols occurring on either side of it. A *context-free grammar* is one which consists of *context-free rules*, and a *context-free language* is a language which can be *generated* by a context-free grammar. *See:* Linguistic form: generative grammar 272

**Context-free grammar:** *see* Linguistic form: algebraic linguistics 270; Linguistic form: generative grammar (M) 272
—, **interlevel of:** *see* Language varieties: register (M) 251
— **of situation:** *see* Context (1), context of situation (G). Language varieties: register (M) 251; Language varieties: stylistics (M) 259; Semantics: introduction (M) 500; Semantics: context and collocation 503; Semantics: meaning and reference 509
—, **phonetic:** *see* Phonology: phonemes and broad transcription (M) 409
**CONTEXT-SENSITIVE.** A *context-sensitive rule* is one which applies only in certain linguistic *environments*. If the rule is a *rewrite rule*, it provides for the replacement of a specified string of symbols only when it occurs in a specified set of environments, defined in terms of the symbols occurring on either side of it. For *context-sensitive grammar* and *context-sensitive languages*, cf. *context-free* (mutatis mutandis). *See:* Linguistic form: generative grammar 272
— **-sensitive grammar:** *see* Linguistic form: generative grammar (M) 272
— **-sensitive languages:** *see* Linguistic form: transformational theory (M) 280
— **-sensitive rules:** *see* Relations between languages: comparative philology (M) 475
— **-sensitive systems:** *see* Linguistic form: system and structure (M) 278
**Contextual meaning:** *see* Semantics: context and collocation 503
— **rule:** *see* Phonology: contrast and opposition (M) 402; Phonology: phonemes and broad transcription (M) 409
**Contextualism:** *see* Semantics: introduction (M) 499
**Contextualist approach:** *see* Semantics: introduction 500
**Continuant features:** *see* Linguistic form: transformational theory 283
**Continuants, frictionless:** *see* Phonetics, articulatory, 395
**Continuum, dialect:** *see* Dialect continuum (G). Language varieties: language and dialect 243
**CONTOID.** Speech-sounds may be classified *phonetically* as either *contoids* or *vocoids;* a contoid is one in which there is some kind of constriction of the *vocal tract*, so that the air either does not leave the mouth without friction or does not leave over the centre of the tongue. *See:* Phonetics, articulatory 393; Phonology: contrast and opposition (M) 401
**Contour tangent elimination:** *see* Optimization of industrial processes 347
**CONTRAST (1).** *Contrast* (1) is synonymous with *opposition*, being the relation among mutually *substitutable items* or *classes*. *See:* Linguistic form: paradigmatic (M) 273
**CONTRAST (2).** A distinction is drawn, especially in *phonology*, between relations of *contrast* (2) and relations of *opposition*. If phonemes are classified according to the *environments* in which they occur, the members of any class, which can all occur in the same environment, are in *opposition*, whereas the relation among the classes themselves is *contrast* (2). *See:* Phonology: contrast and opposition 401
—: *see* Perception of colour 360
—, **phonological:** Phonology: contrast and opposition 401; Phonology: phonemes and broad transcription 409
—, **universal:** *see* Phonology: contrast and opposition (M) 401
**Contrasts, syntactic:** *see* Psychological linguistics: psychological aspects of semantic structure 442
**CONTROL (V).** To send a signal (to a plant or other system) which changes its *state* in such a way as to approach a predetermined goal.
**CONTROL (N).** A *module*, within a plant or other system, which on receipt of a suitable signal will change the *state* of the plant on other systems.
—, **adaptive:** *see* Adaptive control (G).
—: **Basic Elements** 89
—, **bang-bang:** *See* Control, on-off 136
— **by Hybrid Computers** 92
— **by the Maximum Principle** 101
— **by microprogram:** *See* Fixed stores and control by microprogram 181
— **by Model Reference** 106
— **by Stationary Filtering and Prediction (Wiener)** 109
—, **closed loop:** *See* Feedback control (G).
—, **discrete models for:** *See* Discrete models for forecasting and control 162
—, **dynamic optimizing:** *See* Control, predictive, using fast-time models 144
—, **feedback:** *See* Feedback control (G).
— **function, regulatory:** *See* Control, predictive, using fast-time models 141
—, **Hierarchical** 113; *See also:* Control, predictive, using fast-time models 145
—, **Hill-Climbing in** 115
—, **Identification Techniques for** 119
— **in telephony:** *See* Switching and control in telephony 590
—, **input-output:** *See* Computers, multiaccess to 65
—, **Invariance and** 126
—, **motor:** *See* Information theory in psychological measurement 234
— **of Aircraft as two Non-Interacting Systems** 128
— **of billet lengths:** *See* Control by hybrid computers 95
— **of blast furnace:** *See* Control by hybrid computers 95
— **of cement manufacture:** *See* Control by hybrid computers 99
— **of computer peripherals:** *See* Computer peripherals and their control 58
— **of an Economic System** 129
— **of food blending:** *See* Control by hybrid computers 95
— **of a nuclear power plant:** *See* Control by hybrid computers 97

**Control of Respiration, Self-Adaptive** 132
—, **On-Off** 136
—, **open loop:** *See* Feedback control (G). Open loop control (G).
—, **optimal:** *See* Optimal control (G).
—, **optimum:** *See* Control by stationary filtering and prediction 110
—, **order of:** *See* Man-machine communication and ergonomics 304
—, **physiological:** *See* Sensory processes 525; Control of respiration, self-adaptive 132; Homeostasis 213
—, **predictive:** *See* Predictive control (G).
—, **Predictive, using Fast-Time Models** 140
— **problem, general:** *See* Control by the maximum principle 101
—, **process:** *See* Man-machine communication and ergonomics 301
—, **reference model for:** *See* Control by hybrid computers 100
—, **regulatory:** *See* Regulatory control (G).
—, **routing:** *See* Switching and control in telephony 593
—, **schwartz-weiss:** *See* Control, on-off 136
—, **Sensitivity and** 147
—, **Stability and** 149
**CONTROL SYSTEM.** A system for generating control signals, and (some usages) the corresponding controls, and (in some usages) the rest of the system which is being controlled.
— **system:** *See* Eye movements 178
— **system, adaptive:** *See* Adaptive control system (G) Control: basic elements 191
— **system, learning:** *See* Control: basic elements 92
— **system, self-organizing:** *See* Control: basic elements 92
— **systems, digital:** *See* Control systems, sampled-data 155
— **systems, man-machine in:** *see* Man-machine in control systems 307
— **Systems, Multivariable** 151
— **Systems, Sampled-Data** 155
— **switching, common:** *see* Switching and control in telephony 591
— **theory, adaptive:** *see* Adaptive control theory 1
— **theory, stochastic:** *see* Control: basic elements 91
—, **transfer:** *see* Computer peripherals and their control 59
**CONTROL UNIT.** A group of modules, part of a digital computer, whose input is an *instruction* and whose output is the signals necessary to stimulate the circuits by which the instruction will be carried out. These signals perform such tasks as connecting the *registers* to the *arithmetic unit* and the *store*. *See:* Computer peripherals and their control 58
**CONTROL WORD.** A signal usually to be found in a particular store, which determines the next action of a computer or peripheral. *See:* Computer peripherals and their control 59
**CONTROLLABLE.** A system is controllable if each of its *state* variables is influenced by at least one of its *input* variables. *See:* Control systems, multivariable 151
**CONTROLLER.** A system for generating control signals.
—, **adaptive:** *see* Adaptive control theory 1
—, **adaptive, closed-loop:** *see* Adaptive control theory 8
**Controllers, computer linked to:** *see* Control by hybrid computers 95
**Conventional:** *see* Semantics: sign and symbol 510
**Convergence:** *see* Perception, stereopsis as an aspect of 368; Relations between languages: introduction 470
**Conversational mode:** *see* Mode, conversational (G).
**Conversion, antitritanopic:** *see* Perception of colour 363
—, **stratal:** *see* Computational linguistics: introduction 51
**Converter, analog-digital:** *see* Analog-digital converter (G).
—, **digital-to-analog:** *see* Digital signal (G)
**Convolutional coding:** *see* Error correcting codes 175
**CO-OCCURRENCE.** *Co-occurrence* rules are rules specifying which items can occur together in a specified *syntagmatic* relation to each other.
**COORDINATE, COORDINATIVE.** A *coordinate* (or *coordinative*) *construction* is an *endocentric construction* either (or any) of whose *immediate constituents* is *substitutable* for the construction as a whole; otherwise an endocentric construction is *subordinate*. *See:* Linguistic form: syntagmatic 278
— **endocentric:** *see* Linguistic form: syntagmantic 278
**Cord, spinal:** *see* Neuronal nets 320
—, **vocal, frequency of:** *see* Phonetics, auditory (M) 396
**Cords, vocal:** *See* Phonetics, acoustic 391; Phonetics, articulatory 394; Phonetics, experimental (M) 399
**CORE STORE.** An assembly of torcidal magnetic cores, each threaded by three wires, each with two alternative directions of magnetization and thus capable of storing one bit of information. The direction of magnetization of any core is set by passing currents simultaneously through two of the wires. It is 'read' by passing a current through the third wire and detecting whether or not this causes impulsive currents through the other two.
**Corpuscle, Pacinian:** *see* Non-neural elements in receptor systems 337; Receptor (G). Receptors as transducers 456
**CORRELATION ANALYSIS.** The evaluation of the statistical relationship between two analog signals. The correlation coefficient between two signals $x(t)$, $y(t)$ each of whose average value is zero is:

$$r_{xy} = \frac{1}{T}\int_0^T x(t)y(t)\,dt \left/ \left[\frac{1}{T}\int_0^T x^2(t)\,dt\right]^{\frac{1}{2}} \left[\frac{1}{T}\int_0^T y^2(t)\,dt\right]^{\frac{1}{2}}\right.$$

$$= \frac{1}{T\sigma_x\sigma_y}\int_0^T x(t)y(t)\,dt,$$

where $\sigma_x$, $\sigma_y$ are the standard derivations.

The correlation coefficient always lies between $\pm 1$ (Schwartz's inequality). Values near to $+1$ or $-1$ imply that the two signals are closely related. Small values (between $\pm 0.3$ perhaps) imply lack of a close relation.

If one of the original signals is displaced in time, so that they are $x(t-\tau)$, $y(t)$, and $r_{xy}(\tau)$ is evaluated over a range of $\tau$, this is *correlation analysis* and $r_{xy}(\tau)$ is a *correlation function*. Its purpose is to take account of the possibilities of time shifts in the relation between the two signals. P.A.N. Briggs. *See:* Normal distribution (G).

**Correlation analysis of dynamic systems, using pseudorandom binary signals:** *see* Pseudorandom binary signals, use of, in correlation analysis of dynamic systems 433

**CORRELATION COEFFICIENT.** A measure of the correlation between two streams of signals $(\bar{x}+x)$ and $(\bar{y}+y)$, defined as

$$r = \sum xy / (\sum x^2 \sum y^2)^{\frac{1}{2}}$$

(for a definition in terms of time integrals, *see:* Correlation analysis (G)).

— **function:** *see* Correlation analysis (G).

**CORTEX (CEREBRAL).** The skin (like the bark of a tree) of the cerebrum. In man this is the largest of the three easily separable parts of the brain, and it contains about $10^{10}$ neurons all of which have parts, at least, lying in the cortex. The cells are tightly packed in the cortex, with no fluid or tissue between them.

—, **cerebral:** *see* Neuronal nets 321

—, **striate:** *see* Perception, stereopsis as an aspect of 372

—, **visual:** *see* Perception of colour 360

**Corti, organ of:** *see* Receptors: Representation of information about stimuli in populations 469

**CORTICOFUGAL.** (Of a signal or nerve fibre) coming from the cortex. Relating to a centrifugal nerve path, near where it emerges from the cortex.

**CORTICOPETAL.** (Of a signal or nerve fibre) leading towards the cortex.

**COTEXT.** The *cotext* of a particular occurrence of an *item* is the *text* in which it occurs, i.e. its specifically linguistic *context* (1).

**COUNTER.** Component or assembly of logic elements which stores a number, and on receipt of an impulse increases it by $+1$, $-1$, or some other prearranged integer. *Counting modulo n.* At every $n$th impulse the counter reverts to zero and begins again. E.g. the mileage meters on automobiles usually count modulo 100,000 or 1,000,000.

**Coupling, bibliographic:** *see* Bibliographic coupling (G).

**COVARIANCE MATRIX.** Let there be a variable $x$ which may have any of $m$ values and a variable $y$ having any of $n$ values. On any occasion, let the value of $x$ be to some extent influenced by the value of $y$, so that the probability that $x$ has its $i$th value $x_i$ is dependent on $y_j$, the value of $y$ at that time. This is written $P(x = x_i / y = y_j)$ or, more briefly $P(x_i/y_j)$ and is called one of the *conditional probabilities* of $x$, given $y$.

The set of $mn$ conditional probabilities of $x$, given each of the $n$ values of $y$, may be written in the form of a matrix of $m$ rows and $n$ columns. This is the covariance matrix of $x$, given $y$ (sometimes called the covariance matrix of $x$ on $y$). *See:* Adaptive threshold elements 10

**Creativity:** *see* Problem solving 414

**Creole:** *see* Relations between languages: lingua franca 480

**CRISIS TIME.** The interval of time during which a signal from a peripheral is available to a computer; the whole of the signal must be written into the computer within this interval, or part of it will be lost. (Applies also conversely to the time during which a signal from a computer is available to a peripheral.) *See:* Computer peripherals and their control 59

**Criteria, grammatical (language classification):** *see* Relations between languages: typological and areal classifications 486

—, **lexical:** *see* Relations between languages: typological and areal classifications (M) 486

—, **phonological (language classification):** *see* Relations between languages: typological and areal classifications 486

—, **structural:** *see* Relations between languages: typological and areal classifications (M) 486

**Criterion, maximum expected value:** *see* Sensory discrimination, measurement of 513

—, **Neyman-Pearson:** *see* Sensory discrimination, measurement of 513

—, **Nyquist:** *see* Control, stability and 149

—, **Popov's:** *see* Control, stability and 150

—, **Routh Hurwitz:** *see* Control, stability and 149

**CROSS-CORRELATION.** The correlation between two signals, one of which is time-shifted with respect to the other, as in *autocorrelation*. *See also:* Correlation analysis (G). Perception, stereopsis as an aspect of 369

— **-entropy:** *see* Statistics of language: introduction 572

**CROSSTALK.** Leakage of signal transmission from one channel to another; or the resulting confusion of messages.

**Crozier ratio:** *see* Sensory discrimination, measurement of 516

**CRT:** *see* Cathode-ray tube (G).

**Cryptology:** *see* Statistics of language: introduction 569

**CUE.** A signal, relevant or irrelevant, received by an animal during learning and reward experiments. *See:* Animal learning 21

**Cues, depth, binocular:** *see* Perception, stereopsis as an aspect of 368

—, **frequency:** *see* Phonetics, experimental 400

—, **intensity:** *see* Phonetics, experimental 400

—, **time:** *see* Phonetics, experimental 400

**CUMULATION.** The difference in content of a growing text (e.g. an abstracts journal) between any two given dates. *See:* Scientific documentation 496

**Culminative:** *see* Phonology: prosodic features 413

**CUMULATIVE MORPH.** A *cumulative*, or *portmanteau morph* is a morph which represents more than one *morpheme* at the same time. *See:* Grammar (structural) 189

**CURRENT AWARENESS.** Knowledge (by a scientist) of very recent works (usually in published form) in fields of research closely related to his own. *See:* Scientific documentation 496

**Curve, peaked:** *see* Peaked curve (G)

**Cybernetic models:** *see* Psychology, use of models (learning) 447

**CYBERNETICS.** The study of control and communication in the animal and the machine. First used by Norbert Wiener in 1947.

**Cycle:** *see* Loop (G)

—, **transformational:** *see* Linguistic form: transformational theory 284; Transformational cycle (G)

**Cyclopean view:** *see* Perception, stereopsis as an aspect of 372

**Cyclic linear code:** *see* Error correcting codes 174

**DATA.** Signals other than control signals (e.g. from a plant to its controller; subject matter additional to the program, for processing by a computer; output signals from a computer). The Latin singular, *datum*, is not used. Preferred forms are clear from the following acceptable examples: data are available.....; the data is ready.......; and from the following questionable usages: datas are available.....; a data is ready...... *Data sampling.* Conversion of continuous to discrete data by admitting data at a series of instants. *Data logging.* Automatic storing, typing or printing of data from a process.

— **collection systems:** *see* Local networks 288

— **repeating, adaptation with:** *see* Adaptive threshold elements 11

— **repeating, adaptation without:** *see* Adaptive threshold elements 11

—, **representation of:** *see* Data transmission 159

**DATA RETRIEVAL.** Answering questions by computer about a store of data.

— **Transmission** 159

**De Saussure:** *see* Linguistic form: paradigmatic (M) 273; Semantics: sign and symbol (M) 510

**Dead zone:** *see* Adaptive threshold elements 11; Control, on-off 137

**DECIBEL (dB).** A practical unit of change in a quantity, such as acoustic intensity. If a quantity changes in value from $J$ to $K$, it is defined as changing by $10 \log_{10} K/J$ decibels. Thus if a quantity changes in value from $J$ to $10J$ it changes by 10 dB, and if it changes from $J$ to $1.259J$ it changes by 1 decibel. The intensity of a sound is less easy to measure than its sound pressure, which is proportional to the square of the intensity. If $P_1$ and $P_2$ are two sound pressures, the relationship between their intensities is therefore $20 \log_{10} P_1/P_2$ decibels.

**DECISION AXIS (E-VALUE).** In models of sensory discrimination, a magnitude representing the neural effect of a signal. *See:* Sensory discrimination, measurement of 512

**DECISION PROCESS.** A mechanism or program for selecting a sequence of decision-signals or decision-variables; these, in combination with the corresponding state-variables, generate the sequence of outputs of the system. *See:* Dynamic programming 168

— **processes, multistage:** *see* Dynamic programming 168

— **theory, Bayesian:** *see* Pattern recognition 354

**Declarative statement:** *see* Computer language design requirements 54

**Decoder, maximum likelihood:** *see* Error correcting codes 175

**Decoding, sequential:** *see* Error correcting codes 157

**Deep grammatical analysis:** *see* Semantics: introduction (M) 499

— **relations:** *see* Linguistic form: system and structure 279

**DEEP STRUCTURE, DEEP GRAMMAR.** The *deep structure* of an *item* (say, a sentence) is a *representation* of it which shows its *semantic* relations more directly than its *surface structure* does, and which takes the form of a *structural description*—in particular, of a *generalized phrase-marker*. *Deep grammar* is the study and description of those aspects of *linguistic form* (2) which are most directly relevant to meaning. In a *transformational-generative grammar*, a deep structure is related to a surface structure by a set of *transformations*. *See:* Linguistic form: transformational theory 282; Linguistic form; system and structure 279; Psychological linguistics; psycholinguistic studies of syntax 439; Grammar (structural) 186; Relations between languages: typological and areal classifications (M) 486

**DEFECTIVE.** *Paradigms* (1)—sets of words with the same *stem*—can be grouped together into *paradigm-classes*, whose members fall into a certain range of *grammatical classes*; in principle, every stem is found in words of every one of these classes, but there may be exceptions, so that a paradigm has a 'gap' in it, i.e. it lacks a representative in one of the classes, Such paradigms are *defective*.

**Degree, of a differential equation.**
The greatest power to which the highest order derivative in it occurs. E.g. the equation $(d^3y/dx^3)^2 + a(dy/dx)^4 = Q(x)$ has the degree 2.

**Degrees of openness:** *see* Phonology: distinctive features (M) 404

**Deletion:** *see* Linguistic form: transformational theory (M) 280

**DELICACY.** Two *classes* of linguistic items are related in *delicacy* if one is a subset of the other; similarly, one linguistic *description* is more *delicate* than

another if it is more detailed. *See:* Language varieties: register (M)   251
**Demarcation:** *see* Phonology: prosodic features (M)   411
**Demarcative features:** *see* Phonology: prosodic features   412
**DENDROID.** Like a *tree.*
**DENDRITES.** Tree-like processes on a nerve cell body by which signals are collected. *See:* Neuronal nets   321
**DENOTATION.** Linguistic *signs* may be classified as *denotative* (or *referential*) or *connotative* (or *expressive*), according to whether their meaning is intellectual or emotive. *See:* Semantics: introduction   499; Semantics: meaning and reference (M)   507
**DENOTATION OF A NAME.** The set of objects having that name. *See:* Concept formation by artificial intelligence   76
**Denotative meaning:** *see* Semantics: introduction   499
**Dental:** *see* Phonetics, articulatory   394
**DEPENDENCY.** *Dependency* is a *selection relation* between two *items* (or classes of items), which are partners in a *construction;* if one of the partners, but not the other, *substitutes* for the whole construction, then the latter partner is said to *depend* on the former. *See:* Grammar (structural)   202
— **grammar:** *see* Linguistic form: generative grammar (M)   272
**Dependent:** *see* Grammar (structural)   202
**Dephonemicization:** *see* Relations between languages: bilingualism   473
**DEPOLARIZATION OF AN EXCITABLE CELL.** A reduction in the potential difference across its membrane, in or near resting conditions. *See:* Nerve and muscle, initiation and conduction of impulses in   314
**Depth cues, binocular:** *see* Perception, stereopsis as an aspect of   368
— **cues, monocular:** *see* Perception, stereopsis as an aspect of   369
— **perception, binocular:** *see* Perception, stereopsis as an aspect of   368
**DERIVATION (1), DERIVATIONAL HISTORY.** One string of symbols (A) is *derived* from another (B) if there is a *rewrite rule* which will convert (B) into (A). The *derivation* (1) of (A) includes (B) and also (B's) derivation (1). *See:* Linguistic form: transformational theory   281
**DERIVATION (2), DERIVATIONAL AFFIX.** By adding a *derivational affix* to a *root* or *stem,* a new stem can be formed, which is then treated in the same way as a root, in particular, in that it can combine with *inflectional affixes* according to the same rules as apply to roots. *See:* Grammar (structural)   189
**DERIVATION (3).** The *derivation* (3) of a word is its *diachronic* origin—a word in a different language, or an earlier stage of the same language, from which the word in question is considered to be *derived.*
**Derivational affixes:** *see* Grammar (structural)   189
**DERIVED PHRASE-MARKER.** A *phrase-marker* resulting from the application of a *transformation* rule to another phrase-marker is a *derived phrase-marker;* a *final derived phrase-marker* is one which represents a *surface structure,* and is ready to be related to a *phonological representation,* in that no further syntactic transformations apply to it. *See:* Linguistic form: transformational theory   282
**Describing function technique:** *See* Control, stability and   150
**DESCRIPTION.** A *description* of a *language system* is a specification of the rules which must be obeyed in order to produce acceptable *texts* in that language; the form which the description will take depends on the model of language adopted, and the rules may be described in terms of relations rather than as actual instructions. A *description* (or *representation*) of a particular *text* (e.g. of a particular sentence) is a selection, from a particular set of categories, of those categories found in the text in question; this set of categories may be specified by the description of the language system underlying the text, or it may be language independent, as in the case of *phonetic* categories. *Descriptive linguistics* is concerned with producing descriptions of language systems, and is contrasted on the one hand with historical (or *diachronic*) linguistics, which is concerned with the historical development of language-systems, and on the other hand with 'prescriptive linguistics', which is concerned only with certain rather particular areas of a language system, where the language system underlying actual usage is felt to be in some way incorrect. *See:* Linguistic form: system and structure (M)   278; Grammar (structural) (M)   186
**Descriptions, structural:** *see* Linguistic form: generative grammar (M)   272; Psychological linguistics: psycholinguistic studies of syntax (M)   439; Psychological linguistics: theories of learning in relation to language (M)   445
**Descriptive categories:** *see* Grammar (structural)   204
— **linguistics:** *see* Language varieties: register (M)   251
**Descriptively adequate grammar:** *see* Psychological linguistics: theories of learning in relation to language   445
**DESCRIPTOR.** A unit in the description of documents or other 'items of information'. A classification system relies on the use of a restricted set of descriptors to describe a large body of documents or items in a reproduceable (i.e. a retrievable) way. *See:* Information storage and retrieval   225
**Descriptors, relationships between:** *see* Information storage and retrieval   226
—, **semantic association between:** *see* Information storage and retrieval   226
**Design considerations of subscriber's telephone set:** *see* Subscribers telephone set, design considerations of   584
—, **logic:** *see* Logic design, logic (G)
— **requirements of a computer language:** *see* Computer language design requirements   54

**Designation:** *see* Semantics: meaning and reference (M) 507

**Detectors, movement:** *see* Receptors: relation between the stimuli and the activity in single primary units 464

**Determiners of conceptual behaviour:** *see* Conceptual behaviour 85

**Deviation, standard:** *see* Normal distribution (G)

**Device, active:** *see* Active device (G)

**Devices, sensing, computer linked to:** *see* Control by hybrid computers 97

**Devoicing:** *see* Phonology: contrast and opposition (M) 401

**DIACHRONIC.** A *diachronic*, as opposed to a *synchronic*, study of a language is concerned with the way in which the language evolves from one period of history to another. *See:* Grammar (structural) 186; Language varieties: language and dialect (M) 243; Relations between languages: introduction (M) 470

— **semantics:** *see* Relations between languages: semantic change (M) 484

**Diachronical:** *see* Relations between languages: bilingualism (M) 473

**DIALECT (1).** A *dialect* (1) is a *variety* of a *language* (3) defined with reference to the set of people who use it, as opposed to a *register* (1), which is a variety defined with reference to the circumstances in which it is used. The sets of people who use a dialect may differ socially and/or geographically. When the set of people using a dialect only has one member, the dialect is called an *idiolect*. *See:* Language varieties: language and dialect 243; Language varieties: register (M) 251; Relations between languages: comparative philology (M) 475

**DIALECT (2).** A *dialect* (2) is socially different from a *language* (3) in that it is spoken by people with less social prestige; from a purely linguistic point of view, however, they are both dialects (1) and *langauges* (1).

— **atlases:** *see* Language varieties: language and dialect 245

**DIALECT CONTINUUM.** A *language* (3) may be considered as a *dialect continuum*—the *language community* itself can be divided, geographically and/or socially, into smaller communities, each of which speaks a *dialect* (1); the set of dialects comprising the language as a whole is a *continuum* in that dialects tend to merge into their neighbours rather than to be clearly discrete. *See:* Language varieties: language and dialect 243

**DIBIT.** Any pair of binary signals, i.e. any of 11, 10, 01, 00 considered as part of a longer signal. Analogy with *Digraph* (G). *See:* Statistics of language: introduction 567

**Dichotomy.** Two-ness; separation into two.

**Dictionary:** *see* Computational linguistics: introduction 51

**Dictionary, automatic:** *see* Computational linguistics: introduction 51

**Dictionary consultation:** *see* Computational linguistics: machine translation 53

**Diencephalon:** *see* Neuronal nets 320

**Differentiable unimodality:** *see* Optimization, automatic 343

**Differential equation, linear:** *see* Linear differential equation (G)

— **equation, non-linear:** *see* Non-linear differential equation (G)

**DIFFERENTIAL OPERATOR, D.** In mathematical descriptions of control systems, the operator represents differentiation with respect to time.

**'DIFFERENTIATOR'.** In quotes, a receptor which is stimulated by a small class of signals. *'Integrator'*. A receptor which is stimulated by a large class of signals. *See:* Perception of colour 359

**Diffuse features:** *see* Linguistic form: transformational theory 283

**Digital computer, symbol manipulation by:** *see* Symbol manipulation by digital computer 594

— **control systems:** *see* Control systems, sampled-data 155

**DIGITAL SIGNAL.** A signal which must correspond to a number expressible in a limited number of digits in the appropriate scale (e.g. binary, octal, decimal). *Digital to analog converter* (DAC). A module whose output signal is analog, its input being digital.

— **sorting:** *see* Sorting techniques 544

**Diglossia:** *see* Relations between languages: bilingualism 473

**DIGRAPH.** Any pair of printed or written characters, usually taken from a sequence of characters. *See:* Statistics of language: introduction 569

**Dimensionality:** *see* Vector (G)

**DIODE.** Two-electrode valve or semiconductor device, for passing a current which is non-linearly dependent on the potential difference between the electrodes.

**Diphthongal:** *see* Phonetics, auditory 398

**Diphthongization:** *see* Phonetics, auditory 398

**Diphthongs:** *see* Phonetics, auditory 397

**Direct dialled switching:** *see* Switching and control in telephony 590

**Direction:** *see* Writing 628

**DIRECTION, ORIENTATION.** General words drawing attention to the environment components, or *goal* of a system. *See:* Learning machines: a unified view 261

**DISCHARGE.** A sequence of *action potentials*.

**Discontinuous constituents:** *see* Grammar (structural) 195

**DISCOURSE.** A *discourse* is a complete and self-contained *text*, usually consisting of a number of sentences. *See:* Semantics: introduction (M) 499

**Discourse, field of:** *see* Field (1), field of discourse (G); Language varieties: register (M) 251

**Discourse, mode of:** *see* Mode of discourse (G); Language varieties: register (M) 251

**Discourse, style of:** *see* Formality (G). Language varieties: register (M) 251

**Discrete Models for Forecasting and Control** 162

**Discrete-time system:** *see* System (G)
— **units:** *see* Phonetics, experimental (M)  399
**Discriminant functions, Boolean:** *see* Character recognition  42
**Discrimination:** *see* Sensory processes  525
—, **measures of:** *see* Sensory discrimination, measurement of  514
—, **sensory, measurement of:** *See* Sensory discrimination, measurement of  512
—, **wave-length:** *see* Perception of colour  359
**Disparity:** *see* Perception, stereopsis as an aspect of  368
—, **retinal:** *See* perception, stereopsis as an aspect of  368
**DISTANCE (IN INFORMATION SPACE).** A *metric* which is defined so as to be invariant under certain mathematical operations. *See:* Hamming distance (G); Information space (G).
—, **Hamming:** *see* Error correcting codes  173; Hamming distance (G); Information space  221
**DISTINCTIVE, DISTINCTIVE FEATURE.** A *feature* is *distinctive* if its presence or absence cannot be completely predicted from the linguistic *environment*; if it can, it is *redundant*. In particular, *phonemes* can be seen as complexes of *distinctive features*, each of which differentiates the phonemes in question from the other phonemes in the total system. *See:* Phonology: distinctive features  404; Phonology: contrast and opposition  401; Linguistic form: transformational theory  283; Psychological linguistics: psycholinguistic studies of syntax (M)  439; Relations between languages: bilingualism (M)  473; Statistics of language: introduction  567
— **features, prosodic:** *see* Phonology: prosodic features  411
— **phonetic features:** *see* Grammar (structural) (M)  186
— **phonological features:** *see* Linguistic form: transformational theory  283
— **stress:** *see* Relations between languages: typological and areal classifications  486
**DISTINGUISHER.** If an *item*'s *meaning* is analysed into a number of *semantic markers—components* of meaning shared with other items—there may be a residue of meaning which is unique to the item concerned; this is its *distinguisher*. *See:* Semantics: meaning and reference (M)  507
**DISTRIBUTION.** The *distribution* of a linguistic *item* is the set of *environments* in which it can occur; *distributional analysis* is a classification of items according to their distributions in a particular *text*, without reference to meaning. *See:* Grammar (structural)  187; Phonology: phonemes and broad transcription (M)  409; Relations between languages: comparative philology (M)  475; Semantics: introduction (M)  499
**Distribution:** *see* Gaussian distribution, normal distribution (G); Normal distribution (G); Poisson distribution (G)
—, **complementary:** *see* complementary distribution (G); Phonology: distinctive features (M)  404; Phonology: phonemes and broad transcription (M)  409

**Distributional analysis:** *see* Computational linguistics: introduction (M)  49
**DISTRIBUTIVE.** In algebras. Obeying the rule exemplified below:

$$A \times (B+C) = A \times B + A \times C.$$

Here multiplication is said to be distributive with respect to addition, and two operators are concerned. *See also:* Associative (G), Commutative (G), each of which concerns a single operator at a time.
**District switching centre (DSC):** *see* Switching and control in telephony  593
**Disturbance ratio:** *see* Pseudorandom binary signals, use of …  436
**Divergence:** *see* Relations between languages: introduction  470
**Documentation, scientific:** *see* Computational linguistics; introduction  49; Scientific documentation  496
**DOMINATE.** One symbol in a *phrase-structure tree* is said to *dominate* another symbol if the second is attached below the first, either directly or with other symbols in between. If both symbols are *category symbols*, the 'dominates' relation can be interpreted as *constituency:* the dominated symbol *represents* a *constituent* of the item represented by the dominating symbol. *See:* Linguistic form: transformational theory  282; Linguistic form: syntagmatic (M)  277
**Dorsal:** *see* Phonetics, articulatory  394; Phonology: phonemes and broad transcription (M)  409
**Downgraded:** *see* Grammar (structural)  202
**DOWNGRADING.** An *item* is *downgraded* (or *rank-shifted*) if its *rank* (1) conflicts with its *rank* (2). *See:* Grammar (structural)  202
**Drifts:** *see* Eye movements  177
**DUMP.** To remove a program, an instruction, or data from a busy part of a computer (or computer system), to a store from which it can be retrieved when needed.
**Duplexis:** *see* Writing (M)  627
**Duration:** *see* Phonetics, auditory  398
**DYNAMIC.** An adjective used to describe a system in which the instantaneous value of a given *state variable* depends upon the values of the same and other state variables at previous instants.
— **description of a linearized system:** *See* Pseudorandom binary signals, use of …  433
— **optimizing control:** *See* Control, predictive, using fast-time models  140
— **Programming**  168; *see also* Control, stability and  150
**Dynamic systems, correlation analysis of, using pseudorandom binary signals:** *see* Pseudorandom binary signals, use of, in correlation analysis of dynamic systems  433
**DYNAMICS OF A PROCESS OR SYSTEM.** The time relationships between *state variable* of a process, normally expressed in the form of differential equations or equivalent operational expressions.

**E waves:** *see* Neuronal nets 329
**Ear, middle:** *see* Non-neural elements in receptor systems 339
—, **outer:** *see* Non-neural elements in receptor systems 338
— **-training:** *see* Phonetics, auditory 398
**Eardrum:** *see* Non-neural elements in receptor systems 338
**Economy in telecommunication:** *see* Telecommunication, economy in 599
**Economic system, control of:** *see* Control of an economic system 129
**Edge notched card:** *see* Information storage and retrieval 224
**Effect, Abney:** *see* Perception of colour 361
—, **Bezold-Brucke:** *see* Perception of colour 361
—, **Helson-Judd:** *see* Perception of colour 362
— **of hysteresis:** *see* Perception, stereopsis as an aspect of 371
— **of instructions:** *see* Sensory discrimination, measurement of 514
—, **range:** *see* Psychological limiting factors in human performance 437
—, **Stiles-Crawford:** *see* Perception, visual 380
—, **Stiles-Crawford brightness shift:** *see* Perception of colour 363
—, **Stiles-Crawford hue shift:** *see* Perception of colour 363
—, **Troxler's:** *see* Perception, visual 380
**Effectiveness in automata theory:** *see* Automata, infinite-state 36
**Effects, sensorimotor, in sound perception:** *see* Perception of sound 367
**Efferent nerve:** *see* Nerve (G).
**EFFERENT SIGNAL.** Signal from the nervous system to a muscle or a gland or other organ.
**EIGENVECTOR.** If a linear *transformation* $T$ maps vectors in $n$-dimensional space $V$ into the same space, it can be shown that there are directions in space $V$ which are unchanged by the transformation: that is, a vector $X$ in such a direction is transformed into a vector $kX$ in the same direction. These $n$ scalars are in general not all different; a repeated eigenvalue is called *degenerate*. It can be shown that there are exactly $n$ such directions and if no eigenvalues are degenerate, that they are mutually *orthogonal*. The (unit) vectors in the $n$ directions are called the *eigenvectors* (of $V$) with respect to $T$. The $n$ scalar coefficients $k$ are called the *eigenvalues* of $V$ with respect to $T$. In general the transformation $T$ has to be expressed using $n^2$ coefficients, but it can alternatively be expressed using the $n$ eigenvalues alone. Hence their practical importance. P.D.F. Ion.
**Ejectives:** *see* Phonetics, articulatory 396
**Elaborated codes:** *see* Language varieties: register (M) 251
**ELECTROCONVULSIVE SHOCK.** The response of an animal to a suitable electrical potential difference, applied for a suitable short time between an electrode near its brain and another in contact with some other tissue.
**ELECTROCORTICOGRAM. (ECoG).** A record of the summed signals from a large number of neurons picked up by an electrode in contact with the exposed cortex of the brain. *See:* Neuronal nets 327
**ELECTROENCEPHALOGRAM (EFG).** A record of changes in potential of an electrode in contact with a small area of the scalp, usually on a moving chart. *See:* Neuronal nets 326
**Electromyography:** *see* Phonetics, experimental (M) 399
**ELECTRON MICROGRAPH.** A photograph taken by an electron microscope, with a magnification up to about a million times.
**ELECTROTONICALLY.** Involving changes in ionic concentrations and permeability of membrane; e.g. nerve impulse generation and transmission (*see* Action potential (G)).
**ELEMENT (1).** In discussing *syntagmatic* and *paradigmatic* relations the terms of a relation are sometimes referred to as *elements* (1); if the relations are within a *text*, the elements will be *items*, while if they are within a *language-system*, the elements may be *classes*, *features*, *functions* (2) or items, or any other object *generated* by a *grammar* (3). *See:* Relations between languages: semantic change (M) 483; Semantics: field theories (M) 504
**ELEMENT (2), ELEMENT OF STRUCTURE.** A *structure* (2) is represented as a set of *elements of structure* in a specified *syntagmatic* relation to each other; *elements* (2) are thus *elements* (1) which are the terms specifically of syntagmatic relations. Elements of structure may be seen either as *classes* or as *functions* (2); this distinction parallels that between *fillers* and *slots*. *See:* Linguistic form: system and structure 279; Linguistic form: syntagmatic (M) 277
**ELEMENT (3).** A *module* or a connexion between two modules.
—, **adaptive threshold:** *see* Adaptive threshold element (G).
—, **logic:** *see* Logic element (G). Logic design, logic (G).
—, **threshold:** *see* Threshold element (G).
**Elements, non-neural, in receptor systems:** *see* Non-neural elements in receptor systems 337
—, **unreliable, reliable computation with:** *see* Reliable computation with unreliable elements 489
**Elias-Shannon-Gallager bound:** *see* Error correcting codes 174
**Elimination, contour tangent:** *see* Optimization of industrial processes 347
**Embedded sentences:** *see* Linguistic form: transformational theory (M) 280
**EMBEDDING.** An *item* is *embedded* in another item if the first is a *constituent* of the second, and more particularly if it is an *immediate constituent* of the second. It is possible to compare the degree of *embedding* of different items, reflecting the number of *layers of constituency* between each item and the complete sentence.

**Emission, all-or-none:** *see* Neuronal nets 324
**Endocentric constitutes:** *see* Grammar (structural) 196
**ENDOCENTRIC CONSTRUCTION.** *Constructions are either endocentric or exocentric; if one or more of a construction's immediate constituents is substitutable for the construction as a whole, the construction is endocentric; otherwise it is exocentric. Endocentric constructions are further divided into coordinate and subordinate. See:* Linguistic form: syntagmatic 276; Grammar (structural) 186
—, **coordinate:** *see* Linguistic form: syntagmatic 278
**Engineer, human:** *see* Man-machine communication and ergonomics 301
**ENSEMBLE.** The set of possible signals in a *process*. *See:* Random signals and noise 453
**ENTITY.** A symbol taken from an environment, from within a system, or from a store. *See:* Similarity 535
**ENTROPY.** In physics, a measure of the randomness, or degree of disorder, of a chemical system. If $N_1, N_2, \ldots, N_i \ldots$ are the amounts (in moles) of a number of gases, such that $\sum_i N_i = 1$; and if they are mixed, the change in entropy is

$$-R \sum_i N_i \log_e N_i$$

where $R$ is the gas constant.
In information theory, 'entropy' is used for I, the average information content per symbol, for a set of symbols used in a stationary manner to convey information; because

$$I = \sum_i p_i \log_2 p_i$$

where $p_i$ is the probability of choosing the $i$th symbol of the set. *See:* Communication theory 46
— **of the input:** *see* Telecommunication, economy in 599
**ENVELOPE.** The spectrum of a sound, in which amplitude is recorded as a function of frequency. *See:* Speech 546
**ENVIRONMENT (1).** Any *string* of symbols in a *representation* of a linguistic *item* has as its *environment* (1) the remaining symbols in this representation (excluding symbols representing *constituents* of the item it represents); for some purposes not all these symbols may be relevant, in which case they may be excluded from the environment. A particular kind of environment is the *context* (2), which excludes symbols representing items of which the item concerned is itself a constituent. The environment of a string of symbols can also be treated as the environment of the item represented by this string. *See:* Linguistic form: syntagmatic 276; Linguistic form: system and structure (M) 278; Linguistic form: paradigmatic (M) 273; Linguistic from: transformational theory (M) 280; Semantics: context and collocation 503
**ENVIRONMENT (2).** All the possible inputs to a system, including means of generating and modifying the inputs before they finally enter the system.

**Enzymes, feedback inhibition of:** *see* Homeostasis in the single cell 218
**EPSP's (excitatory postsynaptic potentials):** *see* Neuronal nets 322
**Equation, non-linear differential:** *see* Non-linear differential equation (G)
—, **linear differential:** *see* Linear differential equation (G)
—, **Nernst:** *see* Neuronal nets 323
**Equations, implicit and explicit:** *see* Explicit and implicit equations (G)
**Equilibrium, Gibbs-Donnan:** *see* Nerve and muscle, initiation and conduction of impulses in 314
**Equipollent opposition:** *see* Phonology: distinctive features (M) 404
**Equivalent grammars:** *see* Linguistic form: algebraic linguistics 270
**Equivocation:** *see* Telecommunication, economy in 599
**Ergodic process:** *see* Process (G); Random signals and noise 453
**ERGONOMICS.** Application of science to human performance and human factors in work, machine control and equipment design. In the U.S.A., widely accepted titles for the ergonomist are *Human engineer* and *Human factors specialist*. *See:* Man-machine communication and ergonomics 301
**Error correcting codes** 173
**Estimate bias:** *see* Pseudorandom binary signals, use of... 435
—, **Markov:** *see* Control, identification techniques for 121
— **variance:** *see* Pseudorandom binary signals, use of... 435
**Estimation, parameter:** *see* Control, identification techniques for 119
—, **state:** *see* Control, identification techniques for 120
**Evaluation:** *see* Problem solving 415
**EVALUATION METRIC.** An *evaluation metric* is a measure of the simplicity of a *grammar* (3), on the basis of which two different grammars can be compared to find which of them is the better, other things being equal. *See:* Psychological linguistics: psycholinguistic studies of syntax 439
— **of adaptive behaviour:** *see* Adaptive control theory 1
**EVENT.** The broadcasting of a collection of associated signals. *See:* Similarity 535
**EVOKED RESPONSE.** The response in the nervous system to a stimulus applied to a receptor, a particular neuron, or groups of receptors or neurons. *See:* Neuronal nets 327
**Evolutionary operations:** *see* Optimization, automatic 344
**Exchange, local:** *see* Local networks 284
—, **tandem:** *see* Local networks 284
**Executive program:** *see* Computers, multiaccess to 65
**EXOCENTRIC:** *Constructions* are either *endocentric* or *exocentric*: if neither of a construction's *immediate constituents* is substitutable for the construction as a whole, the construction is *exocentric*; otherwise it is *endocentric*. *See:* Linguistic form: syntagmatic 278; Grammar (structural) 196

**Exocentric constitutes:** *see* Grammar (structural)  196
**Expansion, centre of:** *see* Centre of expansion (G)
**Experimental phonetics:** *see* Phonetics, experimental 399; Phonetics, acoustic (M) 391
**Explanations, linear:** *see* Psychological linguistics: theories of learning in relation to language (M)  444
**EXPLICIT.** A *description* is *explicit* if it allows the *generation* of items by a purely mechanical application of rules. A classification of items is explicit if for any contrasting pair of *classes* each class has a different *realization*—even if there is overlap between the classes; that is, the classification is explicit if it makes it possible in every case to decide whether or not a given item is a member of a given class. *See:* Linguistic form: paradigmatic 273; Linguistic form: generative grammar  272
**EXPLICIT AND IMPLICIT EQUATIONS.** When the dependence of a quantity $y$ on a set of parameters $p_1, p_2 \ldots$ can be expressed in the form

$$y = f(p_1, p_2, p_3 \ldots)$$

the equation is explicit.
When it has to be expressed in the form

$$f(y, p_1, p_2, p_3 \ldots) = 0$$

the equation is implicit.
— **characterization:** *see* Psychological linguistics: psycholinguistic studies of syntax (M)  439
**Explicitness:** *see* Linguistic form: generative grammar (M)  272
**Exploration by model:** *see* Computer simulation of human thought processes  60
**Exploratory behaviour, animal:** *see* Animal exploratory behaviour  18
**(Ex)plosion:** *see* Phonetics, articulatory (M)  395
**Exponents:** *see* Relations between languages: introduction (M)  470
—, **phonetic:** *see* Phonology: contrast and opposition (M)  401
**EXPOUND.** A relatively abstract linguistic entity is *expounded* (or *realized*) by a relatively concrete one if the latter can be said to occur because of the former, so that the occurrence of the latter implies the occurrence of the former. In particular, *formal* (or *phonological*) items or *features* can be said to be expounded by *phonetic* items or features.
**Expression:** *see* Form (1) (G); Relations between languages: semantic change (M)  484
**EXPRESSIVE.** A linguistic *sign* is *expressive* if it reflects the feelings of the speaker rather than referring to some object (in which case it would be *referential*). *See:* Semantics: sign and symbol (M)  510
— **features:** *see* Phonology: distinctive features  406
— **resources:** *see* Language varieties: stylistics (M)  259
**Extirpation, hypothalamus:** *see* Animal motivation  24
**EXTRACTION.** Removal of an element (e.g. a vehicle) from a congested region. *See:* Simulation of traffic problems using chain-code random generators  539
**Extrafusal:** *see* Muscle spindles (G)
**Extra-ocular muscles:** *see* Eye movements  176

**Eye, compound:** *see* Perception, visual  373
—, **focal length of:** *see* Focal length of the eye (G)
— **Movements**  176
—, **simple:** *see* Perception, visual  373

**Fact retrieval**  180
**FACT RETRIEVAL.** Answering questions by computer about a store of data. *See:* Fact retrieval  180
**Factor, association:** *see* Association factor (G)
**Factors, psychological limiting, in human performance:** *see* Psychological limiting factors in human performance  437
**Falling:** *see* Phonetics, auditory  398
**Families, language:** *see* Relations between languages: introduction  470; Relations between languages: comparative philology (M)  475
**FAST ACTIVITY.** Relatively fast waves in an *electroencephalogram*, i.e. faster than the *alpha rhythm*. J. D. Cowan.
— **time models for predictive control:** *see* Control, predictive, using fast-time models  140
**FEATURE (1).** The definition of a linguistic *item* or *class* of items can be given as a set of *features*, each of which defines the item or class concerned on one dimension of classification. In *transformational-generative grammars*, features are used in giving both *grammatical* (2) and *phonological* information; in the former case they combine into *complex-symbols*, in the latter into *distinctive feature matrices*; also, grammatical features essentially give *syntactic* (3) information, about the *environments* in which the item or class defined can occur, whereas phonological features give information about its *phonetic realization*. In all models, features are essentially contrastive, but in some models they imply a basically binary contrast—the definition of the item or class either does include the feature or it does not, although it is also possible for the feature to be irrelevant, so neither present nor absent; on the other hand, in other models a feature contrasts, not with its own absence, but with other features defined by the same *system* (2). It is also possible to distinguish between *distinctive* and *redundant* features, according to whether the presence of the feature is predictable from its environment; but the term *distinctive feature* is used especially of the phonetic features which distinguish one *phoneme* from another. *See:* Phonology: distinctive features 404; Phonology: prosodic features 411; Linguistic form: syntagmatic (M) 276; Language varieties: stylistics (M) 259; Linguistic form: paradigmatic (M) 273; Linguistic form: system and structure (M) 278; Semantics: introduction (M)  499
**FEATURE (2).** A characteristic common to different inputs, by virtue of which the inputs can be sorted into classes (e.g. the straight lines, curves, slants, angles etc. by which the brain may possibly identify printed or written characters). A substring of bits which may occur within the original string of a

signal. *See:* Concept formation by artificial intelligence 76; Concept identification — information processing approaches 80; Character recognition 41
**Features, acoustic:** *see* Phonetics, acoustic (M) 391
—, **category:** *see* Linguistic form: transformational theory (M) 281
—, **compact:** *see* Linguistic form: transformational theory 283
—, **compound acoustic:** *see* Speech recognition, automatic 557
—, **configurational:** *see* Phonology: distinctive features 405
—, **consonantal:** *see* Linguistic form: transformational theory 283
—, **continuant:** *see* Linguistic form: transformational theory 283
—, **demarcative:** *see* Phonology: prosodic features 412
—, **diffuse:** *see* Linguistic form: transformational theory 283
—, **distinctive:** *see* Phonology: distinctive features 404; Psychological linguistics: psycholinguistic studies of syntax (M) 439; Relations between languages: bilingualism 473; Statistics of language: introduction (M) 567
—, **expressive:** *see* Phonology: distinctive features 406
—, **flat:** *see* Linguistic form: transformational theory 283
—, **grave:** *see* Linguistic form: transformational theory 283
—, **inherent:** *see* Phonology: distinctive features 406; Phonology: prosodic features 411
—, **juncture:** *see* Linguistic form: syntagmatic (M) 276
—, **lexical:** *see* Language varieties: register (M) 251
—, **nasal:** *see* Linguistic form: transformational theory 283
—, **obstruent:** *see* Linguistic form: transformational theory 283
—, **paralinguistic:** *see* Writing (M) 627
—, **phonemic:** *see* Phonology: distinctive features 408
—, **phonetic:** *see* Phonology: distinctive features 408; Phonology: contrast and opposition (M) 401; Phonology: phonemes and broad transcription (M) 409; Phonology: prosodic features (M) 411
—, **phonetic, distinctive:** *see* Grammar (structural) (M) 186
—, **phonological:** *see* Language varieties: register (M) 251
—, **phonological, distinctive:** *see* Linguistic form: transformational theory 283
—, **prosodic:** *see* Prosodic feature, prosody (G); Phonology: prosodic features 411; Phonology: distinctive features (M) 404
—, **redundant:** *see* Phonology: distinctive features 406
—, **rule:** *see* Linguistic form: transformational theory 282
—, **segmental:** *see* Phonology: prosodic features 411
—, **selectional:** *see* Linguistic form: transformational theory 281
—, **semantic:** *see* Linguistic form: transformational theory (M) 280

**Features, sonority:** *see* Phonology: distinctive features 406
—, **stressed:** *see* Linguistic form: transformational theory 283
—, **strident:** *see* Linguistic form: transformational theory 283
—, **subcategorization:** *see* Linguistic form: transformational theory 281
—, **suprasegmental:** *see* Phonology: prosodic features 411
—, **syntactic:** *see* Computational linguistics: introduction (M) 49
—, **syntactical:** *see* Language varieties: register (M) 251
—, **tense:** *see* Linguistic form: transformational theory 283
—, **tone:** *see* Linguistic form: transformational theory 283
—, **vocalic:** *see* Linguistic form: transformational theory 283
—, **voiced:** *see* Linguistic form: transformational theory 283
**Fechner fraction:** *see* Perception, visual 379
**FEEDBACK CONTROL (closed loop control).** Is exhibited by a system in which the output variable is compared with the input and an error signal is generated. The error signal is used to drive the output variable to equality with the input. Whenever equality is achieved the error and therefore the drive become zero. Power amplification may be used in converting the error signal to the drive signal. Contrast with *Open loop control*. P. H. Hammond.
— **inhibition of enzymes:** *see* Homeostasis in the single cell 218
— **loops, neurally mediated:** *see* Neurally mediated feedback loops (G).
**FEEDFORWARD CONTROL.** A method of control in which disturbances affecting the output variables are anticipated, and compensating fluctuations of the input variables are generated. A knowledge of the *dynamics of the process* is necessary to achieve the correct compensation. P. H. Hammond. *See:* Control, predictive, using fast-time models 140
**Fibonacci numbers:** *see* Optimization, automatic 342
**Fibonacci search:** *see* Optimization, automatic 342
**Fibre diameter, significance of:** *See* Receptors: relation between the stimuli and the activity in single primary units 466
—, **nerve, medullated:** *see* Medullated nerve fibre (G).
—, **nuclear-bag:** *see* Nuclear-bag fibre (G).
—, **nuclear-chain:** *see* Nuclear-chain fibre (G).
—, **sensory nerve:** *see* Receptors as transducers 457
**Fibres, association:** *see* Axonal bundles or fibres (G).
—, **axonal:** *see* Axonal bundles or fibres (G).
—, **commisural:** *see* Axonal bundles or fibres (G).
—, **projection:** *see* Axonal bundles or fibres (G).
**FIELD (1), FIELD OF DISCOURSE.** Non-dialectal *varieties* of language (*registers* (1)) can be classified on a number of dimensions one of which is the *field of discourse* (or *register* (2)). On this dimension regis-

ters are classified according to the type of subject matter (e.g. scientific, religious ...) to which they are appropriate. *See:* Language varieties: register (M)  251; Language varieties: stylistics (M)  259

**FIELD (2), SEMANTIC FIELD.** *Lexical* meaning can be studied by defining, for a given language, a particular set of words which all refer in some sense to the same subject, such as all colour terms. The meanings of these terms taken together constitute a single *semantic field*, and it can be shown how this field is divided up among the words, and how the latter define each other by their mutual oppositions — whereas they do not define words outside this semantic field, at least not so clearly. *See:* Semantics: field theories  504; Relations between languages: loans and loanwords (M)  482; Relations between languages: semantic change (M)  484; Semantics: introduction (M)  499

**FIELD (3).** One of the classes of information in a *file*, e.g. a person's name, or his account number. *See:* Computer language design requirements  45; Information storage and retrieval  223

**FIELD TEST.** A statistically controlled test of a device or idea in the actual environment for which it is designed.

— **theory:** *see* Semantics: field theories  504; Relations between languages: semantic change  484

**Figure, highly compacted:** *see* Highly compacted figure (G).

**Figures of speech:** *see* Relations between languages: semantic change (M)  484

**FILE.** A collection of *records*, each of which has a unique identifier (e.g. a unique number, or a name of an individual), e.g. if a company has 500 employees its payroll file will contain 500 *records. See:* Information storage and retrieval  229; Sorting techniques  543

— **organization:** *see* Information storage and retrieval  229

**FILE UNDER.** To file A under B is to make A an entry in a file among entries having the property B.

**FILLER, FILLER-CLASS.** A *filler* or *filler-class* is the *class* of *items* which occur in a given *slot*. The *filler* and the *slot* together make a *tagmeme*.

**Film, storage on:** *see* Information storage and retrieval  223

**FILTER.** An analog module with a single input and output channel, whose output at any instant is a function of all previous input signals. There are digital filters also. *Linear filter.* A filter whose response (output function) to any number of (possibly overlapping) input functions is the sum of its responses to the individual input functions. *Wiener filter.* A linear filter designed to minimize the *variance* of the output error signal of a controlled system. *Low-pass filter.* Ideally, a filter which transmits undisturbed all components of an input signal with frequency less than a specified 'cut-off' frequency, and which removes all others. *See:* Control by stationary filtering and prediction  109

**Filter, linear:** *see* Filter (G).

—, **low-pass:** *see* Filter (G).

**Filters:** *see* Phonetics, acoustic  392

—, **Wiener:** *see* Control by stationary filtering and prediction  109; Filter (G).

**Final derived phrase marker:** *see* Linguistic form: transformational theory  282

**FINE STRUCTURE OF SPEECH SOUND SPECTRUM.** The sounds in speech which are aperiodic (e.g. those of (v), (s) etc.), or their representation as part of a spectrum. *See:* Speech  545

**Finite automata:** *see* Linguistic form: generative grammar (M)  273

— **-state automata:** *see* Automata, finite-state  32

**FIRE.** A nerve is said to fire when it discharges, a burst of *action potentials*.

**FIXATION.** State of the eyes when a subject, without moving his head, fixes his gaze as accurately as he can upon a well defined target.

**FIXED POINT REPRESENTATION.** The normal way of separating the integral part of a number from the fractional part, e.g. with a decimal point or comma, or by a convention as on a desk calculator. (In contrast with *floating point representation*.)

**FIXED STORE.** In a computer, a store whose information was built in or written at the time of manufacture, to be read but never modified during use. *See:* Fixed stores and control by microprogram  181

— **store, linear matrix type:** *see* Fixed stores and control by microprogram  182

— **Stores and Control by Microprogram**  181

— **store, switch core type:** *see* Fixed stores and control by microprogram  182

**Flap:** *see* Phonetics, articulatory  395

**Flat features:** *see* Linguistic form: transformational theory  283

— **fricatives:** *see* Phonology: contrast and opposition (M)  401

— **random process:** *see* Process (G).

**Flicker sensitivity:** *see* Perception, visual  381

**FLIP-FLOP.** A *monostable* or *bistable* circuit and *trigger;* the context should clarify which alternative it is.

**FLOATING POINT REPRESENTATION.** Most useful numbers, even the very large or small, can be expressed in reasonably small space in the form $a \times 10^b$ or $a \times 2^b$ where $b$ is an integer, and $a$ is the sum of a small integer and a fraction. (E.g. the velocity of light in vacuo $= 2.998 \times 10^{10}$ cm sec$^{-1}$ $= 1.743 \times 2^{34}$ cm sec$^{-1}$.) In computers arranged for the storage and manipulation of numbers in this form, $b$ is called the floating point index. (In contrast with *fixed point representation*.)

**FLUTTER.** In magnetic reproduction, an unwanted signal caused by oscillations set up by friction between the moving tape and the stationary heads. *See:* Magnetic recording  299

**FLUX.** The total flow of signals through a number of input or output channels. *See:* Neuronal nets  320

**FLYING SPOT SCANNER.** A device for converting the light and shade of a picture into a sequence of analog signals. A bright spot of light rapidly traverses the picture, and reflected light in proportion to the reflectivity enters a photoelectric cell, whose voltage output is the required signal.

**FOCAL LENGTH OF THE EYE.** The image and object focal length are not equal, because the image space is a liquid different in refractive index from air. Moreover, the lens system is a 'thick lens' requiring special definitions and measurement techniques. *See:* Perception of colour 359

**FOCUS.** A *focus* is a gap in a *string* of *items* (the *frame*) where items can be added to make the string into a complete and acceptable *utterance*. The items which can occur in a given focus all belong to the same *focus-class* (or *substitution-class*). The technique for classifying items using foci is called the *frame-and-focus* technique.

Fold, venticular: *see* Phonetics, experimental (M) 399

Food blending, control of: *see* Control by hybrid computers 95

Forced choice procedure (FCP): *see* Sensory discrimination, measurement of 518

Forcing function: *see* Autonomous system (G).

Forecasting, discrete models for: *see* Discrete models for forecasting and control 162

**FORGETTING.** Loss by an animal of a behaviour pattern which has been *learned. See:* Animal learning 21

**FORM (1).** *Form* (1) is contrasted in linguistic theory with *content* or with *function;* a linguistic *sign* can be considered to have two parts, of which one is the form—that is, the audible or visible phenomena which are produced whenever the signal occurs. The form is thus the *realization* or *manifestation* of the other side of the sign, its *contents*. Cf. the contrast between *signifiant (form)* and *signifié (content)*.

**FORM (2), LINGUISTIC FORM, FORMAL ITEM.** *Form* is contrasted in linguistic theory with *substance*. The *substance* of language activity includes the movements of the speaker, the actual sounds he produces, or the marks he makes on paper, and also the totality of the situation in which the activity takes place; there is no limit to the points of view from which these can be studied, or to the amount of detail which can be given in describing language activity as substance. (One consequence is that, from this point of view, no two occurrences of language activity are identical.) One point of view from which this activity can be studied is that of *(linguistic) form;* any bit of language activity reflects a particular *language system*, which allows us to represent the activity on a series of *levels of representation (grammar, phonology etc,)*. From this point of view, two occurrences of language activity *can* be said to be identical. The domain of *linguistics* is generally taken to include all of linguistic form, and substance only to the extent to which it has bearing on form; therefore *phonetics* is generally taken to be a different discipline from linguistics. A *formal item* is an *item* (in a particular language) which can be uniquely specified with reference to all the categories set up in a description of the form of the language concerned; it thus represents the intersection of a *grammatical item* and a *lexical item* (but it need not be a 'phonological item', in the sense of representing a *constituent* on the phonological level). *See:* Linguistic form: system and structure 278; Linguistic form: paradigmatic (M) 273; Semantics: sign and symbol (M) 510; Language varieties: stylistics (M) 259; Linguistic form: transformational theory (M) 280

**FORM (3).** A linguistic *form* (3) is a linguistic *item* of some kind, or a set of such items. *See:* Phonetics, experimental (M) 399; Relations between languages: introduction (M) 470; Relations between languages: comparative philology (M) 475; Relations between languages: loans and loanwords (M) 482; Semantics: introduction (M) 499; Semantics: field theories (M) 504; Semantics: meaning and reference (M) 507

—, **Backus normal:** *see* Linguistic form: algebraic linguistics 270

—, **bound:** *see* Bound form (G).

—, **canonical:** *see* Relations between languages: typological and areal classifications 486

**Formal:** *see* Linguistic form: paradigmatic (M) 273; Phonology: contrast and opposition (M) 401; Semantics: sign and symbol (M) 510

**FORMAL COMPUTATION.** One using an algebraic formula rather than simple arithmetic.

— **items:** *see* Linguistic form: paradigmatic 274

— **level:** *see* Semantics: context and collocation (M) 503

**FORMAL LOGIC.** Study of the structure and forms of agreement, using algebraic rather than specific expressions.

— **system:** *see* Linguistic form: generative grammar (M) 272

**Formalism:** *see* Semantics: introduction 499

—, **function-oriented:** *see* Symbol manipulation by digital computer 597

**FORMALITY.** Non-dialectal *varieties* of language (*registers* (1)) can be classified on a number of dimensions, one of which is the dimension of *formality* (or *style of discourse*). On this dimension registers are classified according to the personal relations between the participants with which the registers concerned are compatible (e.g. impersonal, intimate...). *See:* Language varieties: register 251

**Formally undecidable problems:** *see* Unsolvable problems 623

**FORMANT.** A concentration of sound energy in a fairly narrow frequency band, a characteristic of the musical instrument or speaker because it remains largely independent of the note being played or the word being spoken. Detected conveniently by a *sound spectrograph. See:* Phonetics, acoustic 392; Phonetics, experimental 399; Relations between languages: comparative philology (M) 475; Telecommunication, economy in 600

**FORMAT.** The layout of information in a book, a table, or a computer store, input or output. For example a list of coded numbers in a digital computer store, prepared for output by a line printer, might have one number to a computer word, with every sixth word blank, except every 24th word, which is a "new-line" instruction. The printed result would be a table in four columns.

**Formation, concept:** *see* Concept formation (G). Information theory in psychological measurement 235

— **of concept by artificial intelligence:** *see* Concept formation by artificial intelligence 76

**FORMATIVE.** The symbols used in a *representation* of a *deep structure generated* by a *transformational generative grammar* are *category symbols*, *complex symbols* or *formatives*. Formatives represent single non-segmentable *formal items* (i.e. *morphemes* in most cases) or *grammatical features* (when these are not introduced as part of a complex symbol). *See:* Linguistic form: transformational theory 280; Psychological linguistics: psycholinguistic studies of syntax 439

**Formations:** *see* Linguistic form: paradigmatic (M) 273

**FORM-CLASS.** A *class* of mutually *substitutable items*.

**Forms, starred:** *see* Relations between languages: comparative philology 475

**Formula, Pollaczek-Khintchine:** *see* Simulation of traffic problems using chain-code random generators 540

**Fortis:** *see* Phonetics, articulatory 396; Phonology: contrast and opposition (M) 402; Phonology: phonemes and broad transcription (M) 409

**Fovea:** *see* Perception of colour 359

**Fraction, Fechner:** *see* Perception, visual 379

**FRAME.** One technique for classifying *items* in a language is called the *frame-and-focus* technique. A *frame* is a *string* of items with a gap at some point (the *focus*); the items which can occur in this gap to make the string into a complete utterance are all, by definition, mutually *substitutable*, and are all members of the same *focus class* (or *substitution class*).

**Frank and Wolfe method:** *see* Optimization of industrial processes 348

**FREE ASSOCIATION TESTS.** Psychological tests in which the subject is given a word and asked to speak another word, as quickly as possible, without repeating the stimulus word.

**FREE FORM.** A *form* (3), or *item*, is *free* if it can be used, on its own, as a complete *utterance* (2); otherwise it is *bound*. *See:* Grammar (structural) 186

— **root:** *see* Grammar (structural) 189

**FREE VARIATION.** Two *items* are in *free variation* in a given *environment* if one can *substitute* for the other without any change of meaning. If two different *phones* are to be assigned to the same *phoneme*, as its *allophones*, they must be in *free variation* and/or in *complementary distribution*.

**Frequencies, letter:** *see* Statistics of language: introduction 577

**Frequencies, phoneme:** *see* Statistics of language: introduction 577

**Frequency cues:** *see* Phonetics, experimental 400

— **domain techniques:** *see* Control, stability and 150

—, **fundamental:** *see* Phonetics, acoustic (M) 391

— **of vocal cord:** *see* Phonetics, auditory (M) 396

**Freudian unconscious psychology:** *see* Problem solving 416

**Fricatives:** *see* Phonetics, articulatory 395; Phonetics, auditory (M) 396; Phonology: contrast and opposition 401; Speech synthesis 559

—, **flat:** *see* Phonology: contrast and opposition (M) 401

—, **non-sibilant:** *see* Phonology: distinctive features (M) 404

—, **sibilant:** *see* Phonology: distinctive features (M) 404

—, **voiced:** *see* Speech synthesis 559

**Friction:** *see* Phonetics, articulatory 395

**Frictionless continuants:** *see* Phonetics, articulatory 395

**Front:** *see* Phonetics, auditory 397; Phonology: contrast and opposition (M) 401

**Fronted velar plosives:** *see* Phonology: contrast and opposition (M) 401

**FUNCTION (1).** A linguistic sign's function (1) is the part it plays in the *system* of the *language*, i.e. the total set of relations it enters into, and the contribution it makes to the communicative value of any utterance in which it occurs. *See:* Semantics: field theories (M) 504; Semantics: sign and symbol (M) 510; Semantics: meaning and reference (M) 507

**FUNCTION (2), GRAMMATICAL FUNCTION, FUNCTIONAL RELATION.** The *(grammatical) function* (or *functional relation*) of a particular occurrence of an *item* is its *syntagmatic* role in that particular *utterance*, i.e. its relation to other items in the same utterance. (e.g. 'subject' and 'object' are the names of two grammatical functions needed for many languages). *Function* (2) is to be distinguished from *class* or *category* (represented by *category symbols*). *See:* Grammar (structural) 186; Linguistic form: paradigmatic (M) 273; Linguistic form: syntagmatic 276

**FUNCTION (3).** Task, usually of a module rather than of a machine.

**FUNCTION (4).** A signal which varies with time.

**FUNCTION (5).** Part of an instruction to a computer, controlling for example whether it is to add, substract, put into store, etc.

—, **autocorrelation:** *see* Autocorrelation (G).

—, **correlation:** *see* Correlation analysis (G).

—, **forcing:** *see* Autonomous system (G).

**FUNCTION GENERATOR.** An analog module with one or more inputs and outputs, each output being equal to a particular (mathematical) function of the inputs.

—, **grammatical:** *see* Grammar (structural) 186

—, **Liapunov:** *see* Control, stability and 150

—, **objective:** *see* Objective function (G).

**Function, optimal-return:** *see* Dynamic programming 169
—, **-oriented formalisms:** *see* Symbol manipulation by digital computer 597
—, **perfect impulse:** *see* Impulse function, perfect (G).
—, **power:** *see* Power function (G).
—, **random:** *see* Random function (G).
—, **regulatory control:** *see* Control, predictive, using fast-time models 141
—, **source:** *see* Phonetics, acoustic 391
—, **step:** *see* Step function (G).
—, **system:** *see* Phonetics, acoustic 392
—, **transfer:** *see* Transfer function (G).
—, **weighting:** *see* Weighting function (G); Control: basic elements 90
**Functional relations:** *see* Grammar (structural) 186
**Functions, Boolean discriminant:** *see* Character recognition 42
—, **general recursive:** *see* Unsolvable problems 624
— **of statements, Boolean:** *see* Boolean functions of statements (G).
—, **optimal-decision:** *see* Dynamic programming 169
—, **predictably computable:** *see* Automata, infinite-state 37
**Fundamental frequency:** *see* Phonetics, acoustic (M) 391
**FUSED MORPH.** A *fused*, or *portmanteau, morph* is a *morph* which represents two or more *morphemes* at the same time. *See:* Grammar (structural) 186
**Fusimotor:** *see:* Muscle spindles (G)
**Fusion threshold:** *see* Perception, stereopsis as an aspect of 371
**FUSIONAL.** A language is classified *typologically* as *fusional* (or *inflecting*) if the dominant kind of word-structure involves *fused* (or *portmanteau*) *morphs* (i.e. if words are considered to consist of a number of *morphemes*, in addition to the *stem*, but the *phonological representation* of a word cannot be segmented conveniently so that there is a separate string of *phonemes* corresponding to each morpheme). Otherwise, the language is classified as *isolating* or *agglutinative* (or, sometimes, *polysynthetic*). *See:* Relations between languages: typological and areal classifications 486
— **area, Panum's:** *See* Perception, stereopsis as an aspect of 371

**GAIN** (Of a system such as an simplifier), is the ratio of its output to the input, both magnitudes being expressed in the same units.
**GALVANIC SKIN RESPONSE.** A brief change in the potential difference between two electrodes on the skin, used in studies of orienting response and attention. *See:* Attention 28
**Game playing:** *see* Problem solving 415
**GANGLION.** An aggregate of nerve cells, associated with nerve fibre bundles, usually containing synapses (e.g. sympathetic ganglia).
**Garbage collection:** *see* Symbol manipulation by digital computer 597

**GATE.** A *module* made from switches and delays, with a single digital output lead whose activity is determined by the activity of its digital input leads, of which there are two or more. For types of gate, *See:* Logic element (G)
—, **logic:** *see* Logic design, logic (G)
**Gating net:** *see* Modular net (G)
**GAUSSIAN DISTRIBUTION, NORMAL DISTRIBUTION.** The distribution of values of a Gaussian variable among its possible values, on a finite but usually large number of occasions.
— **random process:** *see* Process (G); Random signals and noise 454
**GAUSSIAN VARIABLE.** A variable ($x$) whose probability $x$ of lying in a small range, $P(x$ to $x+dx)$ is a maximum at the mean value $\bar{x}$, and falls away on either side according to the equation

$$P(x \text{ to } x+dx) = (2)^{-\frac{1}{2}} \sigma^{-1} \exp[-(x-\bar{x})^2/2\sigma^2] \cdot dx$$

The shape of the curve is defined by the exponential term, and $\sigma$, the standard deviation, is a measure of its breadth.
**Gender:** *see* Grammar (structural) (M) 205
**General control problem:** *see* Control by the maximum principle 101
— **linguistics:** *see* Foreword XI
— **recursive functions:** *see* Unsolvable problems 624
**Generalization:** *see* Psychological linguistics: theories of learning in relation to language (M) 444
**GENERALIZED PHRASE MARKER.** A *phrase-marker* associated with a *terminal string generated* by the *base component* of a *transformational-generative grammar* is a *generalized P-marker;* together with the terminal string it *represents* the *deep structure* of some sets of sentences. *See:* Linguistic form: transformational theory 282
**GENERALIZED TRANSFORMATION.** A *transformation* operating on pairs of *phrase-markers* rather than on just a single *phrase-marker*. *See:* Linguistic form: transformational theory (M) 284
**GENERATE (1), GENERATIVE GRAMMAR.** A *grammar* (3) (a *description* of a particular *language system*) *generates* (1) the set of *utterances* (usually the sentences) of that language in the sentence that it specifies what the membership of thernc is; more accurately, it generates not the utter levels themselves but *representations* of them on all *levels of representation*. A *generative grammar* is a thing which is *explicit*, and therefore can be said to generate a set of utterances in the above sense. *See:* Linguistic form: generative grammar 272
**GENERATE (2).** A speaker *generates* (2) a textual when he actually produces it in speech or writing.
— **and test:** *see* Problem solving 415
**Generation of sound:** *see* Phonetics, acoustic (M) 391; Phonetics, experimental (M) 399
**Generative:** *See* Linguistic form: paradigmatic 275
— **capacity, strong:** *See* Linguistic form: generative grammar 272; Strong generative capacity (G)

**Generative capacity, weak:** *see* Weak generative capacity (G); Linguistic form: generative grammar  272
— **grammar:** *see* Grammar (structural) (M)  186; Linguistic form: generative grammar  272; Linguistic form: transformational theory (M)  280
**Generator, function:** *see* Function generator (G).
**GENERATOR POTENTIAL.** The potential which may initiate an *action potential*, i.e. if the generator potential exceeds a certain value; it is then responsible for the excitatory depolarization of the nerve fibre membrane. *See also:* Action potential (G). Receptor potential (G).
—, **pulse:** *see* Pulse generator (G).
—, **sequence:** *see* Sequence generator (G).
**GENETIC CLASSIFICATION.** A classification of languages according to whether or not they can be traced back to a common ancestor language is a *genetic*, as opposed to an *areal* or a *typological*, classification. *See:* Relations between languages: introduction  470; Relations between languages: comparative philology  475
— **group:** *see* Relations between languages: typological and areal classifications  486
— **hypothesis:** *see* Relations between languages: comparative philology  476
— **message, transmission of:** *see* Homeostasis in the single cell  218
**Geniculate, lateral:** *see* Sensory processes  528
— **nucleus, lateral:** *see* Perception, stereopsis as an aspect of  372
**Genre:** *see* Role (G). Language varieties: register (M)  253
**Geography, linguistic:** *see* Language varieties: language and dialect  245
**Geometric interpretation of the maximum principle:** *see* Control by the maximum principle  104
**GEOSTATIC SATELLITE.** One which stays in unchanging position relative to the rotating Earth. *See:* Telecommunication, global  606
**Gestalt Psychology**  185
— **view:** *see* Problem solving  416
**Gibbs-Donnan equilibrium:** *see* Nerve and muscle, initiation and conduction of impulses in  314
**Gilbert bound:** *see* Error correcting codes  174
**Gleason:** *see* Linguistic form: paradigmatic (M)  275
**Glides:** *see* Phonology: distinctive features (M)  406
**Gliding:** *see* Phonetics, auditory  398
**Global telecommunication:** *see* Telecommunication, global  604
**Glossematicians:** *see* Semantics: introduction (M)  499
**Glottal:** *see* Phonetics, articulatory  394
— **stop:** *see* Phonology: phonemes and broad transcription (M)  409
**GLOTTAL WAVE.** The sound-wave generated by the larynx, which acts as the carrier-wave for speech. *See:* Phonetics, acoustic  391
**Glottalization:** *see* Phonology: contrast and opposition (M)  401
**Glottalized stops:** *see* Phonology: phonemes and broad transcription (M)  409

**Glottis:** *see* Phonetics, articulatory  394
**GLOTTOCHRONOLOGY.** *Glottochronology* (or *lexicostatistics*) is the comparison of the vocabularies of different languages in order to estimate the closeness of their *genetic relationship*. In the course of time a word may become obsolete in one of its earlier meanings, being replaced in this function by another word; if it is true, as has been suggested, that the rate at which words change in this way is roughly constant, then the length of time since an earlier language split, to produce the languages being compared, can be roughly estimated by seeing what proportion of their vocabularies has changed.
**GOAL.** The desired set of outputs of a machine, or given functions thereof.
The most probable behaviour of an animal in a given *state*, e.g. food ingestion if in a state of hunger. *See:* Animal learning  21
— **structure:** *see* Problem solving  414
**Gödel numbering:** *see* Unsolvable problems  624
**Golay code:** *see* Error correcting codes  173
**Golden blocks:** *see* Optimization, automatic  343
— **section:** *see* Optimization, automatic  343
**GOLGI ENDING (OR GOLGI ORGAN).** An axon ending branching into tufts which flatten as they end on the surface of tendons. *See:* Receptor (G)
**GOVERNMENT.** *Government* is the *selection* of one *grammatical class* by another; the latter is said to govern the former, and in most cases the former *depends* on it as well—thus a preposition or verb is said to govern the case of the noun depending on it. Government also differs from *concord* in that governing and governed classes need not have any *feature* in common. *See:* Grammar (structural)  203; Linguistic form: syntagmatic  278
**Gradient method, hill climbing by:** *see* Control, hill climbing in  117
— **of texture, retinal:** *see* Perception, stereopsis as an aspect of  369
— **projection, Rosen's:** *see* Optimization of industrial processes  348
**Gradual opposition:** *see* Phonology: distinctive features (M)  404
**GRAMMAR (1).** *Grammar* (1) is the study and *description* of the rules underlying the *form* (2) of language in general.
**GRAMMAR (2); GRAMMATICAL ITEM.** *Grammar* (1) can be divided into *grammar* (2), *lexis* and *phonology* (or *graphology*); phonology relates grammar (2) and lexis to the spoken or written substance; the difference between grammar (2) and lexis is that grammar (2) includes the more general rules, involving *closed classes*, while lexis includes less general rules involving *open classes*. A *grammatical item* is a *type* which is a *constituent* on the grammatical *level*, and is uniquely specified as the intersection of a specified set of grammatical *features*; it may or may not be a constituent also on the levels of lexis and phonology, and if it is, it may be possible to further subdivide it *paradigmatically* (i.e. to subclassify it) on

these other levels, i.e. it may or may not coincide with a *lexical item* or a *phonological item*. *See:* Grammar (structural) 186

**GRAMMAR (3), GRAMMATICALITY.** A grammar (3) is a *description* of a particular *language-system* from the point of view of either *grammar* (1) or *grammar* (2). An *item* is (by definition) *grammatical* (or *well formed*) if it conforms to the rules embodied in this *grammar* (3); any discussion of *grammaticality* thus always presupposes a grammar (3) of the language in question. *See:* Linguistic form: generative grammar 272; Linguistic form: transformational theory 280; Linguistic form: system and structure 278; Computational linguistics: introduction 49; Psychological linguistics: psycholinguistic studies of syntax 439

**GRAMMAR (4).** A set of rules which determines the chronological or spatial arrangement of *signals* needed to construct the symbols of a *language* (5). *See:* Computational linguistics: introduction 49; Computational linguistics: machine translation (M) 51; Linguistic form: paradigmatic (M) 273; Linguistic form: syntagmatic (M) 276; Semantics: introduction (M) 499; Writing (M) 627 Linguistic form: algebraic linguistics 270; Unsolvable problems 623

—, **context-free:** *see* Linguistic form: algebraic linguistics 270; Linguistic form: generative grammar (M) 272

—, **context-sensitive:** *see* Linguistic form: generative grammar (M) 272

—, **deep:** *see* Deep structure, deep grammar (G)

—, **dependency:** *see* Linguistic form: generative grammar (M) 272

—, **descriptively adequate:** *see* Psychological linguistics: theories of learning in relation to language 445

—, **generative:** *see* Generate (1), generative grammar (G) Linguistic form: generative grammar 272; Grammar (structural) (M) 186; Linguistic form: transformational theory (M) 280

—, **levels of:** *see* Phonology: phonemes and broad transcription (M) 409

—, **phrase-structure:** *see* Phrase-structure grammar (G); Linguistic form: generative grammar (M) 272; Psychological linguistics: theories of learning in relation to language 445

—, **stratificational:** *see* Computational linguistics: machine translation (M) 51; Linguistic form: generative grammar (M) 272

— **(Structural)** 186

—, **surface:** *see* Surface structure, surface grammar (G)

—, **transformational:** *see* Linguistic form: transformational theory 280; Transformational grammar, transformational generative grammar (G); Computational linguistics: machine translation (M) 51; Linguistic form: generative grammar (M) 272; Phonology: distinctive features (M) 404; Psychological linguistics: psycholinguistic studies of syntax 439

**Grammar, transformational-generative:** *see* Language varieties: stylistics (M) 259; Relations between languages: typological and areal classifications (M) 486

**Grammars, equivalent:** *see* Linguistic form: algebraic linguistics 270

—, **strongly equivalent:** *see* Strongly equivalent grammars (G); Psychological linguistics: psycholinguistic studies of syntax (M) 439

—, **taxonomic:** *see* Grammar (structural) (M) 186

**Grammatical:** *see* Linguistic form: paradigmatic (M) 273; Relations between languages: bilingualism (M) 473

— **analysis, deep:** *see* Semantics: introduction (M) 499

— **categories:** *see* Semantics: context and collocation (M) 503

— **constituents:** *see* Psychological linguistics: psychological aspects of semantic structure 442

— **criteria** (language classification): *see* Relations between languages: typological and areal classifications 486

— **formatives:** *see* Psychological linguistics: psycholinguistic studies of syntax (M) 439

— **function:** *see* Grammar (structural) 186

— **items:** *see* Linguistic form: paradigmatic 274

— **structure:** *see* Relations between languages: comparative philology (M) 475; Semantics: introduction (M) 499; Semantics: field theories (M) 505

— **systems:** *see* Relations between languages: comparative philology (M) 475

— **unit:** *see* Phonology: prosodic features (M) 411; Writing (M) 628

**Grammaticalness:** *see* Statistics of language: introduction (M) 567

**GRAPH (1).** A *graphetically* defined class of written marks standing in the same relation to a *grapheme* as a *phone* does to a *segmental phoneme*. *See:* Writing 627

**GRAPH (2).** A set of *points* (vertices) connected by a set of *lines* (edges). The lines may have directions indicated on them to show that the point at one end is *reachable* from the other end, and they may have quantities indicated on them to show their *capacity* (how much can be pushed through them). Even in their simplest form graphs can be highly efficient in representing which of a set of objects (points) are associated (connected by lines). *See also:* Tree (G). Examples of graphs with four points, the last two being *isomorphic:*

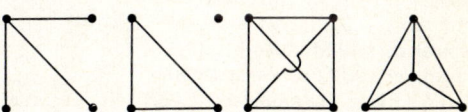

**GRAPHEME.** Any writing-system defines the rules for the use of certain abstract *units* (1) *(graphemes),* which can be combined into strings to produce *graphological representations* of *utterances,* but which are not themselves divisible into smaller units; they are more abstract than *graphs* (1), which are units in a *graphetic* representation, and they may be seen as classes of *allographs*, as *phonemes* can be seen as classes of *allophones*. *See:* Writing   629

**Graphetic structure:** *see* Writing   627

**GRAPHETICS.** *Graphetics* is the study of the visible marks *(graphs)* used in writing from the point of view of their shape and size rather than from that of their use in a particular *system* (1), which is covered by *graphology*; this distinction parallels that between *phonetics* and *phonology*. *See:* Writing (M)   630

**Graphic:** *see* Writing (M)   627

**Graphical Communication**   207

**Graphological layering:** *see* Writing (M)   628

— **structure:** *see* Writing   627

**GRAPHOLOGY.** *Graphology* is the study of *systems* (1) of writing—for each system, graphology describes what *graphemes* are in its vocabulary, and how they are used, as *phonology* does for *phonemes*. *See:* Writing   627

**Graphophonemics:** *see* Writing (M)   627

**Grave features:** *see* Linguistic form: transformational theory   283

**GREY MATTER.** Regions of the brain and spinal cord containing a high proportion of nerve cell bodies and dendrites. (Partly in contrast with *white matter*, which contains myelinated nerve fibres also.)

**Group:** *see* Relations between languages: typological and areal classifications (M)   486

— **codes:** *see* Error correcting codes   174

—, **genetic:** *see* Relations between languages: typological and areal classifications   486

**Switching centre (GSC):** *see* Switching and control in telephony   593

**Grouping:** *see* Linguistic form: syntagmatic   276

—, **areal:** *see* Relations between languages; introduction   470

**Hadamard, conditions of:** *see* Control, sensitivity and   147

— **matrices:** *see* Information space   222

**Hamming bound:** *see* Error correcting codes   173

— **codes:** *see* Information space   222

**HAMMING DISTANCE.** In the theory of codes, a measure of a relationship between two *n*-digit words, which equals the square of the distance between their representations in *n*-dimensional Euclidean space. *See:* Error correcting codes   173; Information space   221

**Hammock net:** *see* Modular net (G).

**Hard palate:** *see* Phonetics, articulatory   394

**HARDWARE.** The modules, collectively or separately, which form a system for computing (data processing) or control, in contradistinction to *software*. The functions of hardware and software may overlap.

**Harmony, vowel:** *see* Relations between languages: typological and areal classifications   486

**HEAD (1).** In a *subordinate construction* one of the *immediate constituents* is substitutable for the whole construction; this is the *head*, and every other immediate constituent is an *attribute*. *See:* Grammar (structural)   196

**Hearing**   211

**HEAD (2).** Small electromagnet used for magnetic recording and reproducing (writing and reading), *See:* Magnetic recording,   291

**Helson-Judd effect:** *see* Perception of colour   362

**Herbrand-Gödel systems:** *see* Unsolvable problems   624

**Hereditary process:** *see* Homeostasis   214

**Hering mechanism:** *see* Perception, visual   378

**HESITATION.** Brief time during which the registers of a computer are being used in moving a word of data to or from a peripheral, delaying the main sequence of operations.

— **phenomena:** *see* Psychological linguistics: psycholinguistic studies of syntax   441

**HEURISTIC.** An aid to discovery. A short cut towards the solution of a problem.

— **search:** *see* Problem solving   445

**Hierarchical control:** *see* Control, hierarchical   113; Control, predictive, using fast-time models   145

**HIERARCHY.** Any system of persons or things in a graded order. *See:* Control, hierarchical   113. *See also:* Tree (G).

**High:** *see* Phonetics, auditory   398

— **frequency radio services:** *see* Telecommunication, global   604

**HIGH LEVEL, LOW LEWEL.** In communication from a human to a computer, the signals are at high level if they are easily translated into natural language, and at low level if they are nearly in the form required by the computer. *See:* Algorithms for processing algorithms   16

**HIGHER CENTRES.** Region in the central nervous system where the most elaborate use seems to be made of incoming and stored information, from which motor activity seems mainly to emanate.

**HIGHLY COMPACTED FIGURE.** In concept formation experiments, a single object containing all the attributes of the concept. *See:* Conceptual behaviour   84

**HILL CLIMBING.** Strategies for adjusting the parameters of a system so that its performance becomes locally optimized. The metaphor is adequate only in simple cases unless the land is considered to be heaving, the hilltop(s) to be changing position, and the climber's information to be limited to proprioception and the readings of a compass and a sluggish altimeter. *See:* Optimization, automatic   342; Control, hill climbing in   115

— **climbing by alternate adjustments:** *see* Controll, hill climbing in   117

— **climbing by gradient method:** *see* Control, hill climbing in   117

— **climbing by steepest ascent:** *see* Control, hill climbing in   117

— **climbing in control:** *see* Control, hill climbing in   115

**HISTOGRAM.** A graphical record in which, for example, the number of occurrences of an event of each range of size is plotted against the size. (The types of objects counted need not be arranged in any particular order.)

**Historical comparison:** *see* Relations between languages: introduction 470

**Hjelmslev:** *see* Linguistic form: paradigmatic (M) 273

**Hold:** *see* Phonetics, articulatory (M) 395

**HOLISTIC.** As a whole; concerning a particular natural group.

**HOMEOSTASIS.** *(Classical)*. The reactions of a living system in maintaining the *internal environment* relatively constant when the external environment changes. *(Modern)*. The behaviour of a multi-level hierarchical organization of self-adaptive control loops in a living organism. I. P. Priban.

**Homeostasis** 213
— **in the Single Cell** 217

**HOMOLATERAL.** On the same side, e.g. in the same cerebral hemisphere.

**Homophones:** *see* Grammar (structural) 188
**Horizontal cells:** *see* Perception of colour 359
**Hubel and Wiesel:** *see* Neuronal nets 332
**Hue:** *see* Perception of colour 361
— **shift effect, Stiles-Crawford:** *see* Perception of colour 363

**Human engineer:** *see* Man-machine communication and ergonomics 301
— **factors specialist:** *see* Man-machine communication and ergonomics 301
— **memory, models for:** *see* Models for human memory 311
— **performance, psychological limiting factors in:** *see* Psychological limiting factors in human performance 437
— **thought process, computer simulation of:** *see* Computer simulation of human thought processes 60

**Hybrid computers, control by:** *see* Control by hybrid computers 92
— **transformer:** *see* Subscriber's telephone set, design considerations of 685

**HYPERCUBE.** A figure in *n* dimensions which corresponds to a cube in 3 dimensions.

**HYPERPLANE.** A surface in *n*-dimensional space, *hyperspace*, corresponding to a plane in 3-dimensional space. There is no apparent difference between a plane and a hyperplane; only between the spaces surrounding them.

**Hyphenation:** *see* Statistics of language: structure of written English words 584
**Hypercorrection:** *see* Relations between languages: bilingualism 473
**Hypothalamus extirpation:** *see* Animal motivation 24
— **stimulation:** *see* Animal motivation 24
**Hypothesis, genetic:** *see* Relations between languages: comparative philology 475
—, **Turing's:** *see* Automata, infinite-state 36
**Hysteresis effect:** *see* Perception, stereopsis as an aspect of 371

**I.C, binary:** *see* Grammar (structural) 195

**ICONIC.** A *sign* is *iconic* if it is similar to what it 'stands for' (its *referent*); otherwise it is *symbolic*. *See:* Semantics: sign and symbol 510

**IDENTIFICATION (1).** A set of measurements or facts necessary to describe a plant or system sufficiently accurately for a mathematical model to be made. *See:* Control, identification techniques for 119; Discrete models for forecasting and control 163

**IDENTIFICATION (2).** A set of attributes, representing a class, from which it can be decided whether or not any entity is a member of the class. *See:* Concept identification—information processing approaches 80

—, **speaker:** *see* Speech recognition, automatic 552

**IDENTIFY (1).** To describe the essential *functions* of (a system or process). *See:* Identification (1) (G)

**IDENTIFY (2).** To describe the essential *attributes* of (a member of a class). *See:* Concept identification —information processing approaches 80

**Identifying:** *see* Lingistic form: paradigmatic (M) 275
**Identity matrix:** *see* Matrix (G)

**IDIOLECT.** The *language* (1) of a single individual at a single time is an *idiolect*. *See:* Language varieties: language and dialect 243; Language varieties: register (M) 251

**IDIOM.** An idiom is a habitual *collocation* of two or more words whose combined meaning is not deducible from a knowledge of the meanings of its component words and of their grammatical *syntagmatic* relations to each other. More generally, any *grammatical item* (whether or not it consists of smaller items) whose meaning cannot be deduced in this way can be called an idiom. *See:* Semantics: context and collocation 503; Relations between languages: loans and loanwords (M) 482

**Illusions:** *see* Perception, visual 386
**Image, sound:** *see* Perception of sound 365
**Images, auditory:** *see* Perception of colour 365
—, **stabilized:** *see* Perception, visual 384
—, **stabilized, perceptual breakdown with:** *see* Perceptual breakdown with stabilized images 388

**IMMEDIATE CONSTITUENT, I.C.** The *immediate constituents* (I.C's) of an *item* are its largest *constituents* on a given *level* (1); any other constituent is a *mediate constituent* of the item in question. An immediate constituent may also be an *ultimate constituent*. Some linguists use the term *immediate constituent analysis (IC analysis)* for a method of segmenting utterances by *binary segmentation*. *See:* Grammar (structural) 194; Linguistic form: syntagmatic 277; Linguistic form: system and structure (M) 279

— **memory:** *see* Information theory in psychological measurement 233

**IMPEDANCE.** Opposition to the flow of alternating current, offered by (a) resistance, (b) inductance, (c) breaks in connexion, ameliorated by capacitance. An inductance or capacitance alone would alter the *phase* of the current by $+90°$ or $-90°$; so the impedance must be expressed by a complex number $R+jX$ corresponding to a resistance of magnitude $(R^2+X^2)^{\frac{1}{2}}$. In another form, the polar form, the impedance is specified by $R$ and an angle which represent the phase shift.

**IMPLICIT EQUATION.** Of the form $f(x, y, \ldots) = 0$ and not usually capable of transformation to an *explicit* form such as $x = F(y, \ldots)$

**Implosives:** *see* Phonetics, articulatory   396

**Improvement of memory:** *see* Models for human memory   311

**IMPULSE.** An *action potential* in nerve or muscle cells.

— **conduction, saltatory:** *see* Medullated nerve fibre (G)

**IMPULSE FUNCTION, PERFECT.** A function (magnitude as a function of time) which has value only at a particular instant in time, but which has a finite integral. The perfect impulse is the formal differential of the *step function*. If a unit impulse function at time $t_0$ is denoted by $\delta(t-t_0)$, and a unit step function by $h(t-t_0)$

then

$\delta(t-t_0) = 0$ when $t \neq t_0$ $\quad h(t-t_0) = 0$ when $t < t_0$
$\quad\quad\quad\quad = \infty$ when $t = t_0$ $\quad\quad \lambda = 1$ when $t > t_0$

and $\quad \int_{-\infty}^{t} \delta(s-t_0)\, ds = h(t-t_0)$.

Mathematical approximations to the perfect impulse usually involve limits of functions whose areas are unity, e.g. $\underset{T \to 0}{Lt}\, \dfrac{1}{2T} e^{-\left|\frac{1}{T}\right|} = \delta t$. Practical approximations are usually fairly simple, for example, the pulse

$p(t-t_0) = 0$ when $t < t_0$ or $t > t_0 + \tau$
$p(t-t_0) = \frac{1}{2}$ when $t_0 < t < t_0 + \tau$

or the triangular function

$\triangle(t-t_0) = 0$ when $|t-t_0| > \tau$
$\triangle(t-t_0) = \tau - |t-t_0|$ when $|t-t_0| < \tau$

Most simplified treatments of dynamic characteristic testing methods use the triangular function as an approximation to the impulse in evaluating the results of cross-correlation. However, the result of these methods is to give the response of the system to a pulse input. P. A. N. Briggs. *See:* Pseudorandom binary signals, use of...  433

**IMPULSE RESPONSE.** The output function (in time) of an analog system when its input is a unit *perfect impulse* (i.e. an infinite amplitude pulse of zero duration). For a *linear system* it is the differential of the unit step response.

**Impulses in nerve and muscle, initiation and conduction of:** *see* Nerve and muscle, initiation and conduction of impulses in   314

**Impulsive:** *see:* Speech synthesis   559

**Incongruities:** *see* Perception, visual   386

**INCORPORATING.** An *incorporating* language is a *polysynthetic* one.

**Independence, binocular vision:** *see* Perception, visual   386

**Independent:** *see* Grammar (structural)   202

**Index, citation:** *see* Citation index (G)

—, **structure:** *see* Structure index (G); Linguistic form: transformational theory   282

**Indicative statement:** *see* Computer language design requirements   54

**Indifference threshold:** *see* Psychological limiting factors in human performance   438

**Induction, scientific:** *see* Statistics of language: introduction   574

**Industrial processes, optimization of:** *see* Optimization of industrial processes   345

**Infinite-state automata:** *see* Automata, infinite-state   35

**INFIX NOTATION.** The usual shorthand for logical operation and statements about sets, in which the operator ($\cap \cup \neq$) appears between the operands. E.g. $P \cap \overline{Q}$ is read as 'P and not Q' or as 'if P then not Q'.

**Infixes:** *see* Grammar (structural)   189

**INFLECTING.** An *inflecting* language is a *fusional* one.

**INFLECTION, INFLECTIONAL AFFIX.** A *class* of words are said to *inflect* if they can be assigned to a number of *grammatical* classes, such that any particular word-*stem* occurs in members of all these classes, and the members of one class are distinguished from those of other classes by their *morphology* (their internal shape) as well as by their *syntax* (the rules for their use). Thus any word belonging to an inflecting class can be *segmented* into two parts: the *stem*, which stays constant from class to class, and any *inflectional affixes* which differ from class to class (but in some *paradigms* (1) of inflecting words—sets of words of different classes but with the same stem—one or more words are distinguished from the others by having no inflectional affix at all). Inflectional affixes are contrasted with *derivational affixes*. See: Grammar (structural)   189; Statistics of language: structure of written English words   584

**Inflectional affixes:** *see* Grammar (structural)   189

— **language:** *see* Relations between languages: introduction (M)   470; Relations between languages: typological and areal classifications (M)   486

**INFORMATION.** The information content of a symbol is the *a priori* uncertainty which exists before it is sent or received, on a logarithmic scale. Here log (uncertainty) is defined to be $-\log$ (probability), and it is always positive. *See:* Communication theory   46

— **flow in nervous system, role of pulse distribution in:** *see* Nervous system, role of pulse distribution in information flow   316

— **items:** *see* Information storage and retrieval   223

— **processing approaches:** *see* Concept identification—information processing approaches   80

—, **rate of transfer of:** *see* Telecommunication, economy in   599

**Information, representation of, about stimuli in populations of receptors:** *see* Receptors: representation of information about stimuli in populations 467
— **selection:** *see* Perception, visual 387
—, **selective dissemination of:** *see* Selective dissemination of information (G)
**INFORMATION SPACE.** The set of all possible values which a named signal may take: e.g. in synoptic meteorology, the force and direction of the wind may have any of 13 force values, multiplied by 8 direction values, namely 104 values in the set. *See:* Information space 221
— **Space** 221
—, **spatial representation of:** *see* Receptors: representation of information about stimuli in populations 469
— **Storage and Retrieval** 223
—, **symbolizing and coding of:** *see* Information storage and retrieval 224
— **Theory in Psychological Measurement** 232
**Informational variables in concept learning:** *see* Conceptual behaviour 86
**Inherent features:** *see* Phonology: distinctive features 406; Phonology: prosodic features 411
**Inherited words:** *see* Relations between languages: comparative philology (M) 475
**Inhibition, feedback, of enzymes:** *see* Homeostasis in the single cell 218
—, **lateral:** *see* Lateral inhibition (G); Neuronal nets 332; Receptors: representation of information about stimuli in populations of receptor units 470
—, **mutual:** *see* Sensory processes 527
**Initiation of impulses in nerve and muscle:** *see* Nerve and muscle, initiation and conduction of impulses in 314
— **of motivational states:** *see* Animal motivation 24
**Inland Trunk Systems** 238
**Inner product** *see:* Vector (G)
**Input, entropy of:** *see* Telecommunicaton, economy in 599
—, **output control:** *see* Computers, multiacess to 65
**processor:** *see* Computational linguistics: introduction 50
— **systems, multiple:** *see* Pseudorandom binary signals, use of... 436
**Institutional linguistics:** *see* Language varieties: language and dialect 243; Language varieties: register (M) 251
**INSTRUCTION.** A signal to the control unit of a computer, which is stored within the computer while the relevant program is running, and obeyed in its proper sequence in the program.
**Instructions, effect of:** *see* Sensory discrimination, measurement of 514
**INTEGRATED CIRCUIT.** A module, containing several components and con hasnexions, which been manufactured in one piece.
**Integration, morphological:** *see* Relations between languages: loans and loanwords 482
—, **phonological:** *see* Relations between languages: loans and loanwords (M) 482

**Integration, semantic:** *see* Relations between languages: loans and loanwords (M) 482
— **with area:** *see* Perception, visual 380
— **with time:** *see* Perception, visual 381
**INTEGRATOR.** An analog module or system whose output is the integral of its input variable with respect to time. Or it may receive two input variables, and its output will be the integral of one with respect to the other, from some time 0 to the time $t$ at which the output is generated. *See also:* Differentiator (G)
**"INTEGRATOR".** A receptor which isstimulated by a large class of signals.
**Intelligence, artifical, concept formation by:** *see* Concept formation by artifical intelligence 76
**Intelligibility, mutual:** *see* Language varieties: language and dialect 243
**Intensity:** *see* Phonology: prosodic features 413
— **cues:** *see* Phonetics, experimental 400
—, **luminous:** *see* Perception of colour 361
**Interchanging pairs, method of:** *see* Sorting techniques 544
**Interdental:** *see* Phonetics, articulatory 394
**INTERFACE.** The total set of channels through which communication occurs between two modules or systems. *Man-machine interface.* The total set of displays or records and controls through which communication is established between a man and a machine. *See:* Man-machine communication and ergonomics 302. *Standard interface.* An agreement which enables modules or systems by different designers to be easily interconnected. *See:* Computer peripherals and their control 60
—, **man-machine:** *see* Interface (G)
—, **standard:** *see* Interface (G)
**INTERFERENCE.** When a speaker of one *language* (3) learns a second language, there is a tendency to generalize some of the rules of the first language to the second language; when these rules conflict with the correct rules for the second language there is *interference*. *See:* Relations between languages: bilingualism 473; Phonology: contrast and opposition (M) 401; Relations between languages: lingua franca (M) 480
—, **semantic:** *see* Relations between languages: bilingualism (M) 473
**INTERFIX (LINK).** When a number of *keywords* are used in the description of a document the librarian may use special marks to show which pairs of keywords are linked, and he calls these marks links or interfixes. *See:* Information storage and retrieval 226
 **erlevel of context:** *see* Language varieties: register (M) 251
**INTERLINGUISTIC.** An *interlinguistic unit* (1) is one which occurs in two or more different languages, i.e. when a unit of one language can be equated with a unit of another. Interlinguistic units are presupposed by *translation*. *See:* Relations between languages: bilingualism (M) 473

**INTERNAL JUNCTURE.** An *internal* (as opposed to a *terminal*) *juncture* is a *juncture phoneme* which does not occur finally in a *string* of phonemes *representing* an utterance, and which determines the *allophones* to be used for adjacent phonemes, but not the pitch pattern *(intonation)* of the preceding stretch of utterance, as do terminal junctures.

**International languages:** *See* Relations between languages: lingua franca  480

— **telecommunication system planning:** *see* Telecommunication system planning, international  607

**Interneurons:** *see* Neuronal nets  330

**Interposition:** *see* Perception, stereopsis as an aspect of  369

**Interpretation, geometric, of the maximum principle:** *see* Control by the maximum principle  104

—, **phonetic:** *see* Linguistic form: transformational theory (M)  283

—, **semantic:** *see* Psychological linguistics: psycholinguistic studies of syntax (M)  439

**Interrogation:** *see* Computer peripherals and their control  60

**INTERRUPT.** An instruction to a computer to suspend the operation of a program transfer control to the program appropriate to a peripheral and return on the proper signal to the original program. *See:* Computer peripherals and their control  59

**Intersensory effects in sound perception:** *see* Perception of sound  367

**INTONATION.** In all languages (presumably) the musical pitch of the voice varies, in speaking, and this variation follows rules which form part of the *language-system*. There are two kinds of rule: *intonation* and *tone;* of these, only intonation seems to be found in all languages. This is variation of pitch which can be related to the *grammatical constructions* with which it is coextensive and/or to the attitude of the speaker. *See:* Phonology: prosodic features  412; Grammar (structural) (M)  186; Linguistic form: syntagmatic (M)  277; Phonetics, auditory (M)  396; Relations between languages: bilingualism (M)  472; Writing (M)  627

— **pattern:** *see* Phonetics, acoustic (M)  393

**Intrafusal:** *see* Muscle spindles (G)

**Introduction to computational linguistics:** *see* Computational linguistics: introduction  49

**Invariance and control:** *see* Control, invariance and  126

—, **principle of:** *see* Control, invariance and  126

—, **selective:** *see* Control, invariance and  127

**INVERSION.** The "solution" of a set of equations in the form

$$y_1 = a_{11}x_1 + a_{12}xx_2 + \ldots$$
$$y_2 = a_{21}x_1 + a_{22}x_2 + \ldots$$
$$\ldots\ldots\ldots\ldots\ldots\ldots\ldots\ldots$$

replacing them by the set

$$x_1 = b_{11}y_1 + b_{12}y_2 + \ldots$$
$$x_2 = b_{21}y_1 + b_{22}y_2 + \ldots$$
$$\ldots\ldots\ldots\ldots\ldots\ldots\ldots\ldots$$

**IPSP's (inhibitory postsynaptic potentials):** *see* Neuronal nets  322

**IS-membrane:** *see* Neuronal nets  323

**ISCHEMIA.** Absence of blood flow.

**ISOGLOSS.** A line which is drawn on a map round the area where speakers live who use a particular linguistic feature (e.g. the area where a particular lexical item, or pronunciation of a lexical item, in used). *See:* Language varieties: language and dialect  245

**Isolated opposition:** *see* Phonology: distinctive features (M)  404

**ISOLATING.** A language is classified *typologically* as *isolating* or *analytic*, (as opposed to *fusional, agglutinative* or (sometimes) *polysynthetic*) if its words tend to consist of only one *morpheme* each, and therefore contain no *morphological markers* of the *grammatical classes* to which they belong. *See:* Relations between languages: typological and areal classifications  486

— **languages:** *see* Relations between languages: introduction (M)  470

**Isolation:** *see* Language varieties: register (M)  251

**ISOMORPHIC.** Of the same form, especially applied to crystals. Two *graphs* are isomorphic if to every point and line of either there corresponds a point and a line of the other. Since the placing of a point and the shape of a line is of no relevance, isomorphic graphs are merely representations of the same graph.

**ITEM, LINGUISTIC ITEM.** Any *constituent* or *constitute* on any *level* (1) is an *item* (on that level); an item may be a *formal item* or a *grammatical, lexical* or *phonological item*. Items are *types*, not *tokens*, so that two or more constituents of an utterance may be tokens of the same item. *See:* Linguistic form: paradigmatic  273; Linguistic form: syntagmatic (M)  276; Computational linguistics: machine translation (M)  51; Phonology: contrast and opposition (M)  401; Phonology: distinctive features (M)  404; Relations between languages: introduction (M)  470; Semantics: field theories (M)  506

**ITEM-AND-ARRANGEMENT (IA).** The *Item-and-arrangement (IA)* model of grammatical description differs from the *Item-and-Process (IP)* model in treating every *morpheme* as having a *phonological realization* which is added to that of any other morpheme with which it combines, whereas I.P. treats some morphemes as being realized by a change in the phonological shape of any morphemes with which they are combined. I.A. differs from the *Word-and-Paradigm (W.P.)* model in not giving the word any special status in the grammatical description. *See:* Grammar (structural)  192

**ITEM-AND-PROCESS (IP).** The *Item-and-Process* (I.P) model of grammatical description differs from the *Item-and-Arrangement* (I.A) model in that it treats some morphemes as changing, rather than simply adding to, the phonological shape of morphemes with which they are combined. It also differs from the *Word-and-Paradigm* (W.P) model in not giving any special status in a grammatical description to the word. *See:* Grammar (structural) 192

**Item, formal:** *see* Form (2) linguistic form, formal item (G). Linguistic form: paradigmatic 274

—, **grammatical:** *see* Grammar (2), grammatical item (G). Linguistic form: paradigmatic 274

—, **lexical:** *see* Lexical item (G). Computational linguistics: introduction (M) 51; Linguistic form: paradigmatic 274; Linguistic form: transformational theory (M) 282; Psychological linguistics: psychological aspects of semantic structure 442; Semantics: context and collocation 503; Semantics: field theories (M) 506

**Items, information:** *see* Information storage and retrieval 223

**Joints, receptors in:** *see* Receptors in joints and muscles 460

**JOURNAL TAPE.** The continuous printed tape from such a machine as a cash register, containing records line by line in chronological sequence.

**Judgement, absolute:** *see* Information theory in psychological measurement 233

**Junction circuits:** *see* Local networks 284

**JUNCTURE.** *Juncture phonemes* are sometimes used in *phonological representations*, in order to show that the *phonetic* transition from the immediately preceding *phoneme* to the immediately following one is different from that which is taken as the normal, i.e. the *allophones* of those two phonemes which occur with a juncture between them are different from those which occur when they are immediately adjacent. Often, but not necessarily, the same allophone occurs before (or after, as the case may be) a juncture as occurs before (or after) a pause; and it may sometimes be possible to represent word-boundaries by a juncture in the phonological representation of a string of words. This kind of juncture is known as *open transition* or *plus juncture* (from the usual symbol used for it: /+/). In addition to *internal juncture*, however, a phonological representation may involve *terminal juncture* (or *terminal contours*); for each language, various kinds of terminal contour can be distinguished, each of which determines some aspect of the change of pitch (i.e. of the *intonation*) during the part of the utterance represented by the preceding string of phonemes. *See:* Grammar (structural) 191

— **features:** *see* Linguistic form: syntagmatic (M) 276
—, **internal:** *see* Internal juncture (G).
—, **terminal:** *see* Terminal juncture (G).

**Kelley's method:** *see* Optimization of industrial processes 343

**Key:** *see* Sorting techniques 544

**KEY-WORDS.** A vocabulary of words chosen so that their presence in a document may be used as criteria of whether the document is needed in response to any particular enquiry. *See:* Scientific documentation 496

**Klüver-Bucy syndrome:** *see* Animal motivation 25

**Knowledge, epistemological:** *see* Psychological linguistics: theories of learning in relation to language 444

—, **psychological:** *see* Psychological linguistics: theories of learning in relation to language 444

**Labial:** *see* Phonetics, articulatory 394; Phonology: phonemes and broad transcription (M) 409

**Labialization:** *see* Phonetics, articulatory 396

**Labio-dental:** *see* Phonetics, articulatory 394

**Labio-velar:** *see* Phonetics, articulatory 394

**Lambda-calculus of Church:** *see* Unsolvable problems 624

**LANGAGE.** De Saussure's term *le langage* is translated as *speech;* it is the name for the general human ability to learn and use particular *languages* (1) *(langues)*.

**LANGUAGE (1), LANGUAGE SYSTEM.** The 'speech-habits' of a given community are its *language* (1); this is the set of rules which a person needs to know in order to speak or write in a way acceptable to other members of that community. These rules constitute a self-contained *system* which is said to 'underlie' all (acceptable) *utterances* made by members of that community. There are, however, rules excluding unacceptable utterances which must be treated not as part of the language system as such, but as part of the general culture of the community; where the dividing line comes is a matter of debate. *See:* Linguistic form: system and structure 278; Linguistic form: transformational theory (M) 280; Psychological linguistics: psycholinguistic studies of syntax (M) 439; Semantics: meaning and reference (M) 507; Writing (M) 627

**LANGUAGE (2).** The set of *utterances* specified by a *language-system* can itself be referred to as a *language* (2); thus a *grammar* (3) can be said to be a *description* of a language (1), but to *generate* (1) a language (2). See Linguistic form: generative grammar 272

**LANGUAGE (3).** Two different *languages* (1) may be different *languages* (3) or different *dialects* of the same *language* (3); this distinction is often made on social as much as linguistic grounds, but the most obvious difference is that monolingual speakers of two *languages* (3) in general cannot understand each other, whereas monolingual speakers of two different *dialects* of the same *language* (3) in general can. *See:* Language varieties: language and dialect 243

**LANGUAGE (4).** A *language* (4) is socially different from a *dialect* (2) in that its speakers have more social prestige, and therefore it is taken as a linguistic model; from a purely linguistic point of view, however, they are both *dialects* (1) and *languages* (1).

**LANGUAGE (5).** Whether natural or artificial, a conventional set of symbols such that a certain *system* (e.g. a human being) can distinguish any one symbol from all the rest. *See:* Similarity 536

—, **algorithmic:** *see* Algorithmic language (G).

— **analyser:** *see* Fact retrieval 180

— **and dialect:** *see* Language varieties: language and dialect 243

— **and social communication:** *see* Information theory in psychological measurement 235

—, **artificial:** *see* Artificial language (1) (G). Artificial language (2) (G). Relations between languages: lingua franca 480; Statistics of languages: introduction (M) 567

—, **assembly:** *see* Assembly language (G).

—, **auxiliary:** *see* Relations between languages: lingua franca 480

—, **command:** *see* Command language (G). Computer operating systems 58

**LANGUAGE COMMUNITY.** A community whose members all claim to speak the same *language* (3) (or languages (3), in cases where one language community represents the intersection of two or more others). *See:* Language varieties: language and dialect 243

—, **computer, design requirements of:** *see* Computer language design requirements 54

—, **contact:** *see* Relations between languages: lingua franca 480

— **families:** *see* Relations between languages: introduction 470; Relations between languages: comparative philology (M) 475

—, **inflectional:** *see* Relations between languages: introduction 470; Relations between languages: typological and areal classifications (M) 486

— **levels:** *see* Semantics: field theories 504

—, **list-processing:** *see* Symbol manipulation by digital computer 596

—, **low-level:** *see* Low-level language (G)

—, **machine:** *see* Object language (G)

—, **morphological system of:** *see* Morphological system of a language (G)

—, **natural:** *see* Natural language (G). Linguistic form: transformational theory (M) 280; Linguistic form: generative grammar (M) 272; Psychological linguistics: psychological aspects of semantic structure 442; Relations between languages: lingua franca (M) 480; Semantics: introduction (M) 499; Statistics of language: introduction (M) 567; Writing (M) 627

—, **object:** *see* Object language (G)

—, **parent:** *see* Relations between languages: introduction 470; Relations between languages: comparative philology 475

—, **procedural:** *see* Computer language design requirements 54

— **processing, automatic:** *see* Computational linguistics: introduction 49

**Language, restricted:** *see* Restricted language (G); Language varieties: register (M) 252; Semantics: field theories 506

—, **self-referencing:** *see* Self-referencing language (G)

—, **semiotic:** *see* Semiotic language (G)

—, **source:** *see* Source language (G)

—, **sources of statistics of:** *see* Statistics of language: introduction 577

—, **standard:** *see* Language varieties: language and dialect 248

—, **standardization:** *see* Relations between languages: lingua franca 480

—, **statistics of:** *see* Statistics of language: introduction 567

—, **system:** *see* Language (1), language system (G). Relations between languages: lingua franca (M) 480; Relations between languages: semantic change (M) 483

—, **target:** *see* Target language (G)

—, **theories of learning in relation to:** *see* Psychological linguistics: theories of learning in relation to language 444

—, **tone:** *see* Phonology: prosodic features 412

—, **trade:** *see* Relations between languages: lingua franca (M) 480

—, **transformational:** *see* Transformational language (G); Linguistic form: transformational theory (M) 280

— **Varieties: Language and Dialect** 243; *See also:* Variety (G)

— **Varieties: Register** 251

— **Varieties: Stylistics** 259

—, **vehicular:** *see* Relations between languages: lingua franca 480

—, **written:** *see* Relations between languages: bilingualism (M) 473

**Languages:** *see* Linguistic form: transformational theory 280

—, **assembly:** *see* Assembly languages 26

—, **context-sensitive:** *see* Linguistic form: transformational theory 280

—, **international:** *see* Relations between languages: lingua franca 480

—, **isolating:** *see* Relations between languages: introduction (M) 470

—, **marginal:** *see* Relations between languages: lingua franca 480

—, **relations between:** *see* Relations between languages: introduction 470

—, **string-processing:** *see* Symbol manipulation by digital computer 597

**(LA) LANGUE.** De Saussure's term *langue* is translated as *language* (1), i.e. it is the *system* of rules rather than the exploitation of this system in actual utterances, which is *parole*. It is also contrasted with *langage*, which is the faculty of language every normal human is born with, as opposed to particular language systems. *See:* Linguistic form: system and structure 279; Language varieties: stylistics (M) 259

**LARYNX.** Cavity in throat holding the vocal cords. *See:* Phonetics, acoustic (M) 391; Phonetics, articulatory 394; Phonetics, experimental (M) 399

**LATERAL GENICULATE BODIES.** Two small terminal swellings of the optic tracts, each containing nerve fibres from both retinas which have passed through the chiasma. In the chiasma the fibres from the right and left half of each retina separate; those from the right halves together enter one tract and those from the left halves enter the other. L. Wheeler. *See:* Perception of colour 360; Sensory processes 528

**Lateral geniculate nucleus:** *see* Perception, stereopsis as an aspect of 372

**LATERAL INHIBITION.** The reduction in activity of receptors adjacent to a field of stimulated receptors; in particular, when this occurs in the retina, it results in enhanced visual contrast and perception of edges. *See:* Neuronal nets 332; Receptors: representation of information about stimuli in populations 470

**Laterals:** *see* Phonetics, articulatory 395; Phonology: contrast and opposition (M) 401

**Lattice, Boolean:** *see* Boolean lattice (G)

**Layered:** *see* Grammar (structural) (M) 199

**LAYERING.** *Layering* is the *constituency* relation among a string of items some of which can be grouped together to form a *constitute*; the *structure* of this constitute is a *layer (of structure)*. *Layered constituents* are sometimes contrasted with *string constituents*: if there are or may be a relatively large number of immediate constituents (IC's) per layer, these IC's are string-constituents, whereas if there must be only two (by the principle of *binary segmentation*) they are layered. *See:* Grammar (structural) 199

—, **graphological:** *see* Writing (M) 627

**Layers of constituency:** *see* Grammar (structural) 198

**Learner, concept:** *see* Concept learner (G)

**LEARNING** by an animal. A persistent change in behaviour in response to a given stimulus; almost certainly involving a change in the nervous system which can occur independently of and prior to its behavioural demonstration. *See:* Animal learning 21

**LEARNING.** By a *self-adaptive machine*. The changes in its *state*, performed by the machine on itself, which tend to improve its speed (or cost) of self-adaptation. *See:* Learning machines: a unified view 261; When the desired response to each input is signalled alongside each actual response:
— by some external agency, this is *Learning with a teacher*;
— by a function of earlier response, this is *Learning without a teacher*. *See:* Pattern recognition 350

**Learning:** *see* Problem solving 414; Psychology, use of models (learning) 447

—, **animal:** *see* Animal learning 21

—, **avoidance:** *see* Animal motivation 24

— **control system:** *see* Control: basic elements 92

— **machines:** *see* Adaptive control theory 9

**Learning Machines: a Unified View** 261

—, **theories of, in relation to language:** *see* Psychological linguistics: theories of learning in relation to language 444

**LEAST SQUARES.** If $a_1, a_2, \ldots a_i \ldots a_n$ are estimates of the value of a quantity and $A$ is chosen so that $\sum_i^n (A - a_i)^2$ is minimum, $A$ is called the *least squares* average. *See:* Optimization, automatic 344

**Length:** *see* Phonology: prosodic features 411

**Lenis:** *see* Phonetics, articulatory 396; Phonology: contrast and opposition 402; Phonology: phonemes and broad transcription 409

**Letter frequencies:** *see* Statistics of language: introduction 577

**LEVEL (1), LEVEL OF REPRESENTATION.** The overall *system* of a *language* can be divided into *levels (of representation)*, each of which is related to the other levels but involves relations, abstractions and/or rules of a different kind; each level can be considered to constitute a separate *system*. Likewise an item can be *represented* on different levels, e.g. it can be represented as a (bracketed) string of *morphemes* or of *phonemes*; hence '*levels of representation*' (cf. *component, stratum, mode*). *See:* Grammar (structural) 186; Psychological linguistics: theories of learning in relation to language 444; Language varieties: language and dialect (M) 243; Language varieties: register (M) 251; Phonetics, experimental (M) 399; Relations between languages: bilingualism (M) 473; Relations between languages: loans and loanwords (M) 482; Relations between languages: semantic change (M) 484; Semantics: context and collocation (M) 503; Semantics: meaning and reference (M) 504; Semantics: sign and symbol (M) 510; Writing (M) 627

**LEVEL (2) SIZE-LEVEL.** *Items* in a given *language*, on a given *level of representation*, can be classified into different *levels*, (2) (or *units* (2)), on the basis of 'size' in the sense that clauses are 'bigger' than phrases or words and therefore belong to a different level (2) from these.

—, **acoustic:** *see* Phonetics, acoustic (M) 391

—, **adapt:** *see* Adaptive threshold elements 11

—, **formal:** *see* Semantics: context and collocation (M) 503

—, **high and low:** *see* High level, low level (G)

—, **morphological:** *see* Semantics: field theories (M) 504

—, **phonological:** *see* Language varieties: stylistics (M) 259

—, **semantic:** *see* Semantics: meaning and reference 508

— **of grammar:** *see* Phonology: phonemes and broad transcription (M) 409

— **of lexis:** *see* Relations between languages: introduction (M) 470

— **of morphology:** *see* Relations between languages: introduction (M) 470

— **of phonology:** *see* Relations between languages: introduction (M) 470

**Levels of language:** *see* Semantics: field theories (M) 504
— **of structure:** *see* Semantics: introduction (M) 499
**Lexeme:** *see* Semantics: introduction (M) 499
**Lexical:** *see* Linguistic form: paradigmatic (M) 273; Relations between languages: bilingualism (M) 473
— **categories:** *see* Linguistic form: transformational theory (M) 280; Psychological linguistics: psycholinguistic studies of syntax (M) 439
— **citeria:** *see* Relations between languages: typological and areal classifications (M) 486
— **environment:** *see* Semantics: context and collocation 503
— **features:** *see* Language varieties: register (M) 251
**LEXICAL ITEM.** An item of vocabulary (usually, but not necessarily, a word). *See:* Item (G). Linguistic form: syntagmatic 276; Semantics: context and collocation 503; Semantics: field theories (M) 506; Linguistic form: paradigmatic 274; Computational linguistics: introduction (M) 51; Linguistic form: transformational theory (M) 282; Psychological linguistics: psychological aspects of semantic structure 442; Relations between languages: comparative philology (M) 475
— **meaning:** *see* Semantics: introduction (M) 499
— **sets:** *see* Linguistic form: paradigmatic 276
— **structures:** *see* Semantics: field theories 505
— **tone:** *see* Relations between languages: typological and areal classifications 486; Tone, lexical tone (tonal) (G)
— **variations:** *see* Relations between languages: semantic change (M) 484
**Lexically conditioned:** *see* Grammar (structural) 188
**LEXICON.** A language's *lexicon* is its vocabulary; the part of a description of a *language-system* which deals with this is also called the *lexicon*. *See:* Linguistic form: transformational theory 282
**Lexicostatistics:** *see* Glottochronology (G)
**LEXIS, LEXICAL.** *Lexis* is the study of the vocabulary of a language; a *lexical item* (with may be a word, or an *item* larger or smaller than a word) is an item which can be uniquely defined in lexical terms (cf. *grammatical item*). A *lexical set* is the set of lexical items which can occur in a particular lexical *environment*. A *lexical category*, in a *transformational generative grammar*, is a *category symbol* which is rewritten as a set of *features* (a *complex symbol*); this complex symbol then permits a *representation* of an appropriate lexical item to be selected from the *lexicon*. *See:* Linguistic form: paradigmatic 274; Psychological linguistics: psychological aspects of semantic structure 442; Semantics: context and collocation 503; Semantics: field theories 505
—, **levels of:** *see* Relations between languages: introduction 470
**Liapunov function:** *see* Control, stability and 150
**LIGHT PEN.** A slim cylindrical device to be held in the hand, containing a photocell which is sensitive to light from only a narrow solid angle. The output signal from the photocell is introduced into the circuitry of a cathode-ray tube, and if sufficiently strong stimulates a spot of light on the screen at the point to which the light pen is pointing
**Lightness:** *see* Perception of colour 361
**Limbs, prosthetic:** *see* Prosthetic limbs 416
**Limen:** *see* Sensory discrimination, measurement of 517
**Limit cycle oscillation:** *see* Control, on-off 136
— **line, vowel:** *see* Phonetics, auditory 397
**Limited register machine (LRM):** *see* Automata, infinite-state 36
**Limits, method of:** *see* Sensory discrimination, measurement of 520
**Line, switch:** *see* Control, on-off 138
**Linear-bounded automata:** *see* Linguistic form: generative grammar (M) 273
— **code, cyclic:** *see* Error correcting codes 174
— **codes:** *see* Error correcting codes 174
**LINEAR DIFFERENTIAL EQUATION.** A differential equation of *degree 1*, such as
$p_0 \, d^n y/dx^n + p_1 d^{n-1} y/dx^{n-1} + \ldots = Q(x)$.
— **explanations:** *see* Psychological linguistics: theories of learning in relation to language (M) 444
— **filter:** *see* Filter (G).
— **group codes:** *see* Information space 222
— **matrix type fixed store:** *see* Fixed stores and control by microprogram 182
**LINEAR OSCILLATOR.** Any device whose output voltage is proportional to sin *wt*, where *w* is a constant and *t* is the time after a suitable instant.
— **perspective:** *see* Perception, stereopsis as an aspect of 369
**LINEAR PROGRAMMING.** Mathematical techniques for optimizing a linear function subject to linear constraints (e.g. in operations research). As a general example, the problem might be to find the non-negative values of $x_1, x_2, \ldots x_i, \ldots x_n$ for which $\sum_{i=1}^{n} a_i x_i$ is a maximum, subject to $m$ linear constraints, namely $\sum_{i=1}^{n} b_{ij} x_i = c_j$, where $j = 1, 2, \ldots m$.
— **regulator:** *see* Control by the maximum principle 103
— **transformation:** *see* Transformation (G).
**Linearized systems, dynamic description of:** *see* Pseudo-random binary signals, use of... 433
**Lingua franca:** *see* Relations between languages: lingua franca 480; Language varieties: language and dialect (M) 243; Relations between languages: introduction 470; Relations between languages: bilingualism (M) 473
**Linguacy:** *see* Writing (M) 627
**Linguistic areas:** *see* Relations between languages: introduction 470
— **form:** *see* Form (2), linguistic form, formal item (G).
— **Form: Algebraic Linguistics** 270
— **Form: Generative Grammar** 272
— **Form: Paradigmatic** 273
— **Form: Syntagmatic** 276
— **Form: System and Structure** 278
— **Form: Transformational Theory** 280

**Linguistic geography:** *see* Language varieties: language and dialect 245
— **research:** *see* Computational linguistics: introduction 50
— **responses:** *see* Speech perception 548
— **structure:** *see* Psychological linguistics: theories of learning in relation to language 444; Phonetics, acoustic 391
— **stylistics:** *see* Language varieties: stylistics 259
— **systems, components of:** *see* Computational linguistics: introduction 50
— **unit:** *see* Unit (1), linguistic unit (G). Psychological linguistics: theories of learning in relation to language 444
— **units, acoustic characteristics of:** *see* Phonetics, acoustic 391
**Linguistics, algebraic:** *see* Linguistic form: algebraic linguistics 270; Linguistic form: generative grammar (M) 272
—, **computational:** *see* Computational linguistics: introduction 49
—, **descriptive:** *see* Language varieties: register (M) 251
—, **general:** *see* Foreword XI
—, **institutional:** *see* Language varieties: language and dialect 243; Language varieties: register 251
—, **sociological:** *see* Language varieties: register (M) 251
— **structural:** *see* Language varieties: stylistics (M) 259; Semantics: field theories (M) 504
**Lining:** *see* Writing 628
**LINK (1).** A computer instruction which enables the main program to be rejoined at the conclusion of a subroutine.
**LINK (2).** *See:* Interfix (G)
—, **mediational:** *see* Mediational link (G).
— **stack, sub-routine:** *see* Stacks 564
**Lip position:** *see* Phonetics, auditory 397
**Liquids:** *see* Phonology: distinctive features (M) 404
**LIST.** The contents of a computer store arranged to receive elements whose size and number are not known in advance. Each element is accompanied by a *pointer* giving the address of the next element in the list. *See:* Algebraic manipulation using lists 12
— **processing:** *see* Symbol manipulation by digital computer 596
— **processing, low-level:** *see* Symbol manipulation by digital computer 597
— **-processing language:** *see* Symbol manipulation by digital computer 596
**LIST STRUCTURE.** A list, any element of which may be either a member of a well-defined set of 'basic' elements (i.e. elements that are not themselves lists) or, recursively, a list structure. *See:* Symbol manipulation by digital computer 595
**Lists:** *see* Algebraic manipulation using lists 12
—, **use of, in algebraic manipulation:** *see* Algebraic manipulation using lists 12
**Literacy:** *see* Writing (M) 631

**Literature:** *see* Language varieties: register 254
**LOAN-EXTENSION.** The extension of the *meaning* of a particular *lexical item* in one language on analogy with the wider meaning or polysemy of the equivalent lexical item in another language. *See:* Relations between languages: bilingualism 473
**LOAN-RENDITION.** Like *loan-translation*, except that the correspondence between the morphemes in the 'source' language and those in the borrowing language is only approximate. *See:* Relations between languages: bilingualism 473
**LOAN-TRANSLATION.** The translation of individual *morphemes* of one language into their nearest equivalent in another language. *See:* Relations between languages: bilingualism 473; Relations between languages: loans and loanwords 482
**Loans:** *see* Relations between languages: introduction 470
**Loans and loanwords:** *see* Relations between languages: loans and loanwords 482
**Loanshifts:** *see* Relations between languages: loans and loanwords 482
**LOANWORD.** A word transferred directly from one *language* (3) to another. *See:* Relations between languages: loans and loanwords 482; Relations between languages: bilingualism 473; Relations between languages: comparative philology 475
**Local area:** *see* Local networks 284
— **exchange:** *see* Local networks 284
— **Networks** 284
**LOCALIZE.** If the function identifying a model with a real system is such that each unit in the model corresponds to some tangible entity (like a neuron or a part of a brain) or to some experimentally manipulable entity (like short term memory) the identification is said to be *localized*. If not, it is said to be *distributed*. *See:* Psychology, use of models (learning) 450
**LOCATION.** A part of a computer store, where signals are written and read by specifying its *address*; unlike a *register* which has no address and is specified implicitly.
**Logging, data:** *see* Data (G).
**LOGIC DESIGN, LOGIC.** Design of the working relations between the components of a switching network (e.g. to achieve the behaviour required from a digital component module). *Logic element*, *Logic gate*. Any of the smallest coherent units, whatever their *Boolean* function, included in a logic design. *Logic symbols*. Representation of logic element used in circuit drawing.
**LOGIC ELEMENT (GATE).** A module which receives a number of digital input signals and generates a single digital output signal, i.e. 0 or 1. The following types have been defined for up to two input signals, but some definitions may be extended to more than two:

| And Element | | Not-and element | | 
|---|---|---|---|
| Input | Output | Input | Output |
| A B | | A B | |
| 0 0 | 0 | 0 0 | 1 |
| 0 1 | 0 | 0 1 | 1 |
| 1 0 | 0 | 1 0 | 1 |
| 1 1 | 1 | 1 1 | 0 |

| Or Element | | Nor Element | |
|---|---|---|---|
| 0 0 | 0 | 0 0 | 1 |
| 0 1 | 1 | 0 1 | 0 |
| 1 0 | 1 | 1 0 | 0 |
| 1 1 | 1 | 1 1 | 0 |

| Equivalence Element | | Non-equivalence Element | |
|---|---|---|---|
| 0 0 | 1 | 0 0 | 0 |
| 0 1 | 0 | 0 1 | 1 |
| 1 0 | 0 | 1 0 | 1 |
| 1 1 | 1 | 1 1 | 0 |

| Not Element | 0 | 1 |
|---|---|---|
| | 1 | 0 |

—, **formal:** *see* Formal logic (G).
**Logico-rhetorical:** *see* Relations between languages: semantic change (M) 483
**Long features:** *see* Linguistic form: transformational theory 283
— **-term memory:** *see* Psychological linguistics: psycholinguistic studies of syntax (M) 439
— **term memory store:** *see* Models for human memory 311
**LOOP.** A sequence of program instructions which must be carried out by a computer a counted number of times, or until some other criterion is satisfied. Each completion of the sequence is called a *cycle*.
   *Closed*: loop, open loop. *See:* Feedback control (G)
—, **closed:** *see* Feedback control (G).
**Loops, feedback, neurally mediated:** *see* Neurally mediated feedback loops (G).
**Loudness:** *see* Phonetics, acoustic (M) 391; Speech perception 548
**Low:** *see* Phonetics, auditory 398
**LOW-LEVEL LANGUAGE.** A language for conveying instructions to a computer which needs only a simple *compiler*. *See:* High level (G).
— **-level list processing:** *see* Symbol manipulation by digital computer 597
— **pass filter:** *see* Filter (G).
**LUMINANCE.** A physical measure of the brightness of an illuminated surface. It is expressed in *candelas per square metre*, and 1 cd/m² may be envisaged as a square metre of the surface giving about the same 'light' as a standard candle. Alternatively, luminance can be expressed in terms of the *foot lambert*, which is 3.426 cd/m².
**Luminous intensity:** *see* Perception of colour 361

**M sequence:** *see* Chain code (G).
**MACHINE.** Any of the tools of man. (E.R.F.W. Crossman. Man-machine communication and ergonomics.)
—, **adaptive:** *see* Adaptive machine or system (G).
—, **automatic:** *see* Automatic machine (G).
— **language:** *see* Object language (G).
—, **limited register:** *see* Automata, infinite-state 36
—, **self-adaptive:** *see* Learning (G).
—, **state of:** *see* State of a machine (G).
—, **theorem proving by:** *see* Theorem proving by machine 616
**MACHINE TRANSLATION, M.T.** Translation of *natural-language texts* by means of a machine (a digital computer). *See:* Computational linguistics: machine translation 51; Computational linguistics: introduction 49; Linguistic form: generative grammar (M) 272
—, **Turing:** *see* Automata, infinite-state 35; Linguistic form: generative grammar (M) 273; Linguistic form: transformational theory (M) 280; Turing machine (G). Unsolvable problems 623
**Machines, learning:** *see* Adaptive control theory 9; Learning machines: a unified view 261
—, **post:** *see* Automata, infinite-state 35
—, **teaching:** *see* Adaptive control theory 9
**MACRO-INSTRUCTION.** In an assembly language, a single instruction which the compiler translates into several machine language instructions. *See:* Assembly languages 27
**Macro-instructions, conditional assembly of:** *see* Assembly languages 27
**Magnetic Recording** 291
— **storage media:** *see* Information storage and retrieval 224
**Man-Machine Communication and Ergonomics** 301
— **in Control Systems** 307
**Management, storage:** *see* Computers, multiaccess to 65
**MANIFEST.** A relatively abstract linguistic entity is *manifested* (or *realized*) by a relatively concrete one if the presence of the latter signals the presence of the former. In particular, a *slot* (or *grammatical function*) is *manifested* in a particular *utterance* by the *item* which 'fills' it (as a noun-phrase can fill the slot 'subject'). *See:* Grammar (structural) 198
**Manipulation, algebraic, using lists:** *see* Algebraic manipulation using lists 12
—, **symbol, by digital computer:** *see* Symbol manipulation by digital computer 594
**MANNER OF ARTICULATION.** An articulatory description of a *contoid* specifies (among other things) its *place of articulation* and its *manner* (or *mode*) *of articulation;* the manner of articulation is the type of constriction of the *vocal tract*—plosive, fricative, etc. *See:* Phonetics, articulatory 395
**Many-one mapping:** *see* Transformation (G).
**Map, topological:** *see* Topological map (G).
**Mapping:** *see* Transformation (G).
**Marginal languages:** *see* Relations between languages: lingua franca 480

**MARKED.** For some sets a distinction can be made between the *unmarked* member and all the other members, which are therefore *marked*. *See:* Psychological linguistics: psychological aspects of semantic structure 443

**Marked member:** *see* Psychological linguistics: psychological aspects of semantic structure 443

**MARKER (1).** The *marker* (1) of a linguistic entity is its *realization;* marker (1) is used especially for the features which identify *grammatical constructions* (1), e.g. '*and*' is treated as a marker of *coordination* in English. *See:* Grammar (structural) (M) 202; Linguistic form: syntagmatic (M) 276; Semantics: meaning and reference (M) 507

**MARKER (2), SEMANTIC MARKER.** An *item's meaning* can, it is said, be analysed into a number of *semantic markers*, which are *components* or *features* also found in the meanings of other items, and a *distinguisher*, which is the residue of meaning after the markers have been deducted. *See:* Psychological linguistics: psychological aspects of semantic structure 442; Semantics: introduction 499; Psychological linguistics: psycholinguistic studies of syntax 439

—, **phrase:** *see* Linquistic form: transformational theory, 282; Psychological linquistics: psycholinguistic studies of syntax (M) 439

—, **phrase, final derived:** *see* Linguistic form: transformational theory 282

**Markers, register:** *see* Language varieties: register (M) 252

—, **syntactic:** *see* Psychological linguistics: psychological aspects of semantic structure 442

**Markov algorithms:** *see* Unsolvable problems 624

— **estimate:** *see* Control, identification techniques for 121

**MARKOV PROCESS (DISCRETE).** A *process* in which each symbol influences, without uniquely determining, the selection of the succeeding symbol, and does *not directly* influence subsequent symbols. *See:* Random signals and noise 454; *Markov process of order m*. A (device that produces a) sequence such that the conditional probability of any symbol being used as the $(2+m)$th symbol.

$P(a_{r+m}/a_1, a_2, \ldots a_{r+m-1})$
$= P(a_{r+m}/a_r a_{r+1} \ldots a_{r+m-1})$

i.e. only the previous $m$ symbols directly influence any symbol. Thus a *random process* is a Markov process of order 0. *See:* Statistics of language: introduction 569

**Masking phenomena:** *see* Perception of sound 367

**Matching:** *see* Problem solving 415

**Mathematical programming:** *see* Optimization of industrial processes 347

**Matrices, Hadamard:** *see* Information space 222

**MATRIX (1).** A *distinctive-feature matrix* (or *structural matrix*) is a two-dimensional *representation* of (a part of) a sentence *generated* by a *transformational-generative grammar;* each column represents one *phonological segment*, and each row represents a *phonetic feature* (3) which is marked as present, absent or irrelevant in that segment. *See:* Linguistic form: transformational theory 280

**MATRIX (2)** An arrangement of numbers in $m$ columns and $n$ rows. For example, in linear transformations, it is used for mapping a vector of $n$ dimensions into a vector space of $m$ dimensions; in bilinear form it is used for expressing a scalar product of two vectors of dimensions $n$ and $m$. *Binary matrix.* A matrix of $m$ columns and $n$ rows, in which every number is either 1 or 0. *Square matrix.* A matrix for which $m = n$. *Symmetric matrix.* A square matrix in which the numbers are equal if they are in positions which are 'reflections' of each other in the *principal diagonal*, i.e. $a_{ij} = a_{ji}$. *Principal diagonal*. The sequence of positions in a square matrix $(1,1), (2,2)\ldots(n, n)$, conventionally running from top left to bottom right. *Identity matrix.* A square matrix, of appropriate size, in which all numbers are zero except those in the principal diagonal, which are all 1.

—, **binary:** *see* Matrix (2) (G).

—, **communication:** *see* Communication matrix (G).

—, **covariance:** *see* Covariance matrix (G).

—, **identity:** *see* Matrix (2) (G).

**MATRIX MULTIPLICATION.** When two matrices have the dimensions $m \times n$ and $n \times q$ they are said to be *conformable* and their product can be defined and found. It is defined as the matrix of dimensions $m \times q$ in which the term in position $(i, k)$ is

$$c_{ik} = a_{i1}b_{1k} + a_{i2}b_{2k} + \ldots a_{im}b_{mk},$$

i.e. $c_{ik}$ is the *inner product* of the $i$th row of the first matrix and the $k$th column of the second.

**MATRIX STORE.** A *core* store in which the cores are arranged in a matrix for convenience and economy of assembly.

—, **phonological:** *see* Matrix (1) (G). Linguistic form: transformational theory (M) 280

—, **square:** *see* Matrix (2) (G).

—, **structural:** *see* Matrix (1) (G). Phonology: contrast and opposition (M) 401

—, **symmetric:** *see* Matrix (2) (G).

— **type fixed store, linear:** *see* Fixed stores and control by microprogram 182

**Maximum expected value criterion:** *see* Sensory discrimination, measurement of 513

— **likelihood decoder:** *see* Error correcting codes 175

— **principle:** *see* Control by the maximum principle 102

— **principle, control by:** *see* Control by the maximum principle 101

— **principle, geometric interpretation of:** *see* Control by the maximum principle 104

— **principle, Pontryagin:** *see* Control, stability and 150

**Meaning:** *see* Computational linguistics: machine translation (M) 51; Linguistic form: paradigmatic (M) 273; Linguistic form: system and structure

(M) 278; Psychological linguistics: psychological aspects of semantic structure 442; Relations between languages: introduction (M) 470; Relations between languages: comparative philology (M) 475; Relations between languages: loans and loanwords (M) 482; Relations between languages: semantic change 484; Relations between languages: typological and areal classifications 486; Semantics: context and collocation 504; Semantics: field theories 505; Semantics: meaning and reference 507
—, **cognitive**: *see* Semantics: introduction 499
—, **conceptual**: *see* Semantics: introduction 499
—, **connotative**: *see* Semantics: introduction (M) 499
—, **contextual**: *see* Semantics: context and collocation 503
—, **denotative**: *see* Semantics: introduction 499
—, **lexical**: *see* Semantics: introduction (M) 499
**Meaningful**: *see* Grammar (structural) 188
**Means-ends analysis**: *see* Problem solving 415
**Measurement of sensory discrimination**: *see* Sensory discrimination, measurement of 512
— **psychological, information theory in**: *see* Information theory in psychological measurement 232
**Measures of discrimination**: *see* Sensory discrimination, measurement of 514
**Mechanics, cochlear**: *see* Cochlear mechanics 44
—, **skin**: *see* Non-neural elements in receptor systems 338
**MECHANISM.** The functioning of a module or a process; a module or process when in operation.
—, **Hering**: *see* Perception, visual 378
—, **speech**: *see* Speech mechanism (G). Phonetics, acoustic 391
—, **transport**: *see* Transport mechanism (G).
**Mechanisms of the colour-vision system**: *see* Perception of colour 362
**Mechanolinguistics**: *see* Computational linguistics: introduction 49
**MECHANORECEPTOR.** A receptor where mechanical energy (more particularly) is absorbed to produce nerve impulses. *See*: Receptors: relation between the stimuli and the activity in single primary units 465; Receptors: representation of information about stimuli in populations 467
**Media**: *see* Writing (M) 627
—, **magnetic storage**: *see* Information storage and retrieval 224
**MEDIATE.** Provide the middle part, e.g. "neurally mediated feedback loops play an important role in speech control".
**MEDIATE CONSTITUENT.** The *mediate constituents* (on a particular *level* (1)) of an *item* are all its constituents on that level except its *immediate constituents*. *See*: Linguistic form: syntagmatic 277
**MEDIATIONAL LINK.** In Stimulus-Response Psychology. An S-R link whose stimulus and response are both entirely internal to the organism.
**MEDIUM.** The base on which signals are recorded and stored, e.g. paper tape, magnetic tape, cathode-ray tube.

**Medium**: *see* Mode of discourse (G); Language varieties: 251; Phonology: contrast and opposition 401; Phonology: phonemes and broad transcription 409
**MEDULLATED NERVE FIBRE.** An axon which is surrounded by a myelin sheath. This is interrupted along its length by *nodes of Ranvier*, and impulse conduction is *saltatory*. *See*: Nerve and muscle, initiation and conduction of impulses in 314; Receptors as transducers 455
**Member, marked**: *see* Psychological linguistics: psychological aspects of semantic structure 443
—, **unmarked**: *see* Psychological linguistics: psychological aspects of semantic structure 443
**Membrane, IS**: *see* Neuronal nets 323
—, **somato-dendritic**: *see* Somato-dendritic membrane (G).
**Memory, human, models for**: *see* Models for human memory 311
—, **immediate**: *see* Information theory in psychological measurement 233
— **improvement**: *see* Models for human memory 311
—, **long-term**: *see* Psychological linguistics: psycholinguistic studies of syntax (M) 439
—, **short-term**: *see* Psychological linguistics: psycholinguistic studies of syntax (M) 439
— **space**: *see* Psychological linguistics: psycholinguistic studies of syntax 440
— **store, long term**: *see* Models for human memory 311
— **store, short term**: *see* Models for human memory 311
— **store, very short term**: *see* Models for human memory 311
**MENTALISM.** *Mentalistic* linguistics tries to study the (postulated) mental states or 'concepts' which are said to be expressed by language. *See*: Semantics: introduction 499
**Mentalistic**: *see* Semantics: introduction 499
**Mentation**: *see* Psychology, use of models (learning) 449
**Merge sorting**: *see* Sorting techniques 544
**MERGING.** The combining of two or more sorted sequences of information so that the final sequence obeys the same rules of sorting as the original sequences. *See*: Sorting techniques 545
**Mesencephalon**: *see* Neuronal nets 320
**METALANGUAGE.** The language used to *describe* a *language system*; a *metalinguistic* statement is a statement about a *language* or *text*.
**METALINGUISTICS.** The study of the relations between a *language system* and all the other cultural systems of the society using it. *See*: Semantics: meaning and reference 509
**Metencephalon**: *see* Neuronal nets 320
**Meter, air-flow**: *see* Phonetics, experimental 400
**Method, comparative**: *see* Relations between languages: introduction 470; Relations between languages; comparative philology 475
—, **Frank and Wolfe**: *see* Optimization of industrial processes 348

**Method, gradient, hill climbing by:** *see* Control, hill climbing in 117
—, **Kelley's:** *see* Optimization of industrial processes 343
—, **Monte Carlo:** *see* Monte Carlo method (G).
— **of constant stimulus differences:** *see* Sensory discrimination, measurement of 517
— **of interchanging pairs:** *see* Sorting techniques 544
— **of limits (ML):** *see* Sensory discrimination, measurement of 520
— **of production:** *see* Sensory discrimination, measurement of 523
— **of reproduction (MR):** *see* Sensory discrimination, measurement of 522
— **of single stimuli (MSS):** *see* Sensory discrimination, measurement of 518
— **of steepest ascent:** *see* Optimization, automatic 343; Optimization of industrial processes 347
—, **simplex:** *see* Optimization of industrial processes 347
—, **staircase:** *see* Sensory discrimination, measurement of 521
—, **staircase, transformed response:** *see* Sensory discrimination, measurement of 521
— **Zoutendyk's:** *see* Optimization of industrial processes 348
**Methods, root locus:** *see* Control, stability and 150
**METRIC.** Any relationship (D) between two points in a space, which is defined in such a way that, for three points $a$, $b$, $c$
$D(a, a) = 0$
$D(a, b) = D(b, a) > 0$ if $b \neq a$
$D(a, b) + D(b, c) \geq D(a, c)$
The last is analogous to the Euclid proposition 'any two sides of a triangle are together greater than the third side'. *See:* Information space 221
—, **evaluation:** *see* Evaluation metric (G); Psychological linguistics: psycholinguistic studies of syntax 439
**MICROELECTRODE.** A fine glass capillary tube containing saline solution, or a fine metal rod insulated except at the tip, suitable for picking up signals passing through a neuron. The diameter of an *extracellular* microelectrode should be 1–5 microns; of an *intracellular* (i.e. for penetrating into a neuron) should not be more than 1 micron.
**MICROFICHE.** A sheet of film, 6in. by 4in., containing the negative images of up to 40 pages of text. *See:* Scientific documentation 497; Information storage and retrieval 223
**MICROFILM.** Transparent photographs, often on rolls of 35 mm film, of the pages of documents. *See:* Scientific documentation 497
**Micrograph, electron:** *see* Electron micrograph (G)
**MICROMINIATURIZATION.** Any of several manufacturing techniques for making connected electronic circuits containing a number of different components in a small volume of material. For example, in a crystal of semiconducting material it is possible to form diodes, resistors, transistors etc, with appropriate electrical connexions between them.

**MICROPROGRAM.** A sequence of instructions, usually contained in a *fixed store* of a computer, necessarily carried out in full as part of an operation of the *control unit;* or the entire set of such sequences stored in any particular computer. *See:* Fixed stores and control by microprogram 181
—, **fixed stores and control by:** *see* Fixed stores and control by microprogram 181
**Mid:** *see* Phonetics, auditory 398
**Middle ear:** *see* Non-neural elements in receptor systems 339
**MINIMAL PAIR.** A pair of *items* differing, at least on the *level* (1) being investigated (usually the *phonological level*), only in one respect, e.g. two words which are phonologically identical except at one place, where one has one *phoneme* and the other has another. *See:* Phonology: phonemes and broad transcription (M) 409
**MINIMAX.** A minimax plan or strategy is one which, in the *mini*mum number of steps, finds the *maxi*mum (or minimum) value of a function of one or more variables.
**Mixed receptor assemblies:** *see* Receptors: representation of information about stimuli in populations 467
**MODALITY.** A mode of manifestation.
**MODE.** If a module or machine has alternative sets of input and output terminals, each operational set of input and output terminals determines a *mode* (of operation).
**MODE, MODE OF DISCOURSE.** Non-dialectal *varieties* of language (*registers* (1)) may be classified on a number of dimensions, one of which is *mode of discourse* (or *medium*). On this dimension registers are classified according to the medium of communication (e.g. printed texts, letters, tape recordings…). *See:* Language varieties: register 251; Language varieties: stylistics (M) 260; Writing (M) 627
**MODE, CONVERSATIONAL.** A way of using a computer, in which, for example, the user sits at a typewriter which records his messages to the computer and the computer's responses to his messages. Or any system of communication between man and computer which produces responses at about the same speed as human conversation. *See:* Computer language design requirements 54
**Mode of Articulation:** *see* Manner of articulation (G)
— **-register:** *see* Language varieties: register 251
**MODEL.** A machine, or a program, or a set of mathematical relations whose response to appropriate inputs approximates to that of an actual system. *See:* Control by model reference 106; Discrete models for forecasting and control 162; Grammar (structural) 192; Linguistic form: system and structure 279
—, **applicational-generative:** *see* Linguistic form: generative grammar (M) 272
— **exploration:** *see* Computer simulation of human thought processes 60
—, **passive:** *see* Speech perception 551

**Model reference:** *see* Control, hill climbing in  119
— **reference, control by:** *see* Control by model reference  106
—, **reference, for control:** *see* Control by hybrid computers  100
— **representation:** *see* Computer simulation of human thought processes  60
**Modela:** *see* Grammar (structural) (M)  186
**Models, computational:** *see* Psychology, use of models (learning)  447
—, **cybernetic:** *see* Psychology, use of models (learning)  447
—, **discrete, for forecasting and control:** *see* Discrete models for forecasting and control  162
—, **fast-time, for predictive control:** *see* Control, predictive, using fast-time models  140
— **for Human Memory**  311
—, **probability:** *see* Models for human memory  312
—, **queueing:** *see* Models for human memory  312
—, **strength:** *see* Models for human memory  312
—, **use of, in psychology:** *see* Psychology, use of models (learning)  447
—, **vocal tract:** *see* Speech synthesis  559
**Modems:** *see* Data transmission  160
**Modifications:** *see* Phonology: prosodic features  411
**MODULAR NET.** A network of *modules* and *connexions*. *Contact net*. A net wherein the output of each module uniquely specifies the input, e.g. relay switching circuits. *Gating net*. A net wherein not every module is such that its output uniquely specifies its input, e.g. it contains AND, OR or NOR *gates*. *Hammock net*. A series-parallel Contact net designed to be either open or closed, as a whole, with minimum chance of an error. *See:* Reliable computation with unreliable elements  485
**MODULATE.** To vary (a stationary process) for the purpose of conveying information, e.g. *pulse-width modulation*, frequency modulated radio waves.
**MODULATION NOISE.** Noise from a magnetic tape which has recorded a signal, caused by imperfections in the coating, such as voids and agglomerations. *See:* Magnetic recording  299
—, **pulse amplitude:** *see* Pulse amplitude modulation (G)
—, **pulse frequency:** *see* Pulse frequency modulation (G)
—, **pulse width:** *see* Pulse width modulation (G)
**MODULE.** Any device, living or mechanical, which receives and emits signals, the emitted signals (output, behaviour) being partly or wholly influenced by the received signals (input). In relation to automata (state-changing machines) a modulate is any one-state component of such a machine.
**MODULO:** *see* Counter (G).
**MONITOR.** To make available for human interpretation or for computation (e.g. to monitor particular data signals from a plant or other process). (Noun) A device used for monitoring.
**Monocular depth cues:** *see* Perception, stereopsis as an aspect of  369
**Monographs:** *see* Statistics of language: introduction  569
**Monophthongal:** *see* Phonetics, auditory  398

**MONOSYSTEMIC,** A *monosystemic* (as opposed to a *polysystemic*) description of a *language* (1) treats it as a single *system* (1), rather than a set of interrelated but relatively independent systems. *See:* Relations between languages: loans and loanwords (M)  482
**MONOTONIC RELATION.** A relation between two variables such that an increase in value of either variable is accompanied usually by an increase and never by a decrease in value of the other.
**MONTE CARLO METHOD.** A method of solving statistical problems by applying mathematical operations to random numbers.
**MORPH.** If an *utterance* is *represented* both as a *string* of *morphemes* and as a string of *phonemes*, a sub-string of phonemes which can be mapped onto a single morpheme is a *morph:* for some linguists the morph is a member (an *allomorph*) of the morpheme, but for others it *realizes* the morpheme. *See:* Grammar (structural)  187
—, **fused:** *see* Fused morph (G)
—, **portmanteau:** *see* Portmanteau morph (G); Grammar (structural)  189
**MORPHEME.** *Morpheme* is the name of the smallest *grammatical unit* (2); it may or may not be possible to map every morpheme onto a string of *phonemes* in the *phonological representation* of the same *utterance*, and for some linguists even *features* can be treated as morphemes. It may or may not be possible to assign a *meaning* to a morpheme. *See:* Grammar (structural)  187; Phonology: contrast and opposition (M)  401; Relations between languages: introduction (M)  470; Relations between languages: typological and areal classifications (M)  486; Semantics: introduction (M)  499; Phonology: distinctive features (M)  404; Phonology: prosodic features (M)  411; Relations between languages: bilingualism (M)  473; Relations between languages: loans and loanwords (M)  482; Writing (M)  627
**Morphemes, surface:** *see* Writing (M)  627
—, **unique:** *see* Grammar (structural)  188
**Morphological integration:** *see* Relations between languages: loans and loanwords (M)  482
**Morphological level:** *see* Semantics: field theories (M)  504
**Morphological structure:** *see* Relations between languages: comparative philology (M)  475
**MORPHOLOGY (1).** *Grammar* (2), is often divided into two parts: *morphology* (1), the rules for forming words, and *syntax* (2), the rules for using words. *See:* Grammar (structural)  189; Phonology: contrast and opposition (M)  401; Relations between languages: lingua franca (M)  480; Relations between languages: typological and areal classifications (M)  486
**MORPHOLOGY (2).** A distinction may usefully be made between the *syntax* (3) of an *item* (describing the rules for using that item) and its *morphology* (2) (describing its own *structure* (2), i.e. the relations among its own parts); for morphology (2) no special

status is given to the word, as opposed to the phrase, clause or sentence, all of which have morphology (2), though they would be excluded from *morphology* (1). See: Linguistic form: paradigmatic  273
—, **comparative:** see Relations between languages: comparative philology  475
—, **level of:** see Relations between languages: introduction  470
**MORPHOPHONEME, MORPHOPHONOLOGY.** *Morphophonology* deals with the relations between *morphemes* and *phonemes*. In order to reduce the number of morphemes which have more than one phonemic 'shape' *(allomorph)* it may be possible to introduce *morphophonemes*, which are of the same size as phonemes, but are *realized* by different *phonemes* according to the *environment*. See: Grammar (structural)  189
**Morphophonemic:** see Phonology: distinctive features (M)  404
**Morphophonology:** see Morphophoneme, morphophonology (G); Grammar (structural)  189
**Morphosemantic approach:** see Relations between languages: semantic change  484
— **theories:** see Semantics: field theories  505
**Morphs, cumulative:** see Grammar (structural)  189
—, **fused:** see Grammar (structural)  186
**Morris:** see Semantics: sign and symbol (M)  510
**Motion parallax:** see Perception, stereopsis as an aspect of  369
**MOTIVATE.** An animal is assumed to be motivated to behave in a particular way when it does so, especially if stimuli are present which have previously been observed to elicit similar behaviour. See: Animal learning  21; Animal motivation  24
**MOTIVATION, MOTIVATED.** A linguistic *sign* is *motivated* if the relation between its *form* (1) and its *content* or *function* follows a general pattern valid for other signs in the language; but even if motivated, a sign may still be *arbitrary*. See: Semantics: sign and symbol  510
—, **animal:** see Animal motivation  24
— **states:** see Animal motivation  24
**Motivational states, initiation of:** see Animal motivation  24
— **states, termination of:** see Animal motivation  25
**MOTONEURON, MOTOR NEURON.** A neuron which carries *motor signals*, i.e. whose outgoing impulses contribute to the control of a muscle, and whose input comes from higher centres and neural feedback loops.
**Motor control:** see Information theory in psychological measurement  234
— **nerve:** see Nerve (G)
— **signals:** see Muscle spindles (G)
— **theory:** see Speech perception  548
**Movement, amoeboid:** see Homeostasis in the single cell  217
— **detectors:** see Receptors: relation between the stimuli and the activity in single primary units  464
— **sensitivity:** see Perception, visual  380

**Movements, eye:** see Eye movements  176
—, **saccadic:** see Eye movements  177
**MULTIACCESS.** A system of computer controls whereby several users can be *on-line* to a computer at the same time. Each user receives reports on errors, need for input data etc. direct from the computer and may be able to respond to them at once. See: Computers, multiaccess to  63
— **to computers:** see Computers, multiaccess to  63
**Multidimensional:** see Dimension (G)
— **classification:** see Dimension (G)
**Multilateral opposition:** see Phonology: distinctive features (M)  404
**MULTINOMIALLY.** As a result of the variations of two or more *independent* variables.
**Multiple input systems:** see Pseudorandom binary signals, use of...  436
**MULTIPLEX TELEMETRY.** The telemetry of many sorts of observables connected with one process, with the help of a *multiplexer*.
**MULTIPLEXER.** A module with many inputs and a single output. It stores the input signals and selects one of them at a time for retransmission unaltered. See: Computers, multiaccess to  63
**MULTIPLEXING.** The technique of replicating modules and connexions to improve the reliability of a system. See: Reliable computation with unreliable elements  487
**Multiplication, matrix:** see Matrix multiplication (G)
**MULTIPLIER (1).** In a digital machine, a module which takes in two digital numeric signals in succession and outputs their product.
**MULTIPLIER (2).** In an analog system, a module which takes in two analog signals simultaneously and continuously, and generates an output signal proportional to their product.
**MULTIPROGRAMMING.** The functioning of a computer when it has several programs in an internal store and switches from one to another to avoid idling. See: Computer operating systems  57
**Multistage decision processes:** see Dynamic programming  168
**Multivariable control systems:** see Control systems, multivariable  151
**MULTIVARIATE CONCEPTS.** Concepts which correspond to a *multidimensional* classification system. See: Concept identification—information processing approaches  82
**Muscle, initiation and conduction of impulses in:** see Nerve and muscle, initiation and conduction of impulses in  314
**MUSCLE SPINDLES (FUSI).** Receptors in muscles, having an afferent nerve supply, i.e. fibres which transmit impulses to the CNS. Efferent fibres *(fusimotor)* transmit signals from the CNS to the *intrafusal* muscle fibres associated with the spindles. See: Receptors in joints and muscles  461
**Muscles, extra-ocular:** see Eye movements  176
—, **receptors in:** see Receptors in joints and muscles  460

**Mutual inhibition:** *see* Sensory processes   527
— **intelligibility:** *see* Language varieties: language and dialect   243
**Mutually expectant elements:** *see* Linguistic form: system and structure (M)   278
**Myelencephalon:** *see* Neuronal nets   320
**Mylar:** *see* Magnetic recording   299

**Naive subject:** *see* Subject (G).
**Name:** *see* Relations between languages: semantic change (M)   484; Semantics: meaning and reference   508; Semantics: sign and symbol   510
**NANOSECOND (ns).** $10^{-9}$ sec.
**NARROWBAND.** Having a narrow range of frequencies.
**NARROW PHONETIC TRANSCRIPTION.** A *narrow* (or *allophonic*) *transcription* differs from a *broad* (or *phonemic*) one in that it uses more symbols for each *phoneme* than the latter, which represents each phoneme by a single symbol in the transcription. Each symbol in a narrow transcription represents an *allophone*, or set of allophones; a narrow transcription is a *phonetic representation* rather than a *phonological* one. *See:* Phonology: phonemes and broad transcription   409; Phonetics: articulatory   393; Phonetics, auditory   396
**Nasal:** *see* Phonetics, articulatory (M)   391; Phonology: contrast and opposition   401
— **features:** *see* Linguistic form: transformational theory   283
**Nasalized:** *see* Phonetics, articulatory (M)   391; Phonetics, auditory   398
— **sounds:** *see* Phonetics, acoustic (M)   391
**Nasalization:** *see* Phonetics, auditory   398
**NATURAL LANGUAGE.** *Language-systems* are either *natural* or *artificial*, according to whether or not they have, or have had, any native speakers. *See:* Linguistic form: transformational theory (M)   280; Writing (M)   627; Linguistic form: generative grammar (M)   272; Psychological linguistics: psychological aspects of semantic structure (M)   442; Relations between languages: lingua franca (M)   480; Semantics: introduction (M)   499; Statistics of language: introduction (M)   567
**Nernst equation:** *see* Neuronal nets   323
**NERVE.** A living cell, whose specific function is the transmission of information. For its structure, *See:* Neuronal nets, Figs. 1 and 2. *Sensory nerve* (or *afferent* nerve). A nerve transmitting information to the *central nervous system*. *Motor nerve* (or *efferent* nerve). A nerve transmitting signal from the *central nervous system*.
— **impulse.** Action potential, q.v.
—, **afferent:** *see* Afferent nerve (G). Nerve (G).
— **and Muscle, Initiation and Conduction of Impulses in**   314
—, **efferent:** *see* Nerve (G).
— **fibre, medullated:** *see* Medullated nerve fibre (G).
— **fibre, sensory:** *see* Receptor as transducers   457

**Nerve, motor:** *see* Nerve (G).
—, **sensory:** *see* Nerve (G).
**Nervous system, central:** *see* Central nervous system (G).
— **System, Role of Pulse Distribution in Information Flow**   316
**Nested sentences:** *see* Linguistic form: generative grammar (M)   273
**NESTING.** A *string* of symbols is *nested* if the symbols within it can be paired off, the last symbol being paired with the first, the penultimate with the second, and so on. *See:* Psychological linguistics: psycholinguistic studies of syntax (M)   439; Writing (M)   627
**Net, contact:** *see* Modular net (G).
—, **gating:** *see* Modular net (G).
—, **hammock:** *see* Modular net (G).
—, **modular:** *see* Modular net (G).
**Nets, neuronal:** *see* Neuronal net (G); Neuronal nets   320
**Networks, local:** *see* Local networks   284
**Neural circuits:** *see* Reverberating activity (G).
**NEURALLY MEDIATED FEEDBACK LOOPS.** *Feedback control systems* (q.v.) in which neural pathways form part of the closed loop.
**NEURON.** Any nerve cell. For its structure, *See:* Neuronal nets, Figs. 1 and 2. *Pyramidal*, *Stellate*. Names and shapes, of two important types of neuron.
—, **accommodation by:** *see* Accommodation by a neuron (G).
—, **adaptation by:** *see* Adaptation by a neuron (G).
**NEURONAL NET.** A network of interacting nerve cells, acting as a *system*. *See:* Neuronal nets   320
— **Nets**   320
**NEUTRALIZATION.** An *opposition* between two categories A and B is *neutralized* under a given set of conditions if, under those conditions, either only one of A and B occurs, or a category occurs which could equally well be identified with either A or B. *See:* Phonology: distinctive features (M)   404
**Neyman-Pearson criterion:** *see* Sensory discrimination, measurement of   513
**Node:** *see* Linguistic form: syntagmatic (M)   277; Tree (G)
**Nodes of Ranvier:** *see* Medullated nerve fibre (G).
**NOISE.** That part of the output of a system which was not influenced by its input. *See:* Communication channel (G); Magnetic recording   299; Random signals and noise   453; Statistics of languages: structure of written English words (M)   581
—, **modulation:** *see* Magnetic recording   299; Modulation noise (G).
—, **white:** *see* Magnetic recording   299; White noise (G).
**Noisy communication channel:** *see* Communication channel (G).
**NOMINALISM.** The fallacy of confusing the attachment of a label (the name for a definitive property of a class of observables) with the provision of a causal explanation.
**NOMINAL VARIABLE.** A variable which is not con-

tinuous and measurable, such as the nationality or the hair colour of a person. *See:* Concept formation by artificial intelligence  76

**Non-interacting systems, control of aircraft as:** *see* Control of aircraft as two non-interacting systems  128

**Non-linear behaviour sequences:** *see* Psychological linguistics: theories of learning in relation to language (M)  444

**NON-LINEAR DIFFERENTIAL EQUATION.** A differential equation not of degree 1, such as

$$a(dy/dx)^2 + b(dy/dx) + c = 0.$$

**NON-LINEAR RELATION.** One in which the dependence of a quantity $y$ on a set of parameters $p_1, p_2, p_3 \ldots$ is not one of simple proportion, i.e. not all of the partial differential coefficients of $y$ with respect to $p_1, p_2, p_3$ are constants. Synonymous with *dynamic relation.*

**Non-linearities of a process:** *see* Dynamics of a process (G)

**Non-Neural Elements in Receptor Systems**  337
— **parts of the ear:** *see* Non-neural elements in receptor systems  338

**Non-sibilant fricatives:** *see* Phonology: distinctive features (M)  404

**NORMAL DISTRIBUTION, GAUSSIAN DISTRIBUTION.** The probability that a signal from such a distribution will have a value between $t$ and $(t + \delta t)$ is

$$p(t)\,\delta t = \frac{1}{\sigma \sqrt{(2\pi)}} e^{-\frac{t^2}{2\sigma^2}} \delta t.$$

The parameter $\sigma$ is called the *standard deviation.*
— **ogive:** *see* Ogive (G).

**Normative conception:** *see* Language varieties: register (M)  251

**Notation, infix:** *see* Infix notation (G).
—, **prefix:** *see* Polish representation (G).
—, **reverse Polish:** *see* Stacks  564

**NRZ RECORDING. NON-RETURN-TO-ZERO.** A binary magnetic recording technique, in which a '1' produces a reversal of magnetization in the tape, and a '0' produces no change. Thus a '1' followed by another '1' produces a return to the original magnetization. *See:* Magnetic recording  295

**NUCLEAR-BAG FIBRE.** Intrafusal *muscle* fibre, the nuclei of whose nerve cells are massed together in a swelling from which a sensory nerve dendrite receives impulses. *See:* Receptors in joints and muscles  460

**NUCLEAR-CHAIN FIBRE.** Intrafusal *muscle* fibre whose nuclei are strung out in a single row. Though they are shorter and narrower than nuclear-bag fibres, their function is similar. *See:* Receptors in joints and muscles  460
— **power plant, control of:** *see* Control by hybrid computers  97

**NUCLEUS.** The granule within a cell enabling it to live.
—, **lateral geniculate:** *see* Perception, stereopsis as an aspect of  372

**Number:** *see* Grammar (structural) (M)  205
—, **wave:** *see* Perception, visual  379

**Numbering, Godel:** *see* Unsolvable problems  624

**Numbers, Fibonacci:** *see* Optimization, automatic  342

**Nyquist criterion:** *see* Control, stability and  149

**Object:** *see* Grammar (structural) (M)  206

**OBJECT LANGUAGE.** The language into which a *translation* is made. In experimental psychology, a language of stimuli and responses appropriate to the organism (not the experimenter). For behaviour models, a language chosen as part of the 'social' language of the modelled species. *See:* Psychology, use of models (learning)  450. In computer science, the language of signals which the computer will obey, or work with, directly, i.e. the *machine language. See:* Computer language design requirements  54

**OBJECTIVE FUNCTION.** A measure of the performance of a system required to optimize several variables at once, such as speed, accuracy and economy. *See:* Man-machine communication and ergonomics  301

**Obligatory tagmemes:** *see* Grammar (structural)  198

**OBSERVABLE.** A system is observable if each of its *state* variables influences at least one of its output variables. *See:* Control systems, multivariable  151

**OBSERVATIONS.** Those signals from an *event* which enter a particular *system. See:* Similarity  535

**Observer, standard:** *see* Perception of colour  360

**Obstruent features:** *see* Linguistic form: transformational theory  283

**Ocean telephone cables:** *see* Telecommunication, global  604

**Off-line computer control:** *see* Control by hybrid computers  95

**'Off' units:** *see* Neuronal nets  331

**Ogden:** *see* Semantics: sign and symbol (M)  510

**OGIVE.** A curve which is *sigmoid* in shape:

*Normal ogive.* A curve whose equation is of the form

$$f(x) = \int_0^x p\,dx$$

where $p$ is the normal or Gaussian probability function proportional to

$$\exp\{-(x-\bar{x})^2/2\sigma^2\}$$

$\bar{x}$ being the mean value of $x$, and $\sigma$ its standard deviation.

**Olfactory brain:** *see* Neuronal nets  320

**One-one mapping:** *see* Transformation (G).

**On-line closed-loop computer control:** *see* Control by hybrid computers  97

**On-line computers for retrieval:** *see* Information storage and retrieval  230

**On-off control:** *see* Control, on-off  136
**On-off control, predictive:** *see* Control, on-off  140
**'On-off' units:** *see* Neuronal nets  331
**ON-LINE.** The relationship of two mechanical systems or of a machine and its user when their signals pass from one to the other without other human intervention.
**'On' units:** *see* Neuronal nets  331
**Open:** *see* Phonetics, auditory  397
**OPEN CLASS.** *Classes* are *open* or *closed;* an open class has a membership which may be definable but is much larger than that of a closed class, and can easily be added to by the addition of new *lexical items* or of new *constructions* (2). *See:* Grammar (structural)  201; Relations between languages: loans and loanwords  482
— **loop adaptive controller:** *see* Adaptive control theory  2
**OPEN LOOP CONTROL.** Is exhibited by a system in which an output variable is controlled directly by an input variable with or without power amplification. Contrast with *Feedback control.* P. H. Hammond.
**OPEN TRANSITION.** *Open transition* (or *plus juncture*) is the *juncture phoneme* found in the middle of strings of *phonemes*, often corresponding to a word or *morpheme boundary* in the grammatical representation, and showing that the phonemes next to it are represented by different *allophones* from those which would occur without the juncture.
**Openness, degrees of:** *see* Phonology: distinctive features (M)  404
**OPERAND.** Part of an instruction to a computer, namely the data to be operated upon or the addresses where these data are to be found. *See:* Computer peripherals and their control  59
**Operating small computers:** *see* Computer operating systems  57
— **systems, computer:** *see* Computer operating systems  57
**OPERATION (1).** Way of working.
**OPERATION (2).** The action of an operator (1)
—, **evolutionary:** *see* Optimization, automatic  344
—, **supervisory:** *see* Supervisory operation (G).
**OPERATOR (1).** Part of an instruction to a computer: the function which it must execute (e.g. plus, minus, read the contents of an address within a store, a place in a table, etc.). The data on which the operation is made consists of one or more *operands*.
**OPERATOR (2).** The human controller of a machine.
—, **differential:** *see* Differential operator (G).
—, **Sheffer stroke:** *see* Sheffer stroke operator (G).
**OPPOSITION.** A distinction is drawn, particularly in *phonology*, between relations of *contrast* (2) and relations of *opposition*. The relation of *substitution* among the members of a set which can all occur in the same *environment* is *opposition*, while the relation between two such sets, whose members cannot all occur in the same environment, is *contrast*. *See:* Phonology: contrast and opposition  401; Phonology: distinctive features  404;

Phonetics, acoustic (M)  391; Semantics: field theories (M)  504
**Opposition, bilateral:** *see* Phonology: distinctive features (M)  404
—, **equipollent:** *see* Phonology: distinctive features (M)  404
—, **gradual:** *see* Phonology: distinctive features (M)  404
—, **isolated:** *see* Phonology: distinctive features (M)  404
—, **multilateral:** *see* Phonology: distinctive features (M)  404
—, **phonological:** *see* Phonology: contrast and opposition  401; Phonology: phonemes and broad transcription  410
—, **privative:** *see* Phonology: distinctive features (M)  404
—, **proportional:** *see* Phonology: distinctive features (M)  404
**OPTIMAL CONTROL.** Operating the controls of a system so as to get the best out of it. *See:* Optimization, automatic  342; Control: basic elements  89; Control by hybrid computers  92; Control by the maximum principle  101; Control by stationary filtering and prediction  109; Control, on-off  136
— **return function:** *see* Dynamic programming  169
— **decision functions:** *see* Dynamic programming  169
— **switching:** *see* Control, on-off  138
**Optimality, principle of:** *see* Dynamic programming  169
**OPTIMIZATION** of a system. It is presupposed that there is a mathematical description of the system and all alternative systems, and that there is a measure of the effectiveness. Optimization is then setting the variables at values (or setting up the system) for which this measure attains the best possible value. *See:* Optimization, automatic  342
—, **Automatic**  342
— **of Industrial Processes**  345
**Optimizing control, dynamic:** *see* Control, predictive, using fast-time models  140
— **control, static:** *see* Control, predictive, using fast-time models  143
**Optimum control:** *see* Control by stationary filtering and prediction  110
— **sampled data system:** *see* Control by stationary filtering and prediction  111
**Optional tagmemes:** *see* Grammar (structural)  198
**Oral:** *see* Phonology: contrast and opposition (M)  401
**ORBIT.** The cavity holding the eyeball, in which it can rotate. *See:* Eye movements  176
**ORDER (1).** If *order* (1) is contrasted (in linguistics) with *sequence* it is taken to cover less superficial *syntagmatic relations* than the latter. Thus the *order* (1) of a set of *items* could include all the *dependency* and/or *constituency* relations among them.
**ORDER (2).** (Of a linear differential equation) the order of the highest order derivative which appears in it (e.g. the derivative $d^3f(x)/dx^3$ is of order 3).

**ORDER CODE.** A set of numbers, each representing one of the possible orders to a computer.

— **of control:** *see* Man-machine communication and ergonomics 304

**ORDERED PAIR.** Two symbols, whose information together is greater than separately; interchanging the symbols would alter the meaning. *See:* Symbol manipulation by digital computer 595

**ORDERED RULES.** If the rules in a *grammar*, or a part of a grammar, are *ordered* they can only be executed in a certain sequence, i.e. any given rule cannot be executed until all the earlier rules have been executed (or by-passed). This restriction may be imposed simply by numbering the rules, or it may be inherent in the conditions for applying each rule.

**Organ of Corti:** *see* Receptors: representation of information about stimuli in populations 469

**Organization, file:** *see* Information storage and retrieval 229

**ORGANIZING SET.** The set of classes to one of which every object in a sample of the universe is stated to belong. *See:* Concept formation by artificial intelligence 77

**Organs of speech:** *see* Phonetics, articulatory 393

**OR-GATE.** A module with a single output lead and two or more input leads. The output lead is active whenever at least one of the input leads is active.

**Orientation:** *see* Direction, orientation (G).

—, **constant, columns of:** *see* Neuronal nets 333

**ORIENTATED.** X-orientated means having closer relationships with X than with anything else.

**ORTHOGONAL.** In a space of *n* dimensions, any number up to *n* of vectors may exist such that no vector has a component in the direction of any other vector. Such sets of vectors or directions are described as orthogonal.

**Oscillation, limit cycle:** *see* Control, on-off 136

**Oscillator, linear:** *see* Linear oscillator (G).

**Outer ear:** *see* Non-neural elements in receptor systems 338

**Overlearned:** *see* Psychological limiting factors in human performance 438


**Pacinian corpuscle:** *see* Non-neural elements in receptor systems 337; Receptor (G); Receptors as transducers 456

**PACKAGE.** A collection of programs for use separately or together in a particular computer application, e.g. information storage and retrieval.

**Pair, minimal:** *see* Phonology: phonemes and broad transcription (M) 409

—, **ordered:** *see* Ordered pair (G)

**Palatal:** *see* Phonetics, reticulatory 395

**Palatalized:** *see* Phonetics, articulatory 396

**Palate, hard:** *see* Phonetics, articulatory 394

—, **soft:** *see* Phonetics, articulatory 394

**Palato-aveolar:** *see* Phonetics, articulatory 395

**Panoramic view:** *see* Perception, stereopsis as an aspect of 369

**Panum's fusional area:** *see* Perception, stereopsis as an aspect of 371

**PARADIGM (1).** A *paradigm* (1) is a set of *items*—often words—which differ in certain respects but are all similar in other respects: usually they all contain the same *stem*. *See:* Linguistic form: paradigmatic. Grammar (structural) 192; Semantics: field theories (M) 504

**PARADIGM (2).** A *paradigm* (2) is a set of *paradigmatically related classes* which may or may not all occur in the same syntagmatic environment; whereas a *system* (2) is a set of such classes which all occur in the same syntagmatic environment. *See:* Linguistic form: paradigmatic 273; Linguistic form: system and structure (M) 278

**PARADIGM (3).** An example, for teaching purposes.

**PARADIGM-CLASS.** A *paradigm-class* is a set of *items*—usually words—distinguished from other such classes by the *paradigms* (1) relevant to their members, e.g. in English one paradigm class could include words to which a singular: plural paradigm was relevant, and another could include those to which a positive: comparative: superlative paradigm applied; the first class would include substantives, the second adjectives. *See:* Linguistic form: paradigmatic 273

—, **word and:** *see* Grammar (structural) 192

**PARADIGMATIC, PARADIGMATIC RELATIONS.** *Paradigmatic relations* subsume all relation of similarity which allow us to classify *items* (in given language) as being the same or different. *See:* Linguistic form: paradigmatic 273; Linguistic form: system and structure 278; Grammar (structural) 192; Linguistic form: syntagmatic (M) 276; Phonology: prosodic features (M) 411

— **class:** *see* Linguistic form: paradigmatic 275

— **relations:** *see* Linguistic form: paradigmatic 274

— **responses:** *see* Psychological linguistics: psychological aspects of semantic structure 442

**Paralinguistic:** *see* Phonetics, articulatory (M) 393

— **features:** *see* Writing (M) 627

**PARALINGUISTICS.** A complete *phonetic representation* of an *utterance* would show some features which are relatable to *segmental phonemes*, and others which are not. Of the latter, some are peculiar to the speaker—his *voice quality*—while others are conventional, in the sense that they occur in the speech of all members of the same *language community*, and are used by all according to approximately the same rules. Of these 'conventional' features, some will be used according to rules which can be seen as relatively well integrated parts of the *language system*—notably features realizing the *phonological* categories of *accent*, rhythm, *tone*, *intonation*—while others cannot; these are the *Paralinguistic features* of the utterance, and the study of them is called *paralinguistics*. They include features such as tremulous voice, clicks of annoyance, etc.

**Parallax, binocular:** *see* Perception, stereopsis as an aspect of 368

**Parallax, motion:** *see* Perception, stereopsis as an aspect of 369

**PARALLEL COMPUTER.** An analog computer which carries out several sets of instructions simultaneously (and usually continously, on continuous streams of input data). A digital computer, programmed to produce two or more output signals from one or more sets of data, and thus to use several of its peripherals 'at the same time'.

**PARAMETER.** A physical quantity or real number whose value within a system is fixed, but which perhaps may be altered by intervention from outside the system. It determines or helps to determine the change in the output or the state of the system in response to a particular change in the input.

— **estimation:** *see* Control, identification techniques for 119

**Parameters, speech:** *see* Speech parameters (G)

**Paratactic constitutes:** *see* Grammar (structural) (M) 186

**Parent language:** *see* Relations between languages: introduction 470; Relations between languages: comparative philology 475

**Pareto law:** *see* Statistics of languages: introduction 575

**Parity binit:** *see* Error correcting codes 174

**PARITY CHECK.** A count of whether the number of bits in a signal is odd or even. If it is a rule, for example, that for every input signal the number shall be even, and a module detects within itself a signal for which parity is odd, the module should output a special signal whose meaning is "parity fail". *See also:* Check-sum (G)

— **-check codes:** *see* Error correcting codes 174

**PAROLE.** De Saussure's term *la parole* is translated as *speaking*, and is contrasted with *la langue*, translated as *language* (1). *Parole* is the use of a *language* to produce *utterances* (or *syntagms*, in de Saussure's terminology); these utterances are not actually part of the language system except by implication: each one is, in principle, created afresh out of the vocabulary provided by the language, according to the rules also provided by the latter. *See:* Linguistic form: system and structure 279

**Paroles:** *see* Language varieties: stylistics (M) 259

**PARSER.** A program that applies a grammatical theory and the known facts of syntax to a text, in order to separate the next into structural units. D. G. Hays. *See:* Computational linguistics: introduction 51

**PARSIMONY.** A principle in the choice of models, that while adequately representing the data they should contain the smallest possible number of parameters.

**Partan:** *see* Optimization, automatic 344

**PARTNER.** A is a *partner* of B in the *constitute* C if A and B are both *immediate constituents* of C. *See:* Grammar (structural) 194

**Parts of the ear, non-neural:** *see* Non-neural elements in receptor systems 338

**Parts of speech:** *see* Statistics of language: structure of written English words (M) 581

**Pass:** *see* Sorting techniques 544

**Passive model:** *see* Speech perception 551

**Patent stereopsis:** *see* Perception, stereopsis as an aspect of 371

**Pathway, afferent:** *see* Afferent pathway (G)

**Pathways, centrifugal:** *see* Sensory processes 533

**PATTERN.** The results of a set of measurements made on a single object (e.g. the $100 \times 100$ values, black or white, of a grid superposed on a photograph). *See:* Pattern recognition 349

—, **behaviour, projection of:** *see* Projecting a behaviour pattern (G)

— **congruity:** *see* Phonology: phonemes and broad transcription 409

—, **intonation:** *see* Phonetics, acoustic (M) 393

**PATTERN RECOGNITION.** The assignment, by man or machine, of different inputs to the same category, by virtue of their having common characteristics. *See:* Pattern recognition 349; Concept identification—information processing approaches 81

— **Recognition** 349; *see also* Perception, stereopsis as an aspect of 369

—, **rhythmic:** *see* Phonetics, acoustic (M) 393

— **-statement:** *see* Computational linguistics: machine translation (M) 51

—, **stress:** *see* Phonetics, acoustic (M) 393

—, **syntactic:** *see* Relations between languages: lingua franca (M) 479

—, **tone:** *see* Phonetics, acoustic (M) 393

**Patterns, shadow:** *see* Perception, stereopsis as an aspect of 369

**Pavlov:** *see* Animal learning 21

**PEAKED CURVE.** A curve containing at least one maximum (e.g. a typical sound spectrum). *See:* Speech 545

**Perception:** *see* Information theory in psychological measurement 234; Perception of colour 358

—, **depth, binocular:** *see* Perception, stereopsis as an aspect of 368

— **of Colour** 358

— **of Sound** 365

— **of speech:** *see* Speech perception 548

—, **sound, sensorimotor effects in:** *see* Perception of sound 367

—, **sound (physiology):** *see* Perception of sound 367

—, **Stereopsis as an Aspect of** 368

— **time (stereopsis):** *see* Perception, stereopsis as an aspect of 371

—, **units of:** *see* Speech perception 550

—, **Visual** 373

**Perceptron:** *see* Concept formation by artificial intelligence 79

**Perceptual Breakdown with Stabilized Images** 388

— **unit:** *see* Psychological linguistics: psycholinguistic studies of syntax (M) 439

**Perfect impulse function:** *see* Impulse function, perfect (G)

**PERFORMANCE (1).** *Performance* (1) is the actual use, or capacity for use, of language, as opposed to *competence*, which is the knowledge of a *language system*, which is presupposed by performance. *See:* Linguistic form: system and structure 279; Psychological linguistics: theories of learning in relation to language 445

**PERFORMANCE (2).** The set of outputs of a machine, considered in relation to the set of inputs and to the required set of outputs.

**Period, refractory:** *see* Refractory period (G)

**Periodicity:** *see* Phonetics, acoustic (M) 391

**PERIPHERAL.** Equipment connected to a computer to provide for the entry of data and for the removal of results. *See:* Computer peripherals and their control 58

— **transfer:** *see* Computer peripherals and their control 59

**Peripherals, computer:** *see* Computer peripherals and their control 58

**PERIPHERY (OF NERVOUS SYSTEM).** Those parts of the nervous system near the outside, i.e. the receptors and motoneurons, up to but not including the spinal column.

**PERMEABILITY.** (Of a membrane.) The rate at which particles, molecules or ions pass through unit area of the membrane when unit force is driving them. A specific case is when unit potential difference is driving ions through the membrane of a nerve cell.

**PERMUTE.** *Permutation* is contrasted in linguistics with *commutation;* the two together are sometimes taken to exhaust possible relations between linguistic *items* or *classes*. Permutation is the relation of interchangeability—A *permutes* with B if the sequence A...B can be reversed to B...A.

**Person:** *see* Grammar (structural) (M) 206

**PERSONAL PROFILE.** The interests (of a scientist) treated as a standing enquiry to a library, to be applied to all incoming documents. *See:* Scientific documentation 496

**Perspective, linear:** *see* Perception, stereopsis as an aspect of 369

**Pharyng(e)al:** *see* Phonetics, articulatory 395

**Pharynx:** *see* Phonetics, articulatory 394

**PHASE.** Two waves of the same velocity and frequency differ in phase at any point of observation if the two disturbances reach their maxima at times which are not coincident. For mathematical reasons, the difference in phase is measured as an angle, in degrees. The interval between the maximum of one wave and the next maximum of the other wave is divided by the interval between successive maxima of either wave, and the result multiplied by 360°. The idea of phase difference is used also to compare the states of the disturbance, at the same instant, at two points of observation where the disturbances are due to the same wave.

— **plane analysis:** *see* Control, on-off 137

**Phasic receptor:** *see* Receptor (G)

**PHASIC SUPERNETS.** Neuronal supernets whose function is to classify and encode specific attributes of a stimulus. *See:* Neuronal nets 328

**Phenomena, hesitation:** *see* Psychological linguistics: psycholinguistic studies of syntax 441

—, **masking:** *see* Perception of sound 367

**Phenomenon, Pulfrich:** *see* Perception, stereopsis as an aspect of 372

—, **Young-Helmholtz:** *see* Perception, visual 378

**Philology, comparative:** *see* Relations between languages: comparative philology 475

**PHONATION.** The production of *voice* by the vocal cords. *See:* Phonetics, articulatory 394; Phonetics, experimental (M) 400

**PHONE.** A *phonetically* defined *type* (i.e. a *class* of sounds) which is of approximately the same duration as a *segmental phoneme*. *See:* Phonetics (G)

**PHONEMATIC UNIT.** Some linguists *describe phonological systems* in terms of two kinds of *unit* (1): *phonematic units*, and *prosodies*. The former correspond *phonetically* to stretches of sound of the length of *segmental phonemes*, whereas the phonetic *features* corresponding to the latter extend over a stretch which may be longer than this, e.g. a syllable or word. Both kinds of unit are defined abstractly, in terms of the *oppositions* they are involved in, which in turn are interrelated in a *polysystemic* description of the phonological system; and although any phonematic unit can be related to some phonetic segment of the utterance, there may be some of the phonologically relevant features of that segment which *realize*, not the phonematic unit, but a prosody.

**PHONEME.** 'A small group of speech sounds, significantly different from all other speech sounds. Two sounds fall into the same phoneme category only if the difference between them never distinguishes two words in the language under consideration.' D. R. Hill. A *phoneme* is a sound type which is defined by a given *language system* and has no relevance except with reference to that language system. Phonemes are either *segmental* or *suprasegmental*, but in either case they are phonological segments which cannot be further segmented, except by analysing them into *distinctive features*. (*Juncture* phonemes are neither segmental nor suprasegmental, since they can never be identified with phonetic segments; *a fortiori*, they can not be further segmented). There are different conceptions of the relation between phonemes and actual speech-sounds: some see it as a class: member relation (a phoneme is a class of *phones*, called its *allophones*); others as a *constituency* relation (a phoneme consists of distinctive features, and each occurrence of the phoneme is marked by the presence of all these features); and others as a *realization* relation (the phoneme is *realized* by a *phone* or some such phonetic unit, the particular phone varying (maybe) according to the environment). *See:* Phonology: phonemes and broad transcription 409; Phono-

logy: distinctive features 404; Relations between languages: introduction (M) 470; Relations between languages: bilingualism (M) 473; Relations between languages: comparative philology (M) 475; Statistics of language: introduction 569; Linguistic form: syntagmatic (M) 276; Phonetics, articulatory (M) 393; Writing (M) 627; Grammar (structural) (M) 186
— **frequencies:** *see* Statistics of language: introduction 577
—, **segmental:** *see* Segment, segmental phoneme (G)
—, **suprasegmental:** *see* Suprasegmental phoneme (G)
— **system:** *see* Phonology: distinctive features (M) 404
**Phonemic:** *see* Relations between languages: bilingualism (M) 473
— **features:** *see* Phonology: distinctive features 408
**PHONEMIC SEQUENCE.** A concatenation of phonemes as the sound signals of speech. D. B. Fry. *See:* Phonetics, acoustic (M) 393
— **structure:** *see* Semantics: field theories (M) 504
— **transcription:** *see* Phonology: phonemes and broad transcription 410
**PHONEMICS.** *Phonemics* is the study of *phonemes:* how the sounds of any given language are to be grouped (as *allophones*) into phonemes, and the rules determining how phonemes combine. The term *phonemics* is sometimes contrasted with *phonology* (2), to refer specifically to studies which treat phonemes as the basic units of a *level of representation* which in principle is independent of the level of *grammar* and is governed by its own system; thus a phonemic description of a language would include *tactic* rules describing the ways in which phonemes combine without reference to the grammatical rules for combining *morphemes* (to be found in the *morphemics*) *See:* Phonology: phonemes and broad transcription 409
**Phonetic:** *see* Phonology: prosodic features (M) 411; Relation between languages: introduction (M) 470; Relations between languages: bilingualism (M) 473
— **change:** *see* Relations between languages: comparative philology 477
— **characterization:** *see* Linguistic form: transformational theory (M) 280
— **context:** *see* Phonology: phonemes and broad transcription (M) 409
— **exponents:** *see* Phonology: contrast and opposition (M) 401
— **features:** *see* Phonology: contrast and opposition (M) 401; Phonology: distinctive features 408; Phonology: phonemes and broad transcription (M) 409; Phonology: prosodic features (M) 411
— **features, distinctive:** *see* Grammar (structural) (M) 186
— **interpretation:** *see* Linguistic form: transformational theory (M) 283
— **quality:** *see* Phonology: distinctive features 404
— **similarity:** *see* Phonology: phonemes and broad transcription 409

**Phonetic structure of speech:** *see* Writing (M) 627
— **substance:** *see* Phonology: phonemes and broad transcription 409
**PHONETIC SYMBOLS.** See p. 718. *See also:* Phonetics, articulatory 393
— **transcription, broad:** *see* Broad phonetic transcription (G)
— **transcription, narrow:** *see* Narrow phonetic transcription (G)
**PHONETICS.** *Phonetics* is the study of speech-sounds not from the point of view of *linguistic form* (as in *phonology*) but from the point of view of *substance*. Thus whereas phonology is concerned with the ways in which sounds are used in one or more particular languages, phonetics is concerned with the ways in which sounds are produced and perceived, and with their analysis and description in acoustic terms. If speech is *segmented* phonetically, the smallest segments are called *phones;* a *phone* may or may not correspond to, and realize, a *phoneme*. A particular phone can be described, or a class of phones can be defined, in *articulatory, acoustic* or *auditory* terms. *See:* Phonetics, acoustic 391; Phonetics, articulatory 393; Phonetics, auditory 396; Phonetics, experimental 399; Phonology: phonemes and broad transcription 409; Phonology: distinctive features 404; Phonology: contrast and opposition 401
—, **Acoustic** 391
—, **Articulatory** 393; *see also:* Phonetics, auditory (M) 396
—, **Auditory** 396
—, **Experimental** 399; *see also:* Phonetics, acoustic (M) 391
**Phonic:** *see* Relations between languages: bilingualism (M) 472
**Phonological:** *see* Linguistic form: paradigmatic (M) 273; Phonology: prosodic features (M) 411
— **component:** *see* Phonology: contrast and opposition 401; Phonology: distinctive features (M) 404
— **contrast:** *see* Phonology: contrast and opposition 401; Phonology: phonemes and broad transcription 409
— **criteria** (language classification): *see* Relations between languages: typological and areal classifications 486
— **features:** *see* Language varieties: register (M) 251
— **features, distinctive:** *see* Linguistic form: transformational theory 283
— **integration:** *see* Relations between languages: loans and loanwords (M) 482
— **level:** *see* Language varieties: stylistics (M) 259
— **matrix:** *see* Linguistic form: transformational theory (M) 280
— **opposition:** *see* Phonology: contrast and opposition 401; Phonology: phonemes and broad transcription 410
— **rules:** *see* Phonology: distinctive features (M) 404
— **structure of speech:** *see* Writing (M) 627
— **structures:** *see* Phonology: phonemes and broad transcription (M) 409

**Phonological systems:** *see* Relations between languages: introduction (M) 470; Relations between languages: comparative philology (M) 475
— **unit:** *see* Phonology: prosodic features (M) 411
**Phonologically:** *see* Phonetics, articulatory (M) 393
— **conditioned:** *see* Grammar (structural) 188
**PHONOLOGY (1).** *Phonology* contrasts on the one hand with *graphology*, in that it deals with spoken, not written, language; and on the other with *phonetics*, in that it deals with *phonological systems* which are parts of particular *language-systems*, rather than with universal phonetic categories. Phonology is *component* (1) or *level of representation* (or, for some linguists, a number of such levels), and the smallest *segments* on this level are generally called *phonemes*. Phonology relates pure *linguistic form (grammatical* and *lexical items)* to phonetic *substance*, but its precise relation to form and to substance is disputed. *See:* Phonology: contrast and opposition 401
**PHONOLOGY (2).** A *description* of the *phonology* (1) of a particular language is the *phonology* (2) of that language. It may take the form of a set of rules for interpreting any *grammatical* and *lexical representation* of a sentence in terms (ultimately) of *universal phonetic* categories *(distinctive features):* or it may take the form of a set of rules which will *generate* strings of *phonemes* without reference to any grammatical or lexical representation of the *items* generated. These two kinds of phonology are sometimes distinguished by reserving *phonology* for the first, and using *phonemics* for the second. *See:* Phonology: phonemes and broad transcription 401; Linguistic form: transformational theory 280; Grammar (structural) 186; Phonology: distinctive features 404; Phonology: prosodic features 411
—: **Contrast and Opposition** 401
—: **Distinctive Features** 404
—, **level of:** *See* Relations between languages: introduction 470
—: **Phonemes and Broad Transcription** 401
—: **Prosodic Features** 411
**PHOTOMULTIPLIER.** A photoelectric cell incorporating a powerful amplifier employing electron multiplication. Its object is to produce an electric current of workable size whenever a brief (or weak) light falls on the photoelectric surface.
**PHRASE-MARKER, P-MARKER.** A *phrase-marker* (P-marker) is a *representation* of a *structure* (2) as a *string* of symbols *(formatives)*, together with the *derivation* (1) of the string; the usual form for a P-Marker is a *tree* whose nodes are labelled with symbols defined by the *rewrite-rules* of the *grammar* (3). A P-marker representing a *deep structure* is a *generalized P-Marker*, and one representing a surface structure is a *final derived P-marker. See:* Linguistic form: transformational theory 282; Psychological linguistics: psycholinguistic studies of syntax 439
— **-marker, derived:** *see* Derived phrase-marker (G)
— **-marker, final derived:** *see* Linguistic form: transformational theory 282

**Phrase-marker, generalized:** *see* Generalized phrase-marker (G); Linguistic form: transformational theory 282
— **structure:** *see* Computational linguistics: machine translation (M) 51; Relations between languages: typological and areal classifications (M) 486
**PHRASE-STRUCTURE GRAMMAR.** A *grammar* (3) consisting of *phrase-structure rules. See:* Linguistic form: generative grammar (M) 272; Psychological linguistics: theories of learning in relation to language (M) 445
**PHRASE-STRUCTURE RULE.** A *phrase-structure rule* is a *rewrite rule* which replaces a single symbol by one or more symbols; in the simplest cases, a phrase-structure rule specifies how a set of items (specified by the symbol to be replaced) is to be *segmented* into *immediate constituents* (each represented by one of the replacing symbols), e.g. 'A → X Y' means 'The immediate constituents of A are X and Y'. *See:* Linguistic form: transformational theory (M) 280
**PHRASE-STRUCTURE UNIT.** A *unit* (1) represented by a single symbol in a *phrase-structure grammar. See:* Psychological linguistics: psycholinguistic studies of syntax 439
**Physiological activity in speech:** *see* Phonetics experimental 399
— **control:** *see* Sensory processes 525; Control of respiration, self-adaptive 132; Homeostasis 213
**PICTOGRAM.** A (stylised) picture of something, used as a linguistic *sign* with that thing as *referent. See:* Semantics: sign and symbol (M) 510
**Pidgin:** *see* Relations between languages: lingua franca 480
**Pidginization:** *see* Relations between languages: lingua franca 480
**Pile:** *see* Stacks 563
**Pitch:** *see* Phonology: prosodic features 411
**PLACE OF ARTICULATION.** An *articulatory* description of a *contoid* specifies (among other things) its *place of articulation* and its *mode* (or *manner) of articulation;* the place of articulation is the point in the *vocal tract* at which the main constriction occurs. *See:* Phonetics, articulatory 394; Phonology: contrast and opposition (M) 401; Phonology: distinctive features 404
**PLAN.** A particular hypothesis of the organization of animal behaviour. *See:* Psychological linguistics; theories of learning in relation to language (M) 444
**Planning:** *see* Problem solving 415
**PLANT SCHEDULING.** Planning in advance and in sequence of the tasks of a plant.
**Playing of games:** *see* Problem solving 415
**Plosives:** *see* Phonetics, articulatory 396; Phonetics, auditory (M) 396; Phonology: distinctive features (M) 404
—, **aspirated:** *see* Phonology: contrast and opposition (M) 401
—, **fronted velar:** *see* Phonology: contrast and opposition (M) 401

**Plosives, retracted velar:** *see* Phonology: contrast and opposition (M) 401
—, **unaspirated:** *see* Phonology: contrast and opposition (M) 401
**Plus juncture:** *see* Open transition (G)
**Pneumograph:** *see* Phonetics, experimental (M) 399
**Point of subjective equality (PSE):** *see* Sensory discrimination, measurement of 517
**POINTER.** In a *list*, the part of a list element which indicates the address of the next element. *See:* Algebraic manipulation using lists 14
**POISSON DISTRIBUTION.** If, in a purely random *process*, a symbol is generated at an average frequency of $\lambda$ times per second, the probability that it will occur exactly $r$ times in a particular interval of duration $\delta t$

is $P(r)\delta t = \dfrac{\lambda^r}{r!} e^{-\lambda \delta t}$.

The distribution of $P(r)$ is called the Poisson distribution.
**Polish notation, reverse:** *see* Stacks 564
**POLISH REPRESENTATION OR PREFIX NOTATION.** An alternative to the *infix notation*, sometimes used in machine languages. In Polish notation, the operator appears before the operands. E.g. $\cap P\bar{Q}$ is read as '*P* and not *Q*'.
**Pollaczek-Khintchine formula:** *see* Simulation of traffic problems using chain-code random generators 540
**Polygraphs:** *see* Statistics of language: introduction 569
**Polynomial approximation:** *see* Optimization, automatic 343
**POLYSYNTHETIC.** A language can be classified *typologically* as *polysynthetic* (or *incorporating*) if its words tend to consist of a large number of *morphemes*, many of which would be translated into any other kind of language as a separate word. Polysynthetic languages are thus at the opposite extreme from *isolating* languages, whose words tend to consist of one morpheme each, but they are merely a special kind of *agglutinative* or *fusional* languages, rather than a different type distinct from either of these. *See:* Relations between languages: typological and areal classifications 486
**POLYSYSTEMIC.** A *polysystemic description* of a *language* (1) differs from a *monosystemic* one in that it comprises a number of different *systems* (2), each applying under a different set of conditions. Every description which has yet been produced is also polysystemic in the sense that it comprises a number of different *systems* (1) *(levels of representation)*. *See:* Linguistic form: system and structure 280; Grammar (structural) 186
**Pontryagin maximum principle:** *see* Control, stability and 150
**Popov's criterion:** *see* Control, stability and 150
**Populations of receptors:** *see* Receptors: representation of information about stimuli in populations 467
**PORTMANTEAU MORPH.** A *morph* which represents two or more *morphemes* at the same time is a *portmanteau*, or *fused*, *morph;* e.g. *we're* could be treated as a single, portmanteau morph representing the same morphemes as are found in *we are*. *See:* Grammar (structural) 189
**Position, lip:** *see* Phonetics, auditory 397
—, **primary:** *see* Primary position (G)
**Post machines:** *see* Automata, infinite-state 35
— **-alveolar:** *see* Phonetics, articulatory 395
**Postsynaptic:** *see* Synapse (G)
— **potentials:** *see* Neuronal nets 322
**Potential:** *see* Action potential (G)
—, **generator:** *see* Generator potential (G)
—, **receptor:** *see* Receptor potential (G)
—, **resting:** *see* Resting potential (G)
—, **slow:** *see* Slow potential (G)
**Potentials, excitatory postsynaptic:** *see* Neuronal nets 322
—, **inhibitory postsynaptic:** *see* Neuronal nets 322
—, **postsynaptic:** *see* Neuronal nets 322
—, **presynaptic:** *see* Neuronal nets 322
**POTENTIOMETER.** An electronic device with 3 terminals and a control. When two of the terminals are at fixed but different potentials, the control sets the potential of the third terminal at values intermediate between the other two.
**POWER FUNCTION.** Function of the form $f(x) = x^a$.
— **plant, nuclear, control of:** *see* Control by hybrid computers 97
**Predictably computable functions:** *see* Automata, infinite-state 37
**Prediction:** *see* Control by stationary filtering and prediction (Wiener) 109
— **and stationary filtering, control by:** *see* Control by stationary filtering and prediction (Wiener) 109
**Predictive analysis:** *see* Computational linguistics: machine translation 53
**PREDICTIVE CONTROL.** Making control decisions on the basis of the predicted behaviour of a system, e.g. by the effects of manual control on a fast model of the system. *See:* Control, predictive, using fast-time models 140
— **control using fast-time models:** *see* Control, predictive, using fast-time models 140
— **on-off control:** *see* Control, on-off 140
**Prefix:** *see* Statistics of language: structure of written English words 582
— **notation:** *see* Polish representation (G)
—, **transformational:** *see* Statistics of language: structure of written English words (M) 583
**Prefixes:** *see* Grammar (structural) 189
**Presbyopia:** *see* Perception, visual 374
**Prescriptive conception:** *see* Language varieties: register (M) 251
**Presynaptic:** *see* Synapse (G)
**Presynaptic potentials:** *see* Neuronal nets 322
**PRIMARY POSITION OF THE EYES.** With their two visual axes horizontal and parallel to the plane of symmetry of the body. The subject is supposed to be erect. *See:* Eye movements 176

**Primitive acoustic features (PAF's):** *see* Speech recognition, automatic  556
**Principal diagonal:** *see* Matrix (G)
**Principle, maximum, control by:** *see* Control by the maximum principle  101
—, **maximum, geometric interpretation of:** *see* Control by the maximum principle  104
— **of invariance:** *see* Control, invariance and  126
— **of optimality:** *see* Dynamic programming  169
**PRINT-THROUGH.** In magnetic reproduction, unwanted signals caused by self-remagnetization during storage of a reel of recorded tape, successive turns being so close. *See:* Magnetic recording  299
**Privative opposition:** *see* Phonology: distinctive features (M)  404
**Probability, conditional:** *see* Conditional probability (G)
— **density, conditional:** *see* Conditional probability density (G)
— **models:** *see* Models for human memory  312
**Problem, general control:** *see* Control by the maximum principle  101
— **Solving**  413
—, **species:** *see* Statistics of language: introduction  575
—, **two-point boundary-value:** *see* Control by the maximum principle  105
**Problems, formally undecideable:** *see* Unsolvable problems  623
—, **unsolvable:** *see* Unsolvable problems  623
**Procedural language:** *see* Computer language design requirements  54
**Procedure, forced choice:** *see* Sensory discrimination, measurement of  518
—, **rating:** *see* Sensory discrimination, measurement of  520
—, **yes-no:** *see* Sensory, discrimination, measurement of  519
**PROCESS (1).** A *process* (1) is an operation to be performed on one linguistic entity in order to turn it into a different, but comparable, entity; for instance, a rule of the form: '*a* becomes *an* before a vowel' specifies a process. *See:* Grammar (structural)  186
**PROCESS (2).** *Process* (2) (or *text*) is contrasted with *system* (1) or *language* (1), to refer to the *utterances* which are produced by applying the rules of the language system. *See:* Linguistic form: system and structure  278
**PROCESS (3).** To change, by a *module*, a set of inputs into a set of outputs.
**PROCESS (4).** The mechanism which governs the selection of a signal; sometimes the signal itself. If a wide view is taken of the signals and their means of selection, a process can be, for example, a manufacturing process. The signals are then the end-products, together with the results of acceptance tests, productivity estimates, and so on. The term is also applied sometimes to spontaneous events which might be mistaken for a signal (e.g. radio waves from outer space, noise).

*Stationary process.* A *process* (4) in which there is no change with time of the mechanisms governing the selection and the generation of the signal.
*Ergodic process.* A *stationary process* in which any one signal is typical of all possible signals. (An infinitely long message, all in one language, would be non-ergodic if the language had not been decided in advance.)
*Purely random process.* A *stationary process* in which each symbol is independently selected, irrespective of the others.
*Flat random process.* Purely random, and all symbols are equally probable.
*Gaussian random process.* A *stationary process* in which all signal amplitudes are Gaussian variables.
— **control:** *see* Man-machine communication and ergonomics  301
—, **decision:** *see* Decision process (G)
—, **dynamics of:** *see* Dynamics of a process (G)
—, **ergodic:** *see* Process (G)
—, **flat random:** *see* Process (G)
—, **Gaussian:** *see* Process (G)
—, **Gaussian random:** *see* Gaussian random process (G)
—, **hereditary:** *see* Homeostasis  214
—, **item and:** *see* Grammar (structural)  192
—, **Markov:** *see* Markov process (discrete) (G)
—, **non-linearities of:** *see* Dynamics of a process (G)
—, **purely random:** *see* Process (G)
—, **random:** *see* Markov process (G)
—, **stationary:** *see* Process (G).
**PROCESS (STRUCTURAL).** Part of a cell or organ which projects out from the main body.
**Processes, human thought, computer simulation of:** *see* Computer simulation of human thought processes  60
—, **industrial, optimization of:** *see* Optimization of industrial processes  345
—, **sensory:** *see* Sensory processes  525
**Processing, batch, of requests:** *see* Information storage and retrieval  229
—, **language, automatic:** *see* Computational linguistics: introduction  49
—, **list:** *see* Symbol manipulation by digital computer  596
— **of algorithms by algorithms:** *see* Algorithms for processing algorithms  15
—, **string:** *see* Symbol manipulation by digital computer  596
**Processor, input:** *see* Computational linguistics: introduction  50
**Production, method of:** *see* Sensory discrimination, measurement of  523
**PRODUCTIVE.** A *construction* (1) is *productive* if its members do not need to be learned individually, i.e. if it can be generalized beyond any members which are already known to occur. *See:* Relations between languages: loans and loanwords (M)  482
— **patterns:** *see* Relations between languages: comparative philology (M)  475

**PROFILE.** The interests of an individual or a group, expressed for example in *descriptors* or *key words*, for the purposes of *information retrieval. See:* Scientific documentation   496; Information storage and retrieval   223

—, **personal:** *see* Personal profile (G)

**PROGRAM.** A stream of *instruction* signals to a computer; each instruction controls what operation is to be performed, and what data to perform them on (or what address where the required data are stored). Thus a program changes the *state* of a computer, and when it is presented with appropriate input data it will produce the required output data.

—, **assembly:** *see* Assembly program (G)

—, **executive:** *see* Computers, multiaccess to   65

—, **systems:** *see* Systems program (G)

**PROGRAMMING (1).** Setting the *state* of a (computing) machine. When the program is introduced, the machine becomes capable of performing a particular type of operation.

**PROGRAMMING (2).** Designing a program, e.g. linear programming, dynamic programming.

—, **dynamic:** *see* Control, stability and   150; Dynamic programming   168

—, **linear:** *see* Linear programming (G)

—, **mathematical:** *see* Optimization of industrial processes   347

Project: *see* Psychological linguistics: theories of learning in relation to language (M)   444

**PROJECTING A BEHAVIOUR PATTERN.** Finding a set of rules for selecting the pattern out of the totality of all possible behaviours. Especially when the behaviour pattern is a set of utterances. *See:* Psychological linguistics: theories of learning in relation to language   444

Projection fibres: *see* Axonal bundles or fibres (G)

**PROJECTION RULE.** A rule for assigning a *semantic* interpretation (a *reading*) to a *deep structure. See:* Linguistic form: transformational theory   282

Prominence: *see* Linguistic form: syntagmatic (M)   277

Pronunciation, received: *see* Received pronunciation (G); Language varieties: language and dialect   250

Proper part: *see* Psychological linguistics: psychological aspects of semantic structure (M)   442

Properties, universal: *see* Phonology: distinctive features (M)   404; Semantics: introduction (M)   499

Proportional opposition: *see* Phonology: distinctive features (M)   404

Prosodemes: *see* Phonology: prosodic features   411

Prosodic distinctive features: *see* Phonology: prosodic features   411

**PROSODIC FEATURE, PROSODY.** The *phonetic features* in an utterance which can be related to *phonological* categories are either *phonemic* or *prosodic*; they are phonemic if they can be related to *segmental phonemes*, otherwise they are prosodic (unless the description involves *suprasegmental phonemes*, in which case the 'prosodic' features can be related to them in the same way that the 'phonemic' features can be related to segmental phonemes). The features most generally classed as prosodic are length, *stress* and pitch, but some linguists treat other features too as prosodic, provided they can extend over stretches of speech longer than segmental phonemes. Prosodic features can be referred to as *prosodies*, and in the sense where they can include features other than length, stress and pitch they are contrasted with *phonematic units. See:* Phonology: prosodic features   411; Phonology: distinctive features   404

Prosthetic Limbs   416

**PROTOCOL.** The original which is being simulated or compared with a model.

**PROTOLANGUAGE.** A language of which there are no recorded *texts* but which is assumed to have been the ancestor of two or more languages of which texts are available. *See:* Relations between languages: comparative philology   475

Protosynthex: *see* Fact retrieval   181

Proving of theorems: *see* Problem solving   414

— of theorems by machine: *see* Theorem proving by machine   616

Pseudo-instructions: *see* Assembly languages   27

— -Noise Sequences   419

— -Random Binary Signals, Use of, in Correlation Analysis of Dynamic Systems   433

**PSOPHOMETRY.** The measurement of noise.

**Psycholinguistic studies of syntax:** *see* Psychological linguistics: psycholinguistic studies of syntax   439

— **theory:** *see* Psychological linguistics: psycholinguistic studies of syntax   439

**Psychological and epistemological knowledge:** *see* Psychological linguistics: theories of learning in relation to language   444

— **aspects of semantic structure:** *see* Psychological linguistics: psychological aspects of semantic structure   442

— **Limiting Factors in Human Performance**   437

— **Linguistics: Psycholinguistic Studies of Syntax**   439

— **Linguistics: Psychological Aspects of Semantic Structure**   442

— **Linguistics: Theories of Learning in Relation to Language**   444

— **measurement, information theory in:** *see* Information theory in psychological measurement   232

— **refractory period:** *see* Psychological limiting factors in human performance   438

**Psychology, experimental terminology and notation:** *see* Sensory discrimination, measurement of (with glossary attached)   512

—, **Freudian unconscious:** *see* Problem solving   416

—, **Gestalt:** *see* Gestalt psychology   185

—, **S-R:** *see* Problem solving   416

—, **Use of Models (Learning)**   447

**Psychophysics of speech:** *see* Speech perception   548

**Pulfrich phenomenon:** *see* Perception, stereopsis as an aspect of   372

**PULSE.** Brief disturbance (e.g. of a voltage in a communication channel). Used in transmission of information. *See:* Control systems, sampled-data   155

**PULSE AMPLITUDE MODULATION.** Insertion of data into a sequence of pulses by adjusting the amplitude (e.g. the voltage) of each pulse in proportion to the measured data-sample.
— **distribution, role of, in information flow in the nervous system:** see Nervous system, role of pulse distribution in information flow  316
**PULSE FREQUENCY MODULATION.** Insertion of data into a sequence of pulses by adjusting the time interval between successive pulses in proportion to the data measurement.
**PULSE GENERATOR.** Device for producing a sequence of pulses to serve as carriers of information, (e.g. of numerical data).
**PULSE SEQUENCE.** Medium for transmitting data by modulating properties of the pulses or their separation. In compound phrases the word 'sequence' is usually dropped.
**PULSE, SQUARE.** Ideal pulse in which the initial rise and final fall in voltage are both instantaneous and the voltage is constant in between.
**PULSE WIDTH MODULATION.** Insertion of data into a sequence of pulses by adjusting the width (i.e. the duration) of each pulse in proportion to the data measurement
**Pure:** see Phonetics, auditory  398
**Purely random process:** see Process (G)
**Pursuit task:** see Man-machine in control systems  307
**PUSHDOWN LIST.** A list of signals (usually in a computer store) which can be altered by only two basic instructions (1) add a new signal to the list (from some other address) (2) remove the last signal from the list (to some other address). See: Algebraic manipulation using lists  14; Stacks  563
— **store:** see Stacks  563
— **store systems:** see Linguistic form: generative grammar (M)  272
**Pyramidal:** see Neuron (G)

**Qualitative stereopsis:** see Perception, stereopsis as an aspect of  371
**Quality, phonetic:** see Phonology: distinctive features  404
—, **voice:** see Voice quality (G); Phonetics, acoustic (M)  391
—, **vowel:** see Phonology: prosodic features (M)  411
**Quantity:** see Phonology: contrast and opposition (M)  401
**Queueing models:** see Models for human memory  312

**R-coloured:** see Phonetics, auditory  398
**R-colouring:** see Phonetics, auditory  398
**Radio services, high frequency:** see Telecommunication, global  604
— **systems (1000 MHz):** see Telecommunication, global  604
**RADIX.** The base of a notation for numbers (e.g. 10 in decimal notation). A number is expressed by a string of integers, each of which must be multiplied by an integral power of the radix determined by its position in the string: and then all are summed.
— **sorting:** see Sorting techniques  544
**RADOME.** A cover for directional transmitting and receiving aerials.
**Random:** see Speech synthesis  559
— **binary signal:** see Pseudorandom binary signals, use of...  433
**RANDOM FUNCTION.** A *random signal* continuously varying as a function of time. See: Random signals and noise  453
— **process:** see Markov process (G).
**RANDOM SIGNAL.** A signal, regarded as the outcome of a statistical *process*.
— **Signals and Noise**  453
— **telegraph signal:** see Pseudorandom binary signals, use of...  434
**Range effect:** see Psychological limiting factors in human performance  437
**Ranges, collocational:** see Semantics: context and collocation  503
**RANK (1), RANK SCALE.** An *item*'s rank (1) is the *unit* (2) of which it is a member. The *rank scale* is an ordered set of all the units (2) of a language; for instance the grammatical rank-scale of English may be taken to be (in descending order): sentence-clause-phrase-word-morpheme. See: Grammar (structural)  186; Writing  627; Relations between languages: typological and areal classifications (M)  486
**RANK (2).** If an *item* A is an *Immediate Constituent* of an item B, and B is a member of (say) the *unit* (1) 'clause', then A's *rank* (2) will be that of the next unit (1) down the rank scale, viz. phrase, irrespective of A's *rank* (1). A is then said to be 'operating at the rank of phrase', or 'functioning as a phrase'. See: Grammar (structural)  186
— **scale:** see Writing  627
**RANKSHIFT.** If an *item*'s *rank* (1) conflicts with its *rank* (2), e.g. if it is a clause (rank (1)) acting at the rank (2) of phrase—then it is said to be *rankshifted;* the phenomenon is known as *rankshift* or *downgrading.* See: Grammar (structural)  187
**Rankshifted:** see Grammar (structural)  187
**Ranvier, nodes of:** see Medullated nerve fibre (G).
**RASTER.** The pattern representing the systematic motion of an electron beam, e.g. the 625 lines and their end connexions on a television screen. See: Character recognition  41
**Rate-aiding:** see Man-machine in control systems  309
**Rate, clock:** see Clock rate (G).
—, **code:** see Error-correcting codes  173
— **of transfer of information:** see Telecommunication, economy in  599
**Rating procedure:** see Sensory discrimination, measurement of  520
**Ratio, Crozier:** see Sensory discrimination, measurement of  516
—, **disturbance:** see Pseudorandom binary signals, use of...  436

45*

**RC.** Using resistors and capacitors only.
**Reaction time:** *see* Information theory in psychological measurement  235
**READ.** To make a copy of the information in a *store* (while either erasing it or leaving it there).
**READING.** A *reading* of a *text* (e.g. a sentence) is a *semantic* interpretation of that text; thus an ambiguous text will have two or more readings. *See:* Linguistic form: transformational theory  282
**REAL TIME.** The timing of signals from an inflexible system (such as a chemical plant or human operator) and of return signals required by it.
**REALIZE, REALIZATION.** A relatively abstract linguistic entity is *realized (or expounded* or *manifested)* by a relatively concrete one if the latter can be said to occur because of the former, so that the occurrence of the latter implies the occurrence of the former. *See:* Grammar (structural)  186; Phonetics, acoustic (M)  391; Phonetics, experimental (M)  399; Phonology: distinctive features (M)  404; Phonology: contrast and opposition (M)  401; Relations between languages; typological and areal classifications (M)  486; Writing (M)  627; Phonology: prosodic features (M)  411
**RECEIVED PRONUNCIATION, R.P.** The pronunciation of English accepted as standard in England. *See:* Language varieties: language and dialect  250
**RECEPTOR.** Ending (or rather, beginning) of a sensory nerve fibre where impulses are initiated by mechanical or chemical abnormality or by mechanical, chemical or electrical changes in the adjacent tissue. *Golgi receptor.* At end of large fibre over 10 $\mu$ in diameter. *Pacinian corpuscle.* Thickly encapsulated receptor to a medium sized fibre 5–10 $\mu$ in diameter. *Ruffini receptor.* A network of fine fibres, surrounded by a thin sheath, receptor to a medium sized nerve fibre 5–10 $\mu$ in diameter. *Phasic receptor.* Responds only to input signals which change with time. *Tonic receptor.* Responds to the steady input signal itself. *See:* Nerve and muscle, initiation and conduction of impulses in  314; Receptors in joints and muscles  460; Receptors: representation of information about stimuli in populations  467
— **assemblies, mixed:** *see* Receptors: representation of information about stimuli in populations  467
—, **Golgi:** *see* Receptor (G).
—, **phasic:** *see* Receptor (G).
**RECEPTOR POTENTIAL.** The potential difference developed across the receptor membrane resulting directly from the *stimulus*. *See:* Receptors as transducers  459. *See also:* Action potential (G). Generator potential (G).
—, **Ruffini:** *see* Receptor (G).
— **systems, non-neural elements in:** *see* Non-neural elements in receptor systems  337
—, **tonic:** *see* Receptor (G).
— **unit:** *see* Receptors as transducers  456
— **unit, single:** *see* Receptors: representation of information about stimuli in populations  467
**Receptors as Transducers**  337
— **in Joints and Muscles**  460
—, **populations of:** *see* Receptors: representation of information about stimuli in populations  467
—: **Relation between the Stimuli and the Activity in Single Primary Units**  463
**Receptors: Representation of Information about Stimuli in Populations**  467
—, **stretch:** *see* Receptors: representation of information about stimuli in populations  467
**Recognizing:** *see* Problem solving  413
**Recognition, character:** *see* Character recognition  41
—, **pattern:** *see* Pattern recognition (G). Pattern recognition  349; Perception, stereopsis as an aspect of  369
—, **speech:** *see* Speech recognition, automatic  552
**Reconstruct:** *see* Relations between languages: comparative philology  475
**RECORD.** A unit block of information in a *file*. It must contain a unique identifier, and may contain information about the values of any of the file's parameters associated with this identifier, e.g. the identifier may be the name of an employee, and the information his age, years of service, tax code etc. Each parameter is called a *field* of the file. *See:* Choosing a computer language  54; Information storage and retrieval  223
**Recording, magnetic:** *see* Magnetic recording  291
—, **NRZ:** *see* NRZ recording (G).
—, **video:** *see* Video recording (G).
**Recoverability:** *see* Linguistic form: transformational theory  283
**Recruiting responses:** *see* Neuronal nets  328
**Recurrent collaterals:** *see* Neuronal nets  330
**RECURSION.** *Recursion* is the property required of any *explicit grammar* (3) if it is to *generate representations* of an infinite number of *utterances* (as in the *description* of any *natural language*). It must be possible for some sub-set of rules in the grammar to generate representations of structures with an indefinite number of *immediate constituents* (as in *linear recursion*, e.g. coordination with 'and'), and it must be possible for some rules to apply more than once in the *derivation* of a string, to produce *embedding recursion* (corresponding to *rankshift*). *See:* Linguistic form: generative grammar  272
**Recursion:** *see* Automata, infinite-state  36
**REDUNDANCY.** In *modular nets*, the replication of identical modules. In a *code*, the ratio $n/k$ where $n$ is the number of symbols transmitted and $k$ is the number of symbols in the decoded message. (Ideally, equiprobable symbols are assumed, or $n$ and $k$ are expressed as numbers of bits of information.) *See:* Reliable computation with unreliable elements  489
—, **rules:** *see* Redundant, redundancy rule (G).
—, **stimulus:** *see* Conceptual behaviour  86
**REDUNDANT, REDUNDANCY RULE.** In any *representation* of a linguistic *item*, or set of items, some part of the representation is *redundant* if it is predictable from the rest of the representation. In particular, a *feature* may be *redundant* in some *environ-*

*ments*, and *distinctive* in others. A *redundancy rule* is a rule which specifies that a given feature is to be added to any representation satisfying a given set of conditions, i.e. in environments in which the feature would be redundant; the feature can then be ignored in all subsequent rules. *See:* Phonology: contrast and opposition 401; Phonology: distinctive features 406; Linguistic form: transformational theory 283; Relations between languages: lingua franca (M) 480
— **features:** *see* Phonology: distinctive features 406
**REFERENCE (1).** In discussing meaning, a distinction may be made between the *symbol* itself, its *reference* (1) (or *thought*) and its *referent*. The reference is the sign's *content*, and the symbol is its *form;* the referent (which may be a particular physical object) is related to the symbol only via the reference. *See:* Semantics: meaning and reference 508; Semantics: introduction 500
**REFERENCE (2), REFERENTIAL.** Linguistic *signs* are sometimes classified as *referential* or *expressive* according to whether they refer to some object in the real world (their *referent*) or express the feelings of the speaker. The former *function* (1) is *reference* (2). *See:* Semantics: sign and symbol 510
—, **model:** *see* Control, hill climbing in 119
—, **model, control by:** *see* Control by model reference 106
— **model for control:** *see* Control by hybrid computers 100
**REFERENT.** The thing, quality etc. in the real world, which is referred to by a linguistic *item. See:* Semantics: meaning and reference 508
**Referential:** *see* Semantics: sign and symbol (M) 510
**Referents:** *see* Semantics: field theories (M) 504
**REFRACTORY PERIOD.** In psychology and physiology, the period after the response to a stimulus during which a second stimulus evokes no response. *See:* Man-machine in control systems 310
— **period, psychological:** *see* Psychological limiting factors in human performance 438
**Regional switching centre (RSC):** *see* Switching and control in telephony 593
**REGISTER (1).** A *register* (1) is a *variety* of a *language* (3) defined with reference to the circumstances in which it is used, and to the purposes for which it is used, as opposed to a *dialect* (1), which is a variety defined with reference to the set of people who use it. Registers may be classified according to a number of different criteria, including *field of discourse, mode of discourse, role, formality*. If a register defined by role is used only for a restricted range of fields of discourse it can be called a *restricted register. See:* Language varieties: language and dialect 243; Language varieties: register 251; Language varieties: stylistics (M) 260; Writing (M) 627; Relations between languages: semantic change (M) 483; Semantics: context and collocation (M) 503; Semantics: field theories 504

**Register (2):** *see* Field (1), field of discourse (G)
**Register (3):** *see* Phonology: prosodic features (M) 413
**REGISTER (4).** A store in a computer, usually one *word* in capcity, for a special purpose such as storing the current instruction, the address of the next instruction, or the result connected with the arithmetic unit.
— **markers:** *see* Language varieties: register (M) 252
—, **-range:** *see* Language varieties: register (M) 251
—, **shift, two-dimensional:** *see* Character recognition 43
**Registers, restricted:** *see* Register (1) (G). Language varieties: register (M) 253
**Registration techniques:** *see* Character recognition 42
**Regulator, linear:** *see* Control by the maximum principle 103
**REGULATORY CONTROL.** Maintaining the outputs of a process as close as possible to their respective set-point values despite the influences of set-point changes and disturbances. *See:* Control, predictive, using fast-time models 140
— **control function:** *see* Control, predictive, using fast-time models 141
**REINFORCEMENT.** An additional signal, in *learning*, designed to encourage a desired persistent change in behaviour. *See:* Psychological linguistics: theories of learning in relation to language (M) 444
**Relation between the stimuli and activity in single primary units:** *See:* Receptors: relation between the stimuli and the activity in single primary units 463
—, **monotonic:** *see* Monotonic relation (G).
—, **non-linear:** *see* Non-linear relation (G).
—, **selection:** *see* Select, selection relation, selection restriction (G).
**Relations between Languages: Introduction** 470
— **between Languages: Bilingualism** 472
— **between Languages: Comparative Philology** 475
— **between Languages: Lingua Franca** 479
— **between Languages: Loans and Loanwords** 482
— **between Languages: Semantic Change** 483
— **between Languages: Typological and Areal Classifications** 486
—, **constituency:** *see* Linguistic form: syntagmatic 277
—, **deep:** *see* Linguistic form: system and structure 279
—, **functional:** *see* Grammar (structural) 186
—, **paradigmatic:** *see* Paradigmatic, paradigmatic relations (G); Linguistic form: paradigmatic 274
—, **structural:** *see* Phonology: constrast and opposition 401; Phonology: phonemes and broad transcription (M) 409
—, **surface:** *see* Linguistic form: system and structure 279
—, **syntagmatic:** *see* Linguistic form: paradigmatic 275; Syntagmatic, syntagmatic relations (G).
**Relationship, anatomical, of channels:** *see* Sensory processes 532
— **between descriptors:** *see* Information storage and retrieval 226

**Relative stability:** *see* Stability (G).
**Release:** *see* Phonetics, articulatory (M)   393
**Relexification:** *see* Relations between languages: lingua franca   480
**Reliable Computation with Unreliable Elements**   485
**RELIABILITY.** A measure or estimate of either (a) the probability of malfunction of a system or (b) the time before a system will fail. *See:* Reliable computation with unreliable elements   489
**Repeat:** *see* Computer peripherals and their control   60
**Repertory:** *see* Language varieties: register (M)   253
**REPRESENTATION.** A *representation* of a stretch of language *(text)* is a *description* of that text in terms of a particular set of categories; any given text can be represented on many different *levels of representation*, some purely linguistic, others not (e.g. an acoustic representation on a spectrograph).
— **by model:** *see* Computer simulation of human thought processes   60
—, **fixed point:** *see* Fixed point representation (G).
—, **floating point:** *see* Floating point representation (G).
—, **level of:** *see* Level (1), level of representation (G).
— **of data:** *see* Data transmission   159
— **of information, spatial:** *see* Receptors: representation of information about stimuli in populations of receptor units   469
—, **Polish:** *see* Polish representation (G).
**Reproduction, method of:** *see* Sensory discrimination, measurement of   522
**Requests, batch processing of:** *see* Information storage and retrieval   229
**Requirements, design, for a computer language:** *see* Computer language design requirements   54
**Research, linguistic:** *see* Computational linguistics: introduction   50
**Residue code:** *see* Error correcting codes   175
**Respiration, self-adaptive control of:** *see* Control of respiration, self-adaptive   132
**Resources, expressive:** *see* Language varieties: stylistics (M)   259
**RESPIRATORY CENTRE.** Part of the medulla oblongata (an expansion of the top of the spinal cord near the centre of the cranial cavity) which initiates, regulates and coordinates respiratory movements.
**RESPONSE.** The change in output signals of a man or animal after a particular *stimulus*. The output of a machine as a result of a particular input.
**Response:** *see* Perception of colour   360; Psychological linguistics: theories of learning in relation to language (M)   444
—, **evoked:** *see* Evoked response (G); Neuronal nets   327
—, **galvanic skin:** *see* Galvanic skin response (G).
—, **impulse:** *see* Impulse response (G); Pseudorandom binary signals, use of...   433
— **surface technique, Carrol's:** *see* Optimization of industrial processes   348
— **system:** *see* Sensory discrimination, measurement of   513
**Response, transient:** *see* Transient response (G).
**Responses, augmenting:** *see* Neuronal nets   328
—, **choice:** *see* Information theory in psychological measurement   234
—, **linguistic:** *see* Speech perception   548
—, **paradigmatic:** *see* Psychological linguistics: psychological aspects of semantic structure   442
—, **recruiting:** *see* Neuronal nets   328
—, **syntagmatic:** *see* Psychological linguistics: psychological aspects of semantic structure   442
**RESTING POTENTIAL.** The normal value of the potential difference across a cell wall (about 50 to 100 mV), the extracellular fluid being positive. *See:* Nerve and muscle, initiation and conduction of impulses in   314; *See also:* Action potential (G)
**Restricted code:** *see* Relations between languages: lingua franca (M)   480; Language varieties: register (M)   251
**RESTRICTED LANGUAGE.** A *restricted language* is a *variety* of a particular *language* (3) (i.e. a *register* (1)) which is appropriate only in a restricted range of *contexts of situations*. *See:* Language varieties: register (M)   252; Semantics: field theories   506
— **register:** *see* Register (1) (G); Language varieties: register (M)   253
**Restriction, selection:** *see* Select, selection relation, selection restriction (G); Psychological linguistics: psychological aspects of semantic structure   442; Semantics: introduction (M)   502
**Restructuring:** *see* Relations between languages: lingua franca   480
**RETICULAR SYSTEM.** (From Latin for 'little net'). The reticular formation is a mixture of grey matter and nerve fibres entering sideways from main afferent tracts. It is located mainly in the brain stem, though its boundaries are ill-defined, and it provides a route whereby afferent signals may reach the cerebral cortex independently of the main sensory pathways. *See:* Neuronal nets   320
**Retinal disparity:** *see* Perception, stereopsis as an aspect of   368
— **gradient of texture:** *see* Perception, stereopsis as an aspect of   369
— **image, stabilized:** *see* Eye movements   178; Perceptual breakdown with stabilized images   388
**Retracted velar plosives:** *see* Phonology: contrast and opposition (M)   401
**Retrieval, fact:** *see* Fact retrieval (G). Fact retrieval   180
— **of data:** *see* Data retrieval (G).
— **of information:** *see* Information storage and retrieval   223
—, **on-line computers for:** *see* Information storage and retrieval   230
**Retroflex:** *see* Phonetics, articulatory   395
**Retroflexed:** *see* Phonetics, auditory   398
**Retroflexion:** *see* Phonetics, auditory   398
**RETROGRADE AMNESIA.** Loss of memory of some of the events close to but preceding some kind of shock, e.g. concussion.

**REVERBERATING ACTIVITY.** Phrase used by Hebb when describing hypothetical *neural circuits* round which signals persist, thus storing information. See: Neuronal nets 320

**Reverse clicks:** *see* Phonetics, articulatory (M) 393
— **Polish notation:** *see* Stacks 564

**REWARD.** Food or other satisfactory signal received by an experimental animal during learning with a teacher.

**REWRITE RULE.** A rule in some kinds of *grammar*, which takes the form: A → B, meaning, given a *string* of symbols including the substring A, this substring is to be replaced by another substring B to produce a different string of symbols. The second string is said to be *derived* from the first. A *rewrite rule* may be *context-free* or *context-sensitive*, and a set of them may or may not be *ordered*. Rewrite rules are the main kind of rule composing a *transformational generative grammar*. See: Linguistic form: generative grammar 272

**Re-writing systems:** *see* Linguistic form: generative grammar (M) 272

**RHEOBASE.** The smallest current which, when applied to a nerve for a sufficient time, will evoke a nerve impulse. See: Neuronal nets 324

**Rhinencephalon:** *see* Neuronal nets 320
**Rhythm:** *see* Writing (M) 627
—, **alpha:** *see* Alpha rhythm (G)
**Rhythmic pattern:** *see* Phonetics, acoustic (M) 393
**Richards:** *see* Semantics: sign and symbol (M) 510
**Ridge:** *see* Optimization, automatic 344; Optimization of industrial processes 347
—, **alveolar:** *see* Phonetics, articulatory 394
— **-following techniques:** *see* Optimization, automatic 344
**Rising:** *see* Phonetics, auditory 398
**Rivalry, binocular:** *see* Perception, stereopsis as an aspect of 372
**Rods:** *see* Perception of colour 359

**ROLE.** Non-dialectal *varieties* of language (*registers* (1)) can be classified on a number of dimensions, one of which is the dimension of *role* (or *genre*). On this dimension registers are classified according to the social or other function of the discourse itself (e.g. informal personal interchange, exposition, literature...). See: Language varieties: register (M) 253

**ROLE INDICATOR.** A mark used by indexers to show the role of a *keyword* or other *descriptor* in the document which it helps to describe. See: Information storage and retrieval 226
— **of pulse distribution in information flow in the nervous system:** *see* Nervous system, role of pulse distribution in information flow 316
— **-register:** *see* Language varieties: register (M) 253

**ROOT.** When a word consists of more than one *morpheme* of which one carries *lexical* rather than *grammatical* information, this morpheme is the word's *root;* any other morphemes in the same word are *affixes*, provided they do not also bear lexical information. See: Grammar (structural) 189

**Root, bound:** *see* Grammar (structural) 189
—, **free:** *see* Grammar (structural) 189
— **locus methods:** *see* Control, stability and 150
**Rosen's gradient projection:** *see* Optimization of industrial processes 348

**ROTE CONCEPTUALIZATION.** Association into categories by mere exercise of memory. See: Concept identification—information processing approaches 80

**Rounded:** *see* Phonology: contrast and opposition (M) 401
**Routh Hurwitz criterion:** *see* Control, stability and 149
**Routing control:** *see* Switching and control in telephony 593
**Ruffini receptor:** *see* Receptor (G).

**RULE.** (In studies of conceptual behaviour). A statement of the manner in which the relevant attributes are combined in examples of a concept, e.g. their joint presence (red triangle), their disjunction (red and/or triangle). See: Conceptual behaviour 84
—, **agreement:** *see* Semantics: introduction (M) 499
—, **base:** *see* Base rule (G); Linguistic form: transformational theory (M) 281
—, **concord:** *see* Semantics: introduction (M) 499
—, **context-sensitive:** *see* Relations between languages: comparative philology (M) 475
—, **contextual:** *see* Phonology: contrast and opposition (M) 402; Phonology: phonemes and broad transcription (M) 409
— **features:** *see* Linguistic form: transformational theory 282
— **(grammar):** *see* Psychological linguistics: psycholinguistic studies of syntax (M) 439
—, **phonological:** *see* Phonology: distinctive features (M) 404
—, **phrase-structure:** *see* Phrase-structure rule (G); Linguistic form: transformational theory (M) 280
—, **projection:** *see* Projection rule (G); Linguistic form: transformational theory 282
—, **redundancy:** *see* Redundant, redundancy rule (G); Linguistic form: transformational theory 283
—, **rewrite:** *see* Rewrite rule (G).
—, **selectional:** *see* Selectional rule (G); Linguistic form: transformational theory 281; Linguistic form: syntagmatic (M) 276
—, **strict subcategorization:** *see* Linguistic form: transformational theory 281; Linguistic form: syntagmatic 278
—, **synthesis by:** *see* Speech synthesis 561
— **-systems:** *see* Psychological linguistics: psychological aspects of semantic structure 442
—, **tactic:** *see* Tactics, tactic rule (G).
—, **transformation:** *see* Relations between languages: typological and areal classifications (M) 486
—, **transformational:** *see* Computational linguistics: machine translation (M) 51; Linguistic form: rtansformational theory (M) 281

**Rules:** *see* Psychological linguistics: theories of learning in relation to language 445
—, **ordered:** *see* Ordered rules (G).

**RUNNING SHORT TERM SPECTRAL ANALYSIS.** Often used on the sound spectrum of speech, it requires a fresh analysis of the speech sounds every time they change. *See:* Speech 545

**Saccadic movements:** *see* Eye movements 177
**SALTATORY CONDUCTION.** The transmission of impulses in myelinated nerve fibres, in which an action potential 'hops' from node to node. *See:* Nerve and muscle, initiation and conduction of impulses in. 316
— **impulse conduction:** *see* Medullated nerve fibre (G).
**SAMPLED DATA.** Information (about the state of a process) at particular instants only. Obtained as if by reading the measuring instruments at prearranged instants. Also, information from particular locations in a store of data. *See:* Control systems, sampled-data 155
— **-data control systems:** *see* Control systems, sampled-data 155
— **-data system, optimum:** *see* Control by stationary filtering and prediction 111
**Sampling, data:** *see* Data sampling (G).
**SANDHI.** *Sandhi* (a term from Sanskrit linguistics) is the influence of one *item* on the *phonetic* or *phonological realization* of another item when the latter occurs next to it: the latter becomes (phonetically or phonologically) more similar to the former than it would be in other environments. *See:* Linguistic form: transformational theory (M) 284
**Sapir (language classification):** *see* Relations between languages: typological and areal classifications 486
**Satellite, geostatic:** *see* Geostatic satellite (G).
—, **synchronous:** *see* Synchronous satellite (G).
**Saturation:** *see* Perception of colour 358
**SCALAR.** A real number, or an undirected quantity such as mass or time (or volume in space of 3 dimensions); distinguished from *vector*.
**Scale, rank:** *see* Writing 627
**SCALING.** The subjective assigning of a numerical value to the 'amount' of a stimulus. *See:* Speech perception 548
**Scanner, flying spot:** *see* Flying spot scanner (G).
**SCANNING.** In a device for reading or writing signals, moving the reading or writing head, or the sensor, in relation to the medium containing the stored information. *See:* Character recognition 41
**Scheduling, plant:** *see* Plant scheduling (G).
**Schwartz-Weiss control:** *see* Control, on-off 136
**Scientific Documentation** 496; *see also:* Computational linguistics: introduction 49
— **induction:** *see* Statistics of language: introduction 574
**SCRIPT.** A linguistic family (or sub-family) of graphs. *See:* Writing (M) 630; Semantics: sign and symbol (M) 510
**SEARCH.** By a learning machine, a change in *state* made either randomly or in a direction predicted to be towards the required state. *See:* Learning machines: a unified view 261
—, **Block:** *see* Optimization, automatic 343
—, **Fibonacci:** *see* Optimization, automatic 342
—, **heuristic:** *see* Problem solving 415
**Searching, binary:** *see* Information storage and retrieval 230
**Secondary articulations:** *see* Phonetics, articulatory 396
— **cardinals:** *see* Phonetics, auditory 397
**Section, golden:** *see* Optimization, automatic 343
**Sectioning:** *see* Optimization, automatic 343
**Security:** *see* Computers, multiaccess to 64
**SEGMENT (NOUN OR VERB), SEGMENTAL PHONEME.** When an *utterance* is analysed *syntagmatically* into parts *(segmented)*, such that each part corresponds to a given stretch of sound (or sequence of letters), these parts are *segments* (or *constituents*) of the utterance. In principle, segments may be of any size, but when a distinction is made between *segmental* and *suprasegmental items* (usually *phonemes*) *segmental* items are the shortest segments into which the utterance can be divided on the *level* in question, whereas *suprasegmental* items are items which extend (or can extend) over a number of segmental items, though they themselves cannot be further divided. *See:* Linguistic form: syntagmatic 276; Grammar (structural) 186; Phonology: prosodic features 411; Phonology: distinctive features 404 (M); Linguistic form: transformational theory (M) 280; Phonetics, articulatory 393; Phonology: contrast and opposition (M) 401; Phonology: phonemes and broad transcription (M) 409; Relations between languages: introduction (M) 470; Relations between languages: comparative philology (M) 475; Relations between languages: typological and areal classifications (M) 486; Sorting techniques 544
**Segmental features:** *see* Phonology: prosodic features 411
**Segmentation:** *see* Linguistic form: paradigmatic (M) 273; Linguistic form: syntagmatic 277; Phonology: distinctive features (M) 404; Relations between languages: typological and areal classifications (M) 486
—, **binary:** *see* Binary segmentation (G).
**SELECT, SELECTION RELATION, SELECTION RESTRICTION.** One kind of *syntagmatic* relation between two *items*, or *classes* of items, is a *selection relation:* one item *selects* another if the first only occurs in the presence of the second. Selection restrictions are restrictions imposed on the *environments* in which a particular item or class of items can occur by the latter's selection relations. *See:* Linguistic form: syntagmatic 277; Linguistic form: system and structure (M) 279; Psychological linguistics: psychological aspects of semantic structure (M) 442; Semantics: introduction (M) 502
**Selection of information:** *see* Perception, visual 387
—, **sorting:** *see* Sorting techniques 544
**Selectional features:** *see* Linguistic form: transformational theory 281

**SELECTIONAL RULE.** *Rewrite rules* which, in a *transformational generative grammar*, can rewrite a symbol as a *complex-symbol* are of two kinds: *strict subcategorization rules* and *selectional rules*. The complex symbol is attached to a *category symbol* which is to be replaced by a *representation* of a particular *item* selected from the *lexicon*, and the purpose of the complex symbol is to give information on the *environment* of this category symbol, in terms of *features* which the lexical item selected must be compatible with. Selectional rules contribute *selectional features* to the complex symbol; these specify the presence in the environment of a certain set of complex symbols, whose *syntagmatic* relations to the complex symbol in question are not subject to the same restrictions as in the case of *subcategorization features*. *See:* Linguistic form: transformational theory 281; Linguistic form: syntagmatic (M) 276

**SELECTIVE DISSEMINATION OF INFORMATION (SDI).** Supplying (to the scientists) all newly received documents, or references to such documents, which match his *personal profile*. *See:* Scientific documentation 496

— **invariance:** *see* Control, invariance and 127

**Self-adaptive control of respiration:** *see* Control of respiration, self-adaptive 132

— **-adaptive machine:** *see* Learning (G).

**SELF-EMBEDDING.** A *grammar* (3) is *self-embedding* if there is a symbol A in its vocabulary which is rewritten, by a *rewrite rule*, as a string of symbols consisting of the same symbol A, and one or more symbols on either side of A. Similarly, an *item* is self-embedding if one of its *immediate constituents*, which is neither its first nor its last immediate constituent, is of the same *class* as the item itself. *See:* Psychological linguistics: psycholinguistic studies of syntax (M) 439

— **-organizing control system:** *see* Control: basic elements 92

**SELF-REFERENCING LANGUAGE.** A language such as human language, in which instructions can be issued for signs and symbols to be adopted. *See:* Psychology, use of models (learning) 450

— **-reproducing automata:** *see* Automata, infinite-state 38

**Semantic:** *see* Linguistic form: paradigmatic (M) 273; Semantics: sign and symbol (M) 510

— **association between descriptors:** *see* Information storage and retrieval 226

— **change:** *see* Relations between languages: semantic change 484

— **component:** *see* Linguistic form: transformational theory (M) 280

— **features:** *see* Linguistic form: transformational theory (M) 280

— **field:** *see* Field (2), semantic field (G); Relations between languages: loans and loanwords (M) 482; Relations between languages: semantic change (M) 484; Semantics: introduction (M) 499; Semantics: field theories 504

**Semantic integration:** *see* Relations between languages: loans and loanwords (M) 482

— **interference:** *see* Relations between languages: bilingualism (M) 473

— **interpretation:** *see* Psychological linguistics: psycholinguistic studies of syntax (M) 439

— **level:** *see* Semantics: meaning and reference 508

— **markers:** *see* Psychological linguistics: psycholinguistic studies of syntax (M) 439; Psychological linguistics: psychological aspects of semantic structure 442

— **structure:** *see* Semantics: field theories 505

— **structure, psychological aspects of:** *see* Psychological linguistics: psychological aspects of semantic structure 442

— **studies:** *see* Language varieties: stylistics (M) 259

**SEMANTICS.** The study of linguistic meaning. *See:* Semantics: introduction 499; Semantics: meaning and reference 507; Relations between languages: semantic change 484; Statistics of language: introduction (M) 567

—: **Introduction** 499

—, **combinatorial:** *see* Combinatorial semantics (G). Semantics: introduction 501

—: **Context and Collocation** 503

—, **diachronic:** *see* Relations between languages: semantic change (M) 483

—: **Field Theories** 504

—: **Meaning and Reference** 507

—: **Sign and Symbol** 510

—, **structural:** *see* Semantics: introduction 499

**Sememic:** *see* Computational linguistics: introduction (M) 49

**SEMIOLOGY, SEMIOTIC SYSTEM.** *Semiology* is a (projected) science of *signs*. A *semiotic system* is any *system* (1) of signs, including *natural languages*. *See:* Semantics: sign and symbol 510

**Semiotic system:** *see* Relations between languages: lingua franca (M) 480

**Semivowels:** *see* Phonetics, articulatory 395; Phonetics, auditory 397

**Sense:** *see* Relations between languages: semantic change (M) 484; Semantics: meaning and reference 508

**Sensing devices, computer linked to:** *see* Control by hybrid computers 97

**SENSITIVITY.** The change in output of a system in response to a small change in an input or a parameter of the system. *See:* Control, sensitivity and 147; Sensory discrimination, measurement of 517

— **analysis:** *see* Control, sensitivity and 147

— **and control,** *see* Control, sensitivity and 147

—, **flicker:** *see* Perception, visual 381

—, **movement:** *see* Perception, visual 380

**Sensorimotor effects in sound perception:** *see* Perception of sound 367

**Sensory Discrimination, Measurement of** 512

— **nerve:** *see* Nerve (G).

— **nerve fibre:** *see* Receptor as transducers 457

— **pathway, classical:** *see* Neuronal nets 328

Sensory Processes 525
**Sentences, embedded:** *see* Linguistic form: transformational theory (M) 280
—, **nested:** *see* Linguistic form: generative grammar (M) 273
**SEQUENCE.** *Sequence* is sometimes contrasted in linguistics with *order;* the sequence of a set of *items* specifies their relations on a single dimension in time or on the page; this is a more superficial ('*surface*') relation than *order*, which can be taken to include any *syntagmatic* relations between the items, including *dependency* and *constituency* relations, and it may be necessary to show this order by using two dimensions, as in a labelled *tree*. *See:* Linguistic form: syntagmatic (M) 276
—, **Bernoulli:** *see* Bernoulli sequence (G).
**SEQUENCE GENERATOR.** Alternative to a fixed store for controlling the operations performed by a computer. *See:* Fixed stores and control by microprogram 181
—, **m:** *see* Chain code (G)
—, **phonemic:** *see* Phonemic sequence (G); Phonetics, acoustic (M) 393
—, **pseudonoise:** *see* Pseudonoise sequences 419
—, **pulse:** *see* Pulse sequence (G).
**SEQUENCING.** Arranging tasks in the order in which they would best be done, e.g. in manufacturing.
**SEQUENTIAL COMPUTER.** Any computer (e.g. a digital computer) which carries out its instructions one by one; but it may have to make a choice of alternative instructions. *See:* Control by hybrid computers 93
— **decoding:** *see* Error correcting codes 157
**Series, time:** *see* Time series (G).
**Services, broadcast, carrier-wired:** *see* Local networks 288
—, **radio, high frequency:** *see* Telecommunication, global 604
**Servicing:** *see* Computer peripherals and their control 59
— **time:** *see* Computer peripherals and their control 59
**SERVOMECHANISM.** A control system in which a signal from a transducer attached to the output device is matched to the input signal. The resulting low-level error signal is amplified to actuate the output variable. *See:* Man-machine communication and ergonomics 301
**SET LEVEL, SET POINT.** The desired value of a variable being controlled by a mechanism.
—, **organizing:** *see* Organizing set (G).
**Sets, lexical:** *see* Linguistic form: paradigmatic 276
**Shadow patterns:** *see* Perception, stereopsis as an aspect of 369
**Shadowing:** *see* Psychological linguistics: psycholinguistic studies of syntax (M) 439
**SHANNON'S CODING THEOREM.** A theorem which proves that noisy channels can be used for almost error-free communication. *See:* Communication theory 46

**SHEFFER STROKE OPERATOR.** From a set of objects which may have either, both, or neither of two properties, this operator selects objects which have not both. Identical with NOT-AND. *See:* Logic element (G).
**Shift register, two-dimensional:** *see* Character recognition 43
**Shifts, sound:** *see* Relations between languages: comparative philology (M) 475
**Shock, electroconvulsive:** *see* Electroconvulsive shock (G).
**Short-term memory:** *see* Psychological linguistics: psycholinguistic studies of syntax (M) 439
— **-term memory store:** *see* Models for human memory 311
**Sibilant fricatives:** *see* Phonology: distinctive features (M) 404
**SIDETONE.** The phenomenon, usually intentional, whereby a telephone speaker hears his own voice in his receiver. *See:* Subscriber's telephone set, design considerations of 584
**SIGMOIDAL.** Shaped like an *ogive*.
**SIGN (LINGUISTIC SIGN)** A *linguistic sign* is the association of some *form* (1), or observable phenomenon, with a *content* or meaning; neither of these on its own constitutes a *sign*. *See:* Semantics: sign and symbol 510; Semantics: field theories (M) 504; Relations between languages: bilingualism (M) 472; Semantics: context and collocation (M) 503
**SIGNAL (1).** A linguistic *sign* whose *function* (1) is *expressive* rather than *referential*. *See:* Semantics: sign and symbol 510
**SIGNAL (2).** The audible or visible evidence of a linguistic *item*'s occurring, e.g. the sounds *manifesting* the item.
**SIGNAL (3).** Any physical representation of information (e.g. spoken word, written symbol, electric current, radio wave).
**SIGNAL (4).** Signal (3) together with the means of carrying it (e.g. radio wave, pulse). *Signal amplitude*. The value of any of those physical variables of a signal (4) which contain information (e.g. voltage, pulse width).
—, **analog:** *see* Analog signal (G).
—, **digital:** *see* Digital signal (G).
—, **random:** *see* Random signal (G)
**Signals:** *see* Semantics: sign and symbol 510
—, **acoustic:** *see* Psychological linguistics: psychological aspects of semantic structure 442
—, **motor:** *see* Muscle spindles (G).
—, **pseudorandom binary, use of, in correlation analysis of binary systems:** *see* Pseudorandom binary signals, use of, in correlation analysis of dynamic systems 433
—, **random:** *see* Random signals and noise 453
**Signifiant:** *see* Signifié (G).
**Significance of fibre diameter:** *See* Receptors: relation between the stimuli and the activity in single primary units 466
**Signification:** *see* Semantics: introduction 499

**SIGNIFIÉ.** A linguistic *sign* is considered to have two parts: the *signifiant*, which is the observable evidence of an occurrence of the sign; and the *signifié*, which is what an occurrence of the sign implies or means, i.e. its '*content*' as opposed to its '*form*'. *See:* Semantics: field theories (M) 505; Semantics: meaning and reference (M) 507

**Similarity** 535

—, **phonetic:** *see* Phonology: phonemes and broad transcription 409

**Simple eye:** *see* Perception, visual 473

**Simplex method:** *see* Optimization of industrial processes 347

**SIMPLICITY METRIC.** A measure of the simplicity of a *grammar* (3).

**Simulation of Traffic Problems using Chain-Code Random Generators** 539

**Single cell, homeostasis in:** *see* Homeostasis in the single cell 217

— **primary units, relation between stimuli and activity in:** *see* Receptors: relation between the stimuli and the activity in single primary units 463

— **receptor unit:** *see* Receptors: representation of information about stimuli in populations 467

— **stimuli, method of:** *see* Sensory discrimination, measurement of 518

**SINGULARY TRANSFORMATION.** A *transformation* operating on a single *string*. (c.f. *generalized transformation*). *See:* Psychological linguistics: psycholinguistic studies of syntax (M) 439

**SINUSOID.** A *wave motion* of a single pure frequency, without harmonics. *See:* Speech synthesis 559

**SITUATION.** The *situation* of an utterance is the totality of circumstances under which it occurs on a particular occasion; the study of situation thus defined goes beyond the study of *linguistic form*, and belongs rather to *substance*. *See:* Semantics: context and collocation 503; Semantics: meaning and reference 507; Language varieties: register (M) 251

**Situation, context of:** *see* Context (1), context of situation (G). Language varieties: register (M) 251; Language varieties: stylistics (M) 259; Semantics: introduction (M) 500; Semantics: context and collocation 503; Semantics: meaning and reference 509

**Skin mechanics:** *see* Non-neural elements in receptor systems 338

**Slicing, time:** *see* Computers, multiaccess to 65

**SLOT.** A *slot* is a grammatical *function*, and defines a place where a *filler* occurs—a class of *items* which can all occur in this *slot*; a slot and its filler together constitute a *tagmeme*. *See:* Grammar (structural) 198

— **-filler analysis:** *see* Grammar (structural) 198

**SLOW POTENTIAL.** The potential in the fluid outside the membranes of cells, fluctuating within the frequency band 10–1000 c/s as a result of their changes in permeability and the action potentials within them. *See:* Neuronal nets, Fig. 16.

**Small computers, operating of:** *see* Computer operating systems 57

— **field tritanopia:** *see* Perception of colour 363

**Smell:** *see* Receptors: representation of information about stimuli in populations 469

**Social communication and language:** *see* Information theory in psychological measurement 235

**SOCIOLECT.** The *dialect* of a *linguistic community* which is separated socially rather than geographically from other linguistic communities. *See:* Language and varieties: language and dialect 243

**Sociolinguistics:** *see* Language varieties: register (M) 251

**Sociological linguistics:** *see* Language varieties: register (M) 251

**Soft palate:** *see* Phonetics, articulatory 394

**SOFTWARE.** Programs controlling the data processing, and input and output signals of a computer, in contradistinction to *hardware*. Particularly the programs for *compiling* and for providing diagnostic reports on failures.

**Solving of problems:** *see* Problem solving 413

**SOMA OR CELL BODY.** The main part of a *neuron* containing the nucleus and other organelles important for cell function, found in large numbers, for example, in the *grey matter* of the brain. *See:* Neuronal nets, Fig. 3.

**Somatic system:** *see* Sensory processes 532

**SOMATO-DENDRITIC MEMBRANE.** Abbreviated to SD-membrane. The membrane of the soma (cell body) and its dendrites, which is very sensitive to incoming impulses via *synapses* with the *axons* of other nerves. *See:* Neuronal nets 322

**Sonority features:** *see* Phonology: distinctive features 406

**SORTING.** The ordering, according to prearranged rules, of items of information no yet in order. *See:* Sorting techniques 546

—, **digital:** *see* Sorting techniques 544

—, **merge:** *see* Sorting techniques 544

—, **radix:** *see* Sorting techniques 544

—, **selection:** *see* Sorting techniques 544

— **Techniques** 543

**Sound changes:** *see* Relations between languages: introduction (M) 470

—, **consonant:** *see* Phonetics, acoustic (M) 391

—, **generation of:** *see* Phonetics, acoustic (M) 391; Phonetics, experimental (M) 399

— **image:** *see* Perception of sound 365

—, **nasalized:** *see* Phonetics, acoustic (M) 391

— **perception:** *see* Perception of sound 365

— **perception, intersensory effects in:** *see* Perception of sound 367

— **perception (physiology):** *see* Perception of sound 367

— **perception, sensorimotor effects in:** *see* Perception of sound 367

— **shifts:** *see* Relations between languages: comparative philology (M) 475

— **-pressure time waveforms:** *see* Hearing 211

**SOUND SPECTROGRAPH.** Device for frequency analysis of sounds so as to show the location on the frequency scale of *formants* and the relative amplitude of the frequency components in the sound being analysed. *See:* Phonetics, acoustic   393

—, **stop:** *see* Speech synthesis   559

— **wave:** *see* Phonetics, experimental (M)   399

**Source function:** *see* Phonetics, acoustic   391

**SOURCE LANGUAGE.** *Translation* is from a *text* in one *language* (3) (the *source language*) into a text in another (the *target language* or *object language*). *See:* Computational linguistics: machine translation   51

**Sources of statistics of languages:** *see* Statistics of language: introduction   577

**SPACE.** The set of all possible values which a quantity or quantities may take. The space has *n* dimensions if *n* numbers, and no more, are needed to specify one element or *point* in the space. *See:* Information space   221

—, **information:** *see* Informational space (G); Information space   221

— **list, available:** *see* Symbol manipulation by digital computer   596

—, **memory:** *see* Psychological linguistics: psycholinguistic studies of syntax   440

— **perception, stereoscopy and:** *see* Perception, visual   385

**Spatial adaptation:** *see* Perception, visual   383

— **representation of information.** *see* Receptors: representation of information about stimuli in populations of receptor units   469

**Speaker identification:** *see* Speech recognition, automatic   552

**SPEAKING.** *Speaking* (translating *la parole*) is contrasted in linguistic theory with *language (la langue)*; *language* is the system of rules a native speaker knows, while *speaking* is the use he makes of this system in talking and listening, reading or writing. (Cf. the distinction between *performance* (speaking) and *competence* (language)). *Speaking* and *language* together constitute *speech*, the general faculty of language acquisition and use. *See:* Linguistic form: system and structure   279

**Specialist, human factors:** *see* Man-machine communication and ergonomics   301

**Species problem:** *see* Statistics of language: introduction   575

**SPECIFIC (1).** Physically separable from the surroundings.

**SPECIFIC (2).** Functionally definable, in terms of those inputs which produce changes in its output in distinction from those which do not.

— **categories:** *see* Grammar (structural)   204

**Spectral analysis, running short term:** *see* Running short term spectral analysis (G).

**SPECTRAL BANDWIDTH.** Range of frequencies of a sound. *See:* Hearing   211

**Spectrograph, sound:** *see* Sound spectrograph (G); Phonetics, acoustic   393

**SPECTRUM.** A way of describing any analog signal, by representing the amplitudes of different aspects of the signal as functions of a measurable attribute (e.g. in light, the amplitude of the signal as a function of the frequency or wave-length). Similarly in sound, and alternating current electricity. Also applicable to the autocorrelation function, and even to mass spectrometry where no wave motion is involved. The alternative way of describing a signal is by its *waveform*, the disturbance at a particular point as a function of time.

—, **speech sound, fine structure of:** *see* Fine structure of speech sound spectrum (G).

**SPEECH (1).** The capacity both for knowledge of a *language (competence)* and for use of it in *speaking (performance)*; *speech* translates de Saussure's term *le langage*.

**SPEECH (2).** The spoken, as opposed to the written, use of language.

**Speech** 545; *see also:* Phonetics, acoustic (M)   391; Phonetics, experimental (M)   399; Writing (M)   627

—, **acoustics of:** *see* Phonetics, experimental   400

— **channel, telephone:** *see* Data transmission   160

—, **figures of:** *see* Relations between languages: semantic change (M)   484

**SPEECH MECHANISM.** The organs used when speaking. *See:* Phonetics, acoustic   391

—, **organs of:** *see* Phonetics, articulatory   393

**SPEECH PARAMETERS.** Experimentally determined components of speech sounds. *See:* Speech synthesis   559

—, **parts of:** *see* Statistics of language: structure of written English words (M)   581

— **Perception**   548

—, **phonetic structure of:** *see* Writing (M)   627

—, **phonological structure of:** *see* Writing (M)   627

—, **physiological activity in:** *see* Phonetics, experimental   399

—, **psychophysics of:** *see* Speech perception   548

— **Recognition, Automatic**   552

— **sound spectrum, fine structure of:** *see* Fine structure of speech sound spectrum (G).

— **Synthesis**   559; *see also:* Phonetics, experimental   400

—, **voiced:** *see* Phonetics, acoustic (M)   391

**Sphere-packed code:** *see* Error correcting codes   173

**SPIKE.** An analog signal whose shape is a spike, plotting voltage against time.

**Spinal cord:** *see* Neuronal nets   320

**Spindles, muscle:** *see* Muscle spindles (G).

**Spirant:** *see* Phonetics, articulatory   396

**Spirometer:** *see* Phonetics, experimental (M)   400

**SPL.** Relative to a sound pressure level $P_{ref} = 2 \times 10^{-5}$; N/m² (Newtons per square metre), e.g. for a sound of 50 dB SPL the sound pressure would be $p$ such that $50 = 20 \log_{10} (p/p_{ref})$ so $p = 2 \times 10^{-5} \times 10^{2 \cdot 5}$ N/m². *See:* Sensory discrimination, measurement of   512

**SPONTANEOUS ACTIVITY.** Action potentials arising

in a nerve fibre, in the absence of an applied stimulus or detectable distortion of the tissue, under normal physiological conditions; sometimes called *noise* (of the fibre). *See:* Receptors: relation between the stimuli and the activity in single primary units 363

**Square matrix:** *see* Matrix (G).

— **pulse:** *see* Pulse, square (G).

**Squares, least:** *see* Least squares (G); Optimization, automatic 344

**S-R psychology:** *see* Problem solving 416

**STABILITY.** Of a *system* which is under *feedback control;* the tendency of the system to settle down into a steady *state* when being designed, a system is said to be stable when the error signal of its feedback control, together with the time-derivatives of the error signal, all go to zero with increasing time. The degree of stability is related to the speed with which these go to zero. *See:* Control, stability and 149. *Stability, relative.* The manner in which the error signal goes to zero after the system has been disturbed, for example, by a 'step input' producing a finite shift in the value of its main input. Also called *transient response.*

— **and control:** *see* Control, stability and 149

—, **relative:** *see* Stability (G).

**Stabilized images:** *see* Perception, visual 384

— **images, perceptual breakdown with:** *see* Perceptual breakdown with stabilized images 388

— **retinal image:** *see* Eye movements 178; Perceptual breakdown with stabilized images 388

**STACK.** A storage module in a digital computer into which items of information may be inserted, and from which items may be extracted (and thereby removed): of the items present in the stack at any time only the last one to have been inserted can be removed. *See:* Stacks 563

—, **arithmetic:** *see* Stacks 564

—, **sub-routine link:** *see* Stacks 564

—, **temporary storage:** *see* Stacks 564

**Stacks** 563

**Staircase method (SM):** *see* Sensory discrimination, measurement of 521

— **method, transformed response:** *see* Sensory discrimination, measurement of 521

**Stammering:** *see* Perception of sound 368

**Standard deviation:** *see* Normal distribution (G).

— **language:** *see* Language varieties: language and dialect 248

— **observer:** *see* Perception of colour 360

**Standardization:** *see* Writing (M) 627

—, **language:** *see* Relations between languages: lingua franca 480

**STARRED FORMS.** In linguistic literature a star (*) is added before a *form* (3) for one of two reasons: (1) in a historical or comparative work the star means that the form is assumed to have occurred in the (dead) language in question, on the basis of evidence from other, later, languages; but there is no direct evidence that the form occurred, such as a written text containing it; (2) in a *description* of a *language system*, the star means that the form is not *grammatical* (3). *See:* Relations between languages: comparative philology 475

**STATE.** Complete description (of a multivariable analog signal). *See:* Perception of colour 358

— **estimation:** *see* Control, identification techniques for 120

— **estimation by inferential means:** *see* Control, predictive, using fast-time models 142

**STATE OF A MACHINE OR SYSTEM.** Its internal condition which can be described, for example, by listing its next state and next output, for any conceivable input. If the state of a machine is never changed by its input, it is a one state machine. *See:* Automata, finite-state 32

**STATE OF AN ANIMAL.** Its internal condition which must be described by its predicted next output, for any input; usually summarized by a few words concerning, e.g. hunger, fear, maternal behaviour. *See:* Animal motivation 24

**STATE SPACE.** The $n$-dimensional space in which *state variables* are represented. *See:* Control systems, multivariable 151

**STATE VARIABLE.** In a physical system the state variables are all its physical variables (i.e. velocities, positions, temperatures etc.). The system (its *dynamic* behaviour) can be completely described by a large enough set of equations involving time and a sufficient number of state variables. P. H. Hammond. *See:* Dynamic programming 168

**STATEMENT (1).** A unit instruction in a programming language. *See:* Algorithms for processing algorithms 15

**STATEMENT (2).** A unit in a theorem proving problem, which may either be an *atomic statement (atom)* or a *Boolean combination* of simpler statements. *Atomic statement (atom).* An expression consisting of a *relation symbol of degree* ($n$) followed by a parenthesized list of $n$ terms. *Term* (in theorem proving). Either a variable, or a function system of *degree* ($n$) followed by a parenthesized list of $n$ terms. *See:* Theorem proving by machine 616

—, **atomic:** *see* Statement (G).

—, **declarative:** *see* Computer language design requirements 54

—, **indicative:** *see* Computer language design requirements 54

**States, autonomous:** *see* Control, on-off 137

—, **motivation:** *see* Animal motivation 24

**Static optimizing control:** *see* Control, predictive, using fast-time models 143

**STATIONARY.** A process is stationary when there is no change with time of the mechanism governing the selection and generation of the signal.

— **filtering and prediction, control by:** *see* Control by stationary filtering and prediction (Wiener) 109

— **process:** *see* Process (G).

**Statistical word associations:** *see* Information storage and retrieval 227

**Statistics of Language: Introduction** 567
— **of language, sources of:** *see* Statistics of language: introduction 577
— **of Language: Structure of Written English Words** 581
**Status:** *see* Computer peripherals and their control 60
**Steepest ascent, hill climbing by:** *see* Control, hill climbing in 117
— **ascent, method of:** *see* Optimization, automatic 343; Optimization of industrial processes 347
**Stellate:** *see* Neuron (G).
**STEM.** Where a word consists of more than one *morpheme*, of which some are *inflexional morphemes*, all but the latter constitute the *stem* of the word. The stem may itself consist of a *root* and one or more *derivational affixes. See:* Grammar (structural) 189; Linguistic form: paradigmatic (M) 273
**STENOTYPING.** A compressed typewritten record of speech (using a special machine) in which each unit of typing corresponds to a spoken syllable. *See:* Statistics of language: introduction 567
**STEP FUNCTION.** An analog signal whose shape is a step, plotting voltage against time. 'Function' is unnecessary. Cf. Spike (G). *See:* Magnetic recording 291
**Stereopsis as an aspect of perception:** *see* Perception, stereopsis as an aspect of 368
—, **patent:** *see* Perception, stereopsis as an aspect of 371
—, **qualitative:** *see* Perception, stereopsis as an aspect of 371
**Stereoscope:** *see* Perception, stereopsis as an aspect of 368
**Stereoscopic acuity:** *see* Perception, stereopsis as an aspect of 371
**Stereoscopy and space perception:** *see* Perception, visual 305
**Stiles-Crawford brightness shift effect:** *see* Perception of colour 363
— **-Crawford effect:** *see* Perception, visual 380
— **-Crawford hue shift effect:** *see* Perception of colour 363
**Stimulation, hypothalamus:** *see* Animal motivation 24
**STIMULUS.** Any input signal to a man or animal, likely to affect its output signals. Any event which disturbs the potential difference across the membrane of the cell. *Sub-threshold (supra-threshold) stimulus.* A stimulus of insufficient (sufficient) strength to start the mechanism whereby a cell transmits a signal along its length. *See:* Nerve and muscle, initiation and conduction of impulses in 314
—: *see* Psychological linguistics: theories of learning in relation to language (M) 444
—, **constant:** *see* Receptors: relation between the stimuli and the activity in single primary units 465
— **redundancy:** *see* Conceptual behaviour 86
—, **sub-threshold:** *see* Stimulus (G).
—, **supra-threshold:** *see* Stimulus (G).
**STOCHASTIC.** *Random.*
— **computers:** *see* Computers, stochastic 66
— **control theory:** *see* Control: basic elements 91

**Stop, glottal:** *see* Phonology: phonemes and broad transcription (M) 409
— **sounds:** *see* Speech synthesis 559
**Stops:** *see* Phonetics, articulatory 395; Phonology: contrast and opposition (M) 401
—, **aspirated:** *see* Phonology: phonemes and broad transcription (M) 409
—, **glottalized:** *see* Phonology: phonemes and broad transcription (M) 409
**Storage management:** *see* Computers, multiaccess to 65
— **of information:** *see* Information storage and retrieval 223
— **on film:** *see* Information storage and retrieval 223
— **stack, temporary:** *see* Stacks 564
**STORE.** Any device where information can be *written* and from which it can be *read*. G. G. Scarrott
—, **buffer:** *see* Buffer store (G).
—, **core:** *see* Core store (G).
—, **fixed:** *see* Fixed store (G).
—, **matrix:** *see* Matrix store (G).
—, **memory, short term:** *see* Models for human memory 311
—, **memory, very short term:** *see* Models for human memory 311
—, **push-down:** *see* Stacks 563
— **systems, pushdown:** *see* Linguistic form: generative grammar (M) 272
**Stores, fixed:** *see* Fixed stores and control by microprogram 181
**Stratal conversion:** *see* Computational linguistics: introduction 51
**Stratificational grammar:** *see* Computational linguistics: machine translation (M) 51; Linguistic form: generative grammar (M) 272
**STRATUM.** A *stratum* is a *level of representation*, i.e. a system within the total *language system*, e.g. *morphology* and *phonology* are two different *strata. See:* Computational linguistics: introduction (M) 49; Computational linguistics: machine translation (M) 51; Language varieties: register (M) 254
**Strength models:** *see* Models for human memory 312
**STRESS.** A syllable is *stressed* if it is pronounced with a relatively large amount of force relative either to the syllables on either side, or to the generally expected amount of force (in which case the syllables on either side will be stressed too). The former is the meaning of *stress* when rules for the placement of stress are given in the *description* of a particular *language system*. Stress is an *articulatory* category, whose *acoustic* and *auditory* correlates may, but need not, be loudness and prominence respectively. *See:* Phonology: prosodic features 411; Grammar (structural) (M) 186; Linguistic form: transformational theory (M) 283; Phonetics, experimental (M) 399; Phonology: distinctive features (M) 404; Relations between languages: bilingualism (M) 473; Statistics of language: structure of written English words (M) 581
—, **accentual:** *see* Phonology: prosodic features 412

**Stress, distinctive:** *see* Relations between languages: typological and areal classifications 486
— **pattern:** *see* Phonetics, acoustic (M) 393
**Stressed features:** *see* Linguistic form: transformational theory 283
**Stretch receptors:** *see* Receptors: representation of information about stimuli in populations 467
**Striate cortex:** *see* Perception, stereopsis as an aspect of 372
**Strict subcategorization rules:** *see* Subcategorization (G); Linguistic form: syntagmatic (M) 278; Linguistic form: transformational theory 281
**STRICTURE.** A complete or partial obstruction to the passage of air through the *vocal tract. See:* Phonetics, articulatory 395
**Strident features:** *see* Linguistic form: transformational theory 283
**STRING (1).** A sequentially ordered set of symbols or *items.*
**STRING (2).** A variable length sequence of elements (symbols) from a well-defined set of basic elements. String elements in a computer are stored sequentially and therefore do not contain internal explicit sequencing information. (Distinct from a *list.) See:* Symbol manipulation by digital computer 595
—, **complex:** *see* Linguistic form: transformational theory 281
—, **consonant:** *see* Statistics of language: structure of written English words (M) 567
**STRING CONSTITUENT.** When a distinction is needed between *immediate constituents* yielded by essentially *binary segmentation* and those yielded by segmentation not subject to the restriction of binarity the former can be called immediate constituents (or IC's) or *layered constituents* and the latter *string constituents. See:* Grammar (structural) 199
— **processing:** *see* Symbol manipulation by digital computer 596
— **-processing languages:** *see* Symbol manipulation by digital computer 597
—, **terminal:** *see* Linguistic form: transformational theory (M) 280; Terminal string (G).
**Strings:** *see* Sorting techniques 544
—, **wellformed:** *see* Linguistic form: generative grammar 272
**STRONG GENERATIVE CAPACITY.** The *strong* (as opposed to the *weak) generative capacity* of a *grammar (3)* is the set of *structural descriptions* generated by the grammar. *See:* Linguistic form: generative grammar 272
— **unimodality:** *see* Optimization, automatic 343
**STRONGLY EQUIVALENT GRAMMARS.** Two *grammars (3)* are strongly equivalent if they have the same *strong generative capacity. See:* Psychological linguistics: psycholinguistic studies of syntax 439
**Structural approach:** *see* Semantics: introduction (M) 499; Semantics: field theories (M) 504
— **background:** *see* Relations between languages: semantic change (M) 484

**Structural criteria:** *see* Relations between languages: typological and areal classifications (M) 486
**STRUCTURAL DESCRIPTION.** A *structural description* of an *item* is a representation of its *structure (2). See:* Linguistic form: generative grammar (M) 272; Psychological linguistics: theories of learning in relation to language 445; Psychological linguistics: psycholinguistic studies of syntax (M) 439
— **grammar:** *see* Grammar (structural) 186
— **linguistics:** *see* Language varieties: stylistics (M) 259; Semantics: field theories (M) 504
— **matrix:** *see* Matrix (1) (G); Phonology: contrast and opposition (M) 401
— **process:** *see* Process (structural) (G).
— **relations:** *see* Phonology: contrast and opposition 401; Phonology: phonemes and broad transcription (M) 409
— **semantics:** *see* Semantics: introduction 499
— **transformation:** *see* Computational linguistics: machine translation 53
**STRUCTURE (1).** The *structure (1)* of a *language* is its *system (1),* i.e. the highly complex set of interrelated rules underlying the utterances of that language. All *models* of language are models of language *structure,* attempting to show how these rules are interrelated. Linguistics (or a branch of linguistics, such as *semantics)* is said to be *structural* if it is based on such a model of language structure; this is usually a question of degree, however, since no completely integrated model has as yet been proposed. *See:* Linguistic form: system and structure 278; Semantics: introduction 499; Relations between languages: comparative philology (M) 475; Relations between languages: loans and loanwords (M) 482; Relations between languages: semantic change (M) 484; Relations between languages: typological and areal classifications (M) 486; Semantics: meaning and reference (M) 507
**STRUCTURE (2).** The *structure (2)* of an *item* is the set of relations among its *constituents;* the only relations taken into account may be *syntagmatic relations,* but the *paradigmatic relations* of its constituents may also be considered relevant. The relevant constituents may include only the item's *immediate constituents,* or may include all its constituents. *See:* Linguistic form: system and structure 278; Grammar (structural) 186; Linguistic form: syntagmatic (M) 276; Computational linguistics: machine translation (M) 51; Phonology: contrast and opposition (M) 401; Relations between languages: introduction (M) 470
—, **deep:** *see* Deep structure, deep grammar (G); Grammar (structural) (M) 186; Linguistic form: transformational theory 282; Psychological linguistics: psycholinguistic studies of syntax 439; Relations between languages: typological and areal classifications (M) 486
—, **element of:** *see* Element (2), element of structure (G). Linguistic form: system and structure 279

**Structure, fine, of speech sound spectrum:** *see* Fine structure of speech sound spectrum (G).
—, **goal:** *see* Problem solving 414
—, **grammatical:** *see* Relations between languages: comparative philology (M) 475; Semantics: introduction (M) 499; Semantics: field theories (M) 505
—, **graphetic:** *see* Writing 627
—, **graphological:** *see* Writing 627
**STRUCTURE INDEX.** The specification, for a given *transformation* of the conditions to be fulfilled in order for the transformation to operate. *See:* Linguistic form: transformational theory 282
—, **level of:** *see* Semantics: introduction (M) 499
—, **lexical:** *see* Semantics: field theories 505
—, **linguistic:** *see* Phonetics, acoustic 391; Psychological linguistics: theories of learning in relation to language 444
—, **list:** *see* List structure (G).
—, **morphological:** *see* Relations between languages: comparative philology (M) 475
—, **phonemic:** *see* Semantics: field theories (M) 504
—, **phonetic of speech:** *see* Writing (M) 627
—, **phonological, of speech:** *see* Writing (M) 627
—, **phrase:** *see* Computational linguistics: machine translation (M) 51; Relations between languages: typological and areal classifications (M) 486
—, **of written English words:** *see* Statistics of language: structure of written English words 581
—, **semantic:** *see* Semantics: field theories 505
—, **semantic, psychological aspects of:** *see* Psychological linguistics: psychological aspects of semantic structure 442
—, **surface:** *see* Surface structure, surface grammar (G); Grammar (structural) (M) 186; Linguistic form: transformational theory 282; Psychological linguistics: psycholinguistic studies of syntax (M) 439; Relations between languages: typological and areal classifications (M) 486
—, **syntactic:** *see* Statistics of language: introduction (M) 567
**Structured:** *see* Linguistic form: system and structure (M) 278; Semantics: field theories (M) 505
**Studies, semantic:** *see* Language varieties: stylistics (M) 259
**Style:** *see* Language varieties: language and dialect 243; Language varieties: register (M) 251; Language varieties: stylistics 259; Semantics: context and collocation (M) 503; Semantics: field theories (M) 504
— **of discourse:** *see* Formality (G); Language varieties: register (M) 251
**STYLISTICS.** The study of *style*, and in particular of literary style. *See:* Language varieties: stylistics 259
**SUBCATEGORIZATION.** *Rewrite rules*, in a *transformational-generative grammar*, which can rewrite a symbol as a *complex symbol*, are of two kinds: *strict subcategorization rules* and *selectional rules*. The complex symbol is attached to a particular *category symbol* which is to be replaced by a *representation* of some *lexical item*, and gives information about the category symbol's *environment*, with which the lexical item must be compatible. The *subcategorization features*, which are introduced by strict subcategorization rules, specify only what other symbols were introduced by the same rule as the category symbol concerned. *See:* Linguistic form: transformational theory 280
— **features:** *see* Linguistic form: transformational theory (M) 281
— **rules, strict:** *see* Linguistic form: syntagmatic (M) 278; Linguistic form: transformational theory 281
**SUBCODE.** The *language-systems* comprising a communication matrix are either different *languages* (3) or different *dialects* (1); in the first case they are called *codes*, in the second case *subcodes*. *See:* Language varieties: language and dialect 249
**SUBJECT.** A person who is given a specific task in a psychology experiment. *Naive subject*. One who has had no opportunity to practise the task. *See:* Speech perception 548
—: *see* Grammar (structural) (M) 206
—, **naive:** *see* Subject (G).
**Subjective equality, point of:** *see* Sensory discrimination, measurement of 517
**SUBORDINATE, SUBORDINATIVE.** A *subordinate (subordinative) construction* is an *endocentric construction* only one of whose *immediate constituents* (the *head*) is *substitutable* for the construction as a whole; otherwise an endocentric construction is *coordinate*. *See:* Linguistic form: syntagmatic 278; Grammar (structural) 196; Psychological linguistics: psychological aspects of semantic structure (M) 442
— **constitutes:** *see* Grammar (structural) 196
**Sub-routine link stack:** *see* Stacks 564
**Subscriber's Telephone Set, Design Considerations of** 584
**SUBSCRIPT.** An integer, or one of a set of integers, describing the position of an entry in an array of entries. For example, if $a_{ij}$ denotes the entry in the $i$th row of the $j$th column of a table, $i$ and $j$ are subscripts. When the address of an entry in a computer store is described, for example, as the $i$th word of the $j$th section of the $k$th block, $i$, $j$, $k$, are also called subscripts.
**SUBSERVE (SOMETHING).** To serve as a means of promoting (something).
**SUBSTANCE.** *Substance* is contrasted in linguistic theory with *form:* substance covers those features of language activity which are independent of the actual language being used, notably the resources of sounds (or written marks) used by the speakers (or writers), and sometimes also the situations in which the language is used; *form* covers the abstractions which can be made from the substance-features, and which constitute the particular *language system* underlying this activity. *See:* Grammar (structural) (M) 186; Phonology: contrast and opposition (M) 403; Writing (M) 627
—, **phonetic:** *see* Phonology: phonemes and broad transcription 409

**Substance, transmitter:** *see* Neuronal nets 322

**SUBSTITUTION, (MUTUALLY) SUBSTITUTABLE.** *Substitution* is a procedure for discovering grammatical similarity, or it is the relation between two *mutually substitutable* items recognized as such by this procedure. If two items both occur in the same environment, then they are mutually substitutable in that environment, since either can be substituted for the other to form a new acceptable sentence. *See:* Grammar (structural) 186; Linguistic form: transformational theory 280

**SUBSTITUTION CLASS.** A *class* whose members are *mutually substitutable* in some or all environments is a *substitution class* (or *focus class*). *See:* Grammar (structural) 200; Linguistic form: generative grammar 273

**SUBSTRATE (1), SUBSTRATUM.** The original language of a community which has adopted a new language, where the latter has been to some extent influenced by the original language. *See:* Relations between languages: lingua franca (M) 480; Relations between languages: introduction (M) 470

**SUBSTRATE (2).** The background material on which something (the *constrate*) is written. *See:* Writing 628

**Subsynaptic:** *see* Synapse (G).

**SUBTENSE (RETINAL).** The total area of retina stimulated when the eye looks at a test object. *See:* Perception of colour 358

**Sub-threshold stimulus:** *see* Stimulus (G).

**Suffix:** *see* Statistics of language: structure of written English words 583; Grammar (structural) 189

**Summation, binocular vision:** *see* Perception, visual 386

**SUPERORDINATE.** Superior in rank. *See:* Psychological linguistics: psychological aspects of semantic structure (M) 442

**SUPERVISORY OPERATION.** The organization and flow-regulation of work in a plant or a data-processing system. *See:* Control by hybrid computers 93

**SUPER-NET.** A constellation or combination of a number of *neural nets*. *See:* Neuronal nets 320

**SUPPLETION.** In some exceptional cases, two *paradigms* (1), each of which is *defective* (lacks representatives for some *grammatical classes*), can be combined into a single paradigm, which is then like other parallel paradigms except that in some of its words one root occurs, and in the others another, e.g. *go-goes-went-gone*, involving two roots: *go-* and *wen-*. Such roots are called *suppletive*. If *go-* and *wen-* are treated as *allomorphs* of the same *morpheme*, then they are *suppletive allomorphs*. *See:* Grammar (structural) 189

**SUPPLY.** Anatomical descriptions of the animal body use the word *supply* to indicate an ordered connexion, in which the more central module supplies the more peripheral module. Thus a nerve fibre supplies a nerve ending.

**Suprasegmental:** *see* Grammar (structural) (M) 186
— **features:** *see* Phonology: prosodic features 411

**SUPRASEGMENTAL PHONEME.** A *suprasegmental phoneme* is one which can be coextensive with more than one *segmental phoneme;* for instance, a phoneme of *stress* or *tone* is generally *realized* by phonetic features extending over a whole *syllable* (or even several syllables). *See:* Phonology: prosodic features 411

**Supra-threshold stimulus:** *see* Stimulus (G).

**Surface morphemes,** *see* Writing (M) 627
— **relations:** *see* Linguistic form: system and structure 279

**SURFACE STRUCTURE, SURFACE GRAMMAR.** The *surface structure* of an *item* (say, a sentence) is a *representation* of it which matches relatively closely its *manifestation* in sound or writing; a *grammar* (3) which is concerned with such descriptions is a *surface grammar*. Surface structure and surface grammar contrast with *deep structure* and *deep grammar*, which are concerned with meaning more than with superficial features of manifestation. In a *transformational generative grammar* there is a clear distinction between deep and surface structures, and deep structures are converted into surface structures by means of *transformations;* a surface structure is shown by a *final derived phrase-marker*. *See:* Linguistic form: transformational theory 282; Linguistic form: system and structure 278; Grammar (structural) (M) 186; Psychological linguistics: psycholinguistic studies of syntax (M) 439; Relations between languages: typological and areal classifications (M) 486

**Switch core type fixed stores:** *see* Fixed stores and control by microprogram 182
— **line:** *see* Control, on-off 138

**Switching and Control in Telephony** 590
— **centre, district:** *see* Switching and control in telephony 593
— **centre, group:** *see* Switching and control in telephony 593
— **centre, regional:** *see* Switching and control in telephony 593
—, **direct dialled:** *see* Switching and control in telephony 590
—, **optimal:** *see* Control, on-off 138

**Syllabary:** *see* Phonology: contrast and opposition (M) 401

**Syllabic:** *see* Phonology: prosodic features (M) 411; Writing (M) 627

**SYLLABIFICATION.** The division of an *utterance* into *syllables*. *See:* Phonetics, experimental (M) 399

**SYLLABLE.** The *syllable* can be defined either *phonetically* or *phonologically;* often the stretches of sounds identified as phonetic syllables correspond to those identified as phonological syllables, but this need not be so. Various phonetic definitions have been suggested, notably with reference to auditory prominence (each peak of prominence marks the centre of one syllable) and to the pressure of air from the lungs (each puff corresponds to one syllable). As a phonological unit, the syllable can be defined, and used, in a variety of ways—often it is the unit with reference to which the *distribution* of *phonemes* is described; similarly, the *graphological* syllable has been suggested as a unit for describing the distribution of *graphemes*. *See:* Statistics of language: structure of written English words 584; Writing 627; Phonology: contrast and opposition (M) 401; Phonology: prosodic features (M) 411

**SYMBOL (1).** A *sign* may be related to its *referent* either conventionally or by virtue of some inherent feature of the sign's *form;* in the first case, the sign is a *symbol* (1) or *symbolic* sign, in the second case an *iconic* sign. *See:* Semantics: sign and symbol 510

**SYMBOL (2).** A written *sign*, as opposed to a spoken one. *See:* Writing (M) 627

**SYMBOL (3)** .The smallest discrete component of a signal. *See:* Process (G); Computational linguistics: machine translation (M) 51; Semantics: meaning and reference (M) 507

—, **category:** *see* Category symbol (G); Linguistic form: transformational theory 281

—, **complex:** *see* Complex symbol (G); Linguistic form: generative grammar (M) 272; Linguistic form: transformational theory 281

— **Manipulation by Digital Computer** 594

**Symbolic:** *see* Relations between languages: typological and areal classifications 486

**Symbolizing and coding information:** *see* Information storage and retrieval 224

**Symbols, alphanumeric:** *see* Alphanumeric symbols (G).

—, **logic:** *see* Logic design, logic (G).

—, **phonetic:** *see* Phonetics, articulatory 393

**Symmetric channel, binary:** *see* Error correcting codes 173

— **matrix:** *see* Matrix (G).

**SYNAPSE.** Space between the axon of one nerve cell and a dendrite or the cell body of another, across which neuronal signals can pass. *Presynaptic.* Relating to a signal approaching a synapse. *Postsynaptic.* Relating to a signal leaving a synapse. *Subsynaptic.* Relating to the part of the dendrite or cell body where signals enter across the synapse.

—, **changes at:** *see* Animal learning 23

**SYNCHRONIC.** A *synchronic*, as opposed to a *diachronic*, study of a language is concerned only with that form of the language which is (or was) current at a given period. *See:* Relations between languages: introduction (M) 470; Relations between languages: comparative philology (M) 475; Relations between languages: loans and loanwords (M) 482

— **analysis:** *see* Relations between languages: semantic change (M) 484

— **approach:** *see* Semantics: introduction (M) 499

**SYNCHRONOUS SATELLITE.** A satellite which remains stationary with respect to the rotating Earth. *See:* Telecommunication, global 606

**Syndrome:** *see* Error correcting codes 174; Information space 222

—, **Klüver-Bucy:** *see* Animal motivation 25

**Syntactic:** *see* Linguistic form: paradigmatic (M) 273; Semantics: meaning and reference (M) 507

— **ambiguity:** *see* Linguistic form: transformational theory (M) 280

**Syntactic complexity:** *see* Psychological linguistics: psycholinguistic studies of syntax 441

— **component:** *see* Psychological linguistics: psycholinguistic studies of syntax (M) 439

— **contrasts:** *see* Psychological linguistics: psychological aspects of semantic structure 442

— **feature:** *see* Computational linguistics: introduction (M) 49

— **markers:** *see* Psychological linguistics: psychological aspects of semantic structure 442

— **pattern:** *see* Relations between languages: lingua franca (M) 480

— **structure:** *see* Statistics of language: introduction (M) 567

**Syntactical features:** *see* Language varities: register (M) 251

**SYNTAGM.** When two or more linguistic *items* are juxtaposed they form a *syntagm. See:* Linguistic form: syntagmatic 277

**SYNTAGMATIC, SYNTAGMATIC RELATIONS.** The relations between an *item* and its *environment* are *syntagmatic relations;* those between it and items with which it may be compared are *paradigmatic relations. See:* Linguistic form: syntagmatic 276; Grammar (structural) 186; Linguistic form: system and structure 279; Linguistic form: paradigmatic 275; Phonology: prosodic features (M) 411; Relations between languages: comparative philology (M) 475

— **relations:** *see* Linguistic form: paradigmatic 275

— **responses:** *see* Psychological linguistics: psychological aspects of semantic structure 442

**SYNTAX (1).** The study and *description* of a *language system* is the *syntax* (1) of that language.

**SYNTAX (2).** *Grammar* (2) is often divided into two parts: *morphology* (1), the rules for forming words, and *syntax* (2), the rules for using words. *See:* Grammar (structural) 190; Phonology: contrast and opposition (M) 401; Phonology: phonemes and broad transcription (M) 409; Relations between languages: typological and areal classifications (M) 486; Statistics of language: introduction (M) 567

**SYNTAX (3).** A distinction may usefully be made between the *syntax* (3) of an *item* and its *morphology* (2); whereas the latter deals with its internal relationships, the former deals with its external relationships, i.e. its relation to other items outside itself, or even to *contexts of situation. See:* Linguistic form: paradigmatic 273

— **of a computer language:** *see* Computer language design requirements 55

—, **psycholinguistic studies of:** *see* Psychological linguistics: psycholinguistic studies of syntax 439

**SYNTHESIS.** The process in *machine translation* of producing a *text* in the target language on the basis of the *analysis* of a text to be translated is called *synthesis. See:* Computational linguistics: machine translation 51

— **by rule:** *see* Speech synthesis 561

**Synthesis, speech:** *see* Phonetics, experimental 400; Speech synthesis 559
—, **system:** *see* System (G).
**Synthesizers:** *see* Speech synthesis 560
**Synthetic:** *see* Relations between languages: typological and areal classifications 486

**SYSTEM (1), SYSTEMATIC, LANGUAGE SYSTEM.**
The *system* of a *language* is the set of rules which the native speaker unconsciously obeys in using the language; these rules say what combinations of sounds (or written marks) are permissible, and under what circumstances they may occur. Linguistics stresses that these rules are inextricably interrelated to make up a single *language system;* but within this overall language system different kinds of rule can be distinguished, (e.g. *grammatical* rules, *lexical* rules, *phonological* rules) so that different *levels* can be distinguished, each having its own system. Moreover, within each level different kinds of rule can be distinguished—*tactic* rules, *realization* rules, etc. *See:* Linguistic form: system and structure 278; Language varieties: register (M) 251; Phonology: distinctive features (M) 404; Relations between languages: bilingualism (M) 473; Relations between languages: typological and areal classifications (M) 486; Semantics: field theories (M) 504; Semantics: meaning and reference (M) 507; Semantics: sign and symbol (M) 510

**SYSTEM (2), SYSTEMIC.** *Systems* (2) are *paradigmatic relations* (or sets of paradigmatically related *classes*) which are not *paradigms* (2), nor *open classes*, nor *clines:* unlike paradigms, systems are restricted to particular *syntagmatic environments;* unlike open classes their membership is clearly definable; unlike clines their members are discrete. Classes which are terms of the same system are said to be systemically related. *See:* Linguistic form: system and structure 278; Grammar (structural) 199; Linguistic form: paradigmatic (M) 273

**SYSTEM (3).** One or more *modules* in communication with each other, considered as a whole with respect to the influence of its input signals on its output signals. Living and mechanical modules are often combined in the same system. *Classification system.* A mechanism or set of rules for assigning every member of a class into one or more of a set of subclasses. *Discrete-time system.* A system which produces an output signal at each instant of a defined sequence of instants. *System synthesis.* The design of a system, including a mathematical study of the interaction of its modules. *See:* Control, stability and 149
—, **adaptive:** *see* Adaptive machine or system (G).
—, **adaptive control:** *see* Adaptive control system (G)
—, **afferent:** *see* Afferent system (G); Sensory discrimination, measurement of 512
— **and structure:** *see* Linguistic form: system and structure 278
—, **auditory:** *see* Sensory processes 530
—, **automatic:** *see* Computational linguistics: introduction (M) 49

**System, autonomous:** *see* Autonomous system (G).
—, **central nervous:** *see* Central nervous system (G).
—, **classification:** *see* System (G).
—, **economic, control of:** *see* Control of an economic system 129
—, **control:** *see* Control system (G); Eye movements 178
—, **discrete time:** *see* System (G).
—, **formal:** *see* Linguistic form: generative grammar (M) 272
— **function:** *see* Phonetics, acoustic 392
—, **grammatical:** *see* Relations between languages: comparative philology (M) 475
—, **language:** *see* Relations between languages: lingua franca (M) 480; Relations between languages: semantic change (M) 483
—, **morphological, of a language:** *see* Morphological system of a language (G).
—, **nervous, role of pulse distribution in information flow:** *see* Nervous system, role of pulse distribution in information flow 316
—, **non-autonomous:** *see* Autonomous system (G).
—, **phoneme:** *see* Phonology: distinctive features (M) 404
—, **phonological:** *see* Relations between languages: introduction (M) 470; Relations between languages: comparative philology (M) 475
—, **response:** *see* Sensory discrimination, measurement of 513
—, **reticular:** *see* Reticular system (G).
—, **semiotic:** *see* Semiology, semiotic system (G); Relations between languages: lingua franca (M) 480
—, **somatic:** *see* Sensory processes 532
— **synthesis:** *see* System (3) (G).
—, **visual:** *see* Sensory processes 528
—, **writing:** *see* Writing (M) 627
**Systematic code:** *see* Error correcting codes 174
— **transcriptions:** *see* Phonology: phonemes and broad transcriptions 410
**Systemic:** *see* Linguistic form: system and structure (M) 278
**Systems, alarm concentration:** *see* Local networks 288
—, **colour-vision, mechanism of:** *see* Perception of colour 362
—, **computer operating:** *see* Computer operating systems 57
—, **content:** *see* Relations between languages: introduction (M) 470
—, **context-sensitive:** *see* Linguistic form: system and structure (M) 278
—, **control, man-machine in:** *see* Man-machine in control systems 307
—, **data collection:** *see* Local networks 288
—, **digital control:** *see* Control systems, sampled-data 155
—, **dynamic, correlation analysis of, using pseudorandom binary signals:** *see* Pseudorandom binary signals, use of ... 433
—, **Herbrand-Gödel:** *see* Unsolvable problems 624
—, **inland trunk:** *see* Inland trunk systems 238

46*

—, **linearized, dynamic description of:** *see* Pseudorandom binary signals, use of ... 433
—, **linguistic, components of:** *see* Computational linguistics: introduction 50
—, **multivariable control:** *see* Control systems, multivariable 151
—, **non-interacting:** *see* Control of aircraft as two non-interacting systems 128
**SYSTEMS CONSULTANT.** A firm which specializes in the application of computers to special tasks.
**SYSTEMS PROGRAM.** A computer program for reorganizing the instructions, data etc. after they have been read into the computer. *See:* Sorting techniques 543
—, **radio:** *See* Telecommunication, global 604
—, **receptor, non-neural elements in:** *See* Non-neural elements in receptor systems 337
—, **re-writing:** *See* Linguistic form: generative grammar (M) 272
—, **sampled-data control:** *See* Control systems, sampled-data 155
—, **writing, alphabetic:** *See* Writing (M) 627

**TABLE LOOK-UP.** As an alternative to computing a function, a computer may store a table of its values for a finite number of values of the arguments. The device of table look-up is also important in abstract discussion. *See:* Automata, infinite-state 38
**TACTICS, TACTIC RULE.** The *tactics* (or *tactic rules*) of a given *level* are rules governing the combination of *items* on that level—what can combine with what, and in what order; thus *phonotactics* is the name of the set of rules governing the combination of *phonemes*.
**TAGMEME.** A *tagmeme* is a *grammatical function* (e.g. subject) together with the *class* of *items* which can have that function (e.g. noun-phrases). *Tagmemic analysis* is grammatical analysis of a language in terms of tagmemes. *See:* Grammar (structural) 198
**Tagmemes, obligatory:** *see* Grammar (structural ) 198
—, **optional:** *see* Grammar (structural) 198
**Tamber:** *see* Phonology: prosodic features 411
**Tandem exchange:** *see* Local networks 284
**Tape, journal:** *see* Journal tape (G).
**TARGET.** An object to be viewed in visual experiments. *See:* Eye movements 176
**TARGET LANGUAGE.** *Translation* is from a *text* in one *language* (3) (the *source language*) into a text in another (the *target language* or *object language*).
**TASK.** Required behaviour of an animal to obtain a reward or to avoid a punishment. *See:* Animal learning 21
—, **compensatory:** *see* Man-machine in control systems 307
—, **pursuit:** *see* Man-machine in control systems 307
**Taste:** *see* Receptors: representation of information about stimuli in populations 468
**Taxonomic grammars:** *see* Grammar (structural) (M) 186

**TAXONOMY.** The principles of classification.
**Teacher:** *see* Learning (G).
**Teaching machines:** *see* Adaptive control theory 9
**Techniques, buffering:** *see* Computer operating systems 60
—, **Carrol's response surface:** *see* Optimization of industrial processes 348
—, **describing function:** *see* Control, stability and 150
—, **frequency domain:** *see* Control, stability and 150
—, **identification, for control:** *see* Control, identification techniques for 119
—, **registration:** *see* Character recognition 42
—, **ridge-following:** *see* Optimization, automatic 344
—, **sorting:** *see* Sorting techniques 543
—, **time domain:** *see* Control, stability and 150
**Telecommunication, Economy in** 599
—, **Global** 604
— **System Planning, International** 607
**Telegraph cables:** *see* Telecommunication, global 604
— **signal, random:** *see* Pseudorandom binary signals, use of ... 434
**Telemetry, multiplex:** *see* Multiplex telemetry (G).
**Telencephalon:** *see* Neuronal nets 320
**Telephone cables, ocean:** *see* Telecommunication, global 604
— **set, subscriber's, design considerations of:** *See* Subscriber's telephone set, design considerations of 584
— **speech channel:** *see* Data transmission 160
**Telephony, switching and control in:** *see* Switching and control in telephony 590
**Temporal adaptation:** *see* Perception, visual 382
**Temporary storage stack:** *see* Stacks 564
**Tenor:** *see* Language varieties: stylistics (M) 260
**Tense:** *see* Linguistic form: paradigmatic (M) 273
— **features:** *see* Linguistic form: transformational theory 283
**Tenue:** *see* Phonetics, articulatory (M) 395
**Terahertz:** *see* Perception, visual 379
**TERMINAL.** A module through which a user sends messages to a computer and receives messages from the computer. A particular class of *peripheral*. *See:* Computers, multiaccess to 63
— **contour.** *See* Terminal juncture (G).
**TERMINAL JUNCTURE.** A *terminal* (as opposed to *internal*) *juncture* (or *terminal contour*) represents a part of the *intonation* of the stretch of speech represented by the preceding string of phonemes, namely, whether the pitch rises, falls or is constant at the end of this stretch.
**TERMINAL STRING.** A *string* of *formatives* generated by the *base component* of a *transformational-generative grammar*. *See:* Linguistic form: transformational theory (M) 280
**Termination of motivational states:** *see* Animal motivation 25
**Test and generate:** *see* Problem solving 415
—, **chi-squared:** *see* Statistics of language: introduction 571
—, **field:** *see* Field test (G).
**Tests, free association:** *see* Free association tests (G).

**TEXT.** A stretch of speech or writing of any length, seen as a *type* or as a *token*. *See:* Linguistic form: system and structure 278; Language varieties: stylistics (M) 259; Linguistic form: paradigmatic (M) 273; Phonology: phonemes and broad transcription (M) 409; Computational linguistics: introduction (M) 49
—, **augmented:** *see* Computational linguistics: machine translation 53
**Texture, retinal gradient of:** *see* Perception, stereopsis as an aspect of 369
**Theorem, Bayes':** *e see* Bayes' theorem (G).
—, **Bernoulli:** *se*3 Bernoulli's theorem (G).
— **proving:** *see* Theorem proving by machine 616; Problem solving 414
— **Proving by Machine** 616
—, **Shannon's coding:** *see* Shannon's coding theorem (G)
—, **Wiener-Khintchine:** *see* Wiener-Kintchine theorem (G).
**Theoretical categories:** *see* Grammar (structural) 204
**Theories, conceptual:** *see* Semantics: field theories (M) 504
—, **field:** *see* Semantics: field theories 504
—, **morphosemantic:** *see* Semantics: field theories 505
— **of learning in relation to language:** *see* Psychological linguistics: theories of learning in relation to language 444
**Theory, active:** *see* Speech perception 551
—, **adaptive control:** *see* Adaptive control theory 1
—, **auditory:** *see* Hearing 211
—, **automata, effectiveness in:** *see* Automata, infinite-state 36
—, **communication:** *see* Communication theory 46
—, **decision, Bayesian:** *see* Pattern recognition 354
—, **field:** *see* Relations between languages: semantic change 484
—, **information, in psychological measurement:** *see* Information theory in psychological measurement 232
—, **motor:** *see* Speech perception 548
—, **psycholinguistic:** *see* Psychological linguistics: psycholinguistic studies of syntax 439
—, **stochastic control:** *see* Control: basic elements 91
—, **transformational:** *see* Linguistic form: transformational theory 280
—, **Weiner:** *see* Control, basic elements 91
**THERMORECEPTOR.** A receptor at which heat flow, caused by a temperature change, initiates nerve impulses. *See:* Receptors: relation between the stimuli and the activity in single primary units 465
**Thesaurus construction:** *see* Information storage and retrieval 227
**Thesis, Church's:** *see* Automata, infinite-state 36; Unsolvable problems 624
**Thinking:** *see* Problem solving 414
**Thought processes, human, computer simulation of:** *see* Computer simulation of human thought processes 60
**THRESHOLD.** In sensory discrimination, the 'just noticeable difference' in sensation. *See:* Sensory discrimination, measurement of 512

**Threshold, absolute:** *see* Sensory discrimination, measurement of 512
**THRESHOLD ELEMENT.** A module made to receive a number of input signal simultaneously. Its output signal can have two values, zero and non-zero. It is non-zero if and only if the sum of every input multiplied by a constant (the *weight*, which may differ among the different input signals) exceeds a given value (the *threshold*).
— **element, adaptive:** *see* Adaptive threshold element (G); Adaptive threshold elements 9
—, **fusion:** *see* Perception, stereopsis as an aspect of 371
—, **indifference:** *see* Psychological limiting factors in human performance 438
**Time, crisis:** *see* Crisis time (G).
— **cues:** *see* Phonetics, experimental 400
— **domain techniques:** *see* Control, stability and 150
—, **integration with:** *see* Perception, visual 381
—, **perception (stereopsis):** *see* Perception, stereopsis as an aspect of 371
—, **reaction:** *see* Information theory in psychological measurement 235
**TIME SERIES.** A sequence of signals recurring at defined intervals of time.
—, **servicing:** *see* Computer peripherals and their control 59
**TIME SHARING.** The use of a computer or other data processing unit by various programs in interwoven succession, in a sequence which is controlled automatically. *See:* Computer operating systems 57; Computers, multiaccess to 63
— **slicing:** *see* Computers, multiaccess to 65
**Timetabling** 619
**TOKEN.** A distinction is made between *types* and *tokens*, the latter being occurrences of the former: for instance, in the sentence *The dog bit the man* there are four word types *(the, dog, bit, man)*, but there are two *tokens* of the word-type *the*, and one token each of the other three word-types *See:* Statistics of language: introduction 567; Linguistic form: paradigmatic 274; Linguistic form: transformational theory 283
**Tomography:** *see* Phonetics, experimental 400
**TONE (1), LEXICAL TONE, TONAL.** *(Lexical) tone* is the use of musical pitch in speech in association with particular *lexically* defined *items* rather than with particular *constructions* or general 'attitudinal' meanings, as in the case of *intonation*. *Tonal languages* are languages in which (lexical) tone is used; most European languages (including English) are not tonal. *See:* Phonology: prosodic features 411; Relations between languages: typological and areal classifications 487; Phonetics, auditory 398; Phonology: distinctive features (M) 404; Writing 627
**TONE (2).** The ability of a muscle to maintain a given tension between the points of attachment of its end. *See:* Eye movements 176
—, **accentual:** *see* Phonology: prosodic features 412
— **features:** *see* Linguistic form: transformational theory 283

— **language:** *see* Phonology: prosodic features   412
— **pattern:** *see* Phonetics, acoustic (M)   393
**Tongue:** *see* Phonetics, articulatory   394
— **advancement:** *see* Phonetics, auditory   397
— **height:** *see* Phonetics, auditory   396
**Tonic receptor:** *see* Receptor (G).
**Top, Benham's:** *see* Perception of colour   363
**TOPOLOGICAL MAP.** A description of the connexions between, e.g. a neural net and a receptive field. Adjacent neurons in the net are stimulated by receptors which are adjacent in the map of the receptive field. *See:* Neuronal nets   320
**TORSION.** Rotation of an eye about the visual axis. *See:* Eye movements   176
**TRACKING.** The response of an operator or control system intended to nullify the effects of some external disturbance (e.g. to adjust a potentiometer to keep a wandering spot of light on an oscilloscope screen as close as possible to a reference point). *See:* Psychological limiting factors in human performance   437
**Tract, vocal:** *see* Phonetics, acoustic (M)   391; Phonetics, experimental (M)   399
**Trade language:** *see* Relations between languages: lingua franca (M)   480
**Traffic problems, simulation of:** *see* Simulation of traffic problems using chain-code random generators   539
**TRAINING.** Of an adaptive system. The manipulation of the inputs in order to force it into a *state* in which it produces the desired set of outputs for given set of inputs. *See:* Adaptive control theory   7
**Transcription, alphabetic:** *see* Phonology: phonemes and broad transcription (M)   409
—, **broad:** *see* Phonology: phonemes and broad transcription   409
—, **narrow phonetic:** *see* Narrow phonetic transcription (G).
—, **phonemic:** *see* Phonology: phonemes and broad transcription   410
**Transcriptions, systematic:** *see* Phonology: phonemes and broad transcription   410
**TRANSDUCER.** System with a single input and a single output channel such that the output signals use energy different in form from the input signals, e.g. a microphone, or a biological receptor.
**Transducers, receptors as:** *see* Receptors as transducers   455
**Transduction:** *see* Perception of colour   361
**Transduction capacity.** The number of different states (2) of stimulus energy which can be transduced into different signals (by the human visual system). L. Wheeler.
**Transfer:** *see* Psychological linguistics: theories of learning in relation to language (M)   444
—, **chained:** *see* Computer peripherals and their control   60
— **control:** *see* Computer peripherals and their control   59
**TRANSFER FUNCTION.** (*See also:* Weighting function) The ratio between two variables in a system or plant which obeys (to a close enough approximation) a set of time-invariant differential equations; normally expressed in terms of Laplace or Heaviside operator. E.g. in a system in which $x$, $y$ are two variables it might be that $x = a\dfrac{d^2y}{dt^2} + b\dfrac{dy}{dt} + cy$; if $s$ is the Laplace operator, $x = as^2y + bsy + cy$, from which the transfer function $y/x(s) = 1/(as^2 + bs + c)$; calling the expression $F(s)$, the relationship is often written $y(s) = x(s)F(s)$. In the steady state $s$ has diminished to zero and the transfer function has become constant: $y/x(O) = 1/c$. P. H. Hammond.
— **of information, rate of:** *see* Telecommunication, economy in   599
—, **peripheral:** *see* Computer peripherals and their control   59
**TRANSFORMATION (1).** A *transformation* (1) is a particular kind of *paradigmatic relation:* given the acceptability of a member $Ai$ of a set $A$, and a transformation $A : B$, we can predict the acceptability of a member $Bi$ of set $B$, and vice versa. (It is not necessary that $Ai$ and $Bi$ be mutually *substitutable*.) In such cases, $Ai$ and $Bi$ are said to be transformationally related, but neither need have priority over the other (cf. transformation (2)). *See:* Linguistic form: paradigmatic   275
**TRANSFORMATION (2).** An operation to be performed on a *string* of symbols, under a specified set of conditions, to convert it into a second string. If such an operation is part of a *transformational (-generative) grammar*, it will be unidirectional, and it will affect not only a string of symbols, but also the *phrase-marker* associated with that string. *See:* Linguistic form: transformational theory   280
**TRANSFORMATION (3).** A set of rules for changing a set of signals of a given kind into a different set of signals. If it is a *one-one transformation*, there is no loss of information, and there exists a set of rules which will change the signals back again, called the *inverse transformation*. *Linear transformation*. A transformation which, for any two input signals, is such that (a) the transform of the sum is the sum of the transform, i.e. $T(A+B) = T(A) + T(B)$, and (b) $T(\lambda A) = T\lambda(A)$, regarding an input signal as a vector and multiplying it by any scalar, $\lambda$. A linear transformation of a set of vectors can be represented by a set of linear equations, one for each member of the set of outputs, e.g.

$$y_1 = a_{11}x_1 + a_{12}x_2 + \ldots\ldots + a_{1m}x_m$$
$$y_2 = a_{21}x_1 + a_{22}x_2 + \ldots\ldots + a_{2m}x_m$$
$$. = \ldots\ldots\ldots\ldots$$
$$. = \ldots\ldots\ldots\ldots$$
$$y_n = a_{n1}x_1 + a_{n2}x_2 + \ldots\ldots + a_{nm}x_m$$

Here $x_1, x_2 \ldots x_m$ are the inputs and $y_1, y_2 \ldots y_n$ are the outputs. The $a$'s are constants specified by the rules of the transformation. *Mapping*. Linear transformations may be visualized geometrically. For example the above transformation may be regarded as changing in input vector (set of signals) in $m$-dimensional space into a vector in a different space of $n$ dimensions. An input vector, for example, is completely specified by the point $(x_1, x_2, \ldots x_m)$ in the input space. The transformation is therefore often described as *mapping* points or vectors in the input space, *to* (or *into* or *onto* with special connotations) the output space. *One-one mapping.* A one-one transformation. *Many-one mapping or transformation.* It frequently happens that the same output signal is derived from more than one input signal. In such cases information is of course lost, and no rules exist for the inverse transformation. Such operations are known as *many-one*, and the output space is called *degenerate*. P. D. F. Ion.

**Transformation:** *see* Computational linguistics: machine translation (M) 51; Linguistic form: transformational theory 280

—, **generalized:** *see* Generalized transformation (G); Linguistic form: transformational theory (M) 284

—, **linear:** *see* Transformation (3) (G).

—, **singulary:** *see* Singulary transformation (G); Psychological linguistics: psycholinguistic studies of syntax (M) 439

—, **structural:** *see* Computational linguistics: machine translation 53

**Transformational:** *see* Grammar (structural) (M) 186; Linguistic form: paradigmatic 275

— **component:** *see* Grammar (structural) (M) 186; Linguistic form: transformational theory 282

**TRANSFORMATIONAL CYCLE.** Certain sets of *transformations* (2) apply in a cycle: the set is applied first to the smallest relevant *string* of symbols, then to the next smallest, and so on until no more strings satisfy the conditions for applying the transformations concerned. *See:* Linguistic form: transformational theory 284

— **-generative grammar:** *see* Language varieties: stylistics (M) 259; Relations between languages: typological and areal classifications (M) 486

**TRANSFORMATIONAL GRAMMAR, TRANSFORMATIONAL-GENERATIVE GRAMMAR.** A *grammar* (3) in which *transformations* (2) are included among the rules by which the set of *grammatical items* are specified is called a *transformational-generative*, *transformational*, or *T.G.* grammar. *See:* Linguistic form: transformational theory (M) 280; Linguistic form: generative grammar (M) 272; Psychological linguistics: psycholinguistic studies of syntax 439

**Transformational grammar:** *see* Computational linguistics: machine translation (M) 51; Phonology: distinctive features (M) 404

**TRANSFORMATIONAL LANGUAGE.** A *language* (2) which can be *generated* only by a *transformational grammar*. *See:* Linguistic form: transformational theory (M) 280

— **prefix:** *see* Statistics of language: structure of written English words (M) 583

— **rules:** *see* Computational linguistics: machine translation (M) 51; Linguistic form: transformational theory (M) 280; Relations between languages: typological and areal classifications (M) 486

— **theory:** *see* Linguistic form: transformational theory 280

**Transformed response staircase method (TRSM):** *see* Sensory discrimination, measurement of 521

**Transformer, hybrid:** *see* Subscriber's telephone set, design considerations of 685

**TRANSIENT RESPONSE.** If an input to a control system is suddenly changed from one steady value to another, the output may approach its new final value in various ways. For example, as in a dial reading instrument, it may be 'overdamped' and exponential in form, or 'underdamped', oscillating about the final value with exponentially diminishing amplitude. Transient responses of this sort are calculated during the design of most engineering control systems. *See also:* Impulse function, perfect (G).

**Transition, open:** *see* Open transition (G).

**TRANSLATE (1), TRANSLATION.** *Translation* is the replacement of a *representation* of a text in one *language* (3) by a representation of an equivalent text in a second language. Texts in different languages can be equivalent in different degrees (fully or partially equivalent), in respect of different *levels of representation* (equivalent in respect of *context*, of *semantics*, of *grammar* (2), of *lexis*, etc.) and at different *ranks* (1) (word-for-word, phrase-for-phrase, sentence-for-sentence). The rank, or level of representation, at which equivalence is sought will depend to some extent on the purposes of the translation but also on the possibility of identifying *interlinguistic units;* the more different the cultures of the *language-communities* of the two languages concerned, the harder it will be to find interlinguistic units on the level of context, especially at the rank of word. The languages from which and into which the translation is made can be called, respectively, the *source language* and the *target language. See:* Language varieties: register (M) 251; Language varieties: stylistics 259

**TRANSLATE (2).** In computer technology, to express information in machine language *only*, to *compile. See:* Computational linguistics: machine translation 51; Computer language design requirements 54

—, **machine:** *see* Computational linguistics: introduction 49; Computational linguistics: machine translation 51; Linguistic form: generative grammar (M) 272

**Transmission of data:** *see* Data transmission 159

— **of the genetic message:** *see* Homeostasis in the single cell 218

**Transmitter substance:** *see* Neuronal nets 322

**TRANSPARENT (PROGRAMMING LANGUAGE).** One in which the intended relation between input and output is easily perceived for any subroutine. *See:* Algorithms for processing algorithms 16

**TRANSPONDER.** A device using its own power supply to receive and re-emit signals.

**Transport:** *see* Character recognition 41

**TRANSPORT MECHANISM.** In a device for reading or writing signals, the mechanism for moving the medium past the reading or writing head, punch or sensor.

**TREE, TREE-DIAGRAM.** A graph with no loops, e.g. each of the three graphs illustrated, which are *isomorphic.* The *nodes* (or points) are in some cases joined by *edges* (or lines).

Trees (b) and (c) are arranged as *hierarchies,* showing different *levels* and different *depths.* Trees consist of a set of nodes linked by branches. In linguistics a *tree-*diagram is a means of showing visually a set of *constituency* relations; each *constituent* is represented by a node in the tree, and the relation between every constituent and its *constitute* is represented by a branch in the tree. The nodes may or may not be assigned labels giving further information about the constituents they represent. *See:* Linguistic form: transformational theory (M) 280; Grammar (structural) 186; Linguistic form: syntagmatic (M) 276

—, **binary:** *see* Binary tree (G).

**TREMOR.** An irregular muscular movement of small amplitude (e.g. smaller than 1 min arc for eye tremor). Any irregularity in a train of control signals to a muscle, causing such irregular movements. *See:* Eye movements 177

**TRIGGER.** A device whose input is a single pulse or step, and whose output is to permit or stop the flow of signals in another circuit; a switch.

**Trigraphs:** *see* Statistics of language: introduction 569

**Trills:** *see* Phonetics, articulatory 395

**Tritanopia, small field:** *see* Perception of colour 363

**Troland:** *see* Perception, visual 378

**Troxler's effect:** *see* Perception, visual 380

**Trunk systems, inland:** *see* Inland trunk systems 238

**TRUTH VALUE, TRUTH FUNCTION.** The value 0 or 1, of a proposition, indicating that it is false or true, respectively.

**Tube, cathode-ray:** *see* Cathode-ray tube (G).

**Turing's hypothesis:** *see* Automata, infinite-state 36

— **machine:** *see* Automata, infinite-state 35; Linguistic form: generative grammar (M) 273; Linguistic form: transformational theory (M) 280; Unsolvable problems 623

**Two-dimensional shift register:** *See:* Character recognition 43

— **-point boundary-value problem:** *See* Control by the maximum principle 105

**TYPE.** A linguistic *item* can be considered either as a *type* or as a *token;* seen as a *type*, it is an object *generated* by the *grammar* (3) of the language concerned, which can 'occur' (i.e. can be used or produced) any number of times; seen as a *token*, it is an occurrence of a type, and can therefore only occur once. E.g. in the preceding sentence there are four tokens of the type '*as*'. *See:* Linguistic form: paradigmatic 273

**Typographic composition, automatic:** *See* Computational linguistics: introduction 49

**Typography:** *See* Writing (M) 627

**Typological:** *See* Semantics: sign and symbol (M) 510

**TYPOLOGICAL CLASSIFICATION.** A classification of languages according to their structural characteristics is a *typological*, as opposed to an *areal* or a *genetic*, classification. A well-known classification of such characteristics is into *isolating, agglutinative, fusional* (and sometimes, *polysynthetic*): languages differ in the degree to which they show these characteristics, rather than in showing one to the exclusion of all the others, so a language is classified typologically according to which of these characteristics is dominant. *See:* Relations between languages: typological and areal classifications 486; Relations between languages: introduction 470; Relations between languages: semantic change (M) 484; Writing (M) 627

— **comparison:** *See* Relations between languages: introduction 470

**ULTIMATE CONSTITUENT.** A *constituent* of an *item* may or may not itself have contituents; if it does not, it is an *ultimate constituent.* An ultimate constituent may also be either an *immediate constituent* or a *mediate constituent* of the item in question. *See:* Grammar (structural) 194; Linguistic form: syntagmatic 277

**Unaspirated plosives:** *see* Phonology: contrast and opposition (M) 401

**Unburdening:** *see* Man-machine in control systems 309

**Undecidability:** *see* Automata, infinite-state 37

**Unimodality:** *see* Optimization, automatic 342

—, **differentiable:** *see* Optimization, automatic 343

—, **strong:** *see* Optimization, automatic 343

**Unique morphemes:** *see* Grammar (structural) 188

**UNIT (1), LINGUISTIC UNIT.** A *linguistic unit* is some kind of abstract entity defined by a *language system*—'*linguistic unit*' may mean an individual *item* or a set of such items or a feature of some kind abstracted from such a set. *See:* Phonetics, acoustic (M) 391; Phonetics, experimental (M) 399; Relations between languages: introduction (M) 470; Semantics: introduction (M) 499; Semantics: field theories (M) 504

**UNIT (2).** In every language, any *constituent* or *constitute* can be assigned (according to some linguists) to one of a small number of sets, called *units* (2)—

that is, it can (in many languages) be classified as a sentence or a clause or a phrase or a word or a morpheme. The units (2) of a language are interrelated by *rank* (1), which in the simplest cases is a relation of *constituency*—sentences consist of one or more clauses, clauses of one or more phrases, and so on. *See:* Grammar (structural)  186

UNIT (3). A *module* or small system of modules.

—, **afferent:** *see* Afferent unit (G)

—, **arithmetic:** *see* Arithmetic unit (G)

—, **control:** *see* Control unit (G)

—, **grammatical:** *see* Phonology, prosodic features (M) 411; Writing  628

—, **linguistic:** *see* Unit (1) (G); Psychological linguistics: theories of learning in relation to language  444

—, **perceptual:** *see* Psychological linguistics: psycholinguistic studies of syntax (M)  439

—, **phonematic:** *see* Phonetic unit (G).

—, **phonological:** *see* Phonology: prosodic features (M) 411

—, **phrase-structure:** *see* Phrase-structure unit (G); Psychological linguistics: psycholinguistic studies of syntax (M)  439

—, **receptor:** *see* Receptors as transducers  456

—, **single receptor:** *see* Receptors: representation of information about stimuli in populations  467

Units, **discrete:** *see* Phonetics, experimental (M)  399

—, **interlinguistic:** *see* Relations between languages: bilingualism (M)  472

Units, **linguistic acoustic characteristics of:** *See* Phonetics, acoustic  391

— **of perception:** *see* Speech perception  550

—, **'on-off':** *see* Neuronal nets  331

UNIVERSAL. A *universal* category is one which is valid for all *language systems*.

— **characteristics:** *see* Linguistic form: transformational theory (M)  280

— **contrast:** *see* Phonology: contrast and opposition (M)  401

— **properties:** *see* Phonology: distinctive features (M) 404; Semantics: introduction (M)  499

UNMARKED. For some sets one member can be considered as in some way neutral, normal or basic compared with the other members; this is the *unmarked* member of the set, other members being *marked*. *See:* Psychological linguistics: psychological aspects of semantic structure  443

Unreliable elements, reliable computation with: *see* Reliable computation with unreliable elements  489

Unrounded: *see* Phonology: contrast and opposition (M)  401

Unsolvable Problems  623

Use of citations: *see* Information storage and retrieval  228

UTTERANCE (1). A *text* which is long enough to be relatable directly to a *context of situation*. *See:* Semantics: context and collocation  503

UTTERANCE (2). A *text* which is preceded and followed by pauses and is therefore considered to be complete and self-contained.

UTTERANCE (3). A particular occurrence *(token)* of a spoken *text*, or the activity involved in producing it. *See:* Linguistic form: syntagmatic (M)  276; Semantics: meaning and reference (M)  507; Psychological linguistics: theories of learning in relation to language (M)  445; Semantics: introduction (M)  499

UTTERANCE. (4) An accredited statement, irrespective of the *characters* and *language* used. *See:* Computational linguistics: introduction (M)  49

Uvula: *see* Phonetics, articulatory  394

Uvular: *see* Phonetics, articulatory  395


VALUE. A linguistic *sign* has a *value* by virtue of its relations to other such signs in a *language-system*. *See:* Grammar (structural)  186; Semantics: field theories  504

Variable: *see* Linguistic form: transformational theory  282

—, **Gaussian:** *see* Gaussian variable (G)

— **mark space** *see:* Pulse width modulation (G)

—, **nominal:** *see* Nominal variable (G)

—, **state:** *see* State variable (G)

Variables, **canonic:** *see* Canonic variables (G)

VARIANCE. A parameter describing the range of signal amplitudes of a stationary *process*: the mean of the sequence of the differences from the average, or

$$\frac{1}{\tau} \int_0^\tau (x - \bar{x})^2 \, dt.$$

—, **estimate:** *see* Pseudorandom binary signals, use of...  435

Variants, **allophonic:** *see* Phonology: phonemes and broad transcription (M)  409

Variations, **calculus of:** *see* Calculus of variations (G)

—, **lexical:** *see* Relations between languages: semantic change (M)  484

VARIETY. A *language* (3) can be seen, not as a single homogeneous *language system*, but as a set of language systems, which are sufficiently similar to be considered by their speakers as the same language (3). Each of these language-systems defines a different *variety* of the language (3). Varieties may differ as to their users or their uses and are called *dialects* (1) in the first case, and *registers* (1) in the second. However, the dialects of a language are not discrete and form a *dialect continuum*, and its registers are not easy to distinguish either, so it is hard to see whether a different language system can be postulated for each variety and, if so, what the relations between these language-systems could be. *See:* Language varieties: language and dialect  243; Language varieties: register  251

VECTOR. An ordered set of quantities (variables) which, for instance, describes a particular input or output of a system, or its state. The value of any variable is called a *component* of the vector. The number of components is sometimes called the dimensionality of the vector. *Inner product of two vec-*

*tors*, having the same number of components. The sum of the products of corresponding components, a *scalar* quantity.

**VECTOR PRODUCT.** A product of two vectors defined in such a way that it, too, is a vector. It is only used in 3 dimensions, and is defined for the vectors $\mathbf{a} = (a_1 a_2 a_3) = a_1 \hat{i}, a_2 \hat{j}, a_3 \hat{k}$ and $\mathbf{b} = (b_1, b_2, b_3) = b_1 \hat{i} + b_2 \hat{j} + b_3 \hat{k}$ by $\mathbf{a} \times \mathbf{b} = (a_2 b_3 - a_3 b_2) \hat{i}$, an expansion most easily remembered as the formal determinant $\begin{vmatrix} \hat{i} & \hat{j} & \hat{k} \\ a_1 a_2 a_3 \\ b_1 b_2 b_3 \end{vmatrix} = \mathbf{a} \times \mathbf{b}$; note $\mathbf{a} \times \mathbf{b} = -\mathbf{b} \times \mathbf{a}$ and that the direction of $\mathbf{a} \times \mathbf{b}$ is that of the perpendicular to the plane defined by the two vectors $\mathbf{a}$ and $\mathbf{b}$. In the above expression $\hat{i}, \hat{j}$ and $\hat{k}$ are called the standard basis unit vectors (and their directions are perpendicular). The multipliers $a_1, a_2 \ldots b_3$ are scalars. The vectors $a_1 \hat{i}, a_2 \hat{j}, a_3 \hat{k}$ are called the *components* of the vector $\mathbf{a}$. P. D. F. Ion.

**Vehicular language:** *see* Relations between languages: lingua franca 480

**Velar:** *see* Phonetics, articulatory 395; Phonology: phonemes and broad transcription 409

— **plosives, fronted:** *see* Phonology, contrast and opposition (M) 401

— **plosives, retracted:** *see* Phonology: contrast and opposition (M) 401

**Velarized:** *see* Phonetics, articulatory 395

**Velum:** *see* Phonetics, articulatory 394

**Ventricular fold:** *see* Phonetics, experimental (M) 399

**VERGENCE.** Relative directions of the two eyes when fixing on a near object. *See:* Eye movements 176

**Vernier acuity:** *see* Perception, stereopsis as an aspect of 378

**Very short term memory store:** *see* Models for human memory 311

**VIDEO RECORDING.** Very high frequency signals (up to 10 Mc/s) recorded magnetically for reproduction of television. *See:* Magnetic recording 291

**View, cyclopean:** *see* Perception, stereopsis as an aspect of 372

—, **Gestalt:** *see* Problem solving 416

—, **panoramic:** *see* Perception, stereopsis as an aspect of 369

**VIEWER.** Any device for making the contents of microfilm or microfiches readable. *See:* Scientific documentation 397

**Visceral brain:** *see* Neuronal nets 320

**Vision, acuity of:** *see* Perception, visual 379

**Visual acuity:** *see* Perception, stereopsis as an aspect of 371

— **adaptation:** *see* Perception, visual 373

**VISUAL AXIS.** Imaginary line marking the 'line of sight' of an eye.

— **capabilities, binocular:** *see* Perception, visual 385

— **cortex:** *see* Perception of colour 360

— **perception:** *see* Perception, visual 373

— **system:** *see* Sensory processes 528

**VOCABULARY.** Usually a list of words restricted in some way (e.g. to a particular speaker, to a book etc). *See:* Semantics: field theories 505

**Vocal cords:** *see* Phonetics, auditory (M) 396; Phonetics, acoustic 391; Phonetics, articulatory 394; Phonetics, experimental (M) 399

**VOCAL TRACT.** The passage through which air is allowed to pass in order to make a speech sound. *See:* Phonetics, articulatory 393; Phonetics, acoustic (M) 391; Phonetics, experimental (M) 399

— **tract models:** *see* Speech synthesis 559

**Vocalic:** *see* Vowel (1) (G); Vowel (2) (G); Phonology: distinctive features (M) 406

— **features:** *see* Linguistic form: transformational theory 283

**Vocoder:** *see* Speech synthesis 560; Telecommunication, economy in 600

**VOCOID.** Speech sounds may be classified *phonetically* as either *contoids* or *vocoids (vowel sounds)*. A vocoid is a sound produced without any constriction in the *vocal tract* such as would produce a *contoid. See:* Phonetics, auditory 396; Phonetics: articulatory (M) 395; Phonology: contrast and opposition (M) 401

**VOICE.** The speech-sound produced when air is forced through the vocal cords so that they vibrate. *See:* Phonetics, articulatory 394

**VOICE QUALITY.** The *phonetic features* of *voice quality* in an utterance are those features in it which are peculiar to the speaker and make it possible to recognize him by his voice. They are thus the features which cannot be related either to *phonological* or to *paralinguistic* categories. *See:* Phonetics, acoustic (M) 391

**Voiced features:** *see* Linguistic form: transformational theory 283

— **fricatives:** *see* Speech synthesis 559

— **speech:** *see* Phonetics, acoustic (M) 391

**Voicing:** *see* Phonology: distinctive features (M) 404

**VOWEL (1), VOWEL-SOUND.** Speech-sounds can be classified as either *vowel-sounds (vocoids)* or *consonant-sounds (contoids)*; this is a *phonetic* distinction, in contrast with that between *vowels* (2) and *consonants* (2), which is a *phonological* distinction. *See:* Phonetics, acoustic (M) 391; Phonetics, auditory 396; Phonology: distinctive features 404

**VOWEL (2).** In most (or all) languages *segmental phonemes* fall into two (or maybe more) classes on the basis of their *distribution;* one of these classes includes phonemes most of which are *realized* as *vocoids*, and another (or the other) includes phonemes most of which are realized as *contoids*. The name *vowel* (2) will then be given to the former, and *consonant* (2) to the latter. *See:* Phonology: contrast and opposition 402; Phonology: phonemes and broad transcription (M) 409; Statistics of language: structure of written English words (M) 581; Writing (M) 627

—, **cardinal:** *see* Cardinal vowel (G); Phonetics, auditory 397

**VOWEL HARMONY.** In some languages, the *vowel-phonemes* of one *class* do not occur in the *environment* of the vowels of another class; in many cases, this means that any word will contain members of one of these classes, but not of both. This phenomenon is called *vowel harmony*. *See:* Relations between languages: typological and areal classifications   487
— **limit line:** *see* Phonetics, auditory   397
— **quality:** *see* Phonology: prosodic features (M)   411
**VOWELS:** *see* Phonology: contrast and opposition 402; Phonology: prosodic features (M)   411

**WAVE.** A disturbance of an observable $y$, which depends on the distance $x$ of the point of observation from a particular point 0 (the origin of the wave) and on the time interval $t$ after a chosen time, according to the following relation, or one of its modifications:

$$y = A \sin 2\pi \left( \frac{t}{\tau} - \frac{x}{\lambda} \right),$$

where $A$ is the amplitude, $1/\tau$ the *frequency*, and $\lambda$ the *wave-length*. The complete disturbance, sometimes called the wave train, can be looked at in two ways: (1) at any point of observation it is a sinusoidal variation of $y$, repeating itself $1/\tau$ times a second; (2) at any time the graph of $y$ as a function of $x$ is a sine curve, the distance between successive peaks being $\lambda$. The wave is said to be *propagated* with a velocity $\lambda/\tau$.
—, **carrier:** *see* Carrier wave (G)
**WAVE FORM.** The value of a variable (e.g. voltage) considered as a function of time. *See also:* Spectrum (G)
— **forms, sound-pressure time:** *see* Hearing   211
—, **glottal:** *see* Glottal wave (G); Phonetics, acoustic 391
— **-length discrimination:** *see* Perception of colour   359
— **number:** *see* Perception, visual   379
—, **sound:** *see* Phonetics, experimental (M)   399
**Waves, E:** *see* Neuronal nets   329
**WEAK GENERATIVE CAPACITY.** The *weak* (as opposed to the *strong*) *generative capacity* of a *grammar* (3) is the *language* (2), i.e. the set of sentences or other *items*—which it *generates;* the *structural descriptions* of the items generated are not part of the grammar's weak generative capacity. *See:* Linguistic form: generative grammar   272
**WEIGHTING FUNCTION.** The weighting function is equivalent to the unit-impulse response function, that is the response of a linear dynamic system to a Dirac delta function at time $t = 0$. It can be shown to be the Laplace transform inverse of the *transfer function*, i.e. the transfer function

$$F(s) = L[W(t)]$$

$$= \int_0^\infty W(t) \exp(-st) dt$$

where $W(t)$ is the weighting function. P.H. Hammond. *See:* Control: basic elements   90
**WELL-DEFINED, WELL-FORMED.** Defined or formed in accordance with the appropriate collection of rules. In linguistics, a *well-formed* (or *grammatical* (3)) *item* is one which is *generated* (1) by a *grammar* (3)—but note that it is *well-formed* only with reference to that *grammar*. *See:* Linguistic form: generative grammar   272
— **-formed strings:** *see* Linguistic form: generative grammar (M)   272
**Whispering:** *see* Phonetics, articulatory (M)   393
**WHITE NOISE.** An ideal stationary analog signal which, on spectral analysis, includes all frequencies within a given range at equal amplitude. *See:* Magnetic recording   299
**WIDE-BAND.** Having a wide range of frequencies.
**Wiener filter:** *see* Filter (G); Control by stationary filtering and prediction (Wiener)   109
**WIENER-KHINTCHINE THEOREM.** Theorem relating autocorrelation function and the distribution of power in the frequency spectrum. A systematically low autocorrelation corresponds to the spread of power over a wide band of frequencies. *See:* Random signals and noise   455
— **theory:** *see* Control: basic elements   91
**Wiesel and Hubel:** *see* Neuronal nets   332
**Willis law:** *see* Statistics of language: introduction 575
**WIRING-DIAGRAM.** The actual interconnexions of a (neural) circuit, rather that a drawing of them. *See:* Neuronal nets   320
**WORD (1).** There is no one definition of the *word* valid for all languages. In *describing* many, perhaps most, languages it is useful to have a *unit* (1) which can be called the word, but for some languages it will be defined *phonologically*, in others *grammatically;* it may be necessary to have two units, one phonological, the other grammatical, which correspond in most but not all cases. 'Institutionalised' words, i.e. those separated by word-spaces in writing—are often based on a number of such criteria, which sometimes lead to conflict and uncertainty, as with English compound words. *See:* Grammar (structural)   186; Relations between languages: typological and areal classifications (M)   486
**WORD (2).** A string of *characters*. A unit of computer storage, consisting perhaps of 24, 32 or 48 bits.
— **accent:** *see* Phonology: prosodic features (M)   411
**WORD-AND-PARADIGM (WP).** *Models* of linguistic *description* have been divided into *item-and-arrangement* (I.A.) models, *item-and-process* (I.P.) models, and *word-and-paradigm* (W.P.) models. The third differs from the first two in distinguishing between grammatical relations above the word and those below the word (i.e. between *syntax* (2) and *morphology* (1)); the internal features (morphology (2)) of words are shown by the use of *paradigms* (1) rather than by treating words as segmentable into *morphemes*. *See:* Grammar (structural)   192

— associations, statistical: *see* Information storage and retrieval 227
—, control: *see* Control word (G).
**Words, inherited:** *see* Relations between languages: comparative philology (M) 475
—, **written English, structure of:** *see* Statistics of language: structure of written English Words 581
**WOW.** In magnetic reproduction, an unwanted signal caused by variations in speed of transport of the tape. *See:* Magnetic recording 299
**WRITE.** To insert information into a *store* (destroying the information previously there).
**Writing** 627
— **system:** *see* Writing (M) 627
— **systems, alphabetic:** *see* Writing (M) 627
**Written English words, structure of:** *see* Statistics of language: structure of written English words 581

— **language:** *see* Relations between languages: bilingualism (M) 473

**Yes-no procedure:** *see* Sensory discrimination, measurement of 519
**Young-Helmholtz phenomenon:** *see* Perception, visual 378

**Z-TRANSFORM.** A mathematical change in variable, used in processing data at regular intervals.
**ZERO. (ANTIFORMANT, ANTIRESONANCE).** In the spectrum of a speech sound, a short range of frequencies at which the energy is low. *See:* Speech synthesis 559
**Zipf-law:** *See* Statistics of language: introduction 575
**Zone, dead:** *See* Adaptive threshold elements 11
**Zoutendijk's method:** *See* Optimization of inndustrial process 348

## THE INTERNATIONAL PHONETIC ALPHABET.
(Revised to 1951.)

|  |  | Bi-labial | Labio-dental | Dental and Alveolar | Retroflex | Palato-alveolar | Alveolo-palatal | Palatal | Velar | Uvular | Pharyngal | Glottal |
|---|---|---|---|---|---|---|---|---|---|---|---|---|
| **CONSONANTS** | Plosive | p b |  | t d | ʈ ɖ |  |  | c ɟ | k g | q ɢ |  | ʔ |
|  | Nasal | m | ɱ | n | ɳ |  |  | ɲ | ŋ | N |  |  |
|  | Lateral Fricative |  |  | ɬ ɮ |  |  |  |  |  |  |  |  |
|  | Lateral Non-fricative |  |  | l | ɭ |  |  | ʎ |  |  |  |  |
|  | Rolled |  |  | r |  |  |  |  |  | R |  |  |
|  | Flapped |  |  | ɾ | ɽ |  |  |  |  | ʀ |  |  |
|  | Fricative | ɸ β | f v | θ ð s z ɹ | ʂ ʐ | ʃ ʒ | ɕ ʑ | ç ʝ | x ɣ | χ ʁ | ħ ʕ | h ɦ |
|  | Frictionless Continuants and Semi-vowels | w ɥ | ʋ |  | ɻ |  |  | j (ɥ) | (w) | ʁ |  |  |
| **VOWELS** | Close |  | (y ʉ u) |  |  |  |  | Front i y | Central ɨ ʉ | Back ɯ u |  |  |
|  | Half-close |  | (ø o) |  |  |  |  | e ø | ə | ɤ o |  |  |
|  | Half-open |  | (œ ɔ) |  |  |  |  | ɛ œ | ɐ | ʌ ɔ |  |  |
|  |  |  |  |  |  |  |  | æ | ɐ |  |  |  |
|  | Open |  | (ɒ) |  |  |  |  | a | ɑ ɒ |  |  |  |

(Secondary articulations are shown by symbols in brackets.)

OTHER SOUNDS.—Palatalized consonants: ț, d̦, etc.; palatalized ʃ, ʒ: ɕ, ʑ. Velarized or pharyngalized consonants: ɫ, d̴, z̴, etc. Ejective consonants (with simultaneous glottal stop): p', t', etc. Implosive voiced consonants: ɓ, ɗ, etc. ɼ fricative trill. σ, ʚ (labialized θ, ð, or s, z). ʮ, ʯ (labialized ʃ, ʒ). ʇ, ʗ, ʖ (clicks, Zulu c, q, x). ɹ (a sound between r and l). ŋ̍ Japanese syllabic nasal. ʓ (combination of x and ʃ). ʍ (voiceless w). ɩ, ʏ, ɷ (lowered varieties of i, y, u). ɜ (a variety of ə). ɘ (a vowel between ø and o).

Affricates are normally represented by groups of two consonants (ts, tʃ, dʒ, etc.), but, when necessary, ligatures are used (ʦ, ʧ, ʤ, etc.), or the marks ͡ or ͜ (t͡s or t͜s, etc.). ͡ ͜ also denote synchronic articulation (m͡ŋ = simultaneous m and ŋ). c, ɟ may occasionally be used in place of tʃ, dʒ, and ʓ, ʒ for ts, dz. Aspirated plosives: ph, th, etc. r-coloured vowels: eɹ, aɹ, ɔɹ, etc., or eʴ, aʴ, ɔʴ, etc., or ę, ą, ǫ, etc.; r-coloured ə: əɹ or əʴ or ɹ or ɐ̴ or ɝ.

LENGTH, STRESS, PITCH.— : (full length). · (half length). ' (stress, placed at beginning of the stressed syllable). ˌ (secondary stress). ˉ (high level pitch); ˍ (low level); ´ (high rising); ˏ (low rising); ˋ (high falling); ˎ (low falling); ˆ (rise-fall); ˇ (fall-rise).

MODIFIERS.— ~ nasality. ˳ breath (l̥ = breathed l). ˬ voice (s̬ = z). ʻ slight aspiration following p, t, etc. ˶ labialization (n̫ = labialized n). ̪ dental articulation (t̪ = dental t). ˙ palatalization (ź = ʒ). ˌ specially close vowel (ę = a very close e). ˛ specially open vowel (ę̞ = a rather open e). ˔ tongue raised (e˔ or ę = ẹ). ˕ tongue lowered (e˕ or ę = ɛ̞). + tongue advanced (u+ or u̟ = an advanced u, t̟ = t̟). - or ˗ tongue retracted (i- or i̠ = i̵, t̠ = alveolar t). ˒ lips more rounded. ˓ lips more spread. Central vowels: ï (= ɨ), ü (= ʉ), ë (= ə˕), ö (= ɵ), ɛ̈, ɔ̈. (e.g. ṇ) syllabic consonant. ˘ consonantal vowel. ʃʻ variety of ʃ resembling s, etc.

# ASSOCIATIONS BETWEEN ARTICLES

*Any article may have something in common with those near it, and with those whose numbers follow the title.*

1. Adaptive control theory 10, 26, 64
2. Adaptive threshold elements 57, 82
3. Algebraic manipulation using lists 17, 138
4. Algorithms for processing algorithms 17, 33, 138
5. Animal exploratory behaviour
6. Animal learning 9
7. Animal motivation 9
8. Assembly languages 4, 17, 138
9. Attention 48, 78
10. Automata, finite-state 64
11. Automata, infinite-state 22, 65, 144
12. Character recognition 82, 131
13. Cochlear mechanics 54, 84
14. Communication theory 47, 59, 105, 139
15. Computational linguistics: introduction
16. Computational linguistics: machine translation 138
17. Computer language design requirements 3, 4
18. Computer operating systems 4, 53
19. Computer peripherals and their control
20. Computer simulation of human thought processes 23, 24, 64, 82
21. Computers, multiaccess to 18, 96
22. Computers, stochastic 10, 27, 33, 78, 117
23. Concept formation by artificial intelligence 20, 64, 82
24. Concept identification—information processing approaches 20, 82
25. Conceptual behaviour 59
26. Control: basic elements 1, 38
27. Control by hybrid computers 31, 35, 36
28. Control by maximum principle 42, 81
29. Control by model reference 1, 33, 45
30. Control by stationary filtering and prediction (Wiener) 39, 43, 57, 105
31. Control, hierarchial 27, 81
32. Control, hill-climbing in 1, 80
33. Control, identification techniques for 45, 64, 99
34. Control, invariance and 40
35. Control of aircraft as two non-interacting systems 41
36. Control of an economic system
37. Control of respiration, self-adaptive 34, 56
38. Control, on-off 80, 81
39. Control, predictive, using fast-time models 30, 31
40. Control, sensitivity and 29, 34
41. Control, stability and 26, 34, 36
42. Control systems, multivariable 46, 81
43. Control systems, sampled-data 30, 74
44. Data transmission 72, 139, 140
45. Discrete models for forecasting and control 1, 29, 32, 33
46. Dynamic programming 30, 81
47. Error correcting codes 14, 105, 117
48. Eye movements 74, 87
49. Fact retrieval 58
50. Fixed stores and control by microprogram 133
51. Gestalt psychology 9, 78, 83
52. Grammar (structural)
53. Graphical communication 18, 21
54. Hearing 13, 84
55. Homeostasis 6, 14
56. Homeostasis in the single cell 37
57. Information space 14, 47
58. Information storage and retrieval 49, 118, 134
59. Information theory in psychological measurement 14, 73, 104, 134
60. Inland trunk systems 71, 141
61. Language varieties: language and dialect 111, 113
62. Language varieties: register
63. Language varieties: stylistics
64. Learning machines: a unified view 1, 10, 23, 82, 129
65. Linguistic form: algebraic linguistics 10, 11, 16, 144
66. Linguistic form: generative grammar
67. Linguistic form: paradigmatic
68. Linguistic form: syntagmatic
69. Linguistic form: system and structure
70. Linguistic form: transformational theory 93
71. Local networks 60, 137
72. Magnetic recording 44
73. Man-machine communication and ergonomics 21, 53, 100, 131
74. Man-machine in control systems 43, 48
75. Models for human memory 24
76. Nerve and muscle, initiation and conduction of impulses in 106, 107, 108, 125